Henry Mc

# A First Sketch of English Literature

Henry Morley

# A First Sketch of English Literature

Reprint of the original, first published in 1883.

1st Edition 2023  |  ISBN: 978-3-38510-555-3

Verlag (Publisher): Outlook Verlag GmbH, Zeilweg 44, 60439 Frankfurt, Deutschland
Vertretungsberechtigt (Authorized to represent): E. Roepke, Zeilweg 44, 60439 Frankfurt, Deutschland
Druck (Print): Books on Demand GmbH, In de Tarpen 42, 22848 Norderstedt, Deutschland

# A FIRST SKETCH

OF

# ENGLISH LITERATURE.

A

# FIRST SKETCH

OF

# ENGLISH LITERATURE.

BY

## HENRY MORLEY,

LL.D., PROFESSOR OF ENGLISH LITERATURE AT UNIVERSITY. COLLEGE, AND
EXAMINER IN ENGLISH LANGUAGE, LITERATURE, AND HISTORY TO
THE UNIVERSITY OF LONDON.

*TENTH EDITION.*

CASSELL & COMPANY, LIMITED:

*LONDON, PARIS & NEW YORK.*

1883.

# PREFACE.

BASIL VALENTINE said, in his *Triumphant Chariot of Antimony*, " The shortness of life makes it impossible for one man thoroughly to learn Antimony, in which every day something of new is discovered." What shall we say then of all the best thought of the best men of our nation in all times? Let no beginner think that when he has read this book, or any book, or any number of books for any number of years, he will have thoroughly learned English Literature. We can but study faithfully and work on from little to more, never to much. Basil Valentine felt in his own way with that teacher of the highest truth who wrote, " If any man think he knoweth anything, he knoweth nothing yet as he ought to know."

This book is but a first sketch of what in " English Writers " it is the chief work of my life to tell as fully and as truly as I can. But no labour of this kind is intended to save any one the pains of reading good books for himself. It is useful only when it quickens the desire to come into real contact with great minds of the past, and gives the kind of knowledge that will lessen distance between us and them. As far as our wit serves, we understand the books of our own day because we live with them. Knowledge common to us as the air we breathe will hereafter be a part of the detail necessary to make that fresh and pleasant to a student in the future, which the idler may enjoy now without trouble.

Together with a first outline of our literature, some account of the political and social history of England should be read ; and while each period is being studied, direct acquaintance should be made with one or two of its best books. Whatever examples may be chosen should be complete pieces, however short, not extracts, for we must learn from the first to recognise the unity of a true work of genius. A short Appendix gives the names and prices of a few of the books suitable for use in this way, and contains a page to be read with the chapter upon Chaucer and his time.

H. M.

*University College, London.*

# CONTENTS.

## CHAPTER I.

PAGE

THE FORMING OF THE PEOPLE : CELTS . . . 1—11

## CHAPTER II.

THE FORMING OF THE PEOPLE : FIRST ENGLISH . 11—39

## CHAPTER III.

TRANSITION ENGLISH . . . . . . . 39—94

## CHAPTER IV.

CHAUCER AND HIS CONTEMPORARIES . . . . 94—170

## CHAPTER V.

THE FIFTEENTH CENTURY . . . . . . 170—209

## CHAPTER VI.

FROM THE YEAR 1500 TO THE YEAR 1558 . . 210—316

## CHAPTER VII.

THE REIGN OF ELIZABETH . . . . . 316—491

## CHAPTER VIII.

PAGE

FROM ELIZABETH TO THE COMMONWEALTH   .   .   491 -594


## CHAPTER IX.

THE COMMONWEALTH   .   .   .   .   .   .   594  628


## CHAPTER X.

FROM THE COMMONWEALTH TO THE REVOLUTION .   628—735


## CHAPTER XL

UNDER WILLIAM III. AND ANNE   .   .   .   .   735—794


## CHAPTER XII.

FROM ANNE TO VICTORIA   .   .   .   .   .   794—895


APPENDIX .   .   .   .   .   .   .   .   .   896—901

INDEX .   .   .   .   .   .   .   .   .   903—914

# A FIRST SKETCH

OF

# ENGLISH LITERATURE.

————◆————

## CHAPTER I.

### THE FORMING OF THE PEOPLE : CELTS.

1. THE Literature of a People tells its life. History records its
deeds; but Literature brings to us, yet warm with their first
heat, the appetites and passions, the keen intellectual debate,
the higher promptings of the soul, whose blended energies
produced the substance of the record. We see some part of
a man's outward life and guess his character, but do not
know it as we should if we heard also the debate within, loud
under outward silence, and could be spectators of each conflict
for which lists are set within the soul. Such witnesses we are,
through English Literature, of the life of our own country. Let
us not begin the study with a dull belief that it is but a bewilder-
ment of names, dates, and short summaries of conventional
opinion, which must be learnt by rote. As soon as we can feel
that we belong to a free country with a noble past, let us begin
to learn through what endeavours and to what end it is free.
Liberty as an abstraction is not worth a song. It is precious
only for that which it enables us to be and do. Let us bring
our hearts, then, to the study which we here begin, and seek
through it accord with that true soul of our country by which
we may be encouraged to maintain in our own day the best
work of our forefathers.

The literature of this country has for its most distinctive
mark the religious sense of duty. It represents a people
striving through successive generations to find out the right and
do it, to root out the wrong, and labour ever onward for the

*B*

love of God.   If this be really the strong spirit of her people, to show that it is so is to tell how England won, and how alone she can expect to keep, her foremost place among the nations.

2.  Once Europe was peopled only here and there by men who beat at the doors of nature and upon the heads of one another with sharp flints.   What knowledge they struck out in many years was bettered by instruction from incoming tribes who, beginning earlier or learning faster, brought higher results of experience out of some part of the region that we now call Asia.  Generation after generation came and went, and then Europe was peopled by tribes different in temper : some scattered among pastures with their flocks and herds, or gathering for fight and plunder around chiefs upon whom they depended ; others drawing together on the fields they ploughed, able to win and strong to hold the good land of the plain in battle under chiefs whose strength depended upon them.  But none can distinguish surely the forefathers of these most remote forefathers of the Celt and Teuton, in whose unlike tempers lay some of the elements from which, when generations after generations more had passed away, a Shakespeare was to come.

Their old home may have been upon the plains and in the valleys once occupied by the Medes and Persians, and in the lands watered by those five rivers of the Punjaub which flow into the Indus.  We may look for it westward from the Indus to the Euphrates ; northward from the shores of the Persian Gulf and the Arabian Sea to the Caucasus, the Caspian, and the river Oxus.

Through the passes of the Caucasus it may be true that those known as the Celts first migrated to the region north of the Black Sea.  Ezekiel, 600 years B.C., named Gomer as a nation, placing it in the north quarter, that is, south of the Caucasus.   Æschylus, about 130 years later, placed the Cimmerians (whose name lives with our Welsh countrymen as Cymry) about the Sea of Azov and in the peninsula called from them the Crimea.  We are told that in Assyrian inscriptions the Sacan or Scythian population which spread over the Persian Empire was called Gimiri ; and the two words (each, perhaps, meaning " rover ") were applied afterwards to separate branches of the same national stock.  North of the Black Sea, between the Danube and the Don, were the Cimmerian or Cymric Celts. East of the Don were the Scyths, whose name may live among ourselves as Scot, since they are thought to be forefathers of those Gaels who are of our nation as the Celts of Ireland and the Scottish Highlands.

Then came the migrations in which, it is said, the Scythian or Gaelic Celts, pushing westward across the Don, forced the Cymry before them. The Cymry, crossing the Danube, ravaged part of Asia Minor, and spread into Europe. The Gaels who followed them spread also into Europe, and were also driven westward as more tribes came after them.

These next tribes appear to have been men of another stock, who held by the eastern plains of Europe, and there established the Slavonic populations.

Then came the Teutons. First, perhaps, came those from about the upper waters of the Tigris and Euphrates and the northern part of the plateau of Iran, who went north-westward towards the shores of the North Sea and western Baltic, there to become forefathers of Low German populations. From the coasts of France and Spain they were shut out by the strong Celtic occupation ; and behind them pressed men of another branch of their own stock—men, perhaps, who had once occupied the highlands of Southern Iran. These established themselves on the higher lands of Central Europe, and were, if the theory be true, ancestors of the High Germans.

3. Gaelic Celts, migrating by sea from Spain, struck on the western coast of Ireland and on our south-western shores. Thence they spread over these islands, of which the first thin peopling seems to have been by a Celtic population of the Gaelic branch.

Low Germans afterwards crossed the Rhine, and made their way by Belgium along North France to the Seine, expelling Cymry whom they found there in possession. These Cymry, driven across the Channel, landed on the eastern part of our south coast, and forced Gaels there in occupation westward. The Low Germans, who had formed a Belgic Gaul, crossed also, and were strong enough to form a Belgic England. Low Germans and Scandinavians from all lands opposite our eastern coast came over as colonists. The Gaels went westward before pressure of the Cymry, as the Cymry were pushed westward by incoming Teutons. At last the main body of the Gaels of Southern Britain had been forced to join their countrymen across the Irish Sea. The Cymry held the pasture land among the mountain fastnesses of Western England, and the Teuton ploughed the plains.

This process of change was continuous, and may have been so for some centuries before the hundred years between the middle of the fifth and the middle of the sixth century after Christ, during which there were six Teutonic settlements thought worthy of especial record. The six settlements were thus distinguished because they established sovereignties and began the strong uprearing of the nation which took from a great immigrant Teutonic tribe its name of English.

4. As tribe pressed upon tribe, lands were not yielded without struggle. These changes and recombinations in the chemistry of nations were accompanied with a quick effervescence; there was war. War and the common needs of life were foremost in man's thought. We have in this country two famous traditional periods of Celtic literature. One belongs to the Gael, the other to the Cymry; and each centres in a battle.

5. About the **Battle of Gabhra,** said to have been fought A.D. 284, is gathered the main body of old GAELIC tradition. **Fionn** (which means "Fair-haired"), the son of Cumhaill, known in modern poetry as Fingal, had a son **Oisin** (which means "The Little Fawn"), who is known in modern poetry as Ossian. Fionn's father, Cumhaill, had been slain in battle by Goll Mac Morna, who, as Fionn's mortal enemy, and afterwards his friend, has an important place in the old traditions. Fionn led one of the four bands into which the Gaels were parted, that of Leinster, known as the Clanna Baoisgne. His clan attained to so much power that the other three combined against it, and then Fionn and his family had to fight for their lives against all the forces of Erin armed against them, except those of his friend the King of Munster. Stirred to the depths by a struggle that compelled them to put out all strength in the defence of what they held most dear, they felt keenly, reached the highest level of the life of their own time, and poured its music out in song. Fionn's cousin, **Caeilte Mac Ronan,** was warrior and bard. **Oisin,** the son of Fionn, was warrior and bard. The brother of Oisin, Fergus the Eloquent (**Fergus Finnbheoil**), was chief bard, and bard only.

More or less changed by time, some fragments of the singing of these men remain on the lips of country folks among the Scotch and Irish Gaels. Only eleven of them are to be found in records older than the fifteenth century; but others were collected from the lips of the people by a Dean of Lismore in Argyllshire, before the days of Queen Elizabeth.

Of the old Gaelic poems and histories Ireland has many remains, such as the tale of *The Battle of Moytura*, and the *Tain Bo*, or *Cattle Plunder of Chuailgne.* In the *Senchus Mor* are ancient laws of Ireland, ascribed sometimes to the third century, sometimes to the fifth, and certainly known as ancient in the days of Alfred. But the chief feature in old Gaelic literature is the development of song during the struggle that ended a year after the death of Fionn in the crushing of his tribe at the battle of Gabhra, which is said to have been fought in the year 284.

Oisin is said to have had a warrior son, Oscar, killed in the battle, and to have himself survived to an extreme old age, saddened by change of times. The name of Oisin was even blended in tradition with that of St. Patrick, who came to Ireland about a century and a half after the battle of Gabhra. Patrick is made to say to Oisin, " It is better for thee to be with me and the clergy, as thou art, than to be with Fionn and the Fenians, for they are in hell without order of release ;" to which Oisin is made to answer, " By the book and its meaning, by thy crozier and by thine image, better were it for me to share their torments than to be among the clergy continually talking. . . Son of Alphinen of the Wise Words, woe is me that I am near the clergy of the bells ! For a time I lived with Caeilte, and then we were not poor."

6. The flowering of the other branch of our old Celtic literature—the CYMRIC—is associated also with a struggle that brought out the noblest life of men touched to the quick and concentrating all their powers for defence of home and liberty. Here also was a struggle against overwhelming force, closed with a ruinous defeat in battle. This was the **Battle of Cattraeth,** said to have been fought in the year 570 by confederate Cymry to resist the advance of the Teuton inland, after the last of the six settlements upon our eastern shores. They were, indeed, men of the sixth settlement, who had landed (A.D. 547) in the north-east, under Ida, and then spread from the sea inland across a part of the land we now call Northumberland, Durham, and Yorkshire. They took certain lands of the Gododin (Otadini of the Romans), which the Cymry made a last great effort to wrest from them. The scene of battle was probably Catterick Bridge, a few miles from Richmond, in Yorkshire. The Cymric tribes were gathered at the call of the Lord of Eiddin, which means, perhaps, not Edinburgh, but the

region of the river Eden, flowing from a source near that of the Swale, through Westmoreland and Cumberland, into the Solway Frith. They came from districts now known by such names as Dumbarton, Wigtown, Kirkcudbright, and Ayr, from Morecambe Bay and all surrounding regions, gathered their force on the hills about the sources of the Eden and the Swale, and thence marched (A.D. 570) down through Swaledale, some five and twenty miles, to Catterick, or Cattraeth. **Aneurin**, one of the chief of the bards inspired by the great life-struggle, sang the disasters of the battle in a poem called the *Gododin*, of which ninety-seven stanzas yet remain. Gray found in a translation of it the passage which he thus put into music of his own :—

> "To Cattraeth's vale in glittering row
> Twice two hundred warriors go ;
> Every warrior's manly neck
> Chains of regal honour deck,
> Wreathed in many a golden link :
> From the golden cup they drink
> Nectar that the bees produce,
> Or the grape's ecstatic juice.
> Flush'd with mirth and hope they burn ;
> But none from Cattraeth's vale return,
> Save Aeron brave and Conan strong
> (Bursting through the bloody throng).
> And I, the meanest of them all,
> That live to weep and sing their fall."

The battle began on a Tuesday, and continued for a week The Cymry fought to the death, and of three hundred and sixty-three chiefs who had led their people to the conflict, only three, says Aneurin, besides himself, survived. " Morien lifted up again his ancient lance, and, roaring, stretching out death towards the warriors, whilst towards the lovely, slender, blood-stained body of Gwen, sighed Gwenabwy, the only son of Gwen. . . . Fain would I sing, 'would that Morien had not died.' I sigh for Gwenabwy the son of Gwen." Thus Aneurin ends his plaint over the crowning triumph of the Teuton. But hearts had beaten high among the Cymry, and from souls astir song had been poured throughout the days of long resistance that had come before. Urien was the great North of England chief who led the battle of the Cymry for their homes and liber-ties against invading Angles. Llywarch the Old (**Llywarch Hen**) Prince of Argoed, whom the remains of verse ascribed to him show to have been first in genius among the Cymric bards. was Urien's friend and fellow-combatant at Lindisfarne, betweer

the years 572 and 579. There, after the death of Urien, he carried
the chief's head in his mantle from the field. "The head," he
sang, "that I carry carried me; I shall find it no more; it will
come no more to my succour. Woe to my hand, my happiness
is lost!" After Urien's death Llywarch joined arms with Cyndyllan, Prince of Powys, at his capital, where Shrewsbury now
stands. Cyndyllan fell in a battle at Tarn, near the Wrekin.
"The hall of Cyndyllan," then sang his friend Llywarch, "is
gloomy this night, without fire, without songs—tears afflict
the cheeks! The hall of Cyndyllan is gloomy this night, without fire, without family—my overflowing tears gush out! The
hall of Cyndyllan pierces me to see it, roofless, fireless. My
chief is dead, and I alive myself." Twelfth century tradition says that this bard was for a time one of King Arthur's
counsellors. Llywarch had many sons; he gave to all of them
his heart to battle for their country, and lost them all upon the
battle-field. "O, Gwenn," he sang of his youngest and last
dead, "O, Gwenn, woe to him who is too old, since he has lost
you. A man was my son, a hero, a generous warrior, and he
was the nephew of Urien. Gwenn has been slain at the ford of
Morlas. . . Sweetly sang a bird on a pear tree above the
head of Gwenn before they covered him with the turf. That
broke the heart of the old Llywarch."

**Taliesin** (Shining Forehead) was another of those Cymric
bards who sang in the hall of Urien. He was bard only,
chief bard, and sang Urien's victories over Ida at Argoed, at
Gwenn Estrad, and at Menao, between the years 547 and 560.
After the death of Urien, he was the bard of Urien's son, Owain,
by whom Ida was slain. After the death of all Urien's sons,
Taliesin ended a sad life in Wales, and was buried, it is said,
under a cairn near Aberystwith.

Myrddhin, or **Merlin**, was another of these bards, the one
who became afterwards one of the chief figures in Arthurian
romance. He was born between the years 470 and 480; served
first the British chief Ambrosius Aurelianus, from whom he took
the name of Ambrose before his own name of Merlin; then
served as bard with Arthur, leader of the Southern Britons. That
was the **King Arthur** who fought as Urien fought, and who,
though seldom named in our oldest Cymric remains, became afterwards typical hero of the contest, Arthur, the King of that heroic
myth which runs through our literature and is made part of the life
of England. Merlin, one day, between the years 560 and 574,

in a field of slaughter on the Solway Firth, lost reason at sight
of the miseries and horrors that surrounded him, broke his sword,
and fled the society of man. Thenceforth he poured lament
through all his music, and at last he was found dead by the banks
of a river. Of other bards the memories survive, but these were
the chief; and if the records of their lives be blended with
much fable, they do, nevertheless, retain truths out of the life of
that great time of effervescence which preceded in this country
a blending of the elements of English strength.

7. Influence of the Celt on English literature proceeds not
from example set by one people and followed by another, but in
the way of nature, by establishment of blood relationship, and
the transmission of modified and blended character to a succeeding generation.

The pure Gael—now represented by the Irish and Scotch
Celts—was, at his best, an artist. He had a sense of literature,
he had active and bold imagination, joy in bright colour, skill in
music, touches of a keen sense of honour in most savage times,
and in religion fervent and self-sacrificing zeal. In the Cymry
—now represented by the Celts of Wales—there was the same
artist nature. By natural difference, and partly, no doubt,
because their first known poets learnt in suffering what they
taught in song, the oldest Cymric music comes to us, not like
the music of the Irish harp, in throbbings of a pleasant tuneful-
ness, but as a wail that beats again, again, and again some
iterated burden on the ear.

The blending of the Celt and Teuton had begun in the north
even before the days of the great battle at Cattraeth. Some
passages in Aneurin's Gododin show that Celts of part of the
Northumberland, Durham, and Yorkshire coast, the men of
Deivyr and Bryneich (Deira and Bernicia), had remained there
and become incorporated with the new possessors of the soil.
There never was repulse of the whole body of the Cymry into
Wales. Bede, writing a hundred and fifty years after the battle
of Cattraeth, speaks of the Britons of Northumberland as being
in his day partly free and partly subject to the Angles. In the
hill-country of the north and west, to which the Teuton did not
care to follow with his plough, and in the fens, were independent
Celts. The drone of a Lincolnshire bagpipe is one of Falstaff's
similes for melancholy. The familiar presence of the bagpipe
indicates a former Celtic occupation of the fens. In the West of
England the Celts were so far from having been entirely driven

into Wales that in King Alfred's time, three centuries after the
struggle ended at Cattraeth, a line from north to south, dividing
England into equal parts, had on the west side of it a country
in which Celts abounded. They were the chief occupants of the
five south-western counties. In Athelstane's time, Celts and
Teutons, Britons and Englishmen, divided equal rule in Exeter.
Neither in the West nor in the North of England were the Celts
enslaved. Wales they had to themselves; and there they
cherished British nationality. But where they lived among the
English they accepted, when outnumbered, the established
power; or, if in equal force, divided rule, and lived in either
case as fellow-citizens with their Teutonic neighbours.

In the fusion of the two races, which then slowly began
among the hills and valleys of the North and West of England,
where the populations came most freely into contact, the gift
of genius was the contribution of the Celt. The writer of our
latest and best history of Architecture, when preparing the
ground for his work by a survey of the characteristics of
different races in relation to his art, says that " the true glory
of the Celt in Europe is his artistic eminence. It is not,
perhaps," adds Mr. Fergusson, " too much to assert that without his intervention we should not have possessed in modern
times a church worthy of admiration, or a picture or a statue
we could look at without shame."

8. The sense of literature was shown in the earliest times by
the support of a distinct literary class among the Celts who
then possessed this country. In Erin, the first headquarters of
song and story, even in the third century, there was the poet
with his staff of office, a square tablet staff, on the four sides of
which he cut his verse; and there were degrees in literature.
There was the Ollamh, or perfect doctor, who could recite seven
fifties of historic tales; and there were others, down to the
Driseg, who could tell but twenty. As we travel down from the
remotest time of which there can be doubtful record, we find the
profession of historian to be a recognised calling, transmitted in
one family from generation to generation, and these later
professors of history still bore the name of Ollamhs. Of the
active and bold fancy that accompanied this Celtic sense of
literature as an art, and of the Celt's delight in bright colour,
almost any one of the old Gaelic poems will bear witness. The
delight in colour is less manifest in the first poems of the
Cymry. For them the one colour was that of blood; they are

B *

of the sixth century, and sing of men who died in the vain fight against the spreading power of the Teuton. Of those Gaels who were known as Gauls to Rome, Diodorus, the Sicilian, told, three centuries before the time of Fionn and Oisin, how they wore bracelets and costly finger-rings, gold corselets, and dyed tunics flowered with colours of every kind, trews, striped cloaks fastened with a brooch and divided into many parti-coloured squares, a taste still represented by the Highland plaid. In the old Gaelic tale of the "Tain Bo," men are described marching : "Some are with red cloaks ; others with light blue cloaks ; others with deep blue cloaks ; others with green, or grey, or white, or yellow cloaks, bright and fluttering about them. There is a young, red-freckled lad, with a crimson cloak, in their midst ; a golden brooch in that cloak at his breast." Even the ghost of a Celt, if it dropped the substance, retained all the colouring of life. The vivacity of Celtic fancy is shown also by an out-pouring of bold metaphor and effective simile :—

> "Both shoulders covered with his painted shield
> The hero there, swift as the war-horse, rushed.
> Noise in the mount of slaughter, noise and fire ;
> The darting lances were as gleams of sun.
> There the glad raven fed. The foe must fly
> While he so swept them as when in his course
> An eagle strikes the morning dews aside,
> And like a whelming billow struck their front.
> Brave men, so say the bards, are dumb to slaves.
> Spears wasted men, and ere the swan-white steeds
> Trod the still grave that hushed the master voice,
> His blood washed all his arms.  Such was Buddvan,
> Son of Bleedvan the Bold."

Here, in a mere average stanza, containing one of the ninety celebrations of the Cymric chiefs who fell at Cattraeth, we have more similes than in the six thousand and odd lines (English measure) of "Beowulf," the first heroic poem of the Teutonic section of our people. The delight in music—among the old Irish Celts in the music of the harp and tabor, among the old Welsh Celts in music of the harp, the pipe, and the crowd—is another characteristic. It is noted also that the music of the Gaels was sweet, lively, and rapid ; and that the music of the Cymry was slower and more monotonous.

In the old Gaelic story of the first appearance of their people in Erin, we read how the Milesians landed unobserved, marched upon Tara, and called on the three kings of the Tuatha de Danaan, who then held the country, to surrender. The kings answered that they h¹d been taken by surprise, and that the invaders ought to re-embark, retire nine waves, and try whether they could make good their landing in fair fight. The Milesians agreed that this was just, and did try back. We are not bound to believe that such things were ever done ; enough for us that there is the temper of the people indicated by the character of its inventions. And they are suggestions of a chivalrous ideal in old days of savage artist life, when the Celt was a pagan gentleman very much in the rough; savage times when, says another of these old tales, the Ulster men mixed the brains of their slain enemies with lime, and played with the hard balls they made ot them. Such a brainstone is said to have gone through the skull of Conchobar, who lived afterwards seven years with two brains in his head, always sitting very still, because it would be death to shake himself. The Ollamh of old told, doubtless, this story with a roguish twinkle of the eye that has descended to his children's children.

The self-sacrificing zeal that entered into the religion of the Celts bore fruit in the first Christianising of the English.

———.

## CHAPTER II.

### THE FORMING OF THE PEOPLE : FIRST ENGLISH.

1. THE First English, who are commonly known by the school-name of Anglo-Saxons, but who called themselves, as we call ourselves now, the English people (*Englisc folc*), were formed by a gradual blending of Teutonic tribes. They came, at different times and in different generations, from different parts of the opposite coast. On our eastern shores, from the Moray Firth to below Whitby, the land lay readiest of access to men from the opposite side of the North Sea, among whom Scandinavians were numerous ; accordingly, the Scandinavian element is chiefly represented in the character, form, face, and provincial dialects of our north country. The part of our east coast belonging now to Lincolnshire was readiest of access to the Danes ; and in Lincolnshire the Danish element is strongly represented. Farther south, our coast was opposite the Frisian settlements ; therefore, among the immigrants over the North Sea to Southern England, the Frisians, forefathers of the

modern Dutchmen, would predominate. Adventurers of many tribes might join in any single expedition. When they had formed their settlements, the Teutonic spirit of co-operation, and the social progress that came of it, produced changes of home, intermarriages, community of interests, community of speech in a language proper to the cultivated men of the whole country. This manner of speech, First English (or Anglo-Saxon), was not brought complete from any place upon the Continent, but it was formed here by a fusion of the closely-related languages or dialects of the Teutonic immigrants. The Teutons of the coast being chiefly the Low Germans, our first English were chiefly a Low German people. The language formed by them, and written with care as they advanced in culture, was mainly Frisian in structure. They called it English. It was English. Let us call it, then, **First English,** and avoid the confusion of ideas produced by giving it—as if it were the language of another people—the separate name of Anglo-Saxon. Their educated men wrote it with much regard to uniformity of practice and grammatical accuracy. The main body of the people spoke it, as they still do, with less regard to grammar, and with great diversities of vocabulary, idiom, and pronunciation. Those diversities are still sharply defined, though in the course of centuries they have been softened by continuance of free communication, and by intermarriage between men and women of all English provinces. The provincial dialects still bear very distinct witness to the original diversity of the Teutonic colonists ; but these differences are not expressed by the Latin words, *Anglus* and *Saxo*. *Anglus* was only a Latin form of *Englisc* (pronounced English), the name by which the people called itself ; and Saxon was the name which others gave to them. This might readily come into some formal use in the south, where Church-bred statesmen had a Roman education ; but in the north it might be less familiar, because there the first educated priestly class was not formed on the Roman model. Thus Bede, a north countryman, tells of English or Angle settlements in his own part of the country ; but, being informed by a southern correspondent of the Saxon settlements of Southern England, supposes that the difference of word means difference of people. Difference there was—in the north were more Scandinavians, in the south more Frisians—but they all took English for their common name ; and when they were first incidentally called Anglo-Saxons by Bishop Asser, the biographer of King

Alfred, the compound word was not meant to represent a race compounded of Angles and of Saxons, but the English part of that great Teutonic population which there was a growing tendency among foreign writers to call, without discrimination of tribes, by the common name of Saxon. Anglo-Saxons meant, therefore, those Saxons who called themselves the Angles ; but Angle is no more than an imperfect re-translation of the Latinised name of the English.

2. Many Celts in our island had been converted to the Christian faith when the last strong settlements were being established here by pagan Teutons. The Teutonic settlers brought with them battle-songs and a heroic legend of a chief named **Beowulf.** This legend was afterwards put into First English verse, probably in the seventh century, perhaps earlier or later, and remains to us, under the name of its hero, one of the earliest monuments of English literature ; a poem of 6,357 short lines, the most ancient heroic poem in any Germanic language. Its hero sails from a land of the Goths to a land of the Danes, and there he frees a chief named Hrothgar from the attacks of a monster of the fens and moors, named Grendel. Afterwards he is himself ruler, is wounded mortally in combat with a dragon, and is solemnly buried under a great barrow on a promontory rising high above the sea. " And round about the mound rode his hearth-sharers, who sang that he was of kings, of men, the mildest, kindest, to his people sweetest, and the readiest in search of praise." In this poem real events are transformed into legendary marvels ; but the actual life of the old Danish and Scandinavian chiefs, as it was first transferred to this country, is vividly painted. It brings before us the feast in the mead-hall, with the chief and his hearth-sharers, the customs of the banquet, the rude beginnings of a courtly ceremony, the boastful talk, reliance upon strength of hand in grapple with the foe, and the practical spirit of adventure that seeks peril as a commercial speculation—for Beowulf is undisguisedly a tradesman in his sword. The poem includes also expression of the heathen fatalism, " What is to be goes ever as it must," tinged by the energetic sense of men who feel that even fate helps those who help themselves, or, as it stands in Beowulf, that " the Must Be often helps an undoomed man when he is brave."

The original scene of the story of this poem was probably a corner of that island of Sæland upon which now stands the capital of Denmark, the corner which lies opposite to Gothland, the southern promontory of Sweden.   But if so, he who in this country told the old story in English metre did not paint the scenery of Sæland, but that which he knew.   A twelve-mile walk by the Yorkshire coast, from Whitby northward to the top of Bowlby Cliff, makes real to the imagination all the country of Beowulf as we find it in the poem.   Thus we are almost tempted to accept a theory which makes that cliff, the highest on our eastern coast, the ness upon which Beowulf was buried, and on the slope of which—Bowlby then being read as the corrupted form of Beowulfes-by—Beowulf once lived with his hearth-sharers.   High sea-cliffs, worn into holes or "nickerhouses many," with glens rocky and wooded running up into great moors, are not characters of the coast of Sæland opposite to Sweden, but they are special characters of that corner of Yorkshire in which the tale of Beowulf seems to have been told as it now comes to us in First English verse.

To the same part of England, and to a date between the years 670 and 680, certainly belongs the other great First English poem, known as Cædmon's " Paraphrase," a paraphrase of some parts of the Bible story.   This poem arose out of the Christianising of the English of the north by Celtic missionaries.

3. There are doubtful traditions which even brought the Apostle Paul to Britain ; which found this country a first bishop in Aristobulus, one of the seventy disciples whom St. Paul mentions in his Epistle to the Romans ; and made a King Lucius who died A.D. 201, the first Christian King, founder also of the first church, St. Martin's, at Canterbury.

But we know more certainly from the evidence of Eusebius, towards the beginning, and of Chrysostom, towards the close of the fourth century, that Christian teachers then visited Britain and made converts.   Alban is said to have been the first British martyr, and the date assigned to his martyrdom is the year 305. In 314 three British bishops were among those present at the Council of Arles.   British bishops were also at the Council of Rimini, in 359.   Between the years 394 and 415, a British Christian scholar, of independent mind and earnest piety, named Morgan, or Morgant (who transformed his Cymric name, which means " one born by the sea-shore," into its classical synonym, **Pelagius**), maintained opinions upon sundry points which were hotly opposed by the Augustine of the primitive Church, and by the great body of the Roman clergy, as the Pelagian heresy.

Patricius, the St. Patrick of the Irish, was Morgan's contemporary, but a younger man, born on the Clyde, near Dumbarton, in the year 372, and active during the former half of the fifth century. His work among the Gaelic Celts aided the efforts of the small communities of Celtic missionaries, called Culdees. St. David, who is remembered as the most famous teacher of the Welsh, was an austere and able priest of the school of the Egyptian monks, son of a Cymric prince, and by tradition uncle to King Arthur. He was at work during the former half of the sixth century. But the chief missionary work was then being done by the Culdees of the Irish Church. Columba, an Irish abbot of royal descent, after founding monasteries in the North of Ireland, passed in the year 563 to Scotland, and for the next thirty-four years laboured there as a missionary on the mainland and in the Hebrides, making his headquarters upon one of the Hebrides, the rocky island of Iona. Iona then became the most important of the Culdee missionary stations. It was not until Columba had been thus at work for three and thirty years that Pope Gregory I. sent the Italian Augustine into this country, where he acted as a missionary from Rome to the South of England, and became the first Archbishop of Canterbury.

The Celtic missionaries had then been at work for generations among the English of the north. They had received their own teaching rather from the Eastern than from the Western Church, and followed, therefore, the practice of the Eastern Church in fixing the time for Easter, and in points of ceremonial wherein that Church differed from the Church of Rome. As the influence of teachers from Rome spread northward, hot conflict was raised between the teachers of the south and of the north upon these points of ceremonial. They appeared more vital questions to the Rome-bred clergy than to those trained in the schools of the Culdees, at Iona or at Lindisfarne. In the year 634 Oswald became king over the rude population of Deivyr and Bryneich, among whom there had been that early fusion of Celts with the incoming English settlers which is referred to by Aneurin in the Gododin (ch. i. § 7). King Oswald sent for missionaries to Iona.

This was two years after the death of the Arabian prophet, Mahomet.

The first of the teachers who came from Iona to the Northumbrians went back and made hopeless report of the people.

Then **Aidan** volunteered for the work, and led a religious colony to Lindisfarne, which is at low water a peninsula, at high water an island, nine miles to the southward of our present Berwick-upon-Tweed. At Lindisfarne, where Oswald founded for him a bishopric, Aidan formed the great missionary station for Northumbria. He gave his goods to the poor, travelled on foot among the people whom he sought to bring to Christ, and won their hearts by simple truth and self-denying earnestness. More Culdees passed through Lindisfarne to join the work, and thus the place came to be known as Holy Isle. For the next thirty years the Celts were in all this region spiritual teachers of the English, and it was out of the midst of this great North of England movement, in the newly-established monastery of Whitby, that the English heart sang through the verse of Cædmon its first great hymn based on the Word of Truth.

4. The Whitby monastery was founded by the Abbess Hilda, in the year 657. She then moved to it from the religious house at Hartlepool, over which she had presided, and into which she had received, two years before, Elfleda, the one-year-old daughter of King Oswald's brother and successor. In thanksgiving for a victory, Elfleda's father had devoted the child to religious life. With a community of both sexes, bound less by formal ties than by a common wish to serve God and aid one another in His service while they diffused Christianity among the people, Hilda lived in the first simple abbey built on the high cliff at Whitby, maintained by a grant of surrounding lands. That which maintained her maintained also the poor about her. She had been taught by Aidan ; had been for some years at Hartlepool much trusted, visited, and counselled by Aidan and other chief teachers of the Celtic Christians. Under her roof, in the year 664, when Whitby Abbey was but seven years old, there was held the Synod of Whitby, for settlement of the questions of ceremonial between the Celtic and the Roman Churches, and peace was secured by concession of the points upon which Rome insisted. At Whitby Hilda was as mother to the child-princess, who grew up under her care and became next abbess after her ; was as mother in her little community, and among the rude people round about, who long preserved the belief that her form is at certain times to be seen in a vision of sunshine among the ruins of the later abbey built upon the site of hers. She so much encouraged the close study of Scripture that in her time many worthy servants of the Church and five

bishops are said to have come out of her abbey. Afflicted during the last six years of her life, she never failed in any duty ; and her last words to her people were that they should preserve the peace of the Gospel among themselves and with all others. At the time of her death, in 680, **Cuthbert**, who died in 686, was Bishop of Lindisfarne.   He also left the mark of a true Christian's life among the people, and was remembered as an angelic missionary priest, who had deep sympathy for the neg·lected poor.   He would seek them in their most craggy and inaccessible homes, to dwell with them by the week or month— their bishop and their brother.   Such stir of human energies produced a poet worthy of the time.   All that we know of him was told by Bede, who was also a north countryman, and who was born about the time when Cædmon's Paraphrase was written.

5. From Bede's account, without adopting its suggestion of miracle in the gift of song to the poet, we may infer that **Cædmon** was a tenant on some of the abbey lands at Whitby, and one of the converts who had a poet's nature stirred by Christian zeal.   One day he joined a festive party at the house of some remoter neighbour of the country-side.   The visitors came in on horseback and afoot, or in country cars, drawn some by horses and some by oxen.   There was occasion for festivity that would last longer than a day.   The draught cattle of the visitors were stabled, and would need watching of nights, since in wild times cattle-plunder also was a recreation, and one that joined business to pleasure.   The visitors took turns by night in keeping watch over the stables.   One evening when Cædmon sat with his companions over the ale-cup, and the song went round, his sense of song was keen, but, as a zealous Christian convert, he turned with repugnance from the battle-strains and heathen tales that were being chanted to the music of the rude harp which passed from hand to hand.   As the harp came nearer to him he rose, since it was his turn that night to watch the cattle, and escaped into the stables.   There, since we know by his work that he was true poet born, his train of thought doubtless continued till it led to a strong yearning for another form of song.   If for these heathen hymns of war and rapine, knowledge and praise of God could be the glad theme of their household music, and if he, even he—perhaps we may accept as a true dream the vision which Bede next tells as a miracle. Cædmon watched, slept, and in his sleep one came to him and said, " Cædmon sing." He said, " I cannot.   I came hither out of

the feast because I cannot sing." "But," answered the one who came to him, "you have to sing to me." "What," Cædmon asked, "ought I to sing?" And he answered, "Sing the origin of creatures." Having received which answer, Bede tells us, he began immediately to sing, in praise of God the Creator, verses of which this is the sense :—" Now we ought to praise the Author of the Heavenly Kingdom, the power of the Creator and His counsel, the deeds of the Father of Glory: how He, though the eternal God, became the Author of all marvels ; Omnipotent Guardian, who created for the sons of men, first Heaven for their roof, and then the Earth." "This," adds Bede, "is the sense but not the order of the words which he sang when sleeping." Cædmon remembered upon waking the few lines he had made in his sleep, and continued to make others like them. The vision seems to have been simply the dream-form given to a continuation of his waking thoughts ; and Cædmon may well have believed, accord-ding to the simple faith of his time, that in his dream he had received a command from heaven. He went in the morning to the steward of the land he held under the abbey, and proposed to use his gift of song in aid of the work that was being done by Abbess Hilda and her companions. Hilda called him to her, up the great rock, and, to test his power, caused pieces of Scripture story to be told to him, then bade him go home and turn them into verse. He returned next day with the work so well done that his teachers became in turn his hearers. Hilda then coun-selled him to give up his occupations as a layman, and received him with all his goods into the monastery. There sacred history was taught to him, that he might place the Word of God in pleasant song within their homes, and on their highways, and at festive gatherings, upon the lips of the surrounding people. He was himself taught by religious men trained in the Celtic school, which was more closely allied to the Eastern than the Western Church. They knew and read the Chaldee Scriptures, and as their new brother began his work with the song of Genesis, the name they gave him in the monastery was the Chaldee name of the book of Genesis, derived from its first words, " In the beginning," that being in the Chaldee b'Cadmon.

6. Cædmon sang, in what is now called his *Paraphrase*, of the Creation, and with it of the War in Heaven, of the fall of Satan, and of his counsellings in Hell as the Strong Angel of Presumption. Thus Cædmon began, first in time and among the first in genius, the strain of English poetry :

> " Most right it is that we praise with our words,
> Love in our minds, the Warden of the skies,
> Glorious King of all the hosts of men;
> He speeds the strong, and is the Head of all
> His high Creation, the Almighty Lord.
> None formed Him, no first was nor last shall be
> Of the eternal Ruler, but His sway
> Is everlasting over thrones in heaven."

Cædmon paints "The Angel of Presumption," yet in heaven
questioning whether he would serve God:

> " ' Wherefore,' he said, ' shall I toil?
> No need have I of master. I can work
> With my own hands great marvels, and have power
> To build a throne more worthy of a God,
> Higher in heaven. Why shall I, for His smile,
> Serve Him, bend to Him thus in vassalage?
> I may be God as He.
> Stand by me, strong supporters, firm in strife.
> Hard-mooded heroes, famous warriors,
> Have chosen me for chief; one may take thought
> With such for counsel, and with such secure
> Large following. My friends in earnest they,
> Faithful in all the shaping of their minds;
> I am their master, and may rule this realm.

And thus, to quote one passage more, Cædmon, a thousand
years before the time of Milton, sang of Satan fallen:

> " Satan discoursed, he who henceforth ruled hell
> Spake sorrowing.
> God's Angel erst, he had shone white in heaven,
> Till his soul urged, and most of all its pride,
> That of the Lord of Hosts he should no more
> Bend to the word. About his heart his soul
> Tumultuously heaved, hot pains of wrath
> Without him.
> Then said he, ' Most unlike this narrow place
> To that which once we knew, high in heaven's realm,
> Which my Lord gave me, though therein no more
> For the Almighty we hold royalties.
> Yet right hath He not done in striking us
> Down to the fiery bottom of hot hell,
> Banished from heaven's kingdom, with decree
> That He will set in it the race of man.
> Worst of my sorrows this, that, wrought of eart.
> Adam shall sit in bliss on my strong throne;
> Whilst we these pangs endure, this grief in hell.
> Woe! Woe! Had I the power of my hands,
> And for a season, for one winter's space,
> Might be without; then with this host, I——
> But iron binds me round; this coil of chains
> Rides me; I rule no more—close bonds of hell
> Hem me their prisoner."

Cædmon, when he has thus told the story of Creation and the Fall of Man, follows the Scripture story to the Flood, and represents with simple words the rush of waters, and the ark "at large under the skies over the orb of ocean." So he goes on, picturing clearly to himself what with few words he pictures for his hearer. The story of Abraham proceeds to the triumph of his faith in God when he had led his son Isaac to the top of a high mount by the sea, "began to load the pile, awaken fire, and fettered the hands and feet of his child; then hove on the pile young Isaac, and then hastily gripped the sword by the hilt, would kill his son with his own hands, quench the fire with the youth's blood." From this scene of God's blessing on the perfect faith of Abraham, Cædmon proceeds next to the passage of the Red Sea by the Israelites, a story of the power of God, who is able to lead those who put their faith in Him unhurt through the midst of the great waters. And the next subject of the extant Paraphrase is taken from the book of Daniel, to show the same Power leading Hananiah, Azariah, and Mishael, with their garments unsinged, through the furnace fire. This paraphrase closes with Belshazzar's feast. The rest is from the New Testament, inscribed in the one extant manuscript less carefully, and by a later hand. It has for its subject Christ and Satan; it is fragmentary, and perhaps no part of it is by Cædmon, except that which describes the fasting and temptation in the wilderness.

7. As to their mechanism, there is one measure for Beowulf, Cædmon's Paraphrase, and all subsequent First English poems. There is no rhyme, and no counting of syllables. The lines are short, depending upon accent for a rhythm varying in accordance with the thought to be expressed, and depending for its emphasis upon alliteration. Usually in the first of a pair of short lines the two words of chief importance began with the same letter, and in the second line of the pair the chief word began also with that letter, that is to say, if the alliteration were of consonants; in the case of vowels the rule was reversed, the chief words would begin with vowels that were different.

8. As to their matter, if we except Cædmon, in whom there was an artistic power perhaps to be accounted for by the beginning of some mixture of blood between the northern English and their Celtic fellow-citizens, the First English writers, whether of verse or prose, were wanting in vivacity of genius. They were practical, earnest, social, true to a high sense of duty,

and had faith in God. They used few similes, and, although
their poetry is sometimes said to abound in metaphor, its metaphors were few and obvious. By metaphor a word is turned out
of its natural sense. There is little of metaphor in calling the
sea the water-street, the whale-road, or the swan-road; the ship
a wave-traverser, the sea-wood, or the floating-wood; a chief's
retainers his hearth-sharers, or night the shadow-covering of
creatures. This kind of poetical periphrasis abounds in First
English poetry, but it proceeds from the thoughtful habit of
realisation, which extends also to a representation of the sense
of words by some literal suggestion, that will bring them
quickened with a familiar experience or human association to
the mind. There is in the unmixed English an imagination
with deep roots and little flower, solid stem and no luxuriance of
foliage. That which it was in a poet's mind to say was realised
first, and then uttered with a direct earnestness which carried
every thought straight home to the apprehension of the
listener. The descendants of those Frisians who did not cross
to our shores resemble the First English before they had been
quickened with a dash of Celtic blood. Both Dutch and
English, when the seed of Christianity struck root among them,
mastered the first conditions of a full development of its grand
truths with the same solid earnestness, and carried their convictions out to the same practical result. Holland, indeed, has
been, not less than England, with England and for England, a
battle-ground of civil and religious liberty. The power of the
English character, and, therefore, of the literature that expresses
it, lies in this energetic sense of truth, and this firm habit of
looking to the end. Christianity having been once accepted,
aided as it was greatly in its first establishment among us by
zeal of the Gael and Cymry, the First English writers fastened
upon it, and throughout the whole subsequent history of our
literature, varied and enlivened by the diverse blending of the
races that joined in the forming of the nation, its religious
energy has been the centre of its life.

9. Cædmon's Paraphrase, written certainly during Abbess
Hilda's rule over Whitby, between 657 and 680, was probably
being produced during the last ten years of her life, or between
the years 670 and 680. Aldhelm, born in 656, was then a
youth, well-born, and well-taught by the learned Adrian, spending alike his intellectual and his material wealth at Malmesbury
for the love of God. In Cædmon's time, in the year 672,

Aldhelm, a youth of sixteen, joined the poor monastery which had been founded by a Scot more learned than rich, named Meldum, after whom the place had its name of Meldum's Byrig, or Malmesbury. The place was so poor that the monks had not enough to eat. Aldhelm obtained a grant of the monastery, rebuilt the church, gathered religious companies about him, and inspired in them his zeal for a pure life. He was a musician and a poet; played, it is said, all the instruments of music used in his time. His letters, and his Latin verse, chiefly in praise of chastity, survive, but those English songs of his which were still on the lips of the people in King Alfred's day are lost to us. William of Malmesbury has recorded, on King Alfred's authority, that Aldhelm was unequalled as an inventor and singer of English verse; and that a song ascribed to him, which was still familiar among the people, had been sung by Aldhelm on the bridge between country and town, in the character of an English minstrel or gleeman, to keep the people from running home directly after mass was sung, as it was their habit to do, without waiting for the sermon. Another story is, that on a Sunday, at a time when many traders from different parts of the country came into Malmesbury, Abbot Aldhelm stationed himself on the bridge, and there, by his songs, caused some of those who would have passed to stay by him and, leaving their trade until the morrow, follow him to church.

10. **Bede**, born in 673, was a child in arms when Cædmon sang the power of the Creator and his counsel, and the young Aldhelm had begun his work at Malmesbury. When seven years old—that is to say, about the time of the death of Abbess Hilda—Bede was placed in the newly-founded monastery of St. Peter, at Wearmouth. Three years later the associated monastery of St. Paul was opened at Jarrow, on the banks of the Tyne, about five miles distant from St. Peter's. Bede, then aged ten, was transferred to the Jarrow monastery. There he spent his life, punctual in all formal exercises of devotion, and employing his whole leisure, pen in hand, for the advancement of true knowledge. He digested and arranged the teaching of the fathers of the Church, that others might with the least possible difficulty study the Scriptures by the light they gave. He produced, in a Latin treatise on *The Nature of Things*, a text-book of the science of his day, digested and compacted out of many volumes. His works are almost an encyclopædia of the know-

ledge of his time. He drew it from many sources, where it lay
hidden in dull, voluminous, or inaccessible books, and he set it
forth in books which could be used in the monastery schools, or
be read by the educated for their own further instruction. The
fame of the devout and simple-minded English scholar spread
beyond our shores. A pope in vain desired to have him brought
to Rome. He refused in his own monastery the dignity of abbot,
because "the office demands household care ; and household
care brings with it distraction of mind, which hinders the pursuit of learning." He was thus at work in his monastery, thirty-
six years old, at the time of the death of Aldhelm.

It was in those days that Roderick the Goth lost Spain to
the Arabs.

In 731, when in his fifty-ninth year, Bede finished the most
important of his works, that known as his *Ecclesiastical History.*
That History of the English Church was virtually a History of
England brought down to the date of its completion, and based
upon inquiries made with the true spirit of a historian. Bede did
not doubt reported miracles, and that part of the religious faith
of his time supplies details which we should be glad now to exchange for other information upon matters whereof he gives too
bare a chronicle ; but, whatever its defects, he has left us a
history of the early years of England—succinct, yet often warm
with life ; business-like, and yet child-like in its tone ; at once
practical and spiritual, simply just, and the work of a true scholar,
breathing love to God and man. We owe to Bede alone the
knowledge of much that is most interesting in our early history.
Where other authorities are cited, they are often writers who,
on the points in question, know no more than Bede had told them.
Bede died in the year 735, three years after the completion
of his History. He wrote in Latin, then the language of all
scholars ; but in his last days, under painful illness, he was
urging forward a translation into English of the Gospel of St.
John. One of his pupils said to him, when the end was near,
"Most dear master, there is still one chapter wanting ; do you
think it troublesome to be asked any more questions?" He
answered, "It is no trouble. Take your pen and make ready,
and write fast." Afterwards, says the pupil, who gave, in a
letter that remains to us, the narrative of Bede's last days,
when the dying scholar had been taking leave of his brethren
in the monastery, and bequeathing among them his little wealth
of pepper, napkins, and incense, "the boy said, 'Dear master,

there is yet one sentence not written.' He answered, 'Write quickly.' Soon after the boy said, 'The sentence is now written.' He replied, 'It is well. You have said the truth. It is ended. Receive my head into your hands, for it is a great satisfaction to me to sit facing my holy place, where I was wont to pray, that I may also sitting call upon my Father.' And thus on the pavement of his little cell, singing 'Glory be to the Father, and to the Son, and to the Holy Ghost,' when he had named the Holy Spirit he breathed his last, and so departed into the heavenly kingdom."

11. The year of the death of Bede, 735, is the supposed date of the birth of **Alcuin**. Alcuin was bred from infancy in the monastery of York. He was there in the time of Egbert, who, in 735, received the pall as second Archbishop of York, and who is said to have founded in York monastery the famous school in which Alcuin was taught. The fame of the York school and library spread to the court of Charlemagne. Noble youths came from afar to be taught theology by Egbert, and other knowledge by his vice-master Albert who in the year 766 succeeded him in the archbishopric. Albert, with Alcuin's help, increased the fame of the school, and continued to be zealous beyond all others for the enrichment of the library. During the fourteen years of the archbishopric of Albert, Alcuin had in the York monastery immediate charge over the school and library. What he learnt from the books he told in his own words to his pupils, and with some of the best of them he established life-long friendships. One of his friends and pupils, Eanbald, in 780 became Albert's successor in the archbishopric. Alcuin had once been to Rome with Albert on a search for books ; now he was sent again, that he might use the opportunity of a mission to fetch the archbishop's pall, and bring with it more books to the York library. Thus Alcuin chanced to be, in 781, at Parma when Charlemagne was passing through that town on the way home from the crowning of his infant son Louis, afterwards Louis le Débonnaire, as King of Aquitaine, and of his second son, Pepin, as King of Lombardy.

Alcuin then was, what Bede had been, the foremost scholar of his time, and Charlemagne sought aid from him as an intellectual ally. He invited Alcuin to his court, where in the winter, when fighting was not in season, Charlemagne studied himself and compelled all his family to study, and whence he would compel his people also to receive instruction under Alcuin's directions. Having returned to York and obtained leave of absence from his superior, Alcuin went, therefore, in 782, to the court of Charlemagne, and took with him some of his best pupils as assistants. In the empire of Charlemagne his work was virtually that of a Minister of Public Instruction, the emperor supporting with despotic power every act of his for the establishment of well-disciplined schools throughout the land. There was also Charlemagne's own Palace School, which some believe to have been the germ of the first university, that of Paris. But 1215 is the date of the earliest record of a place of education called the University of Paris, and Alcuin went to the court of Charlemagne in the year 782. He remained with Charlemagne eight years, and then returned to York; Charlemagne, who had sought to retain him, still maintaining direct relations by investing Alcuin with the office of ambassador to Offa, King of Mercia. After a stay of not quite two years in England, Alcuin returned in the year 792, and spent the rest of his life in the service of Charlemagne, as faithful friend to him and to his empire. Wealth and power were at Alcuin's disposal, but he spoke of himself as "the humble Levite," and was single-hearted in austere performance of his duty. He was strict in discipline, and faithful in counsel to his headstrong master, as his extant correspondence shows. In his theological writing, Alcuin chiefly occupied himself with attack on heresy; but he wrote also text-books to provide means for efficient teaching in his schools, and he was energetic in repression of the love of wine and of the chase that had defied Church discipline.

The scriptorium, or writing-room in the monastery—which once was what the printing-office is to us—Alcuin developed with an energy that ensured rapid multiplication of good books. The hunting monks were bribed to industry by being allowed to chase as many beasts as would yield skins to meet the demand from the scriptorium for parchment. Wine-bibbing monks were told that it was better to copy books than to tend vineyards, by as much as reading lifted the soul higher than wine. But the books to be copied must be those which directly sought to raise men to a contemplation of the God of Christians. As a youth at York, Alcuin had hidden Virgil under his pillow from the eyes of the brother who came with a cane to rouse the sleepers to nocturns; in his later years Alcuin could see in Virgil no more than a heathen liar. "The good monk," he said, "should find enough to content him in the Christian poets." Throughout

Alcuin's writings, which include 232 letters, and some inscriptions, epigrams, and poems, there is a hard sense of duty for the
love of God, but there is little liveliness of fancy.  He was a
thoroughly practical man, who carried into the empire of Charlemagne the same administrative ability which he had shown as
schoolmaster and librarian in the monastery of York, labouring
always with all his powers to bring men to knowledge, that they
might come near to God.   He worked on difficult material, a
fact which may account for some of his severity ; and when he
died, in 804, he was in some trouble with his imperial master for
misconduct of the monks in his own abbey of St. Martin's, at
Tours.

12. Meanwhile, the spirit of the people was expressed also in
song.  Apart from " Beowulf," and Cædmon's " Paraphrase,"
each existing in a single manuscript, the main body of the
First English poetry that has come down to us has been preserved
in two collections, known as the *EXETER BOOK* and the *VERCELLI
BOOK.*  Each is named from the place where it was found.  The
Exeter Book is a collection of poems given, with other volumes,
to the library of his cathedral by Leofric, Bishop of Exeter,
between the years 1046 and 1073.  The other volume was discovered in 1823, in a monastery at Vercelli, in the Milanese,
where it had been mistaken for a relic of Eusebius, who was
once Bishop of Vercelli, and died in 371.

Among the pieces in these volumes are three of considerable
length, by a poet named **Cynewulf.**  His name comes down to
us, because he had a peculiar way of distributing the letters of it
among the verses in some part of each of his poems.  In the
Vercelli Book is Cynewulf's *Elene*, a poem of 2,648 lines, on the
legend of St. Helen, or the Finding of the True Cross by the
mother of Constantine.  In the Exeter Book we have Cynewulf's
legend of *Juliana*, martyr in the days of Emperor Maximian,
and a series of poems which have unity among themselves, and
have been read as a single work, Cynewulf's *Christ.*  Cynewulf
deals with Scripture history and legend in a devout spirit, and
his poems are interesting, although their earnestness is not
quickened by any touch of genius.  He was probably, as Jacob
Grimm suggests, a Cynewulf, Bishop of Lindisfarne, who died in
the year 780 ; certainly of that century, and not Cynewulf,
Abbot of Peterborough, who died Bishop of Winchester in 1008.

Among other poems in the two collections we have in the
Exeter Book the *Traveller's Song*, which is sometimes thought

to be the oldest of First English poems. In it Widsith names the places through which he has wandered. He has witnessed the wars of an Ætla. Some say that this means Attila, the Hun. Another interpretation places the scene of the wandering in our own country, between the years 511 and 534. The Exeter Book contains also the legend of *St. Guthlac*, and a poem on the myth of *The Phœnix*, as an allegory of the life of the Christian; another of its poems is a fable of *The Panther*, applied to the resurrection of our Lord, and another is of *The Whale*, who attracts fishes by sweet odour from his mouth, " then suddenly around the prey the grim gums crash together. So is it to every man who often and negligently in this stormy world lets himself be deceived by sweet odour. . . Hell's barred doors have not return or escape, or any outlet for those who enter, any more than the fishes, sporting in ocean, can turn back from the whale's grip." The jaws of the whale were the accepted symbol of the mouth of hell. They stand for that in tenth century pictures which adorn the manuscript of Cædmon. In later years we still find them so accepted in the scenery of the miracle plays.

This method of reading natural history into religious parable occurred in scattered passages of many early fathers of the Church. By degrees a fixed association was established between the asserted properties of certain animals and the religious meaning given to them, and the collection of such parables into a religious manual of natural history was made at an early date in the Eastern Church, under the name of *Physiologus*. There was a Physiologus denounced as heretical by a council held in the year 496. Fisolog, or Physiolog, came to be quoted as man or book, and we have it as a book in Latin manuscripts of the eighth century. Out of this form of literature sprang the Bestiaries of the Middle Ages.

*An Address of the Soul to the Body*, a poem on *The Various Fortunes of Men*, *Proverbs*, and (Cynewulf's) *Riddles*, were also among the inventions copied into the Exeter Book. The collection includes a few pieces not exclusively devotional, and it represents in fair proportion the whole character of First English poetry. Since it was produced by an educated class, trained in the monasteries, the religious tone might be expected to predominate even if this were not also the literature of a religious people. The domestic feeling of the Teuton is tenderly expressed among these poems in a little strain from shipboard on the happiness of him whose wife awaits on shore the dear bread-winner, ready to wash his travel-stained clothes and to clothe him anew by her own spinning and weaving.

In the Vercelli Book, beside Cynewulf's *Helen*, there is a still longer legend of *St. Andrew*, with a *Vision of the Holy Rood*, the beginning of a poem on *The Falsehood of Men*, a poem on *The Fates of the Apostles*, and two *Addresses of the Soul to the Body*, one corresponding to that in the Exeter Book. . Such poems, in which the Soul debates with the Body as chief cause of sin, remained popular for centuries.

13. Among the remains of First English poetry, outside the Exeter and the Vercelli Book, the most interesting of those which seem to have been produced before the end of the eighth century is a fragment of old battle-song, known as *The Fight at Finnesburg*, discovered in the seventeenth century by Dr. George Hickes, on the cover of a manuscript of Homilies in Lambeth Palace ; also a fine fragment of a poem on *Judith* in the same manuscript which contains Beowulf. Along the margin of a volume of Homilies in the Bodleian Library there is written also a fragment of a gloomy poem on *The Grave.*

14. When Alcuin died, in the year 804, the blending of the elements which were to build up a strong nation had advanced almost to the fusion of states into a single kingdom, with the name of England. The spirit of liberty had from oldest times been common to the Celt and Teuton. When Lucan, who lived in the first century, sang of the liberty, and with that the great-ness, of Rome lost at Pharsalia, he said—

> "That liberty, ne'er to return again
> And flying civil war, her flight has ta'en
> O'er Tigris and the Rhine : and can be brought
> No more, though with our bloods so often sought.
> Would we had ne'er that happiness possessed
> Which Scythia and Germany has blest !
> (*Book. VII. May's Translation.*)

But the steady spirit of association which knits men together for the creation and maintenance of a free state against all adverse influences from without or .from within, that was espe-cially the contribution of the Germans to our strength. Their name of Germans meant "brothers-in-arms." Tacitus, when he described their customs at the end of the first century, told how among them the young member of a household was advanced, when able to bear arms, into the rank of member of the Commonwealth : how chiefs deliberated about minor matters, but about the more important the whole tribe; though when the final decision rested with the people, the affair was always thoroughly discussed before them by their chiefs. There is the germ here of Parliamentary government; and the true home life, from which national life draws its strength, was indicated in the respect of the Germans for their women. " Almost alone among the barbarians," said Tacitus, "they are content with one wife. No one in Germany," he added, with a bitter thought of Rome, "no one in Germany laughs at vice, nor do they call it the fashion to corrupt and be corrupted." The first suggestion even of the spirit which led the Church Reformation of an after age is to be found when Tacitus says of the old German tribes that they " do not consider it consistent with the grandeur of celestial beings to confine the gods within walls, or to liken them to the form of any human countenance. They consecrate woods and groves, and they apply the names of deities to the abstraction which they see only in spiritual worship." Of a mind so characterised in its days of heathendom we have traced the later forms through " Beowulf," Cædmon's " Paraphrase," and other verses, and through the work of Bede and Alcuin, to the time when distinct communities are about to join in regarding England as their common country.

15. But they owed much to the fervour of the Celt. **Dicuil,** an Irish monk, who, in the year 825, at the age of seventy, wrote a Latin description of the earth, says he had spoken with Culdees, or Celtic missionary priests, whose zeal penetrated beyond the Faroes to distant Iceland.

The livelier genius, also, of the Celt, with its audacity of thought, is shown by the writer who best represented English intellect in the generation after Alcuin. This was **John Scotus Erigena,** whose names of Scot and of Erigena—whether that mean born in Erin or in Ayrshire—indicate with the form of his genius that Celtic blood flowed in his veins. He lived at the court of Charlemagne's grandson, Charles the Bald, King of France, who looked upon him as a miracle of wit and wisdom. He was a little man, and once, when he sat at dinner between two very fat monks, the king sent a dish from his own table of three fishes, one large and two small, which he was to share equally with his two neighbours. He gave to each of the fat monks a little fish, and took the big fish for himself. " That is not equal division," said the king. " It is," said Erigena. " There is a little one for a big one, there is a little one for a big one, and I'm a little one for a big one." Such stories indicate lively familiarity of intercourse between the king and the philosopher. Erigena was distinguished for his knowledge of Greek, and he translated for Charles into Latin certain works ascribed to Dionysius the Areopagite, a traditional convert of St. Paul's, and first Bishop of Athens. These were mystical, half Platonic writings, first produced at an Eastern Church conference in the year 532, and there used to support opinions which the theologians of the Western Church denounced as heretical as soon as Erigena's translation made the nature of the teaching known. Erigena produced also a great work of his own in Latin *On the Division of Nature*, in the form of dialogue between pupil and master, which, placing reason higher than authority, set out with the doctrine that there is a perfect harmony between reason and revelation ; and that all philosophy tends to a knowledge of the unity of the Creator, in whom all things begin and end. Evil, Erigena taught, being the opposite to the eternal God, could not be eternal. " A vice," he said, " is a spoilt virtue that can have no separate existence." In eternal fire he saw a material adapta- tion of spiritual thought to the unstrengthed faith, and he idealised some parts of Old Testament story into spiritual symbols. The pure study of Plato, the quick fancy, the bold speculation, brought John Scotus Erigena within the censure of the Pope and of two councils ; but as long as Charles the Bald lived, there was shelter in his court. When Charles the Bald died, in 877, Erigena returned to England ; and it is said that, about the year 884, when he was teaching in the monastery at Malmesbury, his pupils attacked his theology by stabbing him to death with the pointed iron styles used for school writing.

16. About this time, perhaps, there was produced by a Celtic writer a Latin *History of the Britons*. In a prologue which began to appear before the twelfth century copies of the history, its author's name is said to be **Nennius.** Nothing is known of Nennius, and the date of his writing is variously inferred from internal evidence to have been 796, or 800, or 879, or 980. This history tells of the contests of the Britons with the Romans and the Saxons. It derives their name from Brutus, a Roman Consul, and it thus names King Arthur to recite his twelve great battles against the Saxons :—" There it was that the magnanimous Arthur, with all the kings and military force of Britain, fought against the Saxons. And though there were many more noble than himself, yet he was twelve times chosen their commander,

and as often conqueror." Here follow the old names of the places where the twelve battles were fought—1, at the mouth of the river Gleni ; 2, 3, 4, 5, by the river Dulas, in the region Linius ; 6, by the river Bassas ; 7, in the wood Celidon ; 8, near Gurnion Castle, where, it is said, Arthur bore the image of the Virgin on his shoulders ; 9, at Caer Leon ; 10, by the river Trat Treuroit; 11, on the mountain Breguoin ; and, 12, a severe battle in which Arthur penetrated to the hill of Badon (Bath ? Badbury Hill, Dorsetshire ? Bowden Hill, on the Avon, near Linlithgow ?). " In this engagement," adds Nennius, " nine hundred and forty fell by his hand alone, no one but the Lord affording him assistance." No more is said about King Arthur in this early history, and when he is there spoken of it is in association with the year 452. The history of Nennius was ascribed in some manuscripts to Gildas, in whose name there remains a slighter British chronicle, and who is said to have been a fellow pupil of Llywarch Hen, and a brother of Aneurin. But the writer of this chronicle or *The Subjection of Britain* was evidently not one of the Cymry ; he speaks of them with contempt, under the cloak of brotherly reproof. He was a monk of Teutonic race, who lived before the writer of that history ascribed to Nennius in which King Arthur is first mentioned. The two chronicles differ much in spirit, and cannot be by the same writer. In Gildas, who has been sometimes confounded with Nennius, there is no mention of Arthur. But the history of Nennius has some importance in our literature, as evidence that a tradition of King Arthur and his twelve great battles was extant among us in King Alfred's time.

17. In the year of the death of Erigena, 884, Alfred was king of England ; indeed, it is he who is said to have invited Erigena back to his own country. When Alfred became king, in 871, the same races which, by their settlements three or four centuries earlier had laid the foundations of England, were again descending on the coasts of the North Sea and the Atlantic. They spread their ravages from Friesland to Aquitaine, and pushed inland by way of the Rhine, the Seine, the Loire, and the Garonne. In England they were called the Danes, in France the Normans. In 845 Regner Lodbrok and his Danes entered Paris, and took for ship's timber the beams of the church of St. Germain-des-Prés. These bold seafarers had long occupied Shetland, Orkney, and the Hebrides, and formed settlements in Ireland, which in 852 obeyed a chief of their own, who ruled in Dublin. There were minor chiefs of the same race ruling in

Waterford and Limerick. In 860 one of the northern Vikings, on his way to the Faroe Islands, discovered Iceland. In and after 870 Iceland was colonised by northmen of mark, whose power at home was being crushed by Harold Harfagr, then making himself paramount in Norway. These men took with them to Iceland the old language, customs, and traditions of their country, which have there suffered less change than on the mainland.

In the autumn of 866 the Danes occupied in strength part of our eastern coast, and in the following spring they plundered and burnt churches and monasteries of East Anglia. The Abbess Hilda's was among the monasteries burnt in 867, and it was then that a Danish settlement gave to the place, formerly called, from its sacred treasures, Streoneshalh, the name it has since borne—Whitby ; "by" being the commonest of those endings which denote a Danish settlement.

In 876, when our Alfred, aged twenty-seven, had been for five years an unlucky king, with Healfdene strong at the head of his Danes in the North of England, and Guthrum in the South, Rolf (called also Rollo and Rou) entered the Seine. He and his brother Gorm had, like others, contended with their own king at home. Gorm had been killed, and Rolf had gone into independent exile as a bold adventurer by sea. He had sought prizes in England and Belgium before he went up the Seine, and was then invited to take peaceful occupation of Rouen. In 879 King Alfred obtained peace by his treaty with Guthrum. Thirty-two years afterwards, in 911, the land of the Normans, afterwards called Normandy, was yielded to Rollo and his followers.

Thus we see that King Alfred in his struggle with the Danes was battling only with one part of a great movement akin to that which had first brought the English into Britain; and that the foundation of Normandy about ten years after King Alfred's death, is but another of its incidents, although an incident of first importance in the history of Europe.

18. **King Alfred** having secured some peace with the new settlers on his coast, proceeded to restore strength to his people with the help of the best advisers he could gather to his court. Churches and monasteries had suffered for their wealth, but their plunder and destruction meant also destruction of their schools. "There are only a few," said Alfred, "on this side of the Humber who can understand the Divine service, or even translate a Latin letter into English; and I believe not many on

the other side of the Humber either. They are so few, indeed, that I cannot remember one south of the Thames when I began to reign." Alfred re-established monasteries, and took pains to make them efficient centres of education for his people. Partly because the knowledge of Latin had to be recovered, partly because good knowledge is most widely diffused through a land when it is written in the language of the people, Alfred made, or caused to be made for him, translations of the books which had been most valued when they were among the Latin text-books of the days of Bede and Alcuin. One of these was *Bede's Ecclesiastical History*, or History of England, translated into English without any of the added information with which it could have been enriched. Perhaps a reverence for Bede's work caused Alfred to present it to his countrymen without change or addition.

The same feeling would not stand in the way of a free handling of the Universal History of *Orosius*. This had been the accepted manual in monastery schools for general history from the Creation to A.D. 416. Its author was a Spanish controversial Christian of the fifth century, and it was written at the suggestion of St. Augustine of Hippo. Augustine was himself writing "De Civitate Dei" to sustain the faith of Christians who had seen Alaric sack Rome, by showing from Church history that the preaching of the Gospel could not add to the world's misery. He suggested to Orosius, who just then came to consult him on some question of heresy, that he might show from profane history the same thing for the reassurance of the faithful. Orosius produced, therefore, in Latin, a dull book, written, as Pope Gelasius I. said, "with wonderful brevity against heathen perversions," and it became in the monastery schools the chief manual of universal history. King Alfred, in giving a free translation of it to his people, cleared the book of Church controversy, omitted, altered, and added, with the sole purpose of producing a good summary of general history and geography. He made these three special additions :—1. Much from the knowledge of his own time on the geography of Europe, which he called Germania, north of the Rhine and Danube. 2. A geographical sketch of two voyages : one from Halgoland on the coast of Norway, round the North Cape into the White Sea ; the other from Halgoland to the Bay of Christiania, and thence to Slesvig : these being taken from the lips of Ohthere, a rich Norwegian, who made voyages for love of adventure and discovery, for the

C

sake also of taking walrus and for whale-fishing. 3. A geographical sketch of a voyage in the Baltic from Slesvig to Truso in Prussia, taken from the lips of Wulfstan, who was perhaps a Jutlander, and who enriched his dry detail with a lively account of the manners and customs of the Esthonians.

King Alfred's other work in aid of a right knowledge of history was, probably, the establishment of that national record of events which was kept afterwards for a long time from year to year, and is now commonly known as the *Anglo-Saxon Chronicle.* It begins, after a brief account of Britain, with Cæsar's invasion; is in its earlier details obviously a compilation, and that chiefly from Bede, but begins to give fuller details after the year 853; and so, from a date within Alfred's lifetime, begins to take rank rank with Bede as one of the great sources of information on the early history of England. It may be supposed that, for the keeping of this annual record of the nation's life, local events were reported at the headquarters of some one monastery in which was a monk commissioned to act as historiographer; that at the end of each year this monk set down what he thought most worthy to be remembered, and that he then had transcripts of his brief note made in the scriptorium of his monastery, and forwarded to other houses for addition to the copies kept by them of the great year-book of the nation. Geoffrey Gaimar, writing in the twelfth century, says that King Alfred had at Winchester a copy of a chronicle fastened by a chain, so that all who wished might read. In some such way as this the Anglo-Saxon Chronicle was kept up until the time of the Norman Conquest, and for three generations after that. Its last record is of the accession of Henry II. in the year 1154.

King Alfred not only tried to make his countrymen acquainted with the world in which they lived, but he sought also to aid each in acquiring a firm rule over the world within himself. For this reason he turned into English the famous Latin work of *Boëthius,* the last man of genius produced by ancient Rome. Boëthius, a Roman senator, lost the favour of Theodoric by a love for his country, which his enemies called treason, was imprisoned, and from prison led to execution, about the year 525. In prison he wrote his noble work called *The Consolation of Philosophy,* in five books of prose, mixed with verse. The first of its five books recognised as the great source of consolation that a wise God rules the world; the second argued that man in his worst extremity possesses much, and ought to fix his mind on the imperishable; the third maintained that God is the chief good, and works no evil; the fourth, that, as seen from above, only the good are happy; and the fifth sought to reconcile God's knowledge of what is necessary with the freewill of mankind. The charm of a philosophic mind expressed through a pure strain of natural piety had made this dialogue between Philosophy and the Prisoner so popular that the Church justified its use of the volume in schools by claiming Boëthius as a Christian martyr. He was canonised as a saint in the eighth century, though in his book he turns from the depth of worldly calamity to explore all sources of true consolation, and does not name Christ. Alfred believed, as he was told, that Boëthius suffered as a Christian under Theodoric, and told it again when he gave the " Consolations of Philosophy" in English to his people.

King Alfred also, with the same desire to give men inward strength, translated into English a famous book by Pope Gregory the Great. This book, known as the " Regula Pastoralis," showing what the mind of a true spiritual pastor ought to be, was made English as *Gregory's Book on the Care of the Soul.* It is in the preface to this that King Alfred tells of the decay of learning in his kingdom, and of his desire for its true restoration.

19. We cannot know with certainty whether much of the work ascribed to King Alfred was done by his own hand, or whether he may rather be said to have encouraged, by strong fellowship in industry, the labours of those good men whom he gathered to his court, and who worked under his direction, giving and receiving counsel, for the furtherance of his most royal enterprise. What we do know with certainty assures us that, although King Alfred lived a thousand years ago, a thousand years hence, if there be England then, his memory will yet be precious to his country.

The oldest account of the *Life of Alfred* is that ascribed to his fellow-worker **Asser**, a Welsh monk of St. David's, who died Bishop of Sherborne. This Life comes down to us only in late manuscripts, with interpolations from a "Life of St. Neot," which probably was not written until sixty-four years after Asser's death. A manuscript as old as the tenth century existed until 1731, when it was burnt in the fire at the Cotton Library; but from printed references to its contents we learn that it did not contain those passages from the St. Neot's chronicle and idle legends which have caused some to deny that Asser could have been the writer of this Life. There are other reasons for believing

that what we now receive as a Life of Alfred by Asser, his friend
and fellow-worker, is really Asser's Life of him with later interpolations.

20. There is little to be said of our First English Literature
after the time of King Alfred. Ethelwold became in 947 a
monk at Glastonbury, when Dunstan, aged two-and-twenty,
was made abbot there. Dunstan and Ethelwold sought the
establishment of utmost strictness in monastic rule. Ethelwold
restored the decayed abbey at Abingdon, became in 953 Bishop
of Winchester, bought and rebuilt the ruins of Medeshamstead,
now called Peterborough, and rebuilt Winchester Cathedral.
Some fragments of First English in the chapter library at
Gloucester have been partly published in fac-simile as *Gloucester
Fragments*, and include a detail of miracles that preceded and
directed the dedication, by Archbishop Dunstan, of Ethelwold's
restored cathedral of Winchester to St. Swithin, who had been
Bishop of Winchester a hundred years before. In aid of his
own work as a Church reformer, Ethelwold translated into
English Benedict's *Rule of a Monastic Life*. Dunstan wrote
an adaptation of the same rule for the use of English monks,
and also a large *Commentary on the Benedictine Rule*, doubtless
from notes of the lectures given by him to his pupils in the
monastery schools.

21. No vigour of independent genius was developed by this
movement towards greater strictness of monastic rule. The
best intellectual effort among us in the century following the
death of Alfred took the same direction. Earnest and religious
men felt in their youth an enthusiasm stirred by the re-founding
of those monasteries in which they were trained ; and, looking
only to the farthest limit of their little world, they devoutly
sought to raise their country by putting purer and intenser life
into the men who were its teachers. But the nation was advancing, through much stir of blood, into a new age of its life,
and could be little helped by a fixed reproduction of past forms.

Alfred's grandson Athelstane, attacked by Danes from Ireland and Danes of the North of England, with allies from
among the Gael and Cymry, overcame his enemies in the year
937 at the great battle of Brunanburh, a place unidentified,
which may be Brunton, a few miles from Newcastle, by the
Roman wall. This victory over Anlaf the Dane from Ireland,
Constantine of Scotland, and Owen of Cumberland, caused the
writer of the national record for the year 937 to break into song.

The account given in the Anglo-Saxon Chronicle of *The Battle of Brunanburh* is a poem ; and a precedent having thus been established, scraps of verse of less mark occur now and then in the chronicle at the later dates 941, 942, 958, 973, 975, and 1002. Trouble with Danes continued, till there was more quiet in the reign of Edgar, who began to rule at the age of sixteen, and from the outset of his reign took Dunstan for chief counsellor. Edgar, therefore, supported the great efforts made for a revival of monasticism. He died in the year 975, after sixteen years of rule, and was called Lord of the whole Isle of Albion. Blending of all constituents of the great nation of the future was still going on. An England had been formed, and now came the foreshadowing of a Great Britain. The days of the first generations of English are therefore drawing to a close.

Meanwhile Denmark, Sweden, and Norway had grown also into compact powers, and in the reign of Ethelred the Unready England was not merely disturbed by the Danes settled on her shores, but had to face their power as invaders. In the year 994 they attacked Ipswich, ravaged the surrounding country, and were met unsuccessfully at Maldon in Essex by the patriotic bands which had been trained and led by Byrhtnoth, who fell in the battle. There remains to us, nearly complete, a First English poem on *The Battle of Maldon*, or, as it is also called, *The Death of Byrhtnoth*, warm with the generous love of independence, and yet simply honest in its record of defeat, through which we feel, as it were, the pulse of the nation beating healthily.

22. These were the days of outward tumult in which Ælfric wrote his Homilies. Ælfric was one of the first pupils of Ethelwold at Abingdon. When Ethelwold became Bishop of Winchester, Ælfric acted as chief of the teachers in his diocese, and wrote for the use of schools a lively little book of Latin *Colloquy*. It was afterwards enlarged and republished by Ælfric Bata, who had himself been taught Latin by it at Winchester. Latin being in his time, and long before and after, spoken and written as the common language of the learned, colloquy was a common way of teaching. Ælfric represents in his dialogue pupils, who beg to be taught, answering questions as to their respective trades; and thus he brings out in a few pages a very large number of words that would be used by them in talk over the daily business of life. Ælfric wrote also for his pupils a *Glossary* in Latin and English. He was removed from Winchester to the Abbey of Cerne in Dorsetshire by the wish of its founder, and there it

was that, at the request of the founder's son, Ælfric produced his *Homilies*, compiled and translated from the Fathers, in two sets each of forty sermons. The first set was completed in the year 990, and is a harmony of the opinions of the Fathers on all points of faith, as the English Church of his time accepted them. It was made public by the authority of Sigeric, then Archbishop of Canterbury. The other set tells of the saints whom the Church then revered. Ælfric also began a translation, in abridgment, of the Bible into English, and completed in this way the whole Pentateuch, as well as the Book of Job. About the year 1005 Ælfric became an abbot; and 1006 was the year of the death of Ælfric, Archbishop of Canterbury, with whom the Ælfric of literature has, by mistake, usually been identified.

23. Some months after the death of Ethelred, Canute King of Denmark was also King of England. A monk of Ely, who wrote, after 1166, a history of his church, records a scrap of song said to be of Canute's composing. When he was going by boat to Ely to keep a Church festival, he ordered his men to row slowly and near shore, that he might hear the psalms of the monks; then he called to his companions to sing with him, and invented on the spot a little song :

> "Merie sungen the Muneches binnen Ely
> Tha Cnut ching reu therby;
> Roweth cnites ner the land
> And here ye thes Muneches sang.
> (Pleasantly sang the monks in Ely
> When Canute the King rowed by;
> Row, boys, near the land,
> And hear ye the song of the monks).'

With other following words, said to have been still remembered and sung a hundred years after the Conquest.

Earl Godwin was a strong man in the days of Canute's two weak Danish successors; and after the death of Hardicanute, in 1042, he led the English party, and secured for his countrymen an English king in Edward the Confessor, who in 1045 married the great Earl's daughter Edith. The story of First English Literature ends with the work of an unknown writer, who knew intimately Harold and Tostig, who was a loving dependant on their sister Edith, by whom he had first been saved from want, and who wrote in Latin prose, intermixed with verse, a *Life of Edward the Confessor*, which he dedicated to his patroness when she was Edward's widow. This writer was an honest man and clever, with personal affection for Earl Godwin and his household added to his patriotic sympathies. He put his heart into a narrative of those events before the Norman Conquest in which Godwin and his sons Harold and Tostig were chief actors.

## CHAPTER III.

### TRANSITION ENGLISH.

1. DURING the four centuries from Cædmon to the Conquest, the language of books written in English may be said to have been fixed. Among the First English themselves, mixtures of race and tribe from the Continent varied in different parts of the country, and in each place the constituents and the proportions of the mixture were shown by the form of speech. Our provincial dialects were thus established. Then, as now, the spoken language of the country had its local differences, only more strongly marked than they now are; and the untaught multitude was careless about grammar, while the cultivated class, which produced books, maintained in them a standard of the language, being careful to preserve accuracy in use of inflexion, discrimination of gender, and upon all other such points. Even the vocabulary of First English literature remained for those four centuries very uniform; so that, with a few traces of provincialism which may point towards the birthplace of a writer, and perhaps some looseness of grammar towards the close of the period, during the four centuries of First English Literature all English thought written in English may be said to have come down to us in one language as fixed as that which we now speak.

But during the three centuries from the Conquest to the time of Chaucer there was continuous change. The language then was in transition to the later form, in which again it became fixed. In race the Normans were another combination of the English elements. Even the part of France on which they had established themselves was Teutonized before they came to it, for it was that which had in Cæsar's time a population traceable to a Teutonic immigration, and to which there had come in the fifth century the Franks—Teutons again. As far as concerned race only, there was quite as much of original kindred in the blood of those whom we call Normans and Saxons as between fellow-Englishmen now living in Yorkshire and in Hampshire. But the energetic Normans had been drawing, for the subsequent advantage of the world, their own separate lessons from the school of life. They had dropped in France their own language, their sons learnt speech of the mothers found in the new country, and when they first came over here as rulers, gave us kings who spoke only French; ecclesiastics whom their kings could trust, French-speaking abbots at the head of the monasteries, which were the only conservators of knowledge and centres of education; and French-speaking knights in their castles, as centres of influence among the native rural population.

French was the language of the ruling class in Church and State. Latin was used in books habitually, as the common language of the educated throughout Europe; the only language in which a scholar might hope to address not merely the few among a single people, but the whole Republic of Letters. English remained the language of the people, and its predominance was sure.

But there was no longer in the monasteries a cultivated class maintaining a standard of the language. The common people were not strict in care of genders and inflexions. Those new-comers who sought to make themselves understood in English helped also to bring old niceties of inflexion to decay. At the same time old words were modified, and some were dropped, when their places were completely taken by convenient new words that formed part of the large vocabulary wherewith our language was now being enriched. In large towns change was continuous and somewhat rapid; in country districts it was slow. Thus, while the provincial distinctions all remained, local conditions, here advancing there retarding the new movement, caused increase of difference between the forms of speech current in England at one time.

The books written in English during this transition period of the language are usually said to be in Early English. The Early English Text Society, by including Anglo-Saxon, or First English, among its publications, has wisely recognised the fact that English before the Conquest has as much right to be called Early as the English after it. We will take the name, then, as a good general term for the English of all books written before our language had in most respects attained its present form. If we give this sense to the current term of EARLY ENGLISH, there will be a natural division of the Early English period into its two parts ; and as we have spoken of *First English* (or Anglo-Saxon) Literature, we come now to speak of the literature of *Transition English.* Various suggestions have been made for the subdivision of this period. Sir Frederick Madden has called our language Semi-Saxon from 1100 to 1230, Early English only from 1230 to 1330, and Middle English from 1330 to 1500. It is better to shun vagueness. Having a piece of Transition English to place in its proper subdivision, we will therefore simply say that it is Transition English of the former or the latter half of such a century, or of a given date, if date can be more nearly given ; and that it is Northern, Midland, or Southern, or of a given county or town, if we can tell more nearly where its author wrote.

2. In the years next following the Conquest the chief authors were ecclesiastics, and their language Latin. The books were usually Chronicles and Lives of Saints ; but there was representation also of the love of travel, and already a faint indication of the new spirit of free inquiry that was to break the bonds of ancient science.

To the reign of William the Conqueror (1066—1087) belongs the History by **Marianus Scotus,** who was born in 1028, went to Germany in 1052, became a monk at Cologne, and died at Mayence in 1086. He compiled a *History* from the Creation to the year 1083. In the same reign a translation of *Lives of Native Saints* from First English into Latin was made by **Osbern** of Canterbury, who tells that he saw Canterbury Cathedral burnt in the year 1070; and a work was produced on the *Computus,* or Calculation of Easter, by **Gerland,** our earliest mathematician, who observed an eclipse of the sun in the year 1086.

During the reign of William II. (1087—1100), **Turgot,** who had assisted in the rebuilding of the ruined monastery of Jarrow, became prior of the greater monastery of Durham, to which Bede's twin monasteries of Jarrow and Wearmouth then became cells. Turgot's *History of the Monastery of Durham,* in four books, begins with its foundation, and passes into a vivid sketch of what he had himself seen of its history within the stir of his own time. It ends with the year 1096, and has been wrongly ascribed to Simeon of Durham.

3. In the reign of Henry I. (1100-1135), **Sæwulf,** a merchant, the first English traveller who followed in the track of

C *

the Crusaders, went to the East, escaped by accident from a
great storm at Joppa, which destroyed a thousand persons, and
lived to produce a lively record of all that he saw in Palestine
during the years 1102 and 1103. When he came home, Sæwulf
withdrew from the world, and became a monk of Malmesbury,
where the best of the chroniclers after Bede was then librarian.

Our Monastic Chronicles were at their best in Henry I.'s
reign. Then were produced the Chronicles of Ordericus Vitalis
and of William of Malmesbury. To record the deeds of the
history makers, sing the glories of their warrior chiefs, had
been a foremost occupation of the Celtic and First English bards
and gleemen. The history-making Normans gave from the first
much occupation for the pen of the good monk in his Scriptorium. In that room he copied the desirable things that were
not bought for the monastic library : works of the Fathers,
writings in defence of orthodox belief; a good book on the right
computation of Easter; a treatise on each of the seven steps of
knowledge which led up to Theology, namely, Grammar,
Rhetoric, and Logic, forming the Trivium of Ethics, with
Arithmetic, Geometry, Music, and Astronomy, the Quadrivium
of Physics. There would be need also of a fresher history than
Orosius could furnish. The framer of such a history might
begin with Adam, and cause any short sketch of the History of
the World from the Creation to be copied, or a larger history to
be reduced in scale. As he proceeded towards his own time, he
would give out now this now that accepted history of a particular period, to be copied literally or condensed. But when he came
down to a time within his own memory, or that of men about
him, he began to tell his story for himself, and spoke from living
knowledge ; from this point, therefore, his chronicle became for
after-times an independent record of great value. In days when
the strong sought conquest, and lands often changed masters,
the monasteries, with wide-spread possessions, had reason to
keep themselves well informed in the history-making of the
great lords of the soil. The Chronicle, which faithfully preserved
a record of events in the surrounding world during the years last
past, would be one of the best read and most useful books in the
monastic library. Monasteries were many, and the number also
of the chroniclers was great. In England they were usually men
whose hearts were with the people to which they belonged. Not
brilliant, like those chroniclers of France who gave their souls up
to outside enjoyment of court glitter and the pomp of war ; but

sober and accurate recorders of such matter as concerned realities of life, they saw in England the home of a people, not the playground of a king.

**Florence of Worcester** was a brother of the monastery in that town, where he died on the 7th of July, 1118. He wrote a *Chronicle*, which at first was a copy from that of Marianus Scotus, with inserted additions to enlarge the record of English events. His additions he took chiefly from the Anglo-Saxon Chronicle, Bede, Lives of Saints, and Asser's " Life of Alfred." From 1082, where Marianus Scotus ended, Florence continued the work on the same plan, noting events abroad, although chiefly concerned with English history. He brought his record down to 1117, the year before his death; and it was continued to 1141 by other brethren of his monastery.

**Eadmer,** one of the Benedictines of Canterbury, who says that from childhood he was in the habit of noting and remembering events, wrote, in six books, a History of his own Time—*Historia Novorum*—from the Conquest to the year 1122. Eadmer wrote also a life of his friend Anselm, Archbishop of Canterbury, and other ecclesiastical biographies. He was a bright enthusiastic churchman, who refused a bishopric in Scotland because he might not subject it to the Primacy of Canterbury. Archbishop Anselm is the central figure of his History.

But the chief chroniclers who wrote in the time of Henry I., and also during the first seven years of the reign of Stephen, were Ordericus Vitalis and William of Malmesbury. Orderic was by about twenty years the elder man, but as authors they were exactly contemporary, and they both ceased to write—probably, therefore, they both died—in the same year, 1142.

4. **Ordericus Vitalis,** born during the reign of William the Conqueror, near Shrewsbury, at Atcham on the Severn, was the son of Odelire, a married priest from Orleans, who had come over to England with Roger de Montgomery, made Earl of Shrewsbury. Orderic was the name given to the child by the English curate who baptised him. When Orderic was ten years old he had lost his mother, and his father retired, as a monk of the strict Benedictine rule, into a monastery which he had caused the earl to found. Half his estates Odelire gave to the abbey, and the other half as a fief to be held under the abbey by his second son, Everard, who remained outside in the world. Orderic was taken into the monastery with a father who soon found it to be too much indulgence of the flesh to have a

beloved child for his companion. Odelire sent him, therefore, a boy of eleven, to the Benedictine abbey of Ouche, buried among forests in Normandy, and known afterwards by its founder's name, as the Abbey of St. Evroult. There the child, in his twelfth year, received the tonsure on the day of the Feast of St. Maurice, and changed his lay name of Orderic for that of Vitalis, who was one of the two lieutenants of St. Maurice, named with him in the Church celebration of their martyrdom with the whole Roman legion under their command. Ordericus Vitalis spent all the rest of his life at St. Evroult, where there was a great library, as simply as the venerable Bede had spent his life at Jarrow. His work was an *Ecclesiastical History of England and Normandy*, in thirteen books. It begins with brief compilation, and becomes full from the year 1084, early in the seventh book. The first two books, written while Orderic was at work upon a later portion of his narrative, gave a compilation of Church History from the birth of Christ to the year 855; with the addition of a list of Popes from that date to the year 1142. The next four books, setting out with the foundation of monasteries in Normandy, are a history of the Abbey of St. Evroult, and of ecclesiastical affairs immediately concerning it. This was the part of the work first written. Then come the seven books (vii.—xiii.) which are now most to be valued, giving Orderic's conscientious and trustworthy, though confused record of the political events of his own time in Normandy and England. He is chronicler, not historian; shows no artistic faculty in the arrangement of his work. But it abounds in trustworthy suggestive facts, genuine copies of letters, epitaphs, and proceedings in council; shows good sense, as well as piety, in its judgments, and some skilful suggestion of character in the speeches which the author now and then attributes to his heroes. The time of Orderic's death is inferred from the date of the conclusion of his history, 1142, when he was sixty-seven years old.

5. The artistic faculty wanting in Orderic was not wanting in **William of Malmesbury**, who almost rose from the chronicler into the historian. He was born probably about the year 1095, and of his parents one was English and one Norman. He went as a boy into the monastery at Malmesbury, was known there as an enthusiast for books, sought, bought, and read them, and gave all the intervals between religious exercises to his active literary work. He was made librarian at Malmesbury, and would not be made abbot. Robert, Earl of Gloucester, that

natural son of Henry 1. who fought afterwards for his sister against King Stephen, was a man of refined taste, and, among our nobles, then the great patron of letters. To him William of Malmesbury dedicated his chief work, the *History of the Kings of England* (" De Gestis Regum"), as well as other writings. The History of English Kings is in five books, beginning with the arrival of the First English in 449, reaching to the Norman Conquest by the close of Book 2, giving the third book to William the Conqueror, the fourth to William Rufus, and the fifth to Henry I., as far as the twentieth year of his reign. Under a separate title, *Historia Novella*—Modern History—William, at the request of Robert of Gloucester, continued his record of current events, in three short books, to the year 1142, where he broke off in the story of his patron's contest with King Stephen at Matilda's escape over the ice from Oxford to Wallingford. " This," he said, " I purpose describing more fully if, by God's permission, I shall ever learn the truth of it from those who were present." As he wrote no more, the time of William of Malmesbury's death is inferred from the date of the conclusion of his history, 1142, when his age was about forty-seven. So able a scholar had, of course, many commissions from the other monasteries to produce Lives of their Saints. He wrote also in four books a *History of the Prelates of England*—" De Gestis Pontificum."

6. We have interesting evidence of the impulse given by the Arabs to the advance of Science, in the literature of this country during the reign of Henry I. The old school may be said to be represented by continued work on the calculation of Easter, and in 1124 **Roger Infans,** who says that he was then very young, produced a *Computus*, following and connecting that of Gerland. The new school is now represented in its first faint dawn by **Athelard of Bath,** born some time in the reign of William the Conqueror. He studied at Tours and Laon, taught at Laon, and went eastward; made his way to Greece and Asia Minor, perhaps even to Bagdad; and coming home to England in the reign of Henry I., on his way home taught the Arabian sciences, which he then discussed in a book of *Questions in Nature*—" Quæstiones Naturales". In this book Athelard represented himself, on his return to England, hearing from his friends their complaint of " violent princes, vinolent chiefs, mercenery judges," and more ills of life. These ills, he said, he should cure by forgetting them, and withdrawing his mind to the

study of Nature. His nephew, interested also in the causes of things, asked Athelard for an account of his Arabian studies, and the book was his answer. He had left his nephew, seven years ago, a youth in his class at Laon. It had been agreed then that the uncle should seek knowledge of the Arabs, and the nephew be taught by the Franks. The nephew doubted the advantage of his uncle's course of study. What could he show for it? To give proof of its value, Athelard proceeded to results: "And because," he said, "it is the inborn vice of this generation to think nothing discovered by the moderns worth receiving; whence it comes that if you wish to publish anything of your own you say, putting it off on another person, It was Somebody who said it, not I—so, that I may not go quite unheard, Mr. Somebody is father to all I know, not I." He then proposed and discussed sixty-seven Questions in Nature, beginning with the grass, and rising to the stars, the nephew solving problems in accordance with the knowledge of the West, the uncle according to knowledge of the East, where the Arabians were then bringing a free spirit of inquiry to the mysteries of science. Athelard of Bath wrote also on the Abacus and the Astrolabe, translated an Arabic work upon Astronomy, and was the first bringer of *Euclid* into England by a translation, which remained the text-book of succeeding mathematicians, and was among the works first issued from the printing-press.

7. Athelard of Bath expressed his love of science in a little allegory, *De Eodem et Diverso*—"On the Same and the Different" —published before 1116. The taste for allegory was now gathering strength in Europe. It had arisen in the early Church, especially among the Greek Fathers, with ingenious interpretation of the Scriptures. Bede, following this example, showed how in Solomon's Temple the windows represented holy teachers through whom enters the light of heaven, and the cedar was the incorruptible beauty of the virtues. When the monasteries passed from their active work as missionary stations into intellectual strife concerning orthodoxy of opinions, volleys of subtle interpretation and strained parallel were exchanged continually by the combatants. As the monasteries became rich, wealth brought them leisure and temptation of the flesh, but still they were centres of intelligence; and as, in Southern Europe, along the coasts of the Mediterranean, contact with tuneful rhyming Arabs was awakening a soft strain of love music, the educated men of leisure in the monasteries must also exercise their skill

Love, it was said, after the Arabs, is the only noble theme of song. We also, said the church-bound, obey poet's law and sing of love; but when we name a lady we mean Holy Church, or we mean the Virgin, or we mean some virtue. It is earthly love to the ear, but there is always an underlying spiritual sense. Thus we shall find, in a few generations more, the taste for allegory colouring almost the whole texture of European literature, and then remaining for a long time dominant. Athelard's little allegory is the first example in our literature of what afterwards became one of the commonest of allegoric forms. He represents Philosophy and Philocosmia, or love of worldly enjoyment, as having appeared to him, when he was a student on the banks of the Loire, in the form of two women, who disputed for his affections until he threw himself into the arms of Philosophy, drove away her rival with disgrace, and sought the object of his choice with an ardour that carried him in search of knowledge to the distant Arabs.

8. We now pass from the literature of the reign of Henry I. to that of Stephen (1135—1154), remembering that the last seven years of the work of Ordericus Vitalis and William of Malmesbury, and some years of the work of Athelard of Bath, fall within Stephen's reign. Five years after Orderic and William of Malmesbury had ceased to write, **Geoffrey of Monmouth** completed his Latin *History of British Kings*. The patron of William of Malmesbury was the patron also of Geoffrey of Monmouth; the "History of the Kings of England" and the "History of British Kings" are both dedicated to Robert Earl of Gloucester. In one of these works William of Malmesbury brought chronicle writing to perfection; in the other Geoffrey of Monmouth produced out of the form of the chronicle the spirit that was to animate new forms of literature, and opened a spring of poetry that we find running through the fields of English Literature in all after time.

Geoffrey was a Welsh priest, in whom there was blood of the Cymry quickening his genius. He had made a translation of the *Prophecies of Merlin*, when, as he tells us, Walter Calenius, Archdeacon of Oxford, found in Brittany an ancient History of Britain, written in the Cymric tongue. He knew no man better able to translate it than Geoffrey of Monmouth, who had credit as an elegant writer of Latin verse and prose. Geoffrey undertook the task, and formed accordingly his History of British Kings in four books, dedicated to Robert Earl of Gloucester.

Afterwards hè made alterations, and formed the work into eight
books ; to which he added Merlin's Prophecies, translated out
of Cymric verse into Latin prose.  The History, as finally completed by him in 1147, is in twelve books, and the whole work was
a romance of history taking the grave form of authentic chronicle.
Geoffrey closed his budget with a playful reference to more exact
historians, to whom he left the deeds of the Saxons, but whom
he advised "to be silent about the kings of the Britons, since
they have not that book in the British language, which Walter,
Archdeacon of Oxford, brought out of Brittany."  There is a sly
vein of banter in this reference to the mysterious book upon
which Geoffrey fathered his ingenious invention of a list of
British kings, who did wonderful deeds, gave their names to this
place and that, reigned each of them exactly so many years and
months, and made an unbroken series from Brut, great-grandson
of Æneas, through King Arthur to Cadwallo, who died in the year
689.  "It was Somebody who said it, not I."  We first read in
this fiction of Sabrina, "virgin daughter of Locrine;"of Gorboduc,
whose story was the theme of the earliest English tragedy; of
Lear and his daughter ; and, above all, of KING ARTHUR as the
recognised hero of a national romance.  Geoffrey obtained the
by-name of Arturus, and was said to have "made the little finger
of his Arthur stouter than the back of Alexander the Great."
So wrote a painstaking unimaginative chronicler of the next
generation, William of Newbury, who considering "how saucily
and how shamelessly he lies almost throughout," and not caring
to specify "how much of the acts of the Britons before Julius
Cæsar that man invented, or wrote from the inventions of others
as if authentic," said of Geoffrey, "as in all things we trust Bede,
whose wisdom and sincerity are beyond doubt ; so that fabler
with his fables shall be straightway spat out by us all."  Far
from it.  The regular chronicler was scandalised at the pretensions of a perfectly new form of literature, a work of fancy
dressed in the form of one of his own faithful records of events.
But the work stirred men's imaginations.  It was short as well as
lively, the twelve books being no longer than two of the thirteen
books of Orderic's Ecclesiastical History.  Short as it was,
**Alfred of Beverley,** charmed with it, in a copy which he had
with difficulty borrowed, at once made an abridgment of it,
because he had not time to copy all, or money to pay for a full
transcript.  In the household of Ralph Fitz-Gilbert, a strong
baron of the North, lived **Geoffrey Gaimar.**  Constance, the

baron's wife, could read no Latin, but desired to read the much-talked of chronicle. Gaimar undertook, therefore, to translate it for her into French verse, and made his translation perhaps from the book written by Geoffrey himself for his patron, since the copy used was obtained through a friendly Yorkshire baron from the Earl of Gloucester himself. Gaimar continued his chronicle, in French or Anglo-Norman verse,. by adding the series of Saxon kings; and this latter part of his work was all that survived when Wace's more popular version of the famous history into French verse for the use of the court, caused that of Gaimar to be neglected by the copyists.

**Wace** (who has been miscalled Robert Wace through a mis-understanding of five lines in his " Life of St. Nicholas") was born at Jersey, educated at Caen, and was a reading clerk and a romance writer at Caen in the latter part of Stephen's reign. He shared the enthusiasm with which men of bright imagina-tion received Geoffrey of Monmouth's Chronicle, and reproduced it as a French metrical romance, the *Brut*, in more than 15,000 lines. Sometimes he translated closely, sometimes paraphrased, sometimes added fresh legends from Brittany, or fresh inven-tions of his own. His work was completed in 1155, immediately after the accession of Henry II., who gave him a prebend at Bayeux. Wace afterwards amplified a Latin chronicle of the deeds of William the Conqueror, by William of Poitiers, that king's chaplain, into a *Roman de Rou*. But there was no con-tinuance of royal favour, and he died unprosperous in England, in 1184. He was eclipsed at court by Benoit de St. Maure, the author of the " Geste de Troie."

The Welsh priest whose bright invention had thus broken fresh ground in literature was made Bishop of St. Asaph six years after the appearance of his Chronicle. He died in 1154, about a year after he had obtained his bishopric.

9. It was in the time also of Stephen that there was an Englishman in France, **Hilarius**, who had gone to be taught by Abelard at Paraclete, and from whom we have our earliest known *Miracle Plays*. The acting of such plays seems to have been introduced into this country soon after the Conquest. Matthew Paris, a chronicler who lived in the thirteenth century, refers to a miracle-play of St. Katherine, written some years before 1119, by Geoffrey of Gorham, who became afterwards prior, and was in 1119 made Abbot of St. Alban's. Geoffrey had been invited from Normandy by Richard, the preceding abbot, to establish a

school at St. Alban's. He arrived too late, and settled at Dunstable, where there was a school subordinate to that of St.
Alban's, while waiting for the possible reversion of the office
which had then been given to another. Meanwhile he composed at Dunstable his miracle-play, and, when it was ready,
borrowed copes from St. Alban's for the decoration of it. But
on the following night his house was burnt, together with the
copes and all his books. This is the earliest allusion to the
acting of such pieces in this country. They had arisen out of
the desire of the clergy to bring leading facts of Bible history
and the legends of the saints home to the hearts of the illiterate.
A great church was dedicated to some saint. The celebration
of the saint's day was an occasion for drawing from afar, if
possible, devout worshippers, and offerings to the shrine. Some
incidents from the life of the saint, enforcing perhaps his power
to help those who chose him for their patron, it was thought
good to place, at some part of the Church service of the day,
with dramatic ingenuity, before the eyes of the unlettered
congregation.

Take, for example, one of the three plays by Hilarius,
written in France in the time of Stephen, or not later than the
beginning of the reign of Henry II. In a church dedicated to
*St. Nicholas,* upon St. Nicholas's Day, the Image of the Saint
was removed, and a living actor, dressed to represent the statue,
was placed in the shrine. When the pause was made in the service
for the acting of the Miracle, one came in at the church door
dressed as a rich heathen, deposited his treasure at the shrine,
said that he was going on a journey, and called on the Saint to
be the guardian of his property. When the heathen had gone
out, thieves entered and silently carried off the treasure. Then
came the heathen back and furiously raged. He took a whip
and began to thrash the Image of the Saint. But upon this the
Image moved, descended from its niche, went out and reasoned
with the robbers, threatening also to denounce them to the
people. Terrified by this miracle, the thieves returned trem-
blingly, and so, in silence, they brought everything back. The
statue was again in its niche, motionless. The heathen sang his
joy to a popular tune of the time, and turned to adore the
Image. Then St. Nicholas himself appeared, bidding the
heathen worship God alone and praise the name of Christ.
The heathen was converted. The piece ended with adoration
of the Almighty, and the Church service was then continued.

It was probably with such plays that the practice of acting in churches was begun by the clergy in France, where the delight in dramatic entertainment had remained strong since the Roman time. Against the theatres of failing Rome the early Fathers of the Church had battled as against idolatry These things, they said, have their rise from idols, and are baits of a false religion. The Roman stage fell into ruin ; but the dramatic instinct is part of man's nature. At the close of the second century Ezekiel, a tragic poet of the Jews, put the story of the Exodus into the form of a Greek drama. In the fourth century Gregory Nazianzen, as Patriarch of Constanti· nople, attacked the Greek theatre there flourishing by substituting for the heathen plays plays of his own on stories of the Old and New Testament. They were written to the pattern of those of Sophocles and Euripides, Christian hymns taking the place of the old choruses. In humbler fashion, prompted perhaps by the success of their miracle plays, well-meaning priests endeavoured, on those great days of the Church which commemorate the birth or death of our Lord, or any other of the sublimer mysteries of Christian faith, to bring forcibly before the very eyes of the congregation the events told in the Bible lesson of the day. When, in the course of the service, the time came for the reading of the Lesson, it was not read but realised within the church. Such a play was called, not a MIRACLE PLAY but a MYSTERY ; because it dealt not with the miracles of saints, but with the great mysteries of Christianity drawn from the life of Christ. In what way they were at first represented is shown clearly by that one of the three plays of Hilarius which happens to be not a miracle-play but a mystery. Its subject is the *Raising of Lazarus*—mystery of the resurrection of the dead. Its incidents having been realised to the utmost, and its dialogues set to popular tunes of the day, the officiating priest who, as Lazarus, has risen from the tomb, turns in that character to admonish the assembled people. He turns then to the representation of Jesus, whom he adores as master, king, and lord, who wipes out the sins of the people, whose ordinance is sure, and of whose kingdom there shall be no end ; and the closing direction of the author is, that " This being finished, if it was played at matins, Lazarus shall begin ' Te Deum Laudamus ;' but if at vespers, ' Magnificat anima mea Dominum ;'" and so the Church service proceeds. The last of the three plays by Hilarius was designed for a pompous Christmas

representation of the story of *Daniel*, and at its close the
Church service was to be continued by the priest who played
Darius. Such were the miracle and mystery plays written in
France by Hilarius, an Englishman, in or a few years after the
reign of King Stephen.

10. One other book written in Stephen's reign points also to
the future course of thought. This was a little treatise by
**Henry of Huntingdon**, entitled "De Contemptu Mundi"
(On Contempt of the World). Its author was the son of a
married clerk, and was trained in the household of a Bishop of
Lincoln, who remained his patron. He wrote verse and prose
on divers subjects, compiled a *Chronicle* in seven books, which
ended with the death of Henry I., and then added an eighth
book on the reign of Stephen. It was at the end of Stephen's
reign, when he was Prior of Huntingdon, that this busy writer
closed his career with a treatise *On Contempt of the World*,
addressed to the same friend Walter to whom his youthful
poems had been dedicated : "A youth to a youth I dedicated
juvenilities ; an old man to an old man I destine now the
thoughts of age." He recalled in this little book the friends
they had both lost. Men rich in luxury were gone, so were the
wise, so was the strong man who was cruel in his strength.
Of the great kings also who are as gods the lives are vanity
Men of great name were recalled and passed before the imagination in a spirit kindred to that of books of later time which
yielded Tragedies to dramatists when they arose.

11. We pass now from the reign of Stephen to the reign
of Henry II. (1154—1189), a time of great interest in the
early story of our literature. Throughout Europe there was
a new activity of thought among the foremost nations, and
that which was partly represented by the contest between
Henry and Becket was in the general life of the time. Contest
upon the limit of authority, which in its successive forms is the
most vital part of our own history, and has been essential everywhere to the advance of modern Europe, became active in many
places in the days of Henry II. As we shall find the course of
English Literature illustrating throughout a steady maintenance
of the principle out of which this contest arises, let us at once
settle the point of view from which it will be here regarded.

No two men think alike upon all points, and some part of
the difference is as distinctly natural as that which distinguishes
one man from another by his outward form and face. It is

part of the Divine plan of the world that we should not all have the same opinions. If we observe in one man the group of ideas forming his principles of thought, we find that they have well-marked characters, which are common to him and to many others. One might even imagine an arrangement of men by their way of thought, as of plants by their way of growth, into primary classes, sections, alliances, families, genera, and species. And as the two primary classes of the flowering plants are exogens and endogens, so the two primary classes of civilised men are (1) those in whom it is the natural tendency of the mind to treasure knowledge of the past, and shun departure from that which has been affirmed by wise and good men throughout many generations, those, in short, who find rest and hope of unity in the upholding of authority ; and (2) those in whom it is the natural tendency of the mind to claim free right of examining and testing past opinions, who seek the utmost liberty of thought and action, holding that the best interests of the future are advanced when every man labours for truth in his own way, and holds sincerely by his individual convictions. Look where we may, to parties in the Church, to parties in the State, or any chance knot of a dozen men collected at a dinner-party, the form of debate invariably shows this natural division of men's minds, serving its purpose for the thorough trial of new truth. No bold assertion is allowed to pass unquestioned. Whoever states a fact must also be prepared to prove it against ready opponents, who produce all possible grounds of doubt and forms of evidence against it. Thus men are trained in the right use of reason; their intellectual limbs gather strength by healthy exercise ; and wholesome truths come out of the ordeal, as the pure grain winnowed from the chaff. Instead of wishing that all men were of our minds, we should account it one of the first blessings of life that there are men who don't agree with us. The currents of the air and sea are not more necessary and more surely a part of the wise ordinance of the Creator than those great currents of thought which, with all the storms bred of their conflict, maintain health in man's intellectual universe.

When the millions lie in darkness and are thought for by the few, they need the guidance of an absolute authority. As the light grows on them, each becomes more able to help himself. External aids and restrictions become gradually less and less necessary ; exercise of authority falls within narrower limits, and exercise of individual discretion takes a wider range.

This constant readjustment of the boundary-line between individual right and the restraint of law must needs advance with civilisation, as keen intellectual debate prepares the way for every change. In England such a process has gone on so actively and freely that our political institutions, which have grown and are growing with our growth, are strong also with all our strength.

In the time of Henry II. the contest between the king and Becket represented what was then the chief point to be settled in the argument as to the limit of authority. It was a question of supremacy between the two great forms of authority to which men were subjected. Was the Church, representing God on earth, to be, through its chief, the pope, a supreme arbiter in the affairs of men—a lord of lords and king of kings? Or was the king alone supreme in every temporal relation with his subjects? Becket devoutly battled for supreme rule of the Church. Henry maintained the independence of his crown. That battle won, the next part of our controversy on the limit of authority would concern the relations between king and people. When Henry's cause was stained with the crime of Becket's murder, the Church had an advantage of which it understood the value. All that was done to make the shrine of the martyred Becket a place of pilgrimage and to exalt the saint was exaltation of the name inseparable from the cause of an unlimited Church supremacy.

After his murder, in 1170, *The Life of Thomas à Becket* was written by **William Fitzstephen,** a Londoner, who had been a trusted clerk in the Archbishop's household, and was witness to his death. Fitzstephen's life of Becket includes an interesting account of London as it was in Henry II.'s time, with incidental evidence of the growing interest in miracle-plays. London, he says, instead of the shows of the ancient theatre, "has entertainments of a more devout kind, either representations of those miracles which were wrought by holy confessors, or those passions and sufferings in which the martyrs so rigidly displayed their fortitude." It may be observed that Fitzstephen's definition of these entertainments limits them to the miracle-play; there is no reference to any acting of a mystery. When, afterwards, both forms were common, no distinction of name was made between them in this country. All were called miracle-plays; doubtless, because that name alone had become familiar during a long period, in which the only plays acted were miracles. Perhaps a sense of reverence delayed the introduction of the mystery.

12. Outside England the literature of Europe was now taking forms more and more representative of the advance of thought. There was what may be called a Court literature, concerned only with the pleasures of the rich; and there was a National literature, through which men, thinking with or for the people, showed their sense of life and its duties. The famous beast epic of "Reynard the Fox" and Isegrim the Wolf, still vigorous and fresh, first came into literature as a Flemish poem of "Reinaert" in the year 1150, or towards the close of the reign of Stephen. During the reign of Henry II. it was popular abroad as a keen satire from the side of the people on the current misuse of authority. The essence of the work in its first form, and in all early adaptations of it to other countries, was a homely spirit of freedom. The reign of Henry II. was also the time when the Germans gathered fragments of romance into their great national epic of the Nibelungen. It was at the close of the same period that the Spaniards poured out their national spirit in the poem of the Cid. Crusades had brought men into contact with the bright imagination of the East. Romances, brisk with action, were recited or sung to the Norman lords; and southern poets were taught by the Arabs to rhyme tunefully on love. The oldest extant troubadour verse dates from a year after the accession of King Henry II.; and his were the times in which were born the Suabian Minnesänger Hartmann von Aue and Walther von der Vogelweide. Their master, Barbarossa, was then bringing Germans into Italy, and forced the states of the Lombard League into that patriotic contest which, in 1182, left them free republics, with a nominal allegiance to the empire. In Italy the conflict was begun that should stir presently a mighty soul to song.

13. At home, in good harmony with the spirit of Reinaert, or Reineke Fuchs, we have, among the books written in Henry II.'s reign, the "Brunellus" of **Nigel Wireker.** Nigel Wireker was precentor in the Benedictine monastery at Canterbury, friend to William de Longchamp, afterwards Bishop of Ely, to whom he dedicated a treatise *On the Corruptions of the Church.* Wireker's minor writings were attacks upon self-seeking and hypocrisy among those who made religion their profession; for the movement towards reformation in the Church was now begun. Wireker's chief work, *Brunellus*, or

*Speculum Stultorum* (The Mirror of Fools), is a satirical poem in about 3,800 Latin elegiac lines, which has for its hero an Ass, who goes the round of the monastic orders. His name, Brunellus, a diminutive of Brown, is taken from the scholastic logic of the day. It was first applied to the horse when a particular idea—say this horse Brunellus—had to be discussed instead of the general idea,· represented, say, by horse. But when the logicians took to calling the particular idea Bucephalus, the old names of Brunellus and Favellus were transferred to the ass ; and a logician would write thus : " Grant there are two men, say Socrates and Plato, of which each has an ass ; precisely, Socrates Brunellus, Plato Favellus," and so forth. Taking the name of his hero, then, from the jargon of the schools he meant to satirise, Nigel Wireker represented that the Ass Brunellus found his tail too short, and went to consult Galen on the subject. The author explained that his " Ass is that monk who, not content with his own condition, wants to have his old tail pulled off, and try by all means to get a new and longer tail to grow in its place—that is to say, by attaching to himself priories and abbeys." Brunellus was unlucky with his medicines, and had part of his tail, short as he thought it, bitten off by four great mastiffs. He could not go home to his friends in that state. He felt that he had an immense power of patient labour. He would go and study at the University of Paris. After seven years of hard work there, he could not remember the name of the town in which he had been living. But he was proud of his erudition. He did also remember one syllable of the town's name, and had been taught that part may stand for the whole. The sketch of Brunellus at Paris is a lively satire upon the shortcomings of the schools. Brunellus having gone straight through the sciences, it was only left for him ιο perfect himself in religion. He tried all the orders in succession, and ended in the resolve to construct for himself out of them a new composite order of his own. Meeting Galen, Brunellus entered into discussion with him on the state of the Church and of society, until he fell into the hand of his old master, and returned to the true duties of his life.

14. Nigel Wireker did not fight unaided in this battle against the corruption which had come into the Church with wealth and idleness. A like battle formed part of the work of the man of greatest genius among those who wrote in the time of Henry II. This was **Walter Map**, sometimes called Mapes, because

the Latinised form of his name was Mapus. Walter Map had, like Geoffrey of Monmouth, Celtic blood in his veins. Born, about the year 1143, on the borders of Wales, he called the Welsh his countrymen, and England "our mother."

Map studied in the University of Paris, which was then in the first days of its fame. Students were gathered there from many lands ; English enough were among them to form one of the four schools into which it became divided. We know what it was from Wireker's "Brunellus;" and Map tells that he saw, when he was there, town and gown riots: but an ordinance of Innocent III., dated 1215, five-and-twenty years after the death of Henry II., is the first official document in which we find the body of teachers and students gathered in Paris to have been formally called a University. The first document which speaks formally of a University of Oxford is dated 1201; and the University of Cambridge first appears by that name in a document of the year 1223. At the time, therefore, of which we now speak. the Universities were first ceasing to be places in which individual teachers and students came together for their common advantage, and they were acquiring recognition of their corporate existence by the application to them of a name at first not limited to places of education, but applied also to other organised bodies, as to a corporate town, or to an incorporated trade within a town.

After his studies in Paris, Walter Map came home, and was at Court in attendance on King Henry II., who had received much good service from Map's family. In 1173, when his age was about thirty, Map was presiding at the Gloucester assizes as one of the king's ambulant judges, justices in eyre. In the same year he was with the court at Limoges, host, at the king's cost, to a foreign archbishop. He attended Henry II., probably as chaplain, during his war with his sons; represented the king at the court of Louis VII., where he was received as an intimate guest; was sent to Rome to the Lateran Council of 1179, and was hospitably entertained on the way by Henry Count of Champagne.

At that Council appeared some of the Waldenses, or followers of Peter Waldo, with a Psalter and several books of the Old and New Testament in their own tongue, which they wished the Pope to license. Although Map fought stoutly against fleshly corruption of the clergy, and was an earnest Church reformer, he was not advanced beyond the dread of danger from giving the Scriptures in their own tongue to the common people. "Water," he said, "is taken from the spring, and not from the broad marshes." But the question was so far new that this Council of 1179 did not interdict Peter Waldo's Bible. Waldo himself may be remembered as another sign of the growing life of Europe in the days of Henry II. After he had become rich, as a merchant of Lyons, he gave his goods to the poor, gathered followers about him as Poor Men of Lyons, who preached in the villages, opposing a simpler faith and purer rule of life to the corruptions of the Church, and labouring to give the Bible itself to the people as the one authority in matters of religion. Waldo died in 1179, the year of Map's attendance at the Council before which some of the Waldenses came to ask for the Pope's license to their translation of Scripture. The use of it was not forbidden until fifty years afterwards.

After his return from Rome, Map was made a canon of St. Paul's, and also precentor of Lincoln. He held also the parsonage of Westbury, in Gloucestershire, but still was in attendance on the king, and especially attached to the young Prince Henry, after he had been crowned by his father. In the reign of Richard I., and the year 1196, when his age was about fifty-three, Map was made Archdeacon of Oxford, but beyond that date nothing is known of him.

Walter Map was a bright man of the world, with a high purpose in his life; poet and wit, a spiritual man of genius. He fought with his own weapons against the prevalent corruption of the clergy. While he was at court, there began to pass from hand to hand copies of Latin verse purporting to be poems of a certain Bishop Golias, a gluttonous dignitary, glorying in self-indulgence, his name probably derived from gula, the gullet. The verses were audacious, lively, and so true to the assumed character that some believed them to come really from a shameless bishop. Here was the corruption of the Church personified and made a by-word among men. The poems gave a new word to the language—"goliard." Walter Map was the creator of this character; but the keen satire of his lively Latin verse bred imitators, and Father Golias soon had many sons. A fashion for Golias poetry sprang up, and then the earnest man of genius had fellow-labourers in plenty. In one of Map's poems, called the *Confession of Golias*, the bishop is supposed to be confessing himself with the candour of despair. He reveals first the levity of his mind; he who should make his seat upon a

rock is as a ship without a mariner, a lost bird borne through
pathless air.  He next declares his lust.  And then he remembers the tavern he has never scorned, nor ever will scorn till he
hears the angels sing his requiem.  Here Map, with a terrible
earnestness of satire, images the heavens opening upon the
drunkard priest, who lies in a tavern, where, too weak himself to
hold the wine-cup, he has it put to his lips, and so dies in his
shame.  "What I set before me," he says, "is to die in a
tavern; let there be wine put to my mouth when I am dying,
that the choirs of the angels when they come, may say, 'The
grace of God be on this bibber!'"

> *Meum est propositum in taberna mori,*
> *Vinum sit appositum morientis ori,*
> *Ut dicant cum venerint angelorum chori,*
> *Deus sit propitius huic potatori.*

Somebody having set these four lines to light music as a drinking
song, without a suspicion of their meaning, somebody else,
equally wise, has made them a reason for ticketing Walter Map
as "the jovial archdeacon."  Jovial, however, Walter Map may
have been, for he was keen of wit, and knew how to make a
light jest do the work of earnest argument.

15. Another of Map's books took one of the names of a work
written at the beginning of Henry II.'s reign by **John of
Salisbury**, a man of considerable learning, who was born
about the year 1120.  He also had studied at Paris.  He had
attended Abelard's lectures on Mont St. Geneviève, and was
fellow-pupil afterwards with Thomas à Becket under an English
pupil of Abelard's.  John of Salisbury studied on, and as he
advanced in knowledge, sought to make a living by the teaching
of young noblemen.  After twelve years of study and teaching,
he was a penniless scholar whom a kindly French abbot took
for his chaplain, and in about three years more, in 1151, was
able to help to the post of secretary to Theobald, Archbishop of
Canterbury.  When Becket became archbishop, John of Salisbury remained in office, and was his devoted follower.  He
shared Becket's exile, and narrowly escaped sharing his fate at
the assassination.  After this, John of Salisbury remained as
secretary with the next archbishop, and in 1176 was made Bishop
of Chartres, where he died in 1180.  John of Salisbury's book
was entitled *Polycraticus, or De Nugis Curialium et Vestigiis
Philosophorum* (On the Trifles of the Courtiers and Tracks of
the Philosophers).  It is in eight books, which were finished in

1156. The first treats with much erudition of the vanities of hunting, dice, music, mimes, minstrelsy, magic, soothsaying, and astrology, which his second book argues to be not always contemptible. In the third book he treats of flatterers and parasites, and then comes to the remarkable feature of his work, its argument for tyrannicide, which is scholastic altogether in its tone. The fourth book argues that it is only for the Church to say what tyrants shall be slain, and enters into learned disquisitions on the state and duties of a king. The fifth book treats of the king and great officials in their relation to the commonwealth. In his sixth book, John of Salisbury treats of the duties, privileges, and corruptions of the knights; and in the last two books follows the tracks of the ancient philosophers in discussing virtue and vice, true and false glory, with return at last to the doctrine of tyrannicide under the guidance of the Church. In its pedantic way, the "Polycraticus" is interesting as a clumsily aimed return shot in the controversy between Church and State, levelled at the corruption and levity of kings and courts, and claiming for the Church a power to destroy kings at discretion.

16. The second title of this book by John of Salisbury—*De Nugis Curialium* (On the Trifles of the Courtiers)—was that taken by Walter Map for a book of his own, which was very different in texture. He had been asked, he says, by a friend, Geoffrey, to write something as a philosopher and poet, courtly and pleasant. He replied that poetical invention needs a quiet, concentrated mind, and that this was not to be had in the turmoil of a court. But he did accept a lighter commission, and "would endeavour to set down in a book whatever he had seen or heard that seemed to him worth note, and that had not yet been written, so that the telling should be pleasant, and the instruction should tend to morality." His work, therefore, which is in five divisions, is a volume of trustworthy contemporary anecdote by the man who knew better than any other what was worth observing. There is no pedantry at all, no waste of words. There is not a fact or story that might not have been matter of table talk at Henry's Court. Anecdotes on subjects allied to one another are generally arranged together; but there is a new topic in every chapter, and the work is a miscellany rich in illustration of its time, and free enough in its plan to admit any fact or opinion or current event worth record. It includes bold speaking against crusading zeal, that left home duties unper-

formed ; against the vices of the court of Rome ; even against
that vice in the kings of England which caused their people to
be oppressed by unjust game-laws. Under this head King
Henry II. is himself the subject of a warning anecdote.

17. But Map's great work was that which justified his friend
Geoffrey in demanding of him " something as a philosopher and
poet." He it was who first gave a soul to the KING ARTHUR
legends, and from whom we date the beginning of a spiritual harmony between the life of the English people and the forms given
to the national hero by our poets. The Latin races have made
no such use of Charlemagne or Roland as we shall find the
English to have made of the King Arthur myth. The cycle of
the Charlemagne romances offers a wide field for study, bright
with life and colour derived from the active genius of the
*trouvères.* But these tales remain what those of the Arthurian
cycle were before the genius of Walter Map had harmonised
them with the spirit of his country. The Normans had brought
a song of Roland to the battle-field of Hastings, and it was
during the reign of our Henry I., that in 1122, Pope Calixtus II.
officially authenticated the Latin " Life of Charlemagne and
Roland," which was said to have been written by one of Charlemagne's companions, Turpin, who was Archbishop of Rheims
in the eighth century. This book, which became a source of
Charlemagne romance, and earned the title of " Le Magnanime
Mensonge," may possibly have been invented by the order of
the pope who guaranteed the authorship of Turpin. Its object
was to increase the number of the pilgrims to the shrine of St.
James of Compostella. Thenceforth, the Charlemagne romances
multiplied, and side by side with them sprang up stories of
Arthur, a hero popular among the Bretons, for whom the hills
of Wales and Cornwall were a playground of romance. The
*trouvères* of northern France, who catered for energetic men,
ill satisfied with the mere love music of the southern *troubadours,* had tales, no doubt, of Arthur, Merlin, and Lancelot,
which had been partly founded upon Cymric traditions. Thus
L'Ancelot, a diminutive form of Ancel (*ancilla*) a servant, might
be a translation of the Cymric Mael, which also means a servant ;
and there is Cymric tradition of a Mael, king of the native
tribes in the year 560, famous for strength and crimes of un-
chaste violence ; the Meluas who carried off Guinever, wife of
his uncle Arthur, and with whom Arthur made disgraceful
peace. The old tales were tales of animal strength, courage,

and passion. The spiritual life was added to them when Walter
Map placed in the midst of them the Holy Graal, type of the
heavenly mysteries.

Geoffrey of Monmouth's Chronicle had suddenly made King
Arthur famous in England. Wace's romance version had
quickened the interest in his adventures, and then it seems to
have occurred to Walter Map, or to have been suggested to him,
to arrange and harmonise, and put a Christian soul into the
entire body of Arthurian romance. For this purpose he would
associate it with the legend of the Holy Graal, and that legend
itself became the first piece in the series of prose romances,
now produced and written to be read aloud, forming the groundwork on which metrical romances afterwards were based.
These French prose romances seem to have been translated
from Latin originals; and Robert de Borron, to whom it is
ascribed, may rather have been translator than author of (1)
the first of the series, *The Romance of the Holy Graal*, sometimes also called *The Romance of Joseph of Arimathea*, which
was written at least twenty years later than Geoffrey of Monmouth's Chronicle. It is professedly told by a hermit, to whom
in the year 717, appeared, in England, a vision of Joseph of
Arimathea and the Holy Graal. The hermit set down in Latin
what was then revealed to him, and his Latin Robert de Borron
said that he proposed to set forth in French. The Graal, according to its legend, was the Holy Dish (low Latin, *gradale*) which
contained the paschal lamb at the Last Supper. After the
supper it was taken by a Jew to Pilate, who gave it to Joseph of
Arimathea. It was used by Joseph of Arimathea at the taking
down of our Lord from the cross, to receive the gore from his
wounds; and thus it became doubly sacred. When the Jews
imprisoned Joseph, the Holy Graal, placed miraculously in his
hands, kept him from pain and hunger for two-and-forty years.
Released by Vespasian, Joseph quitted Jerusalem and went with
the Graal through France into Britain, where it was carefully
deposited in the treasury of one of the kings of the island, called
the Fisherman King. The Latin adaptation of this legend to
the purpose it was to serve, in the addition of the Graal as a
type of the mystery of godliness to the mere animal life of the
King Arthur romances, we may suppose to have been the work
of Walter Map; Robert de Borron putting into French not
that only, but also the next part of the series, (2) the romance of
*Merlin.* Then followed (3) the romance of *Lancelot of the*

*Lake,* ascribed always and only to Walter Map. In it, while developing the Arthur legend, Map idealised that bright animal life which it had been the only object of preceding stories to express. The romance is rich in delicate poetical invention. Lancelot is the bright pattern of a knight according to the flesh, cleared in one respect of many scattered offences, which are concentrated in a single blot, represented always as a dark blot on his character, the unlawful love for Guinevere. Next in the series comes (4) the Romance of the *Quest of the Holy Graal,* written also indisputably by Walter Map. From Lancelot, who had been painted as the ornament of an unspiritual chivalry, Map caused a son to spring, Sir Galahad, the spiritual knight, whose dress of flame-colour mystically typified the Holy Spirit that came down in tongues of fire. The son and namesake of Joseph of Arimathea, Bishop Joseph, to whom the holy dish was bequeathed, first instituted the order of the Round Table. The initiated at their festivals sat as apostle knights, with the Holy Ghost in their midst, leaving one seat vacant as that which the Lord had occupied, and which was reserved for the pure Galahad. Whatever impure man sat there the earth swallowed. It was called, therefore, the Seat Perilous. When men became sinful, the Holy Graal, visible only to pure eyes, disappeared. On its recovery (on the recovered purity of its people) depended the honour and peace of England ; but only Sir Galahad—who at the appointed time was brought to the knights by a mysterious old man clothed in white—only the unstained Sir Galahad succeeded in the quest. Throughout the " Quest of the Graal," Map knitted the threads of Arthurian romance into the form which it was his high purpose to give them, and made what had become the most popular tales of his time in England, an expression of the English earnestness that seeks to find the right, and do it for the love of God. All their old charm is left, intensified in the romance of Lancelot ; but all is now for the first time shaped into a legend of man's spiritual battle, and a lesson on the search, through a pure life alone, for the full revelation of God's glory upon earth. After this, it remained only to complete the series of the romances by adding (5) the *Mort Artus,* the Death of Arthur ; this also was written by Walter Map, and as a distinct romance, although combined in the printed editions with his Lancelot. The spiritual significance thus given by Walter Map to King Arthur, as the romance hero of the English, he is so far from having lost among us, that we shall find great phases in

the history of English thought distinctly illustrated by modifications in the treatment of the myth.

18. Meanwhile, the demand for Arthurian romances grew;
and when Map's work was done another Englishman, **Luces de
Gast,** living near Salisbury, wrote, probably towards the close
of Henry II.'s reign, the first part of *Tristan,* or Tristram.
The second part was added by Helie de Borron. Popular as it
became, this romance is, in spirit and execution, of inferior
quality. Sir Tristram and the fair Isoude are but coarse doubles
of Map's Lancelot and Guinevere.

A Frenchman, Chrestien of Troyes, who began writing before
the close of Henry II.'s reign, was, in Arthurian romance, the
ablest of the contemporaries and immediate followers of Walter
Map. He began, about the year 1180, with the romance of
"Erec and Enid," and produced metrical versions of Map's
Lancelot and Graal romances. He wrote also the romance of
Percival le Gallois.

Not long afterwards a German poet, Wolfram von Eschenbach, fastened upon the Graal story in the true spirit of Map's
work. Taking the sight of the Graal as the symbol of nearness
to God, he painted in his romance of "Parzival" the soul of
a man striving heavenward, erring, straying, yielding to despair,
repenting, and in deep humility at last attaining its desire.
The Graal, thus become famous, was said to be made of one
emerald lost from the crown of Lucifer as he was falling out of
heaven. Is it a sign of the improvement of the world that a
hexagonal dish of greenish glass, called emerald, which is said
to be the Graal itself, is now visible to all eyes in the treasury of
the Cathedral of San Lorenzo at Genoa?

19. In the earlier part of Henry II.'s reign, **Ailred of Rievaulx** wrote a *Rule of Nuns,* thirty-three *Homilies,* and other
books, including a chronicle which described Stephen's *Battle
of the Standard.* Ailred was born in the north of England, and
educated with the King of Scotland's son, but he left the
Scottish court to become a Cistercian monk in Rievaulx Abbey.
In 1146 he became Abbot of Rievaulx, and he died, aged fifty-
seven, in 1166. Five-and-twenty years afterwards he was
canonised as a saint, for he was so holy that he forbade nuns to
teach little girls, because they could not do so without carnally
patting and fondling them.

**Thomas of Ely** also wrote, early in Henry II.'s reign, a
*History of the Church of Ely.*

20. In the latter part of this reign **Ralph Glanville** wrote his Latin treatise *Upon the Laws and Customs of the Kingdom of England* (Tractatus de Legibus et Consuetudinibus Regni Angliæ), which was completed towards the close of Henry's reign, and is the first treatise on English law.  Ralph, or Ranulph de Glanville, famous as a lawyer and a soldier, was appointed, in 1180, Chief Justiciary of England under Henry II. He distinguished himself by valour in repelling the invasion of William King of Scotland, who was taken prisoner while besieging Alnwick Castle.  After the death of Henry II., Richard I. is said to have extorted from Glanville £15,000 towards the expenses of the crusade in which he accompanied his new master.  He was killed at the siege of Acre, in 1190.  Glanville's authorship of the book attributed to him has been questioned, but is not open to much doubt.  He says that the confusion of our laws made it impossible to give a general view of the whole laws and customs of the land ; he sought rather to give a practical sketch of forms of procedure in the king's courts, and of the principles of law most frequently arising ; discussing only incidentally the fiist principles upon which law is based.

21. Latin poems also were produced in the closing years of Henry II.'s reign by Joseph of Exeter and Alexander·Neckam. **Joseph of Exeter,** or Josephus Iscanus, dedicated to Archbishop Baldwin a Latin poem, in six books, *On the Trojan War*, founded on Dares Phrygius, and finished when Henry II. was preparing for the crusade that Baldwin preached.  He wrote also an *Antiocheis*, of which there remains only a fragment. Joseph of Exeter's Latin poem on the Trojan war was written about the same time as the French metrical romance, the "Geste de Troie," by that Benoit de St. Maure who supplanted Wace in the favour of King Henry II.  Geoffrey of Monmouth's chronicle, and Wace's romance version of it, called the "Brut," had brought Troy stories, as well as King Arthur stories, into fashion among us.  For we had now been taught that the British were descended from the Trojans.  After his escape from Troy with his son Ascanius and their followers, his establishment in Italy and marriage with Lavinia the daughter of King Turnus, Æneas died.  Ascanius, the son of Æneas, had a son, named Silvius, who secretly loved Lavinia's niece.  To this couple a son was born, of whom it was foretold that he should slay his father and his mother, and be driven from the land.  The son was called Brutus ; was the Brut who gave his name to Britain.

D

His mother died in giving birth to him. At the age of fifteen he accidentally shot his father when they were out hunting together. He was banished, went to Greece, and there found kindred Trojans who were slaves. He stirred them to revolt, was made their duke, compelled the King of Greece to give him his daughter Ignogen to wife, and freedom to the Trojans; also to give them all the ships of Greece in which to depart and establish themselves in a new country. On their way from Greece these Trojans landed in the island of Leogice, where Brutus sought counsel in the temple of Diana, and was directed to seek beyond France a winsome land named Albion, surrounded by the sea. So he sailed on, and added to his company, from Spain, a fourfold host of Trojans born of those who had been led thither by Atenor after the fall of Troy. Their chief was Corineus, he who gave his name to Cornwall. After many adventures, Brutus, Corineus, and their Trojans reached this country, landed at Dartmouth, destroyed a few giants who were then the sole possessors of the land, and founded London as New Troy, or Troynovant. Such stories quickened interest in the affairs of Troy, and we have evidence of the new interest in Joseph of Exeter's Latin poem, and the French romance of Benoit de St. Maure. They both based their Troy legends upon the narratives ascribed to Dares and Dictys. Homer was no eyewitness of the siege; he was a partisan, too, of the Greeks. Dares, to whom a Phrygian Iliad was ascribed as early as the year 230, an account said to have been written before Homer's, was a Trojan priest of Vulcan, who warned Hector not to kill Patroclus, and was himself killed by Ulysses. His book existed only in a Latin version, said to have been made by Cornelius Nepos from the Greek autograph found at Athens. This prose history of the fall of Troy was usually associated with the six books on the history of the Trojan war ascribed to Dictys of Gnossus, the companion of Idomeneus. His narrative, said to have been written at the request of Idomeneus, on tablets of bark, in Phœnician characters, was further said to have been buried with its author in a leaden box, and disclosed by an earthquake in the thirteenth year of the reign of Nero. Nero caused the work to be translated into Greek, and from that Greek the Latin version was said to have been made by one Q. Septimius Romanus. In and long after the time of Henry II., Dictys and Dares were regarded as the chief original authorities for the story of the siege of Troy.

It is in Benoit de St. Maure's " Geste de Troie," based chiefly upon Dictys, that we have the germ of the tale, afterwards famous in literature, of Troilus and Cressida.

**Alexander Neckam** was born at St. Albans, in September, 1157, on the same night as King Richard, and was the king's foster brother. He was educated at St. Albans, and early entrusted with the school at Dunstable, dependent on St. Albans Abbey. In 1180, at the age of twenty-three, he was in Paris, distinguished as a teacher. He wrote, within the next ten years, a *Treatise on Science*, in ten books of Latin elegiac verse, wherein he treated of creation, the elements, water and its contents, fire, air, the earth's surface, its interior, plants, animals, and the seven arts. He wrote a similar book in prose, besides other Latin poems, grammatical and theological treatises, and commentaries upon works of Aristotle. Neckam lived on through the reigns of Richard I. and John. In 1213 he became abbot of the Augustines at Cirencester, and he died in 1217.

22. We now pass from the reign of Henry II. to that of Richard I. (1189—1199). In this reign Walter Map was adding to the anecdotes in his " De Nugis Curialium." Towards the close of it, in 1198, **William of Newbury** wrote his Latin chronicle, the *History of English Affairs*. He was a Yorkshireman born and bred ; born at Bridlington, and educated by the Austin canons at Newbury, in the North Riding. As a monk in their abbey he became known for his industry and skill as a writer ; and it was at the request of the Abbot of Rievaulx that he wrote his " Historia Rerum Anglicarum," of which the preface hotly denied Geoffrey of Monmouth's credibility, and the substance proved himself to be a trustworthy chronicler of facts. Beginning at the Conquest, he ran through the events before his own time in a very short summary, and occupied himself almost wholly with the careful record of contemporary events. He died in 1208, aged seventy-two.

Another chronicler of this time, also a Yorkshireman, was **Roger of Hoveden**, or Howden, in the East Riding. He was attached to the household of Henry II., who employed him in collection of the revenues due to the crown from abbeys without abbots or priors. Roger of Hoveden is said to have been at one time a Professor of Theology at Oxford. He was writing in the time of Richard I. his *Annals*, which extend to the year 1201. They begin at the year 732 with a compilation which professes to be planned as a continuation of Bede's History, and come in the second part to a more valuable history of the reigns of Henry II. and Richard I., continued to the third year of John, 1201. For their last nine years Hoveden's Annals are a minute and diffuse contemporary record of events.

23. To the reign of Richard I. belongs also our earliest piece of literary criticism, the treatise of **Geoffrey de Vinsauf** on the New Poetry, *De Nova Poetria.* This writer is called also Galfridus Anglicus. He was educated in the priory of St. Frideswide at Oxford, and in the nascent Universities of France and Italy. He was at Rome when, about the year 1195, he dedicated to his patron there, Pope Innocent III., his Latin critical didactic poem on the New Poetry. His new poetry was the old revived; Joseph of Exeter's Latin poem on the Trojan war was an example of it. Geoffrey of Vinsauf warned men back to the ancient measures, and to the critical standard of Horace. He condemned the Latin rhymes by which they had been superseded. There was, at least, some sign in the book of a tendency to the revival of scholarship. Geoffrey of Vinsauf probably was not the author of an *Itinerary of King Richard* and others to Jerusalem, which has been ascribed to him, and which sets forth that it had been written by Richard the Canon. This is the lively chronicle of an eyewitness, who went himself with King Richard, and saw the last flash of the crusading enthusiasm that Rome afterwards wanted power to sustain in Europe.

24. There is no more to be said of our literature in the reign of Richard I., except in discussion of one writer of mark, who began to use his pen at the close of the reign of Henry II., was writing throughout the reign of Richard I., and continued to write until the reign of John (1199—1216) was nearly ended. This was Gerald du Barri, or Gerald of Wales, commonly known as **Giraldus Cambrensis.** He was born in 1147, and died in the same year as King John, 1216. Gerald came of a fighting family, whose home was in the Castle of Manorbeer, four miles from Pembroke Castle, and who were among the chief helpers in Strongbow's conquest of Ireland. There was an uncle David, Bishop of St. David's, who cherished the young Gerald's turn for study. Study in Wales was continued abroad, and Gerald came home from Paris when his age was about twenty-five, to be entrusted at once with a share in the work of managing wild Wales by a well-organised ecclesiastical discipline. Gerald

came of a Norman father and Welsh mother; he was tall, stalwart, and bold of spirit. As an archdeacon he laboured to re-establish Church discipline among clergy as well as laity, with a fiery zeal that proved inconvenient to many. He was unflinching in performance of his own duties, and in claim of his own rights ; played a bold match of excommunication against a bishop himself, and told his story to the king, who heard it with shouts of laughter, but saw, nevertheless, that this hot Welsh enthusiast for right and duty would not much help the English Church and State as a Welsh bishop. After the death of Gerald's uncle there was a strong desire in Wales to get the vacant see of St. David's restored to its old metropolitan dignity. Archdeacon Gerald, who shared this desire, was elected bishop by the chapter ; but King Henry was for the repression of Welsh national enthusiasm. The election was not confirmed, and soon afterwards Gerald went to Paris for more study. He came home and worried away from St. David's the feeble man to whom that bishopric had been given. In 1184 Henry II. invited the clever Welshman to Court, made him one of his chaplains, and used him in the pacification of Wales, but gave him no substantial reward. In the following year Gerald was ordered to attend upon Prince John, then eighteen years old, in his unsuccessful Irish expedition; for Gerald's counsels would be vigorous, and he had intimate connection with many leading Irish families. It was then that he wrote his *Topography of Ireland*, and this was presently followed—both books, and all other writings of Gerald, being in Latin—by his *History of the Conquest of Ireland*, the best of his writings. The Irish chiefs had their names made classical—Fitzstephen became Stephanides—and they were furnished with ornamental orations, but their characters were described by a lively and shrewd observer, events were told after a careful sifting of evidence, and careful observation of the ground in the case of battles, sieges, &c. At Easter, 1186, Gerald returned to England, and soon afterwards went home to Wales, where he worked on at his "Topography of Ireland." This he published by reading it at Oxford in 1187. The three divisions of the work were read on three successive days, and Gerald entertained at his lodgings on the first day, the poor of the town; on the second day, the doctors and the more eminent pupils; on the third day, the other scholars and many citizens. The capture of Jerusalem by Saladin stirred Europe in the latter part of this year. In 1188 Gerald was by the side

of Archbishop Baldwin when, with a train of clergy, he preached
a crusade through Wales. This caused him to write his
*Itinerary of Wales.* In the following year, 1189, Gerald seems
to have been present at the death of Henry II. He returned to
Wales, and refused the bishopric of Bangor, which fell vacant
while Prince John, during his brother Richard's absence, was
managing the kingdom. His assigned reason for the refusal
was a desire to resume study at Paris; the real reason a desire
to wait for the bishopric of St. David's, that he might battle
from that vantage-ground for the independence of the Welsh
Church. War stopped him on the road to Paris, and Welsh
Gerald then withdrew to Lincoln, at that time famous for its
theological school. There he remained until 1198, when the see
of St. David's again became vacant. The chapter of St. David's
again elected Gerald, but the Archbishop of Canterbury refused
to ratify the election. No Welshman, least of all Welsh Gerald,
was to have the see. Gerald struggled against the archbishop's
decision, travelled alone to the pope through a country
made dangerous by war which had broken out between Philip
Augustus and the Earl of Flanders, and reached Rome in November, 1199. Innocent III. there trifled with his suit; his zeal
for the honour and independence of St. David's became a pontifical joke; and at home Gerald was attainted of treason. But
when he found his cause to be helpless, Gerald's prompt energy
of character enabled him to throw its burden off. He suddenly
reappeared in England, frankly conceded the point he had been
unable to gain, was repaid the costs of his suit, received sixty
marks a year of preferment, and passed the remaining seventeen
years of his life in peace. Among the many books produced by
Gerald's active mind was one written in the reign of Richard I.,
called *Gemma Ecclesiastica*, or Jewel of the Church. He wrote
also, in the reign of John, an autobiographical sketch, in three
parts, *De Rebus a se Gestis* (Of the Things done by Himself), and
when near the close of his life, a *Symbolum Electorum*, in four
parts, containing (1), his Letters; (2), his Poems; (3), the
descriptions of characters given in his works, and the orations
put by him in the mouths of persons of his story; and (4), a
collection of his prefaces.

25. The patriotic feeling which dictated the chief ambition
of Gerald du Barri's life was strong in Wales in his time. Endeavours of our Norman kings to bring the Welsh into subjection
produced in them an energy of contest for the rights and liberties

which men hold dear. Whenever the soul of a people is stirred by a contest that brings out the nobler energies of men, its voice, the literature of the people, acquires higher dignity and power. Struggle for life and liberty against the force of Persia gave to Greece the full expression of her genius. The blossom time of our old Gaelic poetry, in the days of the battle of Gabhra, came of the struggle of a clan against the force which threatened its extinction. The blossom time of the old Cymric poetry, in the days of the battle of Cattraeth, came of the struggle of the Celts against invading Teutons. And thus it is that we find a famous second period of Cymric poetry which corresponds exactly to the time of the Welsh struggle for independence against the power of the Anglo-Norman kings, or from the latter part of the reign of Stephen to the extinction of Welsh independence at the death of Llewellyn in 1282. During this period **Meilyr, Gwalohmai, Owain Prince of Powis, Prince Howel, Kynddelw, Llywarch ab Llywelyn,** and many others became famous for the songs through which they poured the spirit of their countrymen. It was also during this period that Welsh fancy fastened upon the King Arthur stories, and told those and others in the language of the Cymry, as the romances of *the Mabinogion.* That word is the plural of the Cymric word Mabinogi, which (from Mab, a child) means entertainment or instruction for the young.

What is here said of Welsh literature is true not only of the reign of John and the preceding years, but also of the succeeding reign of Henry III., and of the earlier part of the reign of Edward I. We have now to complete the sketch of English literature in King John's time.

26. **Gervase of Tilbury** studied in foreign schools, and served abroad the Emperor Otho IV., for whom he wrote, about the year 1211, his *Otia Imperialia,* full of learning borrowed without acknowledgment from Petrus Comestor, but also an amusing book, most rich in illustration of the traditions, popular superstitions, history, geography, and science of its time.

27. There was no service of the foreigner in **Robert Grosseteste,** a man twenty-eight years younger than Gerald du Barri, who contended for the independence of the English Church as heartily as Gerald wished to contend for the independence of the Church of Wales. Grosseteste, whose name was variously spelt, and who was called also Grosthead, made himself famous

among the English people, by continuing in his own way the labour towards Church reform, which had already found expression in the writings of Nigel Wireker and Walter Map.  Robert Grosseteste was born of poor parents at Stradbrook, in Suffolk, about the year 1175.  He studied perhaps at Paris as well as at Oxford, where he graduated in divinity, and became master of the schools.  Grosseteste was contemporary with the founders of those orders of friars, the Franciscans and Dominicans, who represented, in their first institution, a strong effort to give to the Church unity of faith and a pure Christian discipline.  Dominic was five years older, Francis of Assisi seven years younger than Robert Grosseteste, who became, in 1224, at the request of Agnellus, the provincial minister of the Franciscans in England, their first rector at Oxford.

Francis of Assisi, the son of a rich merchant, gave himself to the service of God by visiting with Christian love the leprous and plague-smitten haunts of the very poor and ignorant, from which the clergy held too much aloof.  By his example he gathered others to his work of bringing religion home to the hearts of wretched men by works of love.  Francis and his brethren were first organised into a distinct body about the year 1209, when John was King of England.  They abjured wealth and learning of the schools, that they might draw nearer to the poor, and trust the strength of Christian sympathy and Christian deeds for winning souls to God.  It is remarkable that this abjuration of book learning opened a way to knowledge.  Their mission of healing to the poor made the Franciscans students of Nature.  In energetic and devoted men the intellect could not remain inactive, and the Franciscans became good physicians.  To the best of their opportunity they explored secrets of Nature; and we shall find them presently yielding to England in a pupil of Grosseteste's her first great experimental philosopher.

Side by side with the Franciscans arose the Dominicans or Preaching Friars.  The Spaniard Dominic was a devout theologian, whose deep conviction it was that, as there could be no salvation in heaven so there should be no mercy on earth for the heretic; that heresy already formed must be uprooted; and that its formation in after time was to be checked or prevented by the labours of a devout and well-trained order of preachers, able to demonstrate the truth of orthodox opinions and, by Church scholarship and strength of argument, to confute doubts as they arose. For this reason Dominic set on foot the work of his Dominicans, which also was begun in the days when John was King of England, and was organised by Pope Innocent III. at the close of that crusade against Waldensian heresy in Languedoc, in which, when one of the leaders of the bloody work asked a Cistercian abbot how, after the storm of a town, he was to know heretic from faithful, "Slay them all," said the abbot, "and the Lord will know his own." King John had been dead eight years when Robert Grosseteste became head of the Franciscans at Oxford. During John's reign he had written Latin books of philosophy and Latin verse. The more important part of his life will have to be told in association with the other evidences of the course of English thought in the reign of Henry III.

28. One other feature of our literature in the reign of John remains to be described, and that is the appearance of books written in the language of the people. Hitherto, since the Conquest, nearly all writing of mark had been in Latin; and those books which were not in Latin were in French. But we begin now to find writers in English, and the earliest of these is **Layamon.** Layamon, the son of Leovenath, called in the later text of his poem, Laweman, the son of Leuca, was a priest who read the services of the Church at Ernley, now Areley Kings, three or four miles from Bewdley, in Worcestershire. Living in the days when Geoffrey of Monmouth's Chronicle and Wace's French metrical version of it were new books in high fame among the educated and the courtly, " it came to him in mind, and in his chief thought," that he would tell the famous story to his countrymen in English verse. He made a long journey in search of copies of the books on which he was to found his poem; and when he had come home again, as he says, "Layamon laid down those books and turned the leaves; he beheld them lovingly; may the Lord be merciful to him!" Then, blending literature with his parish duties, the good priest began his work. Priest in a rural district, he was among those who spoke the language of the country with the least mixture of Norman French, and he developed Wace's " Brut " into a completely English poem, with so many additions from his own fancy, or his own knowledge of West country tradition, that, while Wace's " Brut " is a poem of 15,300 lines, in Layamon's *Brut*, the number of lines is 32,250. Layamon's verse is the old First English un-rhymed measure with alliteration, less regular

D *

in its structure than in First English times, and with an occasional slip into rhyme. Battles are described as in First English
poems.  Here, as in First English poetry, there are few similes,
and those which occur are simply derived from natural objects.
There is the same use of a descriptive synonym for man or
warrior.  There is the old depth of earnestness that rather gains
than loses dignity by the simplicity of its expression.  From
internal evidence, it appears that the poem was completed about
the year 1205.   It comes down to us in two thirteenth-century
MSS., one written a generation later than the other, and there
are many variations of their text ; but the English is so distinctly
that of the people in a rural district, that in the earlier MS.
the whole poem contains less than fifty words derived from the
Norman, and some of these might have come direct from Latin.
In the second MS. about twenty of those words do not occur,
but forty others are used.   Thus the two MSS., in their 56,800
lines, do not contain more than ninety words of Norman origin.
In its grammatical structure Layamon's English begins for us
the illustration of the gradual loss of inflexions, and other
changes, during the transition of the language from First English
to its present form.   It has been called semi-Saxon.  It is better
called Transition English of Worcestershire in the beginning
of the thirteenth century.

29. A writer named **Ormin**, or Orm, began also, in the
reign of King John, another English poem of considerable
extent, called, from his own name, the *Ormulum*.  He tells of
himself in the dedication of his book that he was a regular
canon of the order of St. Augustine, and that he wrote in
English at the request of Brother Walter, also an Augustinian
canon, for the spiritual improvement of his countrymen.  The
plan of his book is to give to the English people in their own
tongue, and in an attractive form, the spiritual import of the
Church Services throughout the year.   He gave first a metrical
paraphrase of the portion of the Gospel assigned to each day,
and added to each portion of it a metrical Homily in which it
was expounded doctrinally and practically, with frequent borrowing from the writings of Ælfric, and some borrowing from
Bede.   The metre is in alternate verses of eight and seven
syllables, in imitation of a Latin rhythm ; or in lines of fifteen
syllables with a metrical point at the end of the eighth, thus :—

> " This boc iss nemmned Ormulum,
> Forrthi that Orrm itt wrohhte."

Of the homilies provided for nearly the whole of the yearly service nothing remains beyond the thirty-second, and there remains no allusion that points to the time when the work was written.   Its language, however, places it with the earliest examples of Transition English, and it belongs, no doubt, to the reign of John, or to the first years of the reign of Henry III. It seems to be the Transition English of a north-eastern county, and the author had a peculiar device of spelling, on the adherence to which by copyists he laid great stress.   Its purpose evidently was to guide any half Normanized town priest in the right pronunciation of the English when he read these verses aloud for the pleasure and good of the people.   After every short vowel, and only then, Orm doubled the consonant.

30. In the reign of Henry III. (1216—1272), which we have now reached, the production of books in the English language became more and more common.   Some hold that a short Proclamation issued in this reign, in the year 1258, should be taken as representing the change from that form of Transition English which we have in Layamon, to a form which they call English, as distinguished from semi-Saxon.   This shows how an ill-chosen name is able to confuse the understanding.

There is a bright English poem called *The Owl and the Nightingale*, which tells how those birds advanced each against the other his several claims to admiration and the demerits of his antagonist ; and how they called upon the author, **Nicholas of Guildford**, to be judge between them.   Master Nicholas lets us know that from a gay youth in the world, he had passed into the Church, where his merits had been neglected, and that he was living at Portsham, in Dorsetshire.   In this poem we have the rhyming eight-syllabled measure of many a French romance, but it is so distinctly English of a rural district, that its 1,792 lines contain only about twenty words which are distinctly Norman in their origin.   It remains to us in two transcripts made in the West of England, both of the thirteenth century. One of them is the same which contains the earliest MS. of Layamon, followed by a brief chronicle to the beginning of the reign of Henry III , and " The Owl and the Nightingale " in the same handwriting.   There is reference in the poem to the death of a King Henry, who probably was Henry II.   There can be very little doubt that " The Owl and the Nightingale " is rightly assigned to the reign of Henry III.

Another of the early pieces of Transition English, of much

interest to students of the language, but of slight interest
as literature, is the *Ancren Riwle* (Rule of the Anchoresses),
which seems to have been written by a Bishop Poor, who died
in 1237. It was intended for the guidance of a small household of women withdrawn from the world for service of God, at
Tarrant Keynstone, in Dorsetshire.

To the reign of Henry III., and about the year 1250, belongs an English poem kindred in spirit to the " Ormulum,"
and, indeed, illustrative of the same feature in English character
which was marked at the outset of our literature by Cædmon's
"Paraphrase." This is a version of the Scripture narrative of
*Genesis and Exodus.* Like " The Owl and the Nightingale," it
illustrates the adoption of rhyme into our native poetry, by use
of the octosyllabic rhyming verse common in many French
romances. The poem of " Genesis and Exodus " is by an unknown author, and represents East Midland Transition English
of the middle of the thirteenth century. It has been suggested
that the author of the " Ormulum " belonged to Lincolnshire ;
the author of the " Genesis and Exodus " to Suffolk. In the
4,162 lines of " Genesis and Exodus," there are only about fifty
words of Norman origin. The writer begins by saying that
men ought to love those who enable the unlearned to love and
serve the God who gives love and rest of the soul to all
Christians, and that Christian men should be glad as birds are
of the dawn to have the story of salvation turned out of Latin
into their own native speech.

The same spirit among the people is represented, from the
date of Layamon onward, by *Homilies*, metrical *Creeds, Pater-
nosters, Gaudia, or Joys of the Virgin*, and short devotional or
moral poems, of which MSS. remains. There is also a *Bestiary*,
in English, apparently of the same date, and produced in the
same part of England as the metrical story of " Genesis and
Exodus." The " Bestiary" is a version from a Latin "Physiologus,"
by a Bishop Theobald, and in its 802 lines, except one or two
Latin names of animals, which had already been adopted in
First English, there are not more than eight words of Romance
origin. To what has been said of the early origin of books
of this kind, when we found them imitated in First English,
(ch. ii. § 12), it may be added that Epiphanius, a Jewish Christian
bishop and opponent of Origen, referred, at the close of the
fourth century, in his book against heresies, to the two natures
of the serpent, with the phrase " as the Physiologues say ;" and

that, as collections of such natural history allegories multiplied, there came to be a sort of canonical rule as to the moral allegory connected with each animal. There was a "Physiologus" ascribed to Epiphanius. In the year 496 Gelasius II. declared at a Church Council that a "Physiologus," then ascribed to St. Ambrose, was apocryphal and heretical; and Latin MSS. of such work date from the eighth century. Early in the twelfth century, a metrical "Bestiary" was written in French by Philippe de Thaun, and in the time of which we are now speaking, there was produced in France, "Le Bestiaire Divin de Guillaume, Clerc de Normandie."

31. There was translation also of popular romances from French into English verse during the reign of Henry III. The most notable of these were "King Horn" and the "Romance of Alexander."

*King Horn* belongs to an Anglo-Danish cycle of romance, from which the Norman trouvères drew material. Another of the tales of this cycle was "Havelok the Dane," formed into a French lay in Henry I.'s time, but translated some years later than "King Horn." Another tale of the same group, afterwards translated into English as a metrical romance, was that of "Guy of Warwick and Colbrond the Dane." Horn put to sea in a small boat, landed in Westernesse, where he became page to King Aylmer, and loved Aylmer's daughter Rimenhild. He was dubbed a knight, and achieved great things. Banished for his love, he bade Rimenhild wait for him seven years. Many things happened before and after King Horn's marriage with Rimenhild. While he was gone to recover his native land from the infidel, a false friend, Fykenild, seized his wife. But Horn went as a harper into Fykenild's castle, killed him, and recovered Rimenhild.

*King Alexander* was a very famous subject of romance poetry. A Greek romance upon him had been written about the year 1060 by Simon Seth, keeper of the imperial wardrobe in the palace of Antiochus at Constantinople, founded upon Oriental legends that abounded among the Persians and Arabians as "Mirrors of Iskander," "The Two-Horned Alexander," &c. This Greek romance was translated into Latin, and from Latin even into Hebrew. It became also the groundwork of many French and English poems. In the year 1200 Gaultier de Chatillon turned it into an "Alexandreis," which was one of the best Latin poems of the Middle Ages, and about the same time, at the beginning of the reign of John in England, the great French romance of Alexander was composed in nine books, containing altogether about 20,000 of the twelve-syllabled lines since known, from their use in that poem, as Alexandrines. All the lines in one of its paragraphs, even though they may be a hundred, rhyme together. The Alexander romance was adopted in Spain, Italy, and even in Scandinavia. A German Alexandries, in six books, was produced during our Henry III.'s reign by a Suabian, Rudolph of Hohenems; and towards the close of the same reign, about the year 1265, there was produced an English free version of the famous poem as the Romance of King Alexander, which has been ascribed without good reason, to an Adam Davie, Marshal of Stratford-at-Bow.

To the reign of Henry III. also may belong the English metrical version of the romance of Sir Tristrem, ascribed to **Thomas of Erceldoune,** in the county of Berwick, the earliest Scottish poet, who was born about 1219, alive in 1286, and dead before 1299. He was in repute in his own day not only as poet, but as prophet also.

32. From the rapid development of an English literature in the language of the people, we now pass to other illustrations of the energy of English thought during the reign of Henry III., and return to **Robert Grosseteste,** whom we left (§ 27), at the date of his appointment, in 1224, as the first rector of the Franciscans in Oxford. He had been Archdeacon of Wilts, was then Archdeacon of Northampton, and became afterwards Archdeacon of Leicester. At one time he was rector of St. Margaret's, Leicester. In 1232, after a severe illness, Grosseteste, who would no longer be a pluralist, gave up all his preferments except a prebend at Lincoln; and in 1235 he was made Bishop of Lincoln, then the largest and most populous diocese in the country, and very famous for its theological school. It was as Bishop of Lincoln that Grosseteste began the most energetic part of his career as Church reformer. Strictly interpreting the duties of his office, he devoted himself to the suppression of abuses. Within a year of his consecration he had, after a visitation of the monasteries, removed seven abbots and four priors. Next year he was, in a Council held in London, supporting the proposal to deprive pluralists of all their livings except one. His strictness produced outcry. The canons preached against their bishop in his own cathedral; a monk tried to poison him. In 1245 Grosseteste obtained the support of the pope for his visi-

tations; and in 1246 he obtained another bull from the pope to prevent scholars at Oxford from graduating in arts without examination. When his visitations were resumed, his unreserved inquiry into the morals of those who undertook the spiritual guidance of his diocese produced so much scandal that appeal was made to the king to check it. The king interfered by forbidding laymen to give evidence in such matters before Grosseteste's officials. Grosseteste battled against the greed of monks who seized for their monasteries possessions and tithes of the Church meant for the use of resident priests. But the monks made it worth the pope's while to be deaf to all the bishop's arguments upon that head. As he left the pope, Grosseteste said aloud, so that his holiness might hear, " O money, money, how much you can do! especially at the court of Rome." In 1252 Grosseteste caused a calculation to be made of the income of the foreign clergy thrust by the pope on English maintenance. It was 70,000 marks, three times the clear revenue of the king. In the following year, 1253, the last year of his life, Grosseteste made a famous stand against the avarice of Rome by refusing to induct one of the pope's nephews into a canonry at Lincoln. He died in the autumn of that year, accusing Rome of the disorders brought into the Church. He left his library to the Franciscans. The mere list of his own writings occupies three and twenty closely-printed quarto pages. He wrote a book of husbandry in Latin, of which there are also MSS. in French. He wrote sermons, treatises on physical and mental philosophy, commentaries on Aristotle, Latin and French verse, including a religious allegory of the *Château d'Amour.* He applied also a rare knowledge of Greek and Hebrew to the minutest study of the Scriptures. He battled against the corruption of the Church, not in the narrow spirit of an ascetic. Three things, he once told a Dominican, are necessary for temporal health : food, sleep, and liveliness. Heartily in accord with the movement represented by the poverty of the Franciscans, he said that he liked to see the friars' dresses patched. But when one of them, mistaking a particular means for the great end that was sought thereby, praised, in a sermon, mendicancy as the highest step towards the attainment of all heavenly things, Grosseteste told him that there was a step yet higher, namely, to support one's self by one's own labour. One intimate friend of Grosseteste's was especially struck by his courage in facing both the king and the pope to maintain right ; another, the most famous of his pupils, Roger Bacon, was impressed most by his marvellous and almost universal knowledge.

33. **Roger Bacon,** born in 1214, was in his cradle in Somersetshire when the barons obtained from King John his signature to Magna Charta. He belonged to a rich family, sought knowledge from childhood, and avoided the strife of the day. He studied at Oxford and Paris, and the death of his father may have placed his share of the paternal estate in his hands. He spared no cost for instructors and transcribers, books and experiments ; mastered not only Latin thoroughly, but also Hebrew and Greek, which not more than five men in England then understood grammatically, although there were more who could loosely read and speak those tongues. He was made Doctor in Paris, and had the degree confirmed in his own University of Oxford. Then he withdrew entirely from the civil strife that was arising, and joined the house of the Franciscans in Oxford, having spent all his time in the world and two thousand pounds of money in the search for knowledge. Roger Bacon's family committed itself to the king's side in the civil war which Henry III.'s greed, his corruption of justice, and violation of the defined rights of his subjects, brought upon him. The success of the barons ruined Bacon's family, and sent his mother, brothers, and whole kindred into exile. Meanwhile the philosopher, as one of the Oxford Franciscans, had come under Grosseteste's care, had joined an order which prided itself in the checks put by it on the vanity of learning. But, in spite of their self-denials, the Franciscans, at Oxford and elsewhere, included many learned men who, by the daily habit of their minds, were impelled to give to scholarship a wholesome practical direction. They were already beginning to supply the men who raised the character of teaching at the University of Oxford till it rivalled that of Paris. Friar Bacon was among the earliest of these teachers, so was Friar Bungay, who lives with him in popular tradition. Roger Bacon saw how the clergy were entangled in barren subtleties of a logic far parted from all natural laws out of which it sprang. He believed that the use of all his knowledge, if he could but make free use of it, would be to show how strength and peace were to be given to the Church. And then the pope, who had been told of his rare acquirements and his philosophic mind, bade Roger Bacon, disregarding any rule of his order to the contrary, write for him what was in his mind. Within his

mind were the first principles of a true and fruitful philosophy. But to commit to parchment all that he had been pining to say would cost him sixty pounds in materials, transcribers, necessary references, and experiments. . He was a Franciscan, vowed to poverty, and the pope had sent no money with the command to write. Bacon's exiled mother and brothers had spent all they were worth upon their ransoms. Poor friends furnished the necessary money, some of them by pawning goods, upon the understanding that their loans would be made known to his holiness. Bishop Grosseteste was now dead, and there was a difficulty between the philosopher and his immediate superiors, because the Pope's command was private, and only a relief to Bacon's private conscience. His immediate rulers had received no orders to relax the discipline which deprived Franciscans of the luxury of pen and ink. But obstacles were overcome, and then Roger Bacon produced within a year and a half, 1268-9, his *Opus Majus* (Greater Work), which now forms a large closely-printed folio ; his *Opus Minus* (Lesser Work), which was sent after the Opus Majus to Pope Clement, to recapitulate its arguments and strengthen some of its parts ; and his *Opus Tertium* (Third Work), which followed as a summary and introduction to the whole, enriched with further novelty, and prefaced with a detail of the difficulties against which its author had contended—details necessary to be given, because, he said, that he might obey the pope's command the friar had pawned to poor men the credit of the Holy See. These books, produced by Roger Bacon at the close of Henry III.'s reign, and when he was himself fifty-three years old, rejected nearly all that was profitless, and fastened upon all that there was with life and power of growth in the knowledge of his time. They set out with a principle in which Bacon the Friar first laid foundations of the philosophy of Bacon the Chancellor of later time. He said that there were four grounds of human ignorance : trust in inadequate authority ; the force of custom ; the opinion of the inexperienced crowd ; and the hiding of one's own ignorance with the parading of a superficial wisdom. Roger Bacon advocated the free honest questioning of Nature ; and where books were requisite authorities, warned men against the errors that arose from reading them in bad translations. He would have had all true students endeavour to read the original texts of the Bible and of Aristotle. He dwelt on the importance of a study of mathematics, adding a particular consideration of optics, and ending with the study of Nature by experiment, which, he said, is at the root of all other sciences, and a basis of religion. Roger Bacon lived into the reign of Edward I., and died in the year 1292.

Contemporary with him was **Michael Scot**, of Balwirie, who travelled abroad, was honoured at the Sicilian court of Frederick II., translated into Latin the Arabian Avicenna's "History of Animals," and wrote a *Mensa Philosophica* about the time when Bacon was working upon his "Opus Majus." Michael Scot, the date of whose birth is unknown, died in 1291, a year before Roger Bacon.

34. Side by side with this development of a true spirit in philosophy, the steady endeavour towards right and justice which arose out of the character of its people had enabled England to maintain the rights of subjects against all wrong doing of their kings. Progress made since the days of Henry II. is illustrated in the reign of Henry III. by the appearance of a jurist, **Henry of Bracton,** who wrote a book with the same title as Glanville's, written in Henry II.'s reign, *Upon the Laws and Customs of England.* Of Bracton himself it is only known that he wrote his treatise in the reign of Henry III., probably between the years 1256 and 1259, that it proves him to have been a lawyer by profession, deeply read in Roman law, and that he must have been the Justiciary Henry of Bracton mentioned in judicial records of 1246, 1252, 1255, and other years, to 1267 inclusive. He was a judge therefore from 1245 to 1267, if not longer. There is reason to think he was a clerk in orders before he became a lawyer. In his treatise he does not, like Glanville, avoid dealing with first principles. English law had, during the seventy years between Glanville's book (ch. iv. § 20) and Bracton's, been developed into a science, and the time was come for the first scientific commentary on its rules. Bracton painted accurately, in the five books into which his work is divided, the state of the law in his time, and he digested it into a logical system. The king's place in its system Bracton thus defined: "The king must not be subject to any man, but to God and the Law; for the Law makes him king. Let the king, therefore, give to the Law what the Law gives to him, dominion and power; for there is no king where Will, and not Law, bears rule."

35. There is the same evidence of national growth in the increasing boldness of the chroniclers. **Roger of Wendover,**

in Buckinghamshire, was a monk of St. Albans, who became precentor of the abbey, and afterwards prior of Belvoir, a cell attached to St. Albans, from which office he was, about the year 1219, deposed for his extravagance. Recalled to St. Albans, Roger of Wendover died there about the year 1237. He wrote under the name of Flowers of History (*Flores Historiarum*) a History of the World from the Creation, in two books, the first extending to the birth of Christ ; the second to the 19th year of Henry III. The latter part of the chronicle, describing the forty or fifty years before 1235, is his own manly and impartial history of his own time.

**Matthew Paris** a younger man, and also monk of St. Albans, who perhaps was called of Paris ' from having been there for study, made free use of Roger of Wendover's " Flowers of History " in his own larger chronicle, which he called *Historia Major.* Indeed, for his detail of events before 1235 he simply annexed Roger of Wendover with a few variations and additions. From that date to 1273 Matthew Paris wrote his own fully detailed journal of the history of his own times, and claimed unsparing liberty in the discussion of events. Monk as he was, he spoke plain language of "the pope and the king, who favoured and abetted each other in their mutual tyranny."

36. We now pass from the reign of Henry III. to that of Edward I. (1272—1307), at whose accession Dante was a child of seven years old. We must, therefore, glance abroad again before discussing the next stage of our own literature. We have seen (ch. iii. § 2) how, in our Henry II.'s time, throughout Europe writers were arising who spoke for the people ; and it has been said that there was in Europe a Court literature for the luxurious few, as well as a National literature for the many. The tales of the trouvères of Northern France, if written for the rich, were astir with action which gave pleasure to all lively minds, and they could be recited to the people at their merrymakings. The love-singing of the troubadours had no such currency. It was a part of the idleness of the idle.

In the twelfth century a chaplain at the French Court named André wrote a book on the " Art of Loving," wherein he cited and described incidentally the Courts of Love, with which, in Northern and Southern France, great ladies amused themselves, from the middle of the twelfth century until the end of the fourteenth. André quotes, among others, the Courts of Love of the ladies of Gascony ; of Ermengard, Viscountess of Narbonne; of Queen Eleanor of Aquitaine, married in 1137 to Louis VII. of France, and afterwards wife of Henry II. of England. The troubadours and their historian, Jean of Notre Dame, speak of the Courts of Love established in Provence, at Pierrefeu, at Signe, at Romanin, at Avignon. Love verses were sung before these courts, love causes were heard with mock legal formalities, and judgments delivered with formal citations of precedents. These courts had also a code, said to have been established by the king of love, and found by a Breton knight and lover in King Arthur's court tied to the foot of a falcon. Most noticeable in the decisions of these Courts of Love is the care taken by the ladies to divide their jest from earnest. The very first law of the code was that marriage does not excuse from love ; and the interpretation of the ladies' courts laid down that love and marriage are things wholly different. Sometimes the playful singing of a lady's praise, the jest of love which was sharply distinguished from all serious suit for marriage, did become serious. One case before the courts was that of a knight, A, who had sought from a lady leave to love after the playful fashion, and had been told by her that she had already a lover, B, but that she would willingly take A whenever B was lost to her. In her case the jest became earnest, and she married B. Then immediately A claimed his right to be her lover, according to her promise. She wished to withdraw from this kind of amusement, but was sued before Queen Eleanor's Court of Love, which decided in the prosecutor's favour, saying, "We do not venture to contradict the decision of the Countess of Champagne, who, by a solemn judgment, has pronounced that true love cannot exist between those who are married to each other." But the nature of women does not change with the centuries ; and it is not possible that in these playful decisions, courts consisting of ten, twelve, or fourteen ladies of chief rank in a district meant to disgrace their sex. They meant the reverse. The love discussed in their courts and sung to them by the troubadours was idle amusement only ; and they took care that no lady who was chosen as the object of a rhymer's love verses should, therefore, be regarded as the object of his serious suit. If the suit was serious that was a private matter, and so was the relation between husband and wife. The distinction was made mockingly, but very firmly ; and the consequence was that the poet always addressed his public exercises on the theme of love to some lady whom he had no thought whatever of marrying. The lady, who was often a married lady, looked upon her place in his verse simply as that of one who had received the high compliment of a dedication. No poet amused the public with his suit to the woman whom he sought to marry, or said to his own wife in his verses what it became him to say only in his home. Thus the ladies enjoyed the polite entertainment of love poetry, and kept it free from risk of compromising them before the world.

The southern poets had taken from the Arabs their belief that love is the essential theme of song. Only love poems were knightly, chevaleresques ; all others, even those of religion, were " sirventes," songs for squires. Thus it became an exercise of ingenuity to express the sentiment of love with all possible variety. After Peter de Vinea had, in our Henry III.'s time, invented what we now know as the sonnet, that form of poem became especially devoted to the use of those who exercised their ingenuity in expressing all phases of love : love in its first emotions ; love, happy, jealous ; the loved one walking, sitting, sleeping ; in health, in sickness, dead ; the lover in despair. Long sequences of sonnets so designed, or still more artificially ingenious in their way, had become common in the time of Dante's youth, and for many generations afterwards were written on this plan. There was so little call for real and earnest thought in such love-singing, that men of rank who had no poetry in their souls learnt to arrange the conventional ideas into musical word patterns. Henry VI., the son of Barbarossa, and the father of Frederick II., at whose Sicilian court, the spirit of song was fostered, this Henry VI. was a famous troubadour, and he gouged out women's eyes when, in 1194, he kept cruel Christmas at Palermo. The character of this form of literature is also indicated by the edict of Clementina Isaure, Countess of Toulouse, who in 1324 instituted what were called the Floral Games. These games assembled at Toulouse the poets of France, and housed them in artificial arbours dressed with flowers. A violet in gold was the reward for the best poem, and the degree of Doctor. was conferred on any one who was three times a prizeman.

During more than thirty years of the reign of Henry III. literature was being fostered at the Apulian Court of Frederick II. Frederick cared little for pope or Church, or for crusading ; but when he found it worth his while to go to Jerusalem, where the sultan gracefully yielded to him the Holy City by the treaty of 1229, Frederick took possession as with the shrug of a philosopher and man of the world who had a high respect for the learning and civilization of the Arabs. At his court in Sicily there was a welcome for all poets and all men of learning, whether Christians, Saracens, or Jews. For the Saracens he had especial liking, and took pains to maintain a good knowledge of Arabic in his dominions. To him Michael Scot dedicated his translation of Avicenna's work upon Animals, and at his request Michael composed a treatise upon Physiognomy. Grosseteste was among Frederick's correspondents. Of the University of Naples Frederick was the founder. He had weaknesses and vices, but his free encouragement of learning, alike of the East and West, the wholesome companionship at his Court of men who had much to learn one from another, and the gay encouragement of song, made Sicily, in the days of our Henry III., the birthplace of modern Italian literature.

Fifteen years after Frederick's death Dante was born. With Frederick II. had arisen the Italian form of the old German struggle between Ghibelline (to the Germans Waiblingen) and Guelf. In the summer of 1236, at the head of the Ghibelline party, Frederick prepared war against Northern Italy—against that part of Italy in which not only the Lombard League, but also the very rivalries and dissensions among and within its free cities, testified to the spirit of freedom that set noblest minds at work. Barbarossa had in vain struggled to force back the leagued Italian free cities under feudal government. In vain Frederick allied himself to the Italian feudal party. The popular party, then called that of the Guelfs, were without a leader, but it suited the pope's policy to befriend it. Its strength was drawn from the growing spirit of independence which caused prisoners of Brescia, bound to the machines advanced against the town, to bid their townsfellows strike fearlessly and count no man's safety of more worth than their country's honour. After Frederick's death, the pope and the Guelfs led armed revolt against the Italian rule of the House of Suabia. But the policy of Rome placed always the feuds and immediate worldly interests of the Papal Court above the larger interests of Italy ; and in 1264, the year before the birth of Dante, Pope Urban IV. brought the dull, cruel, and grasping Charles of Anjou into Italy, as King of Naples, and allied the name and cause of the Guelfs to the lowest forms of foreign tyranny. The political theory of the Ghibellines was now that by acceptance of a strong imperial rule unity was to be secured, and a liberal chief, strong to contend against usurping tyrannies of priestcraft, would give life and law to society. The political theory of the Guelfs was that the proposed head of society would be a foreign master. They declared strongly for the citizen's individual right of self-government, and watched so jealously over municipal privileges, and each city's, each family's right to equality with its neighbour, that feuds between city and city, family and family—to which the Ghibellines pointed as justification of their different political view—arose out of the very energies that gave to Italy a Dante for her son. Men's souls were deeply stirred in contest upon questions involving the essential problems of society ; and out of the energy so roused, there came, as usual, the best expression of man's genius. The development of commerce in North Italy, which had been quickened by the Crusades, brought citizens into wholesome contact with all forms of life ; gave vigour of mind, quickened enterprise, and widened the sense of the worth of civil rights. Thus Florence throve. Within a generation before Dante's birth, its streets had been paved with stone, the Palace of Justice, the prisons, and the Bridge of the Trinity had been built. Greek painters also had been brought to Florence, whom young Cimabue saw at work in the chapel, and whose art was transcended by the genius of that Florentine. Dante was seventeen in the year of the Constitution of Florence, that expressed the political mind of this Athens of the Middle Ages. The Palazzo Vecchio was built when Dante was twenty-four years old. Five years later the builders were at work on the Baptistry and Cathedral ; and Dante was but in his thirty-fifth year when there were cast for the Baptistry Ghiberti's brazen gates, which Michael Angelo declared "worthy to be the gates of Heaven."

If we look out of Italy to France we find there also the independent stir of thought. Guillaume de Lorris had begun, as a troubadour, between the years 1200 and 1230, or in the days of our King John and the earlier years of Henry III., an allegorical love poem, called the "Roman de la Rose." He died, leaving it a fragment of 4,070 lines, which had no special popularity. But in the days of Dante's childhood and youth, between the years 1279 and 1282, Jean de Meung, a poet, born, like Guillaume of Lorris, in the valley of the Loire, but no mere troubadour, took up the unfinished " Romaunt of the Rose," and, by the addition of 18,000 lines, completed it in a new spirit. The timid grace of one young poet was followed by the bold wit of another, who was crammed with the scholarship of his time and poured it out in diffuse illustration of his argument, but who, a man of the people, alive with the stir of his time against polished hypocrisy, annoyed priests with his satire and court ladies with a rude estimate of their prevailing character. Underlying all Jean de Meung's part of the " Romaunt of the Rose " is a religious earnestness that gave its verses currency, and made them doubly troublesome to those who dreaded free thought and full speech.

Into the midst of all this energetic life *DANTE* was born in Florence, a lawyer's son, in the year 1265, seven years before the close of the reign of our King Henry III. His father died during his early childhood, and he was left to the care of a rich mother, who caused him to be liberally trained. Lombardy was without a written language, and the choice of language for the poets of North Italy was between Provençal and Sicilian. Dante chose Sicilian, and blended music of the South with Northern energy. At first, in his early manhood, he wrote the " Vita Nuova "—the New or the Early Life—connecting, with a narrative of aspiration towards Beatrice, as the occasion of them, sonnets, and canzone, representing artificially, according to the manner of that time, various moods of love. Fifty yards from the house in which Dante lived was the house of Folco Portinari, father of the little Beatrice on whom Dante founded, not a set of personal love sonnets, but his ideal of a dawn of life and love distinguished by the chastest purity. When the actual Beatrice died, in the year 1290, she was the young wife of Simon dei Bardi ; but this fact nearly concerned neither Dante nor the poem. At the very outset he describes his ideal as " the glorious lady of my mind," for she represented the pure Spirit of Love, Beatrice, the Blesser ; earthly love in the " Vita Nuova," heavenly love in the " Divine Comedy." There is the most careful exclusion of all fleshly longing from Dante's picture of the Spirit of Love that walks abroad on the same earth with us, while yet, to our hearts, the world is young. When, by the spiritual eye, she is seen no more in the street, Dante's small treason to her memory is checked by a dream of her as the nine years' old child in the crimson dress, who represented the warm glow of love in the heart blessed with a child-like innocence. Dante's unfinished "Convito," continues the allegory of the "Vita Nuova" by showing how, after the actual vision of love in youth and early manhood has departed, the poet, or the soul of man, turns to a new love, and seeks consolation in philosophy. And so the spiritual sense of these works proceeds by definite steps upward to the higher mysteries of the "Divine Comedy." Here, after the early days of faith and love, and when, after the first passage from emotions of youth to the intellectual enjoyments of maturer years, enthusiasm also for philosophy has passed away, Dante, or the Soul of Man represented in his person, passes through worldly life (the wood of the first canto) into sin, and, through God's grace, to a vision of his misery—to the "Hell." But by repentance and penance—"Purgatory"—the marks of the seven deadly sins are effaced from his forehead, and the bright vision of Beatrice—heavenly love—whose handmaids are the seven virtues, admonishes him as he attains to "Paradise." There Beatrice, the Beatifier, Love that brings the Blessing, is his guide to the end of the Soul's course, the glory of the very presence of the Godhead, where a love that is almighty rules the universe. The date of the action of the "Divine Comedy" is in the year 1300; and the whole development of the genius of Dante, which laid the foundation of Italian influence upon literature almost throughout Europe, belongs to a time corresponding to that of the reign of King Edward I. in England.

Towards the end of that reign, Dante still living, Petrarch was born. As Dante was a child of seven at the accession of King Edward I., so Petrarch was a child of three at the accession of King Edward II. Early in the reign of Edward II. Boccaccio was born ; and in the reign of Edward III. we shall begin to find how great was the influence of these Italian writers upon English literature.

37. **John of Oxnead,** a monk of the Abbey of St. Benet Holme, was our chief Latin chronicler who lived in the reign of Edward I. His *Chronicle* began with the year 449 and ended with the year 1292. For events after the Conquest he chiefly followed Roger of Wendover, with interpolations, which became long and important in the reigns of Richard I., John, and Henry III. He gave particular account of the injustice and cruelty with which the Jews were treated in his time, was full in his account of the barons' war with Henry III., and detailed from contemporary knowledge the wresting of Wales from the

last of the Llewellyns in 1282, and the coming out of the London citizens with horns and trumpets to meet the head of the slain patriot.

**Nicholas Trivet,** son of one of the king's justices in eyre, was born about the year 1258, and became one of the Dominican or Preaching Friars.   He wrote Latin *Annals of the Six Kings of the House of Anjou,* ending in 1307 at the death of Edward I. His chronicle is well written, religious in its tone, and very trustworthy in its citation of testimony or transcripts of historical documents.

**Peter Langtoft,** of Langtoft, in Yorkshire, a regular canon of Augustinians at Bridlington, wrote in French verse a *Chronicle of England,* from Brut to the end of the reign of Edward I. His inaccurate French was that of an Englishman who had not lived in France ; the first part of this chronicle abridged Geoffrey of Monmouth, professing to omit what Peter Langtoft took for fable, and to repeat only so much as he thought true. He then gave, from various authorities, the history of First English and Norman kings, down to the death of Henry III., and in the third part of his chronicle became a contemporary historian of the reign of Edward I.   Writing in French for noblemen and gentlemen of England, Langtoft took especial care to make out the best case he could for the justice of King Edward's Scottish wars.

38. Writing in English for the English common people, **Robert of Gloucester,** a monk of the abbey in that town, produced at the same time a rhymed *Chronicle of England,* from the siege of Troy to the death of Henry III. in 1272.   It was in long lines of seven accents, and occasionally six, and was the first complete history of his country, from the earliest times to his own day, written in popular rhymes by an Englishman.   The language is very free from Norman admixture, and represents West Midland Transition English of the end of the thirteenth century.   Part of the work must have been written after the year 1297, because it contains a reference to Louis IX. of France, as Saint Louis, and it was in 1297 that he was canonised.   Robert of Gloucester wrote also, perhaps, *Lives and Legends of the English Saints* in rhyme.

Among other books written in English during the reign of Edward I., was the English version of *The Lay of Havelok the Dane,* which was made about the year 1280, and is one of the brightest and most interesting examples of the English of that time. It told how the young royal Havelok was saved by the fisherman Grim from the usurping Godard, and how, he had landed with Grim and all his family at the spot in England now called, after Grim, Grimsby. There he became a stalwart youth, and served as cook's boy in the kitchen of a usurping Earl Godrich at Lincoln, who held the English princess Goldeburgh much as Godard in Denmark had held Havelok. Havelok proved to be the stoutest man in England, and Earl Godrich, who had promised to wed the princess to the best man in the land, thought treacherously to keep the letter and to break the spirit of his promise, by making her the wife of the cook's boy. But then the royal virtues of young Havelok displayed themselves. Both the usurpers were in due time confounded, and Havelok and Goldeburgh reigned sixty years in England. They had also fifteen sons and daughters, whereof every son became a king, and each daughter a queen. The seal of the borough of Grimsby to this day connects the town with the legend by showing a bold figure of Grim, with his defending sword over a small figure of the royal Havelok and his defending shield over a small figure of the royal Goldeburgh. From old time to this day, the boundary stone between Grimsby and Wellow has been called Havelok Stone, and Grimsby also contains an old Havelok Street.

To the legend of Michael belongs *A Fragment on Popular Science*, which colours with religious thought an attempt to diffuse knowledge of some facts in astronomy, meteorology, physical geography, and physiology. *A Metrical Version of the Psalms* into English was another of the productions of this time. It is known as the *Northumbrian Psalter*. Luxury of the monks was attacked with satire in an English poem of the *Land of Cockaygne* (named from Coquina, a kitchen), a form of satire current in many parts of Europe, which told of a region free from trouble, where the rivers ran with oil, milk, wine, and honey; wherein the white and grey monks had an abbey of which the walls were built of pasties, which was paved with cakes and had puddings for pinnacles. Geese there flew about roasted, crying " Geese, all hot ! " and the monks—as the song went on, it did not spare them. To the close of the reign of Edward I. belongs also a set of moralized proverbs, called the *Proverbs of Hendying*, in a Southern English dialect. Each proverb forms an appendix to a six-syllabled rhyming stanza, with the refrain added, " Quoth Hendying."

39. Less homely philosophy is represented by the writings of Duns Scotus and William Occam. **Duns Scotus** was the elder of the two. He died in 1308, and his work falls wholly within the period of Edward I.'s reign. Occam survived him nearly forty years. John Duns, called Scotus, and by the Parisians the Subtle Doctor, was, like Roger Bacon, a Franciscan friar. He was first educated by the Franciscans of Newcastle, who sent him to Oxford. There he first studied, and then taught, for three years, opposing the doctrines of Thomas Aquinas with a success that is said (fabulously) to have attracted to Oxford 30,000 students. The Franciscans then sent Duns to Paris, where he took the degree of Doctor. In 1307 he had charge of the Theological School at Toulouse—less liberal than that of Paris—and there he sustained, with two hundred arguments, the Immaculate Conception. In 1308 Duns Scotus died. The followers of Thomas Aquinas, who called themselves Thomists, called the followers of Duns Scotus Scotists, or, with a contemptuous application of their chief's name, Dunces. Thomas Aquinas held that the faculties were distinguished, not only from each other, but from the essence of the mind, really and not nominally. Duns Scotus denied all real difference either between the several faculties or between the faculties and the mind, allowing only a nominal distinction between them.

**William Occam** was a pupil of Duns Scotus, and also a Franciscan. As his master was called the Subtle, so he was called the Invincible Doctor, and he carried on, with a broader spirit of philosophy, the war of the Nominalists against the Realists. The doctrine of Scotus and Occam is that which has prevailed in the latter ages of philosophy. Occam especially distinguished himself by the practical good sense which he brought into acute discussions of logic and metaphysics, and those studies owed much of their safe advancement in his day to contact with the English character. Occam's philosophy was not all speculative. While he attacked powerfully the despotism of mere dogmas, and encouraged each thinker to individual inquiry, he gave a workaday turn to his philosophy by boldly arguing against the domination of the Pope in temporal affairs. He was persecuted, but he never flinched; and he died firm to his sense of truth, at Munich, in 1347.

40. We have passed with Occam from the reign of Edward I. through that of Edward II. (1307-1327), and shall do the same

when speaking of **Robert of Brunne**, whose *Handlynge Synne*, written soon after the year 1300, is the last book of Edward I.'s time that has yet to be described. Robert Mannyng, of Brunne, now Bourn, seven or eight miles from Market Deeping, in Lincolnshire, was a canon of the Gilbertine order, who, from 1288 to 1303, professed in the priory of Sempringham, where nuns and monks fulfilled in one house a common vow. Afterwards he was removed to other Lincolnshire priories of the same order at Brimwake and Sixhill. "Handlynge Synne" is his translation of the French words, "Manuel des Péchés," forming the title of a book in French verse ascribed to Bishop Grosseteste, but really written in French by another Englishman, William of Waddington, a Yorkshire town two or three miles from Clitheroe. Of this book Robert of Brunne made a free amplified translation into English verse for the edification of the common people at their games and festivals. He omitted what he thought dull in his original, and added new stories ; the purpose of the work being to give religious instruction in the form of moral anecdotes or tales on the subject of the Ten Commandments, the seven deadly sins, sacrilege, the seven sacraments, and the twelve graces of thrift. Some years afterwards, between 1327 and 1338, Robert of Brunne, then living in the house of Sixhill, made, at the request of his prior, Robert of Malton, a popular translation into English verse of the French rhyming *Chronicle* of Peter Langtoft. It was begun at the time of the death of Edward II., written in the first years of Edward III., and designed, like the "Handlynge Synne," for wholesome recreation of the people at their merry meetings, because it became all Englishmen to know the history of their own land.

To the fourteenth century belongs a Northumbrian poem in about 24,000 lines, called *Cursor Mundi ; or, the Cursur o' the World*, which carries the Scripture story of the world, with curious intermixed legend, through seven ages, from Creation to the other side of Doomsday. During this century also there was continual translation of the most famous French *Metrical Romances*.

41. Richard Aungervyle was born in the year 1281, at Bury St. Edmund's, in Suffolk, and has therefore usually been called, from his birthplace, **Richard de Bury**. His father was a Norman knight, who died in middle life, and left him to the care of his maternal uncles, who sent him to continue his studies at Oxford. There he distinguished himself so much by his acquire-

ments that he was appointed tutor to Prince Edward, afterwards King Edward III.    In that office Richard of Bury preserved at court, for some time, a discreet silence between conflicting parties, while he won the hearty goodwill of his pupil.    In 1325, when Queen Isabel betook herself to Paris, Richard of Bury happened to be serving Edward II. as his treasurer, in Guienne. The time was now come for safe and energetic action in his pupil's interest.    Richard Aungervyle at once gave up to the queen, for advancement of her cause, the money which he had collected in Guienne for Edward II.    Edward's lieutenant in Guienne sent a troop of lancers to arrest the disloyal treasurer, who was pursued by them to the very gates of Paris, where he took refuge with the Franciscans.    In September, 1326, Queen Isabel and her son landed in Suffolk with an army.    Their declared object was the removal of the king's favourite Hugh de Spenser.    Lancastrians and royalists, therefore, alike flocked to their standard ; but the result of the movement was the deposition of King Edward II. by the next Parliament that met ; and thus, in January, 1327, the prince whom Richard Aungervyle had sedulously served, became, early in his fifteenth year, King Edward III.    Eight months later, the deposed king was murdered in Berkeley Castle by two of his keepers, his son ruling at that time under the control of Isabel and Mortimer.    Three years later, in 1330, Mortimer was impeached and hanged as a traitor, and Edward III. was king, free from dictation.

# CHAPTER IV.

## CHAUCER AND HIS CONTEMPORARIES.

1. EDWARD III., aged fifteen, came to his throne in the year 1327.    Geoffrey Chaucer was born in the year 1328.    Some think that the date of his birth should be placed about eleven years later, for a reason that will presently appear.    Other men of great mark were Chaucer's contemporaries, differing little from him in age : John Gower, William Langlande, author of "The Vision of Piers Plowman," and John Wiclif.

In their young days, Richard of Bury rose to the height of his good fortune, and produced a Latin treatise on the love of

books and the right use of them, called *Philobiblon*, which is a
pleasant prelude to the noble strain of literature that was about
to follow. Whether Isabel and Mortimer ruled Edward, or
Edward acted for himself, there was only favour and a full
reward for his past services to be enjoyed by the king's old
tutor who, at a critical time, had committed himself to the cause
of queen and prince. He was at once made Steward of the
Palace and Treasurer of the Wardrobe ; that office he resigned
when in 1329 he was made Lord Keeper of the Privy Seal. In
1330, when his age was forty-nine, he was sent in great state as
ambassador to Pope `John XXII., at Avignon, and there met
Petrarch, who was at that time twenty-six years old. Petrarch,
knowing that Richard of Bury was a great scholar, who had collected the largest library in England, asked him for some information on the subject of the "farthest Thule," which Richard
said that he thought he could find in one of his books when he
got home, and promised to send, but, as Petrarch told one of
his correspondents, he forgot to send it. He might well forget,
for he was very busy. The pope had promised him the next
bishopric vacant in England, and that proved to be the bishopric
of Durham. Pope and king nominated Richard of Bury, but
the Chapter resisted the pope's interference, and elected a very
fit man from among themselves. The king was determined,
and Richard of Bury, forced upon Durham as its bishop,
was consecrated in December, 1333. Not long before this he
had been appointed Treasurer of the Kingdom, and not
many months later he was made Lord Chancellor. He was
employed afterwards by the king as his ambassador, that he
might use his wit in carrying out the peaceful policy that he
advised. His wealth and influence were very great, and he
made generous use of them. In politics his voice was on the
side of peace and goodwill. When his desires for peace were
frustrated, he closed his career as a statesman. In his diocese
he was a most liberal friend to the poor. As a scholar he was
the friend of all who sought knowledge, and gave to all true
students who asked for it—with his hospitality while they were
studying at Durham—free access to that valuable library which
it had been the chief pleasure of his life to collect. He had
used his private fortune and his influence in Church and State
as a collector of books, applying to them the counsel of Solomon,
"Buy wisdom, and sell it not." Travelling friars searched for
him among the book chests of foreign monasteries. Suitors in

Chancery knew that the gift of a rare volume would induce the
Chancellor, not to pervert justice but to expedite the hearing of
their suits. The books, collected with enthusiasm, were not
treasured as a miser's hoard. When he withdrew from participation in the too warlike policy of Edward III., Richard de Bury,
confining himself to the duties of his diocese, lived retired among
his beloved parchments, still drawing to himself as chaplains
and companions the most learned English scholars of his time.
To be his chaplain, and by scholarship to win the household
affection of a man so influential with the king, was a step to
promotion sure enough to satisfy ambitious minds ; while life
with Richard Aungervyle housed the scholar among books, and
gave him hourly access to the best library in England. " It is
to be considered," said this Bishop of Durham, in his Latin
*Philobiblon*, written when Geoffrey Chaucer was sixteen years
old, "what convenience of teaching is in books—how easily,
how secretly, how safely in books we bear, without shame, the
poverty of human ignorance. These are masters who instruct
us without rod and cane, without words and wrath, and for no
clothes or money. If you approach them they are not asleep ;
if you question them they are not secret ; if you go astray they
do not grumble at you ; they know not how to laugh if you are
ignorant. O books, ye only are liberal and free who pay tribute
to all who ask it, and enfranchise all who serve you faithfully !"
In his *Philobiblon*, Richard de Bury enforced the right spirit of
study and right care of books, and it is noticeable that, orthodox
bishop as he was, no book of the time spoke more severely than
his of the degradation of the clergy, of the sensuality and ignorance of monks and friars. The main object of Richard de
Bury's work was practical. He was within a year of his death
when he wrote it, and he desired not only to justify his life-long
enthusiasm as a book collector, but to make the treasures which
he had held in his lifetime as a trust for the benefit of all good
scholarship in England, useful after his death for ever.
*Philobiblon* ended, therefore, with a plan for the bequest of his
books to Oxford on conditions that were to secure their perpetual usefulness, not merely to the particular hall which he
proposed to endow in association with his library, but to the
whole University. He did accordingly endow a hall, which the
monks of Durham had begun to build in the north suburbs of
Oxford, and did leave to it his famous library. Aungervyle's
library remained at Durham College for the use of the university

until that college was dissolved in the time of Henry VIII. Some of the books then went to Duke Humphrey's library, and some to Balliol College ; some went to Dr. George Owen, the king's physician, when he and William Martyn obtained the site of Durham College—afterwards used for the foundation of Trinity College—from King Edward VI.

2. Among the men of mark who passed through Richard of Bury's house as chaplains, the most famous were Thomas Bradwardine and Robert Holcot.

**Thomas Bradwardine,** of an old family named after a village on the Wye still called Bredwardine, was born either at Chichester, or at Hartfield, in the diocese of Chichester, about the year 1290. He graduated from Merton College, and became afterwards Divinity Professor, and Chancellor of the University of Oxford. He was already chancellor of his university when he lived as chaplain and friend with Richard Aungervyle, Bishop of Durham. Through his friend's influence he became chaplain and confessor to Edward III., whom he attended during his wars in France. There the uncouth scholar, whose clumsiness of manner was a jest to the pope's nephew at Avignon, would address, as priest and patriot, the English army on the eve of battle. The king annulled the election when Bradwardine was first chosen archbishop by the monks of Canterbury, saying that he " could ill spare so worthy a man, and never could see that he wished himself to be spared." But very soon the see fell vacant a second time, and then, in the year 1349, when Chaucer's age was twenty-one, Bradwardine was again elected. This time the office was accepted, and Bradwardine came to England, where, forty days after his consecration, and before he was enthroned, he died of the Great Plague, then traversing Europe. At Oxford Bradwardine had written on speculative geometry and arithmetic, on proportions of velocities, and had formed a rather thick volume of astronomical tables. But his great work was founded on University lectures against the Pelagian heresy, written later in life, and this was his *De Causa Dei*— " On the Cause of God against Pelagius," in which he treated theological questions mathematically, and was considered to have produced a masterpiece of doctrinal argument. As the book is now printed, it forms a massive folio of 876 closely-filled pages. Bradwardine thus earned from the pope the title of the Profound Doctor, and from Chaucer the allusion in his Nun's Priest's Tale :

E

> " For I ne cannot bolt it to the bran
>    As can the holy Doctor Augustin,
>    Or Boece, or the Bishop Bradwardin."

**Robert Holcot,** who was also one of Richard of Bury's chaplains, also was among the victims of the Plague in 1349. He was born and educated at Northampton, became a Dominican, taught theology at Oxford, and, when he died, was general of the order of the Austin Friars. He wrote many volumes. In those on scholastic philosophy he followed Duns Scotus and William Occam as a defender of Nominalism, and he contributed to mediæval theology a famous work in four books, *Super Sententias* (On Opinions), in which he undertakes to answer a series of questions upon points of faith. Holcot also wrote while Chaucer, a bright student, was growing into manhood.

Another of Richard de Bury's chaplains was **Walter Burley,** who produced a library of treatises, was an expert scholar in Aristotle, and, like Holcot, maintained the more healthy philosophy of what might be called the English school against the realists.

3. **John of Gaddesden,** in Hertfordshire, had been physician to Edward III. when he was prince, and when he had Richard of Bury for his tutor. In the reign of Edward III. he was the king's physician; and he was the first Englishman who held that office. He wrote a famous compilation of the whole mediæval practice of physic, chiefly as derived from the Arabians by himself and by Gilbertus Anglicus and others of his predecessors, with additions from his own experience. He called his book the " English Rose "—*Rosa Anglica*—because a treatise of medicine published some years before in France had been called the Lily. His book is shrewd, learned, and amusing to the moderns, who laugh at such a remedy for epilepsy as a boar's bladder boiled, mistletoe, and a cuckoo.

4. Monastic chroniclers were active still during the reign of Edward III. **John of Trokelowe** wrote, very early in this reign, some valuable *Annals* of the reign of Edward II. from 1307 to 1323. From that date they were continued by **Henry of Blaneford** with a fragment that came to an abrupt end in the year 1324. Some years later **Robert of Avesbury,** who kept the Register of the Archbishop's Court at Canterbury, began a history, *De Mirabilibus Gestis Edwardi III.* (Of the Admirable Deeds of King Edward III.), which carried from the

birth of Edward III. In 1313 to 1356 a short detail of public events, with simple transcripts of original documents and extracts from letters.

John of Fordun, a village in Kincardine, was a patriotic Scot, secular priest and chaplain of the cathedral of Aberdeen. He had not graduated in the schools. In the reign of Edward III. John of Fordun wrote a *Scotichronicon*, or Chronicle of Scotland. It began with Shem, Ham, Japheth, and the origin of the Scots, and was brought down to the year 1360, in a manner that in some degree forsook the method of monastic annals, and made an approach to a formal history.

In England **Ralph Higden** finished his *Polychronicon* about the year 1361; and at the close of the reign of Edward III. **William Thorn** was at work on a Latin *Chronicle of Canterbury Abbey*.

5. **Ralph Higden** has interest for us not only as a chronicler. His name has been variously spelt. Ranulphus or Ralph, appears sometimes as Radulphus or Randall; and Higden, by transition from Higgeden, has become Higgened or Higgenet, if the common belief be true that Ralph Higden, who wrote in his later years the "Polychronicon," is the Randall Higgenet who in his earlier days wrote the Chester miracle plays. Ralph Higden became a Benedictine monk of St. Werburgh in Chester about the year 1299, and he is believed to be the Randall Higgenet of the same abbey, of whom there was a tradition that he thrice visited Rome to get the Pope's leave for the acting of his miracle-plays at Chester in the English tongue. Leave having been obtained, the plays were said, in a note added at the end of the sixteenth century to a MS. copy of the proclamation of them, to have been first acted at Chester in the mayoralty of Sir John Arnway (1327—1328), which would be about the date of Chaucer's birth. Higden's *Polychronicon*, in seven books, was so called, he says, because it gave the chronicle of many times. Its first book described the countries of the known world, especially Britain; its second book gave the history of the World from the Creation to Nebuchadnezzar; the next book closed with the birth of Christ; the fourth book carried on the chronicle to the arrival of the Saxons in England; the fifth proceeded to the invasion of the Danes; the sixth to the Norman Conquest; and the seventh to Higden's own time in the reign of Edward III., his latest date being the year 1342. He died in

1363, and long after his death the "Polychronicon" stood in high credit as a sketch of universal history, with special reference to England.

Although not beyond doubt, it is very likely that the date assigned to the first acting at Chester of MIRACLE PLAYS in English is right, and that Ralph Higden was the author of the series. Since the days of Stephen and Henry II. religious entertainments of this form had been growing in popularity. A twelfth-century MS., found in the town library of Tours, contains three Anglo-Norman miracle-plays, as old, or nearly as old, as the plays of Hilarius, already described (ch. iii. § 9). The stage directions illustrate the first removal of the acting from the inside to the outside of the church. This must soon have become necessary, if it were only for accommodation of the increasing number of spectators. For the acting of those plays of which a MS. was found at Tours, scaffolding was built over the steps of the church, and the audience occupied the square in front. Out of the heaven of the church, Figura—God—passed to Adam in Paradise, upon a stage level with the highest steps of the church door. From that Paradise Adam and Eve were driven down a few steps to the lower stage that represented Earth. Below this, nearest to the spectators, was hell, an enclosed place in which cries were made, chains were rattled, and out of which smoke came ; out of which also men and boys dressed as devils came by a door opening into a free space between the scaffolding and the semicircle of the front row of spectators. They were also directed now and then to go among the people, and passed round by them sometimes to one of the upper platforms. The original connection of these plays with the Church service was represented by the hymns of choristers.

The next step in the development of the miracle-play was hastened by the complaint that the crowds who came to witness the performance, on an outside scaffolding, attached to the church, trampled the graves in the churchyards. Decrees were made to prevent this desecration of the graves, and the advance probably was rapid to the setting up of detached scaffolding for the performance of the plays—still by the clergy, choristers and parish clerks—upon unconsecrated ground.

In London the parish clerks had formed themselves into a harmonic guild, chartered by Henry III. in 1233, and their music was sought at the funerals and entertainments of the great. As miracle-plays increased in popularity, the parish clerks occupied themselves much with the acting of them. Chaucer's jolly Absalom, of whom we are told that

> " Sometimes to shew his lightness and maistrie
> He playeth Herod on a scaffold high,"

was a parish clerk. The strongest impulse to a regular participation of the laity in the production of these plays seems to have been given by the Church when, in 1264, Pope Urban IV. founded, and in 1311 Clement V. firmly established, the festival of Corpus Christi in honour of the consecrated Host. This was the one festival of the Church wherein laity and clergy walked together. The guilds of a town contributed their pictures, images, and living representatives of Scripture characters to the procession, and the day was one of common festival. From the parade of persons dressed to represent the Scripture characters, it was an easy step to their use in the dramatic presentation of a sacred story. The festival of Corpus Christi, always held on the first Thursday after Trinity Sunday, which is eight weeks after Easter, was a holiday of brightest summer time. It came but a fortnight after the older and yet more popular festivities of Whitsuntide, and Whitsuntide and Corpus Christi soon were established as customary times for the out-of-door performance of mysteries or, as we called them, miracle-plays, by guilds of towns.

But, even in Chaucer's lifetime, such plays were still being acted by the clergy. Both clergy and laity were actors in the middle of the thirteenth century, when in that " Manuel des Pèchés " (ch. iii. § 40) which in the year 1303 Robert of Brunne translated as " The Handlyng Synne," it was declared to be .sin in the clergy to assist at any other plays than those which belonged to the Liturgy and were acted within the church at Easter and Christmas. This author especially condemned participation by the clergy in plays acted in churchyards, streets, or green places. A century later, in 1378, when Chaucer was fifty years old, the choristers of St. Paul's Cathedral petitioned Richard II. to prohibit the acting of the History of the Old Testament, to the great prejudice of the clergy of the Church, who had spent considerable sums for a public representation of Old Testament plays at the ensuing Christmas.

In the hands of the English guilds—which stood for the rising middle classes of the people—miracle-plays received a development peculiar to this country. Instead of short sequences of three or four plays, complete sets were produced, and they told what were held to be the essential parts of the Scripture story from the Creation of Man to the Day of Judgment. The number in each set may have corresponded to the number of guilds in the town for which it was originally written. Each guild was entrusted permanently with the due mounting and acting of one play in the set. Thus, at Chester, the tanners played "The Fall of Lucifer;" the drapers played "The Creation and Fall, and the Death of Abel;" "The Story of Noah's Flood" was played by the water leaders and the drawers of Dee. Among the possessions of each guild were the properties for its miracle-play, carefully to be kept in repair, and renewed when necessary. Actors rehearsed carefully, and were paid according to the length of their parts. They wore masks, or had their faces painted in accordance with the characters they undertook. The player of the devil wore wings and a closely-fitting leather dress, trimmed with feathers and hair, and ending in claws over the hands and feet. All the other actors wore gloves, or had sleeves continued into hands. The souls of the saved in the day of judgment wore white leather ; the others, whose faces were blacked, wore a linen dress suggestive of fire, with black, yellow, and red. Thus we have, among the miscellaneous items in old books of the Coventry guilds, a charge for souls' coats ; one for a link to set the world on fire ; and "paid to Crowe for making of three worlds, three shillings." The stage furniture was as handsome in thrones and other properties as each company could make it. They gilded what they could. Hell mouth, a monstrous head of a whale, its old emblem (chap. ii. § 12), was painted on linen with open jaws—sometimes jaws that opened and shut, two men working them—and a fire lighted where it would give the appearance of a breath of flames. By this way the fiends came up and down.

The acting of one of these great sequences of plays usually took three days, but was not limited to three. In 1409, in the reign of Henry IV., the parish clerks played at Skinner's Well, in Islington, for eight days, "matter from the Creation of the World." In this country the taste for miracle-plays was blended with the old desire to diffuse, as far as possible, a knowledge of religious truth ; and therefore the sets of miracle-plays, as acted by our town guilds, placed in the streets, as completely as might be, a living picture Bible before the eyes of all the people. Such sequences of plays were acted in London, Dublin, York, Newcastle, Lancaster, Preston, Kendal, Wakefield, Chester, Coventry, and elsewhere. The set used in one town might be adopted by another. Many sets must have been lost, but three remain to show how thoroughly the English people sought to use the miracle-play for the advancement of right knowledge. These three are known as the *Chester, Wakefield,* and *Coventry* plays. Those which were acted at Wakefield have been called the "Towneley" Mysteries, because the sole existing MS. of them belonged to the Towneley family.

The *Chester Plays* were a series of twenty-four, written, as we have seen, by a monk of St. Werburgh's in Chester, probably Ralph Higden, and first acted in 1327 or 1328.

There is some reason to think that the *Wakefield Plays* were produced by a monk of the cell of Augustinian canons at Wood-kirk, four miles north of Wakefield, and there is clear evidence that they were written to be acted by the Wakefield guilds. There are thirty-two plays in the Wakefield series, perhaps not all from the same hand, but most of them distinguished among other plays of the kind by unusual ability ; there is breadth of humour where that was called for, and in other places a true natural pathos.

The *Coventry Plays* are forty-two in number, the work of a duller mind. Of the three sets they are the least interesting, and there is reason to doubt the statement, first made in the seventeenth century by a librarian on a fly-leaf of the MS., that these were the plays acted at Coventry. The guilds of Coventry did act plays ; and it is to Coventry that we are indebted for much valuable information on the details of the acting from the entries still preserved in its guilds' books. But this evidence proves also that the plays acted by the guilds of Coventry were not those which we now call Coventry mysteries. A religious house at Coventry may possibly have produced a second set. Wherever written, they came, no doubt, from a house dedicated to the Virgin Mary; for in the pains taken to give prominence to the Virgin we find the most characteristic feature of this series of plays.

The spectator who had taken his place betimes—by six o'clock in the morning—at a window or upon a scaffolding, to see the miracle-plays, would have first the great decorated stage upon six wheels, which was to present the Creation, rolled before him. He would receive from that such living impression as it was meant to convey, and when it rolled away to begin the

series at some other part of the town before another concourse
of spectators, the next pageant would follow to present to him
the story of the death of Abel. That would pass, and then
would come a lively presentment of the story of the Flood.
Sometimes more than one stage was necessary to the acting of a
play. The Old Testament series would be founded on those
parts of Scripture which told of the relations between God and
man, and pointed to the Saviour. The New Testament series
would represent the life of Christ, still showing what the Church
taught to be man's relation to the world to come, and closing
with the Day of Judgment. The acting was not confined to the
stages, but in some places blended with the real life of the town.
The Magi rode in through the streets, sought Herod on his
throne, and addressed him from their horses ; then rode on and
found the infant Christ. At another time a procession travelled
through the streets leading the Lord before the judgment seat of
Pilate. Everything that was a part of Bible story was presented
and received with deep religious feeling. The coarseness of
coarse men, slayers of the Innocents, tormentors, and executioners, was realised in a way that—whatever we may now think
of it—had no comic effect upon spectators. If in France the
manner of acting which brought those who performed devils'
parts into too constant and familiar relations with the audience
deprived them of terror, it was not so in England. Our evil
spirits came only when there was fit occasion, as tempters, as
bringers of evil dreams, as the possessors of lost souls. But
since the strain of deep and serious attention for three long
successive days could not be borne by any human audience,
places of relaxation and laughter were provided, always from
material that lay outside the Bible story. Thus Cain might
have a comic man ; Noah's obstinate wife was an accepted
comic character ; and between the Old Testament and New
Testament sections of the series there was a distinctly comic
interlude, the Shepherd's Play.

*The Shepherds' Play* perhaps arose out of a custom, which
certainly existed in the Netherlands, of blending the performance of a great mystery in the church with the daily life of the
people in the world outside. On Good Friday the scenes of the
Passion were represented in the church ; on Easter day, the
Resurrection : on the intervening Saturday, there came, in the
Netherlands, with the throng of the fair that gathered about
every great Church celebration, criers who sold salves to women

dressed as the three Marys ; while, always with some ultimate reference to the sacred time, there were acted in the open market, peasant comedies, with thumping and abuse. So, when the Nativity was acted in church on Christmas morning, the Shepherds' Plays may have been at their beginning acted out of doors on Christmas Eve. The first notion of the Shepherds' Play was a homely realisation of the record that " there were in the same country, shepherds abiding in the field, keeping watch over their flocks by night." Simple shepherds were represented first, talking together, and their talk was sometimes of the hardships of the poor, of wrongs to be righted ; then came one who was especially the comic shepherd, and jesting began, with wrestling or some other rough country sport. After that, each would bring out his supper. They were shepherds of the same country with the spectators of the play. In the Chester play they spoke of eating meat with Lancashire bannocks, and of drinking Alton ale. Jest having been made over the rude feast, there floated through the air, from concealed choristers, the song of the angels. At first the shepherds were still in their jesting mood, and mimicked the singing ; then they became filled with religious awe, went with their rustic gifts to the stable in which the infant lay, and, after they had made their offerings, rose up exalted into saints. In the Wakefield series there are two Shepherds' Plays, so that the actors might take either. In one of them the comic shepherd is a sheep-stealer, and an incident which must have excited roars of laughter from a rough and hearty Yorkshire audience, is so cleverly dramatised, that, apart from the religious close which can be completely separated from it, this Wakefield Shepherds' Play may justly be accounted the first English farce. Nevertheless, as we shall find, the origin of the modern drama must not be traced to the miracle-play. There is no more than a distant cousinship between them. The miracle-plays, as thus adopted by the English people, remained part of the national life of England, not only throughout Chaucer's lifetime, but long afterwards. In Chaucer's time, even the Cornishmen had such plays written for them in the old Cymric of Cornwall ; and miracle-plays were still acted at Chester as late as the year 1577 ; at Coventry as late as 1580, when Shakespeare was sixteen years old, and the true drama was rising from another source.

6. There will be little more to say of our home literature during the former half of the reign of Edward III., that is

E *

during the boyhood and youth of Chaucer, when two North of England men, Laurence Minot, and Richard Rolle, of Hampole, have been included in the sketch.    One wrote of war, the other of religion.

**Laurence Minot** was a poet who in Northern English celebrated victories of Edward III. over the Scots and the French, from the battle of Halidon Hill, in July, 1333, to the capture of Guines Castle, in January, 1352.* His war-songs were linked together by connecting verses.    When he had celebrated the defeat of the Scots at Halidon Hill, which caused the surrender of Berwick, he exulted in his second song over the avenging of Bannockburn ; then celebrated the king's expedition to Brabant, in 1338 ; proceeded to the first invasion of France ; the sea-fight of Sluys or of the Swyne ; the siege of Tournai ; a song of triumph for the great battle of Crécy, in 1346 ; songs of the siege of Calais, and of the battle of Neville's Cross (October, 1346), in which David King of the Scots was taken prisoner.    Then followed his celebrations of victory at sea over the Spaniards in 1350, and lastly, of the taking of Guines Castle, in 1352, when Chaucer was twenty-four years old. Probably Minot died soon afterwards, as he did not sing of the memorable events of the next following years.    He was our first national song writer, and used with ease a variety of rhyming measures, while he retained something of the old habit of alliteration.

7. **Richard Rolle**, known also as the Hermit of Hampole, was born, about the year 1290, at Thornton in Yorkshire.    He was sent to school, and from school to Oxford, by Thomas Neville, Archdeacon of Durham, and made great progress in theological studies.    At the age of nineteen, mindful of the un-

* *New Style.*—An Act of Parliament of the year 1752 introduced "New Style" by bringing the English reckoning of dates into conformity with that of countries which had adopted Pope Gregory XIII.'s reform of the calendar, a reform first instituted in 1582, and then at once adopted in France, Italy, Spain, Denmark, Flanders, and Portugal. Protestant Germany did not accept this reformation by a pope till 1699 ; Protestant England held aloof till 1752.    Besides the rectification of the day of the month, which then was eleven days behind the reckoning in foreign countries, the Act of 1752 abolished the custom, begun in the twelfth century, and until then in use in England, not in Scotland, of reckoning the 25th of March as the first day of the legal year, while the 1st of January was, according to the popular reckoning by the Julian Calendar, accounted New Year's Day.    Before 1752, therefore, any date in a public record or official document, falling in January or February, or in March, to the 24th inclusive, would be ascribed to the year preceding that in which we should now reckon it.    Thus the capture of Guines Castle was dated January, 1351.    I give all such dates according to the present way of reckoning.

certainty of life, and fearing the temptation to sin, he returned home, and one day told a beloved sister that he had a mighty desire towards two of her gowns, one white the other grey. Would she bring them to him the next day in a neighbouring wood, and bring with them a hood her father used in rainy weather? When she did so, he took off his own clothes, put on his sister's white dress next his skin, drew over it the grey dress with its sleeves cut off, thrusting his arms through the armholes, hooded himself with his father's rain-hood, and having thus made himself look as much like a hermit as he could, ran away, while his sister cried, " My brother is mad !" He went then, so dressed, on the vigil of the Assumption, into a church, and placed himself where the wife of a Sir John de Dalton used to pray. When Lady de Dalton came with her servants, she would not allow them to disturb the pious young man at his prayers. Her sons, who had studied at Oxford, told her who he was. Next day he assumed, unbidden, the dress of an assistant, and joined in the singing of the service ; after which, having obtained the benediction of the priest, he mounted the pulpit, and preached such a sermon that many wept over it and said they had never heard the like before. After mass, Sir John de Dalton invited him to dinner ; but he went, because of humility, into a poor old house at the gate of the manor, till he was urged by the knight's own sons to the dinner table. During dinner he maintained a profound silence; but after dinner, Sir John, having talked with him privately, was satisfied of his sanity ; he therefore furnished the enthusiast with such hermit's dress as he wished for, gave him a cell to live in, and provided for his daily sustenance. The Hermit of Hampole, thus set up in his chosen vocation, became, while Minot was singing the victories of Edward III., the busiest religious writer of his day, and continued so till 1349, when he died, and was buried in the Cistercian nunnery of Hampole, about four miles from Doncaster, near which he had set up his hermit's cell, and which after his death derived great profit from his reputation as a saint. He wrote many religious treatises in Latin and in English, and he turned the *Psalms of David* into English prose. A version of the Psalter into English had been made about nine years before, in 1327, by **William of Shoreham. Richard Rolle** also versified part of the book of Job, and produced a Northern English poem in seven books, and almost ten thousand lines, called *The Pricke of Conscience* (Stimulus Conscientiæ). Its seven books

treat—1. Of the Beginning of Man's Life. 2. Of the Unstable-
ness of this World. 3. Of Death, and why Death is to be
Dreaded. 4. Of Purgatory. 5. Of Doomsday. 6. Of the Pains
of Hell. 7. Of the Joys of Heaven. The poem represents
in the mind of an honest and religious monk that body of
mediæval doctrine against which, in some of its parts—and
especially its claim for the pope or his delegates of power to
trade in release from the pains of purgatory—the most vigorous
protest of the English mind was already arising.

8. To the year 1340, which is about the date of Hampole's
" Pricke of Conscience," belongs a prose translation by **Dan
Michel** of Northgate, into Kentish dialect, of a French treatise,
" Le Somme des Vices et des Vertues," written in 1279 by Frère
Lorens (Laurentius Gallus) for Philip II. of France. The
English translation is entitled *The Ayenbite* (Again-bite, Re-
morse) *of Inwit* (Conscience). It discusses the Ten Command-
ments, the Creed, the seven deadly sins, how to learn to die,
knowledge of good and evil, wit and clergy, the five senses, the
seven petitions of the Paternoster, the seven gifts of the Holy
Ghost, and other such subjects, with more doctrine and less
anecdote than in the " Manuel des Péchés " or " Handlynge
Synne," which was a work of like intention.

9. In the year of the death of Richard Rolle of Hampole, 1349,
John Wiclif was five-and-twenty years old, William Langland
little younger, Geoffrey Chaucer about one-and-twenty, John
Gower little older, and a famous Scottish poet of their day, John
Barbour, was thirty-three years old, according to the earliest
date assigned to his birth, nineteen according to the latest. It
was then also seven-and-twenty years since Sir John Mandeville
set out upon his adventures in the world. Young Chaucer had
begun to sing when Mandeville, by nearly thirty years his senior,
wrote the story of his travels. In the same year, 1349, Dante
had been dead twenty-eight years, but the vigour of Italian
literature was being maintained by Petrarch and Boccaccio,
Petrarch then forty-five years old and Boccaccio six-and-thirty.

**Geoffrey Chaucer** was probably the son of a Richard
Chaucer, vintner, of London, who lived in the Vintry ward, and
had a house and tavern in Royal Street, now College Hill, not
far from the church of St. Mary Aldermary. In that church he
was buried in 1349, when Geoffrey, if born in 1328, would have
been twenty-one years old. Richard had a son John, who was
also a vintner, and who may have been Geoffrey's elder brother.

Chaucer's arms did not connect his family with any noble house. A perpendicular line divided the shield into halves, and it was crossed by a transverse bar. On one side of the middle line the bar was red on a white ground, on the other side white on a red ground. Thomas Fuller says that some wits had made Chaucer's arms to mean "the dashing of white and red wine (the parents of our ordinary claret), as nicking his father's profession." Probably they were right. Arms were not granted to merchants until the reign of Henry VI. ; but long before that time wealthy merchants of the Middle Ages bore their trade-marks upon shields. The vintners, or wine-tunners, to whose body Richard Chaucer belonged, were in the days of Edward III. a prosperous body, merchant vintners of Gascoyne yielding to London several mayors, one of whom, in 1359, feasted together at his house in the Vintry the four kings of England, France, Scotland, and Cyprus.

The date usually assigned to Chaucer's birth, 1328, is inferred from the inscription on his monument in Westminster Abbey. This monument, an altar tomb under a Gothic canopy, was not erected until the year 1556, when Nicholas Brigham, a small poet who reverenced the genius of Chaucer, built it at his own expense. But we know from Caxton that there was an earlier inscription on a table hanging on a pillar near the poet's burial-place; and Brigham can hardly have done otherwise than repeat on his new tomb the old record that Chaucer died on the 25th of October, 1400, and that his age was then seventy-two. This date is in harmony with what we know of Chaucer's life and writings.

Chaucer's writings show him to have been a student to the last ; we cannot therefore ascribe all his knowledge to the education he had as a youth. But his early writings show a range of culture that could have come only of a liberal education. There is no direct evidence that he studied at Oxford or Cambridge. If he went to either University, probably it was to Cambridge, for in his "Court of Love" he makes his Philogenet describe himself as "of Cambridge, clerk ;" and in the opening of his Reve's tale he alludes familiarly to the brook, mill, and bridge, which were "at Trompington, not far fro Cantebrigge." But there are no such familiar references to Oxford in his verse, though it must not be forgotten that the poor scholar sketched with sympathetic touches in the Prologue to the "Canterbury Tales" was a clerk of Oxenforde.

Nothing trustworthy is known of Chaucer's occupation in the world during the first years of his manhood.  He was a poet, we know, and perhaps while he was translating the famous "Roman de la Rose" (ch. iii. § 36)—he tells us himself that he was its translator—he may have been earning money in the Vintry ward.  Chaucer read in the earlier part of his life the French literature then most in request, and by his translations earned a balade of compliment from Eustache Deschamps with the refrain "Grant translateur, noble Geoffroi Chaucier."  It is very likely that Chaucer worked at his translation of the *Romaunt of the Rose* when he was training himself in his vocation as a poet, and that he laid it aside as he felt more and more strongly the impulse towards independent song.  He did not translate selections, but went straight on with the work till he abandoned it.  Of the 4,070 lines which were the work of Guillaume de Lorris, Chaucer gave, in 4,432 lines, a complete translation into English verse, of the same metre, happily fitting English to the French, or now and then expanding the original thought in a version that is close without servility.  Of the 18,002 lines which were the work of Jean de Meung, Chaucer translated on as far as verse 5,169 of the whole poem fully, and even with slight amplification.  There he left off, only appending one passage levelled against hypocrisy in friars, from a much later part of the work.  A fellow-feeling with Jean de Meung may have caused young Chaucer to translate this in advance, while he was still labouring towards a complete version of one of the most famous poems in the fashionable literature of his time.  The fashionable taste for French court poetry is reflected from the greater part of the verse written by Chaucer in his early manhood.  But it is with the higher strain of the Italian literature that his genius feels its affinity as he attains full strength.  Every young poet must acquire the mechanism of his art by imitation, and the fashion among poets in his younger days caused Chaucer to learn his art, in the first instance, as an imitator of the trouvères.  Before the age of forty he had perhaps not fully outgrown the influences of his early training.  But when he had passed the age of forty Chaucer's writing shows, with the best qualities of his own independent genius, that where he looked abroad at all for a quickening influence it was not to France, but to the great Italian writers, Dante, Petrarch, and Boccaccio.

Besides the " Romaunt of the Rose," we may probably place

Chaucer's *Translation of Boëthius,* who had been translated 450 years earlier by King Alfred (ch. ii. § 18), as a work of his youth. It reads like a student's exercise; and it is very remarkable that the interspersed "metra" of the original did not tempt the young poet to exercise his skill in verse. Chaucer's first original work was probably *The Court of Love,* a poem which so clearly derives its allegorical form from a study of the "Roman de la Rose," that it might most naturally have come into the mind of Chaucer while he was at work on his translation of that poem. But, through forms which he was to outgrow, Chaucer already spoke like himself. In this "Court of Love" he struck the key-note of his future harmonies. The most characteristic feature of his poetry at once appears in it. The author is represented as "Philogenet, of Cambridge, clerk," ashamed to think that he is eighteen years old and has not yet paid service at the Court of Love. He journeys thither, and what does he find? Venus, of course, is the goddess worshipped. But under her, the mythical Admetus and Alcestis, through whom marriage was idealized, are King and Queen of Love, and they live in a castle painted within and without with daisies. This reading of love, and the use of the daisy as its type, is Chaucer's own, repeated sometimes in form, and in spirit pervading all the work of his life. For Chaucer aloᵤe in his time felt the whole beauty of womanhood, and felt it most in its most perfect type, in wifehood with the modest graces of the daisy, with its soothing virtues, and its power of healing inward wounds. Physicians in his day ascribed such power to the plant which, by Heaven's special blessing, was made common to all, the daisy, outward emblem also of the true and pure wife in its heart of gold and its white crown of innocence. That is what Chaucer meant when he told in later writing of his reverence for the daisy, and identified Alcestis with it. Why Alcestis? The old fable said that Admetus was the son of Pheres, founder of Pheræ, and one of those who took part in the Calydonian boar hunt and the Argonautic expedition. He sought marriage with Alcestis, daughter of Pelias, and was accepted by her father on condition that he came to claim her in a chariot drawn by lions and boars. This he did by help of Apollo. But, because he forgot to sacrifice to Diana, he found in his bridal chamber snakes rolled in a lump. Apollo appeased the goddess, and also obtained of the Fates deliverance from death for his friend

Admetus if, when the last hour came, his father, mother, or wife would die for him. This Alcestis did ; but she was brought back from the dead by Hercules. In this fable, the lions and boars, which were to be obedient to the rein before the bride was claimed, meant passions to be tamed ; and the next incident was of like significance, the story being, to its close in an ideal of wifely devotion, throughout a mythical upholding of true marriage. In his " Court of Love" Chaucer worked upon the lines of the French poets, introduced even a code distinctly founded upon that of the Courts of Love, which were in his time still popular in France (ch. iii. § 36); but it was not in him to adopt the playful fiction of these Courts. He had what we might now call his own English sense of the domestic side of their one courtly theme, not represented even by the English literature of his day ; and at once he became, alone in his own time, and more distinctively than any who followed him, the reverencer of the daisy as he understood his flower, the poet of a true and perfect womanhood.

Of less interest, but still important, is another point to be noted in Chaucer's Court of Love. It includes stanzas translated from one of those poems with which Boccaccio was then delighting every educated reader of Italian who could buy or borrow copies. It is also in the peculiar seven-lined stanza which should be called Chaucer's stanza, since, probably in the course of such translation, it was evidently formed by him out of the octave rhyme which Boccaccio was then first introducing into literature.

10. We are now passing gradually from that first of the FOUR PERIODS OF ENGLISH LITERATURE which may be called, from its most obvious external character, *the Period of the Formation of the Language* ; and we enter gradually upon a second, which we may call *the Period of Italian Influence.*

The spirit of our literature remains the same from first to last. But in outward fashion—in costume of thought as of bodies—there are marked variations in the course of time. As a student of the history of dress could tell, sometimes very exactly, from the clothes worn by the figure in a portrait when the person lived who was there painted, so the student of the history of literature learns to tell, sometimes very exactly, from the dress worn by a thought—that is to say, from the fashion of its utterance—at what time it was spoken. If a book be written in Early English, which we can interpret only after special study, we

have, of course, an outward sign that it was written during the
Period of the Formation of the Language.  Minuter study of the
language in its early stages will make it possible to infer from
the language of the book, often with great accuracy, at what
date, and even in what part of England, it was written.  In
Chaucer's time the English of our towns had approached so
closely to the modern form that, with slight help from a
glossary, poems of his may be widely enjoyed by those who
have no critical knowledge of the English of the fourteenth
century; but English of the rural districts, older in form
although the same in date, they find it much less easy to understand.  We cannot say that we have passed out of the Period of
the Formation of the Language at the time when a new outward
characteristic, afterwards to become the one most prominent, is
beginning to appear.  At first, in the time of Chaucer, we see
this only as an influence of the best writers of Italy upon the
best writers in England.

With Dante, Petrarch, and Boccaccio began the widespread
influence of Italy over the forms of literature almost throughout
Europe.  When Chaucer was born, in 1328, Dante (ch. iii. § 36)
had been dead seven years, but Petrarch and Boccaccio were
then living—one a young man and the other a boy—each with
his work before him.  At that date Petrarch was twenty-four
years old, Boccaccio fifteen.  They were Chaucer's contemporaries, but were older men, the work of whose manhood came
with the fresh impulse of a new delight upon the mind of
Chaucer in his youth.  Although Boccaccio was nine years
younger than Petrarch, he survived him but a year, Petrarch
dying in 1374, Boccaccio in 1375, when Chaucer was within
three or four years of fifty.

11. *Francis Petrarch*, born at Arezzo, was, like Dante, of
the Florentine Republic.  He was born in a time of party strife,
which caused his family to settle, with many other Italians, at
Avignon, when he was nine years old, and about four years after
a papal court had been established there.  Young Petrarch
studied old Latin authors with the patriotic sense that they were
the forefathers of his countrymen.  From the age of fourteen to
the age of eighteen he was at Montpellier to study law, but he
neglected law and gave his heart to the old Latins, taking, then
and always, a particular delight in collecting manuscripts of
their works.  From the age of eighteen to the age of twenty-one
or twenty-two Petrarch was studying law at Bologna.  Then

his father died, and he returned to Avignon. His mother died soon afterwards, and both Francis and his brother Gerard were robbed of their inheritance by a dishonest executor. From about this time—from the age of twenty-three—Petrarch began to write sonnets to Laura. For means of livelihood he was obliged to look to the patronage that would give him a benefice in the Church, and this he found in the friendship of a young member of the powerful Colonna family who had been his fellow-student at Bologna. His friend, young as he was, came as a bishop, to Avignon ; Petrarch and he became comrades again, and through him Petrarch obtained the help he needed. He travelled. When he was thirty-one his friend and old fellow-student gave him a canonry at Lombès—the place of which he was bishop—and wrote to him about the same time of the Laura whom he had been celebrating in his sonnets, that many believed her to be a work of his imagination, and that his love was the Laurea, the laurel crown, for which he laboured.

The lady to whom these exercises in love-poetry were dedicated in the usual way was a Laurette de Noves, who, at the age of eighteen, married Hugues de Sade, a young gentleman of twenty. He belonged to one of the chief families in Avignon, and she was married two years before Petrarch first met her. While Petrarch sang of Laura, she became the mother of eleven children—seven sons and four daughters. We have seen (ch. iii. § 36) that the customs of the Courts of Love completely shut out any notion of a personal suit towards the lady who was complimented by the dedication to her of a series of pieces of this sort. If doubt on the matter had been possible, Madame de Sade's position at Avignon would, in the case of Petrarch, have effectually settled it. Perhaps she owed, in some degree, the compliment of dedication to the fact that she gave the poet the right name for the ideal of his verse. As Dante's ideal would be best expressed through the name of Beatrice (ch. iii. § 36), so Petrarch's may have caused him to seek some lady who was worthy of his compliment, and who was named Laura. Boccaccio, who is the oldest good authority concerning Petrarch, believed with his friend the Bishop of Lombès, that Laura was an allegory for the Poet's Laurel. When at the age of thirty-three Petrarch bought himself a cottage and two little gardens at Vaucluse, about three miles from Avignon, and settled there, he was not himself single. There was born to him in that year a son, who lived to the age of twenty-four. There was born to him also, some years afterwards, a daughter, Francesca. The rest of Petrarch's life was that of a poet, patriot, and scholar. His heart glowed, and his verse glowed often, with love of his country. He was ashamed of the corruptions of the papal court at Avignon, and earnest for the pope's return to Rome. At the age of thirty-seven he was crowned at Rome as Poet Laureate, and received at Paris the like honour, so winning his Laurel. There was a tradition that Virgil, Horace, and Statius had been so crowned in the Roman Capitol, and the custom, said to have vanished by decay of the Roman Empire, was alleged to have only been revived in the thirteenth century. But it was Petrarch who thus first gave life to the office of Poet Laureate. At that time Petrarch was at work upon a Latin epic on the deeds of the elder Scipio. On this Latin poem—his " Africa "—he chiefly relied for the immortality which he did not suppose that what he wrote in his own mother tongue could give. Seven years after he was laureated, Petrarch throbbed with hope for Italy. Cola Rienzi then became master of Rome, as tribune of the people. Petrarch could live no more in papal Avignon, and he went to his own country. At Parma he heard of the downfall of the tribune, whom the people had deserted. The Colonnas, too, were fallen. " No other ruling family on earth is dearer to me," he said; " but dearer to me is the public, dearer is Rome, dearer is Italy." In 1350, when his age was forty-six, and Chaucer, a youth of two-and-twenty, was training himself in song, translating " The Romaunt of the Rose," and adventuring a sustained flight of his own in " the Court of Love," Petrarch first visited the Florence from which his father had been exiled. Thence Boccaccio, who had long admired his genius, sent forward a Latin poem to welcome him, then came himself to meet him, took him to his house, and established a friendship that continued to the end of Petrarch's life. Boccaccio was, in those days, at work on his " Decameron ;" and by two narrative poems in Italian had already laid the foundation of an influence yet stronger than Petrarch's on the literature of succeeding times.

12. *GIOVANNI BOCCACCIO* was the son of a Florentine merchant. His mother was a Parisian, and his father had lived for a time in Paris. At seven years old Boccaccio had made verses ; but his father meant that he should thrive by trade, and he was placed under a trader, with whom he lived six years, and travelled much. His master said that he was of small capacity,

because he was not apt for the business he was then learning. He was set, therefore, to study canon law, that being a very lucrative profession, and spent nearly another six years in proving himself to be unsuited for that. But the new studies had enabled him to master Latin. As he would not make a lawyer, young Boccaccio's father put him back into trade, and sent him to Naples, where King Robert held court in a spirit that would have tempted men less apt than Boccaccio to a career of letters. At the court of King Robert he heard Petrarch discourse of poetry before his crowning with the laurel wreath. There also Boccaccio sang in praise of Fiammetta, for whom he then wrote his " Filocopo," a version of one of the current French metrical romances—that of " Flore and Blanche-fleur"—into Italian prose, prolix with invocation, love discourse, and episode. But this was followed by another work, dedicated to Fiammetta, telling in Italian and in octave rhyme, under the title of the " Teseide," that story of Palamon and Arcite, which was Englished afterwards by Chaucer, and leads the series of his " Canterbury Tales," as " The Knight's Tale." Boccaccio was in his twenty-eighth year when he produced this poem. Chaucer was then a boy of thirteen. Boccaccio's Italian Theseid was in modern literature the first long narrative heroic poem by a man of genius told straight through without allegory, without verbiage, with simple reliance on its human interest. Its charm was felt wherever Italian was read, and the music also of its new stanza, the octave rhyme. It laid the foundation of modern epic romance. After writing this, Boccaccio, who had returned to his father in Florence, laid the foundation also of pastoral poetry in his " Ameto," "Admetus, Comedy of the Nymphs of Florence " in prose, mixed with rhyme. He represented Admetus as one of rustic unformed mind, civilised by the contemplation of the highest earthly beauty, Lucia or Lia ; discoursing with seven nymphs, by whose names and descriptions known ladies were figured, but who allegorically represent the seven sciences ; and raised by his sense of earthly beauty, Lucia, to a sense and worship of the heavenly beauty, Fiammetta.

The polished Latin eclogue and rude farces of Italian villagers blended in the foundation of these first pastoral dialogues which, according to Boccaccio's example, were produced in Italy during the next hundred years, with speakers who were nymphs, shepherds, satyrs, demigods.

In 1344, when his old father married again, Boccaccio returned to Naples. King Robert was dead, and his immoral granddaughter Giovanna reigned in his stead. She encouraged men of letters in her way, and sought of Boccaccio licentious tales. She revived all literary love-fashions. Justice was dead in Naples, but the queen's authority was upheld in the Courts of Love. In one of those Courts a question arose one day as to which one of three wishes, if he might have one only, a true lover should desire : sometimes to see his lady, sometimes to discourse of her, or to think softly of her within himself. Boccaccio argued for the thinking ; but when his lady left Naples he questioned the truth of his judgment, and produced, in her absence, his second epic romance, his " Filostrato." This was on the love-story of " Troilus and Cressida," once more a sustained tale in octave rhyme, told rapidly and gracefully, depending wholly upon human interest, but reflecting the low morals of the court for which it was produced. The charm of manner was undeniable, and by his two narrative poems, the " Teseide" and " Il Filostrato," Boccaccio established in Italy octave rhyme, a measure of his own creation, though there had been an occasional chance use of it, as by Jehan de Brienne, King of Jerusalem, more than a century before Boccaccio was born. Boccaccio alone established it as the national measure for use in the telling of heroic or romantic tales by the great poets of later time. Boccaccio was about thirty-four or thirty-five years old when he wrote his " Filostrato," Chaucer about twenty.

13. In Chaucer's " Court of Love" there is a close translation of two stanzas from the " Filostrato," besides fainter echo of its music and of that of the " Teseide" here and there. Chaucer afterwards gave his own English rendering of both these poems, and may have begun in his youth to practise himself in verse by translation of some parts of them. In doing so he gave seven lines of English to the eight lines of Italian, and formed out of the octave rhyme of Boccaccio by striking out its fifth line, a measure of his own, not less complete in its harmony. In each measure the lines are of ten syllables. Putting like letters to stand for rhymes, the rhyming in the eight lines of Boccaccio's stanza runs a b a b a b c c, in which the system of the harmony is obvious. In the old Sicilian octave rhyme the verse had simply alternated. Boccaccio turned the closing lines into a couplet, and so gave to the whole measure a sense of perfectness, while adding to its music. Omission of Boccaccio's fifth

line and its rhyme made, Chaucer's stanza run a b a b b c c. Here there are seven lines, three on each side of a middle line, which is that upon which all the music of the stanza turns. It is the last of a quatrain of alternate rhymes, and first of a quatrain of couplets. The stanza thus produced has a more delicate music than the Italian octave rhyme out of which it was formed, and it remained a favourite with English poets till the time of Queen Elizabeth. Because it was used by a royal follower of Chaucer's, it has been called " rhyme royal." Let us rather call it Chaucer's stanza.

14. Boccaccio's " Filostrato " was soon followed by " The Decameron," which he was writing at Florence when, in 1350 Petrarch became his guest there for a time, and the friendship between them was established. The terrible days of the Great Plague of 1348-9 were fresh in men's minds. It was the same plague of which, in England, Bradwardine and Holcot died. Madame de Sade—Petrarch's Laura—had been also among its victims. Boccaccio made this plague-time in Florence the groundwork of his plan for a collection, in Italian prose, of the best stories he could find to tell. He imagined that during the ravages of plague, seven fashionable ladies and three fashionable gentlemen withdrew from its perils, and killed time in telling stories to one another as they lounged in a beautiful garden some miles distant from the town. Each told a tale on each of the ten days of " The Decameron," and this was Boccaccio's contrivance for linking together a series of a hundred tales, which became widely famous, called forth many imitations, and produced a form of literature to which we owe the design of Chaucer's " Canterbury Tales."

The literature of many succeeding generations also bears witness to the influence of Boccaccio's Latin prose treatises, and of those of Petrarch in a less degree, upon imaginations of the poets.

15. Chaucer's " Court of Love " was court poetry ; and the next evidence we have of the course of his life shows that he had obtained footing at court as an attendant upon the young princes, Lionel and John. Lionel of Antwerp, second son of Edward III., was eight years younger than his brother Edward the Black Prince, and two years older than his next brother, John, born at Ghent, in 1340, and called, therefore, John of Gaunt. The king had a fourth son, Edmund, who was a year younger than John, and a fifth son, Thomas, who was an infant when his

brothers were young men.  So far, as regards his court service, Chaucer's life and poetry are especially associated with the friendship and patronage of John of Gaunt ; and we come now to a group of his poems which seems to have been distinctly written for this prince.  Prince Lionel was married, when but a boy, in 1352, to Elizabeth Countess of Ulster; and in a fragment of a household book of hers, containing entries of some expenses in the years 1356-9, the name of Chaucer occurs only in 1357—once in April, once in May, and once in December—at a time when another entry shows that John of Gaunt was a visitor at Hatfield.  The first entry points to preparations for court ceremonies of St. George's Day, in 1357, against which day the Round Tower at Windsor had been completed in order that the feast of the Round Table of the Knights of the Garter might be celebrated with an unexampled splendour for the two prisoner guests, King John of France and King David of Scotland, who were both, at that festival, among the tilters in the lists.  Chaucer's service may only have been transferred for the occasion by Prince John to grace the following of his sister-in-law ; but it may be that Chaucer was attached first to the service of Prince Lionel and thence transferred to that of John of Gaunt.  In the entries of 1358 and 1359 upon the fragment of the Princess Elizabeth's household book, Chaucer's name does not appear ; and 1359 was the date of the marriage of John of Gaunt, with which a group of Chaucer's poems seems to be connected.

On the 19th of May, 1359, John of Gaunt, under his first title as Earl of Richmond, and being then nineteen years old, married Blanche, aged also nineteen, second of two daughters of Henry Duke of Lancaster, the first prince of the blood after the children of the king.

16. Chaucer's *Assembly of Foules* was most probably a poem written for John of Gaunt in 1358, during his courtship of this lady.  If so, the argument implies that when she was eighteen there were three noble suitors for the hand of the great heiress ; that one of them, whose cause the poet advocates, was the king's son ; and that her marriage was postponed for a year.  The poem is, like " The Court of Love," in Chaucer's stanza, and is in the form of a dream, opening and closing with suggestion of the author as a close student of books.  He always reads, he says ; he surely hopes so to read that some day he shall be the better for his study, "and thus to read I will not spare."

In the opening of his poem, Chaucer represents himself as reading with delight a beautiful fragment of the sixth book of Cicero on the Republic, which contains the doctrine of the soul's immortality in "The Dream of Scipio" (Somnium Scipionis). To this fragment a wide influence was given among educated readers of the Middle Ages—an influence which even Dante felt —through the commentary made upon it by Macrobius, a Neoplatonist grammarian of the fifth century, who connected with it his discourses on the constitution of the universe. "The Dream of Scipio" may, therefore, be named with "The Romaunt of the Rose," as the work which, next to it, had chief influence in determining a fashion of court literature for allegorical incidents in form of dream. We find the fashion illustrated in "The Assembly of Foules" and other of the earlier works of Chaucer, and in the literature of succeeding time, until the great development of new thought and new forms of writing in the days of Queen Elizabeth.

In telling the dream which forms the story of "The Assembly of Foules," Chaucer shows, as in "The Court of Love," the enjoyment with which he had then received the narrative poems of Boccaccio. Sixteen stanzas of the "Teseide," which describe Cupid at a fountain tempering his arrows, and the crouched Venus herself, are translated in sixteen stanzas of "The Assembly of Foules," and they are translated in a way that places beyond question Chaucer's knowledge of Italian. The turns of phrase make it quite evident that Chaucer wrote with the Italian original before him.

In the dream story of his poem, Chaucer personified Nature as she had been personified in the thirteenth century by Alain de l'Isle in a popular Latin book of his, written in prose mingled with verse, and called the "Book of the Complaint of Nature" (De Planctu Naturæ). The character of Genius who comes to confess Nature in the latter part of the "Roman de la Rose" was taken from this work. It was the origin also of Genius who acts as the confessor in John Gower's "Confessio Amantis." Chaucer frankly cited Alain as his authority for the personification of Nature in his poem, where she sits enthroned, on Valentine's Day, calling the birds to choose their mates. The first hint of Chaucer's plan seems to have come to him from a passage in Alain's book, which describes Nature's changing robe as being in one of its forms "so ethereal that it is like air, and the pictures on it seem to the eye a Council of Animals. Here

the eagle "—and so forth.  In Chaucer's "Assembly of Foules,"
or, as it is sometimes called, " The Parliament of Birds," Nature
held as chief of the birds to be mated a female eagle, of which
the poet celebrates the grace and beauty.  The worthiest was to
begin the suit.  There spoke then " a tercel eagle, as ye know
full well, the fowl royal, above you all in degree," through whom
Chaucer expressed in allegory the suit of John of Gaunt.  And
when this eagle had declared his love, "another tercel eagle
spake anon, of lower kind," and yet again a third.  Hereupon
Chaucer exercised his sense of humour by representing the
opinions of other classes of birds upon this suit in particular and
love in general.  Nature, bidding the quarrel cease, called on
the lady eagle to speak for herself, but counselled her to take the
royal tercel.  She answered, timidly, that she must wait another
year.  Nature, therefore, counselled the three suitors to wait
patiently—" A yere is not so longë to endure "—and proceeded
to the pairing of the other birds.  Since we have direct evidence
that a year before John of Gaunt's marriage Chaucer was in the
service of one of the young princes—for he was in attendance
upon Lionel's wife—it is almost a matter of course that he should
have exercised his known skill as a poet for the pleasure of his
friends at court in gracing the suit of Prince John for the hand
of Lady Blanche.

    Chaucer's *Complaint of the Black Knight*, which is also
written in Chaucer's stanza, professes to record what the poet
heard of the complaint of a knight whom false tongues had
hindered of his lady's grace.  The poem ends with a direct
appeal to her for whom it was written on her knight's behalf—
" Princess, pleaseth it your benignity," &c.  This, probably, was
a poem designed for John of Gaunt to present to his lady
on occasion of some small misunderstanding incident to days of
courtship.  It is a court poem of French pattern, thoroughly
conventional, expressing unreal agonies by the accepted formulas.
It is conventional even in the use of the usual " Envoy," with
no more change of form than transformation of the customary
" Prince " into " Princess."   In every French province there
used to be a sort of courtly academy of verse-writers, called the
" Puy d'Amours," of which the president was called the Prince.
Poets recited to him their verse, and addressed him in these
last lines, which were called "l'Envoy," or " le Prince."  In the
" Complaint of the Black Knight," the natural genius of Chaucer
appears only in some touches at the close.

17. But throughout the poem known as *Chaucer's Dream*
there is a delicate play of fairy fancy.  It is in the light octosyllabic rhyme, which came in almost with the first English
poems written after the Conquest (ch. iii. § 30), telling how the
poet found himself in dream the only man in a marvellous island
of fair ladies, whose queen was gone over the sea to a far rock to
pluck three magic apples, upon which their bliss and well-being
depended.  But she returned, and with her came the Poet's
Lady, by whom the Queen of that Isle of Pleasaunce had found
herself forestalled.  The Poet's Lady had been found already on
the far rock with the magic apples in her hand.  A Knight also
had there claimed the unlucky Queen as his ; but the Poet's
Lady had comforted her : had graciously put into her hand one
of the apples, and had brought in her own ship both Queen and
Knight home to the pleasant island.  There its fair ladies all
knelt to the Poet's Lady.  The Knight would have died of the
Queen's rigour if she had not revived him by some acts of kindness, after which she was resolved to bid him go.  But then
there were seen sailing to that island ten thousand ships ; and
the God of Love himself made all resistance vain.  Many
Knights landed, and the Queen of the Isle, being overcome,
presented to the Lord of Love a bill declaring her submission.
The God of Love also paid homage to the Poet's Lady, and
himself pleading to her the Poet's cause, laughed as he told her
his name.  The first of the two dreams which form the poem
ended with a festive gathering before the Lord of Love, visible
in the air, and the departure of the Poet's Lady, to whom the
Queen of the Island offered to resign her power if she would but
stay.  The despairing poet followed her ship through the water ;
was rescued, was comforted, and came happily home.  But
with that the first dream ended.  In the next he was again upon
the island, where, between the knights and ladies, marriage was
arranged.  The Queen's Knight, who was a prince, was to go
home and make ready for the wedding.  The poet travelled
with him in a barge—

> "Which barge was as a mannès thought,
> After his pleasure to him brought."

But there were delays, and when the knights returned, behind
their time, they found the Queen and many of the ladies dead of
despair, while those who were not dead were dying.  The Prince
hereupon stabbed himself, and also died.  The Prince, and the

Queen, and the dead ladies were all carried over the sea for burial within a royal abbey.  There, as the dead lay in state, a bright bird perched on the hearse of the Queen and sang three sweet songs.  An old knight, by a sudden movement of his hand, startled the bird, which, in its haste to fly out, beat itself dead against a painted window.  Other birds gathered outside with noise of lament.  One presently brought a green flowerless herb.  The herb grew suddenly, flowered, and yielded seed. One of the seeds was put by a bird into the beak of the dead songster, who at once stood up and pruned himself.  The abbess, with the other seeds, restored the dead Prince, Queen, and ladies to life.  There was, three months after this, a marriage festival; and all, except the Poet, had been thus happily married, when, during a whole day, they besought of the Poet's Lady grace for him also.  She yielded, and their marriage was to be that night.  Then the happy poet was led by the host of the happy in joyous procession into a great tent that served for church, and there was solemn service, with rejoicing afterwards, of which the loud sound woke him from his dream.  He was alone then, in the old forest lodge, where he had slept, and was left in grief to pray that his Lady would give substance to his dreaming, or that he might go back into his dream and always serve her in the Isle of Pleasaunce.  He ended his verse with a balade, bidding his innocent heart go forth to her who may " give thee the bliss that thou desirest oft."

Although this brief note of its plan does not suggest the delicate grace of the poem, it is enough to show that Chaucer's Dream could not have been intended, as some have thought it was, for a celebration of the marriage, in May, 1359, of John of Gaunt, represented by the Knight, to Lady Blanche, represented by the Queen of the Island.  If that had been its purpose, Chaucer would not have made it a chief feature of the poem that he places his own lady high above the Lady Blanche.  If the poem had any personal reference at all, it must have been written for the pleasure of Philippa, daughter of Sir Paon de Rouet, of Hainault, who was king-at-arms for the province of Guienne. This young lady was in the service of Philippa Queen of England, who also was of Hainault.  Queen Philippa was the daughter of a Count of Hainault, and after her, following a common fashion of loyalty, the lady who became the wife of Chaucer seems to have been named.

18. Five months after John of Gaunt's marriage Chaucer

bore arms.   Laurence Minot did not live to include among his
war-poems a celebration of the Battle of Poitiers, fought in September, 1356.   In May of the next year the Black Prince entered
London in triumph, with John King of France his honoured
guest and prisoner.   France was distracted by the Jacquerie,
bred of the utter misery and ruin of her peasantry, and by the
contending factions of her nobles.   But the regency of France
refused to endorse her captive king's assent to the hard conditions of peace offered by his conqueror, and at the end of
October, 1359, Edward III. sailed again to France, with the
largest and best army raised in England for more than a century.   In the ranks of that army every able-bodied courtier must
have been compelled to march.   Geoffrey Chaucer was enrolled
in it, and then he first bore arms.

Evidence of this fact is associated with a statement upon
which those critics rely who do not accept the year 1328 as the
date of Chaucer's birth, but hold that he was born many years
later.   There was in Chaucer's time a long suit, still famous in
heraldic records, between Richard Lord Scrope, of Bolton, and
Sir Robert Grosvenor, of Cheshire, as to the right of bearing
certain arms ; azure, a bend or.   The Constable and Marshal of
England pronounced, in 1390, a decision, with a saving clause
which permitted the loser of the suit, in consideration of the
goodness of his case, to bear the disputed arms within a bordure
argent.   This was disallowed by the king.   Record remains that
at one of the many sittings of the heralds to hear evidence upon
this much ado about nothing, Geoffrey Chaucer was a witness.
He gave his evidence on the 12th of October, 1386, when
his age, if he died in 1400 at the age of seventy-two, was fifty-
eight.   But in the record of his evidence he is described as
" Geffray Chaucere, Esquier, del age de xl ans et plus, armeez
par xxvij ans" (aged forty and more, and having borne arms for
twenty-seven years).   Here it will be observed that upon the
point essential to the cause the record is exact.   Chaucer was
asked how long he had borne arms, and his answer is precisely
entered, twenty-seven years.   According to that reckoning his
bearing of arms dated from 1359, and the evidence he proceeded
to give on Scrope's behalf did, in fact, go back to what he saw
in the year 1359, when he was with Edward's army in Brittany,
and before he was taken prisoner.   But we know that Chaucer
was not asked his age, for upon that point, which was not at all
material to the case, no definite statement was set down.   The

reporter perhaps glanced at the witness, and set down for age "forty and more," before putting the more material question. Upon the age of a man in middle life the estimates differ widely, according to the sense and eyesight of those who make them, and as men differ widely in the period at which they begin to show signs of decay. Chaucer was healthy, genial, and cheerful. It may well have been enough for a rough estimate of his age to set down that he was on the wrong side of forty—"forty and more." Whatever the cause, this document contains even ridiculous blunders in its record of the age of witnesses, and is of no authority on that point. (See Appendix.)

19. The great army with which Geoffrey Chaucer marched, when he first bore arms, in 1359, laid unsuccessful siege to Rheims, advanced on Paris, of which it burnt the suburbs, and there suffered famine so severe that it was forced to a retreat, hasty as flight, towards Brittany, leaving a track of dead upon its way. Over the suffering host then broke, near Chartres, a great storm, in which King Edward vowed to God and the Virgin that he would make peace. It was in Brittany that Chaucer became prisoner to the French. King Edward fulfilled his vow. The Peace of Bretigni was signed in May, 1360, and solemnly ratified at Calais in the following October. The peace would cause release of prisoners; but nothing is known of Chaucer's life for the next seven years. At the end of that time, in 1367, when he was thirty-nine years old, he was still attached to the king's household, and he received in that year a salary of twenty marks for life, or until he should be otherwise provided for, in consideration of his former and future services. The buying power of money changes with the course of time; and Chaucer's twenty marks under Edward III. would be worth about £140 under Victoria.

20. In 1369 John of Gaunt lost his mother, his brother Lionel, and his wife. In service of her mistress, Queen Philippa, the Philippa to whom Chaucer was married had obtained, three years before the queen's death, a pension of ten marks. The death of John of Gaunt's wife, Duchess Blanche, in September, 1369, after ten years of marriage, was lamented by Chaucer in his *Book of the Duchess*, a court poem, in eight-syllabled rhyming verse, with the customary dream, May morning, and so forth, the romance figure of Emperor Octavian, from the tale of Charlemagne, and a chess play with Fortune imitated, almost translated, from a favourite passage of the "Roman de la Rose." Thus far a follower of

the court fashions, Chaucer is in this poem himself a celebrater
of that home delight of love over which Alcestis was queen under
Venus. It is faithful wedded love that the "Book of the
Duchess" honours. We have here also the individual portrait
of a gentlewoman who had been the poet's friend, and in whom
he had seen a pattern of pure womanly grace and wifely worth.
The Duchess Blanche left one son, about three years old, who
became King Henry IV. To him, in his childhood, Chaucer
must have been familiar as his father's household friend, and,
doubtless, often welcome as a playfellow.

21. In the spring and summer of 1370 Chaucer was abroad
on the King's service. In 1370 John of Gaunt married again.
Enriched by the inheritance of his first wife, he had become,
after her father's death in the Plague of 1361, the greatest land-
owner in England, with estates in eighteen English counties, besides several in Wales, and the most beautiful of English palaces,
that of the Savoy, which his late father-in-law had rebuilt from the
ground. Then he was made Duke of Lancaster, was Earl also
of Richmond, Leicester, Lincoln, and Derby. By right of his
second wife he claimed new dignity, and called himself a king.
Pedro the Cruel, whom the Black Prince, at the cost of his own
health and life, replaced on the throne of Castile and Leon, had
been unable to retain it. He was assassinated. His throne was
usurped; but he left two daughters in Aquitaine, the elder of
whom, Constance, was his lawful heir. Her John of Gaunt
married, and at once called himself, as her husband, King of
Castile and Leon. His brother Edmund secured at the same
time the reversion of this chance of a throne by marrying Isabel,
the other daughter of King Pedro. Chaucer and his wife were
both in the service of the titular King and Queen of Castile. Of
Castile and Leon, John of Gaunt had the title of a king without
the rule; but of England, he obtained the rule without the royal
title, and while this power of his lasted his goodwill made
Chaucer prosperous.

In November, 1372, Chaucer—henceforth entitled an esquire
—was made one of a Commission that was to proceed to Italy
and treat with the duke, citizens, and merchants of Genoa for
the choice of some port on the English coast at which the
Genoese might establish a commercial factory. Upon such
business he was in Italy, both at Florence and Genoa, in the
year 1373. This was a year before the death of Petrarch: the
year also in which Petrarch wrote that moralised Latin version

of Boccaccio's tale of Griselda, which was afterwards followed by
Chaucer in his " Clerk's Tale," and of which he made his Clerk say
that it was "learned at Padua of a worthy clerk   . . .   Francis
Petrarch, the laureate poet." Chaucer is likely to have sought
speech with so great a master of his art.   He might also, during
this visit to Italy, have spoken with Boccaccio, then living at
Venice, and within but two years of his death, for Petrarch died
in 1374, Boccaccio in 1375.   Our own poet was home again at
the close of November, 1373, and was paid for his service and
expenses £92, which would be worth more than £900 in present
value.   In April of the next year, 1374, on St. George's Day, a
grant was made to Chaucer of a daily pitcher of wine from the
hands of the king's butler.   This he received till the accession of
Richard II., when, instead of the wine, twenty marks a year were
paid as its money value.   Less than two months after the grant
of daily wine, Chaucer owed also to John of Gaunt's goodwill a
place under Government as Comptroller of the Customs and
Subsidy of Wool, Skins, and Tanned Hides in the port of London.
The rolls of his office were to be written with his own hand, and
none of his duties might be done by deputy.   Only three days after
he had been enriched with this appointment, John of Gaunt
made in his own name a personal grant to Chaucer of £10 (represented now by £100) a year for life, payable at the manor of
Savoy, in consideration of good service rendered by Chaucer and
his wife Philippa to the said duke, to his consort, and to his
mother the queen.   In November of the following year, 1375,
Chaucer received, from the crown, custody of a rich ward, Edmund Staplegate, of Kent ; and this wardship brought him a
marriage fee of £104, represented now by ten times that
amount.   Two months later Chaucer obtained another wardship
of less value ; and in another half-year he was presented with
the fine paid by an evader of wool duties, a gift worth more
than £700 of our money.

22. This was just after the death of the Black Prince, who
had used some of his last remaining strength in opposition to
his father's government as wielded by his brother John.  He had
been in opposition, partly because he shared the popular dislike
of the court party, and resented his father's vassalage to Alice
Perrers, partly because he felt the interests of his son Richard
to be crossed by the ambition of his brother John.   The foreign
wars had been costly and disastrous, the people had made John
of Gaunt answerable for England's failure and distress.   A Par-

liament supported by the Black Prince had opposed him, and was called by the people the " Good Parliament ;" but after the death of the king's eldest son, its last independent act was to resist effectually John of Gaunt's endeavour to procure the exclusion of female heirs to the throne, and so make himself next in succession to his nephew Richard. During the last year of the reign of Edward III., from the close of 1376 to June, 1377, when the king died, Chaucer was twice employed on secret service ; the second time with Sir Thomas Percy, afterwards Earl of Worcester, upon a mission to Flanders.

John of Gaunt seems to have had no love for the wife Constance whom he married only for hope of a kingdom. Chaucer's wife had a sister Catherine, young widow of a Sir Hugh Swinford, of Lincoln, and she also became attached to the household at the half-royal court of the Savoy. She had charge of the children. Catherine Swinford became John of Gaunt's third wife after the death of Constance in 1394. The relation between them was then hardly closer than it had been, but Catherine's children, three sons and a daughter, born before marriage, were then declared legitimate ; and through them Chaucer's sister-in-law became great-grandmother of Margaret Countess of Richmond, mother of Henry VII., and ancestress of the later sovereigns of England.

23. The works of Chaucer hitherto described form a distinct group, marked by the predominating influence of French court poetry. His individuality is shown from the first, as in the honour paid to marriage, though his models are not of the best, and they do not quicken the development of independent strength. But as Chaucer became more and more familiar with the great poets of Italy, their vigorous artistic life guided his riper genius to full expression of its powers. When he had passed forty, and his visit to Italy had quickened his sense of Italian literature, he was, from that time forth, at work with matured power outside the limits of the fashionable French writing of his time. His genius, more akin to that of the great poets of Italy, acquired new freedom of expression. In his *Troilus and Cressida,* which is a free version of Boccaccio's " Filostrato," out of octave rhyme into Chaucer's seven-lined stanza, the English poet not only so dealt with the baser incidents as to breathe pure air through an unwholesome tale ; and even somewhat spoilt the first charm of the story-telling by interpolation of good counsel ; but, for love of honesty, he so transformed the character of

Pandarus in every respect as to make of it a new creation, rich with a dramatic life that is to be found, outside Chaucer, in no other work of imagination before Shakespeare. Chaucer may have been at work upon his poem, which is in five books, and 8,251 lines, in the last years of the reign of Edward III. Ripeness of age is indicated not only by the breadth and depth of insight shown in the character painting, but may be inferred also from the grave didactic tone that interrupts from time to time the light strains of a love-story. " Such fine hath Troilus for love," says Chaucer, at the close :—" Young fresh folks, he or she, look Godward, and think this world but a fair. Love Him who bought our souls upon the cross, and whose love never will be false to you. Such stories as this, the old clerks tell of the world's wretched appetites, and of the guerdon for travail in service of the heathen gods :

> "O moral Gower, this book I direct
> To thee, and to the philosophical Strode,
> To vouchsafe there need is to correct,
> Of your benignities and zealês good."

And the book ends with a prayer that Christ may make us worthy of His mercy.

24. Before carrying this outline of Chaucer's work into the reign of Richard II., we have to complete our sketch of English literature in the time of Edward III. The " Moral Gower" and the " Philosophical Strode," to whom Chaucer dedicated -" Troilus and Cressida," do not come down to posterity with equal fame. **Ralph Strode** has an undying name only because Chaucer has mentioned him, and there is reason to think that he taught one of Chaucer's sons. He was a Dominican of Jedburgh Abbey, who had sought knowledge in France, Germany, and Italy, had visited the Holy Land, and was in highest credit as a theologian and philosopher about the year 1370. He wrote verse also, both Latin and English. Some of his books have been printed in Germany, but none in England.

25. **John Gower** was a gentleman of Kent, close kindred to a knight, Sir Robert Gower, who had property in Suffolk and elsewhere, and who was buried in Brabourne Church, five miles from Ashford. The date of John Gower's birth is not known, but he survived Chaucer eight years. If Chaucer died at the age of seventy-two, and his friend was of equal age with him, Gower died at the age of eighty. It is more likely that he was younger than older. John Gower was well educated, wrote with

F

ease in French, Latin, or English, and used coat armour at a
time when such matters were looked to. In 1365 he was a
feoffee of the manor of Aldington in Kent, and had a rental of
ten pounds out of the manor of Wigborough, in Essex. In 1368
and 1369 he was acquiring the manor of Kentwell, in Suffolk,
which had formerly been the property of Sir Robert Gower.
Towards the close of the reign of Edward III., Gower signed a
deed relating to that manor of Kentwell, and another of his
manors fifteen miles from Kentwell. In that deed he was
described as of Otford, Kent. Among the pleasant hills, then,
of Otford, where in his time the Archbishops of Canterbury
had an old favourite seat, Gower was at home in the reign of
Edward III., as a country gentleman, who had neither wish nor
need to live at court. He wrote in these his earlier days verse
not merely according to the fashion of France, but in French.
There remains a collection of his French exercises in love-poetry,
*Balades*, a form of Provençal verse not in the least related to the
Northern ballad. A balade is a love-poem in three stanzas of
seven or eight (usually seven) lines, and a final quatrain. The
last syllables of the two first lines of each balade are rhymed
with throughout the whole poem, except in the refrain that
should be repeated at the close of every stanza. That iterated
last line usually has a distinct rhyming sound, and one of the
two next preceding lines rhymes with it. Thus the rhyming
might run a b a b c b c | a b a b c b c | a b a b c b c | b c b c.
There were many such elaborate devices for the rhyming of
short pieces by the Provençal and other singers of the South.
Of these the sonnet only can be said to have survived. Gower
wrote five of his balades for those who "look for the issue of
their love in honest marriage." The other forty-five are of the
usual kind, mere variations on the given theme, "universal to
all the world, according to the properties and conditions of
lovers who are diversely experienced in the fortune of love."
Gower wrote also three long poems ; one in French, one in
Latin, one in English. The one in French is lost. It was
divided into twelve books, treating of the vices and virtues, and
of the various degrees of men seeking—as a contemporary described it—to teach, by a right path, the way whereby a trans-
gressed sinner ought to return to the knowledge of his Creator.
That first work, called the *Speculum Meditantis* (Mirror of one
Meditating), was written, no doubt, in the reign of Edward III.,
for the second work was produced early in the reign of

Richard II. The lost French poem would, in that case, be the book which earned for the poet from his friend Chaucer the name of "Moral Gower."

26. **John Wiclif**, born in Yorkshire about 1324, was in 1361 master or warden of Balliol College, Oxford, and was in that year presented by his college to the rectory of Fylingham, in Lincolnshire. Soon afterwards he resigned his mastership, and went to reside on his living. He was presently made Doctor of Divinity. He had a quick mind in a spare, frail body, and at the time when William Langland, of whom we shall have next to speak, was writing in like spirit his "Vision of Piers Plowman," Wiclif was showing his pure desire to restore a spiritual Church. John of Gaunt was then ready, as head of the feudal party at court, to humble the pride of the prelates who claimed temporal power. He welcomed, therefore, the most innocent and self-denying Wiclif as a fellow-combatant; and when, in 1376, at the close of the reign of Edward III., Wiclif was cited as a heretic to appear at St. Paul's before the appointed ecclesiastical judges, he went thither with John of Gaunt and Percy, the Earl Marshal of England, as supporters. This led to a brawl. The populace judged Wiclif by his companions, and saw in him one of the people's enemies. Yet he was already quietly engaged with others upon that *Translation of the Bible* which was not completed until after the death of Edward III. As nothing came of the proceedings at St. Paul's, the monks, who also looked on Wiclif as their enemy, obtained the pope's injunction to the prelates and the university to renew process against him; but before the pope's bulls could reach England Edward III. was dead, and the next following changes were in Wiclif's favour.

27. Of like mind with Wiclif was **William Langland**, who, in Edward III.'s reign, was essentially the poet of the people. William Langland, the author of the *Vision of Piers Plowman*, is said, in a handwriting of the fifteenth century upon one of the MSS. of that poem, to have been born in Oxfordshire, at Shipton-under-Wychwood, the son of a freeman named Stacy de Rokayle, who lived there as a tenant under Lord le Spenser. On another MS. the author of the poem is named William W., possibly William of Wychwood (?) John Bale, writing in the middle of the sixteenth century, made the poet's Christian name Robert, wherein certainly he erred; and said that he was born at Cleobury Mortimer, in Shropshire, wherein, perhaps, he erred

also.  The opening of his poem leads us to infer that William Langland was bred to the Church, and was attached at one time to the monastery of Great Malvern.  But he married, and seems only to have performed minor offices of the Church.  The forty-three remaining MSS. of his great poem represent it, with many variations, in three well-defined stages of completeness, indicating that throughout his life the author was extending and enriching it.  In the portion first written there are references to the Treaty of Bretigny, in 1360, to the great pestilence of 1361, and to a great storm which occurred in the evening of Saturday, January 15th, 1362.  The work must, therefore, have been begun about that time.  In the later continuation of the poem there is reference to a day in April, in 1370, and to the accession of Richard II., in 1377.  As in this part of the poem Langland calls his age forty-five, he was not born earlier than 1332.  He came to London, for in the latest continuation of the poem he speaks of himself as living poorly in Cornhill by the performance of small clerical duties.  If Langland was the author of a poem on the *Deposition of Richard II.*, which has been not unreasonably ascribed to him, he was alive in 1399.

28. *The Vision of Piers Plowman* speaks the mind of the main body of the English people of its time.  It is a vision of Christ seen through the clouds of humanity—a spiritual picture of the labour to maintain right and uphold the life spent upon duty done for love of God.  The poem is in the mystical number of nine dreams, and, in its completest form, twenty-three "passus." A passus is a division of a poem so named from the Latin *pandere* (to spread out, unfold); hence, to unfold in speaking, as when in the "Æneid" it is said of Anchises, "Ordine singula pandit." Without rhyme, unless by accident, and with alliteration in First English manner, a national poet of vivid imagination has here fastened on the courtly taste for long allegorical dreams, and speaks by it to the humblest in a well-sustained allegory, often of great subtlety, always embodying the purest aspirations. Everywhere, too, it gives flesh and blood to its abstractions by the most vigorous directness of familiar detail, so that every truth might, if possible, go home, even by the cold hearthstone of the hungriest and most desolate of the poor, to whom its words of a wise sympathy were recited. Langland dreamt of a fair field full of folk—the World and its people—among whom the maid Meed (worldly reward) was about to be wedded to Falsehood. Theology forbad the marriage, and the question of it was tried

before the king in London. The allegory is the first of the sequence of dreams forming the whole vision, rich in lively picturing of the conditions of men in the world, and plain of speech as to the duties of kings.

The poet slept again, and saw in his second dream again the fair field full of folk, to whom now Reason was preaching that the pestilence and the south-west wind on Saturday at even came to warn them of their sin and pride. After a time Repentance prayed, and then Hope blew a horn, at which the saints in heaven sang, and a thousand men cried up to Christ and His pure mother that they might know the way to Truth. They inquired of a pilgrim fresh from Sinai, who said that he had never heard such a saint asked after. Then suddenly a Plowman put forth his head and said that he knew Truth as naturally as a clerk his books. Piers Plowman is thus first introduced in the poem as type of the poor and simple to whom the things of God are revealed, and gradually, within fifty lines, passes into the Christ who came as one of low estate to guide the erring world. Truth granted a bull of pardon to those who had worked faithfully with Piers the Plowman at the half-acre he had to plough and sow by the highway. The terms of this bull lead to the allegorical search for Do-well, since they are based on the text of Matthew xxv. 46—"They who have done well shall go into life eternal." A priest impugned the worth of such a pardon, and raised a dispute that awoke the dreamer by its noise.

What meant the dream? The pope granted passes into heaven ; but to trust to these

> Is noght so siker for the soul,
> Certes, as is Do-well.

He would search, therefore, for Do-well ; and in his next dream, the third, was told by a man like himself, whose name was Thought, what were Do-well, Do-better, and Do-best. Do-well, man's natural goodness, follows him who is true of tongue and earns his bread by honest labour, takes only that which is his own, and is not drunken or disdainful. Do-better adds to these qualities of natural right and justice the higher Christian graces ; he is meek as a lamb, helpful to others, has broken the bags of Avarice, and has given the Bible to the people. Do-best is above both, and bears a bishop's cross. Him Do-well and Do-better have crowned as their king. Thought sent the dreamer to Wit (knowledge), who told him that Do-well lives in the Castle (of Man's Body) made by Kynde (Nature) who dwells there with his bride Anima (the Soul). Anima has Do-well to defend her borders ; Do-better, daughter of Do-well, for her handmaid ; and Do-best for her spiritual guide. Dame Study, the wife of Wit, was displeased at the telling of these mysteries to the unlearned ; but she was appeased, and passed the dreamer on to Clergy, who told him of the evils and abuses in the Church, and prophesied that there should come a King who would put monks to penance for the breaking of their rule. "And then shall the abbot of Abingdon and all his issue for ever have a knock of a king and incurable the wound."

William Langland was, we shall find, not alone in the forecast of the inevitable issue of the growing worldliness among those who should have been the guardians of religion.

From his third dream the poet was awakened by a sense of shame while he was disputing with Reason. One came to him, Imagination, when he was awake, and told him that if he had been patient he would have heard from Reason what he had been told by Clergy. In his next dream, the fourth, Conscience comforted him, and took him to dine with Clergy, where the meats were psalms and texts, and there was talk again of Do-well, Do-better, and Do-best, Clergy referring to one Piers Plowman, who had made light of all knowledge but love, and saying that Do-well and Do-better were finders of Do-best, who saves men's souls. Patience said he had been told that Disce (learn) was Do-well, Doce (teach) was Do-better, and Dilige (love) was Do-best. The dreamer went on, with Conscience and Patience, to discover more. Then he met on the way Haukyn the Active Man, too busy to clean his coat : he sleeps in it. But Conscience told him how it might be cleaned, and Patience told him of a meat that never failed, though no man ploughed or sowed for it. The dreamer looked and saw that it was a piece of the Paternoster, called Thy-Will-be-Done. "Take it, Haukyn," said Patience, "and eat this when thou hungerest, or when thou art chill or wet ; fetters shall never chafe, nor great lords anger, nor prison harm thee." The sound of Haukyn's weeping broke the dream.

In the next dream, the fifth, Anima (the Soul) spoke with the poet, and after lamenting the avarice and luxury of churchmen. bade him go straight to Christ, figured in

Piers the Plowman.<br>
Petras in Christus.

the allegory passes to the tree bearing the fruit of Charity, which grows in a garden held by Freewill, under Piers the Plowman.

The next dream, the sixth, introduces Faith and Hope, with Charity in the person of the Good Samaritan.

In the seventh dream the poet saw one like both to the Samaritan and to Piers Plowman riding barefoot on an ass's back, and was told by Faith that it was Jesus gone to joust with the foul fiend in the garb of Piers the Plowman. The rest of his dream was the story of Piers the Plowman as the Saviour.

In the eighth dream this identification was continued. Christ was identified also with Do-well in His natural childhood ; with Do-better when He healed and helped all that asked Grace of Him ; with Do-best from the time when His wounds were touched by the doubting Thomas. And Grace, it was said, gave to Piers the Plowman on earth a team of four oxen, which were the Four Evangelists, and four stots, Austin, Ambrose, Gregory, and Jerome, who, with two harrows, an old and a new (Testament), followed Piers's plough. And Grace gave the seed that should be sown : the spirits of prudence, and of temperance, and of fortitude, and of justice. Thus ended the spiritual search ; but over the heavenly vision of Piers Plowman there again rolled the dark mists of earth. Piers was attacked by Pride. Conscience counselled his followers to defend themselves in the Castle of Unity (the Church). The pope, whom " God amend," plundered the Church. The king claimed all he could take.

In the next and last dream, the ninth, Antichrist came in a man's form to waste the crop of Truth. Within the Castle of Unity Flattery got entrance as a physician. Thus Conscience was ousted, saying—

> " Now kynde (*i.e.*, nature) me avenge,
> And send me hap and heele,
> Till I have Piers the Plowman."

So, with the object of his search yet unattained, through the turmoil and disaster of those days of Richard II., in which the poem was completed, the poet sent his last thought heavenward, and built his last hope for the world upon a search for Christ.

29. In completing the account of this important poem we have passed out of the reign of Edward III. into that of his grandson ; but we are not free to discuss the reign of Richard II. while the famous traveller, **Sir John Mandeville**, remains unnoticed. He represented in the reign of Edward III. the English spirit of adventure. By five-and-twenty years and more an

older man than Chaucer, Gower, Wiclif, and Langland, he was born at St. Albans in the beginning of the fourteenth century, and it was in the reign of Edward II., on Michaelmas Day, 1322, that he set out upon his *Travels.* Five years later, when Edward III. became king, Sir John Mandeville was still abroad. He tells us that he visited Tartary, Persia, Armenia, Lybia, Chaldea, and a great part of Ethiopia, Amazonia, India the Less and the Greater, and isles that are about India. For more than thirty years he had been absent, when he came home, as he said, in spite of himself, to rest ; "for rheumatic gouts that distress me fix the end of my labour against my will (God knoweth)." On his way home he showed to the pope what he had written in Latin about the marvels and customs he had seen or heard of. The pope showed the book to his council, and it was approved. After his return Sir John Mandeville employed his forced leisure in turning his Latin book into French, and then again into English. This he did in 1356, thirty-four years after he had sailed from England ; and at a time when Chaucer, at court, had perhaps done little more than translate the "Roman de la Rose," and write his "Court of Love ;" when Gower might have written a balade or two ; and Wiclif and Langland, one at Oxford, and the other possibly at Malvern, were two young and earnest men, with the chief labours of their lives before them.

Mandeville's book was planned with distinct reference to the wants of pilgrims to Jerusalem, and contrived to subordinate accounts of the remotest travel to the form of what we might call a Travellers' Guide to Jerusalem by four routes, with a Handbook to the Holy Places. The wonderful things told do not in themselves convict Mandeville of any wilful untruth. He tells of what was seen by him as matter of knowledge ; in the miracles narrated to him he put faith ; and all other marvels of which he heard he tells only as matter of hearsay. He says that he and his men served the Sultan of Babylon in war against the Bedouins, and had from him letters which gave admission to the least accessible of the Holy Places at Jerusalem. He says also that for fifteen months he and his men served the Great Chan of the Tartars of Cathay (China).

But if Sir John Mandeville visited Cathay and India, and wrote from his own knowledge of what he saw there, he must then have had for a travelling companion a Lombard Franciscan friar, Odoric of Pordenone, in Friuli. Odoric was about fourteen years older than Mandeville, and he started on his travels about five years earlier, remaining absent until 1330. He was in Western India soon after 1321, and spent three of the years between 1322 and 1328 in Northern China. In much of his travel he had an Irish friar for companion. On his return to Italy, in 1330, Odoric told the story of his travels, and it was set down in Latin by a brother of his order. He died in the following year. The resemblance between the narratives of Odoric and Mandeville concerning travel in the far East is so very close that the two men have been spoken of as travelling companions. Mandeville, in describing the Perilous Valley, says that he had with him " two worthy men, friars of Lombardy, who said if any man would enter they would go in with us." Sir John Mandeville's " Travels" were written more than twenty years later than Odoric's, and it is in the resemblances between these two books that we find most reason to doubt Sir John's veracity. It is not unreasonable to ask whether he saw more of Cathay or India than he found upon the pages of the Lombard friar.

30. We may now pass into the reign of Richard II. (1377-1399). The first event in its literary history is the completion by **John Wiclif** (§ 26) of his *Translation of the Bible*. In the year 1360 the English people had in their own current language no part of the Bible but the Psalter. Twenty years afterwards, in 1380, the devoted labour of Wiclif and his fellow-workers had produced a complete English Bible, including the Apocrypha. Wiclif began with Comments on the Gospels, and in the Prologue to the Gospel by Matthew strongly urged that the whole Scripture ought to be translated for the use of the laity. Then he translated Clement of Lanthony's "Harmony of the Gospels." Versions of the Epistles followed. The version of the Gospels was taken out of Wiclif's " Commentaries;" Acts, Epistles, and Apocalypse were added; names of translators being studiously kept out of sight, for this was a labour against custom and against authority disposed to argue by oppression. It was while finishing his translation that Wiclif, whose chief work had been a Latin one, " De Dominio Divino," began to forsake the use of Latin, and wrote English tracts. In 1381 he issued a paper of twelve propositions against transubstantiation. In 1382 the Dominicans, or Black Friars, who were the custodians of orthodoxy, had in their house at London a Council at which twenty-four conclusions selected from Wiclif's writings were condemned. He was banished from the University. In 1384 Wiclif was

F *

summoned to appear before the Pope; but he was then dying
from paralysis, and on the last day of that year he obeyed his
summons to appear before a higher judgment seat.

31. **John Gower** (§ 25) in the earlier days of Richard II.
was still a wealthy country gentleman at home in Kent. He was
acquiring two new manors in Norfolk and Suffolk, and he had
still an interest in land near Wigborough, in Essex, when the
men of Kent, under Wat Tyler, and the men of Essex, with Jack
Straw for their priest, the excommunicated priest John Ball
being also one of the company, rose in rebellion. Gower's
home was in the midst of the district out of which, in May, 1381,
the tumult sprang.

The boy Richard, but eleven years old, had come, in 1377,
to a troubled throne. The people were suffering. The French
and Spaniards harassed the English coasts, destroying towns
and interrupting trade. John of Gaunt urged to Parliament the
needs of the country; and the Parliament, forgetting all old
grudges, voted liberal supplies, only appointing two merchants
as treasurers to protect the public money from misuse. John
of Gaunt then achieved in Brittany a costly failure. The Scots
broke truce. The Government had spent all, and was heavily in
debt. Parliament now resolved to meet two-thirds of the debt
with a poll-tax of three groats upon each person above fifteen
years of age. It was the second poll-tax within five years, and
the sufferings of the people had then brought them to the verge
of the next of the three great plague years of the fourteenth
century. Each is associated with a piece of literature. The
Great Plague of 1348-9, which killed Holcot and Bradwardine
(§ 2), and Petrach's Laura, suggested the groundwork of Boccaccio's "Decameron." The plague of 1360-1 was one of the
miseries which caused William Langland to write the "Vision
of Piers Plowman." The state of England immediately before
the plague of 1382 is the subject of the poem written by John
Gower on the occasion of the Jack Straw rebellion. There were
other bad years, notably one in 1373, and there was no year in
which the plague was altogether absent. But in 1381 the people
had suffered patiently, until the farming of the heavy poll-tax
gave them to be ground under it by men who looked, of course,
to their own want of mercy for the profits of their speculation.
But when, stung to rebellion, this English mob swarmed out of
Kent and Essex to Blackheath, and threatened London, its
demands were simply: that all should be free; that they should

not be restrained from buying and selling wherever they could find a profitable market ; that there should be a fixed rental of land ; and a general pardon. Later experience condemns but one of their four points. These unhappy men, of whom many were seeking honestly to find the right, and some sought no more than a mischievous revenge on those whom they believed to be oppressors, poured into Southwark on the 12th of June, destroyed the Marshalsea, sacked the archbishop's palace, crossed London Bridge next morning, destroyed Newgate, laid waste John of Gaunt's rich palace of the Savoy, and threw into its flames one whom they found taking to himself some of its gold and silver. At the worst they were not thieves, but wild and ignorant avengers. On the 14th. the young king met the rebels at Mile End, and conceded their demands. The great body of them at once retired. But the men stung to a fierce despair by private suffering, with all the baser portion of the crowd, remained. These, breaking into the Tower, where the men of mark in the state had taken refuge, murdered the Archbishop of Canterbury and other lords. This was the rabble met by the king at Smithfield on the 17th of June, when Wat Tyler was stabbed by Walworth the mayor, and the young king, only fifteen years old, won the generous trust even of this worst remnant of the rioters. When they bent their bows, crying "They have killed our captain, slay them all," young Richard galloped up to them and said, "What are you about, my friends? Tyler was a traitor; I am your king. Follow me." They followed, and he led them into the clutch of a troop of soldiers, whom he would have set upon them if Sir Robert Knolles had had not been more merciful and wise than his young master. But submission was made, the concessions were revoked; the insurrection was avenged with cruelty upon the people. Then came on them the terrible plague year, 1382.

32. These were the events which drew from John Gower his best poem, the *Vox Clamantis* (Voice of One Crying), in seven books of Latin elegiacs. In its first book Gower told of the revolt allegorically, in the form of a dream of beasts who have changed their nature. But if, he says, he is in an island of discord, let there be strife without and peace within his doors, and let him seek the less for worldly occupation. A voice admonished him quickly to write what he had seen and heard ; for dreams often contain warnings of the future.

In his second book, being awake, he did begin to write, in·

voking no muse but the Holy Spirit. If he seem unpolished to the reader, let the reader spare the faults, and look to the inner meaning of his work. And again and again he asks that the soul of his book, not its mere form, be looked to. The eye is blind, he says, and the ear deaf that convey nothing down to the heart's depths ; and the heart that does not utter what it knows is as a, live coal hid under ashes. The Voice of One Crying shall be the name of his volume, because there are written in it the words that come of a fresh grief. Then he went on to utter what was in his heart. There is no blind fortune ruling the affairs of men ; they go ill or well according to the manner in which men fulfil their duties before God. As we do, so we rejoice or suffer. There is no misfortune, no good luck. Whatever happens among us, for good or ill, comes with our own doing—"nos sumus in causa." The object of Gower's "Vox Clamantis" was, therefore, to set the educated men, readers of Latin, to the task of finding that disease within our social body of which the Jack Straw rebellion was but a symptom ; his plan was to go through all orders of society, and ask himself wherein each fell short of its duty.

This he began to do in the third book, which has, like the second, a most earnest prelude. "I do not," Gower says, "affect to touch the stars, or write the wonders of the poles ; but rather, with the common human voice that is lamenting in this land, I write the ills I see. In the voice of my crying there will be nothing doubtful, for every man's knowledge will be its best interpreter." Then follows a passage which ought to be quoted by all teachers who would train young Englishmen to write. Gower prays that his verse may not be turgid ; that there may be in it no word of untruth ; that each word may answer to the thing it speaks of pleasantly and fitly ; that he may flatter in it no one, and seek in it no praise above the praise of God. "Give me that there shall be less vice, and more virtue for my speaking."

Then he divided society into three classes, represented by clerk, soldier, and ploughman, and began with an unsparing review of the vices of the higher clergy of his time. Christ was poor ; they heap together wealth. Christ gave on earth peace ; they only stir up wars. Christ gave freely ; they are as locked boxes. He lived to labour, but they take their ease ; Christ was gentle, they are impetuous. He walked in humility ; they walk in pride. Christ was full of pity ; they wreak vengeance. Christ was chaste; they seldom live modest lives.  He was a good shepherd, but they devour the sheep.  They with full stomach praise the fasting of our Lord.  We seek and worship wealth. The poor man shall be a fool, though he speak with the lips of Cato, and Dives shall be a wise man although he know nothing. There is no poor wise man.  If the poor man be wise, he is a poor man and nothing else.  " To this mind," said John Gower, " the prelates conform themselves more than to the mind of Christ."  He referred to the split in the papacy ; and, orthodox conservative country gentleman as he was, he cried, " O head of the Church, recall the times of Christ, and see whether there be in them any example like that which ye follow.  A clergy withdrawn from the law of piety has made that the tail of the Church which used to be its head; its health is its disease ; its life its death ; its lifting up its fall; its law its error ; and its own father its enemy."

The fourth book of the " Vox Clamantis," as well as the third, was given to a review of the corruption of all orders of the clergy. In speaking of the friar, Gower wrote, " A man may serve one of three masters, God, the world, or the Apostate Devil.  We see that the friar does not obey God's rule.  He says that he is not of the world, that he should do a layman's duties to his country.  It is the devil's yoke, then, that he wears.  The only order true to its decretals is that consecrated once on a time by Brother Brunellus" (ch. iii. § 12).

In the fifth book of his " Vox Clamantis," Gower turned to the soldier, and to the pure idea of his knightly honour.  Then he spoke of the serf, dull in ignorance and vice, who tilled the earth ; and of the hired servants, who could scarcely be held for a month to their engagements.  "They disdain to eat common food, find salt meat hurtful, quarrel with the cooking, grumble when there is no roast, say they are none the better for their beer or pease, and will not come again if you do not set a better dinner before them to-morrow.  The poor son of poverty creates himself a lord out of his own stomach, and obeys none other. Loving no man, and not knowing that there is a God, if justice were not armed with terror, he would soon trample like a beast over his master."  So wrote even a generous and true-hearted gentleman, in the days of Richard II.  Alas for the poor, when the best minds are more conscious of the need of the strong hand to keep them down than of the duty of the helping hand to raise them !  The fruits of the earth, gathered by the labourers, are passed from land to land by the merchants.  Gower went on, therefore, to review the merchants and their frauds.

The sixth book of his poem he gave to the lawyer; and from condemnation of injustice in high places, turned with direct address towards the king himself.  "An unlearned boy-king," said Gower, "is negligent of the moral deeds by which the man grows out of the boy.  A youthful assembly follow him as their leader, with such counsels as he wills to have.  Elder men humour him for their greed, and the king's court contains all that is vicious.  Error encompasses the boy on every side."  In plain and direct words the boy was warned of his duty.  His notorious addiction to the pleasures of the table was not forgotten.  "Be free also, O king," said the poet, "from the sin of gluttony; drive out the inertness and oppose the promptings of the flesh, and strongly lay hold on the good way."  The example of his father the Black Prince was set before Richard.  Avoiding war without just cause, kind rather than austere, seeking wisdom, subject to God, who alone is to be feared, let him live in love of God and of his neighbour ; ready for death ; great in the eyes of his subjects as he was found humble in the eyes of God.

The seventh and last book of Gower's "Vox Clamantis" applied Nebuchadnezzar's dream to the state of society in England ; man's hard avarice being the iron in the feet of the image, and his lusts the clay.  Man being the microcosm, the world around him will be good or bad, as he is good or bad.  Prelates, curates, priests, scholars, monks, friars, soldiers, merchants, lawyers, were degenerate.  Gower declared, with this, his especial love for the land of his birth.  He repeated that what he had written was not his own complaint, but the voice of the people revealed to him in his dream.  It touches only the guilty ; and may each correct his own fault where he finds it.  "Here," he says, "is the voice of the people ; but often where the people cries, is God."  And in the "Vox Clamantis" we do hear the voice that throughout the literature of the English people labours to maintain the right and to undo the wrong.

33.  But why did Gower, a true son of the Church, speak as he spoke in this poem of the pope?  In this he shared a widespread feeling that, as William Langland represented, ruin must come to the pope and a "knock of a king" to the Abbot of Abingdon, unless the lives of pope and clergy were amended.  Seventy years of the popes at Avignon—begun in 1309—were followed by a schism in the Church.  The years at Avignon and

the succeeding schism quickened the stir of independent thought against a pope's claim to hold absolute and irresponsible authority.   The removal to Avignon had been provoked by the absolutism of Boniface VIII.   He had written to Philip the Fair of France, " We will you to know, that you are subject to us, in things spiritual and things temporal."   Philip had answered, " Be it known to your supreme fatuity, that in things temporal we are subject to no one."   In his bull "Unam Sanctam," Boniface had set forth obedience to the pope as necessary to salvation.   He had afterwards put Philip under ban.   Perhaps his energy was tainted with the madness which became declared in his last days.   It awakened reasoning as to the pope's position in the Church, and created a division of Church politics into French and Italian.   French policy prevailed.

The Archbishop of Bordeaux, bribed with the papacy to serve the King of France, as Clement V. refused to go to Rome.   Thus began the seventy years of a French papacy, which had a court more scandalous than that of Rome, and set up claims of absolute dominion as loud as those of Boniface, though mainly urged, in servitude to France, against the German Emperor.

The intellect of France, then represented by the University of Paris, laboured to restore peace to the Church.   In his " Defensor Pacis," Marsilius of Padua, who had been rector of the Paris University, argued that it was heresy in the pope to claim against the German Emperor a power to absolve from obedience to laws of God.   He condemned as devilish a pope's absolution of subjects from oath of allegiance to their sovereign.   " Christ only," said Marsilius, " is the rock on which the Church is built."   Peter was not the chief apostle.   No bishop of a particular province is declared by the Gospel to be Peter's successor ; but, rather, he is the true successor to Peter and the other apostles who comes nearest to them in holiness of life.   As for the popes of his time, shutting their doors against humility and poverty—the true companions of Christ—" they," said Marsilius, " are not friends, but enemies of the Bridegroom."

Gregory XI. died in 1378, two years after his return to Rome with those cardinals who would follow him.   His Italian successor, Urban VI., disappointed expectation.   Pride and passion took the place of his peaceful asceticism, and the cardinals, being mostly French, declared by a majority that his election was invalid, because made under constraint. So they forbade obedience to him, and in 1378—three years before the date of the "Vox Clamantis"—made Robert of Cambray Pope Clement VII.

For the next forty years there were two popes at a time. Many in Europe were then ready to say, "If two popes, why not twelve?" and the most earnest defenders of the principle which had based safety of the Church upon the maintenance of one supreme visible head saw no way to peace but by submitting rival claims of irresponsible authority to the judgment of a general council of men who were less than popes.

It was about three years after the beginning of the schism that John Gower, a devout orthodox churchman, hostile to Lollards, declared in his *Vox Clamantis*, that a clergy withdrawn from the law of piety had made that the tail of the Church which used to be its head. "Its health," he said, "is its disease; its life its death; its lifting up its fall; its law its error; and its own father its enemy." The *Concilium Pacis* of Henry of Langenstein, a professor of theology in Paris, is of the same date as the event which produced Gower's *Vox Clamantis*. It urged the healing of schism by a general council, taking its authority from the Divine Head of the Church, and passing resolutions only in His name; and said, "See to it whether horses, hounds, falcons, and the useless servants of the clergy be not now, far more than the Christian poor, eating up the heritage of the Church." Of Boniface IX., who, in 1389, succeeded Urban VI., one record tells that even during mass this or that secretary would be coming to him with some report about money, his living god. He it was who despatched into all countries that enormous staff of hucksters in indulgences upon whom, Chaucer poured scorn in the Prologue to his "Canterbury Tales."

Meanwhile the University of Paris urged that both popes should resign, or else submit their claims to arbitration, and that if they would do neither of these things a General Council should be called; but the pope who rejected all the three paths towards peace should be declared a heretic.

In the first year of the fifteenth century, Nicholas of Clamanges, Bachelor of Theology in the Paris University, and not long afterwards secretary to Benedict XIII., issued a book, *De Ruina Ecclesiæ*, in which he declared the evil of the Church to have grown from the depraved lives of the clergy, and discussed the vices of the various orders, as John Gower had done in the *Vox Clamantis.*  He saw, like Gower, cause and effect in the world's affairs ; and, failing immediate reform, he looked forward to the day of a sharp remedy for evils that had grown with wealth and luxury of the high clergy.  Timely reform alone could avert the issue of all this misdeed in persecution of the Church by the secular power, and its deprival of usurped rights and possessions. For this revolution Nicholas of Clamanges urged that men less blinded might see the foundations laid in divers ways.  The chief duty, he said, of the theologian is to preach from the study of the Scriptures, looking at the Fathers but as rivulets descending from that fountain head.  The doctrine was, according to the spirit of the University of Paris working through the natural diversity of minds, expressed by one party with moderation, by another with uncompromising purpose of subjecting papal absolutism to control of Councils and producing other of the changes sought by more advanced reformers.  The University of Toulouse represented those who maintained faith in the pope's supreme authority, and resisted changes in the Church law of a former time.  And so the controversy stood during the later days of Gower and of Chaucer.

34.  But the best as well as the worst mind of Europe found its voice upon the lips of cultivated churchmen.  In Scotland **John Barbour**, Archdeacon of Aberdeen, had, in the year 1375, half written his poem of the *Bruce.*  This work, complete at the beginning of the reign of Richard II., represented the bright spirit of liberty maintained by that Scottish war of independence (A.D. 1294—1324) which had produced in the days of Edward I. a Wallace, in the days of Edward II. a Bruce, and in the days of Edward III. a poet in John Barbour, who, as he turned Bruce into a hero of romance, wrote with full heart :

> " Ah, Freedom is a noble thing !
> Freedom makes man to have liking ;
> Freedom all solace to man gives :
> He lives at ease that freely lives."

John Barbour, born perhaps in 1316, possibly as late as 1330, was, in 1357, Archdeacon of Aberdeen, and so remained until his death, in 1396.   King Robert II. of Scotland gave him two pensions, one of £10 a year for life, payable out of the customs of Aberdeen, the other, in reward for his poem, 20s. a year, payable for ever from the rent of the land and fisheries which Aberdeen held from the crown.  Besides his *Bruce,* which is a romance of more than 13,000 rhyming eight-syllabled lines, Barbour wrote a book, which is lost, of the " History of Scottish Kings," from Brut and his son Albanac downward. He wrote also many thousand lines of *Lives of Saints*, which have been lately found.

In his great poem on King Robert the Bruce Barbour dealt with events so recent that he could quote for one incident the authority of an eye-witness, Sir Allan Cathcart, by whom he had heard it told. Bruce died in 1329, or less than fifty years before Barbour sang of him. He came to life again in the poem as a knightly hero, able to defend a pass against 300 men of Galloway ; and the true course of his story was followed faithfully, though rather with the freedom of a poet than the literalness of a chronicler. Beyond his day in contempt of astrology, and otherwise very free from superstition, Barbour yet boldly gave a touch of the diabolical to the policy of King Edward II. by making him take counsel with a fiend.

35. While in the North this vigorous Archdeacon of Aberdeen still lived and wrote, and the other famous poets of the South were Langland and Gower, **Geoffrey Chaucer** was, during the reign of Richard II., chief in renown. Of his ditties and glad songs the land full filled was over all. Then it was that he wrote the *House of Fame*. The poem, in three books of octosyllabic rhyme, opened with a dream of the Temple of Venus, which is of glass, in a wide wilderness of sand. The poet, praying to be saved from phantom or illusion, was carried up by an eagle like that which swooped in dream upon Dante in the ninth canto of the " Purgatory." We have passed into the second period of Chaucer's life, when the great Italian poets are far more to him than the small singers of France ; and in the " House of Fame " we find very distinct traces of the influence of Dante on the mind of a great fellow-poet. In Chaucer there was, indeed, no gloom ; but he penetrated none the less deeply to the heart of human life because he had faith in God's shaping of the universe, was kindly and even cheerful, and knew how to be wise without loss of the homely playfulness that comes of bright fancy and a heart at ease. The eagle of the poem declared himself the poet's friend, though he was heavy to carry. Was Jove going to make a star of him ? Chaucer asked. No, said the eagle ; Jove has no thought yet of making a star of you. But you have taken pains with your love-singing, and have been a quiet student, therefore you are being taken up to see the

House of Fame. You hear little about your neighbours, said the eagle to him. When you have done the reckonings of your day's office work (over the books relating to the customs and subsidy of wools, skins, and tanned hides in the port ot London)

> "Thou goest home to thine house anone,
> And allso dumb as a stone
> Thou sittest at another book
> Till fully dazed is thy look,
> And livest thus as an hermite,
> Although thine abstinence is lite " (*i.e.* little).

Chaucer enjoyed life and good fare ; but the man of genius wins only by hard work a fame that is to live through many centuries, and Chaucer, happy among books, which are men disembodied, as among men in the flesh, was a hard-working student. As for the House of Fame, which he was permitted to look into, he found it, he said, the place between heaven, earth, and sea, to which all rumours fall ; and his description of it began with a reminiscence of the invocation at the opening of Dante's " Paradise." But in invoking " Apollo, God of Science and of Light," Chaucer modestly avoids following Dante in the suggestion that he will crown himself with a few leaves of Apollo's laurel. He says only that he will go

> " Unto the next laurèr I see
> And kiss it, for it is thy tree."

Then Chaucer described the House of Fame as he saw it on a rock of ice, inscribed with names of men once famous. Many were melted or melting away ; but the graving of the names of men of old fame was as fresh as if just written, for they were " conservèd with the shade." The description of the House is one of the brightest creations of Chaucer's fancy. There is a grand suggestiveness, a true elevation of thought, in the plain words that conjure up images, clearly defined and brightly coloured, which do not rise only to melt in air and be no more. They pass into the reader's inner house of thought and live there. Of the goddess who sat within, some asked fame for their good works, and were denied good or bad fame. Others who had deserved well were trumpeted by slander. Others obtained their due reward. Some, who had done well, desired their good works to be hidden, and had their asking. Others made like request, but had their deeds trumpeted through the clarion of gold. Some who had done nothing asked and had fame for deeds only to be done by labour ; others who had asked like favour, were

jested at through the black clarion.    Chaucer himself refused to
be petitioner.    Enough, if his name were lost after his death,
that he best knew what he suffered, what he thought.    He would
drink, he said, of the cup given to him, and do his best in his own
art.    From the House of Fame he was taken by the eagle to the
whirling House of Rumour, full of reports and of lies shaped as
shipmen and pilgrims, pardoners, runners, and messengers.
Every rumour flew first to Fame, who gave it name and duration.    In a corner of this House of Rumour Chaucer saw men
crowding about one who told love-stories.    The clamour about
this shadow of himself awoke him from his dream.    Then being
awake he remembered how high and far he had been in the
spirit.

> " Wherefore to study and read alway
> I purpose to do day by day."

36. Among the love-songs which made Chaucer famous were
his translation from "The Romaunt of the Rose" and his
"Troilus and Cressida."    Not content with all that he had done
to give womanly delicacy to the character of Cressida in the
earlier part of the poem, and to draw the noblest moral from her
fall, he felt even yet that the beauty of pure womanhood was
clouded by her story.    He set to work, therefore, upon *The
Legend of Good Women* with the avowed purpose of satisfying
by his writings his own sense of what is good and just.    But the
suggestion even of this series of poems Chaucer derived from
Boccaccio, whose collection of 105 stories of Illustrious Women,
told briefly and pleasantly in Latin prose, includes nearly all of
those whom Chaucer celebrated ; a remarkable omission being
that ideal wife Alcestis, long since enshrined in our poet's verse
as Queen of Love.    Chaucer's stories of good women probably
were written in various years, and represent the steadiness with
which he paid, through life, what he calls reverence to the Daisy.
The Prologue, written in or after 1382, says that it was his delight
to read in books, and that he was not easily drawn from his
studies except in May, when the flowers begin to spring.    And
then of all the flowers it was above all the Daisy that he loved—

> So glad am I, when that I have presènce
> Of it, to doon it allè reverènce
> As she that is of allè flourès flour,
> Fulfillèd of all virtue and honòur,
> And ever alike fair and fresh of hue,
> And I love it, and ever alike new,
> And evor shall, till that mine hertè die.'

Chaucer alone, among those who wrote ditties to the Marguerite or Daisy, sang of the flower as an emblem of womanly truth and purity, of a gentle and devoted wife, with heart of gold and a white crown of innocence. As he sought his Daisy, and greeted it as he could—

> " Kneeling alway till it unclosèd was
> Upon the smalë, softë, swotë grass "—

he heard (here varying his allegory in the praise of woman's innocence) the birds escaped from the net of the fowler who would have betrayed them with his sophistry ; and then the poet, who sang " I ne clepe not innocence folye," feigned that he slept near the daisy on fresh turfs, and saw in dream the God of Love leading a Queen, Alcestis, like the daisy, clad in royal

> " habit green.
> A fret of gold she haddë next her hair,
> And upon that a white coroune she bare,
> With flourouns small."

After Alcestis came " the ladies good nineteen," who were said in Chaucer's " Court of Love " to form her following. These all, when they saw the daisy, knelt and sang with one voice hail and honour to the flower that bare the praise of them all in its white emblem crown. But then the God of Love saw where the poet lay too near to his own flower. He had translated " The Romaunt of the Rose ;" he had sung of the faithless Cressida. Alcestis pleaded for him that he might have been falsely accused. He had served as he could, and here follows a list of some of Chaucer's earlier writings. It includes already that version of Boccaccio's " Teseide "—the story of Palamon and Arcite—which the poet afterwards placed first in the series of Canterbury Tales. It includes also another of the Canterbury Tales, " The Life of Saint Cecile." This is a metrical translation from the Golden Legend, which appeared in the collection as " The Second Nun's Tale." Alcestis obtained grace for the poet on condition that year by year as he lived he should spend time in making a glorious legend

> " Of goodë women, maidenës, and wives,
> That weren true in loving all their lives."

As it was added that the book, when finished, was to be given, on behalf of Alcestis, to the Queen at Eltham or at Shene, we know that this Prologue could not have been written before 1382, when Richard II. married Anne of Bohemia.

: 37. The next work of mark completed in the reign of

Richard II. was a *Translation of Higden's Polychronicon* (§ 5), completed in 1387 by John Trevisa. Trevisa was a Cornishman, educated at Oxford, who became vicar of Berkeley, in Gloucestershire, and chaplain to Thomas fourth Lord Berkeley. Afterwards he was canon of the collegiate church of Westbury. As a clergyman he was no friend to the monks. In the course of his life he had been to Germany and Italy, but he spent most of his days in Gloucestershire, where he occupied his leisure in translation of useful books out of Latin into his mother tongue. He is said to have died in 1412. Trevisa's translation of the "Polychronicon" was made for Lord Berkeley, and was preceded by Trevisa's own *Dialogue on Translation between a Lord and a Clerk;* that is to say, his patron and himself. Trevisa translated from Occam "A Dialogue between a Soldier and a Clerk," and from Fitzrauf, Archbishop of Armagh, a sermon preached at Oxford in 1357 against the Mendicant Friars. Fitzrauf was, in his day, one of the friends of Richard of Bury (§ 1), and was accused to the pope by the Mendicant Friars, against whom he preached this sermon about two years before his death. Caxton, who first printed Trevisa's translation of the "Polychronicon," said that he had also translated the Bible ; and it is thought possible that this translation may be still extant at Rome. Trevisa, who was a shrewd man, added a few short explanatory notes to his translation of the "Polychronicon," which is notable as one of the earliest specimens of English prose.

38. Chaucer and Gower were supreme and almost alone as representatives of English Literature during the second half of the reign of Richard II. The year in which Trevisa finished his translation of Higden was a critical time for the king and country, and for Chaucer too. Thus far Chaucer had prospered. In 1378, within a year after the accession of Richard II., he had been twice sent abroad on diplomatic service—in January, with the Earl of Huntingdon to France, to treat of the king's marriage; and in May, with Sir Edward Berkeley to Lombardy, to treat on affairs concerning the king's war, when the shores of England lay at the mercy of the French and Spaniards. In 1382 the friendship of John of Gaunt had procured for Chaucer another office under Government. Retaining his post as Comptroller of Wool Customs, he became also Comptroller of the Petty Customs in the port of London, with liberty to do the work of that office by deputy. In February, 1385, he was

released from all compulsory work for his salaries by being allowed to appoint a permanent deputy in the office of Wool Customs. Such was the course of Chaucer's outward life at the time when he wrote "The Legend of Good Women." In 1386 he sat as one of the members for Kent in the Parliament which met on the 1st of October, he and his colleague being allowed for their expenses at the rate of eight shillings a day (money of that time) for sixty-one days. The French were then threatening England with invasion ; and the great barons, headed by the king's uncle, the Duke of Gloucester, were active for the overthrow of the king's corrupt administration. John of Gaunt was then away with an army in Portugal, upon affairs arising out of his relation to Castile.

In the Parliament which had Chaucer—acting, of course, with the king's party—among its members, there arose a trial of strength. After three weeks of struggle, Richard was compelled to abandon his Chancellor, the Earl of Suffolk, to a prosecution by the Commons, and to submit himself for twelve months to a Commission of Regency. Two famous noblemen of the day, the Earl of Gloucester and the Earl of Arundel—whom Gower celebrated as the "Swan" and the "Horse" when afterwards he followed the course of their policy with patriotic sympathy in his "Tripartite Chronicle"—as leaders of the Opposition, were included in this Commission. It was to inquire into the conduct of officials of all kinds, and into gifts and pardons granted in the name of the Crown ; it was to hear and decide on all griefs of the people which could not be redressed by common course of law ; and to provide for all abuses such remedies as might seem to it good and profitable. The Commission was appointed on the 19th of November. It began with an examination of the accounts of officers employed in the collection of the revenue. On the 10th of December it dismissed Chaucer from his office of Comptroller of the Wool Customs. Ten days later it dismissed him also from his other office of Comptroller of the Petty Customs.

Chaucer and Gower were old friends, good friends together ; but in relation to the politics of the time so differently placed that Gower, in his country-house, a quiet and independent looker-on, hailed with enthusiasm the success of those whose day of power brought ruin to Chaucer.

39. During at least a part of the year's rule of this Commission of Regency Chaucer seems to have been in Guienne with

John of Gaunt, who was there marrying Philippa, his daughter by his first wife, Duchess Blanche, to King John I. of Portugal. The marriage was graced by Chaucer with his poem of *The Flower and the Leaf.* The Flower and the Leaf represented two of the badges usual in mediæval heraldry. A flower, the rose, is the badge of England ; a leaf, the shamrock, is the badge of Ireland. In Chaucer's time there was a current argument in chivalry as to the relative significance of leaves and flowers. Eustache Deschamps, nephew and pupil of Guillaume Machault, with an eye to the roses of England, wrote in honour of Philippa, upon the occasion of the wedding, a poem giving to the flower superiority over the leaf, as having fairer scent, colour, and promise of fruit. There can be but little doubt that Chaucer's poem was, from the English side, a return compliment to the bridegroom. John of Portugal, a man of thirty, had fought for his throne, and owed both that and his wife to success in battle. He was a soldier king, who lived to be called John the Great ; and Chaucer's poem, written in the person of a lady—the bride elect—gives the chief honour to the laurel, meed of mighty conquerors. " Unto the leaf," she says, " I owe mine observaunce."

40. To this part of Chaucer's life may belong also the poem of *The Cuckoo and the Nightingale.* Master Nicholas of Guildford had sung (ch. iii. § 30) of the contest overheard by him between the owl and nightingale about two hundred years before Chaucer sang of what he also had overheard between the nightingale and cuckoo. But two hundred years before Chaucer the birds were rude ; each bragged of himself, and made contemptuous attacks upon the other. The only question was, which is the better bird? Now, in the contest between nightingale and cuckoo, the cuckoo indeed is a bird of bad manners, but he does not affront the nightingale with personalities. He is rude because he flouts at love, which is the subject of discussion. The poem is based on a popular superstition that they will be happy in love during the year who hear the nightingale before the cuckoo. If they hear the cuckoo first it is the worse for them. No date can be suggested for the poem, which seems to belong to Chaucer's second period, and like " The Flower and the Leaf," which was no doubt written in 1387, during the days of terror for the king's party, shows that Chaucer was a man whom no adversity could sour.

41. On the 19th of November, 1387, the year's power of

the Commission was to expire. Richard, resolving to arrest and send for trial his most obstinate opponents, entered London on the 10th. Next morning he learned that his uncle Gloucester, with the Earls of Arundel and Nottingham, was advancing in force upon London. Before London these lords were joined by John of Gaunt's son, Henry Earl of Derby. They were joined also by the Earl of Warwick, whom Gower in his "Tripartite Chronicle" has celebrated as the Bear. In England there was civil war. The insolent court favourite, Robert de Vere, Duke of Ireland, marching to the king's aid with troops raised near Chester, was met and defeated at Radcot Bridge by young Henry Earl of Derby. The king, preparing to keep Christmas safely in the Tower, was surrounded by troops, when the Londoners fled, and he was soon compelled to make submission. Next year, at the beginning of February (1388), a Parliament met in London, which some called "The Merciless," and some "The Wonderful Parliament," and which sat till Whitsuntide. It hanged Chief Justice Tresilian and the ex-Mayor Sir Nicholas Bramber; hanged or beheaded many more; banished obnoxious justiciars; and compelled the king to swear assent to all these judgments.

If Chaucer wrote *The Testament of Love* during this reign of terror for the men of the king's party, Chaucer was among the imprisoned, and but narrowly escaped the gallows. Whoever wrote that book, which has been long ascribed to Chaucer, was arrested and imprisoned by this Parliament; when in prison was ever sought to declare against his late associates, and had such evidence of murderous designs produced to him that "if they were not seen they might be felt." The prisoner, whoever he was, therefore, told frankly as much as he knew; which, he adds, was no more than those who said he had played false to them owned to be true. Whether the prisoner was Chaucer or not Chaucer, he must have felt that life and liberty were not worth giving for such men as those were shown to be who had been chief plotters on the king's side during the past year. John of Gaunt's son Henry, whom Chaucer had known from childhood, though he had not then influence enough with the Parliament to save old Sir Simon Burley from the scaffold, could speak with effect to Chaucer if he was the prisoner, who in this prose work, "The Testament of Love," solaced captivity after the manner of Boëthius (ch. ii. § 18), by feigning that Love came to him in his cell and held discourse with him, preaching the divinity in manhood, and saying to him, "If thou work, thou art above all things save God alone." Let him seek the Pearl beyond price. The prisoner complained of the hard dealings of fortune. They have taught him, said Love, to know his friends; and if that Pearl shine to himward, he is more blessed than in worldly joy. The spiritual teaching of the book includes a passage that might be Chaucer's in its respect for women. These are its closing words: "He that them annoyeth doth his own shame; it is a comfortable pearl against all teens (sorrows). Every company is mirthed by their present being. Truly I wist never virtue but a woman was thereof the root." The author of "The Testament of Love" was a Londoner, and had also been, like Chaucer, employed under Government; for he says, "While I administered the office of common doing, as in ruling the stablishments emonges the people, I defouled never my conscience for ne manner deed, but ever by wit and by counsel of the wisest, the matters weren drawn to their right ends."

If Chaucer did not write "The Testament of Love"—and it is likely that he did not—we have no evidence of his imprisonment by those who had deprived him of his Government offices. But we have evidence that he was pinched severely in his fortunes at the time of the sitting of the Merciless Parliament; for on May Day in this year, 1388, he was obliged to raise money on his two pensions, which were then cancelled and assigned to a John Scalby. What matter? Chaucer dined worse, and set to work upon the "Canterbury Tales."

42. In Guienne his friend John of Gaunt was repeating the last move in his chess play with fortune, and securing in 1388 a political match for Catherine, only daughter of his wife Constance, and inheritor of her pretensions to the Spanish crown. He married her to Henry, son and heir of the reigning King of Castile; and from this couple, established thus as Prince and Princess of Asturias, the line came down of Spanish sovereigns for many generations.

King Richard, in May, 1389, suddenly asked his uncle Gloucester how old he was; and, being told that he was in his twenty-second year, said he must then certainly be of age to manage his own concerns. So he dismissed his council, took the Government into his own hands, and left his uncle Gloucester to retire into the country, while John of Gaunt was desired to return to England. By this court revolution Chaucer profited. On the 12th of July in the same year he was appointed Clerk of the Works at the Palace of Westminster, Tower of London, Castle of Berkhampstead, and at about a dozen royal manors and lodges, and at the mews for the king's falcons at Charing Cross. He might serve by deputy, and his salary was two shillings a day, which would be about twenty in present value. In November of the same year John of Gaunt returned to London.

During the next eight years of his reign, until the *coup d'état* of 1397, Richard II. remembered the rough lesson he had received. Living in some fear lest he might lose his crown, he was careful to avoid acts that would stir men to rebellion. John Gower was, during much of this time, like other patriots, loyally paying him the honour due to his apparent good intentions, and—considering his youth and noble birth, as son of the Black Prince—due also to the possible ripening of character, now that he had bought much hard experience with the follies of his earlier years.

In 1391 Chaucer, for some unknown reason, ceased to hold office as clerk of the king's works. His means were then very small; indeed it does not appear that he had other income than the £10 a year (say, now £100) for life, granted in 1374 by John of Gaunt, and his allowance of 40s. (say £20) half-yearly for robes as the king's esquire. And it was at this date, 1391, that he wrote for his son Lewis, ten years old, a book of instruction, *Bread and Milk for Babes*, or the *Conclusions of the Astrolabie;* simply and tenderly—true to the pure domestic feeling that shines through his verse—employed in a father's duty of encouraging his child's taste for ennobling studies. He had given the boy an astrolabe, and the little treatise was to show him how to use it, as far as a child could. Some of its uses, he said, "be too hard for thy tender age of ten years to conceive. By this treatise, divided in five parts, will I show thee wonder light rules and naked words in English, for Latin ne canst thou yet but small, my little son. But, nevertheless, sufficeth to thee these true conclusions in English, as well as sufficeth to those noble clerks, Greeks, these same conclusions in Greek; and to the Arabians in Arabic; and to Jews in Hebrew; and to the Latin folk in Latin ; which Latin folk had them first out of divers other languages, and wrote them in their own tongue, that is to say in Latin. . . . . And, Lewis, if it so be that I show thee in my little English as true conclusions touching this matter, and not only as true, but as many and subtle conclusions, as he should in Latin in any common treatise of the astrolabe, con me the more thanks, and pray God save the king that is the Lord of this language."

43. Meanwhile **John Gower** (§ 32) had been living in outward peace, and still was, as far as we know, unmarried. There was an old friendship between him and Chaucer. When, in the first year of Richard's reign, Chaucer went with a mission to Lombardy, he had left the care of his private interests in the hands of two friends, one of whom was John Gower. Chaucer had dedicated to Gower his " Troilus and Cressida," and had then joined to his friend's name a word of honour, as " the moral Gower," which cleaves to it still. Presently we come to a poem of Gower's from which we learn that this friendship remained unbroken to their later days.

In 1389 King Richard had taken the Government into his own hands, and, living in fear of his people, made some effort to rule also himself. For a few following years men who, like Gower, had their country's welfare at heart, credited the king with good intentions, and gave him loyally their friendship. In 1390 John Gower received from the Crown the rectory of Great Braxted, in Essex, a mile distant from the parish of Wigborough, where he had property. John Gower's name is on the list of rectors of this parish, not as priest—for he was not an ordained priest—but as clerk. In 1393 John Gower, rowing to town from his house in Kent or Essex by the river highway, then commonly used as the great London road, met the king's barge. At the invitation of Richard—who was at that time twenty-six years old, while the poet's age was nearer sixty-six—Gower left his boat and conversed with the king, who, in the course of conversation, asked him to write a new book for himself to read. Gower had been suffering from a long illness, and still was ill, but he undertook to write such a book in English for King Richard, to whom his allegiance and heart's obedience were due; and he resolved to write so that his words might be as wisdom to the wise and recreation to the idle. Thus Gower began his " Confessio Amantis" (Confession of a Lover), at a time when his friend Chaucer was at work upon the " Canterbury Tales;" and thus each poet in his latter years was following the example which had been set by Boccaccio in his " Decameron," except that they used verse instead of prose in stringing a chain of tales on a slight thread of story. But as to the spirit of their work our English poets differ much from the Italian.

In the *Confessio Amantis,* Gower's notion of a poem that should be—

> "Wisdom to the wise,
> And play to them that list to play,"

was as serious as Hampole's " Prick of Conscience." He began by telling its origin, and dedicating it to the king. But in a revision of his book, made when Richard had cast down the hope of those who credited him, for a few years after 1389, with the desire to do his duty, Gower expunged his words of allegiance, said in place of them, " What shall befal here afterward God wot!" and transferred the dedication to Henry of Lancaster. For the fashionable device of his poem Gower, infirm and elderly, cared little. To the best of his power he used it as a sort of earthwork from behind which he set himself the task of digging and springing a mine under each of the seven deadly sins. There were eight books, with a Prologue. The Prologue repeated briefly the cry of the "Vox Clamantis." The eight books were, one for each of the seven sins, with one interpolated book, seventh in the series, which rhymed into English a digest of the " Secretum Secretorum." This was a summary of philosophical and political doctrine wrongly supposed in the Middle Ages to contain the pith of Aristotle's teaching, as drawn out by himself for the use of Alexander. The second part of it, " De Regimine Principum," on the duties of kings, or " Governail of Princes," as the English writers called it, enabled Gower to edify the unteachable Richard with much argument upon the state and duties of a king.

But how can " The Confession of a Lover" give occasion for seven sets of stories against the seven deadly sins? Gower feigns that he went to the woods on a May Day, as Lover, and called upon Cupid and Venus. Cupid and Venus came, but he was old, and they showed him no kind cheer, although he said that he was dying of love. If dying, then, said Venus, let her Confessor come and shrive him. The Confessor was Genius, the Priest of Nature, her own clerk, as appointed in " The Romaunt of the Rose," but who had first found his way into literature through " The Plaint of Nature," by Alain de l'Isle (§ 16). To this Confessor the Lover knelt in due form, and begged of Dominus his holy father Genius, as he was himself disturbed at heart, and had his wits greatly astray, that he would put before him the several points of his shrift, that there might be nothing forgotten. He was, in fact, to put, according to the manner of the confessional, his searching questions; and he began in due form with questions as to the Lover's use of his five senses, especially of sight and hearing. The thread was now made ready for the stringing of the chain of stories. The tales lie close together, connected throughout, sometimes skilfully, sometimes with an obvious strain of ingenuity, by passages of dialogue between the Confessor and the Lover whom he systematically questions. Having discoursed on the delusions of the senses, the Confessor called his son's attention to the "deadly vices seven:" pride, envy, anger, sloth, avarice, gluttony, and lust; each classified into its chief forms, and every form illustrated with incident or tale. In the last book Gower elaborated the story of Apollonius of Tyre, which is in the "Gesta Romanorum," an old collection of stories, arranged according to subjects, with allegorical religious applications suitable for use in the enliven-ment of sermons; and called "Deeds of the Romans," because every tale is associated with some real or fictitious Roman emperor. It is also in the "Pantheon" of Godfrey of Viterbo, whence Gower says that he took it. From Gower came the story of "Pericles" among the plays of Shakspeare—a play opened by Gower as chorus, with lines illustrating the use once made of stories furnished in this manner by the poets:

> " To sing a song of old was sung,
>   From ashes ancient Gower is come;
>       .    .    .    .    .
>   It hath been sung at festivals,
>   On Ember eves, and holy ales,
>   And lords and ladies in their lives
>   Have read it for restoratives."

Gower ended his "Confession of a Lover" by reverting to the love-plaint with renewed appeal to Venus, who then told him that his complaints were against Nature. He should re-member his age. Cupid came by with the mirthful band of the young lovers. Age followed with a smaller company of old men who had been servants to Love. These pleaded for the poet. Cupid drew the dart out of his breast. Venus put cold ointment over his heart, and held to him a mirror in which he saw his faded colour, dim sad eyes, face wrinkled with age, and hoary hair. Then, laughing, she asked him what love was; and he replied that he knew not. So he had absolution from his Con-fessor, the Priest of Nature, and was dismissed from the Court of Venus with advice from her to go, "where moral virtue dwelleth." He was to take also a message from Venus to her disciple and poet Chaucer, who in the flower of his youth made ditties and glad songs wherewith, said Venus,

> " The land fulfilled is over all ;
> Whereof to him in special,
> Above all others I am most hold ;
> Forthi now in his daies old,
> Thou shalt him tellé this message : "

That he was to crown his work by making his Testament of Love as Gower had made his shrift, so that her Court might record it. Here it is quite evident that Gower, speaking of himself as one old man, turns with playful compliment to his friend Chaucer as another. A few years later this passage was omitted from a revised copy of the " Confessio Amantis ;" for it would have been out of place—almost a trivial impertinence—when Gower had learnt how Chaucer was in his old days fashioning the crown of his life as a poet, with the " Canterbury Tales." In them we have indeed his Testament of Love to God and Man.

44. Contemporary with the " Confessio Amantis" was a poem of 850 lines, in the measure and outward manner of " The Vision of Piers Plowman," called *Piers Plowman's Crede*, and levelled with much bitterness of feeling against all orders of friars. In this poem an ignorant man who had learnt his Paternoster and Ave Mary wished to be taught his Creed, and, after seeking knowledge in vain of the friars, met with a common ploughman, who explained to him that the friars, although their orders were founded by good men, had become children of the devil, reminded him how they persecuted Wiclif, and himself gave the instruction sought. The ploughman in the poem was simply a poor rustic. There was no high allegory, as in the " Vision," and the antagonism to Church corruption was that of a lower and a harsher mind. The poem was written in or about the year 1394, and the author of it seems to have been the author of " The Plowman's Tale."

45. Geoffrey Chaucer was at work upon the " Canterbury Tales" during the last years of his life, and left them unfinished when he died. He must have lost his wife within a year after his loss of fortune by deprival of his offices in the Customs, for after June, 1387, the receipt of her pension by Philippa Chaucer ceased. But she left him at least two sons, an elder son, Thomas, and the Lewis for whom Chaucer wrote his treatise on the astrolabe. It is probable also that when, in 1381, John of Gaunt paid a substantial sum for the noviliate of an Elizabeth

Chaucer in the Abbey of Barking, he was dealing generously by one of the children of his friend. Chaucer's elder son Thomas, who was born about the year 1367, was advanced in his fortunes both by King Richard and by John of Gaunt. In some year between 1392 and 1404 he married an heiress, who brought him estates in Oxfordshire and other counties. In Thomas's daughter Alice, Geoffrey Chaucer was grandfather to the grandmother of John de la Pole, Earl of Lincoln, whom Richard III. declared heir apparent if the Prince of Wales died without issue. John de la Pole died childless. He was killed at the battle of Stoke, in 1487.

It was in the sixteenth year of Richard, 1393, that Gower, invited courteously into the king's barge, was commissioned to write a new poem for his Majesty. It was in the seventeenth year of King Richard, 1394, that Chaucer, whose means then were very small, received from the king a pension of £20 (equal to £200) a year for life, payable half-yearly, at Michaelmas and Easter. In 1395 Chaucer's straitened means were indicated by four borrowings from the exchequer of money in advance. There was but one such borrowing in 1396; but there were four again in 1397, the year in which King Richard II. cast himself out finally from the hearts of any who had thus far struggled to retain hope of his future.

In 1396, when Richard, aged twenty-nine, was about to ally himself by marriage with an eight-year old French princess, Froissart tells that this king of England spoke to the Count of St. Pol, the French king's representative, of his uncles, among whom Gloucester was opposed to the French match. St. Pol advised dissimulation till the match was made, telling how, " that done, he would be of puissance to oppose all his rebels, for he might rely on aid from the French king." "Thus shall I do," said Richard, and thus he did.

When the discrowning treachery of the *coup d'état* was in preparation, Gower, aged about seventy, resigned the living that he held at Richard's gift, and withdrew from the outer life of the world. The Priory of St. Mary Overies, on the Southwark side of London Bridge (of which the chapel is now represented by the parish church of St. Saviour), was being rebuilt in the reigns of Richard II. and Henry IV. The masons were still at their work when John Gower, who was the most liberal contributor towards the cost of re-building, established lodgings and a chapel of his own in the new priory, and withdrew from the world to spend his last years peacefully, a clerk among clerks, within shadow of the church of which he was an honoured benefactor.  Gower's faith in Richard was gone, and the public events which immediately followed his retirement caused the old poet to write in Latin leonine hexameter his *Tripartite Chronicle.*  This is the sequel to his " Vox Clamantis," since it tells the issue of the mis-government against which that earlier work had been a note of warning.  The Chronicle was called " Tripartite " because it told the story of Richard's ruin in three parts, of which the first, said Gower, related human work, the second hellish work, the third a work in Christ.  Human work was the control of Richard by his uncle Gloucester when the Commission of Regency was estab-lished ; hellish work was the *coup d'état;* the work in Christ was the consequent dethronement of King Richard.

In July, 1397, having secured the French alliance, the king invited the Earl of Warwick (the Bear) to dine with him, and by a treacherous breach of hospitality arrested him, seized his lands, and made him prisoner in the Isle of Man.  The Earl of Arundel (the Horse) was invited to a conference, assured by the king's oath that he should not be injured in person or property. He was seized at the conference, sent to prison in the Isle of Wight, and afterwards beheaded.  By treachery as false, the Duke of Gloucester (the Swan) was seized, imprisoned, and, Gower says, smothered at Calais with a feather bed, by murderers whom his nephew had sent over for the purpose.  Gloucester was murdered in September, 1397.  At the same time there was obtained from a servile parliament a statute (of the twenty-first year of Richard II.) which was virtually abnegation of the power of the Lords and Commons, and its transfer to a junta of the creatures of the king.  Richard was during the next year (1398) supreme, for there was no immediate resistance to his personal government.  In that year Chaucer was very poor.  In January of the same year John Gower had been married in his own chapel under his rooms in the priory.  He doubtless felt need of a kindly woman's care in his old age, and married to obtain good nursing, for his health was weak, and two years later he entirely lost his sight.  While the rich Gower was thus housed, and spending liberally on the building-works of the priory in which he lodged, his friend Chaucer obtained, in May, 1398, the king's letters of protection from arrest, on any plea except it were connected with land, for the next two years, on the ground of " various arduous and urgent duties in divers parts of the

G

realm of England." After this Chaucer, on account either of sickness or occupation, did not apply for money personally ; but in July, 1398, within three months of his obtaining letters of exemption from arrest, he sent to the exchequer for a loan of 6s. 8d.—say £3 6s. 8d. present value.

In the following September lists were set at Coventry for combat between John of Gaunt's son, Henry, and the Duke of Norfolk. Richard, staying the combat, banished both. John of Gaunt survived his son's banishment but a few months, and, dying in 1399, was buried near the high altar in St. Paul's, by the side of his first wife, the Duchess Blanche. Then King Richard added to all other acts of rapacity, by which he was making his name daily more infamous, the seizure of the large inheritance of John of Gaunt's son Henry. In the summer Richard spent in Ireland upon war against the Irish some of the wealth he had wrung by acts of tyranny out of the English. The new Duke of Lancaster was then summoned by his friends from France, and John of Gaunt's son, to whom Chaucer was as an old household friend, landed at Grimsby to claim his inheritance. He had taken to himself the well-known badge of his murdered uncle Gloucester, the Swan. The end soon followed. In September, 1397, the Duke of Gloucester was murdered ; in September, 1398, John of Gaunt's son was banished ; in September, 1399, Richard II. publicly surrendered his crown to the returned exile.

The Act of the Deposition of Richard II. was read in Westminster Hall on the last day of September, and on the 3rd of October the new king granted to Chaucer forty marks a year, in addition to the smaller annuity that King Richard had given him. The old poet had then only a year to live, but his last year was freed from care. At Christmas he took the lease of a house in the garden of the chapel of St. Mary, Westminster, and there he died, aged seventy-two, on the 25th of October, 1400.

John Gower, who needed no money, received from the new king recognition of his hearty sympathy with what he looked upon as Christ's work in the overthrow of tyranny. In the year of Chaucer's death Gower became blind ; but he lived on in the priory till 1408, and after his death in that year, considering his liberal aid to their building-works, his brethren there honoured his memory with a painted window and a tomb upon which his effigy is still to be seen lying, adorned with the Lancastrian collar of SS, with an appended badge of the Swan. This was the

valued gift of the new king, Henry IV.  When in his blindness
his hand touched it, the moralist might now and then recall the
past, and blend hope for the future with abiding faith that "often
where the people cries there is God."

46.  Such work as that upon the unfinished *Canterbury Tales*
could not have been laid aside by Chaucer for work of less
account.  This must have been the main occupation of the poet's
latter days, and the last words of the last tale in the papers
gathered together by the hand of his son Thomas may have been
the last words from his pen.  They look up to heaven where
" the body of man, that whilom was sick and frail, feeble and
mortal, is immortal, and so strong and so whole that there may
no thing impair it : there is neither hunger, nor thirst, nor cold,
but every soul replenished with the sight of the perfect knowing
of God.  This blissful reign may men purchase by poverty
spiritual, and the glory by lowness, the plenty of joy by hunger
and thirst, and rest by travail, and the life by death and mortifi-
cation of sin.  To this life He us bring that bought us with His
precious blood.  Amen."  Chaucer was one of the few greatest
poets of the world who rise to a perception of its harmonies and
have a faith in God forbidding all despair of man.  No troubles
could extort from him a fretful note.  Wisely, kindly, with
shrewd humour and scorn only of hypocrisy, he read the characters of men, and seeing far into their hearts was, in his " Canterbury Tales," a dramatist before there was a drama, a poet who
set the life of his own England to its proper music.  In this
complete work, had it been completed, the whole character of
England would have been expressed, as it is already expressed
or implied in the great fragment left to us.  Boccaccio, who
died twenty-five years before Chaucer, placed the scene of his
" Decameron" (§ 14) in a garden, to which seven fashionable ladies had retired with three fashionable gentlemen during the
plague that devasted Florence in 1348.  They told one another
stories, usually dissolute, often witty, sometimes exquisitely
poetical, and always in simple charming prose.  The purpose of
these people was to forget the duties on which they had turned
their backs, and stifle any sympathies they might have had for
the terrible grief of their friends and neighbours who were dying
a few miles away.  For these fine ladies and gentlemen, equal
in rank and insignificance, Chaucer gave us a group of about
thirty English people, of ranks widely different, in hearty human
fellowship together.  Instead of setting them down to lounge in

a garden, he mounted them on horseback, set them on the high
road, and gave them somewhere to go and something to do.
The bond of fellowship was not a common selfishness. It was
religion ; not, indeed, in a form so solemn as to make laughter
and jest unseemly, yet, according to the custom of his day, a
popular form of religion—the pilgrimage to the shrine of Thomas
à Becket (ch. iii. § 11)—into which men entered with much
heartiness. It happened to be a custom which had one of the
best uses of religion, in serving as a bond of fellowship wherein
conventional divisions of rank were for a time disregarded ;
partly because of the sense, more or less joined to religious
exercise of any sort, that men are equal before God, and also, in
no slight degree, because men of all ranks, trotting upon the
high road with chance companions, whom they might never see
again, have been in all generations disposed to put off restraint
and enjoy such intercourse as will relieve the tediousness of
travel. Boccaccio could produce nothing of mark in description of his ten fine gentlemen and ladies. The procession of
Chaucer's Pilgrims is the very march of man on the high road
of life.

From different parts of London or the surrounding country
Canterbury pilgrims met in one of the inns on the Southwark side
of London Bridge, to set forth together upon the Kent road.
Chaucer's Pilgrims started from the " Tabard," an inn named
after the sleeveless coat once worn by labourers, now worn only
in a glorified form by heralds. Chaucer feigns that he was at the
" Tabard " ready to make his own pilgrimage, when he found a
company of nine-and-twenty on the point of starting, and joined
them, so making the number thirty. Harry Bailly, the host of the
'' Tabard," also joined the party, so making thirty-one. When
Chaucer describes the pilgrims in his Prologue to the " Canterbury Tales," his list contains thirty-one without reckoning the
host. This little discrepancy is one of many reminders in the
work itself that Chaucer died while it was incomplete. As he
proceeded with his story-telling he probably was modifying, to
suit the development of his plan, several of the first written
details of his Prologue. The Pilgrims were : 1, 2, 3, a knight,
his son, and an attendant yeoman ; 4, 5, 6, 7, 8, a prioress,
another nun, who was her chaplain, and three priests ; 9, 10, a
monk and a friar ; 11, a merchant ; 12, a clerk of Oxford ; 13, a
serjeant-at-law ; 14, a franklin, that is, a landholder free of
feudal service, holding immediately from the king ; 15, 16, 17,

18, 19, a haberdasher, a carpenter, a weaver, a dyer, and a tapestry maker ; 20, Roger, or Hodge, of Ware, a London cook ; 21; a sailor from the West country ; 22, a doctor of physic ; 23, Alisoun, a wife of Bath ; 24, 25, two brothers: a poor town parson and a ploughman ; 26, a reeve, or lord's servant as steward or overseer ; 27, a miller ; 28, a sompnour, or summoner of delinquents to the ecclesiastical courts ; 29, a pardoner, who dealt in pardons from the pope ; 30, a manciple of a lawyer's Inn of Court (a manciple was a buyer of victuals for a corporation); 31, Chaucer himself, who is described by 32, Harry Bailly, the host, as one who looked on the ground as he would find a hare, seemed elvish by his countenance, for he did unto no wight dalliance, yet was stout ; for, says the host, " he in the waist is shape as well as I."

Harry Bailly, large, bright-eyed, bold of speech, shrewd, manly, well-informed, had a shrew of a wife. He gave his guests a good supper, and jested merrily when they had paid their reckonings. It was the best company of pilgrims that had been at his inn that year, he said, and he should like to secure them mirth upon the way. They were all ready for his counsel; and it was that each of them should tell two tales on the way to Canterbury, and two other tales on the way home. The one whose tales proved to be " of best sentence and of solas " should have a supper in that room at the cost of all when they came back from Canterbury. He was to be their guide; and whoever gainsaid his judgment was to pay for all they spent upon the way. All agreed, and appointed the host governor, judge, and reporter of the tales. Then wine was fetched, they drank, and went to bed. The host roused them at dawn next morning, the 28th of April (our 7th of May), when the length of day was a few minutes over fifteen hours. The company rode slowly to the watering of St. Thomas—that is to say, of the Hospital of St. Thomas the Martyr in Southwark, which may be called, in the series of Church stations, the London terminus of the line of pilgrimage to St. Thomas the Martyr's shrine at Canterbury. Here the host reminded the companions of their undertaking; and all, at his bidding, drew out slips by way of lot. Whoever had the shortest should begin. This wholesome device excluded all questions of precedence of rank among the fellow-pilgrims. The lot fell to the knight, whereat all were glad; and with the courtesy of prompt assent he began.

47. The knight's tale is the tale of " Palamon and Arcite,"

Englished by Chaucer, in spirit as well language, from the
"Teseide" of Boccaccio. The monk is asked for the next story,
but the miller is drunk, and forces on his companions what he
calls a noble tale. This is a coarse tale told with vivid master-
touches; and, as its jest is against a carpenter, Oswald the
reeve is provoked to match it with a coarser jest against a
miller. An honest warning of their nature is placed by Chaucer
before these two stories, which belong to the broad view of life,
but show the low animal part of it :

> " And therefore whoso list it not to hear
> Turn over the leaf and choose another tale ;
> For he shall find ynow both great and smale
> Of storial thing that toucheth gentilesse,
> And eke morality and holiness. "

In plainest words the reader is warned beforehand by the pure-
hearted poet of the character of these two stories; in order that
they may be passed over by those who would avoid their theme.
The miller's tale has in its coarseness a rough moral at the close.
The reeve's tale paints a form of life that we can well spare from
the picture. Yet it is taken from the "Decameron," and was
put by Boccaccio not, as by Chaucer, in a churl's mouth, but upon
the lips of one of his fine ladies. After this, we find throughout what we found in the knight's tale, Chaucer's sense of the
pure beauty of womanhood. There is the whole range of character to be included in his picture, but on the fleshly side most
natural and genial are the touches with which he gives the wife
of Bath her place among the company. Chaucer began a cook's
tale of a riotous apprentice, as if he meant to read a lesson to
the Perkin revellers of the day, but he broke off, weary of low
themes. The *Tale of Gamelyn*, a bright piece of the class of
poetry to which the Robin Hood ballads belong, is here placed,
as a cook's tale, in Chaucer's series. It may have been among
his papers, but it probably is from another hand. There is in
this tale an Adam Spencer—that is Adam the butler or cellarer
—who, with certain changes, reappeared after many years in
"As You Like It," and whose part Shakespeare himself is said
to have acted. The "Man of Law's Tale" is of a good woman,
the pious Constance, and seems to have been taken from the
second book of Gower's "Confessio Amantis." The "Wife of
Bath's Tale" of a knight, Florentius, who by obedience won a
perfect bride, is again one of the tales of the "Confessio
Amantis." The "Friar's Tale" contemns the cruel rapacity of

sompnours; and the "Sompnour's Tale" scorns hypocritical rapacity in friars. The "Clerk's Tale" is the story of the patience of Griselda, the last tale in the "Decameron," and one which Petrarch said none had been able to read without tears. With the last letter he ever wrote, Petrarch sent to Boccaccio his own Latin prose version of it, as a religious allegory, made in 1373, the year before his own death, and two years before the death of Boccaccio; the year also of Chaucer's visit to Italy. It was "De Obedientia et Fide Uxoria, Mythologia" (A Myth upon Wifely Obedience and Faith), and Chaucer's poem is distinctly founded not on the tale as it stands in the "Decameron," but upon Petrarch's moralised version. This we find throughout, from the form of opening down to the religious application at the end, and the citation of the general Epistle of St. James, in the stanzas beginning—

> " For sith a woman was so patiènt
> Unto a mortal man, well more we ought,
> Receiven all in gree that God us sent."

But the poetical treatment of the story is so individual that it all comes afresh out of the mind of Chaucer. Its pathos is heightened by the humanising touch with which the English poet reconciles the most matter-of-fact reader to its questionable aspects. He feels that the incidents of the myth are against Nature, and at every difficult turn in the story he disarms the realist with a light passage of fence, and wins to his own side the host of readers who have the common English turn for ridicule of an ideal that conflicts with reason. Chaucer's "Merchant's Tale" is that afterwards modernised by Pope in his "January and May." His "Squire's Tale" is of the Tartar Cambys Kan, or Cambuscan, of his two sons Algarsif and Camballo, and of his daughter Canace, who had a ring enabling her to hear the speech of birds, and a mirror which showed coming adversity, or falsehood in a lover. This is a tale of enchantment, left unfinished, with stately promise of a sage and solemn tune, and which suggested to Milton the wish that the grave spirit of thoughtfulness would raise Musæus or Orpheus—

> " Or call up him that left half told
> The story of Cambuscan bold,
> Of Cambell and of Algarsife,
> And who had Canace to wife,
> That owned the virtuous ring and glass;
> And of the wondrous horse of brass
> On which the Tartar king did ride."

The " Franklin's Tale," to be found also in the " Decameron"
(fifth of the tenth day), was of a wife true of word as true of heart.
The second " Nun's Tale " was of St. Cecilia, from the " Golden
Legend," a treatise on Church Festivals, written at the end of
the thirteenth century by an Archbishop of Genoa, Jacobus à
Voragine, and translated into French by Jehan de Vignoy. The
" Pardoner's Tale" (eighty-second in the " Cento Novelle Antiche")
is a lesson against riotous living. Three profligates would slay
Death, the slayer of the young. An old man said they would
find him under an oak in the wood. They found there nearly
eight bushels of gold florins. At this they rejoiced, and cast lots
which of them should go to the town to fetch bread and wine
while the others watched the treasure. The lot fell on the
youngest. While he was gone his comrades plotted to kill him
on his return, that the gold might be divided between two only ;
and he himself plotted to poison two of the bottles of wine he
brought, that all the gold might belong to himself alone. So they
slew him, and had short mirth afterwards over the wine he had
poisoned.

The " Shipman's Tale " was from the " Decameron " (first of
the eighth day), of a knavish young monk. The prioress told
the legend of a Christian child killed by the Jews in Asia. The
child when living loved the Virgin, who appeared to it when
dying and put a grain under its tongue, so that the dead child-
martyr still sang " *O alma Redemptoris Mater.*" Until the grain
was removed the song continued. Chaucer himself began " The
Rime of Sir Thopas," a merry burlesque upon the metrical
romances of the day, ridiculing the profusion of trivial detail
that impeded the progress of a story of tasteless adventures. Sir
Thopas rode into a forest, where he lay down, and as he had
dreamed all night that he should have an elf queen for his love,
got on his horse again to go in search of the elf queen ; met a
giant, whom he promised to kill next day, the giant throwing
stones at him ; and came again to town to dress himself for the
adventure. The pertinacity with which the rhyme proceeds to
spin and hammer out all articles of clothing and armour worn by
Sir Thopas makes the Host exclaim at the story-teller, " Mine
earës aken for thy drasty speech," and cry " no more." The
device, too, is ingenious which puts the poet out of court in
his own company, so far as regards the question who won the
supper. His verse having been cried out upon, Chaucer answers
the demand upon him for a tale in prose with the tale of

Melibæus, a moral allegory upon the duties of life, translated from the Latin of Albertano de Brescia, or its French version, the "Livre de Melibée et de Dame Prudence." Only this and the " Parson's Tale" are written in prose. The "Monk's Tale" is of men in high estate who have fallen into hopeless adversity—a series of short "tragedies," suggested by a popular Latin prose book of Boccaccio's, on the " Falls of Illustrious Men" (De Casibus Illustrium Virorum). Among the Monk's examples is that of Ugolino, whereof Chaucer writes that they who would hear it at length should go to Dante, " the gretê poete of Itaille," as he had said of any reader curious to hear more of Zenobia, " Let him unto my maister Petrarch go." The Host at last stopped Piers the Monk because his tales were dismal ; and Sir John, the Nun's Priest, asked for something merry, told a tale of the Cock and the Fox, taken from the fifth chapter of the "̤ Roman de Renart."

Thus the pilgrims made for themselves entertainment by the way till they reached Boughton-under-Blean, seven miles from Canterbury, where they were overtaken by a Canon's Yeoman, who was followed by his master. These had ridden after the pilgrims for three miles. They seem to have followed them from Faversham, where the Canon—a ragged, joyless alchemist, who lived in a thieves' lane of the suburb—was on the watch for travellers whom he might join and dupe with his pretensions to a power of transmuting metals. This Canon, said his man, after other flourishing as herald of his master, could pave all their road to Canterbury with silver and gold. " I wonder, then,"̤ said Harry Bailly, "that your lord is so sluttish, if he can buy better clothes. His overslop is not worth a mite; it is all dirty and torn." Chaucer proceeds then skilfully to represent the gradual but quick slide of the yeoman's faith from his master, who, when he caught up the company, found his man owning that they lived by borrowing gold of men who think that of a pound they can make two :

> " Yet it is false ; and ay we have good hope
> It is for to doon, and after it we grope."

The Canon cried at his man for a slanderer. The Host bade the man tell on, and not mind his master, who then turned and fled for shame, leaving the company to be entertained with the "Canon's Yeoman's Tale," preluded with experience of alchemy.

The Manciple related after this the tale from Ovid's " Metamorphoses" of the turning of the crow from white to black for having told Apollo of the falsehood of his Coronis. There is

G *

then an indication of the time of day, four o'clock in the afternoon, before the "Parson's Tale," which evidently was meant to
stand last, for it is a long and earnest sermon in prose on a
text applying the parable of a pilgrimage to man's heavenward
journey. The text is from Jeremiah vi. 16 : "Stand ye in the
ways, and see, and ask for the old paths, where is the good
way, and walk therein, and ye shall find rest for your souls."

## CHAPTER V.

### THE FIFTEENTH CENTURY.

1. THE fifteenth century, which added to our literature not one
masterpiece, fed with its very mists the great streams of the
future. Scattered personal interest sped over the scene as a
wild mass of clouds, and rolled at times into a tempest to which
mists of darkness seemed to be reserved for ever. But in the
clods of the earth—among its unconsidered people—there lay
forces to which even mist and storm gave energy; and still
over all there shone the light of Him whose strength is in the
clouds. The vigour of a nation lies, at all times, in the character
and action of the common body of its people. The highest
genius, which implies good sense, true insight, and quick sympathy, must draw its sustenance from the surrounding world of
man and Nature. When it mistakes, if it ever can mistake, the
conventional life of a court for the soul of a nation, seeking to
strike root down into that only and draw support from that, it
must be as good seed fallen among stones. When it mistakes,
if it ever can mistake, the mere dust of the high road, the day's
fashions blown about by every wind, for source of life, it dies
under the feet of the next comer. The good soil is everywhere
in the minds of men. Culture may be confined to a few patches,
but everywhere in the common ground lies that of which fruit
shall come.

2. When Chaucer died, in the year 1400, the first printers
were unborn. John Gutenberg may, indeed, have been an infant
in the first year of the fifteenth century. John Faust was not born
until three years after Chaucer's death ; and his son-in-law, Peter
Schœffer, was some twenty years younger than Faust.

In Spain the Moors held Granada, and the Christians were

divided under the three kingdoms of Leon and Castile, Navarre, and Aragon.

In Germany, the nobles, in the year of Chaucer's death, deposed Emperor Wenzel, and, choosing for themselves a ruler as conveniently incapable but less inconveniently drunken and self-willed, made the Count Palatine of the Rhine Emperor Rupert. To Wenzel they left, for the nineteen remaining years of his life, the sovereignty of Bohemia. A sister to this Wenzel was our Richard II.'s " Good Queen Anne," who died six years before the beginning of the fifteenth century ; and it was to this Wenzel's wife that John Huss, ordained priest in the year 1400, was made confessor.

The marriage between our King Richard and Anne of Bohemia had brought Bohemians to England. One of them, who had been studying at Oxford, took home and communicated to his friend Huss some of the books of Wiclif. The social corruptness of the clergy in Bohemia had prepared the suffering people for an effort to cast out the money-changers from the temple. Huss looked upon his meeting with the works of Wiclif as the happiest event of his life ; and, through him, Wiclif raised revolt of the Bohemians against Italian trading on the national religion. Huss restored also to the University of Prague its nationality. The Archbishop of Prague, called Alphabetarius because his scholarship stopped short at A B C, burned the books of Wiclif, which he could not read, and interdicted the preaching of Huss. But Huss's gospellers sustained him against excommunication by the pope, and their chief battle was not on grounds of controversial theology. Its energies were quickened by the striving of the English people towards national independence in Church matters, and for a religion that no man in Church authority might follow as a knavish trade. The followers of Huss continued, indeed, in a modified and not unorthodox form, Wiclif's attack upon adoration of the host; but otherwise their assault was upon simony in the Church and upon adding belief in the pope to a belief in the three persons of the Trinity. The pope's claim to unlimited obedience, his indulgences, his abuse of excommunication, and the false faith in him, were four of " the six errors " posted by Huss on the gate of the Chapel of Bethlehem. Simony, and the belief that priests made the body of Christ in the mass, were the other two. The argument upon this last head (which did not include denial of transubstantiation itself) was so far an open one that when Huss went, in 1414, to the Council of Constance, he took with him a declaration from the Inquisitor-General of Heresy in Bohemia that, as far as the Inquisitor knew, Huss had shown no disposition to impugn any article of the Christian faith. Condemned as " a disciple of Wiclif, of damnable memory," John Huss, aged forty, whose worst heresy was the belief that liberty of conscience is a right of man, was burnt at Constance, on the 6th of July, in the year 1415, three or four months before the battle of Agincourt. From among the fagots rose a steady hymn of trust in God, till the smoke and the flames choked the firm voice and concealed the singer from the people while his soul was passing to its rest. Huss was afterwards reported to have said, playing upon his own name, which, in Bohemian, means goose : " To-day you burn a goose ; in a hundred years a swan shall arise whom you cannot burn." A hundred and two years after the burning of Huss, Luther affixed to the church-door at Wittenburg his ninety-five theses against indulgences.

3. The heat of struggle against heresy had become fiercer, while effort was made to end that schism in the papacy which had encouraged opposition to its rule (ch. iv. § 33). The Council of Constance that burnt Huss was also to restore unity by subjecting the claims of rival popes to a decision of the Church. In 1406 the death of the Italian, Innocent VII., gave hope to the cardinals at Rome. They elected a quiet old man of eighty pope for Italy, as Gregory XII., with a provision that he was to hold office only till he could arrange with the French pope, Benedict XIII., for a simultaneous abdication. Gregory was at first true to the understanding. Some months after his election he refused to give benefices, saying that he was not made pope for that, but only to end the schism. His friends and kinsmen, who flocked round him clamouring for loaves and fishes, caused him to halt on the way. He became rich in excuses for inaction; and, when nothing else availed, could stop and pray, in high pontifical state, for the peace of the Church, and so dispose of the time he did not wish to spend in action for securing it. Benedict, on the other side, though equally determined to do nothing, professed great readiness to meet Gregory and fulfil the desires of good churchmen. Europe was little edified to see the dance accordingly set up by the two aged popes, who poussetted to each other about France and Italy, but took care never to come near enough to join hands. One professed

fear of hostile ships, and would not approach the coast; the other professed fear of ambuscades, and would not venture far inland. So that, as Aretin wrote, one was a water animal to whom dry land was death; the other a land animal who looked with profound horror at water. By this trifling, and by yet more open swerving from the policy dictated by a true sense of religion, each lost friends. The Italian pope had Italy and the cardinals against him; the French pope was opposed by the French king and the University of Paris. Forsaken by the Church of France, Benedict went to his native Aragon, and then joined Gregory in the convocation of a General Council; this was to meet at Pisa, in the year 1409, for the establishment of unity and good religious order in the Church. It was opened by Jean Charlier, better known as Gerson, Chancellor of the Church and University of Paris, with his essay on the Unity of the Church. The council took into its own hands a power supreme over the popes', thus carrying out the principle advocated by the University of Paris. Gerson and the party represented by him held the whole Church to be bound by what they called essentials of theology, but were so tolerant of minor differences that they were not without hope of reuniting the Eastern with the Western Church. The two popes refused to recognise a council that usurped · papal authority; therefore they were deposed, and in their place was set up a third pope, an Alexander V. This added to the confusion. The new pope owed his rise to a cardinal ex-pirate, Balthazar Cossa, the most infamous man of his order, whose influence came of vast wealth ill-gotten, whose ambition was unscrupulous, and whom it suited at that time to place a creature of his own upon the vacant throne of Christendom. A year afterwards, when Alexander V. died, it was widely believed that the Cardinal Balthazar Cossa had sent him to heaven as soon as he was himself disposed to fill his place in this world. The belief shows what was thought of the man who, in 1410, as John XXIII., inherited the pledge to labour for a reformation of the Church. It was in his time that the reformatory council, which he was at last obliged to summon, met at Constanĉe. It began work in November, 1414, declaring itself to be a continuation of the Council of Pisa. Within four months it had received accusations of deep crime against Pope John. The Council maintained Gerson's principle that the pope is subject to a Church assembly. It tried and deposed

Pope John, humoured Gregory into abdication, left Benedict, deserted by his followers, pope only in his own esteem, and made Cardinal Otto of Colonna, Pope Martin V. The streets of Constance bore daily a shameful witness to the corruption widely spread among the clergy who attended at this Council, and who witnessed the execution of their sentence for the burning of John Huss.

Meanwhile a large part of Europe was fairly upon the way from Huss to Luther. The relation of earnest educated churchmen to the pope, as pope, in the early years of the fifteenth century, remained what it had been in the latter years of the fourteenth (ch. iv. § 33). We find it expressed by Chancellor Gerson in his treatise on the Methods of Uniting and Reforming the Church. "A pope," he said, "is a man, descended from men, earth from earth, a sinner and subject to sin. A few days ago the son of a poor peasant, he is exalted to the papal chair. Does such a one become a sinless man, a saint, without the least repentance for his sins, without confessing them, without contrition of heart? Who has made him a saint? Not the Holy Ghost; for it is not dignity of station that brings the influences of the Holy Ghost, but the grace of God and love; not the authority of the office, for it may be enjoyed by bad men as well as good." This was the free speech of one who avoided the free speculations of the English, and saw no security outside the system of theology accounted orthodox in his own time and country. "Where," he asked, "will you find charity in a pope? At the Roman court the daily talk is of castles, of territorial domains, of the different kind of weapons, of gold; but seldom or never of chastity, alms, righteousness, faith, or holy manners: so that the court, once a spiritual one, has become a secular, devilish, tyrannical court, and worse in manners and civil transactions than any other." This had been the language of Gower's *Vox Clamantis*, and the language used by many educated earnest men whom the Church never accused of heresy, but who belonged to the most faithful of her sons.

4. From King Henry IV. (1399—1413) the English Church reformers, like all other reformers, looked for support; but he had not long worn his crown before he leagued with the clergy against them. As it had been settled by statute of the fifth year of Richard II., so it was confirmed by statute of the second year of Henry IV., that part of the sheriff's oath when he took office was to be that he should seek to redress all errors and heresies,

commonly called Lollards.  This indicates the early sense of
the word which, though otherwise derived from an Englishman,
Walter Lollardus, burnt for heresy at Cologne in 1322, was then
held to be derived from the Latin *lolia* or *lollia* ("tares"); and
that Walter probably was called Lollardus for his sowing of
tares among the good wheat of the Church.   In the second year
of Henry IV. heretics were also left to be dealt with by the
clergy at their own discretion, provided always that the proceedings against them were publicly and judicially ended within
three months.   The end might be a sentence of imprisonment
or fine to any extent, or a delivering over to the secular power
to be burnt to death before the people.   No time was lost by
Archbishop Arundel in exercising this new privilege.   In
February, 1401, William Sawtree (Salter), priest of St. Osyth's
in London, was burnt alive in Smithfield.  In 1410 the Commons
of England prayed the king for repeal or mitigation of the statute
against the Lollards.   The king said that he wished it had been
more severe, and immediately signed a warrant for the burning
of a blacksmith named John Badby.

   **Henry Knighton,** who wrote during this reign a Latin
chronicle of events in England from the time of King Edgar
to the death of Richard II., is full of bitterness against the
Lollards.   He was a regular canon of the abbey of Leicester;
and of Wiclif's translation of the Bible into English his
chronicle said: "This Master John Wiclif translated into the
Anglic—not angelic—tongue the Gospel that Christ gave to
the clergy and the doctors of the Church, that they might
minister it gently to laymen and weaker persons, according to
the exigence of their time, their personal wants, and the hunger
of their minds, whence it is made vulgar by him, and more
open to the reading of laymen and women than it usually is
to the knowledge of lettered and intelligent clergy; and thus
the pearl of the Gospel is cast forth and trodden under feet
of swine."

   There was only one other writer who produced a book of
any note during the reign of Henry IV., and he was a Dominican
—**John of Bromyard**—bitter as Knighton in assault upon
the Lollards.   John of Bromyard, in Herefordshire, taught
theology at Cambridge, and his great work, among others upon
theological, civil, and moral law, was a *Summa Predicantium,*
an alphabetical compilation of material for use in preaching,
arranged under such heads as Abstinence, Absolution, Avarice, ·

and ending in Xhristus ; a work upon so large a scale that when first printed at Nürnberg, in 1485, it filled a thousand large folio pages of double-column black letter. It is an earnest, erudite, and interesting mass of mediæval practical theology.

5. Of our three poets of chief mark during the former half of the fifteenth century, two, John Lydgate and Thomas Occleve, were men about thirty years old at the time of Chaucer's death. They were more than forty when Henry IV. died ; but neither of them seems to have attempted to produce any important work during his reign. The third poet, a younger man, was **James I. of Scotland,** whom Henry IV. made his prisoner in 1405.

The father of James I. was John, who, in 1390, succeeded his father, Robert II., as Robert III. The Scottish nobles had been bred by the long contest with England to use of arms, and were not nice as to the amount of liberty they took. Robert III. was weak, and the Estates of Scotland in Parliament assembled made him answerable for all that the people suffered by misgovernment. In 1398 they transferred his power to his son, whom they made acting-lieutenant for his father, with the title of Duke of Rothsay. Robert III. had also a brother, who was made at the same time Duke of Albany. In 1402 the Duke of Albany contrived to get his nephew the acting-lieutenant into a prison, from which he was soon afterwards brought out for burial. The king had another son, the boy James ; but Albany became sole Governor of Scotland in a time of trouble. The Percys were preparing insurrection against Henry IV. ; they were in secret alliance with Owen Glendower, who had so headed a Welsh struggle for independence as to be for a time King of Wales. Percy, in defiance of a royal order, released Douglas and other Scots taken at Homildon Hill. Douglas marched into England, joined Percy, and shared defeat with him at Shrewsbury. Albany had raised an army, and masked his designs ; but if he had meant to join Percy he was too late. He then favoured the fiction, or maintained the fact, that in Scotland King Richard II. was still living. Either Henry IV. had produced some other body as that of the dead Richard in St. Paul's ; or Albany was showing somebody else as the live Richard in Scotland, for his own future benefit as ruler there. Probably it was Albany who, in 1405, contrived that his nephew James, then a boy of eleven, should, during a time of truce, be intercepted by an armed ship of the English when upon his voyage to France, whither he was being sent for education. In the following year King Robert died, and the boy of twelve became King James I. ; but the Duke of Albany, aged sixty-seven, with a son, Murdoch, to leave in his place, was actually reigning sovereign of Scotland. Thus the boy-king, James I., received his education as a prisoner at the English court, and was a young man of about nineteen, with some genius as a poet and much energy of character, when Henry IV. died and bequeathed the care of him to his son Henry V. Henry V. was also counselled by his father to divert the attention of the English from domestic griefs by foreign war.

Before the death of Henry IV. in England, the northern districts of the Scottish Lowlands were, in 1411, threatened with a descent of Highland marauders in unexampled force, under Donald, the Lord of the Isles. There was a hasty gathering of defenders under Alexander Stewart, Earl of Mar, who checked the advance of the Highlanders at the *Battle of Harlaw.* Poems were written on this battle ; Scottish schoolboys took sides, and played at it. Harlaw remained the name of a tune in the beginning of the seventeenth century.

6. During the reign of Henry V. (1413—1422), James I. of Scotland remained prisoner at the English court ; well educated, trained in English laws and customs, and to be released when further bound by marriage with a lady of the royal family of England. Nature assisted Henry's policy, for a true affection sprang up between King James and the Lady Jane Beaufort, daughter of the Earl of Somerset, niece to King Henry IV., and first cousin to Henry V. The love was celebrated in a poem known as *The King's Quair,* that is, "King's Little Book," from the old French *quayer* or *cayer,* modern French *cahier.* This is a graceful piece of court poetry, inspired by love and a study of Chaucer, and written in Chaucer's own seven-lined stanza, which long remained a favourite with his successors. It has been called rhyme royal, because this particular disciple used it. The "King's Quair" is in six cantos. It begins with (1) the poet in his bed at midnight reading Boëthius, thinking of the wheel of fortune, and likening his own life to a ship among black rocks with empty sail; proceeds (2) to tell of his capture in boyhood, his listening from his prison window to the love-songs of the birds, his wonder what love is, till looking down he saw walking under his tower, newly come to make her morning orisons, the lady whose thrall he became. When she was gone

he lamented, till at evening he lay with his head against a stone, half sleeping, half in swoon with sorrow. Then (3) a dazzling light seemed to come in at the window whereat he leant, and a voice said, "I bring thee comfort and heal; be not afraid." The light went out, and he rose through sphere and sphere to Venus, with her allegorical court, and made his plaint to her. She sent him to Minerva. He went then (4) to Minerva, who bade him base his love on virtue, be true, and meek, and steadfast in his thought, doing fit service to his lady in word and work, and so abide his time. The poet declared in three stanzas that his love was pure as his desire was great.

> " 'Desire,' quod she, 'I nyl it not deny,
> So thou it ground and set in Christin wise.' "

Then at the bidding of Minerva the poet went (5) to Fortune, whose dwelling is, of course, allegorically described. Fortune placed him on her wheel, bade him take heed, and took him by the ear " so earnestly that therewithal I woke." The next and last canto (6) tells how the poet rose from his uneasy sleep and went to the window, where a white turtle-dove, the bird of Venus, alighted on his hand, and turning to him showed him in her bill a fair branch of red gilly-flowers with their green stalks, which had written in gold on every leaf a message of glad comfort to the lover. King James I. ended his poem with a strain of true love, thanked the prison wall from which he had looked forth and leaned, and rejoiced in the unfading flower of his love. An epilogue, or "excusation of the author," represents James, king though he be, acknowledging his "masters" in three poets, whose royalty was more than the inheritance of worldly rank, Gower and Chaucer, and next to these John Lydgate, who, when the young king wrote his poem, was first in repute among men of the generation after Chaucer.

7. **John Lydgate** was born not later than 1370, in Suffolk, at the village of Lydgate, six or seven miles from Newmarket. In the Benedictine Monastery of Bury St. Edmunds he was ordained subdeacon in 1389, deacon in 1393, and priest in 1397. After studying at Oxford, Paris, and Padua, he opened a school of rhetoric at his monastery of Bury St. Edmunds, where Dan (that is Dominus) John Lydgate, the Monk of Bury, became a famous teacher of literature and the art of versifying. He was well read in ancient lore, mathematician also and astronomer as well as orator and poet; a bright, pleasant, and earnest man,

who wrote clear fluent verse in any style then reputable, but who was most apt at the telling of such moral stories as his public liked. Sometimes he was as prolix, and he always was as musical, as the old romancers who had been satirised by Chaucer in Sir Thopas ; but he preferred to take his heroes and heroines out of the Martyrology, and he could write pleasantly to order for the library of any monastery the legend of its patron saint. Since he wrote so much (there are not less than 250 works bearing his name), and almost always as a story-teller, he found many readers, and his rhyming supplied some of the favourite tales of his time. He turned into smooth English verse the tales of Troy and Thebes. He elevated into an English poem that best of the Latin works of Boccaccio which tells and moralises tales of the mutations of affairs of men from Adam downward. These were his three chief works ; but they were written in the reign of Henry VI. Lydgate wrote for Henry V. the " Life of our Lady ;" he sang the tale of St. Alban, the English protomartyr, of his own St. Edmund, and of many a saint more. He could catch the strain of popular song, and satirize the licking up of money which leaves the poor man hopeless of justice in his *London Lickpenny*, whereof the measure is enlivened with the street-cries of his time. He could write morality in the old court allegorical style ; he could kneel at the foot of the Cross and offer to his God the sacrifice of a true outburst of such song as there was in him. John Lydgate was not a poet of great genius, but he was a man with music in his life. He was full of a harmony of something more than words, not more diffuse than his age liked him to be, and, therefore, with good reason, popular and honoured among English readers in the fifteenth century.

8. **Thomas Occleve**, the other chief poet of the generation after Chaucer, was of the same age as Lydgate, and, like Lydgate, about thirty years old when Chaucer died. He was a Londoner, and knew Chaucer ; evidently he refers to a personal relation between them when he speaks of himself as Chaucer's disciple. In his earlier years he lived in the Strand, at Chester's Inn, one of the buildings pulled down for the site of Somerset House. He says that his life was ill regulated in his youth, but says this in a poem designed for moral counsel to young men—*La Male Regle de T. Hoccleve*—of which the purpose doubtless led to a half-artistic exaggeration of self-censure. We know Occleve tolerably well through his chief poem, for the long original

introduction to his version of the *De Regimine Principum*, or
" Governail of Princes" (ch. iv. § 43), consists wholly of moral reflections on the manners of his time, interspersed with references
to his own position in a government office as clerk of the  Privy
Seal.  He was married, had a household to provide for, and could
not get his salary paid, or an annuity for life of twenty marks which
had been  nominally granted  him.   Therefore  he took a melancholy morning walk and met an old man, who asked what was
his trouble.  Was it love, was it care of abundance, was it care of
poverty, was it heresy?—and here six stanzas are given to a recollection of the burning of John Badby, at which Henry V., then
prince, showed his humanity.   When Badby was brought to the
stake, and a barrel was prepared in which to burn him, the prince
spoke to him kindly and urged recantation.   Badby, remaining
firm, was put into the barrel, and the burning fuel was heaped
round it.   The prince, moved by his cries of  agony, caused  the
fuel to be cleared from about him, and again, when he was half
dead, spoke to him, offering to procure pardon and even a
pension.   Badby still was firm; the prince, with some anger,
ordered the fuel to be heaped round him again, and he was
burned to ashes as a hopeless heretic.   When the old man  had
preached upon the sin of heresy, Occleve answered that this was
not his trouble.   The old man was pleased, and urged next that
his counsel was not to be despised for his poor habit; this text
giving occasion for much moral satire on extravagance of costume
in Henry V.'s time.   Then the moralist turned from his poverty to
his age, and found occasion to touch on the riotous excesses of the
young.   Finally he got from the poet a full account of the cause
of his trouble.  A lively dialogue followed on that, giving occasion, as that was taken throughout, for earnest words upon all evils
of the time, from the self-seeking churchmen to the length of
side sleeves.   The old man's advice was that Occleve should
write to the prince something in English, but "write to him no
thing that sowneth to vice," and  show himself to be a man who
deserved payment of arrears of salary.   In obedience to this
counsel, he translated for Henry V. the book "De Regimine
Principum," digested into practical counsel, not without reminder
of the unpaid annuity, and towards the  end with deprecation of
the wars between the Kings of France and England, and an invocation of peace for the land.  " Let Christian kings," he says,
" war only on the enemies of Christ."

   Were they the  men accused of heresy?   Occleve—earnest

and liberal in many things, and in this lighter poem, written in English and in Chaucer's stanza, seeking to find out the wrong and get it undone, with as much earnestness as Gower in his "Vox Clamantis," while he pointed to the corruption of the clergy—was, like Gower, an orthodox maintainer of Church doctrine. We find, therefore, that he assented to the new endeavour to save as it was thought many from the everlasting fire by giving some to be burnt publicly in this world.

9. In the second year of Henry V., in 1414, a new law passed against the Lollards, which ordained that they should forfeit all the lands they had in fee-simple, and all their goods and chattels, to the king. The same Act decreed that whatsoever they were that should read the Scriptures in their mother tongue, they should forfeit "land, catel, lif, and godes from their heyres for ever, and so be condempned for heretykes to God, enemies to the crowne, and most errant traitors to the lande."

On Christmas morning, in 1417, Sir John Oldcastle, Lord Cobham, a brave knight of unblemished life, who held the tenets of Wiclif, and had opened his doors at Cowling Castle to the persecuted teachers of the Lollards, was hung up by the middle in an iron chain upon a gallows in St. Giles's Fields, and burnt alive while thus suspended. The last words heard from him were praise of God, into whose hands he resigned his soul.

Chichele was then primate, violent as Arundel in vindictive dread of Lollard attacks on the Church temporalities. It was he who led his clergy when they urged the ready King Henry V., who was twenty-five years old and had a military genius, to follow his father's counsel, and divert attention of the people from domestic needs by foreign war. The war was based upon unjust claims of dominion over France; claims which the English primate and his party declared to be just and lawful.

Henry V., although essentially a soldier and intemperate in war, was temperate in life, well taught, and had respect for scholars. His ambassador in Spain in 1422 was **William Lindwood,** an Oxford divinity professor, who wrote the *Constitutions of the Archbishops of Canterbury, from Langton to Chichele.* Lindwood was made Bishop of St. Davids in 1434, and died in 1446. He had been preceded in his bishopric by an astronomer, named Rocleve, who had been among the friends of Henry V., and to whom the king gave that see. But most closely attached to Henry V. was the most famous English theologian of his day. **Thomas Notter,** of Saffron Walden, in

Essex, who was born in 1380, and educated at Oxford, where he was Doctor of Divinity, and publicly disputed against Wiclif's doctrines.   He became a Carmelite in London, went to the Council of Pisa, in 1414 became Provincial of the Carmelites in England, and as such was a distinguished member of the Council of Constance (§ 3).   Thomas Netter, of Walden, was regarded by the orthodox as prince of controversialists in the fifteenth century.   The chief of his numerous works was a *Doctrinale*, which is a long and systematic theological assertion of Church doctrine against Wiclif heresies.   He also put together *Fasciculi Zizaniorum*—Bundles of Master John Wiclif's tares with wheat—which contain the statute for the burning of heretics; the bull of John XXIII. against Wiclif's heresies ; condemned opinions of Wiclif ; sentence passed on him and on John Huss ; accusations against Jerome of Prague ; divers condemned errors of Lollards and others; the latest topic being the examination of William White, September 13th, 1428, at which Thomas of Walden was himself present, two years before his death.   This theologian was Inquisitor-General in England for the punishing of heretics.   He had business in Lithuania after the close of the Council of Constance, in 1418, and upon his return was made confessor to King Henry V.

10. In August, 1415, Henry had crossed to France.   On the 25th of the following October he won the battle of Agincourt, and closed the victory with a barbarous massacre of prisoners. Two chroniclers of English history were present at the fight. One, John de Wavrin, fought on the French side, but two years later joined the French allies of England.   He wrote afterwards a chronicle of English history from the earliest years, which he brought down to the year 1471.   He is also probably the anonymous continuer (from 1443) of the chronicle of Monstrelet, who died in 1453.   The other soldier of Agincourt who has left us a chronicle was an Englishman, **John Harding.**   He was born in 1378 ; at the age of twelve was admitted into the house of Sir Henry Percy, known as Hotspur, and served as a volunteer under Percy in the battle of Homildon.   After Percy's death John Harding followed the banner of Sir Robert Umfraville, who died in 1436, and became constable of one of his castles.   John Harding, in and after the reign of Henry V., was much employed in procuring documents—some of them forgeries—in support of the claim on the kings of Scotland for homage to the kings of England.   His English rhyming *Chronicle* was not written

until after the reign of Henry V. But Henry V. was King of England when a rhyming chronicle was written in English of the north, the *Oryginale Cronykil of Scotland*, by **Andrew of Wyntoun**, a regular canon of St. Andrew's, and prior of one of the five subordinated monasteries of St. Andrew's, that of St. Serf, in the island of Lochleven, once a religious house of the Culdees. Andrew of Wyntoun crowded into his nine books of ingenious eight-syllabled doggrel a great number of facts and traditions.

11. We had English verse also from **William of Nassington**, in Northamptonshire, a proctor in the Ecclesiastical Court of York, who translated into English rhyme a Latin metrical treatise on the Trinity and Unity, called *The Mirror of Life*. The translation was made before the year 1400. The original, in several thousand verses, was by John of Waldly, in Yorkshire, an Augustine Friar, provincial of his order in England, and active in controversy against Wiclif.

12. The chief Latin chronicler of the reign of Henry V. was **Thomas Walsingham**, precentor and chief copyist, or scriptorarius, in St. Albans Abbey, where in his time, by his advice, a new Scriptorium was built. He used records produced in the form of chronicle by preceding monks of St. Albans—**William Rishanger, John of Trokelowe, Henry of Blaneford, William Wyntershylle,**—in the formation of an English history, *Historia Anglicana*, which extends from 1272 to the end of the reign of Henry V., in 1422. He also compiled, about the year 1419, his *Ypodgima Neustriæ*, or "Demonstration of Events in Normandy," dedicated to Henry V. in compliment upon his recent conquests of Normandy; but the affairs of Normandy form only a small portion of the work.

13. We may now pass out of the reign of Henry V., who died at the end of August, 1422. When the penitential psalms were being read to him on his death-bed, the words "Thou shalt build the walls of Jerusalem" put into his head more fighting, and he said, "If I had finished the war in France, and established peace, I would have gone to Palestine to redeem the holy city from the Saracens."

He left an infant son, Henry VI. (1422—1461), King of England, and he named his brother Humphrey, Duke of Gloucester, regent of England. Parliament gave chief power to the Duke of Bedford, who was made Regent of France, and the Duke of Gloucester was made President of the Council, as "Protector of the Realm and Church of England," when Bedford was away in France.   This Humphrey, Duke of Gloucester, was the patron of **John Lydgate,** who died about 1460.

For him Lydgate wrote, in the reign of Henry VI., his *Falls of Princes*, a long poem in Chaucer's seven-lined stanza, founded upon Boccaccio's Latin prose work in nine books, "De Casibus Illustrium Virorum;" but Lydgate said that he followed Boccaccio through the version of a Frenchman, Laurent, that is Laurent de Premierfait, who translated also the "Decameron" for Jeanne, Queen of Navarre.   Lydgate interspersed his work with occasional prologues and balades of his own, while he retold the stories, not as a mere rhyming translator, but as a man who had an honest gift of song and felt their poetry.   There passes through the reader's mind a funeral pomp of men who have been carried high on Fortune's wheel, and then been bruised to death by its descending stroke.   The poem warns the mighty to be humble, and the lowly to be well content.

*The Storie of Thebes* is told by Lydgate as another "Canterbury Tale."   After a sickness he went in a black cope, "on palfrey slender, long, and lean," with rusty bridle, and his man before him carrying an empty pack, to the shrine at Canterbury, and by accident put up there at the inn where Chaucer's pilgrims were assembled.   There he saw the host of the "Tabard," who thought him lean for a monk, prescribed nut-brown ale after supper, with anise, cummin, or coriander seed at bedtime. But the best medicine was cheerful company.   So Dan John supped with the pilgrims, went home with them next day, and helped to amuse them with the story of the "Thebaid" of Statius, as it had been manipulated by the romancers of the Middle Ages.

Lydgate's *Troy Book* is a metrical version from a French translation of the "Historia Trojana" of Guido della Colonna, a Sicilian poet and lawyer of Messina, who came to England in 1287 with Edward I., when he returned from his war in Asia. Colonna's "Trojan History" was a version from the "Fall of Troy" ascribed to Dares (ch. iii. § 21).

14. The author of the "King's Quair," **James I.** of Scotland, went home to his Scotch throne not very long after the death of Henry V.   His love was first crowned by marriage to Jane Beaufort with royal state; he was then allowed to proceed to his kingdom, and was crowned at Scone in May of the year 1424.   He sought to maintain peace and order in his kingdom,

endeavoured to bring law and justice within reach of the poor, regulated weights and measures, established a survey of propert; with a view to justice in taxation, and made careful inquiry into titles. He tried to suppress with a strong hand the violence of faction. But the enlarged liberties of the people pressed on the feudal rights of the nobles. Many a rough-handed chief looked also with concern at the inquiry into titles. Sir Robert Graham, who had denounced the king as a tyrant for his encroachment on the nobles, at last broke in upon him with three hundred Highlanders, on the 20th of February, 1437, caught him unarmed, and killed him. He defended himself bravely, and his wife Jane, who sought to shelter him, was wounded in the struggle. He had written of her truly in the "King's Quair:"

> "And thus this floure . . .
> So hertly has unto my help attendit,
> That from the deth hir man sche has defendit."

There remained only a six year old son to be the king's successor.

Some writers ascribe to James I. of Scotland, and some to James IV., two humorous old Scottish poems describing the rough holiday life of the people. They are called *Peeblis to the Play* and *Christis Kirk of the Green.* If they were really by James I., he must have had a range of power that would place him first among the poets of his time.

15. The death of Charles VI. of France made the infant Henry VI. of England, by the Treaty of Troyes, sovereign of France; but this claim was resisted. Then followed contention, wasting life and honour; the patriotic inspiration, the success, and the disgrace to England of the burning of Jeanne d'Arc, after her abandonment and sale by men of her own country. Slowly the French ground was reconquered by the French, and England fell under the plague of civil war. In this contest between the rival lines of York and Lancaster first blood was drawn in the battle of St. Albans, on the 22nd of May, 1455; but after this there was, during four or five years, rest from the actual clash of arms, while strife continued for supremacy under the feeble rule of a king whose mind, weak through disease, swayed in its clearer hours towards a kindly piety.

16. During this interval **Reginald Pecock,** author of the most important English prose work written in the reign of Henry VI., was called to account for the free spirit shown not

in attack upon the higher clergy, but in defence of them. Reginald Pecock, probably a Welshman, was born towards the end of the fourteenth century, studied at Oriel College, Oxford, and was admitted to priest's orders in 1421. In 1431 John Lydgate's patron, the Protector, Humphrey Duke of Gloucester, made Pecock Master of Whittington College, and Rector of St. Michael in Riola. For the next thirteen years he lived in London, taking active interest in the religious controversies that were still astir, and seeking by many tracts, written in English, to convince the Lollards. About 1440 he produced a *Donet*, or introduction to the chief truths of Christianity, in a dialogue between father and son. The second part was against the Lollards. A *Follower of Donet* appeared some years later. In 1444, Humphrey of Gloucester, a lover of books and patron of learning, made Pecock Bishop of St. Asaph. At the same time he became Doctor of Divinity. Bishop Pecock undertook to defend his order against popular aspersions, and in 1447 preached at Paul's Cross a sermon arguing that, although he often preached in his own diocese, bishops were free from the burden of preaching, because they had duties of a higher character ; and that when they were non-resident they had good reason for being so. This sermon was the beginning of a course of offence against the Church, consisting mainly in a defence based upon arguments addressed to the reason. About the year 1449 Pecock was busy upon his chief work, *The Repressor of Overmuch Blaming of the Clergy;* and in the same year he was raised from the Bishopric of St. Asaph to that of Chichester. His "Repressor," although wholly meant as a defence of the higher clergy against those who were called the Bible men, increased the hostility of his own party against him. He undertook to justify eleven, but did in fact restrict himself to six, of the practices for which the clergy incurred blame among the people : these were, the use of images ; the going on pilgrimage; the holding of landed possessions by the clergy ; the various ranks of the hierarchy ; the framing of Church laws by papal and episcopal authority ; and the institution of the religious orders. For discussion of the other five points he referred to other books of his, written or about to be written. Upon the topics it discussed the book was a repertory of fifteenth century argument. The offence was that the whole subject was argued out in homely English for discussion by the English people ; for while Pecock exalted the pope's supremacy, he conceded to his opponents that in Scripture was the only rule of faith, and urged that doctrine should be proved therefrom by reason. This, however, he did while opposing the demand of the Lollards— Puritans of the fifteenth century—for authority of Scripture in less important matters of usage, lay or clerical. There could be no real conflict between reason and Scripture, Pecock taught, and the clergy, he said, shall be condemned at the last day " if by clear wit they draw not men into consent of true faith otherwise than by fire, sword, and hangment ; although I will not deny these second means to be lawful, provided the former be first used." A bishop who thought for himself after this fashion ; denying to the Lollards that deductions from their reading of the Bible were infallible, denying also to his brethren of the hierarchy the right to claim an uninquiring faith in dogmas of the Church ; opposed himself to the passions of the combatants on either side, and had no partisans. In 1457 a council was held at Westminster, in which all temporal lords refused to speak till Pecock had been expelled from it. The divines at this council appointed four-and-twenty doctors to examine Pecock's books. The books were reported against, Pecock was declared a sickly sheep, and called upon to abjure or be burnt. He had admitted the right of the Church thus to compel opinion, and he submitted. The executioner burnt, instead of the bishop, his works in three folios and eleven quartos, including a copy of that " Repressor " of his, a piece of natural fifteenth century English, which yet survives as one of the best and most considerable specimens of early prose among the treasures of our literature. After some months Bishop Pecock was deprived of his see, and secluded in the abbey of Thorney in Cambridgeshire, where he was confined to a private room within sight of an altar, was forbidden ever again to put pen to paper, and was to have access to no books but a breviary, a mass-book, a psalter, a legend, and a Bible. The doors of Thorney Abbey closed on him.

17. There is little more to record of our literature in the reign of Henry VI. Dame **Juliana Berners**, lady prioress of the nunnery of Sopwell, near St. Albans, who was living in 1460, wrote in English verse a *Book of Hunting*, and in English prose the *Art of Hawking* and the *Laws of Arms*.

18. **John Capgrave**, born in 1393, at Lynn in Norfolk, died in 1464 Provincial of the Austin Friars. He excelled all men of the reign of Henry VI. in the industry of a great erudition without genius. He was a hearty orthodox churchman,

who detested Wiclif and his followers, but as an Englishman sympathised with resistance to aggressions of the papal see upon his king's prerogative or the just rights of his countrymen. His chief works are a *Book of the Noble Henries*, dedicated to King Henry VI., and a *Chronicle of England*, dedicated to King Edward IV.

19. Throughout the reign of Henry VI., and on into the reign of Henry VII., extends, from 1422 to 1505, the large body of family and friendly correspondence known as the *Paston Letters*. Most of them are addressed to John Paston, Esq., of Norfolk, who died in 1466; to Sir John Paston, his son, who died in 1479; and to John Paston of Gelston, who died in 1503. They abound in interesting illustrations of our civil and social history during the Wars of the Roses.

20. A most valuable record of the Transition English of Norfolk in the year 1440 is the *Promptorium Parvulorum*, an English-Latin Dictionary, compiled by one of the Dominicans, or Black Friars, of Bishop's Lynn. He was known as **Geoffrey the Grammarian**, and is believed to have been also the author of a Latin-English Dictionary, which he called the *Medulla Grammatices*. The Latin interpretations in the *Promptorium* enable us to define the meaning of many now obsolete words in books written before the Commonwealth.

21. **John Tiptoft, Earl of Worcester**, whom Henry VI. made Lord Deputy of Ireland, and who afterwards was Lord High Constable and Lord High Treasurer, had scholarly tastes, and was translating *Cicero on Friendship* at the time when the first printers with movable types were establishing their art in Mayence. During the short interval of restored rule to Henry VI., breaking the reign of Edward IV., John Tiptoft was accused of cruelty in his Irish administration, and he was executed on Tower Hill in October, 1470.

**Benedict Burgh**, Archdeacon of Colchester, was then at work upon his translation of Cato's "Morals" into English stanzas, for the use of his pupil Lord Bourchier, son of the Earl of Essex. Benedict Burgh is said also to have finished a metrical version of the *De Regimine Principum*, which Lydgate had left incomplete. Burgh himself died in 1488. ·

22. **Thomas Chestre**, who wrote for the minstrels in the reign of Henry VI., Englished the *Lay of Sir Launfal;* but the most famous minstrel of this time was a Scottish rustic, blind from birth, known as Henry the Minstrel, or Blind

**Harry,** who obtained food and clothing by recitation of stories before men of the highest rank. He was one of an order of men who sang or chanted tales to the harp, in verses often of their own composing, enlivened with mimicry and action. Blind Harry, who understood Latin and French, produced a long poem on his nation's hero, *Wallace,* in or about the year 1461. He was the first who followed Chaucer in use of the heroic couplet; and he calls his poem a chronicle derived chiefly from the Latin of John Blair, who had been Wallace's schoolfellow.

23. Of our literature during the reign of Edward IV. (1461—1483) there is only one thing more to be said that is not connected with the introduction of the art of printing with movable types into this country. Even when distracted by contending factions, England was advancing towards freedom. The laws of the country were not based like those of France upon the principle that the will of the monarch is law, but on the will of the people through their representatives. An English lawyer, **Sir John Fortescue,** born in Devonshire, and Chief Justice of the King's Bench from 1442 to 1460, fought at Towton, and fled with King Henry VI. to Scotland and Wales. The exiled king made him his nominal Lord Chancellor. The actual king confiscated his possessions as those of a traitor. As an exile in Lorraine with the queen and prince, he wrote, about the year 1463, for the use of the young prince, a Latin book in praise of the laws of England (*De Laudibus Legum Angliæ*) in dialogue between himself and the prince. It is a simple sketch of the first principles of law. He wrote afterwards in like spirit an English book on the *Difference between Absolute and Limited Monarchy,* his chief object being to show the superiority of a constitutional over a despotic government. After Henry VI. and the prince were dead, Sir John Fortescue acknowledged Edward IV.'s title to the crown, and thus he obtained in 1473 the reversal of his attainder. He is said to have lived to the age of ninety. The strength of constitutional feeling in this chief English lawyer of the fifteenth century may be inferred from his manner of dating the absolute regal dominion from Nimrod, who "first acquired to himself a kingdom, though he is not called a King in the Scripture, but a Mighty Hunter before the Lord. For," says Fortescue, "as a Hunter behaves towards Beasts, which are naturally wild and free ; so did he oblige Mankind to be in servitude and to obey him." He went back even to the mythical

time for the free spirit of the English body politic. " The kingdom of England," he says, " had its original from Brut and the
Trojans who attended him from Italy and Greece, and became
a mixed kind of government, compounded of the regal and
political." Going as far back as he could, he was unable to
find or -conceive an English people passively obedient to any
one irresponsible master. The nation was advancing slowly in
his days; there was social confusion, and intellectual life seemed
to be numbed, while events of great moment were happening abroad. But if there was no guiding light of genius, there
was the sense of God and duty in the people which enabled
them to find their own way till the next guides came.

The rise in Florence of the Medici family; the Capture of
Constantinople by the Turks; and the Invention of Printing,
were, during the reigns of Henry VI. and Edward IV., the
events abroad which had most influence upon the course of
thought in England.

24. It had been to Florence that the pope elected by the
Council of Constance (§ 3), Martin V., finding himself one
of four, and unable to get immediate possession of his rights
at Rome, betook himself in the year 1419. This was when
Henry V. was King of England; and about the time when
Occleve was writing his chief poems, and James I. of Scotland
was writing the " King's Quair." For a year and a half a papal
court was added to the pomps of the free city. The deposed
pope, John XXIII., presently came to Florence, made his submission, and died there, leaving the founder of the great Medici
family, Giovanni de' Medici, one of his four executors. At this
time the wealth of trading Florence was augmented by the purchase of Leghorn and its port from Genoa. The free commonwealth was unrivalled in commercial prosperity. Its citizens
were active in all quarters of the world. There was a treaty
even with the Soldan of Babylon for currency within his realm
of the coin of Florence. The strength thus gathered was soon
to be absorbed and exhausted in the domination of the Medici;
but the founder of that family, the rich banker Giovanni, made
Gonfaloniere in 1421, owed his political rise to his goodwill
towards the people. The war with Filippo Visconti, Duke of
Milan, begun by Florence in 1423, was to check aggression upon
the free cities of Tuscany. But the war began ill, and Florence
might have fallen in the fight for liberty if Venice had not at last
consented to alliance with her. Victory cost Florence three and

a half millions of florins ; and the popular Giovanni de' Medici, who had been at the head of a peace party, obtained political supremacy by the invention and establishment of an equitable income-tax for payment of the public debts. The tax was half per cent. on incomes, as a forced loan to the Government at five per cent. ;. or a third part of the tax might be paid, with abandonment of right to interest and repayment. Money was worth much more than five per cent. to the traders of Florence ; but the deductions allowed before charging for this income-tax secured to every one untaxed his house, his horse, and two hundred florins a year for each mouth in his household. Thus there was a protection against general discontent, and licence for irregular taxation. The half per cent., or decima, was soon taken as the mere unit of calculation, and forced loans of this or that number of decimas, for this or that new exigence of the State, might afterwards be raised at the discretion of the ruler. Such loans were raised now and then as often as twelve times a year, to feed the magnificence of one man at the expense of commerce which had given freedom and strength to the city, and which had sent up that strong shoot of artistic life whereof the later Medici consumed the fruit.

In 1429 Giovanni died, "enormously rich in treasure, but richer still in good repute," lord only of his counting-house. He had steadily rejected the advice of his son Cosmo that he should take advantage of his position in the city by placing himself at the head of the popular party against the weaker faction of the aristocracy, and so rise to political power.

When Cosmo became chief of his house he became chief also of the popular party, which he made a faction. It was faction against faction, chief against chief, and some began to ask themselves to which of the chiefs Florence would have to yield her independence. Cosmo's antagonists achieved his banishment, and thereby added to his strength. Venice welcomed him, Florence missed him. Friends and poor citizens suffered for want of access to the purse by which he made himself beloved. A signory favourable to the Medici was voted into office ; the aristocratic faction failed in an attempt at armed resistance ; and Cosmo was recalled, to enter Florence in great triumph as the father of his country. His first care was for the exile, fine, imprisonment, or death of the stronger men of the opposite side. Having weeded out enemies, or suspected enemies, he and his comrades strengthened new men into serviceable

friends, divided the goods of the outlawed, made new and convenient laws, suppressed elections of unfriendly magistrates, and
took means, by bribing and by tampering with the purses from
which names of magistrates were drawn, to confine to men of
their own faction all offices in which power of life and death
was vested. Power of life and death was given to the eight ;
chance of return was almost wholly cut off from the exiles. Thus
the faction led by Cosmo was supreme. It has been said that
to a remonstrance on the ruin caused to the city by so many
deaths and fines and banishments of worthy citizens, Cosmo
replied that a city ruined was better than a city lost, and that
it cost only a few yards of red cloth to make more citizens
worshipful. Twenty families, says one old historian, were
banished by the Medici for every one that suffered with them.
The exiled leader of the aristocratic faction invited the arms of
the tyrant of Milan to an attack on Florence ; and the city again
fought manfully against foreign despotism while her liberties
were sickening at home.

Then came the time when the fall of Constantinople was
impending. Greek Christians, who sought aid from the nations
of the West, made politic effort to heal the division upon
points of ceremonial between the Eastern and the Western
Churches. The Council of Basle, transferred to Ferrara, and
again to Florence, brought together in Florence, in the year
1439, the Pope Eugenius IV. and the Patriarch Joseph of Constantinople, with many Greek bishops and scholars, and also
the unfortunate Greek Emperor, John Palæologus. Talk of
Plato thus first became familiar to the chiefs of Florentine
society. The Eastern Church assented in five articles to
Western opinion, and united itself to the Church of Rome. But
as this act of union did not secure the desired end of saving
Constantinople from the Turk, after the fall of the Eastern
capital the two Churches fell back into their old state of schism.
More came of the intellectual appetite of the rich merchants
and bankers of Florence for commerce with men who had something new to traffic in—Greek manuscripts worth reading, and
the skill to read them.

25. The Byzantine Empire had in 1425, by a treaty of the
Emperor John Palæologus II., been reduced to Constantinople
and its environs, with some outlying places. These were held
subject to a yearly tribute, which transferred the larger part of
their revenues to the Turk. The treaty was observed by

Sultan Amurath II.  But his son Mohammed II., in the third year of his reign, began, at the age of about three-and-twenty, his career of conquest by overthrowing all that remained of the Roman Empire in the East.  After fifty-eight days' siege, he took Constantinople by storm, on the 29th of May, in the year 1453.  Five years later he made himself master of the Morea.  Occupation of Greece by the Turks drove the Greek patriots and scholars into exile.  They sought a livelihood in foreign capitals by teaching their old language, and diffusing knowledge of the treasures of its literature.  Thus Greek became a part of European scholarship, and Plato lived again, to join the ranks of the reformers.

It was of a Spartan in Paris, who supported himself also by skill with his pen as a copyist, that John Reuchlin had learnt, before he sought more at Florence from Argyropoulos its first famous teacher there, Greek enough to surprise the patriot with speech in his own tongue from a German, and cause him to say, "Alas, Greece is already banished beyond the Alps." Argyropoulos, fugitive to Florence after the capture of Constantinople, had been welcomed by Cosmo de' Medici, appointed tutor to his sons Lorenzo and Pietro, and established as a professor of Greek, with pupils, among whom was Politian.  Among other Greeks who came to Florence was the venerable George Gemisthus Pletho, whose long life had been spent in enthusiastic study of Plato, and who lectured upon him to the Italians, maintaining his philosophy as partisan of Plato against Aristotle.  Cosmo de' Medici, his constant hearer, received his opinions.  While he was steadily pursuing his design to become sovereign in Florence, the head of the great banking-house which spread its branches over Europe set a fashion for the collecting of Greek manuscripts, proceeded towards the establishment of a Platonic academy in Florence, and educated young Marsilio Ficino specially in Platonism, that he might become its head.

John Argyropoulos worked at Aristotle; but the new teachers were generally Platonists, reading their Plato with the glosses of the mystical school of Neoplatonists, whose philosophy had been in the third, fourth, and fifth centuries at war with Christianity; but in this fifteenth century became indirectly an aid in the reformation of the Christian Church.  To the corrupt society of Italy Platonism gave some grace of heathendom and many affectations.  To men of the Teutonic or English race, and others who

H

went to Florence to learn Greek, the new study gave something more. Earnest minds that were battling with the strong animal nature of the Church passed, through the new study, to works of a heathen philosopher who saw a divine soul in the world towards which by heavenward aspiration souls of men could rise. " But if the company will be persuaded by me," wrote Plato, in the tenth book of the Republic, " considering the soul to be immortal and able to bear all evil and good, we shall always persevere in the road which leads upwards, and shall by all means follow justice with prudence; that so we may be friends to ourselves and to the gods, both while we remain here, and when we afterwards receive its rewards, like victors assembled together; and so both here and in that journey of a thousand years we shall be happy." The Neoplatonists had grafted extreme doctrines of purification and subjection of man's animal nature upon the teaching in Plato's " Phædo," that a soul given to fleshly pleasures takes taint of the flesh. They were connected by their faith with the divine essence, and upon many of the best minds of Europe the new study of Greek through such reading of Plato came as a new impulse to conflict with the sensuality which had become the scandal of the Church of Rome. Plato was thus associated among such men with the cause of progress; while Aristotle, of whose teaching the knowledge had been long since diffused by the Arabians through translation, supplied forms for conventional thought, and, eager pioneer as he had been, was made the idol of the schoolmen who stood on the ancient ways. The fall of Constantinople made Plato a power in Europe. So it was that those of the clergy who shrank from the quickened tendency among good scholars to attack their flesh-pots, gave currency to the proverb, " Beware of the Greeks, lest you be made a heretic."

26. It was at this time that the future influence of every wise thought was enlarged by the Invention of Printing. In the year of the battle of St. Albans, 1455, the Bible called the Mazarin Bible, because it was first found in the library of Cardinal Mazarin, was printed at Mayence by John Gutenberg. In the year of the condemnation of Reginald Pecock for declaring that all truth would bear the test of reason and inquiry, John Fust, or Faust, and Peter Schœffer printed a magnificent edition of the Psalter.

Stamping with ink from blocks on which letters had been carved in relief had already been tried when, in 1438, John

Gutenberg, of Mayence, first thought of the use of movable types to save the great labour of cutting a fresh block for every page. He had gone from Mayence to Strasburg as a block printer, become impoverished by a lawsuit, returned to Mayence, and worked at his press in partnership with a wealthy goldsmith, named John Faust, or Fust. After many experiments, so much success was obtained that, as before said, the printing of the Mazarin Bible was completed with movable type in 1455. The partnership was dissolved, and Gutenberg, unable to repay advances of money, made over his types to Faust, who at first printed copies of the Bible to imitate those sold as MSS., and gave for sixty crowns what copyists required five hundred for producing. Then he took into partnership his son-in-law, Peter Schœffer; and in the colophon to the Psalter produced by them in 1457, Faust and Schœffer boasted openly the power of their new art. In 1462 Mayence, which had been for some years a free imperial city, was taken and sacked by its archbishop, Adolphus. This event, by scattering the pupils and workmen of Faust and Schœffer, dispersed through Europe the knowledge of their art. It was carried from Mayence to Haarlem and Strasburg; from Haarlem to Rome, in 1466, by Sweynheym and Pannartz, the first users of Roman type. It reached Paris in 1469; Cologne in 1470; and England, through William Caxton, about 1475. There was no printer in Scotland until after the close of the fifteenth century.

27. **William Caxton,** born about 1422, in the Weald of Kent, was apprenticed to a wealthy London mercer. After his master's death, in 1441, he lived chiefly in Brabant, Flanders, Holland, and Zealand, for thirty years and more. In 1464 he was employed by Edward IV. as one of two commissioners for the settlement of a treaty of commerce with Philip the Good, Duke of Burgundy. That Philip was succeeded, in 1467, by his eldest son Charles, called the Bold, who in the following year, 1468, married Edward IV.'s sister Margaret. Caxton was then in Margaret's service, and received from her a yearly fee. On the 1st of March, 1469, he began a translation from Raoul le Fevre, of the *Recuyell of the Historyes of Troye*, a work suspended by him for two years, and then finished at Margaret's command. In October, 1470, when Warwick, the Kingmaker, was moving Henry VI. up from the Tower to the Palace of Westminster, Edward IV., paying his fur gown for his passage, came as a fugitive to Bruges, with seven or eight hundred hungry

followers.  He was at Bruges five months, and then returned to
become king again.  Among the companions of Edward in this
brief exile to the city in which Caxton served the king's sister, was
his brother-in-law, **Anthony Woodville, Lord Rivers**, translator, from the French, of a book of *Dictes and Sayings of the
Philosophers.*  He submitted his translation to Caxton's criticism.  Having achieved his own version of the *Recuyell of the
Historyes of Troye*—a work afterwards occupying 778 folio pages
of print—Caxton says that he "practised and learnt at great
charge and expense" the art of printing, to enable him to strike
off in one day many copies.  He seems to have learnt the art at
Cologne, of Conrad Winters, who had set up his press there in
1470.  Caxton's translation of the "Histories of Troy" was,
he says, finished at Cologne, September 19, 1471; and then he
began to print.

The first book printed by him was his translation, also from
the French, of a moral treatise, *The Game and Playe of the
Chesse.*  Of this there are two editions, the first said to have
been finished on the last day of March, 1474.  It is assumed to
be the first book printed in this country.  Perhaps it was; but
there is no evidence that Caxton did not print it at Cologne.
It is to the printed copy of the translation of "Les Dictes
Moraux des Philosophes," as *The Dictes and Sayings of Philosophers,* by Anthony Woodville, Earl Rivers, that Caxton first
added, "imprynted by me, William Caxton, at Westmynstre;"
and the date of it is 1477.  A book of 1480 specifies the Abbey
as the place where Caxton had his press.  Resort to the Abbey
scriptorium for copies of books had led to a settlement of
copyists within the Abbey precincts.  Among the "Paston
Letters" is a book bill, dated 1468, from a copyist named W.
Ebesham, who said that he was living at some expense in
the Sanctuary, Westminster.  The new-born giant was in its
mother's lap when Caxton, who had learnt the new art as a
business speculation, worked his press at Westminster Abbey
among the professional transcribers whom he found there busy
with their pens.

28.  In those days Lorenzo de' Medici ruled Florence.
Michael Angelo and Ariosto were both born in one year; and
the year, 1474, was that in which Caxton completed the printing
of his "Game and Play of Chess."  Italian fine gentlemen had
begun to affect far-fetched conceits and ingenuities of speech.
Lorenzo himself, who set forth Platonism in his *Altercazione,*

was writing love sonnets and canzone in a style that would tell how the rays of love from the eyes of his lady penetrated through his eyes the shadow of his heart, like a ray of sun entering the dark beehive by its fissure; and how then, as the hive wakes, the bees fly, full of new cares, hither and thither in the forest, sip at flowers, fly out, return laden with odorous spoil, sting those who are seen idle, so the spirits stir in his heart, fly out to seek the light, &c. &c. But in these days Florence had other poets. Then it was that Luigi Pulci, born in 1432, cleverest of three verse-writing brothers, wrote in the fashionable strain of the flowing of the river Lora in the Apennines into the Severus, in his poem of "The Dryad of Love." The nymph Lora was loved by the satyr Severus. Diana changed him to a stag, then hunted him, and changed him into a river; but the loving nymph, changed also into a stream, ran to her union with him. Luigi Pulci wrote also in a far different vein. Spanish romance was influenced by Vasco de Lobeira, a Portuguese of Chaucer's time, who had been knighted on the battle-field by the King John to whom John of Gaunt married his daughter Philippa. Lobeira, who may have met Chaucer on the occasion of that marriage (ch. iv. § 39), died in 1403, and had written towards the close of the fourteenth century his "Amadis of Gaul," a long prose romance of original invention, which, about 1503, was turned into Spanish, and established in Spain a new form of knightly prose romance. "Amadis" itself had and deserved more popularity than most of its successors. But an earlier impulse from Spain quickened development in Italy of chivalrous romance, and caused Luigi Pulci to produce, in octave rhyme, a prelude of Italian Charlemagne poetry in the irreligious and half-mocking "Morgante Maggiore," of which the first canto has been translated into English by Lord Byron. Then it was also that in Florence the pastoral strain, of which Boccaccio, in his "Admetus," sounded the first note, was taken up by Agnolo of Monte Pulciano. Agnolo, called Politianus— Poliziano—was a marvellous young man of twenty when Caxton finished the printing of his "Game and Play of Chess." He was born in 1454, and had been educated at the expense of Cosmo de' Medici. He studied Greek under Andronicus of Thessalonica, Plato under Marsilius Ficinus, Aristotle under Argyropoulos; he became professor of Latin and Greek at Florence, and was sought as a teacher even by the pupils of Chalcondylas, for he was poet as well as scholar, and could put true life into his teaching. He was but forty when he died, and among his poems he has left us the pastoral tale of Orpheus, his " Orfeo," in *terza rima*, the first pastoral in modern literature with a story in it. Niccolo da Correggio called his "Cefalo," in octave rhyme, recited at Ferrara in 1486, also a story—" Favola "—and in the following years others appeared as rustic comedies, eclogues, or pastoral eclogues. When long, they were divided into acts. And here we are at the source of the taste for pastoral poetry which we shall find after some years coming by way of France to England.

29. These were the days also of Christopher Columbus, born in Italy in 1445. He went to sea about the time when, in 1462, the printers of Mayence were first scattered; and was voyaging northward beyond Iceland, and southward to the coast of Guinea, while the printer's press was being first set up in sundry capitals of Europe.

The short reign of Edward V., in 1483, from April 9 to June 25, and the reign of Richard III. (1483—1485), yielded no work of any mark to English literature. But in 1483 Luther and Raffaelle were born.

During the early part of the reign of Henry VII. (1485—1509) the New World was discovered. Sebastian Cabot, born at Bristol, the son of a Venetian pilot, was but twenty years old when, on a voyage with his father and two brothers in the service of Henry VII., for the discovery and occupation of new lands, he first saw the mainland of America, in 1497. Columbus, in the service of Ferdinand and Isabella of Spain, had found for Spain in 1492 the West India Islands. On his third voyage in search of new lands and their wealth, in 1498, he saw the mainland of America, which had been seen by the Cabots in 1497, and which was named after Amerigo Vespucci, a Florentine, who did not visit it till 1499. "Spain, that used to be called poor, is now the most wealthy of kingdoms," Columbus wrote ; but in his old age he had for one ornament of his home the chains in which he had been sent home from Hispaniola by men weary of one who vexed them with restraints of honesty. "For seven years," he wrote to Ferdinand and Isabella, "was I at your royal court, where every one to whom the enterprise was mentioned treated it as ridiculous ; but now there is not a man, down to the very tailors, who does not beg to be allowed to become a discoverer. There is reason to believe that they make the voyage only for plunder, and that they are permitted

to do so, to the great disparagement of my honour, and the
detriment of the undertaking itself.  It is right to give God his
due, and to receive that which belongs to one's self. . . . I
was twenty-eight years old when I came into your highnesses'
service, and now I have not a hair upon me that is not grey; my
body is infirm, and all that was left to me, as well as to my
brothers, has been taken away and sold, even to the frock that
I wore, to my great dishonour." So Columbus wrote from the
Indies, in July, 1503, when absent on his fourth and last voyage
to the New World, the voyage following that from which he
had returned in chains.  With a pure heart and noble mind
he had served the greed of men ; and to his death, in 1506, he
still found Mammon an ungrateful master.

30. The influence of the capture of Constantinople, in 1453,
upon the development of scholarship in Europe was evident in
England during the last years of the fifteenth century.  The
study of Greek was introduced among us first at Oxford, by
William Grocyn and Thomas Linacre.

William Grocyn, eldest of a group of English classical
scholars, was born at Bristol in 1442, educated at Winchester
School, and thence passed to New College.  The relation between Winchester and New College remains as of old, for it
was in connection with New College that the school had been
founded, in 1387, by Bishop William Long—William of Wyke-
ham.  William Grocyn became, in 1479, rector of Newton Long-
ville, in Buckinghamshire, and afterwards prebendary of Lincoln.
He went to Italy, learnt Greek from Demetrius Chalcondylas
and Politian (§ 28), and in 1491 settled at Exeter College,
Oxford, as the first teacher of Greek.  In 1490 he had exchanged
his living for the Mastership of All Hallow's College at Maid-
stone, where he died in 1522.  Grocyn differed from the common
fashion as a Greek scholar in giving most of his time to the
study not of Plato but of Aristotle, whom he began to translate.
He left his papers and part of his property to Linacre, his
executor, and William Lily.

Thomas Linacre, born at Canterbury, and about eighteen
years younger than Grocyn, was educated at Canterbury and at
Oxford, became fellow of All Souls in 1484, and early in the
reign of Henry VII. was sent on a mission to the Court of
Rome.  He stayed by the way at Florence, and, like Grocyn,
studied Greek under Demetrius Chalcondylas.  After his return
he became M.D. of Oxford, read lectures on physic, and taught

Greek and.Latin.   He was physician and tutor to Henry VII.'s
son, Prince Arthur.

In the year 1500, Grocyn was fifty-eight years old, Linacre
about forty.   John Fisher, who became in 1504 Bishop of
Rochester, was forty-one years old in the year 1500, John
Colet was thirty-four, William Lily was over thirty, and Thomas
More was a young man of twenty.   These men were to be
chief promoters of English scholarship at the beginning of the
sixteenth century.   Scholarship abroad had its best representative in Erasmus, who had come to England in 1497, when he
was thirty years old.   During 1496 he had been supporting
himself in Paris by private teaching.   His fame was in the
future; and the fame of Oxford, as one of the few places
in which Greek could then be learnt, had drawn him to the
place.   There he not only learnt Greek, but he also found
Greek scholars who welcomed him to an enduring friendship.

31. In the year 1500 Michael Angelo was twenty-six years
old, and Ariosto twenty-six; Raffaelle was seventeen, and
Luther seventeen.

Lorenzo de' Medici had died in 1492.   During the latter
years of his rule, Matteo Maria Boiardo, Count of Scandiano
and Governor of Reggio, wrote that poem of "Orlando Innamorato" (Orlando Enamoured) which is of most interest for its
relation to the later work of Ariosto.   Boiardo died, sixty years
old, in 1494, leaving his poem unfinished in his own opinion,
and by several cantos more than finished in the opinion of
others.   This poem dealt more seriously, if less cleverly, than
Pulci's "Morgante" with the Charlemagne romance.   Boiardo
set up Charlemagne's nephew Roland, or Orlando, as true
knight enamoured of a fascinating Angelica, who had been
brought from the far East to sow dissension among the Christians
with whom infidel hosts were contending.   Boiardo was succeeded in his command of the fortress of Reggio by Ariosto the
father, and in his conduct of the story of Orlando by Ariosto
the son, who took up the tale where Boiardo ought to have
dropped it, not where he actually did leave off.

32. During those earlier years of the reign of Henry VII.,
when in Florence Boiardo was giving a new point of departure
to the metrical romance of chivalry, the poetical literature of
this country was most vigorous in the north.   Good poets were
then living, who gave the best evidence of their power in the
first years of the sixteenth century.   John Skelton was about

forty, William Dunbar about forty, and Gavin Douglas about twenty-six years old, in the year 1500. Skelton, in England, and Dunbar, in Scotland, had begun to write before the close of the fifteenth century; but our only poet of mark who then closed his career was **Robert Henryson**, schoolmaster of Dunfermline. He lived to be old, and was among those named as dead in Dunbar's "Lament for the Makers," printed in 1508. The number of Scottish singers named in that piece by Dunbar bears witness to the diffused activity of thought in Scotland at the time when Robert Henryson "compiled into eloquent and ornamental metre" *The Morall Fables of Esope the Phrygian.* There are thirteen fables here versified, including one that has once or twice since taken a place of note in literature, the fable of the "Town and Country Mouse," or, as Henryson had it, the "Taill of the uponlandis Mous and the burges Mous." Another fable of "The Dog, the Wolf, and the Sheep" is treated as an exposure of the abuses in procedure of the ecclesiastical courts. Henryson wrote a prologue to the collection, and another to the fable of "The Lion and the Mouse," which represents himself wandering into a wood on a June morning, sleeping under a hawthorn, and visited in dream by "Maister Esope, poet laureate," who says that he is of gentle blood, and that his "natal land is Rome withouttin nay." Nay, the schoolmaster was asleep when he made Æsop a Roman poet; and asleep after the fashion of many English and other poets since the days of the "Romaunt of the Rose." He used also Chaucer's seven-lined stanza here and in his *Testament of Cresseid;* for this measure had become current among our poets as the English represen tative of octave rhyme. Henryson's "Testament of Cresseid" is a moral sequel to Chaucer's "Troilus and Cressida." Abandoned by Diomede, and become a leper among lepers, she saw Troilus pass on his way back from a brilliant attack upon the Greeks. As she looked at him, although he did not recognise her through her leprosy, yet her presence filled his mind with thought of the fair Cresseid, and in memory of her he threw a rich purse to the leper. Cresseid learnt, after he had passed, that this kind-hearted knight was Troilus; and then, lamenting her inconstancy, she uttered her last Testament and died. Henryson is the author also of our first pastoral poem, *Robene and Makyne,* a work that has much natural and simple beauty, and is not, like most of his writings, too diffuse. *The Bludy Serk* is a good example of the religious earnestness that under-

H •

lies his work, and of the continuance of the old taste for allegory. A prince saved a princess from a dungeon into which she had been cast by a giant, and shut the giant up in his own prison-house. He restored the princess to her father, and then died of a wound received in the conflict, bequeathing to the lady the shirt stained with the blood shed for her, which she was to look at when approached by a new lover. The lady, it is explained, is the Soul of Man, God's daughter, and His handiwork; the giant, Lucifer; the champion, Christ. And, therefore—

> " For His lufe that bocht us deir,
> Think on the bludy serk."

The next men of whom we have to speak represent part of the larger life and energy of England under the Tudors.

33. Owen Tudor, a private Welsh gentleman in the service of Henry V.'s widow, Catherine of Valois, became her second husband. Tudor in Welsh (Tueddwr) means one who inclines, or has a bias. Owen was imprisoned in Newgate and Walling-ford Castle for his inclination towards a royal widow; but Catherine abided by her second husband, and gave him three sons—Edmund, whom Henry VI. made Earl of Richmond; Jasper, Earl of Pembroke; and one who became a monk. Edmund Tudor, Earl of Richmond, married (when she was but ten years old) Margaret, daughter and heiress of John, Duke of Somerset, whose father, John, Earl of Somerset, had been one of the children of John of Gaunt and Chaucer's sister-in-law, Catherine Swinford (ch. iv. § 22). Edmund Tudor died at the age of twenty-five, leaving his wife Margaret, Dowager Countess of Richmond, a young widow with one son, Henry. This was the Henry Tudor, Earl of Richmond, who became chief of the Lan-castrian party, and king after the battle of Bosworth Field, in August, 1485, as Henry VII., then twenty-eight years old. In the following year King Henry married, as policy dictated, Elizabeth of York, eldest daughter of Edward IV.; but was a hard hus-band to her, incapable of love to any of the house of York. In the year 1500, when his own age was forty-three, Henry VII. and his wife had four children living, of six who had been born. Arthur, Prince of Wales, his eldest son, was then fourteen years old; Margaret, his eldest daughter, was eleven; Henry, his second son, nine; Mary, his second daughter, two years old.

The Stuart family retained the throne of Scotland. In that part of our country, during the whole fifteenth century, kings were rebuked freely by the people. But while they suffered insult, and even death, at the hands of turbulent men whom they were unable to control, there was unswerving fidelity to the principle of monarchy, and even to the luckless house of Stuart. Its rule begÀn in 1370, when Robert, the High Steward, so named from his court office, succeeded his cousin David as Robert II. His eldest son succeeded him in 1390. During the troubled reign of that Stuart the second, his son James became prisoner at the English court ; but though a prisoner abroad, he was proclaimed king as James I. of Scotland, Stuart the third, in 1406. He earned fame as a poet, and sought, as a prince, to subject his rough lords to more law than they liked, and he was murdered (§ 6, 14). He was loved by the people, who avenged his death upon his murderers. His eldest son was but six years old at the time of the murder ; but none disputed the throne with him, though rival chiefs were ready enough to seize him, and through him play king. That child, as James II., Stuart the fourth, lived to be thirty, when he was accidentally killed by a wedge blown out of the ring of a gun at the siege of Roxburgh. The son he left for successor was again a child but eight years old, yet his right of succession was respected, and in 1460 he became King James III., Stuart the fifth. He was abundantly afflicted by high-handed lords ; his subjects did not relish his inclination towards artists and musicians, and thought him a coward. Finally, it was believed that he was ready to oppose his troublers by the inbringing of Englishmen, and the perpetual subjection of the realm. He was accused by the Estates ; risen against by barons, with his own son at their head. His friends were routed in a skirmish at the Sauchie Burn, and he was treacherously stabbed during his flight by an unknown assassin. The son, who, being only sixteen years old, joined the confederates against his father, became in the same year, 1488, King James IV., Stuart the sixth. He had been king, then, for about twelve years in 1500.

34. **John Skelton** is the English poet of chief mark whose name is associated with the reign of Henry VII. He was born either in Cumberland or Norfolk, and not before the year 1460 ; educated at Cambridge, where he appears to have taken his degree of M.A. in 1484, and to have written a poem *On the Death of King Edward IV.* Like one of the old metrical tragedies of men fallen from high estate, it tells—the dead king speaking—how the days of power, of wealth wrung from the commonalty, of

costly works under a rule pleasing to some, to others displeasing, are at an end :

> " Mercy I ask of my misdoing ;
> What availeth it, friends, to be my foe,
> Sith I cannot resist nor amend your complaining ?
> *Quid, ecce, nunc in pulvere dormio* "

The last line, suggesting royal pomp asleep in dust, is the refrain to every stanza. In 1489 Skelton wrote, in Chaucer's stanza, an *Elegy upon the Death of the Earl of Northumberland,* who was killed by an insurgent populace in Yorkshire. In the following year, 1490, Caxton spoke of John Skelton, in the preface to his version from the French of a prose romance founded upon the "Æneid," as " Mayster John Skelton, late created poete laureate" in the University of Oxford. Caxton prayed that Skelton, who had translated Cicero's Letters and Diodorus Siculus and divers other works from Latin into English, would correct any mistakes he found. Of Skelton's translations, and of Skelton himself— then about thirty years old--Caxton wrote in the same preface to " The Boke of Eneydos, compyled by Vyrgyle, " that he had translated from the Latin, " not in rude and olde langage, but in polysshed and ornate termes craftely, as he that hath redde Vyrgyle, Ovyde, Tullye, and all the other noble poets and oratours, to me unknowen. And also he hath redde the nine muses, and understande theyr musicalle scyences, and to whom of theym eche scyence is appropred. I suppose he hath dronken of Elycon's well."

The degree of poet laureate was then a recognised degree in grammar and rhetoric with versification. A wreath of laurel was presented to each new " poeta laureatus ;" and if this graduated grammarian obtained also a licence to teach boys, he was publicly presented in the Convocation House with a rod and ferule. If he served a king, he might call himself the king's humble poet laureate ; as John Kay, of whom no verse remains, was, as far as we know, first to do, in calling himself poet laureate to Edward IV. Before obtaining this degree the candidate would be required to write a hundred Latin verses on the glory of the University, or some other accepted subject.

John Skelton, poet laureate of Oxford in 1493, and also of Louvain, was admitted to the same title at Cambridge eleven years later. He had written a poem, now lost, on the creation of Prince Arthur, Henry VII.'s eldest son, as Prince of Wales, in 1489 ; and he wrote Latin verses, also lost, on the creation of the infant Prince Henry (afterwards King Henry VIII.) as Duke

of York, in 1494.   Skelton was in favour with Henry VII., and
also with that king's mother, Margaret Countess of Richmond,
and of Derby by her second marriage.   The Lady Margaret is
remembered as a patroness of learning.   In 1498 Skelton took
holy orders, and at this time he was tutor to Prince Henry;
Bernard André, another poet laureate, being tutor to Prince
Arthur.   As John Skelton himself afterwards wrote:

> " The honor of Englond I lernyd to spelle
>   In dygnite roialle that doth excelle :
>           *       *       *       *       *
>     It plesyth that noble prince royálle
>     Me as hys master for to calle
>     In his lernyng primordialle."

He produced for his pupil a treatise, now lost, called the
*Speculum Principis,* the Mirror of a Prince.   At the end of
the century, when Prince Henry was nine years old, Erasmus,
in dedicating to the boy a Latin ode in " Praise of Britain, King
Henry VII., and the royal child:en," congratulated him on
being housed with Skelton, a special light and ornament of
British literature (" unum Britannicarum literarum lumen et
decus "), who could not only kindle his desire for study, but
secure its consummation.   In the ode itself Erasmus again
spoke of Skelton as Prince Henry's guide to the sacred sources
of learning.

35. **John Fisher,** a native of Yorkshire, a learned and
religious man, born at Beverley in 1459, was, at the end of
the fifteenth century, confessor to Margaret Countess of Richmond, and earnestly abetted her good disposition towards those
engaged in the pursuit of knowledge.

36. In Scotland **William Dunbar** received in the year 1500
a pension of £10 Scots from James IV.   Dunbar was born in
Lothian about the year 1460.   He studied at St. Andrew's, where
he was one of the " determinantes," or Bachelors of Arts, at St.
Salvator's College, in 1477, and took his degree in arts in 1479.
He was a small man, jested at in playful controversy as a dwarf.
For a time he was a Franciscan or Grey Friar, and preached in
Engla.d and in Picardy.   In 1491 he was one of an embassy to
France, a lettered priest acting as secretary under the Earl of
Bothwell.   After this he was abroad for some years in the King
of Scotland's service, and he probably had written, with other
verse, his poem of the *Golden Terge* (first printed in 1508), when
in 1500 he received his small pension of £10 Scots.

Thus Dunbar and Skelton were two men of ripened power, ready to take rank as our chief poets of the North and South at the beginning of the sixteenth century.

37. To the close of the fifteenth century belong also the earliest remaining traces of old English Ballad Literature. Wynken de Worde, born in Lorraine, came to England with Caxton ; and after Caxton's death, in or about the year 1491, succeeded him in his printing-office, and styled himself printer to Margaret Countess of Richmond. He settled afterwards in Fleet Street, and lived until 1534. One of Wynken de Worde's earliest publications was a collection of *Robin Hood Ballads* into a continuous set called *A Lytel Geste of Robyn Hode.* In "The Vision of Piers Plowman," Robin Hood is named as one who was already, in the second half of the fourteenth century, a hero of popular song, Sloth there says :

> " I kan noght parfitly my Paternoster,
> As the priest it syngeth ;
> But I kan rymes of Robyn Hood,
> And Randolph, Erl of Chestre."

We learn also from the " Paston Letters " that in Edward IV.'s time Robin Hood was a hero of one of the popular mummeries. So he remained. A sermon of Latimer's shows with much emphasis the popularity of country sports on a Robin Hood's Day in the time of Edward VI. There are manuscripts also of the ballads of *Robin Hood and the Potter* and *Robin Hood and the Monk*, not older than the last years of the fifteenth century.

The tradition is that Robin Hood was a name corrupted from that of Robert Fitzooth, reputed Earl of Huntingdon, who was born about the year 1160, in the reign of Henry II. After Robin had, in the wildness of youth, consumed his inheritance, he was outlawed for debt, lived in the woods on the king's game, and by his open defiance became an impersonation of the popular feeling against forest laws, which, under the Norman kings, were cruelly iniquitous. Among the woods of England Robin Hood is said to have chiefly frequented Sherwood in Nottinghamshire, Barnsdale in Yorkshire, and Plompton Park in Cumberland. His most trusty friends were, it is said, John Nailor, known as Little John ; William Scadlock, called also Scathelock and Scarlet ; George à Green Pinder (that is, pound-keeper), of Wakefield ; and Much, a miller's son. But he gathered also, tradition says, a stout company of a hundred archers, equal to any four hundred who could be brought against them. The ballads and tales that made Robin Hood representative of English popular feeling not only gave him courage and good-humour, and connected his name with the maintenance of archery for national defence, but also gave him Friar Tuck for chaplain, and blended in him religious feeling with resistance to oppression:

> " A good maner then had Robyn
> In londe where that he were,
> Every daye ere he wolde dine
> Three masses wolde he hear."

His religion took especially the form, once dear to the people, of that worship of the Virgin which softened the harsh temper of mediæval doctrine:

> " Robyn loved our dere lady ;
> For doute of dedely synne,
> Wolde he never do company harme
> That ony woman was ynne."

Maid Marian being added to his company, fidelity to her would express English domestic feeling ; while the same battle against corrupt luxury in the Church which had been represented for the educated courtier by Walter Map's Golias poetry (ch. iii. § 13), was rudely expressed to the people in Robin Hood's injunction to his men:

> " These byshoppes and these archebyshoppes,
> Ye shall them bete and bynde."

Robin Hood pitied the poor, and gave them part in the wealth stripped from those who lived in sensual excess. The chief representative of rich ecclesiastics in the Robin Hood ballads was the Abbot of St. Mary's at York ; and the oppressions of secular authority were especially defied in the person of the Sheriff of Nottingham. Robin Hood is said to have escaped all perils of his way of life, and to have been more than eighty years old when he went to his aunt, the prioress of Kirklees Nunnery, in Yorkshire, to be bled. She treacherously let him bleed to death. As he was thus dying, Robin bethought him of his bugle-horn, and " blew out weak blasts three." Little John came to his rescue, and asked leave to burn the nunnery, but Robin said:

> " I never hurt fair maid in all my time,
> Nor at my end shall it be."

He asked only to shoot an arrow from the window, that he might be buried where the arrow fell ; and so, says tradition, he was buried on a height that overlooks the valley of the Calder, at the distance of a mighty bow-shot from Kirklees.

To the end of the fifteenth century belongs the charming dialogue-ballad of *The Nut Brown Maid.*  She was a baron's daughter, and her love had been won by a suitor who came as "a squyer of lowe degree."  Her faith was tried by her lover's feigning himself one who must die or fly as an outlaw to live by his bow like, Robin Hood.  As he urged the difficulties and dangers that must part them, in stanzas ending with the refrain, "For I must to the greenwood go, alone, a banished man," the Nut Brown Maid met every argument with faithful resolve to bear all and follow him, the stanzas in which she answered closing steadily with the refrain, "For in my mind, of all mankind, I love but you alone."  When she had borne the trial of her faith, she learnt that "the squire of low degree" was neither squire nor banished man, but an earl's son, come to marry her and take her to Westmoreland, which was his heritage.  The ballad ended with a moral like that attached by Petrarch and Chaucer to Boccaccio's tale of the "Patient Griselda" (ch. iv. § 46):

> "For sith men wolde that wymen sholde be meke to them eche on,
> Much more ought they to God obey, and serve but hym alone."

The ballads of *The Battle of Otterburn* and *Chevy Chase* do not remain to us in their first form.  There is no copy of them written so early as the fifteenth century, to which doubtless they belong.  The battle of Otterburn was fought on the 19th of August, 1388, between Scots under James Earl of Douglas, and English under the two sons of the Duke of Northumberland.  It began with a sudden entering of England by the Earl of Douglas with 3,800 men, who advanced to Brancepeth, ravaging the country they passed through.  In the warfare against English settlements in France, such a raid was called by the French allies of Scotland a *chevauchée*, and, by a common process, that name was corrupted into Chevy Chase.  It lives yet among schoolboys as a "chivy."  Now, since there are in Northumberland Cheviot Hills as well as an Otterburn, Chevy Chase was interpreted into the Hunting of the Cheviot.  The old ballad of the "Battle of Otterburn," or "Chevy Chase"—the battle of the *chevauchée* which was its crowning incident—was therefore recast as *The Hunting of the Cheviot*, always with some confused sense of identity between one incident and the other.  The battle of Otterburn is an incident minutely described

by Froissart; but there is no record whatever of any similar
battle that arose out of a Hunting on the Cheviots.   The author
of the ballad of the " Hunting" was, in fact, quite right when he
said :

> " This was the Hontynge of the Cheviot ;
>   That tear began this spurn :
>   Old men that knowen the grownde well yenough
>   Call it the Battell of Otterburn."

The ballad literature to which these poems belong came into
strong life in Europe during the thirteenth, and especially the
fourteenth and fifteenth centuries.   In the thirteenth century
Spain uttered through national ballads the soul of freedom in
her struggle against the Moors.   Our English ballads are akin
to those which also among the Scandinavians became a
familiar social amusement of the people.   They were recited by
one of a company with animation and with varying expression,
while the rest kept time, often with joined hands forming a
circle, advancing, retiring, balancing, sometimes remaining still,
and, by various movements and gestures, followed changes of
emotion in the story.   Not only in Spain did the people keep
time by dance movement to the measure of the ballad, for even
to this day one may see, in the Faroe Islands, how winter
evenings of the North were cheered with ballad recitations,
during which, according to the old northern fashion, gestures
and movements of the listeners expressed emotions of the story
as the people danced to their old ballads and songs.   From this
manner of enjoying them the ballads took their name.   *Ballare*
is a Middle Latin word, meaning to incline to this side and that,
with which the Italians associate their name for dancing, and we
the word " ball " for the name of a dancing party.   The *balade*
of Southern Europe (ch. iv. § 25), a wholly different production,
which is not in the least remarkable for life and energy, took
its name from the same word for another reason.   It inclines to
this side and that, in see-saw with a single pair of rhymes.
There is some reason to think that educated gentlewomen were
often the unknown writers of the ballads of England and the
North of Europe.

# CHAPTER VI.

## FROM THE YEAR 1500 TO THE YEAR 1558.

1. OF the reign of Henry VII. (1485—1509), the last nine years have now to be accounted for. They were a time of rest from the feud between the English crown and Scottish people. Perkin Warbeck was, in 1495, a visitor at the court of James IV. of Scotland, and he was there married to a lady of the royal family. James made some attempts to maintain his guest's quarrel with England, but they came to little ; and Henry VII. worked for a reversal of the policy that made an enemy of Scotland. Scotland, during the English civil wars free from attack, had increased in prosperity and power. Henry VII.'s England needed peace at home ; and in 1502, Margaret Tudor, Henry's daughter, aged thirteen, was affianced to King James IV. of Scotland, then aged thirty. The princess entered Edinburgh a year later, marriage took place on the 8th of August, 1503, and was celebrated by **William Dunbar** (ch. v. § 36), in his poem of *The Thistle and the Rose*, not without the home-speaking which usually passed between a Scottish subject and his sovereign. For Dame Nature says to "the thistle keepit with a bush of spears :"

> " And sen thou art a king, be thou discreet :
> Herb without virtue hald not of sic price
> As herb of virtue and of odour sweet ;
> And let no nettle vile and full of vice
> Her fellow to the guidly flour de lis,
> Nor let no wild weed full of churlishness
> Compare her to the lilie's nobleness."

James IV. of Scotland, to whom such counsel was given, was a handsome man with uncut hair and beard, liberal, active in war or chase, familiar with his people, brave to rashness, well read, and of good address. He could speak Latin, French, German, Flemish, Italian, Spanish, Gaelic, and broad Scotch. He was attentive to priests, and gave by his life good reason for Dunbar's especial warning in " The Thistle and the Rose " of the Thistle's solemn trust to

> " Hold no other flow'r in sic deuty
> As the fresh rose, of colour red and white ;
> For gif thou does, hurt is thine honesty."

Through this weak side of his nature he is said to have been cajoled in his youth by those who led him to unite with them against his father.

Dunbar's poem of " The Thrissil and the Rois," upon the marriage of James IV. of Scotland to Margaret Tudor, is a court poem in Chaucer's stanza, planned to a form that had already become traditional in Chaucer's time (ch. iv. § 13, 16, 20). When he was in bed on a May morning, Aurora looked in at his window, with a pale green face, and on her hand a lark, whose song bade lovers wake from slumber.  Fresh May stood then before his bed, and bade the sluggard rise and write some-thing in her honour.  Why should he rise, he asked, for few birds sang, and May brought only cold and wind that caused him to forbear walking among her boughs?  She smiled, and yet bade him rise to keep his promise that he would describe "the rose of most pleasaunce."  So she departed into a fair garden; and it seemed to him that he went hastily after her, among the flowers, under the bright sunrise, where the birds sang for com-fort of the light.  They sang Hail to the May, Hail to the Morning, Hail to Princess Nature before whom birds, beasts, flowers, and herbs were about to appear, "as they had wont in May from year to year," and pay due reverence.  First *f* the beasts came the Lion, whom Dunbar's description pleasantly associated with the lion on the arms of Scotland.  Nature, while crowning him, gave him a lesson in just rule.  A like lesson she gave to the Eagle, when she crowned him King of Birds ; and, as we have seen, to the Thistle, who personified King James of Scotland, when she "saw him keepit with a bush of spears," crowned him with ruby, and bade him defend all others in the field.  Then came the poet's welcome of the Tudor Margaret, when Nature glorified her as the Rose, the freshest Queen of Flowers ; and the poem closed with a song of hail and welcome to her from the merle, the lark, the nightingale, and from the common voice of the small birds, who, by their shrill chorus, woke the poet from his dream.

2. In this poem, as in "The Golden Terge," Dunbar was a follower of Chaucer, constructing his own work on a time-honoured model.  The " Thistle and the Rose" was written in 1503 ; *The Golden Terge* was first printed by Chepman and Myllar, in 1508, when the printing-press was new to Scotland, Printing did not begin in Edinburgh till about thirty years after Caxton brought it to London.  The art is said to have been taken to Scotland by the priests who fled thither from persecu-

tion in the Low Countries.   But the first patent for establishing a press in Scotland was granted, in 1507, by James IV., to Walter Chepman, a merchant, and Andrew Myllar, a working printer.   Poems of Dunbar were among the first works of their printing.   "The Golden Terge" is in stanzas of nine ten-syllabled lines, forming a peculiar measure allied to that of the balade, each stanza having a musical cadence of two rhymes thus interlaced—a a b a a b b a b.   This poem also begins with the conventional May morning.   The poet rose with the sun, saw the dew on the flowers, heard the songs of the birds, while a brook rushed, over pebbles and little waterfalls, among the bushes. The sound of the stream and song of the birds caused him to sleep on the flowers.   In dream he then saw the river, over which there came swiftly towards him a sail, white as blossom, on a mast of gold, bright as the sun.   A hundred ladies in green kirtles landed from the ship.   Among them were Nature and Queen Venus, Aurora, Flora, and many more.   May walked up and down in the garden between her sisters April and June, and Nature gave her a rich, painted gown.   The ladies saluted Flora, and sang of love.   Cupid and Mars, Saturn, Mercury, and other gods were there, also playing and singing, all arrayed in green.   The poet crept through the leaves to draw nearer, was spied by love's queen, and arrested.   Then the ladies let fall their green mantles, and were armed against him with bows, but looked too pleasant to be terrible.   Dame Beauty came against him, followed by the damsels Fair Having, Fine Portraiture, Pleasaunce, and Lusty Cheer.   Then came Reason in plate and mail, as Mars armipotent, with the Golden Targe, or shield, to be his defender.   Youth, Innocence, and other maids did no harm to the shield of Reason.   Sweet Womanhood, with all her good company, Nurture and Loveliness, Patience, Good Fame and Steadfastness, Benign Look, Mild Cheer, Soberness, and others, found their darts powerless against the Golden Targe.   High Degree failed also; Estate and Dignity, Riches, and others, loosed against him in vain a cloud of arrows.   Venus then brought in allegorical recruits, and rearranged her forces. But Reason, with the Shield of Gold, sustained the shock, till Presence threw a powder in his eyes that blinded him.   Then Reason was jested at, and banished into the greenwood.   The poet was wounded nearly to the death, and in a moment was Dame Beauty's prisoner.   Fair Calling smiled upon him; Cherishing fed him with fair words; Danger came to him

and delivered him to Heaviness.   But then the wind began to
blow, and all, flying to the ship, departed.   As they went they
fired guns, by which the poet was awakened to the renewed
sense of the fresh May morning.   This kind of invention is as
old as " The Romaunt of the Rose" (ch. iii. § 36), but Dunbar
took it from Chaucer.   Though Chaucer had been dead a hundred
years, no poet had yet succeeded to his throne.   The land was
still "full filled with his songs."   Gower and Lydgate were still
named after him in courtly verse as the two other chief poets of
the past ; but of Chaucer men thought as Dunbar wrote in one
of the closing stanzas of his " Golden Terge :"

> " O reverend Chaucer ! rose ot rhetoris all ;
> As in our tongue ane flower imperial,
>   That raise in Britain ever who reads richt,
> Thou bears of makars the triúmph riall ;
> Thy fresh enamellit termes celical
>   This matter could illuminat have full bricht :
>   Was thou nocht of our English all the licht,
> Surmounting every tongue terrestrial
> Als far as Mayes morrow does midnicht."

3. " The Flyting of Dunbar and Kennedy" and Dunbar's
" Lament for the Makars " were also first printed in 1508.   The
genius of Dunbar is, of course, most evident where he is least an
imitator.   In " The Thistle and the Rose" and "Golden Terge"
he is gracefully conventional ; in all his other poetry he is himself ; he utters thoughts of his own life, and illustrates the life
of his own time.

Dunbar's *Lament for the Makars*, or Poets (ποιητής—maker),
was written in 1507, when he lay dangerously ill.   It is in
musical four-lined stanzas, each ending with the refrain, " Timor
mortis conturbat me." (The fear of death disquiets me).   Warm
with religious feeling and a sense of human fellowship, speaking
high thought in homely phrase, with a true poet's blending of
pathos and good-humour, it bows to the supremacy of death
while Dunbar joins lament with kindly memories of poets who
have died before him.

> " And he has now ta'en last of aw
> Gude gentle Stobo, and Quintine Schaw.
> Of whom all wichtis has pitie :
> *Timor mortis conturbat me.*

> " Gude Maister Walter Kennedy
> In point of deid lies verily ;
> Great ruth it were that so suld be .
> *Timor mortis conturbat me.*

" Sen he has all my brether ta'en
He will not let me live alane ;
On forse I maun his next prey be :
*Timor mortis conturbat me.*

" Sen for the death remeid is none,
Best is that we for death dispone,
After our death that live may we :
*Timor mortis conturbat me.*"

The " Good Master Walter Kennedy," to whom Dunbar has
here given a kindly stanza, was his playfellow, for the amusement
of lookers-on, at the *Flyting of Dunbar and Kennedy.* This
metrical scolding-match belongs to a form of literature descended
from the " tenson " or " jeu parti" of early Provençal poetry.
The tenson was a song in dialogue of contention which found its
way into European literature from wit-combats of the Arabs on
nice points of love and philosophy. But the fifteenth century
advanced by many ways to a rough heartiness in dealing with
realities of life. Thus, in a flyting, which takes its name from
our old name for contention, "flit," the two poets, who, if they
had lived some centuries earlier, would, through a tenson, have
been attacking and defending castles in the air, were down upon
earth belabouring each other with the pen as heartily as if they
had come into the tilt-yard, and the pens were lances with
which they were engaged, each in the playful endeavour to
knock down his friend.

Walter Kennedy, who joined in flyting with Dunbar, was the
sixth son of Gilbert, first Baron Kennedy. He acquired, in
1504, the lairdship of Glentig ; and it seems to have been
between this date and 1508 that Dunbar wrote the greater
part of his share in the rough whimsical scolding-match.

With the vigorous homeliness a certain coarseness was then
often associated—coarseness which was not immorality, but consisted in plain utterance of truths belonging to the grosser side of
life. This was common in Dunbar's humorous poetry. It was
used with noble purpose in his *Dance of the Seven Deadly Sins,*
written in 1507, a piece in which new life was given to the old
forms of allegorical poetry by the genius of a master. On the
festival night before Lent, Dunbar saw heaven and hell, in a
trance ; and it seemed to him that Mahoun called for a dance
among the fiends. As the Seven Deadly Sins joined in the
dancing, the allegorical description of each one became vivid
with intensity of life, and was realised to the imaginations of
the people by a profound earnestness expressed with playful

humour.  This poem was followed by one purely humorous,
which described another of the sports called for by Mahoun,
*The Joust between the Tailor and the Soutar* (shoemaker).  And
this, again, was followed by an ironical *Amends to the Tailors
and Soutars*, with the refrain, " Tailors and soutars, blest be ye !"
which was but a new form of flyting.  You tailors and soutars
can shape anew a misfashioned man, cover with crafts a broken
back, mend ill-made feet—

> " In erd ye kyth sic miracles here
> In heaven ye sall be sancts full clear,
> Though ye be knaves in this countrie :
> Tailors and soutars, blest be ye !"

Humour abounded, but it was the humour of a man essentially
earnest.  No poet from Chaucer till his own time equalled
Dunbar in the range of genius.  He could pass from broad jest
to a pathos truer for its homeliness ; he had a play of fancy
reaching to the nobler heights of thought, a delicacy joined with
a terse vigour of expression in short poems that put the grace of
God into their worldly wisdom.

4.  **Gavin Douglas** was another Scottish poet who wrote
during the last nine years of the reign of Henry VII. ; and,
like Dunbar, lived on into the days when Henry VIII. was
King of England.  Gavin Douglas was born about the year
1474, son of that Archibald Earl of Angus who was known as
Bell-the-Cat.  He took holy orders, and became, in the year
1509, the last year of the reign of Henry VII., rector of Hawche
(Prestonkirk).  He had written the longest of his original poems
probably in 1501, when he was about twenty-seven years old.
It was called *The Palace of Honour*, and was, in the measure of
" The Golden Terge," a court poem dedicated to James IV., an
allegory imitated in the usual way from poems that remained
in fashion.  On a May morning the poet entered a garden,
swooned, and dreamt of a procession of Minerva and her court,
Diana and her followers, Venus and all her train, with the court
of the Muses, to the Palace of Honour.  The palace was built
on a high slippery rock with many paths, and but one leading
to the summit.  After much detail, classical and allegorical,
after seeing the Muses cull flowers of rhetoric, Gavin Douglas
awoke, wrote a lay in praise of Honour, and dedicated his
poem to the king.  Steady maintenance of right and duty,
which runs through the literature of our country, is here no
doubt.  We find it also in Gavin Douglas's better poem of

*King'Hart*, an allegory of life, the heart personified as Man ;
but the gathering energies of the nation have not yet raised
up the thinkers who shall cast into new forms the thoughts
of a new day.

5. In England **John Skelton** (ch. v. § 34) may have produced during the latter years of the reign of Henry VII. his
*Bowge of Court.*  It was an allegorical court poem against court
follies and vices.   Bowge is the French *bouche* (the mouth); and
bowge of court was the old technical name for the right to feed
at a king's table.   Skelton here told, in Chaucer's stanza, how in
autumn he thought of the craft of old poets who

> " Under as coverte termĕs as could be
> Can touche a trouth, and cloke it subtylly
> With fresshe utteraunce full sentencyously."

Weary with much thinking, he slept at the port of Harwich in
mine host's house called "Power's Keye ;" and it seemed to him
that he saw sail into harbour a goodly ship, which cast anchor,
and was boarded by traders who found royal merchandise in
her.   The poet also went on board, where he found no acquaintance, and there was much noise, until one commanded all to
hold their peace, and said that the ship was the "Bowge of
Court," owned by the Dame Saunce-pere (Peerless) ; that her
merchandise was called Favour, and who would have it must
pay dear.   Then there was a press to see the fair lady, who sat
enthroned.   Danger was her chief gentlewoman, and taunted the
poet for being over-bold in pressing forward.   Danger asked
him his name, and he said it was Dread.   Why did he come?
Forsooth, to buy some of her ware.   Danger then looked on
him disdainfully ; but another gentlewoman, named Desire, came
to him and said, " Brother, be bold.   Press forward, and speak
without any dread.   Who spares to speak will spare to speed."
He was without friends, he said, and poor.   Desire gave him a
jewel called "bonne aventure."   With that he could thrive ; but,
above all things, he must be careful to make a friend of Fortune,
by whom the ship was steered.   Merchants then thronged,
suing to Fortune for her friendship.   What would they have?
" And we asked favour, and favour she us gave."   Thus ended
the prologue.   Then Dread told how the sail was up, and
Fortune ruled the helm.   Favour they had ; but under honey
oft lies bitter gall.   There were seven subtle persons in the
ship :

" The first was Favell, full of flatery,
  With fables false that well coude fayne a tale;
The seconde was Suspecte, which that dayly
  Mysdempte eche man, with face deedly and pale;
And Harry Hafter, that well coude picke a male;
  With other foure of theyr affynite,
Dysdayne, Ryotte, Dyssymuler, Subtylte."

Harry Hafter in that stanza derives his name from the old English *hæftan* (to lay fast hold of anything). These seven sins of the court had for their friend Fortune, who often danced with them; but they had no love for the new-comer, Dread. Favell cloaked his ill-will with sugared speech. Dread thanked him, and was then addressed in turn by the other vices, each in his own fashion; and at last Dread, the poet, was about to jump out of the ship to avoid being slain, when he awoke, " caught penne and ynke, and wrote this lytyll boke."

But Skelton's fame does not rest upon good thought put into this conventional disguise. He felt with the people; and in the reign of Henry VIII. we shall find him speaking with them, and for them, by putting bold words of his own upon the life of his own day into a form of verse borrowed from nobody. This form of verse, which has been called Skeltonical, appeared in the delicately playful *Boke of Phyllyp Sparowe*, the lament of a simple-hearted maid, Jane Scrope, one of the young ladies who were being educated by the Black Nuns at Carow, near Norwich, for Philip, her pet sparrow, killed by a cat. The lament ended with a Latin epitaph to the bird, and it was followed by dainty commendations of its mistress. This poem, suggested no doubt by the sparrow of Catullus, was written by Skelton before the end of 1508, for it is included among follies at the end of Barclay's "Ship of Fools."

6. **Alexander Barclay,** whose place and date of birth are unknown, was of Oriel College, Oxford. After leaving college he travelled abroad, and then became one of the priests of the college of St. Mary Ottery, in Devonshire. He was afterwards a Benedictine monk of Ely, then among the Franciscans of Canterbury. In 1546 he obtained the livings of Baddow Magna, in Essex, and of Wokey, in Somersetshire; and he had also the living of All Saints, in Lombard Street, when he died, an old man, at Croydon, in 1552. He translated from some of the best authors of the Continent; and the most famous of his translations was that of Sebastian Brandt's "Narrenschiff," done into Chaucer's stanza, with an occasional variation, and pub-

lished in 1508, with some additional home-thrusts of his own, as Barclay's *Ship of Fools.* Sebastian Brandt, born at Strasburg, in 1458, and educated at Basle, became syndic of his native town, and was in 1508 a living writer. He died in 1520. His "Narrenschiff," supposed to have been first published in 1494, though the Latin version of it, "Navis Stultifera," appeared in 1488, led the march of sixteenth century satire in Germany. Brandt called his book "The Ship of Fools" because no cart or coach was big enough to hold them all. The ship once ready, there was a great thronging for berths in her; but nobody was admitted who had sense enough to call himself a fool. Whoever set up for a wit was welcome. One hundred and thirteen several forms of folly were at last entered, with Brandt himself for their leader, as the Bookish Fool, who had many books, and was continually buying others, which he neither read nor understood. Various forms of human folly, among misers and spendthrifts, labourers, gamblers, beggars, huntsmen, cooks, &c., were passed in good-humoured satirical review, with incidental bits of counsel upon the training of children and other subjects. The book was rhymed with homely vigour, and many a proverbial phrase in the Alsatian dialect; it had, therefore, wide currency as a picture of manners, and a wholesome satire on the follies of the day. It went through many editions, was translated into French in 1497; and, while still in the first flush of its fame, was also in 1508 translated into English as the "Ship of Fools" by Alexander Barclay, then signing himself priest and chaplain in the College of St. Mary Ottery. Alexander Barclay's other writings were produced after the death of Henry VII.

7. Another English poet of the reign of Henry VII. was **Stephen Hawes,** a Suffolk man. Like Barclay, he was educated at Oxford, and then travelled. He was well read in the poets of England, France, and Italy, could repeat much of the verse of Lydgate, whom he called especially his master, and, perhaps for his good knowledge of French, was made by Henry VII. groom of the privy chamber. Like Alexander Barclay, Stephen Hawes was a poet without independent genius, a clever man who took delight in literature, and was active with his pen. In 1500 his *Temple of Glass,* an imitation of Chaucer's "House of Fame," was printed by Wynken de Worde. His chief work, first printed by Wynken de Worde in 1517, was finished in 1506, and dedicated to King Henry VII. as "*The Pastime of Pleasure; or, the History of Graund Amoure and La*

*Bel Pucell:* containing the Knowledge of the Seven Sciences
and the Course of Man's Life in this World.   Invented by
Stephen Hawes, groom of King Henry VII. his chamber."   It
is an allegory of the old form, chiefly in Chaucer's stanza.
Graund Amoure passed through the fair meadow of youth,
and then came to the choice between two highways of life, the
way of Contemplation—that was life in a religious order—and the
way of Active Life.   He took the way of Active Life, met Fame
with her two greyhounds, Grace and Governaunce, who told him
of La Bel Pucell.   In her Hawes represented the true aim of
life, only attainable through many labours.   Then he first
visited the Tower of Doctrine, and was introduced to her seven
daughters.   These were the seven sciences, arranged of old into
three, Grammar, Logic, Rhetoric, forming what was called the
"Trivium;" and four, Arithmetic, Music, Geometry, Astronomy,
which formed the "Quadrivium."   When, in his introduction
to these seven daughters of Doctrine, Graund Amoure had
advanced to Music, he found her playing on an organ in her
tower, and it was then that he first saw his ideal, La Bel Pucell.
He told his love to her, and danced with her to sweet harmony.
This means that the youth who has advanced far enough in the
pursuit of knowledge to have ears for the grand harmonies of
life is for a time brought face to face with the bright ideal to be
sought through years of forward battle.   La Bel Pucell went to
her distant home; and Graund Amoure, after receiving counsel
from Geometry and Astronomy, proceeded to the Castle of
Chivalry, prayed in the Temple of Mars, within which was
Fortune at her wheel, and on his way to the Temple of Venus
met Godfrey Gobilive, who spoke ill of women.   This part
is in couplets.   They went to the Temple of Venus; but
Godfrey was overtaken by a lady named Correction, with a
knotted whip, who said that he was False Report, escaped in
disguise from his prison in the Tower of Chastity.   To that
tower the lady Correction introduced Graund Amoure.   As
the adventurer proceeded on his way he fought a giant with
three heads, named Falsehood, Imagination, Perjury, and cut
his heads off with the sword Claraprudence.   Then he proceeded
through other adventures, which carried on the allegory of steadfast endeavour till Graund Amoure saw the stately palace of La
Bel Pucell upon an island beyond a stormy ocean.   After the
water had been crossed, there was still to be quelled a monster
against which Graund Amoure could only defend himself by

anointing his sword with the ointment of Pallas. The last victory achieved, Graund Amoure was received into the palace by Peace, Mercy, Justice, Reason, Grace, and Memory; and he was married next morning to La Bel Pucell by Lex Ecclesiæ (Law of the Church). After his happy years with her, Old Age came one day into Graund Amoure's chamber, and struck him on the breast; Policy and Avarice came next. Graund Amoure became eager to heap up riches. Death warned him that these must be left. After the warning, Contrition and Conscience came to him before he died. Mercy and Charity then buried him. Fame wrote his epitaph. Time and Eternity pronounced the final exhortation of the poem.

Among the other books by Stephen Hawes was a *Conversion of Swearers*, printed in 1509. He wrote also in verse, *A Joyful Meditation of All England*, on the Coronation of King Henry VIII.

8. The chroniclers of English history who wrote in the latter part of the reign of Henry VII. were Robert Fabyan, a Londoner; Polydore Vergil, an Italian; and Bernard André, a Frenchman.

**Robert Fabyan,** son of John Fabyan, of a respectable Essex family, was born in London, and apprenticed to a draper; he became a member of the Draper's Company, Alderman of the Ward of Farringdon Without, and, in 1493, served in the office of sheriff. In September, 1496, in the mayoralty of Sir Henry Colet, Robert Fabyan was chosen, with the Recorder and certain commoners, to ride to the king "for redress of the new impositions raised and levied upon English cloths in the archduke's land," namely, the newly-appointed Philip's charge of a florin for every piece of English cloth imported into the Low Countries; a charge withdrawn in July, 1497. Soon afterwards Fabyan was an assessor upon London wards of the fifteenth granted to Henry VII. for his Scottish war. In 1502, Fabyan resigned his alderman's gown to avoid the expense of taking the mayoralty, for, although opulent, he had a large family. His wife, with four sons and two daughters, from a family of ten boys and six girls, survived him. He died in 1512.

Robert Fabyan was a good French and Latin scholar; and, in using monkish chronicles as material for his own compilation of history, was a devout adopter of the censures of all kings who were enemies to religious places. Of Becket he spoke as a "glorious martyr" and a "blessed saint;" of Henry II. as a "hammer of Holy Church;" but he was not credulous of miracles and marvels. His *Concordance of Histories*, afterwards called "New Chronicles of England and France, in Two Parts," opened with a prologue in Chaucer's stanza, which represented its author as one who prepared material for the skilled artist or historian who should come after him to perfect what he had rudely shaped. The prologue ended with an invocation to the Virgin for help, and the seven parts of the chronicle, which brought the history from Brut to the year 1504, ended with seven metrical epilogues, entitled the "Seven Joys of the Blessed Virgin." The chronicle itself was in prose, with translation into English verse of any Latin verses that were cited. A notable example of this was Fabyan's English version of the Latin verses said to have been made by Edward II. in his imprisonment.

Polydore Vergil, born at Urbino, had won fame in Italy before he came to England for Peter's Pence, and was here made Archdeacon of Wells. He returned to Italy, and died there in 1555. Among his works, all written in Latin, is an English Chronicle, in twenty-seven books, begun by him in the latter years of Henry VII., and finished in the earlier years of the reign of Henry VIII.

Bernard André, born at Toulouse, was an Austin Friar, who was present at Henry VII.'s entry into London after Bosworth Field. Soon afterwards André, who was blind, styled himself Henry VII.'s poet laureate. In 1496 he was made tutor to Arthur, Prince of Wales. John Skelton, also poet laureate, was, as we have seen, tutor to Prince Henry. André had retired from court, and was receiving some small Church preferments, when, in 1500, he began to work at his Latin "Life of Henry VII.," finished in 1502, with a preface in which he undertook to write every year for the king. He seems to have written, in pursuance of this promise, yearly accounts of the chief events of his time; but for the reign of Henry VII. only two of these are extant. André lived on into the reign of Henry VIII., and there remain accounts by him of two years of that reign, 1515 and 1521, the last date at which he is known to have been living. This blind French poet and historiographer, naturalised in England, although no genius, had much repute in his own day.

9. The representatives of the new energy of English scholar

ship, Grocyn, Linacre, Lily, Colet (ch. v. § 30), lived through the reign of Henry VII. into that of Henry VIII.

**John Fisher** (ch. v. § 35), by his influence with Margaret Countess of Richmond, obtained the establishment of Lady Margaret Divinity Professorships in both universities. He became Doctor of Divinity in 1501. In 1502 he was the Lady Margaret's First Divinity Professor at Cambridge. In 1504 he was made Bishop of Rochester. Through his influence Christ's College, Cambridge, was founded by the Lady Margaret, and completed under his care in 1505. He procured in the same way the foundation of St. John's College, finished in 1515. Between 1505 and 1508, Bishop Fisher was the head of Queen's College. He invited Erasmus to Cambridge, offered him an appointment as Lady Margaret's Divinity Professor, and supported him in the endeavour to teach at Cambridge the Greek he had learnt at Oxford. Erasmus persevered only for a few months in the endeavour to form a Greek class. Failing with Chrysolora's Grammar, he tried Theodore Gaza's, and then left the labour to be continued by Dr. Richard Croke. Even at Oxford the new study of Greek was fighting its way slowly against strong opposition of two parties : idlers who called themselves Trojans, and who under leaders whom they called Priam and Hector battled with the Greeks ; and the timidly religious men who cried, " Beware of the Greeks, lest you be made a heretic." There was called forth, indeed, a royal declaration that no student of Greek should be molested; and there was open rebuke of some court preachers who made bold, in the king's presence, to denounce Greek in their sermons.

10. We pass now to the reign of Henry VIII. (1509—1547). When Henry came to the throne, in 1509, a handsome youth of eighteen, well educated and self-willed, Martin Luther was a young man of six-and-twenty, and it was the year of Calvin's birth.

**John Colet**, born in 1466, was the son of Sir Henry Colet, a wealthy city knight, who was twice Lord Mayor of London. Dame Christian, his mother, had eleven sons and eleven daughters, of whom John was the sole survivor. She lived with him during the last nine years of his life, after her husband's death in 1510 ; and, says Erasmus, " being come to her ninetieth year, looked so smooth, and was so cheerful, that you would think she had never shed a tear ; and, if I mistake not, she survived her son, Dean Colet. Now that which supplied a

woman with so much fortitude was not learning, but piety to
God." John Colet had seven years' training at Magdalene
College, Oxford ; then studied in Paris, and then went to Italy
and learnt Greek. While absent from England he was receiving
Church preferment, for his family had interest. After his return he
went to Oxford, and there gave free lectures on St. Paul's Epistles.
In 1504 he became Doctor of Divinity, and in 1505 Dean of St.
Paul's. Inquiry into Scripture was then made by him part of
the Cathedral service ; he preached generally in exposition of
St. Paul's Epistles, his favourite study. He was handsome,
earnest, eloquent, outspoken against corrupt lives of the clergy,
against the confessional, image worship, belief in purgatory,
and thoughtless repetitions of fixed quantities of prayer. The
Bishop of London would have brought him into trouble as a
heretic if he had not been protected by Archbishop Warham.
Among Colet's works were a treatise on the Sacraments of the
Church, and two treatises on the Hierarchies of Dionysius, of
which the latter have been published from the MS. in the library
of St. Paul's School. Other works of his—comments on St.
Paul—remain in manuscript at Oxford. He died in September,
1519. Dean Colet spent his ecclesiastical income on his household and in hospitality ; his large private fortune he spent in
the foundation of St. Paul's School. The foundation of this
school was begun by him in 1510, the year in which his father's
death gave him, at the age of forty-four, a large inheritance. He
appointed his friend William Lily, an excellent Greek scholar,
to be the first head master.

11. **William Lily**, born at Odiham, Hants, in 1468, was
about two years younger than Colet, and had also been educated
at Magdalene College, Oxford. After taking his first degree,
Lily went on a pilgrimage to Jerusalem. It was on his way
back that he studied Greek at Rhodes, and afterwards at Rome.
He had been head master of St. Paul's School for twelve years,
when he died of the plague. His most famous book was the
*Latin Grammar*, produced for the use of the new school,
and familiar to boys of many English schools for many
generations. It was first published in 1513. The preface to
the book was written by Thomas Wolsey, not yet cardinal, but
in the year of its publication Dean of York. The English
"Rudiments" were written by Dean Colet, who wanted confidence in his own Latinity. The English Syntax and the rules
in Latin verse for genders, beginning "Propria quæ maribus,"

and for past tenses and supines, beginning "As in præsenti," were by William Lily. The Latin Syntax was chiefly the work of Erasmus ; and the great currency of the book was the work of Henry VIII., who established its orthodoxy by declaring it penal publicly to teach any other.

12. **Thomas Linacre** (ch. v. § 30), who survived his friends Grocyn and Lily little more than a year, died in 1524, and was buried in St. Paul's. He also produced an Elementary Latin Grammar, which was written in English for the use of the Princess Mary, and was preparatory to his more important work in Latin, " De Emendata Structura Latini Sermonis Libri VI." As a physician he founded not only three lectureships on physic, two at Oxford and one at Cambridge, but he was chief founder also of the Royal College of Physicians, which held its first meetings at Linacre's house, and for which he obtained a charter in 1518. Linacre took orders, and obtained prebends in Wells, York, and Westminster, also the rectories of Mersham, Hawkhurst, Holsworthy, and Wigan.

13. **Sir Thomas More** was another of the Oxford scholars active during the earlier part of the reign of Henry VIII. Born in 1478, he was thirty-six years younger than Grocyn, about eighteen younger than Linacre, and twelve younger than Lily and Colet. Thomas More was the son of Sir John More, knight, a justice of the King's Bench, who was three times married, though he used to say that marriage was like dipping the hand into a bag where there are twenty snakes and an eel—it was twenty to one that you did not get the eel. Thomas More's birthplace and early home being Milk Street, in the City of London, he was sent to St. Anthony's, in Threadneedle Street, then chief in repute among the London schools. More next entered the household of Cardinal John Morton, Archbishop of Canterbury and Lord Chancellor.

Morton had been one of the foremost of Oxford scholars when William Grocyn was a child. He was Doctor of Laws and Vice-Chancellor of the University in 1446. He practised law, and obtained many Church benefices ; was Master of the Rolls in 1472, Bishop of Ely in 1479—the same Bishop of Ely of whom the Protector Richard, about to seize the crown, said :

> "My lord of Ely, when I was last in Holborn,
> I saw good strawberries in your garden there ;
> I do beseech you send for some of them ; "

an hour before he sent him to the Tower. When afterwards

released, and transferred to the custody of the Duke of Buckingham, Morton helped to organise the insurrection which cost
Buckingham his head; and, being himself safe in Flanders, was
thenceforth busy as a negotiator on the side that triumphed
at Bosworth Field. Thus Morton became the trusted friend of
Henry VII., who at the beginning of his reign made him, in
1468, Lord Chancellor of England, and nine months afterwards
Archbishop of Canterbury. In 1489 Morton obtained a bull
from Pope Innocent VIII. authorising him, as visitor, to
exercise authority within the monasteries; in which, the bull
said, there were many who, giving themselves over to a reprobate
mind, and having laid aside the fear of God, were leading a
wanton and dissolute life, to the destruction of their own souls
and the dishonour of religion. While upholding the sovereignty
of the archbishop in spiritual things, Morton, as Henry VII.'s
chief adviser, maintained in temporal affairs the absolute
sovereignty of the king. He greatly enriched himself, but was
liberal with his wealth. He helped the king, more narrowly
avaricious, to draw money, by benevolences or otherwise, from
his subjects; and he shared the king's unpopularity. Morton was
a vigorous old man of between seventy and eighty, whose life
was blended with the history of half a century, when young
Thomas More was placed in his household, and found him a
generous patron and appreciative friend. A son of one of lower
rank was often received of old into a great man's house. He wore
there his lord's livery, but had it of more costly materials than
were used for the footmen, and was the immediate attendant of
his patron, who was expected to give him a start in life when
he came of age. When at Christmas time a Latin play was
acted, young Thomas More could step in at will among the
players, and extemporise a comic part. "Whoever liveth to
try it," Morton would say, "shall see this child here waiting at
table prove a notable and rare man." Dean Colet used to say,
"There is but one wit in England, and that is young Thomas
More." About the year 1497 the archbishop sent the youth to
Oxford, where he was entered to Canterbury College, now
included in Christ Church. There he learned Greek of Linacre
and Grocyn. In 1499 he removed thence to London, and proceeded to study law at Lincoln's Inn. In 1500 Archbishop
Morton died.

While studying law, More, who was earnestly religious, tried
on himself for a time the experiment of monastic discipline,

I

wore a hair shirt, took a log for a pillow, whipped himself on Fridays. At the age of twenty-one he entered Parliament, and soon after he had been called to the bar he was made an Under-Sheriff of London. In 1503 he opposed in the House of Commons Henry VII.'s proposal for a subsidy on account of the marriage portion of his daughter Margaret ; and he opposed with so much energy that the House refused to grant it. One went and told the king that a beardless boy had disappointed all his expectations. During the last years, therefore, of Henry VII., More was under the displeasure of the king, and had thoughts of leaving the country. But in the first years of the reign of Henry VIII. he was rising to large practice in the law courts, where it is said he refused to plead in cases which he thought unjust, and took no fees from widows, orphans, or the poor. He would have preferred marrying the second daughter of John Colt, of New Hall, in Essex, but chose her elder sister, that he might not subject her to the discredit of being passed over. In 1513, Thomas More, then Under-Sheriff of London, is said to have written his *History of the Life and Death of King Edward V., and of the Usurpation of Richard III.*, first printed in 1557, from a MS. in his writing. The book seems to contain the knowledge and opinions of More's patron, Morton, who, as an active politician in the times described, was in peril of his own life from Richard III. When, in describing the death of Edward IV., and reporting his last words to the by-standers, it is said, " He laid him down on his right side with his face toward them," Morton, an eye-witness, rather than More, who was then a five-year-old child, seems to be speaking. Sir George Buck, in a eulogy of Richard III. published in 1646, says that Morton " wrote a book in Latin against King Richard, which came afterwards into the hands of Mr. More, some time his servant ;" and adds a note that "the book was lately in the hands of Mr. Roper, of Eltham, as Sir Thomas Hoby, who saw it, told me." There is some reason, then, to think that More's MS. may have been a translation of his patron's Latin history, and therefore a contemporary record, though ascribed to More by the son-in-law who first printed it, twenty-two years after More's death. The work which comes down to us in Latin and in English, if wholly More's, is mainly based on information given to him by his patron Morton.

14. In the year 1513, when More's "History of Edward V. and Richard III." is said to have been written, Henry VIII.

was launching against France a war of which the details were managed by Thomas Wolsey. Wolsey, the son of a well-to-do butcher of Ipswich, was five years younger than Dean Colet, seven years older than More, and twenty years older than King Henry VIII. From Ipswich Grammar School he went to Magdalene College, Oxford, and there took his B.A. degree so early that he was called the Boy Bachelor. He became Fellow of Magdalene, then master of Magdalene School, where three sons of the Marquis of Dorset were among his pupils. When the sons went home for their Christmas holidays the master was invited with them, and he was so much liked that, in 1500, the marquis gave him the rectory of Lymington, in Somersetshire. Wolsey then obtained the post of chaplain to Henry Dean, Morton's successor in the Archbishopric of Canterbury, the prelate who in November, 1501, married the Princess Katherine of Aragon to young Arthur, Prince of Wales, four months before the boy's death. Henry VIII. married her in 1509, about six weeks after his accession. Dr. Dean was archbishop only for two years, and died in February, 1503, not long after Wolsey had become his chaplain. Wolsey next became one of the chaplains to an old knight, Sir John Nephant, governor of Calais, and managed all his affairs for him so well that when Sir John was, at his own request, called home, he specially commended Wolsey to the notice of the king, and procured for him the post of a court chaplain. Then Wolsey made friends at court, obtained employment on a foreign service, and performed his duty with a rare despatch. The king rewarded him, in 1508, with the deanery of Lincoln. After the accession of Henry VIII., Wolsey obtained the living of Torrington, in Devon, was made also Registrar of the Garter, Canon of Windsor, Dean of York. Dr. Fox, Bishop of Winchester, was Secretary of State and Lord Privy Seal. To him Wolsey in part owed his advancement. Thomas Howard, Earl of Surrey, was Lord Treasurer, and had more of the new king's confidence than the Bishop of Winchester thought good for his own interests. Therefore Dr. Fox sought to advance Wolsey, as a creature of his own, in the king's personal favour ; and, to place him in closer relations with the king, obtained for him the post of Royal Almoner. From that point Wolsey's rise was rapid. He made his society delightful, knew how to win the king to his own counsels, and never flinched from work. In 1512 Henry made an inglorious attempt against France. Ten thousand

Englishmen intended for attack upon Guienne went to Spain, under the Marquis of Dorset, became insubordinate, and returned to England in defiance of the king's commands. Wolsey, the royal almoner, took charge of the victualling of the forces, and laboured indefatigably at the preparation for an attack upon France in 1513, the next year, which should not fail. Henry was leagued against France with Pope Leo X. and the Emperor Maximilian. He crossed to France in the summer of 1513, and the campaign satisfied him, since he won the Battle of the Spurs, took Terouenne and also Tournay, of which place he gave to Wolsey the rich bishopric. Before Henry returned to England, in November of that year, James IV. of Scotland had been slain at Flodden. Wolsey had been in France with the king, counselling and aiding with his great administrative power. Soon after their return the king made his friend Bishop of Lincoln. Before the end of the year 1514 the see of York fell vacant, and Wolsey was made Archbishop of York. Lavish gifts of the king followed rapidly. Wolsey obtained administration of the see of Bath and Wells, the temporalities of the Abbey of St. Albans ; soon afterwards in succession there were added to his archbishopric the bishoprics of Durham and Winchester. He had the revenues of a sovereign, lived pompously, and favoured learning. From 1515 to 1523 no parliament was summoned; Henry and Wolsey held absolute rule. In November, 1515, Wolsey formally received, in Westminster Abbey, from Leo X., the rank of cardinal, which had been granted in September. Dean Colet preached the installation sermon. Towards the close of December, in the same year, Warham, Archbishop of Canterbury, after a vain struggle against usurpations of his power by the strong rival archbishop, yielded to him the office of Lord Chancellor. It was in these days that Thomas More, not knighted yet, wrote his " Utopia."

15. In May, 1515, More had been joined in a commission with Cuthbert Tunstal and others, to confer with the ambassadors of Charles V., then only Archduke of Austria, upon a renewal of alliance. Tunstal, a rising churchman, then held several preferments, and was chancellor to Warham, Archbishop of Canterbury. He was made in that year, 1515, Archdeacon of Chester, and in May, 1516, Master of the Rolls. In the same year, 1516, he was again sent with More on an embassy to Brussels, and lived there under the same roof with Erasmus, who was indebted much to the generous friendship of Archbishop

Warham, and something to the help of English friends, among whom was More, for the leisure which enabled him to produce, in 1516, his New Testament. On the first embassy More was absent more than six months, and during that time he established friendship with Peter Giles (Latinised, Ægidius), a scholarly and courteous young man, who was secretary to the municipality of Antwerp.

More's *Utopia* is in two parts, of which the second, describing the place (Οὐτόπος—or Nusquama, as he called it sometimes in his letters—" Nowhere "), was probably written in the latter part of 1515; the first part, introductory, early in 1516. The book was first printed at Louvain, late in 1516, under the editorship of Erasmus, Peter Giles, and other of More's friends in Flanders. It was then revised by More, and printed by Frobenius, at Basle, in November, 1518. It was reprinted at Paris and Vienna, but was not printed in England during More's lifetime. Its first publication in this country was in the English translation made in Edward VI.'s reign ( 1551) by Ralph Robinson. The name of the book has given an adjective to our language—we call an impracticable scheme Utopian. Yet, under the veil of a playful fiction, the talk is intensely earnest, and abounds in practical suggestion. It is the work of a scholarly and witty Englishman, who attacks in his own way the chief political and social evils of his time. Having commended the book in a witty letter to his friend Giles, More tells in the first part how he was sent into Flanders with Cuthbert Tunstal, "whom the king's majesty of late, to the great rejoicing of all men, did prefer to the office of Master of the Rolls ;" how the commissioners of Charles met them at Bruges, and presently returned to Brussels for instructions ; and how More then went to Antwerp, where he found a pleasure in the society of Peter Giles, which soothed his desire to see again his wife and children, from whom he had been four months away. One day, when he came from the service in Antwerp Cathedral, More fables that he saw his friend Giles talking to " a certain stranger, a man well stricken in age, with a black sunburnt face, a long beard, and a cloak cast homely about his shoulders," whom More judged to be a mariner. Peter Giles introduced him to his friend as Raphael Hythloday (the name, from the Greek ὕθλος and ὅδιος, means " knowing in trifles"), a man learned in Latin and profound in Greek, a Portuguese wholly given to philosophy, who left his patrimony to his brethren, and, desiring to know far countries, went with Amerigo Vespucci in the three last of the voyages of which an account had been printed in 1507. From the last voyage he did not return with Vespucci, but got leave to be one of the twenty-four men left in Gulike. Then he travelled on until having reached Calicut he found there one of the ships of his own country to take him home. So it was that in the course of travel Raphael Hythloday had visited the island of Utopia, unknown to other men ; had dwelt there for five years, and had become familiar with its customs. More's book, which expresses much of the new energy of independent thought, was thus associated with the fresh discovery of the New World. The Cabots had reached the continent in 1497, on the coast of Labrador. Columbus reached it in 1498, near the Island of Trinidad, off the northern coast of South America. The Florentine, Amerigo Vespucci, made his first expedition in 1499, under command of Ojeda ; his second in 1500. His third and fourth voyages were made in 1501 and 1503 in Portuguese ships in the service of King Emanuel of Portugal. In 1505 he re-turned into the service of Spain, but made no more voyages; he prepared charts, and prescribed routes for voyages of other men to the New World. The fame of Amerigo's description of his voyages caused a German geographer to call the newly-founded continent, after his name, America. He died three or four years before Thomas More wrote his " Utopia."

After the greeting in the street, Raphael Hythloday and Peter Giles went with More to his house ; "and there," says More, "in my garden, upon a bench covered with green torves, we sat down talking together." The talk was of the customs among men, and of the government of princes. Why would not Hythloday give his experience as counsellor of some great prince, since " from the prince, as from a perpetual well-spring, cometh among the people the flood of all that is good or evil ?" Thomas More had withheld himself from such service ; and he put two reasons for doing so into the mouth of Hythloday. First, that " most princes have more delight in war (the knowledge of which I neither have nor desire) than in the good feats of peace ; and employ much more study how by right or wrong to enlarge their dominions than how well and peaceably to rule and govern that they have already." Secondly, because "every king's coun-sellor is so wise in his own eyes that he will not allow another man's counsel, if it be not shameful, flattering assent." More had in mind the supreme counsels of Wolsey, abetting Henry VIII.'s

war policy, and doing little to secure peace and well-being
for the English people. Had Hythloday ever been in England,
he was asked. Yes, for a few months, not long after the insurrection of the Western Englishmen (in 1496), "which by their
own miserable and pitiful slaughter was suppressed and ended."
He was then much beholden to Cardinal Morton; and here
More put into Raphael's mouth eulogy of Morton, with an
account of discourse at his table which set forth some of those
social miseries, the amending of which would better become a
prince than foreign war. Some one at Morton's table praised
the strict execution of justice which showed felons hanging
usually by twenty at a time upon one gallows. Hythloday said
he argued that death was too great a penalty for theft. Those
cannot be kept from stealing who have no other way whereby
to live. "Therefore in this point not you only, but also the
most part of the world, be like evil schoolmasters, which be
readier to beat than to teach their scholars." There were
the broken soldiers who came from the wars maimed and
lame. There were the crowds of idle retainers nourished
in the households of great men, these were thrust out of doors,
capable of nothing, when their masters died, or they fell
sick. In France there was what More thought the worse
plague of a standing army, then a new invention, for which
war must be found "to the end they may ever have practised soldiers and cunning man-slayers." A thousand times
more regard ought to be had, said Hythloday, to needs of peace
than to the needs of war. Then there was the destruction of
tillage and increase of pastures for the sheep of the rich abbots.
"They inclose all into pastures; they throw down houses, they
pluck down towns, and leave nothing standing but only the
church to be made a sheep-house." Thus husbandmen were
thrust out of their own; thus victual had grown dear. Many
were forced into idleness, yet the sheep suffered from murrain,
and the price of wool had risen. " Let not so many be brought
up in idleness ; let husbandry and tillage be restored ; let cloth-
working be renewed, that there may be honest labours for this
idle sort to pass their time in profitably, which hitherto either
poverty hath caused to be thieves, or else now be either vagabonds or idle serving men, and shortly will be thieves. For by
suffering your youth wantonly and viciously to be brought up,
and to be infected even from their tender age by little and little
with vice, then a' God's name to be punished when they commit

the same faults after being come to man's estate, which from their youth they were ever like to do,—in this point, I pray you, what other thing do you than make thieves and then punish them?" Such passages indicate the spirit and the purpose of the book concerning which Erasmus wrote to a friend, in 1517, that he should send for More's "Utopia" if he had not read it, and "wished to see the true source of all political evils." And to More Erasmus wrote of his book, "A burgomaster of Antwerp is so pleased with it he knows it all by heart." When Raphael Hythloday's talk in the garden had excited curiosity by its frequent reference to the way things were done in Utopia, he was persuaded to give an account of that wonderful island. His description forms the second part of the little book. It is designedly fantastic in suggestion of details, the work of a scholar who had read Plato's "Republic" and had his fancy quickened after reading Plutarch's account of Spartan life under Lycurgus. But never was there in any old English version of "The Governail of Princes" (ch. iv. § 43) a more direct upholding of the duty of a king in his relation to the country governed than in Thomas More's "Utopia." Beneath the veil of an ideal communism, into which there has been worked some witty extravagance, there lies a noble English argument. Sometimes More puts the case as of France when he means England. Sometimes there is ironical praise of the good faith of Christian kings, saving the book from censure as a political attack upon the policy of Henry VIII. Thus protected, More could declare boldly that it were best for the king "to content himself with his own kingdom, to make much of it, to enrich it, and to make it as flourishing as he could, to endeavour himself to love his subjects, and again to be beloved by them, willingly to live with them, peaceably to govern them, and with other kingdoms not to meddle, seeing that which he hath already is even enough for him, yea, and more than he can well turn him to." But Hythloday added, "'This mine advice, Master More, how think you it would be heard and taken?' 'So, God help me, not very thankfully, quod I.'" The prince's office, in More's "Utopia," "continueth all his lifetime, unless he be deposed or put down for suspicion of tyranny." In the chapter on the Religions in Utopia, More wrote of King Utopus, who conquered the country because it was distracted with quarrels about religion, that "first of all he made a decree that it should be lawful for every man to favour and follow what religion he would, and that he might do the best he could to bring other to his opinion, so that he did it peaceably, gently, quietly, and soberly, without hasty and contentious rebuking and inveighing against each other. If he could not by fair and gentle speech induce them unto his opinion, yet he should use no kind of violence, and refrain from displeasant and seditious words. To him that would vehemently and fervently in this cause strive and contend was decreed banishment and bondage. This law did King Utopus make, not only for the maintenance of peace, which he saw through continual contention and mortal hatred utterly extinguished, but also because he thought this decree would work for the furtherance of religion."

16. More wrote when the days were at hand that would have yielded many bondsmen had Utopus given laws to Europe. The invention of printing had caused a wide *DIFFUSION OF THE BIBLE* in the received Latin version, known as the Vulgate. Eighty editions of it were printed between the years 1462 and 1500. The new impulse given to scholarship was felt by the great scholars of the Church. In 1502, Ximenez, then Primate of Spain and founder of the University of Alcala, projected an edition of the Scriptures known from Complutum, the Latin name of Alcala, its place of publication, as the *Complutensian Polyglot.* He proposed to correct the received version of the books of the Old Testament by the Hebrew text, and those of the New Testament by the Greek text. " Every theologian," he said, " should also be able to drink of that water which springeth up to eternal life at the fountain-head itself. This is the reason why we have ordered the Bible to be printed in the original language with different translations. . . . To accomplish this task we have been obliged to have recourse to the knowledge of the most able philologists, and to make researches in every direction for the best and most ancient Hebrew and Greek manuscripts. Our object is to revive the hitherto dormant study of the Sacred Scriptures." This work was prepared at the university of Alcala by some of the best scholars of Spain, who worked under his direction, and were maintained by his liberality. Leo X. became pope in March, 1513, and the printing of the first part of the Polyglot (dedicated to him), the New Testament, was completed in folio in January, 1514. There were letters and prefaces of St. Jerome and others ; there was a short Greek grammar on a single leaf, and there was a short lexicon : but although money had lavishly been spent in procuring manuscripts for the

I *

determination of the text, there was no description of them, there were no specific references to their authority, no various readings.   In the whole of the New Testament folio there were only four critical remarks upon the text.   The second of the six folio volumes was ready in May, 1514, and served as an Introduction to the Old Testament, containing a Hebrew-Chaldee lexicon, a Hebrew grammar, and other aids.   The other four volumes gave the books of the Old Testament in five forms, the Septuagint, the Vulgate, the Hebrew, the Chaldee text, or Targum of Onkelos, and a Latin version of the Targum. The publication was completed in July, 1517, only four months before the death of its promoter.   The pope's permission for the publication of the work did not appear till March, 1520, and another year elapsed before any one of the six hundred copies printed was allowed to pass the Spanish frontier.

The year of the publication of Utopia, 1516, was also the year in which *Erasmus* turned study of Greek to account by publishing his *New Testament* with the Greek text revised from collation of MSS., a Latin version, which corrected mistranslations in the Vulgate, and appended notes to explain changes of reading.   In the Introduction to this work Erasmus said that the Scriptures addressed all, adapted themselves even to the understanding of children, and that it were well if they could be read by all people in all languages ; that none could reasonably be cut off from a blessing as much meant for all as baptism and the other sacraments.   The common mechanic is a true theologian when his hopes look heavenward, he blesses those who curse him, loves the good, is patient with the evil, comforts the mourner, and sees death only as the passage to immortal life.   If princes practised this religion, if priests taught it instead of their stock erudition out of Aristotle and Averroes, there would be fewer wars among the nations of Christendom, less private wrath and litigation, less worship of wealth.   " Christ," added Erasmus, " says, He who loves me, keeps my commandments.   If we be true Christians, and really believe that Christ can give us more than the philosophers and kings can give, we cannot become too familiar with the New Testament."   This new edition of it was received with interest by many who soon afterwards were in strong opposition to the claims of the reformers.   It was revised, and several times reprinted, while Erasmus followed up his work by the issue of Latin *Paraphrases* of the books of the New Testament, which expanded here and there for the sake of interpretation, and put into a fresh and flowing Latin style, the sense of the text, so as to bring it home at once to the less learned, and even to the learned give sometimes a livelier perception of its meaning. The first Paraphrase was of the Epistle to the Romans, and was first published in 1518. In 1519 followed the Epistle to the Corinthians. The demand for more caused Erasmus to paraphrase other epistles. At the beginning of 1522 appeared his Paraphrase of Matthew's Gospel, dedicated to Charles V. That of John's Gospel followed, with a dedication to Ferdinand I. In 1523 the Paraphrase of Luke's Gospel was published. It . was dedicated to Henry VIII. ; and the Paraphrase of Mark's Gospel, published in 1524, was inscribed to Francis I. In these dedications of the Gospel of Peace to the chief authors of discord there was something akin to the spirit of More's Utopia.

17. It was but a year after the publication of Utopia and of Erasmus's New Testament when, on the 31st of October, 1517, *MARTIN LUTHER* began his career as a reformer by affixing his Ninety-five Theses against Indulgences to the church door at Wittenberg. He was then a pious, preaching monk, a Doctor and Professor of Divinity in the University of Wittenberg, aged thirty-four, desiring to be faithful alike to his Church and to his conscience. Leo X., to meet the expenses of the Roman Court, and for the completion of St. Peter's at Rome, raised money by an indiscriminate sale of indulgences. His commissary, John Tetzel, had told the people that when one dropped a penny into the box for a soul in purgatory, so soon as the money chinked in the chest the soul flew up to heaven. Luther opposed: Tetzel replied. Luther dutifully submitted his propositions to Pope Leo X. The papal legate, Caietan, foiled by Luther's firm placing of Scripture above the pope, when he had thought to bring the poor monk to reason, said, " I will not speak to the beast again ; he has deep eyes, and his head is full of speculation." Leo X. forced Luther into open opposition to the see of Rome by issuing, in November, 1518, a bull declaring the pope's power to issue indulgences which will avail not only the living but also the dead who are in purgatory. Luther still held by his Church, but appealed from the pope to a General Council. Thus the first movements in the public career of Luther corresponded in time with the work of Erasmus upon the New Testament.

When the outcry against Luther became violent, Erasmus

urged moderation ; and, as he said in May, 1519, endeavoured to carry himself as evenly as he could with all parties, that he might more effectually serve the interests of learning and religion.

In June, 1520, Leo X. published a bull formally condemning as heretical forty-one propositions collected from Luther's writings. The pope gave the heretic sixty days within which he was to recant if he would not suffer punishment for heresy. The breach then was complete. Luther denounced "the execrable bull of Antichrist," and wholly separated himself from communion with the Church of Rome. He had denied, he said, Divine Right in the papacy, but now he knew it to be the kingdom of Babylon. In October, 1520, Charles V. was crowned emperor. At the Diet of Worms, held in the beginning of 1521, the pope's bull was about to be confirmed against Luther in his absence, when the Elector of Saxony and other of his friends urged that he should not be condemned unheard. He was summoned, and went boldly, saying that if he knew there were as many devils at Worms as tiles upon the houses, he would go. It is said by a Romanist biographer, Audin, that when, in April 1521, on his way to the Diet of Worms, where he maintained his cause before the assembled cardinals, bishops, and princes of Germany, as the towers of Worms came in sight, Luther stood up in his carriage and first chanted his famous hymn, " Eine feste Burg ist unser Gott " (A mighty stronghold is our God), which Audin called the " Marseillaise of the Reformation."

18. **William Tyndal** was of about Luther's age, born probably in 1484, at Stinchcomb, or North Nibley, Gloucestershire. He was educated at Magdalen Hall, Oxford, graduated at Oxford, was then for some years at Cambridge, and, about 1519, became tutor in the family of a Gloucestershire gentleman, Sir John Walsh, of Little Sodbury. He translated into English the Enchiridion of Erasmus, which argues that Christian life is a warfare against evil, sustained rather by obeying Christ than by faith in scholastic dogmas. As the controvery about Luther gathered strength, Tyndal supported Luther's cause so earnestly that he was cited before the Chancellor of the Diocese of Worcester, and warned. In dispute afterwards with a Worcestershire divine, he said, "If God spare my life, ere many years I will cause a boy that driveth the plough shall know more of the Scriptures than thou dost."

About 1523—the year in which Lord Berners published his

translation of Fioissart's Chronicle—Tyndal came to London, where More's friend, Cuthbert Tunstal, who was at the Diet of Worms in 1521, had been made bishop in October, 1522, and became Keeper of the Privy Seal in the following May. Tyndal failed to obtain, through the good offices of Sir Harry Guilford, one of Sir John Walsh's friends, appoint· ment as one of Tunstal's chaplains ; but he preached some sermons at St. Dunstan's, and was received into the house of Humphrey Monmouth, a rich draper, liberal of mind and purse. There he was for about half a year, and, as Monmouth said afterwards, when in trouble for his own opinions, "he lived like a good priest, as methought. He studied most part of the day and of the night at his book, and he would eat but sodden meat by his good will, nor drink but small beer." Tyndal was a small and thin man, who lived sparely and studied without stint. He must have been already at work in Monmouth's house on his *translation of the New Testament* from Greek into English. Finding, as he said afterwards of himself, " not only that there was no room in my Lord of London's palace to translate the New Testament, but also that there was no place to do it in all England," Tyndal left England for Hamburg, where he increased his knowledge of Hebrew. He was skilled in Hebrew, Greek, and Latin, in Italian, Spanish, French, and German. Although no copies of such an edition are now extant, there is reason to believe that Tyndal at once printed, somewhere on the Continent, his translation into English of two of the Gospels, those of Matthew and Mark. He then, in 1525, secretly printed, beginning to print at Cologne and finishing at Worms, 3,000 copies of his translation of the New Testament into English, in a quarto edition, of which only one fragment remains. There was added to it immediately a second edition of 3,000 copies in octavo, printed at Worms. This was three years after Luther's publication, in September, 1522, of his translation of the New Testament into German.

19. Edicts against the issue of his New Testament caused Luther to write a treatise on "The Secular Power," in which he held that princes were usually paltry fools, ordained only to serve God as a dignified sort of executioners for punishment of the wicked, and not even themselves carrying their artifice so far as to pretend to be good shepherds of the flock. But **Henry VIII.** did so pretend. He had written against Luther, whom he styled " the arch-heretic," a Latin treatise on *The Seven Sacraments*

published in London in 1521, and at Antwerp in 1522, for which Pope Leo X. conferred on Henry the title of "Defender of the Faith," which was confirmed to him by Leo's successor. In 1523 Luther was in full activity, and two of his followers were burnt at Brussels. In October, 1524, Luther abandoned the monastic habit; and in 1525, while Tyndal was printing his New Testament, Luther, aged forty-two, married Catherine Bora, who had been a nun.

20. Tyndal was aided in his work by **William Roy,** a Minorite Friar educated at Cambridge, whose help he needed but whom he did not like; for he described him as "a man somewhat crafty when he cometh unto new acquaintance and before he be thorough known." Tyndal adds concerning Roy that "as long as he had gotten no money, somewhat I could rule him; but as soon as he had gotten him money he became like himself again. Nevertheless, I suffered all things till that was ended which I could not do alone without one both to write and to help me to compare the texts together. When that was ended I took my leave, and bade him farewell for our two lives and, as men say, a day longer." The same William Roy, aided by Jerome Barlowe, another Minorite, published at Strasburg, in 1528, a satire in verse known as *The Burying of the Mass,* with "Rede me and be not wroth" for the first words upon its titlepage, and a woodcut of a satirical shield of arms with two fiends as supporters, for Wolsey, who is styled "the vile butcher's son" and "the proud cardinal." It contains axes to signify cruelty, bulls' heads for sturdy furiousness, a club for tyranny, and in the centre a figure described as

"The mastiff cur bred in Ipswich town
Gnawing with his teeth a kingës crown."

The arms have this couplet above them, signifying Wolsey's pride :

"I will ascend, making my state so high
That my pompous honour shall never die;"

and these below :

"O caitiff, when thou thinkest least of all,
With confusion thou shalt have a fall."

This was in 1528, when Wolsey felt so strong in his supremacy that he could venture, without the king's knowledge, to order heralds to declare war against Spain. His fall was in October, 1529.

21 Meanwhile, copies of Tyndal's translation of the New

Testament, printed in 1525 at the cost of English merchants abroad, had, by their agency, reached England in March, 1526. In the same month Henry VIII. received Luther's second letter to His Majesty, written in the preceding September, and printed before it reached the king.  In the autumn of 1526, in a sermon at Paul's Cross by Cuthbert Tunstal, then Bishop of London, Tyndal's New Testament was officially denounced, and copies of it were then publicly burnt.  In December, 1526, appeared in Latin King Henry's answer to Luther, printed with Luther's letter and an address to the pious readei.  At the beginning of 1527 there was published also in English *A Copy of the Letters wherin the most Redoubted and Mighty Prince our Soverayne Lorde Kynge Henry the Eight, Kynge of Englande and of France, Defensor of the Faith, and Lorde o, Ireland, made Answer unto a certayne Letter of Martyn Luther,* &c.  This had a special preface, in which it was said that Luther "fell into device with one or two lewd persons born in this our realm for the translating of the New Testament into English, as well with many corruptions of that holy text, as certain prefaces and pestilent glosses in the margins, for the advancement and setting forth of his abominable heresies ; intending to abuse the good minds and devotion that you our dearly-beloved people bear toward the Holy Sçripture, and to infect you with the deadly corruption and contagious odour of his pestilent errors.  In the avoiding whereof, we, of our especial tender zeal towards you, have, with the deliberate advice of the most reverend father in God, Thomas Lord Cardinal, Legate *de Latere,* of the see apostolic of York Primate, and our Chancellor of this realm, and other reverend fathers of the spiritualty, determined the said and untrue translations to be burned, with further sharp correction and punishment against the keepers and readers of the same ; reckoning of your wisdoms very sure that ye will well and thankfully perceive our tender and loving mind toward you therein, and that ye will never be so greedy upon any sweet wine, be the grape never so pleasant, that ye will desire to taste it, being well advertised that your eremy before hath poisoned it."  In this year 1527, Henry VIII., with his eye upon Anne Boleyn, began questioning the lawfulness of his marriage to Katherine of Aiagon.

22.  Tyndal doubtless referred to Luther's version of the New Testament into German while he was making his own from the Greek.  More than half of Luther's short preface to his New Testament is incorporated in the prologue to the New Testament

of Tyndal, who used also, with a few additions, Luther's marginal references, simply translated some of his glosses, gave the sense of others, and added many of his own. It was asserted, also, by the English bishops that there were 3,000 errors in Tyndal's translation. Warham, Archbishop of Canterbury, bought up all copies that he could find. In March, 1528, **Sir Thomas More** (§ 13) was licensed by his old friend Tunstal to have and read Lutheran books in order that he might confute them, "forasmuch as you, dearly-beloved brother, can play the Demosthenes both in this our English tongue and also in the Latin." More had been made Treasurer of the Exchequer in 1520, had become Sir Thomas in 1521, a month after his appointment as Master of the Requests. In 1523 he was chosen Speaker of the House of Commons, when a Parliament was summoned to raise money for a war with France, and he had then offended Wolsey by opposing an oppressive subsidy. Henry VIII. delighted in his society, and would pay him unceremonious visits in the house at Chelsea to which he had removed from Bucklersbury. "Great honour," said one of his family, "was this to him." "Yes," answered More, "the king is my very good master; but if my head would win His Majesty a castle in France, it would not fail to be struck off my shoulders." In 1527 Tunstal and More were joined with Wolsey in an embassy to France. On their return Wolsey opened a court for the remedy of abusions in the Church. One of the first called before it, in November, 1527, was Thomas Bilney, whom Tunstal persuaded at that time to recant; and he was released after carrying a fagot in procession, and standing bareheaded before a preacher at Paul's Cross. In 1528 the king made More Chancellor of the Duchy of Lancaster. This was his position, and he was forty-eight years old, when he was licensed by Tunstal to read Lutheran books that he might use his skill in argument against them. He produced in the same year, and published in 1529, a *Dialogue* in four books, being in form of the report to a friend of dialogue between himself and a confidential messenger whom the friend had sent to question More upon religious controversies of the day. The discussion was of image-worship, prayer to saints, going on pilgrimages, and other topics to be met with argument against the views of Luther and Tyndal. The new English translation of the Testament More would take as a New Testament only in the sense of its being Tyndal's or Luther's. More illustrated his complaint against the text by citing Tyndal's substitution of the words congregation, elder, favour, knowledge, repentance, for church, priest, grace, confession, and penance. In this Dialogue More maintained that the English ought to have the Bible in their mother tongue; and said that "to keep the whole commodity from any whole people because of harm that by their own folly and fault may come to some part, were as though a lewd (unlearned) surgeon would cut off the leg by the knee to keep the toe from the gout, or cut off a man's head by the shoulders to keep him from the toothache." A trustworthy version might, he thought, be used prudently for distribution by the clergy. More published also, in 1529, a *Supplication of Souls*, in reply to a short invective called "The Supplication of Beggars," written by Simon Fyshe. He answered John Frith's tract on "The Sacrament of the Altar," and remained active in controversy with the Reformers from 1529 until 1533, appealing to the people through the press with tracts designed to meet and confute those of Tyndal and others. Tyndal produced *An Answer unto Sir Thomas More's Dialogue*, written in 1530, and published in the spring of 1531: and in 1532 appeared More's *Confutation* of Tyndal's answer The spirit of Tyndal's argument for the impugned parts of his translation was expressed in his saying that the clergy had led men to "understand by the word church nothing but the shaven flock of them that shore the whole world;" but that it "hath yet, or should have, another signification, little known among the common people nowadays. That is, to wit, it signifieth a congregation; a multitude or a company gathered together in one, of all degrees of people." In short, he avoided words to which a special and, as he thought, false meaning had become attached; and thus incurred strong condemnation as a partisan translator from those who believed such special meanings to be true. More in his rejoinder, and elsewhere in his controversial writing of these years, was at times false to the principles laid down in his Utopia and illustrated by the main course of his life. He was not himself a persecutor, but he was defending his own Church at a time when it believed that thousands might be saved from everlasting fire by terror of the burning of a few. He flinched from the practical enforcement of that doctrine when he himself wielded the terrors of the law. But abroad and at home it was enforced by governments, when, in reply to Tyndal's sentence, "If our shepherds had been as willing to feed as to shear, we had needed no such dispicience, nor they to have burnt so many as they have," More admitted that there would have been less heresy if there had been more diligence in preaching, and said, " Sure if the prelates had taken as good heed in time as they should have done, there should peradventure at length fewer have been burned thereby. But there should have been more burned by a great many than there have been within this seven year last passed ; the lack whereof, I fear me, will make more burned within this seven year next coming than else should have needed to have been burned in seven score." Let us be just to More, without forgetting that he has left this sentence, written in 1532, to be quoted against him. He was then Lord High Chancellor, and while he held that office, from October, 1530, until 1533, although unjustly accused of cruelties, he did support in controversy—and that not in a single passage—the fierce policy of persecution. If he did not himself light martyr fires, he at least publicly assented to the argument by which they were sustained. By zeal for his Church, when days of conflict came, More's calm philosophy was passed as through a furnace, and did not come out unsinged.

23. More was made Chancellor after the fall of Wolsey, whose condemnation by the English people after he became in their eyes an impersonation of ecclesiastical pride was expressed most vigorously in the satire of **John Skelton** (ch. v. § 34). During the earlier part of Henry VIII.'s reign Skelton was in favour with his old pupil. He was rector of Diss, in Norfolk, as early as 1504, and remained so nominally until his death, though he is said to have been suspended from his functions by Dr. Richard Nix, his diocesan, for inclination towards the opinions of the Reformers. The particular offence said to have been charged against John Skelton by the Dominicans was that he had violated the rule of celibacy, by secret marriage to the mother of his children. Among his lesser poems were four against a Sir Christopher Garnesche, gentleman usher to Henry VIII., with whom Skelton had a flyting, after the manner of that between Dunbar and Kennedy in Scotland (§ 3), or that in France of Sagon with Marot. In Wolsey's earlier days, when he was simply a rising churchman (who early in 1514 became Bishop of Lincoln, and before the close of the year Archbishop of York, and who in 1516 began to build for himself at Hampton Court), Skelton was among his friends. So he remained until a short time after Wolsey had been appointed the pope's sole legate *a latere*, in June, 1519. But in that year Warham, Archbishop of Canterbury, complained to the king of Wolsey

as oppressor of the clergy; and in 1522, when the election of Adrian VI. disappointed him of the papacy, Wolsey, who was maintaining war against France without a Parliament, levied a loan of a tenth on lay subjects, and a fourth on the clergy. In 1523, when Wolsey's illegitimate son, Thomas Winter, was made Archdeacon of York, and again Wolsey was disappointed of the papacy by election of Clement VII., Convocation and Parliament both met. From the clergy Wolsey then got a subsidy of half their annual revenue; from the laity he asked four shillings in the pound, and got half that amount. The supreme minister, then rising yearly in power and wealth, was housed luxuriously in his palace at Hampton Court; the English people suffered from his exactions, and he was daily pointed at by Church reformers, who inveighed against the "pomp and pride" of a high clergy, more ready to shear than feed their sheep. Then it was that John Skelton, who felt with the people, poured upon Wolsey from the voice of one the wrath of many. His form of verse was itself popular—earnest, whimsical, with torrents of rhyme added to short lines kindred in accent and alliteration to the old national form of verse. His *Speke Parrot*, in Chaucer's seven-lined stanza, spoke its satire through a medley of apt sayings, jumbled together and pleasantly blended with scraps from the parrot's feast of languages. The parrot appeared frequently as a court bird in the European literature of these times; and although parrots had been brought into Europe by the followers of Alexander the Great, many centuries before, their diffusion in the earlier years of the sixteenth century was due to the followers of Columbus, for it was one of the smaller results of the discovery of the New World. Skelton's Parrot was gaily painted as a ladies' pet, and a philologist who picked up phrases in all tongues, and also, as he said,

> "Such shredis of sentence, strowed in the shop
> Of auncyent Aristippus and such other mo
> I gader togyther and close in my crop."

Whatever else may be obscure in his whimsically disjointed oracles, it is clear that he meant Henry VIII. and Wolsey by the dogs Bo-ho and Hough-ho (Bow-wow and Wow-wow), when he said:

> "Bo-ho doth bark well, but Hough-ho he ruleth the ring;
> From Scarpary to Tartary renown therein doth spring,
> With, He said, and We said, I wot now what I wot
> *Quod magnus est dominus Judas Scariot.*"

Elsewhere Wolsey was he who makes men to jumble, to stumble, to tumble down like fools, to lower, to drop, to kneel, to stoop, and to play couch-quail. " He carrieth a king in his sleeve, if all the world fail." Since Deucalion's flood, spoke the Parrot, there were never seen " so many noble bodies under one daw's head ; so many thieves hanged and thieves never the less ; so much prisonment for matters not worth an haw ; so bold a bragging butcher, and flesh sold so dear ; so many plucked partridges, and so fat quails ; so mangy a mastiff cur the great greyhound's peer ; so fat a maggot bred of a flesh-fly ; was never such a filthy Gorgon, nor such an epicure, since Deucalion's flood I make thee fast and sure."

The same public scorn of Wolsey was poured in Skeltonic rhyme through Skelton's "*Why Come ye Not to Court ?*" All was wrong in the land ; the English nobles were extinguished under the red hat. " Our barons be so bold, into a mouse-hole they would run away and creep, like a mayny of sheep ; dare not look out at door, for dread of the mastiff cur, for dread of the butcher's dog would worry them like an hog." " I pray God save the king," says Skelton, " wherever he go or ride, I pray God be his guide." But " once yet again of you I would frayne (ask), Why come ye not to Court? To which court? To the King's Court, or to Hampton Court ? Nay, to the King's Court : the King's Court should have the excellence. But Hampton Court hath the pre-eminence, and Yorkës Place with my lordës grace, to whose magnificence is all the confluence, suits, and supplications, embassades of all nations. A straw for law, it shall be as he will. He regardeth lordes no more than potshordes ; he is in such elation of his exaltation, and the supportation of our sovereign lord, that, God to record, he ruleth all at will without reason or skill. Howbeit the primordial of his wretched original, and his base progeny, and his greasy genealogy—he came of the sang-royal that was cast out of a butcher's stall." In more than 1,200 of such short lines Skelton's " Why Come ye Not to Court ?" poured out the anger of the people against Wolsey.

> " He maketh so proude pretens
> That in his equipolens
> He jugyth him equivalent
> With God omnipotent :
> But yet beware the rod,
> And the stroke of God."

Skelton felt deeply, or he could not have braved Wolsey in his day of power with so bold a satire. In this poem he painted the condition of the court.

There was yet another piece, his *Colin Clout*, which also denounced Wolsey, but of which the main purpose was to paint the condition of the country. Colin Clout represented in his poem the poor Englishman of the day, rustic or town-bred. The name blends the two forms of life: Colin is from *colonus*, (tiller of the soil), whence clown; Clout, or Patch, sign of a sedentary calling, stands for the town mechanic, such as Bottom the Weaver, and his "crew of patches, base mechanicals." In Skeltonic verses, about equal in number to those of "Why Come ye Not to Court?" Colin Clout uttered his simple thought upon the troubles of the Church, and all the evil that had come of the corruption of the bishops and high churchmen. "That the people talk this, somewhat there is amiss," said Skelton. In this poem the reference to Wolsey was only incidental, and the desire was to sustain the Church by showing what reform of discipline it needed if it was to "let Colin Clout have none manner of cause to moan." While bishops' mules eat gold, "their neighbours die for meat." Heresies multiply.

> " Men hurt their souls.
> Alas, for Goddes will,
> Why sit ye, prelates, still,
> And suffer all this ill?
> Ye bishops of estates
> Should open the broad gate:
> Of your spiritual charge,
> And come forth at large,
> Like lanterns of light,
> In the people's sight,
> In pulpits awtentyke
> For the weal publyke
> Of priesthood in this case."

Colin Clout closed his rhyming with a prayer to Christ:

> " Such grace that He us send
> To rectify and amend
> Things that are amiss
> When that His pleasure is. Amen."

Among Skelton's other poems two have yet to be named. One of these was a coarse humorous piece upon the Brewing or *Tunning of Elynour Rummyng*, who kept an ale-house on a hill by Leatherhead, and became known to the courtiers of Henry VIII. when the court was at Nonsuch, about six miles off. The other poem was a Morality Play called *Magnificence*.

Skelton died in June, 1529, before the fall of Wolsey, sheltered from his wrath by the sanctuary of Westminster, where he was befriended by John Islip, the Abbot. The old privileges of sanctuary were abridged in the latter years of Henry VIII.'s reign, and abolished in the last year of the reign of James I.

24. The **Morality Play** does not represent a transition from the miracle-play to the true drama, but was simply one of the forms taken by that allegorical literature (ch. iii. § 7 ; ch. iv § 9, 16, 27 ; ch. vi. § 2) which had its narrative form in poems like the " Bowge of Court " (§ 5), or the " Pastime of Pleasure " (§ 7). Miracle-plays (ch. iii. § 9 ; ch. iv. § 5) remained miracle-plays, and were still being acted. These allegorical plays were also written to be acted. There the resemblance ends, except as to that earnestness of purpose which they have in common with most forms of English Literature. There were no morality-plays before the reign of Henry VI., and they did not become widely popular until their personification of the virtues and vices in action could be used for an appeal to the people on great public questions in debate among them. They had a use of their own when, north and south, in the days of Henry VIII., they were planned by men who sought the reformation of abuses ; they helped them to express or form opinions of the people. The best examples of this kind of literature belong, therefore, to the reign of Henry VIII. They are the " Magnificence" of Skelton, and Sir David Lindsay's " Satire of the Three Estates," written in Scotland about six years later. Of these two, Lindsay's work is the more important, and will presently be dwelt upon. Skelton's *Magnificence*, in verse humorous and earnest, showed how Felicity argued with Liberty, who was over-impatient of restraint ; how Measure entering, set forth that " Liberty without Measure proveth a thing of nought ;" how wealthful Felicity and Liberty allowed Measure to guide them, and resolved that—

> " There is no prince but he hath need of us three—
> Wealth, with Measure and pleasant Liberty."

Magnificence then entered, and took them discreetly for companions, but was presently beguiled by the vice Fancy, and practised upon by Fancy himself, under the name of the virtue Largeness, and by the vices Counterfeit Countenance, Crafty Conveyance, Cloked Collusion, Courtly Abusion, and Folly, under the names of Good Demeanaunce, Surveyance, Sober Sadness (Seriousness), Pleasure, and Conceit. They separated

Magnificence from Measure, Liberty, and Felicity, then left him to be beaten down by the blows of Adversity. He was next visited by Poverty, mocked by the vices that betrayed him, and left to give entrance to Despair. Upon Despair followed Mischief, and fallen Magnificence was about to slay himself, when Good Hope entering put to flight those tempters, arrested the sword, and told the sufferer that his physician is the Grace of God. Then came Redress and Sad Circumspection; and finally, by help of Perseverance, he rose to a higher than his old estate, after he had been taught—

> " How suddenly worldly wealth doth decay;
> How wisdom, through wantonness, vanisheth away;
> How none estate living of himself can be sure,
> For the wealth of this world cannot endure."

25. Wolsey, in June, 1529, when Skelton died, was near his fall. It was the month in which Queen Katherine was called before that legatine court of Cardinals Wolsey and Campeggio, which, at the end of July, thwarted the king's impatience by declaring that no judgment of divorce could be pronounced until the pope's assent had been received. On the 17th of the following October Wolsey was deprived of his office of Chancellor, stripped of his wealth, and ruined utterly. He died next year.

**George Cavendish,** who had entered Wolsey's service as a gentleman usher about the year 1519, and had been faithfully attached to him during the last ten years of his life, spoke with the king immediately after Wolsey's death. He was invited into Henry's service, but presently retired to his own little estate in Suffolk, with the wages due from the cardinal, a small gratuity, and six of the cardinal's best cart-horses to convey his furniture. Cavendish wrote, about the year 1554, an interesting *Life of Wolsey*. It was used as a source of information by the chroniclers whom Shakespeare read, but was not itself printed until 1661, a hundred years after its author's death.

**Thomas Cranmer** was, at the time of the fall of Wolsey, forty years old, Doctor of Divinity, Archdeacon of Taunton, a Theological Examiner at Cambridge, and a known expert in Canon Law. There being plague at Cambridge in August, 1529, Dr. Cranmer was then staying with two pupils at the house of their father, Mr. Cressy, at Waltham, in Essex. The king happening to come to Waltham, his almoner and secretary, Edward Fox and Stephen Gardiner, who had been to Rome upon the matter of the king's divorce, were lodged with Mr. Cressy. At supper Dr. Cranmer argued that if the king's marriage was null by any Divine law, the pope could not uphold it, since he could not cancel any law of God. The question might, therefore, be settled on its own merits by learned men. Report made to the king of this opinion of Cranmer's caused him to be sent for, and in or before February, 1530, Dr. Cranmer published in support of his argument a treatise, of which no copy remains. The king at the same time made this new ally one of his chaplains, and gave him a benefice. At the end of 1530 Cranmer went to Rome with Sir Thomas Boleyn (become Earl of Wiltshire and Ormond) and with others. There his book was presented to the pope, and he undertook to dispute openly against King Henry's marriage with Queen Katherine. He returned to England in 1531, and was much with the king at Hampton Court. In August of that year Thomas Bilney, who, being resolved to recant his recantation, had preached publicly in Norfolk, was, on the writ of Dr. Nix, the bishop of the diocese, burnt for his faith at Norwich. Dr. Nix was a man eighty years old, infirm and blind. At this time one Richard Byfield, who had been Chamberlain of the Benedictine Monastery of Bury St. Edmunds, was engaged in the introduction of the numerous Reformation tracts issued by Tyndal and others in Latin and English. He had landed a supply at Colchester, in Midsummer, 1530 ; a second supply at St. Catherine's, in November, 1530, which was seized ; a third supply he brought to London in the spring of 1531 ; but in the beginning of November, 1531, he was arrested, and before the end of the month burnt.

Among the Reformation tracts brought into England in the year 1530 was a little book of Tyndal's on the question of the king's divorce. It was called *The Practice of Prelates; whether the King's Grace may be Separated from his Queen because she was his Brother's Wife.* Ascribing to Wolsey's ambition the sufferings of the people and the scheme for the king's separation from his wife, it declared the scheme to be without warrant from Scripture, and one against which the most glorious king might be warned by one, however mean, who spoke with the authority of God's word, which is "the chiefest of the Apostles, and Pope, and Christ's Vicar, and Head of the Church, and the Head of the General Council."

26. Tyndal issued this tract from Marburg, in Hesse, where, in the same year, 1530, on the 17th of January, he finished

printing his *Translation of the Pentateuch*. He had completed this with the help of **Miles Coverdale**, a Yorkshireman, then forty-three years old, who had been an Austin Friar at Cambridge. The prior of Coverdale's house was Dr. Robert Barnes, a good scholar, who had cultivated scholarship in those about him, reading Plautus, Terence, and Cicero, lecturing upon St. Paul's Epistles, and encouraging discussions upon Scripture. Dr. Barnes had become a leader in arguments of Reformation held by Cambridge men of different colleges at a house called the "White Horse." Compelled by Wolsey, Barnes recanted; but being a second time in extreme peril, he escaped to Germany, where he found friends in the Lutheran chiefs. While resident at Wittenberg he was employed in several negotiations. His friend Coverdale also escaped to the Continent, where he joined Tyndal in his work as a translator of the Scriptures.

In January, 1532, Henry VIII.'s new favourite, Cranmer, was sent as king's orator to the Imperial Court. He was six months at Nuremberg associated with the English ambassador, **Sir Thomas Elyot**, who had it among his instructions to seek the arrest of Tyndal. This Thomas Elyot, a Suffolk man, whom Henry VIII. had knighted, was a writer of mark. In the preceding year, 1531, his chief book, named *The Governor*, had been published—a prose treatise on education, generous and wise in its tone, which opposed the custom of ill-treating schoolboys. He also translated Plutarch's treatise upon Education, and other moral and thoughtful pieces from the Greek, published in 1533 *The Castle of Health*, and in 1538 produced the first *Latin and English Dictionary* published in England. Elyot died in 1546, having published in the preceding year a *Defence or Apology of Good Women*. We return to the time of his embassy to the Emperor, in 1532. On the 22nd of August in that year Warham, Archbishop of Canterbury, died. Then Cranmer was summoned home to be his successor. King Henry had been privately married to Anne Boleyn when Cranmer was installed in his archbishopric, the last Archbishop of Canterbury who took the oath of obedience to the see of Rome. He took this oath on the 30th of March, 1533, after a protestation that it did not bind him to do anything contrary to the laws of God, the king's prerogative, or the commonwealth and statutes of the kingdom. Anne Boleyn's daughter Elizabeth, afterwards Queen Elizabeth, was born on the 7th of September in the same year, 1533.

**John Bourchier, Lord Berners,** the translator of Froissart into some of the best prose English of his time, died in 1532, at the age of sixty-five. He was born at Therfield, in Hertfordshire, was educated at Oxford, travelled abroad, distinguished himself in the king's service when there was insurrection in Devonshire, earned the favour of Henry VII., and was made by Henry VIII. his Chancellor of Exchequer for life. He was lieutenant of Calais and the Marches when he died at Calais, in 1532. He translated Froissart's Chronicle (published by Pynson, in 1523), the "Golden Book" of Marcus Aurelius, and other works, wrote also a Latin sacred play, *Ite in Vineam Meam,* which was acted in church at Calais after vespers.

For some time **Tyndal** was effectually shielded from designs against him by the English Government. His best friends abroad were members of the English Company of Merchant Adventurers. These also supplied money wherewith to keep the press at work. In 1535 Tyndal was living with Thomas Poyntz, an English merchant, at Antwerp, when he was arrested while his watchful host was gone to a great annual fair. After long detention in the Castle of Vilvorde, he was condemned by the Privy Council of Brussels, under a decree against heresy which had been issued in 1530, on the Emperor's authority. Tyndal was strangled and burnt at Vilvorde, on the 6th of October, 1536, and his last words were, "Lord, open the King of England's eyes."

27. While Tyndal was in his prison at Vilvorde, the King of England had been active at home. Fisher, More, and Anne Boleyn were during that time condemned and executed. Cranmer, when made archbishop, had held an ecclesiastical court at Dunstable, and in May, 1533, pronounced sentence of divorce between King Henry and Queen Katherine, whose daughter Mary was then seventeen years old. The pope by a brief declared this divorce to be illegal. Katherine went to Kimbolton, and claimed still to be a queen. The stately coronation of Anne Boleyn followed; then in September the birth of her daughter Elizabeth. Parliament had passed, in the same year 1533, an Act against appeals to Rome, asserting the king's supremacy within his realm. Another statute declared it to be no heresy to speak against the pope; but as to other points heretics had their judges at home, and upon lawful conviction and refusal to abjure, or relapse after abjuration, they were to be "committed to lay power to be burned in open places, for example of other, as hath been

accustomed." Cranmer took part in the examination of John
Frith, and assented to the sentence by which he was burnt in
Smithfield, in July, 1533, together with Andrew Hewit, a tailor's
apprentice. The learned **John Fisher** (ch. v. § 35, ch. vi. § 9),
Bishop of Rochester since 1504, had used earlier than More his
skill in controversial tracts against the Lutherans. A sermon of
his "against the pernicious doctrine of Martin Luther" had been
printed by Wynken de Worde, in 1521. A sickly servant-girl,
named Elizabeth Barton, had lived at Aldington, within twenty
miles of Rochester, and claimed prophetic powers. They were
used and, it may well be, sometimes prompted, against en-
croachers on the pope's authority. She became a nun in
Canterbury, was known as the Holy Maid of Kent, and was
much quoted without serious hurt to herself, until she began to
prophesy against the king's divorce. She was then joined with
others in a charge of treasonous conspiracy, and she was executed with five monks at Tyburn, in April, 1534. The Bishop
of Rochester, who had spoken with her, was attainted for misprision of treason. He was sentenced to forfeiture of his goods,
and imprisonment for life. Meanwhile, an Act had been passed
"for the establishment of the king's succession," which declared the first marriage "unlawful and void;" the second
marriage "undoubtful, true, sincere, and perfect," and its
children heirs to the crown. To write or print an opposite
opinion was declared to be high treason, and to say otherwise
by word of mouth was misprision of treason. All nobles of the
realm, temporal and spiritual, were by the same Act required,
when called upon, to take oath that they would maintain and
defend it. Incidentally this Act included in its preamble a
renunciation of the pope's authority in England. John Fisher
and **Sir Thomas More** were called upon to take the oath, and
after their refusal to swear assent to the preamble of the Act,
though they were ready to accept its substance, and swear fealty
to the succession it established, they were committed to the
Tower.

An Act of the Parliament which met in November, 1534, made
Henry VIII. absolute master of the Church of England, with
"authority to reform and redress all errors, heresies, and abuses
in the same." In 1535, on the 22nd of June, John Fisher, then
seventy-six years old, was beheaded on Tower Hill. A fortnight
afterwards, on the 6th of July, followed the execution of Sir
Thomas More. In the same summer there was commenced a

visitation of the monasteries. It was followed by an Act, passed in March, 1536, which dissolved and confiscated to the king religious houses of less value than two hundred pounds. The members of these monasteries were to be removed into the larger houses. On the 19th of May, 1536, Anne Boleyn was executed upon Tower Hill, and on the 20th Henry was married to Jane Seymour. Queen Katherine had died on the preceding New-year's day. Her daughter Mary, who had held by her mother, made submission to her father in all things after the execution of Anne Boleyn, and was restored to favour.

28. At this time **Hugh Latimer,** aged about forty-five, was newly-made Bishop of Worcester. He was born about 1491, and was the only son among seven children of Hugh Latimer, a yeoman, who rented a farm at Thurcaston, in Leicestershire. When fourteen years old, he went to Clare Hall, Cambridge, obtained a fellowship of his college while yet undergraduate, took his degrees of Bachelor of Arts and Master of Arts in 1510 and 1514, and at the age of about twenty-four was ordained priest at Lincoln. At the age of thirty he graduated Bachelor in Divinity, and his speech on the occasion was against opinions of Melancthon, for he was then active in argument against those who opposed the pope's authority. Bilney, being among those who heard the speech, went to Latimer's rooms afterwards and argued with him. To the influence of Bilney Latimer in later years ascribed his great change of opinion. This change soon caused him to be summoned before Wolsey on a charge of heresy; but he was then content to subscribe such articles as were proposed to him. Latimer's opposition to the pope, which involved support of the king's supremacy, was made known to Henry VIII. by his physician, Dr. Butts, and in March, 1530, Latimer was called to preach before the king at Windsor. Henry then made Latimer his chaplain; and, not offended by his letter written in December, "for restoring again the liberty of reading the Holy Scriptures," in the following year, 1531, he gave Latimer, at the suggestion of Dr. Butts, the rectory of West Kington, in Wiltshire. The new rector's preaching was soon declared to be heretical; he was summoned before Stokesley, Bishop of London, and afterwards before Convocation. He was excommunicated and imprisoned, but made his submission, and by special request of the king went home absolved. A year afterwards, Cranmer became archbishop, and was Latimer's friend. In 1534,

Latimer preached before Henry VIII. on Wednesdays in Lent ; and in the autumn of 1535, when, by Act of Parliament, an Italian, who was non-resident, had been deprived of the bishopric of Worcester, Hugh Latimer was elected in his place.

29. At this time **Miles Coverdale** (§ 26) was printing at Zurich a complete translation of the Bible into English. At the close of 1534 the English clergy had carried in Convocation against a strong party headed by Stephen Gardiner, Bishop of Winchester, a petition to the king for a translation of the Scriptures into English. Thomas Cromwell, the fuller's son, who had once been clerk in the factory of English merchants at Antwerp, and is said in his earlier days to have learnt by heart Erasmus's translation of the New Testament during a journey to and from Rome, had passed from Wolsey's service into that of King Henry. He became, in 1534, Secretary of State, and actively supporting the vote of Convocation, was in search of an English Bible which might go among the people and escape the charge of containing heresies. Coverdale's translation was submitted to the English bishops, who said that it had many faults. "But," said the king, "are there any heresies maintained thereby ?" And when they said that they had found none, he answered, "Then, in God's name, let it go among the people." The royal licence was obtained, but the introduction of Coverdale's translation, printed in 1535, was delayed by the necessity of striking out the name of the king's "most dearest, just wife, Anne," which stood with his own in the dedication. The first printed copies of the whole Bible were admitted into England in 1536, the year of the burning of Tyndal, the year also in which Tyndal's New Testament was first printed in England. Coverdale's translation was described on the title-page as having been made from the German and Latin—"faithfully and truly translated out of Douche and Latin into English." He said that he had five several translations by him, and followed his interpreters. A new edition, revised and corrected, appeared in 1537, printed in England. In July of the same year, 1537, there was published abroad a complete Bible in folio, professing to be "truly and purely translated into English by Thomas Matthew." This was formed out of the translations of Tyndal and Coverdale, under the superintendence of **John Rogers,** who assumed the name of Matthew. He was the son of a John Rogers, of Deritend, in Birmingham, was born there about 1509, educated at Pembroke Hall, took his

B.A. in 1526, and afterwards became chaplain to the English merchants at Antwerp, where Tyndal and Coverdale found in him a friend and ally. His Bible, known as *Matthew's Bible*, included all that had been done by Tyndal, namely his Pentateuch followed by other translations of his down to the end of the second book of Chronicles, and his New Testament. The other canonical books Rogers gave in a strict revision of Coverdale's translation, and the Apocrypha he gave in a translation of his own. Having issued his Bible, Rogers married in the same year, and went to Wittenberg, where he was minister of a congregation during the rest of the reign of Henry VIII. In 1538 Thomas Cromwell had become Lord Cromwell of Oakham, Lord Privy Seal, and the king's vicegerent in all causes touching ecclesiastical jurisdiction and the godly reformation of heresies and abuses in the Church. By virtue of this office he sat in Convocation above the archbishops. Since Henry agreed that diffusion of an English Bible was good policy against the pope, Cromwell, in 1538, was planning a re-publication at Paris of Tyndal's translation in a form that would adapt it for free use. Miles Coverdale had looked to Thomas Cromwell as his friend and patron even when Cromwell was Wolsey's retainer. In February and March, 1538, he was in Berkshire, officially examining church service books to see that the pope's name had been duly erased from their pages. He was then sent by Cromwell to Paris, where he was to superintend the printing of the Bible known as Cromwell's, and there he was in some peril from the Inquisition; the printing begun at Paris was therefore finished in London. Cromwell also employed **Richard Taverner**, an Oxford Reformer who was then attached to the court, on a careful revision of Matthew's Bible. *Taverner's Bible* was published in folio in 1539, with a dedication to the king; and in April of the same year, 1539, appeared Coverdale's revision of Tyndal's work and his own, in the folio known as *Cromwell's (or the Great) Bible*. Cromwell then was Lord Great Chamberlain, and he, in the following year, 1540, was made Earl of Essex, when there appeared the most authoritative of the versions made in Henry VIII.'s reign. It was a revision of Tyndal, planned by Cranmer as Archbishop of Canterbury, and made by direct collation with the Hebrew and Greek texts. It was first published in April, 1540, with a prologue by Cranmer, and is known as *Cranmer's Bible*. This became, and remained till 1568, the translation appointed to be read in churches. Its version of the Psalms is retained to this day by the Church of England in its Book of Common Prayer.

But heresy, especially that of the Sacramentarians, who denied real presence in the Eucharist, was still being attacked with fire and fagot. John Nicholson, known as Lambert, was publicly argued with by the king himself and bishops in Westminster Hall, silenced, and burnt. Cromwell read the sentence. An Observant Friar, named Forest, was burnt alive in an iron cage for denial of the king's ecclesiastical supremacy, after **Hugh Latimer**, Bishop of Worcester (§ 28), had argued with him in vain. The final Act for the Dissolution of Abbeys was passed and enforced in the same year, 1539, in which Cromwell's Bible appeared, and in which also appeared "An Act Abolishing Diversity of Opinions." This law was dictated in person by the king to a "tractable Parliament." It became known as the "Act of the Six Articles," or "Whip with the Six Strings." It declared for transubstantiation, auricular confession, vows of chastity, and private masses, against communion in both kinds, and against marriage of priests. To the king's opinion upon these six points Englishmen were to conform their teaching upon pain of death. Latimer, who could not so teach, resigned his bishopric of Worcester, and was placed in custody of Dr. Sampson, Bishop of Chichester. But in the next year, 1540, Dr. Sampson became himself a prisoner.

The year 1540 was the last year of the life of Thomas Cromwell. Jane Seymour, married in 1536, had died in 1537, soon after giving birth to her son Edward. Henry's next marriage was chiefly forwarded by his friend Thomas Cromwell. It was with Anne of Cleves, whom he found less fascinating in person and character than in her portrait by Holbein. Henry married her in 1540, divorced her in a few months, extended to Thomas Cromwell his disgust at the new wife, and, on a charge of treason and heresy, sent him to execution in July of the same year.

30. During this time **John Leland,** the King's Antiquary, was travelling about England and gathering such information as is left to us in his *Itinerary.* Leland was born in London about 1506. He was one of the boys under William Lily (§ 11) at St. Paul's School. Thence he proceeded to Christ's College, Cambridge. He took his degree of B.A. early in 1522, went then to Oxford, thence to the University of Paris. He became chaplain and librarian to Henry VIII., who gave him, in June, 1530, the rectory of Poppeling, in the Marches of Calais. About 1533

he obtained the title of King's Antiquary; three years later he had special licence to keep a curate at Poppeling, and work in England. Then he was for six years, by royal commission, travelling over England, taking a particular account of the cities, towns, and villages of each county; describing also the situation, soil, course of the rivers, and number of miles from place to place. He set down the several castles, religious houses, and other public and private buildings, with account of the families of best note resident therein. He recorded windows and monuments of antiquity belonging to the several cathedrals, monasteries, &c. He inspected also their libraries, took exact catalogues of books, even made transcripts of matter useful to his purpose of setting forth a trustworthy account of the history and antiquities of the kingdom. Leland, although a Church reformer, lamented the havoc made of valuable libraries at the dissolution of the monasteries, and he did what he could to bring into safe keeping the treasures of literature that he found. Foreign scholars were eager in search. Leland did what he could for England, and was thus employed in 1540, for that was the fourth of his six years of exploration.

31. We look northward again. Before the voice of Dunbar was silent, Lindsay took up the strain and was free Scotland, canny, humorous, sincere, with a direct earnestness that brings out notes of the deeper poetry of life ; the voice for Scotland of that spirit of reformation which had grown up, as we have seen, among true men of all theological creeds during the fifteenth century, and had been strengthened by all influences of the time. Whatever makes a man most man brings out the voice that reaches far beyond the present. The foundations of Scottish literature were laid by our Edward I., when he forced on the Scotch their war of independence, and so gave to their countrymen a Wallace and a Bruce (ch. iii. § 25 ; ch. iv. § 34); their countrymen and ours, the Lowland Scots, being, in fact, most English of the English. Their country, an old place of refuge for the patriotic fugitives from Norman rule, was little oppressed with castles of early Norman build. The Norman castles of which ruins are now to be found in Scotland show their later date almost invariably by the more ornamented style of Edward I.

**David Lindsay,** born about 1490, was the eldest of five sons. His father, also a David, was son to the second son of a Lord Lindsay of Byres, and inherited a smaller estate in Haddingtonshire, which he left when he bought house and land

known as the Mount, upon Mount Hill, five or six miles to the
north-west of Cupar, county town of Fife. It was after the marriage of the Thistle and the Rose (§ 1) that David Lindsay began
his court life. Prosperous Scotland was then busy in her dock-
yards; and King James IV. achieved the construction of what
passed as a monster vessel, the *Great Michael*, 240 feet long, its
hull cannon-proof because ten feet thick and of solid oak. In 1509,
Henry VII. died, and the new King of England promised to give
more trouble to his neighbour. Young David Lindsay was then
leaving college. He had been sent to school in Cupar, and had
seen sometimes the Mysteries and Moralities there acted upon
ground near the Castle Hill, which is still called the Play Field.
In 1505, the year of the birth of John Knox, Lindsay proceeded
to the University of St. Andrew's, and while he was a student
there, about seventeen years old, the death of his father gave
him the Mount for inheritance. He stayed another two years
at St. Andrew's, and was altogether four years in the University,
under the rectorship of the Reverend David Spens. There was
in his time only one college at St. Andrew's, that of St. Salvador.
St. Leonard's was founded about three years after Lindsay left.
After study of books came, perhaps, study of men by travel; but
Lindsay was soon in service at the Scottish court. When, on
the 12th of April, 1512, the prince who became James V. was
born, on the same day David Lindsay, aged about twenty-two,
was one of those appointed to attend upon him. In the following
year Henry VIII. was going to war with France, and France
knew how to procure again the help of her old Scottish ally.
For love of freedom, because the kings of England sought to
subdue Scotland, Scotland had become the natural ally of France.
Every venture made by England in war of ignoble ambition
against France, brought the Scots over the border to enjoy the
opportunity of England's weakness, and create diversion on
behalf of their ally. Until Henry VII.'s time the policy of our
kings maintained Scotland in a constant league with France,
so close that French words, clipped and nationalised, became
familiar on Scottish lips; and even the national "great chieftain
of the pudding race"—notwithstanding all scornful comparison of
it with French *ragoûts*—the haggis, was given to Scotland by the
French allies. Its name is the French *hachis*. Following the
old usage, in 1513, King James IV. resolved, in aid of France,
to invade England. Having come, on his way, to Linlithgow,
with Lindsay in attendance on him, he was there sadly praying

for success in his adventure, when a man in a blue gown, bare-headed, and apparently fifty years old, came rapidly forward among the lords to the desk where the king was at his prayers. There, without homage or salutation, he leaned on the desk and said, "Sir king, my mother has sent me to thee, desiring thee not to go where thou art purposed, which if thou do thou shalt not fare well in thy journey, nor none that is with thee. Further, she forbade thee to mell nor use the counsel of women, which if thou do thou wilt be confounded and brought to shame." Even-song was then near done; the king paused as if to answer, but in the meantime, before the king's eyes and in the presence of all, this man vanished away and could be no more seen. "I heard," says Lindsay of Pitscotie, who tells the tale, a tale which Buchanan records upon Sir David Lindsay's personal testimony; "I heard Sir David Lindsay, lion herald, and John Inglis, the marshal, who were at that time young men and special servants to the king's grace, thought to have taken this man but they could not, that they might have speired further tidings at him, but they could not touch him." In August, 1513, King James, at the head of an army, entered England; on the 9th of September he was one of the ten thousand dead Scots upon whom the night fell over Flodden Field.

Lindsay's young prince, aged one, became King James V.—Stuart the seventh. The child's mother, Henry VIII.'s sister, aged but twenty-four, was made Regent and, being a Tudor, lost no time in marrying again. She gave birth to a posthumous child in the following April; and four months after that, since she might not leave Scotland, became wife to the handsome young Archibald, Earl of Angus, grandson to the Earl of Angus known as "Bell the Cat," and nephew to Gavin Douglas, the poet. At a later date Lindsay reminds King James of state service rendered to him at the beginning of his reign :

> "How as ane chapman beris his pack
> I bure thy grace upon my back,
> And sumtymes stridlingis on my nek,
> Dansand with money bend and bek :
> The first sillabis that thou did mute
> Was 'Pa—Da—Lyn.' Upon the lute
> Then playit I twenty springis perqueir (*Aar cœur*)
> Quhilk was great plesour for to heir
> Fra play thou leit me never rest,
> But 'Gynkertoun' thou luffit ay best;
> And ay, quhen thow come fra the scuel
> Then I behaffit to play the fule."

32. **Gavin Douglas** (§ 4), rector of Hawick, who had become provost of the church of St. Giles in Edinburgh, finished in July, 1513, about two months before the disaster at Flodden, a complete *Translation of the Æneid* into heroic couplet. This is our earliest translation of the "Æneid," or of any Latin classic, into verse. It gave all the twelve books of Virgil, and joined to them a version of the supplementary thirteenth book added by Maphæus Vegius, a pious and clever author, native of Lodi, who died a canon of St. Peter's at Rome, in 1458. Gavin Douglas showed himself a poet with fresh energy, not only in his translation, which has the strength of simplicity, but also in original prologues that introduce the several books. He was ready also, even out of season, to mind his office as a clergyman, as when he translated the sybil into a nun who advised Æneas, the Trojan baron, to persevere in counting his beads. Two months after this work was finished, the poet lost his two elder brothers at Flodden; his father died within twelve months afterwards of grief at their loss. The title and estates descended to the old earl's grandson, Gavin Douglas's nephew, that Archibald whom the widowed queen married within the year of her mourning. The Archbishop of St. Andrew's (a natural son of the late king's) also fell at Flodden, and Queen Margaret nominated Gavin Douglas to the primacy. He took possession of the archbishop's palace, and was besieged in it by one of the other claimants; but a third claimant obtained the pope's grant of the see, and Douglas yielded. The remaining disputants opposed armed followings to one another in the cathedral, but came to a compromise. In 1515 the bishopric of Dunkeld became vacant, and queen and pope both nominated Gavin Douglas to the see; but he was accused of procuring bulls from Rome, and was made to feel the authority of his old rival at St. Andrew's, who imprisoned him for about a year. He was released when the Duke of Albany became regent; and he got his bishopric by David Beaton's mediation, although Andrew Steward did hold out against him, and fire on him from palace and cathedral. The new bishop carried his cathedral, like a fort, by force of arms, but without serious bloodshed. In 1521 the strife of parties compelled Gavin Douglas to take refuge in England. He was well received, and pensioned at the court of Henry VIII. In February, 1522, he was in Scotland declared a traitor. The revenues of his see were sequestrated, and the pope was appealed to lest by chance there might be given to Douglas

the Archbishopric of St. Andrew's, then again vacant. James
Beaton (uncle to David) was made Archbishop of St. Andrew's,
and in the same year, 1522, Gavin Douglas died in London of
the plague.

33. William Dunbar, of whose last years nothing is known,
was then living. He died, an old man, before 1530.

**John Mair** (Latinised Major) taught both Knox and
Buchanan. He was a scholastic theologian, born near North
Berwick, in 1469, who went early in his life to Paris, taught
there philosophy and theology ; became in 1506 a doctor of the
Sorbonne ; became in 1519 Professor of Divinity at St. Andrew's,
afterwards went again to Paris, but returned to St. Andrew's,
and there spent the last twenty years of his life. His writings
were in Latin, theological and moral treatises, and a *History of
Great Britain*, in six books, which joined the chronicles of England and Scotland, and was published at Paris in 1521, the year
in which Luther appeared at the Diet of Worms. This book, by
a Scottish Doctor of the Sorbonne, was not sparing in condemnation of the corruptions of the clergy and the usurpations of
the court of Rome. For each period Mair gave first the English history and then the Scottish. For its free speech, Mair's
history was placed by the orthodox abroad below its author's
scholastic writings. Mair died in 1550.

34. The successor to Dunbar and Douglas was David
Lindsay, whose work as a poet is inseparably associated with
the social history of Scotland in his time.

In 1515, Francis I. came to the throne of France, ratified
peace with England (his predecessor, Louis XII., had married
a sister of Henry VIII.) ; and, with little consultation, included
Scotland in the treaty, on condition of her good behaviour.
This, after Flodden, piqued the Scots ; but they accepted the
apologies of France. In May, 1515, the Duke of Albany, son
to a younger brother of James III., came, with a fleet of escort
and a small court of gay French companions, to be regent of Scotland. He came from a life of luxury, had been Lord High Admiral
of France, and had been bred to French despotic ideas of the
relation between ruler and people. The Scot throve often in
France ; but the Frenchman could not so well make himself at
home in Scotland. The new regency proposed to take the royal
children from the queen. The queen showed them defiantly to
the commissioners from behind the portcullis of Edinburgh
Castle, and took them to Stirling. But a besieging force obliged

her to give up the king and his infant brother Alexander to the custody of Parliament.   In the next year, 1516, feud of Douglases or Anguses against Hamiltons, and other contests, filled the land with slaughter.   The regent tried main force; could not manage the people in that way; sent to France for men, and thereby almost raised an insurrection.   Angus was overmastered and dispatched to France, where he was kept close.   The queen escaped to England, where she bore a daughter.   Her husband, escaping from France, joined her, and became for Henry VIII. an instrument wherewith to vex the Scots.   Upon plea of negotiation necessary for protection against England, the Duke of Albany returned to France when he had been little more than a year in Scotland.   The Estates gave him but four months' leave of absence.   He left Frenchmen in charge of Dumbarton, Dunbar, and Inchgarvie, and a trusted French favourite, La Bastie, acting as warden of the marches.   There La Bastie was killed next year.   The Scots made great parade of a search for the murderers, without meaning to catch them.   Yet the alliance with France had just been renewed.   The regent overstayed his time, and was reminded of the fact.   He was wanted at home.   The party of Angus, that is to say, the Douglases, battled again for predominance, and, with the help of fighting borderers, almost raised a civil war. During these days of confusion, James V. was a child, and David Lindsay faithful in attendance on him.

In April, 1520, Arran and many of the western nobility met at Edinburgh, in the house of Bishop James (not David) Beaton, to plan the seizure of the Earl of Angus.   Angus, informed of this, asked his uncle, Gavin Douglas, Bishop of Dunkeld, to calm the resentment of his enemies.   The bishop met James Beaton in the church of the Black Friars, and urged him to be peacemaker.   Beaton protested that he knew of no design to break the peace, and striking his breast with too much animation, to enforce his denial on his conscience, the blow rang on a coat of mail under the sacred vestments.   " My lord," said Gavin Douglas, " I perceive your conscience is not good; I hear it clattering."   The word " clattering " had a double sense, for in Scottish dialect it meant also "telling tales."   There was presently a battle in the street, after which seventy-two lay dead; and Bishop James Beaton, who had taken refuge behind the altar, owed his life to the intervention of Douglas.   Angus then held Edinburgh by an armed force.   But his Tudor wife had turned against him, was tired of him, and laboured to bring Albany back. In November, 1521, after more than five years' absence, Albany returned. The orders of the Estates had become threatening, for they had declared that if he was not in Scotland by Midsummer, Scotland would declare him infamous, deprive him of office, break with France, make peace with England; and even join Henry VIII. against France. When Albany came back, the queen's warm welcome was imputed to dishonest motives. He was essentially a Frenchman, disliked by the people. The death of the infant prince, Alexander, was ascribed to him. Some asked, was the king safe? Would Albany kill him to rule in his place, or carry him to France and make another Frenchman of him? Scotland had no pleasure in the unnatural alliance forced upon her by the English crown; dislike for it was becoming active. But then Henry VIII. threatened the Scots, and commanded them to turn out Albany; so they were driven to stand by him. Henry had broken with France; he had joined Spain and the pope. Scotland was not to be driven; and thus King Henry's threat checked the rise of an English party. In the following year, 1522, an army of 80,000, raised in Scotland, moved towards the border, causing fear in England. But it did nothing. The insulting threat was withdrawn, and the Scottish leaders were now for a policy of strong defence, not of invasion. Albany went, by his own desire, to France; and thither also went his rival Angus. Still there was border war with England. In September, 1523, Albany returned from France with 3,000 footmen and 500 men-at-arms in 50 vessels. He gathered much of the disbanded army. It was ready to serve Scotland by acting as a check on England's border war, but it would not again play into the hands of France by invading England. Nothing was done, and Albany lost credit still. In May of the next year, 1524, Albany and nearly all the Frenchmen went to France for good, leaving Scotland headless and distracted. Wolsey then wrote to the queen that Henry VIII. meant only love to his nephew. The desire was to win Scotland from France. There was even talk of an eventual union of crowns, by marriage of James V. with the Princess Mary of England. Queen Margaret, the Rose of Dunbar's poem, having shifted her love, in hate of Angus denounced war on him if he should enter Scotland.

James V. was then in his thirteenth year, and it seemed that the best way to check the French party and keep out Albany, was "the erection" of the boy as king by the Estates. The king himself rebelled at confinement. A gentleman who opposed him he struck through the arm with his dagger; and he raised his dagger to a porter who restrained his going forth. Then it was settled that the Earl of Cassilis and three others should ride with the king, and that he might ride with them where he would, so that they brought him at night into Stirling Castle; but they never ventured out more than a mile from Stirling. A letter of liberal promise was conveyed from Henry VIII. to his nephew, and suddenly, one day in August, 1524, the king was brought from Stirling to Edinburgh, where he received sceptre, crown, and sword of honour in the old Tolbooth. Many leaders in the Estates signed a bond to stand by "the erection," and this was the Revolution of 1524. Wolsey and Henry VIII. highly approved of the whole proceeding.

The young king was flattered into love of his uncle, and had no goodwill to France. Meanwhile emissaries of France were active. In the following year, 1525, the capture of Francis I., at Pavia, excited generous sympathy of Scotland for the old ally. The English emissaries were unpopular, and were abused by women in the street. In 1526 the Earl of Angus came to Scotland, humbling himself to his queen. The boy king, told that he might choose his own guardians, took Angus for one of three. Each was to be guardian for three months at a time. Angus, at the end of his first three months, would not give up his office, but kept the king in merciless restraint. Forcible attempts were made in vain for his release. Angus said, "If his enemies got hold of him by one side, his friends would keep him by the other, so that he should be torn in twain."

35. It was during this time that **Hector Boece** (Boyce), Professor of the College of Montacute, published at Paris, in 1526, his Latin *History of the Scots*, in nineteen books. Boyce was born at Dundee about 1465, educated at Aberdeen and Paris, where he taught philosophy, and afterwards was Principal of King's College, Aberdeen. Erasmus corresponded with him, and the King of Scotland pensioned him. He died about 1536, in which year a free prose translation of Boece's History by **John Bellenden**, as the *Hystory and Chroniklis of Scotland*, was printed at Edinburgh. This forms one of the most important pieces of old Scottish prose. Boece's History,

which started from mythical times, was rich in entertaining
fable told with zest ; two mysterious authorities, Veremund and
Campbell, doing for its author the same service done for
Geoffrey of Monmouth by his Breton books (ch. iii. § 8). Boece,
indeed, may have received his inspiration from an edition of
Geoffrey of Monmouth, which had been published at Paris in
1517. John Bellenden, the translator of Boece, matriculated as
a student of St. Andrew's in 1508. He was liberally educated,
and obtained much credit as a poet at the Scottish court. Like
Lindsay, he was in James's service from the time of the
king's infancy. His translation of Boece was made at request
of the king, for whom also he began a translation of Livy, of
which he only completed the first five books. Bellenden, when
he published his translation of Boece, was a doctor in the
Church, Archdeacon of Moray, and Canon of Ross; but he
added to his translation an earnest letter to James V. on the
miseries of wicked princes and the duty of a king. Bellenden's
chief poem was a *Proheme of the Cosmographé*, written for the
king's instruction. He died at Rome, in 1550, an earnest honest
man, and stout opponent of the Reformation.

36. In May, 1528, King James escaped to Stirling ; he was
then seventeen years old, and thenceforth his own master.
When he ceased to hold the person of the king, Angus was
ruined. In the same year Queen Margaret succeeded in
obtaining her divorce from him, and married the new man of
her choice, young Harry Stewart, son of Lord Evandale. King
James applied himself vindictively to the punishment of
Angus. His estates were forfeited, and he was driven to
England, where Henry VIII. received him kindly, but His
Majesty had then no time for Scotch affairs.

While Angus and the English party held possession of the
king, he had been separated from the patriotic **David Lindsay**
(§ 31), although Lindsay's payment as one of the king's personal
attendants was not stopped. When King James broke bounds
and became independent, Lindsay again was by his side, and
thenceforth stood by him always as a faithful counsellor. He
sought incessantly to use his genius as a poet and his influence
as a friend, for the benefit alike of James V. and of Scotland.
Never had king a poet friend who preached to him more indefatigably. First, there was *Lindsay's Dream*, the first of his
longer works, written apparently in 1528, the first year of the
king's independent rule. It contains 1,134 lines, and is through-

out in Chaucer's stanza.  In a prefatory epistle to the king, he reminded his master how

> " Quhen thou wes young, I bure ye in myne arm,
> Full tenderlie, tyll thou begouth to gang,
> And in thy bed oft happit thee full warme ,"

how he had been his playfellow in childhood, and had told him in his youth " of antique stories and deeds martial ;" but now, he said, with the support of the King of Glory, he would tell a story altogether new.  He told, in a prologue of the usual fashion, how, after he had lain sleepless in bed, he rose and went out, on a January morning, to the seashore, there climbed into a little cave high in a rock, and sat with pen and paper, meaning rhyme.  But instead of rhyming, he wrapped himself well up, and after a wakeful night, was lulled to sleep by the sound of the waves, which he had been comparing to this false world's instability.  " Heir endis the proloug, and followis the dreme."  A fair lady, Dame Remembrance, came into Lindsay's Dream, and took him with her first to hell, where they saw popes, emperors, kings, conquerors, cardinals, archbishops, " proud and perverse prelates out of number," with many other churchmen. They suffered, Remembrance said, for covetousness, lust, and ambition; also because they had not taught the ignorant, "provoking them to penance by preaching;" and because they had not made equal distribution of the patrimony and rent of holy kirk, but misspent temporally all that they should have divided into three parts, one for the maintainance of the Church, one for themselves, one for the poor.  There also were captive kings and nobles who suffered for their pride or cruelty, or who had given up eternal bliss for the delights of earth.  From hell, Remembrance took the poet up, through earth, water, and the upper air, beyond the moon and sun and planets, to the firmament "fixit full of sterries brycht," and to the ninth sphere, prime mover of the rest ; although the planets have also a motion in their proper spheres from west to east, some swift, some slow,

> " Quhose motioun causès contynewallie,
> Rycht melodious harmonie and sound,
> And all throw mouying of those planetès round."

On they went, through the crystalline heaven, to the empyrean, where they saw the happiness of heaven.  Returning thence against his will, the poet questioned his companion about the earth ; was told its shape, size, divisions, and subdivisions;

J *

then he asked about Paradise, and passed, with a significant transition, from Paradise to Scotland. Scotland, at his request, was shown to him by Dame Remembrance, and when he saw that it was a fair country, he says, " I did propone ane lytill questioun :

> " ' Quhat is the cause our boundës ben so bair ?'
> Quod I ; ' or quhate does mufe our miserie ;
> Or quareof does proceëd our pourtie ? ' "

Scotland had natural wealth, and a people both ingenious and strong to endure. Lindsay asked, therefore, to be told " the principal cause wherefore we are so poor." The answer to this question brought him to the purpose of his poem, as a warning to James V., now master of his realm. Remembrance said, " The fault is not—I dare well take on hand—nother in to the peple nor the land. The want is of justice, policy, and peace." " Why then," asked Lindsay, " do we want justice and policy more than they are wanted by France, Italy, or England ?" " Quod sche : ' I fynd the falt in to the heid. For they in whom does lie our whole relief, I find them root and ground of all our grief.'" " The poverty of the nation comes," said Remembrance, " from the negligence and insolence of infatuate chiefs,

> " Hauand small ee unto the common weill,
> Bot to thare singulare proffect euerilk deill. "

As Lindsay and his guide thus talked, there came a lean and ragged man, with scrip on hip and pikestaff in his hand, as one who is leaving home. This was the well-being of Scotland, John the Common Weal. Few cared for him, he said in Scotland ; the spiritual estate never paid heed to his complaint, and among the laity there was nought else but each man for himself; so John the Common Weal must leave the land. " But when will you come back again ? " asked Lindsay.

> " ' That questionn, it sall be sone desydit,'
> Quod he : ' there sall na Scot have confortying
> Off me, tyll that I see the countre gydit
> Be wysedome of ane gude auld prudent kyng,
> Quhilk sall delyte him maist, above all thyng,
> To put justice tyll executioun,
> And on strang traitouris mak puneisioun.
> Als yit to the I say ane uther thyng :
> I se, rycht weill, that prouerbe is full trew :
> Wo to the realme that hes ouër young ane kyng.' "

This text from Ecclesiastes x. 16, " Woe to thee, O land, when thy king is a child," was often quoted by our English writers in the earlier part of the reign of Richard II. The course of Scottish history now brought it home to Lindsay, and he did not refrain from uttering it, although it was to a young king of seventeen or eighteen that he told the dream of which this was the pith. Remembrance seemed to the poet to have brought him back to the cave in which he slept, and there, when a passing ship seemed to discharge all its cannon, he awoke and besought God to send grace to the king to rule his realm in unity and peace. " Heir endës the dreme and begynnis the exhortatioun to the kyngë's grace." " Sir," it begins, " since God of His preordinance hath granted thee to have the governance of His people and create thee a king, fail not to print in thy remembrance that He will not excuse thine ignorance if thou be reckless in thy governing . . . and since that thou must reap as thou hast sown, have all thy hope in God, thy Creator, and ask Him grace that thou may be His own." With Lindsay for unwearied counsellor, James V. could not plead that he was uninformed as to his duties. This poem ended in reminder of what paths were to be followed, and what shunned, with a warning of the evil end of those who had not condescended to good counsel. " And, finally, remember thou mon dee . . . Quhar have they gone, thir papis and empriouris ? " For some of them that question had been answered in the beginning of the poem. The visions of hell and heaven were no purposeless opening to Lindsay's Dream of a king's duty to John the Common Weal.

Lindsay's next poem was *The Complaint*, also addressed to the king, and written, probably in 1529, the year of Skelton's death, soon after James escaped from thraldom. It is in 510 lines of octosyllabic rhyme, and professed to complain that, now the king was his own master, greedy men sought and had gifts from him, while his old friend " Da Lyn " was overlooked. This may have been seriously meant, and the " Complaint " may be associated with the fact that in 1530, Lindsay, then about forty years old, was knighted, and made Lion King of Arms, with lands and produce of lands assigned to secure payment of salary. But in his poem named the " Complaint," Lindsay chiefly recalled with strong censure the history of the " erection " of the young king at the age of twelve by new rulers, " for commoun weill makand no cair ; " and what Lindsay regarded as the wilful endeavour of those who then possessed him to corrupt and cheat him by base flatteries and allurements to a self-indulgence that would make him weakly

subject to their will.   The prelates who then ruled should have
shamed to take the name of spiritual priests:

> " For Esyas in to his wark
> Calles thame lyke doggis that can nocht bark,
> That callit ar preistis, and can nocht preche,
> Nor Christis law to the people teche.
> Geve for to preche bene thare professioun,
> Quhy sulde thay mell with court or sessioun,
> Except it war in spirituall thyngis."

There was discord among great lords, till suddenly the king
escaped:

> " Then rais ane reik, or ever I wyste,
> The quhilk gart all thare bandës bryste :
> Than thay allone quhilk had the gyding,
> Thay could nocht keip thare feit frome slyding ;
> Bot of thare lyffës thay had sic dreid,
> That thay war faine tyll trott over Tweid."

John Upland was blithe, said Lindsay, to see order restored; but
it had yet to be restored in the spiritualty.   The king was
admonished, therefore, to have an eye to the clergy, and make
their lives better conform to their vocation, make them preach
earnestly, and leave their vain traditions, which deceived the
simple sheep for whom Christ shed his blood—

> " As superstitious pylgramagis
> Prayand to gravin ymagis,
> Expres againis the Lordis command."

Lindsay added a warning to the king of the fate of Jeroboam, and
many more, princes of Israel, who assented to idolatry.   Sir David
Lindsay has been rightly called the poet of the Scottish Reformation ; but the reformation sought by him in the most active
years of his life was far more social than doctrinal.   He had
bitter cause to direct the king's attention to the pride of prelates
who, in the year of the king's escape from the hands of Angus,
first lighted a martyr fire in Scotland.   It was rare in Scotland
to hear any preaching, except from the Black and Grey Friars.
George Crichton, who succeeded the scholar and poet, Gavin
Douglas, as Bishop of Dunkeld, once thanked God that he knew
neither the Old Testament nor the New, but only his breviary
and his pontifical.   For this he passed into a proverb with the
people, who would say, " Ye are like the Bishop of Dunkeld, that
knew neither the new law nor the old."   But when Tyndal's New
Testament was ready, traders from Leith, Dundee, and Montrose
smuggled copies of it into Scotland; Lutheran opinions spread;

and on the 29th of February, 1528, young Patrick Hamilton, not
twenty-five years old, born of a good Scottish house, an abbot and
a scholar, who had learnt to think in Paris and in Germany, was
burnt for his religion at St. Andrew's.   In the midst of the flames
he was called upon by some spectator, if he still held to his faith
to give a last sign of his constancy.   At once he raised three
fingers of his half-burnt hand, and held them raised until he died.
Each fagot kindled a new fire of zeal.   " Gif ye burn more," said
a friend to one of the bishops, " let them be burnt in the cellars,
for the reik of Mr. Patrick Hamilton has infected as many as it did
blow upon."   Calvin was then only nineteen years old, John Knox
but three-and-twenty.   Lindsay's " Complaint" was followed, in
1530, by *The Testament of the Papingo*, or Popinjay, in 1,183 lines
of Chaucer's stanza, a Scottish " Speke Parrot ' (§ 23).   In this
poem, Lindsay, after a preface in praise of the poets who preceded
him and Scottish poets of his time, feigned that he had the care
the king's parrot, and took her, one bright morning, into a garden,
There he set her on a branch, from which, in spite of warning,
"Thou art right fat, and not well used to fly," the ambitious bird
must needs climb to " the highest little tender twist."   A gust of
wind broke the branch under her ; she fell, swooned, recovered
voice, and blamed false Fortune, who had brought her to court to
be ruined by ambition.   Then she desired, before her death, to
send some counsel to the king.   " Heir followis the first Epystyll
of the Papingo, direct to Kyng James the Fyft."   The Parrot
bequeathed to the king her true unfeigned heart, with much
serious advice to him as to the performance of his duties, for

> " Be thov found sleuthfull or negligent,
> Or iniuste in thyne exicutioun,
> Thov sall nocht faill devine puneissioun."

Let him take note that he was the last king of five score and
five—

> " Off quhose number fyftie and fyve bene slane,
> And, most parte, in thare awin mysgouernance."

The Parrot then dictated a second letter to her brethren of the
court, against ambition, and the misuse of prosperity, against court
vices and court perils.   She recalled the unhappy ends of the last
four Scottish kings from James I. to James IV. ; the recent fall
of Wolsey (in October, 1529) ; and the fall from power of the Earl
of Angus (in 1528).   To the courtiers, therefore, the Parrot said,
there is no constant court but one, where Christ is King, whose
time interminable and high triumphant glory is never gone.

" Heir followis the commonyng betvix the Papingo and hir holye execvtovris." The Magpie, a canon regular and prior, seeing the Parrot in pain, flew down, and asked for bequest of her goods ; the Raven came, too, as a black monk ; and the Kite, as a friar. The Parrot expressed doubt as to the Kite's good conscience, though his raiment was religious like : " I saw you," she said, " privily pick a chicken from a hen under a dyke." " I grant," said the Kite, " that hen was my good friend, but I only took the chicken for my tithe." Let Parrot confess, and the three religious birds would give her worthy funeral. The Parrot longed for better friends to comfort her. Then said the Kite, " We beseech you, ere you die, declare to us some causes reasonable why we ben holden so abominable." Thus Lindsay introduced into the poem, after his plain counsels to the king, an earnest setting forth of the corruption of the clergy. This had come, he said, since Constantine in Rome divorced the Church from Poverty and married her to Property. The children of that marriage were two daughters, Riches and Sensuality, who grew to power and took whole rule of the spiritual state. The clergy who paid court to these ladies soon forgot to study, pray, and preach, " they grew so subject to Dame Sensual, and thought but pain poor people for to teach." Were it not for the preaching of the begging friars, all faith would be extinct among the seculars. When the Parrot had spoken at some length her mind upon such matters, she was shriven by the Kite, and, for want of better, made the Kite and Raven her executors, with the Magpie for overman. She bequeathed her green dress to the owlet, her eyes to the bat, her beak to the pelican, " to help to pierce her tender heart in twain," her voice to the cuckoo, and her eloquence to the goose, her bones to be burnt with those of the phœnix when she next renewed her life, her heart to the king, and the rest of her inside to her executors. Then she commended her spirit to the Fairy Queen. She died ; and her executors fought over her remains.

In 1531, Sir David Lindsay, of the Mount, joined officially as Lion King of Arms in an embassy to Charles V. It was for the renewal of an old treaty of Commerce between Scotland and the Netherlands. In 1533 he was married to a Janet Douglas. That was the year of the divorce of Henry VIII. from Queen Katherine, and the year of the birth of the Princess, afterwards Queen, Elizabeth. No children were born to David Lindsay. In 1535, he was sent with Sir John Campbell to the Emperor to ask in marriage one of the princesses of his house for James V. No marriage came of that negotiation.

37. In the same year, 1535, Lindsay produced in the Play Field at Cupar the most interesting of his works, the Morality Play (§ 24) called *A Satire of the Three Estates.* This was a public setting forth of the condition of the country, with distinct and practical suggestion of the reforms most needed. Diligence first entered, as messenger from King Humanity, who was at hand. The people might now be assured of Reformation. The Three Estates of the nation were warned, in the king's name, to appear. Spectators were invited to be patient for some hours, and exhorted

> "That na man tak our wordis intill disdaine,
> Althocht ye hear, be declamatioun,
> The common-weill richt pitiouslie complaine."

The King then entered, with a prayer that he might use his diadem to God's pleasure and his own great comfort. But he was met and enticed by Wantonness and Placebo, and by Sandie Solace, fresh from a visit to fair Lady Sensuality, whose charms he praised. Sensuality then entered, the king was attracted by her song; she was commended and brought to him. Then came Good Counsel, after long banishment from Scotland, meaning to save King Humanity, who was thus overset in the beginning of his reign. But next came the Vices, Flattery, Falsehood, and Deceit, resolved to seek the King, and to devise some subtle way of keeping him from the guidance of Good Counsel:

> "Wee man turne our claithis and change our stiles,
> And disagyse vs, that na man ken vs.
> Hes nà man clarkis cleathing to len us?"

Flattery, disguised as a friar, took the name of Devotion; Deceit called himself Discretion; and Falsehood, Sapience, but being little wise he presently forgot his name, and confounded it with "thin drink"—"sypeins," the leakage from a cask. The disguised Vices met and beguiled the King. When the greybeard Good Counsel entered they turned him out, and agreed together to make haste with their own profit while the King was young. With aid from Wantonness and Solace, they had the King in attendance on a song from Sensuality, when Dame Verity entered with a call for the spirit of judgment to him that sitteth in judgment:

> "Let not the fault be left into the head
> Then sall the members reulit be at richt."

Especially "the Princes of the Priests" should let their light shine before men, who will pay more heed to their deeds than to their words, and follow them in both.   The Vices spying Verity, resolved together that she must not come to the King's presence. They accused her to the spiritual lords :

> "O reverent fatheris of the Spirituall Stait,
> Wee counsall yow, be wise and vigilant.
> Dame Veritie has lychtit, now of lait,
> And in hir hand beirand the New Testament."

An Abbot advised that she be held prisoner till the third day of the Parliament, and then accused of heresy ; a Parson advised, now that the King was guided by Dame Sensuality,

> "To tak your time, I hauld it best for me,
> And go distroy all thir Lutherians,
> In speciall, yon ladie Veritie."

The spiritual lords then sent the Parson, with Flattery as the Friar, to Dame Verity.   The Parson asked what right she had to preach, and said :

> "I dreid, without ye get ane remissioun,
> And, syne, renunce your new opiniones,
> The spritual stait sall put yow to perditioun
> And in the fyre will burne yow, flesche and bones."

Verity would not recant, and told her inquisitors that if the king knew her they would all be defamed for their traditions.   Then suddenly cried Flattery, the Friar :

> "Quhat buik is that, harlot, into thy hand?
> Out! walloway! this is the New Test'ment,
> In Englisch toung, and printit in England!
> Herisie! herisie! fire! fire! incontinent."

This Morality was acted at Cupar in 1535, the year before the martyrdom of Tyndal.   In 1534 the Convocation of the English clergy had asked the king for an authorised translation of the Scriptures into English ; and in 1535 Coverdale's translation was printed and licensed, though its introduction was delayed till 1536, which was the year also of the appearance of the first copies printed in England of Tyndal's New Testament (§ 29). The outcry of Falsehood may have referred to the current news that the King of England was allowing English Bibles to be printed, but perhaps it was added at some time between 1535 and the second acting of the play in 1539.   So Verity was haled to the stocks, saying :

> "Howbeit ye put ane thousand to torment,
> Ten hundreth thowsand sall rise into thair place."

and praying to God for some reasonable reformation. Chastity entered next, and fared no better than Truth. Neither Estates nor people would receive her, and after some jest by a tailor's wife and a shoemaker's wife, both Verity and Chastity were put in the stocks. Then entered a varlet to announce the coming of Divine Correction. The Vices resolved upon flight, but first quarrelled over the stealing of the King's box, which Deceit made off with. Divine Correction came resolved, with help of the Three Estates, to make Iniquity his thrall. Good Counsel welcomed him. Verity and Chastity were released from the stocks, and with these three in his company, Correction came near to the sleeping King. They drove from him Dame Sensuality, who went to the spiritual lords, and was welcomed by them as their day's darling. The King then received his fit companions and guides, humbly embraced Correction, and having conditionally pardoned Solace and Placebo, so long as they confined themselves to innocent amusements, he proclaimed that there should be a Parliament of all the Three Estates for the redress of wrongs.

Here ended the first part of the satire. The audience ate and drank, and while the actors were gone from their seats there was an interlude. Pauper, the poor man, came into the field, and, in spite of Diligence, who played prologue, climbed into the chair of the player King. After sundry antics, he told that he was from Lothian, and was going to St. Andrew's to seek law. He had kept his old father and mother by his labour, and then had a mare and three cows. When his father and mother died, the landlord took the mare for heriot—that was the fine of a beast of any kind that the tenant died possessed of, which became due, after the tenant's death, to his superior. The vicar had taken from the poor man the best cow when his father died, the next best when his mother died, and then, when his wife Meg had mourned herself to death, the vicar got the third cow; while, by like custom, their umest clayis—outer clothes—went to the clerk. When there was nothing left, the poor man and his bairns must needs go beg. "But," asked Diligence, "how did the parson, was not he thy good friend?" "He," said the poor man, "cursed me for my tithes, and still denies me sacrament at Easter." An English groat was all that he had left, and that was for a man of law. Pauper could not be made to understand that there was no law for him, and that his cows had gone, if not by law, yet by sufficient and good custom, to the vicar—

> " Ane consuetude against the Common Weill
> Sould be na law, I think, be sweit Sanct Geill !"

Not being allowed to ask unwelcome questions about the prelates, Pauper lay down in the field. Presently there came by
him a Pardoner, crying up relics, and abusing the New Testament
that spoilt his trade. There followed some rough jesting at the
Pardoner's expense, and then the poor man woke from dreaming
of his cows, blessed himself, and prayed St. Bride to send his
kye again. Seeing the Pardoner, he looked to him for help. The
Pardoner found that he had a groat, took it, and gave a thousand
years of pardon for it. The poor man was not satisfied unless
he saw what he got for his money, and the interlude closed with
a wrestle between the Pardoner and the poor man, in the course
of which the bag of relics was thrown into the stream that ran
across the Play Field.

Diligence then opened the second part of the Morality, by
proclaiming the arrival of the Three Estates, who marched from
the Pavilion, walking backwards, led by their Vices. The Three
Estates of the Scottish Parliament were the lords spiritual and
temporal and the burgesses, or representatives of cities and
boroughs, who had been added as a third estate in the days of
Robert Bruce. They greeted the King, explained that it was
usual with them to walk backwards, took their seats, and were
told by the King that it was his will to reform all abuses. Every
oppressed man was summoned by Correction to give in his bill.
Then entered, as complainant, John the Common Weal of fair
Scotland, ragged, lame, and sad. He was sad, he said, because
the Three Estates walked backwards, led by their several Vices,
Spirituality by Sensuality and Covetousness, Temporality by
Public Oppression, and the Burgesses by Falsehood and Deceit:

> " Quhat mervell thocht the thrie estaits backwart gang,
> Quhen sic an vyle cumpanie dwels them amang,
> Quhilk has reulit this rout monie deir dayis,
> Quhilk gars John the Common Weil want his warme clais !"

The Vices were presently put in the stocks ; Sensuality and
Covetousness were banished, to the great grief of the Spiritual
Lords; Good Counsel was seated in honour to advise the Parliament ; while John, tne Common Weal, and Pauper, the poor
man, were set to keep the door. Good Counsel then began the
argument of Reformation, with note of the sufferings of the
oppressed poor. John Common Weal complained of treacherous
border thieves, and held that the chiefs who harboured them

ought to be hanged.  He complained of idlers, strong beggars, fiddlers, pipers, and pardoners, of discords raised by the great fat friars, who laboured not and were well fed.  He complained of judgment without mercy upon petty thieves, while a cruel tyrant who wronged all the world—a common, public, plain, oppressor—could by bribery compound with law.  Correction bade the temporal lords put down oppression, bade the bur- gesses avoid deceit, and bade the spiritual lords rent land to men who laboured for their bread.  The temporal lords and burgesses embraced· John the Common Weal, but the spiritualty still stood aloof.  Correction then asked John the Common Weal what more he had to say against the spiritual lords.  There was much more, and he said it, Pauper the poor man heartily backing him with the complaint for his lost cows.  All that fol- lowed was debated and resolved with the assent of Two Estates and the dissent of the Lords Spiritual : reforms as to the corpse present and cow, as to the money spent at Rome in bribery, as to pluralities.  Each priest was to have but a single benefice; the bishops and the clergy were to preach and teach, for what else were they paid in tithes ?  The spiritual lords asked where there was any such duty enjoined on them.  They were referred by Good Counsel to what Saint Paul wrote to Timothy :

> " 'Tak, thair, the buik : let se gif ye can spell.'
> 'I never red that.  Thairfoir, reid it yoursel.' "

Good Counsel then read the passage aloud (1 Timothy iii. 1, 2, 3). Spiritualty hinted that it had been good that Paul had never been born.  John Common Weal thought that if King David, who founded so many abbeys, could look down and see the abominations in them, he would wish he had not narrowed his income threescore thousand pounds a year.  King James I. called him a dear saint to the crown.  For this suggestion Spiritualty held that John Common Weal deserved to be incon- tinently burnt.  Called upon to make his confession of faith, John gave for it the Apostle's Creed, adding that he believed in Holy Church, but not in these bishops and friars : upon which Correction held him to be a good Christian.  It was further resolved that no clergy should judge of temporal causes.  Verity and Chastity then claimed that fit clergy should replace those who were enemies to them, and said that poor ignorant men understood their own crafts better than the clergy theirs ; in witness whereof the shoemaker and tailor were produced and examined in their trades.  Then Diligence was sent to search

for a good preacher.  While he was gone Theft entered, and
Mighty Oppression, who was in the stocks, contrived to slip out,
leaving Petty Theft in his place.  Diligence came back with a
Doctor of Divinity and two Licentiates.  There followed examination of a Bishop, of an Abbot, of a Parson, of a Prioress, and
the sermon was called for.  This the Doctor preached.  His
argument was that Christ through love died to save man, and
that God asks of us only love for love.  Love, he taught, is the
ladder with but two steps by which we may climb to heaven, the
first step being Love of God, the second Love of our Neighbour.
The Parson and the Abbot scoffed at this doctrine, and called
the Doctor down out of the pulpit.  When the two Licentiates
had dwelt presently upon the poverty of Christ and the great
wealth of his successors, Flattery, in the friar's dress, was seized
for giving evil counsel to the Prelates.  Then came the unfrock-
ing and disclosure of the Vices, the deprivation of three perverse
prelates, and the setting of the three wise clergy in their places.
John the Common Weal was gorgeously clothed, and seated in
the Parliament, before which there were read the Acts resolved
upon.  The reading thus introduced by earnest dramatic satire,
interspersed with some rough jesting to amuse the people, was a
reading, in fifteen metrical clauses, of what might be called Sir
David Lindsay's draft of a Reform Bill for Scotland.  Theft,
Deceit, and Falsehood were then taken from the stocks and
hanged, but Flattery escaped.  Then entered Folly to jest, with
a basketful of fools' caps.  When he found that the King gave
bishoprics to preachers, Folly hung his fools' caps round the
pulpit, and preached a satirical sermon to commend them to all
purchasers.  They were commended to the merchant discon-
tented with abundance, who torments himself for gain ; to the
rich old widower who has children and weds a girl ; to the clergy
who take cures only for pelf ; to the princes who shed innocent
blood in labour merely of "ilk Christian prince to ding down
uther."  After Folly's sermon, Diligence spoke a short epilogue,
and the play was over.

38. In 1536, Lindsay wrote for the king two little pieces.  One
was in *Answer to the King's Flyting*, a playful warning answer
to the king's attack on his strict preaching of continence.  The
other was a *Complaint and Public Confession of the King's Old
Hound, Bagsche*, who petitioned on his own behalf the king's
new favourite, Bawte, and the other dogs, his companions.
Bagsche had worried lambs and sheep, had attacked men

savagely, every dog trembled when he was near ; but at last, for his misuse of power, he was cast off, and barely escaped hanging. Prosperous brother Bawte was admonished to take warning, and any strong man who enjoyed court favour might take to himself the auld hound's warning against harsh use of his strength. Within the next three or four years Lindsay wrote also a satire on the long trains worn by ladies, *Ane Supplicatioun against Side Taillis*, and *Kittie's Confession*, an attack on the Con· fessional. Its doctrine is :

> " To the great God omnipotent
> Confess thy sin, and sore repent,
> And trust in Christ, as writis Paul,
> Who shed His blood to save thy soul;
> For none can thee absolve but He,
> Nor take away thy sin from thee."

In 1536 there was an embassy to France, attended by Sir David Lindsay as Lion King of Arms, to ask in marriage for James V. a daughter of the house of Vendôme. That embassy was detained until the king himself arrived, when he chose for himself Magdalene of France, the consumptive eldest daughter of King Francis. She was married to James with much banqueting. On the 28th of May the king and queen arrived at Holyrood. On the 5th of July the bride was dead. Lindsay then wrote *The Deploration of Queen Magdalene*, dwelling at large upon the pomps of her reception, and then passing in one stanza from the festal music to the music of her requiem. Within a year there was another bride to greet. On the 10th of June, 1538, Mary, widow of the Duke of Longueville, and daughter of the Duke of Guise, landed at Fifeness. She was received with triumphs of Lindsay's devising. The genius of Scotland, in angelic form, delivered to her the keys of Scotland from a cloud above an arch. There were forty days of sport. Occasion came of this for Lindsay's short piece on *The Jousting between James Watson and John Barbour*.

In the following year, 1539, five men were burnt for heresy at Edinburgh ; and David Beaton, who had taken part in their condemnation, and had in the preceding year been made a cardinal, became, by the death of his uncle James, Archbishop of St. Andrew's. In the same year, 1539, at the Feast of Epiphany, the king had Lindsay's " Satire of the Three Estates " acted at Linlithgow, before himself and his queen, and the whole council, temporal and spiritual. At the end of the piece James warned some of the bishops who were present that, if they did not take heed, he would send some of the proudest of them to be dealt with by his uncle of England. In the following year, 1540, the Estates, while they maintained the pope's authority, so far followed Lindsay's lead as to pass a friendly Act of Reformation for abatement of " the unhonesty and misrule of kirkmen, baith in wit, knowledge, and manners," as " the matter and cause that the kirk and kirkmen are lightlied and condemned."

We have now followed the main currents of our literature, north and south, to the year 1540. Lindsay was then about fifty years old, Luther was fifty-seven, John Knox was thirty-five years old, and George Buchanan thirty-four.

39. In the year 1540 Rabelais was living, and was forty-five years old. Ariosto died and Montaigne was born in 1533. Italy still had the strongest literary influence upon surrounding nations. Pastoral poetry, which old fable traced to a source in the Sicilian Daphnis, son of Mercury, was at this time passing from Italy and Spain into France. After the " Orfeo " of Poliziano and the " Cefalo " of Niccolo da Correggio (chap. v. § 28) pastorals multiplied ; but the work that concerns us most was the *Arcadia of Jacopo Sanazzaro*, who was born at Naples in 1458, and died in 1532. The "Arcadia" was first published complete in 1504, and was in prose and verse—twelve pieces of prose, each introducing an eclogue. In joining a literary academy its author had transformed his name to Azio Sincero. Under the name of Sincero, he spoke of himself with an Arcadian shepherd in two of the prose introductions; under the name of Ergasto, he lamented the death of his mother, in the tenth and eleventh prose pieces. His mother died in 1490, and his " Arcadia " was then, perhaps, more than half written. There was no continuous narrative, but the prose introductions, and the accord of personal feeling and allusion, gave more than usual coherence to the eclogues.

The influence of Italy on Spain was very strong at the beginning of the sixteenth century. Naples was delivered to Spain after the successes of Gonzalvo de Cordova and the Treaty of 1503. In 1522 Spain was in Italy at the battle of Pavia. In 1527 the pope was a prisoner in Spain. In 1530, Charles V. was in Italy, surrounded by a Spanish court. Sanazzaro himself was descended from a Spanish family settled in Naples. Italian forms of literature were more and more copied in Spain, until, in 1526, Juan Boscan, of Barcelona, distinctly imitated the Italian poetry, and used Italian measures. The strength of Italian

influence on Spanish literature dates from Boscan, who died in
1540, and from his friend Garcilasso de la Vega, who was
killed in 1536, at the storming of a village during Charles V.'s
disastrous invasion of Provence.  Charles executed all the
survivors of the fifty peasants who, in defending their homes,
killed Garcilasso.  Garcilasso's works include three eclogues,
written after 1526, equal in bulk to his other poems.  In the
first and best of them, two shepherds, Salicio (himself) and
Nemoroso (Boscan), complain of love; Salicio mourns a mistress who is dead, Nemoroso one who is faithless.  Like Boscan,
Garcilasso wrote also sonnets in the Italian manner, imitating
Petrarch, but among the poets of his time he showed a chief
delight in Sanazzaro.  The growing taste for pastoral poetry, as
well as Sanazarro's popularity, is shown by the fact that sixty
editions of his "Arcadia" were published in the sixteenth century.

In France, the first eclogue of mark was produced in 1531.
This was *Clement Marot's Complaint of Louise of Savoy*, a
pastoral lament on the death of the mother of Francis I. In
other pastorals of his the great god Pan became the God adored
by pastors of the Church; and he sang of the good and bad
shepherd, and the sorrows of the flocks, in direct sympathy with
the best aspirations of the Church reformers.  Marot was living
in 1540.  He died in 1544.

George of Montemayor, near Coimbra, a Portuguese, was
then a young man.  He wrote in his young days an imitation of the
"Arcadia" of Sanazzaro, "Diana Enamorada." *Montemayor's
Diana* was first printed at Valencia in 1542.  He was himself its
hero, under the name of Sereno; and it gave in form of pastoral
romance events from his own life or experience of his friends.
Under the mountains of Leon shepherds and shepherdesses on
the banks of the Ezla met, and told their stories in seven books
of prose mixed with verse.  The work, which had more story in
it than Sanazzaro's "Arcadia," was left unfinished.  A second
part in eight books was published in 1564, by Alonzo Perez, to
whom Montemayor had told his plan.  Perez promised a third
part, but lived another thirty years without producing it.

40. From the rise of the modern pastoral let us turn now to
the development of the romance of chivalry.  Ludovico, son of
Niccolo Ariosto, who continued with *Orlando Furioso*, the
" Orlando Innamorato " of Boiardo (ch. v. § 31), was born in
1474, at Reggio, where his father was governor.  He was eldest
of ten children, in a household of moderate means.  He was sent

to Ferrara to study law, but gave his time chiefly to the study of
the Spanish and French romances, tales chiefly of Charlemagne,
King Arthur, and their knights.    The original "Amadis of Gaul"
(ch. v. § 28), produced by Vasco de Lobeira in or a little before
1390, existed only in a manuscript now lost.    It was translated
out of Portuguese into Spanish between 1492 and 1504, by
Garcia Ordoñez de Montalvo, governor of Medina del Campo.
It was first printed early in the sixteenth century, but the earliest
known printed edition is of the year 1519, four years after the
printing of "Orlando Furioso."    Young Ariosto, since he failed
as a law student, was allowed to train himself for literature.    He
was but twenty when his father died, and he then devoted himself with good sense and energy to the guardianship of his
brothers and sisters.    Worldly success from the pursuit of literature could, in those days, come only by the way of patronage.
Ariosto submitted to the patronage of Cardinal Ippolito d'Este,
brother to the Duke of Ferrara.    The life of the cardinal, from
whom Ariosto received slender payment while he wrote his
famous poem, was an example of the gross corruption of society
in the Italian courts.    Ariosto broke with him at last, gave him
—and Leo X. also—a place in his satires ; and after the cardinal's death had a friend in the duke.    The ease and playful
grace of Ariosto's masterpiece was the result of that great labour
without which few masterpieces are achieved.    The poet was of
large robust body and healthy mind ; frank, genial, and a hater
of ceremonies ; true to the sisters who depended upon him,
moderate in all things, though tainted with the licence of his
time and country.    As an intent thinker and sturdy pedestrian,
he found himself one day half way to Ferrara when he had but
gone out from Carpi for a breath of morning air in dressing-
gown and slippers ; being so far on the road, he went on to
Ferrara.    From Carpi to Ferrara is a walk of rather more than
thirty miles.    What Ariosto did he did with determination.    He
had read every attainable romance.    He pondered his "Orlando"
well before a word of it was written, rejecting Cardinal Bembo's
advice to make of it a Latin epic.    In writing he would often spend
a day upon the polishing of a few verses written in the morning ;
and having begun his "Orlando" at the age of twenty-nine, by
great industry, in eleven years he was able to issue forty cantos.
That was in 1515.    Six more cantos Ariosto added to the poem
in his lifetime, five he left to be added after his death.    A re-
polished edition of the "Orlando" was issued by him in 1532, the

year before his death.   To this edition he had given with anxious care his last corrections.   The book went to him full of misprints.   " The printer," he cried, " has assassinated me !" Books were then as liable to misprints as men to the plague, but the book disease was curable, and Ariosto's poem lives.   Boiardo, taking for his subject fabulous wars with the Saracens, represented Paris besieged by two hosts of infidels, who menaced the kingdom of Charlemagne, and (Orlando Innamorato) Orlando enamoured of a fascinating Angelica, brought from the far East to produce discord among the Christians.   Ariosto made Angelica herself love and marry Medoro, a young squire, whereby she drove (Orlando Furioso) Orlando mad, until he was healed by Astolfo, who brought his wits back in a phial from the moon. Editions of Ariosto's poem appeared written in his lifetime, in 1515, 1516, 1521, 1526, 1530, and 1532.   In Italy, about the year 1540, stanzas of Ariosto's playful octave rhyme were familiar among the people.   Bernardo Tasso wrote that there was not an artisan, not a boy, girl, or old man, ignorant of the " Orlando Furioso ;" that the lonely traveller relieved the toil of his journey by singing its stanzas ; and that persons of all classes might be heard repeating them in the streets and fields.

Of *Amadis of Gaul* (ch. v. § 28), first printed in Spain in or before 1519, a French translation appeared in 1540.   Amadis itself was followed up by its translator in 1521, with an original romance of his own on the adventures of " Esplandian," son of the perfect knight, Amadis of Gaul (*i.e.* Wales), and the peerless Oriana, who was daughter of Lisuarte, King of England. Of Amadis there were twelve Spanish editions within half a century.   Esplandian was received with favour, and was followed in 1526 by " The History of Florisando," nephew of Amadis.   Then came a " Lisuarte of Greece," son of Esplandian. The new suit was followed with an " Amadis of Greece."

Another Spanish romance hero was *Palmerin*, written by a carpenter's daughter at Burgos, and first printed in 1511.   This hero was called Palmerin de Oliva, because he was found exposed in an osier cradle among olive trees.   He married the daughter of the Emperor of Germany; and in 1516 appeared from the same authoress the second book of " Palmerin," telling the adventures of his sons Primaleon and Polendos.   In 1533 followed the adventures of Palmerin's grandson, Platir.   Other Spanish romances of chivalry competed for attention.   They were a chief source of delight to many readers in the middle of the sixteenth century.

The romance which ranks next in merit to the original "Amadis" is *Palmerin of England*, by Luis Hurtado, and the first part of that appeared in the year of the death of Henry VIII.

41. Ariosto wrote in his youth two Italian comedies, after the manner of Plautus and Terence, and afterwards three more were produced in a theatre fitted up by him for the Duke of Ferrara. The *RISE OF THE MODERN DRAMA* was not from a modification of the miracle-plays, but came, with the revival of letters, almost everywhere from imitation of the Latin dramatists. First, they were Latin imitators of the Latin. Albertino Mussato, of Padua, who died in 1330, produced two tragedies in such Latin as an Italian audience might partly understand; one was an "Achilleis," the other an " Eccerinis," on a native theme, Ezzelin, tyrant of Padua. For the latter play his compatriots gave him a laurel crown. The story of Mussato's Ezzelin was told in five acts, each consisting of a narrative spoken in character—1, by the mother of Ezzelin; 2, by a messenger; 3, by dialogue between two brothers, interrupted by a messenger; 4 and 5, each by a messenger. Single speakers addressed the Chorus, which occasionally asked a question, and at the close of each act lamented or moralised. Each of the five acts of a tragedy by Seneca was usually closed in this way by the chorus. Petrarch said that he wrote when young a comedy, called " Philologia," but kept it to himself. Pier Paolo Vergerio, born in Capo d'Istria, about 1349, a philosopher, jurisconsult, and orator, who assisted at the Council of Constance, wrote in his youth a Latin comedy, named " Paulus," which is not lost, and of which the professed object was to correct the manners of the young. Italy, in the fifteenth century, had the pompous acting of mysteries, the Rustic Farces and Dramatic Pastoral of " Orfeo" (ch. v. § 28), in which Poliziano first gave dramatic action to a pastoral written in the language of the people, and still from time to time a Latin tragedy or comedy. One of these Latin comedies, the " Lusus Ebriorum," by Secco Polentone, was translated into. Italian, and printed in 1472, named afresh *Catinia*, from a chief actor in the story. This seems to have been the earliest printed comedy in any of the modern languages of Europe.

In 1486 there were plays acted in Ferrara before its duke. First, there was acted a translation of the " Menæchmi " of Plautus; then the pastoral " Cefalo," by Niccolo da Correggio; then the " Amphitryon " of Plautus, translated into terza rima; then a sacred comedy on the story of Joseph. For the same

Duke Ercole I., and in the same theatre at Ferrara, were acted
new Italian plays by Antonio da Pistoja; one was *Panfila,* a
tragedy in terza rima (first printed at Venice in 1508), also a
comedy in five acts, and in terza rima, called *Timone,* by Boiardo,
who died in 1494. In 1494, Giacomo Nardi, translator of Livy,
produced in Florence an Italian comedy, in various metres,
called *Amicizia.*

Pomponius Lætus in those days had taught lay youths to
act Plautus and Terence in the houses of great men. In the
chief towns of Italy, in the earlier years of the sixteenth century,
cardinals and other dignitaries frequently had plays of Seneca,
Plautus, and Terence acted before them. Tommaso Inghiramo,
a reverend canon and professor of rhetoric, acquired the surname
of Phædra for his excellent acting of the part of the wife of
Theseus, in Seneca's "Hippolytus," on a stage before the palace
of the Cardinal Raffaelle San Giorgio. The best of the Latin
plays written in Italy was the "Golden Shower" (*Imber Aureus*)
of Antonio Tilesio, a tragedy on the story of Danae, produced in
1529, often acted with great applause, and first printed in 1530.
At that time Coriolano Martirano, Bishop of San Marco, in
Calabria, was producing excellent versions into Latin of the
"Electra" of Sophocles; of the "Prometheus Bound" of
"Æschylus;" of the "Medea," "Hippolytus," "Bacchæ,"
"Phœnissæ," and "Cyclops," of Euripides; and of the
"Plutus" and "Clouds" of Aristophanes.

Native Italian comedy was represented in the first years of
the sixteenth century by Ariosto. His earliest comedy was *I
Suppositi* ("The Substitutes"), where master and man change
places; and in this Ariosto himself said that he followed the
"Eunuch" of Terence and the "Captives" of Plautus. To the
same period of his youth belongs Ariosto's *Cassaria,* where the
plot turns on a box deposited with Crisobolo, and passed by his
son into the power of the master of a fair slave, Eulalia. The
characters here are like those of the Latin comedy, but the plot
is his own. These comedies were first written about 1498, in
prose, but afterwards rewritten into unrhymed verse. His
other comedies, *Lena, Scolastica,* and *Il Negromante* ("The
Magician"), were also in unrhymed verse; the last-named was
sent to Leo X. in 1520, and acted in Rome.

An Italian tragedy on the story of Sofonisba, by Galotto del
Carretto, was acted before Isabella Marchioness of Mantua, in
1502; but *Trissino's Sofonisba,* dedicated to Leo X. in 1515, and

printed in 1529, was the first Italian tragedy of mark. This also was in unrhymed verse. Giovan Giorgio Trissino, born in 1478, of a noble and wealthy family in Vicenza, had a keen delight in Greek, and a genius for poetry and architecture ; he had also means that gave him leisure to indulge his tastes. He went to Rome, and wrote " Sofonisba " to employ his mind when he was in deep grief after the loss of his first wife.

In the year 1540, Trissino lost his second wife. He was then at work on a long epic poem, *Italia Liberata da i Goti* (" Italy Freed from the Goths "), upon the production of which he spent twenty years. It is chiefly famous as the first attempt in modern literature to produce a long epic in unrhymed verse. The first nine books of Trissino's epic appeared at Rome in 1547, the rest followed in 1548.

Of three *Comedies by Machiavelli* (who was born in 1469, and died in 1527), one is a free version of the " Casina" of Plautus, another is a closer version of the " Andria " of Terence; and the third, *Mandragola*, had a plot of its own, illustrating the degradation of society in Florence.

42. The degradation of political life is shown also in his famous treatise " Del Principe "—*Machiavelli's Prince*—first published in 1532. It was a shrewd man's embodiment of the political doctrines of Italian courts, written to please the house of Medici, and showing how a prince, whose territory was newly acquired, not inherited, might master not only Florence, but all Italy. Machiavelli was the best Italian prose writer of that time, and in private life of more than average worth among his countrymen ; but he does not seem to have meant satire when he wrote of Italian state policy, " A prince who would maintain his power should learn to adapt the morality of his actions to the dictates of necessity, and not to study merely what is agreeable to virtue." The same corruption was shown in the remorseless *Satires of Pietro Aretino* on the licentious lives of nuns and cardinals, and the misdeeds of princes, of whom he was called the Scourge. He was himself an example of the degradation he exposed. Pietro of Arezzo, thence called Aretino, was in 1540 forty-eight years old, and writing comedies. He died in 1557. There was also Theophilus Folengo, better known as Merlin Cocaie, the inventor of that odd mixture of Latin with a homely dialect, which takes from a book of his its name of *Macaronic Poetry*. He was born in 1491, of a noble family in Mantua, was baptised Girolamo, but took the name of Theophilus when he

joined the Benedictines of Monte Cassino. In 1509 he became a regular Benedictine, afterwards left the order, roamed about for ten years with a noble lady, stopped work on a serious Latin poem and took to writing a Macaronic Work, which told in the rustic dialect of Mantua, whimsically twisted into burlesque Latin, the adventures of a burlesque hero named Baldus, with lively satire on the vanities of life and Church abuses. He called the parts of his poem " Macaronea Prima," " Macaronea Secunda," &c.— the dish of the people yielding to Italy the name of Maccherone for a booby, as the sausage gives to Germany its Hans Wurst, and we have Jack Pudding. There were seventeen such sections of Jack Pudding verses in the first edition, published in 1521, and in later editions twenty-five. Folengo wrote afterwards a satirical "Orlandino," on the youth of Orlando, in eight cantos of Italian, as Limerno (anagram of Merlino) Pitocco (beggar) ; and when he went back into his religious order, in 1526, he wrote a medley of poems, songs, and tales in Latin, Italian, and the form called, from his "Opus Macaronicum," Macaronic. This he named the " Chaos of Three for One " (*Il Chaos del Triperuno*)—namely, Theophilus Folengo, Merlin Cocaie, and Limerno Pitocco. He wrote afterwards an Italian religious poem, in ten books of octave rhyme, on the " Humanity of the Son of God," and died in 1544.

43. A writer on English poetry, in 1589, says that in the latter end of Henry VIII.'s reign " sprang up a new company of courtly makers, of whom Sir Thomas Wyatt the elder, and Henry Earl of Surrey were the two chieftains; who, having travelled into Italy, and there tasted the sweet and stately measures and style of the Italian poesy, as novices newly crept out of the schools of Dante, Arioste, and Petrarch, they greatly polished our rude and homely manner of vulgar poesy "—(*i.e.*, poetry in the language of the people)—" from that it had been before, and for that cause may justly be said to be the first reformers of our English metre and style."

Sir Thomas Wyatt the elder was born in 1503, at Allington Castle, in Kent, son of Sir Henry Wyatt, who was high in the king's favour, and who died in 1538. Thomas Wyatt entered St. John's College, Cambridge, at the age of twelve, took his Bachelor of Arts degree at fifteen, and was Master of Arts at seventeen. He became a gentleman of the king's bedchamber, and married Elizabeth, daughter of Lord Brook of Cobham. His eldest son, Thomas Wyatt the younger, was born about 1520. In 1533, Wyatt was ewerer at the coronation of his friend, Anne Boleyn. In 1537 he was knighted. He was tall and handsome; his friend Surrey praised his form as one where "force and beauty met." He was skilled in exercise of arms, spoke French, Italian, and Spanish, was apt at kindly repartee, played on the lute, and at the age of five-and-twenty, had been honoured by Leland as the most accomplished poet of his time. The king found pleasure in his conversation. Soon after a short imprisonment in the Tower during the king's pleasure, Sir Thomas Wyatt was sent as ambassador to the Emperor Charles, in Spain, and did not obtain until April, 1539, the recall he wished for. He had to deal with the personal questions between the two sovereigns arising out of the divorce of Queen Katherine, the position of her daughter, the Princess Mary; and the birth of Jane Seymour's son, Edward, afterwards King Edward VI., in the autumn of 1537. There was also the argument of the King of England's next marriage after the death of Jane Seymour. There was also the war between Charles V. and Francis I., closed by the Peace of Nice, in 1538, during Wyatt's tenure of office as English ambassador in Spain. Wyatt followed the emperor, posted to England, was wise and active, but too good a man for diplomatic work in which he was not free to be true.

**Reginald Pole** went to Spain during Wyatt's embassy, and Wyatt's duty was to stand between him and the emperor. Pole's father was cousin to Henry VII., and his mother was a niece of Edward IV. In 1525, Reginald Pole, aged five-and-twenty, returned from foreign universities high in Henry VIII.'s favour, and enriched with pension and Church preferment. But he did not approve of the divorce of Katherine, or of King Henry's repudiation of the pope's authority over the Church. The king, who sought in vain to win him, sent him a pamphlet written by Dr. Sampson, Bishop of Chichester. His reply was a Latin treatise, addressed to the king, in four books, in *Defence of Church Unity*, published in 1536. It condemned the secession of England from Rome. For this he was deprived of his pension and preferments, and compelled to leave England. Henry persecuted his family, and even executed his mother. He was made a cardinal in December, 1536, and afterwards employed as papal legate.

**Sir Thomas Wyatt** was a reformer, liberal and thoughtful, able to appreciate the sincerity of Pole, while he fulfilled his

duty by procuring for him a cool reception at the court of
Charles. The death of Wyatt's father during the time of his
embassy gave him reason to be urgent for a recall, that he might
attend to his own family affairs ; but he was told that his private
affairs were not neglected, since His Majesty had set aside for
him the house of the Friars at Ailesford, in Kent, which
adjoined his own estate at Allington, and was disposed to
continue "good lord unto him." From Spain, Wyatt wrote
earnest letters to his son, on the model of Seneca's epistles.
Here are a few sentences from them:—" Make God and goodness
your foundations. Make your examples of wise and honest
men; shoot at that mark. Be no mocker; mocks follow them
that delight therein. He shall be sure of shame that feeleth no
grief in other men's shames. Have your friends in a reverence;
and think unkindness to be the greatest offence, and least
punished, among men; but so much the more to be dread, for
God is justicer upon that alone. . . . . If you will seem
honest, be honest ; or else seem as you are." Not many months
after his return to Allington, Wyatt's good sense and experience
were again called for by the course of public events. The
Emperor's journey through France to the Netherlands, against
revolted Ghent, was to be watched for any under-currents in its
policy. Wyatt, therefore, was appointed for four months to be
with Charles as Ambassador Extraordinary. He went, and he
sent home faithful reports, with acute comments and sensible
suggestions. His recall was delayed, though again he urged for
it ; but he was able to return to Allington by the middle of May,
1540. In the following July came the fall of Thomas Cromwell,
and after this Sir Thomas Wyatt, who had been one of Cromwell's friends, was sent in the winter 1540-1 to the Tower,
charged with disrespect to the king, and traitorous correspondence with Cardinal Pole. There he wrote :

> " Sighs are my food ; my drink they are my tears;
>     Clinking of fetters such music would crave :
> Stink and close air away my life wears ;
>     Innocency is all the hope I have.
> Rain, wind, or weather I judge by mine ears;
>     Malice assaults that righteousness should have.
> Sure I am, Bryan, this wound shall heal again;
>     But yet, alas ! the scar shall still remain. "

About June, in 1541, Wyatt was tried and acquitted. In July
the king made some amends to him by a grant of lands in
Lambeth, and he showed him afterwards substantial kindness.

Sir Thomas Wyatt went again to Allington, attended personally
to the education of a nephew, wrote a rhymed *Paraphrase of the
Seven Penitential Psalms,* with a prologue of his own before
each of them, and wrote also, in terza rima, three noble satires,
two imitated from Persius and Horace and one freely translated
from Italian. The first and second were addressed to his
friend, John Poyntz, (1.) "of the mean and sure estate,"—a new
elaboration from Horace (Sat. ii. 6) of the story of the town and
country mouse; (2.) of the courtier's life, from the Italian of
Alamanni; the third, to Sir Francis Bryan, entitled, "How to
Use the Court, and Himself Therein," was a paraphrase of a
satire of Horace (Book ii. Sat. 5), wherein, following Horace
closely and bitterly, Wyatt applied to court life the principles of
Macchiavelli:

> "Use virtue as it goeth nowadays
> In word alone, to make thy language sweet,
> And of thy deed yet do not as thou says,
> Else, be thou sure, thou shalt be far unmeet
> To get thy bread."

His second satire, a free translation from Alamanni, told his
friend why he sought to fly the press of courts, and live at
home:

> "My Pointz, I cannot frame my tongue to feign—
> To cloke the truth for praise, without desárt,
> Of them that lust all vices to retain.
> I cannot honour them that set their part
> With Venus and Bacchús all their life long;
> Nor hold my peace of them, although I smart.
> I cannot crouch or kneel to such a wrong,
> To worship them as God on earth alone
> That are like wolves these sely lambs among.
> I cannot with my words complain, and moan,
> And suffer nought; nor smart without complaint;
> Nor turn the word that from my mouth is gone.
> *        *        *        *
> I am not he that can allow the state
> Of high Cæsár, and doom Cató to die,
> That by his death did scape out of the gate
> From Cæsar's hands, if Livy doth not lie,
> And would not live where liberty was lost:
> So did his heart the common weal apply."

In these adaptations from Italian and Latin, Wyatt uncon-
sciously was summing up his life towards its close. In the
autumn of 1542, Henry VIII. was plotting with Charles V. war
against Francis I. Charles sent an ambassador to England. Sir
Thomas Wyatt was ordered to meet him at Falmouth, and bring
him to London. Wyatt rode fast in bad weather, was seized with

a fever on his way, and died at Sherborne, only thirty-nine years old.  His friend, John Leland, published Latin- *Næniæ* (funeral songs) upon his death.  His friend, the Earl of Surrey, then aged about twenty-five, mourned his loss in a little elegy, and drew his portrait, flattered, of course, but true to the main features, in a few stanzas, of which these are three :

> " A visage stern and mild ; where both did grow
> Vice to contemn, in virtue to rejoice :
> Amid great storms whom grace assured so,
> To live upright, and smile at Fortune's choice.

> " A tongue that served in foreign realms his king ;
> Whose courteous talk to virtue did inflame
> Each noble heart ; a worthy guide to bring
> Our English youth by travail unto fame.

> " A heart where dread was never so imprest
> To hide the thought that might the truth advance;
> In neither fortune loft nor yet represt,
> To swell in wealth or yield unto mischance."

Wyatt's songs and sonnets, balades, rondeaux, complaints, and other little poems, closely and delicately imitate, with great variety of music, the forms fashionable in his time among poets of Italy and France.  His sonnets, accurate in their structure, are chiefly translated from Petrarch, many of his epigrams are borrowed from the "Strambotti" (fantastic conceits) of Serafino d'Aquila, a Neapolitan poet, who died in 1500, and whose poems were printed in 1503.  Dante had paraphrased the penitential Psalms; and in 1532 there appeared another version of them into Italian, by Luigi Alamanni, a Florentine poet, born in 1495.  Exiled from Italy after joining in a plot for the death of Cardinal Giulio de' Medici, Alamanni was for some years established at the court of Francis I., to whom he dedicated, in 1532, the volume of his Tuscan works—" Opere Toscane."  This was a collection of sonnets, balades, and other amatory poems in rhyme ; eclogues after the manner of Theocritus, and many other poems in blank verse ; hymns in imitation of Pindar, the first of their kind ; the penitential Psalms; and satires in terza rima, of which the tenth is that freely translated by Wyatt, who doubtless was led by imitation of Alamanni to the choice of the rhyme for his own three satires.  The two longest of Wyatt's amatory odes were taken from two canzoni of Petrarch.  With all this, there is evidence in Wyatt's poetry of strain for ingenuity of word and phrase, for the *concetti* or ingenious conceits which had been developed

K

in Italian literature by imitators of Petrarch, and which had even begun to form a part of polite conversation in the chief Italian cities.

44. **Henry Howard, Earl of Surrey,** born about 1517, was some fourteen years younger than Sir Thomas Wyatt, the poet, and but a few years older than Wyatt's son. He was himself the grandson of that Earl of Surrey to whom the dukedom of Norfolk, forfeited by his father, was given again, in 1514, for his services at Flodden Field. The father of the poet inherited the dukedom in 1524; and Henry Howard, his eldest son, became Earl of Surrey at the age of seven. He was cupbearer to the king in 1526; and in 1533, when Wyatt, aged thirty, served as ewerer at the coronation of Anne Boleyn, the Earl of Surrey, aged about sixteen, carried one of the swords before the king. Early in 1532 he had been contracted in marriage to the Lady Frances Vere, daughter to John, Earl of Oxford. He was married to her in 1535, at the age of about eighteen. In March of the following year his eldest son, Thomas, was born, and Surrey was knighted in October. His second son, Henry, was born in 1539. Early in 1542, Queen Catherine Howard, a cousin of Surrey's, whom the king married within a fortnight after his divorce from Anne of Cleves, was executed in the Tower; but on the following St. George's Day, Surrey was made a Knight of the Garter. In July of the same year, the Earl of Surrey was imprisoned in the Fleet for seeking fight with a gentleman of Middlesex, an offence which he admitted, and ascribed to "the fury of reckless youth." He was released early in August, and crossed the border with his father, who had command of that expedition against Scotland which clouded with disaster the last hours of the Scottish James V.

45. Henry VIII.'s sister, Queen Margaret, for whom in her youth Dunbar had written "The Thistle and the Rose," died in 1541, after wild endeavours to obtain divorce from her third husband. In the same year died the two infant boys born of the marriage of James V., in 1538, with Mary of Guise (§ 38). James was perplexed at home. His uncle Henry was imperious. He demanded in vain that all religious refugees from England to Scotland should be delivered up to him. He proposed to meet his nephew at York, went thither in state, found there no King of Scots, was furious, accused James of breaking faith and of connivance with the Irish rebels, and resolved to assert forcibly his claim to be master of Scotland. There was also the fact

that Beaton, become a cardinal, had gone, in 1541, from Scotland to Rome on a secret embassy. On such grounds Henry VIII. declared war, and the Earl of Surrey's father was sent, with Surrey among his forces, to harry the Scots across the border. A dash of three thousand against Jedburgh failed, six hundred were taken prisoners. Henry sent thirty thousand men to the North, without caring how they were to be fed. That army did some mischief, but could not be kept together, and James V. might have retaliated upon England; but the Scots abided by the policy of simple defence to which they had held since Flodden. Ten thousand were, nevertheless, dispatched across the border. On English ground they were in tumult of wrath at finding that an unworthy favourite of King James was their commander. Into the midst of the confusion thus caused a troop of English soldiers dashed, and the Scots army was dispersed at Solway Moss. The king, whose strength had long been failing, was not far distant, and news of this disaster came to him on the 7th of December, 1542, side by side with announcement of the birth of a daughter. He said, despondingly, of his kingdom, "It came with a lass, and it will go with a lass;" and died on the 14th of the same month, leaving that infant, a week old, Mary Queen of Scots.

**James V. of Scotland**, with vices of a kind too easily forgiven, did with rough energy seek to work out the problem of society, and, while cruelly satisfying his own hatreds, do some good to John the Common Weal (§ 36, 37). The poor man had access to him. The power of the great lord was severely curbed. James V. was called the King of the Commons; has been credited with the authorship of *Christis Kirk of the Green*, and *Peblis to the Play*, or of "Christ's Kirk of the Green" as an imitation of the other poem, which might then be ascribed to James I., his predecessor. He certainly did write verse, and the original conception of two songs, which come to us only in a later Scottish dialect, the *Jollie Beggar* and the *Gaberlunzie Man*, has been ascribed to him.

46. **The Earl of Surrey,** after his return from the northern expedition, was, in April, 1543, summoned before the Privy Council on a charge laid against him by the Mayor, Recorder, and Corporation of London, for going about the streets at midnight in unseemly manner, with Thomas Wyatt the younger and another companion, breaking windows of the citizens with stone bows. He pleaded guilty, and was again sent to the Fleet.

There he wrote a whimsical little *Satire against the Citizens of London*, arguing that his object was to warn them of their sins and, since preaching failed,

> " By unknown means it likèd me
> My hidden burthen to express
> Whereby it might appear to thee
>     That secret sin hath secret spite ;
> From justice' rod no fault is free,
>     But that all such as work unright
> In most quiet are next ill rest :
>     In secret silence of the night
> This made me with a reckless breast
> To wake thy sluggards with my bow."

After his second penance in the Fleet, Surrey went a second time to the wars. In October, 1543, he joined as a volunteer the English force encamped before Landrecy, near Boulogne, in aid of the Emperor. After a month's study of the art of war, Surrey came home, when the army went into winter quarters. Then he began to build a great house, Mount Surrey, at St. Leonards, near Norwich. In July, 1544, he went to the wars again, and aided his father in the siege of Montreuil, while Henry VIII. in person invested and took Boulogne. The siege of Montreuil was then raised, and Surrey, as marshal of the English camp, conducted the retreat. At the end of the year he and the Duke of Norfolk, his father, were again in England. In August, 1544, the Earl of Surrey crossed the Channel again ; this time as commander of the vanguard in an expedition for the defence of Boulogne. He was presently in command at Boulogne, and so remained till April, 1546, when he was recalled. He returned, spoke angrily of the Earl of Hertford (afterwards Protector Somerset), whom the king had placed over him, and who was at feud with the Howards. For this Surrey underwent a short imprisonment in Windsor Castle but on the 12th of December both he and his father were arrested and sent, one by land the other by water, to the Tower. They were of royal blood, and could be ruined easily by the suggestion to King Henry of any shadow of suspicion that after his death they might aspire to the throne during the minority of his son Edward. Mainly upon a question of the royal quartering in his arms, as he had borne them for years with assent of the heralds, the Earl of Surrey was condemned to death as a traitor. His death warrant was nearly the last signed by Henry VIII.; signed with a stamp, since the dying king was himself become unable to write. Surrey was but thirty years old when he was beheaded on Tower

Hill, on the 21st of January, 1547, and the king died within a week, leaving the Duke of Norfolk's death warrant unsigned.

Henry Howard, Earl of Surrey, was impetuous and lively, less inclined than Sir Thomas Wyatt to side with the Church Reformers, but liberal of mind, bold, frank, incapable of subterfuge or falsehood. His *Paraphrases* of the first five chapters of *Ecclesiastes*, and of the 8th, 55th, 73rd, and 88th *Psalms*, show the religious side of his English character. The Paraphrases of the Psalms were made, as a little poem tells, when justice had impressed him with some error of his reckless youth, and

> " Began to work despair of liberty,
> Had not David the perfect warrior taught
> That of my fault thus pardon should be sought."

Surrey's complaints, sonnets, and other poems in the Italian manner, all of love, are more various in their interest but less various in their music than those of Wyatt, and contain a few touches of mirth, as in the pleasant poem of "A Careless Man Scorning and Describing the Subtle Usage of Women towards their Lovers," which ends thus:

> " Lord ! what abuse is this; who can such women praise,
> That for their glory do devise to use such crafty ways ?
> I, that among the rest do sit and mark the row,
> Find that in her is greater craft than is in twenty mo';
> Whose tender years, alas ! with wiles so well are sped,
> What will she do when hoary hairs are powdered in her head ?"

Two of Surrey's sonnets have made it possible to identify the Geraldine to whom they were addressed. She was Elizabeth, second daughter of Gerald Fitzgerald, ninth Earl of Kildare ; a child whose family was attainted for revolt against the crown, and whose father was in the Tower when she was brought to Hunsdon to be cared for by her second cousin, the Princess Mary. This little homeless child was seven years old in the year of Surrey's marriage, eight years old when his first son was born. According to the custom of addressing sequences of love sonnets to anybody whom it was desired to honour, and towards whom there was no personal love-suit (ch. iii. § 36; ch. iv. § 11) the Earl of Surrey, with kind feeling towards the child, made her his Geraldine. When she was about fifteen (in 1543) she married, and became Lady Brown. She was but nineteen in the year of Surrey's execution, and that was in the lifetime of his wife, who survived him twenty years.

Wyatt and Surrey are said to have been the introducers of

the sonnet into English literature, but this credit is due especially to Wyatt, not only as the elder man and earlier writer, but as the one of the two who alone gave accurate models of the structure of that form of poem. Surrey did not take the trouble to observe the rule of rhyming in the octave of two quatrains and the sestette of two terzettes which constitute the typical Italian sonnet, and his rhymes do not once accord with the system from which Petrarch hardly more than once departed, even in a slight degree. The true sonnet consists of two quatrains and two terzettes. In the two quatrains forming the first eight lines there are only two rhymes, with their order fixed for the first quatrain, where it is a b b a, but not for the second. These quatrains open the subject. The expression of the thought for which the sonnet is written falls within the two terzettes, and here vigour of expression is less cramped by restriction in the rhyming ; while there are but six lines there are three rhymes, and they may be arranged at the discretion of the poet, energy of expression being at its height in the last line. Although Surrey's sonnets are in fourteen lines, and closely imitate Petrarch's forms of thought, yet as to their mechanism they are all at fault. Wyatt studied the form of the verse before he imitated, and the true sonnet was introduced into our literature by him alone.

47. The Earl of Surrey, however, stands alone as the first English writer of Blank Verse. He translated two books of the "Æneid," the second and fourth, into ten-syllabled lines of metre without rhyme, and this experiment was founded upon one of the new fashions in Italian literature. It may have been immediately suggested to him by a translation into Italian blank verse of the same two books of Virgil by Cardinal Ippolito de' Medici, or more probably by the poet Francesco Maria Molza, who allowed the cardinal to take the credit of it. Molza was a bright poet in Latin and Italian, who closed in 1544 a life shortened by dissipation. The taste for unrhymed verses, called *versi sciolti* (untied or free verses) was new even in Italy. In Tuscan literature, unrhymed verse existed, indeed, at the outset. It has been said that the prose of Boccaccio in the " Decameron " was largely intermixed with " versi sciolti," not distinguished from prose in the writing, or afterwards in the printing. Among the most notable of early examples was the *Cantico del Sole* ("Canticle of the Sun") by St. Francis of Assisi (ch. iii. § 27), which, although written as prose, admits of an arrangement into lines of seven and eleven syllables. The

brethren were also taught to sing it by Fra Pacifico, a poet and musician of that time.   But the Provençals being incapable of this form of verse, the Tuscans almost ceased to use it.   At the beginning of the sixteenth century, it appeared in Italy with the new birth of the drama.   The final vowel in Italian makes the blank verse answering to ours of ten syllables eleven syllabled, with the last syllable short.   Ariosto gave in his comedies great lightness to his verse by making at the end of a line two short syllables, instead of one, trip after the last accent. This blank measure of his own device is said to be of *endecasillibi sdruccioli* (sliding hendecasyllables).   Trissino used unrhymed lines of eleven syllables, with the last unaccented, in his tragedy of *Sofonisba,* begun about 1515, and printed in 1529 (§ 41).  Alamanni was another active cultivator of blank verse, and used it freely in his *Opere Toscane,* published in 1532 (§ 43).  All this was known to the Earl of Surrey, as a reader of the best Italian literature of his time.   Trissino's attempt to extend the use of blank verse to the epic poem in his *Italia Liberata,* which nobody wished to imitate, could have had nothing to do with any writing of the Earl of Surrey's, for the first part of that poem was not published until some months after Surrey's execution. But there were Ariosto's comedies ; there was Trissino's tragedy ; there were Alamanni's elegies ; and more particularly there was the version of the same two books of Virgil, in Italian blank verse, ascribed to the Cardinal Ippolito de' Medici. Boscan was introducing blank verse into Spain, among his other imitations of Italian fashions (§ 39), at the time when Surrey was first writing it in England.   The first blank verse in Spain was Boscan's version of the story of Hero and Leander, some 3,000 lines long, published in 1543.

In Surrey's translation there are passages which seem to show that he was acquainted with Gavin Douglas's version of the "Æneid" into heroic couplet, although that work was not printed till 1553.  Nor were any of the poems of Wyatt or Surrey printed before the death of Henry VIII.  They were handed about and read in written copies.  The first collection of them in print was made, we shall find, with verse of other poets of less mark, in 1557,

48. There can be no doubt that the first known English comedy, although not printed until 1566, was produced in the latter part of the reign of Henry VIII.   Its author was **Nicholas Udall,** born in Hampshire, in 1505 or 1506.  In 1520 he was admitted a scholar of Corpus Christi College.

Oxford. He took his degree of B.A. at Oxford, but his known goodwill to the Lutherans kept him from proceeding to his M.A. until 1534. At Oxford, Leland was among his friends; and in 1532, Leland and Udall jointly wrote the Pageant exhibited by the Mayor and Citizens of London when Anne Boleyn entered the City after her marriage. Udall was at that time a schoolmaster. In 1533 he published and dedicated to his boys, *Floures for Latin Spekynge*, selected and gathered out of Terence, and the same translated into English. The selections were made from the first three comedies of Terence. In 1534, Udall, who was highly esteemed for his scholarship, was made head master of Eton School; and in 1538 appeared a newly-corrected edition of his " Flowers for Latin Speaking," enlarged from 110 to 192 pages. It was the custom at Eton for the boys to act at Christmas some Latin stage-play, chosen or written for them by the master. Among the writings ascribed to Udall about the year 1540 were several Latin comedies, and a tragedy on the Papacy, written probably to be acted by his scholars. When it occurred to him to write for his boys an English comedy, wherein, as its Prologue says,

> " All scurrility we utterly refuse,
> Avoiding such mirth wherein is abuse,'

and avowedly following Plautus and Terence, " which among the learned at this day bears the bell," he produced what is, as far as we know, the first English comedy. Its name is *Ralph Roister Doister*, and it professed to be a wholesome jest against vain-glory. " Roisterer " is still northern English for a swaggerer, but the word came in from the old French *rustre* (" a ruffian "). The *rustarii* were French freebooters of the eleventh century. Ralph Roister Doister of Udall's play is a swaggering simpleton, a feeble conceited fop of the days of Henry VIII., who is played upon and lived upon by Matthew Merrygreek, a needy humourist. The jest of the play was in the absurdities of Ralph's suit to Dame Christian Custance, " a widow with a thousand pound," already betrothed to a merchant, Gavin Goodluck, away at sea. The play, in lively rhyming couplets, interspersed with a few merry songs, was written with so good a sense of the reverence due to boys that it may be read by boys of the present day. The incidents provided good matter for merry acting, with an occasional burst of active fun, as in a brisk battle lost by Ralph and his men to Custance and her women, armed with broomsticks. The comedy showed also its origin in a schoolmaster, by including a good lesson on the importance of right pauses in reading. A love-letter sent by Ralph to Dame Christian Custance was read to her, with its sense reversed by putting the stops in the wrong places, thus :

> " Now by these presents I do you advertise
> That I am minded to marry you in no wise.
> For your goods and substance I could be content
> To take you as ye are. If ye mind to be my wife,
> Ye shall be assured for the time of my life
> I will keep ye right well from good raiment and fare.
> Ye shall not be kept but in sorrow and care.
> Ye shall in no wise live at your own liberty ;
> Do and say what ye lust, ye shall never please me,
> But when ye are merry, I will be all sad ;
> When ye are sorry I will be very glad ;
> When ye seek your heart's ease I will be unkind ;
> At no time in me shall ye much gentleness find ;"

and so forth, all reversible by change of punctuation. The last-quoted lines seem to be a play upon a verse of Sir Thomas Wyatt's—

> " When ye be merry then I am glad,
> When ye be sorry then I am sad ;
> Such a grace or fortune I would I had,
> You for to please howe'er I were bestad."

If this comedy, as there can be little doubt, was written for the Eton boys, its date must be during Udall's time at Eton, between 1534 and 1541, when the result of an inquiry into what was called a robbery of silver images and plate from the College (but the question being of images suggests another view of the matter) was Udall's dismissal from the mastership. He was then Vicar of Braintree, in Essex, and remained so until December, 1544, when he resigned. In 1542, Udall published an English translation of the third or fourth books of the "Apophthegms of Erasmus," with an introduction and colloquial notes. He was still schoolmaster somewhere. Between 1542 and 1545 he was translating the *Paraphrase of Erasmus* upon Luke, which he dedicated to Henry's last queen, Catherine Parr, by whose "procurement and charge" the other parts of the Paraphrase of Erasmus upon the New Testament were being Englished. The Princess Mary undertook and partly translated the Paraphrase of St John's Gospel, but falling ill, left it to be finished by her chaplain. The first volume, containing the Gospels and the Acts, was published after King Henry's death, in January, 1548.

K *

49. There were Masques and Interludes during the reign of Henry VIII. Disguisings formed part of the pleasures of a court even so early as the reign of Edward III., who kept Christmas at Guildford in 1348 with mumming in masks and fancy dresses. Francis I. and Henry VIII. took pleasure in costly entertainments; and the more elaborate Masque, introduced from Italy very early in Henry VIII.'s reign, with characters assumed by lords and ladies, first became an important feature in court entertainments. The chronicler Edward Hall has recorded that, at Greenwich, in 1512, "on the day of the Epiphany at night, the king, with eleven others, was disguised after the manner of Italy, called a Mask, a thing not seen before in England; they were appareled in garments long and broad, wrought all with gold, with visors and caps of gold. And after the banquet done, these masquers came in with six gentlemen disguised in silk, bearing staff torches, and desired the ladies to dance; some were content, and some refused; and after they had danced and communed together, as the fashion of the mask is, they took their leave, and departed." Holinshed has described a masque at Greenwich in Henry VIII.'s time, with mechanical contrivances, and action in dumb show. A castle was built in the hall of the palace, with towers, gates, battlements, and mimic preparations for a siege. It was inscribed on the front "Le Fortresse Dangereux." Six ladies, clothed in russet satin, overlaid with leaves of gold, and with gold coifs and caps, looked from the castle windows. The castle was so made that it could be moved about the hall for admiration by the company. Then entered the king with five knights in embroidered vestments, spangled and plaited with gold. They besieged the castle until the ladies surrendered, and came out to dance with them. The ladies then led the knights into the castle, which immediately vanished, and the company retired.

In these Masques there was dumb-show and dancing, but no speaking. Another form of entertainment, "after banquet done," or between meat and the banquet or dessert, was the Interlude. This was satire in dialogue, ingeniously written for the entertainment of the company, and spoken by persons who assumed different characters; but there was no working out of a dramatic fable. Generation after generation of Italian villagers had been thus entertained in rustic farces. In Spain the Constable de Luna, who was executed in 1453, was said by his chronicler to have had a great deal of inventive faculty, and to have been " much given to making inventions and (*entremeses*) interludes for festivals." In France there was the fraternity of the *Enfants sans Souci*, formed of lively young men of good society, who acted jests upon the follies of their day. They were an offshoot from the French Festival of Fools, which burlesqued religion in the churches about Christmas time; but passing from the Church to the world, they called Humanity " Folly," and their President the "Prince of Fools." Charles VI., about the time of the death of Chaucer, had given them special privilege to act their jests in public places. There were also the Clerks of the Bazoche; these were the law clerks of the palace, whom Philip the Fair had formed in 1303 into a half-burlesque guild, called the Bazoche, for judgment of disputes between attorneys' clerks, or between them and other people. The Clerks of the Bazoche acted farces before the king on a marble table at the end of the great hall of the palace. In 1516 the Bazoche was forbidden to refer to princes and princesses of the court; in 1536 all personality was forbidden under penalties; and in 1538 it was required that the players of these entertainments should submit their manuscript to the court fifteen days before acting, and omit passages marked by the court censor, on pain of prison and corporal punishment. Such entertainments, of which, in France, very free use was made for political and social satire, were represented at Henry VIII.'s court by the Interludes of **John Heywood.** Two printed in 1532 were *The Play of Love; or, a New and a very Mery Enterlude of all Maner Weathers;* and *A Mery Play between the Pardoner and the Frere, the Curate and Neybour Pratte.* One published in 1535 was called *Of Gentylnes and Nobylyte: a Dyaloge between the Marchaunt, the Knyght, and the Plowman, compiled in maner of an Enterlude, with divers Toys and Gestis added thereto to make Mery Pastyme and Disport.* Of another, published without date, and called *The Foure P.s: a very Mery Enterlude of a Palmer, a Pardoner, a Potecary, and a Pedlar*, the jest was, that after each had shown his humours—and here Heywood, although firm to the old Church, wrote as contemptuously as Sir David Lindsay of the Pardoner's traffic—first rank was to be adjudged by the Pedlar to whichever of his three companions excelled in lying, since that was, in the way of business, common to all. The Palmer won with this:

" And this I would ye should understand,
I have seen women five hundred thousand ;
And oft with them have some time tarried.
Yet in all places where I have been,
Of all the woman that I have seen,
I never saw nor knew in my conscience,
Any one woman out of patience."

John Heywood was born perhaps at North Mims, in Hertfordshire, where afterwards he certainly had a home. He was
opposed to Lutheranism; and his friendship for Sir Thomas
More having brought him into the king's favour, he retained it
by his wit. He remained at court when Edward VI. was king,
and under Queen Mary, for whom, when a young princess, he
had shown a particular respect; but on the accession of Elizabeth he went abroad, and died at Mechlin, in 1565. Besides his
Interludes, John Heywood wrote six hundred Epigrams. Italian
influence had bred lively demand at court for ingenious quips
and turns of speech, which Henry VIII. was clever enough to
relish. To this reign belonged the collection of *A Hundred
Merry Tales*, first printed about 1525, by John Rastell—a learned
printer, and author too, who married a sister of Sir Thomas
More—and the *Merry Tales and Quick Answers*, printed about
1535, by Thomas Berthelet.

50. Another writer of Interludes was **John Bale,** born in
1495, at Cove, in Suffolk, educated among the Carmelites in
Norwich, and then at Jesus College, Cambridge. Heywood
was not a Protestant, but Bale became one, and escaped from
under the papacy of Henry VIII. in England, to live in
Holland during the last six years of his reign. Henry condemned with equal severity the religious heresy of Lutherans,
and the political heresy of those who in matters of faith placed
the pope as an authority above himself. A new edition of
Fabyan's Chronicle (§ 8), published in 1542, was adapted to the
times by transforming Becket's epithet of " blessed saint " into
"traitorous bishop." The word "pope" was changed in it
throughout to " Bishop of Rome." Everything was omitted or
altered that tended to encourage houses of religion, penance,
pilgrimages, or the preservation of relics, or spoke of the contempt of shrines as an offence.

A later chronicler than Fabyan was **Edward Hall,** born
in Shropshire at the end of the fifteenth century. He was in
1514 scholar of King's College, Cambridge, but removed to
Oxford; about 1518, Hall entered at Gray's Inn, was called to

the bar, became Common Serjeant and Under Sheriff, and in 1540 one of the judges of the Sheriff's Court. His career belonged entirely to the reign of Henry VIII., and he died in 1547. His history of *The Union of the Two Noble and Illustre Families of Lancastre and Yorke,* commonly called Hall's *Chronicle,* ended with the year 1532. It was first published in 1548, after its author's death, by Richard Grafton, who said that " Hall dying, and being in his latter time not so painful and studious as he ought to have been," Grafton himself undertook the completion of it. This was a forbidden book under Philip and Mary.

51. English scholarship was best represented in the latter part of Henry VIII.'s reign by Roger Ascham, with whom we shall presently pass to later times ; and by **John Cheke** and **Thomas Smith,** neither of them knighted before Henry's death. They were born in the same year, 1514 ; Cheke at Cambridge, Smith at Saffron Walden, in Essex. Both studied at Cambridge, Cheke at St. John's College, and Smith at Queen's ; both became famous at the University as students—and, while still young men, teachers—of Greek. They worked together as reformers of the method of pronunciation, and excited a warm controversy on the subject. Greek, as received into England from the teaching of the learned refugees (ch. v. § 25, 30), was pronounced after their fashion ; β was pronounced like our *v,* *ι* and *αι* were pronounced alike, and *ι, ι, υ* had the same sound. Cheke and Smith declared this to be a modern Greek corruption of the ancient language, and proposed to give each letter value. They began by partial use of their new system of pronunciation in the course of lectures. When this had provoked question, each appointed a day for the explanation of his views, and both won followers. Students of Cambridge then acted the " Plutus " of Aristophanes pronounced in the new manner, and, six years later, when Dr. Ratcliff tried the old way he was hissed. He appealed to the Chancellor of the University. This was Stephen Gardiner, Bishop of Winchester, who addressed to Cheke an admonition that conceded high respect to him as a scholar, but condemned the youthful fervour with which he was spreading heresy against the established form of Greek pronunciation among students of the University. Gardiner then exercised his authority as Chancellor by issuing, in 1542, an edict settling the true faith in Greek vowels and diphthongs as absolutely as King Henry VIII.

settled it for his subjects in all other matters. Cheke held his own, and replied with a treatise, *De Pronuntiatione Lingua Graca,* which was published afterwards in 1555. Smith wrote also a sensible letter on the subject, and the Chancellor's decrees were not obeyed.

At the age of two-and-twenty, Cheke had published an English tract, called " *A Remedy for Sedition,* wherein are contained many things concerning the true and loyal obeisance that Commons owe unto their Prince and Sovereign Lord the King." In later days his loyalty and his fame as a scholar caused him to be appointed tutor to Prince Edward.

52. **Sir David Lindsay,** of the Mount, after the death of James V., went officially to deliver back to Charles V., in the Netherlands, the late king's badge of the order of the Golden Fleece. In 1544-6 he sat in three Parliaments as member for Cupar. Luther died on the 18th of February, 1546. On the 28th of May, in the same year, occurred the event moralised by Lindsay in his poem called " *The Tragedie of the vmquhylle* " (whilom) " *maist reverend father, David, be the mercy of God, Cardinal and Archibyschope of Sanct Androvs,*" &c. Here Lindsay told in Chaucer's seven-lined stanza how, when he was sitting in his oratory, reading Boccaccio on the " Falls of Illustrious Men " (ch. v. § 13), there appeared to him

> " Ane woundit man, aboundantlie bledyng,
> With visage paill, and with ane dedlye cheir,
> Semand ane man of two-and-fyftie yeir ;
> In rayment reid clothet full curiouslie,
> Off vellot and of saiting crammosie."

" With feeble voice, as man opprest with pain," he declared himself to be the late Cardinal Beaton, and told the story of his life, and of his fall from the height of power. He was slain, and his body, salted and closed in a box, lay for seven months in a dunghill without Christian burial. Let all my brother prelates, said the ghost, amend their lives, remembering that they will be called to account for everything belonging to their cures :

> " Ye prelat, quhilk hes thousandis for to spende,
> Ye send ane sempyll freir for you to preche :
> It is your craft—I mak it yow to kend—
> Your selfis in your templis for to teche."

The death of Beaton brought together Knox and Lindsay, for Lindsay was then among those who persuaded Knox to his first preaching.

53. **John Knox** was born in 1505, at Gifford, in East Lothian. He was educated in the Grammar School at Haddington, and in 1522 matriculated in St. Andrew's University, which then had John Mair (§ 33) for its provost. He took priests' orders, but was drawn to the side of the Reformers; and became the friend and follower of George Wishart, a Scottish schoolmaster, who, about 1536, began to preach as a Reformer. Wishart went to England and recanted, but, recovering more than his old boldness, came back to Scotland in 1543, and, though of gentle character, preached with intense enthusiasm. Thus he stirred among the people violent antagonism to the practices that he denounced, so that they wept over them in themselves, and raged at them in others. John Knox, to protect his beloved preacher, whose assassination had been once attempted, waited upon him bearing a two-handed sword. Flesh and blood went for little in the growing heat of spiritual conflict. On the 20th of November, 1541, at Geneva, Calvin's ecclesiastical and moral code was established. Under this code it was forbidden to read "Amadis of Gaul," or any romances. Three children were solemnly punished for stopping outside to eat apples after service had begun. In 1568 a child was beheaded for having struck her parents. A lad of sixteen was sentenced to death for only threatening to strike his mother. And this was called the "Yoke of Christ." Knox was tutor to the sons of the lairds of Niddrie and Ormiston. When Wishart was seized as a heretic, Knox desired to share his fate; "Nay," said Wishart, "return to your bairns" (his pupils), "and God bless you. One is enough for a sacrifice." Wishart's martyrdom, in March, 1545, witnessed by Beaton from his velvet cushions at a window of the castle of St. Andrew's, was followed in May, 1546, by the murder of Beaton. This had been for two years the subject of a conspiracy, of which both Wishart and King Henry VIII. had an assenting knowledge. To Wishart and others plot of such a murder was honest question of hewing Agag in pieces. Beaton's deathblow was prefaced by the man who dealt it with a deliberate speech, declaring it to be about to fall "only because thou hast been, and remainest, an obstinate enemy against Christ Jesus and His Gospel." The sixteen men who had surprised Beaton in his castle held it, and welcomed into it all.men whose zeal for Reformed opinions brought them within the danger of the Scottish hierarchy. The chief murderers of Beaton, Henry's most vigorous political

antagonist in Scotland, received pensions from the King of England; and the garrison—Castilians as they were called—in the strong castle by the sea, received also supplies of money and victuals from Henry VIII.   In April, 1547, Knox joined the Castilians.   Sir David Lindsay also went among them.   Their chaplain had been worsted in argument by an orthodox dean. Knox came to the rescue with his pen.   Then many of them urged Knox to preach.   He had renounced his priests' orders, and said he had no vocation; but it was urged on him that every congregation has an inherent right to call any qualified person to be its teacher.   So Knox began his preaching.   In August of the same year a French squadron obliged the garrison to capitulate, and Knox became for two years a prisoner in the French galleys.   When on one occasion an image of the Virgin was brought round for the prisoners to kiss, Knox said, "Trouble me not.   Such an idol is accursed, therefore I will not touch it."   When it was forced on him, he threw it into the river, saying, "Let Our Lady now save herself.   She is light enough; let her swim."

54. The Scottish Reformers of those days completed "*A Compendious Book of Godly and Spiritual Songs*, collected out of sundrie parts of Scripture, with sundrie of other ballates changed out of prophaine sangis," and set the best of the gay tunes to new words, breathing love of God or defiance of the pope, in this fashion :

> " The paip, that pagane full of pryd,
>    Hee hes us blinded lang ;
> For where the blind the blind doe gyde,
>    No wonder both goe wrang.
> Of all iniquitie,
> Like prince and king, hee led the ring.
> Hay trix, trim goe trix, under the greenwode tree."

On New Year's-day, 1540, when Francis I. and Charles V. rode into Paris together, and Sir Thomas Wyatt (§ 43), Ambassador Extraordinary from England, was commissioned to search quietly into the minds of those two princes, Clement Marot presented to King Francis his translation of thirty of the Psalms of David set to light song tunes or airs from the vaudevilles. Marot translated twenty more ; they became even fashionable substitutes for songs on idler themes.   Calvin adopted them— when set to graver strains, written specially for them by Guillaume Franc—for use in the churches of Geneva, and published them with a preface of his own, in which he commended the fit use of Church music. In England **Thomas Sternhold** felt the new impulse, and translated during Henry VIII.'s reign some of the Psalms into English. Sternhold was born in Hampshire, and after education at Oxford, became groom of the robes to Henry VIII., who liked him well enough to bequeath him a hundred marks. He desired to do with his psalms in England what had been done in France by Marot, "thinking thereby that the courtiers would sing them instead of their sonnets, but did not, only some few excepted," whose religion we respect more than their taste.

55. We now pass out of the reign of Henry VIII. with **Roger Ascham**, who was born, about the year 1515, at Kirkby Wiske, near Northallerton, in Yorkshire. His father, house steward in the family of Lord Scrope, had two daughters and three sons. Young Roger Ascham was educated by Sir Humphrey Wingfield, of whom he said afterwards, "This worshipful man hath ever loved, and used to have many children brought up in learning in his house, amonges whom I myself was one, for whom at term times he would bring down from London both bow and shafts. And when they should play he would go with them himself into the field, see them shoot, and he that shot fairest should have the best bow and shafts, and he that shot ill-favouredly should be mocked of his fellows till he shot better. Would to God all England had used or would use to lay the foundation of youth after the example of this worshipful man in bringing up children in the Book and the Bow; by which two things the whole commonwealth, both in peace and war, is chiefly valid and defended withal." Sir Humphrey was enforcing the spirit of the law that required all boys between seven and seventeen to be provided with a long-bow and two arrows; every Englishman older than seventeen to provide himself with a bow and four arrows; and every bowyer to make at least two cheap bows for every dear one. At fifteen Roger Ascham became a student at St. John's College, Cambridge. He took his B.A. in 1534; obtained a fellowship in his college; and in 1537 became a college lecturer on Greek. He was at home for a couple of years after 1540, during which time he obtained a pension of forty shillings from the Archbishop of York. It ceased at the archbishop's death, in 1544. In that year, 1544, Ascham wrote *Toxophilus*, and lost his parents, who both died on the same day. In 1545, being then twenty-nine years old, he presented "Toxophilus"

to the king, at Greenwich, and was rewarded with a pension of ten pounds.

"Toxophilus" was a scholar's book, designed to encourage among all gentlemen and yeomen of England the practice of archery for defence of the realm. The treatise was divided into two books of dialogue between Philologus and Toxophilus; the first book containing general argument to commend shooting, the second a particular description of the art of shooting with the long-bow. Ascham argued for it as a worthy recreation— one very fit for scholars—that in peace excludes ignoble pastimes, and in war gives to a nation strength. Men should seek, he said, to excel in it, and make it a study. Then he proceeded in the second part of his work to treat it as a study. The book was published in 1545, with a dedication to Henry VIII., and a preface, in which Ascham justified his use of English. To have written in another tongue would, he said, have better advanced his studies and his credit; but he wished to be read by the gentlemen and yeomen of England. He could not surpass what others had done in Greek and Latin; while English had usually been written by ignorant men so meanly, both for the matter and handling, that no man could do worse. Ascham was, in his preface to "Toxophilus," the first to suggest that English prose might be written with the same scholarly care that would be required for choice and ordering of words if one wrote Latin. "He that will write well in any tongue," said Ascham, "must follow this counsel of Aristotle, to speak as the common people do, to think as wise men do; and so should every man understand him, and the judgment of wise men allow him. Many English writers have not done so, but using strange words as Latin, French and Italian, do make all things dark and hard. Once I communed with a man which reasoned the English tongue to be enriched and increased thereby, saying, 'Who will not praise that feast where a man shall drink at a dinner both wine, ale, and beer?' 'Truly,' quod I, 'they be all good, every one taken by himself alone, but if you put malmsey and sack, red wine and white, ale and beer, and all in one pot, you shall make a drink neither easy to be known, nor yet wholesome for the body.'" The manly simplicity of Ascham's own English is in good accord with his right doctrine. His Latin was so well esteemed that in the year after the appearance of "Toxophilus" he succeeded Cheke as Public Orator, and wrote the official letters of the University.

Ascham was famous also for his penmanship, and taught writing to the prince whose reign we now pass into, Edward VI. (1547-1553), at the date of his accession, between nine and ten years old. The Earl of Hertford was made Protector, as Duke of Somerset. Under Edward VI., Ascham had his pension confirmed and augmented. In 1548 he became tutor to the Princess Elizabeth, at Cheston, but he was annoyed by her steward, and had therefore returned to the University when, in 1550, he was through Cheke's good offices appointed secretary to Sir Richard Morison, then going as Ambassador to Charles V. He reached Augsburg in October, was away more than a year, and published in 1553 a *Report and Discourse written by Roger Ascham, of the Affairs and State of Germany and the Emperor Charles his Court, during certain years while the said Roger was there.*

56. **John Cheke** (§ 51), who had assisted for the last three years in Edward's education, was a great scholar himself, and a cause of scholarship in others who earned reputation and looked back to him with gratitude. He was knighted by King Edward, and had grants of land. He became also in this reign a privy councillor and secretary of state. Sir John Cheke drew force for the real work of life out of his studies. He was especially familiar with Demosthenes, and said that the study of him taught Englishmen how to speak their minds.

**Thomas Smith** (§ 51), who had been travelling among the Universities of France and Italy towards the close of Henry VIII.'s reign, and took the doctor's degree at Padua, was, after the accession of Edward VI., made Provost of Eton; in 1548 he was knighted. Sir Thomas Smith became, like his friend Sir John Cheke, a secretary of state under Edward, and he was employed as an ambassador.

57. In the first year of the new rule the Protector Somerset endeavoured to compel the union of North and South by enforcing Henry VIII.'s policy of a marriage between Edward of England and Mary Queen of Scots. "If we two," he wrote, of the two countries, "being made one by amity, be most able to defend us against all nations, and having the sea for wall, the mutual love for garrison, and God for defence, should make so noble and well-agreeing a monarchy that neither in peace we may be ashamed nor in war afraid of any worldly or foreign power, why should not you be as desirous of the same and have as much cause to rejoice at it as we?" John Knox was in the

French galleys; the old hierarchy ruled in Scotland. There Reformation was under foot; in England its friends were supreme. Accord was impossible. There was one more shock of arms, and a defeat of Scots at the Battle of Pinkie.

Of **Sir David Lindsay** there is little more to tell. He had written, probably before the accession of Edward VI., his *Historie of Squire William Meldrum,* umquhile laird of Cleische and Bynnis, a whimsical burlesque romance that is not all burlesque, of a valiant Scottish squire of Lindsay's own time, with a taste in it of Chaucer's Sir Thopas, or rather of the Italian half-mocking treatment of heroic song, and an after relish of strong national self-satisfaction. This is the best of Lindsay's lighter strains. His last work was his longest, and supremely grave—*The Monarchie: a Dialogue betwixt Experience and a Courtier, of the Miserable Estate of the World* —finished in 1553. The first line of its Epistle to the Reader called it a "lytil quair of mater miserabyll." There was, alas, no king to dedicate it to, but it was submitted to the rulers and priests, praying them to Christianise the laws, and remember that Scotland suffered war, famine, and pestilence for sin. The Word of God must be taught, and the people repent of sin, before their enemies could have no might against the Christian banner. He divided his poem into a Prologue and Four Books. The Prologue, in Chaucer's stanza, told how the poet went into a park on a May morning, and, delighted with the beauty of Nature, dwelt upon the miseries of man. He invoked no pagan muse, for he had never slept upon Parnassus, or drunk with Hesiod of Helicon, the source of Eloquence. If any Muse were invoked it might be Rhamnusia, Goddess of Dispute; but, he said:

> " I mon go seik ane muse more confortabyll,
>   And sic vaine superstitioun to refuse,
>   Beseikand the gret God to be my muse."

The mount to which he betook himself was not Parnassus but Calvary; his fountain was the stream that flowed, and flows yet through the world from wounds of Christ upon the Cross. In that stream bathe me, he prayed, and make me clean from sin—

> And grant me grace to wrytt nor dyte no thing
>   Bot tyll his heych honour and loude louyng ;
>   But" (*i.e.*, without) " whose support thare may na gud be wrocht
>   Tyll his plesûre, gude workis, word nor thocht."

After such Prologue, Lindsay told in his first book—this and the rest of the poem being in octosyllabic rhyme—how there came to him, the Courtier, walking in the park, an old man named Experience, of whom he asked comforting counsel. Experience taught that the love of God and of Christ, who died for men, gave comfort among the troubles that have come by sin. After an exclamation to the reader, on his writing in his mother tongue, which led to a requirement that the clergy should teach, and that the books necessary to the spiritual life of men should be translated into the language of the people, Lindsay made Experience tell the Courtier in the rest of Book I. how Adam fell, and the Flood came, through sin ; in Book II., how in the great monarchy of Nineveh the first war was begun "by cruel, prideful, covetous kings" seeking wrongfully to plunder one another. There were four great monarchies—the Assyrian, Persian, Greek, and Roman. Ninus also invented image-worship ; and thus Lindsay passed to long lament for the idolatry in Scotland of his time. Of Ninus and his burial, and of the miserable ends of Semiramis and Sardanapalus, Lindsay told in his second book. In his third book he told of the destruction of Sodom and Gomorrah and the cities of the plain, and shortly of the second, third, and fourth monarchies, with the miserable destruction of Jerusalem ; and lastly, of the spiritual and papal monarchy. Under this head appeared again the grief of the poor man whose three cows would be taken by the Church if he, his wife, and their eldest child should die, so that the little children would be left orphan and destitute. Lindsay's third book of the Monarchy ended with a description of the court of Rome. The fourth book, after dialogue on duty and on death, described Antichrist, the day of judgment, bliss of heaven, and the final monarchy of Christ. David Lindsay was a poet of the same national type as John Gower. He had not the artistic genius of Dunbar, as Gower had not the artistic genius of Chaucer ; but Gower and Lindsay had a like sense of God and duty, a depth of earnestness that was itself a power, a practical aim, and a directness in pursuit of it, that caused each in didactic poetry to "write the ills he saw." The points of difference are manifest ; especially there was in Lindsay a vein of humour, which also belongs to the people whom he represented, but of which Gower seems to have had less than his share.

Sir David Lindsay, as Lion King of Arms, held a chapter of

heralds in January 1555, and that is the last record of his life. It is not known when he died, or where he was buried; but it may be added that in that year 1555 his "Satire of the Three Estates" was acted again before Queen, Court, and Commons.

58. The general pardon usual at a coronation ended at the coronation of Edward VI. the persecution under the Six Articles. A *Book of Homilies*, which had been suggested in the preceding reign to secure uniformity of preaching, was now executed by Archbishop Cranmer and his colleagues. Twelve Homilies were produced and "appointed by the king's majesty to be declared and read by all parsons, vicars, or curates, every Sunday, in their churches where they have cure." There was an English visitation during the Scotch war to ascertain how far in each parish images were removed; pilgrimages, offerings, and superstitious holidays abolished; the Lord's Prayer, and the Ten Commandments, and the Articles of Faith taught to the young; and the great Bible, in English, made accessible in some convenient part of every church. Some associated the two facts that ten thousand Scots fell at Pinkie, and that there was a great destruction of images in London upon the same day. Cranmer had chosen *Erasmus's Paraphrase* of the New Testament for translation. It had been for some time in hand, and was now to form two folio volumes produced at the public expense, and set up in churches for an aid in the instruction of the people. Upon this work we left **Nicholas Udall** busy (§ 48). The first volume, containing the Gospels and the Acts of the Apostles, appeared in January, 1548. Udall, who had translated the Paraphrase of St. Luke's Gospel, placed the texts throughout that Gospel, and the others (except Mark), to show how they corresponded with the Paraphrase. He wrote also an Introduction to the Gospels, in three letters, one to King Edward, one to the Reader, and one to Queen Catherine Parr. The other volume appeared in August, 1549, with a preface by **Miles Coverdale** (§ 26, 29) and John Olde. Coverdale was now Almoner to Queen Catherine, and in 1551 was made Bishop of Exeter.

The first measure of the Parliament of 1549 was an Act for Uniformity of Service, which established the use of an English *Book of Common Prayer* (known as "The First Service Book") in English Churches. Richard Grafton (§ 50) was one of its two authorised printers, and the issue began in March, 1549. With some variations made in an edition of 1552, called "The Second

Service Book," this volume was in its main features that which is still used by the Church of England. In the First Book the service began with the Lord's Prayer. All that now stands before this was added in the Second Book. The reading of the Ten Commandments was placed in the Communion, and there were other occasional changes, such as that in the Burial Service, of prayers for the dead into thanksgivings.

On Whit-Sunday, 1549, the Act for Uniformity of Service came into operation. In Devonshire the people forcibly opposed the disuse of the old method of religious service, which had become associated with their daily sense of God. Exeter itself was besieged. There was armed insurrection, cruelly suppressed. In Norfolk rebellion began in July, and under Robert Ket, tanner, of Wymondham, there was war against the system of enclosures that oppressed the poor. Sir Thomas More had dwelt on this evil in his " Utopia;" Simon Fyshe had touched upon it in his "Supplication for the Beggars"—men made beggars by the religious orders (§ 22). A supplication to Parliament in Henry VIII.'s time showed that in Oxfordshire there were fewer ploughs by forty than there had been. A plough kept six persons ; and where those forty ploughs had fed 240 persons there were only sheep. The disuse of tillage and the throwing of fields together into large pasturages was to a small class a source of wealth, obtained by the service of few shepherds, instead of many ploughmen and field-labourers. Old farm-servants were turned out, and their homes were levelled. It was said that in each of fifty thousand towns, villages, and hamlets, there was an average loss of one plough since the beginning of the reign of Henry VII. That, it was argued, meant three hundred thousand broken men, some driven to beg, others to steal and die upon the gallows. When the religious houses had joined lands together, and helped to create the suffering, they yet, by their systematic almsgiving, and by serving as hospitals, chance lodgings and asylums for the sick and destitute, allayed the pain of wounds that were in part of their own making. The breaking up of such houses destroyed their charitable organisation, and though laws were made to require employment of field-labour, these were evaded, and the people suffered on without assuagement of their griefs. This was what caused the poor people of Norfolk to feel that they were being devoured by the rich ; to pull down the enclosures to which they attributed their misery, gather themselves into

camp on Mousehold Heath and Mount Surrey, there holding
rude council under an oak, which they called "The Tree of
Reformation." Their hopeless protest ended in disaster on the
27th of August.    Upon the claim of the Devonshire men for
restoration of the Mass, of the abbey lands, and of the law of the
Six Articles, **Nicholas Udall** (§ 48) published in 1549 "*An·
Answer to the Articles of the Commoners of Devonshire and
Cornwall,* declaring to the same howe they have been seduced
by evell persons, and howe their consciences may be satysfyed
and stayed concerning the sayd artycles, sette forth by a countryman of theirs, much tendering the wealth bothe of their bodyes
and solles." Udall at this time preached actively. He translated
in 1551 Peter Martyr's tract on the Eucharist, and in the same
year was admitted to a Prebend of Windsor.    He published
Latin letters and poems; edited also a folio of T. Geminie's
"Anatomy;" still preaching constantly: and in March 1553,
was made rector of Calbourne, in the Isle of Wight.

**Thomas Sternhold** (§ 54), who died in 1549, published in
1548 *Certayne Psalms,* only nineteen in number.    In 1549 there
appeared, with a dedication to Edward VI., a new edition of *All
such Psalms of David as Thomas Sternhold, late grome of the
Kinges Majestyes robes, did in his lyfe time drawe into Englysshe
metre.*    This contained thirty-seven Psalms by Sternhold, and
seven by **John Hopkins,** a Suffolk clergyman and schoolmaster, who joined in his labour.    To an edition of 1551, Hopkins
added seven more psalms of his own.    Hopkins and others then
worked on with the desire to produce a complete version of the
Psalms of David into a form suited for congregational singing.

59. **Hugh Latimer** (§ 28, 29), when Edward VI. came to
the throne, was released from the Tower, and preached at Paul's
Cross his first sermon after an eight years' silence, on the first
of January, 1548.    A few days later the House of Commons
proposed his restoration to the Bishopric of Worcester ; but
this he declined.    In March of the same year Latimer began to
preach before larger audiences, from a pulpit set up in the
king's private garden at Westminster.    His extant *Sermon on
the Ploughers*—the teachers and preachers of religion—was
delivered at St. Paul's, in January, 1549.    In March and April of
the same year—on the Fridays in Lent—he preached *Seven
Sermons before Edward VI.,* two on "The Duty of a King," one
on "The Unjust Judge," two on "The Lawfulness of Kings," and
one on "The Agony in the Garden."    These were followed by his

farewell sermon before Edward. Latimer seems to have been in Lincolnshire during the rest of the reign of Edward VI., and there, in the autumn of 1552, at Grimsthorpe Castle, before the Duchess of Suffolk, he preached his *Seven Sermons on the Lord's Prayer*, which, with another series of twenty-one *Sermons preached in Lincolnshire*, have been preserved. Latimer's preaching was essentially English ; homely, practical, and straight to its purpose. There was no speculative refinement, but a simple sense of duty to be done for love of God. He pointed distinctly to the wrongs he preached against. After three of his Lent sermons before the king, three hundred and seventy-three pounds retained dishonestly were restored to the State by certain of the king's officers. He enlivened his admonition with shrewd sayings, recollections of life, genial humour. In many respects Latimer personified the spiritual life of the work-a-day Englishman. In his fifth sermon on the Lord's Prayer, when he was arguing that the true religious houses had not been pulled down, he said, " I read once a story of a holy man, some say it was St. Anthony, which had been a long season in the wilderness, eating nor drinking nothing but bread and water ; at the length, he thought himself so holy that there should be nobody like unto him. Therefore, he desired of God to know who should be his fellow in heaven. God made him answer, and commanded him to go to Alexandria, there he should find a cobbler which should be his fellow in heaven. So he went thither and sought him out, and fell acquainted with him, and tarried with him three or four days to see his conversation. In the morning his wife and he prayed together, then they went to their business, he in his shop, and she about her housewifery. At dinner-time they had bread and cheese, wherewith they were well content, and took it thankfully. Their children were well taught to fear God, and to say their Paternoster, and the Creed, and the Ten Commandments, and so he spent his time in doing his duty truly. I warrant you he did not so many false stitches as cobblers do nowadays. St. Anthony perceiving that, came to the knowledge of himself, and laid away all pride and presumption. By this example you may learn that honest conversation and godly living is much regarded before God, insomuch that this poor cobbler, doing his duty diligently, was made St. Anthony's fellow."

Edmund Spenser was born in 1552 or 1553.

60. In the reign of Queen Mary (1553—1558), soon after her

proclamation, Latimer was brought from Lincolnshire, and lodged on the 13th of September in the Tower.   On the 14th Cranmer also was sent to the Tower.   As Latimer passed through Smithfield he said that the place had long groaned for him.   In the following March, 1554, Hugh Latimer, with Thomas Cranmer, Archbishop of Canterbury, and Nicholas Ridley, Bishop of London, was tranferred to a prison at Oxford.   There were to be public disputations between those in power and the accused prisoners.   Latimer was baited on the 18th of April. Age and infirmity, a mind never practised in scholastic disputation, and the practical fact that the dispute was a form with its end predetermined, caused Latimer to content himself with a declaration that he held fast by his faith.   After trial, under a commission issued by Cardinal Pole, Latimer and Ridley were burnt at Oxford, on the 16th of October, 1555.   When the lighted fagot was placed at the feet of Ridley, Latimer exclaimed: " Be of good comfort, Master Ridley, and play the man.   We shall this day light such a candle, by God's grace, in England as I trust shall never be put out."

**Miles Coverdale** (§ 26, 29, 58), made Bishop of Exeter under Edward VI., was deprived and imprisoned by Queen Mary before he went abroad; and after many wanderings, settled at Geneva, where he was still active in Bible translation.

**John Fox,** who in later years compiled a painful record of the persecutions for religion in his time, was born in 1517, at Boston, in Lincolnshire.   He was educated at Brazenose College, Oxford, and became fellow of Magdalene.   He wrote Latin plays on Scriptural subjects before he devoted himself wholly to the great religious controversies of his day.   Then he studied Hebrew, read the Greek and Latin fathers, was accused in 1545 of heresy, and was expelled from college.   He next lived with Sir Thomas Lucy, of Charlcote, near Stratford-on-Avon, as tutor to his children ; then he came to London, and after the execution of the Earl of Surrey, John Fox was employed as tutor to his children.   At the beginning of Mary's reign Fox was protected by the Duke of Norfolk, but he presently escaped to Basle, where he lived as correcter of the press for the printer Oporinus, and resolved to write his Martyrology.

We need not dwell on the reaction against Church Reformers in the reign of Mary.   The best thought of the country was not with it, and it gave nothing to English literature but the quicker spirit of antagonism that embittered controversy in succeeding years. In January, 1554, Sir Thomas Carew failed in a demonstration against Queen Mary's union with Philip of Spain, son of the Emperor Charles V. Before the end of the month, Sir Thomas Wyatt the younger, son of the poet, headed insurrection against the proposed marriage, marched to London, and there yielded himself prisoner on the 7th of February. He was executed on the 11th of April. Mary was married to Philip of Spain on the 25th of June. In 1555 seventy-one heretics were executed ; in 1556, eighty-three ; in 1557, eighty-eight ; in 1558, forty.

John Heywood (§ 49), who had not been banished from court in the reign of Edward VI., and who had shown real liking for Queen Mary when she was a princess, in her father's lifetime, remained at her court, and had her confidence. After her death he went abroad, and died at Mechlin in 1565.

Nicholas Udall (§ 48, 58) also retained Mary's good-will. He had spoken highly of her in a special Prologue to her part of the translation from Erasmus's New Testament Paraphrase, and he was employed, by her warrant, in directing a dramatic entertainment for the feast of her coronation ; also in preparing dialogues and interludes to be performed before her. In 1554 or 1555, Udall was made head master of the school settled at Westminster by Henry VIII., in 1540. In November, 1556, Mary re-established the monastery, and there was an end of Udall's office, but a month later there was an end also of his life.

Sir Thomas Smith (§ 51, 56) under Mary was deprived of all his offices, but had for his learning a pension of £100.

Sir John Cheke (§ 51, 56), at the death of Edward VI., was one of those who sought to secure the succession of Lady Jane Grey. He was sent to the Tower, but for his learning his life was saved, and he was permitted to leave England. While abroad his estates were confiscated. He was seized by Philip at Brussels, and sent to England, where he escaped death by recantation. The queen then gave him means of life, but made life a torture by compelling him to sit on the bench at the judgment and condemnation of those heretics who did not faint in the trial of their faith. His age was but forty-three when he died, in September, 1557.

Two books were printed by Richard Tottel in 1557, namely, *Tottel's Miscellany*, and a *Hundreth Good Pointes of Husband-*

*rie*, by **Thomas Tusser**. Tottel's Miscellany was a collection of verses, known in society, but never before published, by the Earl of Surrey, Sir Thomas Wyatt, and others. Thomas Tusser's poem was the first edition of a work afterwards much enlarged. These were new books at the accession of Elizabeth, and are related to the early literature of her reign.

---

## .CHAPTER VII.

### THE REIGN OF ELIZABETH.

**1.** On New Year's-day, 1540, when Francis I. and Charles V. rode into Paris together (ch. vi. § 43, 54), the Emperor was on his way through France to punish Ghent. The Netherlands passed in 1477 to Austria, by marriage of Mary of Burgundy with Archduke Maximilian. Charles V. was born of marriage between Archduke Philip, heir by right of his mother to the Netherlands, and Joanna, who being the second daughter of Ferdinand and Isabella, was, after the death of intervening persons, heir to the monarchies of Spain. Thus Charles acquired by inheritance both Spain, which was essentially Catholic, and the Netherlands, with a population kindred to our own.

The seventeen provinces of the Netherlands differed in character and constitution, but they all sent deputies to a States-General, which had no power of taxation, and acknowledged appeals to a Supreme Tribunal at Mechlin. Four of these provinces were duchies—Brabant, Limburg, Luxemburg, and Guelderland; seven were counties—Flanders, Holland, Zealand, Artois, Hainault, Namur, and Zutphen; five were seigniories—Friesland, Mechlin, Utrecht, Overyssel, and Groningen; and the seventeenth—Antwerp—was a margraviate. Charles was himself born and bred in Flanders; he talked Flemish and favoured Flemings. The Netherlanders, therefore, liked him, though their temper was republican, and his was a despotic rule. He taxed them heavily because they were more prosperous than their neighbours. It was revolt in Ghent against an excessive tax that Charles went to put down in 1540. He did put it down with a strong hand, compelling the chief citizens to kneel before him in their shirts, with halters round their necks.

The spirit of the Reformation spread also among these people of the Netherlands ; and Charles V. battled in vain against it. He sought to bring into Flanders the Inquisition, which had been re-instituted in Spain by Ferdinand and Isabella in 1480 ; but the people rose and expelled the Inquisitor-General who had been sent to them by the pope. A modified Inquisition was established, with provision made in 1546 that no sentence of an inquisitor should be carried out until it had the sanction of a member of the Provincial Council. Thus in the Netherlands thousands died for their faith, while the English Reformers were during the reign of Edward VI. gathering strength.

In October, 1555, Charles V., aged about fifty-six, abdicated at Brussels in favour of his son Philip II., then twenty-eight years old, a small, thin, sullen man, fair-haired and blue-eyed, with a great mouth, a protruding lower jaw, and a digestion spoilt by pastry. He had been married about fifteen months before to Queen Mary of England ; and Sir Thomas Wyatt the younger had been executed for rebellious objection to the wedding (ch. vi. § 60). Philip received from his living father Spain, with all its outlying dominion, a month after the sovereignty of the Netherlands had been transferred to him. His dignity as head of the Holy Roman Empire, Charles resigned in favour of his brother Ferdinand. In September, 1556, Charles sailed for Spain, and he died in his seclusion at Yuste about two months before Anne Boleyn's daughter became Queen of England.

If Charles had been in some respects a Fleming among the Spaniards, Philip, born and bred in Spain, was a Spaniard among the Flemings. His court in Brussels was almost wholly Spanish, his advisers were Spanish grandees ; the chief of them, Philip's pliant favourite, Ruy Gomez, afterwards Prince of Eboli, who usually counselled peace, and the Duke of Alva, counsellor of war. Philip had remained in England with Queen Mary after his marriage to her in July, 1554, until some weeks before his father's abdication. He did not return to England until March, 1557, when, for reasons of his own, as King of Spain, he urged England into war with France. Paul IV. was seeking, by alliance with France, to loosen the hold of Spain upon Italian soil. Philip, therefore, caused England, in June, 1557, to declare war against his enemy of France, and in July, having gained his point, left England never to return. On the other side, Mary of Guise, then Regent of Scotland, was incited by King Henry II. of France to attack England. The Duke of Savoy, with the Spanish army of the Netherlands and

English reinforcements, gained in August a great victory over the Constable Montmorenci, at St. Quentin, and then, through advice of Philip, lost the opportunity of pressing victory by an advance. He stayed to press siege of the town, which was not taken till a fortnight later. The Duke of Guise, coming from Italy, was made Lieutenant-General of France, assembled a fresh army, and by surprise took Calais and Guines from the English in January, 1558, thus making a happy end of English domination on French soil. On the 24th of the following April, Guise's niece, Mary Stuart, the Queen of Scots, then about sixteen years old, was married to Francis, the French dauphin, a youth of her own age ; and by a secret article of the marriage contract, Scotland and France were to be united under one sovereign if Mary died childless. When Mary of England died, on the 17th of November, 1558, Elizabeth was twenty-five years old, and the Queen of Scots was held by many in England, and by most in France, to have a more legitimate right to the throne. The new queen took for her chief counsellor Sir William Cecil, then aged thirty-eight, the Lord Burleigh of after years, and made Cecil's brother-in-law, Sir Nicholas Bacon (they married two daughters of Sir Anthony Coke) her Lord Keeper. Philip of Spain, her sister's widower, thought it good policy to offer his hand to Elizabeth of England, on condition that she would profess the same religion he professed, and maintain it and keep her subjects true to it. Elizabeth dead, the English throne would pass to the Queen of Scots—through her to France. The marriage of Elizabeth, though not to Philip, was therefore desired by her people. Spain was the first power of the world, and France the second. England had declined during the reign of Mary. Her active fleet consisted of seven coast-guard vessels, and eight small merchant brigs and schooners altered for fighting, besides twenty-one vessels in harbour, of which all but six or seven were sloops and boats. But Spain and France were rival powers, and for a time Elizabeth could make the jealousies of one serve to protect England from the other. The endeavours of Spain and England to procure restitution of Calais were suspended for some months ; and in April, 1559, the belligerents, Spain helping England in negotiation, made peace in the Treaty of Cateau-Cambresis. In the following July, at festivities in celebration of this peace, Henry II. of France was killed by an accident, and was succeeded by the eldest of his seven children, the young husband of Mary Queen of Scots, who was ruled by the Guises, through their niece, his wife, during the seventeen months of his reign. Francis and Mary called themselves King and Queen of England, Scotland, and Ireland. The chief endeavour of the Guises was to subdue the Church Reformers, or Huguenots, as they were called, from "Eguenots," a French corruption of the German "Eidgenossen" (sworn associates). Oppression by the Guises produced organised resistance, part political, and part religious. Elizabeth in England had restored Cranmer's liturgy; established in the Prayerbook a choice of prayers to meet differences of opinion, and other compromises; dissolved the monasteries which Mary had refounded; sent to the Tower, where they were well lodged and had no axe to fear, those bishops who refused allegiance to her supremacy; and held her own, although the Protestantism of the English towns was represented by much smaller numbers than Catholicism of the rural districts. To foreign menace the young queen could reply with spirit that "her realm was not too poor, nor her people too faint-hearted, to defend their liberties at home and to protect their rights abroad." In December, 1560, Francis II. died, and the next brother, a boy in his eleventh year, became king as Charles IX. His mother, Catherine de' Medici, ruled in his name, at first with a desire to please all parties, and allay their strife.

Soon after the Treaty of Cateau-Cambresis, which ended war between France and Spain, King Philip left the Netherlands under the regency of his half-sister, the Duchess Margaret of Parma, natural daughter of Charles V. Philip parted from the Netherlands in August, 1559, with a "Request" for three millions of gold florins; and information that he had commanded the Regent accurately and exactly to enforce every existing edict and decree for the extirpation of all sects and heresies. The Request was not assented to without an emphatic counter-request from each of the provinces, and a remonstrance from the States-General, signed by the Prince of Orange, Count Egmont, and others, urging the withdrawal of Spanish troops out of the Netherlands. Very soon after Philip had returned to Spain, at an *auto-da-fé* in October, he swore by the cross of his sword to give all necessary favour to the holy office of the Inquisition; and to a young man, one of thirteen then burnt alive before him, who asked how he could look on and suffer such things to be done, he answered, "I would carry the wood to burn my own son withal, were he as wicked as you."

2. **John Knox,** after his imprisonment in the French galleys (ch. vi. § 53), had been in England from 1549 to 1554, and as one of Edward VI's chaplains had been associated with men of the English Reformation. He spent two of the five years in Berwick, two in Newcastle, and one in London. He found his first wife at Berwick, and married her before he was driven out of England by the persecutions under Mary. He was then in different places on the Continent, at Dieppe, at Frankfort, until 1555, when, after a short visit to Scotland, he became the pastor of an English congregation at Geneva. There he worked with Calvin, who had become supreme, and made the city what Knox took to be "the most perfect school of Christ that ever was on earth since the days of the Apostles." It was from Geneva, just before the accession of Elizabeth, that Knox issued, without his name, his *First Blast of the Trumpet against the Monstruous Regiment of Women.* His wrath was against the rule of the three Marys, Mary of Guise, queen dowager and regent of Scotland, Mary Queen of Scots, and Queen Mary of England, and on behalf of "so many learned and men of grave judgment as this day by Jezebel are exiled." In his preface he said that men had offended "by error and ignorance, giving their suffrages, consent and help to establish women in their kingdoms and empires, not understanding how abominable, odious and detestable is all such usurped authority in the presence of God ; " and he ended with this sentence : "My purpose is thrice to blow the trumpet in the same matter, if God so permit : twice I intend to do it without name, but at the last blast to take the blame upon myself, that all others may be purged." After such preface he began his book, a small quarto, about as big as a man's hand, with the assertion that "to promote a woman to bear rule, superiority, dominion or empire above any realm, nation, or city, is repugnant to nature, contumely to God, a thing most contrarious to His revealed will and approved ordinance, and finally it is the subversion of good order, of all equity and justice." Women are not worthy to rule. "I exempt," said Knox, "such as God, by singular privilege and for certain causes known only to Himself hath exempted from the common rank of women, and do speak of women as nature and experience do this day declare them. Nature, I say, doth paint them further to be weak, frail, impatient, feeble and foolish : and experience hath declared them to be unconstant, variable, cruel, and lacking the spirit of

counsel and regiment." He quoted Aristotle's opinion, "that wheresoever women bear dominion there must needs the people be disordered, living and abounding in all intemperancie, given to pride, excess, and vanity ; and finally, in the end, that they must needs come to confusion and ruin." He argued for the subjection of woman from Scripture and the Fathers, adding, as he quoted Chrysostom, " Beware, Chrysostom, what thou sayest ; thou shalt be reputed a traitor if Englishmen hear thee, for they must have my sovereign lady and maitresse, and Scotland hath drunk also the enchantment and venom of Circes." Instances of exceptional women like Deborah, Knox argued, will no more prove the right of a woman to judge Israel, than the instance of Solomon will prove polygamy a right of man. "Moreover," he said, " I doubt not but Deborah judged what time Israel had declined from God : rebuking their defection and exhorting them to repentance, without usurpation of any civil authority. And if the people gave unto her for a time any reverence or honour, as her godliness and happy counsel did well deserve, yet was it no such empire as our monsters claim." " Let all men," he said at the end, " be advertised, for the trumpet hath once blown." Knox blew no other blast, and would have recalled this if he could, although he did state in advance that the argument of his " Second Blast " was well to proclaim how through one woman England had been betrayed to Spain, and Scotland to France through another. That the issuing of such a book should coincide in time with the accession of Queen Elizabeth was unlucky for the argument of the Reformer. Knox had cut off retreat from his position. He might rank Elizabeth with Deborah ; but he had refused to clothe even Deborah with civil authority, not doubting that she had " no such empire as our monsters claim." Moreover, he had pledged himself to two more blasts from the same trumpet; and if his argument was good, the elevation of yet another woman to supremacy would make its enforcement only the more necessary.

A reply to Knox was published at Strasburg by John Aylmer, in the spring of 1559, called "*An Harborowe for Faithful and True Subjects against the late blown Blast concerning the Government of Women, wherein be confuted all such reasons as a stranger of late made in that behalf, with a brief Exhortation to Obedience.*" It ended with praise of Elizabeth's simplicity of dress as a princess, her disregard of money, love

L

of books.   Her first schoolmaster said to the writer that he
learnt of her more than he taught.   " ' I teach her words,' quod
he, 'and she me things.   I teach her the tongues to speak, and
her modest and maidenly life teacheth me works to do.' "   She
had patiently borne affliction.   " Let us help her who is come to
be our Judith and our Deborah; help with our means, with
hearts that will either win or die, and with obedience to God's
lieutenant, our sovereign."   England calls to her children—
England, of whom came that servant of God, their brother,
John Wiclif, "who begat Huss, who begat Luther, who begat
Truth.   Let us seek to requite her with thankfulness, which
studieth to keep us in quietness."   John Aylmer, the author of
this answer to Knox, was born in 1521.   He had been tutor to
Lady Jane Grey, and made study so pleasant to her that he was
the cause of her delight in it.   In 1553 he was Archdeacon of
Stow.   In the reign of Mary he was a Protestant exile at
Zurich.   Having returned to England after the accession of
Elizabeth, he made himself agreeable to the queen.   In 1562 he
became Archdeacon of Lincoln, and in 1576 Bishop of London.
In that character we shall meet with him again.

3. **John Knox,** who had not made himself agreeable to the
queen, and could not obtain from her, in 1559, a passport through
England to Scotland, was obliged to go by sea.   His presence
in Scotland had been called for, in March, 1557, by the nobles
who favoured the Reformation.   He had consulted Calvin, and
parting from his congregation at Geneva, had come as far on his
way home as Dieppe, when he found that his friends had lost
courage, and no longer sought a thorough reformation.   From
Dieppe he wrote, in October, 1557, an earnest letter to the
Lords whose faith had failed; another to the whole nobility of
Scotland; others to special friends.   His letters revived zeal.
In December, 1557, the Scottish Reforming nobles met in Edinburgh, and drew up an agreement known as the First Covenant.   It bound them to strive even to death " to maintain, set
forward, and establish the most blessed Word of God and His
congregation."   The Scottish Reformers, who had resolved to
abstain from Mass, formed small congregations in private
houses; the word Congregation thus became common among
them, and the Earl of Argyll and other Reforming nobles who had
signed this covenant were now called Lords of the Congregation.
They advised and ordained that the Missal be put aside, and
that the Common Prayer be read in all parishes; but as this

would not be immediately done, they added counsel that
" doctrine, preaching, and interpretation of Scriptures be had
and used privately in quiet houses, without great conventions of
the people thereto, till God move the prince to grant public
preaching by faithful and true ministers." The book of Common
Prayer here intended was King Edward's service-book. The
Archbishop of St. Andrews met this movement by burning for
heresy Walter Mill, a pious parish priest, eighty-two years old,
who said from the flames, "I trust in God that I am the last
that shall suffer death in Scotland from this cause." He was
the last ; last of about twenty. His death quickened reaction.
Adherents of the Congregation multiplied. A petition was
presented to the queen-regent for freedom of worship, and the
sacraments of Baptism and the Lord's Supper in the vulgar
tongue ; freedom to all for exposition of the Scripture ; and .
amendment of the scandalous lives of the clergy. Mary of
Guise, personally amiable, though not trustworthy, assented on
condition that the Reformers did not preach publicly in Edinburgh or Leith. In November, 1558, the Lords of the Congregation sought to obtain right of worship in the language of the
people from a convention of the Roman clergy, and would have
succeeded if they had consented to retain in the services the
Mass, with faith in purgatory and prayers for the dead. In
November, 1558, the Estates were to meet in Edinburgh, and
to Parliament also the Lords of the Congregation were resolved
to carry an appeal. They sought of it suspension and modification of Acts against heresy, sought check upon the power of the
spiritualty. The queen-regent, in good temper and good policy,
spoke them fair until she had secured the aid of the Protestant
nobles for the marriage of her daughter with the dauphin,
which took place in April, 1558; also till she had won
from them, in the Parliament which met in November, their
consent to the conferring of the crown of Scotland on the dauphin
as king-consort. That was the state of affairs in Scotland when
Mary of England died, and Elizabeth became queen in her stead.

But then there was a new hope for the Guises. Since
Elizabeth had been declared illegitimate, the Queen of Scots
was Queen also of England. In England itself there was a
large Catholic rural population; and the Guises governed Scotland on one side of her, France on the other. A Scottish synod
in March, 1559, repelled the petition of the Congregation ; the
queen-regent supported the synod, and summoned Reformir

preachers to appear at Stirling on the 10th of May. Their friends determined to come with them, unarmed protectors. The regent, alarmed, checked their approach, and caused them to stop at Perth, by promise to withdraw the summons. Then she commanded that the preachers should be declared rebels because they did not come to Stirling. That was the state of affairs in Scotland when John Knox landed at Leith.

He went to Perth, and in the church there preached against idolatry. After his congregation had dispersed, a priest prepared to celebrate Mass ; this fired the magazine of zeal. All images and ornaments within the church were broken to pieces; the monasteries of the Black and Grey Friars and the Charter-house were sacked. For this excess armed force was brought against the excited citizens. They shut their gates and issued letters to the queen-regent, the nobility, and "to the generation of Antichrist, the pestilent prelates and their shavelings within Scotland." The Earl of Glencairn with two thousand men checked the queen's troops, and Perth was opened to her on condition that none of the inhabitants should be molested on account of their religion. The Lords of the Congregation quitted Perth next day, after entering into a second Covenant for mutual support and defence. The queen-regent did not keep faith with the citizens of Perth, and thereby lost more of the confidence of Scotland. Knox went into Fife. More churches had their images and altars broken. He went boldly to St. Andrew's. The archbishop left the town, Knox preached in the cathedral church on the driving of traffickers from the temple, and after his sermon the people proceeded to deface all churches in the town and destroy the Dominican and Franciscan monasteries. The queen threatened again with troops. The people flocked together and were formidable. The queen temporised. The people marched on Perth, compelled the new garrison to surrender, and then burnt the beautiful Abbey of Scone, in which from ancient time the kings of Scotland had been crowned. Destruction of monasteries went on. The cry was, " Down with the crows' nests, or the crows will build in them again." Finally, the Lords of the Congregation were in Edinburgh, whence the queen-regent had fled. They claimed the Reformation of Religion and expulsion of the French, who were said to have devoted the land to their own uses, and already to have set up a Monsieur d'Argyll among themselves. Edinburgh was surrendered upon favourable terms, and the

Lords of the Congregation went to Stirling. There they signed their names to a third Covenant, designed to check the tampering of the queen-regent with individuals. They pledged themselves not to treat with her separately.

Francis and Mary having become King and Queen of France, French soldiers landed at Leith, also a legate from the pope, and three doctors from the Sorbonne. Now, therefore, the Lords of the Congregation looked to England, and corresponded much with Sir William Cecil. In July, 1559, John Knox enclosed to Cecil a letter for Queen Elizabeth, expressing his attachment to her and her government, though he abided, he said, by the general principles laid down in his "First Blast." Cecil, in answer, simply began his letter with the text, " There is neither male nor female, but we are all one in Christ," and then passed to other matters. Elizabeth still kept Knox at a distance. Correspondence was continued by the Scottish Lords. The Scottish movement for Church Reform and against French rule went on with the knowledge of Elizabeth, and with the aid of English money. It took presently the form of a plan for replacing the queen-regent by the Earl of Arran. In October, 1559, with open concurrence of Knox, the queen-regent was deprived of her office by "us the Nobility and Commons of the Protestants of the Church of Scotland." But the Reforming barons were unable to hold their ground against disciplined troops. They left Edinburgh, and acted each in his own country, looking still to England for help difficult to give, since Scotland and England were at peace. But Elizabeth did, on the ground of danger to England from a French conquest of Scotland, undertake by secret treaty at Berwick to assist in expelling the French. In April, 1560, the English besieged Leith, while the Lords of the Congregation signed a fourth Covenant, pledging themselves to pursue their object to the last extremity.

The queen-regent died in the midst of these troubles. France and England agreed on a treaty by which soldiers were withdrawn on both sides. Strife was ended, and peace was proclaimed at the Edinburgh market cross in July, 1560. Nothing was said about Church Reformation, but the way was laid open for it. The Three Estates met on the 1st of August, and on the 17th adopted for the nation a Confession of Faith in twenty-five articles, which embodied the opinions of John Knox. On the 24th the Estates added to their work three Acts, 1, annulling all previous Acts regarding censures of the Church or worshipping of saints ; 2, abolishing the pope's jurisdiction within the realm ; and, 3, making it criminal to say a Mass or hear a Mass. The first offence was to be punished with confiscation of goods, the second with banishment, the third with death. Edmund Spenser was at this time about seven years old.

4. The sweet spirit of song rises in the early years of Elizabeth's reign like the first chirping of the birds after a thunderstorm. *Tottel's Miscellany*, issued in June, 1557, as *Songes and Sonnettes, written by the Ryght Honorable Lorde Henry Haward, late Earl of Surrey, and other* (ch. vi. § 60), was as a brake from which there rose, immediately before the reign began, a pleasant carolling. Among the smaller song-birds there were two with a sustained rich note, for in this miscellany were the first printed collections of the poems of Sir Thomas Wyatt (ch. vi. § 43) and the Earl of Surrey (ch. vi. § 44, 46). This is our earliest poetical miscellany, if we leave out of account the fact that pieces by several writers had been included, in 1532, in the first collected edition of Chaucer's works. Tottel's first edition contained 271 poems, the second contained 280; but 30 poems by Grimald, which appeared in the first edition, were omitted in the second, which appeared a few weeks later, so that between the two there were 310 poems in all. In 1559 there was a third edition of the "Miscellany ;" in 1565, the year after Shakespeare's birth, a fourth ; the eighth, and last of the Elizabethan time, in 1587. During the reign of Elizabeth other books of the same kind appeared : *The Paradise of Dainty Devices*, collected by Richard Edwardes, of Her Majesty's Chapel, then dead, for a printer named Disle, and published in 1576 ; *A Gorgious Gallery of Gallant Inventions*, edited by Thomas Proctor, in 1578, with help from Owen Rawdon ; *A Handefull of Pleasant Delites*, by Clement Robinson and divers other, in 1584 ; *The Phœnix Nest*, edited by R. S., of the Inner Temple, gentleman, in 1593 ; *England's Helicon*, edited by John Bodenham, in 1600 ; and *A Poetical Rhapsody*, edited by Francis Davison, in 1602. The most popular of these was *The Paradise of Dainty Devices*. In the first edition of *Tottel's Miscellany* there were thirty-six poems by the Earl of Surrey, to which four were added in the next issue ; ninety by Sir Thomas Wyatt, to which six were added ; forty by Nicholas Grimald ; and ninety-five by unnamed authors, among whom were Thomas Church-

yard, Thomas Lord Vaux, Edward Somerset, John Heywood, and Sir Francis Bryan. **Nicholas Grimald** was born about 1519, in Huntingdonshire, was educated at Christ's College, took his B.A. in 1540, in 1542 was incorporated at Oxford, and elected a probationer fellow of Merton College, Oxford. In 1556, Tottel published for him a translation of " Tully's Offices." His connection with Tottel at this time, omission of so much of his verse from the second edition of the " Miscellany," and reduction of his name in that edition to the initials N. G., make it possible that Grimald edited the "Miscellany." In 1558, Tottel issued a second edition of Grimald's translation of the " De Officiis." Grimald was dead in May, 1562. Two poems of his which were not omitted in the second edition have especial interest as the first specimens in English of original blank verse (ch. vi. § 47). One was a piece of one hundred and fifteen lines, on *The Death of Zoroas, an Egyptian Astronomer, in First Fight that Alexander had with the Persians,* beginning :

> " Now clattering arms, now raging broils of war,
> Can pass the noise of taratantars' clang "—

("taratantars" altered in the next edition to "dreadful trumpets "). The other was a somewhat shorter piece, upon the *Death of Cicero.*

5. In 1559, Richard Tottel printed " in Flete Strete, within Temple Barre, at the signe of ' The Hand and Starre,' " a translation into English verse of "the sixt tragedie of the most grave and prudent author, Lucius Anneus Seneca, entituled *Troas*, with divers and sundrie additions to the same, newly set forth in Englishe by **Jasper Heywood**, student in Oxforde." John Heywood (ch. vi. § 49) had two sons—Ellis, the elder, a good scholar, who joined the order of the Jesuits in 1560 ; and Jasper, who was born about 1535, was educated at Oxford, and, some months before the publication of his version of the *Troas*, being twenty-three years old, had resigned a fellowship at Merton College for fear of expulsion. He was elected to a fellowship of All Souls', but left the University, and in 1561, having held by his father's faith, became a Roman Catholic priest. He joined the Jesuits, studied theology for two years, and, after some time abroad, returned to England as Provincial of the Jesuits in 1581. He went abroad again, and died at Naples in 1598. Some poems of his are in the *Paradise of Dainty Devices;* and he translated from Seneca, in the first years

of Elizabeth's reign, not only the *Troas*, but also the *Thyestes*, in 1560, and the *Hercules Furens*, in 1561. Other men set to work on other tragedies. Alexander Neville published, in 1563, a translation of the *Œdipus;* John Studley translated four— *Hippolytus, Medea, Agamemnon,* and *Hercules Oetæus;* Thomas Nuce translated *Octavia*, and the *Thebais* was trans- lated by Thomas Newton, who, in 1581, collected the ten translations into a single volume, published as *Seneca: his Tenne Tragedies, translated into Englysh.* These translations indicate the strong influence of the Latin tragedy upon the minds of scholars and poets in the birthtime of our native drama. There is no blank verse in them. Jasper Heywood opened his *Troas* with a preface in Chaucer's stanza, but he wrote his dialogue chiefly in couplets of fourteen-syllabled lines. Thus, for example, Hecuba begins :

> " Whoso in pomp of proud estate or kingdom sets delight,
> Or who that joys in princes' court to bear the sway of might,
> He dreads the fates which from above the wavering gods down flings,
> But fast affiance fixed hath in frail and fickle things ;
> Let him in me both see the face of Fortune's flattering joy,
> And eke respect the ruthful end of thee, O ruinous Troy ! "

Sometimes the measure of the dialogue changes to four-lined elegiac stanza, which is the measure also of a chorus added by Jasper Heywood himself to the first act :

> " O ye to whom the Lord of land and seas,
> Of life and death, hath granted here the power,
> Lay down your lofty looks, your pride appease,
> The crowned king fleeth not his fatal hour."

At the opening of the second act of the " Troas," Jasper Hey- wood raised the sprite of Achilles, and made him speak in Chaucer's stanza :

> " The soil doth shake to bear my heavy foot,
> And fear'th again the sceptres of my hand,
> The poles with stroke of thunderclap ring out,
> The doubtful stars amid their course do stand,
> And fearful Phœbus hides his blazing brand ;
> The trembling lakes against their course do flyte,
> For dread and terror of Achilles' sprite."

The other translators followed Jasper Heywood's lead. With some further variety in the choruses, these are the metres into which the poets of the first years of Elizabeth translated the tragedies of Seneca.

6. In the earlier years of Elizabeth's reign the revived taste

for classical literature not only, through Plautus and Seneca, became part of the early story of our drama, but showed itself variously in the form of bright translations from the Latin. Gavin Douglas's translation of the Æneid (ch. vi. § 32), finished in 1513, was first printed in 1553. Thomas Phaer, who was born at Kilgarran, in Pembrokeshire, studied at Oxford and at Lincoln's Inn, became advocate for the marches of Wales, afterwards doctor of medicine at Oxford. In May, 1558, in the days of Philip and Mary, six months before Elizabeth's accession, there appeared, " *The Seven First Books of the Eneidos of Virgil,* converted in Englishe meter by Thos. Phaer, Esq., sollicitour to the King and Queenes Majesties, attending their honourable. counsaile in the Marchies of Wales." He continued the work, and had begun the tenth book, when he died, in 1560, and was buried in Kilgarran Church. In 1562 there were published, dedicated to Sir Nicholas Bacon, Lord Keeper, Phaer's *Nyne First Books of the Eneidos.* The translation was completed with less ability by Thomas Twyne, a Canterbury man, practising as a physician at Lewes, and published in 1573. Phaer, who was a fair poet, wrote also on law and medicine. His "Virgil" is in the same fourteen-syllabled rhyming measure which we have seen used in the translation of Seneca.

The other chief translation from the Latin poets in the early part of Elizabeth's reign was Arthur Golding's "Ovid," also translated into fourteen-syllabled lines. Arthur Golding was a Londoner, of good family, and lived at the house of Sir William Cecil, in the Strand. He translated Justin's " History" in 1564, and " Cæsar's Commentaries" in 1565, which was the year of the publication of " *The Fyrst Fower Bookes of the Metamorphoses,* owte of Latin into English meter, by Arthur Golding, gentleman." Ten years later, when Shakespeare was eleven years old, Arthur Golding published his complete translation of *The XV. Bookes of P. Ovidius Naso, entytuled Metamorphoses,* dedicated to Robert, Earl of Leicester. This was the book through which men read the "Metamorphoses" in English till the time of Charles I.

7. The fourteen-syllabled line is one of the favourite measures in the completed version of " *The Whole Booke of Psalmes* (ch. vi. § 54), collected into English metre by T. Sternhold, L. Hopkins, and others, conferred with the Ebrue, with Apt Notes to sing them withall." This appeared in 1562, and was then attached for the first time to the Book of Common Prayer.

L *

Among the "apt tunes" is that to which the 100th Psalm was sung, now known as "The Old Hundredth." It had been one of the tunes made by Goudimel and Le Jeune for the French version of the Psalms by Clement Marot.

8. Among the "others" who translated was **Thomas Norton**, whose initials were appended to twenty-eight of the Psalms, and who had a hand with **Thomas Sackville** in the writing of the first English tragedy. Thomas Norton, eldest son of a small landed proprietor, of Sharpenhoe, in Bedfordshire, was born in 1532. He became a good scholar and zealous Protestant, served in his youth the Protector Somerset, and then, in 1555, entered himself as a student of the Inner Temple. In 1561 he published a *Translation of Calvin's Institutes*, which went through five editions in his lifetime ; and it was in this year that Norton, aged twenty-nine, joined Sackville in the production of the tragedy of *Gorboduc*. He was translating Psalms also, for it was in the following year, 1562, that the completed Psalter of Sternhold and Hopkins appeared. Thomas Sackville was four years younger than Norton. He was born in 1536, at Buckhurst, in Sussex, and was the son of Sir Richard Sackville, whom we shall find befriending Roger Ascham. Thomas Sackville went to Oxford at the age of fifteen or sixteen, and thence to Cambridge, where he took his degree of M.A. His University reputation as a poet was referred to by Jasper Heywood, before his version of Seneca's "Thyestes," published in 1560 :

> "There Sackville's sonnets sweetly sauste,
> And featly fyned bee."

Thomas Sackville married, at the age of nineteen, the daughter of a privy councillor, and sat in a Parliament of Philip and Mary at the age of twenty-one, as member for Westmoreland. In the first year of the reign of Elizabeth he was member for East Grinstead, and took part in business of the House. When he left the University, Sackville had entered himself to the Inner Temple. Thus it was that he joined Norton, also of the Inner Temple, in the writing of *Gorboduc* for Christmas recreation of the Templars. Great lords had for many years kept servants paid to provide them with amusement. Records of the Augustine Priory at Bicester show that, in 1431, minstrels of different lords visited the monastery. In a like record of another house of the Augustines, such entertainers were before 1461 called mimes and players. A MS. of the time of Henry VI. laid against those old entertainers a complaint raised also against the first professional actors in Elizabeth's day, that they profaned the holy days.

"Goddis halidays non observantur honeste,
For unthrifty pleyes in eis regnant manifeste."

From that time till the first years of Elizabeth's reign there had been itinerant performers, acting as retainers of the nobility. In the north, in 1556, there were six or seven persons acting in the livery of Sir Francis Leek. Sir Robert Dudley, afterwards Earl of Leicester, had such theatrical servants, and wrote in April, 1559, to the Earl of Shrewsbury, Lord President of the North, for their licence to play in Yorkshire, they having already leave to play in divers other shires. Mary suppressed plays which contained attacks upon her Church, and gave impulse to the production of miracle-plays. In 1556 the " Passion of Christ" was acted at Greyfriars in London, before the Lord Mayor and Privy Council. It was repeated in 1557, and in the same year, on St. Olave's night, the "Life of St. Olave" was acted in his church in Silver Street. Elizabeth on her accession required the licensing of plays and interludes, with refusal of licence to those touching questions of religion and government.

Court entertainments had been placed in 1546 under the management of Sir Thomas Cawarden, probably the first Master of the Revels; and at Christmas there was a Lord of Misrule. At Christmas in 1551, Holinshed says that in the place of the Lord of Misrule "there was, by order of the Council, a wise gentleman and learned, named George Ferrers, appointed to that office for this year, who being of better credit and estimation than commonly his predecessors had been before, received all his commissions and warrants by the name of Master of the King's Pastimes." But Sir Thomas Cawarden was Master of the Revels—or, in official language, Magister Jocorum, Revellorum et Mascorum—until 1560, when he died, and was succeeded by Sir Thomas Benger. Elizabeth reduced the cost of her amusements. Mary had paid two or three thousand a year in salaries to her theatrical and musical establishment; Elizabeth reduced this, but still had salaried interlude players, musicians, and a keeper of bears and mastiffs. The gentlemen and children of the Queen's chapel were also employed as entertainers.

At Christmas, 1561, many of the queen's council were

present at the festivities of the Inner Temple; and the Lord of Misrule rode through London in complete harness, gilt, with a hundred horse and gentlemen riding gorgeously with chains of gold, and their horses goodly trapped. The play produced on this occasion was Sackville and Norton's *Gorboduc;* and on the 18th of January it was presented upon a great decorated scaffold in the queen's hall in Westminster by the gentlemen of the Inner Temple, after a masque. An unauthorised edition of it was published in 1565, as *The Tragedy of Gorboduc.* Our first printed tragedy appeared, therefore, when Shakespeare was one year old. "Ralph Roister Doister," our earliest comedy, was first printed in 1566, when Shakespeare was two years old. Thus Shakespeare and the English drama came into the world together. On the title-page of this unauthorised edition of "Gorboduc" it is said that the three first acts were by Norton. The authorised edition did not appear until 1571, and in that the name of the play appeared as *Ferrex and Porrex.* The argument was taken from Geoffrey of Monmouth's "History of British Kings" (ch. iii. § 8), and was chosen as a fit lesson for Englishmen in the first year of the reign of Elizabeth. It was a call to Englishmen to cease from strife among themselves, and knit themselves into one people, obedient to one undisputed rule. Each act is opened with a masque, or dumb-show; and as the play was modelled on the Tragedies of Seneca, there was at the close of every act except the last a chorus. Except for the choruses, Sackville and Norton used the newly-introduced blank verse as the measure of their tragedy. Hitherto this measure had been little used by us, and never in an original work of any magnitude. The plot of "Gorboduc" is very simple. Act I.—After a dumb-show of the bundle of sticks which could be broken only when they were no longer bound together, Videna, the wife of King Gorboduc, tells Ferrex, her eldest son, with "griefful plaint," that his father intends to deprive him of his birthright by equal division of his kingdom between both his sons. King Gorboduc will seek that day the consent of his council. Gorboduc then himself unfolds his plan to his council. One councillor argues at length that the king does wisely; another argues at length that equal division between the two sons is good, but not good to be made in their father's lifetime; a third, the good councillor, Eubulus argues at length that division of rule is bad for Gorboduc, bad for Ferrex and Porrex :

" But worst of all for this our native land.
Within one land one single rule is best :
Divided reigns do make divided hearts ;
But peace preserves the country and the prince."

He recalls the civil wars that had been :

" What princes slain before their timely hour !
What waste of towns and people in the land !
What treasons heap'd on murders and on spoils!
Whose just revenge ev'n yet is scarcely ceas'd ;
Ruthful remembrance is yet raw in mind.
The gods forbid the like to chance again."

Gorboduc having listened to his councillors, does what he meant
to do. He assigns England north of the Humber to Porrex,
and the south to Ferrex. A chorus then in four stanzas points
the moral of this portion of the story. Act II.—After a dumb-
show of a King who refused the good wine offered by age and
experience, and took the poison offered by one who looked plea-
santer, there are two scenes. One shows Ferrex between two counsellors, of whom one is a parasite, the other trustworthy. The
parasite humours wrath against father and brother ; the good
counsellor seeks to prevent dissension. Ferrex resolves to
prepare himself in arms against the possible devices of his
brother, and leaves the stage in company with the bad counsellor. Porrex is then shown also between two counsellors ; one
of whom tells him that his brother is arming against him, and
promoting a strife which the other counsellor endeavours to
prevent. Porrex will not give Ferrex leisure to prepare his force,
but will at once attack him. He also leaves the stage in company
with his bad counsellor, and the good counsellor resolves to
haste to Gorboduc "ere this mischief come to the likely end."
Chorus then in four stanzas deplores the rashness of youth, and
condemns the false traitor who undermines the love of brethren.
Act III.—After a mask of mourners clad in black, who pass
thrice about the stage, Gorboduc is shown as he lays before his
best and worst councillor the tidings of the strife between his
sons, tidings brought to him promptly by the peacemaker from
each. While he is being counselled to use his authority as a
father, and to make his power seen, a messenger comes to tell
that Porrex has already carried out his threat, and slain his
brother Ferrex. The father breathes revenge against the
traitor son, and Chorus ends the act with moralising on the
lust of kingdoms and the cruelty of civil strife. Act IV.—After
a masque of the three Furies, each driving before her a king and

queen who had unnaturally slain their own children, Queen
Videna laments for her firstborn, and breathes vengeance against
Porrex :

> "Changeling to me thou art, and not my child,
> Nor to no wight that spark of pity knew."

King Gorboduc then has his son Porrex brought before him by
Eubulus. Porrex expresses deep repentance, does not ask to live,
but shows how the bond of love had been unknit by the division
of the kingdom. His brother, he says, had hired one of his own
servants to poison him. Gorboduc sends Porrex from his
presence as an "accursed child" until he shall have determined
how to deal with him. Then, while he laments to his councillors, a woman of the queen's chamber enters in distraction, and
tells how Porrex has been stabbed in his sleep by his mother. At
the close of the act the meditation of the chorus harmonises as
usual with the matter of the dumb-show that preceded it. Act V.
—After a dumb-show of war and tumult, the Dukes of Cornwall,
Albany, Lloegria, and Cumberland possess the stage, and we
learn that the people have risen and slain both Gorboduc and
his queen. The lords, therefore—Eubulus one with them—are
armed against the people, for, says Eubulus :

> "Though kings forget to govern as they ought,
> Yet subjects must obey as they are bound."

A long argument of Eubulus upon the best way to deal with
"skilless rebels," is followed by the marching off of all the
lords, except Fergus Duke of Albany, who stays to meditate the
raising of himself to supreme rule. Fergus proceeds to his own
kingdom to buy arms. Eubulus relates, with moralising, the
misery and destruction of the people ; the great lords return from

> "The wide and lasy fields
> With blood and bodies spread of rebels slain ;
> The lofty trees clothed with the corpses dead,
> That, strangled with the cord, do hang thereon."

But a messenger brings news of the advance against them all of
Albany with twenty thousand men. They hasten to more
conflict

> "Upon the wretched land
> Where empty place of princely governance,
> No certain stay now left of doubtless heir,
> Thus leave this guideless realm an open prey
> To endless storms and waste of civil war."

One argues that for the welfare of their native land the crown be adjudged to one of their own country by common counsel of them all:

> " Such one, my lords, let be your chosen king,
> Such one so born within your native land :
> Such one prefer, and in no wise admit
> The heavy yoke of foreign governance."

The play ends with a long moralising on the situation by Eubulus, which includes a glance at the danger to the kingdom:

> " When, lo, unto the prince,
> Whom death or sudden hap of life bereaves,
> No certain heir remains."

Thus our first tragedy distinctly grew out of the life of its own time, and gave expression to much that lay deep in the hearts of Englishmen in the first years of Elizabeth's reign. The best poetry of the play is in the fourth act, which certainly is Sackville's; and the fifth may well represent the youth of one who gave his after life to state affairs.

9. With one other work of mark in the Elizabethan time, Sackville's name was associated before he turned from poetry, as pleasure of his youth, and gave his life to politics. This was the *Mirror for Magistrates*, a work that expanded as the reign went on into a long series of poems moralising those incidents of English history, which warn the powerful of the unsteadiness of fortune by showing them as in a mirror that " who reckless rules, right soon may hap to rue." A printer in Queen Mary's time seems first to have designed a long sequence of narrated Tragedies, as all tales of the reverse from high and happy fortune were then called. From the Conqueror downward, a series of poems from English history suggested by Boccaccio's "Falls of Illustrious Men" (ch. v. § 13) was to moralise the past for the use of the present, and teach men in authority to use their power well. In Sackville's mind, the plan of a mere rhyming sequel to Lydgate's " Falls of Princes " took shape nobly, and he meant himself to write a sequence of the tragedies, but he wrote only two poems, an *Induction*, which was designed as general introduction to the series of his own writing, and the *Complaint of Henry Stafford, Duke of Buckingham.* The Induction is the best of Sackville's poetry. It follows the old forms, and is an allegory in Chaucer's stanza. Opening, not with a spring morning, but with winter night and its images of gloom and desolation, the poet represents himself abroad, mourning the death and ruin of all summer glory, when he meets a woebegone woman

clad in black, who is allegorically painted as Sorrow herself. Her home is among the Furies in the infernal lake.

> " Whence come I am, the dreary destiny
>    And luckless lot for to bemoam of those
> Whom fortune, in this maze of misery,
>    Of wretched chance, most woeful mirrors chose
>    That, when thou seest how lightly they did lose
> Their pomp, their power, and that they thought most sure,
> Thou may'st soon deem no earthly joys may dure

By Sorrow the poet was to be taken

> " First to the grisly lake,
> And thence unto the blissful place of rest,
>    Where thou shalt see, and hear, the plaint they make
> That whilom here bare swing among the best."

The descent of Avernus and the allegorical figures within the porch and jaws of hell—Remorse of Conscience, Dread, Revenge, Misery, Care, Sleep, Old Age, Malady, Famine, War, Deadly Debate, Death—are described with dignity and energy of imagination. In reading Sackville's Induction we find ourselves, indeed, very far on the way from Stephen Hawes (ch. vi. § 7) to Spenser. The poet, and Sorrow his guide, were ferried across Acheron, passed Cerberus, and reached the horror of the realm of Pluto. At the cry of Sorrow the rout of unhappy shades gathered about them; and first Henry Stafford, Duke of Buckingham, when he could speak for grief, began his plaint, bade Sackville mark well his fall,

> " And paint it forth, that all estates may know ;
> Have they the warning, and be mine the woe."

Sackville wrote in the series no other Tragedy than this, perhaps because his way of life drew him from literature, perhaps because he was too good a poet to be satisfied with this manner of work. His complaint of Henry Stafford, Duke of Buckingham, abounds in poetry of thought and musical expression, but the essential difference between a history and a poem makes itself felt. The unity of the piece as a poem is marred by faithful adherence to historical detail, and Sackville no doubt felt that he must either illustrate the good doctrine of Aristotle in his poetics, and write poems that were not exactly histories, or he must write histories that were not exactly poems. The very excellence, also, and intensity of his Induction struck a note which the sequence of tragedies, unless they were true poems, would not sustain.

Sackville left, therefore, to Baldwin and his friends the

working out of the printer's first idea.  The work had been
undertaken by William Baldwin, with aid chiefly from George
Ferrers.  In his hands the "Mirror for Magistrates" meant
simply a long English sequel to Boccaccio, as versified in Lydgate's "Fall of Princes."  It was a series of metrical biographies,
begun and part printed in 1555, but stopped by the intervention
of Stephen Gardiner, who was then Lord Chancellor, and who
died in November of that year.  After the accession of Elizabeth,
a licence was obtained, in 1559, and in that year the "Mirror
for Magistrates" was first issued.  It had a prose introduction,
showing how it was agreed that Baldwin should take the place
of Boccaccio, that to him the wretched princes should complain,
and how certain friends "took upon themselves every man for
his part to be sundry personages."  Then they opened books
of chronicles, and "Maister Ferrers (after he had found where
Bochas left, which was about the end of King Edward the
Third's reign) said thus :—' I marvel what Bochas meaneth, to
forget among his miserable princes such as were of our own
nation. . . . Bochas, being an Italian, minded most the
Roman and Italian story, or else, perhaps, he wanted the knowledge of ours.  It were, therefore, a goodly and notable matter
to search and discourse our whole story from the first beginning
of the inhabiting of the isle.  But seeing the printer's mind is
to have us follow where Lydgate left, we will leave that great
labour to other that may intend it, and (as one being bold
first to break the ice) I will begin at the time of Richard the
Second, a time as unfortunate as the ruler therein.'"  Ferrers
began, therefore, with the fall of Robert Tresilian, Chief Justice
of England, in Chaucer's stanza, with the lines lengthened from
ten syllables to twelve.  There are some other measures, but the
greater part of "The Mirror of Magistrates" is in Chaucer's
stanza, with prose talk by the company between the tragedies.
The work, as published in 1559, contained nineteen tragedies;
beginning with "Tresilian" and ending with "Edward IV."  The
greater number of these were written by Baldwin ; Ferrers wrote
three ; and one, on Owen Glendower, was written by Phaer, the
translator of Virgil.  In 1563 another edition appeared, in which
eight tragedies were added, one being Sackville's "Complaint
of Buckingham," with the "Induction" placed before it, and
another, the story of Jane Shore, by Thomas Churchyard.

**William Baldwin**, chief editor of "The Mirror for Magistrates," was an ecclesiastic, whose father had worked in a printing-

office. He graduated at Oxford, about 1532 was a schoolmaster. He wrote a metrical version of Solomon's Song, and was appointed in 1552 to set forth a play before the king.

**George Ferrers** was born at St. Albans, educated at Oxford, then student of Lincoln's Inn. He was in Parliament under Henry VIII., was patronised by Thomas Cromwell, imprisoned in 1542. He translated Magna Charta and some other statutes from French into Latin and English, was of the suite of the Protector Somerset, and is said to have compiled the part of Grafton's Chronicle which tells the history of Mary's reign. He composed interludes for the court ; in 1553 he was the king's Lord of Misrule at Greenwich for the twelve days of Christmas (§ 8) ; he wrote other rhyme than that in the "Mirror for Magistrates;" and he died in 1579.

In 1574, **John Higgins** published *The First Part of the Mirror for Magistrates*, containing sixteen legends of his own, for the period from Brut to the birth of Christ. He opened his work with a general Induction in Chaucer's stanza, which was suggested to him by Sackville's. John Higgins was a clergyman and schoolmaster at Winsham, in Somersetshire, who wrote some scholastic books, and was alive in 1602, when he joined in a theological controversy. Editions of the "First Part" and of the "Last Part" of the "Mirror of Magistrates" were in demand till 1578, when there appeared a *Second Part of the Mirror for Magistrates*, containing twelve legends by Thomas Blenerhasset, and filling up in the wide scheme the period from Cæsar's Invasion to the Norman Conquest.

An edition of the "Mirror for Magistrates," in 1587, united the work of Baldwin and Higgins, adding chiefly new legends by John Higgins, but also a legend of Wolsey by Thomas Churchyard. This was the most complete form attained by the work during the reign of Queen Elizabeth. It was popular throughout the reign, and one of the sources from which dramatists, when they arose, drew plots for plays.

**Thomas Sackville** was knighted in 1567, the year after his father's death, and made a baron as Lord Buckhurst. He rose in the state, and after the death of Lord Burghley, in 1599, succeeded him as High Treasurer of England. Early in the next reign, in 1604, Sackville was made Earl of Dorset, and in 1608, being then seventy-two years old, he died while sitting at the Council Table.

10. **Thomas Churchyard,** born at Shrewsbury about 1520,

and a soldier in his earlier years, was not only the author of two of the better class of tragedies in "The Mirror for Magistrates" —"Jane Shore" and "Wolsey"—but a busy poet, whose literary activity began with Elizabeth's reign, and continued to its close. He died in 1604, after an unprosperous life of dependence upon patrons, and had these lines for epitaph:

> " Poverty and poetry his tomb doth inclose;
> Wherefore, good neighbours, be merry in prose."

His *Davie Dicar's Dream*, published in 1563, produced from Thomas Camel a metrical "Rejoinder to Churchyard," and led to a controversy of wits. Among Churchyard's numerous publications were, in 1575, " *The First Part of Churchyard's Chips, containing Twelve Labours* —not Herculean," a collection of twelve pieces; in 1578, *Praise and Report of Frobisher's Voyage,* a *Description of the Wars in Flanders,* a translation of the *Three First Books of Ovid de Tristibus,* and a description of his own devices for the entertainment of the queen in Norwich in that year. In 1579 he published *A Welcome Home to Frobisher;* the *Services of Sir William Drury, Lord Justice of Ireland;* and a piece on the *Miserie of Flaunders, Calamitie of France, Misfortune of Portugal, Unquietness of Ireland, Troubles of Scotland, and the Blessed State of England.* The chief of many works by Churchyard after 1579 was his patriotic poem on Welsh worthies, *The Worthiness of Wales,* published in 1587, with a dedication to the queen.

11. We will take the year 1579 as a dividing line between the earlier and latter part of Elizabeth's reign. The whole reign covered a period of forty-four years four months and a week. In 1579 a child born at Elizabeth's accession came of age; she had then reigned twenty-one years, and those who had grown up under the influences of her reign formed the new generation of Englishmen. Then the Elizabethan time bore fruit abundantly. In 1579, Spenser produced his first published work; the drama had just sprung into independent life; and young John Lyly published the "Euphues" which gave its name to an external fashion of Elizabethan literature. Before 1579, while the number of works of genius was yet small, both history and literature show how England was still gathering the force that after 1579 found its own various ways of intense expression.

12. John Bale was sixty-three years old, John Fox forty-one, John Jewel thirty-six, at the accession of Elizabeth. John Bale

(ch. vi. § 50) had printed at Ipswich, in 1548, and presented to Edward VI., the first edition of his (Latin) " Summary of the Illustrious Writers of Great Britain." In 1552, Edward VI. made him Bishop of Ossory ; and he afterwards painted his difficulties with a flock of antagonist faith to his own, in a book called *The Vocation of John Bale to the Bishopric of Ossory in Ireland ; his Persecutions in the same, and his Final Deliverance.* After the accession of Mary, Bale escaped to Switzerland, but he came to England upon the accession of Elizabeth, obtained in 1560 a prebend in Canterbury Cathedral, and died in 1563. The completed edition of John Bale's account of English Writers—*Scriptorum Illustrium Majoris Brytanniæ Catalogus*—expanded from five centuries to fourteen, was published in folio by Oporinus, at Basle, in 1557 and 1559. It is our first literary history, inaccurate and warped by the controversial heat of the time, but important as an aid to study of our early literature.

13. **John Fox** (ch. vi. § 60) had in the reign of Mary worked as corrector of the press for Oporinus, of Basle, to whom he introduced himself by presentation of the first sketch of his history of the Church, warped also by the heat of conflict, and first suggested to him by Lady Jane Grey. At this he proceeded to work, writing it then in Latin. The first sketch was published in octavo in 1554. John Aylmer (§ 2), and more particularly Edmund Grindal, also exiles, aided Fox with information received out of England concerning the martyrs for their faith. At the accession of Elizabeth, Fox was in Basle with a wife and two children, poor, but with a more settled employment than he could afford immediately to leave. His friend Grindal went back to England, but Fox remained another year at Basle, and for a time suspended, as Grindal advised, the production of his enlarged history of troubles in the Church, because new matter in abundance would now surely come to light. This enlarged book appeared, in its first Latin form in folio, from the press of Oporinus, in August, 1559, and containing some facts that were omitted in the translations. In the following October, John Fox had returned to London, where he was housed by Aldgate at Christchurch, the manor-place of his old pupil the Duke of Norfolk. From Aldgate he went every Monday to the printing office of John Day, whence early in 1563 appeared in folio the first edition of his work in English as *Acts and Monuments of these latter and perillous Dayes, touching matters of the Church, wherein are comprehended and described the great Persecutions*

*and horrible Troubles that have been wrought and practised by the Romishe Prelates, especiallye in this Realme of England and Scotlande, from the Yeare of our Lorde a Thousande unto the Tyme now present.  Gathered and collected according to the true Copies and Wrytinges certificatorie, as wel of the Parties themselves that suffered, as also out of the Bishops' Registers which were the doers thereof, by John Foxe.*  To a right student the value of such a book is rather increased than lessened by the inevitable bias of a writer who recorded incidents that had for him a deep, real, present interest, and who had his own part in the passion of the controversy he describes.  It vividly represents one aspect of the strong life of the sixteenth century.  The book, dedicated to the queen, was ordered to be set up in parish churches for the use of all the people, except in times of Divine service.  From the Duke of Norfolk's, Fox went to live near John Day, for whom he worked as author, translator, and editor.  John Day, a Suffolk man, had been busy in Edward VI.'s time as a printer of Bibles.  Under Mary he was at one time a prisoner, at one time an exile.  Under Elizabeth he had a printing-office, growing in size, against the city wall by Aldersgate, and shops for the sale of his books in several parts of London.  Letters to Fox are extant addressed to him as "dwelling with Master Day, the printer, at Aldersgate;" and also to "Master John Fox, at his house in Grubbe Street."  In Grub Street, then, we have, during the early years of Elizabeth, John Fox, the martyrologist, housed in a quality not unlike that of the bookseller's hack, though he and his bookseller and printer were actually fellow-workers with a common aim, and that the noblest, whereby they were to earn bread in service of their country.  Captain Pen had already taken precedence of Captain Sword.  Fox held a prebend at Salisbury, although he was opposed to the compromise with old forms in the ecclesiastical system of the Church, and refused to subscribe to anything but the Greek Testament.  He preached at Paul's Cross and elsewhere; but his most important work was that done with John Day.

John Day, the printer, was the only man of his calling who had types in the First English (or Anglo-Saxon) characters.  One incident of the English Reformation was a revived study of First English, because that was a way to evidence of the antiquity of the Reformed Church.  Sermons and writings of its first clergy would show that the Church of the Reformation was in agreement with the Church of England in its earliest state, before corruption had crept in. Fox, therefore, studied First English, and one use made by him of Day's types was to produce, in 1571, dedicated to the queen, an edition of the *Saxon Gospels.* John Fox died in 1587.

14. **John Jewel,** born in Devonshire in 1522, had been tutor and preacher in his University of Oxford, and rector of Sunningwell, near Oxford. He bent under persecution after the accession of Mary, and subscribed to the Church of Rome; but was distrusted and went abroad. He returned to England at the accession of Elizabeth, and stood forward as one of the sixteen Protestants appointed to dispute before the queen with sixteen Catholics. He was in 1559 one of the commissioners for the extirpation of Catholicism in the West of England, and a few months later was made Bishop of Salisbury. His Latin Apology for the English Church—*Apologia Ecclesiæ Anglicanæ* —published in 1562, was accepted as a representative book of its time, and was in the same year translated into English by Lady Anna, the wife of Sir Nicholas Bacon. John Jewel died in 1571, at the age of fifty, having broken his health by reducing hours of sleep to the interval between midnight and four in the morning.

15. The chief promoter of Fox's edition of the Saxon Gospels was Archbishop Parker. **Matthew Parker,** born in 1504, at Norwich, was the son of a merchant. At the age of twelve he lost his father, but he was educated carefully by his mother, who sent him to Corpus Christi College, Cambridge. There he obtained a fellowship in 1527. In 1533 he preached his first sermon before the University, and obtained the good-will of Cranmer, who brought him to court. Anne Boleyn made him her chaplain, and tutor to her child Elizabeth. In 1537 he was made chaplain to Henry VIII., and then D.D. In 1541 he got a prebend in Ely, and soon afterwards a rectory in Essex. In 1544 he was Master of Corpus Christi College, and he held that office for nine years. In 1545 he was made Vice-Chancellor of the University, and rector of Landbeach, in Cambridgeshire. At the accession of Edward VI. Matthew Parker married. In 1552, King Edward gave him a prebend at Lincoln, having already made him his chaplain. During his exile, in the reign of Mary, Parker translated the Psalms into English verse, for comfort to himself like that of David, for whom in a time of trouble, as Parker says in his metrical preface:

"With golden stringes such harmonie
His harpe so sweete did wrest,
That he reliev'd his phrenesie
When wicked sprites possest."

This version of the Psalter, finished in 1557, was printed about 1560 by John Day. Parker published also, "against a civilian naming himself Thomas Martin, Doctor of the Civil Laws, going about to disprove the said marriages lawful," *A Defence of Priestes Marriages*, written by a learned man who died in the reign of Philip and Mary; with addition of his own "History of Priests' Marriages from the Conquest to Edward VI.'s Reign," which contains several quotations from First English. Upon her accession, Queen Elizabeth entrusted to Matthew Parker the revision of Edward VI.'s Service Book, and made him Archbishop of Canterbury in the place of Reginald Pole (ch vi. § 43), whose religious zeal had been in accord with the endeavours to suppress Protestant heresies, who had been made archbishop on the day after the burning of Cranmer, and who died a day after Queen Mary. For some time Matthew Parker objected to the appointment of himself, and it was not completed until 1559. He was zealous in the conflict of his time, learned in Church antiquities, and firm in support of the ecclesiastical system in the English Church.

There were produced early in the reign of Elizabeth two English versions of the Bible, which remained during the rest of her life commonly in use. These were the Geneva Bible, which appeared in 1560, and the Bishops' Bible, which appeared in 1568. *The Geneva Bible* was produced by the English congregation at Geneva during the reign of Mary, chiefly at the cost of John Bodley, the father of Sir Thomas Bodley. In 1557 the New Testament, translated by William Whittingham, Calvin's brother-in-law, was first published. It was translated from the Greek text as published by Erasmus, and revised from manuscripts collected by Genevan scholars. Calvin prefixed to it an "Epistle declaring that Christ is the End of the Law." Whittingham, then, with the aid of fellow-exiles, Gilby, Sampson, and others, turned to the Hebrew text, and instead of coming to England after the death of Mary, these labourers remained at Geneva to complete their work Hebrew scholarship had advanced, and the Geneva Bible, completed in 1560, four years before the birth of Shakespeare, was as faithful as its translators could make it. Various readings were given in the margin, and there were notes on points not only of history and geography but also of doctrine, which distinctly bound this version to the religious school of Calvin.   In the Geneva Bible appeared, for the first time, as a plan to secure facility of reference, the now familiar division of the text into verses.   This was the household Bible of those whom we may call—using the phrase in a broad sense—the Eliza-bethan Puritans.   In the dedication of it to Queen Elizabeth, the zeal of the Genevan Reformers was not less harsh than that from which they had suffered themselves in the reign of Mary.   Elizabeth was reminded how the noble Josias " put to death the false prophets and sorcerers, to perform the words of the law of God.  .  .   Yea, and in the days of King Asa, it was enacted that whosoever would not seek the Lord God of Israel should be slain, whether he were small or great, man or woman."

The zeal of Elizabeth was not so fierce.   Her supremacy had been assured in civil and ecclesiastical matters, and uniformity in religion had been established by law.   All persons in the Church, all graduates in the Universities, and all persons holding office of the crown, were required to take the oath of supremacy. A clergyman who did not use *The Book of Common Prayer*, or who spoke against it, was fined for the first offence a year's value of his living, and was liable also to six months' imprisonment.   For the second offence his living was forfeited ; and a third offence subjected him to imprisonment for life. The book had been prepared from a comparison of the first and second Service Books of Edward.   Its introduction had been opposed, but when introduced there were, of 9,400 clergymen then in England, only 189 who became Noncon-formists, and gave up their livings.  Among the laity deprecia-tion of the Book of Common Prayer was also liable to heavy punishment ; and there was a fine of a shilling upon all persons who did not attend their parish church or some recognised place of worship on Sunday unless reasonable cause for absence could be shown.   There was established also a High Court of Commissioners appointed under the Great Seal of England, to determine upon questions of " error, heresy, or schism." Roman Catholics were thus liable to punishment if they disparaged the services of the Reformed Church, and to fine if they stayed away from them ; while the Puritans who objected to the retained forms of Catholicism in the English

Church might be compelled by the High Court of Commission to accept whatever doctrine or practice the commissioners declared to be sanctioned by Parliament, by a general Council, or by the canonical Scriptures. Any three of the forty-four members of this Court might inquire concerning heretical opinions, seditious books, &c., contrary to the Acts of Supremacy and Uniformity; any three, a bishop being one, might try cases of wilful absence from church, and punish offenders by church censures or fines, or might try a clergyman on matters of doctrine. The commissioners might summon any one upon suspicion, and put him to his oath. Elizabeth had also, like the Tudors before her, the sovereign's own court of Star Chamber. Once this had been useful in overruling feudal power when it thwarted the due course of justice, but it had become a convenient instrument of personal rule. Troublesome members of Parliament and jurors could be imprisoned by it or fined; it undertook censorship of the press, and in Elizabeth's time prohibited the circulation of Roman Catholic works. This machinery was worked with various degrees of energy. John Fox, as we have seen, was Nonconformist, and though honoured by the queen, and free, of course, from persecution, he was left in poverty until Cecil contrived that he should have, on his own terms, a prebend in Salisbury Cathedral. Sampson, one of the translators of the Geneva Bible, refused the bishopric of Norwich because he would not take the prescribed oaths, but he was made at Oxford Dean of Christchurch; and Humphrey, another of the early Puritans, was at the same time made President of Magdalene College. Different degrees of objection to Church ceremonial produced also a diversity of practice, which was made in 1564 the subject of special inquiry by the High Court of Commission. Thus the clergy were said to officiate " some with a square cap, some with a round cap, some with a button cap, some with a hat." Such inquiry led to the deprival and imprisonment of Sampson and Humphrey. The London clergy were called before the Commissioners, commanded thenceforth "that strictly ye keep the unity of apparel," and summoned singly to conform or lose their livings. Of ninety-eight London clergymen sixty-one subscribed, and thirty-seven were suspended for three months with threat of deprivation if they did not within that time conform. The objection of those whom Archbishop Parker called "the precise brethren" was to the creation by human authority of laws as part of their religion which were not derived from the authority of the Bible, the one source of law in matters of religion, but from the ceremonial of a church which had assigned a superstitious value to its clothes. Each clergyman with cure of souls was then required to swear obedience to all the queen's injunctions; to all letters from Lords of the Privy Council; to all articles and injunctions from the metropolitan; to all articles and mandates from his bishop, archdeacon, and other ecclesiastical officers. **Miles Coverdale**, as a Nonconformist, had been neglected in the first years of Elizabeth, until Edmund Grindal, then Bishop of London, obtained for him in 1562 the London parish of St. Magnus, without oaths required. He was now, at the age of eighty, obliged to give up his living, and was until his death, in 1567, a preacher unattached.

Archbishop Parker was thoroughly sincere in carrying out this policy. There was a wide-spread reverence for the old forms of the Church in rural England; many scholars and students of the past shared in the reverential feeling, and wished to secure essentials of reform with least possible disturbance of forms and customs that had been blended with the worship of God by their forefathers. Respect for the past was natural to **Matthew Parker.** In his household all servants when they had nothing else to do were required to bind books, to copy or paint from manuscripts, or engrave on copper. He took pains to collect manuscripts scattered at the destruction of the monasteries, especially the most ancient of those that related to our own Church. He caused four old historians to be edited, Matthew Paris, Matthew of Westminster, Thomas Walsingham, and Asser's "Life of Alfred." In 1566 he issued Ælfric's Homily on the Lord's Supper, to be read to the people at Easter, before sacrament. The tendency of all his labour is indicated by his own work, a folio printed in Latin, in 1572— *De Antiquitate Britannicæ Ecclesiæ,* &c.—on the antiquity of the Church of Britain and privileges of the Church of Canterbury, with its seventy archbishops. Parker represented honestly, and maintained in the manner of the time, the principle of authority within the Church. His friend Queen Elizabeth liked Puritans rather less than Catholics, because their opposition to authority in many of its forms implied, if it spread and took other shape, a possible abridgment of the power of the crown.

For the Geneva Bible, John Bodley obtained in 1561 a patent, giving exclusive right to print that version for seven years. In 1566, a revised edition being ready, an extension of the licence was applied for, and permitted for twelve years longer, on condition that no impression should pass without the direction, consent, and advice of the Archbishop of Canterbury and Bishop of London. John Bodley would not consent to that ; and the Geneva Bible was printed abroad for English use until the death of Archbishop Parker. Parker, meanwhile, produced, with conscientious care, a version which was to supersede in churches Cranmer's Bible (ch. vi. § 29). About 1564, in the year of Shakespeare's birth, he distributed the work of translation among fifteen learned men, most of them bishops, urged on them to do their work "in such perfection that the adversaries can have no occasion to quarrel with it," and published the result in 1568. This translation, from the number of bishops who took part in it, and from the fact that it became, for Elizabeth's reign, the authorised version for church use, was known as *The Bishops' Bible.* It put aside, for example, Tyndal's word " congregation," against which More had contended, and which had remained in Cranmer's Bible, giving the word "Church," that Tyndal had avoided (ch. vi. § 22). But tendencies of thought are indicated by the fact that of eighty-five editions of the English Bible published in Elizabeth's reign, sixty were of the Geneva version.

16. On the way from the monastic chronicle to later forms of history, we have now come to a form of chronicle in which the design of Robert of Gloucester (ch. iii. § 38) is carried out with simple directness. The Latin monastic chronicle (ch. iii. § 3) was to enable studious brethren to connect their lives with the great life of the world, and the history and interests of the abbey itself usually in this chronicle lay at the heart of all the business of the world. But now we have in our own tongue abstracts and chronicles of past events at the heart of which there lies only the desire that Englishmen should know what it concerns them to know of the life of their own country. There is no attempt at a minute tracing of cause and effect—that was to follow; no rhyming to recommend the story to the ears of an uneducated people—that had gone before. In the stir of life at the beginning of the sixteenth century, there was not only a desire but a need simply to know what had been done in the past.

**Richard Grafton,** who completed Hall's Chronicle, (ch. vi. § 50) produced, therefore, in 1563, *An Abridgment;* and in

1565 *A Manual of the Chronicles of England,* from the Creation to the date of publication ; and in 1568 and 1569, in two folios, *A Chronicle at large and meere History of the Affayres of Englande and Kinges of the same.*

John Stow, born in Cornhill about 1525, was a tailor's son, and for a few years himself a tailor. But the life of the time stirred in him an enthusiasm for the study of English history and antiquities. He produced, in 1561, *A Summary of English Chronicles,* and gave time and labour in travel about the country to produce for posterity a larger record ; but he would have given up the delight and chief use of his life, to go back to tailoring for need of bread, if he had not been encouraged by occasional help from Archbishop Parker. His history first appeared in 1580, a quarto of more than 1,200 pages, as *Annales, or a Generale Chronicle of England from Brute unto this present yeare of Christ,* 1580.

Ralph Holinshed had produced, with help of John Hooker, Richard Stanihurst, Boteville, Harrison, and others, his Chronicle three years before, in 1577, when Shakespeare was thirteen years old. Prefixed to it was a "Description of Britaine," valuable as an account of the condition of the country at that time. It was in two folio volumes, with many woodcuts. The second edition, which contained some passages that displeased the queen and required cancelling, appeared in 1586 and 1587, when Shakespeare's age was about twenty-three. It was chiefly in Hall and Holinshed that Shakespeare read the history of England. Of Holinshed himself little more is known than that he came of a respectable family at Bosley, in Cheshire, and that he was, in the latter part of his life, steward to a Thomas Burdet, of Bromcote, Warwickshire.

When the Chronicles of Holinshed and Stow appeared, in 1577 and 1580, William Camden had been appointed second master of Westminster School, and was at work on his *Britannia.* Camden was a Londoner, born in 1551, or about two years older than Spenser. He was educated at Christ's Hospital and St. Paul's School, entered as a servitor at Magdalene College, Oxford, whence he removed to Broadgate Hall (now Pembroke College), and then to Christchurch. He graduated in 1573, and in 1575 became second master at Westminster School, where he spent all leisure in the studies by which he served his country in the latter part of Elizabeth's reign, and in the reign of her successor.

To this record of the cultivation of English history by men of the people—a poor scholar, a gentleman's steward, a tailor, at a time, too, when there was another tailor, John Speed, gathering enthusiasm for such studies—we may add note of the service done to literature by **George Bannatyne.** He was the seventh child of a family of twenty-three, born in 1545, and bred to trade. In 1568 he was a young man of twenty-three, at home because it was a time of pestilence, when work was stopped. He amused himself in his forced leisure by copying all the pieces of good Scottish poetry he could meet with. His collection was so well taken care of that it has come down to our own time, a MS. of 800 closely-written pages, now in the library of the Faculty of Advocates, at Edinburgh.

17. We return to the poets, and take poetry on the side nearest to trade—with still a chief regard for the material well-being of England—in **Thomas Tusser,** whose *Hundreth Good Pointes of Husbandrie,* the first form of a larger book, appeared in 1557, the year before Elizabeth's accession (ch. vi. § 60). Thomas Tusser was born about 1515, at Rivenhall, in Essex, was first a chorister at St. Paul's, and then was placed at Eton under Udall (ch. vi. § 48, 58, 60), of whom he says :

> " From Paul's I went, to Eton sent,
>   To learn straightways the Latin phrase,
>   Where fifty-three stripes given to me
>   At once I had.
>   For fault but small, or none at all,
>   It came to pass thus beat I was :
>   See, Udall, see, the mercy of thee
>   To me, poor lad."

Tusser went from Eton to Cambridge, was fourteen years at Court under the patronage of Lord Paget, then took a farm in Suffolk, and rhymed about farming. He first broke out in 1557 with his "Hundred Good Points," but his crop of rhyming maxims had increased fivefold by the year 1573, when Richard Tottel published Tusser's *Five Hundreth Points of good Husbandry,* giving the round of the year's husbandry month by month, in a book of 98 pages, six and a half quatrains to a page. Tusser's strength may have been in high farming, it was not in high poetry. Nevertheless, there is a musical sententiousness in his terse rhymes, and an air of business about them; his Pegasus tugged over the clods with his shoulder well up to the collar, and the maxims were in a form likely to ensure for them wide currency among the people. While less practical poets might bid their readers go idly a Maying with Maid Marian. Tusser advised otherwise :

> " In May get a weed-hook, a crotch, and a glove,
> And weed out such weeds as the corn doth not love.
> For weeding of winter corn now it is best,
> But June is the better for weeding the rest."

Thomas Tusser died in 1580.

18. **George Turbervile** was about fifteen years younger than Tusser. He was born at Whitchurch, in Dorsetshire, educated at Winchester and New College, Oxford, became secretary to Sir Thomas Randolph, ambassador at the Court of Russia, and lived into the latter part of Elizabeth's reign. He published, in 1567, two translations—one of *The Heroical Epistles of Ovid*, six of them translated into blank verse, and the others into four-lined stanzas ; the other of the Latin *Eclogues of Mantuan*, an Italian poet, who had died in 1516. In 1570 there appeared a volume of his own poems as *Epitaphes, Epigrams, Songs, and Sonets; with a Discourse of the friendly Affections of Tymetes to Pindara his Ladie*. Turbervile takes a pleasant place among the elder Elizabethan poets. He wrote also books of *Falconrie* and *Hunting*, and made versions from the Italian, notably ten *Tragical Tales translated by Turbervile, in Time of his Troubles, out of sundrie Italians, with the Argument and L'Envoye to each Tale;* published in 1576.

From Italy, with French intervention, the story of "Romeo and Juliet" first came into English verse in 1562, two years before Shakespeare's birth, as *The Tragicall Historye of Romeus and Juliet, written first in Italian by Bandell, and now in English by Ar. Br.*, that is, **Arthur Brooke**. Arthur Brooke took his poem from a French variation on the story by Bandello, himself altering and adding. In 1567, "Romeo and Juliet" appeared again in English, this time in prose, as the twenty-fifth novel of the second volume of *The Palace of Pleasure*, a collection of tales from the Italian, by **William Paynter**. Shakespeare afterwards founded his play on the tale as told by Arthur Brooke. Thus Ar. Br. wrote :

> " ' Art thou,' quoth he, ' a man ?  Thy shape saith so thou art ;
> Thy crying and thy weeping eyes denote a woman's hart :
> For manly reason is quite from of thy mind outchased,
> And in her stead affections lewd and fancies highly placed ;
> So that I stoode in doute this howre at the least,
> If thou a man or woman wert, or els a brutish beast.' "

Which became in Shakespeare's verse :

> "Art thou a man? Thy form cries out thou art :
> Thy tears are womanish ; thy wild acts denote
> Th' unreasonable fury of a beast."

William Paynter, Clerk of the Office of Arms within the Tower of London, produced in 1566 the first volume of the " Palace of Pleasure," containing sixty novels translated from Boccaccio's " Decameron." In the following year he published, in a second volume, thirty-four more novels, partly taken from Bandello, whose tales first appeared at Lucca, in 1554. There were nine volumes of them, and it indicated the corruption of Italian life that some of the most licentious were inscribed to ladies of good fame.

19. **Roger Ascham** (ch. vi. § 55) made this in " The Schoolmaster," one ground of his argument against the " manners and doctrine our Englishmen fetch out of Italy." Ascham, although a Protestant, had escaped persecution in the reign of Mary ; his pension had been renewed, and in May, 1554, he had been appointed Latin secretary to the queen, with a salary of forty marks. In that year also he gave up his fellowship, and married Margaret Howe. By Queen Elizabeth, Roger Ascham, who had been one of her teachers in Greek, was still continued in his pension, and retained in his post of Latin Secretary. In 1560 the queen gave him the prebend of Wetwang, in York Minster. The archbishop had given it to another, and Ascham did not get his dues without a lawsuit. In 1563, Ascham, as one in the queen's service, was dining with Sir William Cecil, when the conversation turned to the subject of education, from news of the running away of some boys from Eton, where there was much beating. Ascham argued that young children were sooner allured by love than driven by beating to obtain good learning. Sir Richard Sackville, father of Thomas Sackville (§ 8), said nothing at the dinner-table, but he afterwards drew Ascham aside, agreed with his opinions, lamented his own past loss by a harsh schoolmaster, and said, Ascham tells us in the preface to his book, " ' Seeing it is but in vain to lament things past, and also wisdom to look to things to come, surely, God willing, if God lend me life, I will make this, my mishap, some occasion of good hap to little Robert Sackville, my son's son. For whose bringing up I would gladly, if it so please you, use specially your good advice. I hear say you have a son much of his age (Ascham had three little sons) ; we will deal thus together. Point you out a schoolmaster who by your order

shall teach my son and yours, and for all the rest I will provide, yea, though they three do cost me a couple of hundred pounds by year : and besides you shall find me as fast a friend to you and yours as perchance any you have.' Which promise the worthy gentleman surely kept with me until his dying day." The conversation went into particulars, and in the course of it Sir Richard drew from Ascham what he thought of the common going of Englishmen into Italy. All ended with a request that Ascham would "put in some order of writing the chief points of this our talk, concerning the right order of teaching and honesty of living, for the good bringing up of children and young men." That was the origin of Ascham's book called *The Schoolmaster.* Ascham wrote in Latin against the mass, and upon other subjects connected with religious controversy. His delicate health failed more and more. He became unable to work between dinner and bed-time, was troubled with sleep-lessness, sought rest by the motion of a cradle, and ended his pure life as a scholar in 1568, at the age of fifty-three. His "School-master" was left complete, and published in 1570 by his widow, with a dedication to Sir William Cecil. Beseeching him, she said, to take on him "the defence of the book, to avaunce the good that may come of it by your allowance and furtherance to publike use and benefite, and to accept the thankfull recognition of me and my poore children, trustyng of the continuance of your good memorie of M. Ascham and his, and dayly com-mendyng the prosperous estate of you and yours to God, whom you serve, and whose you are, I rest to trouble you. Your humble Margaret Ascham." The treatise is in two parts, one dealing with general principles, the other technical, as in "Tox-ophilus ;" the first book teaching the bringing up of youth, the second book teaching the ready way to the Latin tongue. Great stress is laid in Ascham's "Schoolmaster" on gentleness in teach-ing. As to the true notes of the best wit in a child, Ascham will take, he says, "the very judgment of him that was counted the best teacher and wisest man that learning maketh mention of, and that is Socrates in Plato, who expresseth orderly these seven plain notes to choose a good wit in a child for learning." He was to be (1) Euphues ; (2) of good memory ; (3) attached to learning ; (4) prepared for labour and pains ; (5) glad to learn of another ; (6) free in questioning ; and (7) happy in well-earned applause. The first of these qualities, Ascham describes at especial length ; and the embodiment of the description, in a character wanting some of the other qualities, is, as we shall presently see, John Lyly's hero Euphues, described in a tale which has for subordinate title, "The Anatomy of Wit." Ascham's "Schoolmaster" was first published by his widow in the year 1570. The first part of Lyly's "Euphues" appeared in 1579 ; the other part, "Euphues and his England," in 1580.

"Ευφυἡς," the Schoolmaster said, "is he that is apt by goodness of wit, and appliable by readiness of will, to learning, having all other qualities of the mind and parts of the body that must another day serve learning, not troubled, mangled, and halved, but sound, whole, full, and able to do their office : as a tongue not stammering, or over hardly drawing forth words, but plain and ready to deliver the meaning of the mind; a voice not soft, weak, piping, womanish, but audible, strong, and manlike ; a countenance not werish and crabbed, but fair and comely ; a personage not wretched and deformed, but tall and goodly : for surely a comely countenance, with a goodly stature, giveth credit to learning and authority to the person ; otherwise, commonly, either open contempt or privy disfavour doth hurt or hinder both person and learning. And even as a fair stone requireth to be set in the finest gold, with the best workmanship, or else it loseth much of the grace and price, even so excellency in learning, and namely divinity, joined with a comely personage, is a marvellous jewel in the world. And how can a comely body be better employed than to serve the greatest exercise of God's greatest gift, and that is learning? But commonly the fairest bodies are bestowed on the foulest purposes. I would it were not so ; and with examples herein I will not meddle ; yet I wish that those should both mend it and meddle with it which have most occasion to look to it, as good and wise fathers should do," &c.

In illustration of the force of gentleness in teaching, Ascham cited in "The Schoolmaster" his finding of Lady Jane Grey, when he called on her at Broadgate, in Leicestershire, before his going into Germany, reading Plato's Phædo in Greek, "and that with as much delight as some gentlemen would read a merry tale in Boccaccio." He asked her how that was; and she said it was because God had given her severe parents and a gentle schoolmaster. At home she was so continually under punishment and censure that she longed for the time when she must go to Mr. Aylmer (§ 2) "who teacheth me so gently, so pleasantly, with such fair allurements to learning, that I think

M

all the time nothing whiles I am with him. And when I am
called from him I fall on weeping, because whatsoever I do
else but learning is full of grief, trouble, fear, and whole mis-
liking unto me." For Italy, said Ascham, the best that it could
teach of the joining of learning with comely exercises was to
be found in the "Courtier" (*Cortegiano*) of Count Baldassar
Castiglione (the original published in 1516), "which book,
advisedly read and diligently followed but one year at home in
England, would do a young gentleman more good, I wis, than
three years travel abroad spent in Italy." "And I marvel,"
adds Ascham, "that this book is no more read in the court
than it is, seeing it is so well translated into English by a
worthy gentleman, Sir Thomas Hoby" (translation published
1561). Italy, said Ascham, is not what it was wont to be.
"Virtue once made that country mistress over all the world.
Vice now maketh that country slave to them that before were
glad to serve it. . . . If a gentleman must needs travel into
Italy, he shall do well to look to the life of the wisest traveller
that ever travelled thither, set out by the wisest writer that ever
spake with tongue, God's doctrine only excepted, and that is
Ulysses in Homer." The "Schoolmaster" observed that
Ulysses "is not commended so much nor so oft in Homer,
because he was πολύτροπος, that is, skilful in men's manners and
fashions, as because he was πολύμητις, that is, wise in all purposes
and ware in all places." Against Circe's enchantment Homer's
remedy was the herb Moly, "with the black root and white
flower, sour at the first but sweet in the end, which Hesiodus
termeth the study of virtue." This was of all things most
contrary to what Ascham called "the precepts of fond books
of late translated out of Italian into English, sold in every shop
in London. . . . Ten sermons at Paul's Cross do not so
much good for moving men to true doctrine as one of these
books do harm with enticing men to ill living."

Let our young men, then, go to Italy under the keep and
guard of one "who by his wisdom and honesty, by his example and
authority, may be able to keep them safe and sound in the fear
of God, in Christ's true religion, in good order and honesty of
living." Ascham quoted to his countrymen the Italian proverb
that "an Italianate Englishman is an incarnate devil." The
readiest way, he said, to entangle the mind with false doctrine
is first to entice the will to wanton living. Ascham dwelt on
the outcome of a sensual life in the contempt by Italians alike

of the pope and of Luther; "they allow neither side : they like none but only themselves.  The mark they shoot at, the end they look for, the heaven they desire, is only their own present pleasure and private profit ; whereby they plainly declare of whose school, of what religion they be : that is Epicures in living, and *ἄθεοι* " (atheists, the word was now being Anglicised) "in doctrine.  This last word is no more unknown now to plain Englishmen than the person was unknown sometime in England, until some Englishmen took pains to fetch that devilish opinion out of Italy."

20. Roger Ascham's "Schoolmaster" produced both name and substance of the "Euphues" of young **John Lyly.** Lyly was born in the Weald of Kent, about 1553; became a student of Magdalene College, Oxford, in 1569; took his degree of B.A. in 1573, and of M.A. in 1575; and was incorporated as M.A. of Cambridge in 1579.  It was in the spring of the year 1579 that he published *Euphues; or, the Anatomy of Wit.*  This earnest book, written at the age of five-and-twenty, made Lyly's reputation as a wit.  It evidently was suggested by the reading of Ascham's "Schoolmaster."  From citation of the anatomy of a teachable child's wit, as set forth by Socrates, and from Euphues, the first of the discriminated qualities, it obtained, as we have just seen, both its titles.  Its form is that of an Italian story, its style a very skilful elaboration of that humour for conceits and verbal antitheses which had been coming in from Italy and was developing itself into an outward fashion of our literature.  In form and style, therefore, it sought to win a welcome from those fashionable people upon whose minds there was most need to enforce its substance.  In substance it was the argument of Ascham's "Schoolmaster" repeated: corruption of English life by the much going of our young men to Italy ; the right development of the young mind by education on just principles, to a worthy life and a true faith in God.

21. It was not by right of their literature alone that the Italians of the sixteenth century, claiming the first rank in civilisation, spoke of the outer nations, after the old Roman fashion, as barbarians.  Jerome Cardan, describing to his countrymen his visit to the court of Edward VI., said of the English that "in dress they are like the Italians, for they are glad to boast themselves nearly allied to them, and therefore study to imitate as much as possible their manner and their clothes.  Certain it is that all the barbarians of Europe love the Italians more

than any race among themselves." He hinted that "perhaps these people do not know our wickedness."

The prevalence of a poetic element in the Italian character was of itself dangerous to foreigners of colder blood who went to Italy for inspiration. In that land of song, at the beginning of the sixteenth century, there was still to be heard the complaint made by Petrarch generations earlier, that the very tailors and shoemakers stitched rhymes and cobbled verse. Commentators upon Petrarch issued forth out of the printing-offices by dozens at a time, and were to be heard by thousands discoursing in society. His words were picked over for allegories, and his book of verse, weighted with fanciful interpretations, was disgraced into a pattern-book for all tailors of rhyme, a *Follet* for the literary milliner who set the fashion after which the luxury of idleness should be attired. Thus Petrarch unwittingly became a father of conceits. When, after the death of Leo X., the Florentine academicians, sorely punished for political conspiracy, were forced to confine their energies to literature, verbal haggling over Petrarch was their chief delight. Great poets were arising. The romantic epic, the pastoral, the satire, even the drama, were all dropping their first-fruits upon the rich Italian soil; but ready rhetoric, of sentiment determined to be clever and not caring to be true, still yielded the husks eaten by the mob alike of the palace and the street.

But upon the fashion of speech at Elizabeth's court there were other influences of which we have not yet taken account. Some of its peculiarities, together with the very name that gave the term of Euphuism to its affectations, are to be traced to the Platonists, who were strong in the days of Henry VIII. But Platonism also came to us from Italy. It was in Florence that the refugee Greeks, after the fall of Constantinople, were first welcomed as revealers of Plato and Aristotle (ch. v. § 25). In Italy Plato, in France Aristotle, was preferred. Neoplatonists had given interests to the Rabbinical doctrine of the Cabbala, then received by many a good Christian scholar. It was joined to principles of an occult philosophy, partly derived from the same source, but enriched from teaching of the Arabs; and it was confirmed by marvellous recitals in the "Natural History" of Pliny. "The mysteries of Nature," one of her students then said, "can no otherwise than by experience and conjecture be inquired into by us." Until the asserted experience of ancient naturalists had been disproved by the experience of later times,

it was not very unreasonable to assume that the science of the
ancients equalled their philosophy and poetry. To deny virtues
assigned to certain stones, plants, animals, or stars, simply
because they were wonderful, certainly would not have been
wise. Even in the magical doctrines then widely accepted
there was reasoning entitled to respect. Their basis, it may be
observed, was so far from being diabolical, that they set out
with a demand for purity of life, and for a high spiritual adoration of the source of all the harmony they laboured to find in
the wonders of creation. It is to be remembered, therefore, that
those marvellous properties of things, honestly credited and freely
used in the fashioning of ornaments of speech, had not for the
reader of their own time that inherent absurdity which now
attaches to them. It is very difficult indeed now to read in the
old sense the kind of writing in which Lyly was master, " talking," as Drayton said,

> "Of stones, stars, plants, of fishes, flies,
> Playing with words and idle similies."

We must not forget that before the idlers went to Italy our
scholars as well as our poets had been there. In Italy, Colet,
Linacre, Grocyn, Lily, and Latimer, had learnt their Greek.
Even after Elizabeth's day, Platonism survived to the time of
the Commonwealth, in Henry More, who wrote Platonic songs
of the Soul's Life and Immortality, and dedicated to his friend
Cudworth a defence of the Threefold Cabbala. But Henry
More's spiritual conceits have no concord with courtly affecta-
tions. " If," he says, " by thoughts rudely scattered in my verse
I may lend men light till the dead night be gone,"

> "It is enough I meant no trimmer frame,
> Nor by nice needlework to seek a name."

To that taste for " nice needlework " Camden objected in
" our sparkful youth," ready to " laugh at their great-grand-
fathers' English, who had more care to do well than to speak
minion-like."

22. In the dedication of his *Euphues* to Lord de la Warre, Lyly
suggests that there may be found in it " more speeches which
for gravity will mislike the foolish than unseemly terms which
for vanity may offend the wise." He anticipates some little
disfavour from the " fine wits of the day ; " and his allusions to
" the dainty ear of the curious sifter," to the use of " superfluous
eloquence," to the search after " those who sift the finest meal

and bear the whitest mouths," sufficiently show that his own manner was formed on an existing fashion. " It is a world," he says, " to see how Englishmen desire to hear finer speech than their language will allow, to eat finer bread than is made of wheat, or wear finer cloth than is made of wool ; but I let pass their fineness, which can no way excuse my folly." But Lyly being a master of the style he had adopted, his ingenious English was taken as the type of successful writing in the fashionable manner, and from the title of his novel, the name of " Euphuism " was derived for the quaint writing, rich in conceit, alliteration, and antithesis, which remained in favour during the rest of the period of Italian influence on English literature.

Lyly's novel itself was in design most serious. He represented Euphues as a young gentleman of Athens, who corresponded in his readiness of wit and perfectness of body to the quality called Euphues by Plato. He went to Italy, to Naples, " a place of more pleasure than profit, and yet of more profit than piety, the very walls and windows whereof showed it rather to be the tabernacle of Venus than the temple of Vesta. . . a court more meet for an atheist than one of Athens." There he showed so pregnant a wit that Eubulus, an old gentleman of the place, was impelled to warn him at length against the dangers of the city in words ending with the solemn admonition, " Serve God, love God, fear God, and God will so bless thee as either heart can wish or thy friends desire." Young Euphues disdained counsel of age, and bought experience in his own way. He found a friend in a young and wealthy town-born gentleman, named Philautus. Euphues and Philautus " used not only one board but one bed, one book (if so be it they thought not one too many)." Philautus was supplanted by Euphues in the light love of Lucilla, daughter of Don Ferardo, one of the chief governors of the city. This parted the friends ; until Euphues was in his turn cast off for one Curio, a gentleman of little wealth and less wit. Then Euphues lamented his rejection of the fatherly counsel of Eubulus, and his spending of life in the laps of ladies, of his lands in maintenance of bravery, and of his wit in the vanities of idle sonnets. The greatest wickedness, he found, is drawn out of the greatest wit, if it be abused by will, or entangled with the world, or inveigled by woman. He would endeavour himself to amend all that is past, and be a mirror of godliness thereafter, rather choosing to die in his study amidst his books than to court it in Italy in the company of

ladies. The story was here at an end, although the volume was
not and Lyly's idler readers, who had caught at his bait of a
fashionably conceited tale, might now begin to feel the hook with
which he angled.  Philautus and Euphues renewed their friendship; and Euphues, having returned to Athens, sent to his friend
in Naples "a cooling card for Philautus and all fond lovers."
Then followed a letter "to the grave matrons and honest maidens
of Italy," in the spirit of one who, as Euphues wrote, "may
love the clear conduit water, though he loathe the muddy ditch.
Ulysses, though he detested Calypso, with her sugared voice, yet
he embraced Penelope, with her rude distaff." It should no
more, said Lyly, grieve the true woman to hear censure of
woman's folly "than the mint master to see the coiner hanged."
Increasing in earnestness, the book then gave, under the heading
of " Euphues and his Ephebus " (Ephebus meaning a youth come
to man's estate, which was for boys in Athens the age of seventeen), a systematic essay upon education, sound as Ascham's in
its doctrine ; dealing with the management of children from their
birth, and advancing to the ideal of a university.  Rising still in
earnestness, as he showed his Euphues growing in wisdom, Lyly
made a letter to the gentlemen scholars of Athens preface to a
dialogue between Euphues and Atheos, which was an argument
against the infidelity that had crept in from Italy.  It is as
earnest as if Latimer himself had preached it to the courtiers of
King Edward.  Euphues appeals solemnly to Scripture and the
voice within ourselves.  In citation from the sacred text consist
almost his only illustrations ; in this he abounds.  Whole pages
contain nothing but the words of Scripture.  At a time when
fanciful and mythological adornment was so common to literature that the very Bible Lyly read—the new Bishops' Bible (§ 15)
—contained woodcut initials upon subjects drawn from Ovid's
" Metamorphoses," and opened the Epistle to the Hebrews with
a sketch of Leda and the Swan, Lyly does not once mingle false
ornament with reasoning on sacred things.  He refers to the
ancients only at the outset of his argument, to show that
the heathen had acknowledged a creator : mentions Plato
but to say that he recognised one whom we may call God
omnipotent, glorious, immortal, unto whose similitude we that
creep here on earth have our souls framed; and Aristotle, only
to tell how, when he could not find out by the secrecy of
nature the cause of the ebbing and the flowing of the sea, he
cried, with a loud voice, " O Thing of Things, have mercy upon

me!" In twenty black-letter pages there are but three illustrations drawn from supposed properties of things. The single anecdote from profane history may here be quoted from a discourse that introduces nearly all the texts incorporated in our Liturgy:—" I have read of Themistocles, which having offended Philip, the King of Macedonia, and could no way appease his anger, meeting his young son Alexander, took him in his arms, and met Philip in the face. Philip, seeing the smiling countenance of the child, was well pleased with Themistocles. Even so, if through thy manifold sins and heinous offences thou provoke the heavy displeasure of thy God, insomuch as thou shalt tremble for horror, take his only-begotten and well-beloved Son Jesus in thine arms, and then He neither cah nor will be angry with thee. If thou have denied thy God, yet if thou go out with Peter and weep bitterly, God will not deny thee. Though with the prodigal son thou wallow in thine own wilfulness, yet if thou return again sorrowful thou shalt be received. If thou be a grievous offender, yet if thou come unto Christ with the woman in Luke, and wash His feet with thy tears, thou shalt obtain remission."

The first part of Euphues—*Euphues; or, the Anatomy of Wit*, published in 1579—is a complete work. The second part— *Euphues and his England*, published in 1580—was apparently designed to mitigate some of the severity of the first, which had given offence at Oxford, and indirectly deprecate, in courtly fashion, a too ruinous interpretation of the author's meaning. In the first part Lyly satisfied his conscience ; in the second part, but still without dishonesty, he satisfied the court. He had ended the first part with an intimation that Euphues was about to visit England, and promised, within one summer, a report of what he saw. In his second part, therefore, Euphues, bringing Philautus with him, lands at Dover, after telling a long moral story on the sea. The two strangers pass through Canterbury, and are entertained in a roadside house by a retired courtier. This personage keeps bees and philosophises over them; from him we hear the lengthy story of his love, enriched with numerous conceited conversations. In London the travellers lodge with a merchant, and are admitted to the intimacy of a lady named Camilla, who is courted and who finally is married, though she be below his rank, by noble Surius. With Camilla and the ladies who are her friends, the strangers converse much in courtly fashion. Philautus of course falls in love with her, and worries her with letters; but he is at last led by Flavia, a prudent matron, to the possession of a wife in the young lady Violet. Every Englishwoman is fair, wise, and good. Nothing is wrong in England ; or whatever is wrong, Lyly satirises with exaggerated praise. The story is full of covert satire, and contains much evidence of religious earnestness. It is designedly enriched with love-tales, letters between lovers, and ingenious examples of those fanciful conflicts of wit in argument upon some courtly theme, to which fine ladies and gentlemen of Elizabeth's court formally sat down as children now sit down to a round game of forfeits. Having saved to the last a panegyric upon Queen Elizabeth, which blends an ounce of flattery with certainly a pound of solid praise in its regard for her as the mainstay of the Protestant faith, Euphues retires to Athens, where, he says, " Gentlemen, Euphues is musing in the bottom of the mountain Silixedra, Philautus is married in the Isle of England : two friends parted, the one living in the delights of his new wife, the other in contemplation of his old griefs."

After a few more words, Lyly parted from his readers by committing them to the Almighty.

23. Such were the times wherein Spenser and Shakespeare grew to their full powers : Spenser representing England with its religious sense of duty combative, bitterly combative, in all the struggle of the time ; Shakespeare enabled by that English earnestness to speak through highest poetry the highest truth, to shape in immortal forms the very spirit which we lose too often while we fight to make it ours.

**Edmund Spenser** was born in or about the year 1552. He belonged to a branch of the family of the Spencers of Althorpe, Northamptonshire, and, though born in London, his home as a boy was in the North of England, probably upon the Yorkshire border of Lancashire. In 1569 he entered Pembroke College, Cambridge, as a sizar. In the same year there was published a book devised by S. John van der Noodt, a refugee from Brabant, called, *A Theatre wherein be represented as well the Miseries and Calamities that follow the Voluptuous Worldlings, as also the great Joys and Pleasures which the Faithful do enjoy. An Argument both Profitable and Delectable to all that sincerely love the Word of God.* The book opened with six pieces, which were the first six of the *Visions of Petrarch* translated by Spenser, and they were followed by some translations which, with later change from blank verse into rhyme, may be identified

M *

among Spenser's *Visions of Bellay.* Spenser's participation as a youth in such a work as Van der Noodt's, agrees with what we learn of him in later years. Spenser graduated as B.A. in 1573, and as M.A. in 1576.

24. In that year, when Spenser's age was about four-and twenty, a friend and fellow-student of his at Pembroke Hall, **Gabriel Harvey,** was lecturing on rhetoric at Cambridge. The introductory lecture of Harvey's course in 1577, apparently his second course, was published under the name of *Ciceronianus;* and his two first lectures of the course for 1578 were also published, under the name of *Rhetor.* He had then advanced from a close following of Bembo and other Italians, who exalted above all things the Ciceronian style, and had received an impulse to the appreciation of individuality in other authors, from the reading of Jean Sambuc's " Ciceronianus." He had learnt, within that year, to look for the whole man in a writer as the source of style, and, still exalting Cicero, to attend first to the life and power of the man, and not to the mere surface polish of his language. " Let every man," he said, "learn to be, not a Roman, but himself." Gabriel Harvey then, the friend of Spenser and of Sidney, was no pedant. He was the eldest of four sons of a prosperous rope-maker at Saffron Walden. Two other brothers, Richard and John, followed him after a long interval to Cambridge ; Richard, the elder, coming to Pembroke Hall as a boy of fourteen, in 1575, and finding in his brother Gabriel a guide and tutor.

An obscure book of Gabriel Harvey's enables us to understand the way of Spenser's introduction into life. In July, 1578, Queen Elizabeth visited Audley End, the great house in the neighbourhood of Saffron Walden. Cambridge being close by, the University paid homage to the queen on that occasion. Gabriel Harvey, being a Saffron Walden man, made much of the event. When the great scholar, **Sir Thomas Smith,** who was of Saffron Walden and a kinsman, (ch. vi. § 51, 56), who had become a Secretary of State under Elizabeth and Chancellor of the Order of the Garter, and had written a Latin book upon England—*De Republicâ Anglorum*—died, in 1579, Harvey wrote his lament called *Smithus.* A series of Latin poems celebrating notabilities of the queen's visit to Saffron Walden was written by **Gabriel Harvey,** and published under the name of *Gratulationes Waldenses* ("Walden Gratulations"). Two were upon words spoken by the queen concerning Gabriel himself. He pressed forward with his homage, and the Queen said, "Who is this? Is it Leicester's man that we were speaking of?" Being told that it was, she said, "I'll not deny you my hand, Harvey." Again, as the subject of another set of verses, "Tell me," the queen said to Leicester, "Is it settled that you send this man to Italy and France?" "It is," said he. "That's well," she replied, "for already he has an Italian face, and the look of a man ; I should hardly have taken him for an Englishman" —like an Italian for the dusky hue which Thomas Nash afterwards compared to rancid bacon. Here, then, we learn that Harvey was in Leicester's service, and about to be sent abroad by him. But Harvey just after this time wrote to his friend Spenser, who had left college upon taking his M.A. degree, and who seems to have been living as a tutor in the North of England, bidding him leave "those hills were harbrough nis,"

> " And to the dales resort, where shepherds rich
> And fruitful flocks bene everywhere to see."

The common friend of Harvey and Spenser who wrote the original gloss on this passage says, "This is no poetical fiction, but unfeignedly spoken of the poet self, who for special occasion of private affairs (as I have been partly of himself informed) and for his more preferment, removing out of the north parts came into the ·south as Hobbinol" (that is the name given in "The Shepherds' Calendar" to Gabriel Harvey) " advised him privately." Now, the advancement was by introduction to the Earl of Leicester, by whom, either in place of Harvey, or as well as Harvey, Spenser was sent abroad. In October, 1579, there were addressed to Gabriel Harvey some affectionate hexameters by Edmund Spenser, then on the point of travelling into France. "Dispatched by my lord, I go thither," Spenser said, in the postscript dated from Leicester House "as sent by him and maintained (most what) of him ; and there am to employ my time, my mind, to his honour's service." Clearly, then, the introduction to Leicester, which determined the whole future of Spenser's life, he had obtained from his friend Harvey. As "Leicester's man," Harvey had become acquainted with Philip Sidney, Leicester's nephew. Likeness in age and love of literature had developed between them a friendship in which Spenser now was joined. It was in the year 1579, when he was in Leicester's service and Sidney's society, a frequent guest at Penshurst, and a young man with a career opening before him, that Spenser, aged twenty-seven, published his first book, *The Shepherds' Calendar.*

25. **Philip Sidney** was born at Penshurst, in November, 1554, eldest child of Sir Henry Sidney, who was at the time of his son's birth twenty-five years old, and had been knighted four years before, in company with Sir William Cecil. His mother. had been Lady Mary Dudley; she was daughter to the Duke of Northumberland and sister to Sir Robert Dudley, who, in 1564, was created Earl of Leicester. The next child of the household was a daughter, Mary, one year younger than Philip, his companion in childhood and the only sister who lived to become a woman. At the accession of Elizabeth, Sir Henry Sidney was Lord Justice of Ireland; he then served as Lord President of Wales, and in October, 1565, still acting as President of Wales by deputy, he was appointed Lord Deputy of Ireland. There " O'Neil the Great, cousin to St. Patrick, friend to the Queen of England, and enemy to all the world besides," seizing the occasion given in 1560 by the attempt of the Earl of Sussex to enforce Protestantism on the Irish Catholics, had made himself master of the north and west. Sir Henry battled bravely and generously with the real difficulties of his position, while his credit at court in London was being impaired by complaints that arose from selfish jealousies of the Earls of Ormond and Desmond in the south. As Lord President of Wales and the Marches of the same, namely, the four counties of Gloucester, Worcester, Hereford, and Shropshire, having his court at Ludlow Castle, Sir Henry Sidney had sent his son Philip, a grave, studious boy, to Shrewsbury school. In 1568 he went to Oxford, where Christchurch was his college. Sir Henry Sidney was during his son's Oxford days Lord Deputy of Ireland, and sometimes at home in Ludlow as Lord President. Sidney remained three years at Oxford, where one of his chief friends was a student of his own age, who had been his schoolfellow at Shrewsbury, **Fulke Greville.** Greville, who was of an old Warwickshire family, afterwards became an ornament of Elizabeth's court, and lived into the time of Charles I., being throughout his life the influential friend of many poets and scholars. He was knighted by Elizabeth in 1591, and was raised to the peerage, as Lord Brooke, in 1627. In 1571, during a time of plague, **Philip Sidney** left Oxford, in his seventeenth year, without having taken a degree. In the same year his father, who had prayed for

recall from Ireland if he could not be more firmly supported in his office, obtained leave of absence. His post in Ireland was then given to another; and the queen, who had the year before raised Sir William Cecil to the peerage, as Lord Burghley, offered a peerage also to Sir Henry Sidney. But Sidney was three thousand pounds the poorer for his Irish duties, and declined an honour he had not means to sustain. He remained Lord President of Wales ; and his son Philip, after leaving Oxford, was for a time probably with his uncle Leicester at court. In May, 1572, Philip Sidney went with the embassy of the Earl of Lincoln to treat on the question of Elizabeth's marriage to the Duke of Alençon. He went commended by his uncle's letters to the friendship of Francis Walsingham, English Ambassador in Paris. He did not return with Lord Lincoln, but remaining in Paris, he was there on the 24th of August, sheltered in Walsingham's house, during the time of the Massacre of St. Bartholomew.

26. Twelve years before, when Charles IX., ten or eleven years old, became king, his mother, Catherine de' Medici, had begun rule for him with a policy of conciliation. But the strife of souls was too intense to endure compromise. In March, 1562, it sprang into civil war at the Massacre of Vassy. The Huguenots rose to arms, under the Prince of Condé as head of the Protestant league. Philip of Spain aided the Catholics with troops and money. Elizabeth of England aided the French Protestants with troops, who garrisoned Havre, Rouen, and Dieppe. The King of Navarre having received a mortal wound at the siege of Rouen, the Duke of Guise became sole head of the French Catholic party. His assassination left open the way to a peace, by the Edict of Amboise, in March 1563, which was needed for the safety of the throne. In the following year Catherine was visited by her daughter Elizabeth, whom, in 1560, Philip of Spain, aged thirty-four, had married, her age being then fifteen, and she betrothed to his son Don Carlos. With Elizabeth came Philip's counsellor of war, the Duke of Alva. Between Catherine and Alva there was at that time much private discourse, of which one phrase was overheard by young Henry of Béarn. The Duke of Alva was exhorting Catherine to get rid of a few leaders of the Huguenots, and said, " One head of salmon is worth ten thousand heads of frogs." Still Catherine kept peace. In December, 1565, a new pope, Pius V., became head of the Catholic Church, austere, devout,

inflexible in a resolve to support Christendom against the Turks armed in the Mediterranean, and to put forth all his might against the heretics.    New prisons had to be built in Rome, and Italian men of genius who thought too freely were among his victims.    In the summer of 1567 the Duke of Alva was allowed to march an army through France to the Netherlands, where the spirit of independence had been gaining strength.

In March, 1563, the nobles of the Netherlands, guided chiefly by William, Prince of Orange, who had for supporters the Counts Egmont and Horn, had formed themselves into a league against the government of Cardinal Granvella, who was forced to retire in March, 1564.    Meanwhile, Calvinism had spread in the Low Countries, and the regent Margaret, who inclined towards the nobles, was urged by Philip to strong measures.    In October, 1565, Philip wrote a letter requiring that the edicts against heresy should be enforced as heretofore. The Prince of Orange and the nobles obtained from the regent its immediate publication, and a storm of feeling was excited that caused Margaret to ask leave to resign.    Flemings began to emigrate by thousands into England, where they set up looms.    On the 11th of November, François Dujon, called Francis Junius, preached at Brussels before the Flemish nobles.    This Junius was an ardent scholar, who had been studying at Geneva, when his father was slain by a fanatic crowd while he was inquiring into a massacre of Huguenots within their place of worship at Issoudun.    Francis Junius forswore France, lived for a time at Geneva by giving lessons in Greek, Latin, and Hebrew, and had then been called to the Netherlands as pastor of the Huguenot congregation which met secretly at Antwerp.    After the sermon of Junius some Flemish nobles formed a distinct league against oppressions of the government, and Philip van Marnix, Lord of Mont Saint Aldegonde, a young man of twenty-seven, who had been trained at Geneva, where he was the friend of Calvin, drew up what was known as the "Act of Compromise."    This Act, in January 1566, set forth the mind of the league by denouncing the Inquisition as illegal and iniquitous, and binding the subscribers to defend one another in a resistance that was not against allegiance to the king.    The league was formed without the knowledge of the Prince of Orange, and discountenanced by him; but he at the same time, as Governor of Holland and

Zealand, resisted the king's letter. The strong feeling and strong action of the native population produced what was called a "moderation" of the law against heresy—hanging was put for burning. Then missionaries preached to crowds of the people in woods, plains, villages, and suburbs of towns; and this was the state of things in the Netherlands in the first year of the papacy of Pius V. Philip made some illusory concessions while he levied troops; contests arose in the Netherlands between royalist troops and insurgent people; but presently the King of Spain was again master, Holland being last to yield. Meanwhile there was continued passage of Protestant Netherlanders into England, quickened by dread of the approach of Alva with a Spanish force. Alva was urged by Pope Pius V., as he passed near Geneva, to "clean out that nest of devils and apostates," but he marched steadily on, and entered Brussels with his Spaniards on the 22nd of August, 1567. This was when Edmund Spenser was a boy of fifteen, in his northern home, when England was filled with the reports of persecution in the Netherlands from refugee Flemings, who were bringing into England industry of the loom and wealth of commerce, with new impulse to the love of liberty; and when one of the refugees, John van der Noodt, was presently to cause the young poet to write his first lines for the printer in a declaration of the miseries and calamities that follow worldlings, and the joys and pleasures which the faithful do enjoy.

Joys of the faithful,—although Alva garrisoned the towns of the Netherlands with a licentious Spanish soldiery, seized Egmont and Horn, prohibited emigration, organised the Council of Tumults, known as the "Council of Blood." Margaret retired; Alva succeeded to her powers as regent and governor-general. On the 16th of February, 1568, a sentence of the Inquisition condemned all the inhabitants of the Netherlands to death, except a few specially named. In a letter to Philip, Alva reckoned at 800 heads the executions to take place after Passion-week. Money was raised by confiscation. In the summer of that year, 1568, the Prince of Orange published his justification against condemnation passed upon him, repudiated the Council of Tumults, and declared that he had become a Protestant. By sentence of the Council of Tumults, the Counts Egmont and Horn were executed on the 5th of June. The Duke of Alva took two "heads of salmon." Alva's troops had then a victorious campaign against armed opposition, and their leader praised himself for having trampled down heresy and rebellion.

News like this from the Netherlands stirred the blood of the French Huguenots, and, at the close of the year 1567 a second civil war began. In 1568 there was a pause ; but early in the spring of 1569 war was resumed, and then young Walter Raleigh came to share in the struggle as one of a company of English volunteers.

27. **Walter Raleigh** was of the same age as Spenser, born in 1552, at the manor-house of Hayes Barton, about a mile from Budleigh, in Devonshire. In 1566 he was sent to Oriel College, Oxford, where he remained three years; and at the age of seventeen he left college without a degree to join as a volunteer the Protestants in France. His mother was third wife of Walter Raleigh, of Hayes Barton. Her maiden name was Champernon, and by a former marriage with Otho Gilbert, of Greenway, she had three sons, of whom one became famous as Sir Humphrey Gilbert, the great navigator. Her relative, Henry Champernon, raised a troop of a hundred mounted Englishmen to aid the Huguenots in France ; and Walter Raleigh, who had gone before his cousin in 1569, shared the defeats of the Huguenots at Jarnac and Moncontour, shared their successes of 1570, had interest in the treaty of August, 1570, which conceded much to the Reformers, and which was protested against by Pius V. and Philip II. In the spring of 1571 a Synod of the Reformed Church was held, by the king's permission, at Rochelle. Admiral Coligny was welcomed at court, and the king even prepared an expedition in aid of the persecuted Reformers in the Netherlands. The expedition was begun. The king seemed ready to take Coligny's advice, and declare war with Spain, against the counsel of his mother. On the 18th of August, 1572, Henry of Navarre was married to Marguerite of Valois. The 24th was St. Bartholomew's-day, the day of the concerted massacre of Huguenots in Paris and the provinces of France, which happened at the time when Philip Sidney was in Paris.

28. No peace was secured ; Rochelle revolted, and Raleigh remained to fight awhile in France, while **Philip Sidney** travelled on alone to Strasburg and Frankfort. In Frankfort he lodged at a printer's ; and the youth of eighteen drew to himself the friendship of a French Huguenot of fifty-five, Hubert Languet, who had once been a Professor of Civil Law in Padua, but who went from Paris to Frankfort as secret minister of the

Elector of Saxony. Languet saw in the grave young Englishman, who had high birth, genius, and manly feeling, who was
possible heir of his uncle Leicester, possibly the future minister
of England, hope of his cause in Europe. The elder Reformer, therefore, loved the youth, counselled him, and watched
over him with fatherly solicitude, of which his extant Latin
letters (first published in 1632) bear witness. Sidney wrote of
him afterwards in the "Arcadia:"

> " The song I sang old Languet had me taught—
>   Languet, the shepherd best swift Ister knew,
> For clerkly reed, and hating what is naught,
>   For faithful heart, clean hands, and mouth as true
>   With his sweet skill my skilless youth he drew
> To have a feeling taste of Him that sits
> Beyond the heaven—far more beyond our wits."

With Languet, Philip Sidney went, in 1573, from Frankfort to
Vienna ; thence, after an excursion into Hungary, he went on
to Italy, having for one of his companions Lewis Bryskett,
afterwards a friend of Spenser's. After eight weeks in Italy,
with Venice for head-quarters, and giving six weeks to Padua,
but urged by the anxious Languet not to visit Rome, he returned through Germany, and was back in England by June,
1575. In July he was with the court, and shared *The Princely
Pleasures at the Court at Kenilworth*, as they were called by
George Gascoigne when he next year published an account of
them.

29. **George Gascoigne**, son and heir of Sir John Gascoigne, was born about the year 1536, perhaps in Westmoreland, educated at Cambridge, admitted to Gray's Inn in 1555,
and called as an Ancient of his Inn in 1557. At the accession
of Elizabeth, George Gascoigne was an ardent youth of about
twenty-two, disinherited by his father, caring more for literature
than for common law. In 1566 there were represented at Gray's
Inn two plays of his preparing, both translations. One, called
*The Supposes*, was a prose translation of Ariosto's comedy, " Gli
Suppositi " (ch. vi. § 41) ; the other was *Jocasta*, an adaptation
from the "Phænissæ" of Euripides. This, the first acted
version of a Greek play, was, like "Gorboduc," written in blank
verse, and with a dumb-show before every act. In 1572, Gascoigne published *A Hundreth Sundrie Floures bound up in one
small Poesie.* He had then Lord Grey of Wilton, a strict Calvinist, for patron, and was, at the time of publication, a captain

in the Netherlands under William of Orange, who, in July of
that year, was declared by the deputies of eight cities Stadtholder of Holland.    Brabant and Flanders were in that year
cruelly subdued to Spain, but in Holland the revolt was maintained steadfastly.    Haarlem stood a siege of more than eight
months, with three hundred women among its defenders.  When
the town was at last brought to surrender, after solemn assurance
that none should be punished except those who, in the opinion
of the citizens themselves, deserved it, two or three thousand of
the inhabitants were treacherously slaughtered, and three
hundred were drowned in the lake, tied by twos back to back.
In December of that year, 1573, the Duke of Alva was, by his
own wish, recalled, and boasted on his way home that he had
caused 18,600 Netherlanders to be executed.   Gascoigne's adventures in the Netherlands were over, and he was living at
Walthamstow in 1574, when he described " The Princely Pleasures at Kenilworth," began his satire called " The Steele Glass,"
and prefixed verses of commendation to a book of Turbervile's.
In 1576, George Gascoigne published *The Steele Glas* and *The
Complaint of Philomene,* besides *A Delicate Diet for Daintie-
mouthde Droonkards,* and in October, 1577, he died.    The
" Complaint of Philomene " is, in form of elegy, the fable of
" The Nightingale."   " The Steel Glass " is a clever satire, which
upholds with religious earnestness a manly and true life.    Satire,
who has Plain Dealing for father, Simplicity for mother, and
Poesy for sister, complains here that his sister has been married
to Vain Delight, and that every man will have a glass " to see
himself, yet so he seeth him not."

> " That age is dead and vanished long ago
> Which thought that steel both trusty was and true,
> And needed not a foil of contraries,
> But showed all things as they were in deed.
> Instead whereof our curious years can find
> The christal glass which glimseth brave and bright,
> And shows the thing much better than it is,
> Beguiled with foils of sundry subtle sights,
> So that they seem, but covet not to be."

Gascoigne's Satire therefore resolves to hold up the faithful
glass of burnished steel, and from it show true images of men.
The poem is in about 1,100 lines of blank verse, and is the first
example in our language of a poem of any length, and not
dramatic, written in that measure.    It is also the only example
before Milton's " Paradise Lost " of an English poem of any

length in blank verse, except an insignificant work by W. Vallans, published in 1590, as "The Tale of the Two Swans, wherein is comprehended the original and increase of the River Lea, commonly called Ware River ; together with the Antiquities of sundrie Places and Towns seated upon the same."

30. **Philip Sidney** (§ 25), at the close of 1575, was living in London with his mother.   Need of his father's good service in Ireland had been felt, and Sir Henry Sidney had left London in August, again to labour in Ireland as Lord Deputy.   In 1577, though but twenty-two years old, Sidney was sent as ambassador to the new Emperor of Germany, Rudolph II., with formal letters upon his accession, and with private instructions to do what he could towards the promotion of a Protestant League among the princes of the Continent.   Hubert Languet was active about him.   He came home through the Netherlands, to convey to William of Orange Queen Elizabeth's congratulations on the birth of his first child; and he saw on the way Don John of Austria, that illegitimate son of Charles V. of whom, when he had in 1571 triumphed over the Turks in the Gulf of Lepanto, Pope Pius V. said, " There was a man sent from God, and his name was John."   When Sidney spoke with him, Don John had been sent from the King of Spain, and had just entered Brussels as Governor-General of the Provinces of the Netherlands.

Sidney found when he came home, in June, 1577, his sister, Mary, married.   At the age of twenty she had become in the preceding February the third wife of Henry Herbert, Earl of Pembroke, a quiet and good man of forty.   Sidney was now in favour at court.   In April, 1578, when the queen visited Leicester, at Wanstead, he contrived for her pleasure a little occasional masque called *The Lady of May*, after this fashion.   A masquer, dressed like an honest countrywoman, appeared before the queen as she was walking with her train in Wanstead gardens, and complained of a daughter who was troubled with two suitors.   Then six shepherds came out of the wood with the Lady of May, "hauling and pulling to which side they should draw her."   An old shepherd in absurd words, complained that a woman of a minsical countenance had disannulled the brainpain of two of their featiest young men; but produced Master Rombus, the schoolmaster, who could better, " disnounce the whole foundation of the matter."   Master Rombus " disnounced " pedantry and dog-Latin, in a style very like that afterwards used by Shakespeare's Holofernes, in " Love's Labour's Lost."   The May Lady stopped him, and left it to the queen to decide, after hearing their contest in song, which of the shepherds was to be preferred. Then came the rural songs. When the queen was to give judgment, an old shepherd and a forester intervened with argument in comic prose whether the estate of shepherds or of foresters were the more worshipful. Rombus, the schoolmaster, interposed again with his pedantry, and was about to judge for the queen, when the May Lady again stopped him. The queen gave what judgment she thought best, the masquers all struck up their music, the one who was declared victor by Her Majesty expressed his joy in song, and the May Lady spoke a little epilogue.

In July, 1578, Philip Sidney was one of the men of mark who followed Queen Elizabeth to Audley End, and received honours of verse from Gabriel Harvey in the "Walden Gratulations." But Sidney was weary of idleness at court. His friend, Fulke Greville, returning from a foreign mission, received on his way from William of Orange a message for Elizabeth, craving leave of her freely to speak his knowledge and opinion of a fellow-servant of his who lived unemployed under her. He had had much experience, had seen various times and things and persons, but he protested that Her Majesty had in Mr. Philip Sidney one of the ripest and greatest statesman that he knew of in all Europe. If Her Majesty would but try the young man, the prince would stake his own credit upon the issue of his friend's employment about any business, either with the allies or with the enemies of England. And this was said, not without reason, by William the Silent of a young man of four-and-twenty, who seems to have been the type of what was noblest in the youth of England during times that could produce a Shakespeare.

31. This was said of Sidney at the time when **Edmund Spenser** came to London, and after he had been abroad on Leicester's errand, and finished his "Shepheardes Calender" where he had Sidney for companion. The little book was published anonymously,. with a dedication to the noble and virtuous gentleman, most worthy of all titles, both of learning and chivalry, Master Philip Sidney. *The Shepheardes Calender: conteyning Twelve Æglogues proportionable to the Twelve Monethes*, and dedicated to Philip Sidney, was introduced by "E. K."—Edward Kirke, an old college friend of Spenser's and Harvey's—with a letter to Gabriel Harvey, in which "the new poet" was said to have begun with eclogues, "following the example of the best and most ancient poets, which devised this

kind of writing, being so base for the matter and homely for the
manner, at the first to try their abilities," and to have other works
by him sleeping in silence, " as his ' Dreams,' his 'Legends,' his
' Court of Cupid,' and sundry others." " E. K." added a postscript, urging Gabriel Harvey to give to the world also his own
"gallant English verses." A "glosse," of small value, was added
by " E. K." to each eclogue.

In his "Shepheardes Calender," Spenser derived from Skelton
the name of Colin Clout, which he applied to himself also in later
poetry. The Colin Clout of Skelton (ch. vi. § 23) was a homely
Englishman, who felt that many wrongs were waiting to be
righted, and especially condemned luxury and self-seeking of the
higher clergy. Spenser was of one mind with Skelton upon this,
and took his side at once in the Church controversies of the time,
although in doing so he boldly placed himself beside one who was
at that time under the Queen's displeasure. In the seventh
eclogue, Thomalin sees the elevation of Morrell, whose herd is
astray among rank bushes, and refuses to go up the hill to him.
Morrell sings in the praise of holy hills, but Thomalin replies:

> " To kerke the narre, from God more farre,
>   Has bene an old-sayd sawe,
> And he that strives to touch a starre
>   Oft stombles at a strawe.
> " Alsoone may shepheard clymbe to skye
>   That leades in lowly dales
> As goteherd prowd that, sitting hye,
>   Upon the mountaine sayles."

Thomalin then enforces the lesson of humility with teaching
derived from old Algrind:

> " Such one he was (as I have heard
>   Old Algrind often sayne),
> That whilome was the first shepheard
>   And lived with little gayne;
> And meeke he was, as meeke mought be,
>   Simple as simple sheepe;
> Humble, and like in eche degree
>   The flocke which he did keepe.
>     *       *       *       *
> Like one (sayd Algrind) Moses was
>   That sawe hys Maker's face."

Those old true shepherds loved their flocks, and simple was their
weed, but now

> " They bene yclad in purple and pall,
>   So hath theyr God them blist;
> They reigne and rulen over all,
>   And lord it as they list."

A shepherd who has been to Rome saw their misusage.  Their sheep have crusts and they the bread.

> " They han the fleece and eke the flesh,
>  (O seely sheepe the while !)
>  The corne is theyres, let others thresh,
>  Their handes they may not file.
>  They han great stores and thriftye stockes,
>  Great freendes and feeble foes;
>  What neede hem caren for their flocks
>  Their boyes can looke to those."

Morrell replies to all this with a suggestion that harm may come of meddling, and that in blaming the wealth of shepherds Thomalin meddles more than he shall have thanks for.  But say, Morrell asks, who is that Algrind whom you so often name ?  The reply figured to every reader of that day Archbishop Grindal, then under the Queen's heavy displeasure for acts heartily approved by Spenser.  In this eclogue Spenser, indeed, simply transferred the syllables of the names of Elmer or Aylmer, in 1579 Bishop of London, and Grindal, then Archbishop of Canterbury.

32. **John Aylmer**, the gentle tutor of Lady Jane Grey (§ 19), and the author of the reply to Knox's " First Blast of the Trumpet " (§ 2), had been made Bishop of London in 1576.  He upheld Elizabeth's own policy, and was as zealous against those who were now becoming known for Puritans or Precisians as against the Catholics.  In 1578 the Stationers' Company, of which Richard Tottel was then master, had by suit to the Lord Treasurer, got out of Newgate a young bookseller whom Bishop Aylmer had imprisoned for reprinting a book that objected to the management of the Church by its bishops.  In 1579, at the time when the " Shepheardes Calender " appeared, Aylmer had brought before the High Court of Commission, Mr. Welden, a gentlemen of Cookham, in Berkshire, who strongly objected to a minister sent by the Bishop of London in place of one who had been ejected as a Puritan.  Mr. Welden had said of Bishop Aylmer, to his poursuivant sent down to Cookham, " What was he before but a private man ?  But he must be lorded, ' An, it please your lordship' at every word, and that there was never bishop so vilely esteemed as he was, and that he was as ill thought of as ever was Bonner."  Aylmer urged that he could not remain in his see if the High Court of Commission did not support him, and was doing this at the very time when Spenser looked up at him and asked, " Is not thilke same a goteherde prowd?"  But Spenser, in this his first book, not

merely contemned Aylmer; he declared his reverence for
Grindal.

33. **Edmund Grindal,** born in 1519, had been in 1550
chaplain to Ridley. In 1553 he fled from Mary to Strasburg. In
1558 he was one of those who drew up the new Liturgy. In 1559
he was made Master of Pembroke Hall, Spenser's own college,
and Bishop of London. In 1570 he became Archbishop of York,
and in 1575 Archbishop of Canterbury. He used his influence
in the Church to increase the number and efficiency of those
whom he looked upon as faithful preachers, and he refused
livings to those whom he did not find learned and able. The
particular cause of his unpopularity at court was his encouragement of what were called "prophesyings" for the higher educa-
cation of the clergy in the duties of their office. The word
"prophesying" was used with the sense of interpretation of the
Scriptures given to it in St. Paul's epistles. Such meetings of
the clergy, for the purpose of interpreting difficult passages, or
considering how to explain clearly and rightly passages that
might raise question among their flocks, had sprung up in several
parts of England, especially Northamptonshire, when Grindal
used his influence to encourage them. The custom was that the
ministers within a precinct met on a week-day in some principal
town, where there was some ancient grave minister that was
president, and an auditory admitted of gentlemen or other persons of leisure. Then every minister successively, beginning at
the youngest, did handle one and the same part of Scripture,
spending severally some quarter of an hour or better, and in the
whole some two hours. And so the exercise being begun and
concluded with prayer, and the president giving a text for the
next meeting, the assembly was dissolved. Archbishop Grindal
thought these meetings serviceable, and believed that the mis-
management accidental to them might be readily avoided.
Queen Elizabeth held that they encouraged novelty, caused
people to ramble in their fancy, and neglect their affairs. She
told Grindal that there was too much discussing and explaining;
it would put an end to unity of opinion. She would have no
more prophesyings; as for preachers, there were by far too many,
three or four in a county would suffice; and the authorised
Homilies were to be read instead of original sermons. That
was the only way to keep the people of one mind (ch. vi. § 58).
The First *Book of Homilies,* issued in 1547, was adopted by Elizabeth in 1559, and enlarged with a Second Book in 1563. Grindal

replied in a letter loyal to the queen, but loyal also to his conscience. He argued to her from Scripture that the Gospel should be plentifully preached ; met the objections to the prophesyings; declared that Scripture and experience showed them to be profitable ; and said, " I am forced, with all humility, and yet plainly, to profess that I cannot with a safe conscience, and without the offence of the majesty of God, give my assent to the suppressing of the said exercises; much less can I send out my injunction for the utter and universal subversion of the same. I say with St. Paul, ' I have no power to destroy, but to only edify ;' and with the same apostle, ' I can do nothing against the truth, but for the truth.' If it be your Majesty's pleasure, for this or any other cause, to remove me out of this place, I will, with all humility, yield thereunto, and render again to your Majesty that I received of the same. . . . Bear with me, I beseech you, Madam, if I choose rather to offend your earthly majesty, than to offend the heavenly majesty of God." In June, 1577, Grindal was, for this persistence in what he believed to be his highest duty, by order of the Privy Council confined to his house and sequestered for six months. Lord Burghley instructed him how he was to make formal submission to the queen. He did not make it. There was question of depriving him, but for that he was too popular with a large section of the clergy and the people. Nevertheless, he remained under sequestration, and these were the relative positions of Morrell and of the wise Algrind, when Spenser's " Shepheardes Calender " appeared. At a Convocation in the following year, 1580, the archbishop being still under sequestration, Aylmer presided. Some of the clergy were unwilling to proceed to business without the archbishop, but a petition was sent to the queen, also a letter signed by twelve bishops, both without effect. Grindal at this time was becoming blind. At last, it has been said, being really blind, more with grief than age, he was willing to put off his clothes before he went to bed, and in his lifetime to resign his place to Dr Whitgift, who refused such acceptance thereof. And the queen, commiserating his condition, was graciously pleased to say that as she had made him so he should die, an archbishop ; as he did, July 6th, 1583.

34. In his reference through pastoral forms to the great questions that concerned the flocks and shepherds of the Church, especially in the fifth and seventh eclogues, Spenser followed the example of Clement Marot (ch. vi. § 39): indeed, the study

of Marot led Spenser to shape two of his eclogues, the eleventh and twelfth, distinctly upon eclogues by the poet of France and the French Reformers. Spenser's eleventh eclogue, between Colin and Thenot, was a free version of Marot's lament between Colin and Thenot for Louise of Savoy, whom Spenser transformed into Dido, changing also her son, Francis I., into "the great shepherd, Lobbin." Spenser's twelfth eclogue was a paraphrase of Marot's upon the course of his own life, called his "Eclogue to the King under the names of Pan and Robin." Spenser's sincerity in speaking his mind upon Church matters, without regard to interest at court, gave value to his poetical homage to the queen in the fourth eclogue. The element of love was necessary in a set of pastorals, and cruel Rosalind inspired the song in the first and sixth eclogues. "E. K." tells us that there had been a real Rosalind. Very likely; Spenser's age was twenty-seven. But if there had been no love fancy within his experience it would still have been in the poem, since in poetry this must needs be one ingredient of a Shepheardes Calender. In his English, Spenser here and everywhere set his face against all affectation of his time, whether it were the pedantry which Sidney ridiculed in Master Rombus (§ 30), or the dainty alliteration and antithesis, with ingenuity of simile, for which the taste came in from Italy, and wherein Lyly's "Euphues" (§ 22), published in the same year as the "Shepheardes Calender," showed mastery. Spenser used homely English, and looked back to Chaucer as his chief. Homage was paid by the new poet to Chaucer, under the pastoral name of Tityrus, in the second, the sixth, and the twelfth eclogues ; in the second eclogue also there was place found for an attempt at story-telling in Chaucer's manner. The rustic English of the shepherds assumed a few forms which had become obsolete at court, and which, simple as they were, "E. K." in his "Gloss" interpreted ; but here, and in later poetry of Spenser's, much of the antique air came from the poet's use of his own north-country English, that still retained, as our rustic English even at this day retains, what townspeople regard as obsolete words and forms of inflection. But there was a direct strengthening of Spenser's genius by study of Chaucer. The laboriously small literature of Italy, which then set the fashion in England, Spenser disdained ; and there was something combative in his upholding of Chaucer, and his use of the simplest one and two-syllabled English words at a time when the new energies of thought were busy, among other things, with the invention of new words derived from

Greek and Latin. Ten years after 1579, George Puttenham, in writing upon English Poesie, cited among new words thus introduced, placation, assubtiling, numerosity, facundity, implete, words which did not take root in the language; and others which did—method and methodical, prolix, compendious, function, impression, indignity, penetrate, delineation, dimension, compatible, egregious, audacious. Increasing wealth of thought required enlargement of the language. Word-coining of the Elizabethan time was not all affectation, although at court there was much good breath wasted in that way. Spenser disliked it, and opposed it by his practice to the last. Chaucer it was, says Colin Clout, "Who taught me, homely, as I can, to make" The god of shepherds, Tityrus, is dead—

> " And all hys passing skil with him is fledde,
> The fame whereof doth dayly greater growe;
> But if on me some little drops would flowe
> Of that the spring was in his learned hedde—"

Such was the first aspiration of the poet who was to make for himself a name often to be coupled with Chaucer's, and like his, a name "the fame whereof doth daily greater grow."

35. But if Spenser was out of sympathy with the small writers of Italy, he took delight in Ariosto (ch. vi. § 40), and there was one great poet then living and suffering in Italy, *TORQUATO TASSO*, with whom he came to feel the fellowship of noble minds. Tasso was born in 1544, ten or eleven years after the death of Ariosto. He was eight or nine years older than Spenser, and his influence on Spenser's later work was that of one great living poet upon another who was some years younger than himself. Tasso died in 1595, Spenser in 1599. Torquato Tasso was a poet's son, a child with a passion for learning and rare depths of devotional feeling; a youth studying with his father the best writers of his own country, for, said the father wisely, men should not so study as to become like citizens abroad and strangers at home. In the year of Elizabeth's accession Torquato Tasso was fourteen, and his father, Bernardo, published a poem on the romance of Amadis of Gaul, the "Amadigi." At seventeen Torquato published his "Rinaldo;" the son's fame at once rivalled the father's, and thenceforth he made poetry his work in life. In 1579, when Spenser's "Shepheardes Calender," and Lyly's "Euphues" appeared, Tasso had written at the court of Ferrara courtly poetry, and earned repute in Italy, especially by a pastoral drama called *Aminta*, published in 1573. He had been long engaged on his

great poem, which was written but not yet published.  For some years also the taint of melancholy madness in his nature had made itself known, and in that year, 1579, Tasso was treated by the Duke of Ferrara as a confirmed lunatic, in a hospital for madmen. Those were dark ages in our social history, so far as concerned the treatment of insanity.  When Tasso could utter his distress, " Alas, alas," he wrote, " I had determined to write two epic poems on noble subjects, four tragedies of which I had formed the plan, and much in prose, to be eternally remembered of me in the world."  But what was thirst for immortality when in his misery he said he sought no higher happiness than freedom to slake that animal thirst by which he was tormented?  He yearned, he said, if not for liberty, the right of man, at least for the brute's right, " to quench freely in the streams and fountains that thirst with which, it soothes me to repeat it, I am burnt up."

In 1579 there had lately appeared in France a poem called " La Sepmaine, ou Creation du Monde," by *Guillaume de Saluste du Bartas,* a French Huguenot noble, who was born in the same year as Tasso, and was educated as a soldier.  His religious poem on the "Divine Week of the Creation" abounded in those overstrained conceits which the example of Italy had introduced into the polite language of surrounding countries.  For this reason, and for its religious spirit, " La Sepmaine"(Semaine) became so famous that it went through thirty editions in six years, and was translated into Latin, Italian, German, and English; generally more than once into each language.  The name of "Saluste of France" became coupled with that of " Tuscan Arioste," and remained great until the passing away of the form of taste it satisfied.  But we shall find in the days of his currency an English minor poet seeking immortality as the translator of Du Bartas.

36.  In 1579, when Shakespeare was fifteen years old, and Francis Bacon was nineteen, **Sir Thomas North** published his translation of *Plutarch's Lives.*  This was not from the original Greek, but from the delightful Plutarch in thirteen volumes (six for the Lives and seven for the Morals), published in and after 1567 by Jacques Amyot, who was in those days the prince of French translators.  Amyot lived to within a year of fourscore, and died in 1593.  Sir Thomas North was himself an active member of the English band of translators produced by the revival of letters.  Among his other translations was, in 1570, one from the Italian version of a famous Arabian fable book called

"Calilah i Dumnah," as "The Morale Philosophie of Doni."
But he is here named because it was chiefly in North's Plutarch,
published in 1579, that Shakespeare, as a playwright, learnt his
history of Rome.

37. **William Shakespeare** was born at Stratford-on-Avon,
in April, 1564; perhaps on the 23rd of April, for he was baptised on
the 26th.   There is a tradition that he died on his birthday, and
he died on the 23rd of April, 1616.   His father was John Shakespeare, a glover in Henley Street, and probably the son of Richard
Shakespeare, farmer, at Snitterfield.   John Shakespeare was
living in Henley Street in 1552.   In 1556—the year of the birth
of Anne Hathaway, the poet's future wife—John Shakespeare
was sued in the bailiff's court, and described as a glover.   In
that year also the copyholds of a house in Greenhill Street, and
of another in Henley Street, were assigned to him.   In 1557
John Shakespeare married Mary, the youngest daughter of
Robert Arden, of Wilmcote, "husbandman."   Her father had
died a month before the marriage, leaving to Mary by his will
a small property at Wilmcote, called Ashbies, of about fifty-four
acres, with two houses, and interest in other land at Wilmcote ;
also two tenements at Snitterfield, and £6 13s. 4d. in cash.   That
was Mary Arden's fortune, and it helped John Shakespeare for
some years.   In 1558 the first child of the marriage was born, a
girl, Joan, who died.   In 1562 another child was born, a girl,
Margaret, who died.   In 1564 another child was born, and that
was William Shakespeare.   His father was not then in want.
The plague was in Stratford in 1564, and John Shakespeare
made a fair donation for relief of the poor.   In 1566 a second
son, Gilbert, was born.   In 1569 a daughter was born, who lived
to be married ; she was christened by the name of the first
daughter, who had died, Joan.   In 1570, John Shakespeare rented
Ington Meadow, a farm of fourteen acres.   The meadow-land
would feed sheep ; sheep are shorn for wool, and eaten for mutton:
hence John Shakespeare, glover, in Henley Street, has also been
called farmer, butcher, and dealer in wool.   He could not live
by gloves alone, the large coarse gloves used in country work,
which are still in chief demand at Stratford.   In 1571 another
girl was born, Anne.   In 1573 another boy was born, Richard.
In 1575 John Shakespeare bought the two freehold houses in
Henley Street, with garden and orchard.

In 1576, as we shall see presently, the first theatres were
built, but not until later the Blackfriars.   In that year William

Shakespeare was a boy of twelve, the eldest of five children, in a household from which prosperity was on the point of departing.

In 1577, John Shakespeare, as an alderman of Stratford, was excused half his payment towards furnishing pike and bill men, that is to say, half his police rate. Other aldermen paid 6s. 8d. he only 3s. 4d. In the following year, 1578, John Shakespeare and his wife (John Shakespeare was then, in a deed, styled "yeoman.") were obliged to mortgage the little property at Ashbies for £40, to Edmund Lambert. Money was raised also by selling for £4 to Robert Webbe immediate interest in the tenements at Snitterfield. At this time John Shakespeare was defaulter also in the levy for armour and defensive weapons; and while he was thus troubled for want of money, he lost his younger daughter Anne, a child of about eight years old. So matters stood with the Shakespeares in 1579, when William was fifteen years old, and the number of the children was reduced to four—three boys and a girl. It is likely that William Shakespeare had been taught in the Stratford Grammar School; it could not well be otherwise, but there is no direct evidence of the fact. There is direct evidence of the poverty of his home in 1579, and afterwards, till he himself repaired its fortunes.

38. **Francis Bacon**, three years and three months older than William Shakespeare, was the son of Queen Elizabeth's Lord Keeper, Sir Nicholas Bacon, and was born in London, at York House, in the Strand, on the 22nd of January, 1561. Sir William Cecil, afterwards Lord Burghley, and Sir Nicholas Bacon, married two daughters of Sir Anthony Cooke (§ 1). The sister, Anne, married by Sir Nicholas, was his second wife. She was an educated woman, with strong religious feeling, who took strong interest in the reformation of the Church, and inclined to the Puritan side in later questions of its internal policy. It was she who translated Jewel's "Apology" into English (§ 14). Sir Nicholas Bacon had by his former wife, six children, and by his second wife two, Anthony and Francis ; Anthony two years older than Francis, who was thus the youngest of eight in a household living sometimes in London, at York House, sometimes at Gorhambury, near St. Albans. In April, 1573, when Anthony was fourteen and Francis twelve, the two boys were entered as fellow-commoners at Trinity College, Cambridge. Of Francis Bacon's career at college, ending in his sixteenth year, we have only two notes. They are from Dr. Rawley, his chaplain of after days. One is that Queen Elizabeth "delighted much then to

confer with him, and to prove him with questions ; unto which
he delivered himself with that gravity and maturity above his
years, that Her Majesty would often term him ' the young Lord
Keeper.'  Being asked by the queen how old he was, he answered
with much discretion, being then but a boy, ' That he was two
years younger than Her Majesty's happy reign ;' with which
answer the queen was much taken."  The other record is this :
"Whilst he was commorant in the University, about sixteen
years of age (as his lordship hath been pleased to impart unto
myself), he first fell into the dislike of the philosophy of Aristotle ;
not for the worthlessness of the author, to whom he would
ascribe all high attributes, but for the unfruitfulness of the way ;
being a philosophy (as his lordship used to say) only strong for
disputations and contentions, but barren of the production of
works for the benefit of the life of man ; in which mind he continued to his dying day."

In September, 1576, Sir Amyas Paulet went to Paris to
succeed Dr. Dale as English Ambassador.  Francis Bacon, who
was to be trained for diplomatic life, entered at Lincoln's Inn,
and proceeded to France, where he was one of the suite of Sir
Amyas.  Those were in France the first days of the League.
Charles IX. had died less than two months after the Massacre
of St. Bartholomew.  His brother, the Duke of Anjou, licentious
and effeminate, had become king, as Henry III.  In February,
1575, the Huguenots, under the Prince of Condé, signed a league
with the liberal Catholics, under the Marshal de Damville.  The
Duke of Alençon also joined the insurgents in the south ; and in
1576, Henry of Navarre, afterwards to be Henry IV., escaped
from the surveillance of Catherine, and joined the conflict.  Full
concession to the Reformers was extorted, and obtained in May,
1576.  This roused the Catholics, who, seeing what had been
done by the strength of one league, resolved on a combination
of their own ; and Henry, the young Duke of Guise, who was
now leader of the Catholics, organised, by means of the association
of the clergy and Jesuits throughout the country, a great Catholic
League, which in a few months enrolled thirty thousand members.
This was a confederation to maintain the Church in its old form,
the king's authority, and that of the head of the league, by
whose ambition the king's authority was threatened.  This league
was just formed, when Francis Bacon, a youth of sixteen, was
first in Paris with Sir Amyas Paulet.  He was in the summer
and autumn of 1577 with Sir Amyas in the French court at

Poitiers. After a little more than two years of this training in France to diplomatic life, there came a cloud over the prospects of Bacon in the year 1579. In the February of that year his father died, after a few days' illness, before completing the provision he had meant to make for the younger son by his second marriage. Francis Bacon, then eighteen years old, came to London at the end of March, with commendations to the queen from Sir Amyas Paulet, and settled down at Gray's Inn to study of the law as a profession.

In 1579, then, we have Spenser, aged about twenty-seven, publishing his first book, *The Shepheardes Calender;* Lyly, aged twenty-five or twenty-six, publishing *Euphues;* Bacon, aged eighteen, thrown on his own resources by his father's death, is beginning study of law as the profession by which he must live; and Shakespeare, aged fifteen, is eldest of a family of young children in a household that begins to feel the pinch of poverty.

39. In January, 1562, as we have seen (§ 8) "Gorboduc," our first tragedy, was presented before Queen Elizabeth by the gentlemen of the Inner Temple. A fortnight later, the queen saw a play on the subject of Julius Cæsar. Companies formed for the entertainment of great lords, acted as servants of this or that lord, for their own profit and the public entertainment, in inn yards (§ 8). In 1563 the plague destroyed in London 21,530. Archbishop Grindal advised Sir William Cecil to inhibit all plays for a year, and, he said, if it were for ever it were not amiss. In the summer of 1564, Queen Elizabeth visited Cambridge, and was entertained with Udall's (ch. vi. § 48, 58, 60) play of *Ezechias* in English. In the following Christmas what is called a tragedy, perhaps *Damon and Pithias*, by Richard Edwards, a musician and writer of interludes, was acted before Her Majesty by the children of the Chapel Royal, Richard Edwards being then their master. For its happy end and its intermixture of farcical matter, as in the shaving of Grim the Collier by the court lackeys, that rhyming play is a comedy, but it includes a tyrant and a hangman. Edwards was born in Somersetshire, and was a student at Corpus Christi College, Oxford, before he became attached to the court. That to the court he looked for his advancement we may infer from the form of his father's blessing, given in a poem of his in the "Paradise of Dainty Devices:"

"My son, God guide thy way, and shield thee from mischance,.
And make thy just deserts in court thy poor estate advance."

In 1561, Elizabeth made him a gentlemen of the Royal Chapel, and master of the singing boys. He was in very high repute for his comedies and interludes. On the 3rd of September, 1566, Edwards's *Palamon and Arcyte* was acted before Elizabeth, in the hall of Christ Church, Oxford. At the beginning of the play part of the stage fell in ; three persons were killed and five hurt ; but the play was acted and the queen enjoyed it, giving eight guineas to one of the young actors who pleased her much. Dr. James Calfhill's Latin play of *Progne*, acted two days later, was less successful. It was in the same year that Gascoigne's *Supposes* and *Jocasta* (§ 29), from Ariosto and Euripides, were played during the revels at Gray's Inn.

At court it was the business of the Master of the Revels to have plays rehearsed before him, and to choose the best. In the course of 1571 the plays acted before the queen were *Lady Barbara*, by Sir Robert Lane's men ; *Iphigenia*, by the children of Paul's ; *Ajax and Ulysses*, by the children of Windsor ; *Narcissus*, by the Children of the Chapel ; *Cloridon and Radiamanta*, by Sir Robert Lane's men ; *Paris and Vienna*, by the Children of Westminster.

In 1572 it was enacted that all fencers, bear-wards, common players in interludes, and minstrels not belonging to any baron of this realm, or to any other honourable personage of greater degree, should be treated as rogues and vagabonds if they had not the licence of at least two justices of the peace. This requirement was renewed twenty-five years later.

40. In May, 1574, the Earl of Leicester procured, as special privilege for his own servants, James Burbadge, John Perkyn, John Lanham, William Johnson, and Robert Wylson, the first royal patent " to use, exercise, and occupy the art and faculty of playing Comedies, Tragedies, Interludes, Stage Plays and such other like as they have already used and studied, or hereafter shall use and study, as well for the recreation of our loving subjects as for our solace and pleasure when we shall think good to see them," within the City of London and its Liberties, or in any other city, without let ; " provided that the said Comedies, Tragedies, Interludes, and Stage Plays be by the Master of the Revels (for the time being) before seen and allowed ; and that the same be not published or shown in the time of Common Prayer, or in the time of great and common Plague in our City of London." The city authorities opposed the concession of this patent ; but in July, 1574, a letter was

written from the Privy Council requiring the Lord Mayor " to admit the comedy players within the City of London, and to be otherwise favourably used." In 1575 the Common Council framed regulations that were in effect prohibitory ; for they required not only that a licence should be obtained from the Lord Mayor for every exhibition, but also that half the players' profits should be given up for charitable uses.

As yet no theatre had been built. Actors produced their entertainments upon scaffolds set up for the purpose in convenient places. In a town there was no place more convenient than the inn yard, as the inn yard used to be when there was much travelling by coach and on horseback. The large inner square of the building, entered by an archway, had, at least on the first floor, often on other floors, a gallery round it, into which rooms opened. The stage built against one side of the yard had close above it a piece of gallery which could be, and was, curtained off with it for use. It would serve for a window or a balcony, from which a king or a fair lady looked down ; it would serve for the battlements of a castle, from which an attacking force could be defied ; it would serve for the top of his palace, from which David observed Bathsheba. In the unenclosed part of the gallery above, on each side of the curtains, was the music. The trumpet sounded thrice, and at the third sound of the trumpet the curtain before the stage was drawn to either side, thus framing it in drapery. Upon the stage there was no scenery. A bed, or a table and chair, might be produced if necessary, or a god might be let down in a chair if the arrangement of galleries and windows in the place of performance made it easy to do that ; but the play itself was the whole entertainment. The players did their best in dressing and in acting ; the poet did his best to entertain the people and provide the players with effective parts. What scenery the poet wanted he could always paint for himself in words. A large part of the audience stood on the ground in the open yard—groundlings of the original pit, for whom at first there were no seats provided. The galleries surrounding the old inn yard were the first circles of boxes, and the rooms of the inn, which could be taken for solace of the more luxurious, were the first private boxes. After theatres had been built, those boxes were for some time called " rooms." The acting was at first on holidays, because on working days, when most people were about their business, only the few idlers

N

could afford to give attention to the play; for there was no acting after dark. The play was always over in time to enable playgoers to get back home before sunset. Following the old usage, in accordance with opinion of the Roman Catholic Church that after hours of service sports lawful on other days were lawful on Sundays, the afternoon of Sunday was at first a recognised time for such entertainments, but this was strongly opposed by the Puritans. . The Corporation of London, Puritan in its tendency, battled against the players, and supported its case with various arguments: as, desecration of Sabbath and saints' days; bringing of young people together under conditions that would favour the forming of unmeet contracts; temptations from the inns; chance of seditious matter in the plays; idle waste of money that, if superfluous, should be given to the poor; hurt of people by the fall of scaffolding, and by the weapons and gunpowder used in the performances; chance of diffusing plague, by bringing people together in great crowds. In December, 1575, the authorities of the City of London prohibited altogether the acting of plays within their jurisdiction as ungodly, and made humble suit for like prohibition in all places near the city. The queen's players then petitioned the Privy Council against the procedure of the Corporation of London, and of the justices of Middlesex, who also had opposed them. The city argued in reply to the players "how unseemly it is for youth to run straight from prayer to plays, from God's service to the devil's." Among other of its suggestions, one was that since the death-rate, in absence of plague, was forty or fifty a week, acting of plays in London should be forbidden wherever the death-rate exceeded fifty. The population of London was then about 150,000.

In 1576 the city desired that the players should act only in private houses, or if elsewhere, then only on condition that the death-rate had for twenty days been under fifty; that they should never act on the Sabbath, nor on holy-days till after evening prayer, and always early enough to allow the spectators to return home before dark; also, that none but the queen's players should be thus licensed, and that not only the number of these, but their names, should be specified. If they infringed these regulations there was to be an end of toleration. Hostility of the Common Council at last drove the actors into parts of London that were not within its jurisdiction; and in this year, 1576, James Burbadge bought

a site for his first house, *The Theatre.* Evidence, published by
Mr. Halliwell in 1874, proves that the *Blackfriars Theatre* was
not built until about twenty years later. In these contests
the Earl of Leicester was, among men in power, the most active
supporter of the players. In, or soon after 1576, the second
theatre was built beyond the jurisdiction of the Mayor and
Corporation. Both were outside the walls, in the fresh air of
Shoreditch. The Londoner who passed out through the town
walls at Bishop's Gate had before him a suburban street of good
houses and gardens, running between the clear green space of
the Spital Field and the open Finsbury Field, in which were
three windmills. That line between fields of Bishopsgate Street
Without the town gate, continuing the line of Bishopsgate Within,
led to the pleasant country houses of Shoreditch, and these were
good houses, chiefly in favour with foreign merchants resident in
London. In Shoreditch, beyond the walls, but with a well-
inhabited town road—Bishopsgate Street Without—leading
through the fields to it, were built *The Theatre* and *The
Curtain.* These seem, therefore, to have been the theatres which,
in 1576, first gave a home of its own to the English drama.
William Shakespeare was at Stratford then, aged twelve.

41. Among the first writers and actors in these first theatres
was **Stephen Gosson**, a young Oxford graduate, born in Kent
in 1555, who studied at Christ Church. After taking his B.A.
degree, he came to London in 1576, aged twenty-one, attached
himself at once to the new theatres, and wrote plays, which are
now lost—*Catiline's Conspiracies; Captain Mario,* a Comedy;
*Praise at Parting,* a Moral. Meanwhile the opposition of the
Puritans continued. A sermon at Paul's Cross, preached by
T. Wilcocks, on Sunday, Nov. 3, 1577, in a time of plague,
exhorted the people to "look but upon the common plays in
London, and see the multitude that flocketh to them and followeth
them : behold the sumptuous theatre houses, a continual monument of London's prodigality and folly. But I understand," said
the preacher, "they are now forbidden because of the plague. I
like the policy well, if it hold still ; for a disease is but botched
or patched up that is not cured in the cause, and the cause of
plagues is sin, if you look to it well; and the cause of sin are
plays : therefore the cause of plagues are plays." Mention is
made of the Theatre and Curtain by name in the Rev. John
Northbrooke's *Treatise wherein Diceing, Dauncing, vaine Plays
or Enterludes, with Idle Pastimes, &c., commonly used on the*

*Sabbath-day are reproued by the authoritie of the Worde of God
and auncient writers. Made Dialogue wise.* This was entered
at Stationers' Hall at the beginning of December, 1577.

Young Stephen Gosson, who earned credit also as a writer of
pastorals, was moved by the controversies of the time not only
to abandon his new calling as a writer for the stage, but to join
in attack upon the theatres.   This he did in 1579, by publishing
a short prose book called *The School of Abuse, containing a
Plesaunt Invective against Poets, Pipers, Plaiers, Jesters, and
such-like Caterpillers of a Commonwelth ; setting up the Flagge
of Defiance to their mischievous exercise, and overthrowing their
Bulwarkes, by Profane Writers, Naturall Reason, and Common
Experience: a Discourse as pleasaunt for Gentlemen that favour
Learning, as profitable for all that wyll follow Vertue.*  This
was entered at Stationers' Hall in July.   "Euphues" had been
published in the spring.   There was just time for Gosson to have
read "Euphues" before writing his own little treatise, which was
produced under the influence of the same fashion which Lyly's
book illustrated.   The dedication to Sir Philip Sidney might, for
its style, have been signed "John Lyly" instead of "Your Wor-
shippes' to command, Stephen Gosson."   For example, after
citing Caligula's great preparation to invade England, where
he only "charged every man to gather cockles," Gosson says,
"The title of my book doth promise much, the volume you
see is very little : and sithens I cannot bear out my folly by
authority, like an emperor, I will crave pardon for my phrensy
by submission, as your worships' to command.  The school which
I build is narrow, and at the first blush appeareth but a dog-
hole ; yet small clouds carry water ; slender threads sew sure
stitches ; little hairs have their shadows ; blunt stones whet
knives ; from hard rocks flow soft springs ; the whole world is
drawn in a map, Homer's 'Iliad' in a nut-shell, a king's picture in a penny," and so on.   Philip Sidney, we learn, was ill-
pleased with the dedication to him of a book that set out with an
attack on poetry, and Gosson's "School of Abuse" is believed to
have prompted Sidney to the writing of his "Apology for Poetry."
From the poets Gosson went on to the musicians, and then to
the players.   One passage in his attack upon them is worth
notice.   He said it might be urged that, whatever were the
immoralities of ancient comedy, "the comedies that are exercised
in our days are better sifted, they show no such bran."   After
comparing the immorality of the old plays with the morality of

the new ones, he said, "Now are the abuses of the world revealed; every man in a play may see his own faults, and learn by this glass to amend his manners." But admitting this, he added, "If people will be instructed (God be thanked) we have divines enough to discharge that, and more by a great many than are well hearkened to." So that even in these days of its first infancy there was the earnest spirit of the time in the Elizabethan drama; the same earnest spirit that in another form laboured for its destruction. Stephen Gosson having left the stage, added to his invective a short *Apology for the School of Abuse*, and went into the country as a tutor.

42. **Thomas Lodge**, son of Sir Thomas Lodge, a London grocer who was Lord Mayor in 1563, was a fellow-student of Gosson's, a young man of his own age. He wrote at once a reply to Gosson, "Honest Excuses" on behalf of the stage. Early in 1582 the players also defended their calling in their own way by acting *a Play of Plays*. **Stephen Gosson** then produced at once a five-act answer, entitled, *Plays Confuted in Five Actions, &c., proving that they are not to be suffered in a Christian Commonwealth; by the way both the cavils of Thomas Lodge and the Play of Plays written in their defence, and other objections oj Players' friends, are truly set down and directly answered.*

In 1591, Gosson was made Rector of Great Wigborough, in Essex. In 1600, by an exchange of livings, he came to town, aged forty-five, as Rector of St. Botolph, Bishopsgate, and there he officiated for nearly a quarter of a century, until his death in 1624.

**Thomas Lodge** made for himself a name of honour among the men who were creating a poetical drama when Shakespeare began his career in London. Lodge was a Roman Catholic and a good scholar. From Oxford he went to Avignon, where he graduated as doctor of medicine. On his return he was incorporated at Cambridge; and he became in London not only a successful dramatist and poet, but also a thriving physician, with a practice chiefly among those of his own religious faith. **John Lyly**, a year or two older than Lodge and Gosson, we shall also find to be in the first group of Elizabethan dramatists. **Robert Greene** was a few years younger, perhaps not more than two or three years older than William Shakespeare; and **Christopher Marlowe** was born in the same year as Shakespeare. Two other dramatists of this group, **Thomas Kyd** and **Henry Chettle**, may have been of about the age of Robert Greene.

43. On the 6th of April, 1580, there was a considerable shock of earthquake felt in many parts of England. It produced a *Discourse upon the Earthquake*, from Arthur Golding (§ 6), the translator of Ovid; *A Warning on the Earthquake*, from Thomas Churchyard (§ 10), and with a preface, dated June 19, 1580: *Three proper and wittie familiar letters lately passed betweene two University men, touching the earthquake in April last, and our English reformed versifying, with the preface of a well-wisher to them both.* The two University men were **Edmund Spenser** and **Gabriel Harvey.** As to the earthquake, Harvey described the effect of it on minds at Cambridge, and protested against the practice of converting natural events into Divine warnings, and associating them with predictions. He had a strong sense of the emptiness of this part of the supposed knowledge of the time, the stronger because one of his brothers gave much attention to the study of astrology. The "English reformed versifying" meant a fancy of the day among some University men who discussed literature together — Harvey, Spenser, Sidney, and Sidney's friends and college companions, Edward Dyer and Fulke Greville, with others—for the abolishing of rhyme and introduction of the Latin system of quantity into English verse. They were amusing themselves with English hexameters, sapphics, and other forms derived from the old Latin poetry. Spenser sent Harvey four lines of hexameter as a sample, and asked, "Seem they comparable to those two which I translated you extempore in bed the last time we lay together in Westminster?" He observed difficulties in accent, and desiring a fixed system to work upon, wished Harvey would send him " the rules and precepts of art which you observe in quantities, or else follow mine that M. Philip Sidney gave me, being the very same which M. Drant devised, but enlarged with M. Sidney's own judgment, and augmented with my observations, that we might both accord and agree in one, lest we overthrow one another and be overthrown of the rest." He said that Dyer had liked Harvey's satirical verses, and that he himself was about to write *Epithalamium Tamesis* (its idea seems to have been worked afterwards into the "Faerie Queene," Book IV., canto xi.); his *Dreams* and *Dying Pelican* were about to be printed; and he was already at work upon *The Faerie Queene.* The *Dreams* were not published ; perhaps Spenser withdrew them because they were exercises of ingenuity, according to a fashion of the time with which his own taste as a poet was not in unison.

Because they were after the manner of the time they delighted
Harvey, who was clever and liberal of mind, with a quick-witted
delight in literature, but who was simply a clever man of his own
day. Harvey worshipped Euphuism in its sources: " I like your
' Dreams' passingly well," he told Spenser, "the rather because
they savour of that singular and extraordinary vein and invention
which I ever fancied most, and in a manner admired only in
Lucian, Petrarch, Aretino, and all the most delicate and fine-
conceited Grecians and Italians (for the Romans, to speak of,
are but very ciphers in this kind), whose chief endeavour and
drift was to have nothing vulgar, but in some respect or other,
and especially in lively hyperbolical amplification, rare, quaint,
and odd in every point, and, as a man would say, a degree or
two above the reach and compass of a common scholar's
capacity." Spenser had written at this time nine comedies after
the manner of Ariosto, and these also he probably withheld from
publication because they had the qualities that caused Harvey
to write, " I am void of all judgment if your nine comedies
whereunto, in imitation of Herodotus, you give the names of the
nine Muses (and in one man's fancy not unworthily) come not
nearer Ariosto's comedies, either for the finesse of plausible
elocution or the rareness of poetical invention, than the Elvish
Queene doth to his ' Orlando Furioso,' which, notwithstanding,
you will needs seem to emulate and hope to overgo, as you flatly
professed yourself in one of your last letters." Spenser then had
begun his " Faerie Queene," and begun it with high aspiration.
He went on with it undaunted by his friend Harvey's warning,
" If so be the ' Faerie Queene' be fairer in your eye than the
nine Muses" (the comedies) "and Hobgoblin run away with the
garland from Apollo, mark what I say—and yet I will not say that
I thought. But there, an end for this once, and fare you well till
God or some good angel put you in a better mind." It was really
" fare you well," for in this year Spenser went to Ireland.

44. At the beginning of 1580, **Philip Sidney** had addressed to the queen a wise and earnest written argument
against the project of her marriage with the Duke of Anjou.
His uncle, Leicester, whose secret marriage with Lettice, Countess
of Essex, had become known, was already under the queen's
displeasure; and Sidney, after writing this letter, found it best
to withdraw from court. Towards the end of March, 1580, he
went to stay at Wilton with his sister, the Countess of Pembroke,
whom Spenser afterwards honoured as

> " The greatest shepherdess that lives this day,
> And most resembling both in shape and spright
> Her brother dear ; "

and upon whose death, when her course was ended, Ben Jonson
wrote :

> ' Underneath this sable herse
> Lies the subject of all verse,
> Sidney's sister, Pembroke's mother ;
> Death, ere thou hast slain another
> Learn'd and fair and good as she,
> Time shall throw a dart at thee."

Sidney's sister became " Pembroke's mother " in that spring of
1580 when her brother Philip was staying at Wilton.   He remained there about seven months.   Brother and sister worked
together at that time upon a joint translation of *The Psalms of
David* into English verse.   It was then also that Sidney occupied hours of his forced idleness by beginning to write for the
amusement of his sister a long pastoral romance, in prose mixed
with verse, according to Italian fashion, with abundance of
poetical conceits—his *Arcadia.*   It was done at his sister's wish,
and as he wrote to her, " only for you, only to you. . . . .
For, indeed, for severer eyes it is not, being but a trifle, and that
triflingly handled.   Your dear self can best witness the manner,
being done in loose sheets of paper, most of it in your presence, the rest by sheets sent unto you as fast as they were done."
This romance was not published by Sidney.   Not long before
his death he said that he wished it to be burnt.   But it belonged
to his sister, who valued it, and by her it was, after his death,
prepared for the press, and published in 1590.   Much of it was
written during the summer of 1580, and the rest chiefly, or
entirely in 1581.   Though long, Sidney's " Arcadia " is unfinished except by the addition of a hurried close.   It is a pastoral of the school of the " Arcadia " of Sanazzaro, and the
" Diana Enamorada " by George of Montemayor (ch. vi. § 39),
but its intermixture of verse and prose develops more completely a romantic story, and it adds to the pastoral a new
heroic element.   This was suggested partly by the Spanish romances of "Amadis" and " Palmerin " (ch. vi. § 40), partly by the
*Æthiopian Historie* of Heliodorus, lately translated from the
Greek by Thomas Underdown.   Heliodorus, Bishop of Tricca, in
Thessaly, who lived at the end of the fourth century, wrote, under
the name of " Æthiopica," ten books of romance on the loves of
Theagenes and Chariclea.   Sidney had been enjoying this in

Underdown's translation.   In his " Defence of Poesy," written in 1581 (although not published until 1595), after saying that Xenophon had " in his portraiture of a just empire under the name of Cyrus (as Cicero saith of him), made therein an absolute heroical poem ; so," he added, " did Heliodorus in his sugared invention of that picture of love in Theagenes and Chariclea, and yet both these writ in prose : which I speak to show that it is not rhyming and versing that maketh a poet, no more than a long gown maketh an advocate, who, though he pleaded in armour, should be an advocate and no soldier." Sidney's *Arcadia* may be, in this sense, taken as all poet's work ; giving a new point of departure for heroic romance grafted upon pastoral.   As he was writing for his sister a romance after the fashion of his day, Sidney, in the " Arcadia," would amuse himself by showing how he also could be delicate and fine conceited. This is the groundwork of its story.   Two cousins and close friends, Musidorus, the elder, Prince of Thessaly, and Pyrocles, the younger, Prince of Macedon, are wrecked on the Spartan coast.   Musidorus is saved and taken to the delicious pastoral land of Arcadia.   His friend is supposed to have been lost. Musidorus is sheltered by Kalander, an Arcadian noble.   Presently he leads an Arcadian force against Helots of Sparta, who have made Kalander's son their prisoner, and at the close of combat with a mighty captain of the Helots, finds him to be his lost friend Pyrocles.   Peace is made.   Kalander's son is released, and the two friends begin a course of love adventures. Basilius and Gynecia, king and queen of Arcadia, have two daughters—majestic Pamela, and sweet Philoclea.   To keep men away from his daughters, Basilius has built two lodges in a forest.   In one he lives with his wife and his younger daughter Philoclea ; in the other Pamela lives under the care of a clown Dametas, who has an ugly wife, Miso, and an ugly daughter, Mopsa.   The only men who may come near are a priest and some shepherds skilled in music.   Musidorus now loves Pamela ; he is disguised as a shepherd, Dorus, and affects passion for Mopsa.   Pyrocles loves Philoclea ; he is disguised as an Amazon, Zelmane, and inspires love in King Basilius, who takes him for a woman, as well as in Queen Gynecia, who sees that he is a man.   Many troubles and adventures, episodes of romance, conceited dialogues and songs, including experiments in " our English reformed versifying," are built upon this groundwork.   The king's sister-in-law, Cecropia, desires to set up her

N *

son Amphialus as King of Arcadia, that she may rule through him.   Cecropia carries off Pamela, Philoclea, and Zelmane. She fails to bend Philoclea to assent to the love of her son, goes to the chamber of Pamela, hoping to prevail over her, and hears her praying to heaven for succour.   We shall meet again with Pamela's prayer.   The Arcadian army battles for the rescue of the captives, and in the course of this contest Amphialus slays Argaluš, the husband of Parthenia. She afterwards arms herself to avenge her husband, comes as a stranger knight, and is herself slain by Amphialus, who suffers grief and shame for his victory.   The latter part of the " Arcadia" is less fully worked out.   The princesses and Pyrocles, still as the Amazon Zelmane, are again at home.   Musidorus escapes with Pamela to Thessaly.   Pyrocles remains, troubled by the affections of the king and queen, but he brings both to their senses, they resume their royal duties, and the lovers are made happy.

There is much difference between the style of Sidney's " Arcadia," and that of his *Apologie for Poetrie*, written in 1581, although not published until 1595, when Sidney was dead.   This little treatise, in simple English, maintains against such attacks as Gosson's (§ 41) the dignity of the best literature.   The " Apologie for Poetrie " is the first piece of intellectual literary criticism in our language ; it springs from a noble nature feeling what is noblest in the poet's art, is clear in its plan, terse in its English, and while all that it says is well said, it is wholly free from conceits.   The conceited style, indeed, it explicitly condemns, as eloquence disguised in painted affectation, " one time, with so far-fetched words, they may seem monsters, but must seem strangers to any poor Englishman; another time, with coursing of a letter, as if they were bound to follow the method of a dictionary ; at another time with figures and flowers extremely winter-starved.   But I would this fault were only peculiar to versifiers, and had not as large possession among prose printers ; and (which is to be marvelled) among many scholars ; and (which is to be pitied) among some preachers. . . .   For now they cast sugar and spice upon every dish that is served to the table ; like those Indians, not content to wear earrings at the fit and natural place of the ears, but they will thrust jewels through their nose and lips, because they will be sure to be fine."

45. In 1576, Pope Gregory XIII. had issued a bull depriving

Elizabeth of all title to Ireland, and releasing her Irish subjects
from allegiance. Sir Henry Sidney had returned to England,
and resigned his office as Lord Deputy of Ireland in the autumn
of 1578. In 1578, James Fitzmaurice, who had been for two
years seeking aid from the Catholic powers, got from the pope
some arms, ammunition, and money, sailed to Ireland with
adventurers, chiefly Spaniards and Italians, commanded by an
Italian, landed at Smerwick Bay, in Kerry, and began to construct a fort there, which was called Del Oro. A great part of
Ireland was in insurrection when the English Government at last
appointed as successor to Sir Henry Sidney, Arthur Lord Grey
of Wilton, a strict Puritan, whom we have already met with as
a patron of the poet Gascoigne (§ 29). He arrived at Dublin
August, 1580, having with him **Edmund Spenser** as his
private secretary. The patronage of Leicester, and the good
word of Philip Sidney through his father, would suffice as introduction for a man in himself welcome, since the secretary was
upon matters of policy of like mind with his chief. On the
7th of September, Lord Arthur Grey assumed his office. On
the 14th a fresh force of six or seven hundred Spaniards disem-
barked, repaired and took possession of the Fort del Oro. The
Earl of Desmond was ready with his followers to join them and
act with them if he could. Lord Grey marched promptly on
Del Oro, Admiral Winter co-operating with him at sea. On the
2nd of November Lord Grey pitched his camp within eight
miles of the fort. Within the fort was an advanced guard of
the power of Spain, seeking through Ireland to oppose the
heresies of England. Lord Grey had with him his secretary
Spenser, and in his camp was Captain **Walter Raleigh**. The
garrison of the fort was in a few days forced to surrender at
discretion; Lord Grey telling its captains, who pleaded obedience
to authority, that he "would not greatly have marvelled if men
commanded by natural and absolute princes did sometimes take
in hand wrong actions ; but that men of account, as some of
them made show of being, should be carried into unjust, wicked
and desperate actions, by one that neither from God nor man
could claim any princely power or empire, but, indeed, a detestable shaveling of the Antichrist and general ambitious tyrant
over all principalities, and patron of the diabolical faith, I could
not but greatly wonder." The fort was given up, and on the 10th
of November two officers, one of them Captain Raleigh, were
sent in to massacre the prisoners. "I put in certain bands."

wrote Lord Grey, "which straightway fell to execution. There were six hundred slain." Spaniards and Italians of rank were spared, and distributed among officers, who were to make prize-money by their ransoms. Such was the bitterness of the strife which Spenser witnessed, and which he was then expressing through sweet music of his verse ; sweet music from a soul pure, earnest, but strongly sharing in the conflict of its time. To Spenser, as to his chief, Catholicism was "the diabolical faith," the pope "a detestable shaveling of the Antichrist."

46. These also were the events which first brought Edmund Spenser and Walter Raleigh together. Raleigh had come back to London from his service with the Huguenots, and lived for a short time in the Middle Temple, where he wrote a poem of compliment, prefixed in 1576 to Gascoigne's "Steel Glass" (§ 29). In 1578, Sir John Norris crossed to the Low Countries with a small force, of which Raleigh was one, to join in the con-test against Don John, who, after his triumph over infidels at Lepanto, was to master heretics as Governor of the Netherlands. Early in 1578 the Netherlanders had been banned by the pope as unbelievers. There was appeal to arms. The forces of Spain had from their Church the privileges of crusaders. The Spaniards obtained a great victory over the army of the States at Gemblours. War went on nevertheless. In Holland and Zealand the Reformation was in 1578 formally established by civic revolution, that placed Protestants instead of Catholics in the magistracy at Amsterdam and Haarlem. Raleigh took part in a success of arms on Lammas-day; and Don John died on the 1st of October, at a time when Raleigh was busy on another enterprise. On the 19th of November he sailed from Plymouth with his half-brother, Sir Humphrey Gilbert, who took seven ships and 350 men on an expedition that was foiled. They fell in with a Spanish fleet, lost one of their ships, and Gilbert and his brother-in-law, Walter Raleigh, came back to England in the early summer of 1579, with the wreck of their small force. After a few months of London life, Raleigh then sailed for Ire-land, in January, 1580. His energy was overbearing, and weak leaders did not love the bold, proud, and plain-spoken captain, who shone in conflict with the rebels, and in suggestion of policy for quelling the rebellion ; until, in December, 1581, he was sent back to the Court at London with despatches.

After the massacre at Del Oro, Spenser returned with Lord Arthur Grey to Dublin. In 1581, Spenser was made Clerk of Degrees and Recognisances in the Irish Court of Chancery, and received also a lease of the lands and abbey of Enniscorthy, in Wexford county. He transferred the lease within a year ; and in 1582, Lord Arthur Grey, "after long suit for his revocation, received Her Majesty's letters for the same." Spenser remained in Ireland as an English Government official. In 1588 he vacated his post in the Irish Court of Chancery, on being appointed clerk to the Council of Munster. In 1589 he came to London with Sir Walter Raleigh, to present to the queen the first three books of *The Faerie Queene*, which were first published in 1590. Before speaking of this, we trace the other outlines of our sketch from 1579 to 1590.

47. **William Shakespeare** (§ 37) was in 1579 fifteen years old, and his home had fallen into poverty. In 1580 his father's name appeared in a list of gentlemen and freeholders in Barlichway hundred ; but poverty still pressed, and John Shakespeare sold his reversionary interest in the Snitterfield tenements for £40 to R. Webbe. In the same year, 1580, another son, Edmund, was born. The 28th of November, 1582, is the date of the preliminary bond with a notary, for marriage licence of William Shakespeare and Anne Hathaway, daughter of Richard Hathaway, "husbandman," of Shottery. Her father had been dead a twelvemonth. The marriage would have followed immediately, but before marriage there was, in those days, a more binding ceremony of betrothal than is customary now. Thus, in a play of George Peele's, " The Old Wives' Tale," there is a magic light to be blown out by a woman who is neither maid, wife, nor widow. The light is blown out by Venelia, not maid because she is betrothed, not wife because she is not married, and not widow because he lives to whom she was betrothed. Shakespeare's age when he married was eighteen years and seven months; Anne Hathaway was six-and-twenty. There is no evidence whatever that this marriage was other than a happy one. On the 26th of May, 1583, Shakespeare's first child, Susanna, was baptised. On the 2nd of February, 1585, there were twins to baptise. They were named Hamnet and Judith ; no doubt after Hamnet and Judith Sadler, bakers, friends of the Shakespeares. (Hamnet Sadler, when he died, left Shakespeare 36s. 8d. to buy a ring.) In some way Shakespeare must have endeavoured to support his little family ; his father could not help him. In 1585, John Shakespeare was arrested for lack of goods to distrain on. In 1586, John Shakespeare was twice

arrested for debt; and, on the ground of his constant absence
from the meetings of the Corporation, he was deprived of his
alderman's gown. He was an unprosperous man, of at least
fifty-six, with five children, the youngest six years old. William,
the eldest, was then about twenty-two, had been four years
married, and his wife had three babies to feed and train—
Susanna, three years old; the twins, Hamnet and Judith, two.
How could he best maintain them? He was a poet. Players
had been to Stratford. He would go to London, and would
seek his fortune by steady work in association with the rising
power of the stage.

His wife and babies he would not take with him into the
unwholesome atmosphere of the great town, or bring into contact
with the wild life of the playhouse wits. The children would
be drawing health from the fresh breezes of Stratford; the wife
would be living a wholesome life among her old friends, neighbours, and relations; while he worked hard for them where money
could be earned, took holiday rests with them when theatres
were closed, and hoped that he might earn enough to enable him
to come home for good before he was very old, and live a natural
and happy life among the quiet scenes of his birthplace, among
relatives who loved him, and among the old friends of his childhood and his youth. The man of highest genius is the man also
of highest sanity. In lower minds unusual excitement of the
brain may lead to bold or eccentric forms of expression, with
half-bred resemblance to originality and energy of thought.
Ephemeral and even lasting reputations may be founded on this
form of wit; but the greatest among poets, a Chaucer or a
Shakespeare, is calm and simply wise. He is greatest of poets
not because he does not, but because he does feel, and that
more intensely and more truly than his neighbours, the natural
ties of life. He has keen happiness in the home circle, in the
scenes associated with his childhood, in the peaceful fellowship
of man. His old friends, Judith and Hamnet Sadler, the bakers,
were more, not less, to the author of "King Lear" than they
would be to the citizen with less perception of the harmonies of
life. Of all that it is natural and fit for common men to say
and do, Shakespeare had, because of his transcendent genius,
only a simpler, truer sense than any of his neighbours.

Shakespeare came to London, then, in or about the year
1586; and, Shakespeare though he was, he did not leap to instant
fame, but worked his way to a front place in his profession by

six years of patient industry. He was so ready to do any honest work, that at the end of six years we have the first indication of his rise in the complaint of a competitor, that he is a Johannes Factotum (Jack of all Trades). This was the position of William Shakespeare in 1592, when he was twenty-eight years old. In studying Shakespeare's life it is needful to distinguish firmly between facts of which there is evidence and idle fancies: as of Shakespeare having in his youth stolen deer from a park in which there were no deer to be stolen; of his having been a butcher, and, when he killed a calf, having done so with a grand air; with other small-talk of dead gossips.

48. **Francis Bacon** (§ 38), aged eighteen at the time of his father's death in 1579, studied at Gray's Inn, was admitted an utter barrister in June, 1582; and about this time, aged twenty-one, sketched briefly in a Latin tract, called *Temporis Partus Maximus* (The Greatest Birth of Time), the first notion of his philosophy. In November, 1584, Bacon took his seat in the House of Commons, as member for Melcombe Regis, in Dorsetshire. In the next Parliament, which met in October, 1586, he sat for Taunton, and was one of those who presented a petition for the speedy execution of Mary Queen of Scots. He was then member for Liverpool, active in public affairs, and presented to the ministry a wise paper of his own called, *An Advertisement Touching the Controversie of the Church of England.* Its topic was the Marprelate Controversy, presently to be described, and it contained the germ of his essay " Of Unity in Religion." In October, 1589, there was given to Bacon the reversion of the office of Clerk of the Council in the Star Chamber, with £1,600 or £2,000 a year, and the further advantage that its work was done by deputy. But for this Bacon had twenty years to wait; the holder of it lived till 1608. If that office had fallen to him early in life, Bacon might possibly have given up his career as a lawyer, and devoted himself wholly to the working out of his philosophy.

49. Let us turn now to the controversies of the Church, first going back a little way to trace events in Scotland. There, as we have seen (§ 3), the confession of John Knox was established by the Three Estates in 1560 as the confession of the Scottish people; by three Acts the rule of the pope was abolished, and the Reformation was established. There was a new sense of fellowship between England and Scotland; the patriotic Scot of the Reformed Church no longer looked upon France as his

country's natural ally; but the Scottish Catholics looked both to France and Spain. In 1561 there was a systematic demolition of monasteries, and of images and altars in the cathedrals. In August of that year, Queen Mary, who had become a widow at the end of 1560 by the death of Francis II. of France, returned to Scotland, aged nineteen. On the first Sunday after her arrival she heard Mass; and, by the new law of Scotland, that was a crime, with penalty for the first offence of confiscation of goods, for the second of banishment, and for the third of death. At a banquet to the queen and her court in Edinburgh, entertainment was provided in presentment of a mystery of Korah, Dathan, and Abiram, who were destroyed for burning strange fire on the altar. It included parody of the Mass, and burning of a priest in effigy. The Earl of Huntly, leader of the Romanist party, stopped the performance. Guises and Frenchmen were in Scotland, and the question was raised of Mary's succession to Elizabeth upon the throne of England. With this in view, Mary served the time, and showed herself well-disposed towards the Protestantism of the people. Knox maintained his cause in plain words, both in his preaching and in interviews with the queen. He wished that she could hear the preaching too: " If your grace," he said, " please to frequent the public sermons, then doubt I not but ye shall fully understand both what I like and mislike, as well in your Majesty as all others." And of his bold preaching he said, " Why should the pleasing face of a gentlewoman affray me? I have looked on the faces of many angry men, and yet have not been affrayed above measure." In May, 1564, about a month after the birth of Shakespeare, Calvin died. In July, 1565, Queen Mary married, without advice of Parliament, her cousin Henry Stuart, Lord Darnley; and proclaimed her husband King of the Scots. He also was Roman-Catholic, and the marriage was according to the rites of the Church of Rome. In March, 1566, Darnley, with Lord Ruthven and others, seized and murdered David Rizzio in the queen's rooms. Knox approved the deed in his history, where he said, " That great abuser of this commonwealth, that poltroon and vile knave, Davie, was justly punished for abusing of the commonwealth, and for his other villany which we list not to express." With Darnley the queen dissembled, and he meanly turned with her against his associates. " As they have brewed," he said, " so let them drink." On the 19th of June, 1566, Mary's son was born, afterwards to become James VI. of Scotland and James I. of England. His father was then detested by his mother. Soon afterwards there was a gunpowder plot against Darnley, directed by the Earl of Bothwell. On the 9th of June, 1567, Darnley was murdered. Early in May, Bothwell was divorced from his wife, and on the 15th of May, Queen Mary married him. The Barons rose; Bothwell and Mary were parted. The queen was brought back to Edinburgh, thence she was removed to Lochleven ; and at Lochleven she was compelled to sign an abdication in favour of her son, and appoint the Earl of Moray regent during the child's minority. Thus James Stuart, when not quite a year old, became King James VI. of Scotland; and John Knox preached the sermon at his coronation.

In the last years of Knox there was not only political confusion, but there were defections from the cause for which he lived, and there were differences of opinion between him and his brethren in the General Assembly. In 1568, in an answer to a letter written by James Tyrie, a Jesuit, he wrote himself "John Knox, the servant of Jesus Christ, now weary of the world, and daily looking for the resolution of this my earthly tabernacle." In these his latter days, Knox, somewhat palsied, went to preach, supported by a staff in one hand, and his servant Richard Bannatyne upon the other side. "In church," wrote one who knew him then, "he was by the said Richard and another servant lifted to the pulpit, where he behoved to lean at his first entry ; but ere he had done with his sermon he was so active and vigorous that he was like to ding the pulpit in blads " (break it in pieces) " and fly out of it." In September, 1572, he preached in the Tolbooth, then a dying man, upon the horror of that year, the Massacre of St. Bartholomew. He died on the 24th of the following November. John Knox's *Historie of the Reformation of Religioun within the Realm of Scotland* first appeared twelve years after his death, in 1584, published in Edinburgh, but printed in London, and afterwards partly suppressed in 1587 by the seizure and destruction of copies, at the order of the Archbishop of Canterbury. The whole grim energy of Knox's character animates this recital of events in which and for which he lived.

50. Of the learned men employed in education of the young King James of Scotland, there is one, **George Buchanan,** historian and poet, who has a place of honour in our literature. He was was born at Kellerne, Lennoxshire, in 1506. His father

died, leaving his mother almost destitute, with five boys and three girls; and George was sent by James Heriot, a brother of hers, to Paris for his education.  There he already wrote much Latin verse.  His uncle's death, two years afterwards, obliged him to come back without health or money.  He made a campaign with French auxiliaries in sharp weather, lost health again, was in bed the rest of the winter, went to St. Andrew's to study under old John Mair (ch. vi. § 33), with whom he went to Paris. There he became Lutheran, was for two years very poor, then for two years and a half he taught grammar at the College of St. Barbe.  He was then in France as tutor and companion for five years to the young Earl of Cassillis, and went back with him to Scotland.  He there acted as tutor to the king's natural son, James, afterwards Earl of Moray.  But he attacked the monks in Latin satires, especially in his *Franciscanus* and *Fratres Fraterrimi*, was denounced by Beaton, and compelled to leave Scotland again. He went to England; but there, he says, he found Henry VIII. burning men of both parties, more intent on his own interests than on purity of religion.  So being half at home in France— though Buchanan carried Scotland about with him wherever he went—he went to Paris, found his enemy Cardinal Beaton there also in his way, and was invited by a learned Portuguese, Andrew Goveanus, who resided at Bordeaux, to teach there.  Thus he became Professor of the Humanities at Bordeaux, where he had Montaigne in his class, and where he wrote two Latin tragedies of his own, on *Jephthah* and *John the Baptist*, and translated into Latin the *Medea* and *Alcestis* of Euripides.  These were written, year by year, as they were required—the translations first—to be acted, according to custom, by the students of Bordeaux.  Goveanus was at last summoned to Portugal by his king, and invited to bring with him men learned in Greek and Latin, to join in the work of the newly-founded University of Coimbra.  All Europe was involved in war.  Buchanan was glad to find in Portugal a quiet corner.  There he was very happy, with bright associates, and his brother Patrick among them, till the death of Goveanus.  A persecution then began, some teachers were imprisoned; for a year and a half Buchanan was worried, and inquired into; and then he was confined for a few months in a monastery.  There he occupied himself by making his famous poetical paraphrase of the Psalms into Latin verse—*Paraphrasis Psalmorum Davidis poetica*—first published at Paris in 1564.  When he left Portugal, Buchanan came first to England—it was in the time of Edward VI.—then he went to France; then was called to Italy by Marshal de Brissac, and was for five years with the marshal's son, sometimes in France, sometimes in Italy. During that time he made a special study of the religious controversies of the day. In 1566, at the age of sixty, Buchanan was made Principal of St. Leonard's College, in the University of St. Andrew's. In the earliest childhood of James VI., Buchanan became his tutor. George Buchanan was the best Latin poet this country had produced. He would seek to instil scholarship and theology of the Reformed Church into the boy whose father was murdered, and whose mother was in England. Mary had escaped from Lochleven in 1568, nobles had gathered force to rally round her; they had been defeated at Langside by the Regent Moray, and the queen then fled across the border into England. There Elizabeth detained her. Mary's party and her cause were the party and cause of Catholicism. The Scottish Reformers under Moray's regency acted with Protestant England, and fell into disrepute even of subserviency to England. The question of Mary's complicity in the murder of Darnley was in agitation at Elizabeth's court, and in the case against her a chief part was played by eight letters and some verses cut into lengths of fourteen lines, and called sonnets of hers, said to have been found on the 20th of June, 1567, in a casket that Bothwell left behind him in Edinburgh. After the assassination of the Regent Moray in 1570, civil discord between the two parties in Scotland rose to an extreme height. The friends of Mary were active; a messenger from the Duke of Alva was in Scotland; and a new Catholic rebellion broke out in the North of England. Lennox, next regent, perished in the Scottish turmoil, in 1571; he was succeeded by young James's governor, the Earl of Mar. Then came, in 1572, the Massacre of St. Bartholomew, to deepen the sense of danger from Catholicism. Sentence of death was resolved by Elizabeth's advisers upon Mary of Scotland, as a foremost cause of peril to the country. Elizabeth was not to be answerable for the act, but Mary was to be returned to Scotland with a secret understanding that she was returned for execution. Then it was that the Casket Letters were first published to the world. George Buchanan published anonymously in Latin, an enforcement of the charges against Queen Mary. It was published in London, and there appeared immediate translations of it into French and Northern English, the latter as *Ane Detec-*

*tioun of the Doingis of Marie Quene of Scottis, twiching the
Murthir of hir Husband, &c., Translatit out of Latin quhilk
was written be M. G. B. Sanctandrois, be Robert Leckprevik.*
The Latin translation of the Casket Letters is here rendered
into Scottish dialect; and there is a rendering of nearly all into
French. We now have them in no other shape. The originals
are lost; it is not an improbable supposition that they were
destroyed by Mary's son. During the last twelve or fourteen
years of his life, Buchanan employed his mastery of Latin,
and his knowledge of events, in writing a Latin History of
Scotland—*Rerum Scoticarum Historia*—in twenty books. It
connected with the past the life of his own day, gave unity to
all, and placed at the head of it the sense of nationality.
It was in his nature to care rather to mark the progress of a
people than to celebrate the power of a chief. This was distinctly shown in a sort of Socratic dialogue, published by him
in Latin, in 1579, on the law as it relates to government among
the Scots—*Jus Regni apud Scotos*—which ends by replying to
their neighbours who called the Scots seditious, "What is that
to them? We make our tumults at our own peril. No people
were ever less seditious, or more moderate in their seditions.
They contend much about laws, royal rights, and duties of
administration; not for destruction and hatred, but for love of
country and defence of law." Buchanan's history was first published in 1582, the year of its author's death.

51. Meanwhile, Buchanan and others had been doing their
best for the education of young **James VI.** He was a clumsy
boy, with ungainliness produced by physical defect, a tongue
too large for his mouth, and a mind in which all depths that
there could ever be must be made artificially. Good workmen
dug and shaped; the boy was good-tempered, picked up some
shrewdness, lived a creditable life, had respect for knowledge,
and good appetite for it, though bad digestion. He had a
pleasant type of it before him in cheery, impressible George
Buchanan; a Presbyterian, austere but half way through, with
a face like a Scotch Socrates, although more apt than Socrates
to take offence, familiar with Latin as with his native tongue,
full of anecdote and good talk, familiar also with languages
and people round about, and liking Scotland all the better for
experience in other lands. But for James the horizon did not
widen as he climbed the hill of knowledge, his heart did not
swell as he rose to higher sense of harmony and beauty; he

hammered at the big lumps about him, and was proud of
being so far up. In 1585, when his age was but nineteen,
he published at Edinburgh *The Essayes of a Prentise in the
Divine Art of Poesie.* In preliminary sonnets of compliment,
the Muses, through various courtly representations, sought to

> " Tell how he doth in tender yearis essay
>   Above his age with skill our arts to blaise
> Tell how he doeth with gratitude repay
>   The crowne he won for his deserved praise.
> Tell how of Jove, of Mars, but more of God
> The glorie and grace he hath proclaimed abrod."

The " Essayes " opened with twelve sonnets of invocations to
the gods, namely, Jove, Apollo, each of the four Seasons, Neptune,
Tritons and their kind, Pluto, Mars, Mercury, and finally, for
the twelfth sonnet :

> " In short, you all fore named gods I pray
>   For to concur with one accord and will
> That all my works may perfyte be alway :
>   Which if ye doe, then swear I for to fill
> My works immortall with your praises still :
>   I shall your names eternall ever sing
> I shall tread downe the grass on Parnass hill
>   By making with your names the world to ring ;
> I shall your names from all oblivion bring ;
> I lofty Virgill shall to life restoirr."

Buchanan was for three years dead, and there were few left
who would tell a young king that his works were not " perfyte
alway." Then followed a translation of *L'Uranie,* or " The
Heavenly Muse," from Du Bartas, original and translation
printed upon opposite pages, with a modest preface in admiration of " the devine and illuster poete, Salust du Bartas " (§ 35),
by the " oft reading and perusing " of whom James was moved
" with a restless and lofty desire to preas to attaine to the like
virtue." To the level of Du Bartas he could not at all aspire in
his own verse ; let him, he said, follow imperfectly as a translator.
This represented only the common admiration of his time
which Du Bartas enjoyed. In a copy of " Quintilian," annotated by Gabriel Harvey when the *Sepmaine* of Du Bartas
was a new book, Harvey wrote in the margin, beside a mention
of Euripides, " Euripides, wisest of poets : except now at length
the divine Bartas." After his version of one of the shorter
poems of Du Bartas, King James gave for his next essay a
dim allegory, smoothly versified, in Chaucer's stanza, " Ane

Metaphoricall Invention of a Tragedie called Phœnix," with a
preface of eighteen bad lines, arranged first as shaped verse, in
the form of a lozenge upon a little pedestal, then as a compound acrostic. Then followed a short bit of translation out
of the fifth book of Lucan; and then, lastly, " Ane Schort
Treatise, containing some Reulis and Cautelis to be observit
and eschewit in Scottis Poesie." Here we find, among other
things, that the technical name then given to Chaucer's stanza
was derived from Chaucer's most popular example of it. It was
called " Troilus Verse."

52. We glance abroad to connect the narrative with facts
in foreign literature which concern our story. *Michel de
Montaigne*, who had been among George Buchanan's students
at Bordeaux, produced the first edition of his Essays in 1580.
There was a second edition in 1588. This first of the great
essayists had learnt Latin as a mother tongue, had seen much
of the world in his youth; and he died in 1592, aged fifty-nine,
after much enjoyment and half philosophical half gossiping
discussion of life, at his seat of Montaigne, near Bordeaux.

In 1581, when *Torquato Tasso* was still a prisoner with
the insane, appeared his great heroic poem in twenty-four books,
on the First Crusade, and recovery of Jerusalem from the
Saracens, at the end of the eleventh century. The poem had
two names, *Goffredo*, from its hero, Godfrey of Bouillon, and
*Gerusalemme Liberata* (" Jerusalem Delivered "), from its action.
There were eight independent and sometimes conflicting issues
of this poem in Italy within nine months of its first publication.
One of these had an essay prefixed on the question of the two
titles. To one of the last of them there was appended an allegorical interpretation. The old relish for allegory in literature,
which we have traced down from early Christian days, was in
Elizabeth's time unabated.

But for some years after 1581 the fame of the now obscure
*Du Bartas* rose higher than that of Tasso. The " Divine Week "
of Du Bartas was followed by a " Second Week " (*Second
Sepmaine*), in 1584. This divided into seven periods, poetically
called days, the religious history of man expressed in the successive histories of Adam, Noah, Abraham, David, Zedekiah,
the Messiah, and, for seventh " day," the Eternal Sabbath.
Du Bartas only lived to complete four of the seven sections of
this work, but he wrote also many other moral and religious
poems. He also repaid the royal compliment of a translation

of *L' Uranie* by translating into French, as *La Lepanthe*, the poem on the battle of Lepanto which King James of Scotland wrote soon after publishing his " Essayes of an Apprentise." This appeared with a preface of the translator to the author, wherein James was honoured with the name of a Scotch Phœnix, and the divine Du Bartas himself declared that he could not soar with him, could only stand on earth to see him in the clouds. Du Bartas wished he had only so much of James, as to be but the shadow of his shape, the echo of his voice.

> " Hé ! fusse ie vrayment, O Phœnix Escossois,
> Ou l'ombre de ton corps, ou l'echo de ta voix ! "

There was another Frenchman then in high and deserved repute among English Reformers, one of Philip Sidney's friends, *Philip de Mornay, Seigneur du Plessis.* He was not much older than Sidney, for he was born in 1549 ; and he would have been endowed with good things in the Church by family influence, if his mother had not become Protestant, and trained her child from ten years old in the Reformed opinions. He served awhile in the army, went to Geneva, studied law in Heidelberg, travelled in Italy, Germany, the Netherlands, and England. He went in 1576 to the court of King Henry of Navarre, became one of his nearest friends, and helped to make him Henry IV. of France. Philip du Plessis Mornay was an accomplished man of the world, with tact, experience, and a practical mind, as well as religious earnestness and a delight in literature. He became known as an envoy at Elizabeth's court, where the best men were his companions. The influence obtained by his high character, his skill in management of affairs, and the pure tone of his writings, caused him to be called sometimes the Pope of the Huguenots. In 1587, **Arthur Golding** (§ 6) published a translation of *Du Plessis Mornay on the Truth of Christianity.*

53. There were still also translations from the ancient poets. **Richard Stanihurst,** who was son of a Recorder of Dublin, had written at University College, Oxford, a system of logic, in his eighteenth year, had studied law also at two Inns of Court, had been married to a knight's daughter, and was living at Leyden, when he published in 1582 a translation of the first four books of Virgil's " Æneid " into English hexameters. This was made at the time of the small war against rhyme, and fashion for this sort of " new English versifying " (§ 43); and Stanihurst was accounted a fine scholar. His attempt at an

English "Virgil" in Virgil's own measure was praised by those who encouraged the experiment, attacked by others. Had Virgil himself written in English in 1582, he would hardly have expressed Jupiter's kiss to his daughter by saying, as Stanihurst made him say, that he " bussed his pretty prating parrot," or written hexameters of this sort to describe Laocoon's throwing his spear at the great wooden horse:

> "' My lief for an haulfpennie, Troians,
> Either heere ar couching soom troups of Greekish asemblie,
> Or to crush our bulwarcks this woorck is forged, al houses
> For to prie surmounting thee town : soom practis or oother
> Heere lurcks of coonning : trust not this treacherus ensigne ;
> And for a ful reckning, I like not barrel or herring ;
> Thee Greeks bestowing their presents Greekish I feare mee.'
> Thus said, he stout rested, with his chaapt staffe speedily running,
> Strong the steed he chargeth, thee planck ribs manfully riding.
> Then the iade, hit, shivered, thee vauts haulf shrillie rebounded
> With chush clash buzzing, with droomming clattered humming."

Richard Stanihurst published in 1584, in Latin, four books of an Irish chronicle, *De Rebus in Hibernia Gestis Libri IV.* He had been at work on this since the close of his college days, and though born in Dublin he had been bred in England, and was trained into the prevalent opinion then held by the English of the native Irish race. It is not necessary to believe that he desired to write only what would please his English patrons. He afterwards took orders in the Catholic Church, and, it is said, undertook to recant the errors in his "Irish Chronicle." In 1587 he published at Antwerp, in two Latin books, a *Life of St. Patrick*, the apostle of Ireland, and his later writings were religious. He lived on through a great part of the reign of James I., and died in 1618.

The first attempt at a translation of Homer into English Alexandrine verse was begun in 1563, and published in 1581. This appeared in *Ten Books of Homer's Iliades.* It was not translated from the Greek direct, but chiefly through the French version of Hugues Salel, by **Arthur Hall**, of Grantham, a member of Parliament. The fact that this is the first Englishing of Homer gives the book importance.

54. **Barnaby Googe**, born about 1540, at Alvingham, and son of the Recorder of Lincoln, was a translator from the moderns. In 1560 he issued the first three books, and in 1565 all twelve books of an English version of the Italian Manzolli's satirical invective against the Papacy, *The Zodiac of Life.* In

1570, Google published a translation of another Latin invective, written by Thomas Kirchmeyer, which he called *The Popish Kingdome; or, Reigne of Antichrist.* In 1577 he published a translation from the Latin of the *Four Bokes of Husbandrie,* by Conrad Heresbach. He also translated from the Spanish; and a little volume of his own verse, *Eglogs, Epytaphes, and Sonettes,* was issued in 1563. Google died in 1594.

**George Whetstone,** a minor poet of this time, who was in repute with his contemporaries as "one of the most passionate above us to bewail the perplexities of love," wrote under a name taken from the popular story-book of Marguerite of Navarre, *A Heptameron of Civil Discourses.* This also is a book of tales. Among those which he took from the "Hecatommithi," or "Hundred Tales," of Giraldi Cinthio, first published in 1565, tales which deal with the tragic side of life, is one that was used by Shakespeare for the plot of his *Measure for Measure.* Whetstone had himself written a play on the same subject, *Promos and Cassandra,* in two parts, printed in 1578.

**Anthony Munday** was a minor writer, whose literary activity in verse and prose, as playwright, ballad writer, and pamphleteer, began in 1579, and extended through the rest of the reign of Elizabeth, and the whole reign of her successor. He died in the reign of Charles I., in 1633. He was bred in the English college at Rome, and afterwards turned Protestant. His earliest introduction to literature was as a player and a writer for the stage. In 1582 he gave great offence to the Catholics by publishing *The Discoverie of Edmund Campion, the Jesuit,* which provoked reply. After this he was in the service of the Earl of Oxford, and was also a messenger of the queen's bedchamber. He had reputation among our first dramatists for skill in the construction of a comic plot. His earliest printed book is religious in its tendency; and so indeed was a great part of the drama during Elizabeth's reign. Its title explains its purport. It was in verse, and called *The Mirror of Mutabilitie; or,* Principal Part of the Mirrour of Magistrates : Selected out of the Sacred Scriptures. The titles of his next two books may be taken as examples of Euphuism; they are both dated in 1580, the year of the second part of Lyly's Euphues (§ 22). One is *The Fountaine of Fame, Erected in an Orchard of Amorous Adventures;* the other, *The Paine of Pleasure, profitable to be perused of the Wise, and necessary to be by the Wanton.*

Munday took violent interest in the arrest and execution of

the Jesuits sent by the pope as devoted missionaries for the re-conversion of England. Edmund Campion had been an Oxford student and a Protestant. He changed his faith from con-viction, became a Jesuit, and exposed himself to death in Eng-land for devotion to what seemed to him the highest duty he could find. In his torture and execution, and in the other exe-cutions of like men, we feel painfully, as elsewhere proudly, the intensity of conflict in their day. They did not, it was said by those who sent them to death, suffer for their faith, but for their political assent to the pope's right to depose the Queen of England. They did suffer for that assent; but then unhappily it was a part of their religious faith. There were high principles, momentous interests of the future, then at stake; the immediate issues of the struggle were uncertain, peril was great, on each side temper rose with the excitement of a noble energy: but we need not now read with the pleasure that was taken in the writing of it, Anthony Munday's *Breefe and True Reporte of the Execution of certaine Traytours at Tiborne, the xxviii. and xxx. Dayes of May,* 1582; though we can understand the ground of his *Watchwoord to Englande, to beware of Traytors and Tretche-rous Practises, which have beene the Overthrowe of many famous Kingdomes and Commonweales* (1584); and see the harmony between this strength of public feeling and the religious tempera-ment which caused him to print in 1586 a book of *Godly Exercise for Christian Families, containing an Order of Praires for Morning and Evening, with a little Catechism between the Man and his Wife.* Such men were of the common crowd of English dramatists of Elizabeth's day, and there was a bright spirit of song in them all. Munday's next book (in 1588) was *A Banquet of Dainty Conceits; furnished with verie delicate and choyce Inventions to delighte their Mindes who take Pleasure in Musique; and there withall to sing sweete ditties, either to the lute, bandora, virginalles, or anie other Instrument.*

55. **George Peele,** a playwright with genius, who belonged also to this early group, was born in 1558, a gentleman's son, and said to be of a Devonshire family. He became a student of the University of Oxford, at Broadgates Hall, now Pembroke College, took his degree of B.A. in June, 1577, became M.A. in 1579, when twenty-one years old. He remained another two years in the University, thus having been a student there for nine years, when he married a wife with some property, and went to London. While in the University he was esteemed as a poet,

made a version (now lost) of one of the two Iphigenias of
Euripides into English, and probably then wrote his *Tale of
Troy*, in one book of heroic couplets; but this was first printed
in 1589. In London, Peele took his place, probably at once,
among the poets.

They were almost without exception University men who
were writing for the players. It was pleasant work and profitable. Hitherto everywhere, and still outside the theatre, the
man with ability to be useful or pleasant—and to be whole-
somely pleasant is also to be useful—as a writer, could not
expect to live by the use of his pen, unless he received indirect
aid from the patronage, or direct aid from the purse, of a great
lord or of the sovereign. Without help of the patron, or hope
of such help, many works of genius could never have been
written in a world where daily bread costs daily money. Such
patronage took many gracious forms ; often it was ungracious.
It offered only a precarious support, and lured sensitive men
through years of vain anxiety and hope to a sorrowful old age.
Spenser described it in his " Mother Hubbard's Tale:"

> " So pitiful a thing is suitor's state !
> Most miserable man, whom wicked fate
> Hath brought to court, to sue for had ywist
> That few have found, and many one hath m.._t !
> Full little knowest thou that hath not tried,
> What hell it is in suing long to bide :
> To lose good days that might be better spent ;
> To waste long nights in pensive discontent ;
> To speed to-day, to be put back to-morrow ;
> To feed on hope, to pine with fear and sorrow :
> To have thy princes' grace, yet want her peers';
> To have thy asking, yet wait many years ;
> To fret thy soul with crosses and with cares :
> To eat thy heart through comfortless despairs ;
> To fawn, to crouch, to wait, to ride, to run,
> To spend, to give, to want, to be undone."

But there was no large public of readers, and there was no
possible escape from the patron till the theatres began to rise.
Then those who would now be readers became hearers, and
paid for hearing as they would now pay for reading. From the
money taken for each performance, there was pay to the author,
pay to the actors ; pay earned as simply and independently by
the use of a craft, as money earned by carpenter or smith. A
short experience of this made known to the clever men who
came to London from the Universities to make their way in

life how they could run alone at once, and remain masters of
themselves.  If they chose to seek a patron, they might do that
also, but they were not compelled to feed on hope; there was
money for their bread, unless they spent all upon sack.  In later
years, when the stage had a less direct relation to all classes of
the people, but was itself debased by court patronage, this way
of escape from the patron became but a narrow one.  All hope
of independence for the men of genius rested then upon the
slow advance of education, till the readers could do gradually,
now for one, then for another, and at last for all forms of literature, what in Elizabeth's day the hearers did for one form only.
The young men thus established in London, drawing money
from the theatres, could add also to their reputations and their
incomes by writing for the booksellers tales, poems, or pamphlets upon stirring questions of the day.  This they did, and
there were some who flung themselves with high glee into paper
wars, ready to profit in all possible ways by skill in the amusement of the town.

Peele's acquired knowledge caused him to be employed in
Oxford, in 1583, as acting manager for two Latin plays, by his
friend Dr. Gager, presented at Christ Church before a Polish
prince.  His first published verse was prefixed to Thomas
Watson's " Passionate Centurie of Love," published in 1583.

56. **Thomas Watson** was of about Peele's age, and died
in 1592.  The thirty-five years of his age were all lived in
Elizabeth's reign.  He was born in London, studied in Oxford,
then in London again, and applied himself to common law;
was in Paris for a time before 1581, in which year he published
a version in Latin of the *Antigone* of Sophocles.  A scholar
and a poet; at first writing chiefly in Latin, afterwards in English verse; appreciated as he deserved to be by Sidney, Lyly, and
Peele; a friend of Spenser's; Watson was the sweetest of the
purely amatory poets of Elizabeth's reign.  In 1582 appeared
his book with a Greek and English title—Greek titles were then
becoming fashionable—'Εκατομπαθία (*The Passionate Centurie of
Love*), that is to say, a Love Passion in a Hundred Sonnets.
According to the old Italian method, which had been revived
by Surrey (ch. vi. § 46), exercises upon various phases of the
passion of love in sequences of sonnets were still in fashion;
these poems were known as Passions.  Each of Watson's
hundred passions has a prose explanation before it; and
each consists of three of the six-lined stanzas then called

Common Verse, the stanza which, as King James VI. recorded, poets were to use " in materis of love." Take one of Watson's for example :

> "Tully, whose speech was bold in ev'ry cause,
> If he were here to praise the saint and serve,
> The number of her gifts would make him pause,
> And fear to speak how well he doth deserve.
> Why then am I thus bold, that have no skill?
> Enforced by love, I show my zealous will."

In 1585 appeared Watson's Latin Poem, *Amyntas*, from which his fellow poets took the name they gave him in their rhymes; and in 1595—after Italian Madrigals Englished and other works—appeared his *Teares of Fansie; or, Love Disdained.* From Watson we return to his friend,

57. **George Peele**, who published anonymously, in 1584, *The Araygnement of Paris: a Pastorall, presented before the Queenes Maiestie by the Children of her Chapell.* It is a pastoral play in five acts, not the less but the more poetical for a child-like simplicity of dialogue. It is written at first in various rhymed measures, which run into musical songs, passions, and complaints that sing themselves, but the metre becomes blank verse when the arraigned shepherd Paris has to defend himself before the council of the gods against the charge of unjust judgment. The gods, greatly puzzled, leave Diana to settle the question, and she settles it by compromise. In the fifth act she comes with Juno, Pallas, and Venus, all content to present the apple to Elizabeth, before whom also the three sisters, " Dames of Destiny," yield up their distaff, reel, and fatal knife. By way of epilogue, the performers at the end of the play poured the good wishes of men and gods on Her Majesty in two Latin hexameters.

In 1585, George Peele was the deviser of a Lord Mayor's pageant. Of his other plays, there were none printed before 1590, the year in which Spenser published the first three books of the "Faerie Queene," and which we take as a convenient dividing point for study of the second part of the reign of Elizabeth.

58. **John Lyly**, after the publication of the two parts of his "Euphues," in 1579 and 1580, was paying suit and service to Lord Burghley. Sir Thomas Benger, Master of the Revels, had died in 1577, and the place, which remained for a time vacant, was desired by Lyly. But Edmund Tylney was

appointed in July, 1579. Lyly now became a dramatist, and wrote plays for the court on classical or mythological subjects, nine plays in all, seven in prose, one of the later ones—*The Woman in the Moon*—in blank verse, and another of the later ones—*The Maid's Metamorphosis*—chiefly in rhyme. The prose is laboured to the fashion of the day; a Euphuism, rich in far-fetched, whimsical, and delicate conceits, play upon words, and antithesis with alliteration, interspersed with songs which now and then are excellent. In each play the plot, characters, and dialogues are alike artificial; the poet's aim is not to stir the soul, but to provide a pleasant entertainment for the fancy. The first printed of Lyly's plays, in 1584, was *Campaspe*, played before the queen by Her Majesty's children, and the children of Paul's. It was acted both at court and at the Blackfriars' theatre. In this play is Lyly's well-known song of Apelles— founded on a conceit, of course:

> "Cupid and my Campaspe played
> At cards for kisses, Cupid paid;
> He stakes his quiver, bow and arrows,
> His mother's doves, and team of sparrows.
> Loses them too; then down he throws
> The coral of his lip, the rose
> Growing on's cheek (but none knows how),
> With these the crystal of his brow,
> And then the dimple of his chin:
> All these did my Campaspe win.
> At last he set her both his eyes,
> She won, and Cupid blind did rise.
> O Love! has she done this to thee?
> What shall, alas, become of me?"

In the same year was printed *Sapho and Phao*, which had been played before the queen on Shrove Tuesday, by the children of her chapel and the boys of Paul's. These were the only plays of Lyly's printed before 1590. But we shall find him presently supposed to contribute a tract called *Pap with a Hatchet*, in the paper war of 1589, which gave rise to Bacon's "Advertisement Touching the Controversies of the Church of England."

59. **Robert Greene** was novelist as well as dramatist, and as a novelist he was a follower of Lyly. He was born at Norwich, educated at St. John's College, Cambridge, took his degree of B.A. in 1578. Peele taking his at Oxford in 1577, there probably was little difference between the ages of those poets; and Greene may have been born about 1559 or 1560. After

1578, Greene visited Italy and Spain, before graduating as M.A. in 1583. In 1584 he published three prose love-pamphlets, in the style of Euphues, *The Myrrour of Modestie; Morando, the Tritameron of Love;* and *Gwydonius, the Carde of Fancie.* On the title-page of his little book of 1585, *Planetomachia,* he wrote himself, "Student in Physicke." In the same year he satisfied the natural interest of the public in what was for that time of conflict with Catholicism one of the great topics of the day, the death of the pope, by translating through the French, *An Oration, or Funerall Sermon, uttered at Roome, at the Buriall of the Holy Father, Gregorie the XIII., who departed in Christ Jesus, the 11th of Aprill,* 1585. In this or the next year Greene married. He himself told, in one of his last writings, of the vicious way of life into which he had now fallen. Dramatists and players enjoyed jovial fellowship at the tavern, the money soon earned was soon spent; temptations pressed on the weak will, and more than one fine mind sank under them. Greene's wife, a gentleman's daughter, endeavoured in vain to part him from bad company; he says that he spent her marriage portion, and after the birth of a child forsook her ; she going into Lincolnshire, he working on in London, " where in short space I fell into favour with such as were of honourable and good calling. But here note that though I knew how to get a friend, yet I had not the gift or reason how to keep a friend." In these and all such words we must not omit to observe that Greene's object in accusing himself was to warn others to keep in the right way. He was, like Occleve in one of his poems (ch. v. § 8), seeking to win hearts to his cause by holding a brief against himself as advocate for virtue. But Greene was actually sinking low in 1590, and within two years of death. His plays remained unprinted until after his death. The actors were unwilling to chill interest in a play, while it was still upon the stage, by publication of its dialogue. The date, therefore, of the first printing of any good Elizabethan play is often much later than that of its first performance. Love-pamphlets Greene was issuing steadily. In 1587, *Euphues, his Censure to Philautus,* was followed by an *Arcadia.* In 1588 he printed *Pandosto; or, the Triumph of Time,* the story upon which Shakespeare founded his "Winter's Tale." In the same year followed a collection of stories, poems, and reflections, called *Perimedes, the Blacke-Smith: a Golden Methode how to vse the Mind in Pleasant and Profitable Exercise.* If Greene was himself falling from the true standard of life, yet to the last he laboured to maintain it in his writings. Perimedes was followed, still in the same year, by *Alcida*, or *Greene's Metamorphosis;* and, in 1589, by the *Spanish Masquerado, Tullie's Love,* and *Orpharion.*

60. **Christopher Marlowe,** who advanced the Elizabethan drama to the point from which Shakespeare rose to the supreme heights of poetry, was six years younger than George Peele. He was but two months older than Shakespeare ; born at Canterbury in Shakespeare's birth-year, 1564, one of several children of John Marlowe, shoemaker, and clerk of St. Mary's, and he was baptised on the 26th of February. He was educated first at the King's School, Canterbury, and then at Corpus Christi (Benet) College, Cambridge. For his University education he must have been indebted to the kindness of some liberal man who had observed his genius. He did not go with a scholarship from the King's School. He graduated as B.A. in 1583, as M.A. in 1587, by which time he had achieved great success at a stroke with his play of *Tamburlaine the Great.* The theme, like the grievance of Mycetes, with which it opened, required " a great and thundering speech," and Marlowe did not, like Mycetes, find himself " insufficient to express the same." The old British public had enjoyed for centuries, in Herod of the miracle-plays (ch. iv. § 5), the character of a pompous braggart, who could rant well. In one of the sets of plays Herod's speeches were crowded with words that began with "r," for greater convenience of r-r-rolling them well in his mouth. Marlowe gave them a Tamburlaine who could out-herod Herod, and he roared Marlowe into sudden fame. The desire indeed was so great to hear him roar, that Marlowe let him roar again, and maintained his success by the production of a *Second Part of Tamburlaine.* The two parts were first printed in 1590, without author's name. These plays were founded on the story of Tamerlane, or Timour the Tartar, who after leading his countrymen to their own deliverance from foreign oppression, was crowned at Samarcand in 1370, and presently set forth on a career of conquest. In 1402, he made the great Ottoman sultan, Bajazet, his prisoner. He had set out in winter weather, at the age of seventy, for the addition of China to his conquests, when he died. In the embodiment of this notion of an all-devouring conqueror, "the scourge of God," Marlowe used the blank verse, which had not then secured its footing on the public stage. Our first tragedy was in that new

measure ; but it was written for Christmas entertainment at the
Inner Temple.  Blank verse was used in the last two acts of
"The Arraignment of Paris ;" but that was written for the queen
and court.  The plays for the public were in prose or rhyme,
till the Prologue of Tamburlaine said to the people :

> " From jigging veins of rhyming mother wits,
> And such conceits as clownage keeps in pay,
> We'll lead you to the stately tent of war,
> Where you shall hear the Scythian Tamburlaine
> Threaten the world with high astounding terms,
> And scourging kingdoms with his conquering sword."

Marlowe, by his "Tamburlaine," and by the better plays
which followed it, developed blank verse as the measure for
English dramatic poetry, made its worth felt, and was among
dramatists the first cause of its general adoption.

"Tamburlaine" is rant glorified.  It was enjoyed even by
those who laughed at it.  The boldest stroke was in the opening
of the 3rd Scene of the 4th Act of Part II.  "Enter Tamburlaine, drawn in his chariot by the Kings of Trebizon and Soria
with bits in their mouths, reins in his left hand, and in his right
hand a whip with which he scourgeth them."

> " ' Holla, ye pamper'd jades of Asia !
> What ! can ye draw but twenty miles a day,
> And have so proud a chariot at your heels,
> And such a coachman as great Tamburlaine ?'"

Marlowe's *Tragical History of Doctor Faustus* probably
appeared on the stage in 1589, in blank verse intermixed with
scenes of prose ; but it was not printed in the lifetime of its
author.  The hero of this famous legend, which is said by some
to have been grafted upon Faust the printer (ch. v. § 26), seems
to have been really a man who, at the beginning of the sixteenth
century, affected pre-eminence in necromancy, astrology, and
magic, and took as one of his sounding names, "Faustus," for
its Latin meaning—favourable, or auspicious.  About him, as a
centre of crystallisation, tales ascribed in the first instance to
other conjurors arranged themselves until he became the popular
ideal of one who sought to sound the depths of this world's
knowledge and enjoyment without help from God.  But in the
religious controversies of the sixteenth century, the connection
between Faustus and Satan associated this legend in the minds
of ardent Reformers with the Church of Rome ; and in 1587
there appeared at Frankfort, written with a strong Protestant

O

feeling, the first elaborated " History of Dr. Faustus," told as a
terrible example to all high-flying, headstrong, and Godless men.
It gathered about Faustus more old tales of magic, and was so
popular that it was reprinted in 1588.    From this edition of
1588 an English story-book of Dr. Faustus was translated.
This book Marlowe also translated in his nobler way, taking the
plot of his play either from the German original, or from this
first translation, perhaps while it was yet in hand.

Marlowe, in telling this tale on the stage, made no division
into acts.   Using the chorus as narrator of any part of a tale
that was not to be shown or told during the action, Marlowe
first brought in Chorus to tell how Faustus was born of poor
parents, at Rhodes, in Germany, taught at Wittenburg made
Doctor of Divinity, and excelled all in dispute,

> " Till swoln with cunning of a self conceit,
> His waxen wings did mount above his reach,
> And melting, heavens conspired his overthrow."

He turned to magic—"And this the man that in his study sits."
Chorus then left the audience to hear Faustus condemn each of
the sciences in turn, discard the Bible, and swell with desire for
the magician's power, stretching as far as doth the mind of man.
The people saw his good and evil angels stand beside him, as he
heard one warn, the other tempt.   They saw him yield himself to Valdes and Cornelius, to be taught magic arts ; saw
Mephistophiles appear to his incantation in his own natural
ugliness, but, at Faust's bidding, reappear in the shape of a
Franciscan Friar.   Compelled to answer, Mephistophiles spoke
truth.   The people heard Faustus disdain the fear of God :

> " But leaving the vain trifles of men's souls,
>   Tell me what is that Lucifer thy lord ?
> *Meph.* Arch-regent and commander of all spirits.
> *Faust.* Was not that Lucifer an angel once ?
> *Meph.* Yes, Faustus, and most dearly-loved of God.
> *Faust.* How comes it, then, that he is prince of devils ?
> *Meph.* Oh, by aspiring pride and insolence ;
>   For which God threw him from the face of heaven.
> *Faust.* And what are you that live with Lucifer ?
> *Meph.* Unhappy spirits that fell with Lucifer,
>   Conspired against our God with Lucifer,
>   And are for ever damned with Lucifer.
> *Faust.* How comes it, then, that thou art out of hell ?
> *Meph.* Why this is hell, nor am I out of it ;
>   Think'st thou that I, that saw the face of God,
>   And tasted the eternal joys of heaven,
>   Am not tormented with ten thousand hells ?

> In being deprived of everlasting bliss?
> O Faustus, leave these frivolous demands
> Which strike a terror to my fainting soul.
> *Faust.* What! Is great Mephistophiles so passionate
> For being deprived of the joys of heaven?
> Learn then of Faustus manly fortitude,
> And scorn those joys thou never shalt possess."

Boldly Faustus sends an offer of his soul to Lucifer, for four-and-twenty years of his own will. At midnight he expects the answer. Midnight approaches, and again his good and evil angels speak at either ear. The guardian angel's voice is heard in vain. The bond is signed with blood stabbed from the arm. Upon the first hour of its enjoyment a touch of repentance breaks. Again his good angel pleads with him; his evil angel seeks to harden him against the warning voice. His heart is hardened, he cannot repent. He questions Mephistophiles upon the heavenly spheres; and he is answered. He asks, "Who made the world?" and his familiar will not tell. Again comes the pang of conscience. He cries to himself, " Think Faustus upon God who made the world!"

> "*Re-enter* Good Angel *and* Evil Angel.
> " *E. Ang.* Too late.
> . *G. Ang.* Never too late, if Faustus will repent.
> *E. Ang.* If thou repent, devils will tear thee in pieces.
> *G. Ang.* Repent, and they shall never raze thy skin.
>     [*Exeunt* Angels.
> *Faust.* O Christ, my Saviour, my Saviour,
> Help thou to save distressed Faustus' soul!"

But Lucifer and Beelzebub now stand with Mephistophiles before him; hold him to his bond; will show him pastime. They introduce to him the seven deadly sins. Chorus explains now to the people that we shall see Faustus next at Rome, and straightway the pomp of the court of Rome is marshalled out for mockery. Pope Adrian in supreme pride ascends his chair, by using for a footstool Saxon Bruno, whom the Emperor appointed. Adrian will depose the Emperor, and curse his people. Then Faustus and Mephistophiles beguile him in his policy; scatter confusion in his court; snatch, being invisible, his dishes and his cup; box his ears; and beat the friars, who come in with bell, book, and candle, to sing maledictions on them. Other scenes follow to represent incidents in the life for which a soul was paid. Touches of farce lie by the tragic scenes. Then Faustus is in his study again. His end is near. To some of his scholars he shows a fair vision of Helen. They depart. An old man enters who, with loving words, warns Faustus of his peril. Faustus despairs. Mephistophiles gives him a dagger. " Oh, stay ! " cries the old man :

> " Oh, stay, good Faustus, stay thy desperate steps !
> I see an angel hover o'er thy head,
> And with a vial full of precious grace
> Offers to pour the same into thy soul :
> Then call for mercy, and avoid despair."

He repents, yet he despairs ; he cannot escape from the toils of Mephistophiles. Helen is brought to him between Cupids, He leaves the stage worshipping her, and then the thunder rolls ; the Powers of Evil enter, and from the background Lucifer and Beelzebub keep grim watch over their victim. With changed looks Faustus parts from his scholars, and they leave him to his last agony on earth. The poet makes its horror felt. The good and evil angels speak again. His good angel sets before him and before the audience, while music sounds, a vision of the heavenly throne among the saints which he has forfeited. His Evil Angel then sets before him and the audience a vision of that " vast perpetual torture-house " to which he goes :

> " Those that are fed with sops of flaming fire
> Were gluttons, and loved only delicates,
> And laughed to see the poor starve at their gates.
> But yet all these are nothing ; thou shalt see
> Ten thousand tortures that more horrid be.
> *Faust.* Oh, I have seen enough to torture me !
> *E. Ang.* Nay, thou must feel them, taste the smart of all ;
> He that loves pleasure must for pleasure fall."

The clock strikes eleven, and the terror of the last hour is then painted. In language drawn from Scripture, Faustus cries in his despair :

> " Mountains and hills, come, come, and fall on me,
> And hide me from the heavy wrath of heaven !
> No !
> Then will I run headlong into the earth ;
> Gape earth ! Oh, no, it will not harbour me ! "

The terror grows, and the clock strikes the half hour. Faustus now cries in his anguish :

> " Cursed be the parents that engender'd me !
> No, Faustus, curse thyself, curse Lucifer,
> That hath deprived thee of the joys of heaven."

The clock strikes twelve, and the audience sees the terrible fulfilment of the bond. Depths of religious energy were stirred when this was the new play, and the last great event in the real world had been the defeat of the Spanish Armada.

Marlowe's *Faustus* represents the highest point reached by the Elizabethan drama before 1590. Shakespeare, who had come unknown and poor among the dramatists and actors, with credentials from no University, was then quietly and surely working his way up. Bound to the truth of nature, he could not rise by an audacity like that of Marlowe, who in 1590 had a higher public reputation. There is no genuine evidence that Shakespeare had shares in a theatre until he was one of " those deserving men " who were made partners in the profits of *The Globe*, which was built of the materials of *The Theatre* in the beginning of 1599.

61. **Philip Sidney,** at court again, after the months of retirement at Wilton, during which he wrote " Arcadia," was knighted by Elizabeth in January, 1583, when his age was about twenty-eight. In the following March he was married to Frances, eldest daughter of Sir Francis Walsingham, and the next year was spent in married peace. Sidney wrote sonnets in those days —" Passions " of the old conventional type—meaning, as usual, to address them to some lady who deserved compliment, and of whom his conventional rhapsodies could not very well be taken seriously. As the Earl of Surrey addressed his love exercises to a child for whom the court felt sympathy, Sidney paid the like compliment to an unhappy wife. Penelope Devereux, daughter to his old friend the late Earl of Essex, had once been talked of as his own possible wife. Her father said that he would have been proud of Philip Sidney for a son-in-law. And if so why had the match not taken place? If Sidney had been really devoted to the lady he could have married her. He did not marry her because he did not wish to do so, and in his own day no reasonable being ever supposed that he paid suit to her except in the way of verse. Towards the close of 1580, Penelope, then about eighteen, was married by her guardian against her will to Lord Robert Rich, heir to the ill-gotten wealth of Lord Chancellor Rich. That chancellor, the grandson of two thriving London mercers, had risen by his want of principle, and had secured to himself great bargains at the suppression of the monasteries. He grasped wealth enough to endow two earldoms acquired by his descendants. The chancellor died in 1568, and his son Robert, second baron Rich, died in 1581, leaving his son and heir, another Lord

Robert, the rich man to whom Penelope was sold.  She protested even at the altar.   The contractor for her is described as "of an uncourtly disposition, unsociable, austere, and of no very agreeable conversation to her."   The unhappiness of her forced marriage made Lady Rich at this time an object or considerate attention.   Philip Sidney was an old friend of her father's, and he gave her the place of honour in his sonnet-writing, wherein she was to be Stella (" the Star "), he Astrophel " the  Lover of  the Star ") ; and certainly, as all the court knew, and as the forms of such ingenious love-poetry implied, so far as love in the material sense was concerned, with as much distance between them as if she had shone upon him from above the clouds.   Sidney's *Astrophel and Stella* sonnets were being written at the time when he was about to marry Fanny Walsingham ; and in those earnest Elizabethan days, at the fitfully strict court of Elizabeth, since the character of such poetical love-passions was then understood, they brought upon Sidney's credit not a breath of censure.   As for Lady Rich, she gave herself to Sir Christopher Blount, who became Lord Mountjoy in 1600, and after divorce from her husband she married him.   But that was a real passion, and what each felt in it was not told for the amusement of the public.

In 1584 the course of events led Sir Philip Sidney to advocate direct attack by sea upon the Spanish power.  He would have Elizabeth come forward as Defendress of the Faith, at the head of a great Protestant League.  He was a member of the Parliament that met in November, 1584, and in July, 1585, he was joined with the Earl of Warwick in the Mastership of the Ordnance.   His strongest desires caused him to look in two directions for his course of action : he might aid in direct attack on the Spanish possessions, which, as source of treasure, were a source of power ; he might aid in the rescue from Spain of the Netherlands.  During a great part of the year 1585 his mind was very much with Drake and Raleigh.

62. Naval enterprise had advanced rapidly in England since the days of the Cabots (ch. v. § 29).   In 1574, George Gascoigne (§ 29) obtained from **Sir Humphrey Gilbert**—who had been knighted for his services against the Irish—his *Discourse to prove a Passage by the North-West to Cathay and the East Indies.*   He first sought to prove that America was an island ; and then brought together the reports of voyagers by whom a North-West Passage to Cathay and India had been attempted.

By this route only, he argued, we could share the wealth derived by Spain and Portugal from traffic with the East ; be unmolested by them in our course; and undersell them in their markets, besides finding new sources of wealth, and founding colonies for the relief of overcrowded England.

This treatise revived interest in the subject. It passed from hand to hand in M.S., and was printed in 1576, the year in which Martin Frobisher started, on board the *Gabriel*, of twenty-five tons burthen, upon the first of his three voyages in search of a North-West Passage. He entered the bay called Frobisher's Straits, and believed that through this he should find a passage. He was away four months, and from a piece of stone brought back with him it was inferred that he had found a region rich in gold. A "Company of Cathay" was formed, with Frobisher for Captain-General by Sea, and Admiral of the ships and Navy of the company. This company received its charter in March, 1577 ; and in May Frobisher started on his second voyage. The chief aim now was to secure a gold district on the north shore of America. He took possession of Meta Incognita for Queen Elizabeth, and carried home 200 tons of the supposed ore, reaching England again at the close of September. The adventurers did not find satisfaction in their ore ; it was admitted to be "poor in respect of that brought last year, and of that which we know may be brought the next year." At the end of May, 1578, Frobisher started again. He found the channel afterwards known as Hudson's Straits, but was obliged to hold to the search for gold, and his little fleet brought home, after many perils, a good supply of the stones, out of which no gold could be got. The Cathay Company broke up in quarrel and confusion, and Frobisher himself was brought low by the unlucky bit of stone on which he stumbled. It had excited thirst for gold, which ruined both his enterprise and him. Francis Drake, a Devonshire sailor's son, had been a sea-captain at the age of twenty-two. He had served against the Spaniards, under Sir John Hawkins ; had damaged them much in an expedition of his own in 1572. In November, 1577, he had been entrusted with a little fleet of five vessels to attempt a voyage into the South Seas through the Straits of Magellan, and in November, 1580, he returned in his own ship, the *Pelican*, from his memorable voyage round the globe. The queen knighted him in April, 1581, and ordered his ship to be preserved.

In June, 1578, Sir Humphrey Gilbert obtained a charter for

discovery and occupation of distant and barbarous lands, and for the planting of a colony which he was to rule "as near as conveniently might be according to the laws of England." His half brother, **Sir Walter Raleigh,** went with him on his first unlucky voyage (§ 46), and returned with him to Plymouth in May, 1579. After this, Gilbert fought in Ireland and the Netherlands. In the summer of 1583, having raised money by admitting others to a share in the adventure, Gilbert and Raleigh started again, and arrived at St. John's Harbour, in Newfoundland, where were some six-and-thirty vessels of merchants and fishermen. There Gilbert determined to set up his colony. The traders agreed to join the colonists in paying their tax to the governor; but of the colonists brought with him, most were men from whom the steadier sort asked to be taken away home. After many misfortunes, Gilbert on the homeward voyage went down with his vessel, the last words heard from him by those on board a companion ship being his cry to them, as he stood firm to the helm of his own little craft—the *Squirrel,* of ten tons—" Courage, my friends, we are as near heaven by sea as on the land."

Such letters-patent as Gilbert had held were given by the queen, in March, 1584, to his half-brother, Walter Raleigh. In April he sent out Captains Barlow and Amadas, in two vessels, to explore the coast of America from Florida northward, and report promptly upon any region he found fit for colonising. They returned in September, after a fortunate voyage, and Captain Barlow gave an excellent account of the shores to which our maiden queen was pleased to give the name of " Virginia."

In the spring of 1585, Raleigh sent a fleet of seven vessels to Virginia, in charge of his cousin, Sir Richard Grenville, with Ralph Lane, who was to be governor of the colony they went to found. Lane was left with 105 colonists on the island of Roanoake. In the same year Sir Francis Drake was sent as admiral, with a fleet of twenty-one ships, against the Spaniards in the West Indies. **Sir Philip Sidney** helped towards the fitting of this expedition, and was bent on taking part in it himself, sharing authority with Drake after they had put to sea. Sidney went to Plymouth; but his secret plan became known, and his sailing with Drake's fleet was stayed by the queen's absolute command. Drake, therefore, sailed without him in September; and soon afterwards a daughter was born to Sir Philip Sidney, who was baptised Elizabeth, the queen standing as sponsor. Then he went to his death in the Low Countries.

63. The seven northern provinces of Holland had declared their independence on the 29th of September, 1580. In 1584, William of Orange had been assassinated. In 1585, the ten southern provinces were conquered by the Prince of Parma. Catherine de' Medici was in that year proposing to Philip of Spain invasion of England for the crushing of heresy. Philip pointed to heretics nearer home. Protestants of the Netherlands appealed to England, and on the 10th of August, 1585, a treaty was signed at Nonsuch, stipulating that England should provide 5,000 foot-soldiers and 1,000 horse to aid war in the Netherlands, while, as security for expenses, and as headquarters for troops, temporary possession was to be taken of Flushing, Brill, and the Castle of Rammekins. Then England declared war for three objects: to secure peace to all of the Reformed Faith; restoration to the Netherlands of ancient rights; and the safety of England. The English went out with the Earl of Leicester for their leader; Sir Philip Sidney as Governor of Flushing and of Rammekins; and Sir Thomas Cecil, eldest son of Lord Burghley, as Governor of Brill. Sidney went to his post in November, 1585; the earl followed in December, and spent over-much time in feasting. Sidney's heart was in his duty; he planned work in vain, and he sought in vain to protect the poor soldiers against chiefs who enriched themselves out of their pay and their supplies. In January, Leicester offended Elizabeth by accepting from the States the rank of Governor-General of the United Provinces. Sir Philip Sidney fretted at inaction. His wife joined him at Flushing. In May, 1586, Sidney received news of the death of his father. In July, he had a chief part in the capture of Axel. In August his mother died. In September he joined with Sir John Norris and Count Lewis William of Nassau, in the investment of Zutphen. On the 22nd of that month Sir Philip Sidney received his death wound in a gallant assault made by a few hundred English against a thousand cavalry, and under fire from walls and trenches. A musket-ball from one of the trenches shattered Sidney's thigh-bone. His horse took fright and galloped back, but the wounded man held to his seat. He was then carried to his uncle, asked for water, and when it was given, saw a dying soldier carried past, who eyed it greedily. At once he gave the water to the soldier, saying, "Thy necessity is yet greater than

o *

mine." Sidney lived on, patient in suffering, until the 17th of
October. When he was speechless before death, one who stood
by asked Philip Sidney for a sign of his continued trust in God.
He folded his hands as in prayer over his breast, and so they
were become fixed and chill when the watchers placed them by
his side, and in a few minutes the stainless representative of the
young manhood of Elizabethan England passed away.

64. In the same year Ralph Lane and his colonists were
brought back from Roanoake, rescued by Drake, as he returned
from his West Indian expedition. The colonists had ruined
themselves by ill-treatment of the friendly natives, whom they
had converted into foes. They brought tobacco back with
them, and were the first to teach England the art of smoking
it. **Thomas Hariot**, one of their number, published in 1588
*A Briefe and True Report of The New Found Land of Virginia,
&c.*, in which he described the cultivation by the natives of the
herb which they called *appowoc*, but the Spaniards, *tabacco.*
" They use to take the fume or smoke thereof by sucking it
through pipes made of claie into their stomacke and heade,"
with wonderfully good results. " We ourselves," Hariot added,
" during the time we were there, vsed to suck it after their
maner, as also since our returne, and have found manie rare
and wonderful experiments of the vertues thereof; of which
the relation would require a volume by itselfe: the vse of it by
so manie of late, men and women of great calling as else, and
some learned phisitions also, is sufficient witnes."

The year of the death of Sidney, and the return of Drake
from his success in the West Indies, 1586, was the year also
of the plot known as Babington's Conspiracy, for the murder
of Elizabeth and setting of Queen Mary upon the throne.
Elizabeth's secretary, Walsingham, gave Mary full opportunity
of committing herself to this scheme before it was disclosed.
She was then tried, under a commission issued in October.
That she had plotted for her own rescue by a Spanish invasion,
Mary did not deny. She denied privity in the conspiracy for
assassination, but was declared guilty of that, the sentence being
without derogation to James King of Scots. On the 8th of
February, 1587, Mary Queen of Scots was executed in the
Great Hall at Fotheringay. A week afterwards there was in
London a funeral pageant for Sir Philip Sidney.

**Raleigh** was growing rich by his adventures. Sir Richard
Grenville, who arrived too late at Roanoake for the relief of

Lane and his party, obtained great booty from Spain on the way home.  One of Raleigh's privateers took a Spanish ship in the Azores with great treasure of gold, jewels, and merchandise.  Two barks of his in the Azores made more prizes than they were able to bring home.  Raleigh was in favour too, at court, knighted (1585), enriched with 12,000 acres of forfeited land in Ireland (1586), with a lucrative licence for the sale of wines, with the profits on over-lengths of cloth, alone worth more than £4,000 a year.  He was made Captain of the Guard, Gentleman of the Privy Chamber, Lord Warden of the Stannaries, and Lord-Lieutenant of Cornwall.  Money was sunk in the attempts to colonise Virginia, but it was only a part of the money made by Spanish prizes.  Another expedition to Virginia was sent out by Raleigh in 1587; it was unsuccessful, and, in March, 1589, Raleigh transferred his patent to a company of merchants.  In 1588, Raleigh was at work with all his might upon the raising of a fleet to resist Spanish invasion.  Elizabeth was excommunicated by Pope Sixtus V.  Crusade was preached against England; the Armada came.  On board one of its ships was Cervantes.  On Sunday, the 24th of November, 1588, Queen Elizabeth went in state to St. Paul's, to return thanks for the defeat of the Armada.  Shakespeare, with his career before him, was at work in London in those days, with his great successes all to come, but sharing the deep feelings that bred noble thought in the Elizabethan time.

The narratives of our adventurous seafarers were in those days treasured for posterity by **Richard Hakluyt**, who was born at Eyton, Herefordshire, in 1553.  He was educated at Westminster School, and Christchurch, Oxford, and delighted always in tales of far countries and adventure by sea.  He entered the Church, went to Paris in 1584, as chaplain to the English Ambassador, and was made prebendary of Bristol.  In 1582, when he was twenty-nine years old, Hakluyt issued his first publication, *Divers Voyages Touching the Discoverie of America, and the Lands adjacent unto the same, made first of all by our Englishmen, and afterward by the Frenchmen and Bretons: and certain Notes of Advertisements for Observations, necessarie for such as shall hereafter make the like attempt.*  Hakluyt also translated books of travel from the Spanish, but his great work was that which first appeared in folio in 1589—*The Principal Navigations, Voyages, and Discoveries made by the English Nation.*

65. In such times **William Camden** (§ 16) published his *Britannia*, which described the country that had risen to its front place in the world ; and **William Warner**, born in London in the year of Elizabeth's accession, a poetical attorney, celebrated *Albion's England* in thirteen books of fourteen-syllabled rhyming verse, first published in 1586. His poem was of Albion's England, because it did not, like Albion, include Scotland. It was an easy, lively, homely history of England, from the Deluge down to Warner's own time, homely in use of simple idiomatic English, full of incidents and stories, often rudely told, and often with a force or delicacy of touch that came of the terse directness with which natural feeling was expressed. Warner's poem had for a time great popularity. He was not a great poet, but the times were stirring, and they drew ten thousand lines of lively verse upon his country, even out of an attorney.

66. But the Elizabethan time, like any other, had its surface follies and its varieties of fashion. In 1583 the Reverend **Philip Stubbes** published *The Anatomie of Abuses : conteyning a Discoverie or Briefe Summarie of such Notable Vices and Imperfections as now raigne in many Christian Countreyes of the World : but especialie in a very famous Ilande called Ailgna* : *Together with most fearful Examples of God's Judgementes executed vpon the wicked for the same as well in Ailgna of late, as in other places elsewhere.* Ailgna, of course is Anglia, and a second part of " The Anatomie of Abuses " appeared in the same year. The book is in dialogue between Philoponus and Spudeus. Ailgla, says Stubbes, is a famous and pleasant land, with a great and heroic people, but they abound in abuses, chiefly those of pride ; pride of heart, of mouth, of apparel. In pride of apparel they pane, cut, and drape out with costly ornaments the richest material, and spread out ruffs with supportasses—wires covered with gold or silk— and starch. Philip Stubbes denounced starch as "the devil's liquor," and told of a fair gentlewoman of Eprautna (Antwerp) upon whom a judgment had fallen for her vanity in starched ruffs, even so lately as the 22nd of May, 1582. She was dressing to attend a wedding, and falling in a passion with the starching of her ruffs, said what caused a handsome gentleman to come into the room, who set them up for her to perfection, charmed her, and strangled her. When she was being taken out for burial, the coffin was so heavy that four

strong men could not lift it. It was opened. The body was gone; but a lean and deformed black cat was sitting in the coffin, "a setting of great ruffs and frizzling of hair, to the great fear and wonder of all the beholders."

67. The days that were to produce great poets produced also discussions on the Art of Poetry. Young King James of Scotland had tried his 'prentice hand at this (§ 51); Sidney had written "An Apologie for Poëtrie" (§ 44). **William Webbe**, of whom little is known, was a Cambridge man, who took his B.A. in 1573, and was a friend of Harvey and Spenser. He was afterwards private tutor in the Sulyard family, at the manor-house of Flemings, near Chelmsford, and there he wrote in the summer evenings *A Discourse of English Poetrie*, which was printed in 1586. Webbe shared Gabriel Harvey's interest in the reformed English versifying. His book, which dwells much on Phaer's "Virgil," and most upon Spenser's "Shepheard's Calender" (§ 31), leads up to a discussion of metres, with special reference to Latin models and to his own translation of the first two Eclogues of Virgil into English hexameters; beginning thus:

> "Tityrus, happilie thou lyste tumbling under a beech tree,
> All in a fine oate pipe these sweete songs lustilie chaunting."

Webbe added to his little book a summary of Horace's "Art of Poetry," taken from George Fabricius, of Kemnitz, himself a very good poet in Latin, who died in 1571. Another Elizabethan book upon the art of verse was by **George Puttenham** — *The Art of English Poesie, in Three Books; the first of Poets and Poesye, the second of Proportion, and the third of Ornamente*—written about 1585, and published in the spring of 1589. The author, who cited a dozen other works of his own which are lost, was born about 1530, had been a scholar at Oxford, had delighted in verse and written it, had seen the courts of France, Spain, Italy and the Empire, and was skilled in French, Italian, and Spanish, as well as in Greek and Latin. There was no author's name on the title-page of his book; but as early as 1605 it was said to be by George Puttenham, one of the queen's gentlemen pensioners. The book is a systematic little treatise of some extent, dealing with the origin and nature of poetry; its several forms, as satire, comedy, tragedy, &c.: its several metres and proportions, including the various ways of writing verse in shapes, as the lozenge, or rombus; the fuzie spindle, or romboides; the triangle, or tricquet; the square; the pillar, pilaster, or cylinder; taper, or piramis; rondel, or sphere; egg, or figure oval; with many of these reversed and combined; a fashion then coming into use from Italy and France. Puttenham says that an Eastern traveller whom he met in Italy told him that this fashion was brought from the courts of the great princes of China and Tartary. The introducer of "shaped verses" into Europe is said to have been a Simmias of Rhodes, who lived under Ptolemy Soter, about 324 B.C. Puttenham's argument concerning metres includes, of course, some reference to the question of Latin quantity applied to English verse. The last book discusses the language of the poet; tropes and figures of speech, with examples; fitness of manner, and the art that conceals art. Among illustrations of poetical ornament is a poem by Queen Elizabeth herself, written when the presence of Mary Queen of Scots in England was breeding faction; and the Queen of England, "nothing ignorant in those secret favours, though she had long, with great wisdom and pacience, dissembled it, writeth this ditty most sweet and sententious, not hiding from all such aspiring minds the daunger of their ambition and disloyaltie:"

> " The doubt of future foes exiles my present joy,
> And wit me warns to shun such snares as threaten mine annoy.
> For falsehood now doth flow, and subject faith doth ebb,
> Which would not be if reason ruled or wisdom weaved the web.
> But clouds of toys untried do cloak aspiring minds,
> Which turn to rain of late repent by course of changed winds
> The top of hope supposed the root of ruth will be,
> And fruitless all their graffed guiles, as shortly ye shall see.
> Then dazzled eyes with pride, which great ambition blinds,
> Shall be unsealed by worthy wights, whose foresight falsehood finds;
> The daughter of debate, that eke discord doth sow,                .
> Shall reap no gain where former rule hath taught still peace to grow,
> No foreign banished wight shall anchor in this port,
> Our realm it brooks no stranger's force, let them elsewhere resort.
> Our rusty sword with rest shall first his edge employ
> To poll their topes that seek such change and gape for joy."

68. The year of the publication of George Puttenham's book, 1589, was the year of chief activity in the *Martin Marprelate* Controversy. Martin Marprelate was the name under which first one epistle writer then many companions of his in the work of " Pistling the Bishops "—nearly all these writers being deprived ministers—waged war against that which Elizabethan Puritans condemned in Episcopacy. Government sought to suppress their publications. They were " printed in Europe not fur from some bouncing priests;" or " over sea, in Europe, within two

furlongs of a bouncing priest, at the cost and charges of Martin
Marprelate, gent." The first tract was temperately answered
by Thomas Cooper, Bishop of Winchester, in *An Admonition
to the People of England.* This made Cooper himself an object
of attack. The Martinists were earnest men, who affected light
speech to win light minds of the many to their side. The books
were printed at a wandering press, hunted by the Government
from Moulsey, near Kingston-on-Thames, where it was first set
up, to Fawsley, in Northamptonshire, thence to Norton, thence
to Coventry, thence to Welstone, in Warwickshire, whence
letters were sent to another press in or near Manchester, which
was found printing *More Work for a Cooper.* The chief Martinists were John Penry, John Udall, John Field, and Job
Throckmorton, who wrote, *Hae ye any Work for Cooper.* John
**Penry,** a Welshman, bred at both Universities, and earnestly
devoted to his cause, was hurried to the gallows for his writings.
Yet, as he wrote before his execution, " I never did anything in
this cause for contention, vain-glory, or to draw disciples after
me. Great things in this life I never sought for: sufficiency I
had, with great outward trouble; but most content I was with
my lot, and content with my untimely death, though I leave
behind me a friendless widow and four infants." **John Udall,**
left unexecuted, died in prison. He was tried for the authorship
of an anonymous book, called, *The Demonstration of Discipline;*
and when he would have called witnesses they were refused
hearing, on the ground that witnesses in favour of the prisoner
were against the queen. " It is for the queen," said John Udall,
"to hear all things, when the life of any of her subjects is in
question." The literary war against the maintainers of Martin
Marprelate was carried on by the wits and playwrights. **John
Lyly** did not write *Pap with a Hatchet; or, a Fig for my Godson; or, Crack me this Nut. To be sold at the sign of the Crab-
tree Cudgel, in Thwack-coat Lane.* "Who," one said in it,
" would curry an ass with an ivory comb? Give the beast thistles
for provender." Conscious of the unseemly tone of the whole
controversy, he wrote towards the end, " If this vein bleed but six
ounces more, I shall prove to be a pretty railer, and so in time
grow to a proper Martinist ; " and he took leave of his adversary
with a " farewell and be hanged." The piece cannot be Lyly's.

Another active writer was a scurrilous and unscrupulous
young wit, **Thomas Nash,** then about twenty-three years old,
beginning to be active as a dashing pamphleteer. One of his

pieces was called *Almond for a Parrot ; or, an Alms for Martin.*
**Francis Bacon** was twenty-nine years old when, in his paper
on these *Controversies of the Church* (§ 48), he reasoned against
contention about ceremonies and things indifferent, strife in a
spirit opposite to that of St. James's admonition, " Let every
man be swift to hear, slow to speak, slow to wrath." Bacon
thought men over-ready to say of their own private opinions,
" Not I, but the Lord," where Paul said " I, and not the Lord,"
or " according to my counsel ; " he desired, therefore, as to the
Church controversies, to point out " what it is on either part
that keepeth the wound green, and formalizeth both sides to a
further opposition, and worketh an indisposition in men's minds
to be reunited." " And, first of all," he said, " it is more than
time that there were an end and surcease made of this immodest
and deformed manner of writing lately entertained, whereby
matters of religion are handled in the style of the stage."
Bitter and earnest writing came, he said, of an enthusiasm not
to be hastily condemned ; but to leave all reverent and religious
compassion towards evils, to intermix Scripture and scurrility
sometimes in one sentence, was far from the manner of a
Christian.  It was an evil, too, " that there is not an indifferent
hand carried towards these pamphlets as they deserve.  For
the one sort flieth in the dark, the other is uttered openly.  And
we see it ever falleth out that the forbidden writing is thought
to be certain sparks of a truth that fly up in the faces of those
that seek to choke and tread it out ; whereas a book authorised
is thought to be but the language of the time."  Bacon thought
that, except Bishop Cooper's, the pamphlets were equally bad
on both sides.  As to the occasion of the controversies, if
any bishops be as all are said to be, let them amend ; men
might abate some of their vanities of controversial zeal, think
less of measuring the value of religion by its distance from the
error last condemned as heresy, and care less about introducing
new forms from abroad.  Bacon, whose mother sympathised
with the Nonconformists, avowed in this paper his own adherence
to the established system in the Church, but he desired to urge
on both parties moderation, a spirit of concession in discussing
mere externals, and a better sense of Christian brotherhood,
for " the wrath of man worketh not the righteousness of God."
" A contentious retaining of custom," he urged, " is a turbulent
thing, as well as innovation."  He agreed " that a character of
love is more proper for debates of this nature than that of

zeal," and trusted that what he had said should "find a correspondence in their minds which are not embarked in partiality,
and which love the whole better than a part."

69. In August, 1589, the rule of the house of Valois came to
an end in France by the assassination of Henry III.  The king
in the preceding December had by assassination got rid of his
powerful opponents, the Duke of Guise, head of the Catholic
League, and the duke's brother, the Cardinal of Lorraine.  The
League was therefore in open revolt against him; the Sorbonne
released Frenchmen from their oath of allegiance to him; the
pope excommunicated him; and he was driven into alliance with
Henry of Navarre and the Huguenots for the recovery of his
capital.  At the beginning of these days Catherine de' Medici
died.  While the King of France and the King of Navarre,
whom the League wished to exclude from the succession, were
besieging Paris, Henry III. was stabbed by an enthusiastic
young Dominican.  Before he died he acknowledged the King
of Navarre his successor.  Henry IV. thus became King of
France, with a promise to maintain the Catholic faith and the
property and rights of the Church.  Many of his Huguenot
followers fell from him, because they looked on this as an
engagement to protect idolatry.  But the League opposed him.
Queen Elizabeth sent succour of men, and £22,000 in money.
In September Henry IV. repulsed the Leaguers at Arques.  At
the end of October he carried the suburbs of Paris.  He then
retired on Tours, making that his capital.  On the 14th of
March, 1590, he obtained a signal victory over the Leaguers
and the Spanish auxiliaries at the battle of Ivry, in which "the
divine Bartas" fought.

Against England Spain was yet gathering force.  He would
persevere, Philip said, even if he sold the silver candlesticks on
his table.  But England had risen to the occasion.  The golden
time of Athens was the time when the soul of the people was
stirred nobly in contest for liberty against the power of the
Persians.  The Netherlands were so much the better for their
life-struggle on behalf of all that men should hold most dear,
that while the southern unemancipated provinces were declining,
the Dutch were adding to the streets of their old towns, new
towns were erected by the industries that flocked in, and in
the year 1586-7 eight hundred ships entered their ports.  So
England, trained for generations in the path of duty, faced the
great peril of these days, held in the world of thought the

ground which she had thus far conquered, and, gathering all her
energies, went strongly forward.   When, in 1589, Drake was
sent as admiral, with Sir John Norris in command of the land
forces, to attack the Spanish power over Portugal, by making
Don Antonio king, **George Peele**, the dramatist (§ 55, 57), sang
*A Farewell, entituled to the Famous and Fortunate Generalls of
our English Forces: Sir John Norris and Sir Francis Drake,
knights, and all theyr brave and resolute followers;* to which he
added his *Tale of Troy* (§ 55), then first printed.   Peele's cry
was:

> " To arms, to arms, to glorious arms !
>   With noble Norris and victorious Drake,
>   Under the sanguine cross, brave England's badge,
>   To propagate religious piety;
>
>    *    *    *    *    *
>
>   Sail on, pursue your honours to your graves :
>   Heaven is a sacred covering for your heads,
>   And every climate virtue's tabernacle.
>   To arms, to arms, to honourable arms !
>   You fight for Christ, and England's peerless queen,
>   Elizabeth, the wonder of the world,
>   Over whose throne the enemies of God
>   Have thunder'd erst their vain successful braves.
>   Oh, ten times treble happy men, that fight
>   Under the Cross of Christ and England's queen,
>   And follow such as Drake and Norris are !
>   All honours do this cause accompany;
>   All glory on these endless honours waits:
>   These honours and this glory shall He send,
>   Whose honour and whose glory you defend.

Thus spoke out of our literature the mind of England; and such
was its mind in the year 1590, to which we have now brought
down this narrative.

70. **Robert Greene** was much occupied during his last
years in exposure of the cheats of London, by his *Notable
Discovery of Coosnage;* also his two parts of *Coney Catching,*
published in 1591, and a third part of " Coney Catching" in the
year of his death, 1592.   In his novel of *Never Too Late,*
published in 1590, he shadowed his relation to his own wife;
and in the *Groat's Worth of Wit Bought with a Million of
Repentance,* he drew from incidents in his own sad life part of
the story of a reprobate Roberto.   His hero, reduced to a single
groat, said, " Oh, now it is too late to buy wit with thee! and
therefore will I see if I can sell to careless youth what I
negligently forgot to buy."   This novel was published after
Greene's death, in September, 1592.   He died at the house of a

poor shoemaker, near Dowgate, to whom he owed ten pounds.
Under the bond for this money, he wrote to his deserted ·wife,
" Doll, I charge thee, by the love of our youth and by my soul's
rest, that thou wilt see this man paid; for if he and his wife had
not succoured me I had died in the streets." These last lines of
of his, in Chaucer's stanza, were written not long before his
death:

> " Deceiving world, that with alluring toys
>     Hast made my life the subject of thy scorn,
> And scornest now to lend thy fading joys
>     T'outlength my life, whom friends have left forlorn;
>     How well are they that die ere they be born,
> And never see thy sleights, which few men shun
> Till unawares they helpless are undone!
>
> " Oft have I sung of Love, and of his fire;
>     But now I find that poet was advised
> Which made full feasts increasers of desire,
>     And proves weak love was with the poor despised;
>     For when the life with food is not sufficed,
> What thoughts of love, what motion of delight,
> What pleasaunce can proceed from such a wight?
>
> " Witness my want, the murderer of my wit:
>     My ravished sense, of wonted fury reft,
> Wants such conceit as should in poems fit
>     Set down the sorrow wherein I am left;
>     But therefore have high heavens their gifts bereft,
> Because so long they lent them me to use,
> And I so long their bounty did abuse.
>
> " Oh, that a year were granted me to live,
>     And for that year my former wits restored!
> What rules of life, what counsel would I give,
>     How should my sin with sorrow be deplored!
>     But I must die, of every man abhorred:
> Time loosely spent will not again be won;
> My time is loosely spent, and I undone."

Here also the depths were stirred; but the earnest spirit of the
time, and the sweet music it drew from the souls of men,
ennobled also the fallen dramatist whom a town ruffian, " Cutting Ball," defended from arrest. Among Greene's plays was
one, written with Thomas Lodge, called *A Looking-Glass for
London and England.* This was not printed until 1594. In it
the corruption of Nineveh stood as a figure for the sins of
England. Oseas the prophet witnessed and warned from the
stage:

> " Look, London, look; with inward eyes behold
> What lessons the events do here unfold.
> Sin grown to pride, to misery is thrall:
> The warning bell is rung, beware to fall."

At the close of the play the prophet Jonas, who had been calling on Nineveh to repent, turned to the audience of islanders, " whose lands are fattened with the dew of heaven," and exclaimed:

> " O London ! maiden of the mistress isle
> Wrapt in the folds and swathing-clouts of shame,
> In thee more sins than Nineveh contains !
> Contempt of God ; despite of reverend age ;
> Neglect of law ; desire to wrong the poor ;
> 　　　*　　　*　　　*
> Thy neighbours burn, yet dost thou fear no fire ;
> Thy preachers cry, yet dost thou stop thine ears ;
> The 'larum rings, yet sleepest thou secure.
> London, awake, for fear the Lord do frown :
> I set a looking-glass before thine eyes.
> Oh, turn, oh, turn, with weeping to the Lord,
> And think the prayers and virtues of thy queen
> Defer the plague which otherwise would fall !
> Repent, O London ! lest, for thine offence,
> Thy shepherd fail—whom mighty God preserve,
> That she may bide the pillar of His Church
> Against the storms of Romish Antichrist !
> The hand of mercy overshade her head,
> And let all faithful subjects say, Amen."

Whereupon there arose, it may be, an emphatic " Amen " from the playhouse benches ; for although many precisians stayed away, a playhouse audience under Elizabeth represented more nearly than it has done at any later time the whole people of England.

There were plays wholly by Greene, on the stories of *Orlando Furioso; Friar Bacon and Friar Bungay; George a Greene, the Pinner of Wakefield; Alphonso, King of Aragon;* and Scottish *James IV.*

His *Groat's Worth of Wit* was published after his death by his friend **Henry Chettle,** a fat and merry dramatist, of whose forty plays about four remain, and who was a printer before he became wholly a playwright.　To the " Groat's Worth of Wit " there was an appended address from Greene to his brother playwrights, Marlowe and Peele, with whom he associated Lodge, which includes this reference to Shakespeare: —" Unto none of you, like me, sought those burrs to cleave ; those puppets, I mean, that speak from our mouths, those antics garnisht in our colours.　Is it not strange that I to whom they all have been beholding—is it not like that you to whom they all have been beholding—shall, were ye in that case that I am now, be both of them at once forsaken ?　Yea, trust them not ;

for there is an upstart crow beautified with our feathers, that, with his *tiger's heart wrapped in a player's hide*, supposes he is as well able to bombast out a blank verse as the best of you ; and, being an absolute Johannes-fac-totum, is in his own conceit the only Shake-scene in a country. Oh, that I might entreat your rare wits to be employed in more profitable courses, and let these apes imitate your past excellence, and never more acquaint them with your admired inventions ! "

71. Here, then, about six years after his coming to London, is, in 1592, the first evidence that **William Shakespeare** has worked his way up to success. It is the first and last unkind word spoken of him, spoken in bitterness of spirit and in sickness, by a fallen man. A few weeks after the appearance of this, **Henry Chettle** took occasion, in a publication of his own, called *Kind-Hart's Dream*, to regret that he had not erased what Greene wrote about **Shakespeare**. " I am so sorry," he said, " as if the original fault had been my fault, because myself have seen his demeanour no less civil than he excellent in the quality he professes ; besides, divers of worship have reported his uprightness of dealing, which argues his honesty, and his facetious grace in writing that approves his art."

Greene's special reference is to Shakespeare's work upon those old plays which are placed among his own as the three parts of King Henry VI. *The First Part of Henry VI.* is doubtless an old play slightly altered and improved by Shakespeare. *The Second Part of King Henry VI.* was Shakespeare's alteration of a drama, printed in 1594 as *The First Part of the Contention betwixt the two famous Houses of York and Lancaster;* and *The Third Part of King Henry VI.* was an alteration from *The True Tragedie of Richard Duke of Yorke, and the Death of good King Henrie the Sixt, with the whole Contentione betweene the two Houses Lancaster and Yorke,* first printed in 1595. This was the play that contained the line preserved by Shakespeare, and turned against him by Greene, " O tiger's heart wrapt in a woman's hide" (Act I., Scene 4). The line may have been Greene's own, for one or two of the plays thus altered may have been written by Greene or by Marlowe.

72. **Greene** died at the age of thirty-two, on the 3rd of September, 1592. **Marlowe** died when he was not yet thirty, on the 16th of June, 1593, stabbed in the eye by Francis Archer, who was defending himself in a brawl after a feast at Deptford. We have spoken of Marlowe's *Tamburlaine,* and of his *Faustus*

His *Jew of Malta* gives in Barabas a powerful picture of the
Jew maligned still by the mediæval prejudices of the Christians.
Marlowe's *Edward the Second* was the nearest approach made
by the year 1590 to a play in which there is a natural development of character.   The last and worst of Marlowe's plays,
and the one that was most. carelessly printed, is his *Massacre
of Paris*, which dramatised the strife in France.   It included
not only the Massacre of St. Bartholomew, but also the death
of Charles IX., the assassination of the Duke of Guise by
Henry III., and the assassination of Henry himself by the
Dominican Friar, Jacques Clement, with the succession of Henry
of Navarre to the French throne.   The dying Henry III. in the
last scene of the play breathed vengeance against the pope, and
said :

> " Navarre, give me thy hand : I here do swear
> To ruinate that wicked Church of Rome,
> That hatcheth up such bloody practices ;
> And here protest eternal love to thee,
> And to the Queen of England specially,
> Whom God hath blest for hating papistry."

In the last lines of the play Henry of Navarre vowed so to revenge his predecessor's death,

> " As Rome, and all those popish prelates there,
> Shall curse the time that e'er Navarre was king,
> And rul'd in France by Henry's fatal death."

A tragedy of *Dido, Queen of Carthage*, left unfinished by
Marlowe, was completed by his friend Thomas Nash, and acted
by the children of Her Majesty's chapel.   **Thomas Nash (§ 68),**
who was baptised at Lowestoft in November, 1567, was dead in
1601.   **Marlowe** made a poor version of *Ovid's Elegies*, first
published in 1596 with the Epigrams of Sir John Davies.   His
beginning of a free paraphrase of the *Hero and Leander* ascribed
to Musæus, was afterwards completed by George Chapman.
**George Peele** died about 1598 ; but **Thomas Lodge,** whose
novel of *Rosalynde*, published in 1590, suggested the plot of
Shakespeare's " As You Like It," lived on throughout the reign
of Elizabeth's successor.

In **Peele's** *Old Wives' Tale*, printed in 1595, there was a sort
of child's story told with a poet's playfulness.   There was no
division into acts.   Three men lost in a wood were met by Clunch,
and introduced to his old wife Madge, who gave them a supper, over which they sang, and then began telling them in old

wives' fashion the "Old Wives' Tale." It is a tale of a king's daughter stolen by a conjuror, who flew off with her in the shape of a great dragon, and hid her in a stone castle, "and there he kept her I know not how long, till at last all the king's men went out so long that her two brothers went to seek her." While the old woman talked, the two brothers entered, and the story-telling passed into the acting of the story : very much as the art of the mediæval story-teller had passed into that of the Elizabethan dramatist. The Princess Delia was sought by her brothers, and sought also by Eumenides, her lover. A proper young man, whom the magician had turned into a bear by night and an old man by day, delivered mystic oracles by a wayside cross. Sacrapant triumphed in his spells, until Eumenides had made a friend of the ghost of Jack by paying fifteen or sixteen shillings to prevent the sexton and churchwarden from leaving poor Jack unburied. The ghost of Jack played pranks, and made an end of Sacrapant, whose destiny it was "never to die but by a dead man's hand." The light in the conjuror's mystic glass had been blown out, as before said (§ 47), by one that was "neither wife, widow, nor maid." The piece included a comic braggart, who could deliver himself—in burlesque of Stanihurst (§ 53)— according to the reformed manner of versifying :

"Philida, phileridos, pamphilida, florida, flortos ;
'Dub dub-a-dub, bounce,' quoth the guns, with a sulphurous huff-snuff."

The piece was a playful child's story, told with child-like simplicity and grace.

73. **William Shakespeare** in 1593, the year of the death of Marlowe, had not yet produced any of his greatest plays. The plays of his own then written were *The Two Gentlemen of Verona* (1591 ?), *The Comedy of Errors* (1592 ?), probably also *Love's Labour's Lost*. In 1593 he first appeared in print by publishing his *Venus and Adonis*, a poem in the six-lined stanza then used as the common measure for a strain of love. It was dedicated to Henry Wriothesley, Earl of Southampton, who in 1593 was twenty years old ; the age of Shakespeare being twenty-nine. The Earldom of Southampton had been given in 1546 by Henry VIII. to the grandfather of Shakespeare's friend and patron. The father of Shakespeare's earl had been a Roman Catholic, and friend to the cause of Mary Queen of Scots. He died when his successor in the earldom (through death of an elder brother) was a child. The young earl, a ward

of Lord Burghley's, had been educated at Cambridge, where he took his degree of M.A. in 1589; he then came to London, joined an Inn of Court, was in favour with the queen, and was a liberal friend of the poets. In his dedication of it to Lord Southampton, Shakespeare called *Venus and Adonis* the "first heir of my invention." To the same patron Shakespeare dedicated in the following year, 1594, his *Lucrece*, in Chaucer's stanza —"Troilus verse." The two poems, one of the passion of love, one of heroic chastity, belong together, and their sweet music spread over the land that once had been filled with the songs of Chaucer. Of the *Venus and Adonis* there were five editions before the close of Elizabeth's reign. *Titus Andronicus*, a play ascribed to Shakespeare, but certainly a piece from another hand which he but slightly touched (in an older form it had been called " Titus and Vespasian "), seems to have been first acted in January, 1594.

74. In 1599 the Blackfriars Company built, as a summer theatre, *The Globe*, on Bankside. It was a wooden hexagon, circular within, and open to the weather; but the stage was sheltered by some roofing. London Bridge was the one bridge of that time, and playgoers crossed to the Bankside theatres by water from various parts of London. Sunday performances had been abolished for the last sixteen years. They had been strongly opposed (§ 40). On the 13th January, 1583, in Paris Garden— an old place of entertainment, where beasts had been baited early in Henry VIII.'s reign—during performance on the Sabbath, a decayed wooden gallery fell down, and many lives were lost. This was looked upon as a judgment from Heaven, and the Privy Council thenceforth enforced an order that the actors should "forbear wholly to play on the Sabbath-day, either in the forenoon or afternoon, which to do they are by their lordships' order expressly denied and forbidden." But there was now no want of audiences on other days. Richard Barbage had leased Blackfriars to one Evans, whose actors were the children of the chapel. Barbage's sons bought in 1596 the remainder of Evans' lease. After this the children of Her Majesty's chapel acted at Blackfriars when the adult company was acting at the Globe. Thus we have prefixed to Lyly's " Campaspe," " the Prologue at the Court," and " the Prologue at the Black Friars."

75. John Lyly in 1590 was famous, but not prosperous in his dependence on court patronage. He had in vain sought office as Master of the Revels, and wrote to the Queen, " If your

sacred Maiestie thinke me vnworthy, and that after x yeares tempest, I must att court suffer shipwrack of my tyme, my wittes, my hopes, vouchsafe in your neuer-erring iudgement some plank or rafter to wafte me into a country where, in my sad and settled devocion, I may in euery corner of a thatcht cottage write praiers in stead of plaies, prayer for your longe and prosprous life, and a repentaunce that I have played the foole so longe." In 1593, in a second petition to the queen, Lyly prayed for " some lande, some good fines or forfeitures that should fall by the iust fall of these most false traitors, that seeing nothing will come by the Revells, I may pray vppon the Rebèlls. Thirteene years your highnes servant, but yet nothing ; twenty freinds that though they saye they wil be sure I find them sure to be slowe. A thousand hopes, but all nothing ; a hundred promises, but yet nothing. Thus casting vpp the inventory of my freinds, hopes, promises, and tymes, the summa totalis amounteth to iust nothing. My last will is shorter than myne invencion; but three legacies—patience to my creditors, melancholie without measure to my friends, and beggerie without shame to my family." Lyly's comedy of *Mother Bombie*, acted by the children of Paul's, was first printed in 1594. Mother Bombie is a fortuneteller, and the scene is laid at Rochester ; but the construction of the plot is artificial, and even the names of the characters show the relation between Plautus and Terence, and the earlier Elizabethan comedy. There are Memphis and Stellio, Prisius and Sperantus, Candius, Mæstius, Accius, Livia, Serena and Silena, even a " Dromio, servant to Memphio," side by side with " Halfpenny, a boy, servant to Sperantus." Lyly, who lived in the parish of St. Bartholomew the Less, had a son born in 1596, who died in 1597, a son born in 1600, and a daughter in 1603; and he died himself in November, 1606, aged fifty-two.

76. **Edmund Spenser** (§ 23, 31, 34, 43, 45, 46), whose " Shepheard's Calender" had been reprinted in 1581 and 1586, came to London at the end of 1589, was introduced by Raleigh to Elizabeth, and published in 1590 the first section, containing the first three books, of *The Faerie Queene, disposed into Twelve Bookes, Fashioning XII Morall Vertues*. It was dedicated to Her Majesty, and had a prefatory letter addressed to Sir Walter Raleigh, dated January 23, 1589 (New Style, 1590). Spenser had been at work on his great poem for more than ten years (§ 43), and the part of it now published was received with an admiration that caused its publisher to get together a volume of

other poems by Spenser, which he published in 1591, under the
title of *Complaints.*   This volume contained Spenser's *Ruines
of Time; Teares of the Muses; Virgil's Gnat; Prosopopoia, or
Mother Hubberd's Tale; The Ruines of Rome, by Bellay; Muiopotmos, or the Tale of the Butterflie; Visions of the World's
Vanitie; Bellayes Visions;* and *Petrarches Visions. The Ruines
of Time,* dedicated to Sidney's sister, the Countess of Pembroke,
was a series of mournful visions, forming a poem in Chaucer's
stanza, on the death of " Philisides" (Sir Philip Sidney).   In the
*Teares of the Muses,* each Muse in turn lamented, in the six-lined
Common Verse, the decay of her just rule.   This poem Spenser
dedicated to the Lady Strange, with whom he claimed kindred,
and whom we shall meet again.   She was Alice, youngest
daughter of Sir John Spencer, of Althorpe,. then married to
Ferdinando Stanley, Lord Strange, who became Earl of Derby
by the death of his father, in September, 1593.   He died himself in the following April, leaving his widow Countess Dowager
of Derby, and the mother of two girls.   *Virgil's Gnat,* done
into octave rhyme, was said to have been long since "dedicated
to the most noble and excellent lord, the Earl of Leicester,
late deceased."   It is a free version of a poem—*Culex*—that
used to be ascribed to Virgil.   *Prosopopoia; or, Mother Hubberd's
Tale,* Spenser dedicated to the Lady Compton and Monteagle,
who was Anne, another of the daughters of Sir John Spencer,
of Althorpe.   It is a pleasant satirical fable, in Chaucer's rhyming ten-syllabled lines, and  written designedly in Chaucer's
manner, showing how the Fox and the Ape, his neighbour and
gossip, went disguised into the world to mend their fortunes.
To begin, they would not be of any occupation, but the free
men called beggars.   But what warrant should they have for
their free life ?   They would protect themselves by the name of
soldiers—" That now is thought a civil begging sect."   The Ape,
as likest for manly semblance, was to act the poor soldier ; the
Fox to wait on him and help as occasion served.   Spenser
having cried shame on this common abuse of an honourable
name, next made the Ape a shepherd, with the Fox for sheep-
dog.   In this character

> " Not a lamb of all their flockes supply
> Had they to shew ; but ever as they bred
> They slue them, and upon their fleshes fed."

The Fox and the Ape, having escaped after a  great slaughter of
the flock entrusted to their care, set up a new calling " much like

to begging, but much better named." They got gown and cassock, and as poor clerks begged of a priest, who reproached them for not seeking some good estate in the Church. Through the counsel given by this priest when the Fox and the Ape asked for advice, Spenser satirised the too easy lives of an indolent, well-to-do clergy.

> " By that he ended had his ghostly sermon
> The Foxe was well induc'd to be a parson,
> And of the priest eftsoones gan to inquire
> How to a benefice he might aspire.
> ' Marie, there,' said the priest, ' is arte indeed :
> Much good deep learning one thereout may read ;
> For that the ground-worke is, and ende of all,
> How to obtaine a beneficiall.' "

They must dress well, wait on some religious nobleman, and affect a godly zeal ; or, if the Fox looked to court for promotion :

> " Then must thou thee dispose another way :
> For there thou needs must learne to laugh, to lie,
> To crouche, to please, to be a beetle-stock
> Of thy great Master's will, to scorne, or mock ;
> So maist thou chance mock out a benefice,
> Unless thou canst one conjure by device,
> Or cast a figure for a bishoprick."

The courtiers also must be bribed. The Fox and Ape were thankful for good counsel, and presently Fox was a priest, with Ape for parish clerk. They behaved so ill in their new calling that they were obliged at last to escape from it, and, by counsel of a fat mule from the court, they next tried life among the courtiers. At court the Ape walked on tiptoe, as if he were some great Magnifico ; and the Fox, as his man, supported him. Here followed Spenser's satire of court vices and follies, with a picture in verse of the true courtly gentleman, for which in Spenser's mind perhaps his friend Sir Philip Sidney sat. It is in this part of " Mother Hubberd's Tale" that we find Spenser's lines upon the pitiful state of the suitor (§ 55). From court also Fox and Ape were obliged to fly ; and next they came upon the Lion sleeping, stole his crown and skin, and assumed royalty. The Ape was king, the Fox his minister. A satire followed on tyrannical misgovernment. Jove saw it ; and Mercury, sent from Jove to make inquiry into it, aroused the sleeping Lion, who reclaimed his own.

> " The Foxe, first author of that treacherie,
> He did uncase, and then away let flie :

> But th' Ape's long taile (which then he had) he quight
> Cut off, and both ears pared off their height ;
> Since which all Apes but halfe their eares have left,
> And of their tailes are utterlie bereft."

*Muiopotmos; or, the Tale of the Butterflie,* Spenser dedicated to the Lady Carey, who was Elizabeth, another of the daughters of Sir John Spencer, of Althorpe.   It is an original allegory in octave rhyme.   The *Ruins of Rome* and the *Visions,* both from Bellay, his own *Visions of the World's Vanity,* and the *Visions of Petrarch,* are alike in form, and written sonnet wise, the "Visions" of Bellay and "Visions" of Petrarch, being chiefly a new version of Spenser's youthful contribution to the *Theatre for Worldlings* (§ 23).   These were the contents of the volume of Spenser's poetry published as *Complaints,* in 1591, the year after the success of the the first three books of the "Faerie Queene."

Spenser wrote also about this time an elegy on the death of the wife of Arthur (afterwards Sir Arthur) Gorges, a "lover of learning and virtue."   The lady was daughter and heir of Henry Lord Howard, Viscount Byndon, and the poem was published separately, under the name of *Daphnaida.*

77.   In February, 1591, Spenser received, as further earnest of success, a pension of £50 a year from Queen Elizabeth.

In October, 1591, a grant was made or confirmed to him of land in Cork, with the old castle of Kilcolman, in which he seems to have lived before his visit to England, and which had belonged to the Earls of Desmond.   It was two miles from Doneraile, on the north side of a lake fed by the river Awbey, Spenser's Mulla.   After his return to Ireland, Spenser dedicated to Sir Walter Raleigh, from his house at Kilcolman, the 27th of December, 1591, his poem entitled *Colin Clout's Come Home Again,* to which additions were made before its publication.   In this poem Colin, having told his fellow shepherds how Raleigh, "the Shepherd of the Ocean," visited him in 1589, and caused him to "wend with him his Cynthia to see," described, in pastoral form, England, the queen herself, and, under pastoral names, celebrated personages of the court and living poets. Among them was he of the name Shake Spear, that doth heroically sound :

> "And there, though last, not least, is Aetion ;
> A gentler shepherd may no where be found :
> Whose Muse, full of high thoughts' invention,
> Doth like himselfe heroically sound."

This was not published until 1595, and in the same year appeared Spenser's sonnets or *Amoretti*, and the *Epithalamium*, an exquisitely musical and joyous bridal song, written about the time of his own wedding. No lady's name is publicly associated with the sonnets, and they were written doubtless for the pleasure of the lady who became his wife. Three or four of them contain personal references, but the rest are of the usual kind. Spenser had been married on the 11th of June, 1594, when his age was about forty, to a lady living near Kilcolman, whose name, like the name of his queen and of his mother, was Elizabeth. In 1595 he had come to England again with the next instalment of three books of the "Faerie Queene," and with a prose *View of the Present State of Ireland*, in a dialogue between Eudoxus and Irenæus, which was circulated in manuscript, but was not printed until more than thirty years after his death. It was hard in the policy it recommended, and about Kilcolman Spenser was not kindly remembered. The *Second Part of the Faerie Queene*, containing the fourth, fifth, and sixth books, appeared in 1596, together with a reprint of the first three books. In the same year Spenser, while in London, added to two hymns of "Love and Beauty," written years before, two other hymns of "Heavenly Love and Heavenly Beauty." These *Hymns* were published at once, and in the same year appeared also his *Prothalamium* on the marriage of two daughters of the Earl of Worcester. Spenser published nothing more before his death. In 1597 he returned to Kilcolman. In 1598 he was named by the queen for Sheriff of Cork. Children had been born to him ; there were two sons living, Sylvanus and Peregrine. In October, 1598, Tyrone's rebellion broke out. Kilcolman was attacked, plundered, and burnt. Spenser and his family were cast out ; an infant child of his is said to have perished in the flames, but that is doubtful. Spenser was thus driven back to England, and died soon after his arrival, on the 13th of January, 1599, at a tavern in King Street, Westminster. King Street was then a very good street, on one side open to fields, and forming the main road between the Abbey and Parliament House and the court, which since Wolsey's forfeiture had been at the old Palace of Whitehall. That palace having been for centuries the residence of the Archbishop of York, was the York House that Wolsey had enriched with his magnificence. Henry VIII. took it in 1529. Elizabeth held court there ; and Spenser had taken his lodging where he might be near the court, to which he looked for repair of his fortunes.

78. Spenser's letter to Raleigh prefixed to the fragment of
the "Faerie Queene," "expounding his whole intention in the
course of this work," said only that he laboured to pourtraict in
Arthure, before he was king, the image of a brave knight, perfected in the twelve moral vertues, as Aristotle hath devised,
the which is the purpose of the first twelve books ; which if I
finde to be well accepted, I may be perhaps encouraged to frame
the other part, of politicke vertues, in his person after that hee
came to be king." It was left for the reader to discover how
grand a design was indicated by these unassuming words.
Spenser said that by the Faerie Queene whom Arthur sought,
"I mean glory in my generall intention, but in my particular I
conceive the most excellent and glorious person of our sove-
raine the queene, and her kingdom in Faeryland." The student
of the "Faerie Queene" must bear in mind that its "general
intention" is its essential plan as a great spiritual allegory; that
this is consistent throughout, is the very soul of the poem, source
of its immortal life ; and that the "particular" significations,
which are frequent and various, are secondary senses lying only
on the surface of the main design, with which they harmonise,
and to which they gave a lively added interest in Spenser's time.
Faery means in the allegory Spiritual. A faery knight is a
spiritual quality or virtue militant, serving the Faerie Queene,
Gloriana, which means in the general allegory Glory in the
highest sense—the glory of God. Read out of allegory, therefore, "The Glory of God" is the name of Spenser's poem.
Again said Spenser, in this introductory letter, "In the person of
Prince Arthure I sette forth Magnificence in particular, which
vertue, for that (according to Aristotle and the rest) is the perfection of all the rest, and conteineth in it them all : therefore
in the whole course I mention the deedes of Arthure applyable
to that vertue, which I write of in that booke ; but of the xii
other vertues I make xii other knights the patrones, for the
more variety of the history." Spenser's ethical system was
bound up with his religion ; he painted, therefore, in his separate knights, each single virtue of a man striving heavenward,
but failing at some point, and needing aid of Divine grace.
This came through Arthur, in whom all the virtues are contained, who is filled with a great desire towards the Faerie
Queene—the Glory of God—and who above all represents, in the
literal sense of the word, Magnificence, since he may be said to
indicate the place of the Mediator in the Christian system. If

we had had all twelve books of the poem, which was left only half finished, they would have been an allegory of man battling heavenward with all his faculties, through trial and temptation. The other poem, had it followed, would have been an endeavour to represent through allegory an ideal citizenship of the kingdom of Heaven.   Because the " Faerie Queene " was published incomplete, Spenser told so much of what its readers could have found in the whole work as was necessary to direct their understanding to the well-head of the history, "that from thence gathering the whole intention of the conceit, ye may as in a handfull gripe at the discourse." He gave the clue into our hands, and then left us to find our own way through the poem upon which he spent the best thought of his life.

Moral philosophy was divided into ethics, which dealt with the individual ; and politics, which dealt with the community. Spenser's project was of two poems, applying each of these to his own sense of the relation between man and God.   In Plato's "Republic" there was mention of four Cardinal Virtues—Courage, Temperance, Justice, Wisdom.   In the "Protagoras," Plato added to these, Holiness.   This Aristotle omitted, because, as studies, he distinctly separated Ethics from Religion.   Aristotle's list in his "Ethics," made without special devotion to the number twelve, was, in Book III., Courage and Temperance ; in Book IV., Liberality, Magnificence, Laudable Ambition (Philotimia), Mildness of a Regulated Temper; Courtesy, or regulated conduct in society; Regulation of Boastfulness, including avoidance of the affectation of humility, that is to say, sincerity of manner ; Social Pliability of Wit (Eutrapelia) ; and Modesty, which Aristotle called hardly a virtue, but rather a feeling.   In the fifth book of his "Ethics," the virtue he discussed was Justice.   In the sixth book he took Intellectual Virtues—Philosophy and Wisdom, including Prudence, Apprehension, and Considerateness.   The seventh book of the "Ethics" was on Pleasure, and dealt also with Incontinence and Intemperance ; the eighth and ninth books were on Friendship.   Upon the groundwork of this treatise of Aristotle's there had been built this classification of the virtues, which was that commonly received in Spenser's time : they were of three kinds—I. Intellectual, II. Moral, III. Theological.   The Intellectual Virtues were — Intellectual Knowledge, producing Art ;   Wisdom, producing Prudence.   The Moral Virtues were—1, Prudence, Mother of All; 2, Justice; 3, Courage ; 4, Temperance.   These

were the four Cardinal Virtues. Then came, 5, Courtesy; 6,
Liberality; 7, Magnificence; 8, Magnanimity; 9, Philotimia
(Laudable Ambition); 10, Truth; 11, Friendship; 12, Eutrapelia
(Social Pliability of Wit). The theological virtues were these
three—Faith, Hope, and Charity. Spenser dealt as a poet with
his subject, and in no way bound himself to the scholastic list.
In the six books of the "Faerie Queen" which are extant, and
the fragment of a seventh, first printed with a new edition of
the poem, in 1611, this is Spenser's order of the virtues:—1,
Holiness; 2, Temperance; 3, Chastity; 4, Friendship; 5,
Justice; 6, Courtesy; and (probably) 7, Constancy. The several
qualities of the true man taken in this order represent fidelity
to God, 1, in soul, and, 2, in body; 3, 4, the bond of love
between man and woman in pure marriage, this form of love
being dealt with especially under the head of Chastity; and
between man and man, this form being dealt with especially
under the head of Friendship. Love, the great bond of humanity,
having been taken first, Spenser then passed to the next great
bond, 5, Justice. Where the supremacy of Love does not
suffice, Justice must govern. Having dealt with these two
great bonds between man and man, Spenser passed next to the
lighter, all-pervading bond of, 6, Courtesy. "Greet kindly,
though ye be strangers," said one of the old Cymric bards.
The recognition of this bond of common kindliness, where there
has been no opportunity for closer ties, was the next condition
in a sequence reasoned out like Spenser's. But Courtesy, which
bids us yield to others on all non-essential points, needs to be
balanced with the virtue that will save us from a careless yielding
of essentials. So after Courtesy came, probably, Constancy, in
Spenser's system. Thus we may trace the mind of the poet
even in the sequence of the six books of his poem.

The more detailed study of English writers, to which this
volume is an introduction, attempts an analysis of the whole
allegory of the "Faerie Queene." Here there can be no more
said than will suffice to show its nature. The form of a
romance of chivalry was in its own day the most popular that
could have been selected. Spenser not only followed Spanish
romances, and Ariosto's "Orlando," but adapted himself to
the humour of his time, as illustrated by the *Famous Historie
of the Seven Champions of Christendome*, a pious romance
of saintly knights and fair ladies, dragons and chivalrous
adventures, told in Euphuistic style, of which the first part,

which Spenser had read, appeared probably about the middle of Elizabeth's reign, the second part certainly in 1597. Richard Johnson, whose name is associated with this book, and who finished re-editing it in the year of Shakespeare's death, was not its author. Shakespeare also had read it; and since Elizabeth's time it has been dear to many generations of children. Spenser formed his allegory out of stock incidents in such romances, but he so told his story as to give to every incident a spiritual meaning. The form of verse contrived by Spenser for exclusive use in this poem is a nine-lined stanza, called "Spenserian." It was made by adding an Alexandrine to the stanza that French poets often used in the *Chant Royal*, a longer form of balade, called "Royal Song," in which God was the King celebrated. That eight-lined stanza was applied also to other uses. Marot, for example, who did not use it for his "Chants Royaux," made it the measure of his poem on the marriage of James V. of Scotland with Magdalene of France. Chaucer and followers of his had used it now and then, as in the "Envoye to the Complaint of the Black Knight," in "Chaucer's A B C," in "The Balade of the Visage without Painting," and "*L'Envoye à Bukton*." It consisted of two quatrains of ten-syllabled lines, with alternate rhyme; the second rhyme of the first quatrain agreeing with the first rhyme of the quatrain that followed, thus, a b a b, b c b c; this could go on indefinitely upon the same system — c d c d, d e d e, e f e f, &c. Now, Spenser's added line follows the system of the verse as to its rhyme, but destroys expectation of continuance by the two extra syllables, which close with a new turn the music of the stanza. Thus the Spenserian stanza becomes as to its rhyming a b a b, b c b c, c. The *Faerie Queene*, it may be added, abounds in graceful imitations or paraphrases from the ancient poets, and from Ariosto and Tasso; incidents are also suggested by Spenser's readings in Arthurian romance, in the first part of "The Seven Champions," in "The Orlando Furioso," and in Tasso's heroic poem.

Let us now lightly illustrate from the first book the manner of the allegory. Twelve Faerie Knights, who represent twelve virtues, were knights of the Faerie Queene; they served the Divine glory. One, a clownish young man—"base things of the world, and things that are despised, hath God chosen"—desired to serve, and rested on the floor, "unfit through his rusticity for a better place." Then came Truth, as a fair lady, to complain

P

of the huge dragon—"the Dragon, that old serpent, which is the Devil"—who besieged her father and mother, an ancient king and queen, Adam and Eve, typifying the race of man. What knight would aid her? Then "that clownish person," who was to represent in the allegory Holiness, or the religion of England in Spenser's time, and that, too, in Spenser's form of it—"upstarting, desired that adventure." The lady told him that unless he could use the armour which she brought, he could not succeed in that enterprise: that was the armour of a Christian man specified by St. Paul: "Wherefore take unto you the whole armour of God, that ye may be able to withstand in the evil day, and having done all, to stand. Stand, therefore, having your loins girt about with truth, and having on the breast-plate of righteousness, and your feet shod with the preparation of the Gospel of Peace; above all, taking the shield of faith, wherewith ye shall be able to quench all the fiery darts of the wicked. And take the helmet of salvation, and the sword of the spirit, which is the Word of God." St. Paul used the image again : "Let us who are of the day be sober, putting on the breast-plate of faith and love; and for an helmet the hope of salvation." When thus armed, the clownish person "seemed the goodliest man in all that company, and well liked of the lady." "If any man," said St. Paul, "be in Christ, he is a new creature." The knight set out to battle with the Dragon, and—so much having been indicated in the letter to Raleigh—here the first book of the *Faerie Queene* begins. The gentle knight was the element of holiness in the Christian soul, seeking conquest of evil, clad in the armour of righteousness, with the cross on his breast and on his shield. His steed represented passions and desires, disdaining the curb, but needing the curb as they carry us upon the chosen path. The knight sought his adventure to win the grace of Gloriana, which of all earthly things he most did crave. "The Lord shall be unto thee an everlasting light, and thy God thy glory." Beside him rode a lovely lady, Truth, on a lowly ass, more white than snow—patient of desire, dispassionate of temper—Truth under a veil. "And by her, in a line, a milk-white Lamb she led," guide and companion of innocence, herself as guileless descended from the angels who knew man in Paradise.

> "Behind her farre away a Dwarfe did lag
> That lasie seemd, in being ever last,
> Or wearied with bearing of her bag
> Of needments at his backe.'

The dwarf was the Flesh, with its needments: sometimes the bodily life of the man; sometimes, when the allegory took a wider range, the common body of the people, with its natural instincts. The theme of the book was opened with a general allegory of the contest with Error; then it became individual and national, painting English religion from the point of view of an Elizabethan Puritan.

The day became troubled, and the knight and his companions found shelter in a wood, whose ways were the ways of the world. The trees in it typified the forms of human life: "the sailing pine" for trade; "the vine-prop elm" for pleasure: "the poplar never dry," freshness of youth; "the builder oak, sole king of forests all," man in mature strength' building his home in the world; "the aspen, good for staves," to support decrepid age; and then the grave, "the cypress funeꞏ al." The other trees typified glory and tears, chase of meat, grinding of meal, griefs of life and their consolations, the shock of war and the wise uses of life, fruitfulness, completeness in form, that which is for us to mould, and that which is often rotten at the core. Losing themselves among the pleasant ways of the world the knight and his companions took the most beaten path, which led them to the den of Error. Before the battle with the monster there was flinching of the flesh, eagerness of the spirit. By the light of his spiritual helps the Red Cross Knight could see the monster as it was; it was a light from his glistening armour which the brood of Error could not bear.

> "Soone as that uncouth light upon them shone
> Into her mouth they crept, and suddain all were gone."

When the knight, in the contest, was wound about with the huge train of the monster, the poet cried, "God helpe the man so wrapt in Errores endlesse traine!" That was the help his lady urged him to secure. "Add faith unto your force, and be not faint." After this general picture of the conquest over Error, Spenser began to sketch, in the bitter spirit of his time, the relation of Catholicism to the Red Cross Knight of England.

The knight's armour was worn that he might stand against "the wiles of the devil." That chief deceiver, Archimago, now appeared, representing as a simple hermit the first stage of what Spenser looked upon as the "diabolical faith" (§ 45). He bade the Red Cross Knight and his companions to rest within his hermitage, and, as they slept there he created by his magic a

deceiving semblance of the lady, now named Una, because of
the singleness of Truth. The deceiving image represented
sensuous religion. The Christian misdoubted the corrupt Church
that yet feigned to be his, and missed the firm voice of his guide
and comforter:

> " 'Why, dame,' quoth he, 'what hath ye thus dismayed ?
> What frayes ye, that were wont to comfort me affrayd !' "

The close of that first canto represented, then, from Spenser's
point of view, the Christian before the Reformation. In the second
canto, simple Truth having been maligned by arts of the devil,
the Christian was stirred to passion against her, she was deserted
by him, body and soul, but at her slow pace she followed the
man carried away by his swift passions. Then the devil, hater
of truth, disguised himself as the Red Cross Knight, and there
was the " diabolical faith " personified. The true Saint George—
the religion of England—parted from Truth, met with a faithless
Saracen, named Sansfoy, Infidelity, strong, careless about God
and man, companion of the woman clothed in scarlet, who was
mitred, jewelled, and borne on a " wanton palfrey "—by wanton
passions. Then followed the shock of battle against infidelity,
which only through the death of Christ has Christianity been
able to survive:

> " 'Curse on that Cross' (quoth then the Sarazin),
> ' That keepes thy body from the bitter fitt !
> Dead long ygoe, I wote, thou haddest bin,
> Had not that charme from thee forwarned itt.' "

The heavenward-striving soul could strike down infidelity;
but then it took the woman clothed in scarlet, named Duessa,
because of the doubleness of Falsehood, for Fidessa, the true
faith. She was another image of the Church of Rome—

> " Borne the sole daughter of an Emperour,
> He that the wide West under his rule has,
> And high hath set his throne where Tiberis doth pas."

Her the knight took for companion; but she appealed rather to
his eyes than to his mind, he was—

> " More busying his quicke eies her face to view,
> Than his dull eares to heare what shee did tell.

He travelled on with his new lady, who could not endure the
heat of the day, and rested with her under shade of trees, from
which he plucked a bough to make a garland for her forehead.
But the tree bled, and uttered a sad voice. It was Fradubio,

thus transformed because he had doubted between the witch
Duessa and Fraelissa. That witch had caused Fraelissa to
appear deformed, Fradubio had then given himself to Duessa,
till one day he saw her in her own true ugliness. Fradubio
and Fraelissa were both turned to trees, and

> "'We may not channge' (quoth he) 'this evill plight,
> Till we be bathed in a living well.'"

Fraelissa being thus transformed, and awaiting such release,
could not herself represent true Christian faith, between which
and the false Church Fradubio was in doubt. Spenser represented by her a pure heathen philosophy, like that of Plato;
purer and fairer than the "diabolical faith" that rivalled and
supplanted it, but no longer an active moving power in the
world. Philosophy must live with its votary a vegetative life
until its powers are renewed by union with the Church of Christ.
"A garden enclosed is my sister, my spouse—a well of living
waters."

In the next canto, forsaken Truth, parted from men,

> " Her dainty limbs did lay
> In secrete shadow, far from all men's sight:
> From her fayre head her fillet she undight,
> And layd her stole aside. Her angel's face,
> As the great eye of heaven, shyned bright,
> And made a sunshine in the shady place;
> Did never mortal eye behold such heavenly grace."

A lion that rushed upon her was subdued to the service of her
innocence. Spenser used here the romance doctrine that a lion
will not hurt a virgin. St. George, in "The Seven Champions,"
recognised the virginity of Sabra by two lions fawning upon her.
Spenser's lion, whose yielded pride and proud submission made
him the companion of Una, represented Reason before the
Reformation serving as ally of Truth against Ignorance and
Superstition. "The lion would not leave her desolate, but with
her went along," and presently they came near the dwelling of
Ignorance and her daughter Superstition. Una called to the
damsel—the voice of Truth calling to Superstition:

> " But the rude wench her answered nought at all:
> Shee could not heare, nor speake, nor understand;
> Till seeing by her side the Lyon stand
> With suddeine feare her pitcher downe she threw,
> And fled away: for never in that land
> Face of fayre Lady she before did view,
> And that dredd Lyon's looke her cast in deadly hew."

She never had seen the fair face of Truth, and dreaded the attack of Reason. The Lion, "with his rude clawes, the wicket open rent," thus representing still the work of Reason at the Reformation. Una and the lion, Truth served by Reason, lay down in the house of Ignorance and Superstition, whither by night came Kirk-rapine with plunder of the Church to his companion, "the daughter of this woman blind, Abessa, daughter of Corceca slow." Kirk-rapine represented theft of sacred things and of the money of the poor, by men who entered the Church only for the goods they could take out of it; by the abbots and high clergy, the hirelings in the Church, false pastors who took no care of the sheep committed to their care, except to fleece them and devour their flesh. Kirk-rapine found in Abessa's den the lion, who,

> " Encountring fierce, him suddein doth surprize;
> And, seizing cruell clawes on trembling brest,
> Under his lordly foot him proudly hath supprest."

Doubtless, the general image of the force of reason in attack on the ill-gotten wealth of those who took to their own use what was given to maintain religion and relieve the poor, was joined here to a particular image of the lion of England, as Henry VIII., with his foot on the suppressed monasteries. Therefore, when it is said of Kirk-rapine that "the thirsty land dranke up his life," there might be reference to the enrichment of the land by restoration of wealth that had been drawn from it to feed the luxury of Churchmen.

Reason had now taken its fit place in the allegory. In Spenser's system it was not by help of Reason, but only by Grace of God, that the last triumph was to be secured. The lion, therefore, fell under the stroke of Sansloy. Reason could not resist the force of lawlessness. Not yet joined to her Red Cross Knight, Una had only the natural heart of man to recognise her beauty. She was adored by the "salvage nation."

> " During which tyme her gentle wit she plyes
> To teach them truth, which worship her in vaino,
> And made her th' Image of Idolotryes."

The Red Cross Knight was taken by Duessa to the House of Pride, thence, warned and aided by the natural instincts of his dwarf, he escaped, wounded by Joylessness; and being weary took his armour off and rested by the way. He sat by a fountain which had been once a nymph—one of Diana's nymphs—

who " satt downe to rest in middest of the race." " Let us not
.be weary in well-doing, for in due season we shall reap—if we
faint not." The Christian warrior, thus resting in midst of his
race, escaped from the pomps of "the diabolical faith " only to
become the thrall to like pomps in another form.   That Spenser
held to be the present danger of the English Church.   The woeful
dwarf, the common body of the people, took up the knight's
neglected arms, carried them on, seeking aid in this distress,
and met with Una.   Then to the aid of Truth and to the rescue
of the religion of England came Prince Arthur, bearing the
shield of Divine Grace.   "Ay, me," now says the poet in the
prelude to the canto which describes Prince Arthur's intervention,—

> " Ay, me ! how many perils doe enfold
> The righteous man, to make him daily fall,
> Were not that heavenly Grace doth him uphold
> And stedfast Truth acquite him out of all."

The wondrous horn blown by Arthur's squire—the faithful
preacher—before the giant's castle, was the horn of the Gospel.

> " Wyde wonders over all
> Of that same hornes great virtues weren told,
> Which had approved bene in uses manifold."

The rescued Christian looking back on his delusions and
misdeeds was tempted by despair, but the voice of Truth
answered to his doubt:

> Come, come away, fraile, feeble, fleshly wight,
> Ne let vaine words bewitch thy manly hart,
> Ne divelish thoughts dismay thy constant sprights
> In heavenly mercies hast thou not a part ?
> Why should'st thou then despeire that chosen art ?
> Where Justice growes, there grows eke greater Grace.

And when the Red Cross Knight was next brought by Una
to the House of Holiness, where Dame Cœlia lived with her
three daughters, Faith, Hope, and Charity, to be prepared for
the last great fight with the Dragon, the opening stanza showed,
again, how carefully Spenser had provided for the most essential
feature of his poem, express declaration of its meaning:

> ' What man is he, that boasts of fleshly might
> And vaine assuraunce of mortality,
> Which, all so soone as it doth come to fight
> Against spirituall foes, yields by and by,
> Or from the fielde most cowardly doth fly!

> Ne let the man ascribe it to his skill,
> That thorough Grace hath gained victory :
> If any strength we have, it is to ill,
> But all the good is God's, both power and eke will."

Spenser believed that he had given aid enough for the interpretation of his allegory.  In the introduction to his second book he told the reader that

> " Of faery land, yet if he more inquyre,
> By certein signes, here sett in sondrie place
> He may it fynd: ne let him then admyre,
> But yield his sence to bee too blunt and bace
> That no'te without an hound fine footing trace."

Spenser's "fine footing" has been traced but carelessly; while all readers have felt the sweetness of music, and enjoyed the feast of imagination that the *Faerie Queene* offers to those who simply yield themselves up to a sense of the surpassing beauty of its pictures and of its deeply earnest spiritual undertone.  Profoundly earnest, and the work of a pure mind, the *Faerie Queene* is yet bitter at core.  It is the work of a great poet, who felt and expressed both the essence and the accidents of the great struggle in which he was himself a combatant.  Through all its delicious melody it breathes a stern defiance of whatever cause was not, in the eyes of a true-hearted Elizabethan Puritan, the cause of God.  The deeper allegory that expresses abstract truth holds on throughout the *Faerie Queene* its steady course, but it is conveyed through many references, in their own time not in the least obscure, to affairs of England, Ireland, France, Spain, Belgium.  For example, in the ninth canto of Book V. Spenser enforced the whole case for the execution of Mary Queen of Scots, and at the beginning of the next canto he spoke his mind, still on the surface of the allegory of Mercilla and Duessa, upon Elizabeth's unwillingness to sentence Mary.  The doom was

> " By her tempred without griefe or gall,
> Till strong constraint did her thereto enforce:
> And yet even then ruing her wilfull fall
> With more than needfull naturall remorse,
> And yeelding the last honour to her wretched corse.

The larger allegory dealt here with the mercy that should season justice ; but the bitterness of conflict was so prominent that, on the publication, in 1596, of the second part of the *Faerie Queene*, which contained this passage and others like it, King James of Scotland desired Spenser's prosecution.  The English ambassador in Scotland wrote to Lord Burghley, in November, 1596, that he had satisfied the king as to the privilege under which the book was published, yet he still desired that Edmund Spenser, for this fault, might be tried and punished.

79. **Samuel Daniel** was born near Taunton, in 1562, the son of a music master. From 1579 to 1582 he was studying as a commoner at Magdalen Hall, Oxford, but he did not take a degree. In 1585, at the age of twenty-three, he translated from the Italian *The Worthy Tract of Paulus Iouius, contayning a Discourse of rare Inuentions, both Militarie and Amorous, called Impresse. Whereunto is added a Preface, contayning the Arte of Composing them, with many other Notable Deuises.* Daniel became tutor to the Lady Anne Clifford, afterwards Countess of Pembroke, and became historian and poet under the patronage of the Earl of Pembroke's family. He began his career as an original poet, strongly influenced by the Italian writers, in 1592, with *Delia: contayning certayne Sonnets, with the Complaint of Rosamond.* This he dedicated to Mary, Countess of Pembroke, Sidney's sister; augmented editions, bringing the number of sonnets to fifty-seven, followed in 1594 and 1595. In 1595, Daniel combined his functions of historian and poet by publishing *The First Fowre Books of the Civille Warres betweene the Two Houses of Lancaster and Yorke.* This poem is in stanzas of the octave rhyme, established by Boccaccio as the Italian measure for narrative poetry (ch. iv. § 12), used by Pulci, Boiardo, Ariosto, Tasso. Strongly influenced by Italian forms, and often paraphrasing and translating from Italian, Daniel took naturally to octave rhyme for his poem on the civil wars. It was, like Sackville's tragedy of Buckingham, in the *Mirror for Magistrates,* too much of a history to be a poem in the true artistic sense, but it was musical in versification, patriotic and religious, and somewhat diffuse in moralising, with so much of the conservative tone that, in Church matters, some thought Daniel inclined towards Catholicism. In 1597 appeared his *Tragedy of Philotas;* in 1599, *Musophilus,* and other *Poetical Essayes.* The poem on the *Civil Wars* was also extended to five books in 1599, a sixth book followed in 1602. Daniel's *Musophilus* was a general defence of learning in dialogue between Philocosmus, a lover of the world, and Musophilus, a lover of the Muses. It has been said that after the death of Spenser, in 1599, Daniel succeeded him as poet laureate. But there was in Elizabeth's time no recognised court office of poet laureate (ch. v. § 34).

P *

80. **Michael Drayton**, born at Harthill, Warwickshire, was of about the same age as Daniel, but a poet with more sensibility, more vigour and grace of thought. Like Daniel, he began to write after 1590, and became a busy poet. He is said to have been maintained for a time at Oxford by Sir Henry Godere, of Polsworth, and he had a friend and patron in Sir Walter Aston, of Tixhall, in Staffordshire. In 1591, Drayton began his career as poet with a sacred strain: *The Harmonie of the Church, containing the Spiritual Songs and Holy Hymns of Godly Men, Patriarchs, and Prophets, all sweetly sounding to the Glory of the Highest.* This was followed, in 1593, by *Idea; The Shepherd's Garland, fashioned in Nine Eclogs; Rowland's Sacrifice to the Nine Muses;* in 1594, by his *Matilda,* and his *Idea's Mirrour, Amours in Quatorzains.* In 1596, *Matilda* reappeared in a volume which showed Drayton's muse to be then running parallel with Daniel's in choice of subject, and to be passing from love pastorals and sonnets to a strain from the past history of England. A year after Daniel's "Civil Wars," appeared Drayton's *Tragical Legend of Robert Duke of Normandy, with the Legend of Matilda the Chaste, Daughter of the Lord Robert Fitzwater, poysoned by King John; and the Legend of Piers Gaveston, the latter two by him newly corrected and augmented;* and in the same year, 1596—year of the second part of the *Faerie Queene,* and of Spenser's last publications— appeared Drayton's *Mortimeriados; The Lamentable Ciuell Warres of Edward the Second and the Barrons*—a poem afterwards known as the *Barons' Wars.* It was in stanzas of octave rhyme, like that poem on the civil wars of Lancaster and York which Daniel had published in part, and was still at work upon. The poets chose these themes because they yielded much reverse of fortune that could point a moral in the spirit illustrated by the still popular *Mirror for Magistrates* (§ 9). In 1598 Drayton again made poetry of history by publishing— their idea taken from Ovid—*England's Heroical Epistles*— letters from Rosamond to Henry II. and Henry II. to Rosamond, with like pairs of letters between King John and Matilda, Mortimer and Queen Isabel, and so forth.

**Henry Constable** published in 1592 twenty-three sonnets, under the title of *Diana; or, the Praises of his Mistres in Certaine Sweete Sonnets:* five were added to the next edition (1594). Other occasional verses and his *Spiritual Sonnets* bear witness to his ingenuity and sense of music. Constable belonged to a good Roman Catholic family, was born about 1555, became B.A. of St. John's College, Cambridge, 1579, and falling, as a Roman Catholic, under suspicion of treasonable correspondence with France, left England in 1595. In 1601 or 1602 he ventured to return, was discovered, and committed to the Tower, whence he was not released till the close of 1604. He was dead in 1616.

81. **John Davies**—who did not become Sir John till after the death of Elizabeth—was born in 1570, third son of John Davies, a lawyer at Westbury, in Wiltshire. He was sent to Oxford at the age of fifteen, as commoner of Queen's College, and thence went to study law at the Middle Temple, but he returned to Oxford in 1590 and took his degree of B.A. He was called to the Bar in 1595, and in 1596 published a poem on the art of dancing, entitled *Orchestra*. In the Middle Temple John Davies had been sometimes under censure for irregularities, and in February, 1598, he was expelled the Society for beating one Mr. Martin in the Temple Hall. John Davies then went back to Oxford and wrote a poem of good thoughts, pithily expressed, in quatrains. The poem was called (Know Thyself) *Nosce Teipsum. This Oracle Expounded in Two Elegies. 1. Of Humane Knowledge. 2. Of the Soule of Man, and the Immortalite thereof;* dedicated to Elizabeth, and published in 1599. Its stanzas of elegiac verse were so well packed with thought, always neatly contained within the limit of each stanza, that we shall afterwards have to trace back to this poem the adoption of its measure as, for a time, our "heroic stanza." The manner of it may be shown in a few quatrains that point the connection between *Nosce Teipsum* (Know Thyself) and its author's recent disgrace at the Middle Temple:

> " If aught can teach us aught, Affliction's looks
> (Making us pry into ourselves so near),
> Teach us to know ourselves, beyond all books,
> Or all the learned schools that ever were.
>
> " This mistress lately pluck'd me by the ear,
> And many a golden lesson hath me taught;
> Hath made my senses quick and reason clear;
> Reform'd my will and rectify'd my thought.
>
> " So do the winds and thunders cleanse the air:
> So working seas settle and purge the wine;
> So lopp'd and pruned trees do flourish fair;
> So doth the fire the drossy gold refine.

> " Neither Minerva, nor the learned Muse,
>   Nor rules of art, nor precepts of the wise,
>   Could in my brain those beams of skill infuse,
>   As but the glance of this dame's angry eyes.
>
> " She within lists my ranging mind hath brought,
>   That now beyond myself I will not go;
>   Myself am centre of my circling thought,
>   Only myself I study, learn, and know."

Thenceforth there was a change in Davies's career. He
was a member of the Parliament which met in October, 1601,
showing liberal interest in the privileges of the House and the
liberties of the people. In Trinity term of that year he was
restored to his old rank in the Temple; and at the death of
Elizabeth stood ready for a rapid rise in his profession.

82. **William Camden** (§ 16, 65), who was second master
of Westminster School when he published, in 1586, the first
edition of his *Britannia*—a work afterwards much expanded—
succeeded Dr. Edward Grant as head master in 1593. In 1597
he published for the use of Westminster boys a *Greek Grammar*,
which in course of time went through a hundred editions. In
the same year he left the school on being appointed Clarencieux
King-at-Arms. Camden was widely famed for learning, and
his purity of life and modest kindliness surrounded him with
friends.

**John Stow** (§ 16) still worked at history, and published in
1598, when more than seventy years old, the first edition of his
*Survey of London*—a book of great value. But he had lost
his best friends, and at the end of Elizabeth's reign he was distressed by poverty.

**John Hayward**—who became Sir John in the next reign—
published, in 1599, the first of his historical biographies, as the
*First Part of the Life and Raigne of King Henrie IIII.
Extending to the end of the first yeare of his raigne.* It was
dedicated, with high admiration, to the Earl of Essex, at a time
when the earl's dealing with the question of King James's succession was bringing his head into peril; and it contained a
passage on hereditary right in matters of succession that caused
Elizabeth to imprison the author and bid Francis Bacon search
the book for any treasonous matter to be found in it. Narratives and stage presentations of the deposition of Richard II.
were at this time supposed to have political significance.
Bacon's report was a good-natured joke : he found no treason
but much larceny from Tacitus.

83. **Francis Bacon** (§ 38, 48, 68), who had sat in Parliament for Melcombe Regis and Taunton, became member for Middlesex in the Parliament that met in February, 1593. One of the first questions before it was the granting of money to provide against danger from the Catholic Powers by which England was threatened. The Lords asked for a treble subsidy, payable within three years, in six instalments. Bacon assented to the subsidy, but raised a point of privilege in objection to the joining of the Commons with the Upper House in granting it. The point of privilege was overruled; the Lords and Commons did confer; the treble subsidy was granted; four years instead of three being allowed for the payment. Bacon had argued that the payment ought to extend over six years, for three reasons—the difficulty, the discontent, and the better means of supply than subsidy. His speeches on this occasion gave serious offence to the queen. He had no longer free access to her at Court, and this displeasure made her less ready to give him, over the heads of older lawyers, the office of Attorney-General, which presently fell vacant. The Earl of Essex, six years younger than Francis Bacon, was then looked to by both Anthony and Francis as their patron, and he did all that he could to influence the queen in Bacon's favour. The queen hesitated; dwelt on Bacon's youth and small experience—he was thirty-three—and in April, 1594, she gave the desired office to Sir Edward Coke, who was already Solicitor-General, who had large practice and high reputation as a lawyer, and was nine years older than Bacon. But Coke's appointment left vacant the office of Solicitor-General. For this suit was made with continued zeal, but in November, 1595, it was given to Serjeant Fleming. Essex, generous and impulsive, wished to make some amends to Bacon for his disappointment, and gave him a piece of land, which he afterwards sold for £1,800—say about £12,000, at the present value of money. Before July, 1596, Bacon was made Queen's Counsel. At the beginning of May in that year, Sir Thomas Egerton, who had been Master of the Rolls, became Lord Keeper. Bacon then sought in vain to succeed Egerton as Master of the Rolls. That was the year in which the Earl of Essex sailed for Cadiz.

84. **Sir Walter Raleigh** (§ 64) went with Essex on that expedition. He and Essex had been volunteers in the expedition of Drake and Norris (§ 69) to Portugal, which came home with much booty. Then the "Shepherd of the Ocean" went to Ireland, and came back with his friend Spenser to Court, after

planting about his own house at Youghal the first potatoes in
Ireland, with roots brought from Virginia. In the spring of
1591 an expedition was sent out under Lord Thomas Howard
and Raleigh's cousin, Sir Richard Grenville, to intercept the
fleet which annually brought to Spain its treasure from the
East. The English cruised about the Azores, where the Spanish
fleets from the East and the West Indies came together. The
Spanish fleet was found to be too strong, and Lord Thomas
Howard ordered his ships to keep together and avoid attack;
but Sir Richard Grenville, in the *Revenge*, believing that others
would follow, boldly dashed into the enemy's armada, where he
was left unaided, and fought desperately for fifteen hours with
fifteen great ships out of a fleet of fifty-five, sinking two and
doing great damage to others. When the *Revenge* must needs
be lost, and Grenville himself was wounded in the brain, he
ordered his surviving men to blow up the vessel. But the
*Revenge* was surrendered, Grenville's wounds were dressed by
the Spanish surgeons, the Spaniards who stood by marvelling
at his stout heart. As death drew near he said to them, in
Spanish, " Here die I, Richard Grenville, with a joyful and quiet
mind, for that I have ended my life as a true soldier ought to do
that hath fought for his country, queen, religion, and honour;
whereby my soul most joyful departeth out of this body, and
shall always leave behind it an everlasting fame of a valiant and
true soldier that hath done his duty, as he was bound to do."
*A Report of the Truth of the Fight about the Iles of Açores
this last Sommer Betuuixt the* Reuenge, *one of her Maiesties
Shippes, and an Armada of the King of Spaine*, was published
by Raleigh in November, 1591.

Raleigh then had Sherborne Castle given to him, but was
soon afterwards in the Tower, under her Majesty's displeasure,
for an amour with Elizabeth Throgmorton, a Maid of Honour,
whom he married after his release. He was in the Parliament
of 1593, when a bill was brought in for suppression of the
Brownists—a sect opposed to prelacy, and claiming equality
and independence of all congregations. " Root them out,"
said Raleigh, " by all means; but there are twenty thousand
of them, and if the men are put to death or banished,
who is to maintain the wives and children?" Raleigh next
planned an expedition to Guiana, tempted by the fables about
El Dorado (the Gilded One, priest or king smeared with oil and
covered with gold dust, an ideal god of wealth, lord of a city

fabulously rich), and sailed with a little expedition in February, 1595, attacked the Spaniards in Trinidad, and destroyed the new city of San José. He then went up the Orinoco, picked up a legend of Amazons, which gave its European name to a great river, and, when the rains set in, came home, bringing a young cacique with him. Raleigh reached England about the end of July, 1595, lived in London in great state, and published, in 1596, *The Discoverie of the Empyre of Guiana, with a Relation of the Citie of Manoa (which the Spanyards call El Dorado), and of the Prouinces of Emeria, Arromaia, Amapaia, &c. Performed in the year* 1595.

In the spring of 1596 the Spanish forces, under Cardinal Albert, Archduke of Austria, Spanish Governor of the Netherlands, took Calais before English aid could be sent to Henry IV. of France. An English fleet, with a Dutch contingent, sailed from Plymouth on the 1st of June, under Essex as commander of land forces and Lord Howard of Effingham as commander at sea, with Sir Walter Raleigh as Rear-Admiral. It entered the harbour of Cadiz, scattered and partly destroyed the fleet—the Spaniards themselves firing the large vessels—and left the Duke of Medina Sidonia to burn the carracks laden with merchandise worth millions, while they were engaged in the capture and sack of the town. Essex counselled that they should proceed to catch the treasure fleet on its way home, but this counsel was overruled, and a few days afterwards the Spanish treasure fleet sailed unhurt up the Tagus. The popularity of Essex was greatly increased, and Bacon wrote him a long letter on the text of Martha troubled about many things when one only was needful, and that one was—win the queen. It was a letter of astute council as to the management of her Majesty.

85. **Francis Bacon** having fallen into debt, cherished, in 1597, a hope of marrying the rich young widow of Sir William Hatton, who died in March of that year. In that year, also, Bacon was returned to Parliament as member for Ipswich. Essex endeavoured to help him in his widow hunt. The lady, in November, 1598, married Sir Edward Coke. In 1597 Essex sailed with another expedition to the Azores, where he was joined by **Raleigh** as Rear-Admiral. Raleigh took the town of Fayal, and was accused of breach of discipline; but nothing more came of that expedition, except the chance capture of a few rich prizes When the fleet returned, in October, there had been alarm at home of Spanish invasion. A Spanish force had been

seen from the coast of Cornwall ; some of its officers had landed on the Scilly Islands.    But again our loyal English weather had confounded the Spaniards, and that danger, the last of its kind, had been averted.

It was in January of this year (1597) that **Francis Bacon** —then thirty-six years old—published, with a dedication to his brother, *Essayes, Religious Meditations, Places of Perswasion and Disswasion.*    The essays in this first edition were only ten in number, and they dealt exclusively with the immediate relations of a man to life ; his private use of his own mind ; his use of it in relation to the minds of others, in relation to' the interests of others, in relation to his own interests—personally, as in case of money, health, and reputation, and also as they were mixed up with the business of mankind.    Thus the ten essays were—1. Of Study; 2. Of Discourse ; 3. Of Ceremonies and Respects ; 4. Of Followers and Friends ; 5. Of Suitors ; 6. Of Expense ; 7. Of Regiment of Health ; 8. Of Honour and Reputation ; 9. Of Faction ; 10. Of Negotiating.    The relation of man to another world was left designedly beyond the range of this first little group of essays ; but that element was supplied in the same book by twelve essays of another kind—the "Religious Meditations" which next followed.    These "Meditationes Sacræ" were in Latin ; their subjects—1. The Works of God and Man ; 2. The Miracles of our Saviour ; 3. The Innocency of the Dove and the Wisdom of the Serpent ; 4. The Exaltation of Charity ; 5. The Moderation of Cares ; 6. Earthly Hope ; 7. Hypocrites ; 8. Impostors ; 9. Several kinds of Imposture ; 10. Atheism ; 11. Heresies ; 12. The Church of the Scriptures.    The third section was formed by a group of what may be called ten essays of another kind—"A Table of Coulers, or Apparances of Good and Euil, and their Degrees as Places of Perswasion and Disswasion ; and their several Fallaxes, and the Elenches of them."    Colours meant circumstances which are likely to produce popular impressions and to sway the judgment of a weak man, or of a strong man not fully considering and pondering a matter.    They persuade to error, and they also quicken the persuasion to accept a truth.    Therefore, said Bacon, "to make a true and safe judgment nothing can be of greater use and defence to the mind than the discovery and reprehension of these colours, showing in what cases they hold, and in what cases they deceive : which, as it cannot be done but out of a very universal knowledge of the nature of things, so

being performed, it so cleareth a man's judgment and election
as it is the less apt to slide into error." Elenches are specious
arguments. Bacon takes a colourable form, such as this—" Let
us not wander into generalities, let us compare particular with
particular," submits it to an intellectual analysis, and points out
where its fallacies may lie; illustrating his argument with
images that would themselves have force to persuade or dis-
suade. Thus the form, " Let us not wander into generalities,
let us compare particulars with particulars," is met in three
ways, which are illustrated by these three examples—" The
blossom of May is generally better than the blossom of March;
and yet the best blossom of March is better than the best
blossom of May." " In many armies, if the matter should be
tried by duel between two champions, the victory should go
on one side, and yet if it be tried by the gross it would go of the
other side." " Generally metal is more precious than stone, and
yet a diamond is more precious than gold."

The little book, no bigger than the palm of a man's hand,
in which Bacon made his first appearance as an essayist, is thus,
throughout, an illustration of that genius for analysis applied to
the life of man which he applied in his philosophy to Nature.
He used the word "essay" in its exact sense. The Latin
*exigere* meant to test very exactly, to apply to a standard
weight or measure. The late Latin word *exagium* meant a
weighing, or a standard weight; thence came Italian *saggio*,
a proof, trial, sample; and *assaggiare*, to prove or try; whence
the French *essay*, and the English double forms, "assay" and
"essay." An assay of gold is an attempt to ascertain and
measure its alloys and to determine accurately its character
and value. An essay of anything in human nature submitted
it to a like process within the mind : it was an "essay of" something, and not as we write, now that the true sense of the word
is obscured, an "essay on." Strictly in that sense Bacon used
the word, and the essays, at which we shall find his work
running side by side with the development of his philosophy,
have therefore a definite relation to it. The style of these brief
essays, in which every sentence was compact with thought and
polished in expression until it might run alone through the world
as a maxim, had all the strength of euphuism and none of its
weakness. The sentences were all such as it needed ingenuity
to write; but this was the rare ingenuity of wisdom. Each
essay, shrewdly discriminative, contained a succession of wise

thoughts exactly worded. Take, for example, the first form of the first words of the first essay in this first edition : " Studies serue for pastimes, for ornaments, and for abilities. Their chiefe use for pastime is in priuateness and retiring ; for ornamente is in discourse, and for abilitie is in iudgement. For expert men can execute, but learned men are fittest to iudge or censure. To spend too much time in them is sloath, to vse them too much for ornament is affectation : to make iudgement wholly by their rules is the humour of a scholler. They perfect Nature, and are perfected by experience. Craftie men contemne them, simple men admire them, wise men vse them : For they teach not their owne vse, but that is a wisedome without them : and aboue them wonne by obseruation. Reade not to contradict, nor to belieue, but to waigh and consider." And so forth ; words like these being themselves considered by their writer and made more weighty in subsequent editions. Small as the book was, the quality of Bacon's mind was proved by this first publication of his essays.

86. Elizabeth's faithful Minister, William Cecil, Lord Burghley, died in August, 1598 ; Philip II. of Spain died a month later. But Spain still threatened England. Hugh O'Neale, Earl of Tyrone, aided by Spain, was in arms in Ireland. Sir John Norris had died under the fatigues of conflict with him. The Earl of Essex—frank and generous, but hot-headed, obstinate, and indiscreet—was made Lord-Deputy of Ireland, with large power. He left London for Dublin, openly confident of his future achievements, at the end of March, 1599. In May he marched out of Dublin with 16,000 men. After showy movements in Munster that seemed purposeless, for his work lay in Ulster, he had, early in September, a force in Ulster facing that of the rebel army ; but after a conference with Tyrone he assented to a six weeks' armistice, and agreed to make known to the English Government such conditions of peace from Tyrone as a conqueror might have dictated. Then he dispersed his army. The queen wrote her disapproval ; Essex left his command to hurry to her, and on the 28th of September, "about ten o'clock in the morning, alighted at the court-gate in post, and made all haste up to the presence, and so to the privy chamber, and stayed not till he came to the queen's bed-chamber, where he found the queen newly up, with her hair about her face .... and he so full of dirt and mire that his very face was full of it." He was commanded in the evening

to keep his chamber.  Next day he was examined before the Council, and was put under easy restraint—first with the Lord-Keeper, then in his own house.  Tyrone rose in rebellion again; another lord-deputy was sent, whose action was efficient.  Essex was then suspended from his offices of Privy Councillor, Lord-Marshal, and Master of the Ordnance.  In August he was released from custody, but forbidden to come to Court.  His monopoly of sweet wines expired, and Elizabeth would not renew the patent.  Then his quick temper became rebellious. He had been in correspondence with James VI. of Scotland— by cypher in the hand of Francis Bacon's brother Anthony—to force from Elizabeth, now sixty-eight years old, a recognition of her successor.  His impulsive dealing with this question perhaps introduced the considerations that had paralyzed his Irish policy.  But Essex now passed into open rebellion.  On the 8th of February, 1601, he and three hundred gentlemen, including Shakespeare's friend, the Earl of Southampton, were at Essex House.  The queen sent the Lord-Keeper and other officers of State to ask the reason of the gathering.  Essex contrived to lock them up in his library, and then, with his adherents, he rode out to raise the Londoners.  His object was to surprise the Court, seize the queen's person, and compel her to dismiss her present advisers and then call a Parliament.  But he overrated his own influence with the people, and after some lives had been lost, retreated by water to Essex House, burnt some papers, and was forced to surrender; that night the Earls of Essex and Southampton were prisoners in the Tower.  Queen's counsel, Bacon one of them, were called upon to inquire into this act of treason, by examining the prisoners.  They worked for seven days, in parties of not more than three, taking the several prisons in succession.  When Essex was arraigned, the evidence against him was produced by Coke, and Coke's way of letting it run off into side issues was rather favourable to the accused. Then Bacon rose, not being called upon to rise, pointed more strongly the accusations against his friend and benefactor, and brought the evidence back into a course more perilous to his life.  "As Cain," said Bacon, "that first murderer, took up an excuse for his fact, shaming to outface it with impudency, thus the earl made his colour the severing some men and councillors from her Majesty's favour, and the fear he stood in of his pre- tended enemies, lest they should murder him in his house." The evidence proceeded, and Coke's method again gave the earl some advantage. Bacon then rose and said, "I have never yet seen in any case such favour shown to any prisoner; so many digressions, such delivering of evidence by fractions, and so silly a defence of such great and notorious treasons." And he proceeded again to urge the main accusation home against Essex. On the 25th of February, 1601, Essex was beheaded, by his own wish privately, within the Tower. Upon Lord Southampton sentence was not executed, but he remained a prisoner during the rest of Elizabeth's reign. Justification of the execution of the Earl of Essex was entrusted to the advocate who had pressed with most energy the case against him at his trial. Materials were supplied in "twenty-five papers concerning the Earl of Essex's treasons, &c., to be delivered to Mr. Francis Bacon, for Her Majesty's service;" and Bacon's hand, following particular instructions as to the manner of treatment, drew up for the public *A Declaration of the Practices and Treasons attempted and committed by Robert late Earle of Essex and his Complices.* Before its publication (in 1601) this declaration was discussed by councillors and queen, and underwent the alterations incident to such discussion. Bacon had been living beyond his means, and was still seeking advancement. In September, 1598, he had been arrested for debt, but in the spring of 1601 his worldly means were somewhat improved by the death of his brother Anthony. He obtained a gift of £1,200, the fine of one of the accomplices of Essex, but he obtained no higher reward of his services before the death of Elizabeth, on the 24th of March, 1603.

87. Francis Bacon, our first essayist, was preceded in European literature only by Montaigne. Montaigne had a translator in **John Florio.** It has been suggested, without reason, that in the Holofernes of *Love's Labour's Lost,* Shakespeare was ridiculing Florio. "Resolute John Florio," as he wrote himself, was an active man of Italian descent, born in London in Henry VIII.'s reign, who taught Italian and French at Oxford, and was in high repute at Court. He published, in 1578, *Florio his First Fruites; which yeelde familiar speech, merie Prouerbes, wittie sentences, and golden sayings. Also, a perfect Introduction to the Italian and English Tongues.* In 1591 followed *Florio's Second Frutes. To which is annexed his Garden of Recreation, yeelding six thousand Italian Prouerbs.* At the end of Elizabeth's reign, in 1603, appeared *The Essays of Michael, Lord of Montaigne, done into English by John Florio.*

Upon a copy of this book Shakespeare's autograph has been found, and Shakespeare's knowledge of Montaigne is shown in the *Tempest,* where the ideal commonwealth of the old Lord Gonzalo (Act ii. sc. 1) corresponds closely, in word as well as in thought, with Florio's Montaigne. Of course, also, the great poems of Ariosto and Tasso were translated.

**Sir John Harington,** born at Helston, near Bath, in 1561, and educated at Eton and Cambridge, published at the age of thirty, in 1591, *Orlando Furioso in English Heroical Verse.* Harington was knighted on the field by the Earl of Essex.

Tasso had in Elizabeth's reign two translators. The first was **Richard Carew,** whose *Godfrey of Bulloigne, or the Recouerie of Hierusalem* appeared in 1594; the second was **Edward Fairfax,** whose translation appeared with the same titles in 1600. It is in the octave rhyme of the original, one of the most musical and poetical of all English translations into verse. Fairfax was the second son, perhaps illegitimate, of Sir Thomas Fairfax, of Denton, in Yorkshire. He lived as a retired scholar at Newhall, in Knaresborough Forest, and, later in life, educated with his own children those of his brother Ferdinand, Lord Fairfax. One of these nephews became famous as the Fairfax of the Civil Wars. Edward Fairfax himself lived into the reign of Charles I., and died in 1632.

88. The literature of the Church of England was represented in the latter years of Elizabeth's reign by **Richard Hooker,** who was born at Heavitree, near Exeter, about 1553. He was to have been apprenticed to a trade, but his aptness for study caused him to be kept at school by his teacher, who persuaded young Richard Hooker's well-to-do uncle, John, then Chamberlain of Exeter, to put him to college for a year. John Hooker, a friend of Bishop Jewel's (§ 14), introduced his nephew to that bishop, who, finding the boy able and his parents poor, sent him at the age of fifteen to Corpus Christi College, Oxford. Edwin Sandys, Bishop of London, heard from Jewel the praises of young Richard Hooker, and though himself a Cambridge man, sent his son to Oxford that he might have Hooker, whose age then was nineteen, for tutor and friend. Other pupils came, and Hooker was on the most pleasant relations with them. In 1577 he became M.A. and Fellow of his college.

89. A friend of Hooker's at college, about four years older than himself, was **Sir Henry Savile,** who had graduated at

Brazenose and was elected to a Fellowship at Merton College. Savile afterwards travelled on the Continent. On his return he gave lessons to the queen in Greek and Mathematics, and became Warden of Merton College. In 1581 Savile published, at Oxford, a translation of *The Ende of Nero and Beginning of Galba, Fower Bookes of the Histories of Cornelius Tacitus; The Life of Agricola.* In 1596, Savile added to his office of Warden of Merton College that of Provost of Eton, and in the same year published *Rerum Anglicarum Scriptores post Bedam præcipui*—a folio containing the works of some of the old historians after Bede; namely, William of Malmesbury, Henry of Huntingdon, Roger Hoveden, Ethelwerd, and Ingulphus of Croyland. The death of his son caused Savile to devote his property to the encouragement of learning, and, in the reign of James I., in 1619, he founded at Oxford the Savilian professorship of Astronomy and Geometry. Sir Henry Savile died at Eton in 1622.

90. **Richard Hooker**, whom we left to follow the career of his friend Savile, was appointed, in 1579, to read the Hebrew lecture in his university, and did so for the next three years. He took holy orders, quitted Oxford, and married a scolding wife. He was shy and shortsighted, and had allowed her to be chosen for him. Of himself it is said that he never was seen to be angry. In 1584 Hooker was presented to the parsonage of Drayton-Beauchamp, near Aylesbury; and there he was found by his old pupil, Edwin Sandys, with Horace in his hand, relieving guard over his few sheep out of doors, and indoors called from his guests to rock the cradle. Sandys reported Hooker's condition to his father, who had become Archbishop of York. In 1585 the office of Master of the Temple became vacant, and Hooker, then thirty-two years old, was, through the Archbishop's influence, called from his poor country parsonage to take it.

When, in 1583, good Archbishop Grindal (§ 33) was succeeded at Canterbury by John Whitgift, there was a return of bitterness against the Nonconformists, with extreme claim of all rights of the Church. This intensified the controversies of the time. The lecturer at the Temple for evening sermons, when Hooker became Master, was Walter Travers, a minister of blameless life, a correspondent of Beza's, and a warm supporter of opinions cherished by the Puritans. He was popular in the Temple, had hoped also himself to be chosen Master, and obtain increase of influence for his opinions. In Hooker the Temple had a Master who was faithful to the ecclesiastical system of the English Church. In the Temple church on Sundays Hooker preached in the morning, Travers in the evening, and, as it was said, " the forenoon sermon spake Canterbury, the afternoon Geneva." This continued until the Archbishop forbade Travers's preaching. Petition was in vain made to the Privy Council; and this led to discontent. The petition was printed privately, and published. Hooker then published an *Answer to the Petition of Mr. Travers*, and was drawn into a controversy, which led his pure and quiet mind to the resolve that he would argue out in detail his own sense of right and justice in the Established Church system of his country, in *Eight Books of the Law of Ecclesiastical Polity*. That he might do this he asked for removal to some office in which he might be at peace. He wrote to the Archbishop, " My Lord, when I lost the freedom of my cell, which was my college, yet I found some degree of it in my quiet country parsonage: but I am weary of the noise and oppositions of this place; and indeed, God and Nature did not intend me for contentions, but for study and quietness. My Lord, my particular contests with Mr. Travers here have proved the more unpleasant to me, because I believe him to be a good man; and that belief hath occasioned me to examine mine own conscience concerning his opinions." Study had not only satisfied him, but he had " begun a treatise, in which I intend a justification of the laws of our ecclesiastical polity; in which design God and his holy angels shall at the last great Day bear me that witness which my conscience now does, that my meaning is not to provoke any, but rather to satisfy all tender consciences; and I shall never be able to do this but where I may study, and pray for God's blessing upon my endeavours, and keep myself in peace and privacy, and behold God's blessings spring out of my mother earth, and eat my own bread without opposition; and, therefore, if your Grace can judge me worthy of such a favour, let me beg it, that I may perfect what I have begun." Hooker accordingly was made, in 1591, rector of Boscombe, in Wiltshire, a parish with few people in it, four miles from Amesbury, and was instituted also, as a step to better preferment, to a minor prebend of small value in Salisbury. At Boscombe Hooker finished the *Four Books of the Lawes of Ecclesiastical Politie*, published in 1594, with " A Preface to them that Seeke

(as they tearme it) the Reformation of Lawes and Orders
Ecclesiasticall in the Church of England." These four books
treated, 1. Of laws in general; 2. Of the use of Divine law contained in Scripture, whether that be the only law which ought
to serve for our direction in all things without exception; 3. Of
laws concerning Ecclesiastical Polity, whether the form thereof
be in Scripture so set down that no addition or change is
lawful; and, 4. Of general exceptions taken against the Lawes
of the English Church Polity as being Popish, and banished
out of certain reformed churches. What Hooker said of
Travers, Travers had like reason to say of Hooker, for this was
the work of a good man, in the eyes of thousands whom it may
not have convinced on points of discipline; a work perfect in
spirit, earnest, eloquent, closely reasoned, and in the best sense
of the word religious. Hooker's opening argument upon the
origin of laws among men has interest from its close relation to
the later arguments of Hobbes and Locke upon the origin and
nature of the rights of kings. After reasoning that we derive
our knowledge from experience and reasoning, and that the
two principal fountains of human action are knowledge and
will, he says that we find out for ourselves laws, by reason, to
guide the will to that which is good, and further to supply those
defects and imperfections which are in us living singly and
solely by ourselves, we are naturally induced to seek communion and fellowship with others. "Thus arose political
societies among men naturally equal. Men reasoned that strifes
and troubles would be endlesse, except they gave their common
consent all to be ordered by some whom they should agree upon,
without which consent there were no reasons that one man·
should take upon him to be lord or iudge over another; because
although there be, according to the opinion of some very great
and iudicious men, a kinde of naturall right in the noble, wise,
and vertuous, to governe them which are of servile disposition;
neuerthelesse for manifestation of this their right, and men's
more peaceable contentment on both sides, the assent of them
who are to be governed seemeth necessary."

In 1595 Richard Hooker left Boscombe for tne rectory of
Bishopsbourne, three miles from Canterbury, where he spent
the rest of his life. In 1597 appeared the fifth book of his
*Ecclesiastical Polity*, which was longer than all the other four
together. He died in 1600, having, while his health failed,
desired only to live till he had finished the remaining three

books of the work, for which his life seemed to have been given him. His health suffered the more for his labour at them, but he did complete the remaining three books, though without the revision given to the preceding five, and they were published, some years after his death, in 1618.

91. There were in Elizabeth's reign two brothers Fletcher, Richard and Giles, whose children are more interesting than themselves. Richard Fletcher became D.D., and bishop successively of Bristol, Worcester, and London. He attended at the execution of Mary Queen of Scots, angered the queen by his second marriage, smoked much tobacco, and was the father of John Fletcher, in the next reign, friend and fellow-writer, as a dramatist, with Francis Beaumont. Richard's brother, Giles Fletcher, became LL.D., was employed by Elizabeth as Commissioner in Scotland, Germany, and the Low Countries, was sent as ambassador to Russia, and published, in 1591, a book *Of the Russe Common Wealth,* with dedication to the queen. It was quickly suppressed, "lest it might give offence to a prince in amity with England." Dr. Giles Fletcher thought he had found in the Tartars the lost tribes of Israel. He became treasurer of St. Paul's, secretary to the City of London, and Master of the Court of Requests. He had two sons, Phineas and Giles Fletcher, afterwards known as poets. These, then, were first cousins of John Fletcher the dramatist.

92. Shakespeare was in his maturity of power, and a new generation of dramatists was growing towards manhood, when **Joseph Hall** published his satires. Joseph Hall was born in 1574, at Bristow Park by Ashby-de-la-Zouch, and educated at Emmanuel College, Cambridge. In 1597, at the age of twenty-three, he published *Virgidemiarum, Six Bookes; First Three Bookes of toothlesse Satyrs:* 1. *Poeticall;* 2. *Academicall;* 3. *Morall.* In the following year the work was completed by *Virgidemiarum: the Three Last Bookes of Byting Satyrs.* It means nothing particular to say that these satires were burnt by order of the Archbishop of Canterbury. Whitgift and Bancroft, Archbishop of Canterbury and Bishop of London, as censors of the press, distinguished themselves, in 1599, by ordering the burning of much literature, Marlowe's *Ovid* and his *Satires,* Marston's *Pygmalion,* Hall's *Satires,* the epigrams of Davies and others, the tracts of Nash and Harvey, and decreeing that no satires or epigrams should be printed for the future

Censorship of the press by the Church came in with printing. The ecclesiastical superintendence introduced in 1479 and 1496, was more completely established by a Bull of Leo X. in 1515, which required bishops and inquisitors to examine all books before printing, and to suppress heretical opinions. At the Reformation this practice was continued, under authority, and assumed now by the Crown as part of its prerogative, and delegated to the Archbishop of Canterbury and Bishop of London. Printing was also restrained by patents and monopolies. In Elizabeth's time it was interdicted in all parts of England, except London, Oxford, and Cambridge, and the presses there were limited in number.

Joseph Hall's six books, *Virgidemiarum, i.e.,* of rod-harvests, stripes or blows, were the work of a clever young man who had read Juvenal and Persius and the satires of Ariosto, and who, because he was the first to write English satire in the manner of Juvenal, ignorantly believed himself to be the first English satirist. "I first adventure," he said in his prologue—

> " I first adventure, follow me who list,
>   And be the second English satirist."

The mistake is of no consequence. Hall's satires are in rhyming couplets of ten-syllabled lines; he thought English rhyme inferior to Latin quantity, but saw that the Latin metres could not be applied to English verse, and laughed at Stanihurst (§ 53).

> " Whoever saw a colt, wanton and wild,
>   Yok'd with a slow foot ox on fallow field,
>   Can right areed how handsomely besets
>   Dull spondees with the English dactylets.
>   If Jove speak English in a thund'ring cloud,
>   Thwick thwack, and riff raff, roars he out aloud.
>   Fie on the forged mint that did create
>   New coin of words never articulate ! "

Hall laughed at the rising drama, crying—

> " Shame that the Muses should be bought and sold
>   For every peasant's brass on each scaffold."

He laughed at what he called "pot fury of the dramatists."

> " One higher pitch'd doth set his soaring thought
>   On crowned kings, that fortune hath low brought :
>   Or some upreared high aspiring swaine,
>   As it might be the Turkish Tamburlaine :
>   Then weeneth he his base drink-drowned spright
>   Rapt to the threefold loft of heaven hight,

> When he conceives upon his feigned stage
> The stalking steps of his great personage,
> Graced with huff-cap terms and thund'ring threats
> That his poor hearer's hair quite upright sets."

But while Hall attacked the "terms Italianate, big-sounding sentences and words of state" upon the stage, he paid homage to Spenser.

> " Let no rebel satyr dare traduce
> Th' eternal legends of thy faerie muse,
> Renowned Spenser: whom no earthly wight
> Dares once to emulate, much less dares despight."

Only he paired in the next line Du Bartas with Ariosto: "Salust of France and Tuscan Ariost." The satirist in the golden time of Elizabethan vigour talked as usual of the good old times that were gone, when luxury was not, and our

> " Grandsires' words savoured of thrifty leeks
> Or manly garlicke.
>    *     *     *     *     *
> But thou canst mask in garish gauderie,
> To suit a foole's far-fetched liverie.
> A French head joyn'd to necke Italian :
> Thy thighs from Germanie, and brest from Spain .
> An Englishman in none, a foole in all :
> Many in one, and one in severall.
> Then men were men ; but now the greater part
> Beasts are in life, and women are in heart."

If we go back to Occleve (ch. v. § 8), or farther back to Gower (ch. iv. § 32), we find that the note has always been the same; sound and true in the steady fixing of attention upon vices and follies to be conquered (since there is small hope for a people that will only praise itself), but with innocent delusion of a bygone golden age. Hall's golden age, however, is not bygone; it is to be found in Spain, if the test of it be a relish for garlic. Joseph Hall obtained the living of Hawstead, Suffolk, but resigned it for the living of Waltham Holy Cross, in Essex. This he held for two-and-twenty years, while obtaining, as we shall find, after Elizabeth's death, other promotions.

93. We part, in Elizabeth's reign, from "Salust of France," at the year 1598, when Joshua Sylvester, then thirty-five years old, translated his *Diuine Weekes and Works* (§ 35, 52). Sylvester had begun in 1590, by publishing a translation of the poem of Du Bartas upon the Battle of Ivry, *A Canticle of the Victorie obtained by the French King Henrie the Fourth at Yvry. Translated by Josua Siluester, Marchant-aduenturer.*

He had added another piece to that in 1592. There had been
other translators from the French poet. In 1584, Thomas
Hudson had published at Edinburgh a translation of his *History
of Judith*, made by command of James VI. Another of these
translators was William Lisle, of Wilbraham, who published a
part of *The Second Week* of Du Bartas in 1596, dedicated to
Lord Howard of Effingham, added the *Colonies* in 1598, and
translated, in all, four books. Another of the translators, at the
end of Elizabeth's reign and beginning of the reign of James
in England, was Thomas Winter. In verses of praise prefixed
to Sylvester's translation, Joseph Hall said—

> " Bartas was some French angel, girt with Bayes:
> And thou a Bartas art in English Layes,
> Whether is more? Mee seems (the sooth to say'n)
> One Bartas speaks, in Tongues, in Nations, twain."

And Ben Jonson wrote (Du Bartas died in 1590)—

> " Behold ! the reverend shade of Bartas stands
> Before my thought and (in thy right) commands
> That to the world I publish for him, This:
> Bartas doth wish thy English now were His.
> So well in that are his inventions wrought,
> As his will now be the Translation thought,
> Thine the Original ; and France shall boast
> No more those mayden glories shee hath lost."

But it is to be remembered that Du Bartas owed his repute
with us not only to his skill as a writer according to the
ephemeral taste of the time, but also as a French Huguenot for
his accord with the religious feeling of the English people, and
because his song was always upon sacred themes.

94. Ben Jonson has just been quoted. In 1598 he had begun
to write. He was ten years younger than Shakespeare, and in
the closing year of Elizabeth's reign, when Shakespeare had
risen to the fulness of his power, Ben Jonson was beginning his
career. We have now to end the sketch of our literature in
Elizabeth's reign with some account of the latter years of the
*ELIZABETHAN DRAMA.* To avoid confusion let us take that
word to mean simply, the English drama during the reign of
Elizabeth. It falls naturally into two sections, which we may
call Earlier and Later Elizabethan. The *Earlier Elizabethan
Drama* dates from the first plays at the beginning of Elizabeth's
reign to the date of Spenser's latest publications, the year of the
second part of the *Faerie Queene*, 1596. It includes *Gorboduc*
and the earliest plays, plays of Lodge, Peele, Lyly, Greene.

Marlowe, and the early works of Shakespeare. The *Later Elizabethan Drama*, from 1596 to 1603, has in its centre Shakespeare, become master of his art; a few of the elder writers who add to the number of their works; with a few younger men, Ben Jonson, Marston, Dekker, and Heywood, who began to write plays under Elizabeth; and one older man, George Chapman, who started later in life as a playwright, and then took his place among Later Elizabethan dramatists. With Shakespeare, these younger men, and George Chapman, passed as active workers into the reign of James the First. But in that reign the number of the dramatists was soon increased by poets who had been young men or children under Elizabeth. These writers were educated more or less by the same influences that had produced the great Elizabethan poets. In their writing there was an Elizabethan character, but they wrote their plays in the reigns of James I. and Charles I. Such were Beaumont and Fletcher, Webster, Massinger, Ford, and Shirley.

95. **William Shakespeare** (§ 37, 47, 71), in 1596, buried at Stratford his only son Hamnet, twelve years old. A grant of arms to his father in that year (about which there was another note in 1599) indicates that the poet was then prospering. In 1597, three plays of his were published in quarto, *Richard II.*, *Richard III.*, and *Romeo and Juliet.* Those plays of Shakespeare which were printed in his lifetime were in quarto form, and known to students as the early quartos. They were not corrected by the author. Even Ariosto, as we have seen (ch. vi. § 40), after the minutest care in writing his *Orlando*, had no oversight of the business of publication. In Easter term of the same year, 1597, Shakespeare began to form the home in his native town to which he had looked forward. He bought for sixty pounds, New Place, the best house in the line of the main street of the town, with two barns and two gardens behind, in the direction of the Avon. It had been built by Sir Hugh Clopton in the time of Henry VII., and it was bought by Shakespeare of William Underhill, a man of good position, whose home was close by, at Idlicote, but who was himself buying land about Stratford, and seeking to establish a family. Underhill died a few months after he had sold the house to Shakespeare. New Place was in Chapel Street, at the corner of a lane, Chapel Lane, leading towards the river. At the opposite corner was, and is, a church called the Guild Chapel, or Chapel of the Holy Cross, from which the street and lane

were named, and founded also in the reign of Henry VII. by
Sir Hugh Clopton. On the other side of the Guild Chapel was
the grammar school. Thus the church stood between Shakespeare and the school. In 1597 also, while Shakespeare was
establishing this home for himself in Stratford he was helping
his father and mother, for there was a bill filed in Chancery
by John Shakespeare and his wife to recover Ashbies (§ 37)
from John, the son of Edward Lambert. There is also other
evidence that by this time Shakespeare's prudent management,
and his success in London, had enabled him—the first man in
our literature who did so—to save money earned, not indirectly,
by the free use of his genius. A record, dated October, 1598,
shows him to have been assessed on property in the parish of
St. Helen's, Bishopsgate. The plays of his printed in quarto, in
1598, were *Love's Labour's Lost* and *Part I. of King Henry IV.*,
but there is other evidence to show what plays of his had by
that date been acted.

John Bodenham published in 1598 a collection of sententious extracts from ancient moral philosophers, &c., called
*Politeuphuia* (*Wits' Commonwealth*). It was designed chiefly
for the benefit of young scholars, was popular, and often afterwards reprinted. In the same year, 1598, Francis Meres,
M.A., published *Palladis Tamia* (*Wits' Treasury, being the
Second Part of Wits' Commonwealth*), 12mo, of 174 leaves,
euphuistic, as its title indicates, and also designed for instruction
of the young. This book contained a brief comparison of English poets with Greeks, Latins, and Italians, and in the course
of it Meres wrote: "As the soule of Euphorbus was thought
to live in Pythagoras, so the sweete wittie soule of Ovid lives in
mellifluous and hony-tongued Shakespeare; witnes his *Venus
and Adonis*, his *Lucrece*, his sugred *Sonnets* among his private
friends, &c. As Plautus and Seneca are accounted the best for
comedy and tragedy among the Latines, so Shakespeare among
the English is the most excellent in both kinds for the stage; for
comedy, witnes his *Gentlemen of Verona*, his *Errors*, his *Love's
Labor's Lost*, his *Love's Labour's Wonne*" [probably a former
name of *All's Well that Ends Well*], "his *Midsummers Night
Dreame*, and his *Merchant of Venice;* for tragedy, his *Richard
the 2, Richard the 3, Henry the 4, King John, Titus
Andronicus*, and his *Romeo and Juliet*. As Epius Stolo said
that the Muses would speake with Plautus' tongue, if they
would speak Latin, so I say that the Muses would speak

---

with Shakespeare's fine filed phrase, if they would speake English."

In 1598 **Shakespeare** was thirty-four years old; he had been at work in London for about twelve years, of which the first six had been years of patient upward struggle, and the other six had been years of increasing power and prosperity. He had written chronicle plays, in which his muse did "like himself heroically sound;" had dealt playfully in *Love's Labour's Lost* with the euphuism of his time; had found out the marvellous wealth of his imagination "glancing from heaven to earth, from earth to heaven" in the *Midsummer Night's Dream;* had shown in *Romeo and Juliet* the innocent beauty of young love breathing its harmonies among the petty feuds and hatreds of mankind; and in the *Merchant of Venice* he had risen to a pure expression of that spirit of religion which, for many in his time was obscured by passions of the conflict between creed and creed. What the Capulets and Montagues meant in *Romeo and Juliet*, the Jew and Christian meant in the *Merchant of Venice;* but in that play the central thought to which every scene relates gave prominence to the relation between Shylock and Antonio.

When he had done his 'prentice work, and become master of his craft, every play of Shakespeare's became a true poem, and had the spiritual unity that is in every great work of art. Each play had its own theme in some essential truth of life, which is its soul expressed in action, and with which every detail is in exquisite accord.

96. In the *Merchant of Venice*, for example, Shakespeare dealt in his own way with the problem of life. It opens with a vague foreshadowing of evil in a merchant with his wealth upon the waves. There is rapid advance of the story, the very first lines pointing towards the event on which the action of the play depends; but the narrative all springs up naturally in a dialogue that represents the cheerful intercourse of life. This genial air is, as it were, the atmosphere of the whole play, softens all its didactic outlines, and pervades especially its opening and close. The dialogue in the first scene, while firm, as it is throughout, to the story-telling, abounds chiefly in suggestion of the different ways in which men variously tempered take what comes to them in life, including those

> " Whose visages
> Do cream and mantle like a standing pond."

And do a wilful stillness entertain,
With purpose to be dress'd in an opinion
Of wisdom, gravity, profound conceit,
As who should say, 'I am Sir Oracle,
And when I ope my lips let no dog bark.'"

The social geniality deepens at the end of the first scene into the close intercourse of friendship between Antonio and Bassanio. There is here a double purpose answered. It pertains to the essence of the play that a firm friendship between man and man should be at the root of it, but this friendship unites also the two men, who serve as centres to the two parts of the story: the old story of the caskets, used by Shakespeare for a solving of life's problem from its human side; and the old story of the pound of flesh, through which he added the diviner sense of duty.

Bassanio sought Portia, that lot in life which is the ideal of us all:

" Nor is the wide world ignorant of her worth,
For the four winds blow in from every coast
Renowned suitors, and her sunny locks
Hang on her temples like a golden fleece;
Which makes her seat of Belmont Colchos' strand,
And many Jasons come in quest of her."

When we pass in the next scene to Belmont the story-telling is continued rapidly, and there is the light genial air of playful intercourse still softening the firm expression of the main idea. Thus the dialogue between Portia and Nerissa plays over the conditions of life and temper that affect right search for a good life. They, it is lightly suggested, who have a right love for it will choose their way in the pursuit of it according to God's meaning, and then follow whimsical sketches of some national ideas of happiness proper to the Neapolitan, the Bavarian, Frenchman, Englishman. The scene ends with mention of Bassanio, " a scholar and a soldier," whole worker, mind and body, through whom we shall get the solution of this part of the problem.

Still never forgetting that he has a story to tell, and that this must not stand still, all thought being expressed in it and none merely scattered round about it, Shakespeare then takes up the second of the two threads from which the plot is woven, advancing rapidly the story of the bond, while he subtly prepares the mind of spectator or reader for the reverse of Antonio's fortune and for the antagonism to come. Then Jew and

Christian are brought face to face, and there is strong marking
of the enmity of each to each. Wrongs suffered by Jews at the
hands of Christians are, in Shylock's speech beginning, " Signor
Antonio, many a time and oft," given as ground for Shylock's
bitterness. Antonio replies with Christian disdain and intolerance. He has called Shylock dog, and says,—

> " I am as like to call thee so again,
> To spit on thee again, and spurn thee too."

The first act closes with Antonio's acceptance of the bond,
suggested in the idleness of malice when there is little or no
prospect of its enforcement. But the scene opens and closes
with a pointing of attention to the ships that bear Antonio's
wealth upon the waves.

In developing his plot Shakespeare produces a fine climax
by so interweaving its two threads that the one which leads to
the human lesson of the way to the true life comes to its end
in the third act; the other is ready to add, in the fourth act,
its diviner lesson, and the fifth act then rises to the height of
heaven itself in expressing the full thought of the whole play.

At the opening of the second act we are in Belmont, and the
vain-glorious Prince of Morocco is to make his choice. Why
Prince of Morocco? Because he is to represent the man whose
choice is of the golden casket, as determined by the outside
pomp and glory of the world; and this view of life men associate
with Eastern splendour. The scene changes to Venice, and
Lancelot Gobbo, the clown—whose change of service is of great
use to the story—stands also, in his relation to the inner thought
of the play, for the raw material of humanity; good-natured, as
Shakespeare always felt men and women, on the whole, to be,
and with the rudiments of two helps to the higher life—conscience
and natural affections. As Bassanio prepares to depart for
Belmont, Gratiano will go too; the genial temper is the right
companion of earnest effort, but it must be kept within due
bounds. Among the many sketches of forms and ways of life
that belong as accessories to the working out of the main
thought in the *Merchant of Venice*, Bassanio's counsel to
Gratiano, " Thou art too wild, too rude, and bold of voice,"
balances Gratiano's former censure of an affected precision. In
the next scene, between Lancelot and Jessica, we have again
Lancelot's natural sympathies, and a suggestion of those cheer-
less restraints of home which made it not unnatural for Jessica's

Q

quick Eastern blood, nourished in Italy, to urge her beyond rule. After this scene, while only a masking is in question, there is preparation for the wrong that will stir Shylock's hatred of the Christian into fury, just at the time when Antonio's bond is forfeit. In the love between Lorenzo and Jessica there is Shakespeare's practical suggestion, as in the love between the Capulet and Montague, that we all are of one race, and should feel our kindred. So when, in *Cymbeline,* Arviragus says to Imogen, " Brother, stay here: are we not brothers?" She replies—

" So man and man should be ;
But clay and clay differs in dignity,
Whose dust is both alike."

It is the clay in us, and not the nobler part, that makes the separation.

In the scene between Shylock and his daughter, again, there are the ungenial home conditions which serve to make her conduct less unnatural, and the story is continued to the flight of Jessica during Bassanio's parting festivities, and to the rapid departure of Bassanio's ship. Then we return to Belmont, and see the Prince of Morocco trust his hope of happiness to that golden casket, which is inscribed, " Who chooseth me shall gain what many men desire." His choice is that of all who place the happiness of life in money-making, or in the luxurious enjoyment of what money buys. Within the golden casket is a carrion death, with the lesson: .

" Many a man his life hath sold
But my outside to behold."

Shakespeare takes us back to Venice, shows us the Jew's fury at the abduction of his daughter—his own flesh has been torn from him, " I say, my daughter is my flesh and blood." His claiming of the bond while in the passion of this wrong brings within bounds of nature an extravagant fable that had been used only as a parable. Suggestion of peril to Antonio in Salanio's

" Let good Antonio look he keep his day,
Or he shall pay for this,

is immediately followed by the first indication of the fall of the merchant's fortunes, coupled with a fresh suggestion of his friendship for Bassanio.

We pass then to Belmont, and see the silver casket chosen by the Prince of Arragon. Why Prince of Arragon? Because the Spaniard was the common type of self-asserting pride, and through the silver casket choice was made of a life happy by attainment of one's own deserts. He will not choose with those whom the gold tempts :

> "I will not choose what many men desire,
> Because I will not jump with common spirits,
> And rank me with the barbarous multitudes."

But he accepts the condition on the silver treasure-house : "Who chooseth me shall get as much as he deserves." We all know the man, not base of mind, who only wants his deserts, and loses precious time over lamenting that he has never got them. If the critics had been just to his books, or his pictures ; if this, and if that, and

> ' Oh, that estates, degrees, and offices
> Were not derived corruptly, and that clear honour
> Were purchased by the merit of the wearer."

But the true life is not so to be won. The silver casket reveals only a fool's head, with a legend that reminds the chooser of the shadow's bliss of him who was in love with his own shadow. The second act ends with the landing of Bassanio at Belmont, and again a glancing forward at the hope inspired by him.

The third act opens with the loss of all Antonio's wealth on the waves, whereby the passion of Shylock is suddenly supplied with power of revenge. Let Antonio look to his bond. What kindness can he ask?

"He hath disgraced me, and hindered me half a million ; laughed at my losses, mocked at my gains, scorned my nation, thwarted my bargains, cooled my friends, heated mine enemies ; and what's his reason? I am a Jew. Hath not a Jew eyes? Hath not a Jew hands, organs, dimensions, senses, affections, passions? fed with the same food, hurt with the same weapons, subject to the same diseases, healed by the same means, warmed and cooled by the same winter and summer, as a Christian is? If you prick us, do we not bleed? if you tickle us, do we not laugh? if you poison us, do we not die? and if you wrong us, shall we not be revenged? If we are like you in the rest we will resemble you in that. If a Jew wrong a Christian, what is his humility? Revenge. If a Christian wrong a Jew, what should his sufferance be, by Christian example?"

Shylock is ready to stand upon the letter of the law, and the story is now ripe for a full expression of the innermost thought of the play, which, deepening as it goes, continues to the end.

Bassanio's choice of the leaden casket is preluded with a song, ringing the knell of trust in the delight of the eyes only. "Who chooseth me, must give and hazard all he hath." That is the legend on the casket of lead, threatening more than it promises, by which alone the true life may be won.  The human lesson of life summed up in it, is like that of the parable of the talents.  A man must exert all his powers ; be the best and do the best that it is in him to be or do ; give all that he hath, and hazard all : not making conditions of reward according to desert ; not asking whether he shall be rich, or praised, or happy, for the simple hearty doing of his duty; but doing it and taking what may come.  So is Portia won, and plighted to Bassanio, as Nerissa to Gratiano, with a ring, never to be lost or given away.  The severe outline of the higher lesson of life is here softened again by the pervading atmosphere of genial intercourse ; but from the human truth so far expressed, Shakespeare passes on at once to the divine truth which is its crown.

Antonio's letter to Bassanio arrives at Belmont.  In Antonio, man—subject to fortune, changeful as the waves—is about to stand between the two principles of justice and mercy, of the Old Testament and of the New, as Shakespeare read them. Out of the lips of Portia, who has represented, in some sense, the natural life, will come most fitly a recognition of the spirit which makes earthly power likest God's.  In the fourth act Shylock holds by the law and by his bond.  When asked, "How shalt thou hope for mercy, rendering none?" Shylock answers, still placing the letter above the spirit, "What judgment shall I dread, doing no wrong?"  He stands for law ; must he be merciful?  "On what compulsion must I, tell me that?" Through Portia's famous answer, Shakespeare sets forth the divine side of his lesson, and

> "Therefore, Jew
> Though justice be thy plea, consider this,
> That, in the course of justice, none of us
> Should see salvation : we do pray for mercy
> And that same prayer doth teach us all to render
> The deeds of mercy.".

But Shylock says,—

> "My deeds upon my head !  I crave the law."

Saint Paul had said, what Shakespeare is here teaching, "By the deeds of the law there shall no flesh be justified ;" and, "Now we are delivered from the law, that being dead wherein we were held ; that we should serve in newness of Spirit, and not in the oldness of the Letter."  Shylock is made to feel that even by the strict letter of his bond he cannot stand : his pound of flesh must be an exact pound, not a hair's weight more or less; and there must be no blood shed, because the letter of the bond does not give him one drop of blood. Shylock is foiled, and sentenced; not harshly, except in the requirement that he undergo the form of being made a Christian; and the genial atmosphere again softens the sharp didactic outline. The manner of this—the success of the disguised ladies in getting from their husbands, as gifts to the learned counsel and his clerk, the rings they had vowed never to part with—prepares the way for a genial close to the whole play. It will supply means for a pleasant, quick, and sure identification; while the incident of the giving of the rings is still, in its own lighter form, in unity with the grand scene on which it follows. For its meaning is, that in little things as in great—even in little promises—we owe allegiance rather to the spirit than to the letter. Bassanio and Gratiano, true as they were pledged to be, had yielded, in spite of the letter of their pledge, all that was due elsewhere to courtesy and friendship.

The great lesson of life is taught, and the last act of the play opens with the Jew and Gentile, representing any two forms of bitter antagonism, in embrace of love under the calm expanse of heaven. The act opens genially, with playful words of love, and rises soon to a sublime earnestness, as Lorenzo looks from earth up to God's universe, of which it is a part:

> " Look how the floor of heaven
> Is thick inlaid with patines of bright gold ;
> There's not the smallest orb that thou behold'st
> But in his motion like an angel sings,
> Still quiring to the young-eyed cherubims ;
> *Such harmony is in immortal souls ;*
> But whilst this muddy vesture of decay
> Doth grossly close us in, we cannot hear it."

Then the musicians, who had been sent for, enter, and with soft strain represent to the ear, as Shakespeare often in his plays has made it represent, immortal harmony. Lorenzo's answer to Jessica's " I am never merry when I hear sweet music," " The reason is your spirits are attentive," &c., still uses music as type of that higher harmony which is within our souls. To want that is to be " the man that hath no music in himself, nor is not moved with concord of sweet sounds." Because of that want, he

> " Is fit for treasons, stratagems, and spoils;
> The motions of his spirit are dull as night,
> And his affections dark as Erebus :
> Let no such man be trusted. Mark the music."

The music, thus associated with the harmony of human souls and of the great visible universe under which the lovers sit, still plays.   Then enters Portia, with Nerissa, and the train of thought is continued in their first natural words by an image that brings the deeper sense of the play to its fit close.   Its meaning is, that man's endeavour to establish the kingdom of heaven within him shines royally, till it has blended with, and is lost in, the supreme glories of eternal love.

> "*Portia.* That light we see is burning in my hall.
> How far that little candle throws his beams !
> So shines a good deed in a naughty world.
> "*Nerissa.* When the moon shone, we did not see the candle.
> "*Portia.* So doth the greater glory dim the less :
> A substitute shines brightly as a king
> Until a king be by, and then his state
> Empties itself, as doth an island brook
> Into the main of waters.  Music !  Hark !"

And then we pass to the playful end, in unaffected chatting of good fellowship—again the kindly air of life encircling all.

John Fox, with controversial bitterness, had registered the pangs of martyrs, and believed all ill of the opponents of his form of faith.   Spenser, with sweetness of voice, had expressed the fierceness of the conflict from which Shakespeare rose to a full sense of the divine harmonies and to a quiet, all-embracing charity.   But there could have been no Shakespeare without the conflict that had stirred men to their depths, or in a country yielding no such combatants as those who, in Tudor times, had, through infirmities of human character, employed their highest energies, given and hazarded all they had, and, zealous to serve God, striven day after day to do their duty.

97.  In 1599 appeared an improved edition of *Romeo and Juliet* and *The Passionate Pilgrim*—a small collection of love poems, all ascribed on the title page, by an adventurous publisher, to Shakespeare, who objected to this use of his name.   The volume includes, with pieces by Shakespeare, others which it is known that he did not write.

In 1600 the plays of Shakespeare first printed in quarto were *The Merchant of Venice, A Midsummer Night's Dream, Much Ado About Nothing*, and *Henry V.*

Shakespeare's father died early in September, 1601.

*The Merry Wives of Windsor* was the only play of Shakespeare's printed in 1602.   There was a tradition current at the beginning of the eighteenth century that this was written at the request of Queen Elizabeth, who was so much pleased ·with Falstaff, in the two parts of *King Henry IV.*, that she commanded a play upon Falstaff in love, being, moreover, in such haste for it that it was to be written in fourteen days. This may or may not be true. " The Diary of John Manningham," a member of the Middle Temple, makes known to us that Shakespeare's *Twelfth Night* was acted in the Middle Temple on the 2nd of February, 1602. In that year *Venus and Adonis* reached a fifth edition.

In May, 1602, Shakespeare continued the investment of his earnings in his native place, by buying of William and John Combe 107 acres of arable land, in the parish of Old Stratford, for £327 ; and later in the year he made two more purchases, one of a cottage and its ground near New Place, the other, for sixty pounds, of a messuage with two barns, two gardens, and two orchards. He was extending his grounds behind New Place towards the river.

It seems to have been in the earlier part of this year, 1602, that Shakespeare's *Hamlet* was first acted. It was entered by a bookseller on the Stationers' Register on the 26th of July, 1602, to be published " as it was latelie acted." Thus, by the date of the death of Elizabeth, March 24, 1603, Shakespeare had risen to the full height of his genius.

98. Of the new dramatists rising around him one, **George Chapman**, was as old as Elizabeth's reign ; and he was not a dramatist only. He was born in 1557 or 1559, at Hitchin, in Hertfordshire. He was called afterwards by William Browne, " The Shepherd of fair Hitching Hill." About 1574 he was sent to Trinity College, Oxford, where he fastened with especial delight on the Greek and Roman classics. After two years at Oxford, he left without a degree. Nothing is known of him as a writer before 1594, when he published Σκιανυκτος, *The Shadow of Night: containing two poetical hymns devised by G. C., Gent.* In the next year, 1595, this was followed by *Ouid's Banquet of Sence, a Coronet for his Mistresse Philosophie, and his amorous Zodiacke.* In 1598 appeared the first section of the main work of George Chapman's life, his translation of Homer in *Seauen Bookes of the Iliades of Homere, Prince of Poetes, translated according to the Greeke, in Judgment of his best Commentaries, by George Chapman, Gent.* The seven books were the first and second, and the seventh to the eleventh. They are in the fourteen-syllabled measure, to which he adhered throughout the

Iliad and Odyssey; but here was a separate issue by him of a version of *The Shield of Achilles*, in 1598, in ten-syllabled verse.

Chapman had now also begun his career as a dramatist, and in 1598 appeared his first printed comedy, the *Blind Beggar of Alexandria*, which had been acted sundry times by the Earl of Nottingham's servants. The same company acted his second comedy, printed in 1599, *An humerous Dayes Myrth.* At the end of Elizabeth's reign, Chapman was at work still on his Homer, but had not yet issued another section of it.

99. **Thomas Heywood** was a native of Lincolnshire and a Fellow of Peterhouse, Cambridge. He joined the players, and was a young man when writing for them in 1596. In 1598 he produced *War without Blows and Love without Suit,* and immediately afterwards *Joan as good as my Lady.* Heywood passed into the next reign as one of the most prolific playwrights of the time. Of about the same age as Heywood was

**Thomas Middleton,** a gentleman's son, born in London in 1570. He was admitted of Gray's Inn in 1593, and published in 1597 the *Wisdom of Solomon Paraphrased;* probably he was also the author of *Microcynicon, six snarling Satires,* published in 1599. In the same year he joined **William Rowley** in writing his first play, the *Old Law.* In 1602, **Middleton** wrote the tragedy of *Randall Earl of Chester,* without help, and the *Two Harpies* in partnership with others; in 1602, also, his *Blurt, Master Constable, or the Spaniard's Night Walk* was printed.

**Thomas Dekker,** who was also born about 1570, began to write in the days of the later Elizabethan drama. His *Phaëton* was acted in 1597; other plays rapidly followed. His comedies of *Old Fortunatus* and the *Shoemaker's Holiday* were printed in 1600, and his *Satiromastix,* presently to be spoken of, in 1602.

**John Marston,** who was educated at Oxford, began in 1598 as a satirist with the *Scourge of Villanie, three Books of Satires,* and the *Metamorphoses of Pigmalion's Image, and certaine Satyres,* one of the books burnt by Whitgift and Bancroft (§ 92) when they forbade the writing of more satire. Marston wrote a tragedy, *Antonio and Mellida,* which had a sequel, *Antonio's Revenge,* and these plays were both printed in 1602.

100. But foremost among these writers of the later Elizabethan

drama, was Ben Jonson. He was of a north country family, son of a gentleman who was ruined by religious persecution in the reign of Mary, who became a preacher in Elizabeth's reign, and who died a month before the poet's birth, in 1573. Ben Jonson's mother took a bricklayer for second husband, and at some time during Ben's childhood she was living in Hartshorn Lane, near Charing Cross. The boy was first taught in the parish school of St. Martin's, and then owed to the kindness of William Camden (§ 82) an admission to Westminster School. He is said to have tried his stepfather's business for a little while, before he went to fight against Spain as a volunteer in the Low Countries. When he came home he joined the players and married. In 1597, when he was twenty-four years old, he was a sharer in the company of the Rose at Bankside. In these early days Ben Jonson acted the old Marshal Jeronimo in Thomas Kyd's *Spanish Tragedy*, and enriched-the play with an effective scene between mad old Jeronimo and a painter, in the manner of the earlier Elizabethan drama. In 1596 Ben Jonson's comedy, *Every Man in his Humour* was produced, with Italian characters and a scene laid at Florence. He then revised it, made the characters all English, and laid the scene in and between Coleman Street and Hoxton. In this, its present shape, it was performed in 1598 by the company to which Shakespeare belonged, the name of Shakespeare himself standing at the head of the list of actors. *Every Man in His Humour* is a true comedy carefully constructed. Its action, contained within a single day, opens at six in the morning and ends with a supper. The course of time is unobtrusively but exactly marked as the story proceeds, and the plot is not only contrived to show varieties of character, each marked by a special humour or predominance of one peculiar quality, but the incidents are run ingeniously into a dramatic knot which the fifth act unties. But Ben Jonson's next three plays were of another character ; they were not so much true comedies as bright dramatic satires, based on a noble sense of life and of the poet's place in it. *Every Man out of his Humour*, produced in 1599, *Cynthia's Revels*, in 1600, and the *Poetaster*, in 1601, were annual satires, the first touching especially the citizens, the second the courtiers, and the third the poets, in as far as any of these lived for aims below the dignity of manhood. Ben Jonson was at that time of his life tall, meagre, large-boned, with a pock-marked face and eager eyes ; a poet and keen satirist

Q *

with a true reverence for all that was noble, a lofty sense of the
aims of literature, and a young zeal to set the world to rights,
with a bold temper and an over-readiness for self-assertion.    In
*Cynthia's Revels* he jested scornfully at the euphuisms and shallow graces of the Court, at lives spent in the mere study of airs
and grimaces.    "Would any reasonable creature," he asked
through one of his characters, "make these his serious studies
and perfections, much less only live to these ends, to be the
false pleasure of a few, the true love of none, and the just
laughter of all?"    He urged for the Court idlers, in words
characteristic of the mind that made him, next to Shakespeare,
foremost among English dramatists,—

> ' That these vain joys in which their wills consume
> Such powers of wit and soul as are of force
> To raise their beings to eternity,
> May be converted on works fitting men ;
> And for the practice of a forced look,
> An antic gesture, or a fustian phrase,
> Study the native frame of a true heart,
> An inward comeliness of bounty, knowledge,
> And spirit that may conform them actually
> To God's high figures, which they have in power.

When Dekker and Marston considered themselves to have been
pointed at in the *Poetaster*, they resolved to give a taste of his
own whip to the too ardent satirist, whose vivid impersonations
of the follies of society were looked upon as personal attacks by
all the men in whom such follies were conspicuous.    Dekker
wrote his *Satiromastix* (whip for the satirist), and it was acted
as a retort on Jonson's *Poetaster*.    But although Ben Jonson's
own admirable bully, Captain Tucca, was reproduced and let
loose upon him to abuse him roughly, yet through the characters
of Demetrius and Crispinus, by whom Dekker and Marston held
themselves to have been attacked, and who were also reproduced,
the retort was made in a tone that showed the quarrel to be, as
a Latin motto to the printed book expressed, among friends
only.    The motto said, "I speak only to friends, and that upon
compulsion."    One passage will serve as sufficient evidence of
this.    Ben Jonson, as Horace Junior, is made to plead for his
satires of citizens and others :—

> " *Horace.* What could I do, out of a just revenge,
> But bring them to the stage ? They envy me,
> Because I hold more worthy company.
> " *Demetrius.* Good Horace, no.   My cheeks do blush for thine
> As often as thou speak'st so.   Where one true

> And nobly virtuous spirit for thy best part
> Loves thee, I wish one ten with all my heart.
> I make account I put up as deep share
> In any good man's love which thy worth earns
> As thou thyself. We envy not to see
> Thy friends with bays to crown thy poesie.
> No, here the gall lies, we that know what stuff
> Thy very heart is made of, know the stalk
> On which thy learning grows, and can give life
> To thy (once dying) baseness, yet must we
> Dance antics on your paper——
>       " *Horace.* Fannius——
>       " *Crispinus.* This makes us angry, but not envious.
> No, were thy warpt soul put in a new mould,
> I'd wear thee as a jewel set in gold."

In that spirit Dekker resolved to let his eager, positive friend
Ben feel in his own person how he liked being held up to the
town as the butt of satire.  Jonson replied with an Epilogue to
his *Poetaster,* and urged, as he had always urged, that his books
were taught "to spare the persons and to speak the vices."
But, in fact, he generously yielded, and said,

> " Since the comic Muse
> Hath proved so ominous to me, I will try
> If tragedy have a more kind aspect.
> Her favours in my next I will pursue,
> When, if I prove the pleasure of but one,
> So he judicious be, he shall be alone
> A theatre unto me."

Thus it happened that Ben Jonson's last work in Elizabeth's
reign was upon his first tragedy *Sejanus.*

---

# CHAPTER VIII.

## FROM ELIZABETH TO THE COMMONWEALTH.

### A.—REIGN OF JAMES I.

1. WHEN Elizabeth died, on the 24th of March, 1603, and
James VI. of Scotland became James I. of England, Shakespeare was thirty-nine years old and Bacon forty-two.  Spenser
had been dead about four years, Richard Hooker three.  Robert
Greene had been dead about eleven years and Christopher
Marlowe ten.  George Peele was dead, and Thomas Nash had
been dead a year or two.  Thomas Sackville, the author of our
first tragedy (ch. vii. § 8), now Lord Buckhurst, and aged 67,

was one of those who, after the queen's death, administered the affairs of the kingdom and proclaimed King James. A year later Sackville was created Earl of Dorset, and he died in 1608. John Lyly, author of *Euphues* (ch. vii. § 20), was living at the accession of James I., fifty years old, and had three years to live.   Gabriel Harvey (ch. vii. § 24), also aged fifty, lived throughout James's reign, a Doctor of Civil Law, practising as advocate in the Prerogative Court. Thomas Lodge (ch. vii. § 42), aged forty-eight, lived on, as a physician in good practice.  John Stow (ch. vii. § 82) was seventy-eight years old, and "as a recompense for his labours and travel of forty-five years, in setting forth the chronicles of England and eight years taken up in the survey of the cities of London and Westminster, towards his relief now in his old age," he asked for, and obtained, the king's letters patent empowering him "to gather the benevolence of well-disposed people within this realm of England; to ask, gather, and take the alms of all our loving subjects." He lived only till 1605 on this boundless reward of his enthusiasm.

Among men who had written in the past reign there also were still alive: Richard Stanihurst (ch. vii. § 53), aged about fifty-eight, he died in 1618; William Camden (ch. vii. § 82), fifty-two; Sir Walter Raleigh (ch. vii. § 84), fifty-one; Anthony Munday (ch. vii. § 54), forty-nine, he lived on until 1633; George Chapman (ch. vii. § 98), forty-six; William Warner (ch. vii. § 65), forty-five, he died in 1609; Samuel Daniel (ch. vii. § 79), forty-one; Michael Drayton (ch. vii. § 80), forty; Joseph Hall (ch. vii. § 92), twenty-nine; Ben Jonson (ch. vii. § 100), twenty-nine; and Marston, Middleton, Heywood, Dekker (ch. vii. § 100), of about Ben Jonson's age.

Among the dramatists born in the reign of Elizabeth who began to write under the Stuarts there were, at the accession of James I., John Fletcher, twenty-seven years old; Francis Beaumont, seventeen; John Webster, perhaps twenty-three; Cyril Tourneur, perhaps twenty; Philip Massinger, nineteen; John Ford, seventeen; James Shirley, nine.   These were Stuart dramatists, and not Elizabethan.   But they were born in Elizabeth's reign, and their plays retain much of the Elizabethan character.

2. We have given the name of *ELIZABETHAN DRAMATISTS* only to those who wrote in the reign of Elizabeth; and we have seen these divided into two sections, the *Earlier and Later Elizabethan* (ch. vii. § 94).   That part of the work of any of

them which was done under the Stuarts we may now place in a third section and call it *Stuart-Elizabethan.* Thus Marlowe's plays are Earlier Elizabethan; Shakespeare's, except his 'prentice work in the Earlier Elizabethan time, rank with the Later Elizabethan if written before March, 1603; after that date they are Stuart-Elizabethan.

Next to these will come the dramatists who wrote all their works under the Stuarts. The oldest of them, those who were born under Elizabeth, form a distinct class of *ELIZABETHAN-STUART DRAMATISTS.* Those who were also born and bred under the Stuarts are the *STUART DRAMATISTS;* the Commonwealth dividing *Earlier* from *Later Stuart.* Thus the division becomes:—

I. *ELIZABETHAN, a.* Earlier; *b.* Later; *c.* Stuart-Elizabethan.

II. *ELIZABETHAN-STUART.*

III. *STUART, a.* Earlier; *b.* Later.

3. Among writers with their work before them who were men or children at the accession of James I., were Lancelot Andrewes, forty-eight years old; John Donne, aged thirty; Robert Burton, twenty-seven; George Sandys, twenty-six; Edward Herbert of Cherbury, twenty-two; James Usher, twenty-three; Richard Corbet, twenty-one; John Selden, nineteen; Phineas and Giles Fletcher, twenty-one and perhaps nineteen; William Drummond of Hawthornden, eighteen; George Wither, fifteen; Thomas Hobbes, fifteen; Thomas Carew, about fourteen; William Browne, thirteen; Robert Herrick, twelve; Francis Quarles, eleven; George Herbert, ten; and Izaak Walton, ten. For so many years had each received his training while Elizabeth was queen.

4. Shakespeare was the great living writer at the accession of James I., when his company became that of the King's Players instead of the Lord Chamberlain's. The children of the chapel, who had acted Ben Jonson's *Cynthia's Revels* and the *Poetaster* at the Blackfriars' Theatre, became at the same time Children of his Majesty's Revels, and usually acted at Blackfriars when the King's Servants were at the Globe. The plays produced by Shakespeare in the reign of James I., and their probable dates, were *Othello*, perhaps;—it was played at Court November 1, 1604;—and *Measure for Measure*, possibly in December, 1604; *Macbeth*, early in 1606; *King Lear*, acted before James, December 26, 1606 (first printed, 1608); *Pericles*

(on work by another hand), 1607 or 1608 (first printed, 1609); *Antony and Cleopatra*, 1608 [in this year Milton was born]; *Troilus and Cressida*, early in 1609 (two editions were printed in that year, one of them before the play had been acted). There were no more of Shakespeare's plays printed in quarto during his life. *Cymbeline* was probably first acted about 1609; *Coriolanus* and *Timon of Athens*, 1610. The earliest notice of a performance of the *Tempest* is of 1611. It is one of Shakespeare's latest plays, perhaps his last, and there may be a reference to this in Prospero's breaking of his wand, burning of his books, and departure from the magic island. The notion of the play is, indeed, that man, supreme in intellect, master of the powers of earth and air, yet yearns for and needs the natural life with its affections. Bad as the world might be, and ill as it had used him, Prospero brought it to his island, with all its incidental treacheries and all its incidental grossness, bound himself with it again, and went home to it. Shakespeare felt only more keenly than his neighbours all the ties of home and kindred. He had been using the profits from his art to make himself a home at Stratford, and while he had still power to enjoy the home life that he had denied himself in part while he was earning, he broke his magic rod, and went home finally to his wife and children when his age was about forty-eight. *King Henry VIII.* was the play being acted when the Globe Theatre was burnt down, June 29, 1613, by the discharge of "chambers" in Act i. sc. 4. Because Sir Henry Wotton speaks of the play then acted as "a new play, called *All is True*," some think that Shakespeare's career closed with the production of *Henry VIII.*, in 1613. It has been said also that Shakespeare's versification falls into three periods: an early period, in which he seldom took liberties with the metre of his ten-syllabled line; a second period, in which eleven-syllabled lines are more frequent; and a late period, in which he used much greater freedom. In *Henry VIII.* extra syllables are more frequent than in any other play, and so distinctly marked, that they are not seldom monosyllables. This peculiarity was introduced deliberately. It is strongly marked in the most characteristic passages, as in the speech of Buckingham before his execution, and in Wolsey's farewell to his greatness. The pomp of the heroic line is broken at its close, and falls succeed each other making a sad music, in harmony with the feeling of the scene and of the play. For the whole play is a lesson on the changing

fortunes of men and their one trust in God. Henry VIII. stands
in the centre as the earthly Fortune, by whose smile or frown
earthly prosperity is gained or lost ; scene after scene shows rise
and fall of human fortunes as of waves of the great sea, and each
fall—Buckingham's, Katherine's, Wolsey's—leads to the same
thought—

" Farewell

The hopes of Court!  My hopes in heaven do dwell."

The play is as true as any sermon could be to such a text on the
world and its pomps as this from the 39th Psalm, " Man walketh
in a vain shadow, and disquieteth himself in vain : he heapeth
up riches, and cannot tell who shall gather them. And now,
Lord, what is my hope : truly my hope is even in thee."

Shakespeare had prepared for retirement by an investment
which would cause him to draw even a main part of his income
from his native place. This was the purchase, in 1605, of a
moiety of a lease granted in 1544 for 92 years—therefore, with
31 years yet to run—of the tithes, great and small, of Stratford,
Old Stratford, Bishopton, and Welcombe. The price paid
for this was £440, and the tithes would produce him £60 a
year, an income with the buying power of, say £300 or £400 a
year at the present value of money. In 1607, on the 5th of
June, Shakespeare married his elder daughter, Susanna, to John
Hall, a prosperous medical practitioner at Stratford.    In
February, 1608, the birth of Mrs. Hall's only child, Elizabeth,
made Shakespeare a grandfather ; and in September of that
year his mother died.   In 1612, at which time probably Shakespeare had retired to New Place, he was engaged in a lawsuit
arising out of his share of the tithes.   His brother Richard died
in February, 1613.  A month afterwards he bought a house
near the Blackfriars Theatre for £140, paying £80 and mort-
gaging for the rest, then paying the mortgage off, and leasing
the house to John Robinson.   In June of the same year, 1613,
the Globe Theatre was burnt down while *Henry VIII.* was
being acted, but he seems then to have had no share in the
property.  In 1614 Shakespeare was active, with others of his
neighbourhood, in protecting the rights to common lands near
Stratford against an enclosure scheme.   In 1615 he was still
interested in the enclosure question.   In 1616, he married his
other daughter, Judith, to Thomas Quiney, a vintner and wine
merchant at Stratford, who was four years younger than herself.
Shakespeare had given directions for his will in the preceding

January, but it was executed on the 25th of March. He died on the 23rd of the following April, 1616, aged fifty-two. An after-thought of a bequest to his wife of " the second best bed " has been weakly taken as evidence of want of affection. It would be at least as reasonable to say that, as the best bed in most houses is that of the guest chamber, the second best becomes that of the husband and wife, and the special bequest was, therefore, dictated by a feeling of domestic tenderness.

Shakespeare's wife survived until 1623. That was the year in which his plays were first collected in a folio, as *Mr. William Shakespeare's Comedies, Histories, and Tragedies. Published according to the True Originall Copies.* The other three folios appeared in 1632, 1663 (with *Pericles* and six spurious plays added, namely, *The London Prodigal, The History of Thomas Lord Cromwell, Sir John Oldcastle Lord Cobham, The Puritan Widow, A Yorkshire Tragedy,* and the *Tragedy of Locrine*), and 1685 (also including the spurious plays).

*Shakespeare's Sonnets,* mentioned by Meres in 1598 (ch. vii. § 95), were first published in 1609. They are 154 in number, and their chief theme is friendship. Various attempts have been made to build sentimental theories upon the sonnets of Shakespeare, as upon those of Surrey (ch. vi. § 46) and of Sidney (ch. vii. § 61). From what has been said in former chapters of the character of sonnet writing, from its origin to the Elizabethan time, it will be understood that I have here nothing to do but endorse (dropping its " well-nigh ") the opinion arrived at by one of the most thorough Shakespeare students of our time, Mr. Dyce, who says, " For my own part, repeated perusals of the *Sonnets* have well-nigh convinced me, that most of them were composed in an assumed character on different subjects, and at different times, for the amusement, if not at the sugges-tion, of the author's intimate associates (hence described by Meres as 'his sugred sonnets among his private friends'); and though I would not deny that one or two of them reflect his genuine feelings, I contend that allusions scattered through the whole series are not to be hastily referred to the personal cir-cumstances of Shakespeare." They are exquisite little pieces, not in the true sonnet measure (ch. vi. § 46), but with a form of their own; for each of them consists merely of three four-lined stanzas of alternate rhyme with a couplet added. Spenser's sonnets keep to the five rhymes, and although they have their own method of interlacement, it is one in full accord with the nature of this kind of poem.   In a sonnet of Shakespeare's there are seven rhymes.   It is in fact simply a little poem in three four-lined stanzas and a couplet.

5. The "Mermaid" was a tavern by Cheapside, between Bread Street and Friday Street, accessible from either ; and here Sir Walter Raleigh is said to have established a club, at which Shakespeare, Ben Jonson, Beaumont, Fletcher, and other wits of the time met.   The club founded by Raleigh is mythical, but the "Mermaid" was a famous tavern, and that the wits of the time frequented it we have witness in Beaumont's lines to Jonson, which recall—

> "What things we have seen
> Done at the 'Mermaid !'   Heard words that have been
> So nimble and so full of subtile flame,
> As if that every one from whom they came
> Had meant to put his whole wit in a jest,
> And had resolved to live a fool the rest
> Of his dull life."

Ben Jonson, under James I., gradually became the con-vivial centre of a group of men of genius, and owed his pre-dominance to a real intellectual power.   The playhouse audience was losing its old national character.   Secession of those men who might have said "Amen" at the close of the *Looking-glass for London and England* (ch. vii. § 70), meant the gradual loss of a main element in the audience—that part of it on which a dramatist who is intensely earnest can rely for sympathy.   The shallowness of the king's character made his patronage of the stage no remedy for this.   Fewer men came to the playhouse with their souls ready to answer to the touch of genius.   The range of Shakespeare's plots was wide as humanity, and in the true Elizabethan drama there is throughout variety of motive for the action of the dramas.   But we have not gone far into the reign of James I. before we find this range becoming narrowed. The lower standard of the audiences for whom the playwright worked limited the expression of his highest power.   In the Elizabethan-Stuart drama the plots nearly all turn upon animal love.   Ben Jonson did not stoop to this.   His plays had variety of theme, and through their wit and humour a vigorous mind was often uttering its wisdom to the deaf.   He and his hearers were out of accord.   He spoke of them and to them with an arrogant disdain, which they in part deserved ; and at last, after years of impatient service, while their degradation had been steadily proceeding, he turned from them with bitter words of loathing. Ben Jonson's self-assertion went too far; but that which provoked it was a real change in the character of the dramatist's public. The growth of Puritanism outside the theatre withdrew, as has been said, an important element from the playhouse audience. Plays were then written to please the class of men who were left as patrons of the stage, and the change thus made in the plays would quicken the defection of the better sort of playgoers. But while Ben Jonson disdained the judgment of these later audiences, there was no disdainful spirit in his dealing with true men. He looked up to Shakespeare, and the fittest eulogy of Shakespeare's genius that any Englishman had written came from Ben Jonson. In his later life young men of genius gathered about him and looked up to him; he called them heartily his sons, and had frank pride in their achievements. Of Shakespeare it was Ben Jonson who sang,

> " How far thou didst our Lyly outshine,
> Or sporting Kyd, or Marlowe's mighty line.
> And though thou hadst small Latin and less Greek,
> From thence to honour thee I will not seek
> For names : but call forth thundering Æschylus,
> Euripides, and Sophocles to us,
> Pacuvius, Accius, him of Cordova, dead
> To live again, to hear thy buskin tread
> And shake a stage; or, when thy socks were on,
> Leave thee alone for the comparison
> Of all that insolent Greece or haughty Rome
> Sent forth, or since did from their ashes come.
> Triumph, my Britain ! thou hast one to show,
> To whom all scenes of Europe homage owe.
> He was not of an age, but for all time !
> And all the Muses still were in their prime
> When, like Apollo, he came forth to warm
> Our ears, or like a Mercury to charm.
> Nature herself was proud of his designs,
> And joyed to wear the dressing of his lines."

. Ben Jonson's tragedy of *Sejanus*, produced in 1603, with work in it from another hand, was not very successful, but it succeeded better after he had recast it in part and made it all his own. It was printed in 1605, and the small criticisms of a pedantic age Ben Jonson forestalled with footnotes citing the authority for all that he had worked into a harmonious and very noble play. Because the footnotes were there, and looked erudite, the superficial thing to do was to pronounce the play pedantic. But it is not pedantic. Jonson was no pedant; he had carried on for himself the education received at Westminster School, was a good scholar, delighted in his studies, and accumulated a good library, which, in the latter part of his life was burnt. But he was true poet and true artist. His lyrics rank with the best of a time when nobody wrote dramas who was not poet enough to produce musical songs. No man can be a dramatist, in any real sense of the word, who cannot produce good lyrics. The greater includes the less. As dramatist Jonson had not Shakespeare's wealth of fancy, his sense of kindred with all forms of life—one source of that more than insight into character, of that power of being in imagination all that man can be, which caused his character painting to stand quite alone in the world's literature. Nobody but Shakespeare ever made men speak as from within, and one might say, betray themselves, as men and women do in real life, so that in his mimic world the persons are as variously judged and tried by as many tests as if one were discussing words and deeds of living people. All other dramatists have painted men and women as they saw them and we see them, from without ; not reproducing life, but drawing pictures of it.

Ben Jonson judged himself aright, and wrote only two tragedies. But each of them has a clear artistic structure, with dignity in its main thought, and vigorous dramatic scenes from which, though it be tragedy, the humour of the satirist is not entirely absent. Sejanus rises by base arts ; he spurns the gods, but has within his house a shrine to Fortune. He scorns the spiritual aims of life, works grossly for material success, and from his pinnacle of state falls to be dashed in pieces.

> " Let this example move the insolent man
> Not to grow proud and careless of the gods."

There is a scene at the opening of the second act in which Eudemus, the physician, is painting the cheeks of Livia. The dialogue blends meanest frivolity with a light planning of the most atrocious crime, and shows how Ben Jonson, following his own bent, could join a stern sense of the tragic in life with the humour of the comic poet. There is a very light touch of the spirit of comedy, suggesting the relation of small men to great events, in the fidgetty movements of Consul Regulus, who has been called out of his bed, in the third scene of the fifth act. In some character of a rough, honest censor, Ben Jonson himself often walked abroad through his own plays. Thus, in *Sejanus,* he may be said to have embodied himself in the part of Arruntius.

In these first years, also, of James's reign there was so little of the ill-will of small minds following the stage controversy raised by Marston and Dekker in *Satiromastix* (ch. vii. § 100), that Jonson and Dekker were working together, in 1603, at a masque for the City of London on his Majesty's accession ; and one of Marston's best plays—the *Malcontent*, written probably in 1602, and certainly published in two editions in 1604—was dedicated to Ben Jonson as his liberal and cordial friend. In 1605, when *Sejanus* was printed, Marston's friendship for Ben Jonson appeared in the front of it ; and in that year also (1605) Ben Jonson was fellow-worker with Marston and Chapman in the play of *Eastward Hoe*. The play contained a sentence— afterwards expunged—that offended the king and brought the writers into trouble; but its whole character of Sir Petronel Flash was a satire upon his Majesty's great cheapening of the honours of knighthood. The play itself, with some freedom of detail, was supremely moral in its design, being a contrast between the careers of the Idle and Industrious Apprentice.

Ben Jonson, who had many friends among the abler men of rank at Court, began at the outset of James's reign to find employment as a writer of Court Masques. In this form of writing—which had been untouched by Shakespeare—he was in his own day easily the first. But his true strength was in a form of comedy exclusively his own, broad and deep, generous in its aim, with scorn for all that is base, lively in its painting of a great variety of characters, each with some one predominating feature which he called its humour, and strong throughout with a manly vigour of thought that gives a bracing sense of intellectual energy to every scene. The reader's mind, after a ramble through *Volpone* or the *Alchemist*, feels as his body might after a wholesome walk in the sea breeze. Ben Jonson, about thirty years old at the accession of James I., was about thirty-two when, after *Sejanus*, he produced *Volpone; or, the Fox*, in 1605 ; then followed two more of his masterpieces, *Epicene ; or, the Silent Woman*, in 1609, and the *Alchemist*, in 1610. His other tragedy came next, the *Catiline*, in 1611. For twelve years, during this earlier part of his life, Ben Jonson had been a Roman Catholic ; but he had by this time rejoined the Church of England. In 1613 he was in France as companion and tutor to Sir Walter Raleigh's son. When he came home he poured scorn upon the outside show of Puritanism in his *Bartholomew Fair*, and produced, in 1616, the year of Shakespeare's death, a comedy called *The Devil is an Ass,* in which the imp Pug, having obtained a holiday on earth, went back a lost fiend as to his character, for said Satan to him :

> " Whom hast thou dealt with,
> Woman or man, this day, but have outgone thee
> Some way, and most have proved the better fiends."

Each party in the rising controversy of the day had its mean rout of camp-followers, serving the times for their own advantage. If Zeal-in-the-Land Busy in *Bartholomew Fair* represented one of the untruths of the time, the truth he parodied was in the good men of all parties. It was in Ben Jonson among the rest, and he uttered it in his own way as a comedian, very distinctly in this play, which followed next after " Bartholomew Fair." In the same year, 1616, Ben Jonson published a folio as the first volume of his *Works,* including not plays only, but epigrams and miscellaneous poems gathered under the title of *The Forest.* In this year of Shakespeare's death, Jonson ceased to write for the playhouse. He continued to produce Court Masques, but wrote no more plays for the public stage until after the death of James I. The degree of M.A. was conferred on him in 1619, by the University of Oxford ; and, at the cost of some trouble, Ben Jonson escaped being knighted by King James.

6. **Francis Beaumont** and **John Fletcher,** whose plays belong entirely to the reign of James I., first appeared together as friends of Ben Jonson, each of them furnishing verses prefixed to the first publication of *Volpone,* in 1607. John Fletcher, the elder of the two friends, was born at Rye, in 1576, when his father—ten years afterwards a bishop (ch. vii. § 91)—was vicar there. He was educated at home and at Benet College, Cambridge ; afterwards came to London, and began his career as a dramatist, at the age of about twenty-seven, with *The Woman Hater* and *Thierry and Theodoret,* both perhaps written before he entered into literary partnership with Beaumont.

Francis Beaumont was ten years younger than Fletcher. He was the third son of Sir Francis Beaumont, Justice of the Common Pleas, was born in 1586, admitted in his thirteenth year a gentleman commoner of Broadgate Hall (now Pembroke College), Oxford, left the University without a degree, and at the age of about seventeen was entered of the Inner Temple. Before he was nineteen he published a paraphrase of Ovid's tale of *Salmacis and Hermaphroditus ;* and in 1607, when he was twenty-one and Fletcher thirty-one, he wrote his lines in praise of Ben Jonson's

*Volpone.* Thenceforth, until the year of Shakespeare's death, Beaumont and Fletcher, close friends, worked together for the players. Beaumont had private means, and married. Fletcher depended on his earnings. Beaumont died a few weeks before Shakespeare, in March, 1616; all plays, therefore, that are the joint work of Beaumont and Fletcher, were produced during the ten years between 1606 and 1616. John Fletcher was not only ten years older than Beaumont, but he survived him nine years, and was sole author of many of the plays known as Beaumont and Fletcher's. Beaumont, as dramatist, wrote probably no work that was all his own, except in 1613 a masque on the marriage of the Princess Elizabeth. Fletcher wrote a play or two of his own before the partnership began; probably four plays wholly his own were produced during the partnership; and he continued to write during the nine or ten years between Beaumont's death, in March, 1616, and his own death by the plague, in August, 1625. Omitting a few doubtful works, about forty plays were written entirely by John Fletcher, and thirteen were the joint work of the partners. These were *Philaster, The Maid's Tragedy, A King and no King, The Knight of the Burning Pestle, Cupid's Revenge, The Coxcomb, Four Plays in One, The Scornful Lady, The Honest Man's Fortune, The Little French Lawyer, Wit at Several Weapons, A Right Woman,* and *The Laws of Candy.* In verses " On Mr. Beaumont, written presently after his death," by his friend John Earle, then a young man, credit is given to Beaumont for the first three plays named in this list. Francis Beaumont and Ben Jonson were hearty friends. The elder poet wrote of the younger,

> " How I do love thee, Beaumont, and thy Muse,
> That unto me dost such religion use !
> How I do fear myself, that am not worth
> The least indulgent thought thy pen drops forth ! "

Tradition, dating from their own time, gave pre-eminence to Fletcher for luxuriance of fancy and invention, and to Beaumont for critical judgment, to which it was said that even Ben Jonson submitted his writings. The wit and poetry of these plays were spent chiefly on themes of love. Their authors, capable of higher flights, so far accommodated their good work to the lower tone of the playhouse as to earn praise for having " understood and imitated much better than Shakespeare the conversation of gentlemen whose wild debaucheries and quickness of wit in repartees no poet can ever paint as they have done. Humour, which Ben Jonson derived from particular persons, they made it not their business to describe ; they represented all the passions very lively." So Beaumont and Fletcher were praised by Dryden in the time of Charles II., when their plays were "the most pleasant and frequent entertainments of the stage, two of theirs being acted through the year for one of Shakespeare's or Jonson's." We shall see how in that later Stuart time *The Maid's Tragedy* was dealt with. As first produced, in 1609, it ended tragically for a king of Rhodes, and its last words were:

> " On lustful kings
> Unlook'd for sudden deaths from Heav'n are sent
> But curst is he that is their instrument."

Here was the good Elizabethan sense of common right and duty, guarded by a line in recognition of the sacredness of royal persons. *The Faithful Shepherdess,* by Fletcher alone, produced early in 1610, was above the playhouse standard of taste and morality, being a pastoral play in praise of maiden innocence, daintily versified and most pure in its design, although its moral is sometimes enforced by scenes which, as men now judge, depict too freely the evil they condemn. That is a question only of change in conventional opinion ; the true mind of the play is absolutely pure.

7. *The Knight of the Burning Pestle,* by Beaumont and Fletcher, was a lively burlesque on the taste for high-flown romances, which Cervantes had attacked only six years before in his "Don Quixote." A citizen, speaking from among the audience, stops the actors at their prologue, says there shall be a grocer in the play, and he shall do admirable things. The citizen's wife says he shall kill a lion with a pestle ; and their man, Ralph, is the man to do it. Ralph, being thus forced on the players, burlesques the taste for Palmerin of England, appears, with squire and dwarf, as a knight, who swears by his ancestor Amadis of Gaul, has an inn described to him by his squire as an ancient castle held by the old knight of the most holy order of " The Bell," who has three squires—Chamberlino, Tapstero, and Ostlero —and when the tapster answers a lance-knock at the door, addresses him in this fashion :

> " Fair Squire Tapstero, I, a wandering knight,
> Hight of the Burning Pestle, in the quest
> Of this fair lady's casket and wrought purse,
> Losing myself in this vast wilderness,

> Am to this castle well by fortune brought,
> Where hearing of the goodly entertain
> Your knight of holy order of ' The Bell'
> Gives to all damsels and all errant knights,
> I thought to knock, and now am bold to enter."

This earliest burlesque in our dramatic literature was evidently following the lead of " Don Quixote."ᵃ It was in 1605, at a time corresponding to the second year of the reign of James I. in England, that *CERVANTES* published the first part of his *Don Quixote;* the second part, still better than the first, was published in 1615. Beaumont and Fletcher's burlesque on the affected forms into which tales of chivalry had degenerated, appeared in 1611.

In the conflict that brought Spain and England into opposition and that touched all Europe to the quick, the two great centres of activity were London and Madrid. The quickened energies developed in each city a vigorous intellectual life, and the Spanish drama rose at the same time with ours to its full height. The great developer of Spanish drama, *Lope de Vega*, was but seventeen months older than Shakespeare. He sailed in the great Spanish Armada, he exulted in a poem of ten cantos—the " Dragontea "—upon the death of Drake, and he called Queen Elizabeth the " Scarlet Lady of Babylon." Lope de Vega lived till 1635, and was writing throughout the reign of James I., while *Calderon*, the next great Spanish dramatist, born at the end of Elizabeth's reign, was growing up to manhood.

8. During the best years of Shakespeare's life as a dramatist, **William Alexander**, of Menstrie, afterwards Sir William Alexander and first Earl of Stirling, wrote four weak plays— *Darius*, first printed in 1603; *Cræsus*, in 1604; *the Alexandrian*, in 1605, and *Julius Cæsar*, in 1607, when the series was published together as *The Monarchic Tragedies*. William Alexander was then a Gentleman of the Chamber to Prince Henry, and a Scotchman in much favour with King James.

**Cyril Tourneur,** a dramatic poet with real tragic power, of whose life little is known, and whose remaining plays are *The Revenger's Tragedy, The Atheist's Tragedy,* and *The Nobleman,* wrote only in the reign of James I.

**William Rowley,** who during the last three years of Shakespeare's life was at the head of the Prince of Wales's company of comedians, wrote, or took part in writing, many plays, chiefly comedies, during the reign of James I. He published also, in 1609, a lively picture of London life, called *A Search* *for Money; or, the Lamentable Complaint for the Losse of the Wandering Knight, Monsieur l'Argent.*

**Thomas Middleton** (ch. vii. § 99) was a dramatist throughout the reign of James I., whom he did not long survive. He died in July, 1627.

**Thomas Dekker** (ch. vii. § 99) remained throughout the reign of James I. an active dramatist and pamphleteer. He lived on into the next reign, and died an old man, not earlier than 1637.

**Nathaniel Field** was one of the Children of the Revels who, in 1601, played in Ben Jonson's " Poetaster." He became known as a very good actor in the Blackfriars company, also as a dramatist. Before 1611 he wrote two plays of his own, *Woman is a Weathercock*, and a second part, called *Amends for Ladies*. He lived, and so did that busiest of playwrights, **Thomas Heywood** (ch. vii. § 99), until about 1641.

9. John Webster and Philip Massinger, true poets both, and dramatists of higher mark than those just named, were nearly of like age. **Philip Massinger** was born at Salisbury, in 1584. His father was in the household of Henry Earl of Pembroke. In the last year of Queen Elizabeth's reign, Massinger became a commoner of St. Alban's Hall, Oxford ; but the death of his father, in 1606, obliged him to leave the University and support himself as he could. Many of his plays are lost, and there is no record of work of his earlier than 1622, when *The Virgin Martyr* was printed. *The Duke of Milan* was printed in 1623. In December, 1623, Massinger's name first appeared in the office book of the Master of the Revels, when his *Bondman* was acted. That play was first printed in 1624. Twelve of Massinger's plays were printed in his lifetime, but only these three in the reign of James I. Massinger remained an active dramatist during fifteen years of the reign of Charles I.

**John Webster,** a master poet in the suggestion of tragic horror, produced in the reign of James I. two of his finest plays, *The White Devil; or, Vittoria Corombona*, printed in 1612 ; and *The Duchess of Malfi*, first acted about the time of Shakespeare's death, but printed in 1619. Webster also wrote in the reign of Charles I. He lived on into the time of the Commonwealth, and died about 1654.

10. **George Chapman**, during the reign of James I., was an active dramatist. In 1606, besides *Eastward Hoe* (§ 5), in which he had a hand, his comedy of *All Fools* was printed ; in 1606 *Monsieur d'Olive* and *The Gentleman Usher;* in 1607 his

tragedy of *Bussy d'Ambois*, which kept the stage for some time
after his death. Other tragedies and comedies followed. But
his chief work was still at the translation of Homer (ch. vii. § 98),
on which he was engaged throughout the reign of James I.
Twelve books of Homer's Iliad, translated by George Chapman, appeared about 1610 ; and in the following year, the whole
twenty-four books of *The Iliads of Homer*, dedicated to Prince
Henry, who died in November, 1611. This was followed by the
twelve first books of the Odyssey, about 1614, and in 1615, the
whole twenty-four books of *Homer's Odysses, translated according to the Greek.* About the year of Shakespeare's death (Chapman's folios are not dated), Chapman's "Iliad" and "Odyssey "
appeared together as *The Whole Works of Homer, Prince of
Poets.* Chapman proceeded then to translate the Homeric Hymns,
and "Battle of the Frogs and Mice," ascribed to Homer. This
translation appeared at the end of the reign of James I., as *The
Crown of all Homer's Workes, Batrachomyomachia, his Hymns
and Epigrams, translated by George Chapman.* Because of the
vigour of the Elizabethan time, and the fact that Chapman was
a poet, this translation is the crown of the works of Chapman.

> "He leapt upon the sounding earth, and shook his lengthful dart,
> And everywhere he breathed exhorts, and stirr'd up every heart.
> A dreadful fight he set on foot. His soldiers straight turned head.
> The Greeks stood firm. In both the hosts the field was perfected.
> But Agamemnon foremost still did all his side exceed,
> And would not be the first in name unless the first in deed."

Thus sang George Chapman, who was himself the Agamemnon
of the host of the translators of Homer.

11. Another good translator of this time was **George
Sandys**, second son of the Sandys, Archbishop of York, whom
Aylmer succeeded in the Bishopric of London. George Sandys
was born at Bishopsthorpe, in 1577, and educated at Oxford. In
1610 he set out upon the travels of which he published an
account in 1615, as *A Relation of a Journey begun A.D. 1610.
Four Books containing a description of the Turkish Empire, of
Egypt, of the Holy Land, of the Remote Parts of Italy, and
Islands adjoining.* He then worked at his translation of Ovid's
*Metamorphoses; The first Five Books* appearing in the reign of
James I. Sandys' travels are told gracefully, in a style less
laboured than that of **Richard Knolles'** *General History of
the Turks*, which first appeared in the year of King James's
accession.

12. Apart from their direct value as record, there is the charm also of an unaffected method in **William Camden's** Latin annals of the reign of Queen Elizabeth —*Annales Rerum Anglicarum et Hibernicarum regnante Elizabetha*—of which the first part, ending at 1589, was first published in 1615, and the second part early in the reign of Charles I., in 1627. An English translation, as *The Historie of the Life and Reigne of the most renowned and victorious Princesse Elizabeth, late Queen of England. . . . Composed by way of Annales by the most learned Mr. William Camden,* was published 1630. The work had been suggested to Camden, the most fit man living, by Lord Burghley, who, says the annalist, " set open unto me first his own and then the Queen's rolls, memorials, records, and thereout willed me to compile in a historical style the first beginnings of the reign of Queen Elizabeth." He studied carefully to carry out this design, procured access to charters, letters patent, letters, notes of consultations in the council chamber, instructions to ambassadors ; looked through Parliamentary diaries, acts, and statutes, and read over every edict or proclamation ; for the greatest part of all which he was beholden, he said, to Sir Robert Cotton, "who hath with great cost and successful industry furnished himself with most choice store of matter of history and antiquity ; for from his light he hath willingly given great light unto me." Camden chose to take, for clearness and simplicity, the form of Annals for his work; but endeavoured so to tell his facts that their relation to each other might be understood, for he liked, he said, that saying of Polybius, "Take from history, why, how, and to what end, and what hath been done, and whether the thing done hath succeeded according to reason, and whatsoever is else will rather be an idle sport than a profitable instruction : and for the present it may delight, but for the future it cannot profit." **Samuel Daniel** (ch. vii. § 79) wrote also as Annals, but in English, his *Collection of the History of England,* first published in 1613 and 1618. It begins with Roman Britain, and ends with the reign of Richard III.

13. **Robert Bruce Cotton,** born at Denton, Huntingdonshire, in 1570, and educated at Trinity College, Cambridge, was knighted by James I. In 1611, when his Majesty had invented the rank of baronet, and began to trade in the new article, Sir Robert Cotton became one of his first customers. King James was aided in his controversies by Sir Robert Cotton's learning, and the treasures of literature rescued by him

from the scattered waste of the monasteries, were at the service of all who could make good use of them. It was in the reign of James I, that an older man, **Sir Thomas Bodley,** founded the Bodleian Library at Oxford. He was born at Exeter, in 1544, the son of that John Bodley who, in exile at Geneva, had been a chief promoter of the translation known as the Geneva Bible (ch. vii. § 15). Thomas Bodley had come to England at Elizabeth's accession, entered at Magdalene College, Oxford, became Fellow of Merton, had been employed by the queen on embassies, was for nine years ambassador at the Hague, but in 1597 he retired from public life, and made it the work of his last years to give to the University of Oxford a library in place of that which it had lost. In 1602 he refitted the dismantled room which had been used for the library founded by Humphrey Duke of Gloucester, and furnished it with ten thousand pounds' worth of books. In July, 1610, he laid the foundation-stone of a new library building; and died in 1612, about a year before the building was completed.

14. The development of England at a time when men felt they were living history, and the lively controversy upon questions in which authority of the past was being constantly appealed to, gave great impulse to historical research. John Stow was followed by another patriotic tailor chronicler, **John Speed,** born in 1555, at Farington, in Cheshire, who, with little education, became enthusiastic in the study of the antiquities of his own country. In 1608 and 1610 he published fifty-four maps of England and Wales. In 1611 he published, in royal folio, his Chronicle, as *The History of Great Britaine under the Conquests of the Romans, Saxons, Danes, and Normans.* In 1611 appeared, in folio, his *Theatre of the Empire of Great Britaine;* and in 1616 the religious side of his English character was shown by the publication of *A Cloud of Witnesses; and they the Holy Genealogies of the Sacred Scriptures, confirming unto us the truth of the histories of God's most holie Word.* Speed married when young, had eighteen children, and passed his golden wedding-day, his wife dying in 1628, and he in 1629.

There were two brothers, William and Robert Burton, of Lindley, in Leicestershire, who both went to school at Sutton Coldfield, and to college at Brazenose, Oxford. **William Burton** became a lawyer, gave his mind to antiquities, and published, in 1622, in folio, a *Description of Leicestershire: containing Matters of Antiquitye, Historye, Armorye, and*

*Genealogy.* **Robert Burton** became a clergyman, and had the livings of St. Thomas, Oxford, and Segrave, in Leicester-shire ; but he still lived a quiet scholar's life at his college, and in 1621, published the *Anatomy of Melancholy, by Democritus Junior.* This discussion of all forms of melancholy, and their remedies, is very quaint and ingenious in thought and expression, and so crammed with pleasant erudite quotations that the book has been to many; later writers, who desired to affect knowledge of books they had never seen, the storehouse of their second-hand learning. Although an original book, its manner was in the fashion of the time, and it is said to have made the fortune of its Oxford publisher. It went through five editions before its author's death, in 1639.

History moralised in the *Mirror for Magistrates,* remained popular after the accession of James I. The last edition of that work appeared in 1610, edited by **Richard Niccols,** *newly enlarged with a last Part, called a Winter Night's Vision, being an addition of such Tragedies, especially famous, as are exempted in the former Historie, with a Poem annexed, called England's Eliza.* This final edition contained ninety-one legends.

15. There was a poet's mind in **Sir Walter Raleigh,** though he shone most as a man of action. Spenser had taken pleasure in his verse. A poet's sense of the grand energies of life was in Raleigh's conception of a History of the World, to keep his busy mind astir during imprisonment. Raleigh's good fortune was at an end when James I. became king. In November, 1603, he was tried at Winchester—there being the plague then in London—and unjustly found guilty of participation in an attempt to place Arabella Stuart on the throne, and of a secret correspondence with the King of Spain. Raleigh was sentenced to death, but reprieved. His personal property, forfeited by the attainder, was also restored, and he was detained a prisoner in the Tower, where his wife obtained permission to live with him, and where his youngest son was born. It was during these twelve years in the Tower that Sir Walter Raleigh wrote his fragment of a *History of the World,* which fills a substantial folio. It contains five books of the first part of the History, beginning at the Creation and ending with the Second Macedonian War. The theme of its opening chapter is " Of the Creation and Preservation of the World," and the argument of its first section, " that the Invisible God is seen in His creatures." Raleigh even discusses fate, foreknowledge, and

free-will, before he begins the story of man's life on earth, and proceeds with historical detail that includes reasonings upon the origin of law and government. This folio was published in 1614, and in 1616, the year of Shakespeare's death, Raleigh, by bribing the king's favourite, and exciting other hopes of gain, obtained liberty without any formal pardon, and a patent under the Great Seal for establishing a settlement in Guiana. The expedition failed, and Raleigh was too faithful to the old traditions of his life. He returned in July, 1618, having lost his eldest son in an attack on the new Spanish settlement of St. Thomas ; and to oblige Spain, James I. then caused him, at the age of sixty-six, to be executed, without trial, by carrying out of the fifteen-year-old sentence, on the 29th of October, 1618. English regard for the Elizabethan voyagers was maintained in this reign by the Rev. **Samuel Purchas**, vicar of Eastwood, in Essex. The Rev. Richard Hakluyt's manuscripts came into his hands, and he resigned his vicarage to his brother, to devote himself to a continuation of the work of Hakluyt. His first volume appeared in folio in 1613, *Purchas his Pilgrimage*. It was followed, in 1625–6, by *Hakluytus Posthumus; or, Purchas his Pilgrimes*, in five folio volumes.

Descriptions of strange lands suggested to **Joseph Hall** (ch. vii. § 92) his Latin satire, first published at Hanover in 1607, *Mundus Alter et Idem*. Another world and the same, which places in the Southern region hitherto unknown, the imagined continent about the south pole, a satirical image of the hitherto known world which occupies the other half of the author's map. In that mirrored southern world there is a Holy Land said to be still unknown, a Crapulia divided into Pamphagonia, the land of gluttons ; with whimsical subdivision into provinces, an account of its laws, religion, and manner of electing a chief ; and Yvronia, the land of drunkards, described in like manner. The land of women is described as Viraginia. Moronia, the land of fools, with its subdivisions, covers a large space. The other region is Lavernia, the land of thieves. The piece has the fault of all satire that dwells exclusively upon the baser side of human life.

16. History and antiquities were much studied by the controversial writers in the reign of James. At the beginning of the reign there was some revival of the old controversy as to the relation of the pope to kings; and this was quickened by the discovery of the Gunpowder Plot, in November, 1605. In 1608,

Cardinal Bellarmin, under the name of his secretary, Matthew
Tortus, answered King James's *Triplici nodo, triplex Cunæus;
or, an Apologie for the Oath of Allegiance against the two
Breues of Pope Pavlvs Qvintvs, and the late Letter of Cardinal
Bellarmine to C. Blackwel, the Arch Priest* (1607). Robert
Bellarmin, an Italian Jesuit, born in Tuscany, in 1542, was
the great controversialist on the side of Rome. He had
taught divinity at Louvain, and read lectures at Rome on points
of controversy, had been sent also as legate to France, when,
in 1599, he was made cardinal, and, in 1602, Archbishop of
Capua. In 1605 he resigned the archbishopric that he might
be near the pope, and do battle for the papacy on the great questions of the day. He was learned, acute, and so honest in avoiding misrepresentation of the arguments he sought to answer, that
his works, in three folio volumes, put very fairly upon record
the positions of his opponents as well as his own. In these
controversies the men of the Reformed Church had hitherto
allowed citations of authority to weigh against them. They had
not matched their antagonists in knowledge of Church history
and of the writings of the fathers; but a great demand for knowledge of this kind was now producing the supply of it. **Lancelot
Andrewes,** on whom the king called for an answer to Bellarmin, and who produced as answer his *Tortura Torti* (1609),
was in this way the most learned Churchman of the days of
James I. He was born in London, in 1555, educated at Merchant Taylor's School, sent for his ability to Pembroke Hall,
Cambridge (Spenser's College), obtained a fellowship, studied
and taught divinity with great success, and was consulted as a
profound casuist. Henry Earl of Huntingdon took him to the
North of England, and there he persuaded some Roman Catholics
to change their faith. Sir Francis Walsingham gave him the
Parsonage of Alton, in Hampshire, and he was then successively
vicar of St. Giles's, Cripplegate, Prebendary of St. Paul's—
where he read divinity lectures three times a week in term time—
Master of Pembroke Hall, Chaplain in Ordinary to Elizabeth,
and Dean of Westminster. The queen would not raise him
higher, because his ecclesiastical view of the rights of bishops
forbade him to alienate episcopal revenues. James I. delighted
in his preaching, which was that of a religious man strongly
tinged with the pedantry of the time, and made him, in 1605,
Bishop of Chichester. He was promoted afterwards through
the bishopric of Ely to that of Winchester, in 1618, and he died

in 1626, aged seventy-one.  *Ninety-six Sermons* of his were
published by command of Charles I., in 1631.

17.  **James Usher,** twenty-five years younger than Bishop
Andrewes, succeeded to his repute as a theologian, and excelled
him in learning.  Usher was born at Dublin, in 1580, son to one
of the six clerks in chancery.  He was taught to read by two
aunts, who had been blind from their cradle, but who knew
much of the Bible by heart.  Trinity College, Dublin, owes its
existence to a grant made by Queen Elizabeth, in 1591, of the
Augustine monastery of All Saints.  The first stone was laid on
New Year's-day, 1593.  It began work in the same year, and
James Usher was one of the first three students admitted.  He
had delight in history, made chronological tables as a boy, and,
as a youth, when the Church controversies became interesting
to him, he resolved to read for himself the whole works of the
fathers whose authority was so continually cited.  He began
at the age of twenty, and, reading a portion daily, finished at the
age of thirty-eight.  Usher's father died when he was about to
be sent to London to study law.  He then abandoned to his
brothers and sisters his paternal inheritance, reserving only
enough for his own support at college in a life of study, obtained
a fellowship, at the age of twenty-one took holy orders, argued
and preached against the Catholics, and opposed toleration of
them.  At the accession of James I. James Usher was twenty-
three years old.  He came to London to buy books for the library
of the new college at Dublin, and found Sir Thomas Bodley
(§ 13) buying books for Oxford.  While he was in London
Usher's mother became Roman Catholic, and all his controversial skill failed afterwards to reconvert her.  In 1606, and
afterwards at regular intervals of three years, Usher was again
book-buying in England.  In 1607, he was made—aged twenty-
seven—Professor of Divinity at Dublin, and Chancellor of St.
Patrick's Cathedral.  In 1612 he became Doctor of Divinity.
In 1613, he published in London, and dedicated to King James
his first book, in Latin, continuing from the sixth century the
argument of Jewel's Apology (ch vii. § 14), to prove that the
tenets of the Protestants were those of the primitive Christians.
In the same year Usher married the well-dowered daughter of
his old friend and associate in book-buying, Luke Chaloner.  In
1615, a convocation of the Irish clergy drew up by Usher's
hand a set of 104 articles for the Irish Church.  Their theology
was Calvin's, and they included an injunction to keep holy the

Sabbath-day: for this and his strong opposition to the Roman
Catholics, it was represented to King James that Usher was a
Puritan. A correspondent of Usher's at this time observed
how easily the king could be set against a clergyman by styling
him a Puritan, " whence it were good," he said, " to petition His
Majesty to define a Puritan, whereby the mouths of those scoffing
enemies would be stopt; and if His Majesty be not at leisure,
that he would appoint some 'good men to do it for him." His
Majesty hated a Puritan as one who did not bow down to the
divine right of rule in bishops and archbishops, and, therefore,
would have but a weak faith in the divine authority of kings.
James had spoken his own mind as a "free king," with weak
notions of freedom in a people, when, in 1598, he published *The
True Law of Free Monarchies; or, the Reciprock and Mutual
Dutie betwixt a Free King and his Naturall Subjectes,* and he
had a sufficiently shrewd sense of the tendencies of Puritan
opinion. When Usher came to England next, in 1619, he
found it necessary to bring with him a certificate of orthodoxy
from the Lord Deputy and his Council, and he had to submit to
the infliction of a private theological examination, with his most
conceited Majesty for the examiner. But Usher was a strong
and conscientious supporter of authority in Church and State,
and passed his examination so well that the king gave him the
bishopric of Meath. As bishop, Usher was still active against
Catholicism, and he published, in English, in 1622, *A Discourse
on the Religion Anciently Professed by the Irish and British,*
to show that Protestant opinions were those of the ancient faith,
and point out how at successive times the practices of the Church
of Rome had been introduced. This work caused King James
to command that Bishop Usher should produce a larger work,
in Latin, on the antiquities of the British Church, with leave of
absence from his diocese for consultation of authorities. He
was a year in England, returned to Ireland in 1624, and, in
reply to William Malone, published an *Answer to a Challenge
of a Jesuit in Ireland* to disprove uniformity of doctrine in the
Roman Catholic Church; thus giving more evidence of his
knowledge of ecclesiastical antiquities. He then returned to
England, and as the Archbishop of Armagh died at that time,
King James, in the last year of his reign, gave the archbishopric
to Usher.

18. The accusation of Puritanism made at one time against
Usher was, as we have seen, partly grounded on the Calvinism

K

of the articles drawn up by him for a convocation of the Irish Church. The Established Church of England was in Elizabeth's time chiefly Calvinist in doctrine; under the Stuarts it was chiefly Arminian. Puritans held generally by the faith of Calvin, but by each road England went the way to her own liberties. *Arminius* was the Latinised name of Jacob Harmensen, who was born in 1560, at Oudewater, in South Holland, where his father was a councillor. Left early an orphan, Arminius was helped by friends to study at Leyden, Marburg, Geneva, and Basle. He went also to Padua and Rome before he returned to Holland, and preached in pulpits of the Reformed Church. In 1588 he became pastor at Amsterdam. Some clergy at Delft then published a volume against Calvin's doctrine of predestination. Arminius was asked to refute their book, examined its arguments, was convinced, and ended not merely by accepting but by developing and enforcing its opinions. Great controversy then arose, but the chair of theology vacant at Leyden by the death of Francis Junius (ch. vii. § 26) was offered to Arminius. There he had to meet the assaults of a Calvinist colleague, Francis Gomarus, and the two parties formed were called Arminians and Gomarists. The good man's life was embittered by this controversy, and he died in 1609, leaving many disciples, who, in 1610, set forth by five articles the opinions of their founder in a Remonstrance to the Estates of Holland. This gave them the name of *The Remonstrants*. They had freedom of opinion until 1618, when it was taken from them by their religious and political enemies at the Synod of Dordrecht, and was not recovered again till the death of Maurice, Prince of Orange, in 1625, the year also of the death of James I.

19. **John Selden** was born in December, 1584, at Salvington, about two miles from Worthing, in Sussex. His father was a musician, who sent him to the free school at Chichester, whence he was sent by the master's advice to Hart Hall, Oxford. In 1602 he became a member of Clifford's Inn; and a year after the accession of King James, being then aged nineteen, he removed to the Inner Temple. John Selden had a strong body, able to sustain incessant studies; he had also a wonderful memory. He practised little at the bar, but was consulted for his knowledge; gathered many books, inquired through them freely, and wrote on the front leaf of most of them, as his motto, in a Greek sentence, "Above all, Liberty." He very soon became solicitor

and steward to the Earl of Kent, and found also a good friend in Sir Robert Cotton, to whom he dedicated his first book, finished in 1607, but not published till 1615, the *Analecton Anglo-Britannicon Libri Duo*, two books of collections, giving a summary chronological view of English records down to the Norman Invasion. In 1610, besides two little treatises, one Latin and one English, on the antiquities of English law, he set forth some results of his reading in a short piece on *The Duello, or Single Combat*, extra-judicial and judicial, but chiefly judicial, with its customs since the Conquest. In 1614, Selden produced his largest English work, *Titles of Honour*, a full study of the history of the degrees of nobility and gentry, derived from all ages and countries, but applied especially to England. In 1617 appeared, in Latin, Selden's treatise on the gods of Syria—*De Deis Syris*—a learned inquiry into polytheism, mainly with reference to that of Syria, for special study of the false gods named in the Old Testament. This book and the *Titles of Honour* had raised and extended beyond England Selden's character for learning, when, in 1618, his way of research crossed dangerous ground, for he then highly offended James I., by publishing *The History of Tithes*. The churchmen who dwelt most upon obedience to authority, whom, therefore, the king preferred, had upheld a divine right of tithes, inherited by the Christian from the Jewish priesthood. Selden's book was not written, he said, to prove a case on either side; it was not "anything else but itself, that is, a mere narrative, and the history of tithes." But in his dedication of it to Sir Robert Cotton he had rightly said that study of the past is to be cherished only for its fruitful and precious part, "which gives necessary light to the present;" and condemned "the too studious affectation of bare and sterile antiquity, which is nothing else than to be exceeding busy about nothing." When, therefore, it appeared that Selden had carefully marshalled and verified authorities on both sides, and that, although he himself gave no opinion, his facts against the theory of a divine right of tithes outweighed his facts in favour of it, there was outcry, and His Majesty had argument with Mr. Selden, who was introduced to him by two friends, one of them Ben Jonson. Selden was called also before members of the High Commission Court, who compelled him to a declaration in which he did not recant anything, but was sorry he spoke. He admitted error in having published "The History of Tithes," in having given "occasion of argument against any right of maintenance, *jure divino*, of the ministers of the gospel," and expressed grief at having incurred their lordships' displeasure. Selden's book was prohibited; all men were free to write against it. Richard Mountagu, afterwards Bishop of Norwich, was encouraged by the king to confute Selden, to whom His Majesty said, "If you or any of your friends shall write against this confutation I will throw you into prison." Dr. Mountagu had it all his own way when, in 1621, he issued his *Diatribe upon the First Part of the late History of Tithes.* Selden confined himself to private comments, and sent to Edward Herbert, afterwards Lord Herbert of Cherbury, some notes on the work of one of his antagonists. He sought also to appease His Majesty by giving him three tracts, to make amends for his inadvertent rudenesses. 1. His Majesty concerned himself about the number of the Beast, and Selden had spoken slightingly of the attempts to calculate it. In one of the three tracts he now restricted his censure, and spoke respectfully of a most acute deduction of His Majesty's. 2. Selden had spoken of Calvin's confession that he could not interpret the Book of Revelation as "equally judicious and modest." But King James was a confident interpreter, and was not he also judicious and modest? Selden explained that all men had not ignorance to confess, and that King James's explanations were "the clearest sun among the lesser lights." 3. Selden had referred in his "History of Tithes" to the want of evidence that Christmas-day was a true anniversary. "This," said King James, "countenances Puritan objection to our way of keeping Christmas." To please the king, Selden in his third tract produced evidence to support the date of the anniversary. It was at the close of James's reign, in 1624, that John Selden first entered Parliament, as member for Lancaster.

20. The keen spirit of inquiry that formed part of the new life of England made, in **Edward Herbert** (afterwards known as Edward Lord Herbert of Cherbury), a bold stride towards denial of all revelations in religion. Edward Herbert was born at Montgomery, in Wales, educated at Oxford, visited London in 1600, went abroad, joined English auxiliaries in the Netherlands, was an intrepid soldier, was knighted on the accession of James I., was sent in 1616 as ambassador to France, was recalled for a bold saying, sent back again, and in 1624 published at Paris a Latin treatise upon Truth—*De Veritate*—in which he denounced those who did not hold his own five fundamental

truths of natural religion. He argued that heaven could not reveal to a part only of the world a particular religion. Yet he said that, to encourage himself to oppose revelation, he asked for a sign, and was answered by a loud yet gentle noise from heaven.

21. The rising spirit of inquiry was now active also for advance of science. John Napier, of Merchistoun, used the same mind which had spent its energies, in 1593, upon "A Plaine Discovery of the whole Revelation of St. John," upon the discovery of the use of Logarithms, and set forth his invention, in 1614, as *Mirifici Logarithmorum Canonis Descriptio.* In the following year, 1615, William Harvey first brought forward, in lectures at the College of Physicians, his discovery of the Circulation of the Blood, afterwards more fully established and set forth in a small book, early in the reign of Charles I. Harvey lost practice by his new opinions, and his doctrine was not received by any physician who was more than forty years old; but he was made, in 1623, Physician Extraordinary (which is less than Ordinary) to James I.

22. Advance of scientific inquiry is a marked feature in the literature of the Stuart times, and it was aided greatly by Francis Bacon (ch. vii. § 85), who during the reign of James I. set forth his philosophy. Bacon now prospered. He was made Sir Francis by his own wish, in July, 1603, that he might not lose grade, because new knights were multiplying, and there were three of them in his mess at Gray's Inn. Essex had been active for James. Bacon told the Earl of Southampton that he "could be safely that to him now which he had truly been before;" and adapted himself to the new political conditions by writing a defence of his recent conduct, as *Sir Francis Bacon his Apologie in certain Imputations concerning the late Earle of Essex.* To the first Parliament of King James, Bacon was returned by Ipswich and St. Albans. He was confirmed in his office of King's Counsel in August, 1604; but when the office of Solicitor-General became vacant again in that year, he was not appointed to it. In 1605, about the time of the discovery of Gunpowder Plot, there appeared, in English, *The Twoo Bookes of Francis Bacon. Of the Proficience and Aduauncement of Learning, Diuine and Humane. To the King.* These two books of the Advancement of Learning—which, in 1623, towards the end of his life, reappeared in Latin, expanded into nine books, *De Augmentis Scientiarum, Libri IX.*—form the first part, or

the groundwork of his *Instauratio Magna*, or "Great Reconstruction of Science." It was dedicated to King James, as from one who had been "touched, yea, and possessed, with an extreme wonder at those your virtues and faculties which the philosophers call intellectual; the largeness of your capacity, the faithfulness of your memory, the swiftness of your apprehension, the penetration of your judgment, and the facility and order of your elocution." Of the "universality and perfection" of His Majesty's learning, Bacon said, in this dedication, "I am well informed that this which I shall say is no amplification at all, but a positive and measured truth; which is, that there hath not been since Christ's time any king or temporal monarch which hath been so learned in all literature and erudition, divine and human." His Majesty stood "invested of that triplicity which in great veneration was ascribed to the ancient Hermes; the power and fortune of a king, the knowledge and illumination of a priest, and the learning and universality of a philosopher." It was fit, therefore, to dedicate to such a king a treatise in two parts, one on the excellency of learning and knowledge, the other on the merit and true glory in the augmentation and propagation thereof. In his first book Bacon pointed out the discredits of learning from human defects of the learned, and emptiness of many of the studies chosen, or the way of dealing with them. This came especially by the mistaking or misplacing of the last or furthest end of knowledge, as if there were sought in it "a couch whereupon to rest a searching and restless spirit; or a terrace for a wandering and variable mind to walk up and down with a fair prospect; or a tower of state for a proud mind to raise itself upon; or a fort or commanding ground for strife and contention; or a shop for profit or sale; and not a rich storehouse for the glory of the Creator and the relief of man's estate." The rest of the first book was given to an argument upon the Dignity of Learning; and the second book, on the Advancement of Learning, is, as Bacon himself described it, "a general and faithful perambulation of learning, with an inquiry what parts thereof lie fresh and waste, and not improved and converted by the industry of man; to the end that such a plot made and recorded to memory may both minister light to any public designation and also serve to excite voluntary endeavours." Bacon makes, by a sort of exhaustive analysis, a ground-plan of all subjects of study, as an intellectual map, helping the right inquirer in his search for the right path. The right path is that by which he has the best chance of adding to the stock of knowledge in the world something worth labouring for, as labour for "the glory of the Creator and the relief of man's estate."

In May, 1606, Bacon, aged forty-six, married Alice Barnham, daughter of a London merchant who was dead, and whose widow had taken in second marriage Sir John Packington, of Worcestershire. The lady had £220 a year, which was settled on herself. In June, 1607, Sir Francis Bacon became Solicitor-General. While rising in his profession he was still at work on writings that set forth portions of his philosophy. In 1607 he sent to Sir Thomas Bodley his *Cogitata et Visa*—a first sketch of the *Novum Organum*. In 1608—the year of John Milton's birth—Bacon obtained the clerkship of the Star Chamber, worth £1,600 or £2,000 a year, of which the reversion had been given him in 1589. In 1612 appeared, in November or December, Bacon's *Second Edition of the Essays;* there had been, since the first, two unauthorised editions, in 1598 and 1606. In Bacon's own second edition the number of the essays was increased from ten to thirty-eight, and those formerly printed had been very thoroughly revised. The range of thought, also, was widened (ch. vii. § 85), and the first essay was "Of Religion." The purpose of dedicating this edition to Prince Henry was stopped by the prince's death, on the 6th of November. In February, 1613, Bacon contrived, for the gentlemen of Gray's Inn and the Inner Temple, a *Masque of the Marriage of the Thames and the Rhine*, on the marriage of the Princess Elizabeth to the Elector Palatine. In October, 1613, Bacon was made Attorney-General. The dispassionate mind that his philosophy required Bacon applied somewhat too coldly to the philosophy of life. Without hatreds or warm affections, preferring always a kind course to an unkind one, but yielding easily to stubborn facts in his search for prosperity, Bacon failed as a man, although he had no active evil in his character, for want of a few generous enthusiasms. Seeking to please a mean master, who was the dispenser of his earthly good, in 1614 Bacon was official prosecutor of Oliver St. John, a gentleman of Marlborough, who had written a letter to the mayor of his town on the illegality of the king's act in raising money by benevolences. In December of the same year the Rev. Edmund Peacham, a clergyman seventy years old, rector of Hinton St. George, Somersetshire, was deprived of his orders by the High Commission for accusations against his diocesan. In searching his house a manuscript

sermon was found, which had been written but not preached.
It censured acts of the king—as sale of Crown lands, gifts to
favourites—and seems to have suggested that the recovery of
Crown lands to the people might cost blood. The old clergyman
was, by the king's desire, accused of treason, and was twice put
to the rack, that accusation of himself or others might be wrung
from him. As Attorney-General, Bacon, serving his master, discussed privately with the judges in furtherance of the king's
desire that Peacham might be convicted of treason for the composition of the sermon without any act of publication. They
would not see with the king's eyes, or follow Bacon, who wrote
to the king of his foregone conclusion as the truth, and expressed
his hope of the judges that "force of law and precedent will
bind them to the truth ; neither am I wholly out of hope that my
Lord Coke himself, when I have in some dark manner put him
in doubt that he shall be left alone, will not continue singular."
As nothing could be done in London, the old clergyman was
sent to Taunton assizes, where a conviction was secured in
August, 1615 ; but the sentence of death was not carried out,
because many of the judges were of opinion that Peacham's
offence was not treason. He died, in 1616, a prisoner in Taunton
gaol. In 1616—the year of Shakespeare's death—Bacon was
made a Privy Councillor. While the Attorney-General was thus
obedient to his master, he was suitor for the office of Lord-
Keeper, which the bad health of Lord Chancellor Ellesmere
would probably soon cause him to resign. This office Bacon
obtained in March, 1617. In January, 1618, he became Lord
Chancellor ; six months afterwards he was made Baron Verulam.
In October, 1620, he presented to the king his *Novum Organum*,
a fragment on which he had worked for thirty years, and which
formed the second and main part of his "Instauratio Magna."
Three months later he was made, on the 27th of January, 1621,
Viscount St. Albans, and had reached his highest point of greatness. Then came his memorable fall.

On the 15th of March the report of a Parliamentary Committee on the administration of justice charged the Lord Chancellor with twenty-three specified acts of corruption. Bacon's
final reply was : "Upon advised consideration of the charge,
descending into my own conscience, and calling my memory to
account as far as I am able, I do plainly and ingenuously confess
that I am guilty of corruption, and do renounce all defence, and
put myself on the grace and mercy of your lordships." He then,

as he had been required to do, replied upon each case, and
pleaded guilty to each. The Lords sent a committee of twelve
to the Chancellor, to ask whether he had signed this, and would
stand by his signature. He replied to the question : " My lords,
it is my act, my hand, and my heart. I beseech your lordships
to be merciful to a broken reed." He was sentenced by the
House of Lords, on the 3rd of May, 1621, to a fine of £40,000,
which the king remitted ; to be committed to the Tower during
the king's pleasure, and he was released next day ; thenceforth
to be incapable of holding any office in the State, or sitting in
Parliament. It was decided by a majority of two that he should
not be stripped of his titles. Of worldly means there remained
what private fortune he had, and a pension of £1,200 a year
that the king had lately given him. The rest of his life Bacon
gave to study, only applying, unsuccessfully, in 1623, for the
provostship of Eton. In 1622 he published, in Latin, as the
third part of his " Instauratio Magna," his Natural and Experimental History—*Historia Naturalis et Experimentalis*, and his
*Historie of the Raigne of K. Henry VII.*, dedicated to Charles,
Prince of Wales. In 1623 appeared, in Latin, his *History of
Life and Death*, as well as the Latin expansion into nine books
of " The Advancement of Learning," as a first volume of his
works. In 1625, Bacon published his own *Third Edition of the
Essays*, with their number increased to fifty-eight, and again
with revision and rearrangement of the earlier matter. The first
essay in this final edition was " Of Truth ;" and the Essay " Of
Religion," with its title changed to " Of Unitie in Religion," was
much enlarged and carefully modified, to prevent misconception
of its spirit. On the 9th of April, 1626, ten years after Shakespeare, Francis Bacon died.

Bacon arranged his writings for the "Instauratio Magna" into
six divisions :—1. The books on the "Dignity and Advancement
of Learning "—the ground-plan. 2. The " Novum Organum," of
which only the first part was executed, showing what was the new
instrument, or method of inquiry, which he substituted for the old
instrument, the " Organon" of Aristotle. 3. The "Experimental
History of Nature ; or, Study of the Phenomena of the Universe."
In this division Bacon's most complete work was the *Silva
Silvarum ; or, Natural History in Ten Centuries*. Then came
the science raised on these foundations, in, 4, the *Scala Intel-
lectus ;* or, Ladder of the Understanding, which leads up from
experience to science. 5. The *Prodromi ;* or, the Anticipations
R *

of the Second Philosophy—provisional anticipations founded on experience, which the investigator needs as starting-points in his research ; and, 6, Active Science—experiment in the fair way to such gains of knowledge as may benefit mankind.

Bacon opposed to the "Organon" of Aristotle, which only analysed the form of propositions, his "New Organon," which sought a method of analysis that would attain discoveries enlarging the dominion of man. "Human science," he said, "and human power coincide." Invention must be based upon experience ; experience be widened by experiment. Bacon's highest and purest ambition was associated with his life-long endeavour to direct the new spirit of inquiry into a course that would enable men "to renew and enlarge the power and dominion of the human race itself over the universe. . . . Now the dominion of men over things depends alone on arts and sciences; for Nature is only governed by obeying her." Bacon had no sympathy whatever with research that consists only in turning the mind back on itself. For him the mind was a tool, and nature the material for it to work upon. The only remaining way to health, he said, "is that the whole work of the mind be begun afresh, and that the mind, from the very beginning, should on no account be trusted to itself, but constantly directed." All knowledge comes to men from without, and the laws to which we can subject natural forces are to be learnt only from the interpretation of nature. In former days invention had been left to chance, and science had been occupied with empty speculations. A way of inquiry should be used that will lead—be inductive—from one experience to another, not by chance, but by necessity. Hence Bacon's method has been called inductive ; but the second and main part of his philosophy was, after arriving by this method at a truth in nature, to deduce therefrom its uses to man. Having found, for example, by inductive experiment, a general truth about electricity, the crowning work of the Baconian philosophy would be to deduce from it the Atlantic cable.

Bacon taught that the inquirer was to take as frankly as a child whatever truths he found. He compared human knowledge with divine, of which it is said, "Except ye become as little children ye shall not enter into the kingdom of heaven." And he too said, "Little children, keep yourselves from idols." "The idols," Bacon said, "and false notions which have hitherto occupied the human understanding and are deeply rooted in it, not only so beset the minds of men that entrance is hardly open to truth, but even when entrance is conceded, they will again meet and hinder us in the very reconstruction of the sciences, unless men, being forewarned, guard themselves as much as possible against them." He therefore classified the common forms of false image within the mind to which men bow down. They are Idols (1) of the Forum or Market-place (*Idola Fori*), when we take things not for what they are, but for what the common talk, as of men in the market-place, considers them to be ; they are Idols (2) of the Theatre (*Idola Theatri*), when we bow down to authority, or fear to differ from those who have played great parts on the world's stage ; Idols (3) of Race or Tribe (*Idola Tribus*) are "founded," says Bacon, "in the very tribe or race of men. It is falsely asserted that human sense is the standard of things," for the human intellect, blending its own nature with an object, distorts and disfigures it. There are Idols also (4) of the Cave or Den (*Idola Specus*) ; these are the accidental faults and prejudices of the individual inquirer.

On his guard against these idols, the philosopher who follows Bacon's teaching trusts to pure experience. Everything in Nature appears under certain conditions. Comparative experiments can be made to determine which of these conditions are essential and which accidental. Thus we may advance from fact to fact, till, by successive testings and comparisons of facts, we reach one of the laws by which the course of nature is determined. So we ascend, by the method of induction, from the experiment to the axiom. But experiment may seem to have found a law with which some fact—some "negative instance"—is at odds. This contradiction must not be put out of sight, but taken simply as against acceptance of the law till it be reconciled with it. Nay, more, the investigator must use all his wit to invent combinations able to disprove his fact, if it be no fact ; he must seek to invent negative instances, acting as counsel against himself until assured that his new fact will stand firm against any trial. " I think," said Bacon, " that a form of induction should be introduced which from certain instances should draw general conclusions, so that the impossibility of finding a contrary instance might be clearly proved." When so assured that it stands firm, the inquirer may announce his new truth confidently, and either deduce from it himself or leave others to deduce its use to man.

In this philosophy Bacon did no more than express formally,

distinctly, and with great influence over the minds of others, what had always been the tendency of English thought. His namesake, Roger Bacon, in the thirteenth century, had pursued science very much in the same spirit, and had nearly anticipated Francis Bacon's warning against the four idols, in his own four grounds of human ignorance (ch. iii. § 33). We must not forget, also, when we find feebleness in the scientific experiments of Bacon and his followers, with the retention of much false opinion about nature, that what Bacon professed was to show, not grand results, but the way to them.  He bade his followers " be strong in hope, and not imagine that our 'Instauratio' is something infinite and beyond the reach of man, when really :t is not unmindful of mortality and humanity ; for it does not expect to complete its work within the course of a single age, but leaves this to the succession of ages ; and, lastly, seeks for science, not arrogantly within the little cells of human wit, but humbly, in the greater world."

23. We finish the sketch of our literature in the reign of James I. with a glance at some of the poets who were not dramatists.  **Michael Drayton** (ch. vii. § 80) wrote, at the king's accession, *To the Majestie of King James: a Gratulatore Poem*, but turned from the king disappointed ; published, in 1604, his fable of *The Owle ;* and in 1607 the *Legend of Great Cromwell*, which appeared again in 1609 as *The Historie of the Life and Death of the Lord Cromwell, some time Earl of Essex and Lord Chancellor of England.*  In 1613 appeared his *Poly-olbion* (the word means Many-ways-Happy), a poetical description of his native land, in nearly sixteen thousand lines of Alexandrine verse, with maps of counties, and antiquarian notes by the author's friend, John Selden.  This poem was another illustration of the quickened patriotism of the English. Thus Drayton sang when he came to his own county of War-wick, that he and Shakespeare loved :

> " My native country, then, which so brave spirits hast bred,
>   If there be virtues yet remaining in thy earth,
>   Or any good of thine thou bredst into my birth,
>   Accept it as thine own, whilst now I sing of thee,
>   Of all the later brood the unworthiest though I be."

**William Browne**, born in 1590, at Tavistock, in Devon-shire, studied at Exeter College, Oxford, then went to the Inner Temple, and in 1613, the year of the appearance of Drayton's "Polyolbion," produced, at the age of twenty-three, the first part of his *Britannia's Pastorals,* partly written before he was twenty. The *Shepherd's Pipe,* in seven eclogues, followed in 1614. In 1616, the year of Shakespeare's death, appeared the second part of Browne's *Britannia's Pastorals.* The two parts were published together about the end of James's reign, and about the same time their author went back to Exeter College as tutor to Robert Dormer, Earl of Carnarvon. His pleasant pastoral strain touched but lightly upon the realities of life. The rustic manner showed the influence of Spenser, but in James's reign this influence was greatest on Giles Fletcher.

24. **Giles Fletcher** (ch. vii. § 91), was at Trinity College, Cambridge, when he contributed a canto on the death of Queen Elizabeth to the collection of verses *Sorrow's Joy,* on the death of Elizabeth and accession of James, published by the printer to the University in 1603. He took the degree of B.D. at Trinity College, and held the living of Alderton, in Suffolk, till his death, in 1623. It was not until after the death of Giles that his elder brother, Phineas, appeared in print as a poet, though at the close of his own early poem Giles spoke of his brother as young Thyrsilis, the Kentish lad that lately taught

> " His oaten reed the trumpet's silver sound."

Giles Fletcher's poem was published at Cambridge, in 1610, when the author's age was about six-and-twenty. It was a devout poem on *Christ's Victory and Triumph in Heaven and Earth over and after Death,* in an original eight-lined stanza, suggested by Spenser's, but not happily constructed. For five lines the stanza followed Spenser, and then came a triplet, of which the last line was an Alexandrine, as in the Spenserian stanza. Thus :

> " At length an aged sire far off he saw
>   Come slowly footing ; every step he guess'd
> One of his feet he from the grave did draw ;
>   Three legs he had, that made of wood was best ;
> And all the way he went he ever blest
>   With benedictions, and with prayers store ;
>   But the bad ground was blessed ne'er the more :
> And all his head with snow of age was waxen hoar."

Christ's Victory in Heaven heralded the work of Christ with long personifications and speeches of Justice and of Mercy, to whom finally all bowed ; the Victory on Earth painted Christ in the wilderness, approached by Satan (the aged sire above mentioned) in the guise of an old Palmer, who so bowed "that at his feet his head he seemed to throw," who led Christ to echoes of Spenser to the cave of Despair, which he would entice him to enter ; to the top of the Temple, also, where personified Presumption tempted in vain ; and then to Pangloretta, on the mountain top, where Giles Fletcher faintly recalled notes from Spenser's bower of Acrasia. The other two books on the Triumph over Death and the Triumph after Death were in like manner.

**Joshua Sylvester** (ch. vii. § 93), about 1620, gratified His Majesty, who had published in 1604 a *Counterblaste to Tobacco*, with a poem of his own, called *Tobacco Battered and the Pipes Shattered (about their Ears that idlely Idolise so Base and Barbarous a Weed; or at least-wise Over-love so Loathesome Vanitie), by a Volley of Holy Shot thundered from Mount Helicon*. This poem was as wise as its title, and suggests the form into which Euphuism degenerated in the time of James I.

25. Strain for ingenious alliteration, and for unexpected turns of phrase or thought, losing much of the grace and strength it had in the Elizabethan time, became more pedantic in the wise, more frivolous in the foolish, often obscure by the excess of artifice and the defect of sense. There was the same degeneration everywhere of the *Earlier Euphuism*, bright with fresh invention and poetical conceits, into the *Later Euphuism* that had to a great extent lost freshness of impulse, and was made obscure by poets who, with less to say than their predecessors, laboured to outdo them in ingenuities of thought and speech. There is no reason in or out of metaphysics why the Later Euphuistic poetry, of which Donne's verse is a type, should be called "metaphysical." It was so called in an age that knew little or nothing of the character of English poetry before the Commonwealth. There is as little reason for the assertion that a change for the worse was made in our literature by the influence of Donne. He only represented change, and he was popular because he followed cleverly the fashion of his day. Precisely what has been said of Donne, in his relation to our English literature, has been said also of Gongora, who died in 1627, and of Marino, who died in 1625—men who went with the same current of literature, one in Spain, the other in Italy, during the reign of James I. in England. In Spain the writers corresponding to our Earlier and Later Euphuists are known as the *Conceptistas*, or "Conceited School," and the *Cultos*, who cherished what they called a "Cultivated Style" in poems and romances. Our later Euphuism was English cousin to the

*cultismo* of Spain, and to the style called, after Marino, by Italians the *stile Marinesco.* Here, also, we are at the beginning of the history of the false worship of diction.

26. **John Donne** was born in 1573, the son of a London merchant. He was taught at home till, in his eleventh year, he was sent to Hart Hall, Oxford. At fourteen he left Oxford for Cambridge, where he remained till he was seventeen, but took no degree, because his family was Roman Catholic, and would not let him take the required oath. He left Cambridge for London, and studied law at Lincoln's Inn. His father died at that time, leaving him three thousand pounds. His mother sought to bring him to the faith of his parents; and unsettlement of mind caused him to make a special study of the controversies of the time between the Roman Catholics and the Reformers. As a storehouse of opinion on the controversy, young Donne fastened upon the works of Cardinal Bellarmin (§ 16). He went with the expeditions of the Earl of Essex, in 1596 and 1597, and spent afterwards some years in Italy and Spain, returned to England, and became chief secretary to Lord Chancellor Ellesmere. He held that office five years, during which he fell in love with Anne More, a niece of Lady Ellesmere, who lived in the family. Her father, Sir George More, heard of this, and carried away the young lady to his house in Surrey; but a secret marriage was effected. When this was told to Sir George, he caused Lord Ellesmere to dismiss his secretary, whom apparent ruin could not keep from a play on words, according to the fashion of the time; for in writing the sad news to his wife he added to his signature the line, "John Donne, Anne Donne, Un-done." Donne was imprisoned for a time, and when he was free his wife was kept from him. He sued at law to recover her. She came to him when his means were almost gone, and a family grew fast about the young couple, who were living in the house of a kinsman, Sir Francis Woolly, of Pirford, Surrey. It was then urged upon Donne that he should take orders in the Church, but he hesitated, and preferred study of civil and canon law. Sir Francis Woolly died, but before his death he had persuaded Donne's father-in-law to cease from wrath and pay a portion with his daughter, at the rate of £80 a year. Donne remained very much dependent on the liberality of friends, and was still studying points of controversy between the English and the Romish Church, when a home was given to him in the house of Sir Robert Drury, in

Drury Lane. Donne came now into contact with King James, discussed theology with him, and wrote, at his request, a book on the taking of the oaths of supremacy and allegiance, called *Pseudo Martyr*, published in 1610. This pleased the king so much that he required Donne to be a clergyman. Donne made what interest he could to have the king's good-will shown in the form of secular employment; but James had made up his mind that Donne should be a preacher, and, in spite of himself, he was forced into the Church as the only way by which he was allowed a chance of prospering. When Donne had at last taken orders, King James made him his chaplain, and in the same month called on Cambridge to make him Doctor of Divinity. In this first year of his prosperity Donne's wife died, leaving him with seven children. Outward prosperity increased. He became a famous preacher and a fashionable poet, was lecturer at Lincoln's Inn till he was joined in a mission to Germany, and about a year after his return was made by the king, in 1623, Dean of St. Paul's, while the vicarage of St. Dunstan's in the West, and yet another good thing, fell to him almost at the same time. Donne survived King James, and died in the year 1631. His lighter occasional poems were not published until after his death. In James's reign he, like other poets, published in 1613 "An Elegy on the Untimely Death of the Incomparable Prince Henry." A severe illness of his own led also to the publication in 1624 of his *Devotions upon Emergent Occasions, and Seuerall Steps in Sickness;* and in 1625 he published a poem upon mortality, since that was not out of harmony with his sacred office. It was called *An Anatomy of the World, wherein, by the untimely Death of Mrs. Eliz. Drury, the Frailty and Decay of this whole World is represented.* From this poem we take, for specimen of artificial diction, a passage that contains by rare chance one conceit rising in thought and expression to the higher level of Elizabethan poetry:

> " She, in whose body (if we dare preferre
> This low world to so high a marke as shee)
> The Western treasure, Easterne spicery,
> Europe, and Afrique, and the unknowne rest
> Were easily found, or what in them was best;
> And when we have made this large discoverie
> Of all, in her some one part then will bee
> Twenty such parts, whose plenty and riches is
> Enough to make twenty such worlds as this;
> Shee, whom had they knowne, who did first betroth
> The tutelar angels, and assigned one, both

> To nations, cities, and to companies,
> To functions, offices, and dignities,
> And to each several man, to him, and him.
> They would have given her one for every limbe;
> Shee, of whose soule, if we may say, 'twas gold,
> Her body was th' Electrum, and did hold
> Many degrees of that; wee understood
> Her by her sight; *her pure and eloquent blood*
> *Spoke in her cheekes, and so distinctly wrought*
> *That one might almost say, her body thought.*
> Shee, shee, thus richly and largely hous'd, is gone."

Unreality of a style that sacrifices sense to ingenuity is most felt in Donne's lighter poems. The collection of the verse of the late Dean of St. Paul's published in 1635, as *Poems by J. D., with Elegies on the Author's Death*, opens with an ingenious piece, of which the sense is, so far as it has any, that a woman's honour is not worth a flea. Donne was unquestionably a man with much religious earnestness, but he was also a poet who delighted men of fashion.

27. The literary affectations of the time were reduced to absurdity by Thomas Coryat, and John Taylor, the Water Poet. **Thomas Coryat**, son of George Coryat, rector of Odcombe, Somerset, and educated at Gloucester Hall, Oxford, lived a fantastic life at court for the amusement of Prince Henry. In 1608 he travelled on foot for five months in France, Italy, and Germany, walking 1,975 miles, and more than half the distance in one pair of shoes, which were only once mended. The shoes, when he came home, were hung up in Odcombe Church, and kept there as the "thousand mile shoes" till 1702. The travel in them was described in a book published in 1611, as *Coryat's Crudities hastily Gobbled Up in Five Months' Travel in France, &c. Introduced by An Odcombian Banquet of nearly Sixty Copies of Verses*, which were praises written in jest by nearly all the poets of the day. This book was followed by *Coryat's Crambe; or, his Colewort Twise Sodden, and now Served with other Macaronicke Dishes as the Second Course to his Crudities.* In 1612, Coryat gathered the people of Odcombe at their market cross, and took leave of them for a ten years' ramble. He visited Greece, Egypt, India, and died at Surat, in 1617. There was the English love of sturdy enterprise and adventure underlying Coryat's endeavour to delight his public.

**John Taylor** was a poor man's son from Gloucestershire, who became a Thames waterman, after he had served under Elizabeth in sixteen voyages; he was with Essex at Cadiz and

the Azores. He read many books, and he wrote sixty-three booklets to amuse the public with their oddities. He made presents of his little books to customers and courtiers, and took whatever they might give in return. One of his books told how he won a bet that he would row in his boat to the Continent and back again within a certain time. It appeared as *Taylor's Travels in Germanie; or, Three Weekes Three Daies and Three Hours' Observations and Travel from London to Hamburg. . . . Dedicated for the present to the absent Odcombian knight errant, Sir Thomas Coriat, Great Britain's Error and the World's Mirror.* This appeared in the year of Coryat's death at Surat. Another of Taylor's freaks was a journey on foot from London to Edinburgh, " not carrying any money to and fro, neither begging, borrowing, nor asking meat, drink, or lodging." This yielded, in 1618, a book, *The Pennyles Pilgrimage ; or, the Moneylesse Perambulation of John Taylor, alias the King's Majestie's Water Poet, from London to Edenborough on Foot.* Another of his adventures was a voyage from London to Queenborough in a paper boat, with two stock-fish tied to two canes for oars. It was celebrated, in 1623, by *The Praise of Hempseed, with the Voyage of Mr. Roger Bird and the Writer hereof, in a Boat of Brown Paper, from London to Quinborough in Kent. As also a Farewell to the Matchless Deceased Mr. Thomas Coriat. Concluding with Commendations of the famous River of Thames.* All this was a little tract of twenty-four leaves. So we come down from Elizabeth to James I.; from Frobisher, and Drake, and Raleigh, to poor Tom Coryat and John Taylor, His Majesty's Water Poet. But although the court lost dignity, the spirit of the people was unchanged.

28. **George Wither** was born in 1588, at Bentworth, near Alton, in Hampshire. At the beginning of the reign of James I. he was sent to Oxford, but was soon recalled to attend to the Hampshire farm land. In 1612, Wither first appeared as a poet by joining in the lament for Prince Henry, adding to his Elegies a "supposed interlocution between the ghost of Prince Henry and Great Britaine;" and in 1613, being then twenty-five years old, he spoke out boldly for England in *Abuses Stript and Whipt; or, Satirical Essayes, by George Wyther, divided into Two Bookes.* The successive satires are under the heads of human passions, as Love, Lust, Hate, Envy, Revenge, and so forth :

" What ? you would fain have all the great ones freed,
They must not for their vices be controll'd :

> Beware ; that were a sauciness indeed ,
> But if the great ones to offend be bold,
> I see no reason but they should be told."

Wither was bold in condemnation as others in offence. While he continued the attack upon self-seeking of the higher clergy, he maintained the office of the bishop, and gave high praise to the Archbishop of Canterbury and Bishop of London. The Satires, although sharp, were generous ; their style was diffuse, but simple, earnest, often vigorous, for Wither had the true mind of a poet. He would tell what he knew,

> " And then if any frown (as sure they dare not)
> So I speak truth, let them frown still, I care not."

The great ones did frown, and Wither was locked up in the Marshalsea. But he was not to be silenced. He sang on in his cage, and sang plain English, contemning the pedantry of fashion. Wither translated in his prison a Greek poem on " The Nature of Man," besides writing the most manly pastorals produced in James's reign, *The Shepheards' Hunting : being certain Eclogues written during the time of the Author's Imprisonment in the Marshalsey*, and a *Satire to the King*, in justification of his former Satires. In the "Shepheard's Hunting," we learn how Wither, as Philarete (lover of Virtue), had hunted with ten couple of dogs (the satires in " Abuses Stript and Whipt ") those foxes, wolves, and beasts of prey that spoil our folds and bear our lambs away. But wounded wolves and foxes put on sheep's clothing, complained of the shepherd's hunting, and caused his imprisonment. In his prison, Philarete talked with his friends, kept up his spirit, and was comforted by song. *Wither's Motto, Nec habeo, nec careo, nec curo* (" I have not, want not, care not ")—a line in it says, " He that supplies my want hath took my care "—was published in 1618. In 1622 Wither's poems were collected as *Juvenilia ;* and in the same year he published *Faire-Virtue, the Mistresse of Philarete, written by Him-selfe.* Virtue is here described as a perfect woman, mistress of Philarete (lover of Virtue). This long poem, in seven-syllabled verse, is musical with interspersed songs, including the famous—

> " Shall I, wasting in despair,
> Die because a woman's fair ?"

and delicately playful with the purest sense of grace and beauty. George Wither takes his own way still, saying :

" Pedants shall not tie my strains
To our antique poets' veins,
As if we in latter days
Knew to love, but not to praise.
Being born as free as these,
I will sing as I shall please,
Who as well new paths may run
As the best before have done."

Wither remained an active writer in the reign of Charles I. ;
and **Francis Quarles**, who was four years younger than
Wither, produced his best work after the death of James I.
Quarles was born in 1592, at Romford, in Essex, educated at
Christ's College, Cambridge, and at Lincoln's Inn.    He was
cupbearer to James's daughter, the Queen of Bohemia, and
afterwards served in Ireland as secretary to Archbishop Usher
(§ 17).    His first publication was in 1620, *A Feast for Wormes
in a Poem on the History of Jonah*, with *Pentalogia; or, the
Quintessence of Meditation.*    In 1621 followed *Hadassa; or, the
History of Queen Esther*, these histories being in ten-syllabled
couplets, and, in the same measure, *Argalus and Parthenia*,
a poem in three books, founded on a part of Sidney's " Arcadia "
(ch. vii. § 44).    Then came in 1624, *Job Militant, with Meditations Divine and Moral ;* also *Sion's Elegies, wept by Jeremie
the Prophet ;* and, in 1625, *Sion's Sonnets, sung by Solomon the
King, and periphrased.*    The writing of Quarles in the reign
of James I. consisted, then, of *Argalus and Parthenia*, and
those pieces which were collected into one volume, in 1630, as
Quarles's *Divine Poems.*

29. **William Drummond**, M.A. of Edinburgh, after four
years in France, inherited, in 1610, at the age of twenty-five, his
paternal estate of Hawthornden, gave up the study of law, took
his ease, and wrote poetry.    He joined in the lament for the
death of Henry, Prince of Wales ; published at Edinburgh,
in 1616, *Poems: Amorous, Funerall, Divine, Pastorall, in
Sonnets, Songs, Sextains, Madrigals, by W. D., the Author
of the Teares on the Death of Meliades*, (Meliades was the
anagram made for himself by the prince from " Miles a Deo ");
and in 1617, upon James's visit to Scotland, published *Forth
Feasting: a Panegyric to the King's Most Excellent Majestie.*
During the greater part of April, 1619, Drummond had Ben
Jonson for a guest, and took ungenial notes of his conversation.
In 1623 he published *Flowvres of Sion, to which is adjoyned his
Cypresse Grove.*    His sonnets were true to the old form of that

kind of poem, and they were not all of earthly love and beauty, for sonnets in the spirit of Spenser's Hymns of Heavenly Love and Beauty (ch. vii. § 77) are among the spiritual poems in Drummond of Hawthornden's "Flowers of Sion."

**Sir Thomas Overbury** was murdered in 1613, when but thirty-two years old.   As a follower of the king's favourite, Carr, he opposed his marriage with the Countess of Essex.   The king, wishing to send Overbury out of the way, offered him an embassy to Russia.   He refused it, and was committed to the Tower for contempt of the king's commands.   There, by the connivance of Lady Essex, Overbury died of poison ten days before the judgment of divorce; and this was followed, as the year closed, by the creation of Carr as Earl of Somerset, and his marriage to the Countess in the Chapel Royal.   Bacon devised a masque at Gray's Inn in honour of the marriage.   He also took part, in May, 1616, in the trial of the earl and countess for the murder of Sir Thomas Overbury.   The victim of this crime was in repute among the writers of his day for a poem on the choice of a wife, called *A Wife now a Widowe*, published the year after his murder, in 1614, and reprinted in the same year with the addition of twenty-one characters.   To write compact and witty characters of men and women was a fancy of the time, derived in the first instance from Theophrastus, and associated with the quick growth of the drama.   Such pithy character writing had been prefixed formally as " The Character of the Persons " to Ben Jonson's "Every Man Out of his Humour;" and the dialogue of the second act of his "Cynthia's Revels," produced in 1600, is chiefly made up of such character writing as that in which Sir Thomas Overbury showed his skill in 1614, and John Earle showed his in 1628.   It was the manner of this character writing that suggested to young Milton his lines on the death of Hobson, the University carrier.

30. **John Milton** was seventeen years old at the end of James's reign, and we may now pass with him into the reign of Charles I.   He was born in Bread Street, Cheapside, on the 9th of December, 1608.   His father, also a John Milton, was son to a Catholic, of Oxfordshire, perhaps a husbandman, perhaps an under-ranger of Shotover Forest, who had cast him off for changing his religion.   Thus the poet's father had settled in London as a scrivener, and prospered.   He had a taste for music.   In 1601 he had been one of twenty-two musicians who

published twenty-five madrigals, as *The Triumphs of Oriana.*
In 1614, when the poet son was about six years old, the musician
father was joined with others in providing music to the *Tears and
Lamentations of a Sorrowful Soul.* Seven years later, as contributor to a book of *Psalms,* he harmonised the tunes still popular
as "Norwich" and "York." Of the tenor part of York tune, it
has been said that at one time "half the nurses in England were
used to sing it by way of lullaby." Thus the poet's father had
musicians among his friends, as well as men like himself earnest
in religious feeling. One of these, Thomas Young, of Loncarty,
in Perthshire, afterwards a minister in Suffolk, and a man of
note among the Puritans, was the boy's first teacher. In 1622,
Young, aged thirty-five, went to be pastor of the congregation of English merchants at Hamburg; his pupil had then
been for a couple of years at St. Paul's School (ch. vi. § 10),
where Mr. Gill was head master, and his son, Alexander Gill,
taught under him. Milton was a schoolboy at St. Paul's from
1620 until a few months before the close of the reign of James I.
His father too readily encouraged the boy's eagerness for study;
he had teaching at home as well as at school, suffered headaches,
and laid the foundation of weak sight by sitting up till midnight
at his lessons.

At St. Paul's School Milton found a bosom friend in Charles
Diodati. The friendship outlasted their boyhood, only death
interrupted it. Charles was the son of Theodore Diodati, a
physician in good practice in London, who had been born in
Geneva, the son of Italian Protestants. His younger brother,
Giovanni, uncle of Milton's friend, was still at Geneva, professor
there of theology, and had published translations of the Bible
into Italian and French. Of such a household came the friend
to whom young Milton spoke his inmost thoughts. Charles
Diodati left school more than two years before Milton, and
went to Trinity College, Oxford, where, in November, 1623, he
joined in writing Latin obituary verse upon the death of William
Camden. But John Milton and Charles Diodati had their
homes in the same town, and their friendship was easily maintained by visits and correspondence. There is a Greek letter
written in London from Diodati to Milton, hoping for fine
weather and cheerfulness in a holiday the two friends meant to
have next day together on the Thames. The surviving children
in Milton's home were Anne, the eldest; John; and Christopher,
seven years younger than John. Towards the close of 1624

Milton's sister, Anne, married Mr. Edward Phillips, of the Crown Office in Chancery.

In February, 1625, John Milton was admitted at Christ's College, Cambridge, aged two months over sixteen; but he had returned to London before the end of the term, and was there on the 26th of March, writing to his old tutor, Thomas Young, an affectionate letter: "I call God to witness how much as a father I regard you, with what singular devotion I have always followed you in thought." The next day, March 27, 1625, was the day of the death of James I.

### B.—REIGN OF CHARLES I.

31. Charles I. came to the throne at the age of twenty-five. Ben Jonson was then fifty years old, Milton not seventeen, and Bacon sixty-four, with but another year to live. John Fletcher (§ 6) died five months after the accession of Charles I.

At the accession of Charles I., Dr. Donne (§ 26) was fifty-two years old, and he lived until 1631; George Chapman (ch. vii. § 98, ch. viii. § 10) was sixty-eight years old, and lived till 1634. John Marston (ch. vii. § 99, 100) died about the same time as Chapman. Thomas Dekker and Thomas Heywood (ch. vii. § 99), who continued to write plays, lived on till about 1641. Heywood had "an entire hand or a main finger" in 220 plays. John Webster (§ 9) lived throughout the reign of Charles I., and died under the Commonwealth, about 1654.

32. **Ben Jonson** (ch. vii. § 100, ch. viii. § 5), after the death of James I., was driven to the stage again by poverty. The town did not receive his play, *The Staple of News*, produced in 1625, with much favour, and at the close of that year the poet had a stroke of palsy. He had bad health during the rest of his life. His play of *The New Inn*, acted in January, 1630, was driven from the stage; and it was then that Jonson turned upon the playhouse audiences with an indignant ode. At the end of 1631 a quarrel with our first great architect of the Renaissance, Inigo Jones, who invented the machinery for the court masques, deprived Jonson of all court patronage, and in 1632 and 1633 he was compelled to write feebly for the public stage his last plays, *The Magnetic Lady* and *The Tale of a Tub*. But after this, court favour and city favour, which also had been withdrawn, were regained for him. He had a pension from court of £100 and a tierce of canary. The favour of all the good poets of the

time was with him always. In the latter part of James's reign Jonson had lodged at a comb-maker's, outside Temple Bar. Just within Temple Bar, and between it and the Middle Temple gate, was a tavern, which had for its sign Dunstan, the saint of the parish, with the devil's nose in his tongs. It was called, therefore, the "Devil Tavern." Here Ben Jonson gathered about him the new generation of poets, in the Apollo Club. In his last days, when disease was closing in upon him, he was all poet again, at work on his pastoral play of *The Sad Shepherd; or, a Tale of Robin Hood*, which he left unfinished. He died in August, 1637, and was buried in Westminster Abbey. There was question of a monument, but none was raised. One Jack Young gave a mason eighteenpence to cut on the stone over the grave "O rare Ben Jonson."

33. **Philip Massinger** (§ 9) lived until 1640, writing many plays, of which only eighteen remain. The public stage under Charles I. was not strongly supported by the king and court, and it was strongly contemned by the Puritans. Good plays were often ill received, and then good poets might hunger. In 1633, when Ben Jonson made his last struggle to please a playhouse audience, Massinger printed that one of his plays which has held the stage to our own time, *A New Way to Pay Old Debts*. In the same year also Ford's *Broken Heart* was first printed.

**John Ford**, born in 1586, at Ilsington, in Devonshire, and bred to the law, began to write plays only two or three years before the accession of Charles I., and was one of the chief dramatists of Charles's reign until his death in 1639. In Ford, as in Massinger, men born in Elizabeth's reign, with grandeur of poetical conception, there is still the ring of Elizabethan poetry.

There is enough of it also in **James Shirley**, who was only about nine years old when Elizabeth died, and who lived into Charles II.'s reign, to justify his place among Elizabethan Stuart dramatists. The reign of Charles I. was Shirley's work-time as a dramatist. He was a Londoner born, educated at Merchant Tailors' School and St. John's College, Oxford, when Laud was its president. He removed to Cambridge, took orders, had a cure near St. Albans, left that because he turned Romanist, and taught, in 1623, at the St. Albans Grammar School. Then Shirley came to London, became a dramatist, and was not unprosperous; his genius and his Catholicism recommended him to Charles's queen. He went to

Ireland in 1637, the year of Ben Jonson's death, and wrote plays for a theatre then newly built, the first in Dublin.  When he came back, a clever dramatist and blameless gentleman, James Shirley took part on the king's side in the Civil War; and when the stage would no longer support his wife and family he taught boys again.

34. In the versification of many Elizabethan Stuart dramatists, and noticeably in Massinger and Shirley, there is further development of the ten-syllabled blank verse into a free measure, with frequent use of additional syllables, often monosyllables (ch. vi. § 47).  The breaks of lines also are often so made as to compel such running of two lines together as deprives the verse of some of its character.  We have begun the descent from poetical blank verse to a loosely metrical form of dialogue, when we find writing like this in Massinger:

> " Speak thy griefs.
> I shall, sir;
> But in a perplexed form and method, which
> You only can interpret: would you had not
> A guilty knowledge in your bosom of
> The language which you force me to deliver."

35. **Thomas May,** born in Sussex, in 1594, came from Cambridge to Gray's Inn, and was the one among Elizabethan Stuart dramatists whose work was least Elizabethan.  His comedy of *The Heir* was printed in 1622, when he also published a translation of *Virgil's Georgics.*  In 1627 appeared his translation of *Lucan's Pharsalia,* which had been preceded, in 1614, by that of Sir Arthur Gorges.  In 1633, May added, in seven books, his own *Continuation* to the death of Julius Cæsar.  May's *Lucan* caused Charles I. to command of him two original historical poems.  These were, *The Reigne of King Henry the Second, in Seven Bookes* (1633), and, also in seven books, *The Victorious Reigne of King Edward the Third.*  In the Civil War, May took part with the Parliament, and was made its secretary and historiographer.  In this character he published, in 1647, in folio, *The History of the Parliament of England which began Nov. 3,* M.DC.XL.; *with a Short and Necessary View of some Precedent Years;* an abridgment of this, in three parts, appeared in 1650, the year of his death.  May also translated a selection from Martial's Epigrams and Barclay's "Argenis" and " Icon Animarum."

36. Stuart dramatists born within a year or two after the

death of Elizabeth were Jasper Mayne, Thomas Randolph, and William Davenant. **Jasper Mayne,** born in 1604, at Hatherleigh, Devonshire, was educated at Westminster School and Christ Church, Oxford. He held the livings of Cassington and Pyrton, in Oxfordshire, till he was deprived of them in 1648. He wrote in the time of Charles I. a comedy called *The City Match* (printed in 1639), and the tragi-comedy of *The Amorous War* (printed in 1648). After the Restoration he became Archdeacon of Chichester and chaplain to Charles II. He lived till 1672.

**Thomas Randolph,** born at Newnham, Northamptonshire, in 1605, was at Westminster School with Mayne. He went to Trinity College, Cambridge, became M.A. and Fellow of his College, was a good scholar and good wit, lived gaily, and died in 1634, before he was thirty. In honour of sack and contempt of beer, he wrote a lively dramatic show, called *Aristippus* (1630), in which the jovial philosopher—whose name was given to sack (sec) or dry sherry—lectured to scholars on the virtues of that source of inspiration till the scholars sang:

> " Your ale is too muddy, good sack is our study,
> Our tutor is Aristippus."

Yet in another of Randolph's plays, *The Muses' Looking-Glass* —" the Ethics in a Play"—there is a moralising of the uses of the drama for the benefit of Puritan objectors; and after a dance of the seven sins, the opposite extremes which have a virtue in the mean—as servile Flattery and peevish Impertinence, extremes on either side of Courtesy; impious Confidence and overmuch Fear, extremes of Fortitude; swift Quarrelsomeness and the Insensibility to Wrong, extremes of Meekness—are cleverly illustrated in successive dialogues. The Golden Mean appears at last, with a masque of Virtues, replying to the Puritans who said that the stage lived by vice—

> " Indeed, 'tis true,
> As the physicians by diseases do,
> Only to cure them."

This was far more rational than Laud's way of answering Prynne. **William Prynne,** born in 1600, at Swainswick, near Bath, educated at Oriel College, Oxford, and then a barrister of Lincoln's Inn, represented Puritan opinion by writing, in 1628, *Health's Sickness,* on the Sinfulness of Drinking Healths, and a tract on *The Unloveliness of Lovelocks.* His tracts in the reign of Charles I. were very numerous, and upon every point of controversy maintained by the Puritans. In 1633 he published, against plays, masques, balls, and other such entertainments, *Histrio-mastix : the Players' Scourge or Actors' Tragedie.* For this book Prynne was committed to the Tower, prosecuted in the Star Chamber, and sentenced to pay a fine to the king of £5,000, to be expelled from the University of Oxford, from the Society of Lincoln's Inn, and from his profession of the law; to stand twice in the pillory, each time losing an ear; to have his book burnt before his face by the hangman; and to suffer perpetual imprisonment.

**Thomas Randolph** wrote also a comedy, *The Jealous Lovers*, acted, in 1632, before Charles and his queen by the students of Trinity College; and a graceful pastoral play, *Amyntas* (1638), acted before the king and queen at Whitehall. Among Randolph's songs and poems is one to Ben Jonson, who loved him and other of the bright young poets of the day, and called them sons. I was not born, he says, to Helicon,

> But thy adoption quits me of all fear,
> And makes me challenge a child's portion there.
> I am akin to heroes being thine,
> And part of my alliance is divine."

**William Davenant**, son of an Oxford innkeeper, was born in 1605, was educated at the Oxford Grammar School and at Lincoln College, went to court as page to the Duchess of Richmond, and was then in the household of Sir Philip Sidney's friend, **Fulke Greville, Lord Brooke,** until his murder in 1628. *Certaine Learned and Elegant Workes*, by Fulke Greville, were published in 1633, including his tragedy of *Alaham Mustapha*, of which a fragment had been printed in 1609. He left behind him also a short life of Sir Philip Sidney, which was published in 1652. **Davenant,** after his patron's death, turned to the stage, and began, in 1629, with a tragedy, *Albovine, King of the Lombards*, followed next year by two plays, *The Cruel Brother* and *The Just Italian.* In 1634, Davenant wrote a masque, *The Temple of Love*, to be presented at Whitehall by the queen and her ladies. In 1635 he published with other poems *Madagascar*, in couplets of ten-syllabled lines, on an achievement at sea by the king's nephew, Prince Rupert. Davenant remained in favour at court for his Masques and Plays; and after the death of Ben Jonson, Davenant took his place. Small-talk has it that disappointment at this turned Thomas May from the king. In 1639, William Davenant

was made governor of the king and queen's company acting
at the Cockpit in Drury Lane. Outbreak of civil war brought
him into danger. He escaped, returned, was the Earl of Newcastle's Lieutenant-General of the Ordnance, and, in 1643, was
knighted for his service at the siege of Gloucester. As exile
in Paris, Sir William Davenant was at the end of the king's
reign writing *Gondibert*, an heroic poem. Davenant resumed
his post as a leading dramatist, and was poet-laureate after the
Commonwealth.

37. **William Habington,** who, like Mayne, Randolph,
and Davenant, was born soon after Elizabeth's death, and was
about twenty at the accession of Charles I., wrote a tragi-
comedy of *The Queen of Arragon*, published in 1640. In that
year appeared also his *Historie of Edward the Fourth, King of
England*, written at the king's request. Habington's father was
a Worcestershire Roman Catholic, condemned to abide always
in Worcestershire, for having concealed in his house persons
accused of complicity in Gunpowder Plot. The father, since he
was to see so much of Worcestershire, wrote a history of the
county. The son, educated at St. Omer's, came home and
married Lucy, daughter of William Herbert, first Lord Powis.
In the name of Castara he paid honour to her through some
lyrics of pure love, as the type of modest, spiritual womanhood.
Habington's *Castara* first appeared in two parts, in 1634; the
second edition, adding three prose characters and twenty-six new
poems, appeared in 1635; and a third in 1640, enlarged with a new
part, containing a Character of "The Holy Man" and twenty-
two poems, chiefly sacred. **John Earle** (§ 29), M.A., Fellow
of Merton, had published, in 1628, his collection of Characters,
as *Micro-cosmographie; or, a Peece of the World Discovered, in
Essayes and Characters.* Earle was then twenty-seven years old.
He became afterwards chaplain to the Earl of Pembroke, and
was Bishop of Salisbury when he died, in 1665.

38. We leave the line of the playwrights, which we have followed down to the young writers of the time of Charles I., and turn
back to the elder men who were in that reign writing poetry.

**Dr. Barten Holyday,** chaplain to Charles, was born in
1593, the son of an Oxford tailor. He was educated at Christ
Church, took orders, went to Spain with Sir Francis Stewart,
and after his return was chaplain to the king and Archdeacon of
Oxford. He was a learned man and timid politician. He is
hardly to be called a dramatist, although he wrote a comedy,

published in 1618, called *Technogamia; or, the Marriage of the Arts.* But he left behind him when he died, in 1661, a translation of *Juvenal and Persius* into poor verse, with many learned illustrative notes. **George Sandys** (§ 11) published his complete translation of *Ovid's Metamorphoses* in 1626, and in 1636 a *Paraphrase of the Psalms,* with music of tunes by Henry Lawes. Sandys died in 1644.

**Thomas Carew,** born in Devonshire in 1589, was gentleman of the privy chamber and sewer in ordinary at the court of Charles I., a lively man, whose little poems were in good request, but, except when set to music, were not published in his lifetime. He died in 1639. The musicians William and Henry Lawes set many songs of Carew's, and were the chief writers of music for the poems that abounded in this reign.

**William Drummond of Hawthornden** (§ 29) lived through the reign of Charles I., and died soon after the king's execution, in 1649. There has been ascribed to him a mock-heroic macaronic poem (ch. vi. § 42) on a country quarrel over muck-carts—*Polemo-Middinia inter Vitervam et Nebernam*—blending Latin with the Scottish dialect in a coarse but comical example of that kind of writing.

**John Taylor,** the Water Poet (§ 27), wrote on through the reign of Charles I., and took part in the Civil War by discharging squibs of verse against the Puritans. He had then an inn at Oxford. When the king's cause was lost, he set up an inn in London, by Long Acre, with the sign of "The Mourning Crown;" but he was obliged to take that down, and set up his own portrait in place of it. He died in 1654.

39. **George Wither** (§ 28), at the beginning of the reign of Charles, was in London during a great plague time, bravely helping its victims, and he published, in 1628, a poem upon his experiences, as *Britain's Remembrancer: containing a Narration of the Plague lately Past; a Declaration of the Mischiefs Present, and a Prediction of Ivdgments to Come (if Repentance Prevent not). It is Dedicated (for the Glory of God) to Posteritie; and to these Times (if they please), by Geo. Wither.* Wither tells the reader of this book: "I was faine to print every sheet thereof with my owne hand, because I could not get allowance to doe it publikely." His verse translation of *The Psalms* was printed in the Netherlands, in 1632; his *Emblems,* with metrical illustrations, in 1635; his *Hallelujah; or, Britain's Second Remembrancer,* in 1641. Wither, of course, was active

in the Civil War, body and mind, becoming captain and major in
the army of the Parliament. When his " Emblems" appeared he
was the king's friend. He was the king's friend even when
opposing him in the first incidents of civil war, as one who hoped
for reconciliation between king and parliament. Wither lived
on, and was an old man in London at the time of the great fire.
He died in 1667.

**Francis Quarles** (§ 28) produced in 1632 *Divine Fancies,
Digested into Epigrammes, Meditations, and Observations;* and
the quaintest and most popular of his books of verse, *Emblems
Divine and Moral,* appeared in the same year (1635) with the
" Emblems" by George Wither. The taste for emblem pictures,
with ingenious and wise interpretation of them, had been
especially established by the Latin verse " Emblems" of the
great Italian lawyer, Andrea Alciati, who died in 1550. These
" Emblems" were translated into Italian, French, and German,
and read in schools. The taste they established was widely
diffused throughout the seventeenth century. The prevalent
taste for ingenious thought, blending with the religious feeling
of the people, helped especially to a revival of emblem writing
in Holland and England, and in Holland the Moral Emblems of
Jacob Cats, statesman as well as poet, who was born in 1577,
came twice as ambassador to England and outlived Quarles,
were in very high repute. Quarles, in Ireland with Archbishop
Usher, suffered by the Irish insurrection of 1641. He came to
England, took part with the royal cause in a book called *The
Loyal Convert,* joined the king at Oxford, and was ruined in
the Civil War. He had been twice married, and had by his
first wife eighteen children. Quarles died, overwhelmed with
troubles, in 1644.

40. **George Herbert,** born at Montgomery Castle, in 1593,
was the fifth of seven sons in a family of ten. His eldest
brother was **Edward Herbert** (§ 20), who returned from
France to England at the beginning of the reign of Charles I.,
was made an Irish baron, and in 1631 an English peer, as Lord
Herbert of Cherbury. In the Civil War, Edward Herbert first
sided with the Parliament, and then went to the king's side at
great sacrifice. He died in 1648, and in the following year
appeared his *History of the Life and Reign of Henry VIII.,*
in which little attention is paid to the religious movements of
the time. **George Herbert,** who was consumptive, died in
1633, fifteen years before his elder brother. His father died

when he was four years old, and till he was twelve he was in the care of a very good mother at home, with a chaplain for tutor. He was then sent to Westminster School, and at fifteen elected from the school for Trinity College, Cambridge. In 1615, George Herbert became M.A. and Fellow of his College. In 1619 he was chosen orator for the University, and so remained for the next eight years. His wit in use of the laboured style of the time delighted King James ; for when his Majesty made the University a present of his " Basilicon Doron," which had been published in 1599, George Herbert ended for the Cambridge authorities his acknowledgement of the royal gift, with the remark, put neatly in Latin verse, that they could not now have the Vatican and the Bodleian quoted against them ; one book was their library. James, upon this, observed that he thought George Herbert the jewel of the University. The Cambridge Public Orator, who was skilled in French, Italian, and Spanish, thought he might rise at court, and was often in London. The king gave him a sinecure worth £120 a year. With this, his fellowship, his payment as Orator, and private income, he could make a good figure at court, and he was usually near the king. But the death of two of his most powerful friends, and soon afterwards of King James himself, put an end to George Herbert's ambition to become one day a Secretary of State. He resolved then to follow his mother's often-repeated counsel, and at the beginning of the reign of Charles I., George Herbert took orders. He obtained, in 1626, the prebend of Layton Ecclesia, in the diocese of Lincoln, and with help of his own friends handsomely rebuilt the decayed church of that village. The Rev. George Herbert, cheerful and kind, tall and very lean, was ill for a year with one of his brothers, at Woodford, in Essex, and then again recruiting health in Wiltshire, at the house of the Earl of Danby, whose brother had become his mother's second husband. He then married, three days after their first interview, a young kinswoman of the earl's, who had been destined for him by her father, and in April, 1630, three months after the marriage, which proved a most happy one, George Herbert was inducted into his living of Bemerton, a mile from Salisbury. He was then thirty-six years old. The pure beauty of the evening of George Herbert's life—the three years at Bemerton before his death in 1633—was expressed in his verse as in his actions. With Hooker's faithful regard for the Church system, he maintained it in his parish according to his own standard of purity, blended with love and a free-handed charity, with poetry and music. He was a skilful musician, and went into Salisbury twice a week on certain days for the cathedral service. In 1631 George Herbert's poems appeared as *The Temple: Sacred Poems and Private Ejaculations.* The forced ingenuity of the time is in them, but the ingenuity so forced is that of a quick wit, and the spirit glorifies the letter; the words, too, are by the writer's sense of harmony tuned often exquisitely to the soul within them. Herbert's *Priest to the Temple; or, Character of a Country Parson,* was first printed under the Commonwealth, in 1652.

41. **Phineas Fletcher,** who had the living of Hilgay, in Norfolk, was born at Cranbrook, Kent, in April, 1582, and went to Cambridge from Eton in 1600. He published in 1627 a satire against the Jesuits, *The Locustes or Apollyonists,* in Latin and English; in 1631, *Sicelides, a Piscatory,* in five acts, as it hath been acted in King's College, in Cambridge; in 1632, a couple of religious pieces; in 1633, Latin poems, *Sylva Poetica* and *The Purple Island.* Phineas Fletcher's "Purple Island" is "the Isle of Man," and the poem is a long allegory in ten cantos of man as the study of mankind, with an allegorical description of his structure, much larger and less poetical than Spenser's in (Book II. Canto 97 of) the "Faerie Queene:" with allegorical description of the passions, desires, virtues lodged in man, as "this Purple Island's nation," and, of course, not wanting the dragon to be fiercely contended with. The poem was written long before it was published, for its flight is said to be that of a "callow wing that's newly left the nest," and it represents a young man's reverence for Spenser. Quarles called its author "the Spenser of this age." The metre of "The Purple Island" is Giles Fletcher's eight-lined stanza (§ 24), with its fifth line gone. **William Harvey** published, in 1628, the little Latin book, *De Motu Sanguinis et Cordis,* which diffused through Europe his discovery of the circulation of the blood. In 1633 the "thousand brooks," which represented veins and arteries, in Fletcher's "Purple Island," were described by Fletcher according to the old doctrine, without knowledge or without recognition of Harvey's discovery. In 1633 Fletcher's Piscatory play was followed by *Piscatorie Eclogs and other Poeticall Miscellanies.* They are seven pastorals, in which the old forms are applied to fishermen. "A fisher lad (no higher dares he look)," or "Myrtel fast down by silver Medway's shore," and

> "On a day
> Shepherd and fisherboys had set a prize
> Upon the shore, to meet in gentle fray,
> Which of the two should sing the choicest lay."

Phineas Fletcher wrote of himself as Thirsil, and figured his father with his troubles at Cambridge as Thelgon of Chame. Among his other poems was *Elisa, an Elegy* for the early death of Mr. St. Antony Irby, as the lament of "his weeping spouse, Elisa."

**Richard Corbet,** born in 1582, was of Phineas Fletcher's age. He was the son of a famous gardener, from whom he inherited some land and money. He was educated at Westminster School and Oxford ; became M.A. in 1605, and was in repute first as a University wit and poet, and then as a quaint preacher, who got patronage at James's court. He married in 1625, became Bishop of Oxford in 1629, of Norwich in 1632, and died in 1635. He was a stout royalist, worked with Laud, but was less bitter, and wrote merry squibs against the Puritans. A poem to his little son, and one on the death of his father, show his kindliness. One of sundry recorded jokes of Bishop Corbet's, is of the upsetting of his coach when he and his chaplain, Dr. Stubbings, who was very fat, were spilt into a muddy lane. Stubbings, the bishop said, was up to his elbows in mud ; and he was up to his elbows in Stubbings. A very small volume appeared in 1648, issued by Corbet's family, entitled *Poetica Stromata ; or, A Collection of Sundry Pieces in Poetry : Drawn by the known and approved hand of R. C.* Written copies of short satires, songs, and other pieces, passed from hand to hand, so that a man might have high reputation in society as wit and poet without the printing of a line of his during his lifetime, except now and then, when Henry Lawes or some other composer had set a song to music.

42. **Edmund Waller** was of the same age as Sir William Davenant, and, like Davenant, lived to take place among the writers under Charles II. He was born in 1605, at Coleshill, Herts. His father died in his infancy, and left him an income of £3,500 a year ; say, ten thousand in present value. His mother was John Hampden's sister. He was educated at Eton and Cambridge, entered Parliament when young, and soon became known at court as a poet. He added to his wealth by marrying a city heiress, who died leaving Waller, in 1630, a gay courtier of five-and-twenty, writing verse-worship of the

8

Earl of Leicester's eldest daughter, Lady Dorothea Sidney, as Sacharissa, and of another lady of the court, perhaps Lady Sophia Murray, as Amoret. The lady whom he took as second wife has no place in his verses. She became the mother to him of five sons and eight daughters. In the Civil Wars, Waller at first took part with his uncle Hampden; but he opposed abolition of Episcopacy, showed goodwill to the king, spoke freely in the Parliament,—by which he was sent, in 1642, as one of the Commissioners to the king at Oxford,—and, in 1643, plotted against it. He saved himself ignobly, and escaped, after a year's imprisonment, with a fine of £10,000 and exile to France, where he lived chiefly at Rouen.

43. **Sir John Suckling** was about four years younger than Waller, and a year younger than Milton. He was born in 1609, the son of the Comptroller of the Household to James I. Suckling was an overtaught child, who could speak Latin at the age of five; but he cast aside, as a young man, his father's gravity, was on active service for six months in the army of Gustavus Adolphus, and in the days of Charles I. lived in London as light wit, light lyric poet, light dramatist, and liberal friend of men of genius. His plays were *Aglaura, Brennoralt,* and *The Goblins.* He spent £12,000 on rich equipment of a troop of 100 horse to aid the king, and died in 1641, of a wound in the heel, some say, caused by a servant who robbed him; but there is more reason to think that he took poison in Paris.

44. **William Cartwright** also wrote plays and lyrics, was about two years younger than Suckling, and also died at the age of thirty-two. He was the son of a Gloucestershire gentleman, who had wasted his means, and lived by innkeeping at Cirencester. William Cartwright was taught in the Cirencester Grammar School, at Westminster School, and Christ Church, Oxford. He became M.A. in 1635, took orders, and was a famous preacher. He studied sixteen hours a day, preached excellent sermons, wrote excellent lyrics, and also four plays; one of them, *The Royal Slave,* a tragi-comedy, acted before the king and queen in 1637, by the students of Christ Church, Oxford. Cartwright was also an admired lecturer at Oxford on metaphysics, worked hard as one of the council of war to provide for the king's troops at Oxford, was beloved of Ben Jonson, who said of him, "My son Cartwright writes all like a man," and was praised by his bishop as "the utmost man could come to." He died in 1643, of the camp fever that killed many at Oxford.

45. Oxford had Cartwright; Cambridge had **John Cleve-land,** for nine years a Fellow of St. John's College, eminent in poetry and oratory, and the first to pour out from the Royalist side defiant verse against the Puritans. Turned out of his fellow-ship, he joined the king at Oxford; then went to the garrison at Newark-on-Trent, where he was made Judge-Advocate, and re-sented the king's order to surrender. He was then in prison at Yarmouth till the Commonwealth, when he obtained his release from Cromwell, lived quietly in Gray's Inn, and died in 1658. Cleveland was the best of those Royalist poets who chiefly wrote partisan satire. The most popular, perhaps, was **Alexander Brome,** an attorney in the Lord Mayor's Court, who was not thirty at the date of the king's execution, and whose songs were trolled over their cups by Royalists of every degree.

46. **Sir John Denham** was born in Dublin in 1615, son of a Baron of Exchequer. He was an idle student at Oxford, and joined gambling with study of law at Lincoln's Inn. But he checked himself, published an *Essay on Gaming,* and in 1636 translated the second book of the "Æneid." In 1638 his father died. In 1641 he produced his tragedy of *The Sophy,* which was acted at a private house in Blackfriars, with so much suc-cess that Waller said he "broke out like the Irish rebellion, three score thousand strong, when nobody was aware, or in the least suspected it." The play was followed, in 1643, by his *Cooper's Hill,* a contemplative poem on the view over the Thames and towards London from a hill in the neighbourhood of Windsor Castle. Denham was actively employed in the king's service, but in the midst of his labours he found time to publish a trans-lation of *Cato Major.* Denham lived to receive homage among poets of the reign of Charles II.

47. **Richard Crashaw,** son of a preacher zealous against Catholicism, was born about the year of Shakespeare's death, educated at the Charterhouse and Pembroke Hall, Cambridge. Before he was twenty he published anonymously sacred epi-grams in Latin. He graduated, became a Fellow of Peterhouse, was expelled from Cambridge in 1644, for refusing to subscribe the Covenant, became a Roman Catholic, and went to Paris. There in 1646, the year of the publication of his *Steps to the Temple,* he was found by Cowley, and commended to the friendship of Queen Henrietta Maria, from whom he had letters to Rome. At Rome he became secretary to a cardinal and Canon of the Church of Loretto. Crashaw died in 1650.

With much more of the later Euphuism than is to be found in lyrics of those Cavalier poets who took active part in the stir of the Civil War, Crashaw's religious poems, " Steps to the Temple," are not less purely devotional, though they have less beauty and force than those of Herbert, whom he imitated, and of whose volume he wrote to a lady, with a gift of it, " Divinest love lies in this book."

**Henry Vaughan** was born in 1622 at Scethrog, in Llansaintfread, Brecknockshire.  He went in 1638 to Jesus College, Oxford ; published love verses in 1646 ; became a country doctor in his native place ; married ; had children ; and produced in 1650 *Silex Scintillans*, the Flint (of the Heart) yielding Sparks (of spiritual fire).  There was a second part in 1655.  This book of religious poems is scarcely inferior to Herbert's *Temple*.  Vaughan published also *Olor Iscanus* in 1651 ; *The Mount of Olives*, 1652 , *Flores Solitudinis*, 1654.  He lived until 1695.  His twin-brother Thomas wrote of magic and alchemy as "Eugenius Philalethes."

48. **Abraham Cowley** was born in 1618, after the death of his father, who was a London stationer.  His mother, who lived to be eighty, struggled to educate him well, and he got his first impulse to poetry as a child from Spenser, whose works lay in his mother's parlour.  His mother got him into Westminster School, where he wrote a pastoral comedy called "Love's Riddle," and in his fifteenth year (in 1633) appeared Cowley's *Poetical Blossoms*, with a portrait of the author at the age of thirteen, and including " The Tragical History of Pyramus and Thisbe," written at the age of ten, and " Constantia and Philetus," written at the age of twelve.  In 1636 he went to Cambridge.  In 1638 the play of *Love's Riddle*, written at school, was published ; and also a Latin comedy, *Naufragium Joculare*, acted at Trinity College in that year.  At the beginning of the Civil War, Cowley's play of *The Guardian* was acted before the prince as he passed through Cambridge.  In 1643, Abraham Cowley, M.A., ejected from Cambridge, went to St. John's College, Oxford, and wrote satire against the Puritans. He went afterwards with the queen to Paris, and was employed in ciphering and deciphering letters between her and the king. His love-poems appeared in 1647, under the title of *The Mistress*.  They are musical, ingenious, and free in tone, but strictly works of imagination.  It is said that Cowley was in love but once, and that he was then too shy to tell his passion Abraham Cowley lived into the reign of Charles II.

49. **Richard Lovelace,** the brilliant and handsome Cavalier poet, died miserably during the Commonwealth. He was born in the same year as Cowley, 1618, the eldest son of Sir William Lovelace, of Woolwich, and was educated at Charterhouse School, and Gloucester Hall, Oxford. Lovelace was so hand-some that, in 1636, though a student of but two years' standing, he was made, at the request of a great lady, M.A., among persons of quality who were being so honoured while the court was for a few days at Oxford. He was the first and last under-graduate who was made Master of Arts for his beauty. Love-lace attached himself to the court, served in 1639 as an ensign in the Scottish expedition, afterwards as captain ; wrote a tragedy called *The Soldier;* retired to his estate of Lovelace Place, at Canterbury ; was elected to go up to the House of Commons with the Kentish petition for restoring the king to his rights, and for this was committed to the Gatehouse Prison at Westminster, April 30, 1642. There he wrote his song, " To Althea, from Prison," which contains the stanza :

> " Stone walls do not a prison make,
>   Nor iron bars a cage ;
> Minds innocent and quiet take
>   That for an hermitage.
> If I have freedom in my love,
>   And in my soul am free,
> Angels alone that soar above
>   Enjoy such liberty."

After some weeks of imprisonment, Lovelace was released on bail, and lived in London beyond his income, as a friend of the king's cause and of good poets. In 1646 he served in the French army, and was wounded at Dunkirk. Report of his death caused Lucy Sacheverell, the Lucasta (*lux casta,* " chaste light ") of his poetry, to disappoint him of her hand by marrying another. In 1648, Lovelace returned to England, and was soon a political prisoner in Peter House, Aldersgate Street, where he arranged his poems for the press—*Lucasta: Epodes, Odes, Sonnets, Songs, &c.,* published in 1649. Richard Lovelace died, it is said, in an alley in Shoe Lane, in 1658.

50. To these poets who were battling, suffering, and singing in the days of Charles I., and out of whose midst rose the first music of Milton, there is one yet to be added—a man twenty-seven years older than Lovelace and Cowley, but who sang when they were singing, and outlived them both. This was the Rev. Robert Herrick, Vicar of Dean Prior, in Devon

shire. **Robert Herrick,** born in 1591, was the fourth son of
a silversmith in Cheapside. His University was Cambridge, and
it was in 1629 that he was presented to his living, in the village
of Dean Prior, four miles from Ashburton, where he spent the
next seventeen years of his life, and said :

> " More discontents I never had
>  Since I was born, than here ;
>  Where I have been, and still am sad,
>  In this dull Devonshire."

There Herrick, with great nose and double chin, lived as a
bachelor vicar, attended by his faithful servant, Prudence
Baldwin, and a pet pig, whom he taught to drink out of a
tankard. In 1648, Robert Herrick was ejected from his living,
and betook himself to London, where he had wits and poets for
companions, and published at once, for help to a subsistence,
his delightful love lyrics, epigrams, and scraps of verse in many
moods ; sometimes reflecting licence of the times, not of the
man ; including also strains of deep religious feeling. These
pieces—many of them only two or four lines long—he had
written in the West of England, and therefore (from *hesperis,*
" western ") he called them *Hesperides ; or, Works both Humane
and Divine."* His pious pieces were arranged under the name
of *Noble Numbers.* The imaginary fair one whom Herrick
celebrated in his lonely vicarage was Julia.

> " Cherrie ripe, ripe, ripe, I cry,
>  Full and faire ones, come and buy,
>  If so be you ask me where
>  They doe grow, I answer, There,
>  Where my Julia's lips doe smile,
>  There's the land, or cherry-isle ;
>  Whose plantations fully show
>  All the yeere where cherries grow."

**51. John Milton** (§ 30) returned to Cambridge and began
his studies there twelve days after the accession of Charles I.
In the following winter his sister's first-born, a daughter,
died in infancy of a cough, and verses upon that family
grief open the series of Milton's poems with a strain of
love. He practised himself as a student, both in Latin and in
poetry, by writing Latin elegies. One, written in September,
1626, was on the death of Bishop Andrewes (§ 16). Throughout his college days Milton retained his old kindness for his
teacher at St. Paul's School, young Alexander Gill, corresponding
with him, praising verse of his, and submitting verse of his own

to his friend's criticism. He retained, also, his old kindness for his first tutor, Thomas Young, who came back from Hamburg to take a vicarage in Stowmarket. In 1629, on the 26th of March, Milton graduated as B.A. On the following Christmas-day, his age being twenty-one, he wrote his hymn, "On the Morning of Christ's Nativity." It may have then come into young Milton's mind to form a series of odes on the great festivals of the Christian Church, for on the 1st of January the ode on the Nativity was followed by one on "The Circumcision;" and when Easter came he began a poem on "The Passion," of which he wrote only eight stanzas and then broke off. "This subject," says the appended note, "the author finding to be above the years he had when he wrote it, and nothing satisfied with what was begun, left it unfinished."

In 1631 the unexpected death of the young Marchioness of Winchester was lamented by poets, and among them by Ben Jonson in his latter years, by Milton at the opening of his career. On his birthday, the 9th of December, in the same year 1631, Milton wrote that sonnet "on his being arrived at the age of twenty-three," which is the preface to his whole life as a man. He refers in it to his boyish aspect, feels his mind unripe, his advance slow, his achievement little, and adds these lines of self-dedication, to which he was true in his whole after life :

> " Yet be it less or more, or soon or slow,
>   It shall be still in strictest measure even
>   To that same lot, however mean or high,
>   Toward which Time leads me, and the will of Heaven :
>   All is, if I have grace to use it so,
>   As ever in my great Task-master's eye."

Already Milton showed himself an exact student of his art. This sonnet, and every other sonnet written by him, was true to the minutest detail in its technical construction (ch. vi. § 46)—true not only in arrangement of the rhymes, but in that manner of developing the thought for which the structure of this kind of poem was invented. The sonnet of self-dedication Milton wrote when his college life was near its close. In July, 1632, he graduated as M.A. At Cambridge, Milton had added seven years of study in the University to seven years of school training. He was not paled by study, but long retained the bloom of youth upon a very fair complexion. He was a little under middle height, slender, but erect, vigorous, and agile, with light brown hair clustering about his fair and oval face, with dark grey eyes.

His voice is said to have been "delicate and tunable." His father, by this time retired from business, and living in the completely rural village of Horton, which is not far from Windsor Castle, had designed his eldest son for a career in the Church ; but Milton felt, he said afterwards, that "he who would take orders must subscribe himself slave and take an oath withal," and by that feeling the Church was closed to him. His choice was to be God's minister, but as a poet. Such a choice produced from his father natural remonstrance. There is reference to this in a Latin poem to his father—"Ad Patrem"—written by Milton at the close of his University training, full of love and gratitude for the education so far finished, with this glance at the kindly controversy that was then between them. The translation is Cowper's :

> " Nor thou persist, I pray thee, still to slight
> The sacred Nine, and to imagine vain
> And useless, powers, by whom inspired ? Thyself
> Art skilful to associate verse with airs
> Harmonious, and to give the human voice
> A thousand modulations, heir by right
> Indisputable of Arion's fame.
> Now say, what wonder is it if a son
> Of thine delight in verse, if so conjoin'd
> In close affinity, we sympathise
> In social arts, and kindred studies sweet ?
> Such distribution of himself to us
> Was Phœbus' choice ; thou hast thy gift, and I
> Mine also, and between us we receive,
> Father and son, the whole-inspiring God."

Milton went home to Horton, and proceeded to add to the seven years of school training and the seven years of university training another seven years of special training for his place among the poets. Nearly six years were spent at Horton, from the end of July, 1632, to April, 1638 ; then followed fifteen months of foreign travel.

Milton's life as a writer is in three parts :—1. The period of his Earlier Poems, in the time of Charles I., including "L'Allegro" and "Il Penseroso," "Arcades," "Comus," "Lycidas;" all written during the training time at Horton. 2. The period of his Prose Works, from 1641 to the end of the Commonwealth. 3. The period of his Later Poems, in the time of Charles II., namely, "Paradise Lost," "Paradise Regained," and "Samson Agonistes." To the reign of Charles I. belong, then, all Milton's Earlier Poems and some of his Prose Works.

52. *L'Allegro* and *Il Penseroso* are companion poems, repre-

senting two moods of one mind, and that mind Milton's. No man can be the one, in Milton's sense, who cannot also be the other. It was part of Milton's training for his work as a poet to study thoroughly the words through which he was to express his thought. Milton's precision in the use of words is very noticeable, and it fills his verse with subtle delicacies of thought and expression. Mirth and Melancholy would not content Milton as titles for these poems, because one word has for its original meaning "softness," and is akin to marrow, the soft fat in bones; the other word, based on an old false theory of humours in a man, traces the grave mood to black bile. The poems themselves use the English words with definition of the sense in which alone each is accepted:

> "These delights if thou canst give,
> Mirth, with thee I mean to live."

> "These pleasures, Melancholy, give,
> And I with thee will choose to live."

The Italian titles to the poems represented in each case the real source of these delights and pleasures. Milton's Mirth was the joy in all cheerful sights and sounds of nature, and in social converse natural to the man whose bosom's lord sits lightly on his throne; and "L'Allegro" is defined in Gherardini's *Supplimento a' Vocabolarj Italiani* (six vols., Milan, 1852) as "one who has in his heart cause for contentment (*che ha in cuore cagione di contentezza*), which shows itself in serenity of countenance." "Il Penseroso," whose name is derived from a word meaning "to weigh," is the man grave, not through ill-humour, but while his reason is employed in weighing and considering that which invites his contemplation. With his companion sketches of this true lightness of heart and this true gravity, Milton blends a banning of the false mirth of the thoughtless —"vain deluding joys, the brood of Folly"—and the black dog, the loathed (from *láth*, meaning "evil") Melancholy "of Cerberus and blackest midnight born." To commendation of the true he thus joins condemnation of the false; and by transferring his condemnation of a baseless joy to the opening of that poem which paints gravity of thoughtfulness, and his condemnation of a Stygian gloom to that poem which paints innocent enjoyment, he heightens the effect of each poem by contrast, and links the two together more completely. The poems are exactly parallel in structure.

8 *

| *L'Allegro.* | *Lines.* | *Il Penseroso.* | *Lines.* |
|---|---|---|---|
| 1. Banning of "loathed" Melancholy ... ... ... | 1—10 | 1. Banning of "vain" Joys ... | 1—10 |
| 2. Invitation to "heart-easing" Mirth ... ... ... ... ... | 11—24 | 2. Invitation to "divinest" Melancholy... ... .. ... | 11—21 |
| 3. Allegorical parentage and companions... ... ... ... | 25—40 | 3. Allegorical parentage and companions... ... ... ... | 22—54 |
| 4. The Morning Song ... ... | 41—56 | 4. The Even Song .. ... ... | 55—64 |
| 5. Abroad under the Sun ... | 57—98 | 5. Abroad under the Moon ... | 65—76 |
| 6. Night, and the tales told by the social fireside ... ... | 99—116 | 6. Night, and lonely study of Nature's mysteries, and of the great stories of the Poets | 77—120 |
| 7. L'Allegro social ... ... ... | 117—134 | 7. Il Penseroso solitary ... ... | 121—154 |
| 8. His Life set to Music... ... | 135—150 | 8. His Life set to Music... ... | 155—174 |

9. Acceptance of each mood—if this be it.

53. The cousin to whom Spenser dedicated "The Tears of the Muses," retaining the higher title that belonged to her as widow of her first husband (ch. vii. § 76), still was called the Countess Dowager of Derby after she had become wife of Sir Thomas Egerton, afterwards Lord Chancellor Ellesmere. Lord Ellesmere, too, had been married before, and his son John married one of the two daughters of the widow who became his second wife. When Milton was at Horton, in Buckinghamshire, the Dowager Countess of Derby, having outlived both her husbands, and bearing the title given by the first of them, lived chiefly at her favourite country house of Harefield, in Middlesex. That was on the borders of Buckinghamshire. At Ashridge Park, also on the borders of Buckinghamshire, and but a few miles from Horton, lived John Egerton, only male heir of Lord Chancellor Ellesmere, who, in compliment to his family, had been made Earl of Bridgewater. He was doubly son-in-law to the Countess of Derby, for she had been his father's wife, and was his own wife's mother. The Earl and Countess of Bridgewater had four sons and eleven daughters, of whom, in 1634, when Milton produced "Comus" for them, ten survived, namely, eight daughters, of whom the eldest was Lady Frances, aged thirty, and the youngest Lady Alice, aged fourteen or fifteen. After the eight girls came two boys—John, the elder and heir, Viscount Brackley, aged twelve or thirteen, and Thomas, aged eleven or twelve. Milton's introduction to this household was probably through Henry Lawes, who, as fashionable composer and musician, taught singing in noble families. Henry and William Lawes were sons of a musician, had been singing-boys in Salisbury Cathedral, and were now prospering in London. Doubtless the elder Milton's interest in music had caused Henry Lawes, eight years older

than Milton, to be one of the poet's friends.  The *Arcades* may
have preceded "Comus."  On some occasion of congratulation,
the old Countess of Derby's numerous family of children and
grandchildren planned a small entertainment in her honour,
to contain only a few songs and a few spoken words of blessing
on her house.  Henry Lawes would be taken into counsel as
musician, and would probably suggest that he had a friend
at Horton, a few miles off, who could write the words.  For
such a purpose, certainly, and probably in some such way,
Milton received the commission which caused him to write
*Arcades* (" The Arcadians").  On the appointed day the old lady
was led to a seat of state—say, in her garden.  Then "some
noble persons of her family" came "in pastoral habit," as
Arcadians, down the garden walk towards her, singing her
praise as they approached.  They arranged themselves before
her, and to pay homage to her one stood forward as the genius
of the wood about her house, who blessed the place with health,
and lived in accord with the celestial harmonies.  Two other
songs then followed, of love and praise to the old lady; the
young members of the family paid homage to her; she would
then kiss them, say "Thank you, my dears," and all was over.
The poem was but a slight piece, contrived according to the
fashion of the time, its simple motive being family affection.

There is no direct evidence that "Arcades" was written
before "Comus;" but it is likely that success in the small occasional masque caused Milton to be joined again with Henry
Lawes when a masque on a much larger scale was required
by the same family for a state occasion.  This was *Comus*.

In June, 1631, John Egerton, Earl of Bridgewater, was
nominated to the office that Sir Henry Sidney had held, of
Lord President of the Council of the Principality of Wales and
the Marches of the same, with a jurisdiction and military
command that comprised the English counties of Gloucester,
Worcester, Hereford, and Shropshire.  Ludlow Castle, in Shropshire, was the seat of government; it was to the Lord-President
of Wales what Dublin Castle now is to the Lord-Lieutenant of
Ireland, and a large hospitality was, of course, one duty of the
Lord-President's office.  The Earl of Bridgewater did not go
to his post till 1633.  In the following year he was joined by
members of his family who had been left at Ashridge or Harefield, and then it became the Lord-President's business to give a
grand entertainment to the country people, and of this a masqu

was to be one feature. The masque of "Comus," by John Milton, with music by Henry Lawes, was accordingly produced in the great hall of Ludlow Castle, on the 29th of September, 1634. Milton was true in " Comus " to the highest sense of his vocation as a poet, while he satisfied all accidental demands on his skill. The masque must include music—with a special song for Lady Alice—dances, and entertaining masquerade. The rout of Comus disguised in heads of divers animals, provided masquerade in plenty. The masque must appeal to local feeling, and did that by bringing in Sabrina, the nymph of the Severn ; must refer, also, with direct compliment, to the new Lord-President, and must provide fit parts for the three youngest children of the family, the Lady Alice, and her brothers John and Thomas, aged from fifteen to twelve. William Prynne had been pilloried, and was then in prison, for his " Histriomastix " (§ 36), produced only two years before. Richard Baxter, two years before, had been a youth of seventeen, living in Ludlow Castle as private attendant upon Mr. Wicksted, the chaplain, when the presidency was in commission, and Baxter told afterwards of the corrupting influences of the place. He knew, he said, one pious youth whom it had made a confirmed drunkard and a scoffer. Something of this Milton may have known when he made his masque a poet's lesson against riot and excess. The reverence due to youth Milton maintained by causing his children-actors to appear in no stage disguise, but simply as themselves. There was on the stage a mimic wood, through which the children passed on the way to their father and mother, who sat in front, and to whom, at the close of the masque, they were presented. As they traversed this wood of the world, typical adventures rose about them, and gave rise to dialogue, in which the part given to Lady Alice made the girl— still speaking in no person but her own—a type of holy innocence and purity.

Since in the same year, 1634, the " Comus" of Ericius Puteanus (first published at Louvain in 1608) was reprinted at Oxford, it may be that this pamphlet had some influence on Milton's choice of subject for his masque. When in London, Milton went to the play, as a letter to his friend Diodati tells us, and the revival of Fletcher's " Faithful Shepherdess " (§ 6) occurred at the beginning of 1634, when it was "acted divers times with great applause" at the Blackfriars Theatre, after its production at court on Twelfth Night. Some influence from

Fletcher's play might blend with some influence from a recent reading of the Dutchman's pamphlet, newly re-issued from an Oxford press, when Milton was determining the subject of his masque. "Comus" is quite original, but it includes distinct evidence of Milton's acquaintance with those works. He may have read, also, Peele's "Old Wives' Tale" (ch. vii. § 72). Ericius Puteanus was the Latinised name of Hendrick Van der Putte, known in France as Henri du Puy, a modest and sound scholar, who was born at Vanloo, in 1574, and after writing about a hundred little books, officiating also as Professor of Eloquence at Milan and Louvain (where he succeeded Lipsius, in 1606), and as Historiographer to the King of Spain, died at Louvain, governor of the citadel there and Councillor of State, twelve years after Milton's "Comus" was produced. The "Comus" of this writer had for its second title, "Phagesiposia Cimmeria"— that is, eating and drinking after the manner of Cimmerians, or those who live in darkness—and under the fiction of a dream, with dialogue of a friend, Aderba, and a wise Tabutius, in a great hall of feasters which has the colossal image of the idol Comus upreared at one end, Van der Putte's book in Latin prose exposed and censured the vices of sensualists.

Comus was a Greek personification of disordered pleasure, "tipsy dance and jollity." The name is derived from the Greek word for a village (κώμη). When the procession at old sacred festivals passed from village to village, with measured step and music, it picked up a disorderly following of merry villagers, who sang and danced wildly and out of measure. This following was called the Comus, and soon yielded a general name for unmeasured festival. The next step was to personification. This we have in the Agamemnon of Æschylus, when Cassandra says of the house of the son of Atreus : "That horrid band who sing of evil things will never forsake this house. Behold Comus, the drinker of human blood, fired with new rage, still remains within the house, kindred of Furies, hard to send away." The last step was to engrave his image, and this was done by representing him as a divinity balanced unsteadily on his crossed legs, with a large stomach, a drooping head, and an inverted torch in his hand—the torch of reason.

54. In 1635 Milton was incorporated as M.A. at Oxford. On the 3rd of April, 1637, his mother died. On the 10th of August, 1637, the son of Sir John King, Secretary for Ireland, Edward King, a young man who was a fellow of Milton's own college a'

Cambridge, who was three or four years younger than Milton, and had been destined for the Church, was drowned when on his way home for the long vacation. The ship in which he sailed from Chester for Dublin struck on a rock, in a calm sea, near the Welsh coast, and went down with all on board. When the next college session began, a little book of memorial verse, in Latin, Greek, and English, was planned, and this appeared at the beginning of 1638, as "Obsequies to the Memorie of Mr. Edward King." It contained twenty-three pieces in Latin and Greek, and thirteen in English, of which thirteen the last was Milton's *Lycidas*, written in November, 1637.

At that time Milton was preparing to add to his course of education two years or more of travel in Italy and Greece. As a poet he did not count himself to have attained, but still pressed forward. In a letter to his friend, Charles Diodati, he had written on the 23rd of September: "As to other points, what God may have determined for me I know not; but this I know, that if He ever instilled an intense love of moral beauty into the breast of any man, He has instilled it into mine : Ceres, in the fable, pursued not her daughter with a greater keenness of inquiry than I, day and night, the idea of perfection. Hence, whenever I find a man despising the false estimates of the vulgar, and daring to aspire, in sentiment, language, and conduct, to what the highest wisdom, through every age, has taught us as most excellent, to him I unite myself by a sort of necessary attachment; and if I am so influenced by nature or destiny, that by no exertion or labours of my own I may exalt myself to this summit of worth and honour, yet no powers of heaven or earth will hinder me from looking with reverence and affection upon those who have thoroughly attained this glory, or appear engaged in the successful pursuit of it. You inquire with a kind of solicitude even into my thoughts. Hear, then, Diodati, but let me whisper in your ear, that I may not blush at my reply—I think (so help me Heaven !) of immortality. You inquire also what I am about? I nurse my wings, and meditate a flight; but my Pegasus rises as yet on very tender pinions. Let us be humbly wise."

The opening lines of Milton's *Lycidas* repeat this modest estimate of his achievement. In "Comus" Milton had produced one of the masterpieces of our literature, but he felt only that the laurels he was born to gather were not yet ripe for his hand, and that when the death of Edward King called from him verse again, and love forced him to write, his hand could grasp but roughly at the bough not ready for his plucking.

> " Yet once more, O ye laurels, and once more
> Ye myrtles brown with ivy never sere,
> I come to pluck your berries harsh and crude·
> And, with forced fingers rude,
> Shatter your leaves before the mellowing year:
> Bitter constraint, and sad occasion dear,
> Compels me to disturb your season due:
> For Lycidas is dead, dead ere his prime,
> Young Lycidas, and hath not left his peer.
> Who would not sing for Lycidas?"

The pastoral name of Lycidas was chosen to signify purity of character. It sprang, probably, from a Greek root (λύκη) meaning light. Like Spenser, Milton looked on the pastoral form as that most fit for a muse in its training time. Under the veil of pastoral allegory, therefore, he told the story of the shipwreck; but in two places his verse rose as into bold hills above the level of the plain, when thoughts of higher strain were to be uttered. The first rise (lines 64 to 84) was to meet the doubt that would come when a young man with a pure soul and high aspiration laboured with self-denial throughout youth and early manhood to prepare himself for a true life in the world, and then at the close of the long preparation died. If this the end, why should the youth aspire?

> " Were it not better done, as others use,
> To sport with Amaryllis in the shade,
> Or with the tangles of Neæra's hair."

(As in Virgil, Ecl. viii., ll. 77, 78; and Horace, Od. III. xiv., ll. 21—24.)

But, Milton replied, our aspiration is not bounded by this life:

> " Fame is no plant that grows on mortal soil,
> Nor in the glistering foil
> Set off to the world, nor in broad rumour lies;
> But lives and spreads aloft by those pure eyes
> And perfect witness of all-judging Jove:
> As he pronounces lastly on each deed,
> Of so much fame, in heaven expect thy meed.

From that height of thought Milton skilfully descended again:

> " O fountain Arethuse, and thou honour'd flood,
> Smooth-sliding Mincius, crown'd with vocal reeds·
> That strain I heard was of a higher mood :
> But now my oat proceeds," &c.:

and we are again upon the flowery plain of the true pastoral, till presently there is another sudden rise of thought (ll. 108—131). The dead youth was destined for the Church, of which he would have been a pure devoted servant. He is gone, and the voice of St. Peter, typical head of the Church, speaks sternly of the many who remain—false pastors who care only to shear their flocks, to scramble for Church livings, and shove those away whom God has called to be His ministers. Ignorant of the duties of their sacred office, what care they? They have secured their incomes; and preach, when they please, their unsubstantial, showy sermons, in which they are as shepherds piping not from sound reeds but from little shrunken straws ("scrannel," from *scrincan*, to shrink, past *scranc*, with diminutive suffix. In Lancashire a "scrannel" is a lean skinny person). The congregations, hungry for the word of God, look up to the pulpits of these men with blind mouths, and are not fed. Swollen with windy doctrine, and the rank mist of words without instruction, they rot in their souls and spread contagion, besides what the devil, great enemy of the Christian sheepfold, daily devours apace, "and nothing said." Against that wolf no use is made of the sacred word that can subdue him, "of the sword of the Spirit, which is the word of God" (Ephes. vi. 17). "But that two-handed engine"—two-handed, because we lay hold of it by the Old Testament and the New:

> " But that two-handed engine at the door
> Stands ready to smite once, and smite no more."

Milton wrote engine (contrivance of wisdom) and not weapon, because "the word of God, quick and powerful, and sharper than any two-edged sword" (Heb. iv. 12), when it has once smitten evil, smites no more, but heals and comforts.

Here again, by a skilful transition, Milton descends to the level of his pastoral or Sicilian (ch. v. § 28) verse. The river of Arcady has shrunk within its banks at the dread voice of St. Peter, but now it flows again:

> " Return, Alpheus; the dread voice is past,
> That shrunk thy streams; return, Sicilian Muse,
> And call the vales," &c.

The first lines of "Lycidas" connected Milton's strain of love with his immediate past. Its last line glances on to his immediate future. Milton was preparing for his travel to Italy and Greece. "To-morrow to fresh woods and pastures new."

55. In April, 1638, Milton, attended by one man-servant, left Horton for his travel on the Continent. His younger brother, Christopher, married about that time, and seems then to have lived at Horton with his father. Milton went to Paris with letters to the English Ambassador there, Lord Scudamore, by whom he was introduced to Hugo Grotius, then ambassador at the French court for the Queen of Sweden. Hugo Groot, born at Delft in 1583, had acquired fame as a youth at the beginning of the century by his Latin tragedies and poems. His career had been that of a patriotic historian, philosopher, and statesman, and he was prosperous at home until he suffered for maintaining the cause of the Arminians (§ 18). For this he was doomed at the Synod of Dort, in 1618, to perpetual imprisonment. In prison he was still a busy writer. After two years' imprisonment his escape was contrived by his wife, but it was not till October, 1631, that he was able to return to his own country. The strength of party feeling caused him to leave Holland again in March, 1632, and he found a friend in the great Chancellor Oxenstiern, who then came to the head of affairs in Sweden. In 1636, Grotius was sent to Paris as ambassador from Sweden, and he retained that office till 1644, the year before his death. From Paris, Milton went to Nice, from Nice by sea to Genoa; he visited Leghorn and Pisa, stayed two months at Florence, then, by way of Siena, went to Rome. At Rome he remained two months, and while there enjoyed and praised in three Latin epigrams the singing of the then famous vocalist, Leonora Baroni. From Rome, Milton, aged thirty, went to Naples, where he was kindly received by Manso, Marquis of Villa, then an old man of seventy-eight, the friend and biographer of Tasso. At his departure he paid his respect to Manso in a Latin poem addressed to him. Milton was about to pass on through Sicily to Greece when, as he wrote afterwards in his " Second Defence of the People of England," " the melancholy intelligence which I received of the civil commotions in England made me alter my purpose; for I thought it base to be travelling for amusement abroad while my fellow-citizens were fighting for liberty at home." He retraced his steps, dwelt on his way back another two months at Rome, where, when attacked for his faith he boldly defended it. " It was," he says, " a rule I laid down to myself in those places, never to be the first to begin any conversation on religion; but if any questions were put to me concerning my faith, to declare it without any reserve or fear." At Florence also he

again stayed for two months; he visited Lucca, Bologna, Ferrara; gave a month to Venice; from Venice he shipped to England the books he had bought in Italy; then he went through Verona and Milan to Geneva, where he was in daily converse with Giovanni Diodati (§ 30), uncle of his old school friend. From Geneva, Milton passed through France, and was at home again in July or August, 1639, after an absence of about fifteen months.  When he returned he found his friend Charles Diodati dead, and poured out his sorrow in a Latin pastoral, "Damon's Epitaph"—*Epitaphium Damonis*—with the refrain:

> "Go seek your home, my lambs; my thoughts are due
> To other cares than those of feeding you."

The flocks, the dappled deer, the fishes, and the birds can find the fit companion in every place:

> "We only, an obdurate kind, rejoice,
> Scorning all others, in a single choice;
> We scarce in thousands meet one kindred mind,
> And if the long-sought good at last we find,
> When least we feel it, Death our treasure steals,
> And gives our heart a wound that nothing heals.
> So, go, my lambs, unpastur'd as ye are,
> My thoughts are all now due to other care.
> Ah, what delusion lur'd me from my flocks,
> To traverse Alpine snows, and rugged rocks!
> What need so great had I to visit Rome,
> Now sunk in ruins, and herself a tomb?
> Or, had she flourish'd still as when, of old,
> For her sake Tityrus forsook his fold,
> What need so great had I t' incur a pause
> Of thy sweet intercourse for such a cause;
> For such a cause to place the roaring sea,
> Rocks, mountains, woods, between my friend and me?
> Else had I grasp'd thy feeble hand, compos'd
> Thy decent limbs, thy drooping eyelids clos'd,
> And, at the last, had said—' Farewell—ascend—
> Nor even in the skies forget thy friend.' "

Into Charles Diodati's ear Milton had whispered his dream of immortality, said that his muse rose yet only on tender wings, unequal to the meditated flight.  In his poem to Manso, Milton indicated that it was in his mind to write a poem of high strain upon King Arthur.  A passage in this "Epitaph of Damon" shows that when he came back to England the design to write an epic upon Arthur took a more definite shape.  Had he taken Arthur for his hero, Milton would, like Spenser (ch. vii. § 78), have turned him to high spiritual use.  He had looked for examples, he said afterwards (in his "Reason of Church Government

against Prelacy"), to Homer, Virgil, Tasso, to the plays of
Sophocles and Euripides, to the odes of Pindar, to the poetical
books of the Old and New Testament, as "the mind at home
in the spacious circuit of her musing" sought to plan its future
work.   He had reasoned to himself whether in the writing of an
epic poem "the rules of Aristotle herein are to be strictly kept
or nature to be followed, which in them that know art and use
judgment is no transgression but an enriching of art."   But
still, and for years yet to come, Milton felt that the work to
which his soul yearned forward was to be achieved only "by
devout prayer to that eternal Spirit who can enrich with all
utterance and knowledge, and sends out His seraphim, with the
hallowed fire of His altar, to touch and purify the lips of whom
He pleases: to this must be added industrious and select reading,
steady observation, insight into all seemly and generous arts and
affairs."   He knew that only hard work could enable him to
make the best use of his genius, hard work and a right life.   In
the "Apology for Smectymnuus" Milton has written, "I was
confirmed in this opinion, that he who would not be frustrate
of his hope to write well hereafter in laudable things, ought
himself to be a true poem."

56. The news that caused Milton to turn back from his
longer travel into Greece was news of trouble with the Scots
which clearly boded civil war.   Milton had left Wentworth and
Laud governing England.   In June, 1638, judgment was given
against John Hampden in the question of ship-money; and law,
physic, and divinity were pilloried in the persons of **William
Prynne,** the lawyer (§ 36), now to be branded on both cheeks
with "S. L." (Schismatic Libeller), and imprisoned for life in
Carnarvon Castle; Robert Bastwick, a physician; and Henry
Burton, a clergyman.   Prynne's controversial activity against
Laud and his policy was met by that of **Peter Heylin,** a divine
of Laud's own school, who had published, in 1621, *Microcosmus,*
a Description of the World, and, in 1629, became chaplain to
Charles I.   Dr. Heylin, who was born in 1600 and died in 1662,
was a prolific writer, bitter against Puritans, and very faithful in
maintaining the Divine authority of Church and king.   Milton
left England in April, 1638, and while he was away Church
controversy had been embittered.   Prelacy had been restored
in Scotland in 1606.   In 1609, King James had further set up in
Scotland the Court of High Commission.   In 1618, King James
had forced the Assembly at Perth to accept for the Scottish

Church Five Articles of his own devising.    This was the year in
which the Synod of Dort declared Calvinism the religion of the
Dutch, and condemned the Five Points in the Remonstrance of
the Arminians (§ 18).    James had not carried out his design of
imposing upon the Church of Scotland a liturgy like that of
the Church of England, in place of Knox's " Book of Common
Order," which some used and some had dropped.    But, in 1636,
Charles I. issued under the Great Seal, by his personal authority,
" Canons and Constitutions Ecclesiastical for the Government
of the Church of Scotland," followed by a " Book of Common
Prayer," prepared by two Scottish bishops, and so revised by
Laud that it came nearer than the Anglican Service Book to
the form of a Roman Missal.    The new Prayer-Book was to be
proclaimed at every market cross, and to come into use at
Easter, 1637.    The people were stirred to excitement.    The
Scottish bishops delayed.    The court forbade farther delay ; the
new service was used for the first time on the 23rd of July, 1637,
and there were riots at Edinburgh in the churches of St. Giles
and the Greyfriars.    The Scottish Council suspended for a time
the use of both the old and the new Service Books.    Laud and
the king would not yield, and there were then riots in Edinburgh.
But the resolve of a nation was not represented only by excesses
of a mob.    The nobles, the middle classes, and the clergy
claimed a right to meet and petition ; and the Privy Council at
Edinburgh then assented to the proposal that they should be
represented by four permanent committees, consisting, 1, of
nobles ; 2, of a gentleman from every county ; 3, of a minister
from every presbytery ; 4, of a burgher from every town ; each
sending representatives to a central committee.    The four
committees sat at four tables in the Parliament House, were
known as the Tables, and formed a central revolutionary committee that soon became the supreme power.

Opposition to the new Prayer-Book was now blended with
opposition to the whole Episcopacy and the Court of High Commission.    It was determined to revive the method of covenanting
used by the Lords of the Congregation, when the Scottish Reformation was established.    A confession which King James VI.
had been made to subscribe in 1581, during a panic against
Romanism, was now revived ; there was added to that, a summary of the Acts of Parliament condemning Romanism and
securing the liberties of the Scottish Church ; and then came,
as third part of the same document, the Covenant itself, in which

the subscribers swore to maintain their religion.  On the 28th of February, the signing of the Covenant began at Edinburgh, in the Greyfriars church and churchyard.  Copies were sent for signature throughout the country.  The cause of prelacy was lost in Scotland.  As the Archbishop of St. Andrews said, the Covenanters had "thrown down in a day what we have been building up for thirty years."

So matters stood when Milton, in the spring of 1638, the year of the Second Scottish Reformation, set out for his travel in Italy.  King Charles partly opposed, partly temporised, and partly yielded ; but the strong will of the Scottish laity bore down all his resistance.  On the 21st of November, 1638, a General Assembly of the Scottish Church met in Glasgow Cathedral, the Marquis of Hamilton sitting as Lord High Commissioner to represent the king.  This Glasgow Assembly swept away King James's Five Articles, swept away King Charles's Canons and the Service Book, and swept away the Bishops, finishing its labours on the 20th of December.  Meanwhile, both sides had been preparing arms in case of need, and news of what seemed to be the inevitable conflict, with a sense of what the letting out of waters might be if the strife began, caused Milton to abridge his term of travel.

In the spring of 1639, King Charles was at the head of an army at York, and the Covenanters were being drilled into an organised force by Alexander Leslie, who had been serving his apprenticeship to battle with the Dutch against Spain, and had been a field-marshal under Gustavus Adolphus in the Thirty Years' War for the defence of German Protestantism, which had yet nine of its thirty years to run.  At the end of May the English and Scottish armies faced each other at Berwick, on opposite sides of the Tweed, every Scottish company having colours inscribed in golden letters, "For Christ, Crown and Covenant."  But no blow was struck, a pacification was agreed upon at Berwick ; and though the king would not recognise any acts of the Glasgow Assembly, he yielded the essential points by promising a free General Assembly, at Edinburgh, on the 6th of August, followed by a Parliament on the 20th, to make its resolutions law.  For a time, then, civil war was averted ; and so matters stood when, at the end of June, or early in July, 1639, Milton returned from his travel in Italy.

In August the General Assembly met in Edinburgh, passed an Act cancelling all that had been done since 1606 for the establishment of Episcopacy in the Church of Scotland, and restored the old Presbyterian system. Having secured their own liberties, the Scottish Presbyterians proceeded to attack the liberties of others ; they renewed the Covenant, required all to swear to it, and asked for civil pains and penalties on Roman Catholics and others who refused. Parliament met on the day after the closing of the Assembly, but King Charles prorogued it.

John Spottiswoode, Archbishop of St. Andrew's, who had lived in London since his deposition, died at the close of this year, 1639, aged seventy-four. He left behind him a *History of the Church of Scotland, beginning the Year of Our Lord 203, and continued to the end of the Reign of King James VI.,* which was first published in folio in 1655. It is an honest book, written by a strong upholder of Episcopacy. Ten years younger than Spottiswoode was another actor in these scenes, David Calderwood, a Presbyterian divine, who told the story as a strong opponent of Episcopacy, and dealt with that part about which he could give valuable information in his *True History of the Church of Scotland from the beginning of the Reformation unto the end of the Reign of James VI.* Calderwood died in 1651.

Charles I. endeavoured to prevent the confirmation of the Acts of the Edinburgh Assembly, by a Scottish Parliament. He therefore prorogued the Parliament to October, then again to November, then to June, 1640. A technical blunder enabled the Scots to turn deaf ears to the next prorogation ; their Parliament met, and soon afterwards their General Assembly met also, at Aberdeen. In August an army, under Leslie, marched southward from Edinburgh, routed the king's troops at Newburn, and on the 30th had possession of Newcastle. In England, Charles, needing money, after governing for eleven years without a Parliament, had summoned one in April to dissolve it in May. It sat for three weeks, and was the Short Parliament. The Covenanters were in Newcastle, and were to be paid £850 a day by the king while the terms of peace were being arranged ; and a new Parliament, to become memorable as the Long Parliament—it sat for thirteen years—was opened on the 3rd of November, 1640. On the 11th of November, it impeached the Earl of Strafford, who was committed to the Tower on the 25th. On the 18th of December, Archbishop Laud was impeached, and on the 1st of March, 1641, he was sent to the Tower. On the 22nd of March, Strafford's trial began, and on the 12th of May, Strafford was executed. Among other early proceedings of this Parliament were the release of political prisoners—that brought **William Prynne** (§ 36), among others, back in triumph to London—abolition of the Star Chamber and of the Court of High Commission ; peace with Scotland ; and discussion of Episcopacy.

In December, 1640, fifteen thousand Londoners petitioned Parliament for the rooting out of the Episcopal system, with all its dependencies. Other petitions followed, and were referred to a Committee of Religion, which was to consider the whole question, and report to the House. **Joseph Hall**, Bishop of Norwich (ch. vii. § 92, ch. viii. § 15), who had published a treatise, in 1640, on *Episcopacy by Divine Right*, issued at the end of January, 1641, his *Humble Remonstrance to the High Court of Parliament. By a Dutifull Sonne of the Church.* The question thus raised occupied many earnest minds in 1641, and was in that year the chief subject of controversy. John Milton took part in the argument.

57. **Sir Henry Wotton**, who had been Provost of Eton since 1624, and who had written a most cordial letter to his young neighbour, John Milton, before he left for Italy, died, at the age of seventy-two, six months after Milton's return. He had been, as a young man, secretary to the Earl of Essex, had then lived in Florence, and served the Grand Duke of Tuscany as a diplomatist. Being sent as ambassador to James VI. of Scotland, Wotton pleased that monarch so well that he was employed by him, when King of England, as his ambassador to Venice, and to princes of Germany. He was made Provost of Eton at the close of James's reign ; and in the same year, 1624, he published his *Elements of Architecture.* Wotton wrote also on the State of Christendom, a Survey of Education, Poems, and other pieces, collected and published in 1651, by Izaak Walton, as *Reliquiæ Wottonianæ; or, a Collection of Lives, Letters, Poems, with Characters of Sundry Personages, and other Incomparable Pieces of Language and Art. By Sir H. Wotton, Knt.*

During the last months of Wotton's life at Eton, the old provost was much comforted by the society of **John Hales** (born in 1584), who had been made Greek professor at Oxford in 1612, and who had then an Eton fellowship. He died in 1656, and his writings were published in 1659, as *Golden Remains of the Ever Memorable Mr. John Hales, of Eton College.* The most interesting part is the series of letters written by Hales

from the Synod of Dort. Having gone to the Hague, in 1616,
as chaplain to the English Ambassador, Sir Dudley Carleton,
Hales went to the Synod of Dort, where his sympathies were
with the Arminians ; and in letters and documents sent to Sir
Dudley Carleton, he has left an interesting narrative of the proceedings of the Synod. Hales was sixteen years younger than
his friend Sir Henry Wotton, and eighteen years older than his
friend **William Chillingworth**, who was born at Oxford, in
1602, and had Laud for his godfather. Chillingworth became a
Fellow of Trinity, was converted to the Roman faith by John
Fisher, the Jesuit, re-converted by Laud, returned to Oxford, inquired freely into religion, and published, in 1637, dedicated to
Charles I., his *Religion of Protestants, a Safe Way to Salvation.*
Chillingworth's inquiry led him to dissent from the Athanasian
Creed and some points of the Thirty-nine Articles. That
stayed his promotion ; but in 1638 he was induced to subscribe
as a sign of his desire for peace and union, but not of intellectual
assent. He then obtained preferment in the Church, and was
in the Civil War so thoroughly Royalist that he acted as engineer
at the siege of Gloucester. He was taken prisoner at the siege
of Arundel, and died in 1644. One of the worst examples of
the bitterness of theologic strife was published immediately after
his death, by Francis Cheynell, in a pamphlet called *Chilling-
worthi Novissima ; or, the Sickness, Heresy, Death, and Burial
of William Chillingworth.* He was the friend of Laud, and
therefore counted as an enemy by Francis Cheynell ; but he was
a man of the best temper, as well as a clear close reasoner.

58. The religious mind of England had in the days of
Charles I., as always, manifold expression. There were many
readers of the *Resolves, Divine, Political, and Moral,* published
in 1628, by **Owen Feltham**, a man of middle-class ability,
with a religious mind, who was maintained in the household of
the Earl of Thomond. His Resolves are one hundred and
forty-six essays on moral and religious themes, the writing of a
quiet churchman, who paid little attention to the rising controversies of his day.

Oriental scholarship was represented by **John Lightfoot**,
born at Stoke-on-Trent, in 1602, who had been of Milton's
college, at Cambridge, then was tutor at Repton School, then
held a curacy in Shropshire, and became chaplain to Sir Rowland Cotton, a great student of Hebrew. This gave Lightfoot
his impulse to a study of the Oriental languages, and in 1629

he published his *Erubhim; or, Miscellanies, Christian and Judaical,* dedicated to Sir Rowland, who gave him, two years afterwards, the rectory of Ashley, Staffordshire.

**Henry More** represented Platonism. He was born in 1614, at Grantham, in Lincolnshire, educated at Eton and Christ's College, Cambridge, where he obtained a fellowship. He abandoned Calvinism, was influenced by Tauler's " Theologia Germanica," and fed his spiritual aspirations with writings of Plato and the Neoplatonists, Plotinus and Iamblichus, and Platonists of Italy at the time of the revival of scholarship. Henry More was for a time tutor in noble families, obtained a prebend at Gloucester, but soon resigned it in favour of a friend. Content with a small competence, he declined preferment, and sought to live up to his own ideal as a Christian Platonist. He lived on through the reign of Charles II., and died in 1687, aged seventy-three. The Platonism which had been a living influence upon Europe at the close of the fifteenth century had its last representative in Henry More. In 1642 he published " Ψυχῶδια Platonica; or, a Platonical Song of the Soul," in four books; with prefaces and interpretations, published in 1647, as "Philosophicall Poems." The first book, "Psychozoia " (the Life of the Soul) contained " a Christiano-Platonicall display of life." The Immortality of the Soul was the theme of the second part, " Psychathanasia," annexed to which was a metrical " Essay upon the Infinity of Worlds out of Platonick Principles." The third book contained " A Confutation of the Sleep of the Soul, after Death," and was called " Antipsychopannychia," with an Appendix on " The Præ-existency of the Soul." Then came " Antimonopsychia," or the fourth part of the " Song of the Soul," containing a confutation of the Unity of Souls; whereunto is annexed a paraphrase upon Apollo's answer concerning Plotinus his soul departed this life. This poem was throughout written in the Spenserian stanza, with imitation also of Spenser's English. The books were divided into cantos, and each canto headed in Spenser's manner. Thus, the first canto of Book I. is headed:

> " Struck with the sense of God's good will
> The immortality
> Of souls I sing; praise with my quill
> Plato's philosophy."

But there is no better reason why it should not have been all written in prose, than the evidence it gives that Platonism came as poetry to Henry More, although he was not himself a great poet. Dr. Henry More also published, with a dedication to Cudworth, the Hebrew Professor at Cambridge, his *Threefold Cabbala*, a triple interpretation of the three first chapters of Genesis, with a *Defence* of it. The Jewish Cabbala (from *kibbal*, "to receive") was conceived to be a traditional doctrine or exposition of the Pentateuch, which Moses received from the mouth of God while he was on the mount with Him. Henry More's "Threefold Cabbala" was, he said "the dictate of the free reason of my minde, heedfully considering the written text of Moses, and carefully canvasing the expositions of such interpreters as are ordinarily to be had upon him." The threefold division of his "Cabbala" was into literal, philosophic, and moral. More wrote also against Atheism, and on theological topics.

Intense religious feeling, Puritan in tone, was expressed in the sermons and books of **Richard Sibbes** (born in 1577), who was Master of Catherine Hall when Milton was at Cambridge, and a frequent preacher in the University. Of the two great English Universities, Cambridge was the stronghold of the Puritans. The persecuted Puritans who had left home for the New World called the town Cambridge in which they founded, in 1638, their first university, named after a private benefactor, John Harvard, a clergyman of Charlestown. Sermons by Sibbes were published as his *Saints' Cordials*, in 1629. To his *Bruised Reede and Smoking Flax*, in which other sermons were collected, Baxter said that he owed his conversion. Richard Sibbes had died in 1635.

59. Two clever clergymen, one aged thirty-three, the other twenty-seven, Thomas Fuller and John Wilkins, were, in 1641 taking opposite sides in the great controversy of the day **Thomas Fuller**, born at Aldwinkle, Northamptonshire, in 1608, was educated at Queen's College, Cambridge. He became a popular preacher at St. Benet's, Cambridge, then obtained a prebend at Salisbury, and became Rector of Broad Winsor, in Dorsetshire, when he married. His first publication, at the age of twenty-three, was a poem, in three parts, *David's Hainous Sinne, Heartie Repentance, Heavie Punishment.* In 1639 appeared, in folio, Fuller's first work of any magnitude, *The History of the Holy Warre.* His wife died, and in 1641 he came to London as lecturer at the Savoy Church, in the Strand, where his vivacity of speech not only brought together crowded audiences within the walls, but also procured him listeners outside

the windows. In 1642, Fuller published one of the most characteristic of his works, *The Holy and Profane State*, a collection of ingenious pieces of character writing, moral essays, and short biographical sketches. Troubled as the times were, the book went through four editions before 1660. The quips and conceits of Fuller's style represent the later Euphuism in its best form, for Fuller had religious feeling and high culture, good humour, liberality, quick sense of character, and lively wit, which the taste of the day enabled him to pour out in an artificial form, with a complete freedom from affectation. Culture and natural wit made his quaintness individual and true. The ingenuity of **John Wilkins** took a scientific turn. He was born in 1614, the son of a goldsmith, at Oxford, was educated in Oxford, graduated, took orders, and was chaplain, first to Lord Say, then to the Count Palatine of the Rhine. When the Civil War broke out, Fuller went to the king, at Oxford ; and John Wilkins took the Solemn League and Covenant. In 1638, Wilkins, aged twenty-four, published anonymously, *The Discovery of a New World; or, a Discourse tending to prove that 'tis probable there may be another Habitable World in the Moon.* In 1640 this was followed by a *Discourse concerning a New Planet: tending to prove that 'tis probable our Earth is one of the Planets.* Wilkins's book on the world in the moon closed with an argument for the proposition "that 'tis possible for some of our posterity to find out a conveyance to this other world ; and if there be inhabitants there, to have commerce with them." His other tract, in support of the doctrine set forth by Copernicus, in 1543, and developed in the time of Charles I. by Galileo, included a temperate endeavour to meet those prevalent theological objections to which Galileo had been forced to bend. It was in 1632 that Galileo published, at Florence, the " Dialogues," in which he proved the double movement of the earth, round the sun and round its own axis. In June, 1637, Galileo, seventy years old, was sentenced to imprisonment by the Inquisition at Rome, and forced to abjure the " heresy " of " holding and believing that the sun is the centre of the world, and immovable ; and that the earth is not the centre, and that it moves." It may be added of Galileo, who, by ground glasses fitted to an organ-pipe, discovered the uneven surface of the moon, and taught his pupils to measure its mountains by their shadows, who discovered Jupiter's satellites, Saturn's ring, the sun's spots, and the starry nature of the Milky Way, that he became blind in 1636, and was living, blind, at his country house near Florence, when, during his Italian journey, Milton spoke with him.

60. Soon after his return to England, **John Milton** settled in London, by taking lodgings for a short time at the house of a tailor in St. Bride's Churchyard, and there he undertook the teaching of his sister Anne's two boys, Edward and John Phillips, aged nine and eight. Edward Phillips, to whom Anne Milton was married in 1624, died in 1631, leaving his widow with these boys, then babies, their only surviving children. Mrs. Phillips had had a considerable dowry from her father, and the bulk of her husband's property was left to her. When her brother John undertook the education of her boys, she had taken for second husband Thomas Agar, a widower, who succeeded also to Edward Phillips's post of Secondary in the Crown Office. While teaching his nephews, Milton, in 1640, was sketching plans of sacred dramas, dwelling especially upon " Paradise Lost " as the subject of a drama: suggesting also as themes, "Abram from Morea ; or, Isack redeem'd," " The Deluge," " Sodom," " Baptistes," noting subjects also from British history. Milton " made no long stay," his nephew tells us, in his lodgings in St. Bride's Churchyard: "necessity of having a place to dispose his books in, and other goods fit for the furnishing of a good handsome house, hastening him to take one ; and, accordingly, a pretty garden-house he took, in Aldersgate Street, at the end of an entry, and therefore the fitter for his turn, besides that there are few streets in London more free from noise than that." There he worked hard, and had his two nephews to board with him. There also he began, in 1641, the second part of his literary life, put aside, at the age of thirty-two, his high ambition as a poet, and, devoting himself to the duty that lay nearest to his hand, gave the best years of his manhood, the twenty years from thirty-two to fifty-two, to those questions of his day that touched, as he thought, the essentials of English liberty.

In 1641 the great argument was for and against Episcopacy. Bishop Hall's *Humble Remonstrance to the High Court of Parliament* appeared at the end of January, in defence of the Liturgy and of Episcopal Government. Towards the close of March appeared *An Answer to a Book entituled an Humble Remonstrance . . Written by Smectymnuus.* This name was compounded of the initials of the five divines who took part in its production, Stephen Marshall, Edmund Calamy,

Thomas Young, Matthew Newcomen, and William Spurstow. Thomas Young, Milton's old tutor, was chief author of the pamphlet. James Usher (§ 17), now Archbishop of Armagh, was urged by Bishop Hall to add the weight of his knowledge of Church antiquities to the argument for Episcopacy, and he published, towards the end of May, *The Judgment of Doctor Rainoldes touching the Originall of Episcopacy, more largely confirmed out of Antiquity.* A week or two later, when the Bishops' Exclusion Bill was awaiting the decision of the Lords, and when the Commons, on the 27th of May, had expressed their mind more strongly by passing the second reading of a "Root and Branch " Bill, " For the utter abolishing and taking away of all Archbishops, Bishops," &c., Milton published his first pamphlet, entitled, *Of Reformation touching Church Discipline in England, and the Causes that hitherto have hindered it : Two Books, written to a Friend.* In the first book he argued that, in and after the reign of Henry VIII., Reformation of the Church was most hindered by retaining ceremonies of the Church of Rome, and by giving irresponsible power to bishops, who, though they had removed the pope, yet "hugged the popedom and shared the authority among themselves." In his second book, Milton argued from history that the political influence of prelacy had always been opposed to liberty. This pamphlet of ninety pages was followed quickly by a shorter pamphlet in twenty-four pages, chiefly in reply to Usher, and entitled *Of Prelatical Episcopacy ; and whether it may be deduc'd from the Apostolical Times by vertue of those Testimonies which are alleg'd to that purpose in some late Treatises, one whereof goes under the Name of James, Archbishop of Armagh.* While the controversy was at its height, Milton's pen had no rest. Bishop Hall had replied promptly to Thomas Young and his fellow-writers, with *A Defence of the Humble Remonstrance against the Frivolous and False Exceptions of Smectymnuus.* This was a thick pamphlet. The Smectymnuans replied again for themselves in a thicker pamphlet ; and Milton aided them with his own third pamphlet, *Animadversions on the Remonstrants Defence against Smectymnuus,* which is a rough pulling to pieces of Hall's pamphlet, with sharp comment upon successive passages and phrases.

On the 1st of December the Grand Remonstrance was presented by the Commons to the king, at Hampton Court. On the 31st of December, the Commons voted that the House be resolved into a committee to take into consideration the militia of the kingdom. On the 3rd of January, 1642, the Attorney-General, at the bar of the House of Lords, accused, in the king's name, of high treason, Lord Kimbolton and five members of the House of Commons—Pym, Hampden, Hollis, Haslerig, and Strode. On the same day the king sent, without warrant of Privy Council or of magistrate, a serjeant-at-arms to the House of Commons to require of the Speaker that the five members be given in custody. On the following day the king came to the House with armed force to take them, but leave had been given to them to absent themselves. On the 10th of January, Charles left Whitehall for Hampton Court. Next day the five members were brought in a popular triumph to the House of Commons. On the 14th of February, the king, who returned no more to London till the end, gave his assent to the Bill which excluded bishops from the House of Lords. On the 16th the queen, taking the crown jewels with her, went to Holland. She was in search of aid for the impending struggle. The king, who refused assent to the Bill for regulating the militia, went to York. On the 23rd of April he appeared, with a body of horse, before Hull, and demanded admission to the town and fortress. The governor replied respectfully that he had sworn to keep the place at the disposal of the Parliament, and could not admit the king. Thirty-two peers and sixty-five members of the House of Commons then joined the king at York; those who remained formed a Parliament no longer asking the king's sanction for its acts. On the 5th of May, Parliament issued its ordinance for the militia. Civil war was inevitable; there was contest between each party for possession of fortified places and gunpowder. On the 22nd of August, the king set up on Nottingham Castle the royal standard, with a red battle-flag over it—a formal act signifying that the kingdom was in a state of war—and called upon his subjects to attend him. Next day the king heard that the army of the rebels—for such he had now declared them—was, horse, foot, and cannon, at Northampton.

While this was the course of events, John Milton continued his discussion of Episcopacy. In the first months of 1642 he published, near the time when the king gave his assent to the Bill excluding bishops from the House of Lords, the fourth of his pamphlets on this subject, now first setting his name upon the title-page. This was *The Reason of Church Government urg'd against Prelaty, by Mr. John Milton: In Two Books*

It was a careful expression of his argument that Church government is necessary, but that Prelacy is not the proper form of it. He suggested rather a government by presbyters and deacons, with free debate and vote in parochial consistories, representing single congregations; and a General Assembly, elected as a parliament for the whole Church. In the opening of the second book he expressed his spirit, as a writer, in the midst of strife on questions of this kind. The duty was burdensome. " For, surely, to every good and peaceable man, it must in nature needs be a hateful thing to be the displeaser and molester of thousands; much better would it like him doubtless to be the messenger of gladness and contentment, which is his chief intended business to all mankind, but that they resist and oppose their own true happiness. But when God commands to take the trumpet and blow a dolorous or jarring blast, it lies not in man's will what he shall conceal." When the Word was in the heart of Jeremiah, as a burning fire shut up in his bones, he was weary with forbearing, and could not stay ; " which might teach these times not suddenly to condemn all things that are sharply spoken or vehemently written, as proceeding out of stomach, virulence, or ill-nature." When there was so strong a resisting power to contend with, " no man can be justly offended with him that shall endeavour to impart or bestow, without any gain to himself, those sharp and saving words which would be a terror and a torment in him to keep back. For me, I have determined to lay up, as the best treasure and solace of a good old age, if God vouchsafe it me, the honest liberty of free speech from my youth, when I shall think it available in so dear a concernment as the Church's good." If the end of the struggle be oppression of the Church, how shall he bear in his old age the reproach of the voice within himself, saying, " When time was, thou couldst not find a syllable of all thou hast read or studied to utter in her behalf? Yet ease and leisure was given thee for thy retired thoughts out of the sweat of other men. Thou hast the diligence, the parts, the language of a man, if a vain subject were to be adorned or beautified ; but when the cause of God and His Church was to be pleaded, for which purpose that tongue was given thee which thou hast, God listened if He could hear thy voice among His zealous servants, but thou wert dumb as a beast ; from henceforward be that which thine own brutish silence hath made thee." In this spirit Milton maintained throughout his prose writing that which he believed to be the cause of liberty. Were he wise only to his own ei ds, he said, he would write with leisurely care upon such a subject as of itself might catch applause, and should not choose " this manner of writing wherein knowing myself inferior to myself, led by the genial power of nature to another task, I have the use, as I may account, but of my left hand." Many a man of genial temper and predominating gentleness of life has gone as a soldier into battle, and struck death about him without stopping to discriminate the true merits of those whose skulls he cleft. He knew only that one of two sides was to prevail, and while the battle raged he was to do his duty as a soldier. In bloodless war of controversy for a vital cause, where the appeal is on a few broad questions to national opinion, there may be like need to beat roughly down opposing arguments, to roll in the dust and march over the credit of opposing reasoners, without staying a blow to an opponent's credit as a reasoner from just consideration of his feelings and impartial weighing of his merits. The day may come when we shall all argue with philosophical precision, and call equal attention to the merits and the faults of those over whom we struggle to prevail. It certainly is nearer than it was in Milton's time. Controversy then was simply a strong wrestle with the single desire in each wrestler to secure the fall of his antagonist. So Milton wrestled, and gave many a rough hug with his intellectual arm, but he sought only the triumph of his cause by strife of mind with mind : his antagonists opposed to him argument rough as his own, with coarse abuse ; and their supporters, when they could, had argued with the prison and the pillory. But Milton never called for pains and penalties on an opponent. That is not true of the Long Parliament. At Christmas, 1641, it sent William, Archbishop of York, and twelve bishops, of whom one was Joseph Hall, Bishop of Norwich (ch. vii. § 92), to the Tower for a protest against acts done in Parliament while they were kept away by force of tumult in the streets. Bishop Hall remained in the Tower till the beginning of May, and during his imprisonment appeared a reply to Milton's " Animadversions." The writer of much of this reply was probably the Rev. Robert Hall, the bishop's son. It was called *A Modest Confutation of a Slanderous and Scurrilous Libell, intituled Animadversions upon the Remonstrant's Defence against Smectymnuus.* This modest confuter says of John Milton that " Of late, since he was out of wit and clothes, he is now clothed in serge and confined to a

parlour ; where he blasphemes God and the king as ordinarily
erewhile he drank sack and swore.    Hear him speak !    . . .
Christian ! dost thou like these passages ?  or doth thy heart rise
against such unseemly beastliness ?    . . .  Nay, but take this
head  . . .  Horrid blasphemy !  You that love Christ, and
know this miscreant wretch, stone him to death, lest yourselves
smart for his impunity." Milton replied with *An Apology
against a Pamphlet call'd A Modest Confutation of the Animadversions of the Remonstrant against Smectymnuus.*  It includes
a dignified reply to the personal slanders, in which Milton expressed the true spirit of his life, and censured the butcherly
speech " against one who in all his writing spake not that any
man's skin should be rased."

61. Five pamphlets within a year had now represented
Milton's part in the argument upon Episcopacy, and he had delivered his mind on the subject.  Among the other writers on the
question there was one man of genius, nearly five years younger
than Milton, opposed to him in opinion but as pure in aspiration, who was made by the king's will Doctor of Divinity, for
a pamphlet called *Episcopacy Asserted.* This was **Jeremy
Taylor.**  He was born at Cambridge, in August, 1613, the son
of a barber, who sent him, when three years old, to a free school
then just founded by Dr. Stephen Perse.  At thirteen, Jeremy
Taylor left this school to enter Caius College as a sizar, or poor
scholar.  He had proceeded to the degree of M.A., and been
ordained by the time he was twenty-one.  A college friend then
asked young Taylor to preach for him at St. Paul's.  He had,
like Milton, outward as well as inward beauty, and a poet's
mind.  Archbishop Laud heard of his sermons, called him to
preach at Lambeth, and became his friend.  Laud having more
patronage and influence at Oxford than at Cambridge, Taylor
was incorporated there, and the archbishop procured for him a
Fellowship of All Souls, by using his sole authority as Visitor of
the College to overrule the statutes which required that candidates
should be of three years' standing in the University.  Laud also
made the young divine his chaplain ; and in March, 1637, when
Jeremy Taylor was not yet twenty-four, obtained for him the rectory of Uppingham, in Rutlandshire.  Two years later, in May,
1639, Taylor was married, in his own church, to Phœbe Langs-
dale.  Three years afterwards his youngest son died, in May,
1642, and his wife died shortly afterwards.  He was left with two
infant sons, at the time when the breach between the king and

T

Commons had become irreparable. Then he was made one
of the king's chaplains, and joined the king; perhaps when, in
August, he was on his way to hoist the royal standard at Nottingham.   The infant boys must have been left to the care of his
wife's relations, and for some years remained with them.   In October, 1642, the Parliament resolved on sequestration of the livings
of the loyal clergy.   Jeremy Taylor, like Herrick and others, was
deprived.   The indecisive battle of Edge Hill was fought in the
same month.   In November, the king marched upon London ;
there was a fight at Brentford.   The Londoners mustered their
trained bands.   It was the occasion of Milton's sonnet, " When
the Assault was Intended to the City."   But the Royalists retired, and at the end of November the king was at winter
quarters in Oxford.   There Jeremy Taylor published his *Episco-*
*pacy Asserted*, and was rewarded, at the age of twenty-
nine, with the degree of Doctor of Divinity.   On the 26th of
January, 1643, Parliament passed a Bill for the utter abolition of
Episcopacy.

62.   **John Milton** took no part in the strife of swords, nor did
he write a syllable to animate it.   His duty to God was to make
full use of his reason.   For him the great inspiring truth was,
not that Englishmen drew swords on one another—glory of
animal battle we share with the dogs and cats—but that they
were drawn to this by a conflict of opinion.   On one side was a
belief that discord would be endless if Englishmen were not in
Church and State bound by allegiance to a single authority,
ordained by God; on the other side, a belief that such authority
in Church and State had claimed for itself too great a power to
restrain men where God made them free.   Authority should
not decree for them the form of their opinions.   Yet very many
fought on this side against authority over themselves who were
too ready to impose their own opinions upon others.   Milton was
true to his own principle.   He was against the Parliament when it
put thought in fetters.   The passions and stupidities of men had
made the Civil War a dread necessity, but the work of bloodshed
was no work for him who "in all his writing spake not that any
man's skin should be rased."   To each man his place ; and
Milton's place was to keep watch over the course of opinion
while the contest raged.   His life would have belied his writing
if Milton had ever shot a man for his opinions.   His own
brother, Christopher, was a Royalist, and difference of opinion
caused no break in the household harmony.   Christopher had

been called to the bar in January, 1640, and in 1641 had settled
at Reading, with his wife and one or two young children. The
father, too, left Horton then, and lived with Christopher at
Reading. In April, 1643, strife was resumed with the siege of
Reading, which on the 24th surrendered to the forces of Parliament. Milton took also about this time—at the end of May
or in June—a wife from a Royalist family with which he had an
old acquaintance. This was Mary Powell, eldest daughter in the
large family of Richard Powell, of Forest Hill, three or four miles
from Oxford, then the head-quarters of the Royalists. The old
home of the Milton family was in the same part of Oxfordshire,
and between Milton and the Powells there had been old neigh-
bourly relations. John Milton, the poet, when at college, had
money of his own. Perhaps the grandfather, who had quarrelled
with his father, did what is not uncommon in family quarrels,
and left property over the son's head to the son's son. At any
rate, John Milton, when at Cambridge, and twenty years old, had
lent £500 to Richard Powell. The Powells, therefore, were old
friends, and to them Milton, aged not quite thirty-five, went for
the wife, then in her eighteenth year, whom he brought home
to Aldersgate Street about the end of June, 1643. Her experience was of a Cavalier country gentleman's way of free
housekeeping and social enjoyment. The philosophic calm of
the house in Aldersgate Street was new to her, and at first
irksome. In the first weeks of marriage those whose lives have
differed must learn how to make their lives agree, and it must
needs take more than a month to do that where home-grown
ways, in many respects opposite, have to be changed or modified,
and brought into accord. Milton's young wife was allowed or
encouraged by her family to fly from the first difficulty. "By
the time," says Milton's nephew, "she had for a month or there-
about led a philosophical life, her friends, possibly incited by her
own desire, made earnest suit by letter to have her company the
remaining part of the summer." She was to return at Michaelmas, but did not. At this time Milton began to receive other
pupils than his two nephews, and through the disestablishment
of Christopher after the surrender of Reading, soon after
Milton's wife had gone back to Forest Hill, his father came to
live with him.

When Milton's newly-married wife went to her home, near
Shotover, the queen had just joined King Charles at Oxford,
bringing more troops with her; the Royalists had been victorious

in Somersetshire and Wiltshire; strife was embittered, Royalist hope was rising.   On the 27th of July, Bristol was taken by Prince Rupert.   A note from Colonel Cromwell, on the 6th of August, recognised "how sadly our affairs stand."   The change of prospect might have led the Powells to prompt or encourage a separation of their daughter from John Milton.   In September there was published by the Parliament the text of the "Solemn League and Covenant," which was to bring in Scottish aid.   Commissioners to Scotland had asked for a Civil League, the Scotch offered a Religious Covenant; the compromise took form that might be made to content both sides, as the Solemn League and Covenant, which, after slight modification by the Westminster Assembly, the Parliament swore to maintain.   In the middle of January, 1644, the Scots, again under Leslie, who was now Earl of Leven, entered England.

Milton sought in vain to win back his wife; and being left with nothing of matrimony but its chain, his mind was turned into a course of thought upon the bond of marriage.   The result was, in 1644, his treatise in two books on *The Doctrine and Discipline of Divorce*, addressed to the Parliament and the Westminster Assembly then sitting, written wholly without passion or personal reference, and arguing from a pure and spiritual sense of marriage as a bond for the mutual aid and comfort of souls rather than of bodies.   He asked that among reforms then under discussion there might be included a revisal of the canon law, which allowed divorce only on grounds less valid than "that indisposition, unfitness, or contrariety of mind, arising from a cause in nature unchangeable, hindering, and ever likely to hinder, the main benefits of conjugal society, which are solace and peace."   When marriage was found to be rather an unconquerable hindrance than a help to the true ends of life, Milton desired that it might be ended by deliberate consent of both husband and wife, religiously, in presence of the Church.   For he said, "It is less breach of wedlock to part, with wise and quiet consent betimes, than still to foil and profane that mystery of joy and union with a polluting sadness and perpetual distemper: for it is not the outward continuing of marriage that keeps whole that covenant, but whatsoever does most according to peace and love, whether in marriage or in divorce, he it is that breaks marriage least; it being so often written that "Love only is the fulfilling of every commandment." Right or wrong in opinion, Milton wrote this treatise in no spirit of bitterness. His last words in it are, "That God the Son hath put all other things under His own feet, but His commandments he, 'nath left all under the feet of Charity." In a second pamphlet, published in the same year, 1644, Milton supported his case by translating and abridging the like opinions of Martin Bucer from a book of his on "The Kingdom of Christ," addressed to Edward VI. This pamphlet was addressed also to the Parliament, as *The Judgment of Martin Bucer concerning Divorce*.

63. But this was not the only nor even the chief subject occupying Milton's thoughts in the year 1644. In that year he addressed to the Parliament another writing, which is the noblest of his English prose works, *Areopagitica; a Speech of Mr. John Milton for the Liberty of Vnlicenc'd Printing, to the Parlament of England*.

John Selden had said in Parliament, in 1628, "There is no law to prevent the printing of any books in England; only a decree of the Star Chamber." Licensing of new books was placed in the power of the Archbishop of Canterbury and his substitutes and dependents, who used, we are told, "that strictness that nothing could pass the press without his or their approbation, but the authors must run a hazard." The Star Chamber, under Charles I., had sought to make more effective the decrees and ordinances of Queen Elizabeth (ch. vii. § 92) for the control of the press, and the suppression of books that contained opinions distasteful to the Government. In July, 1637, a stringent decree was issued for the control of printers, booksellers, and the works issued and sold by them, and to restrain unlicensed importations. All books of Divinity, Physic, Philosophy, and Poetry were to be licensed either by the Archbishop cf Canterbury or Bishop of London, or by substitutes of their appointment. Check was thus put on the reprint of books of divinity formerly licensed. A new licence was denied, for instance, to Fox's "Book of Martyrs." Historical works seem to have been submitted to the Secretary of State for his sanction. To May's "Edward III." is prefixed, "I have perused this book, and conceive it very worthy to be published.—Io. Coke, Knight, Principall Secretary of State, Whitehall, 17th of November, 1634." Besides His Majesty's printers and the printers allowed for the Universities, the number of master printers was, by the decree of 1637, limited to twenty, who were named; and no new

printer could be licensed until the place of one of the twenty was left vacant for him by death, censure, or otherwise. It was decreed also that there should be only four licensed type-founders, also named, and, like the printers, under strictest oversight, and there were arrangements for the hunting out of all unlicensed presses. Now the Long Parliament, which had abolished the Star Chamber, set up a Committee of Examinations for control of printers, search for books and pamphlets disapproved by them, and seizure of the persons by whom such works were published or sold; and on the 14th of June, 1643, the Lords and Commons ordered the publication of their ordinance " for the regulating of printing, and for suppressing the great late abuses and frequent disorders in printing many false, scandalous, seditious, libellous, and unlicensed pamphlets, to the great defamation of religion and Government." Milton met this by publishing, in November, 1644, a noble protest, as his plea for liberty of thought and utterance. " Why," he asked, " should we affect a rigour contrary to the manner of God and of Nature, by abridging or scanting those means, which books freely permitted are, to the trial of virtue and the exercise of truth."
" And now," he says again, " the time in speciall is, by priviledge to write and speak what may help to the furder discussing of matters in agitation. The Temple of *Janus* with his two *controversal* faces might now not unsignificantly be set open. And though all the windes of doctrin were let loose to play upon the earth, so Truth be in the field, we do injuriously by licensing and prohibiting to misdoubt her strength. Let her and Falshood grapple; who ever knew Truth put to the wors, in a free and open encounter. Her confuting is the best and surest suppressing. He who hears what praying there is for light and clearer knowledge to be sent down among us, would think of other matters to be constituted beyond the discipline of *Geneva*, fram'd and fabric't already to our hands. Yet when the new light which we beg for shines in upon us, there be who envy, and oppose, if it come not first in at their casements. What a collusion is this, whenas we are exhorted by the wise man to use diligence, *to seek for wisdom as for hidd'n treasures* early and late, that another order shall enjoyn us to know nothing but by statute. When a man hath been labouring the hardest labour in the deep mines of knowledge, hath furnisht out his findings in all their equipage, drawn forth his reasons as it were a battel raung'd, scatter'd and defeated all objections in his way, calls

out his adversary into the plain, offers him the advantage of
wind and sun, if he please, only that he may try the matter by
dint of argument, for his opponents then to sculk, to lay am-
bushments, to keep a narrow bridge of licencing where the
challenger should passe, though it be valour enough in souldier-
ship, is but weaknes and cowardise in the wars of Truth.  For
who knows not that Truth is strong next to the Almighty; she
needs no policies, no strategems, no licencings to make her
victorious; those are the shifts and the defences that error uses
against her power."

Milton called this tract " Areopagitica," with reference to an
oration of Isocrates, "the old man eloquent" of his sonnet to
Lady Margaret Ley, whom

> " That dishonest victory
> At Chæronea, fatal to liberty;
> Kill'd with report."

Isocrates, who had Demosthenes among his pupils, is said to
have been an old man of ninety-eight when he ceased to take
food after receiving the news of the battle of Cheronea (B.C. 338).
Twenty-one of his sixty speeches are extant, and one of these,
inscribed "Areopagitic," was a polished argument in the form
of deliberative, not popular, oratory designed to persuade the
High Court of Areopagus to reform itself.  Milton was seeking
to persuade the High Court of Parliament, our Areopagus, to
reform itself, by revoking a tyrannical decree against liberty of
the press.  He took, therefore, for his model this noble Greek
oration, written with discretion and high feeling, but without
harshness of reproof.  He uttered nobly his own soul and the
soul of England on behalf of that free interchange of thought
which Englishmen, permitted or not, have always practised,
and by which they have laboured safely forward as a nation.

Milton published also, in 1644, his short letter on "Education," addressed to **Samuel Hartlib.**  Samuel Hartlib was of
a good Polish family; ancestors of his had been Privy Councillors to Emperors of Germany.  He came to England in 1640,
and his active beneficent mind brought him into friendship
with many of the earnest thinkers of the time.  In 1641, Hartlib
published *A Brief Relation of that which hath been lately
attempted to procure Ecclesiasticall Peace among Protestants,*
and a *Description of Macaria,* his ideal of a well-ordered state.
In the midst of the strife of civil war, Hartlib was wholly
occupied with scientific study, having especial regard to the

extension and improvement of education, and the development of agriculture and manufactures. In 1642 he translated from the Latin of a Moravian pastor, John Amos Komensky, two treatises on *A Reformation of Schooles.* His zeal for the better education of the people, as a remedy for their distresses, caused him not only to give thought to the education of the poor, but also to attempt the establishment of a school for the improved education of the rich; and he asked Milton to print his ideas on the subject; hence the tract of eight pages published by Milton, in 1644, without title-page, but inscribed on the top in one line, *Of Education. To Mr. Samuel Hartlib.* In 1645, Hartlib edited a treatise on "Flemish Agriculture," which gave counsel that added greatly to the wealth of England. Among Hartlib's schemes was a plan for a sort of guild of science, which should unite students of nature into a brotherhood while they sought knowledge in the way set forth by Francis Bacon.

64. Bacon's philosophy had arisen out of that part of the energy of thought, quickened along its whole line, which prompted free inquiry into nature. It gave new impulse and a definite direction to the movement that produced it. Scientific studies had new charms for many minds, and there was an enthusiasm for experiment in the Baconian way (§ 22). Many a quiet thinker, to whom civil war was terrible, turned aside from the tumult of the times, and found rest for his mind in the calm study of nature. Such men were drawn together by community of taste, driven together also by the discords round about them; and the influence of Bacon's books upon the growing energy of scientific thought was aided by the Civil War.

Robert Boyle, the chemist, was a young man in these days. The outside dignity of the Boyle family was established by Richard, son of Roger Boyle, of Canterbury. Richard Boyle went to Ireland, married an heiress, who soon died, became secretary for the Government in Munster, used his opportunities of getting estates cheap, became · enormously rich, married another heiress, and died Earl of Cork in 1643, leaving seven sons and eight daughters, with estates enough to provide handsomely for all of them. His fifth son was **Roger Boyle,** born in 1621, who at twenty married a daughter of the Earl of Suffolk, went with his bride to Ireland, defended his father's castle of Lismore in the Rebellion, and often brought armed force to the aid of his neighbours. We shall meet with him again. The seventh son of the Earl of Cork was born in 1626, the year of Bacon's death, and he was **Robert Boyle,** educated between eight and twelve years old at Eton, then at Geneva. When his father died, in 1643, Robert Boyle, aged seventeen, returned to England. By advice of his eldest sister, Lady Ranelagh, he shunned the strife of parties, and devoted himself to study. Lady Ranelagh having become a widow, added her income to Robert's, and kept house for him. In 1644, Robert Boyle became a friend of Hartlib's, and entered heartily into his beneficent schemes. He became also a friend of Milton's, for Lady Ranelagh sent her son and her nephew, the Earl of Barrimore, to Milton's school. Another of Milton's pupils was Sir Thomas Gardiner, of Essex. In Robert Boyle the fresh study of nature quickened love of God; his scientific thought was blended with simple and deep religious feeling.

Dr. Thomas Browne, of Norwich, who did not become **Sir Thomas Browne** until the reign of Charles II., was educated at Winchester and Oxford. He practised physic for a time in Oxfordshire, married, went to Ireland, France, and Italy; on his way home through Holland was made M.D. at Leyden, returned to England, and in 1636 settled at Norwich. In 1642 he published his *Religio Medici* (the Religion of a Physician), rich in the original quaintness that was then especially enjoyed, full of learning, Latinism, acute perception, and courageous ingenuity, and with religious depths where now and then the formalist suspected shallows, with delight in knowledge, acceptance of the scientific errors of the time, and bold feeling in right and wrong directions for new matter of thought. In 1646, Dr. Browne of Norwich published his *Pseudodoxia Epidemica* (Epidemic False Doctrines); *or, Inquiries into Vulgar and Common Errors,* which showed the scientific mind itself accepting uncorrected errors of the learned upon which, in our thoughtless moods, we may now look back with surprise. The men of science had only made a fresh start with more settled determination, and a better guide upon the road to truth. But Bacon knew no better than his neighbours what they would find on the way. Copernicus had reasoned in vain for him as for others. When Bacon rejected the theory of the crystalline spheres, he added, " Nothing is more false than all these fancies, except perhaps the motions of the earth, which are more false still." John Wilkins (§ 59) was even now one of the few men in England for whom Galileo had not spoken in vain. " Smectymnuus," opposing one of Bishop Hall's assertions, took the notion " that the earth moves "

T *

as a commonplace for an absurdity : " We shall show anon that there is no more truth in this assertion than if he had said with Anaxagoras, ' Snow is black,' or with Copernicus, ' The earth moves and the heavens stand still.' " Error so great among the learned showed clearly enough that it was not for science to stand still.

A young man of science who did not separate himself from the contest of the time was the mathematician, **John Wallis,** born in 1616, son of a rich incumbent of Ashford, Kent. His father died when he was six years old, his mother educated him for a learned profession, he went at sixteen to Emmanuel College, Cambridge, and is said to have been the first student who maintained Harvey's new doctrine of the circulation of the blood (§ 41). There was no study of mathematics then in Cambridge ; the best mathematicians were in London, and their science was little esteemed. Wallis graduated, obtained a fellowship at Queen's College, took orders in 1640, and acted as chaplain in private families until the Civil War. He then took the side of the Parliament, and used his mathematical skill in reading the secret ciphers of the Royalists. The ingenious **John Wilkins** had called attention to various methods of cipher-writing, as well as of telegraphing, in 1641, by his *Mercury; or, the Secret and Swift Messenger : Shewing how a Man may with Privacy and Speed Communicate his Thoughts to a Friend at any Distance.* In 1643, **John Wallis,** aged twenty-seven, obtained the living of St. Gabriel, Fenchurch Street. In the same year the death of his mother gave him independent fortune. In 1644 he married, and was one of the secretaries of the Assembly of Divines at Westminster. In 1645 he was among the men of science, and took part in the meetings which led to the formation of the Royal Society. In 1648 he was rector of a church in Ironmonger Lane. He remonstrated against the execution of Charles I., and in 1649 he was appointed Savilian Professor of Geometry at Oxford.

**Sir Henry Spelman,** who died in 1641 at the age of eighty, was only twelve years younger than the founder of that professorship (ch. vii. § 89). He had been employed and knighted by James I. He was an orthodox antiquary, who had written in behalf of tithes when John Selden got into trouble for his account of them, and left behind him a valuable archæological glossary, and a collection in two folios, the first published in 1639, the second after his death, of British Ecclesiastical Laws, *Con-*

*cilia, Decreta, Leges, Constitutiones in Re Ecclesiastica Orbis Britannici.* He had a son, Sir John Spelman, who inherited his tastes, wrote a life of King Alfred, and survived his father but two years. In 1640, Sir Henry Spelman, then eighty years old, founded a lectureship at Cambridge for the study of Anglo-Saxon or First English. Archbishop Usher, at his suggestion, nominated **Abraham Wheloc,** a learned Orientalist, who was already teaching Arabic there. Sir Henry Spelman set apart a portion of his private income and the vicarage of Middleton, as a stipend either for the reading of Anglo-Saxon lectures, or the publishing of Anglo-Saxon manuscripts. Wheloc preferred private study. He edited Bede's History (ch. ii. § 10 ), and gave much of his time to the printing of the gospels in Persian, to be used for missionary enterprise.

65. **John Milton** had no great liking for the Westminster Assembly, in which Wallis, the mathematician, acted as a secretary. The prevailing policy in the Assembly and the Parliament was Presbyterian. Milton's "Reason of Church Government against Prelacy" showed that he had no dislike to the Presbyterian system in itself, but it seemed to him that the Scottish Covenanters and their English allies sought to impose it on all men without regard to their consciences, and to set up a spiritual dominion that differed only in name from that which they had thrown down. Milton's battle was against a despotism from without, forcing the consciences of men. The Westminster Assembly first met in July, 1643, summoned by an ordinance of Parliament, to reconstitute the Church in nearer harmony with the Church of Scotland and other Reformed Churches abroad. There were 121 divines and 30 laymen, among whom was John Selden, who took an active part in the debates. The rising body of the Independents, weakly represented in the Assembly, had a central doctrine that brought Milton into much sympathy with them. They held with the Brownists, who were Independents of Elizabeth's time (ch. vii. § 84), that, given the Bible for a rule of faith, each Christian should draw from it the highest truth that was the truth to him ; that men who agreed sufficiently should form themselves into a congregation, elect and pay their own minister, be independent of all outside interference, and seek in their own way their own spiritual welfare. They would form a united church of all these bodies of Christians, each left free to seek Divine truth in the way that seemed right to its members, and all held together by the Christian charity which bound them

to avoid coercion of their neighbours. That view of a church agreed with Milton's sense of right. In 1643 a pamphlet written in this spirit, *An Apologeticall Narration of some Ministers formerly Exiles in the Netherlands, now Members of the Assembly of Divines,* was answered by A. S. In the Assembly and in his writings **Samuel Rutherford** bitterly attacked the Independents, and **Thomas Edwards** expressed a hate of all who differed from him that, in 1646, was summed up in his *Gangræna; or, A Catalogue of many of the Errours, Heresies, Blasphemies, and Pernicious Practices of the Sectaries of this Time;* **Rutherford** publishing in the same year his *Divine Right of Church Government.* Seeing such things, and attacked himself, **Milton,** in his sonnet on the *New Forcers of Conscience under the Long Parliament,* spoke his mind about the Westminster Assembly that would

> " Adjure the civil sword
> To force our consciences that Christ set free,
> And ride us with a classic hierarchy
> Taught ye by mere A.S. and Rotherford.
> Men whose life, learning, faith, and pure intent
> Would have been held in high esteem by Paul,
> Must now be named and printed heretics
> By shallow Edwards and Scotch What-d'ye-call."

He trusted Parliament would use its civil power to clip, not, as under past tyranny, the ears, but the phylacteries of these new masters :

> " When they shall read this clearly in your charge :
> New Presbyter is but Old Priest writ large."

66. Absolute authority of the king was maintained in the philosophy of **Thomas Hobbes,** who was born in April, 1588, son of a clergyman, at Malmsbury, in Wiltshire. As a schoolboy at Malmsbury he translated the "Medea" of Euripides from Greek into Latin verse. In 1603 he was entered to Magdalene Hall, Oxford ; and in 1608 became tutor to William, Lord Cavendish, son of Lord Hardwicke, soon afterwards created Earl of Devonshire. In 1610, Hobbes travelled with his pupil in France and Italy. When he came home, Bacon, Lord Herbert of Cherbury, and Ben Jonson, were among his friends. In 1626 his patron died, and in 1628 the son whose tutor he had been died also. In that year Hobbes published his first work, a *Translation of Thucydides,* made for the purpose of showing the evils of popular government. Ben Jonson helped in the revision of it. Hobbes next went to France as tutor to the son of Sir Gervase

Clifton, but was called back by the Countess Dowager of Devonshire to take charge of the young earl, then thirteen years old. In 1634 he went with his pupil to France and Italy, returned to England in 1636, and, still living at Chatsworth with the family he had now served for about thirty years, he, in this year, honoured Derbyshire with a Latin poem on the wonders of the Peak, *De Mirabilibus Pecci.* In 1641 Hobbes withdrew to Paris, and in 1642 published in Latin the first work setting forth his philosophy of society. It treated of the citizen—*Elementa Philosophica de Cive.* Hobbes upheld absolute monarchy as the true form of government, basing his argument upon the principle that the state of nature is a state of war. In 1647 Hobbes became mathematical tutor to Charles Prince of Wales.

67. **Nicholas Hunton,** a Nonconformist minister, published in 1643-4 a treatise on Monarchy, in two parts, with a Vindication. Part One inquired into the nature of Monarchy; Part Two argued that the sovereignty of England is in the Three Estates—King, Lords, and Commons. This doctrine was afterwards, in 1683, condemned by the Convocation of the University of Oxford, and the book publicly burnt. Two or three years later it was answered by **Sir Robert Filmer,** an upholder of absolute monarchy, who based it upon patriarchal authority, and combated every form of the assertion that men were born equal. Filmer's reply to Hunton, published in 1646, was entitled *Anarchy of a Limited and Mixed Monarchy.* Sir Robert was the son of Sir Edward Filmer, of East Sutton, in Kent. He entered Trinity College as a student in 1604, and died under the Commonwealth, in 1653. The book for which he is remembered, his " Patriarcha," written about 1642, was not published until 1680 ; but in 1648 he expressed much of his argument in a pamphlet on *The Power of Kings; and in Particular of the King of England,* which sets out with this practical definition of the king's absolute power not subject to any law. " If the sovereign prince be exempted from the laws of his predecessors, much less shall he be bound by the laws he maketh himself ; for a man may well receive a law from another man, but impossible it is in nature for to give a law unto himself." Filmer published also in 1648, *The Freeholder's Grand Inquest touching our Soveraign Lord the King and his Parliament,* endeavouring to prove from history that the king alone makes laws and is supreme judge in Parliament ; that " the Commons by their writ are only to perform and consent to the ordinances of Parliament,"

and that the Lords " are only to treat and give counsel to Parliament."

68. **John Selden** (§ 19), in December, 1621, had joined in a protest of the House of Commons, claiming liberty of speech, and counselling James I. upon his duties as the king of a free people, and for that offence to the king he suffered slight imprisonment. In the Parliament of Charles I. he was opposed to arbitrary government, he supported liberty of the press, and was sent to the Tower for a time by Charles as well as by James. But Selden had the moderation of a scholar, and the regard for old institutions that is strengthened by a study of the past; while, true to his love of liberty, he sought conciliation, and was somewhat suspected by more angry combatants. Usher had been nominated as a member of the Westminster Assembly, but refused to attend, and preached against it at Oxford. On this account it was resolved to confiscate his library, but Selden saved it for him. Selden himself went to the Assembly, and foiled bitter divines at their own weapons. " Sometimes," says his friend Whitelock, " when they had cited a text of Scripture to prove their assertion, he would tell them, ' Perhaps in your little pocket Bibles with gilt leaves,' which they would often pull out and read, ' the translation may be thus, but the Greek or Hebrew signifies thus and thus,' and so would silence them." When, in September, 1645, the House of Commons was debating the proposal to bring in excommunication and suspension from the Sacrament as part of the discipline in the new establishment of religion, Selden marshalled his learning into array against it. The most interesting books of his that appeared in the reign of Charles I. were his account of the marbles brought from the East to the house of the Earl of Arundel, a great patron of art and literature—the *Marmora Arundelliana*, published in 1629; and the *Mare Clausum* (" Closed Sea "), published in 1636—it had been written in the reign of James I. Grotius, in his *Mare Liberum* (" Free Sea "), having contended that the sea was free to the Dutch in the East Indies, where Portugal laid claim to rights in it, Selden argued that the sea round England belonged to the English. The book was not printed in James's reign; but in 1634 disputes arose out of the claim of Dutch fishermen to the right of free sea for the herring fishery by English coasts. Selden's *Mare Clausum* was then published, with its purport set forth in its title-page, " The Closed Sea; or, On the Dominion of the Sea. Two Books. In the first it is demonstrated that the

sea, from the law of nature or of nations, is not common to all men, but is the subject of property equally with the land In the second, the King of Great Britain is asserted to be lord of the circumfluent sea, as an inseparable and perpetual appendage of the British Empire." In 1640, Selden published an elaborate work on the natural and national law of the Jews— *De Jure Naturali et Gentium juxta Disciplinam Ebræorum;* and he added to this, in 1646, *Uxor Ebraica,* which was a work upon the Jewish laws of marriage and divorce.

69. We return now to **John Milton,** and his argument on a like question. In 1645 he met the religious arguments against his doctrine with a pamphlet called *Tetrachordon* (that is, "arranged with four chords") : *Expositions upon the Four Chief Places in Scripture which treat of Marriage or Nullities in Marriage.* To this was added presently *Colasterion* (*i.e.,* "place of punishment"), a reply to an anonymous assailant, with a special word to the Parliament's new licenser, who surpassed the old licenser under the Crown, "for a licenser is not contented now to give his single imprimatur, but brings his chair into the title-leaf, there sits and judges up or judges down what book he pleases." The licenser who cried a book up on its title-page might help the printer to put off wares otherwise unsaleable, which might in time, Milton suggested, bring him in round fees. But upon the subject of divorce, also, Milton had now said what he had to say.

Civil war had advanced. English and Scottish armies were besieging York ; in June, 1644, Prince Rupert marched to relieve the city. He did so, but marched out again ; and on the 2nd of July, at Marston Moor, the charges of Fairfax and Cromwell turned defeat of the Parliamentary army into signal victory. The queen fled to France. On the 10th of January. 1645, the Presbyterians sent Laud to the scaffold—Prynne, his violent opponent, and once his victim, acting as counsel against the helpless old man at his trial. Then followed the failure of an attempt at treaty ; and then, on the 14th of June, the battle of Naseby, in which the king's cause was completely lost, and the success again was mainly due to Cromwell and his Ironsides, This ruin of the king's cause brought the Powells into difficulties. John Milton's wife suddenly appeared to him in 1645, when he was paying a visit to a relative named Blackborough, who lived by St. Martin's-le-Grand. She knelt for forgiveness, had it at once, went back to his home, and we have no reason for doubting that she learnt to understand his gentle nature. He resumed, also, his active good-will to her family, and, with help of his brother Christopher as a lawyer, stood between them and ruin. In the same year, 1645, Milton removed to a larger house in Barbican, and a publisher obtained from him a collected edition of his earlier verse, *Poems both Latin and English, by John Milton.* In the following year, 1646, Milton's first daughter, Anne, was born. She was lame. In the next year, 1647, his second daughter, Mary, was born, and his father died. He moved in that year to a house in Holborn, looking back on Lincoln's Inn Fields. He published no more pamphlets or books during the Civil Wars.

In 1648, Cromwell had defeated, at Darwen Bridge, the Scotch Royalist army brought in by the Duke of Hamilton, and was welcomed in Edinburgh as a deliverer ; and after this Milton addressed to him a sonnet as "our chief of men," who had prevailed, "guided by faith and matchless fortitude ;" but while paying honour to his success in battle, the poet urged that which lay next to his heart

> " Yet much remains
> To conquer still ; Peace hath her victories
> No less renown'd than War ; new foes arise
> Threatening to bind our souls with secular chains."

On the 2nd of May, 1648, the Presbyterians had secured a Parliamentary ordinance enacting that all persons who, "by preaching, teaching, printing, or writing," denied seven specified articles of faith, should, on conviction, if the error were not abjured, "suffer the pains of death, as in the case of felony, without benefit of clergy."

To Fairfax, also, Milton wrote his praise for victory ; but in each sonnet the praise for prowess in battle is the prelude in the two quatrains to the essential thought in the terzettes. This is the essence of Milton's sonnet to Fairfax :

> " Oh, yet a noble task awaits thy hand,
> (For what can war but endless war still breed ?)
> 'Till truth and right from violence be freed,
> And publick faith cleared from the shameful brand
> Of publick fraud. In vain doth Valour bleed,
> While Avarice and Rapine share the land."

70. We look back now with equal reverence to men of all opinion who have been true to the highest life within their souls. **Jeremy Taylor** (§ 61) was, early in 1644, a chaplain with

the Royal army in Wales. He was imprisoned for a time, after the defeat at Cardigan, then married a Welsh lady, Joanna Bridges, who had some property at Llangedock, in Carmarthenshire, and with two companions—William Nicholson, afterwards Bishop of Gloucester, and William Wyatt, afterwards a Prebendary of Lincoln—Jeremy Taylor kept a school, Newton Hall, in Carmarthenshire, at Llanvihangel Aberbythyrch. It lies near Grongar Hill, and the great house of the neighbourhood is Golden Grove, where Lord and Lady Carbery were his warm friends. In this Welsh village Taylor wrote his best works, and first, in 1647, his *Liberty of Prophesying* (ch. vii. § 33), a plea for freedom to all in the interpretation of the Bible, with one simple standard of external authority, the Apostles' Creed. In this book Jeremy Taylor showed, of course, the natural bent of his mind towards authority in Church and State. He would have a church of every country contained within its political boundaries, and allowed the ruler more power to secure uniformity than would be practically consistent with his theory; but this represents only the form of thought which was as natural to him as his different form of thought to Milton. It was warmed in Jeremy Taylor with true fervour of devotion, and brought home to the sympathies of men by a pure spirit of Christian charity. The mischiefs of prevailing discord came, he said, "not from this, that all men are not of one mind, for that is neither necessary nor possible, but that every opinion is made an article of faith, every article is a ground of quarrel, every quarrel makes a faction, every faction is zealous, and all zeal pretends for God, and whatsoever is for God cannot be too much. We by this time are come to that pass, we think we love not God except we hate our brother." And these were the last words in the book: "I end with a story which I find in the Jews' books :— When Abraham sat at his tent door, according to his custom, waiting to entertain strangers, he espied an old man stooping and leaning on his staff, weary with age and travel, coming towards him, who was an hundred years of age; he received him kindly, washed his feet, provided supper, and caused him to sit down; but observing that the old man ate and prayed not, nor begged for a blessing on his meat, asked him why he did not worship the God of heaven. The old man told him that he worshipped the fire only, and acknowledged no other god; at which Abraham grew so zealously angry that he thrust the old man out of his tent, and exposed him to all the evils of the night and an unguarded condition. When the old man was gone, God called to Abraham and asked him where the stranger was? He replied, 'I thrust him away because he did not worship thee.' God answered him, 'I have suffered him these hundred years, although he dishonoured me ; and couldst thou not endure him one night, when he gave thee no trouble?' Upon this, saith the story, Abraham fetched him back again, and gave him hospitable entertainment and wise instruction. 'Go thou and do likewise,' and thy charity will be rewarded by the God of Abraham."

## CHAPTER IX.

### THE COMMONWEALTH.

1. ON the 30th of January, 1649, in weather so cold that the Thames was frozen over, King Charles I., after trial by a High Court of Justice constituted by authority of the House of Commons, was publicly executed at Whitehall. On the 7th of February, the House of Commons abolished the office of King in this nation, and soon afterwards a Council of State was appointed, consisting of forty-one persons, of whom twenty-two, Including Sir Henry Vane, refused to sign a document expressing their approval of the proceedings by which monarchy had been overthrown. It was agreed to let the past be, and take only a pledge of fidelity for the future. To this Council John Milton was appointed Secretary for Foreign Tongues.

With much weakness of character, through which he fell, the king had many merits, and he died asserting that his people mistook the nature of government, for that men were free under a government not by being sharers in it, but by due administration of its laws. He did not understand that form of government towards which England was now tending, as, with advance of civilisation, the old controversy on the limit of authority (ch. iii. § 11) advanced its ground. Some who condemned the king did so in cruelty of zeal ; with others, trial, sentence, and execution of a king by his people, for the first time in the history of man, was a blow struck at the doctrine of an irresponsible monarchy. But thousands had taken the Parliament's side in the Civil Wars who would not have assented to this act. **Dr. John Gauden** published about a fortnight before the execution his *Religious and Loyal Protestation against the present Declared Purposes and Proceedings of the Army and others, about the Trying and Destroying our Sovereign Lord the King. Sent to a Collonell to bee presented to the Lord Fairfax, and his Generall Councell of Officers, the fifth of January,* 1648 (New Style, 1649). This was " Printed for Richard Royston;" and Richard Royston was then printing another work of Gauden's, which was not issued until a few days after the execution, but its appearance at such a time made it a power. It was called " Εἰκὼν Βασιλικὴ" (Eikōn Basilikē, the Royal Image), *The Portraicture of His Sacred Majesty in his Solitudes and Sufferings.* It was written in the first person, professing to be the work of Charles himself, displaying his piety while it set forth an explanation of his policy. It was in 28 sections, as :  1. Upon His Majesties calling the last Parliament. 2. Upon the Earl of Strafford's Death ; and so forth, usually giving, as from the king's own lips, a popular interpretation of his actions, and each section ending with a strain of prayer. One section, the 25th, consisted wholly of " Penitential Meditations and Vows in the King's Solitude at Holmby ;" the 27th was fatherly counsel " To the Prince of Wales ;" and the 28th closed the series with " Meditations upon Death, after the Votes of Non-Addresses, and His Majestie's closer Imprisonment in Carisbrook Castle." The writer of this book (except two of its sections) had, as John Gauden, B.D., preached before the Parliament, in November, 1640, to its great satisfaction, on *The Love of Truth and Peace.* He was chaplain to the Earl of Warwick, a Presbyterian leader, and afterwards held under the Parliament the living of Bocking, in Essex. When he was at work upon his book for the king, he showed his design to Anthony Walker, Rector of Fifield, who agreed with his strong desire to aid the king, but doubted the morality of personating him, to which Gauden replied, " Look on the title, 'tis *The Portraicture,* &c., and no man draws his own picture." Dr. Walker was with Gauden when he called on the Bishop of Salisbury (Dr. Duppa), left Gauden and the bishop to a private talk, and was told afterwards that the bishop had liked the work, but thought there should be sections added on ' The Ordinance against the Common Prayer Book," and " Their Denying his Majesty the attendance of his Chaplains." As bishop and as chaplain to the king, Duppa felt strongly on these points, and he had agreed to write the sections upon them (16th and 24th in the printed book). The book being finished, a copy

of it was sent to King Charles by the hands of the Marquis of
Hertford, when he went to the Isle of Wight. This was the copy
found with corrections upon it in the king's handwriting. Time
pressed, and it was thought the better course to publish at
once, without waiting for His Majesty's permission. The press
was corrected by Mr. Simmonds, a persecuted minister, and the
last part of the manuscript was taken by Anthony Walker on
its way to the printer's on the 23rd of December, 1648. The
Marquis of Hertford afterwards told Mrs. Gauden that the
king had wished the book to be issued not as his own, but as
another's ; but it was argued that Cromwell and others of the
army having got a great reputation with the people for parts and
piety, it would be best to be in the king's name, and His Majesty
took time to consider of it. When the book appeared its authorship was known to the Marquis of Hertford, Lord Capel, Bishop
Duppa, and Bishop Morley. After the Restoration, Dr. Gauden
privately proved his claim to Charles II. and the Duke of York,
and was made Bishop of Exeter before the end of 1660 ; had
in a few months £20,000 in fines for the renewal of leases ;
thought himself poorly rewarded ; pressed for Winchester, got
Worcester, and died six months afterwards. Lord Clarendon,
vexed by Gauden's importunities, wrote to him (March 13, 1661)
when he was Bishop of Exeter : "The particular which you
often renewed, I do confesse was imparted to me under secrecy,
and of which I did not take myself to be at liberty to take
notice ; and truly when it ceases to be a secret, I know nobody
will be gladd of it but Mr. Milton. I have very often wished I
had never been trusted with it." In a sale of books of the
Marquis of Anglesey, a private note was found in his copy of
the "Eikon Basilike," saying that when in 1675 he was showing
to the king and Duke of York the MS. of the work, with some
corrections in their father's own handwriting, they assured
the marquis "that this was none of the said king's compiling,
but made by Dr. Gauden, Bishop of Exeter."

This fact was known to not more than a dozen people when,
a few days after the execution, "Eikon Basilike" appeared.
Charles II. said to Gauden that if it had come out a week sooner
it would have saved his father's life. It would not have done
that ; but it touched the religious feeling of the people, and
excited a strong sympathy. At home and abroad fifty thousand
copies were circulated in a twelvemonth. There were also appended to some of these copies His Majesty's Speeches, Prayers,

Messages for Peace, and Letters.  A " Prayer in Time of Captivity," said to have been delivered to Dr. Juxon, Bishop of London, immediately before the king's death, was an adaptation to his own case of Pamela's prayer, in Sidney's " Arcadia " (ch. vii. § 44).  Charles, no doubt, read novels, rightly thought this prayer good and applicable to himself, adapted it, and used it. Dr. Juxon, who did not read novels, supposed it to be original. Nobody can have intended any fraud, for, as detection was inevitable, it would have been a mere asking for ridicule.

2. The strong feeling excited by the form given to the arguments of the " Eikon Basilike " had to be met, and on the 15th of March, John Milton was called upon by the Council of State to answer it.  He had then already published his " Tenure of Kings and Magistrates," which appeared in February, when the answer to " Eikon Basilike " appeared, later in the same year, 1649, " Published by Authority," as " Εἰκονοκλαστής " (The Iconoclast).  "The Author, I. M."  In his preface Milton said, " I take it on me as a work assign'd rather than by me chosen or affected, which was the cause both of beginning it so late, and finishing it so leisurely in the midst of other employments and diversions."  He treated the book as the king's, and said, " As to the author of these soliloquies, whether it were the late king, as is vulgarly believ'd, or any secret coadjutor, and some stick not to name him, it can add nothing, nor shall take anything from the weight, if any be, of reason which he brings." It was a time for forbearance, but if the king left this new appeal behind him to truth and the world, the adversaries of his cause were compelled " to meet the force of his reason in any field whatsoever, the force and equipage of whose arms they have so often met victoriously."  Milton accordingly replied, section by section, to each of the twenty-eight parts of the " Eikon Basilike."

3. But the chief expression of Milton's thought upon the great event of the time is to be found in his *Tenure of Kings and Magistrates*, which he began to write during the struggle between the Presbyterians and Independents.  The Presbyterians brought Charles to the block, and the Independents executed him.  The Presbyterians sought mastery over the Independents by separating themselves from the act.  As a Royalist said, their grief was " that the head was not struck off to the best advantage and commodity of them that held it by the hair."  Since the deed was done, Milton's desire was that it

should not have been done in vain, but that it should be held
to signify what was for him the central truth of the great
struggle, that the chief magistrate of a nation, whatever he be
called, has no power to dispense with laws which are the
birthright of the people; that he is bound to govern in accordance with them, is himself under them, and answerable for the
breach of them.   Milton sought to give to so momentous an act
its true interpretation, as a violent expression of the principle
towards which the question of the limit of authority was tending,
the principle that, forty years later, was to be finally established
at the Revolution.   This principle, the essence of the struggle,
was what Milton kept in mind, and for this, throughout his
prose writing under the Commonwealth, he sought chiefly to
win assent from wise and simple.   He " wrote nothing," he said
in a later book (his " Second Defence "), " respecting the regal
jurisdiction, till the king, proclaimed an enemy by the Senate,
and overcome in arms, was brought captive to his trial and
condemned to suffer death.   When, indeed, some of the Presbyterian leaders, lately the most inveterately hostile to Charles,
but now irritated by the prevalence of the Independents in the
nation and the Senate, and stung with resentment, not of the
fact, but of their own want of power to commit it, exclaimed
against the sentence of the Parliament upon the king, and
raised what commotions they could by daring to assert that
the doctrine of Protestant divines, and of all the Reformed
churches, was strong in reprobation of this severity to kings,
then at length I conceived it to be my duty publicly to oppose
so much obvious and palpable falsehood.   Neither did I then
direct my argument or persuasion personally against Charles;
but, by the testimony of many of the most eminent divines, I
proved what course of conduct might lawfully be observed
towards tyrants in general.   . . . .   This work was not
published till after the death of the king; and was written rather
to tranquillize the minds of men than to discuss any part of
the question respecting Charles, a question the decision of which
belonged to the magistrates and not to me, and which had now
received its final determination."

Early in 1649, Milton also published *Observations on the
Articles of Peace between the Earl of Ormond and the Irish,*
in which comments of his upon a manifesto of the Presbytery of
Belfast show very clearly the spirit of the relation between the
Presbyterians and Milton as an Independent.   The Indepen-

dents, then predominant, were charged, he said, with having broken the Covenant. "Let us hear wherein. 'In labouring,' say they, 'to establish by law a universal toleration of all religions.' This touches not the State; for certainly, were they so minded, they need not labour at but do it, having power in their hands; and we know of no Act as yet passed to that purpose. But suppose it done, wherein is the Covenant broke? The Covenant enjoins us to endeavour the extirpation first of popery and prelacy, then of heresy, schism, and profaneness, and whatsoever shall be found contrary to sound doctrine and the power of godliness. And this we cease not to do by all effectual and proper means: but these divines might know that to extirpate all these things can be no work of the civil sword, but of the spiritual, which is the word of God" (ch. viii. § 54). "No man well in his wits, endeavouring to root up weeds out of his ground, instead of using the spade will take a mallet or beetle. Nor doth the Covenant any way engage us to extirpate or to prosecute the men, but the heresies and errors in them, which we tell these divines and the rest that understand not, belongs chiefly to their own function, in the diligent preaching and insisting upon sound doctrine, in the confuting, not the railing down, of errors . . . by the power of truth, not of persecution."

It was also in the first months of 1649 that Milton planned and began a *History of England*, which would have expressed his view of the life of the nation if his pen had not been called to the immediate service of his country, and so left it a fragment in six books, extending from the old fabulous times to the Conquest. This was not published until 1670, but four of the six books were written at the beginning of the Commonwealth.

4. When Milton was appointed Foreign Secretary to the Council, he removed, to be near his work, to lodgings, first at Charing Cross, by the opening into Spring Gardens, and afterwards in Scotland Yard. It was here that he wrote his first "Defence of the People of England." One of the foremost scholars of the time upon the Continent had accepted, with a hundred gold jacobuses, the commission to arraign England before the intelligence of Europe for the murder of her king. His book, with the Royal Arms of England on its title-page, appeared towards the end of 1649, in Latin, because addressed to readers throughout Europe, as Salmasius's "Royal Defence of Charles I., addressed to his legitimate heir Charles II."

(*Cl. Salmasii Defensio Regia pro Carolo I.  Ad Serenissimum
Magnæ Britanniæ Regem Carolum II., Filium natu majorem,
Hæredem et successorem legitimum.*)  Claude de Saumaise
was about twelve years older than John Milton, whose age
when he wrote his reply was forty-one.  Saumaise was the
son of a learned member of Parliament for Burgundy, who,
in 1597, translated Dionysius of Alexandria into French verse.
He was educated at home by his father, and, when ten years
old, read Pindar and wrote Greek and Latin fluently.  At
sixteen he was sent to study at Paris, where the influence of
Casaubon made him a Reformer.  He went next to Heidelberg,
there formally renounced Catholicism, worked hard, gave every
third night to study, fell ill, went home and wrote books full of
minute erudition.  In 1622, at the age of twenty-six, he edited
Tertullian on the Pallium, for the sake of producing a minute
treatise upon the dress worn by the ancients.  Milton began
by studying man's inmost soul, Saumaise by studying the
clothes outside the surface of his body.  Saumaise worked at
the "Polyhistor" of Solinus, because that gave him an opportunity for the display of various learning, and he enriched his
exercitations with an appendix on Manna and Sugar.  He
studied Hebrew, Persian, and Arabic; was invited to Venice,
Oxford, even Rome, although he had cast off the pope; but
settled at Leyden, in 1632, with a public salary.  In 1642 his
father died, and he returned to France.  Richelieu and, after
Richelieu's death, in December, 1642, Mazarin pressed the
famous scholar to remain in his own country, but he went back
to Leyden, where he was applied to on behalf of Prince Charles,
and wrote against the English people his Defence of Charles I.
In 1650, while Milton was at work upon his answer, Saumaise
went to the Court of Christina, of Sweden, then about twenty-
five years old, who had said she could not be happy without
him; and there he was in such high favour that the queen
is said to have lighted his fire with her own hands when she
came for confidential morning talks with him.  Saumaise,
under the assumed name of Wallo Messalinus, had attacked
Episcopacy violently, in 1641, in a Latin book on "Presbyters
and Bishops."  Claude Sarrau, a devoted admirer of his genius,
warned him after his "Royal Defence" appeared that he was
contradicting doctrines which he had been honoured for maintaining with fidelity, and said, in reply to his excuses, "I am of
opinion that even a king's advocate ought not, in his master's

cause, to speak in public differently from what he speaks and thinks in private. . . . But you wrote, you say, 'by command.' And was it possible for any commands to prevail on you to change your opinion? Your favourite Epictetus tells us that our opinion is one of those things in our power, and so far in our power that nothing can take it away from us without our consent." There is, of course, no parallel between the beneficent duty of an advocate before a court of justice, who gives to the worst criminal the right of a clear statement of whatever can be urged in his defence, and the act of an independent scholar, who for fame or money will affirm what he does not believe.

Milton was called upon by the Council of State to reply to Salmasius. His health was already weak, the sight of his left eye already gone, and he was told he would lose his eyesight altogether if he undertook this labour. But to maintain before Europe in Latin, as he had maintained before his countrymen in English, what was for him and, as he believed, for England the living truth involved in the great struggle, with all its passions and misdeeds, was the next duty in his intellectual war. Milton wrote his " Defence of the People of England against Claude Saumaise's 'Royal Defence'" (*Defensio pro Populo Anglicano contra Claudii Salmasii Defensionem Regiam*), and the sight of the remaining eye then gradually vanished. Yet he said, in a sonnet to his old pupil, Cyriac Skinner—for Milton loved alike those who had taught him and those whom he had taught :

> " Yet I argue not
> Against Heaven's hand or will, or bate a jot
> Of heart or hope ; but still bear up and steer
> Right onward. What supports me, dost thou ask ?
> The conscience, friend, to have lost them overplied
> In liberty's defence, my noble task,
> Of which all Europe rings from side to side ;
> This thought might lead me through the world's vain mask,
> Content, though blind, had I no better guide."

Milton's reply to Saumaise first gave him European reputation. Queen Christina read his book, delighted in it, and told Saumaise that he was beaten ; upon which Saumaise, whose health had been failing, found that the climate of Sweden disagreed with him. The common question was, "Who is this Milton?" Nicholas Heinsius, in Holland, had asked it of Isaac Voss, who was among the scholars then at the court of this daughter of Gustavus Adolphus ; and Voss at last replied, " I know now about Milton from my Uncle Junius, who is intimate with him (*qui cum eo familiaritatem colit*). He has told me that he serves the Parliament in foreign affairs; is skilled in many languages; that he is not indeed of noble, but, as they say, of gentle birth ; a pupil of Patrick"—(mistake for Thomas)—"Young; kindly, affable and endowed with many other virtues" (*comem, affabilem, multisque aliis præditum virtutibus*").

5. The Francis Junius who gave this information was the son of a Francis Junius who took part in the great religious contest of the Netherlands (ch. vii. § 26). Milton's friend had come to England in 1620, and become librarian to that Earl of Arundel for whom Selden, with aid from Patrick Young, royal librarian, described the Arundel Marbles (ch. viii. § 68). Junius held that office for thirty years, and was known among scholars as an enthusiastic student of the early languages of Europe. For this reason, when Usher, among his searches for books, found a MS. of First English, which proved to be (and is to this day) the only known copy of the work of the "Anglo-Saxon Milton," "Cædmon's Paraphrase" (ch. ii. § 5), he gave it to Francis Junius, as the man most able to make proper use of it. Junius could show it to his friend Milton, who cared much for such things, tell him about it, describe to him notable passages in it, before he left England in 1650. After his departure, Junius printed " Cædmon's Paraphrase" at Amsterdam, in 1655. Certainly, therefore, Milton knew of " Cædmon's Paraphrase" before he began to write " Paradise Lost."

6. The "Defence of the People of England" is, above all things, Milton's argument for the responsibility of kings against the theory of their divine right to an absolute command over their subjects. Salmasius said, "As to the pretended pact between a king and his subjects, certainly there is none in kingdoms born of force of arms, as almost all existing kingdoms are," and he thought it simply ridiculous to say, as the English did, that a king was the minister and servant of his people, and waged not his own wars, but theirs. Milton wrote to convince the many and the few. To the thinkers the great body of argument was addressed ; for them he appealed out of his own highest nature to their highest sense of right ; but he satisfied he many, too, by blending with his answer vigorous combat of the kind that alone would win attention from the thoughtless. On another occasion he had said, "There cannot be a more proper object of indignation and scorn together than a false

prophet taken in the greatest, dearest, and most dangerous cheat —the cheat of souls—in the disclosing whereof, if it be harmful to be angry, and withal to cast a lowering smile, when the properest object calls for both, it will be long enough ere any be able to say why those two most rational faculties of human intellect, anger and laughter, were first seated in the breast of man." And now Milton had not only to cast back the contumelies of Salmasius against the English people, but scorned an advocacy that, upon a question of the welfare of humanity, was on a vital point not what the writer thought, but what he had agreed to say. He trusted still to the fair battle of thought. At the end of the preface to his reply he said, "And now I would entreat the illustrious States of Holland to take off their prohibition, and suffer the book to be publicly sold; for when I have detected the vanity, ignorance, and falsehood that it is full of, the farther it spreads the more effectually it will be suppressed." In the noble close to his Defence, Milton urged on the people of England that they must themselves refute their adversary, by a constant endeavour to outdo all men's bad words with their own good deeds. God had heard their prayers, but now, he said, you must show "as great justice, temperance, and moderation in the maintaining your liberty as you have shown courage in freeing yourselves from slavery."

7. In 1650, the year in which this Defence appeared, there was a son born to Milton, and lost in its infancy. In 1651 he left his lodgings for a pretty garden-house next to Lord Scudamore's, and opening into the Park, now No. 19, York Street, Westminster. In 1652 his third daughter, Deborah, was born there, and at the same time his wife died, on the 2nd of May. In the following year Milton reinstated his wife's family at Forest Hill, by recovering for them, with Christopher's help, part of the exorbitant fines levied on their land.

In the year of his wife's death appeared "The Cry of Royal Blood to Heaven against the English Parricides" (*Regii Sanguinis Clamor*), another Latin appeal to Europe. Saumaise had meant to reply to Milton, but his health was failing still. He died in 1653. The new attack upon the English was written by a Frenchman, Pierre Dumoulin, who wrote afterwards a treatise on Peace of Soul and Content of Mind, and was made a Prebendary of Canterbury; but its actual promoter and nominal author was Alexander More, a Protestant divine, born at Languedoc, where his father, a Scotchman, was principal of the

college. More had been professor of Greek at Geneva, but in
1649 disagreement with colleagues obliged him to leave, and
he went to Middleburg, afterwards to Amsterdam and Paris.
His personal character was notoriously worthless. Milton's
"Second Defence of the People of England," published in 1654,
was followed by a defence of himself. On the 16th of December,
1653, Cromwell had been made Lord Protector of the Commonwealth, and Milton's Second Defence, published in 1654, contains
expression of the nation's faith in him as "father of his country,"
and earnestly admonishes him that his country has entrusted to
his hands her freedom. In the duties before him there are, said
Milton, difficulties to which those of war are child's play. He
must not suffer that liberty for which he encountered so many
perils to sustain any violence at his own hands, or any from
those of others ; and he must look for counsel to men who had
shared his dangers, "men of the utmost moderation, integrity,
and valour ; not rendered savage or austere by the sight of so
much bloodshed and of so many forms of death ; but inclined
to justice, to the reverence of the Deity, to a sympathy with
human suffering, and animated for the preservation of liberty
with a zeal strengthened by the hazards which for its sake they
have encountered." Of his countrymen during the struggle they
had gone through Milton says here, "No illusions of glory, no
extravagant emulation of the ancients influenced them with a
thirst for ideal liberty ; but the rectitude of their lives and the
sobriety of their habits taught them the only true and safe road
to real liberty ; and they took up arms only to defend the
sanctity of the laws and the rights of conscience." Of himself
he says, "No one ever knew me either soliciting anything myself
or through my friends. I usually kept myself secluded at home,
where my own property, part of which had been withheld during
the civil commotions, and part of which had been absorbed
in the oppressive contributions which I had to sustain, afforded
me a scanty subsistence."

8. In 1654, gradual loss of sight in the remaining eye ended
in Milton's complete blindness. Its cause was not in the eyes
themselves, which remained unimpaired, but in the nerve of
sight ; it was a form of blindness then known, from a wrong
theory of its cause, as gutta serena ("drop serene"), but now
called amaurosis. Its predisposing cause in Milton was the
gouty constitution which he must have inherited, and of
which, at last, he died. Its exciting cause was exhaustion

of nervous power by excessive use of his eyes in study from childhood.

In 1654, then, Milton was blind, his wife had been dead two years, and when she died left him in charge of three little girls, of whom the eldest was but six years old, the youngest a new-born infant. But it was not until two years after his blindness became complete, or about four years after the death of his first wife, that Milton—the ages of his three motherless girls being then ten, nine, and four — married again. His second wife was Catherine, daughter of Captain Woodcock, of Hackney. She died in a year, at birth of her first child, and the child followed her. How tenderly Milton had sought to bring into his home with this second wife a companion to himself, with womanly care for his little girls, his sonnet " on his deceased wife" shows. He had dreamt of her one night after her death as coming to him before he awoke to blindness, with veiled face—for he had never seen her :

> " Methought I saw my late espoused saint
> Brought to me like Alcestis from the grave.
> *     *     *     *
> And such as yet once more I trust to have
> Full sight of her in heaven without restraint—
> Came, vested all in white, pure as her mind :
> Her face was veil'd, yet to my fancied sight,
> Love, sweetness, goodness, in her person shined
> So clear, as in no face with more delight ;
> But oh, as to embrace me she inclined,
> I waked, she fled, and day brought back my night !"

9. At this time Milton took reduced pay as Latin or Foreign Secretary, and was assisted in his work by **Andrew Marvell**. Andrew Marvell, born in November, 1620, was son of a clergyman, and master of the Grammar School at Kingston-upon-Hull. He was sent at fifteen to Trinity College, Cambridge. When he was still a youth his father was drowned by crossing the Humber in stormy weather with a young lady, who was resolved to return home after a christening at his house. She was the only daughter of a widow, who, considering how Mr. Marvell's life had been lost, took charge of his son, completed his education, and at her death left him her property. Andrew Marvell graduated as B.A. in 1638, and about 1642 went abroad, spending four years in foreign travel. After his return he was at Bilbrough, in Yorkshire, teaching languages to the only daughter of Lord Fairfax, and his first poems were upon the Hill and

Grove at Bilbrough and upon the House at Nun-Appleton, another seat of Fairfax's, in Yorkshire. In 1653, Milton recommended the appointment of Marvell as his assistant secretary, but at that time without success. He described him, both from report and "personal converse," as of "singular desert;" told that he had been four years abroad, in Holland, France, Italy, and Spain, knew these four languages, and was well read in Latin and Greek. With characteristic kindliness, Milton added to his recommendation of young Marvell, "This, my lord, I write sincerely, without any other end than to perform my duty to the public in helping them to an able servant; laying aside those jealousies and that emulation which mine own condition might suggest to me by bringing in such a coadjutor."

Milton sent, in 1654, his "Second Defence of the People of England" to Cromwell by Andrew Marvell's hand; and in 1657 Cromwell made Marvell tutor to young Mr. Denton, the son of an old friend who had died leaving the Protector his boy's guardian. Andrew Marvell's quality had now made itself known, and in the same year, 1657, he obtained the office of assistant-secretary to Milton for the foreign correspondence. What was written officially for foreigners was Latin; but unofficial correspondence and conversation in the chief languages of Europe would be required also, and for this Milton and Marvell were both qualified.

10. At the beginning of the Commonwealth there were among the young men born in the reign of Charles I., and from seventeen to twenty-one years old at the time of his execution, John Bunyan, George Villiers Duke of Buckingham, Robert Boyle, and Sir William Temple, all born in the year 1628; the divines of after years, Isaac Barrow and John Tillotson, both born in 1630; John Dryden, born in 1631; and John Locke, born in 1632. Isaac Newton, ten years younger, was a child of seven at the beginning of the Commonwealth.

Among men of the elder generations who died during the Commonwealth were the dramatists, John Webster and Thomas Heywood (date unknown); John Selden (1652); James Usher (1656), his last years being occupied in the production of his *Annals*, first in Latin (1650 and 1653), and then in an English translation of his own, published in 1658, as *Annals of the World deduced from the Origin of Time, and continued to the Destruction of the Temple, containing the History of the Old and New Testament.* John Taylor, the Water Poet, died in 1654;

John Hales in 1656; William Harvey in 1657; Richard Love-lace in 1658; John Cleveland in 1659. Among those born under the Commonwealth were no writers of higher mark than Jeremy Collier, John Oldham, and Thomas Otway. ·

A few plays by Elizabethan Stuart dramatists were printed under the Commonwealth, as, in 1656, Ford and Dekker's " Sun's Darling," and " The Old Law," by Massinger, Middleton, and Rowley; but that race of writers survived only in **James Shirley** (ch. viii. § 33), who had served the Earl (afterwards Duke) of New-castle during the wars, and helped him to write plays. Under the Commonwealth, Shirley printed some of his old plays, but theatres being closed, he kept a prosperous school in Whitefriars, and wrote grammars. Shirley had among his friends in trouble **Thomas Stanley** (born 1624), son of Sir Thomas Stanley, of Hertfordshire, who lived in the Middle Temple, and produced under the Commonwealth, in 1655, *A History of Philosophy*, popular in its time, and translated into Latin and Dutch.

**Dr. Jasper Mayne** (ch. viii. § 36), during the Common-wealth, was chaplain to the Earl of Devonshire, where he was brought into the society of Thomas Hobbes, whom he did not like.

11. **Thomas Hobbes** (ch. viii. § 66) was active under the Com-monwealth. In 1650 he published a treatise on *Human Nature; or, the Fundamental Elements of Policy*, and another, *De Corpore Politico; or, the Elements of Law, Moral and Politic*. In the following year, 1651, appeared his *Leviathan; or, the Matter, Form, and Power of a Commonwealth, Ecclesiastical and Civil*. This book he caused to be written on vellum for presentation to Prince Charles; but the divines were in arms against Hobbes for opinions which they considered hostile to religion. Upholder as he was of the supremacy of kings, Charles naturally avoided him. No man can hurt religion by being as true as it is in his power to be; and that Hobbes was. Our judgment of a man ought never to depend upon whether or not we agree with him in opinion. Hobbes was an independent thinker, and retained his independence when he might have lapsed into the mere hanger-on of a noble house, or, by dwelling only on some part of his opinion, have looked for profit as a flatterer of royalty. At Chatsworth he gave his morning to exercise and paying respects to the family and its visitors; at noon he went to his study, ate his dinner alone without ceremony, shut himself in with ten or twelve pipes of tobacco, and gave his mind free play. Hobbes's

*Leviathan,* "occasioned," he says, "by the disorders of the present time," is in four parts, 1, Of Man; 2, Of Commonwealth; 3, Of a Christian Commonwealth; 4, Of the Kingdom of Darkness. Whatever can be compounded of parts Hobbes called a body; man, imitating nature, or the art by which God governs the world, creates "that great Leviathan called the Commonwealth or State, which is but an artificial man, though of greater stature and strength than the natural, for whose protection and defence it was intended." In this huge body the sovereignty is an artificial soul, as giving life and motion to all its parts. (1.) The matter and artificer of it is Man. Men are by nature equal, and their natural state is one of war, each being governed by his own reason, and with a right to everything that he can get. But he may agree to lay down this right, and be content with so much liberty against other men as he would like them to have against himself. Retaining certain natural rights of self-preservation, man makes a covenant which is the origin of government, and injustice then consists simply in breach of that covenant. (2.) For the particular security not to be had by the law of nature a covenant is made, which forms man into the Commonwealth, and is the basis of the rights and just power or authority of a sovereign, who becomes thenceforth as soul to the body. The subjects to a monarch thus constituted cannot without his leave throw off or transfer monarchy, because they are bound by their covenant. "And whereas," says Hobbes, "some men have pretended, for their disobedience to their own sovereign, a new covenant, made not with men but with God; this also is unjust: for there is no covenant with God but by mediation of somebody that representeth God's person; which none doth but God's lieutenant, who hath the sovereignty under God." (3.) Reason directs public worship of God, but since a Commonwealth is but as one person, it ought also to exhibit to God but one worship. There is no universal Church, because there is no power on earth to which all other Commonwealths are subject; but there are Christians in many states, each subject to the Commonwealth of which he is a member. It is the function of the constituted supreme power to determine what doctrines are fit for peace and to be taught the subjects. All pastors in a church exercise their office by Civil Right; the civil sovereign alone is pastor by Divine Right. The command of the civil sovereign, having Divine warrant, may be obeyed without forfeiture of life eternal; therefore not to obey is unjust. All that is necessary to salvation is contained in Faith in Christ and Obedience to Laws. (4.) The "Rulers of the Darkness ot this World" are the confederacy of deceivers that, to obtain dominion over men in this present world, endeavour by dark and erroneous doctrines to extinguish in them the light both of Nature and of the Gospel; and so to disprepare them for the kingdom of God to come.

Much of the detail in "Leviathan" and other writings led to a belief that the doctrines of Hobbes were destructive to Christianity and all religion. This was expressed by Dr. Bramhall, Bishop of Derry, in a book called *The Catching of Leviathan*, to which Hobbes wrote an answer. Hobbes published, in 1654, a treatise written in 1652, *Of Liberty and Necessity, wherein all Controversy concerning Predestination, Election, Free-will, Grace, Merits, Reprobation, &c., is fully Decided and Cleared.* Dr. Bramhall undertook to show him that on these points also he was to be by no means clear of controversy.

**Sir Robert Filmer** (ch. viii. § 67) published, in 1652, *Observations upon Mr. Hobbes's Leviathan, Mr. Milton against Salmasius, and H. Grotius De Jure Belli et Pacis, concerning the Originall of Government.* Filmer repudiated Hobbes's notion of authority established by a covenant among men naturally equal, his own faith being that authority was given by Divine appointment from the first.

12. The writings of **James Harrington** show from another point the energy with which the mind of our British Leviathan was now in debate within itself (ch. i. § 1). James Harrington, born in 1611, eldest son of Sir Sapcotes Harrington, was of a good Rutlandshire family. In 1629 he entered as a gentleman commoner of Trinity College, Oxford. His father died before he was of age. He went to Holland, Denmark, Germany, and France, and to Italy, where he became an admirer of the Venetian Republic. After his return he lived a studious life, and was generous in care for his younger brothers and sisters. At the beginning of 1647 he was appointed to wait on Charles I., after his surrender to the English Commissioners, went with him from Newcastle, and was one of his grooms of the chamber at Holmby House. The king preferred his company, talked with him of books and foreign parts, and was only a little impatient when Harrington, a philosophical republican, entertained His Majesty with a theory of an ideal Commonwealth. Harrington

U

was with Charles in the Isle of Wight, but was afterwards separated from him because he would not take an oath against connivance at the king's escape. After the king's execution Harrington worked out his view of government in the book which he called *The Commonwealth of Oceana.* Oceana was England, and he styled Scotland Marpesia, Ireland Panopæa, Henry VII. Panurgus, Henry VIII. Coraunus, Queen Elizabeth Parthenia, and so forth. Oceàna being island, seems, said Harrington, like Venice, to have been designed by God for a Commonwealth; but Venice, because of its limited extent and want of arms, "can be no more than a Commonwealth for preservation: whereas this, reduced to the like government, is a Commonwealth for increase." At the foundation of Harrington's theory was the doctrine that empire follows the balance of property. He began with a sketch of the principles of government among the ancients and among the moderns, arguing throughout that dominion is property, and that, except in cities whose revenue is in trade, the form of empire is determined by the balance of dominion or property in land. If one man be, like the Grand Turk, sole landlord, or overbalance the people three parts in four, his empire is Absolute Monarchy. If the nobility be the landlords, or overbalance the people to the like proportion, that is the Gothic balance, and the empire is Mixed Monarchy, as that of Spain or Poland, and of Oceana, till "the Statute of Alienations broke the pillars by giving way to the nobility to sell their estates." If the whole people be landlords, or hold the lands so .divided that no one man or small body of men overbalance them, the empire (unless force intervene) is a Commonwealth. Any possible attempt to maintain government in opposition to this principle leads, said Harrington, to disorder. Where a nobility holds half the property, and the people the other half, the one must eat out the other, as the people did the nobility in Athens, and the nobility the people in Rome. After illustrating this position, Harrington cited, under feigned names, nine of the most famous forms of legislation known in history; and out of what he took to be the good points of each, with additions and modifications of his own invention, he produced a Council of Legislators and a Model Commonwealth for his Oceana. Olphaus Megaletor (Oliver Cromwell), the most victorious captain and incomparable patriot, general of the army, was made by its suffrage Lord Archon of Oceana; fifty select persons sat as a Council to assist him. The materials

of a Commonwealth are the people; these the Lord Archon and
his Council divided into freemen or citizens, and servants. The
servants were not to share in the government until able to live
of themselves. The citizens were divided into youths (from
eighteen to thirty) and elders; also, according to their means,
into horse and foot; and, according to their habitations, into
parishes, hundreds, and tribes. A thousand surveyors, each
with a district assigned to him, "being every one furnish'd with
a convenient proportion of urns, balls, and balloting-boxes (in
the use whereof they had been formerly exercised), and now
arriving each at his respective parishes, began with the people
by teaching them their first lesson, which was the ballot; and
though they found them in the beginning somewhat froward, as
at toys, with which (while they were in expectation of greater
matters from a Council of Legislators) they conceived themselves to be abused, they came within awhile to think them
pretty sport, and at length such as might very soberly be used
in good earnest." Then followed an account of the machinery
of balloting in each parish for deputies, only the elders being
the electors; of balloting also for the new pastor by the elders
of the congregation in every parish church, with provision
saving the rights of all Dissenters; and for the election of
justices and high constables, captains and ensigns, coroners
and jurymen, by ballot, among deputies of the parishes, and so
throughout; "the ballot of Venice, as it is fitted by several
alterations, to be the constant and only way of giving suffrage
in this Commonwealth." The method of voting by ballot in the
national Senate was illustrated by a picture. The full scheme
of a Commonwealth was worked out in the "Oceana" with much
detail. Harrington's manuscript was seized and carried to
Whitehall, but pleasantly recovered by appeal to Cromwell
through his daughter Lady Claypole, and published in 1656,
inscribed "to His Highness, the Lord Protector of the Commonwealth of England, Scotland, and Ireland." Like all books
that represented the activity of independent thought on the
great questions of the day, Harrington's "Oceana" produced
pamphlets in attack and in defence. Its chief opponents were
Dr. Henry Ferne, afterwards Bishop of Chester, and Matthew
Wren, one of the votaries of experimental science, out of whose
meetings the Royal Society was presently to spring, and of
whom Harrington said they had "an excellent faculty of magnifying a Flea and diminishing a Commonwealth." Partly to

the opinions of Hobbes and partly to those of Harrington, Richard Baxter opposed his "Holy Commonwealth." Harrington published an abridgment of his political scheme in 1659, as *The Art of Lawgiving;* and established, in the latter days of the Commonwealth, a club called the *Rota*, which met at the "Turk's Head," kept by one Miles, in the New Palace Yard, Westminster, and sat round an oval table, with a passage cut in the middle of it by which Miles delivered his coffee. The Rota discussed principles of government, and voted by ballot. Its ballot-box was the first seen in England. Milton's old pupil, Cyriac Skinner, was one of the members of this Club, which was named from a doctrine of its supporters, that in the chief legislative body a third part of the members should rote out by ballot every year and be incapable for three years of re-election; by which principle of rotation Parliament would be completely renewed every ninth year. Magistrates also were to be chosen for only three years, and, of course, by ballot.

13. **Richard Baxter**, in his *Holy Commonwealth; or, Political Aphorisms, opening the true Principles of Government*, opposed his title to the heathenish Commonwealth of other theorists, and pleaded the cause of Monarchy. Baxter was born in 1615, at High Ercall, by the Wrekin, in Shropshire. After living ten years there with his grandfather, he went to Eaton Constantine, to his father, who had become very devout after loss of much of his estate by gambling. Richard Baxter's chief place of education was the free school at Wroxeter. From Wroxeter he went to be the one pupil of Mr. Wicksteed, chaplain of Ludlow Castle (ch. viii. § 53); then he taught in Wroxeter school for a few months, had cough with spitting of blood, and began the systematic study of theology. "My faults," said Baxter, "are no disgrace to any University, for I was of none; I have little but what I had out of books and inconsiderable helps of country tutors. Weakness and pain helped me to study how to die; that set me on studying how to live." In 1638 Baxter became head master of a free school just founded at Dudley, took orders, went to Bridgenorth, and was forced by Laud's Church policy into Nonconformity. In 1640 he settled in Kidderminster, whence he was driven after two years by Royalist opposition. His life and his thoughts were unsettled by the Civil War. He signed the Covenant, and afterwards repented. He was with the army of the Parliament as military Chaplain, and found there that "the most frequent and vehement

disputes were for liberty of conscience, as they called it—that is, that the civil magistrate had nothing to do to determine matters of religion by constraint and restraint." He battled against their opinions, and was unpopular, but towards the close of the Civil Wars Baxter had a severe illness, and it was during this illness that he wrote his *Saints' Everlasting Rest*, first published in 1650. Under the Commonwealth, Baxter was opposed to Crom-well, argued privately with him on his position in the State, and, as we have seen, supported Monarchy in the political discussions of the day.

**John Howe**, Cromwell's chaplain, was fifteen years younger than Baxter. He was born in 1630, at Loughborough, where his father was minister of the parish. When John Howe was about three years old, his father was suspended and condemned to fine, imprisonment, and recantation by the High Commission Court, for opposing " The Book of Sports," which offended Puritans by encouraging Sunday afternoon amusements, and for praying in his church "that God would preserve the prince in the true religion, which there was cause to fear." King James I.'s De-claration to his subjects concerning lawful sports to be used on Sundays was published in 1618, and professed to have originated in the desire to take away a hindrance to the conversion of Roman Catholics by checking the Puritans in their endeavour to repress "lawfull recreation and exercise upon the Sundayes afternoone, after the ending of all diuine seruice." Charles I. re-issued this declaration in 1633, with an added command for the observance of wakes. The reprint of James's proclamation with the ratification of Charles added was that " Book of Sports " which Howe's father was punished for opposing. He escaped to Ireland, and was there till 1641, when he returned with his boy, and settled in Lancashire. In 1647, John Howe, aged seventeen, entered Christ's College, Cambridge, as a sizar. He took his degree of B.A. at Cambridge, and was at Oxford in the first years of the Commonwealth. He formed there his own system of theology, became M.A. in 1652, was ordained, and became, at two-and-twenty, pastor at Great Torrington, in Devon-shire. The energy with which in these days the religious life of England was animating the great social changes may be illus-trated by Howe's work for his flock on any one of the frequent fast-days. He began with them at nine a.m., prayed during a quarter of an hour for blessing upon the day's work, then read and explained a chapter for three-quarters of an hour, then prayed for

an hour, then preached for an hour and prayed again for half an
hour, then retired for a quarter of an hour's refreshment—the
people singing all the while—returned to his pulpit, prayed for
another hour, preached for another hour, and finished at four p.m.,
with one half-hour more of prayer, doing it all singly, and with his
whole soul in it all.   In 1654 Howe married the daughter of an
elder minister.   In 1656 he happened to be in London on a Sunday, and went, out of curiosity, to Whitehall Chapel, to see the
Lord Protector and his family.   But the Lord Protector saw also
the young divine in his clerical dress ; sent for him after service,
and asked him to preach on the following Sunday.   He preached,
was asked to preach again, and was at last urged by Cromwell
to stay by him as his domestic chaplain.   He took that office,
and was made also lecturer at St. Margaret's, Westminster, the
parish church of the House of Commons.   In three months he
was writing from Whitehall to Baxter, for counsel as to those duties
of which it would be most useful 'for him to remind the rulers,
and he was supporting at head-quarters a plan of Baxter's for
producing a more open fellowship among Christians of hitherto
contending sects.   Zealous and fearless enough to preach before
Cromwell against a point of the Protector's own faith, Howe was
thoroughly tolerant.   When Thomas Fuller had to satisfy the
Triers—a board for examining ministers before they were inducted to a charge—he was hard pressed upon a particular
point, and said to Howe, good-humouredly, " You may observe,
sir, that I am a pretty corpulent man, and I have to go through
a passage that is very strait ; be so kind as to give me a shove
and help me through."   Howe got him through.   John Howe
was Cromwell's chaplain to the last, and remained in the same
office during the nine months' rule of the Protector's son,
Richard.   The best of his many books, *The Living Temple,*
appeared in two parts, in 1676 and 1702.   Howe lived till 1705.

14.  **Thomas Fuller** (ch. viii. § 59), who married, in 1654, a
sister of Lord Baltinglasse, wrote during the Commonwealth his
*Pisgah-Sight of Palestine* (1650), an account of Palestine and its
people, illustrative of Scripture ; his *Abel Redivivus* (1651),
being " Lives and Deaths of the Modern Divines, written by
several able and learned men ;" and (in 1656), in folio, *The
Church History of Britain,* from the Birth of Christ to 1648,
which was not the less a piece of sound, well-studied work for
being quaint in style, good-humoured, and witty

**Jeremy Taylor** (ch. viii. § 70) published, in 1649, *The*

*Great Exemplar of Sanctity and Holy Life, according to the Christian Institution, described in the History of the Life and Death of Christ;* in 1650, his *Holy Living,* with "Prayers for our Rulers," altered afterwards to "Prayers for the King;" in 1651, his *Holy Dying;* and the first volume for the "Summer Half-year" (the second, for the "Winter Half-year," followed in 1653) of *A Course of Sermons for all the Sundaies in the Year.* His friend, Lady Carbery, died in October, 1650, and Taylor preached her funeral sermon with the tender piety of friendship, Jeremy Taylor, when he wrote verse, failed as a poet. He was no master in that form of expression; but natural grace of mind, with a fine culture, liveliness of fancy, the unaffected purity of his own standard of life upon earth, and, in the midst of all the tumult of the time, "the strange evenness and untroubled passage" with which he was himself, as he said of Lady Carbery, "sliding towards his ocean of God and of infinity with a certain and silent motion," has filled his prose with the true poetry of life. In 1655 he applied the name of Lord Carbery's house to a book of devotion, *The Golden Grove; or, a Manual of Daily Prayers and Letanies fitted to the Dayes of the Week: also, Festival Hymns, according to the Manner of the Ancient Church.* Jeremy Taylor was imprisoned twice during the Commonwealth, and brought down on himself a controversy upon original sin, by his *Unum Necessarium; or, The Doctrine and Practice of Repentance.* In 1656 he lost two children by small-pox and fever, and had only one son left of the family by his second marriage. In 1657 he published a *Discourse on the Measures and Offices of Friendship,* addressed to Mrs. Catherine Philips, with whom we shall meet again as the first English-woman who earned good fame as a poetess. At this time Jeremy Taylor was preaching in London, and had John Evelyn among his friends. Lord Conway, who had a residence at Portmore, offered him the post of alternate lecturer at Lisburn, nine miles from his house. Taylor accepted it, and went to Ireland in the summer of 1658. Even then he was not left wholly in peace; "for," he wrote, "a Presbyterian and a mad-man have informed against me as a dangerous man to their religion, and for using the sign of the cross in baptism." He was taken to Dublin, but obtained easy acquittal.

15. **John Bunyan** was born in 1628, the son of a poor tinker, at Elstow, in Bedfordshire. He was sent to a free school for the poor, and then worked with his father. As a youth of

seventeen he was combatant in the Civil War. He was married, at nineteen, to a wife who helped him to recover the art of reading, over the only books she had —" The Practice of Piety" and "The Plain Man's Pathway to Heaven." He went regularly to church, but joined in the sports after the Sunday afternoon's service, which had been a point of special defiance to the Puritans, by the proclamation of James I., in 1618, re-issued by Charles I. in 1633. Once Bunyan was arrested in his Sunday sport by the imagination of a voice from heaven. Presently he gave up swearing, bell-ringing, and games and dances on the green. Then came the time of what he looked upon as his conversion, brought about by hearing the conversation of some women as he stood near with his tinker's barrow. They referred him to their minister. He says that he was tempted to sell Christ, and heard, when in bed one morning, a voice that reiterated, "Sell Him, sell Him, sell Him." This condition was followed by illness which was mistaken for consumption ; but Bunyan recovered, and became robust. In 1657 he was deacon of his church at Bedford, and his private exhortations caused him to be invited to take turns in village preaching. Country people came to him by hundreds. Only ordained ministers might preach. In 1658 complaint was lodged against Bunyan ; but under the Commonwealth he was left unmolested.

16. **George Fox**, founder of the Society of Friends, was about four years older than Bunyan. He was born at Fenny Drayton, Leicestershire, in July, 1624, the son of a respectable weaver. He was taught reading and writing, and then placed with a shoemaker, who also kept sheep. Fox minded the sheep. His mind from childhood was fixed upon Bible study, he was true of word, and as he took the Scripture "Verily" for his most solemn form of assertion, it was understood that, "If George says 'Verily,' there is no moving him." At twenty, in obedience to words that seemed to answer prayer, he left his home, and, having means enough for simple life without a trade, spent about nine months in towns where he was unknown, and free to wander and reflect. He made himself a suit of leather clothes, that would last long without renewal, and gave himself up to intense religious meditation. He came home still unsettled, and again moved restlessly about, profoundly dwelling upon the relation of his soul to God. The result was uttermost rejection of all forms and ceremonies as a part of true religion. "God," he said to himself, "dwells not in temples made with

hands, but in the hearts of His obedient people." The Church of Christ was, he felt, a living church; and he became zealous against reverence paid to churches of brick and stone, which he denied to be churches, and thenceforth called steeple-houses. He not only set himself against those parts of ceremonial which had been a source of contest from the days of Cranmer to the days of Laud, but utterly against all ceremonial, in Church and State. He realised to his own mind a Christian commonwealth in which the civil power is obeyed as far as conscience permits, and, if disobeyed, never resisted; in which the great religious bond of love makes all men equal before God, by teaching man to be the Friend of man. In such a community there should be no untrue forms of ceremonial, no reverence by using the plural pronoun, and addressing one as if he were two, by scraping the foot, or uncovering the head. In all things the simple word of truth was to be all-sufficient, so that Christians would swear not at all, but their word would be simply Yea or Nay. He would have a church of souls with no paid minister, no formal minister of any kind, no formal prayers, and no formal preaching. At the meetings of such a church there should none speak unless it were borne in upon any one that there was something to say fresh from the heart, but in that case each man or woman was free to address the assembled friends. It was in 1647 that Fox began to spread his opinions, and gather friends. Some of their first meetings were held at Dukinfield and Manchester. The protest against formalism was so complete and so unflinching, that it brought the followers of Fox into constant collision with the usages and laws, or supposed laws, of society. If an oath had to be taken it was refused, because it was an oath, and the penalty was borne of the refusal. The hat not removed in church, or in a court of justice, or by a son in presence of his father; the courteous "you" transformed to "thou" in days when "thou," as now in Germany, was used only to an inferior or to an equal friend—offences such as these against the established forms led, Fox says, to "great rage, blows, punchings, beatings, and imprisonments." Fox was imprisoned first at Nottingham, in 1649, because the spire of the great church had caused him to "go and cry against yonder great idol and the worshippers therein." He stopped the preacher with contradiction in the middle of his sermon, and was imprisoned for interruption of the service; but his religious fervour won the heart of one of the sheriffs, and he was quickly released. But

U*

in 1650 he was arrested at Derby for telling " plain and homely truths" at a gathering summoned by Presbyterian preachers, was taken before the magistrates, and suffered much from Justice Gervas Bennet.   It was this justice who first gave to Fox and his friends in derision the name of Quakers, because Fox bade him tremble and quake before the power of the Lord. At Derby, Fox was imprisoned for twelve months in the common gaol on a charge of blasphemy, while his religious life answered the charge, and he, as a guiltless man, refused either to go through the form of being bound to good behaviour, or to allow any one to be surety for him.   At last he was released unconditionally.   He then preached and drew followers to his cause in Yorkshire and Westmoreland; was charged with blasphemy at Lancaster; imprisoned, in 1653, at Carlisle, and released when the case was brought before Cromwell's first Parliament. In his home at Drayton, in 1654, he disputed with the clergy, was arrested on suspicion of holding or encouraging seditious meetings, and was sent to Cromwell, who heard him at length while he was dressing, took his hand as he left, and said, with tears in his eyes, " Come again to my house, for if thou and I were but an hour a day together, we should be nearer one to the other." Fox was free again, but he and his followers were still persecuted. The character of other interviews shows clearly that Cromwell recognised a true man in George Fox.   His intense religious fervour led to acts of seeming insanity, when a sudden impulse, biblical in its form, was taken with simple faith for a Divine prompting, and acted upon straightway.   The body also, both in John Bunyan and in George Fox, was sometimes fevered by the intensity of spiritual life.   George Fox's followers were unflinching in their protest.   In 1659 two thousand of them had suffered more or less in the foul gaols; and 164 of the Friends offered themselves in place of that number of their fellow-worshippers whom they found to be in danger of death from continuance of their imprisonment.   Fox wrote letters, of which many were collected, and about 150 doctrinal pieces.   He lived until 1690, and his *Journal of his Life, Travels, Sufferings, &c.,* was published in 1694.

17.   Everywhere there was in those days the quickened spirit of inquiry.   It entered into politics; and patriotic thinkers, representing many forms of mind, active in fresh examination of the framework of society, sought to find their way to the first principles on whcih established forms of government are

founded, and part false from true.  It entered into religion; and devout men, also representing many forms of mind, went straight to the Bible as the source of revealed truth, seeking to find their way to the first principles on which established forms of faith are founded, and part false from true.  It entered into science; and followers of Bacon, hoping to draw wisdom from the work of the All-wise, went straight to Nature as the source of all our material knowledge, and sought, by putting aside previous impressions where they interfered with a new search for truth, to find their way to the first principles upon which a true science is built.

18. These men of science, who were drawn together in the time of Civil War, were active still under the Commonwealth. There was **Robert Boyle** (ch. viii. § 64), with a special turn for chemical investigation, and an ever-present sense of God in nature.  During the Commonwealth it was chiefly at Boyle's house, in Oxford, with his sister, Lady Ranelagh, for hostess, that the knot of associated men of science had their meetings. There was **Samuel Hartlib** (ch. viii. § 63), one of the first to suggest fellowship in the pursuit of knowledge, a foreigner who spent his whole fortune for the well-being of England, and was still at work under the Commonwealth, issuing practical books that taught the English farmer to improve his crops.  Hartlib's services were recognised by Cromwell with a pension of £300 a year.  This ceased at the Restoration, and Hartlib died poor and neglected.  There was **John Wallis,** Savilian Professor of Geometry at Oxford (ch. viii. § 64), who prepared the way for Newton.  Newton's binomial theorem was a corollary of the results of Wallis on the quadrature of curves.  Wallis published, in 1655, his chief mathematical work, *Arithmetica Infinitorum,* with a prefixed treatise on Conic Sections.  **Thomas Hobbes,** who swam out of his depth in mathematics, supposed himself to have squared the circle.  Wallis commented on this in his *Elenchus Geometriæ Hobbianæ.*  Hobbes, who never took contradiction well, retorted with *Six Lessons to the Professor of Mathematics at Oxford.*  Wallis replied, in 1656, with *Due Correction for Mr. Hobbes ; or, School Discipline for not saying his Lesson right.*  Hobbes rejoined with *Stigmas; or, The Marks of the Absurd Geometry, &c., of Dr. Wallis :* and the controversy went on for some time, Wallis being in the right, and also cleverer than Hobbes in conduct of the controversy. The best of his retorts was *Hobbius Heautontimoroumenos*

(named from one of the comedies of Terence, Hobbes, the Self-Tormentor), published in 1663. Wallis lived till 1703. Another of these comrades in science was **John Evelyn**, born in 1620, the son of Richard Evelyn, of Wotton, Surrey. Evelyn loved art and nature, had ample means, left England because of the Civil War, and travelled in France and Italy; came home in 1651 with his fair and clever wife, and amused himself with the laying out of his famous gardens at Sayes Court, quietly holding stout Royalist opinions, and avoiding a pledge to the Covenant. In 1659 he sketched a plan of a philosophical college, and published also an *Apology for the Royal Party*. There was also, as Evelyn calls him, that most obliging and universally curious **Dr. Wilkins** (ch. viii. § 59, 64), who had wonderful transparent apiaries; a hollow statue which spoke through a concealed tube; also "a variety of shadows, dyals, perspectives, and many other artificial, mathematical, and magical curiosities, . . . . . most of them of his own and that prodigious young scholar, Mr. Chr. Wren." Young Christopher Wren, nephew of the Bishop of Ely, was also in fellowship among these followers of science. There was **William Petty** (knighted in 1661), born in 1623, son of a clothier at Romsey, educated at the Romsey Grammar School, and Caen, in Normandy. He began active life with some experience in the navy, then, after 1643, was in France and the Netherlands for three years, and studied medicine and anatomy. In 1648 he published *The Advice of W. P. to Mr. Samuel Hartlib for the Advancement of some Particular Parts of Learning*, that is, the extension of education to objects more connected with the business of life. He went to Oxford, taught anatomy and chemistry, became in 1649 M.D. and Fellow of Brazenose. Some of the first scientific gatherings were in his rooms. In 1652 he was physician to the army in Ireland; in 1654 obtained a contract for the accurate survey of lands forfeited by the rebellion of 1641, by which he made £10,000 while instituting the first scientific survey of Ireland. Having surveyed the forfeited lands, Petty was a commissioner for parting them among the soldiery, and he enriched himself by profitable purchases. At the end of the Commonwealth his personal dealing with Irish lands was brought in question by Sir Hierom Sankey, but the Commonwealth and the inquiry into Dr. Petty's dealings came to an abrupt end together.

19. The garden and museum at Lambeth of John Tradescant the son, founded by John Tradescant the father, traveller in

Europe, Asia, Africa, and afterwards gardener to Charles I., was one of the scientific curiosities of London under the Commonwealth. Tradescant published, in 1656, a catalogue of the collection, the *Museum Tradescantium.* A great friend of his was **Elias Ashmole** (born 1617, died 1692), who under the Commonwealth studied alchemy; published, in 1652, a *Theatrum Chemicum Britannicum, containing several Poetical Pieces of our famous Philosophers who have written the Hermetique Mysteries in their own Ancient Language;* in 1654, a *Fasciculus Chemicus;* and, in 1658, *The Way to Bliss,* which expressed faith as it is in the Philosopher's Stone. Ashmole published in 1672 a *History of the Garter.*

When John Tradescant the younger died, in 1662, he left his museum to Ashmole, and the widow contested his right unsuccessfully. Ashmole acquired the museum and gave it to Oxford, where, with his own books and papers afterwards added to the gift, it is now known as the Ashmolean Museum.

Ashmole's taste for the marvellous in nature was shared by **Sir Kenelm Digby.** An Everard Digby, who died in 1592, wrote curious books; his son, Sir Everard, knighted by James I., was hanged, drawn, and quartered for giving £1,500 towards expenses of the Gunpowder Plot. The eldest son of that Sir Everard was Sir Kenelm Digby, born in 1603, and educated at Oxford. He travelled in Spain, discovered, as he supposed, a sympathetic powder for cure of wounds, was knighted in 1623, was sent with a fleet into the Mediterranean in 1628, and returned to the faith of his fathers as a Roman Catholic in 1636. In the Civil Wars he helped the king among the Roman Catholics, and was then exile in France until Cromwell's supremacy gave him liberty to revisit England; but he returned to France. He published, in 1644, a mystical interpretation of *The 22nd Stanza in the 9th Canto of the 2nd Book of Spenser's Faerie Queene;* in 1645, *Two Treatises on the Nature of Bodies and of Man's Soule;* took lively interest in Palingenesis; wrote *Observations upon Sir T. Browne's Religio Medici,* and was ingenious in the pursuit of forms of learning which have proved to be more curious than true. He died in 1665.

**William Dugdale,** the antiquary, born in 1605 at Coleshill, Warwickshire, was educated at Coventry Free School, and by his father. In 1644 he was made Chester Herald, and was with Charles I. throughout the Civil Wars. Under the Commonwealth, he produced in 1655, with Roger Dodsworth, the first of the three folio volumes (the others followed in 1661 and 1673) of his *Monasticon Anglicanum*, giving chiefly the foundation charters of the English monasteries. Many Puritans saw in the book a first attempt towards the re-introduction of Catholicism. In 1656, Dugdale published the result of twenty years' research in a learned, accurate, and honest account of his native county, *The Antiquities of Warwickshire*, the best of our old county histories. This was followed, in 1658, by the *History of St. Paul's Cathedral in London, from its Foundation until these Times.* Dugdale was knighted after the Restoration, and made Garter King at Arms. He died in 1686.

John Rushworth, born in Northumberland, in 1607, and educated at Oxford and Lincoln's Inn, was an expert shorthand writer, employed to take down the most important debates in Parliament and in high courts of justice. In 1640 he was one of the clerks of the House of Commons, and afterwards secretary to Fairfax. In 1658 he was member for Berwick. In was in 1659 that he issued, dedicated to Richard, Lord Protector, the first of the seven folios (the last appeared in 1701) of his *Historical Collections of Private Matters of State, Weighty Matters in Law, Remarkable Proceedings in Five Parliaments, from 1618 to 1648. The Tryall of Thomas, Earl of Strafford,* forming an eighth volume, appeared in 1680. From Rushworth to light literature is a stride.

20. Sir Richard Fanshawe, a firm Royalist, and secretary to Charles Prince of Wales, to whom he had dedicated, in 1647, his *Translation of the Pastor Fido of Guarini*, published in 1655 a translation of the national epic of the Portuguese, *The Lusiad* of Camoens. Sir Thomas Urquhart published, in 1653, a translation of Rabelais' *Gargantua and Pantagruel.* Translations of the French romances of Magdeleine de Scuderi, Calprenède, and others, appeared throughout the Commonwealth, and an attempt was made at an original imitation of them by Roger Boyle (ch. viii. § 64) in his *Parthenissa.* But Nathaniel Ingelo, D.D., who looked upon the writing and reading of romances as "impertinencies of mankind," and poetry and romances as "pitiful things," produced, in 1660, an antidote, in form of a romance, called *Bentivoglio and Urania,* wherein Bentivoglio, or Goodwill, born in the higher Theoprepia, or a state worthy of God, is enamoured of Urania, who represents Heavenly Light or Divine Wisdom, and has allegorical experience in divers godly and ungodly states.

21. **Izaak Walton,** born in 1593 at Stafford, was a hosier in the Royal Exchange, and afterwards in Fleet Street, near Chancery Lane, making money enough to retire upon and take life easily. In 1636 he married a descendant of Cranmer. He was left a widower in 1640. In 1647 he married a sister of Bishop Ken, and he had children by each of his wives. He was a hearty Royalist and churchman, who loved God and Nature with simplicity of mind, and greatly relished a day's fishing. In 1653 he gave to his countrymen the first edition of *The Compleat Angler; or, the Contemplative Man's Recreation: being a Discourse of Fish and Fishing,* in form of dialogue, with pictures of the trout, pike, carp, tench, perch, and barbel. In 1655 a second edition appeared, almost rewritten, much enlarged, with three speakers, Piscator, Venator (taking the place of Viator), and Auceps ; Fisher, Hunter, and Birdcatcher ; and with four more plates of fish.

22. We now turn to the poets. **Abraham Cowley** (ch. viii. § 48) remained in France till 1656, and then returned to England, was taken prisoner by messengers in search for another man, and released upon security given for him by a friend. He remained quietly in London till the death of Cromwell, published in 1656, in folio, the first edition of his *Works,* declaring in the preface that his desire had been for some days past, and did still very vehemently continue, to retire himself to some of the American plantations, and forsake this world for ever. In 1657 he was made M.D. of Oxford, and with a poet's sense of the charm of science, he devoted himself to the study of botany. Dr. Cowley took a lively interest in the fellowship of men of science, and the best way of advancing scientific knowledge. At the death of Cromwell he returned to France.

23. **Sir William Davenant** (ch. viii. § 36) was living with Lord Jermyn in the Louvre, when, in January, 1650, he dated the *Discourse upon Gondibert, an Heroic Poem,* addressed to Thomas Hobbes, who had been reading the poem as it was written. It occurred to him to go to the loyal colony of Virginia with a body of workmen, but the vessel in which he sailed was taken by one of the ships of the Parliament, and Davenant carried to the Isle of Wight, where he was imprisoned in Cowes Castle. There he continued "Gondibert" to the middle of the third book, and as that was half the poem—for his plan was to have five books answering to five acts of a play, with cantos answering to scenes—he wrote a "Postscript to the

Reader," dated "Cowes Castle, October 22, 1650," and sent it to
the press. With its prefatory discourse and postscript this half
of the poem, which was left a fragment, appeared in 1651. Of
the two books written at the date of the preface "to his much
Honour'd Friend, Mr. Hobbes," Davenant said, "I delay the
publication of any part of the poem till I can send it you from
America, whither I now speedily prepare; having the folly to
hope that when I am in another world (though not in the
common sense of dying) I shall find my readers, even the
poets of the present age, as temperate and benign as we are
all to the dead whose remote excellence cannot hinder our reputation." In the Postscript to the Reader, written at Cowes Castle,
Davenant believed that he should, in the common sense, speak
from another world, and said, "'Tis high time to strike sail and
cast anchor, though I have but run half my course, when at the
helm I am threatened with Death, who, though he can visit us
but once, seems troublesome; and even in the innocent can
beget such a gravity as disturbs the music of verse." Davenant
was brought to London for trial, and his life was saved, some
say by two Aldermen of York, some say by Milton. He was
detained a prisoner for two years, but treated with indulgence.
Davenant and his "Gondibert" were laughed at, in 1653, by
four writers of *Certain Verses written by several of the Author's
Friends, to be Reprinted in the Second Edition of Gondibert,*
and these critics were not "temperate and benign." But the
book has interest for the student. The long, grave, half-philo-
sophical preface, prosing about rhyming, marks very distinctly
that influence of France upon our literature of which the
grounds were then fully established, and which came in with the
Restoration. As to metre, the use in a heroic poem of what
Davenant called his "interwoven stanza of four" was preferred,
he said, "because he believed it would be more pleasant to the
reader, in a work of length, to give this respite or pause between
every stanza (having endeavoured that each should contain a
period) than to run him out of breath with continued couplets.
Nor doth alternate rhyme by any lowliness of cadence make
the sound less heroick, but rather adapt it to a plain and stately
composing of musick ; and the brevity of the stanza renders it
less subtle to the composer and more easy to the singer, which,
in *stilo recitativo,* when the story is long, is chiefly requisite."
He adds that he was chiefly influenced by hope that the cantos
of his poem might really be sung at village feasts. Dryden for

a time followed Davenant's adoption of this measure as the heroic stanza, which Davenant found ready perfected in Sir John Davies's *Nosce Teipsum* (ch. vii. § 81). In its design, the poem blends something of the political philosophy of Hobbes with the keen interest in Nature quickened by Bacon, and seeks to build on them a song of love and war, designed, as Davenant said of it in his Postscript, " to strip Nature naked, and clothe her again in the perfect shape of virtue." The Lombard Aribert rules in Verona ; his only child is a daughter, Rhodalind. Either Prince Oswald or Duke Gondibert, both mighty in war, might wed the damsel, and succeed to empire. Oswald is brilliant and ambitious of rule ; Gondibert has ambition of a higher kind. Each has his camp and faction. There is a hunting of Gondibert's, leading to an ambush of Oswald's, and a duel, in which Gondibert is wounded, Oswald slain. Then, at the close of the first book, Gondibert is taken, by advice of the aged Ulfin, to the house of Astragon, the wise and wealthy.

> " Though cautious Nature, check'd by Destiny,
>   Has many secrets she would ne'er impart ;
> This famed philosopher is Nature's spie,
>   And hireless gives th' intelligence to Art."

In the next book, after four cantos of events at Verona, the seat of empire, where Rhodalind can give supreme rule with her hand, we find Gondibert in the house of Astragon, which is more full of signs of deep inquiry into Nature than John Evelyn found the lodgings of " the most obliging and universally curious Dr. Wilkins." Over one gate is written, " Great Nature's Office," where old busy men are labouring as Nature's registrars; there is a garden, " Nature's Nursery ;" a skeleton room, called " The Cabinet of Death :"

> " Which some the Monument of Bodies name ;
>   The Arke, which saves from graves all dying kindes;
> This to a structure led, long known to Fame,
>   And call'd the Monument of Vanish'd Minds.

> " Where, when they thought they saw in well-sought books,
>   Th' assembled soules of all that Men hold wise,
> It bred such awfull rev'rence in their looks,
>   As if they saw the bury'd writers rise."

There is also a triple Temple, dedicate " To Days of Praise, and Penitence, and Prayer." In this half mythical house of Astragon there is Birtha, daughter of Astragon, who tends Gondibert's wounds, and whose womanhood is partly an ideal of the simple beauty and beneficence of Nature. Her Gondibert loves, though Aribert had destined him for Rhodalind. When Gondibert seeks Astragon's assent to this love, he has to give an account of himself to the lady's father, and expresses much of the main thought of the poem by telling in what way he is ambitious. He has vanquished the Huns, he would conquer the world, but only because division of interest is the main cause of discord (here Thomas Hobbes approved the writer's principles), and Gondibert wished to bring the universe, for its own peace, under a single monarchy. A great warlike ambition ; but, he says :

> " But let not what so needfully was done,
>    Though still pursued, make you ambition feare;
> For could I force all monarchys to one,
>    That universal crown I would not weare.

> " He who does blindly soar at Rhodalind,
>    Mounts like seeld Doves, still higher from his case ;
> And in the lust of empire he may finde,
>    High hope does better than fruition please.

> " The victor's solid recompence is rest :
>    And 'tis unjust that chiefs who pleasure shunn,
> Toyling in youth, should be in age opprest
>    With greater toyles, by ruling what they wonn.

> " Here all reward of conquest I would finde :
>    Leave shining thrones for Birtha in a shade ;
> With Nature's quiet wonders fill my minde,
>    And praise her most because she Birtha made."

Davenant is artificial in his praise of Nature, but there is true dignity in many passages of " Gondibert," with frequent felicity of expression ; there is such aim at ingenuity as we find in the later Euphuists, modified by the new influence of the French critical school. Its chance of a good reception was not improved by Hobbes's declaration, made in its behalf, that "Gondibert" deserved to last as long as the Æneid or Iliad. The jest was ready against a book not serious enough for one-half of the public and too serious for the other, that said, laughing :

> " Room for the best of poets heroic,
> If you'll believe two wits and a stoic.
> Down go the Iliads, down go the Æneidos :
> All must give place to the Gondiberteidos."

24. **John Dryden**, born August 9th, 1631, at Aldwincle, in Northamptonshire, of good family, was educated at Westminster School, where he wrote some euphuistic verse, and at Trinity College, Cambridge, where he took his degree of B.A. in 1654.

the year of his father's death. He seems to have come to London in the summer of 1657, and was at first in the home of his cousin, and Cromwell's friend, Sir Gilbert Pickering. He was in his twenty-eighth year when Cromwell died, on the 3rd of September, 1658, and he wrote, after the funeral, one of the many tributes to his memory, *Heroic Stanzas on the Death of Oliver Cromwell,* using the measure of " Gondibert." With customary strain to be ingenious, there was a simple close.

**George Wither** (ch. viii. § 39) and **Andrew Marvell** (§ 8) had followed Cromwell's career with their verse. George Wither had published, in 1655, a poem called *The Protector,* upon Cromwell's acceptance of that office. Andrew Marvell had written loyally on the first anniversary of his government, and he was now among the mourners.

25. The fabric held together by the might of Cromwell fell after his death. His amiable son Richard called a Parliament which vanished before the power of the army, and Richard Cromwell passed from the Protectorate to private life. He lived to see the Revolution, and he died a country gentleman, in 1712. The attempt to revive the Long Parliament as a central authority failed also to restrain the army. George Monk marched out of Scotland to subdue, as he said, the military tyranny in England, but it was soon evident that there was no hopeful way out of the discord but a Restoration of the Monarchy.

In these days **John Milton,** first fearing predominance of the Presbyterians, had addressed to the Parliament called by Richard Cromwell *A Treatise of Civil Power in Ecclesiastical Causes,* showing that it is not lawful for any power on earth to compel in matters of religion. To the revived Long Parliament, which succeeded the short-lived Parliament called by Richard Cromwell, Milton addressed *Considerations touching the Likeliest Means to Remove Hirelings out of the Church,* in which he argued that each pastor should be maintained by his own flock. On the 20th of October, 1659, Milton wrote a letter to a friend *On the Ruptures of the Commonwealth,* and addressed a brief letter to Monk on *The Present Means and Brief Delineation of a Free Commonwealth, easy to be put in Practice and without Delay.* A few months later he published a pamphlet called *The Ready and Easy Way to Establish a Free Commonwealth, and the Excellence thereof, compared with the Inconveniences and Dangers of Re-admitting Kingship in this Nation.* His main suggestion was : " Being now in anarchy, without a counselling

and governing power, and the army, I suppose, finding themselves insufficient to discharge at once both military and civil
affairs, the first thing to be found out with all speed, without
which no Commonwealth can subsist, must be a. Senate, or
General Council of State, in whom must be the power, first, to
preserve the public peace; next, the commerce with foreign
nations; and, lastly, to raise monies for the management of
those affairs : this must either be the Parliament re-admitted to
sit, or a Council of State allowed of by the army, since they
only now have the power.   The terms to be stood on are, liberty
of conscience to all professing Scripture to be their rule of faith
and worship ; and the abjuration of a single person." He urged
to the last moment of hope the first principles of what he said
is not called amiss "the good old cause ;" adding, "Thus much
I should perhaps have said, though I was sure I should have
spoken only to trees and stones; and had none to cry to but
with the prophet, ' O Earth, Earth, Earth !' to tell the very soil
itself what her perverse inhabitants are deaf to.   Nay, though
what I have spoke should happen (which Thou suffer not who
didst create mankind free, nor Thou next who didst redeem us
from being servants of men !) to be the last words of our expiring
liberty."

———

## CHAPTER X.

### FROM THE COMMONWEALTH TO THE REVOLUTION.

#### CHARLES II.

1. THE second of the Four Periods into which, with reference
to outward fashion only, English Literature is divided, was
now passing away, and the third—*the Period of French
Influence*—came in rapidly after the accession of Charles II.
We should have felt it sooner if we had been less intent upon
our own affairs during the Civil Wars and Commonwealth, for
the foundations of it were laid while Charles I. was our king.
The English Royalists who lived in France after the failure of
the king's cause were there being educated in its fashions.

   Italian influence in France, blended as elsewhere with influence of Spain, had produced forms answering to English
Euphuism ; but they were of a lower kind, because there was
not then in France, as in England, a time of special literary
energy.  There was a taste for long stories, blending the Spanish

chivalrous romance with the pastoral (ch. vi. § 39, 40), a more
marked classicism, a delight in sounding phrases. In the time
of our Elizabeth, Ronsard (b. 1524, d. 1585) was extending the
use of the ten-syllabled line, rhymed in couplets, which became
to the French what blank verse has become to us. Our poets
were then experimenting, with various success, in the enrichment
of the language with new words from Greek and Latin. Ronsard
carried this far, tried Latin signs of comparison—*docte, doctieun
doctime*—and made a verse of three of the words that he wished
he might use—" *ocymore, dyspotme, oligochronien.*" Malherbe
(b. 1555, d. 1628) followed Ronsard with finer taste, and was,
during the first quarter of the seventeenth century, the most
determined champion of the verbal purity of French. He was
known as the tyrant of words and syllables. " This doctor in
the vulgar tongue," wrote his friend Balzac, "used to say that
for so many years he had been trying to de-Gasconise the
Court, and that he could not do it. Death surprised him when
rounding a period." " An hour before his death," says his disciple Racan, " Malherbe woke up with a start to correct his
nurse for use of a word that was not good French ; and when
his confessor reprimanded him for that, he said that he could
not help himself, and that he would defend to the death the
purity of the French language." We only understand, but
Malherbe felt, the need of earnest critical attention to the
unsettled language of his country as France rose in power.
Deliberation in the choice of words made him a slow writer.
He spent three years in the composition of an ode intended to
console the President of Verdun for the loss of a wife. When
the ode was finished, the president had consoled himself by
marrying another.

Sidney's *Arcadia* (ch. vii. § 44), which first blended the heroic
with the pastoral in a long romance of adventure, had in England no direct imitators ; but in France books of this kind established themselves as the prose fiction of their day, and the best
of them, as we have seen (ch. ix. § 20) were translated into English
during the Civil Wars and Commonwealth. Their line began
with the *Astrée* of Honoré d'Urfé (b. 1567, d. 1625), first appearing in 1608, 10, 19, in three parts. His secretary, Baro, published the rest, completed in 1627. Our version appeared in 1657,
as *Astrea : A Romance written in French, by Messere Honoré
d'Urfe, and Translated by a Person of Quality*. Its primitive
Arcadia was placed in the valley of the Loire ; and its variety of

excellent discourses and extraordinary sententiousness caused
Richelieu to say that " He was not to be admitted into the
Academy of Wit who had not been well read in ' Astrea.'"

In the year 1600, Catherine de Vivonne de Pisani married, at
the age of sixteen, the Marquis de Rambouillet, Grand Master
of the Royal Wardrobe.  In the polite society gathered about
her at the Hôtel Rambouillet ladies predominated; and they
occupied themselves so much with the maintenance of a high
standard of refinement in speech, that they and their imitators
were called, in all gravity, and in their own fine phrase, *Les
Précieuses.*  French was unsettled.  North and south of the
Loire the difference of dialect was almost difference of language.
The court dialect of Henry IV. and his Béarnois shocked all
the polite Parisians; the king's oaths shocked the ladies.  In
those days polite people were reading the polite dialogue of
" Astrée," *Malherbe* was upholding purity of French, *Vaugelas*
(b. 1585, d. 1650) was giving his mind to a refined study of the
language, and the blossom-time of French literature was not far
distant.  But of what use to have a literature where the language
is unsettled, and a hundred years hence its changes will defeat
an author's hope of outliving his body in his books ?  The ladies
of Paris began the movement of reform by exercising social
influence; and the Marquise de Rambouillet, reinforced by four
daughters, was still living at the accession of Charles II.  Many
English " persons of quality " in Paris during the Commonwealth
would be among her guests.  The doings of the *Précieuses,*
though blended with weakness and affectation, had importance
for the history of literature during the first thirty or forty years
of the seventeenth century.  Receiving company while on her bed,
after a fashion of the time and the manner of the whole community of the *Précieuses,* who followed in her steps—so giving
to fashion the phrase " courir les ruelles "—and in winter denying
fire as perilous to the complexion of herself and of her delicate
guests in chamber, corridor, or alcove, the Marquise de Rambouillet welcomed princes and wits at her weekly feasts of verbal
criticism.  Before her circle Pierre Corneille read his tragedies,
and the youth Bossuet first displayed the genius of the preacher.
Purity of speech was demanded of all who frequented the Hôtel
Rambouillet.  There was to be no unclean word, and much that
was common it pleased the particular genius of the house to call
unclean.  The marchioness disdaining her own common name
of Catherine, Malherbe tortured his wit and produced for her

instead of it Arthénice, its anagram. Vaugelas, the grammarian, ranked above princes at the Hôtel Rambouillet. " If the word *féliciter* is not yet French," wrote Balzac, " it will be so next year; M. de Vaugelas has given me his word not to oppose it." Over-familiar words, if tolerated by the French at large, were replaced at the head-quarters of polite speech by delicately-conceited phrases. As the marchioness saw company in her night-cap, and the idea Night-cap might have to be expressed in conversation, while the word was too coarse for choice lips, its association with sleep and dreams suggested that it might be referred to as "the innocent accomplice of falsehood." Laughter was clownish, but if mentioned it might be described as loss of seriousness. Literature itself was not to be debased into a pleasure for the vulgar; it was not to be national, it was to be all polite. In 1629, gatherings allied to these became habitual at the house of Valentine Conrart, one of the king's secretaries, who had a turn for books; and out of these meetings came Richelieu's suggestion that Conrart and his fellow-workers should proceed systematically, following a fashion common in Italy, but chiefly imitating the Academia della Crusca, founded in 1582, and rule over French, under royal letters-patent, as a *FRENCH ACADEMY*, with forty members. The formation of this academy was completed in 1636. It was to meet once a week, to labour with all possible care and diligence to give fixed rules to the language, and to make it more eloquent and fitter for the treatment of the arts and sciences. It was to produce a dictionary. Only words in the dictionary of the Academy were to be esteemed good French. It was to produce also a grammar, a treatise on rhetoric, and a treatise of poetry, establishing its laws for the politest literature of all kinds. The great question of choice of words, and criticism about verse and prose, now occupied many minds; and as Regnier said of the critics of this school, all they did was to prose about rhyme and rhyme about prose.

> " S'ils font quelque chose,
> C'est proser de la rime, et rimer de la prose."

Poets were small and romancers long-winded. The diffuse pastoral romances dealt only with the love and heroism of royal personages. The chief writers of those romances, all born about the beginning of the seventeenth century, were *Marin le Roy de Gomberville*, who wrote " Polexandre," " Cytherée," and " La Jeune Alcidiane;" *Gautier de Costes Seigneur de la Calprenède.*

who wrote " Silvandre," " Cleopatre " (1656), " Cassandre " (1642), and " Pharamond " (1661). Each was in ten or twelve volumes, which came out by instalments, two at a time. A rich lady married Calprenède, on condition that he would finish " Cleopatra," because there had been so long a pause that she feared she might go to her grave without having the last volume. Chief of the company of novelists was a lady, *Magdeleine de Scudéri*, six years younger and six times more clever than her prolific brother Georges, in whose name she published some of her stories. Georges himself wrote, says Boileau, a volume a month in defiance of good sense. Magdeleine, born in 1607, lived till 1701, and was called, with classical elegance, the Sappho of her age, chiefly for her ten-volume romances, " Artamene; ou, le Grand Cyrus" (1650), " Clelie "(1660), "Almahide; ou, l'Esclave Reine" (1660), &c. At the date of the accession of Charles II., French literature was about to pass out of this stage.

The year 1660 was the year in which *BOILEAU*, then twenty-four years old, wrote his first satire. Nicolas Boileau Despréaux, born in 1636, at the same time as the French Academy, was the son of an actuary. His mother died in his infancy; he was a sickly boy, subject to an unfriendly nurse. At twenty he was an advocate unfit for the Bar, turning his mind to theology; but his place not being in the pulpit, he abandoned the Church, and not the Church only, but also a benefice of eight hundred livres that he had been persuaded to hold at least for a certain term of years. In laying it down, he gave to the poor all it had brought him. " But," said an abbé, who himself owned many benefices, " that was a good thing to live upon, M. Boileau." " Not a doubt of it," Boileau answered; " but to die upon, Monsieur l'Abbé—to die upon ! " It was his honesty that gave permanent force to this man's genius. Resenting the degradation of taste in his day, Boileau laughed at the public that could see a rival to Corneille in Georges Scudéri, and could read with delight dainty romance after the manner of the *Précieuses*, by Scudéri's sister, Magdeleine, whose "Almahide; or, The Slave Queen," in eight volumes, appeared when the critic, a young man of four-and-twenty, was bent upon active war against all this emptiness that had usurped the place of honest wit. Chapelain, also, after thirty years' gestation, during which he was well nourished by the Duc de Longueville, had brought to light, when Boileau was a youth of twenty with a lively sense of the dull and absurd, twelve cantos of his " Pucelle." " I will make war against all this," said the young critic. It was urged upon him that he would bring a swarm of enemies about his ears. His answer was, " Well, I shall be an honest man, and never fear them."

It had been in the time of our Commonwealth that *MOLIÈRE* produced, in 1653, the first of his now recognised plays, " L'Etourdi," at Lyons; it was followed by " Le Dépit Amoureux," and by " Les Précieuses Ridicules," in 1659. By this time the *Précieuses* had become ridiculous through weak provincial imitations of the ladies—eight hundred or more—who still discussed polite language and literature in Paris. In 1660, Molière's theatrical company, as the " Troupe de Monsieur," began to act in the hall of the Palais Royal; and the rest of his plays were produced between 1660 and 1673, the year of his death. The elder Corneille was thirty-three years older than Racine; the age of Pierre Corneille being fifty-four, and of *JEAN RACINE* twenty-one, at the date of the Restoration. Racine's first tragedy appeared in 1664. Molière, about this time, when asked who were the chiefs of French literature, said, " Corneille and I. Racine is a 'bel esprit,' whom I have had great trouble in teaching to write verses." As for Corneille, before Molière began he had already written twenty-one pieces and 40,000 verses.

*PIERRE CORNEILLE* (b. 1606, d. 1684) began with comedies, turned to tragedy, in 1635, with his " Medea; " and in 1636 this was followed, when he was thirty, by the " Cid;" over which the French Academy set up a controversy. The academy had its letters-patent registered a few months after the triumphant appearance of the " Cid." Georges de Scudéri, who had written a dozen bad plays, abused the " Cid," and appealed to the academy. Richelieu, founder and "protector" of the academy, disliked the " Cid," and his wish obtained from Corneille the author's assent, which had been made necessary by its rules, before the academy could pass official judgment upon any work. Then the academy appointed a committee, and in due time published its "sentiments," in the midst of a shower of ink from the small critical pens. Study of Lope de Vega and Calderon (ch. viii. § 7) influenced Corneille, and, through him and others, the French drama generally. Their direct and indirect influence is visible in the comedies of intrigue which became common on the English stage after the Restoration. The vapid criticism of the French Academy caused Corneille to turn awhile from his work in disgust; but "Les Horaces" followed in 1639, and "Cinna" but a few months later, then "Polyeucte," &c. Corneille aimed at producing impressions of the heroic, and it was he who gave rise in this country to the Heroic Play that formed one feature in our literature under Charles II. At first there was a simple dignity in Corneille's tragedies; but in his later pieces he sought more intricacy of plot. His plays became less simple in form, more declamatory and inflated. They were, in fact, the progenitors of the heroic plays of Dryden. His measure, alike in comedy and tragedy, was the rhyming couplet of ten-syllabled lines, which now became known, from its use in French tragedies, as the heroic couplet. So it is still called, though with us Chaucer had used it in his "Canterbury Tales" but as an easy form of narrative verse; and Stephen Hawes evidently looked upon it as the measure for familiar and comic narrative (ch. vi. § 7). Corneille's heroic verses were establishing among French critics the measure of their serious drama. Italian criticism, soon to be surpassed in France, was still regarded as the best in Europe; and in Italy, in 1655, Cardinal Sforza Pallavicino published his "Erminigildo," with a long prefatory discourse to recommend the use of rhyme in tragedy. Corneille had at that time ceased awhile to produce dramas. He said that his poetry was decaying with his teeth, and employed himself in writing his three Essays on Dramatic Poetry—one on the Dramatic Poem generally, one on Tragedy in particular, and one on *The Three Unities.* These essays were finished in 1659; and thus it was just at the time of the accession of Charles II. that the much talk of the Three Unities of Time, Place, and Action, was put into the mouths of critics. Though partly drawn from Aristotle and the practice of the Greek theatre, it was from Corneille that they took the form in which they became current. Aristotle dwelt much and rightly upon unity of the fable—that is, Unity of Action—in a tragedy. He said also, incidentally, that "tragedy endeavours, as far as possible, to confine its action within a single revolution of the sun, or nearly so"—that is Unity of Time. As to Unity of Place, Corneille owned that he could not find it required by a single precept either in Aristotle or in Horace. In 1659, Corneille returned to the stage again, with "Œdipe," and wrote seven or eight weak plays between 1660 and 1665.

2. The English drama after the Restoration of the Stuarts, in 1660, was marked strongly by this influence of France.

**Sir William Davenant** (ch. viii. § 36; ix. § 23), after his release
from imprisonment, had evaded the interdict upon dramatic entertainments by opening Rutland House, Charterhouse Yard, on the
21st of May, 1656, for what he called operas. Blending of music
with dramatic action had its origin in Italy. An Italian drama
with musical accompaniments had been represented at the ·
Castle of St. Angelo, in 1480; but the first opera was performed
at Venice, in 1634. Davenant, therefore, was following a new
Italian fashion that had already found its way to France. At
Rutland House, Davenant produced the first part of his *Siege of
Rhodes*, with various scenery, each entry prepared by instrumental music, with dialogue in recitative interspersed with songs
and choruses; his attempt was that of the musician in his *Playhouse to Let*, who says:

> " I would have introduc'd heroique story
> *In stilo recitativo.*"

With the Restoration arose two patented dramatic companies, servants of the king and of his brother, the Duke of
York. Sir William Davenant's company was that of the Duke
of York's players, acting first at a theatre in Portugal Row,
Lincoln's Inn Fields, and afterwards in Dorset Gardens. Thomas
Betterton was the best actor in his company. The king's players
acted at the Cockpit until they were ready, in April, 1663, with a
new Theatre Royal, on the site of the present house in Drury
Lane. Their chief was **Thomas Killigrew** (b. 1611, d. 1684),
son of Sir Robert Killigrew, of Hanworth, near Hampton Court,
chamberlain to Queen Henrietta Maria. Thomas Killigrew had
been page of honour to Charles I., and had married a maid of
honour. He was witty and profligate, amused Charles II., who
made him Groom of the Bedchamber, and was one of the king's
familiar companions. Killigrew published, in 1664, nine *Plays*,
and thought it worth noting that he had written them in nine
different cities—London, Paris, Madrid, Rome, Turin, Florence,
Venice, Naples, and Basle. Killigrew, then, was manager of
the king's company; and **Davenant**, formally appointed Poet
Laureate, manager of the duke's. A clause in his patent said
that, "Whereas the women's parts in plays have hitherto been
acted by men in the habits of women, at which some have taken
offence, we do permit and give leave for the time to come that all
women's parts be acted by women on the stage." The actress's
profession, therefore, became established at the Restoration, and

women acted at both houses.    Actresses began to appear in
the time of Charles I.    In the *Court Beggar*, a comedy by Ben
Jonson's old servant, Richard Brome, acted in 1632, although not
printed till 1653, Lady Strangelove says, "The boy's a pretty
actor, and his mother can play her part.    The women now are
in great request."    Changes of scenery, also, which had been
introduced by Davenant under the Commonwealth, became at
the Restoration an established custom in both theatres.    In 1661,
Davenant revised his *Siege of Rhodes*, and produced the second
part, still including music and variety of measures, but using the
rhymed couplet as the staple of heroic dialogue.    It was the
first English play of its time that did so.    Davenant had, in
his former plays, written what had come to be taken for blank
verse ; but its degeneration had been rapid (ch. viii. § 34), and
blank verse in Davenant yielded such lines as these :

> " How did the governours of the
> Severe house, digest th' employment my
> Request did lay upon their gravities ?"

**3. John Dryden** (ch. ix. § 24) was among those who welcomed the new order of things, and his *Astræa Redux*, in honour
of the Restoration, was published at once by Henry Herringman.    Although this poem follows in Dryden's works the heroic
stanzas on the Death of Cromwell, it must be remembered that
there was an interval of eighteen months between their dates—
months busy with events that would be strong argument to a
mind like Dryden's against the political faith in which he had
been bred.    Until the death of Cromwell, nothing occurred to
change the course of family opinion which Dryden had inherited
and drew from those about him ; but the disposition of his
mind placed him among those whose nature it is to seek
peace by the upholding of authority.    The experience of the
last eighteen months of the Commonwealth made him no
mere flatterer of Monarchy, but, throughout the reign of
Charles II., the most active supporter of its claim to the
obedience of all.    In religion, the same tendency of mind led
him at last to find peace in reliance upon the supreme authority
of Rome.    He left opinions in which he had been bred for those
to which he had been born, and never swerved from them.
Maintenance of one central authority was the principle on which
philosophers, statesmen, poets, and a large part of the common
crowd of men based a consistent view of what was best for the
well-being of society.    The men who laid chief stress upon

the freedom of each to think and speak and act up to his own high sense of right, untrammelled by laws that could serve only to check individual development, had Milton for their chief; and though in apparent disrepute under Charles II., they were still the moving power in the country. But in the continual re-adjustment of the limit of authority made necessary by increasing power of thought in the many, the progress of England has been assured equally by the men of both parties, by the action and reaction on each other of these two natural types of opinion. There would be little use in a watch all spring and no cog-wheel, or all cog-wheel and no spring. Wider and deeper education of the people will some day make freedom in diversity produce a nobler harmony than was conceived by those who, in the time of a low general culture, saw hope of peace only in general sub-mission of all wills to one.

4. In the *Siege of Rhodes*, **Davenant** held by the extension of that theory of Hobbes's to contending nations as well as to contending men of the same country, which he had made the ground of Gondibert's ambition to subdue the world. His life was too much given to low pleasures, and he was called upon to entertain the frivolous. If Davenant could have felt with Milton that he who would excel in poetry should be himself a poem, his genius had wings to bear him higher than he ever reached. Among the musical love-passions of the *Siege of Rhodes*, he was still aiming at some embodiment of his thought that the nations of Christendom fail in their work for want of unity. They let the Turks occupy Rhodes because they could not join for succour. In his dedication of the published play to the Earl of Clarendon, Davenant (referring with honour to " the great images represented in tragedy by Monsieur Corneille ") says : " In this poem I have revived the remembrance of that desolation which was permitted by Christian princes, when they favoured the ambition of such as defended the diversity of religions (begot by the factions of learning) in Germany ; whilst those who would never admit learning into their empire (lest it should meddle with religion, and intangle it with controversie) did make Rhodes defenceless ; which was the only fortified academy in Christendom where divinity and arms were equally professed."

5. Opposite opinions were in conflict then in England ; such conflict, whenever it occurs, breeds thought in men ; and those who in quiet times would have thought with their fathers, often

changed their faith and were zealous in the new cause, as converts are apt to be, because of the strength of fresh conviction.
Dryden, in artificial strain, but not essentially dishonest, wrote
his *Astræa Redux* in 1660; and in 1661 addressed a panegyric
*To his Sacred Majesty*, on his coronation, and New Year's-day
verses, in 1662, *To my Lord Chancellor*, Lord Clarendon.

John Dryden's first comedy, in prose—*The Wild Gallant*,
produced in February, 1663, by the king's company—was a
failure.   He had no aptitude for the licentious light comedy now
in favour; but "The Wild Gallant" was followed, at the same
theatre, before the end of the year, by a tragi-comedy, *The Rival
Ladies*, which brought into play some of his higher powers, and
was a success.   Dryden was at the same time working with
Sir Robert Howard at his play of *The Indian Queen*, which
was produced at the king's theatre, with rich scenery and dresses,
in January, 1664.   Sir Robert Howard, born in 1626, was the
youngest son of the Earl of Berkshire.   He had been educated
at Magdalene College, Oxford, was now member for Stockbridge, and had shown his literary tastes by publishing, in
1660, *A Panegyrick to the King; Songs and Sonnets; the
Blind Lady, a Comedy; The Fourth Book of Virgil; Statius
his Achilleis, with Annotations;* and *A Panegyrick to General
Monk.*   Very complimentary lines by Dryden were prefixed
to that volume.   Sir Robert Howard, who was now one of
the better dramatists of the time, must not be confounded
with his contemporary, the Hon. Edward Howard, who
wrote worse plays, whose poem of *Bonduca, the British Princess*
(1669), became a jest of the wits, and whose verse the Earl
of Dorset called the "solid nonsense that abides all tests."
A friendship had been established between John Dryden
and Sir Robert Howard.   Dryden went with his friend to
the Earl of Berkshire's house at Charlton, in Wiltshire, worked
with him at *The Indian Queen*, and won his sister Elizabeth for
wife.   They were married in December, 1663, and *The Indian
Queen*, all written in heroic couplets, was produced in the
following month.   Dryden's *Rival Ladies* had been written in
blank verse, with some passages of heroic couplet.   In the
dedication of the published play (1664) to Roger Boyle, Earl of
Orrery, Dryden discussed his reasons for this.   Roger Boyle
(ch. ix. § 20), since we last met with him, was secretly helping
Charles under the Commonwealth, till Cromwell called upon
him, showed him intercepted letters, and invited him to choose

between prosecution and fidelity to the Republic. Boyle changed his party, and gave Cromwell the aid of his large Irish influence. In those days he began *Parthenissa*, which was in six volumes, the sixth volume not appearing until 1676. After the death of Cromwell, Roger Boyle worked for the Restoration. Charles II. made him Earl of Orrery and Lord Justice of Ireland. In his dedication of his *Rival Ladies* to this Earl of Orrery, Dryden started an argument upon the comparative merits of rhyme and blank verse in plays. The argument is interesting for the evidence it gives of the depths into which blank verse had fallen while Milton was using it for the measure of his " Paradise Lost." It should be remembered that, with insignificant exception (ch. vii. § 29), blank verse had never been used in our literature as the measure of a great narrative poem. On both sides of the controversy it was being taken for granted that the measure was too mean for that ; the question was only whether its resemblance to common prose did not make it proper for the dialogue of plays. Dryden, following Corneille, though he repudiated a French influence, now began to argue that the dignity of tragedy demanded rhyme. This was not, he said, a new way so much as an old way revived ; "for many years before Shakespeare's plays was the tragedy of 'Queen Gorboduc' in English verse." Gorboduc (ch. vii. § 8) was a king, not a queen; and the play was in blank verse, not in rhyme, as Dryden supposed. But supposing, he went on, the way were new, "Shall we oppose ourselves to the most polished and civilized nations of Europe ?" All the Spanish and Italian tragedies he had seen were in rhyme (but see ch. vi. § 41) ; for the French, he would not name them, because we admitted little from them but "the basest of their men, the extravagance of their fashions, and the frippery of their merchandize." Shakespeare, "to shun the pains of continual rhyming, invented that kind of rhyming which we call blank verse (but see ch. vi. § 47), but the French more properly *prose mesurée.*" Rhyme leads to inversions, but not in a skilful writer, and if they be avoided it has all the advantages of prose besides its own. "But the excellence and dignity of it were never fully known till Mr. Waller taught it ; he first made writing easily an art : first shew'd us to conclude the sense most commonly in distichs, which in the verse of those before him runs on for so many lines together that the reader is out of breath to overtake it."

6. Edmund **Waller** (ch. viii. § 42) was then living; he

died in 1687, aged eighty-two, and he showed his superiority
to predecessors by writing a new fifth act to Beaumont and
Fletcher's *Maid's Tragedy* (ch. viii. § 6). That play was interdicted under Charles II., because it was personal to His Majesty
in the suggestion that

> " On lustful kings
> Unlooked-for sudden deaths from heaven are sent."

Waller reconciled it to the new morality by a new fifth act.
in which the wronged Melantius is overpowered by the con-
descension of the lustful king, who offers him " satisfaction " in
a duel :

> " The royal sword thus drawn, has cur'd a wound
> For which no other salve could have been found.
> Your brothers now in arms ourselves we boast,
> A satisfaction for a sister lost.
> The blood of kings exposed, washes a stain
> Cleaner than thousands of the vulgar slain."

And the stern condemnation of the original play was ingeniously
conjured into

> " Long may he reign that is so far above
> All vice, all passion but excess of love ! "

7. Such were Mr. Waller's couplets with the sense concluded in distichs ; and **Dryden** was here one of the first to
show that ignorance of our literature before the Commonwealth
which characterized the English critics of the French school.
Out of this ignorance arose false estimates which have passed
from book to book, and would lead the unwary to suppose that
the art of writing good English in all its forms was discovered
by men who were alive to flatter one another in the reign of
Charles II. Dryden went on : " The sweetness of Mr. Waller's
lyric poesie was afterwards followed in the epic by Sir John
Denham, in his ' Cooper's Hill ' (ch. viii. § 46) ; a poem which
your lordship knows, for the majesty of the style is, and ever will
be, the exact standard of good writing." **Sir John Denham,**
who died in 1668, was also alive to be praised, and pleased no
doubt to hear his good meditations on the view from Cooper's
Hill described as an epic poem. It was Davenant's turn next.
" But if we owe the invention of it " (*i. e.* the right use of rhyme)
" to Mr. Waller, we are acknowledging for the noblest use of it
to **Sir William Davenant,** who at once brought it upon the
stage and made it perfect in the ' Siege of Rhodes.' " **Dryden**
then specified these advantages of rhyme over blank verse—(1)
aid to memory ; (2) sweetness of rhyme adding grace to the

smartness of a repartee; and (3) that it bounds and circum-scribes the fancy which, without it, tends to outrun judgment. In 1665, Dryden produced with success a play of his own, *The Indian Emperor*, a sequel to "The Indian Queen," but it was not published until 1667. In the same year, 1665, the Plague in London closed the theatres. Dryden's brother-in-law, Sir Robert Howard, publishing in 1665, as *Four New Plays*, his comedies of *The Surprisal* and *The Committee*, and his tragedies, *The Indian Queen* and *The Vestal Virgin*, put into his preface the chief points of his private argument with Dryden on behalf of blank verse in the drama. "Another way," he says, "of the ancients, which the French follow and our stage has now lately practised, is to write in rhyme; and this is the dispute betwixt many ingenious persons, whether verse in rhyme or verse without the sound, which may be called blank verse (though a hard expression), is to be preferred?" He held both proper, "one for a play, the other for a poem or copy of verses; a blank verse being as much too low for one as rhyme is unnatural for the other: a poem being a premeditated form of thought upon design'd occasions, ought not to be unfurnish'd of any harmony in words or sound: the other is presented as the effect of accidents not thought of." He argued that rhyme in a repartee, which should have its charm in sudden thought, makes it "rather look like the design of two than the answer of one." As to the checking of luxuriant fancy, he said, "he that wants judgment in the liberty of his fancy may as well show the defect of it in its confinement." He argued that great thoughts are not "more adorned by verse than verse unbeautified by mean ones, so that verse seems not only unfit in the best use of it, but much more in the worse, as when a servant is called or a door bid to be shut in rhyme. It is true Lord Orrery's plays in verse"—his *History of Henry V.*, *Mustapha*, *Black Prince*, and *Tryphon* were published in 1669—"are all majesty and ease, meeting every conceivable objection; this does not convince my reason, but employ my wonder." Let us share wonder at the verse of Roger Boyle, "all majesty and ease." Mustapha, son of Solyman the Magnificent, addresses the Queen of Hungary, whom he loves:

> "This visit without leave may rude appear:
> Yet, Madam, when you shall vouchsafe to know
> That I to-morrow must tow'rds Syria go,
> The opinion of my rudeness you'l re-call:
> I must attend you now or not at all."

v

Thus it was that French example set our writers prosing about rhyme, and this dignified style replaced the verse of Shakespeare, which had sunk so low in polite estimation. Yet in these days Milton, never to be understood by France, was attuning his divine song to the measure which was not held, even by the chief advocate for its use in tragedy, to be dignified enough for " a paper of verses." For Milton was

Unchanged
" To hoarse or mute, though fallen on evil days,
On evil days though fallen, and evil tongues ;
In darkness, and with dangers compassed round,
And solitude ; yet not alone, while thou
Visit'st my slumbers nightly, or when morn
Purples the east : still govern thou my song,
Urania, and fit audience find, though few."

**8. John Milton** (ch. viii. § 30, 51—55, 60, 62, 63, 65, 69; ch. ix. § 2—8, 25) at the Restoration withdrew from danger to a friend's house in Bartholomew Close, while his prosecution was voted by the Commons, and his " Iconoclastes " and " Defence of the People of England" were ordered to be burnt by the hangman. His friend, Andrew Marvell, was member for Hull; but Anthony à Wood says that Davenant now returned an old obligation (ch. ix. § 23), and saved Milton from being placed among the exceptions to the Act of Oblivion passed on the 29th of August. Milton was nevertheless arrested, but his release was ordered by the House of Commons on the 15th of December, and he appealed against the excessive fees charged for his imprisonment. For about a year he lived in Holborn, near Red Lion Square. In 1662 he was in Jewin Street, whence he removed to a small house in Artillery Walk, by Bunhill Fields, his home for the rest of his life. Robert Boyle's sister, Lady Ranelagh (ch. viii. § 64; ch. ix. § 18), was a kind and active friend, but his daughters were growing up in the home of a blind father without a mother's care, and he, too, needed domestic aid and comfort. In Jewin Street, by the advice of Dr. Paget, his physician, Milton again married. He was then fifty-four years old, and his third wife was a distant relation of the doctor's—Elizabeth, daughter of Mr. Randle Minshull, of Wistaston, Cheshire, born late in 1638, and married Feb. 11, 1663. She devoted herself to her husband; but the addition of a young wife into the household did not benefit the daughters. In 1662, Milton's eldest daughter, Anne, was sixteen ; his second daughter, Mary, was fifteen ; and Deborah, his youngest, ten. Milton's home life was

simple. He rose at four in summer, five in winter, heard a
chapter of the Hebrew Bible, and was left till seven in meditation. After breakfast he listened to reading and dictated till
noon. From twelve to one he walked, or took exercise in a
swing. At one he dined ; then until six he was occupied with
music, books, and composition. From six to eight he gave to
social chat with friends who came to visit him. His youngest
daughter, Deborah, said of Milton, many years after his death,
"that he was delightful company ; the life of the conversation,
not only on account of his flow of subject, but of his unaffected
cheerfulness and civility." At eight Milton supped, then smoked
a pipe, and went to bed at nine.

One of those who read to him was a young Quaker, Thomas
Ellwood. *The History of the Life of Thomas Ellwood . . .
Written by his Own Hand,* is a most interesting record of the
persecution suffered by the Quakers (ch. ix. § 16) in the reign of
Charles II. His troubles had been chiefly at home in Oxfordshire, when his desire to improve himself in knowledge urged on
his friend, Isaac Pennington, of Chalfont, caused Ellwood to
come to London. His "friend had an intimate acquaintance
with Dr. Paget, a physician of note in London, and he with John
Milton, a gentleman of great note for learning throughout the
learned world, for the accurate pieces he had written on various
subjects and occasions. This person having filled a public
station in the former times, lived now a private and retired life
in London, and having wholly lost his sight, kept always a man
to read to him, which usually was the son of some gentleman of
his acquaintance, whom, in kindness, he took to improve in his
learning." Ellwood, when twenty-three years old, obtained in
1662, through Dr. Paget, the liberty of coming to Milton's house
"when I would, and to read to him what books he should appoint me, which was all the favour I desired." Ellwood tells of
his courteous reception ; of Milton's teaching him the foreign
pronunciation of Latin ; and how Milton, "perceiving with what
earnest desire I pursued learning, gave me not only all the encouragement but all the help he could. For, having a curious
ear, he understood by my tone when I understood what I read,
and when I did not ; and accordingly would stop me, examine
me, and open the most difficult passages."

9. In 1665, London was desolated by the plague, and most
people who were able to escape from it into the country did so.
Young Thomas Ellwood, at Milton's request, took a small house

for him in Chalfont St. Giles. When Milton came to it Ellwood was in Aylesbury Prison, under a new and severe law, made specially against the meeting of Quakers for worship. "But now," he wrote, "being released and returned home, I soon made a visit to him to welcome him into the country. After some common discourses had passed between us, he called for a manuscript of his, which, being brought, he delivered to me, bidding me take it home with me and read it at my leisure, and when I had so done return it to him with my judgment thereupon. When I came home, and had set myself to read it, I found it was that excellent poem which he entitled *Paradise Lost.* After I had, with the best attention, read it through, I made him another visit, and returned him his book, with due acknowledgment of the favour he had done me in communicating it to me. He asked me how I liked it, and what I thought of it, which I modestly but freely told him ; and, after some further discourse about it, I pleasantly said to him, 'Thou hast said much here of Paradise Lost, but what hast thou to say of Paradise Found ?' He made me no answer, but sat some time in a muse ; then brake off that discourse, and fell upon another subject. After the sickness was over, and the city well cleansed and become safely habitable again, he returned thither. And when afterwards I went to wait on him there (which I seldom failed of doing whenever my occasions drew me to London), he showed me his second poem, called *Paradise Regained,* and in a pleasant tone said to me, 'This is owing to you ; for you put it into my head by the question you put to me at Chalfont, which before I had not thought of.'" It is still the same John Milton, sociable and kindly to the last. Ellwood's question was not a very wise one, because Milton's first poem did include what he had to say about Paradise Found. But Milton had tried its effect on a simple, pious mind, and Ellwood's question indicated to him that the average mind of a religious Englishman wanted yet more emphasis laid on the place of Christ in his religious system. His fit audience, though few, was of men who would put their souls into the reading of his poem. Ellwood, he knew, had no skill as a critic ; what he would bring to his reading would be a religious mood. It was this which had prompted the question, indicating that in him there was yet a religious want unsatisfied. Milton resolved to make his purpose sure, and wrote the second poem. *Paradise Lost,* then, was finished before the end of 1665 ; and *Paradise Regained* probably was written before April 27, 1667, the date of Milton's agreement with Samuel Simmons to sell him the copyright of " Paradise Lost " for £5, with conditional payment of another £5 when 1,300 copies had been sold, and of another £5 after the sale of 1,300 copies of the second edition, and of the third —each edition to be of not more than 1,500. Milton received altogether in his lifetime £10 for *Paradise Lost;* and his widow received £8 for her remaining interest in the copyright. The poem, divided at first into ten books, was well printed in a little quarto volume, price three shillings. It was without preface or note of any kind, and had no " Arguments " before the books. It was simply *Paradise Lost : a Poem written in Ten Books by John Milton,* and published in 1667. It had to be licensed. Cromwell had got rid of the licenser, but he was now revived, and the Rev. Thomas Tomkyns, chaplain to the Archbishop of Canterbury, suspected a political allusion in the lines

> " As when the sun, new risen,
> Looks through the horizontal misty air,
> Shorn of his beams ; or, from behind the moon,
> In dim eclipse disastrous twilight sheds
> On half the nations, and with fear of change
> Perplexes monarchs."

This perplexed Tomkyns ; but the difficulty was overcome, and Milton, the stronger as a poet for the years of waiting while he did day labour in the service of his country, gave to his countrymen the poem to which he had aspired when in his youth he nursed his wings at Horton, and whispered his dream of immortality into the ears of his friend Diodati (ch. viii. § 54). The subject chosen was the worthiest he had been able to conceive. He would enshrine in his work the religion of his country. Opening with invocation of the Holy Spirit, he made it his labour to

> " Assert Eternal Providence,
> And justify the ways of God to men."

Dryden was among the visitors of the companionable poet in his later years ; and in the preface to his " Fables," Dryden wrote : " Milton is the poetical son of Spenser. Milton has confessed to me that Spenser was his original." Spenser and Milton, indeed, have a distinct relation to each other as combatants on the same side in the same battle at two different points. Each, with his own marked individuality, expressed also, as a representative Englishman, the life of his own time. Different as their two great poems are in form and

structure, there is likeness in the difference; for the *Faerie
Queene,* in which all qualities of mind and soul are striving
heavenward, was a religious allegory on the ways of men to
God. "Paradise Lost" was designed to approach the national
religion from the other side, and show the relation, justify the
ways, of God to men. Milton furnished his epic with sublime
machinery, after the manner of Homer and Virgil, by taking
from the fathers of the Church the doctrine of angels and arch-
angels, and the story of the fall of Lucifer, which had from old
time been associated with the Scripture narrative (ch. iv. § 5).
The legend of Lucifer originated in a cry of the prophet against
Babylon (Isa. xiv. 12—15):—"How art thou fallen from heaven,
O Lucifer, son of the morning! how art thou cast down to the
ground, which didst weaken the nations! For thou hast said
in thine heart, I will ascend into heaven, I will exalt my throne
above the stars of God: I will sit also upon the mount of the
congregation, in the sides of the north: I will ascend above the
heights of the clouds; I will be like the most High. Yet thou
shalt be brought down to hell, to the sides of the pit." From
the time of St. Jerome downward, this symbolical representation of the King of Babylon in his splendour and his fall has
been applied to Satan in his fall from heaven, probably because
Babylon is in Scripture a type of tyrannical self-idolizing power,
and is connected in the book of Revelation with the empire of
the evil one. The use of this machinery, and that of the arch-
angels, enabled Milton to place Adam on earth between the
powers of heaven and hell, and represent the contest vividly
to the imagination. To represent the unseen by new combinations of the seen was inevitable. It is simply impossible to
describe that of which no man has ever had experience on earth.
Therefore Raphael tells Adam—

> " What surmounts the reach
> Of human sense, I shall delineate so
> By likening spiritual to corporal forms
> As may express them best; though what if earth
> Be but the shadow of heaven, and things therein
> Each to other like, more than on earth is thought?"

Milton's poetry shows deep traces of his study of Plato; and this
last question enables the mind of the reader to pass from admission that new combinations of the known must represent
the unknown, through philosophic thought, into a livelier
acceptance of the narrative so prefaced.

The poem, as we now have it in twelve books, falls naturally into three equal parts. We begin in the midst of the story. In the first four books Heaven, Earth, and Hell are opened to the imagination, and man is placed at his creation between the contending powers of good and evil. The next four books (v.—viii.) contain Raphael's narrative of the Past, through which we learn the events that concerned man before Adam was created. In the last four books we have the Fall and its consequence, with Michael's vision of the Future. This includes the Redemption of Man, and the whole dealing of God with him through Christ.

> " Now amplier known, thy Saviour and thy Lord :
> Last, in the clouds, from heaven to be reveal'd
> In glory of the Father, to dissolve
> Satan with his perverted world ; then raise
> From the conflagrant mass, purged and refined,
> New heavens, new earth, ages of endless date,
> Founded in righteousness, and peace, and love ;
> To bring forth fruits, joy and eternal bliss."

*Paradise Lost* is not to be judged prosaically by the standard of each reader's personal opinion on points of faith. It is the religion of its time, intensely biblical, and deals only with great features of national theology. Milton's chief argument for Divine justice is in answer to the questions, "Why was man permitted to fall?" and, " Man having fallen, how has God dealt with him ?" The answer to the first question came from Milton's soul : God made man free. He made a wrong use of his freedom ; but had he been formed capable only of choosing one of two alternatives, he would have had no choice, no liberty, no use of reason. The spirit of Milton's answer to the second question is expressed in the words of Adam :

> " O goodness infinite, goodness immense !
> That all this good of evil shall produce,
> And evil turn to good ; more wonderful
> Than that which by creation first brought forth
> Light out of darkness ! Full of doubt I stand,
> Whether I should repent me now of sin
> By me done and occasion'd ; or rejoice
> Much more, that much more good thereof shall spring ;
> To God more glory, more good-will to men
> From God, and over wrath Grace shall abound."

Not unwilling to dwell on this theme, Milton, in the four books of *Paradise Regained*, represented in another form the contest of Christ with the Power of Evil, by taking for his subject the Temptation in the Wilderness. But this is no sequel to "Paradise Lost," which, including the whole reach

of time, began and ended in infinity. The reader whose form
of religion is not Milton's may find its spirit at the heart of
"Paradise Lost" in the predominant conviction that God is
supreme in Wisdom and Beneficence, and the resolve to draw
for himself and his countrymen this truth of truths out of the
national theology. *Paradise Lost* repays long and close study
of the distribution of its parts, the subtle skill of its transitions,
the blending of sweet echoes from the noblest wisdom of the
past with the fresh thought of a poet who can approach the
Mount of God, hymning His praise, can make the hollow deep
resound with bold defiance of Omnipotence, can sing with
tender grace of Eve in Paradise, and out of his own innocence
can speak her purity. Milton's precision in the use of words,
conspicuous in his early poems, fills "Paradise Lost" with subtle
delicacies of expression. Thus, when it is asked in hell who
shall cross the dark unbottom'd infinite abyss to the new world,

> " Upborne with indefatigable wings
> Over the vast abrupt, ere he arrive
> The happy isle ; "

familiar as we are with books in which we had better not look
at each word with all our understanding, we may not stay to
observe that "arrive" strictly means "come to the shores of."
So Chaucer said of his Knight :

> " In the greete see
> At many a noble arrive hadde he be."

Among passages in "Paradise Lost" interesting for their relation to the life and times of Milton are the reference to his
blindness in the opening of Bk. III., ll. 1—54, the reference to
hirelings in Bk. IV., ll. 183—193, and the opening of Bk. VII.,
ll. 1—39.

10. **John Dryden** (§ 7) also left London during the plague.
He went to the house of his father-in-law, at Charlton, and there
still discussed rhyme and blank verse with Sir Robert Howard.
Dryden's eldest son was born at Charlton, in 1665 or 1666, for
he remained there in 1666, the year of the Fire of London
and of a great sea-fight with the Dutch. Both these events he
celebrated in a poem, "Annus Mirabilis," the wonderful year ;
and his reply to his brother-in-law in discussion of the question
of blank verse, also written at Charlton, formed part of his
"Essay of Dramatic Poesy."

Dryden's *Annus Mirabilis* adopted the name of a Puritan
book published in 1661, "Mirabilis Annus ; or, the Year of Pro-

digies and Wonders," &c., with texts on its title-page pointed
directly against Charles and his court, and in its substance a
marvellous collection of " Prodigies Seen in the Heavens " and
" Strange Accidents and Judgments befalling Divers Persons "
during the first year of the Restoration. The design of the book
was to comfort the faithful with this warning to the rout of ungodly and profane men.  " Let especially the oppressors and
persecutors of the true Church look to themselves, when the
hand of the Lord in strange signs and wonders is lifted up
among them ; for then let them know assuredly that the day of
their calamity is at hand, and the things which shall come upon
them make haste.  The totall and finall overthrow of Pharaoh
and the Ægiptians (those cruell task-masters and oppressors of
the Israelites) did bear date not long after the wonderfull and
prodigious signes which the Lord had shown in the mid'st of
them."  Dryden's "Annus Mirabilis " was a shot from the other
side.  It was treated by him as a year that brought honour and
strength to the king.  The Dutch War, one of its themes, began
with a quarrel between traders.  In 1664, James, Duke of York,
was governor of the African Company, which had been established by charter to import gold-dust from Guinea, and slaves
for the West Indian planters.  The Dutch traders had, during
the Civil War, erected forts along the coast ; hence rivalry.
The African Company, seconded by the East India Company,
complained to Parliament.  James advocated their cause, and
urged that now, while seamen who had been with Blake were
to be had, was the right time for war.  Charles opposed.  The
merchants complained that the Dutch had not executed the
terms of the treaty of April, 1653, with the Commonwealth ;
that they molested the African coast by inciting natives to
destroy English factories, and established fictitious wars for the
sake of excluding English trade by blockades of the most frequented ports, whereby there was a loss of £700,000 to English
merchants, besides four million lost by their not giving up Rou,
a small island in the Indian seas.  Then Parliament addressed
the king, petitioning for redress, and promising to stand by
him.  Charles assented.  De Witt ruled Holland at the head of
the Louvestein faction, which had despised Charles in his exile.
Meanwhile the African Company had sent Sir Robert Holmes
with a few small ships of war to recover Cape Coast Castle that
the Dutch had taken.  He found in a Dutch vessel papers that
induced him to exceed his commission.  In February, 1664, he

v *

reduced Cape Coast Castle, destroyed Dutch factories, took the forts on Goree, then crossed the Atlantic to New Amsterdam, lately recovered to England by Sir R. Nicolas, and named, in honour of his patron the duke, New York. This action brought on the war, and gave to Holmes his character in Dryden's poem as "Holmes, the Achates of the Generals' fight." The allusion is to three lines in the Æneid (Bk. I., ll. 174—6), which tell that when the tempest-tost Æneadæ had landed on the Libyan coast, Achates lighted a fire, and from a little spark made a great flame.

> " And first from flints together clash'd
> The latent spark Achates flash'd,
> Caught in sere leaves and deftly nursed
> Till into flame the fuel burst."
>
> *Conington's Translation.*

So the single act of Sir Robert Holmes spread into a general war. The Dutch ambassadors remonstrated. The king said that the expedition had been sent by private authority of the African Company; that Holmes should be tried when he came back, and justice done. By order of De Witt, De Ruyter, who was cruising with Sir John Lawson in the Mediterranean against Turkish pirates, separated on the plea that he had orders to attack a squadron of pirates in the Canaries, and made reprisals on the English along the coast of Guinea; then crossed to the West Indies, and captured above twenty sail of merchantmen. Lawson, without instructions, took indemnity by sweeping 130 Dutch traders into English ports, and holding them there. Charles now counted cost. A war was estimated at two millions and a half, but the people were ready, and Sir R. Paston, a country gentleman, moved for the vote. A known dependent of the Ministers met the motion with a feigned proposal for a smaller sum. He was eagerly interrupted by two members supposed to be independent, and the vote was obtained by a majority of seventy. The Lords assented, and in February, 1665, Charles declared war. Until this time the clergy had taxed themselves in Convocation. Their right was now waived, though saved by a proviso in the Act. The precedent was stronger than the saving clause, and thus the vote for a Dutch war gave a death-blow to the power of the clergy in Convocation. James, Duke of York, sailed in the *Royal Charles*, with a fleet in three squadrons, and gained a victory over Opdam, on the 3rd of June, 1665, off the coast of Suffolk. The Dutch admiral was blown up with his flag-ship.

11. It was on the eve of this deadly encounter that **Charles Sackville**, Lord Buckhurst, afterwards **Earl of Dorset** (b. 1637, d. 1706), produced his *Song written at Sea, in the First Dutch War*, 1665, *the Night before an Engagement*. Charles Sackville, in these days, was a licentious wit of the court; but he had taste, and came into much honour among patrons of literature. His song before the battle has always passed as his best piece, and it represents him with no thought but of court gallantry to the ladies, on the eve of a conflict that would scatter death around him :

> " To pass our tedious hours away
>   We throw a merry main ;
> Or else at serious ombre play ;
>   But why should we in vain
> Each other's ruin thus pursue ?
>   We were undone when we left you.
>       With a fa la, la, la, la."

It does not follow that the writer had no serious thought when he wrote thus; but serious thought was out of fashion at the court of Charles II.

12. After the Duke of York's victory followed, in history and in Dryden's poem, the attempt on the Dutch merchant fleets in the neutral harbour of Bergen, which Dryden made the best of, but which was alike dishonourable and unsuccessful. In October, 1665, the Parliament at Oxford granted an additional million and a quarter for the war, with a gift of £120,000 to the Duke of York. In January, 1666, the King of France joined the Dutch ; Prince Rupert and General Monk (now Duke of Albemarle) were made generals of the English fleet, and the four days of the sea-fight off the North Foreland, specially celebrated in a hundred stanzas of the *Annus Mirabilis*, were the first four days of June. It was a drawn battle. Rupert was gone with twenty ships in search of the French. Monk found the Dutch, and attacked them ; on the second day the Dutch were reinforced, and Monk had to burn some disabled vessels ; on the third day English ships ran on the Galloper Sands, and the ruin would have been complete if, on the evening of that day, Rupert had not at last come with his twenty sail ; on the fourth day the vessels passed each other five times in line, and separated in a mist. But from the next sea-fight, on the 25th of June, De Ruyter retreated, often turning on the enemy, till he was in safe shelter. Monk and Rupert then interrupted Dutch commerce at will, and Holmes, with a squadron of boats and fire-ships, entered the

channel between Ulie and Schelling, the rendezvous of the Dutch Baltic trade. He burnt two men-of-war, 150 merchantmen, and 3,000 houses of the peaceable and unarmed town of Brandaris. The second battle and this achievement also form part of the subject of Dryden's poem ; and the celebration of battle by sea is broken by a digression upon shipping and navigation, with a glance at triumphs of the future which are to be attained by that study of God and nature for which men of science were now banded together.

Here Dryden introduces an apostrophe to the *Royal Society*, which originated in the peaceful gathering of men of science during the Civil Wars (ch. ix. § 18). In 1645, Wilkins, Wallis, Dr. John Goddard, and others, began to meet, sometimes at Dr. Goddard's lodgings in Wood Street, or some convenient place near, on occasion of his keeping an operator for grinding glasses for telescopes and microscopes ; and sometimes at a convenient place in Cheapside, sometimes in Gresham College, or some place near adjoining. "About the year 1648-1649, Wallis records, "some of us being removed to Oxford—first Dr. Wilkins, then I, and soon after Dr. Goddard—our company divided. Those in London continued to meet there, as before, and we with them when we had occasion to be there. And those of us at Oxford . . . continued such meetings in Oxford, and brought those studies into fashion there, meeting first at Dr. Petty's lodgings, in an apothecary's house, because of the convenience of inspecting drugs and the like, as there was occasion ; and after his remove to Ireland, though not so constantly, at the lodgings of Dr. Wilkins, then Warden of Wadham College ; and after his removal to Trinity College, in Cambridge, at the lodgings of the Honourable Mr. Robert Boyle, then resident for divers years in Oxford. Those meetings in London continued, and after the king's return, in 1660, were increased with the accession of divers worthy and honourable persons, and were afterwards incorporated by the name of the Royal Society." It was incorporated as "The President, Council, and Fellows of the Royal Society for Improving Natural Knowledge," in April, 1662 ; and Dryden, elected a fellow on the 19th of November, 1662, was doubtless present at its first anniversary meeting, on St. Andrew's Day, November 30, 1663. His generous sympathy with the new impulse to science caused him to make occasion for paying honour to the Royal Society in his *Annus Mirabilis* (st. 165, 166).

From the successes at sea Dryden passed to an elaborate depiction of the Fire of London, the generous exertions of the king, and his own prophetic forecast of the greater London that should rise, and of the national prosperities to come. As immediate prophecy, the close was falsified by the disgrace to us in June, 1667, of the Dutch in the Medway, burning English ships at Chatham.

13. These events, and many details of life in the reign of Charles II., are brought near to us by the diary of **Samuel Pepys** (b. 1632, d. 1703), the son of a tailor. He went to St. Paul's School and Cambridge, married at twenty-three a girl of fifteen, and was helped up in life by the patronage of Sir Edward Montagu, afterwards Earl of Sandwich, to whom he was related. He became, as Clerk of the Acts, a busy and useful member of the Navy Board, not unmindful of profits to be made in his position, but watchful over the best interests of the navy. This was his position during the years in which he kept his amusing *Diary.* It extends from January, 1660, when his age was twenty-seven, to May, 1669. The unguarded small-talk of the diary, a mixture of simplicity and shrewdness, which entertains us while it gives life to our knowledge of the past, should not make us forget that Pepys was a sensible and active public servant. The liveliest impression of the Fire of London is that given us in his "Diary," from Sunday, the 2nd of September, when a maid called Mr. and Mrs. Pepys up at three in the morning "to tell us of a great fire they saw in the city ; so I rose and slipped on my night-gown, and went to her window, and thought it to be at the back-side of Mark Lane at farthest," through all the work, misery, and confusion of the week, to the next Sunday, the 9th, when at church they had "a bad, poor sermon, though proper for the time ; nor eloquent, in saying at this time that the city is reduced from a large folio to a decimo-tertio." Pepys's " Diary," in six manuscript volumes, was among the books and papers bequeathed by him to Magdalene College. It was first published by Lord Braybrooke, in 1825.

The *Diary* of **John Evelyn** (ch. ix. § 18) began with his birth, in 1620, became full after the death of his father, at the end of 1640, and was continued to the close of his life, in 1706. It was first published by Mr. William Bray, in 1818. **John Aubrey** (b. 1626, d. 1697), who, in 1646, by his father's death, inherited estates in Wiltshire, Surrey, Herefordshire, Brecknockshire, and Monmouthshire, had a taste for antiquarian gossip, but was so credulous and superstitious that his records are worth little. His "Miscellanies," upon various subjects, first published in 1696, are an amusing gathering of superstitious notes upon Day-Fatalities, Apparitions, &c. Aubrey left behind him a work on *The Natural History and Antiquities of the County of Surrey.* He lost his property, by litigation and otherwise. Anthony à Wood, after twenty-five years acquaintance, said of him, spitefully, "He was a shiftless person, roving and magotie-headed, and sometimes little better than crazed ; and being exceedingly credulous, would stuff his many letters sent to A. W. with folleries and misinformations."

14. **Anthony à Wood** was born in 1632, at Oxford, opposite Merton College, where he afterwards was educated. He was admitted B.A. in 1652, M.A. in 1655, and then began a perambulation of Oxfordshire. He was inspired by Leland's collections in the Bodleian. Anthony à Wood's chief pleasures thenceforth were music and the study of Oxford antiquities. As he says in his own account of his life, "All the time that A. W. could spare from his beloved studies of English history, antiquities, heraldry, and genealogies, he spent in the most delightful faculty of music, either instrumental or vocal." In 1669 he had written, in English, his *History and Antiquities of the University of Oxford,* which was translated into Latin under the superintendence of Dr. Fell, who altered and added at discretion. As Anthony à Wood had not a sweet temper, and was accustomed to speak his mind roughly, he did not take this very kindly. The book appeared, in Latin, in 1674. His chief work, *Athenæ Oxonienses; an Exact History of all the Writers who have had their Education in the University of Oxford: to which are added the Fasti, or Annals of the said University,* was first published, in two folios, in 1691-2. When the second volume appeared he was cited before the Vice-Chancellor's Court for two libellous accusations of corruption (pp. 220 and 269) against the late Chancellor, the Earl of Clarendon. The book was burnt, its author expelled, and gazetted as an infamous libeller, a year before his death, in 1695.

15. **Dryden** published his *Annus Mirabilis* in January, 1667, a heroic poem, in 1,216 lines of Davenant's heroic stanza, in which there is yet some trace of that taste for ingenious conceit, derived of old from Italy, which caused Mr. Pepys's minister to say in his sermon that London had been reduced by the Great Fire from folio to decimo-tertio. But the vigour of a

master's hand appears in this attempt of Dryden's at heroic treatment of events yet fresh, dignifying the king's cause by the places given in the poem to Charles and his brother. In 1667 appeared also Dryden's *Essay of Dramatic Poesie*, a dialogue between Eugenius (Charles Sackville, Lord Buckhurst), Lisideius (Sir Charles Sedley), Crites (Sir Robert Howard), and Neander (Dryden). In June, 1666. he says, they went down the river towards Greenwich to hear the noise of cannon in the sea-fight with the Dutch. As the sound seemed to recede they judged that the Dutch were retreating, and conversation turned on the plague of bad verse that would follow victory. So they passed to an argument on ancient and modern poets, soon limited to Dramatic Poesie. The dialogue so introduced dealt with the subject of a play, "the famous rules which the French call Des Trois Unitez," action, plot, &c. Lisideius spoke of the beauty of French rhyme, and of the just reason he had to prefer that way of writing in tragedies before ours in blank verse, and then the argument went through all its points (§ 30). Crites reproduced Sir Robert Howard's case against rhyme. Neander answered "with all imaginable deference and respect, both to that person from whom you have borrowed your strongest arguments, and to whose judgment, when I have said all, I finally submit." There was no discourtesy here to **Sir Robert Howard.** In the next year, 1668, Sir Robert published his tragedy of *The Duke of Lerma*, and took occasion in its preface to reply, on behalf of blank verse, to the arguments of Dryden in his essay. The controversy amused the polite readers, to whom it supplied matter of talk, but there was not a trace in it of private quarrel; although Shadwell afterwards, in a scurrilous attack on Dryden, said that he and his brother-in-law nearly fought.

16. In the midst of such talk, Milton's " Paradise Lost " (§ 9) came out in blank verse ; for the first time in our literature a great poem, an epic, in blank verse. And there was not a line of explanation or apology. Milton's publisher—in the face of a controversy that on both sides assumed blank verse to be mean —applied to the author and got from him that blunt little preface of three Miltonic sentences, headed "The Verse." It was printed with Arguments to the books, on a leaf added to the volume.

**Sir Charles Sedley,** the Lisideius of the "Essay of Dramatic Poesie," was about twenty-one years old at the Restoration, and another of the dissolute clever light wits of the court. In 1667 he had just written a tragedy on *Antony and Cleopatra* (published 1677), and in 1668, his comedy of the *Mulberry Garden* was very successful. He had skill in frivolous love-verses, of which the Earl of Rochester wrote:

> " Sedley has that prevailing, gentle art
> That can with a resistless charm impart
> The loosest wishes to the chastest heart; "

and died in August, 1701. Both Sedley and the Earl of Dorset, in the next reign, favoured the Revolution.

**Dryden** continued to earn money by writing for the stage. In March, 1667, his *Secret Love* was produced with success at the king's theatre, and printed next year. Nell Gwyn shone in it as Florimel. Dryden's *Sir Martin Marr-all*, a version of Molière's " L'Etourdi," was produced in the same year; and also a new version of Shakespeare's *Tempest*, based upon a suggestion by **Davenant** that Shakespeare's play of a woman who had never seen a man could be improved by adding to it a man who had never seen a woman. This adaptation of Shakespeare to the taste of the court of Charles II. was one of Davenant's latest devices. He died in April, 1668, aged sixty-three, and Dryden succeeded to his dignity as Poet Laureate.

17. At this time **George Villiers**, Duke of Buckingham, whose age was thirty-three at the Restoration, was amusing himself with the production of a burlesque on the heroic dramas of the day, which in due time was to be acted under the name of *The Rehearsal*. He had begun when Davenant was laureate, and given to his hero, Bayes, who wore the laurel, some of Davenant's characteristics. Now Dryden wore the bays, and Dryden presently produced some notable examples of heroic sound and fury. The jest, therefore, was now pointed more especially at Dryden. George Villiers was with Prince Charles in Scotland, was at the battle of Worcester in 1651, came over to England, and, in November, 1657, married Andrew Marvell's pupil (ch. ix. § 9), heiress and only daughter of Lord Fairfax. By this marriage he saved the greater part of his own estate. At the Restoration he had an income of £20,000 a year, became Gentleman of the King's Bedchamber, Privy Councillor, and Master of the Horse. He was lively, careless, extravagant, and variously clever, with taste for chemistry and literature, and music and intrigue.

**Dryden** produced in 1668, with passages showing know-

ledge of astrology, in which art he was really a believer, *An
Evening's Love; or, the Mock Astrologer,* a careless version
of the French comedy *Le Feint Astrologue,* by Corneille's
younger brother Thomas. In 1669 Dryden produced a tragedy,
called *Tyrannic Love; or, the Royal Martyr,* on the story of St.
Catherine. In the prologue to this, he extended Horace's
" *serpit humi tutus* " into

> " He who servilely creeps after sense
> Is safe, but ne'er will reach an excellence."

He knew very well that he was often pleasing his audiences
with ranted nonsense in heroic strain. Porphyrius defying the
tyrant Maximin, at the end of the fourth act, replied to him in
this fashion :

> " *Max* The Sight with which my eyes shall first be fed
> Must be my Empress and this Traitor's head.
> " *Por.* Where'er thou stands't, I'll level at that place
> My gushing blood, and spout it at thy Face,
> Thus, not by Marriage, we our Blood will join :
> Nay, more, my Arms shall throw my Head at thine."

Dryden's next play was *Almanzor and Almahide; or, the Conquest of Granada,* in two parts, of which the first appeared in
1670. In that year his mother died.

In 1671 the Duke of Buckingham's caricature of such plays
in *The Rehearsal* was at last produced, at the King's Theatre, with
immense success. This was really a plea for good sense against
showy nonsense ; merry, and free from the indecency then common in dramatic jests. It was only in the preceding year, 1670,
that Dryden had the grant of the office of Poet Laureate, vacant
in 1668 ; but there was joined to it the office of Historiographer-
Royal, vacant since 1666. In *The Rehearsal,* Smith from the
country and Johnson of the town meet, plays are talked of ;
Mr. Bayes passes across the stage, and is caught as an author.
He has a new play in his pocket, explains his method of producing plays, is going to the Rehearsal of his new play, takes
them to it, instructs the actors, and discourses with Smith and
Johnson over a jumble of burlesque scenes, which would be recognised by playgoers of the time as caricatures of passages in
plays of Davenant, Dryden, Sir Robert Howard, and others.
There is a plot, which is no plot, of their gentleman usher
and physician against the two kings of Brentford ; there is
an army concealed at Knightsbridge ; there is Prince Volscius,
who falls in love as he is pulling on his boots, and makes his

legs an emblem of his various thought; there is a Draw-cansir, whose name pairs with Dryden's Almanzor. Almahide, in *The Conquest of Granada*, says to Almanzor, "Who dares to interrupt my private walk?" Almanzor replies:

> " He who dares love ; and for that love must die,
> And knowing this, dares yet love on, am I."

Usurping King Physician says to Drawcansir, "What man is this that dares disturb our feast?" Drawcansir replies:

> " He that dares drink, and for that drink dares die,
> And knowing this, dares yet drink on, am I."

And so forth. The last words of the Epilogue were:

> " May this prodigious way of writing cease.
> Let's have, at least once in our lives, a time
> When we may hear some Reason, not all Rhyme :
> We have these ten years felt its influence ;
> Pray let this prove a year of Prose and Sense."

That was produced in 1671. In 1672, Dryden printed his " Conquest of Granada," with an essay prefixed to it, "Of Heroick Plays." Here he assumed the question of rhyme in heroic plays to be settled by the fact that " very few Tragedies in this age shall be receiv'd without it." He gave Davenant the place of honour as originator of the heroic play, taking his music from Italian operas, and heightening his style from the example of Corneille. He said that his own plays, with love and valour for their proper theme, were based on principles of the heroic poem, and that he formed his much-abused Almanzor from Homer's Achilles, Tasso's Rinaldo, and Calprenède's Artaban. He might have added that he took the first suggestion of his play from the Almahide of Magdeleine Scudery, which did not appear in its English translation until 1677. Finally, Dryden said, " I have already swept the stakes ; and with the fortune of prosperous gamesters can be content to sit quietly, to hear my fortune curst by some, and my faults arraign'd by others, and to suffer both without reply."

18. In 1671, when the town was being amused with Buck-ingham's " Rehearsal," John Milton published, in one volume, his " Paradise Regained" (§ 9), and *Samson Agonistes*. There is a double sense in the word Agonistes. It may mean a striver in actual contest, or a striver in games for the amusement of the people. Samson was both. Milton at last working out his early notion of a sacred drama moulded on those of the Greek ·

tragedians, took for his theme Samson as a type of the maintainers of what Milton knew as " the good old cause" in England. Their ,party was now as Samson, blind, powerless, the
scorn of the Philistines of Charles II.'s court. Samson was
called to make them sport, was for them Agonistes in the
second sense, while for himself and God true striver ; and he
would yet prevail. Although the mockers had the mastery to-
day, God was not mocked. The drama closely followed the
Greek model, even in the construction of its choruses, which
had only a few rhymes interspersed among their carefully constructed metres. In nearly all the poetry of this last period of
Milton's life, the grandeur of the poet's thought and his supreme
skill in the use of language, caused him almost wholly to put
aside the ornaments of rhyme—" invention," as he now called
it, "of a barbarous age (ch. iii. § 30, 35) to set off wretched matter
and lame metre." Samson's lament for his blindness (ll. 75—109)
could, of course, be realised by the blind poet. He blended
with his argument a thought of his own temperate life ending
in pains of gout, the scourge of the luxurious, when the chorus
gave dramatic expression (ll. 667—709) to the question of God's
dealings with the nation and with many a true Agonistes of
the Commonwealth ; not

> " Heads without name no more remember'd,
> But such as thou hast solemnly elected,
> With gifts and graces eminently adorn'd,
> To some great work, thy glory,
> And people's safety, which in part they effect ;
> Yet toward these thus dignified, thou oft
> Amidst their highth of noon
> Changest thy countenance, and thy hand, with no regard
> Of highest favours past
> From thee on them, or them to thee of service."

They are left open to the hostile sword,

> " Or else captiv'd,
> Or to th' unjust tribunals under change of times,
> And condemnation of th' ungrateful multitude.
> If these they 'scape, perhaps in poverty
> With sickness and disease thou bow'st them down—
> Painful diseases, and deform'd,
> In crude old age :
> Though not disordinate, yet causeless suffering
> The punishment of dissolute days."

But the doubt is expressed only like the doubt in Lycidas :

> " Were it not better done as others use,
> To sport with Amaryllis in the shade ?"

expressed, because the answer is to follow in the last lines of
the play.   And they were Milton's last words as a poet :

> " All is best, though oft we doubt
> What the unsearchable dispose
> Of Highest Wisdom brings about,
> And ever best found in the close.
> Oft he seems to hide his face,
> But unexpectedly returns :
> And to his faithful champion hath in place
> Bore witness gloriously ; whence Gaza mourns.
> And all that band them to resist
> His uncontroulable intent :
> His servants he, with new acquist
> Of true experience, from this great event,
> With peace and consolation hath dismiss'd,
> And calm of mind, all passion spent."

In 1673, the year before his death, there was a second and
enlarged edition—only the second edition—twenty-eight years
after the first, of Milton's *Poems both Latin and English.*   In
the same year he published one more prose tract upon a
question of the day, of *True Religion, Heresy, Schism, and
Toleration.*   The Duke of York, heir to the throne, was a
Roman Catholic.   Protestant England looked with dread to
his succession, and the argument over Catholicism was again
active.   Milton pleaded still for perfect liberty of conscience,
but held that the Roman Catholics, by maintaining a foreign
despotism that weighed alike on civil and religious liberty, shut
themselves out from a full toleration.   He would not have civil
penalties inflicted on them, but he shared the common dread of
their predominance, and wished to restrain them where that
could be done without denying them what they thought necessary to salvation.

In 1674 Milton published the second edition of " Paradise
Lost," almost without change beyond the placing of the
Arguments before the books, and changing the number of the
books from ten to twelve, by dividing what had been the seventh
and tenth books into those which are now the seventh and
eighth, eleventh and twelfth.   There is all the grace of his youth
in Milton's manner of introducing these new breaks.   Raphael's
narrative of the seven days of creation is in the seventh book.
In the first edition the discourse now in the eighth book followed
without break, the lines running together thus :

> " If else thou seek'st
> Aught not surpassing human measure, say.
> To whom thus Adam gratefully replied."

Milton did not make his break by simply writing
" Book VIII.," but made a poet's pause by this fresh opening :

> " The angel ended, and in Adam's ear
> So charming left his voice, that he awhile
> Thought him still speaking, still stood fix'd to hear ;
> Then, as new wak'd, thus gratefully replied."

The first five lines of Book XII. were added for the same good
reason. John Milton, aged sixty-six, died on Sunday, the 8th of
November, 1674.

19. **Jeremy Taylor** (ch. viii. § 61, 70; ch. ix. § 14), aged
forty-seven at the Restoration, published in June, 1660, his
*Ductor Dubitantium; or, the Rule of Conscience in all her
General Measures*, a book of casuistry, which he had designed
to be the great work of his life. It was dedicated to Charles II.,
and followed in two months by *The Worthy Communicant.*
In August he was nominated Bishop of Down and Connor;
he was made also Vice-Chancellor of Dublin University, and
a member of the Irish Privy Council. In April, 1661, he
had the adjacent bishopric of Dromore united with Down
and Connor, in consideration of his "virtue, wisdom, and
industry." At the opening of the Irish Parliament, in May,
1661, Jeremy Taylor preached, and admonished his hearers
to oppress no man for his religious opinions, to deal equal
justice to men of all forms of faith, and "do as God does,
who in judgment remembers mercy." He still lived near Portmore, and made pious use of his newly-acquired wealth. He
apprenticed poor children, maintained promising youths at the
University, and rebuilt the choir of Dromore Cathedral. In
1664 he issued, with addition of a second part, his *Dissuasive
from Popery*, first published in 1647. His son by his second
marriage died before him. Of his sons by the first marriage, the
elder, in the army, was killed in a duel with an officer of his own
regiment ; the younger, destined for the Church, had been drawn
to the court, became secretary to George Villiers, Duke of
Buckingham, was corrupted by court manners of the Restoration, and a profligate life with a consumptive constitution
caused his death about the same time as his father's. Jeremy
Taylor died, aged fifty-five, on the 13th of August, 1667, in the
year of the publication of " Paradise Lost." Of Milton's three
daughters, the eldest, Anne, who had a deformed body and
pleasing face, married an architect, and died at the birth of her
first child ; Mary, the second, did not marry. Deborah, who

loved her father, left home to avoid her mother-in-law, went with a lady to Ireland, married Mr. Clarke, a weaver in Spital-fields, and had ten children.

20. **John Bunyan** (ch. ix. § 15), incurring the penalty for unauthorised preaching, was committed to prison in November, 1660, on the charge of going about to several conventicles in the country, to the great disparagement of the government of the Church of England. He was sent, aged thirty-two, to Bedford Jail for three months. As he would not conform at the end of that time, he was re-committed. He was not included in the general jail delivery at the Coronation of Charles II., in April, 1661. His wife—she was his second wife—appealed three times to the judges, and urged that she had "four small children that cannot help themselves, one of which is blind, and we have nothing to live upon but the charity of good people." She appealed in vain. "I found myself," said Bunyan, "encompassed with infirmities. The parting with my wife and poor children hath often been to me in this place as the pulling of the flesh from the bones, and that not only because I am somewhat too fond of these great mercies, but also because I should have often brought to my mind the many hardships, miseries, and wants that my poor family was like to meet with should I be taken from them, especially my poor blind child, who lay nearer my heart than all besides. Oh, the thoughts of the hardships I thought my poor blind one might go under would break my heart to pieces. 'Poor child!' thought I, 'what sorrow art thou like to have for thy portion in this world! Thou must be beaten, must beg, suffer hunger, cold, nakedness, and a thousand calamities, though I cannot now endure the wind should blow upon thee.'" So felt the great warm heart that was pouring out in Bedford Jail its love to God and man. Depth of feeling, vivid imagination, and absorbing sense of the reality of the whole spiritual world revealed to him in his Bible, made Bunyan a grand representative of the religious feeling of the people. In simple direct phrase, with his heart in every line, he clothed in visible forms that code of religious faith and duty which an earnest mind, unguided by traditions, drew with its own simple strength out of the Bible. Bunyan wrote much, profoundly religious tracts, prison meditations, a book of poems—*Divine Emblems; or, Temporal Things Spiritualised, fitted for the use of Boys and Girls*, and other occasional verse. The whole work of his life was like that indicated in his child's book, a

spiritualizing of temporal things.   Matter for him was the shadow, soul the substance; the poor man whose soul Bunyan leads by thoughts that it can follow, passes through a hard life with its dull realities all glorified.   Look where he may, a man poor and troubled as himself has stamped for him God's image on some part of what he sees.   As Bunyan himself rhymes:

> " We change our drossy dust for gold,
>    From death to life we fly;
> We let go shadows, and take hold
>    Of immortality."

The poor man's child, ill taught, and with small power of advancing in the world, may look at a snail and think of what John Bunyan wrote for children, in his prison, of the snail:

> " She goes but softly, but she goeth sure;
>    She stumbles not, as stronger creatures do:
> Her journey's shorter, so she may endure
>    Better than they which do much farther go.
>    *    *    *    *    *
> Then let none faint, nor be at all dismay'd,
>    That life by Christ do seek, they shall not fail
> To have it; let them nothing be afraid:
>    The herb and flow'r are eaten by the snail."

The first part of *The Pilgrim's Progress from this World to that which is to Come, delivered under the similitude of a Dream, wherein is discovered the Manner of his Setting Out, his Dangerous Journey, and Safe Arrival at the Desired Country*, was written in Bedford Jail, where Bunyan was a prisoner for more than eleven years, from November, 1660, to March, 1672, when a Royal declaration allowed Nonconformists (except Roman Catholics) to meet under their licensed ministers.   His *Holy City* had been published in 1665; and after his release Bunyan published *a Defence of the Doctrine of Justification by Faith*, *a Confession of his Faith*, an appeal entitled *Come and Welcome to Christ*, before that *First Part of the Pilgrim's Progress* appeared in 1678, four years after the death of Milton.   The allegory is realized with genius akin to that of the dramatist. Christian, with the Burden on his back and the Book in his hand, sets out on his search for eternal life, and is at once engaged in a series of dialogues.   Neighbours Obstinate and Pliable attempt to turn him back.   Pliable goes a little way with him, but declines to struggle through the Slough of Despond, and gets out on the wrong side.   Then Christian meets Mr. Worldly Wisemen, from the town of Carnal Policy, hard by, has a talk

with him before he enters in at the Strait Gate, triumphs over
Apollyon, passes through the Valley of the Shadow of Death,
overtakes his townsfellow Faithful, who tells his experiences of
the journey, and they then come upon Talkative, who was also
of their town, son of one Say-well, of Prating Row.   All the
dialogue is touched with humorous sense of characters drawn
from life and familiar to the people, while the allegory blends
itself everywhere with the poor man's Bible reading, and
has always its meaning broadly written on its surface, so that
the simplest reader is never at a loss for the interpretation.
The adventures of Christian in Vanity Fair are full of dramatic
dialogue.   Then there is still talk by the way between Christian
and Hopeful before they lie down to sleep in the grounds of
Doubting Castle, where they are caught in the morning by its
master, the Giant Despair.   There is life and character still in
the story of their peril from the giant, before Christian remembers that he has " a key in his bosom," called Promise, that will
open any lock in Doubting Castle.   And so the allegory runs
on to the end, lively with human interest of incident and shrewd
character-painting by the way of dialogue, that at once chain
the attention of the most illiterate; never obscure, and never
for ten lines allowing its reader to forget the application of it all
to his own life of duty for the love of God.   The story ends
with the last conflict of Christian and Hopeful, when at the hour
of death they pass through the deep waters, leaving their mortal
garments behind them in the river, and are led by the Shining
Ones into the Heavenly Jerusalem.   In 1682 appeared Bunyan's
allegory of the *Holy War;* and in 1684 the second part of
" Pilgrim's Progress," telling the heavenward pilgrimage of
Christian's wife and four children.   England was England
still, under a king who was tainting fashionable literature.   Her
highest culture produced in the reign of Charles II. " Paradise
Lost;" and from among the people who had little culture except
that which they drew for themselves from the Bible, came the
" Pilgrim's Progress."

21. **Richard Baxter** (ch. ix. § 13) was also an active writer
throughout the reign of Charles II.   Soon after the Restoration,
in 1662, there were more than 4,200 Quakers in prison at one
time.   In 1670, **Robert Barclay**, of Ury, near Aberdeen, then
twenty-two years old, defended the Friends, whose society he
had joined, in a treatise, published at Aberdeen, entitled, *Truth
cleared from Calumnies.*   In 1676 he was confined with others in

a prison so dark that unless the keeper set the door open or brought a candle they could not see to eat the food brought in to them.  In the same year appeared Barclay's *Apology for the True Christian Divinity as the same is held forth and preached by the People called in scorn Quakers, being a full Explanation and Vindication of their Principles and Doctrines.*  It was first published in Latin, at Amsterdam, and then, translated by the author, published in England.  The address to Charles II., in the place of a dedication, called upon him for justice on behalf of a most peaceful body of his subjects, and said: " Thou hast tasted of prosperity and adversity; thou knowest what it is to be banished thy native country, to be overruled as well as to rule and sit upon the throne; and being oppressed, thou hast reason to know how hateful the oppressor is both to God and man.  If, after all these warnings and advertisements, thou dost not turn unto the Lord with all thy heart, but forget Him who remembered thee in thy distress, and give up thyself to follow lust and vanity, surely great will be thy condemnation."

22. In the reign of Charles II., the Episcopal Church had among its representatives (besides, for a year, Thomas Fuller) Jeremy Taylor, Cudworth, Barrow, Tillotson, Leighton, Beveridge, and Burnet.  **Thomas Fuller** (ch. viii. § 59) under Charles II. was restored to his prebend of Salisbury, and made D.D. and chaplain to the king; but he lived only until August, 1661.  His *History of the Worthies of England* appeared in 1662, and is the most popular of all his works.

**Ralph Cudworth,** born in 1617, at Aller, Somersetshire, became Fellow of Emmanuel College, Cambridge.  In 1644 he was Master of Clare Hall; in 1645, Regius Professor of Hebrew, and devoted himself to Jewish antiquities.  He became D.D. in 1651; in 1654, Master of Christ's College (meanwhile also rector of North Cadbury, Somersetshire).  He then married, and spent the rest of his life at Cambridge.  In 1678 he published the first part of *The True Intellectual System of the Universe.* The work was planned in three parts, of which this first part was devoted to the refutation of atheism.  The other two parts were to have been on Moral Distinctions and Free Will.  His philosophical method and liberality of mind offended many theologians, who cried out on him as an atheist for his method of refuting atheism.  He died in the year of the Revolution, leaving one daughter, who married Sir Francis Masham.

**Isaac Barrow,** born in 1630, educated at Charterhouse

and Cambridge, became Fellow of Trinity, subscribed to the Covenant, but insisted on the erasure of his name.  He studied science as well as divinity—astronomy, botany, chemistry, and even anatomy.  In 1655 he sold his books that he might have money for travel.  He found friends on his road ; visited Paris, Florence, Venice, and Constantinople, and came home, in 1659, through Germany and Holland.  Then he took orders, was Professor of Greek at Cambridge, next also of Geometry at Gresham College ; and after that Lucasian Mathematical Lecturer at Cambridge until 1669, when he gave place to his friend, Isaac Newton.  In 1672 the king made him Master of Trinity and he was Vice-Chancellor of the University when he died, in 1677, aged forty-seven.  He wrote mathematical works, and sermons full of sense and piety.  A collected edition of Isaac Barrow's works was published by Archbishop Tillotson, in four volumes folio, in 1683-7.

John Tillotson was born in the same year as Barrow (1630), son of a clothier at Sowerby, near Halifax.  He went as a Nonconformist to Clare Hall, Cambridge, and began life as a private tutor and curate to Dr. Wilkins, at St. Lawrence Jewry. He made himself agreeable to authority, both after the Restoration and after the Revolution ; rose in the Church, upholding simple acceptance of the ruling powers ; and was made Archbishop of Canterbury in 1691, after the suspension of Sancroft. He died in 1694, and left to his widow unpublished sermons that fetched 2,500 guineas.  Yet Tillotson was not, like Leighton, a man of genius, capable of deep thought and grand expression.

Robert Leighton (born 1613, died 1684) was the son of a man who in the reign of Charles I. had his nose slit and his ears cut, and was whipped from Newgate to Tyburn for offending Government with two books called " Zion's Plea " and "The Looking-Glass of the Holy War."   Robert Leighton was a Scottish divine, thoughtful as well as eloquent.  He came to London to resign the bishopric of Dumblane, vexed by contention with the Presbyterians, and was sent back Archbishop of Glasgow.   But he could endure the strife against Episcopalians in Scotland only for another year, resigned, withdrew to Sussex, and died there in 1684.  His sermons, published in 1692, are those of the greatest preacher in the Episcopal Church of the later Stuart period.

William Beveridge (born 1638, died 1708), educated at Cambridge, was a Hebrew scholar at eighteen, and published at

the age of twenty, in Latin, a Syriac grammar and treatise on
the excellence and usefulness of Oriental languages. He has
left 150 published sermons, besides theological tracts. Beveridge
became chaplain to William III. at the Revolution, but was not
made a bishop till Queen Anne's reign.

**Gilbert Burnet,** born in 1643, studied at Aberdeen. In
1669 he was Divinity Professor at Glasgow. In 1674 he settled
in London, and became preacher at the Rolls Chapel. In 1677
Burnet published *Memoirs of the Lives and Actions of James
and William, Dukes of Hamilton, &c., in Seven Books,* upon
which he had been at work in Scotland ; and in 1679 appeared
the first of the three volumes of his *History of the Reformation
in the Church of England,* which agreed so well with the feeling
of the time against Catholicism that he received for it the thanks
of both Houses of Parliament, with a desire that he would go
on and complete the work. The second volume followed in
1681 ; the third not until 1715. In 1680 Burnet wrote an account
of the penitent close of the dissolute life of **John Wilmot,
Earl of Rochester,** one of the court wits who trifled in verse,
and whose best piece of verse is upon *Nothing*.

23. A courtier and poet of much higher mark was **Wentworth Dillon, Earl of Roscommon,** born in 1633, nephew
and godson to the Earl of Strafford. He was at the Protestant
College at Caen when, by the death of his father, he became
Earl of Roscommon, at the age of ten. He remained abroad,
travelled in Italy till the Restoration, when he came in with
the king, became captain of the band of Pensioners, took for a
time to gambling, married, indulged his taste in literature,
strongly under the French influence, and had a project for an
English academy like that of France.

*Boileau's* influence became supreme upon the publication of
his "Art of Poetry" (*L'Art Poétique*), in 1673. Its four cantos
embodied his main doctrine as the Poet of Good Sense. In idea
and execution it was inspired by Horace's "Art of Poetry ;" but
its polished maxims, applied specially to French poetry, are more
systematically arranged. The order of its cantos is:—1. General rules, with a short digression on the history of French poetry
from Villon to Malherbe. 2. Rules and characteristics of the
eclogue, elegy, ode, sonnet, epigram, balade, madrigal, satire,
and vaudeville. 3. Rules of tragedy, comedy, and epic. 4.
General advice to poets on the use of their powers ; choice of a
critic ; origin, rise, and decline of poetry ; praise of Louis XIV.

The critical shortcomings of this work, which may be said to have given the law for some years to French and English literature, nearly all proceed from a wholesome but too servile regard for the example of the ancient classic writers. The chief authors of Greece and Rome were to be as much the models of good literature as the Latin language was a standard of right speech. This led, indeed, to a sound contempt of empty trivialities, but it left the critic with faint powers of recognition for a Dante, a Shakespeare, or a Milton. Boileau was even hindered by it from perceiving how far Terence was surpassed by his friend Molière. His discipline thus tended obviously to the creation of an artificial taste for forms of correct writing excellent in themselves, but as means of perfect expression better suited to the genius of the French than of the English people. He was a true Frenchman, and English writers erred by imitation even of his excellence, in adopting too readily for a nation Germanic in origin and language forms that harmonized better with the mind and language of a Latin race. But, at the same time, they shared with their neighbours the benefit of assent to the appeal in his "Art Poétique" on behalf of plain good sense against the faded extravagancies of that period of Italian influence from which life and health had departed :

> " Évitons ces excès.  Laissons à l'Italie
> De tous ses faux brillans l'éclatante folie.
> Tout doit tendre au Bon Sens."

These lines declare the living spirit of the poem, in which, if we are to see only in one foremost work the altered temper of a generation, it may especially be said that the period of Italian influence ended and French influence became supreme.

We are now, therefore, to find in English literature a rising race of critics who test everything by Latin forms. The English must be, for dignity, as Latin as possible in structure, because so the French had determined. That was obedience to them in the letter, not in the spirit. In origin and structure, their language was chiefly Latin : they, therefore, other things being equal, preferred words of Latin origin. In origin and structure our language is Teutonic : and had we really followed their example, we should, other things being equal, have preferred words of Teutonic origin. Critics now abounded in France. *Dominique Bouhours* (born 1628, died 1702), an accomplished Jesuit, wrote criticisms both on style and language. *René le*

*Bossu* (born 1631, died 1680) published in 1675 a treatise on the Epic, which became the critical authority upon that subject. *René Rapin* (born 1621, died 1687), who wrote, in four books, a Latin poem " Of Gardens," was so much esteemed that Dryden said he was "sufficient, were all other critics lost, to teach anew the rules of writing."

The **Earl of Roscommon**, who died in 1684, was bred in the same school, followed its fashions, and wrote about writing. He translated into verse *Horace's Art of Poetry*, translated into verse Virgil's sixth Eclogue, one or two Odes of Horace, and a passage from Guarini's " Pastor Fido." Of his original writing the most important piece is an *Essay on Translated Verse*, carefully polished in the manner of Boileau, sensible, and often very happy in expression. Himself, in a corrupt time, a poet of " unspotted lays," he was true to his doctrine that

> " Immodest words admit of no defence ;
> For want of decency is want of sense."

When he tells the translator that he must thoroughly understand what he is translating, he says :

> " While in your thoughts you find the least debate,
> You may confound, but never can translate.
> You still will this through all disguises show,
> For none explain more clearly than they know."

He pities from his soul unhappy men compelled by want to prostitute the pen ; but warns the rich :

> " Let no vain hope your easy mind seduce,
> For rich ill poets are without excuse."

And let no man mistake every stir to write verse for a sign of power :

> " Beware what spirit rages in your breast ;
> For ten inspired, ten thousand are possest."

With all its great faults, the court of the Restoration must be credited with a good society of men of high rank who made it a point of fashion to cultivate their minds, acquire, according to the new standard of France, a fine critical taste, write verse themselves—as Lord Mulgrave wrote, " Without his song no fop is to be found,"—receive sweet incense of praise from poorer writers, and give in return for it a kindly patronage.

**John Sheffield** (b. 1649, d. 1721) became by his father's death **Earl of Mulgrave**, at the age of nine. At seventeen he was in the fleet against the Dutch, and he served afterwards also in fleet and army.  He was made Duke of Buckinghamshire in 1703, and is, therefore, known to modern literature by that title. In the days of Charles II. he wrote light pieces of verse, and two poems in the new critical fashion, which were his chief efforts— an *Essay on Satire*, in 1675, and an *Essay on Poetry*, which is a little "Art of Poetry" applied to England.  The wholesome stress is still laid on good sense, in strong reaction against the paste brilliants of the decayed Italian school.  "'Tis wit and sense that is the subject here," he writes :

> " As all is dulness where the Fancy's bad ;
> So, without Judgment, Fancy is but mad:
> And Judgment has a boundless influence
> Not only in the choice of Words or Sense,
> But on the World, on Manners, and on Men ;
> Fancy is but the Feather of the Pen ;
> Reason is that substantial, useful part,
> Which gains the Head ; while t'other wins the Heart."

Lord Mulgrave placed Shakespeare and Fletcher at the head of modern drama ; but wrote some years afterwards two tragedies, *Julius Cæsar* and *Marcus Brutus*, in which he set his own taste above Shakespeare's.  Profoundly ignorant of the real unity of plan in Shakespeare's "Julius Cæsar," and of the place of tyrannicide at the heart of the drama, the polite patron and cultivator of literature in the new manner of France saw that Shakespeare could not be saved by the dramatic gospel of Corneille, and reconstructed his "Julius Cæsar," with the unities respected : "This play begins the day before Cæsar's death, and ends an hour after it."  His rebuilding threw out material enough for another play, the tragedy of "Marcus Brutus." Here "the play begins the day before the battle of Philippi, and ends with it ; but Lord Mulgrave regretted the inevitable change scene from Athens to Philippi, whereby, he said, he

> " Commits one crime that needs an Act of Grace,
> And breaks the Law of Unity of Place."

Comparison of Shakespeare in his habit as he lived, with Shakespeare as dignified with a Louis Quatorze wig by Lord Mulgrave, illustrates very well the weak side of the French influence on English literature.   The polite lord even corrected Antony's speech over Cæsar's body.  Shakespeare made him say :

> " The evil that men do lives after them,
> The good is oft interred with their bones."

Bones !  Vulgar and unpleasant.  His lordship polished this

into " The good is often buried in their graves." Each play
has a closing thought to mark the adapter's want of sympathy
with Brutus.   Indeed, Lord Mulgrave had written an ode in
depreciation of Brutus as reply to Cowley's in his praise.

24. **Abraham Cowley** (ch. viii. § 48 ; ix. § 22) published
in 1662 two books in Latin verse *Of Plants*, which sang of
herbs in the manner of the elegies by Ovid and Tibullus.
Four other books were added: two upon flowers in the various
measures of Catullus and Horace ; and two upon trees, in the
manner of Virgil's " Georgics." The last book is patriotic
and political. The British oak, in an assembly of the trees,
enlarges upon the king's troubles and the beginning of the
Dutch War.   This work, *Plantarum, Libri VI.*, was first published complete with Cowley's other Latin poems, in 1678.
Cowley, after the Restoration, was neglected by the court,
and owed his means of retirement to the good-will of Lord
St. Albans, whom he had served as secretary, and the Duke of
Buckingham.   His *Cutter of Coleman Street*, which was his
juvenile play of *The Guardian* in an altered form, was censured
as a satire upon the king's party.   He was also guilty of an ode
in which Brutus was honoured, and it is said that a request to
the king for some recognition of his faithful service to the royal
family in its adversity was met by Charles II. with the answer,
" Mr. Cowley's pardon is his reward."   Cowley translated two
of Pindar's odes, the Second Olympic and the Third Nemean,
turned into a Pindaric ode the thirty-fourth chapter of Isaiah,
and wrote odes of his own in the same manner.   He had
a lively fancy and a generous mind, capable of real elevation
of thought, although for high flight as a poet his wings were too
much clogged with ornament.   He died in July, 1667, the year
of the publication of that *Annus Mirabilis* in which the writing
even of Dryden still had traces of the later Euphuism.   But
the Pindaric ode, as an imitation from the ancients, became one
of the recognised forms of verse under the new influence.   Neither
Cowley nor any other of these new writers of Pindarics came
near to Ben Jonson, whose noble " Pindaric Ode on the Death
of Sir H. Morison " was true to the ancient model.   But now, in
a poet, bound by rule, and condemned to the heroic couplet
as the safe classical measure, wished for a little liberty to be
wilful in metre and audacious in thought, he could still be
polite and classical by taking out his freedom under shadow of
the name of a Pindaric ode.

Cowley said, in his "Ode to Brutus:"

> " From thy strict rule some think that thou didst swerve
> (Mistaken honest men) in Cæsar's blood ;
> What mercy could the tyrant's life deserve
> From him who killed himself rather than serve ? "

Lord Mulgrave, in his argumentative Pindaric " Ode on Brutus,"
in reply to Cowley, followed the poet's ode all through with his
antagonism. When quoting one passage he could not keep
his polite taste from " improving " it, and thus called attention
in a note to the fact that he had done so : " In repeating these
four verses of Mr. Cowley, I have done an unusual thing ; for
notwithstanding that he is my adversary in the argument, and
a very famous one too, I could not endure to let so fine a
thought remain as ill-expressed in this ode as it is in his ;
which anybody may find by comparing them together. But I
would not be understood as if I pretended to correct Mr. Cowley,
tho' expression was not his best talent : For, as I have mended
these few verses of his, I doubt not but he could have done as
much for a great many of mine." Cowley remained true to his
opinions on the great conflict before the Restoration, but he had
nothing in common with this intellectual foppery, or with the
course of life at the court of Charles II. He passed, therefore,
his last seven or eight years by the Thames, " in calm of mind,
all passion spent," away from the stir of London, first at Barn
Elms, where he had a dangerous fever, and then at Chertsey.
The wise thoughtfulness of these last years is shown by Cowley's
*Essays in Verse and Prose.* Although he was a man who found
much pleasure in solitude, and is said often to have left the room
when a woman entered, he animated these essays with the love of
liberty in a social form. Solitude meant liberty to think. " The
first Minister of State," said Cowley, " has not so much business
in public as the wise man has in private." The private station,
not in bonds to poverty nor under the restraints of artificial
form, was his ideal of a freeman's life, "with so much knowledge and love of piety and philosophy (that is, the study of
God's laws and of his creatures) as may afford him matter
enough never to be idle, though without business ; and never
to be melancholy, though without sin or vanity." And again,

> " If life should a well-ordered poem be
> (In which he only hits the white
> Who joins true profit with the best delight),
> The more heroique strain let others take,
> Mine the Pindarique way I'll make :

.The matter shall be grave, the numbers loose and free ;
It shall not keep one settled pace of time,
In the same tune it shall not chime,
Nor shall each day just to its neighbour rhime.
A thousand liberties it shall dispense,
And yet shall manage all without offence
Or to the sweetness of the sound, or greatness of the sense."

One source of the charm of Cowley's Essays is that they came straight from the heart, and that there is this unity of thought in their variety of treatment. Whatever his theme—Liberty, or Solitude, or Obscurity, or Greatness, or Avarice, or the Danger of an Honest Man in Much Company, or the Shortness of Life and the Uncertainty of Riches, or Nature in the Fields and in the Garden, or if he was only giving verse translation of Claudian's "Old Man of Verona," Horace's "Country Mouse,' or those lines from the second book of Virgil's "Georgics" which begin "O fortunatos nimium," or Martial's "Vis fieri Liber?"—the theme is always one,—Peace in the form of life which gives the highest Freedom to fit use of a full mind.

25. In excuse for the king's indifference to Cowley, it may be said that as there was no possible accord in the vibration of the two minds, one could get no tone out of the other. Why, then, did Charles also neglect **Samuel Butler,** who aided the court party with lively jest against the Puritans, and was in much need of friendly patronage? Charles shone in shallow mimicry of earnest men, and could put all his mind into the telling of an idle story ; he enjoyed ridicule of his adversaries, and he therefore found much to enjoy in "Hudibras." But it was the work of a man who laboured and read, and who liked work. His Majesty liked sauntering through life. He preferred the company of Killigrew (§ 2) and men whose jests were idle ; but even then he was apt to forget their faces if they were a week out of his sight, and Butler was too proud to stand in the throng of the court suitors. Samuel Butler was born in February, 1612, at Strensham, Worcestershire, the fifth of seven children of a small farmer, who had sent him to the college school at Worcester. He began life as clerk to a justice of the peace, Mr. Jefferies, of Earl's Croombe, and he then amused himself with music and painting. Probably at this time he compiled in law French a complete syllabus of "Coke upon Littleton ;" there also existed in Butler's handwriting a French Dictionary, compiled and transcribed by him. Afterwards Butler came into the service of the Earl of Kent, at Wrest, in Bedfordshire. He

W

was then about seventeen. Selden (ch. viii. § 19, 68) acting as
solicitor and steward to the family, employed Butler to write
and translate for him. Here Butler had access to books, and
must have been an active and attentive reader. After several
years at Wrest, he passed into the service of Sir Samuel Luke,
at Wood End, or Cople Hoo Farm, three miles from Bedford.
Sir Samuel Luke was a wealthy man, justice of the peace,
colonel in the army of the Parliament, and member for Bedfordshire in the Long Parliament. Sir Samuel Luke and his Puritan
friends seem to have suggested to Butler his burlesque poem ;
indeed, Butler, in closing the first canto of his first part, indicated
Sir Samuel Luke in a blank, when he made *Hudibras*, preparing
" to keep the peace 'twixt dog and bear," say :

> " 'Tis sung there is a valiant Mameluke
> In foreign land, yclep'd ——
> To whom we have been oft compared
> For person, parts, address, and beard ;
> Both equally reputed stout,
> And in the same cause both have fought ;
> He oft, in such attempts as these,
> Came off with glory and success ;
> Nor will we fail in th' execution,
> For want of equal resolution."

After the Restoration, Butler was made secretary to Lord Carbery, and steward of Ludlow Castle ; for Lord Carbery, Jeremy
Taylor's friend, had become Lord President of Wales. In
Ludlow Castle, Butler prepared for the press the first part of
" Hudibras," which appeared in 1663. As a burlesque romance
it is in the octosyllabic rhyme of our old metrical romances
(ch. iii. § 30), with a frequent use of extra syllables for comic
double and treble rhymes, like that which has kept alive the
name of **Alexander Ross,** a busy ephemeral writer, with a
bent towards religious history, who had been master of Southampton School and chaplain to Charles I., and who died in
1654. He had published, in 1617-19, a Latin poem on the
History of the Jews ; in 1634, a Life of Christ, in words and
lines taken from Virgil (*Virgilius Evangelizans*); and after
divers other books, in 1652, *Arcana Microcosmi; or, the Hid
Secrets of Man's Bodie;* in the same year, in six books, a continuation or second part of Raleigh's *History of the World;*
and, in 1653, *A View of All Religions.* It was as Historian of
the World and Viewer of All Religions that **Butler** whimsically cited him, in the lines :

> " There was an ancient sage philosopher
> That had read Alexander Ross over,
> And swore the world, as he could prove,
> Was made of fighting and of love."

So Butler, at the opening of " Hudibras," spoke of the times "when civic fury first grew high :"

> " And pulpit, drum ecclesiastic,
> Was beat with fist instead of a stick."

So of the stocks, described as a castle :

> " In all the fabric
> You shall not see one stone nor a brick."

Or the single rhyme could be made whimsically, as

> " If animal, both of us may
> As justly pass for bears as they ;
> For we are animals no less,
> Although of different specieses."

The form of Butler's mock heroic was influenced by his reading of " Don Quixote," whom he quoted now and then. " Don Quixote " had been translated by Thomas Shelton, from an Italian version, and first published in two quarto volumes, in 1612 and 1620, afterwards in one folio volume, in 1652. Hudibras, on a horse clearly related to Rosinante, went " a colonelling " as a Presbyterian Quixote, and had his Sancho in Squire Ralpho, through whom Butler caricatured the Independents. In the debates between Hudibras and his squire, the points of difference between Presbyterians and Independents are touched lightly ; and what story there is proceeds, in good romance fashion, no faster than Chaucer's " Sir Thopas " (ch. iv. § 47). But the whimsical dialogues, descriptions, and turns of fancy that make up the poem, sparkle with keen wit applied incessantly to the real life and deeper thought of England in its day. The man of true genius never spends his energy on the mere outward fashions of his time. The story of the first part of the poem told how Sir Hudibras and Ralpho went forth to make an end of a bear-baiting, were drubbed in battle with the folk concerned in the bear-baiting, but were left, by the escape of the bear, masters of the field and of a one-legged fiddler, whom they carried off and put in the stocks. The escaped bear having been rescued, his friends came in search of the warriors, beset the house of Hudibras, and when he came out with Ralpho betimes in the morning, being stirred by a sense of victory to present himself with new hope to a disdainful widow who had goods and chattels, he was in trouble again, and finally vanquished in single combat by a woman. Trulla then claimed his arms, adorned him with her petticoat, caused Hudibras and Ralpho to be put in the stocks from which the one-legged fiddler was released. So they were left, Presbyterian and Independent, in high argument together about synods. There was no book so popular at court as "Hudibras" when it came out. The king quoted its couplets; Lord Clarendon hung Butler's portrait on his wall; it was, as Pepys records, the book most in fashion. The second part, equally popular, appeared in the following year, 1664. Butler married, but not money. The king and court did nothing for him, and he was saved from absolute starvation only by the liberality of a bencher of the Middle Temple, Mr. Longueville, who at last paid for his funeral. The discredit of this neglect was felt by other men of genius who were Butler's contemporaries. Dryden, in asking for unpaid arrears of his own salary, wrote, "It is enough for one age to have neglected Mr. Cowley and starved Mr. Butler." Otway, not long before he also died in hunger, wrote in the prologue to a play:

> " Tell 'em how Spenser died, how Cowley mourned,
> How Butler's faith and service were return'd."

And Oldham asked, "On Butler, who can think without just rage?" After publishing two parts of "Hudibras," Butler turned from his labour sick at heart. There was an interval of fourteen years, during which he lived in obscurity, before the third part appeared, in 1678; and he died in September, 1680.

26. Otway, who prospered least among the dramatists of Charles II.'s time, was the least frivolous. **Thomas d'Urfey,** born in Devonshire about 1630, lived to be very old, was known in the reign of George I. as one of the wits of the time of Charles II., and was "Tom" to the last, so that even the stone over his grave recorded of him "Tom d'Urfey: died February 26, 1723." He wrote plays, operas, poems, and songs, and was a diner-out among great people, whom he entertained by singing his own songs to his own music. That was his chief title to honour, and he was so well known that a country gentleman who came to London must not go home till he was able to say that he had met Tom d'Urfey. In 1676, D'Urfey began with *Archery Revived*, a heroic poem; a tragedy, *The Siege of Memphis;* and a comedy, *The Fond Husband; or, The Plotting Sister.* Comedies, with an occasional tragedy or tragi-comedy,

then followed one another fast. In 1682, D'Urfey, who had nothing of Butler's substance in him, published a satire, called *Butler's Ghost; or, Hudibras, the Fourth Part: with Reflections on these Times.* An imitation of Butler by **Samuel Colvil**, *The Mock Poem; or, Whiggs' Supplication*, sometimes called the Scottish " Hudibras," had appeared in 1681, the year after Butler's death. A volume of songs by **D'Urfey** appeared in 1687, and the collection made from time to time was completed in six volumes by 1720, as *Wit and Mirth; or, Pills to Purge Melancholy : being a large Collection of Ballads, Sonnets, &c., with their Tunes.* D'Urfey was of about Dryden's age, or a year or two older. Sir George Etherege was about four years, Thomas Shadwell eight years, younger than Dryden ; and Elkanah Settle was eight years younger than Shadwell.

**Sir George Etherege,** after some University training at Cambridge, some travel abroad, and some reading of law, gave himself to easy enjoyment of life among the men of fashion. He made himself a comrade of George Villiers, Sedley, Rochester, and their friends, by the success of his first comedy, *The Comical Revenge; or, Love in a Tub*, published in 1664. This was followed, in 1668, by *She Would if She Could;* and, in 1676, by his third and last comedy, *The Man of Mode; or, Sir Fopling Flutter.* There was ease and liveliness in these images of the corrupt life gathered about Charles II., by one who found enjoyment in its baseness. Etherege got his knighthood to enable him to marry a rich widow; was sent as English Minister to Ratisbon, and died there about 1694, by breaking his neck in a fall down-stairs when, as a drunken host, he was lighting his guests out of his rooms.

**Thomas Shadwell,** of a good Staffordshire family, was born in 1640, at Stanton Hall, Norfolk. He was educated at Caius College, Cambridge, studied law in the Middle Temple, went abroad, came home, and at once became popular as a dramatist. He began, in 1669, with *The Royal Shepherdess*, a tragi-comedy. This was followed by the comedies of *The Sullen Lovers* and *The Humourists;* and, in 1671, *The Miser*, from Molière. The tragedy of *Psyche*, in 1675, was followed in 1676 by the tragedy of *The Libertine* and the comedy of *Epsom Wells.* In 1678, Shadwell made the requisite improvements in *Timon of Athens*, which he said in the dedication " was originally Shakespeare's, who never made more masterly strokes than in this ; yet I can truly say I have made it into a play.'

Shadwell's *Lancashire Witches* and Teague O'Divelly, the Irish
Priest, first printed in 1682, held the stage for some time,
and contains one of the earliest specimens of the stage Irishman.  This play not only ridiculed the Roman Catholics, but
was spoken of before its production as containing an attack
on many clergy of the Church of England, in the character
of Smerk, chaplain to Sir Edward Hartfort, "foolish, knavish,
Popish, arrogant, insolent ; yet for his interest slavish."  Abuse
of the office of domestic chaplain was satirized in this character,
and also the spirit of Church intolerance against the Nonconformists; a great part of the dialogue that developed Mr.
Smerk was struck out by the Master of the Revels, and appeared only in the published play, where it was printed in italics.
Thus it was said to Smerk :

> " With furious zeal you press for discipline,
> With fire and blood maintain your great Diana,
> Foam at the mouth when a Dissenter's named ;
> (With fierie eyes, wherein we flaming see
> A persecuting spirit) you roar at
> Those whom the wisest of your function strive
> To win by gentleness and easie ways."

The stage Irish of that time had a touch of the stage Welsh.
One says to Teague, " You are a Popish priest ?"  He
answers, " Ah, but 'tis no matter for all daat, Joy : by my shoul,
but I will taak de oades, and I think I vill be excus'd ; but
hark vid you a while, by my trott, I shall be a Papist too for all
dat, indeed, yes."  In such comedies of Shadwell as *Epsom
Wells*, *Bury Fair* (1689), and *The Scowerers* (1690), we have
a clear surface reflection of certain forms of life in the later
Stuart time.

**Elkanah Settle**, born at Dunstable in 1648, studied at
Trinity College, Oxford, but left the University without a degree,
came to London, and in 1673 achieved a great success with his
tragedy in rhyme of *The Empress of Morocco*.  Settle showed
some vanity in the dedication of the play, which was published
with illustrative engravings—a frontispiece of the outside of the
Duke's Theatre, and pictures of the stage set with the chief
scenes.  His fellow dramatists did not admire the young man's
self-satisfied contempt of " the impudence of scribblers in this
age," that "has so corrupted the original design of dedication."
Having no very great genius to be proud of, he sneered at Dryden's critical dedications and prefaces with a "But, my lord,
whilst I trouble you with this kind of discourse, I beg you would

not think I design to give rubs to the Press as some of our tribe
have done to the Stage." Settle's popular play was open to
criticism, and his vanity invited it.  " The Empress of Morocco "
was accordingly pulled to pieces in a pamphlet written chiefly
by John Crowne, with aid from Shadwell and Dryden.  Settle
replied, and the controversy seemed to give him more importance with his public.  Other tragedies by Settle followed :—
*Love and Revenge,* in 1675 ; then *Cambyses; The Conquest of
China by the Tartars; Ibraham, the Illustrious Bassa,* from
Magdeleine de Scuderi's novel (§ i); *Pastor Fido,* from
Guarini's pastoral drama ; *Fatal Love; The Female Prelate,
being a History of the Life and Death of Pope Joan.* All
these were written before 1681.

John Crowne, who had been foremost in attack on Settle's
" Empress of Morocco," was the son of an Independent minister
in Nova Scotia.  He was for a time gentleman usher to an old
lady of quality ; but in 1671 he appeared as a dramatist with
the tragi-comedy of *Juliana,* the first of seventeen plays written
before his death in 1703.  He attached himself to the court
party, and in 1675 satirized the Whigs in a comedy called *City
Politics.*  In the same year he produced at court the masque of
*Calisto.*  In 1677 Crowne brought out a tragedy in two parts
on *The Destruction of Jerusalem.*  It is said that after the
appearance of this play, Rochester, who introduced Crowne at
court, ceased to be his friend ; also that he made enemies and
hindered his future success by attacking the Whigs in his *City
Politics.*  The king promised to do something for him when he
had written one comedy more, and gave him for groundwork, a
Spanish play by Moreto, *No Puede Ser* (" It Cannot Be "),
founded on the *Mayor Imposible* of Lope de Vega.  This was
the origin of Crowne's most successful comedy, *Sir Courtly
Nice;* but Charles II. died on the last day of its rehearsal,
and the dramatist had afterwards to live as he could by his
talent.

There was a marked influence of the Spanish comedy of
intrigue upon our stage after the Restoration, and to the plays
of Lope de Vega and Calderon had now been added those of
*Agustin Moreto,* who died in 1669, aged fifty-one.  Between
1654 and 1681 his works were being printed in three volumes,
besides many detached pieces not included in the volumes.
Moreto, besides religious and heroic plays, wrote comedies of
intrigue which excelled in light character-painting.  His fop,

"the handsome Don Diego," passed into a proverb, and the same kind of light character-painting is a characteristic of much of the later Stuart comedy.

27. Lee and Otway produced their first plays in the same year, 1675. **Nathaniel Lee** (b. 1650, d. 1690), the son of Dr. Lee, Incumbent of Hatfield, was educated at Westminster School and at Trinity College, Cambridge ; but, left to his own resources, he took to the stage, and, in 1672, played at the Duke's Theatre the part of Duncan in "Macbeth." Although an admirable reader, he was unable to get his living as an actor. He then produced, at the age of twenty-five, the first of his eleven plays, *Nero;* and between 1675 and 1684, this was followed by eight other plays of his own, including his two most popular, *The Rival Queens; or, Alexander the Great* (1677), and *Theodosius; or, the Force of Love* (1680). He also joined Dryden in the plays of *Œdipus* (1679) and *The Duke of Guise* (1683). There was a wildfire of imagination in Lee, and he drank too freely. In November, 1684, he was received into Bedlam, where he remained four years. A scribbler said to him when he was there, "It is easy to write like a madman." "No, said Lee, "it is not easy to write like a madman ; but it is very easy to write like a fool." Between his recovery and his death, at the age of forty, Lee wrote, in 1689 and 1690, two more plays, *The Princess of Cleve* and *The Massacre of Paris;* but he was chiefly dependent upon ten shillings a week from the Theatre Royal. He brought elevation of thought and occasional pathos, with frequent passion of love, into the sound and fury of the heroic style. There was more in him of the finer touch of nature than in any other of the dramatists of his time but Otway.

**Thomas Otway,** son of the Rev. Humphrey Otway, Rector of Woolbeding, was born at Trotton, near Midhurst, Sussex, in March, 1651. He was educated at Winchester School, and then at Christ Church ; but left Oxford without a degree, and became an unsuccessful actor in the Duke of York's company, failing at once in Mrs. Behn's tragedy of *The Jealous Bridegroom.* The Earl of Plymouth, one of the king's natural sons, got Otway a commission as cornet of horse in the new levies for Flanders. He came back poor, produced *Alcibiades* in 1675, and soon afterwards, in the same year, *Don Carlos, Prince of Spain,* which was a great success, was played for thirty successive nights, and brought Otway some money. He took his plot (as Schiller did long afterwards) from *Dom Carlos,*

*Nouvelle Historique*, published in 1672 by the Abbé de St. Réal, a clever French writer of that time, who had taste and refinement, and who enjoyed the study of striking passages of history, and like his friend, Varillas, cared rather to make them interesting by the interweaving of fictitious incident than to distinguish himself by fidelity of record. In 1677 Otway published his tragedy of *Titus and Berenice*, from Racine's *Bérénice*, produced at the same time as Corneille's *Tite et Bérénice*, in 1670. The plays of Racine and Corneille were both written to order. Otway followed in his own way Racine's plot, using the same characters, and compressing the piece into three acts. With his version of "Bérénice," Otway published a version from Molière's comedy (first acted in 1671) of *The Cheats of Scapin*. A comedy, *Friendship in Fashion*, which reflected the low morals of the court, was followed, in 1680, by two tragedies very different in character. One of them, *Caius Marius*, illustrated the predominance of the French school and the neglect · of Shakespeare ; for here Otway, not indeed with the self-sufficiency of a Lord Mulgrave, but with expression in the prologue of a poet's reverence for Shakespeare, mixed with his play a great part of "Romeo and Juliet," in a form that suited the new sense of the polite in literature. The classical discords of Marius and Sulla replaced those of the Capulets and Montagues, and Romeo became a Marius Junior. Some speeches of Mercutio were given to Sulpitius; Nurse remained Nurse, but Juliet was changed into Lavinia. Otway's other play, produced in 1680, was *The Orphan*. In both these plays Otway abandoned rhyme, and adopted blank verse as the fit measure for tragedy. In *The Orphan* he abandoned also the French faith in kings and queens, princes and princesses, as the sole objects of tragic interest. Monimia, the orphan daughter of an old brother-in-arms, whose whole wealth and nobility were in his worth as a man, is bred in the house of a nobleman who lives retired from court, with two sons and a daughter. Her brother, an impulsive honourable soldier, comes as guest to the house. These, with the chaplain and various servants in the country house, are all the persons of the play. The tragedy is a domestic drama, written in verse with much care. Animal passion is too obtrusively the mainspring of the plot ; but the appeal was meant to be throughout to the higher feelings of the audience, and *The Orphan* held the stage for years as a touching picture of innocence and beauty cast down into uttermost distress. If the

W *

passions were overstrained, they yet had truth of nature for their starting-point; and Otway drew natural tears from many who found only an artificial excitement in heroic plays which did not " servilely creep after sense." Having found in blank verse the fitting instrument, Otway put out his strength again in a play, *Venice Preserved*, which is still occasionally acted. He took his story from another book of the same French writer to whom he was indebted for the plot of his " Don Carlos." " Venice Preserved" is founded on the best book written by St. Réal, entitled *Histoire de la Conjuration que les Espagnols formerent, en* 1618, *contre la République de Venise*, published in 1674, and, like the " Dom Carlos," a passage of history transformed into historical romance. Otway, who produced in *The Orphan* and *Venice Preserved* the two best plays of the later Stuart drama, and who was a stout supporter of the Royal cause in detached poems as well as through his plays, was suffered to die of want. He died in April, 1685, in a public-house on Tower Hill, in which he had taken refuge to escape a debtor's prison. It is said that, in passion of hunger, he asked a shilling from a gentleman, who gave him a guinea; that he at once bought bread, and was choked in eager swallowing of the first mouthful. Probably that is an invention; but it is an invention founded on the fact of Otway's absolute distress and poverty. In his *Orphan*, although he laid the scene in Bohemia, there was England meant in the old noble's language of devotion to the king, but he said to his sons, bitterly :

> " If you have Children, never give them Knowledge,
> 'Twill spoil their Fortune, Fools are all the Fashion.
> If you've Religion, keep it to yourselves :
> Atheists will else make use of Toleration,
> And laugh you out on't ; never shew Religion,
> Except ye mean to pass for Knaves of Conscience,
> And cheat believing Fools that think ye honest."

Reaction against past restraint, and scorn of a mere self-seeking show of righteousness among the meaner part of their opponents, made it with many a mark of loyalty to seem licentious and profane. The corruption of the time appeared therefore to be more than it was ; but was much more than it would have been if Charles II. could have served his country in any other way than by giving the help of his bad character towards the Revolution.

28. One woman was among those who maintained the more corrupt form of the later Stuart drama. This was Aphra

**Behn,** born at Canterbury, in 1642, daughter of a General Johnson, who obtained through his kinsman, Lord Willoughby, the post of Governor of Surinam and the thirty-six West India Islands. He went when Aphra was very young, and died on the passage; but his widow and family settled in Surinam, where Aphra became acquainted with the African prince, Oroonoko, a slave who suffered torture and death for his love of liberty. Upon his story she founded afterwards the best of her novels. Aphra returned to England after some years in South America, married Mr. Behn, a Dutch merchant in London, and was soon left a widow. Charles II. delighted in her, and sent her in 1666, during the Dutch War, to use her charms of wit and liveliness as a political spy at Antwerp. She obtained an ascendancy over Van der Albert, an influential man, who enabled her to report home De Ruyter's design of coming up the Thames, but her report was not believed. Van der Albert died afterwards when he was about to marry Mrs. Behn. On her way home she was nearly shipwrecked. Her character suffered by the freedom of her manners. She began her career as a dramatist in 1671, and wrote for her livelihood seventeen plays, chiefly comedies, which reflected the gross manners of the court, and now and then belaboured the *Roundheads,* who gave their name to one comedy produced in 1682. Her most popular play was *The Rover; or, the Banished Cavaliers,* in 1677, followed by a second part in 1681. She translated Rochefoucauld's "Maxims" and Fontenelle's "Plurality of Worlds," wrote model love-letters, wrote poems, and was called "the divine Astræa." She wrote also short novels, among which, and among all her writings, *Oroonoko; or, the Royal Slave,* stands foremost, generous in temper, pure in tone, and the first book in our literature that stirred English blood with a sense of the negro's suffering in slavery. The story was a romance founded on fact, told as from the writer's personal experience in Surinam, in clear, good, unaffected English. Mrs. Behn, with a slave for her hero, known as Cæsar among the planters, a slave whose thirst for freedom drew other slaves from their work, who was flogged and rubbed with pepper, and at last was hacked to death limb by limb, represented him as a man with high and tender feeling. Wher she had told of his fortitude, she wrote of the unhappy negro as "this great man." "Thus," she says, "died this great man; worthy of a better fate, and a more sublime wit than mine to write his praise: yet I hope the reputation of my pen is considerable enough to make his glorious name to survive to all ages, with that of the brave, the beautiful, and the constant Imoinda." The second strong call upon Englishmen for sympathy with the slave was produced by this novel. Mrs. Behn died in 1689; in 1696, Southerne's best play, " Oroonoko," founded upon her novel, enforced its argument upon the stage.

Of another lady known as a writer, who died early in the reign of Charles II., and who was praised in style of the *Précieuses* as " the matchless Orinda," none but pleasant memories remain. She was **Katherine Philips**, for whom Jeremy Taylor wrote his treatise on Friendship (ch. ix. § 14), and who was worthy to be Jeremy Taylor's friend. Although praised at court she preferred quiet life with her husband in Wales, and died of small-pox in 1664, when only thirty-one years old. She published nothing in her lifetime. A few months before her death a publisher had collected copies of her poems that had passed among her friends, and issued them without her consent, as *Poems by the Incomparable Mrs. K. P.* Five years after her death a friend edited the first full and accurate edition of her works, as *Poems by the most deservedly Admired Mrs. Katherine Philips, the Matchless Orinda. To which is added Monsieur Corneille's Pompey and Horace Tragedies. With several other Translations out of French.* Cowley was among the writers of the prefatory verses in her honour. There is one note never absent from the praise :

> " She does above our best examples rise
> In hate of vice and scorn of vanities."

The verses themselves, touched by the French school in their manner, are not of the highest mark as poetry, but natural in their topics, and full of the kindly grace of womanhood. Friendship is a prominent theme. The volume includes various poems to special friends, Lucasia (Mrs. Anne Owen, by her second marriage Lady Dungannon) and Rosania (Regina Collier) ; occasional verses upon marriages and deaths among the friends of her home circle ; an epitaph on her mother-in-law ; praise of country life ; of the Welsh language ; lines to her husband upon a short parting ; lines on the last sad parting from two children ;—all that she wrote showing what Cowley called " the tender goodness of her mind." Not long before her own death she lost her first-born, in his thirteenth year, and her lament for him closed thus :

> "Alas! we were secure of our content;
> But find too late that it was only lent
> To be a mirrour, wherein we may see
> How frail we are, how spotless we should be.
> But if to thy blest soul my grief appears,
> Forgive and pity these injurious tears;
> Impute them to Affection's sad excess,
> Which will not yield to Nature's tenderness,
> Since 'twas through dearest ties and highest trust
> Continued from thy cradle to thy dust;
> And so rewarded and confirm'd by thine,
> That (wo is me!) I thought thee too much mine.
> But I'll resign, and follow thee as fast
> As my unhappy minutes will make hast.
> Till when, the fresh remembrances of thee
> Shall be my emblems of mortality.
> For such a loss as this (bright Soul) is not
> Ever to be repaired or forgot."

29. The Life of the Soul had been the chief subject of the poetry of **Henry More** (ch. viii. § 58), who lived throughout the reign of Charles II., and produced, in 1675 and 1679, first his theological works, and then his philosophical works translated into Latin. Henry More died in 1687.

**Robert Boyle**, throughout the reign of Charles II., was still blending religion with his philosophical researches into nature. Henry More, doubtless, was in good sympathy with Robert Boyle's letter on *Seraphic Love*, addressed to a young "Lindamor" disappointed in courtship; a commendation to him of that purely spiritual love to which More found both Christianity and Platonism inviting men. This, although written in 1648, was first published in 1660, a little before the book which set forth Boyle's *New Experiments Physico-mechanical, touching the Spring of the Air and its Effects, made for the most part in a New Pneumatical Engine.*

These were experiments made with the air-pump, a contrivance first suggested, in 1654, by Otto Guericke, a magistrate of Magdeburg, but more perfectly worked out, in 1658 or 1659, by Robert Boyle, with the help of **Robert Hooke**, who was then about twenty-three years old, living with Boyle as a chemical assistant. Hooke was made, in 1662, Curator of the Experiments of the Royal Society; in 1664, its Professor of Mechanics; and, in 1665, Professor of Geometry in Gresham College. He improved the microscope, was at the head of English microscopic research, and published, in 1666, his *Micrographia; or, some Physiological Descriptions of Minute Bodies, made by Magnifying Glasses.* Robert Hooke, who was made

M.D. by Tillotson in 1691 and died in 1702, was one of the best representatives of the activity of scientific thought under Charles II.

**Robert Boyle's** publications continued to witness to his active interest in science. In 1661 he published considerations on the conduct of experiments, and some more experiments of his own, in *Certain Physiological Essays;* published, also, his *Sceptical Chemist,* in argument against those short-sighted philosophers who "are wont to endeavour to evince their salt, sulphur, and mercury to be the true principles of things." In 1663 he published *Some Considerations touching the Usefulness of Experimental Natural Philosophy,* and *Experiments and Considerations touching Colours,* also *Considerations touching the Style of the Holy Scriptures;* and among many other little books, with God and Nature for their theme, was one, published in 1665, but written when he was very young—"in my infancy," he says, writing to his sister, Lady Ranelagh, who had asked him to find it—entitled, *Occasional Reflections upon Several Subjects: whereto is premised a Discourse about such kind of Thoughts.* This was the book afterwards ridiculed by Swift, in his "Meditations on a Broomstick."

There was much ridicule of the Royal Society in its first years, and a belief in many that its new ways of research were destructive of true learning, and even of religion. This caused **Thomas Sprat** to publish, in 1667, his *History of the Royal Society.* Sprat, born in Devonshire in 1636, was a clergyman's son. He studied at Wadham College, Oxford, became M.A. in 1657, and obtained a fellowship. His turn for science meant no more than activity of mind under the influence of Dr. Wilkins (ch. viii. § 59, 64), who was Warden of Wadham. His turn for verse seems to have meant no more than activity of mind under the influence of Cowley, who, since 1657, had been, as Dr. Cowley, one of Wilkins's circle of philosophers. Sprat's last poem was upon Cowley's death, his first was on the death of Cromwell, "To the Happy Memory of the late Lord Protector;" and he published also, in 1659, a Cowleian poem, in thirty-one "Pindaric" stanzas, on *The Plague of Athens,* suggested by the description of it in Thucydides. Sprat took orders at the Restoration, was chaplain to the Duke of Buckingham, and soon afterwards to the king. Cowley, with whom he was intimate, died in 1667; and Sprat's enthusiastic ode on Cowley's poetry was written in the year of the publishing of his "History of the Royal Society." Cowley had entrusted to his friend Sprat the care of his writings, and in 1668 Sprat published Cowley's Latin works, prefaced with a *Life of Cowley*, also in Latin.   This was amplified and prefixed, in 1688, to an edition of Cowley's English works.   Thomas Sprat's life after the age of thirty-two does not concern literature.   In 1688 he had been four years Bishop of Rochester.   He complied as passively as he could with the Revolution, and died at the age of seventy-seven.

In 1668, Dr. John Wilkins (ch. ix. § 18), who had become Dean of Ripon, was made Bishop of Chester; and in the same year his most interesting work, *An Essay towards a Real Character and a Philosophical Language*, was printed by the Royal Society.   This applied natural philosophy to language, and laboured towards the deduction from first principles of quickened intercourse among men, by an easy common language in which significant signs were to build up the meaning of each word.   Bishop Wilkins died in 1672, at his friend Tillotson's house in Chancery Lane.

Robert Boyle's writings chiefly concerned experiments on air and on flame, till 1674, when he published *Observations about the Saltness of the Sea*, and a book written during his retirement from London in the plague-time of 1665, *The Excellency of Theology compared with Natural Philosophy, as both are the Objects of Men's Study*.   In the following year, 1675, appeared his *Considerations about the Reconcilableness of Reason and Religion*.   Robert Boyle, who never named God without a reverent pause, refused to take orders with assurance of high Church promotion ; he said that he could serve religion more effectually as a layman.   He sent to a friend in the Levant, for distribution, Dr. Edward Pocock's translation into Arabic of Grotius on the "Truth of Christianity," printed at Boyle's expense, after a liberal reward to the translator.   Boyle caused also an Irish Bible to be produced, and this too was printed at his expense.   As one of its directors, he was active in urging the East India Company to use its influence in spreading Christianity with trade ; and he was the first governor of a corporation for the propagation of the Gospel and the conversion of the American natives in New England.   For six years he helped to provide Burnet with the means that enabled him to write and publish the first volume of his "History of the Reformation" (§ 22). In 1680 Robert Boyle declined the Presidency of the Royal Society, because he was unwilling to be bound by test and oaths

on taking office.   He was not a Nonconformist, but was zealous
against intolerance.   He also declined the Provostship of Eton,
and several times refused a peerage.   He is said to have spent
£1,000 a year in works of benevolence.   Robert Boyle was tall,
very thin, and of feeble constitution.   He never married.   His
dearest female friend was his sister, Lady Ranelagh, whom he
survived only a week.   He died at the end of December, 1691.

30. **Isaac Newton** (not Sir Isaac till Queen Anne's reign)
was born at the manor of Woolsthorpe, Lincolnshire, on Christmas-day, 1642.   His father's death left the manor to him in his
childhood, and a few years afterwards his mother married again.
He went to the free school at Grantham, and was then taken
home to learn the management of his small property; but his
bent for study caused him to be sent back to Grantham School,
and entered, at eighteen, Trinity College, Cambridge, where he
took his degree as B.A. in 1664.   There his interest in mathematics was quickened by Isaac Barrow, who became, in 1663,
the first Lucasian lecturer in mathematics (§ 22).   From Euclid,
understood at the first reading, Newton turned to Descartes,
whose new methods were then being followed at Cambridge,
and from Descartes passed to the mathematical writings of
John Wallis (ch. viii. § 64; ch. ix. § 18), and these, especially
his *Arithmetica Infinitorum*, were the books that stimulated
Newton's own genius, and led him to his theory of fluxions
(differential and integral calculus) promulgated in 1665, at the
age of twenty-three.   Leibnitz afterwards contested with him
honours of discovery.   This was an addition to mathematical
science which gave the most essential aid to exact calculation of
the movements of the heavenly bodies.   Newton occupied himself, also, at this time, with the grinding of object-glasses.
Observations with a prism led Newton to views upon the
decomposition of light, which were developed into a new revelation of the processes of Nature.   In 1667 he became M.A. and
Fellow of his College.   In 1669 he succeeded his friend Barrow
as mathematical professor; and the course of his researches at
that time caused him to give lectures on optics, in Latin.   In
1671 Isaac Newton became a Fellow of the Royal Society, and
communicated to it his new theory of Light.   His first discovery
of the law of Gravitation was made also in the reign of
Charles II., although not published until 1687.   Newton's marvellous insight into the order of Nature increased his reverence
for the Creator.   He spent much time in study of the Bible

and when he became foremost in fame among philosophers, and there was wonder at the comprehensive character of his discoveries, he said only, " To myself I seem to have been as a child picking up stones on the sea-shore, while the great ocean of truth lay unexplored before me."

31. The busy spirit of inquiry that had advanced from reform of Church discipline to active study of the foundations of religion and government, that sought more and more to interpret and apply to the use of man the laws of external nature, was at the same time occupied with a scrutiny of those natural laws which affect the results of human intercourse and the social well-being of nations. Attempts were made in the direction of a science of Political Economy. In 1664, with some curious documents upon our trade with the East Indies, appeared *England s Treasure by Foreign Trade*, by Thomas Mun, the ablest advocate of the East India Company. He was then dead, and might have written the book five-and-twenty years before. In this work Mun upheld foreign commerce as the best source of a nation's wealth ; and held by an old theory of the balance of trade, that our exports should exceed our imports, so that the difference between them—the balance of trade—should always be coming in as bullion or money. Another of the reasoners on commerce in the reign of Charles II. was Sir Josiah Child (b. 1630, d. 1699), who published, in 1668, a *New Discourse of Trade*. It argued incidentally against the dread of depopulation by colonies, and other errors ; but its main object was to advocate reduction of the legal rate of interest. Sir William Petty (ch. ix. § 18) published, in 1667, a treatise *On Taxes and Contributions*, and in it he was, incidentally, the first to lay down the doctrine that the value of commodities is determined by the labour and time needed for producing them. Petty died in 1687. His widow was made Baroness Shelburne. The elder of his two sons succeeded to that title, and died childless. The title was then revived in Henry, the second son, great uncle of the first Marquis of Lansdowne.

In medicine the advance made by Thomas Sydenham from traditions in the treatment of disease to fresh observation and thought was so great that the modern art of healing was, in a sense, founded by him. Sydenham was born of a good Dorsetshire family in 1624, went to Oxford at eighteen, and at the age of twenty-four, in 1648, took the degree of M.B., and

obtained a fellowship at All Souls. He visited the medical
school at Montpellier, and then practised medicine at Westminster. In 1663 he was made Licentiate of the Royal College
of Physicians. His medical writings are not voluminous, but
they are very practical. He observed nature minutely, and
was a fellow-thinker with Robert Boyle, who had a most lively
interest in the application of the study of nature to the practice
of medicine. Among Boyle's suggestions was an anticipation of
the observing of sounds within the body as a help to a knowledge of the nature of disease. Writing of a certain fever,
Sydenham described his treatment, and said : " Meanwhile I
watched what method Nature might take, with the intention of
subduing the symptoms by treading in her footsteps. . . . .
more could be left to Nature than we are at present in the habit
of leaving her. To imagine that she always wants the aid of
Art is an error—an unlearned error, too." The physician must,
he argued, follow and aid the processes by which Nature relieves
herself of a disease, or else he must discover a specific  The
search for specifics, dwelt upon by Robert Boyle as one duty of
the physician, seemed to Sydenham also of highest importance.
One of the few known specifics, Peruvian bark, which has a
supreme power over ague, Sydenham used with the best effect.
It became known to the Jesuits in 1638, from its use by the
natives when the Countess of Cinchona, wife of the vice-regent
of Peru, was cured of ague by it. In 1639 the Jesuits carried it
to Spain. It was introduced into England in 1653, against medical condemnation as quackery. In 1658 much was said of an
alderman who died of ague with bark, and the prejudice was so
strong that Cromwell died of a tertian ague when bark might
have saved his life. Not long before the use of bark, one in
four and a half of all the deaths in England was from ague.
A century later the proportion of deaths from ague had come
to be one in 3,767. Sydenham established the use of " Jesuits'
Powder" in ague, and was the first to introduce a great
reform into the treatment of small-pox. His medical writings
chiefly dealt with the epidemics that spread death in our towns,
because in this direction he might help to do in his own art
the highest service to society. He died in 1689.

32. Observation of nature was not yet applied to history.
**William Prynne** (ch. viii. § 56), when he had ended his battle
with Episcopacy, and had his revenge on Laud, turned his
bitterness against the Independents. He was strong for recon-

cilement with the king. Under the Commonwealth he was in opposition to the Independents, openly defied Cromwell's authority, and was imprisoned. He assisted in the Restoration, sat for Bath in Parliament, and became under Charles II. Keeper of the Records in the Tower, with a salary of £500 a year. In this reign he published the three folios known as Prynne's Records, *An Exact Chronological and Historical Demonstration of our British, Roman, Saxon, Danish, Norman, English Kings' Supreme Ecclesiastical Jurisdiction in and over all Spiritual or Religious Affairs, &c.* These records of the ecclesiastical jurisdiction of the kings of England extend to the end of the reign of Edward I. Prynne died in 1669.

33. **Edward Hyde** was made at the Restoration Earl of Clarendon and Lord Chancellor. After his fall, in November, 1667, he went to France, and died at Rouen, in December, 1674. His *Brief View of the Pernicious Errors in Hobbes's Leviathan* appeared two years after his death ; but his *History of the Rebellion and Civil Wars in England, begun in the Year* 1641, was first published at Oxford, in three folios, in 1702-4. Still later, in 1727, appeared in folio *A Collection of several Tracts of the Right Honourable Edward, Earl of Clarendon,* containing his " Vindication " from the charge of high treason that closed his political career ; "Reflections upon several Christian Duties, Divine and Moral, by way of Essays," all written after his fall ; a "Dialogue on Education," and a complete set of " Contemplations and Reflections on the Psalms of David." The MSS. of Clarendon's own *Account of his Life, from his Birth to the Restoration in* 1660, and a Continuation from 1660 to 1667, written for the information of his children, were given by Clarendon's descendants to the University of which he had been chancellor, and first published at Oxford in 1759. The *Continuation* serves at the same time as a continuation of the History of the Rebellion, Clarendon's life being as inseparable from the events in which he played a leading part as his history is inseparable from the bias of mind which determined his career.

34. **Thomas Hobbes** (ch. viii. § 66; ch. ix. § 11), living far into the reign of Charles II., published, in 1675, a *Translation of the Iliad and Odyssey* into English verse, after an experiment with four books of the "Odyssey" as *The Voyage of Ulysses.* He died in 1679, at the age of ninety-two. In the year of his death

appeared a Latin poem by him on his own *Life*, written at the age of eighty-four, and his *Behemoth : The History of the Civil Wars of England, and of the Councels and Artifices by which they were carried on, from the Year* 1640 *to the Year* 1660. This is discussed in the form of a dialogue between A and B, and sets forth Hobbes's opinions on the place of the Roman Catholics, Presbyterians, and Independents in their relation to the Civil War, upon ship-money, the action of the Long Parliament and the Commonwealth, and other topics interesting to a philosophical inquirer with some strong opinions of his own.

B says in the course of this dialogue that he should like to see "a system of the present morals written by some divine of good reputation and learning, and of the late king's party." "I think," A answers, "I can recommend unto you the best that is extant, and such a one as (except a few passages that I mislike) is very well worth your reading.   The title of it is, *The Whole Duty of Man laid down in a Plain and Familiar Way.*" This popular book, with prayers appended, including a prayer for the Church and prayers "for those who mourn in secret in these times of calamity," was first published in 1659, was translated into Welsh in 1672, into Latin in 1693, and has been attributed by different speculators to three archbishops, two bishops, several less dignified clergymen, and a lady.

35. **Samuel Parker** was a worldly defender of the Church against Nonconformity.   He was born in 1640, the son of one of Cromwell's committee-men, and a strict Puritan until the Restoration, when he had been a year at Oxford.   In 1665, at the age of twenty-five, he became one of the Fellows of the Royal Society, and carried experimental science into theology with a book in Latin of " Physico-Theological Essays concerning God "—*Tentamina Physico-Theologica de Deo*—which got him the post of chaplain to Archbishop Sheldon, who also made him Archdeacon of Canterbury.   In 1670 he published *A Discourse of Ecclesiastical Polity, wherein the Authority of the Civil Magistrate over the Consciences of Subjects in Matters of Eternal Religion is Asserted;* and in 1672 he wrote a preface to a posthumous work of Archbishop Bramhall's, *A Vindication of the Bishops from the Presbyterian Charge of Popery.* This brought down on Samuel Parker's head the satire of **Andrew Marvell** (ch. ix. § 9), who under the Restoration represented Hull in Parliament, and fought for liberty of conscience with satire, the one weapon effective among triflers in

high places. According to the custom of an older time, Hull
paid its members, and private news-letters then furnishing
what we find now in the newspapers, Marvell maintained a
steady correspondence with his constituents, sending almost
every post-night an account of the proceedings of Parliament.
He seldom or never spoke in the House, but his pen was a
known power. Indolent King Charles relished the sharpness
of it, although his own follies and vices were not spared. The
court party would have been glad to secure the one lively
satirist who was not on their own side. Lord Danby found his
way up to Marvell's second floor in a court leading from the
Strand, with message of regard from the king and expression
of His Majesty's desire to serve him. Marvell answered that
His Majesty had it not in his power to serve him. When a
place at court was suggested, Marvell replied that if he accepted
it he must either be ungrateful to the king in opposing court
measures, or a traitor to his country in complying with them.
His Majesty must believe him a loyal subject, and true to the
king's real interest in remaining independent. Lord Danby
ended with offer of a present of a thousand pounds from His
Majesty, and that was refused as firmly. In one of his verse
satires, " Hodge's Vision from the Monument, December, 1675,"
the member for Hull refers to the bribery of members of
Parliament :

> " See how in humble guise the slaves advance
> To tell a tale of army, and of France,
> Whilst proud prerogative in scornful guise,
> Their fear, love, duty, danger does despise.
> There, in a bribed committee, they contrive
> To give our birthrights to prerogative :
> Give, did I say? They sell, and sell so dear
> That half each tax Danby distributes there.
> Danby, 'tis fit the price so great shall be,
> They sell religion, sell their liberty."

Marvell told the king in his verse that, as the astronomer described spots in the sun, he loyally described his faults, and
pointed out that those who seemed his courtiers were but his
disease. He attacked those who for their own advantage

> " About the common prince have raised a fence ;
> The kingdom from the crown distinct would see,
> And peel the bark to burn at last the tree.
> As Ceres corn, and Flora is the spring,
> As Bacchus wine, the Country is the king.

Let him get rid of his " scratching courtiers "—" The smallest

vermin makes the greatest waste"—let him choose for his
companions and counsellors generous men too noble to flatter,
and too rich to steal :

> " Where few the number, choice is there less hard.
>   Give us this court, and rule without a guard."

The spots in the sun were assuredly not spared in Marvell's
rhymes. In the dialogue between the horses of the two statues,
that of Charles I. at Charing Cross, set up by Lord Danby, and
that of Charles II. at Woodchurch, set up by Sir Robert Viner,
they agreed in lament

> " To see *Dei Gratia* writ on the throne,
>   And the king's wicked life say, 'God there is none.'"

The horse of Charing said to the horse of Woodchurch :

> " Thy rider puts no man to death in his wrath,
>   But is buried alive in lust and in sloth ;"

and thought he "had rather bear Nero than Sardanapalus."

> " *Woodchurch.* What is thy opinion of James, Duke of York?
>   *Charing.* The same that the frogs had of Jupiter's stork.
>   With Turk in his head, and the Pope in his heart,
>   Father Patrick's disciples will make England smart.
>   If e'er he be king I know Britain's doom,
>   We must all to a stake or be converts to Rome.
>   Ah Tudor ! ah Tudor ! of Stuarts enough ;
>   None ever reigned like old Bess in the ruff."

And presently we have this question and answer :

> " ' But canst thou devise when things will be mended?'
>   ' When the reign of the line of the Stuarts is ended.'"

So spoke the verse of Marvell, whose satire both in verse and
prose dealt only with the vital questions of his time. Thus,
when Samuel Parker not only attacked the Nonconformists, but
argued for the supreme power of a king to bind the consciences
of his subjects, he brought Andrew Marvell down in unmerciful
prose satire on himself and his cause. It was in 1672, and the
town was then being amused with Buckingham's " Rehearsal,"
just produced. Marvell at once took from the popular play the
machinery of his satire, and its name, *The Rehearsal Transprosed*, came from a passage in it. Mr. Bayes, explaining to
Smith and Johnson his rules, as a dramatist, says, " ' Why, sir,
my first rule is the rule of transversion, or regulus duplex :
changing verse into prose, or prose into verse, alternative as
you please.' *Smith.* 'How's that, sir, by a rule, I pray ?' *Bayes.*
' Why, thus, sir ; nothing more easy when understood : I take

a book in my hand, either at home or elsewhere, for that's all one. If there be any wit in't, as there is no book but has some, I transverse it : that is, if it be prose, I put it into verse (but that takes up some time) ; if it be verse, put it into prose.' *Johnson.* ' Methinks, Mr. Bayes, that putting verse into prose should be call'd transprosing. *Bayes.* ' By my troth, a very good notion, and hereafter it shall be so.' " Following this notion, Andrew Marvell, when he put the Rev. Samuel Parker into the part of Bayes, and applied the new joke of the town to a comment on the advocate for a royal supremacy over men's consciences, called his book of prose satire *The Rehearsal Transprosed.* It was written against such doctrines as these : That unless princes have power to bind their subjects to that religion they apprehend most advantageous to public peace and tranquillity, and restrain those religious mistakes that tend to its subversion, they are no better than statues and images of authority. That in cases and disputes of public concernment, private men are subject to the public conscience, and if there be any sin in the command, he that imposed it shall answer for it, and not I whose whole duty it is to obey. The commands of authority will warrant my obedience ; my obedience will hallow, or at least excuse my action, and so secure me from sin, if not from error ; and in all doubtful and disputable cases 'tis better to err with authority than to be in the right against it. That it is absolutely necessary to the peace and happiness of kingdoms that there be set up a more severe government over men's consciences and religious persuasions than over their vices and immoralities. Marvell's satire upon Parker and his principles produced various answers, with such titles as, *Rosemary and Bayes, The Transproser Rehearsed, A Commonplace Book out of the Rehearsal Digested under Heads,* and *Stoo him Bayes ; or, Some Animadversions on the Humour of Writing Rehearsals.* **Samuel Parker,** who, as chaplain to the Archbishop of Canterbury, had a voice in licensing, sought to withdraw the licence from Marvell's book. At last he replied to it with a *Reproof to the Rehearsal Transprosed,* and Marvell rejoined at once (in 1673) with "*The Rehearsal Transpros'd : The Second Part.* Occasioned by Two Letters : The first Printed by a nameless Author, Intituled A Reproof &c. The Second Letter left for me at a Friend's House, Dated Nov. 3, 1673, subscribed 'J. G.,' and concluding with these words : ' If thou darest to Print or Publish any Lie or Libel against Doctor Parker, by the Eternal God I will cut thy

Throat.' Answered by Andrew Marvell." That was the title-
page, and where the licenser's imprimatur should be there was
a sentence from the *Reproof* taken in place of license; for the
author of the "Reproof," being the archbishop's chaplain, was
an official licenser, and this was the sentence : " Reproof, p. 67.
If you have anything to object against it, do your worst. You
know the press is open." Under this sentence, therefore,
Marvell wrote " Licensed the 1st of May, 1673. By the Author
and Licenser of the Ecclesiastical Polity." Marvell never lost
sight of the principle for which he was contending in the form
of battle then most likely to prevail. Simply direct reasoning
would have been read only by those who agreed with it already,
but the worrying of Doctor Parker and his cause with reason in
the form of a shrewd bantering satire, not free from a coarseness
and rough personality more pleasant and convincing then than
now, was a delightful spectacle even to Doctor Parker's friends.
There was no better way of knocking the support from under a
shallow and intemperate apostle of a king's right to direct the
consciences of his people. Anthony à Wood says that Parker
"judged it more prudent to lay down the cudgels than to enter
the lists again with an untowardly combatant, so hugely well-
versed and experienced in the then but newly refined art,
though much in mode and fashion ever since, of sporting and
jeering buffoonery. It was generally thought, however, by many
of those who were otherwise favourers of Parker's cause, that the
victory lay on Marvell's side, and it wrought this good effect on
Parker, that for ever after it took down his great spirit." Burnet
says he " withdrew from the town and ceased writing for some
years." But **Samuel Parker**, who was made Bishop of Oxford
by James II., and died in 1687, poured out his impotent rage
against his adversary in a Latin History of his Own Time (from
1660 to 1680). *De Rebus sui Temporis Commentariorum Libri
IV.*, which was not printed until 1726, appeared in an English
translation by Thomas Newlin in 1727, and became known as
" The Tory Chronicle." Marvell's character of Parker, in " The
Rehearsal Transprosed," may not be so very far from the truth
as Parker's account of Marvell in the History of his Own
Time ; but in no case can a man's character be taken from an
antagonist while, in the act of controversy, he is endeavouring
to break his credit. Marvell's next prose satire was called forth
about three years later by Dr. Francis Turner. The Bishop of
Hereford, Dr. Croft, had published a book urging forbearance

and charity upon all the contending parties in religion. This book, called *The Naked Truth; or, the True State of the Primitive Church: by a Humble Moderator,* had been attacked without forbearance or charity by Dr. Turner, Master of St. John's College, Cambridge, in *Animadversions on the Naked Truth.* That was in 1675, when the popular new play (printed in 1676) was Etherege's "Man of Mode" (§ 26). Marvell at once fitted Dr. Turner with a character out of it, as *Mr. Smirke; or, the Divine in Mode,* and again charged home on the court party with allusion fresh from the last new play, and a force of satire that cut off the unlucky Dr. Turner from the support and fellowship he looked for. Marvell added to his "Mr. Smirke" *A Short Historical Essay concerning General Councils, Creeds, and Impositions in Matters of Religion.* In 1677 Marvell defended John Howe (ch. ix. § 13) against three assailants of a book of his on "Divine Prescience," and in the following year he published *An Account of the Growth of Popery and Arbitrary Government in England.* In August, 1678, he died.

36. **John Dryden** (§ 10—12, 15) also was being forced by the new taste of the court into expression of his most vigorous thought through satire. He still wrote for the stage. In 1673, when Settle published his "Empress of Morocco" (§ 26), Dryden wrote a poor tragedy to encourage public feeling against the Dutch after the breaking of the Triple Alliance. This was *Amboyna; or, the Cruelties of the Dutch to the English Merchants.* He printed also *Marriage à la Mode,* acted the year before, in which he blended prose scenes with blank verse again, as well as heroic couplets. Another play, produced in 1672, unsuccessfully, *The Assignation,* was in prose, with a little blank verse, chiefly in the last act. In *Amboyna,* the dialogue is chiefly a loose blank verse printed as prose. In 1674, the year of Milton's death, Dryden published—it was not acted—an opera based on his "Paradise Lost," called *The State of Innocence and Fall of Man.* It is in heroic rhyme, with little provision for song, but much for machinery and spectacle. The adaptation was made in good faith, but it is instructive to compare Milton's dialogue between Adam and Eve in their innocence with Dryden's endeavour to reproduce its effect on the minds of people who enjoyed the comedies of Etherege and Mrs. Behn. John Dryden was among those who had visited John Milton, for, in the preface to his "Fables," Dryden quotes from a conversation

with him. He is said to have asked Milton's leave to adapt "Paradise Lost," and to have been answered with a good-humoured, "Ay, you may tag my verses." In 1675, Dryden produced a heroic play, *Aurenge Zebe; or, the Great Mogul,* which remained popular. It was the last play written by him in heroic rhyme, and he expressed in its dedication to Lord Mulgrave some weariness of play-writing, with a manifest feeling that he had not, as a dramatist, done justice to himself. Instead of rhyming plays, he was hoping for leisure to rhyme a great poem. " If I must be condemn'd to rhime," he said, " I should find some ease in my change of punishment. I desire to be no longer the Sisyphus of the Stage; to rowl up a stone with endless labour (which, to follow the proverb, gathers no moss), and which is perpetually falling down again; I never thought myself very fit for an employment where many of my predecessors have excell'd me in all kinds; and some of my contemporaries, even in my own partial judgment, have outdone me in comedy. Some little hopes I have yet remaining, and these too, considering my abilities, may be vain, that I may make the world some part of amends for many ill plays by an heroick poem. Your lordship has been long acquainted with my design, the subject of which you know is great, the story English, and neither too far distant from the present age, nor too near approaching it. Such, it is my opinion, that I could not have a nobler occasion to do honour by it to my king and country, and my friends; most of our ancient nobility being concerned in the action. And your lordship has one particular reason to promote this undertaking, because you were the first who gave me the opportunity of discoursing it to His Majesty and His Royal Highness. They were then pleas'd both to commend the design, and to encourage it by their commands. But the unsettledness of my condition has hitherto put a stop to my thoughts concerning it. As I am no successor to Homer in his wit, so neither do I desire to be in his poverty. I can make no rhapsodies, nor go a-begging at the Græcian doors, while I sing the praises of their ancestors. The times of Virgil please me better, because he had an Augustus for his patron. And to draw the allegory nearer you, I am sure I shall not want a Mecænas with him. 'Tis for your lordship to stir up that remembrance in His Majesty, which his many avocations of business have caus'd him, I fear, to lay aside." This invocation is not equal to Milton's :

" Chiefly Thou, O Spirit, that dost prefer
Before all temples the upright heart and pure,
Instruct me . . . . . . . . . . .
. . . . . . . . . what in me is dark
Illumine, what is low raise and support."

But no heroic poem came of a looking up to the divine majesty of Charles II.

After " Aurenge Zebe," Dryden did cease for a time from writing plays, his next being in 1678, an ambitious revision of Shakespeare's "Antony and Cleopatra," as *All for Love; or, The World Well Lost.* In his preface, he said, " I have endeavour'd in this play to follow the practice of the ancients, who, as Mr. Rymer has judiciously observed, are, and ought to be, our masters. . . . In my stile I have profess'd to imitate the divine Shakespear; which, that I might perform more freely, I have disincumber'd myself from rhyme. Not that I condemn my former way, but that this is more proper to my present purpose."

37. **Thomas Rymer**, here quoted with respect, was, in 1678 about forty years old, a Yorkshireman, educated at Northallerton School and Cambridge, who had entered at Gray's Inn. When this preface was written, Rymer had just taken a foremost place among the critics who, following Boileau's argument for classical models and good sense, applied French Laws to English Literature, by publishing, early in 1678, *The Tragedies of the Last Age Consider'd and Examin'd by the Practice of the Ancients, and by the Common Sense of all Ages. In a Letter to Fleetwood Shepheard, Esq.* The plays here suggested for criticism were Beaumont and Fletcher's " Rollo," "King and No King," and " Maid's Tragedy;" Shakespeare's " Othello" and "Julius Cæsar;" and Ben Jonson's " Catiline." But Rymer brought his letter to an end when he had criticized the three plays by Beaumont and Fletcher, and summed up with this opinion of the noblest epoch of dramatic literature in the world's history: " I have thought our poetry of the last age as rude as our architecture; one cause thereof might be, that Aristotle's treatise of poetry has been so little studied amongst us." Mr. Rymer reserved the discussion of the other plays, and said, " With the remaining tragedies I shall also send you some reflections on that ' Paradise Lost ' of Milton's which some are pleas'd to call a poem, and assert rime against the slender sophistry wherewith he attacques it." Mr. Rymer called the

poetry of times before the French influence came in "rude as
our architecture." The new polite taste condemned also Gothic
architecture, because it was not based on Greek or Roman
models. St. Paul's Cathedral, at this time being rebuilt after
the Fire of London, is our noblest result of the classical
renaissance that in architecture began in the time of Charles I.,
and had Inigo Jones for its leader. Dryden's plays, in 1679,
were *Œdipus*, with Nathaniel Lee (§ 27), and a reconstruction
of Shakespeare's " Troilus and Cressida," both in blank verse,
with *Limberham*, a comedy in prose. The book of *Troilus
and Cressida* had not only a dedication, with incidental criticism, but also a "Preface to the Play," in which Dryden
discussed at some length the grounds of criticism in tragedy.
The critical discussions in the dedications and prefaces to
Dryden's published plays greatly assisted the sale of his play-
books, and, when printed by themselves, they show their
strength as by far the best and most characteristic criticism
upon forms of poetry produced during the reign of Charles II.
In the preface to " Troilus and Cressida" Dryden no longer
disdained a servile creeping after sense, but wrote, " 'Tis neither
height of thought that is discommended, nor pathetic vehemence,
nor any nobleness of expression in its proper place; but 'tis a
false measure of all these, something which is like 'em and is
not them : 'tis the Bristol stone which appears like a diamond"—
(" Evitons ces faux brillans," Boileau had said)—" 'tis an extravagant thought, instead of a sublime one; 'tis roaring madness, instead of vehemence; and a sound of words instead of
sense "—(" Tout doit tendre au bon sens," Boileau had said).
Dryden felt the genius of Shakespeare, had a sense even of
smallness in the wit of what he held to be his own more
refined age; and if there had been the strength of Dryden in
many writers, our literature would have profited by the just
demand for good sense in poetry as a reaction from the later
Euphuism (ch. viii. § 25), without losing height of thought,
pathetic vehemence, or nobleness of expression. But the times,
and his relation to them, gave Dryden little opportunity of
touching the ideal that lay only half recognised within him. In
December, 1679, he was waylaid and cudgelled by ruffians,
employed, it was believed, by the Earl of Rochester, who wrongly
supposed him to have had a hand in Lord Mulgrave's Essay on
Satire, that contained sharp lines not only on Rochester, but
also on the vices of the king. In 1679 Dryden's salary and

pension began to fall into arrears, and continued to do so during the next four years. In 1679 he produced a translation of the *Epistles of Ovid*, by various hands besides his own. In the spring or summer of 1681, Dryden produced a play addressed to the popular feeling of the day against the Roman Catholic priesthood, called *The Spanish Friar; or, the Double Discovery*. It has earned special praise for the dramatic skill with which it makes an underplot unite with the main action of the piece. This appeared as what Dryden called "a Protestant play addressed to a Protestant patron" a few months before his "Absalom and Achitophel," which was published in November.

38. When Dryden said, in 1675, in the dedication of "Aurenge Zebe," that some of his contemporaries had outdone him in comedy, the men he would have named would doubtless have been Sir George Etherege and William Wycherley, who had been then only three years before the town. In later life he quoted, in an "Epistle to Congreve," Etherege his courtship; Southern's purity; the satire, wit, and strength of manly Wycherley. Southern did not appear as a dramatist till 1682.

**William Wycherley** was born in 1640, at Clive, near Shrewsbury, where his father had some property. After his earliest schooling he was taught in France, and there became a Roman Catholic. At the Restoration he returned to England, became a fellow-commoner of Queen's College, Oxford, and was re-converted to Protestantism. He said afterwards that his first play, *Love in a Wood; or, St. James's Park*, was written at nineteen, when he had just left France; and that he wrote *The Gentleman Dancing-Master* when he had been a year at Oxford. He was at sea with the Duke of York at the defeat of the Dutch off Lowestoft, in June, 1665. Wycherley's "Love in a Wood" was produced in 1672, and, together with his good looks, it won him the favour of one of the king's mistresses, the Duchess of Cleveland. His other play, written at college, *The Gentleman Dancing-Master*, was produced in the following year, 1673. His next acted play was not the next that he wrote, for he had written *The Plain Dealer* just after his experience of the Dutch war, at the end of 1665, but kept it by him in doubt of the town's acceptance of its character of the Plain Dealer—Manly, "of an honest, surly, nice humour, supposed first, in the time of the Dutch war, to have procured the command of a ship out of honour, not interest, and choosing a sea-life only to avoid the world." "The Plain Dealer," therefore, was reserved, and *The Country Wife*, written at the age of thirty-two, when his earlier plays began to appear on the stage, was produced with great success in 1675. Then came, in 1677, *The Plain Dealer* on the stage, and those were the four comedies of Wycherley, all produced in the reign of Charles II. He lived till 1715, but wrote no more plays. After the publication of this play, Wycherley was in a bookseller's shop at Tunbridge Wells with a friend, Mr. Fairbeard, when a rich, handsome young widow, the Countess of Drogheda, came into the shop and asked for "The Plain Dealer." "Madam," said Mr. Fairbeard, since you are for the Plain Dealer, there he is for you," and pushed Wycherley towards her. This introduction led to their marriage. The lady proved a fond and jealous wife. She died soon, leaving Wycherley her fortune; but his title to it was successfully disputed, he was ruined by law-suits, and spent the last years of the reign of Charles II. in a debtor's prison. James II., after witnessing a performance of "The Plain Dealer," rescued its author from prison by giving him a pension of £200 a year and offering to pay his debts. But Wycherley did not venture to name all his debts, and left enough unpaid to weigh him down in after life.

Wycherley was the first vigorous writer of what has been called our Prose Comedy of Manners. In the absence of all that poetry which lies in a perception of the deeper truths and harmonies of life, his plays resemble other comedies of the later Stuart drama. There was little of it even in the metrical heroic plays. But Wycherley's differ from other comedies of their time by blending with surface reflection of the manners of an evil time a larger, healthier sense of the humours of men, caught from enjoyment of Molière. Wycherley's best plays are founded upon Molière—*The Country Wife* upon *l'Ecole des Femmes*, and *The Plain Dealer* on *Le Misanthrope*. They are not translations; but in turns of plot and certain characters the direct and strong influence of Molière is evident. Dryden and others borrowed from Molière; Wycherley was, in a way, inspired by him. He had not Molière's rare genius, and could not reproduce the masterly simplicity and ease of dialogue that is witty, and wise, too, in every turn, while yet so natural as to show no trace of a strain for effect; that is nowhere fettered to a false conventionality, but so paints humours of life as to be good reading for ever, alike to the strong men and to girls and boys. Our English writers of the Prose Comedy of Manners cannot claim readers, like Molière, from civilized Europe in all after time ; but, as compared with other English dramatists of their own time, they did widen the range of character-painting— witness the widow Blackacre and her law-suit in *The Plain Dealer*—and they did take pains to put substance of wit into their dialogue.  Four dramatists are the chiefs of this school of prose comedy—Wycherley, Congreve, Vanbrugh, and Farquhar. Of these Wycherley came first, and wrote his four plays in the reign of Charles II.  His last play was acted sixteen years before the first of Congreve's.  Congreve's plays were all produced in the reign of William III., and those of Vanbrugh and Farquhar in the reigns of William and of Queen Anne.

**Thomas Southern,** whom Dryden afterwards commended for his purity, was born in Dublin in 1660.  He came to London in 1678, and at the age of eighteen entered the Middle Temple.  He was but twenty-two when, in 1682, his tragedy of *The Loyal Brother ; or, the Persian Prince,* was acted.  The controversy over the succession of the king's brother then ran high, and Southern, taking the side of the court, meant his play, of which the plot was from a novel, " Tachmas, Prince of Persia," to be taken as a compliment to James, Duke of York. It was followed, in 1684, by a comedy, *The Disappointment ; or, the Mother in Fashion,* which had a plot taken from the novel in " Don Quixote " of " The Curious Impertinent."

**Thomas Brown,** a witty and coarse writer of trifles, whose name afterwards as Tom Brown became very familiar in society, began his career towards the close of Charles II.'s reign.  He was born in 1663, the son of a farmer, at Shiffnal, Shropshire ; became a clever but discreditable student of Christchurch, Oxford ; acquired skill in French, Italian, and Spanish, as well as Latin and Greek; was obliged by his irregularities to leave the University, and was schoolmaster for a time at Kingston-on-Thames.  Then he came to London, lazy, low-minded, dissolute, and clever, to live as he could by his wit.

39. We now pass out of the reign of Charles II. with those writers who illustrate especially the course of events leading towards the Revolution.

**Sir William Temple,** born in 1628, the son of Sir John Temple, Master of the Rolls in Ireland, studied under Cudworth (§ 22), at Cambridge, in the days of civil war.  After two years at Emmanuel College, he left without a degree, travelled, became master of French and Spanish, married, and towards the close of the Commonwealth lived with his father in Ireland. In 1663 he came to London with his wife, and attached himself to the rising fortunes of Lord Arlington, who sent him during the Dutch war as an English agent, with promise of subsidy, to our ally the Bishop of Munster. He was then made a baronet, and appointed Resident at the viceregal court of Brussels. There he developed his skill in diplomacy. At the time of the Peace of Breda, in July, 1667, which ended war with the Dutch, the ambition of Louis XIV., his lust of conquest, and his impersonation of his own maxim—"The state is myself" (*L'Etat c'est moi*)—caused France under his rule to take the place once occupied by Spain as a public enemy. After the death of Philip IV. of Spain, in 1665, Louis XIV. had claimed Brabant, Flanders, and all Spanish possessions in the Low Countries, by right of his queen, in accordance with a local custom, which placed daughters by a first wife above sons by a second, in questions of inheritance. In May, 1667, in pursuance of this claim, he sent Turenne with an army into Flanders, captured towns, and at the end of August made a three months' truce. Sir William Temple then got leave to make an unofficial tour in Holland. When at the Hague he called on the Grand Pensionary, John de Witt, the active mind of Holland at that time, said that his only business was to see what was worth seeing in Holland, and added, "I should execute my design very imperfectly if I went away without seeing you." Then Sir William Temple talked naturally with De Witt over the relations between England and Holland, and heard simply expressed the wish for a general coalition to save Flanders. Temple urged on unwilling ministers at home accord with this. Charles hoped to rule England by help of the King of France. But public opinion was strong, although he had done what he could towards the suppression of it. Although the fall of Clarendon, at the close of 1667, was forced by popular antagonism to his principles, the court was glad to get rid of him as a grave and steady man. "He had," says Evelyn, "enemies at court, especially the buffoons and ladies of pleasure, because he thwarted some of them and stood in their way." Pepys tells how Lady Castlemaine, whose aviary overlooked the Whitehall Gardens, rushed thither from her bed at noon, "And thither her woman brought her her night-gown, and she stood blessing herself at the old man's going away ; and several of the gallants of Whitehall—of which there were

many staying to see the chancellor's return—did talk to her
in her birdcage." George Villiers, Duke of Buckingham, was
then Chief Minister for a time, with Arlington as Secretary of
State; but the Parliament was still threatening, the foreign
policy of the Government was being censured, and very soon
after the fall of Clarendon the new ministers resolved to bid
for popularity by authorising Sir William Temple to treat with
De Witt. Temple then acted the part of Plain Dealer in the
highest sense of the word, and in five days secured the Triple
Alliance of England, Holland, and Sweden, which could not
have been obtained by the old diplomatic forms within five
months. The result of this alliance was that Louis XIV., who
had already sent his armies into Franche Comté, gave up that
conquest and made peace. England thus won, for the first time
in the reign of Charles II., respect in Europe; Englishmen of
all parties at home were proud of the bloodless victory; and
Sir William Temple, as its author, rose to fame as a great
diplomatist and patriotic statesman. He became Ambassador
at the Hague, and was there when the king, with help of the
Cabal Ministry, resumed the livery of his French master.

40. Anthony Ashley Cooper, first Earl of Shaftesbury—
Dryden's Achitophel—was born in 1621, son of Sir John
Cooper and Anne, heiress of Sir Anthony Ashley, of Wimborne
St. Giles, Dorsetshire. By the death of his father he became
Sir Anthony at ten years old, and inherited the estates of his
father and of Sir Anthony Ashley, which were very large. He
went to study at Oxford in 1636; in 1638 became student of law
at Lincoln's Inn; was member for Tewkesbury in 1640, did not
sit in the Long Parliament, followed the king till 1643, and was
then strong on the side of the Parliament. He raised a force
in Dorsetshire, stormed Wareham, and reduced the surrounding
country. Though suspected of some Royalism, Sir Anthony
Cooper was a member of Cromwell's first Parliament, was appointed one of the Protector's Council of State, and often
opposed his designs. In April, 1660, he was one of those appointed to draw up an invitation to the king, and one of the
commissioners sent over to Breda. Monk made much use of
his counsel. When Charles came over, Sir Anthony was made
Governor of the Isle of Wight, colonel of a regiment of horse,
Lord-Lieutenant of Dorset, Chancellor of the Exchequer, and a
Privy Councillor. In 1661 he was made Baron Ashley, of
Wimborne St. Giles, with acknowledgment that the Restoration

x

was due to "his wisdom in counsels in concert with General Monk." As Chancellor of the Exchequer, serving under Lord Treasurer the Earl of Southampton, his relation and intimate friend, Lord Ashley, who had an intensely active mind in a small body, managed affairs in his own way ; but while Clarendon was in power he belonged to an opposition section of the Ministry. He resisted the Uniformity Bill, and other measures against Dissenters ; opposed the French connection, the sale of Dunkirk, and the war with the Dutch. He spoke, says Clarendon, " with great sharpness of wit, and had a cadence in his words and pronunciation that drew attention." In May, 1667, the Lord Treasurer died. Ashley remained Chancellor of the Exchequer, and was made one of the commissioners for executing the office of Lord Treasurer. This was Lord Ashley's position when he brought John Locke into his house.

John Locke was born at Wrington, Somersetshire, on the 29th of August, 1632. His father served in the Parliamentary Wars under Colonel Popham, by whose advice Locke was sent to Westminster School. In 1651, he was elected student of Christchurch, Oxford, where he turned from the Aristotelian scholastic philosophy, read Bacon, and read also Descartes, through whom, by study of an opposing doctrine, he became more strongly animated with the spirit of Bacon's teaching. The new and growing interest in scientific studies caused Locke to find charm in experimental science. Having taken his degree in arts, he made physic his profession, and practised a little in Oxford. But Locke's health was delicate ; and in 1664 he went abroad as secretary to Sir William Swan, then sent as envoy to some German princes. After a year's absence, he returned to Oxford, and was there when Lord Ashley was sent from London to drink mineral waters at Acton for an abscess in the breast. Lord Ashley wrote to ask Dr. Thomas, a physician at Oxford, to have the waters ready against his coming there. Dr. Thomas, being called away, asked his friend, Mr. Locke, to procure them. He employed somebody who disappointed him, and had to call upon Lord Ashley to make apologies. Lord Ashley kept him to supper, asked him to dinner next day, became fascinated by his liberal and thoughtful conversation; and, in 1667, asked him to stay at his house in London ; he also followed Locke's advice in opening the abscess on his breast, a sore, probably scrofulous, which never healed. Shaftesbury urged upon Locke not to pursue medicine as a profession, beyond using his skill among his friends, but to devote the powers of his mind to study of the great questions in politics.  Locke did so, and was often consulted by a patron who was but an erratic follower of principles which Locke developed and maintained throughout his life with calm consistency.  As one of those included in the grant of Carolina, Lord Ashley employed Locke to draw up a constitution for the new colony ; he did so, and showed in it a strong regard for civil and religious liberty.  In 1668 Locke became one of the Fellows of the Royal Society. Soon afterwards he went abroad with the Earl and Countess of Northumberland ; but the earl. died at Turin, in May, 1670. Locke returned to England, lived again with Lord Ashley, and was asked by him to undertake the education of his only son. About the same time he was present in Oxford at a lively discussion, where it seemed to him that the differences of opinion lay wholly in words.  This thought first turned his mind in the direction of his Essay concerning Human Understanding.

41. In 1670, while Locke was at Turin, there were the negotiations at Dover which led to the secret agreement of Charles II. and his new Cabinet, the Cabal Ministry—Sir Thomas Clifford, Lord Ashley, the Duke of Buckingham, Lord Arlington, and the Duke of Lauderdale—with Louis XIV.  Charles agreed, for an annual subsidy of £120,000 during the war, to abandon his allies, join Louis in invading Holland, make a public profession of the Roman Catholic religion, and encourage it as much as possible in his dominions.  If this led to rebellion in England, Louis promised to help Charles against England with men and money.  Sir William Temple was summoned to London. De Witt doubted the aspect of affairs.  Sir William Temple said, "I can answer only for myself.  If a new system be adopted, I will never have a part in it.  If I return you will know more ; if not, you will guess more."  Temple came home to be civilly slighted until June, 1671, when the secret treaty with France had been ratified, and open action was to follow.  Temple was then formally dismissed from his ambassador's office, and retired into private life at Sheen, where he wrote an *Essay on Government*, and an *Account of the United Provinces.*

In 1670 the Act of 1664 against Conventicles was renewed with increase of severity.  Under this Act, William Penn had been imprisoned.  He was born in 1644, the son of Admiral Sir William Penn, educated at Christchurch, Oxford ; and, having

turned Quaker, was twice turned out of doors by his father.
Then he was tolerated, but not helped, at home, and no effort
was made to release him when he was imprisoned for attendance
at religious meetings.   He began at the age of twenty-four (in
1668) to preach and write.   For his second paper, *The Sandy
Foundation*, he was imprisoned seven months in the Tower, and
he wrote in prison, at the age of twenty-five, his most popular
book, *No Cross no Crown.*   He obtained release by a vindication called *Innocency with her Open Face.*   In 1670 his father
died, reconciled to him.   Penn inherited his estate, then wrote,
travelled, supported his religious faith, and in 1681, for his
father's services and debts to him from the Crown, obtained a
grant of New Netherlands, thenceforward called Pennsylvania.
In 1682, having published his scheme in *A Brief Account of the
Colony of Pennsylvania,* he embarked, and, in 1683, founded
Philadelphia.   In 1684, the last year of Charles II., Penn revisited England.

England and France declared war against Holland in March,
1672 ; and at the same time Charles obeyed that part of his
secret instructions which bound him to aid the Catholics, by
issuing, on his own royal authority, a Declaration of Indulgence in Religion, suspending the execution of all penal laws
against Nonconformists and recusants.   It was this that released **John Bunyan** from his long imprisonment in Bedford
Jail (§ 20).

**John Locke** urged on his patron, who, in April, 1672, was
made Earl of Shaftesbury, the tyranny involved in this claim of
a dispensing power, the sole right to loosen implying also the
sole right to bind.   In November, Shaftesbury succeeded Sir
Orlando Bridgman as Lord Chancellor, and made John Locke
Secretary of Presentations under him.   In June, 1673, he made
him also secretary to a commission of the Board of Trade, over
which Shaftesbury was president.   Locke held the office in
Chancery only while his friend was Chancellor.   The secretaryship, which was worth £500 a year, he retained till the commission expired, in December, 1674.   With little knowledge of
law, and much disrespect for it, Shaftesbury sought, as Lord
Chancellor, to decide honestly and promptly, in accordance with
what seemed to him justice and good sense.   But the lawyers
taught him by incessant arguments upon notices of motion to
discharge his orders.   Dryden, in otherwise pitiless satire against
Shaftesbury, inserted praise of him as a chancellor who strove,

" Unbribed, unsought, the wretched to redress,
Swift of dispatch, and easy of access. "

The House of Commons meanwhile had compelled the king to retract his Declaration of Indulgence, and passed a Test Act, declaring all persons incapable of public employment who did not take the oaths of allegiance and supremacy, and receive the sacrament according to the rites of the Church of England. The Duke of York, who was honest in profession of his faith, had to resign his post of Lord High Admiral. Parliament was prorogued with a motion before it against the French alliance; the Cabal Ministry broke up; Shaftesbury, ceasing to be chancellor, in November, 1673, went into opposition; and there followed a long struggle between the King and the Commons. Charles met his Parliament of 1674—the year of Milton's death —with a direct falsehood. He denied that there was any secret treaty with the King of France. The Commons refused more supplies for the disgraceful war, and Sir William Temple was drawn from his retirement to negotiate a separate peace with Holland. This done, he went back as Ambassador to the Hague, and William of Orange rose equal to the occasion in the fight with France. Then it was found that Charles, in spite of the peace, had left troops with Monmouth to assist the French; but Charles's minister, Danby, smoothed the way with the bribery of members of Parliament that Andrew Marvell satirized (§ 35). Persecution of the Nonconformists was a source of petty plunder. Baxter tells how he was "being newly risen from extremity of pain, suddenly surprised in my house by a poor violent informer and many constables and officers, who rushed in and apprehended me, and served on me one warrant to seize on my person for coming within five miles of a corporation, and five more warrants to distrain for an hundred and ninety pounds, for five sermons." In such days one of the king's mistresses had in a single year £136,668 out of the Secret Service money. In November, 1675, Charles prorogued Parliament for fifteen months, and was paid by the King of France five hundred thousand crowns for that personal service to himself. He took, also, a pension, on condition of dissolving any Parliament that offered to force on him a treaty which had not received the assent of Louis XIV. At the end of December, 1675, the licenses of coffee-houses were withdrawn, and they were shut up, because of the talk in them on the condition of the country. Among others was Will's Coffee-house, kept by William Irwin, at the house on the north side of Russell Street, at the end of Bow Street, which, through Dryden's use of it, had become the great resort of the wits of the time.

42. After private letters and occasional printed pamphlets of news, Mercuries of the Civil War had been the first active beginnings of the newspaper. **Marchmont Needham** had attacked Charles I. in the "Mercurius Britannicus," was imprisoned, pardoned, and set up a "Mercurius Pragmaticus" against the king's enemies. By the king's enemies Needham was imprisoned, pardoned, and then wrote for ten years "Mercurius Politicus" against the Royalists. Charles II. pardoned him, and he died in 1678. **Roger l'Estrange,** youngest son of Sir Hammond l'Estrange, born in Norfolk, in 1616, and educated at Cambridge, had been a friend of Charles I., and narrowly escaped execution in the Civil Wars. In 1663 he published a pamphlet entitled, *Considerations and Proposals in order to the Regulation of the Press; together with Diverse Instances of Treasonous and Seditious Pamphlets, proving the Necessity thereof.* This got him the post of Licenser, in succession to Sir John Birkenhead, and also "all the sole privilege of printing and publishing all narratives, advertisements, Mercuries, intelligencers, diurnals, and other books of public intelligence." He began business at the end of August, 1663, with *The Public Intelligencer,* and introduced it with this doctrine : "As to the point of printed intelligence, I do declare myself (as I hope I may in a matter left so absolutely indifferent, whether any or none) that supposing the press in order, the people in their right wits, and news or no news to be the question, a public Mercury should never have my vote ; because I think it makes the multitude too familiar with the actions and counsels of their superiors, too pragmatical and censorious, and gives them not only an itch, but a kind of colourable right and license to be meddling with the government." Still he would do what he might to "redeem the vulgar from their former mistakes and illusions." As for reports of debates in Parliament, "I have observed," says L'Estrange, "very ill effects many times from the ordinary written papers of Parliament news"—such as Andrew Marvell supplied regularly to his constituents (§ 35)— "by making the coffee-houses and all the popular clubs judges of those councils and deliberations which they have nothing to do withall." In November, 1665, when the plague in London had driven the Court to Oxford, appeared No. 1 of *The Oxford*

*Gazette.* When the Court returned to London, it appeared, on the 5th of February, 1666, as *The London Gazette,* under which name it still exists. It was placed at once under Sir Joseph Williamson, Under-Secretary of State (from whom Addison, now born, had his Christian name), and his deputy writer of it was, for the first five years, Charles Perrot, M.A., of Oriel. L'Estrange set up, in November, 1675, the first commercial journal, *The City Mercury,* and in 1679, an *Observator,* in defence of the king's party. In April, 1680, the first literary journal appeared, as a weekly or fortnightly catalogue of new books, the *Mercurius Librarius.*

Roger l'Estrange was a busy man. He published, in 1678, an abstract of *Seneca's Morals,* and in 1680 a translation of *Tully's Offices.* James II. knighted him, and he published in 1687, in the king's interest, *A Brief History of the Times,* chiefly about what was called the Popish Plot.

43. We return to the time when Charles sought to repress opinion by shutting coffee-houses. Parliament, that had been prorogued for fifteen months in 1675, met again on the 15th of February, 1677. When it met, Shaftesbury argued that it had been dissolved by long suspension. It was voted that he should beg the king's pardon on his knees at the bar. He refused, and was committed to the Tower. The Earl of Salisbury, Lord Wharton, and the Duke of Buckingham were committed also, but made submission in a few months. Shaftesbury held out for a year. In this year, 1677, William of Orange came to England, and on the 4th of November he was married to Mary, eldest daughter of James Duke of York. It was a marriage that Sir William Temple had been active in promoting. In October, 1678, Titus Oates, a man who had been in orders in the English Church, and who, in 1677, had pretended to go over to Rome, and so been admitted as a Jesuit, came back from among the Jesuits with his story of a Popish plot to kill King Charles, because he did not help Catholicism, and put at once on the throne his brother James, who was to produce such a return of England to the true faith as had not been known since the days of Mary. Oates made oath to his narrative before a zealous Protestant justice, Sir Edmundbury Godfrey. A fortnight afterwards Godfrey was found murdered in a ditch near Primrose Hill. Public faith in Titus Oates and fury against the Catholics now rose to a height. **Roger North,** youngest son of Dudley, Lord North, was then a young man of twenty-eight, a

. strong partisan of the Stuarts. He left behind him an "*Examen,* or Inquiry into the Credit and Veracity of a Pretended Compleat History of England." (By White Kennett, a Whig, who became, in 1718, Bishop of Peterborough.) This was not published till 1740, and his *Lives of his Three Brothers* were not published until 1742-4. These books of Roger North's abound in anecdote of his own time. He tells, among other things, that at the funeral of Sir Edmundbury Godfrey "there was all this while upheld among the common people an artificial fright, so as almost every man fancied a Popish knife at his throat. And at the sermon, besides the preacher, two other thumping divines stood upright in the pulpit, one on each side of him, to guard him from being killed while he was preaching, by the Papists." Parliament formally declared its faith in the plot after Oates had been examined before a committee. Then came the rule of this infamous man as a public accuser. In the midst of it all came an exposure in Parliament of some of the king's secret dealing with France. The minister suffered for the king, and Danby was impeached, but during its proceedings against him Parliament was dissolved. The new elections were against the Court. Before the next Parliament met, the Duke of York bent to the storm and consented to go abroad, after providing with his brother that no claims of the Duke of Monmouth should be allowed against him. Monmouth, born at Rotterdam in 1649, was supposed to be the eldest of the king's natural sons. He was a Protestant and a favourite son. He had been made Duke of Monmouth in 1663, was "to take place of all dukes," and was about the same time married to the Countess of Buccleuch. It was said by many that his mother, Lucy Waters, had been married to the king, and if so, Monmouth was true heir. The king, before his brother James left England, made a solemn affirmation to his Council that he never was married to any woman but his wife, Queen Catherine, then living. The new Parliament proceeded with Danby's impeachment; and the king's difficulties were now so great that he looked for essential support to **Sir William Temple,** in whom the people had most faith, and who had never been in active opposition to the king. Three times during the late troubles Sir William had declined to support the king's cause as a Secretary of State. He was now summoned to London, and proposed a new Privy Council of thirty members, half of them great officers of State, the other half independent English gentlemen of property. In accordance with advice from such a council, the king was to pledge himself to govern without any reserve of a secret committee. Charles agreed. The people were content. The new Council was formed in April, 1679, with Shaftesbury for Lord President, placed there by the king, but not the less still leader of the Opposition. The new Council was a failure. Parliament had before it a Bill to exclude the Duke of York from the succession. The king, therefore, prorogued Parliament on the 26th of May, 1679, giving unwilling assent at the same time to its Habeas Corpus Act " for the better securing of the Liberty of the Subject." The prorogued Parliament was dissolved before it met again. Again a new Parliament met, on the 7th of October, 1679. It was still prorogued from time to time. The heat of discussion over, the Exclusion Bill led to invention of party names. The Irish being supporters of the succession of the king's Roman Catholic brother, the opponents of the Exclusion Bill were called Bogtrotters ; then, says Roger North, "the word Tory was entertained, which signified the most despicable savages among the wild Irish." Their adversaries were called Whigs, that being Scottish for the acid whey that settles from sour cream, applied generally by Scottish Episcopalians to Presbyterians, and made familiar at that time by the insurrection of the Scottish Covenanters in 1679. In July, 1679, Charles was ill, and Monmouth near him. The Duke of York suddenly returned from Brussels to protect his rights. The rival candidates for the succession were then sent away, Monmouth to Flanders, James, as Lord High Commissioner, to Scotland. Shaftesbury, dismissed from the Presidency of the Council, promoted great popular demonstrations against Catholicism ; and on the 28th of November Monmouth suddenly returned from Flanders. The king deprived him of his offices, and 'ordered him to quit the country. He remained. Parliament had been prorogued, as usual, and the people poured in petitions against further prorogation when it met. The king forbade petitioning against the known laws of the land.

It was in this year, 1679, that **John Oldham** wrote his satires on the Jesuits. He was born in 1653, son of a Nonconformist minister at Shipton, Gloucestershire. Oldham went to St. Edmund Hall, Oxford, and returned home, after taking his B.A. degree, in 1674. He became usher in a school at Croydon. Verse written by him found its way to the Earls Rochester and Dorset and Sir Charles Sedley, who astonished the poor usher

x *

by paying him a visit. He became tutor to two grandsons of Sir Edward Thurland, a judge living near Reigate, and then to the son of a Sir William Hickes, near London. This occupation over, he lived among the wits in London, was remembered as the poetical usher by Sedley and Dorset; was on affectionate terms with Dryden, and found a patron in the Earl of Kingston, with whom he was domesticated, at Holme Pierrepoint, when he died of small-pox, in December, 1683, aged thirty. His chief production was the set of four *Satyrs upon the Jesuits*, written in 1679, modelled variously on Persius, Horace, Buchanan's " Franciscan," (ch. vii. § 50), and the speech of Sylla's ghost at the opening of Ben Jonson's " Catiline." The vigour of his wit produced a bold piece of irony in an *Ode against Virtue* and its *Counterpart*, an ode in Virtue's praise, with many short satires and odes—one in high admiration of Ben Jonson—paraphrases, and translations. There is a ring of friendship in the opening of Dryden's lines upon young Oldham's death before time had added the full charm of an English style to the strength of wit in his verse :

> ' Farewell ! too little and too lately known,
> Whom I began to think and call my own ;
> For sure our souls were near ally'd, and thine
> Cast in the same poetic mould with mine."

On the 25th of June, 1680, the Earl of Shaftesbury, with others of the Lords and Commons, presented the Duke of York to the Grand Jury of Westminster as a Popish recusant. The Chief Justice averted the consequence of that by discharging the jury. Parliament met on the 21st of October, after seven prorogations. On the 2nd of November the Exclusion Bill was again brought in. Monmouth, called commonly the Protestant Duke, who had made in August a triumphal progress in the West of England, was the desired successor. The Exclusion Bill, passed by the Commons on the 15th of November, was carried by Lord Russell to the peers, and delivered with a mighty shout from two hundred members of the House of Commons, who went with it. It was rejected by the Lords. The Commons resolved to grant no supply until the Duke of York had been excluded from the succession. Parliament was dissolved on the 18th of January, 1681. King Charles made a treaty with Louis XIV., and held to the Catholic succession, for £50,000 a quarter—payment to begin at the end of June, 1681. On the 21st of March the next Parliament met at Oxford. Charles was firm; at the end of a week he smuggled his robes with him into a sedan chair, and suddenly dissolved that Parliament also. He summoned no other during his reign. Having got rid of Parliament, and incidentally struck off the list of his privy councillors Sir William Temple—who now withdrew from public life—the king resolved to proceed boldly, and strike down the Earl of Shaftesbury. He was sent to the Tower on the 2nd of July, upon the testimony of two Irish witnesses, who swore that he had suborned them to bear false witness against the Queen, the Duke of York, and other personages. He was to be indicted for subornation and treason before a London grand jury, and if the grand jury did not ignore the bill of indictment, he would be tried by his peers in the Court of the High Steward, and condemned to death by judges of the king's selection.

44. That was the state of affairs when **John Dryden** supported the king's cause with a political pamphlet in verse, his satire of *Absalom and Achitophel*. Its aim was to assist in turning a current of opinion against Shaftesbury ; to secure, as far as pamphlet could, the finding of a true bill against him. The satire appeared anonymously, on the 17th of November, 1681. The accident of a second poem has caused this to be known as the first part of "Absalom and Achitophel," but it is a complete work. Monmouth as Absalom and Shaftesbury as Achitophel had occurred before in the paper war ; and the use of such allegory was an appeal to the religious feeling of a people among whom those most likely to follow Shaftesbury were those most likely to be persuaded by a Scripture parallel. Charles, therefore, was David ; Cromwell, Saul ; the Duke of Buckingham figured as Zimri ; Titus Oates, as Corah ; the Roman Catholics were Jebusites ; the Dissenters Levites, and so forth. The argument of the poem was to this effect. The outcry over the asserted Popish plot gave heat to faction, and of this Shaftesbury took advantage. He reasoned thus and thus, to persuade Monmouth to rebellion ; Monmouth, answering thus and thus, yielded to the persuasion. Who were the lesser associates in this rebellion, the sprouting heads of the hydra? Here followed sketches from life of other leaders of the opposition, and among them George Villiers, Duke of Buckingham, as Zimri. Monmouth appealed thus and thus to the people. The rebellion grew. What friends had King Charles? Here followed sketches from life of some of the chief

friends of the king.   Next came counsel of the king's friends;
and then the poem ended with the king's own purpose, expressed
in David's speech.   " I have been," he said, " forgiving till they
slight my clemency.   'Tis time to show I am not good by force."

> "Oh, that my power to saving were confined !
> Why am I forced, like Heaven, against my mind
> To make examples of another kind ?
> Must I at length the sword of justice draw !
> Oh, curst effects of necessary law !
> How ill my fear they by my mercy scan !
> Beware the fury of a patient man.
> Law they require : let law then show her face.
>
> *   *   *   *   *   *
>
> He said : the Almighty, nodding, gave consent,
> And peals of thunder shook the firmament.
> Henceforth a series of new time began,
> The mighty years in long procession ran ;
> Once more the godlike David was restored,
> And willing nations knew their lawful lord."

The success of the satire as a poem was all it deserved to be.
At once vigorous and highly finished, its characters of the chief
men on either side, its lines and couplets, neatly fitted to
express much that the king's party had to say, were quoted
and parodied, praised and abused.   Two dozen lines repaid
Buckingham's rehearsal (§ 17) fifty-fold, if Dryden thought at
all—as probably he did not—of a mere jest of the stage, when
dealing with a vital question that seemed to have brought the
nation once more to the verge of civil war, and writing what
might help to send the chief opponent of Charles to the scaffold.
The literary triumph was great, but that was all.   The
prophecy of the closing lines was not fulfilled.   The poem was
published on the 17th of November.   On the 24th the indictment was presented to the grand jury at the Old Bailey, and
returned ignored.   There were great public rejoicings, and a
medal was struck to commemorate the triumph.

45. Of the Whig replies to " Absalom and Achitophel," one,
*Absalom Senior; or, Absalom and Achitophel Transprosed,* was
by Elkanah Settle.   Another, *Azaria and Hushai,* was by
Samuel Pordage, son of the Rev. John Pordage, of Bradfield,
in Berkshire, deprived of his living in 1654, on a charge of
conversation with evil spirits.   Pordage was a member of
Lincoln's Inn, and had published in 1660, with notes, *The
Troades,* from Seneca, and a volume of poems.   He was the
author, also, of two tragedies, *Herod and Mariamne,* in 1673,

and the *Siege of Babylon*, in 1678, and of a romance called *Eliana*. Samuel Pordage replied to Dryden's satire with a temperance rare in the controversies of that time. Unlike other opponents, he gave Dryden credit for his genius ; and the only lines in the reply that have any resemblance to the usual coarseness of abuse are those which comment on the opening lines of Dryden's poem, which were meanly complaisant to the king's vices. Good Mr. Pordage, writing, like Dryden, without a name upon his title-page, said in his preface :—" I shall not go about either to excuse or justifie the publishing of this poem, for that would be much more an harder task than the writing of it. But, however, I shall say, in the words of the author of the incomparable ' Absalom and Achitophel,' that I am sure the design is honest. If wit and fool be the consequence of Whig and Tory, no doubt but knave and ass may be epithets plentifully bestowed upon me by the one party, whilst the other may grant me more favourable ones than perhaps I do deserve. But as very few are judges of wit, so, I think, much fewer of honesty; since interest and faction on either side prejudices and blinds the judgment, and the violence of passion makes neither discernible in an adversary. I know not whether my poem has a genius to force its way against prejudice. Opinion sways much in the world, and he that has once gained it writes securely. I speak not this anyways to lessen the merits of an author whose wit has deservedly gained the bays. . . . The ancients say that everything hath two handles. I have laid hold of that opposite to the author of ' Absalom.' As to truth, who has the better hold let the world judge ; and it is no new thing for the same persons to be ill or well represented by several parties." Absalom was a rebel to his father ; the author of this piece prefers to represent Monmouth through Azaria, who was a good son. Shaftesbury in this poem, therefore, is Hushai. The king is good Amazia, who,

" Tho' he God did love,
Had not cast out Baal's priests, and cut down every grove.

Former rulers had maintained strict laws against idolatry. Cromwell being Zabad, Charles in exile had been Amazia, who

" Over Jordan fled,
Till God had struck the tyrant Zabad dead ;
When all his subjects, who his fate did moan,
With joyful hearts restored him to his throne ;

> Who then his father's murtherers destroy'd,
> And a long, happy, peaceful reign enjoy'd,
> Belov'd of all, for merciful was he,
> Like God, in the superlative degree."

But the Chemarims (Jesuits) and Hell had hatched a plot—

> ' For the good Amazia being gone,
> They had designed a Baalite for the throne.
> Of all their hopes and plots, here lay the store:
> For what encouragement could they have more,
> When they beheld the king's own brother fall,
> From his religion and to worship Baal."

Then Titus Oates revealed the plot.

> " A Levite who had Baalite turn'd, and bin
> One of the order of the Chemarim,
> *    *    *    *
> Libni, I think, they call the Levite s name.

But the faithful Hushai boldly opposed the king's brother, Eliakim—

> " To whom the king ev'n to excess was kind,
> And tho' he had a son, for him the crown design'd."

The friends of Baal now encouraged jealousy of Azaria.

> " If with wise Hushai they the prince did see,
> They call'd their meeting a conspiracy,
> And cry, that he was going to rebell:
> Him Absalom they name, Hushai Achitophel."

Among the friends of Eliakim, Dryden is satirised as " Shimei, the poet-laureate of that age."

> " Sweet was the muse that did his wit inspire,
> Had he not let his hackney muse to hire.
> But variously his knowing muse could sing,
> Could Doeg praise, and could blaspheme the king:
> The bad make good, good bad, and bad make worse,
> Bless in heroicks, and in satyrs curse.
> Shimei to Zabad's praise could tune his muse,
> And princely Azaria could abuse.
> Zimri, we know, he had no cause to praise,
> Because he dub'd him with the name of Bayes."

The closing speech of David Samuel Pordage matched with a closing speech of Amazia, wherein he restored peace, and secured his throne by assenting to the wishes of his people.

In the second edition of Dryden's " Absalom and Achitophel," which appeared in December, 1681, the lines were inserted which praised Shaftesbury's conduct as Chancellor, and also the lines concerning Monmouth:

> " But, oh! that yet he would repent and live!
> How easy 'tis for parents to forgive!
> With how few tears a pardon might be won
> From Nature, pleading for a darling son!"

46. The medal struck to commemorate the rejection of the bill against Shaftesbury was the subject of Dryden's next piece in this series, *The Medal: a Satire against Sedition.—By the Author of "Absalom and Achitophel."* It was published early in March, 1682, with a prefatory " Epistle to the Whigs." It was invective against Shaftesbury, blended with expression of Dryden's faith in the unity maintained by holding firmly to a fixed succession, and believing the inherent right of kings. " If true succession from our isle should fail," the various religious sects, political parties, even individual men, would strive together.

> " Thus inborn broils the factions would engage,
> Or wars of exiled heirs, or foreign rage,
> Till halting vengeance overtook our age,
> And our wild labours, wearied into rest,
> Reclined us on a rightful monarch's breast."

Again the only temperate reply was that of Samuel Pordage. Dryden had dwelt on Shaftesbury, whose image was upon the obverse of the medal. On the reverse side was the Tower, and Pordage took this for his text in *The Medal Revers'd: a Satyre against Persecution.—By the Author of "Azaria and Hushai."* To complete the parallel, this opened with an introductory epistle to the Tories. Dryden was still recognised as " Our Prince of Poets," and there was nothing harder said of him than that he was on the side of the strong with Cromwell, and is so again with Charles. He found on one side of the medal Sedition under a statesman's gown. Reverse the medal, and upon the other side there is an image of the Tower, badge of as bad a hag, Persecution:

> " Let then his satyr with Sedition fight,
> And ours the whilst shall Persecution bite:
> Two hags they are, who parties seem to make:
> 'Tis time for satyrs them to undertake.
> See her true badg, a prison or the Tower;
> For Persecution ever sides with Power."

Very different in its character was Shadwell's answer, *The Medal of John Bayes: a Satyr against Folly and Knavery.* This also had its introductory epistle to the Tories, but not dealing at all with the great controversy before the nation, it was a savage personal attack on Dryden. As for the verses, in some parts unutterably coarse, let their closing triplet indicate their tone:

> " Pied thing ! half wit ! half fool ! and for a knave
> Few men than this a better mixture have :
> But thou canst add to that, coward and slave."

47. This brutal attack provoked a delicate revenge. In October, 1682, appeared *MacFlecknoe.— By the Author of "Absalom and Achitophel."* This was a mock heroic in rhymed couplets, setting forth how that aged prince, Richard Flecknoe, who

> " In prose and verse was owned without dispute
> Through all the realms of nonsense absolute,"

chose in his last days Shadwell for successor.

> " Shadwell alone of all my sons is he
> Who stands confirmed in full stupidity.
> The rest to some faint meaning make pretence,
> But Shadwell never deviates into sense."

The coronation of Shadwell was in the Nursery at Barbican, a theatre established in 1662 for the training of children to the stage ; and there he swore " Ne'er to have peace with wit nor truce with sense." There he received the sceptre, and was crowned with poppies, and " on his left hand twelve reverend owls did fly." Then, in prophetic mood, Flecknoe blessed and counselled his successor, till he was, after the manner of Sir Formal Trifle, in Shadwell's " Vertuoso," let down through a trap-door while yet declaiming.

> " Sinking he left his drugget robe behind,
> Borne upwards by a subterranean wind.
> The mantle fell to the young prophet's part
> With double portion of his father's art."

**Richard Flecknoe** had been dead four years when this poem was written. He was an Irishman, and had been a Roman Catholic priest before the Restoration. His first writings were religious : *Hierothalamium ; or, The Heavenly Nuptials with a Pious Soul,* in 1626 ; *The Affections of a Pious Soul* (1640) ; then came *Miscellanea; or, Poems of all Sorts* (1653) ; *A Relation of Ten Years' Travels in Europe, Asia, Africa, and America* (1654) ; *Love's Dominion : a Dramatic Piece* (1654) ; *The Diarium, or Journal divided in Twelve Jornadas, in Burlesque Rhyme or Drolling Verse* (1651) ; *Enigmaticall Characters, all taken to the Life, from several Persons, Humours, and Dispositions* (1658) ; *The Marriage of Oceanus and Bri-*

*tannia* (1659); *Heroick Poems* (1660); *Love's Kingdom: a Pastoral Tragi-Comedy, with a Short Treatise of the English Stage* (1664); *Erminia: a Tragi-Comedy* (1665); *The Damoiselles à la Mode: a Comedy* (1667); *Sir William Davenant's Voyage to the other World: a Poetical Fiction* (1668); *Epigrams of all Sorts* (1669); *Euterpe Revived; or, Epigrams made at Several Times in the Years* 1672, 1673, and 1674, *on Persons of great Honour and Quality, most of them now living: in Three Books* (1675); *A Treatise of the Sports of Wit* (1675). The catalogue describes the man.

48. In November, 1682, appeared the *Second Part of Absalom and Achitophel*, to which Dryden contributed only 200 lines (ll. 310 to 509), containing a few character sketches, among which by far the most prominent are Elkanah Settle as Doeg, and Shadwell as Og. The second title of Settle's "Absalom Senior, or Absalom and Achitophel transprosed"—a feeble echo from Marvell—was here satirised, together with these opening lines of his poem—

> " In gloomy times, when priestcraft bore the sway,
> And made heaven's gate a lock to their own key,"

which were thus treated by Dryden—

> " Instinct he follows, and no fartner knows,
> For to write verse with him is to transprose .
> 'Twere pity treason at his door to lay,
> Who makes heaven's gate a lock to its own key."

A fairly whimsical misunderstanding of a clumsy sentence. Settle, poor fellow, meant that as the Roman Catholic priests had a key to heaven's gate which did not fit its lock, they made for the gate a new lock that would fit their key. Among other characters sketched or alluded to, Dryden, in this contribution to Tate's poem, passed lightly over Pordage in one line : " As lame Mephibosheth, the wizard's son."

**Nahum Tate,** the author of the rest of the Second Part of " Absalom and Achitophel" (though it had, no doubt, touches from Dryden's hand), was born in Dublin, in 1652, the son of Dr. Faithful Tate, and educated at Trinity College there. He came to London, published in 1677 a volume of *Poems*, and between that date and 1682 had produced the tragedies of *Brutus of Alba* and *The Loyal General; Richard II.; or, the Sicilian Usurper;* an altered version of Shakespeare's *King Lear;* and an application of " Coriolanus " to court politics of the day, as *The Ingratitude of a Commonwealth; or, The Fall* *of Coriolanus.* Tate wrote three other plays before the Revolution. It was not till 1696 that he produced, with Dr. Nicholas Brady (b. 1659, d. 1726), also an Irishman, and then chaplain to William III., a *New Version of the Psalms of David,* and in 1707 one more tragedy of his was acted, *Injured Love; or, The Cruel Husband.*

49. In November, 1682, another poem by **Dryden** appeared, ["A Layman's Religion"] *Religio Laici,* in the style of Horace's Epistles, being a letter written originally to a young man, Henry Dickenson, who had translated Father Simon's "Critical History of the Old Testament." This expression of Dryden's mind upon religion, in 1682, should be impartially compared with that in "The Hind and Panther," written five years later, when he became a Roman Catholic. "Religio Laici" was addressed to the translator of a Roman Catholic book on the Old Testament, which is described by Dryden as a "matchless author's work." In the preface and in the poem Dryden modestly dissented from the preface to the Athanasian Creed, which excluded the heathen from salvation. He took his place in the preface between the Roman Catholics as Papists and the Nonconformists, believing that there was continuous endeavour to restore the pope's authority over the King of England. His argument was solely against the pope's claim to dispense with the obedience of subjects to a heretic king. But that was also an article of the faith Dryden afterwards adopted. When he came to speak of the Nonconformists, he dwelt, in his preface to the *Religio Laici,* on the evil caused by the wresting of texts since the Bible had been translated. "How many heresies the first translation of Tyndal produced in a few years, let my Lord Herbert's 'History of Henry VIII.' inform you," and so forth. He quoted from Maimbourg, a Roman Catholic, that wherever Calvinism was planted, "rebellion, misery, and civil war attended it." And presently he said, "'Tis to be noted, by the way, that the doctrines of king-killing and deposing, which have been taken up only by the worst party of the Papists, the most frontless flatterers of the pope's authority, have been espoused, defended, and are still maintained by the whole body of Nonconformists and Republicans." In the poem so introduced, Dryden argued that Reason is but the dim light of moon and stars, which is lost when the sun rises :

> " So pale grows Reason at Religion's sight,
> So dies and so dissolves in supernatural light."

He argued that before revelation the best men had but imperfect notions of the highest good, that Deism had un-
consciously borrowed from revelation that sense of the One
God to be worshipped by praise and prayer, and of a future
state, which it believed Reason to have discovered. He passed
to the scheme of redemption expressed in the Bible, and, from
objections of the Deist that "no supernatural worship can be
true," and that millions have never heard the name of Christ, he
took occasion to express his faith that

> " Those who followed Reason's dictates right,
> Lived up and lifted high their natural light,
> With Socrates may see their Maker's face,
> While thousand rubric-makers want a place."

He argued that no Church could be an omniscient interpreter of
Scripture, and that the Scriptures themselves might be corrupted, but

> " Though not everywhere
> Free from corruption, or entire or clear,
> Are uncorrupt, sufficient, clear, entire
> In all things which our needful faith require."

He argued that it was for the learned to sift and discuss the
doctrines drawn out of the Bible, but

> " The unlettered Christian who believes in gross
> Plods on to heaven, and ne'er is at a loss :
> For the strait gate would be made straiter yet
> Were none admitted there but men of wit."

If the Bible had been handed down from the past by the church
of the Roman Catholics,

> " The welcome news is in the letter found ;
> The carrier's not commissioned to expound."

Once the clergy had traded with it on the ignorance of the
people; now the ignorance of the people had made it the
common prey: it was misused with great zeal and little thought.

> " So all we make of Heaven's discovered will
> Is not to have it or to use it ill.
> The danger's much the same, on several shelves
> If others wreck us or we wreck ourselves."

What remained, then, but the middle way between those shoals?

> " In doubtful questions 'tis the safest way
> To learn what unsuspected ancients say :
> For 'tis not likely we should higher soar
> In search of heaven than all the Church before :

> Nor can we be deceived unless we see
> The Scripture and the fathers disagree.
>
> *       *       *       *
>
> And after hearing what the Church can say
> If still our reason runs another way,
> That private reason 'tis more just to curb
> Than by disputes the public peace disturb.
> For points obscure are of small use to learn:
> But common quiet is mankind's concern. "

So the poem ended with the desire for peace by resting on authority, and Dryden's " Religio Laici," instead of being an antagonist work, is a natural prelude to " The Hind and Panther." Under the tumult of the time the religious mind of Dryden was steadily on its way to the form of Catholicism in which he died.

50. In February, 1682, when Southern's first play, " The Loyal Brother " (§ 38), was acted, Dryden wrote prologue and epilogue to it. It was the beginning of a friendship. Dryden raised the price of his prologue on this occasion. " The players," he said, " have had my goods too cheap." In December of the same year, 1682, he produced his tragedy of *The Duke of Guise* written with Lee (§ 27). It was designed to apply the story of the French League to the English opposition of that day. With the same allusion he made a *Translation of Maimbourg's History of the League,* and published it in 1684. In 1683 he had contributed a Preface and a Life to a new translation of *Plutarch* by several hands.

51. In July, 1683, upon false accusation of complicity in the Rye House Plot, Lord William Russell was executed in Lincoln's Inn Fields, and, on the 7th of December, Algernon Sidney upon Tower Hill. **Algernon Sidney,** second son of Robert, second Earl of Leicester, and brother to Waller's " Sacharissa " (ch. viii. § 42), had shown throughout his career lively hostility to tyranny. He had been out of England in the earlier years of Charles II.'s reign, but in 1667 came home, at his father's death, and was detained by a Chancery suit. He was an Independent and Republican. For that he died, convicted of treason, says Evelyn, " on the single witness of that monster of a man, Lord Howard of Escrick, and some sheets of paper taken in Mr. Sidney's study, pretended to be written by him, but not fully proved." He left behind him a *Discourse Concerning Government,* first published in 1698.

52. **Dryden** suggested and edited, in 1684, a volume of *Miscellany Poems.—Containing a New Translation of Virgill's Eclogues, Ovid's Love Elegies, Odes of Horace and other*

*Authors; with several Original Poems, by the most Eminent Hands.* This revival of the old Elizabethan plan of gathering into one volume papers of verse from various hands was successful. The volume of 1684 was the first of a new series of such Miscellanies. In this volume itself the chief original poems were reprints—" MacFlecknoe," "Absalom and Achitophel," and " The Medal." The translations were by Dryden, Sedley, Lord Roscommon, the late Earl of Rochester, Otway, Rymer, Tate, Sir Carr Scrope, George Stepney, Thomas Creech, Richard Duke, Mr. Adams, Mr. Chetwood, Mr. Stafford, and Mr. Cooper.

**George Stepney** (b. 1663, died 1707), wrote pleasant occasional verse. He was educated at Westminster School and Trinity College, Cambridge, and owed his political employment after the Revolution to the warm friendship of a fellow-student, Charles Montague, afterwards Lord Halifax.

**Thomas Creech,** born in 1659, near Sherborne, Dorset, studied at Wadham College, Oxford, and got a fellowship for his translation of *Lucretius,* published in 1682. In 1684, the year of the first volume of Miscellany Poems, Creech published a verse translation of the Odes, Satires, and Epistles of Horace, which did not sustain his credit, though he applied the satires to his own times. The end of his life was that, in 1701, Wadham College presented him to the rectory of Welwyn, and he hanged himself in his study before going to reside there. **Richard Duke,** also a clergyman, was a friend of Otway's, and tutor to the Duke of Richmond.

In 1685, **Dryden** published, still with Tonson, *Sylvæ; or, The Second Part of Political Miscellanies.* It contained translations by himself from the " Æneid," and from Lucretius, and from Theocritus and Horace, with short pieces, original and translated by himself and others, including a Latin poem by his eldest son Charles, on Lord Arlington's gardens. Charles Dryden was hardly nineteen, and lately entered at Trinity College, Cambridge. Dryden's second son was at Westminster School, the third and youngest at the Charterhouse.

53. **John Locke** (§ 40, 41) had graduated as M.B. at Cambridge, and gone to Montpellier, where there was a great medical school, and also a southern climate, which his health required, for he was threatened with consumption. He was at work upon his Essay at Montpellier, but when, in 1679, his patron Shaftesbury became president of Sir William Temple's newly-devised Council, he sent for Locke, who returned to England, and was

by his friend's side in the ensuing time of peril. After his escape from the scaffold in 1682, Shaftesbury went to Holland, and died there in 1683. Locke remained in Holland. In November, 1684, by a special order from Charles II., he was deprived of his studentship at Christchurch. But Charles II. died on the 6th of February, 1685

JAMES II

54. **John Dryden,** who had been rehearsing at court an opera of *Albion and Albanius,* in honour of King Charles's triumph over opposition, paid laureate's homage to the deceased king with his imperial mourning song, *Threnodia Augustalis,* published in March. This ode heralds the rule of James II. as that of a warlike prince. He is to be a martial Ancus after Numa's peaceful reign. But James II. warred only on his people. He began by going openly to mass, and staying prosecutions for religion which then pressed only on the Roman Catholics who would not take the oath of supremacy, and on the Quakers, who would not take any oath at all. Some thousands of Roman Catholics and fourteen hundred Quakers were set free. The new king called, by a special letter to Scotland, for new penal laws against the Covenanters. It was made death to preach in-doors or out at a conventicle, and death to attend one in the open air. **Richard Baxter** (§ 21) was tried before Judge Jeffreys for seditious libel in complaint of the wrongs of Dissenters, in his *Paraphrase on the New Testament,* published in 1685. "Leave thee to thyself," said James's judge to the old man, whose friends thronged the court about him, "and I see thou wilt go on as thou hast begun ; but, by the grace of God, I'll look after thee. I know thou hast a mighty party, and I see a great many of the brotherhood in corners waiting to see what will become of the mighty don, and a doctor of the party at your elbow ; but, by the grace of Almighty God, I will crush you all." Baxter, unable to pay a fine of five hundred marks, was for the next eighteen months in prison. On the 14th of June the Duke of Monmouth landed from Holland, at Lyme, in Dorsetshire, with eighty-three followers. Next day he had 1,000 foot and 150 horse. Among those who hurried to his standard was Daniel De Foe, then about twenty-four years old.

55. **Daniel De Foe,** born in 1661, was the son of James Foe, a well-to-do butcher, in the parish of St. Giles's, Cripplegate. His father, a Dissenter, sent him to the school kept at

Newington Green by Charles Morton, a good scholar, who included English among school studies, and afterwards, when driven to America by persecution, became Vice-President of Harvard College. After a full training with Mr. Morton, Daniel Foe began the world in Freeman's Court, Cornhill, as an agent between manufacturers and retailers in the hosiery trade. His strong interest in public events had been shown already in the reign of Charles II., by a tract, *Presbytery Roughdrawn*, published in 1683. After the accession of James II. he was one of those citizens of London who, when they heard Monmouth had landed, rode away to join him. He was with Monmouth at Sedgmoor. Monmouth was executed on the 15th of July, 1685. Then followed the barbarous progress of Judge Jeffreys through the scenes of the rebellion in the West, after which he was made Lord Chancellor. In October of the same year Louis XIV. signed the decree known as the Revocation of the Edict of Nantes. That edict, subscribed by Henry IV. in 1598, secured freedom of worship and equal rights to the French Protestants. They were now prohibited exercise of their religion in France, their places of worship were to be levelled, their ministers were exiled, but the congregations were forbidden to leave the country with their ministers, on pain of confiscation and condemnation to the galleys. They must conform, and thenceforth have their children baptised as Roman Catholics. The decree was carried out with cruelty, but could not stop the emigration. Many came to England, bringing their industries with them. Evelyn at this time noted in his diary a harangue of the Bishop of Valence, who said that this victory over heresy "was but what was wished in England ; and that God seemed to raise the French king to this power and magnanimous action, that he might be in capacity to assist in doing the same here." The English Parliament met in November. The Commons protested feebly, the Lords more stoutly, against the king's violation of the Test Act as avowed in his opening speech. "Let no man," said James, "take exception that there are some officers in the army not qualified according to the late tests for their employments. The gentlemen, I must tell you, are most of them well known to me, and . . . I think them now fit to be employed under me." Parliament was prorogued on the 20th of November, and no supplies had been voted ; but at the outset of his reign James had secured to himself a vote for life of the chief imposts. Parliament was kept in abeyance, twice prorogued in 1686, twice in 1687, and dissolved in July of that year. In 1686 James devised a plan for legalizing by collusion his claim of a right to dispense with the Test Act, which excluded Roman Catholics from civil and military offices. He had appointed a Roman Catholic, Sir Edward Hales, Governor of Dover Castle and colonel of a regiment. Having dismissed four judges and his Solicitor-General, who protested against his course, and secured to himself a servile court, he caused Sir Edward's servant to proceed against his master for not having taken the Sacrament as required by the Test Act. The defence was His Majesty's dispensing power, and this was allowed by a judgment which virtually abolished the Test Act; for, said the court, the king "could pardon all offences against the law, and forgive the penalties, and why could he not dispense with them?" Warrants were next issued authorising members of the Church of Rome to hold benefices in the Church of England. The English clergy were forbidden to preach upon any point of controversy with the Church of Rome. James licensed a king's printer for printing missals, lives of saints, and Roman Catholic tracts, and set up an Ecclesiastical Commission, with Jeffreys for president. At the end of 1686 he appointed a Roman Catholic to the deanery of Christchurch. In February, 1687, he required the University of Cambridge to confer the degree of M.A. on a Benedictine monk. The oaths being refused, the degree was refused. Vice-Chancellor and Senate were summoned before the Ecclesiastical Commission, and the Vice-Chancellor was suspended from his revenue as Master of Magdalene College. In April, 1687, James issued a Declaration for Liberty of Conscience in England. By the exercise of the royal prerogative, all penal laws against Nonconformists were suspended; oaths and tests were abrogated. Baxter was thus released from prison. Presbyterians, Independents, Quakers, were all free to worship as they would. Catholicism was also free from impediment; and there was the king ready to give to its professors the chief places in the Church and the great Universities. Many Dissenters did not see the drift of the king's liberality, or care to remember that the liberality, if wise and good, was in a form that set the English Parliament aside, and made the king absolute source of law.

Daniel Foe, after the battle lost at Sedgmoor, had left England. He had been to Spain and Portugal as a trader, but when the cruel search for Monmouth's followers had long been

over he returned, having picked up abroad the fancy for a " De"
before his name, and now his voice was heard again in three
pamphlets.   One was *A Tract against the Proclamation for the
Repeal of the Penal Laws*, then came *A Pamphlet against the
Addresses to King James*, and yet again *A Tract upon the Dispensing Power*.   These, all published in 1687, were De Foe's
writings in the reign of James II.

56. It was in this year of troubles, 1687, that **Isaac
Newton** published the great work which includes his demon-
stration of the theory of Gravitation (§ 30), commonly known as
" Newton's Principia."

57. **John Dryden** obtained the licence for his *Hind and
Panther*, a defence of the Roman Catholic religion, only a week
after the issue of the Declaration of Indulgence.   It was being
read and talked of when the king, who had in case of need an
army encamped on Hounslow Heath, received on the 3rd of
July a Papal nuncio with great pomp at Windsor, and next day
a proclamation in the *London Gazette* dissolved the prorogued
Parliament.   The publication of *The Hind and Panther* was
deliberately timed to aid King James in his scheme of a
Catholic reaction.   It dealt as distinctly as " Absalom and
Achitophel" did in its day with the essential question of the
hour ; but the point of view was honestly Dryden's.   James
was not liberal to Dryden.   In the renewal of his offices of
laureate and historiographer, the annual butt of canary had
been subtracted from his pay, and the renewal of the pension
of £100, that lapsed at the death of Charles, was neglected for
twelve months after the new king's accession.   There was no
bribe, direct or indirect ; and Dryden was the reverse of a
time-server in staying by King James when nearly all his
friends were leaving him, and prudently trimming their
sails to meet the inevitable change of wind.   But Dryden
had his own convictions, and was true to them.   He said
in his preface to *The Hind and Panther*, " Some of the
Dissenters, in their addresses to His Majesty, have said ' that
he has restored God to His empire over conscience.'   I confess
I dare not stretch the figure to so great a boldness ; but I
may safely say that conscience is the royalty and prerogative
of every private man."   He had said as much in the " Religio
Laici," and the spirit of charity in that poem remained
unaltered in " The Hind and Panther."   This argument for
Catholicism is in three parts, and is the longest of Dryden's poems

The milk-white Hind is the Church of Rome; the Panther is the Church of England, "fairest creature of the spotted kind."

> " A milk-white hind, immortal and unchanged,
> Fed on the lawns, and in the forest ranged ;
> Without unspotted, innocent within,
> She feared no danger, for she knew no sin."

The other beasts had no good-will to her; and Independent, Presbyterian, Quaker, Freethinker, Anabaptist, Arian, are figured under bear, wolf, hare, ape, boar, fox. Then Dryden argues on with little heed to any fable, merely hindered by his clumsy animal machinery where his desire is for direct argument. When he speaks of the persecutions attendant on the Revocation of the Edict of Nantes, he says :

> " Of all the tyrannies on human kind
> The worst is that which persecutes the mind.
> Let us but weigh at what offence we strike :
> 'Tis but because we cannot think alike.
> In punishing of this we overthrow
> The laws of nations and of nature too."

One evening the beasts came down to the common watering-place, and the Hind stood timidly aside, till, with an awful roar, the lion (James II.) bade her fear no more.

> " Encouraged thus, she brought her younglings nigh,
> Watching the motions of her patron's eye,
> And drank a sober draught ; the rest, amazed,
> Stood mutely still, and on the stranger gazed;
> Surveyed her part by part, and sought to find
> The ten-horned monster in the harmless hind,
> Such as the wolf and panther had designed."

On nearer view they admired her ; and when the rest of the herd had gone to their heaths and woods, the Panther

> " Made a mannerly excuse to stay,
> Proffering the hind to wait her half the way :
> That, since the sky was clear, an hour of talk
> Might help her to beguile the tedious walk.
> *    *    *    *    *    *
> After some common talk, what rumours ran,
> The lady of the spotted muff began."

Then the two beasts talked theology, the Hind stating the case for Catholicism, and the Panther stating the objections to be met, until the Hind had reached her lonely cell, and

> " She thought good manner bound her to invite
> The stranger dame to be her guest that night."

The Panther assented, and the Hind wished she would dwell

with her, not for a night, but always.  Then the talk went on
after the Hind's hospitalities, and Dryden laboured to enliven it
with a couple of tedious bird fables ; one told by the Panther of
swallows and martins, and one by the Hind of pigeons and a
buzzard, after which the two beasts went to bed.

> "The dame withdrew, and wishing to her guest
> The peace of heaven, betook herself to rest.
> Ten thousand angels on her slumbers wait,
> With glorious visions of her future state."

58.  While the town was reading this curious pamphlet, one
of the best lay arguments for Catholicism, and, as a poem, full
of good lines, but very clumsy in its structure as a whole,
there suddenly appeared Mr. Bayes's old friends, Smith and
Johnson, hearing Mr. Bayes express his delight at this his new
achievement, in *The Hind and the Panther Transvers'd to
the Story of the Country Mouse and the City Mouse.*  This
caricature, in the manner of "The Rehearsal," was as lively as the
piece it imitated.  Mr. Bayes was now proud not of his play,
but of his fable.  "An apt contrivance, indeed," says Johnson.
"What, do you make a fable of your religion?"  *Bayes :* " Ay,
I'gad, and without morals, too ; for I tread in no man's steps ;
and to show you how far I can outdo anything that ever was
writ in this kind, I have taken Horace's design, but, I'gad, have
so outdone him, you shall be ashamed for your old friend.  You
remember in him the Story of the Country Mouse and the City
Mouse ; what a plain, simple thing it is, it has no more life
and spirit in it, I'gad, than a hobby-horse ; and his mice talk so
meanly, such common stuff, so like mere mice, that I wonder
it has pleased the world so long.  But now will I undeceive
mankind, and teach 'em to heighten and elevate a fable.  I'll
bring you in the very same mice disputing the depth of
philosophy, searching into the fundamentals of religion,
quoting texts, fathers, councils, and all that ; I'gad, as you
shall see, either of 'em could easily make an ass of a country
vicar.  Now, whereas Horace keeps to the dry, naked story, I
have more copiousness than to do that, I'gad.  Here, I draw
you general characters, and describe all the beasts of the
creation ; there, I launch out into long digressions, and leave
my mice for twenty pages together ; then I fall into raptures,
and make the finest soliloquies, as would ravish you.  Won't
this do, think you?"  *Johnson:* "Faith, sir, I don't well conceive
you ; all this about two mice?"  *Bayes:* "Ay, why not?  Is it

not great and heroical?  But come, you'll understand it better
when you hear it ; and pray be as severe as you can; I'gad, I
defy all criticks.  Thus it begins :

> " ' A milk-white mouse, immortal and unchang'd,
> Fed on soft cheese, and o'er the dairy rang'd ;
> Without, unspotted ; innocent within,
> So fear'd no danger, for she knew no ginn.' "

This new jest upon Dryden was by two young men who became
afterwards famous, Charles Montague and Matthew Prior.

**Charles Montague**, born in April, 1661, was the fourth
son of the Hon. George Montague, a younger son of the first
Earl of Manchester.  He was sent at fourteen to Westminster
School, where he formed so intimate a friendship with George
Stepney (§ 52) that he avoided a scholarship at Oxford, and got
leave from his friends to join Stepney at Trinity College, Cambridge.  At the death of Charles II., Montague contributed to
the volume of condolences and congratulations for the new
king that was put together according to custom.  His poem,
" On the Death of His Most Sacred Majesty King Charles II.,"
pleased Lord Dorset and Sir Charles Sedley so well that they
invited Montague to town.  The piece was a clever but unmeasured panegyric, opening with this bold couplet:

> " Farewell, great Charles, monarch of blest renown,
> The best good man that ever fill'd a throne."

Dorset and Sedley were on the popular side, in opposition to
the king's designs, made more alarming by his setting up of
a standing army for aid in suppressing possible resistance to
them.  At their suggestion, Montague joined Prior in reply to
Dryden's " Hind and Panther."

**Matthew Prior**, born in 1664, lost his father when young,
and came into the care of his uncle, Samuel Prior, who kept
the " Rummer " Tavern, near Charing Cross.  It was a house
frequented by nobility and gentry ; so it chanced that the
Earl of Dorset found in it young Prior, who had been taught
at Westminster School, reading Horace for his amusement.
He talked to him, saw him to be clever, and paid the cost
of sending him to St. John's College, Cambridge.  Prior was
then eighteen.  He took his B.A. degree in 1686, returned
to London, and took his place among the young wits of the
Whig party by the brightness of the satire upon Dryden's
" Hind and Panther."  He made friends also by the good

quality of a poem on the Deity, written according to a practice of his college to send every year some poems upon sacred subjects to the Earl of Exeter in return for a benefaction by one of his ancestors.

59. On the 27th of April, 1688, James issued a repetition of his Declaration of Indulgence. By an Order in Council, on the 4th of May, he ordered it to be read in churches and chapels throughout the kingdom on two successive Sundays by ministers of all persuasions, the first reading to be in London on the 20th of May, and in the country on the 3rd of June. On the 18th of May a protest was signed on behalf of a great body of the clergy, by William Sancroft, Archbishop of Canterbury, and six bishops—Thomas Ken, Bishop of Bath and Wells; Francis Turner, Bishop of Ely; Thomas White, Bishop of Peterborough; John Lake, Bishop of Chichester; William Lloyd, Bishop of St. Asaph; and Sir Jonathan Trelawny, Bishop of Bristol—who declared their loyalty, but pointed out that the Declaration was "founded upon such a dispensing power as hath been often declared illegal in Parliament." Of these "seven lamps of the Church," **Thomas Ken** has a place in literature. He was born in 1637, the son of an attorney. His mother died when he was four years old, and his home was then at the haberdasher's shop in Fleet Street kept by Izaak Walton; for his eldest sister, who took charge of him, was Izaak Walton's second wife. Ken was seven when Izaak Walton retired from business; and his home was then in Walton's cottage by the banks of the Dove, in Staffordshire. **George Morley,** Bishop of Winchester, was Izaak Walton's son-in-law; and **Thomas Ken** was sent, at thirteen, to Winchester College. In 1656 he went to Oxford, and joined a musical society formed there, for, like his sister, Mrs. Walton, Ken had a delightful voice, and he played on the lute, viol, and organ. As a student also, Ken began an epic poem on Edmund, the East Anglian king martyred by the Danes. He became M.A. in 1663, and chaplain to Lord Maynard, with the rectory of Easton Parva, just outside Lord Maynard's park, in Essex. Then he became domestic chaplain to George Morley, Bishop of Winchester, in whose household Izaak Walton and his family were already domesticated. Then he obtained a fellowship of Winchester College, and lived in the Wykehamist house. The Bishop of Winchester gave him, in 1667, the living of Brightstone, in the Isle of Wight; and it was in the Isle of Wight, as Rector of Brightstone, that Ken wrote his

*Morning and Evening Hymns,* using them himself, and singing them to his lute when he rose and when he went to rest. In 1669 the Bishop of Winchester gave Ken other promotion, and he left the Isle of Wight. In 1675 he visited Rome with his nephew, young Izaak Walton. In 1681 he published his *Manual of Prayers for the Scholars of Winchester College.* In 1683, Ken went as chaplain-in-chief of the fleet sent to Tangier, and found, when he came home in April, that his brother-in-law, **Izaak Walton,** had died in December, 1683, aged ninety-one.

It had been in 1670 that Walton published in one volume the *Lives*—written from time to time—of Hooker, Sanderson, Wotton, Donne, and Herbert; and in 1676 that **Charles Cotton** (b. 1630, d. 1687), a translator of Corneille's " Les · Horaces" and Montaigne's Essays, and author of a *Travestie of Virgil,* added the "*Second Part of the Complete Angler :* being Instructions how to Angle for Trout or Grayling in a Clear Stream."

In October, 1684, Ken was at the deathbed of his friend **George Morley,** whose writings had been collected in 1683 as " *Several Treatises written upon Several Occasions,* by the Right Reverend Father in God, George, Lord Bishop of Winton, both before and since the King's Restauration : wherein his judgment is fully made known concerning the Church of Rome, and most of those Doctrines which are controverted betwixt her and the Church of England." **Thomas Ken** then became chaplain to Charles II., and was made Bishop of Bath and Wells not many days before the king's death. Ken published a *Manual of Prayer, Seraphical Meditations,* and a poem called *Hymnotheo; or, the Penitent,* but his fame rests on the Morning and Evening Hymns, and on his place among the Seven Bishops.

60. By some means the petition of the bishops was printed and hawked about London. When the appointed Sunday came the Declaration was read only in four London churches. It was read by not more than 200 of the clergy in all England. On the 8th of June the seven bishops were committed to the Tower for seditious libel, but enlarged on recognizances before their trial. They were tried and acquitted. The shouts of popular rejoicing were echoed by the soldiers in the camp at Hounslow. On the 10th of June, two days after the bishops had been sent to the Tower, a son was born to James and his queen. This event might ensure a Roman Catholic succession to the throne, and

gave, therefore, the finishing blow to the king's cause.  The passions of the time produced also a common false impression that the child was an imposture.  But **John Dryden,** as laureate, hailed this event with *Britannia Rediviva: a Poem on the Birth of the Prince.*  Of course there are in this poem of panegyric for the parents and hope for the child indications that Dryden knew as well as other men the dangers of the time :

> " Nor yet conclude all fiery trials past,
> For Heaven will exercise us to the last.
> *      *      *      *      *      *      *
> By living well let us secure his days ;
> Moderate in hopes and humble in our ways.
> No force the free-born spirit can constrain,
> But charity and great examples gain.
> Forgiveness is our thanks for such a day ;
> 'Tis god-like God in his own coin to pay."

On the 30th of June, the day of the acquittal of the seven bishops, a messenger was sent to invite William of Orange to enter England at the head of troops.  On the 5th of November William's fleet entered Torbay, and William landed at Brixham. James found himself deserted.  On the 19th of December the Prince of Orange held a court at St. James's.  On the 13th of February, 1689, William and Mary became king and queen of England.  Conditions and limitations of royal authority embodied in the Declaration of Rights and Liberties of the English People were joined to the offer of the throne.  It was accepted presently with those limitations, and they were afterwards embodied in the Bill of Rights.

## CHAPTER XI.

### UNDER WILLIAM III. AND ANNE.

1. IN the course of English Literature after the Revolution, the old contest about the limit of authority (ch. iii. § 10) became less and less prominent.  For a time the same parties continued the same battle ; the upholders of supreme authority sought to reconquer ground that had been won by their antagonists. There were years even in which many doubted whether we had seen the last of civil war.  But the limitation of the monarchy was maintained.  The machinery of government was brought by degrees into good working order, and slow changes tended

constantly to the removal of undue restraints upon each life within the body of the people.  Meanwhile, also, there was a slow rise in the average power of the unit in the population. We shall find, therefore, in the literature now to be described a gradual abatement of that strife of thought through which we won our liberties, and an increasing sense of the true use of freedom.  A land is free when there is nothing to restrain and much to aid the full development of each one mind in it.

Not many years after the Revolution we shall begin to find encroachment upon the French influence over our literature, by writers who do not address the polite patron, but find readers enough in the main body of their countrymen.  As the natural mind of the people acted upon the Elizabethan dramatists who had England fairly represented in the playhouse audience, we shall find it also using healthy influence upon those writers of the eighteenth and nineteenth century who did not follow the doctrine expressed in the *Poétique* of La Mesnadière, that literature is only for kings, lords, and fine ladies, scholars and philosophers.  As the many-headed monster learns to read, we come into the last of the Four Periods into which our literature falls (ch. iv. § 10), the *Period of Popular Influence*.  This we shall find encroaching more and more on the French influence during many years of its decline.  There will be, indeed, another form of French influence upon our literature, not of polite French on polite English, but of nation upon nation.  Our political settlement of 1689, following that of the Dutch, influenced opinion in other countries.  It was a starting-point of thought which in France, under conditions unlike ours, advanced during the next hundred years to the Revolution of 1789.  Out of intense feeling and quick wit of the French came bold suggestion of social systems that were to solve all problems and go far beyond any results attained by our dull habit of accommodating ourselves to the possible.  We should have been worth little as a people if our neighbours had not stirred us by their noble ardour to achieve, if it might be, a perfect reconstruction of society, based on a complete reconsideration of the rights and duties of the individual in relation to himself, his family, his country, and his Maker if he had one.  That spirit of inquiry which we have seen gathering strength since Elizabeth's time, we shall find active still ; bold in its testing of accepted facts and search after new truth in all the realms of knowledge.  In some directions we shall find it quickened

and emboldened by this new influence of France. We shall
find also the reaction against despotism connected throughout
Europe with the rise of a strong spirit of nationality, strong
in England, aiding the reaction against petty classicism and
Latin-English, and bringing us, as a Teutonic race, to fellow-
feeling with the kindred literature of the Germans at a time
when that was vigorously representing the new impulse of
thought. During all their contests against despotism, we have
felt with our neighbours, but, without need of another revolution
for ourselves, have plodded on, and have not been misguided by
that quiet religious sense of duty which does keep us, with all
our individual stupidities, from first to last as a nation, steady
upon a road that cannot lead to ruin. We have now to trace in
our literature the mind of England passing by natural sequence
to a form of endeavour in our own times as distinctly marked
as that of any one age in its earlier life ; the form of endeavour
towards which all past struggle tended, and which works towards
results that five hundred years hence may be not half attained.

2. John Bunyan and George Villiers, Duke of Buckingham,
who differed only a few months in age, both died in 1688.
Ralph Cudworth also died within the year before the accession
of William and Mary. Edmund Waller, Henry More, and
Sir William Petty had passed away within the last two years.
Aphra Behn, Sir George Etherege, and Sydenham, the phy-
sician, died within the first year of the reign. The great
living writers were John Dryden, who was in the first year of this
reign fifty-eight years old ; John Locke, fifty-seven ; and Isaac
Newton, forty-seven. The oldest living writer was William
Prynne, eighty-nine, and he lived to be ninety-nine. John
Wallis, the mathematician, and Sir Roger l'Estrange were
seventy-three, and both lived through the reign ; so did John
Evelyn, who, at the beginning of the reign of William and
Mary was sixty-nine, and Samuel Pepys, who was fifty-seven.
Sir William Temple and Robert Boyle were sixty-one ; John
Howe and John Tillotson were fifty-nine. Robert South and
Edward Stillingfleet were fifty-four; Gilbert Burnet, forty-six ;
William Sherlock about the same, and William Penn a year
younger. The Earl of Dorset was fifty-two ; Thomas Rymer
was about fifty ; the Earl of Mulgrave forty, and John Dennis,
with fame to come as a critic, thirty-two. Of the dramatists,
past and future, William Wycherley was forty-nine ; John
Vanbrugh, twenty-three ; William Congreve, nineteen ; and

Y

George Farquhar, eleven. Thomas Shadwell was forty-nine ;
Elkanah Settle, forty-one; John Crowne, over forty; Sir
Charles Sedley, about fifty ; Thomas Southern, thirty; Colley
Cibber, eighteen; Nicholas Rowe, fifteen. Jeremy Collier was
thirty-nine; Richard Blackmore, thirty-six. Daniel Defoe and
Charles Montague were twenty-eight ; Francis Atterbury and
Richard Bentley were twenty-seven; Matthew Prior was
twenty-five ; Samuel Garth, about twenty-five ; George Gran-
ville, Lord Lansdowne, twenty-two : and among the young
men and boys, with all their work before them, were Richard
Steele and Joseph Addison, seventeen ; Isaac Watts, fifteen ;
John Arbuthnot, fourteen ; Henry St. John, eleven ; Thomas
Parnell, nine ; Edward Young, five ; Allan Ramsay, four ; Pope
and Gay, babies.

3. When the first Earl of Shaftesbury died, in 1683,
**John Locke** (ch. x. § 53) remained in Holland. James II.
demanded him of the States, on false suspicion of his having
been concerned in Monmouth's invasion, and he was in con-
cealment till the close of 1686. In 1687 he was in safe harbour
at Amsterdam, where his chief friends were the leaders of the
Arminian or Remonstrant school, which had its head-quarters
there. Arminius himself (ch. viii. § 18) had once been pastor at
Amsterdam ; his successor, Simon Bisschop, born at Amsterdam
in 1583, was, under the name of Episcopius, the man who first
expressed, though not systematically, the doctrines of the
Arminians or Remonstrants in various theological writings.
When the persecution of the Remonstrants slackened, after the
death, in 1625, of Stadtholder Maurice, Episcopius, who had
been expatriated by the Synod of Dordrecht, settled at Amsterdam, opened there the Oratory of the Remonstrants, and took
the chair of Theology in their seminary. Episcopius died in
1643 ; his successor was Etienne Courcelles, who collected his
works in two volumes, published at Amsterdam in 1650 and
1663. The successor of Courcelles was Locke's Dutch friend,
Philip van Limborch, nephew of Episcopius, whose life he
wrote. Limborch was born at Amsterdam, and was within a year
of the same age as Locke. In 1668 he had become pastor of
the Remonstrants' church, and next year also Professor of
Theology at the Remonstrants' seminary. He held those
offices until his death, in 1712 ; and Locke, at Amsterdam, was a
member of his congregation. There was also a philosophical
society over which Limborch presided, and of which Locke and

Jean Leclerc were the most important members. The principles of Toleration maintained by Limborch were propagated by Leclerc. Limborch also wrote. His " Theologia Christiana," published in 1686, was the first complete system of Arminian theology ; and in 1692 he published a " History of the Inquisition," which set forth the odiousness of its tyranny. Locke's strong friendship for Limborch was that of a fellow-combatant, and his first letter, *On Toleration*, published in Latin, at Gouda, in 1689—*Epistola de Tolerantia*—was dedicated " Ad clarissimum virum T.A.R.P., T.O., L., A., scripta a P.A., P.O.; J.L., A."—the letters meaning that the piece was addressed to the illustrious Professor of Theology among the Remonstrants, Hater of Tyranny, Limborch of Amsterdam (Theologiæ Apud Remonstrantes Professorem, Tyrannidis Osorem, Limburgum, Amstelodamensem) ; and written by the Friend of Peace, Hater of Persecution, John Locke, Englishman (Pacis Amico, Persecutionis Osore, Johanne Lockio, Anglo).

Locke's other friend, Jean Leclerc, born at Geneva, was a great-nephew of Courcelles, a man of about thirty, who had been turned by the writings of Episcopius from the Calvinism in which he had been bred; had made a stir in his church at the age of twenty-two by publishing theological letters, under the name of " Liberius a Sancto Amore ;" and, after movements which included a short residence in London, settled at Amsterdam, where he was Professor of Philosophy, Belles Lettres, and Hebrew in the Remonstrants' college. He had an active mind, wrote much, and well. A few years before his death, in 1736, he lost his reason, continued to talk, write, and correct proofs, with the steadiness of a sane scholar, but without any sense or order in his thoughts. The papers over which he seemed to himself to be living as of old were burnt by his printer as they were received. In his early manhood, when he was among Locke's friends at Amsterdam, Leclerc was editing his " Bibliothèque Universelle," which extended to twenty-six volumes. Locke's *Essay Concerning Human Understanding* was finished among these friends at Amsterdam in 1687 ; and an outline of it, translated into French by Leclerc, appeared in the " Bibliothèque Universelle " for January, 1688. Other extracts from it afterwards appeared in the same journal. Locke's *New Method of making Common-place Books* was translated into English in 1697, from Leclerc's " Bibliothèque " for 1685.

The English Revolution having been accomplished, John

Locke came over to England in February, 1689, in the fleet that convoyed the Princess of Orange. He was made a Commissioner of Appeals, with a salary of £200 a year; and declined other preferment, including offer of the post of envoy to some court where the air might suit his inferior health. But he found a pleasant home at Oates, in Essex, with Sir Francis and Lady Masham. Lady Masham was Cudworth's only child (ch. x. § 22), and had been trained by her father to scholarship and liberal thought; she and her husband were, therefore, in strong intellectual sympathy with Locke, and established a room as his own in their country house at Oates. In 1691, Locke published *Some Considerations on the Lowering of Interest and Raising the Value of Money*. The practical tendency of his writings caused him to be made, in 1695, a Commissioner of Trade and Plantations; and he surprised merchants by showing them how a philosopher might have wider and clearer views of business than they had themselves. In 1700 he resigned his seat at the Board of Trade, and spent the rest of his life at Oates, in study of the Scriptures. He died there, on the 28th of October, 1704, aged seventy-three. In Locke's personal character there was the simplicity of genius. Living a pure life, with its whole labour given to the highest interests of men, Locke was naturally grave, but his was the gravity of unaffected thoughtfulness, which qualified him but the more for innocent enjoyment. He spoke and wrote plain English, gave himself no airs of artificial dignity, would laugh at those who laboured to look wise, and quote the maxim of Rochefoucauld, that gravity is a mystery of the body contrived to conceal faults of the mind.

4. Locke's most important writings came together with the new order of things in England, and expressed the spirit of the English Revolution. He dealt first with Religious Liberty, in *Three Letters concerning Toleration*. The first was in Latin, addressed, as we have seen, to Limborch, and printed at Gouda, in 1689, translated in the same year into Dutch and French, and then into English, by William Popple. Its argument is that toleration is the chief characteristic mark of the true Church. Antiquity, orthodoxy, and reformed discipline may be marks dwelt upon by men striving for power over one another; but charity, meekness, and goodwill to men are marks of the true Christian. Christianity is no matter of pomp and dominion; its power is over men's lives, to war against their lusts and vices, teach

them charity, and inspire them with a faith working oy love. If persecution be a zeal for men's souls, why does it leave lusts of the flesh unattacked, and only compel men to profess what they do not believe in points of doctrine? It is the duty, Locke argued, of the civil magistrate to secure to every citizen the just possession of the things belonging to this life—his life itself, his liberty, health, and safe possession of his goods. It is not the duty of the civil magistrate to dictate religion to the people. God never gave such authority, and man cannot delegate to another the command over his soul. The power of the magistrate consists only in outward force, which cannot produce inward persuasion. He may argue, indeed, and so may other men; but in this he only is master who convinces. Nor if men's minds were changed would they be probably nearer heaven for adopting the opinions of the court. The Church only is concerned with souls of men, and a church Locke held to be "a voluntary society of men joining themselves together of their own accord, in order to the public worshipping of God in such manner as they judge acceptable to Him and effectual to the salvation of their souls." Each member must worship in accordance with his sense of truth; a man cannot inherit convictions as he inherits house and land. The Church being, therefore, a society of men who join together for the worship they believe will bring them nearest to their God, its laws, said Locke, must be of its own making; they cannot be imposed from without. Those who attach importance to the episcopal rule established by a long series of succession, are right in maintaining for themselves what they judge necessary, "provided I may have liberty at the same time to join myself to that society in which I am persuaded those things are to be found which are necessary to the salvation of my soul." The Gospel frequently declares that the disciples of Christ should suffer persecution, but nowhere that the Church of Christ should persecute; and to those who cried for the Church as the Ephesian silversmith cried for Diana, Locke argued that it might be advantageous to themselves "to require those things in order to ecclesiastical communion which Christ does not require in order to life eternal;" but he added, "how that can be called the Church of Christ which is established upon laws that are not His, and which excludes such persons from its communion as He will one day receive into the kingdom of heaven, I understand not." The end of a religious society, he said, is the public

worship of God, and by means thereof, the acquisition of eternal
life. All discipline should therefore tend to that end, and the
church has no control over the outward goods of its members.
Force belongs wholly to the civil magistrate; the arms of a
church are admonitions, exhortations, and advices. The utmost
force of ecclesiastical power is to cut off a member from the
society which he dishonours, and which refuses any longer to
associate with him. After he has thus been cut off from his
church, all its relation with him and, of course, all power over
him is at an end. A church is free to decline fellowship with
an obstinate offender against its laws, but this must be without
rough usage or civil injury of any kind. " No private person has
a right in any manner to prejudice another person in his civil
enjoyments because he is of another church or religion." His
civil rights are his as a man, Christian or Pagan. We are bound
·to be just ; " nay, we must not content ourselves with the narrow
measure of bare justice—charity, bounty, and liberality must be
added to it. This the Gospel enjoins, this reason directs, and
this that natural fellowship we are born into requires of us." What
is true of private persons is equally true of particular churches,
"which stand as it were in the same relation to each other as
private persons among themselves ; nor has any one of them
any manner of jurisdiction over any other—no, not even when
the civil magistrate (as it sometimes happens) comes to be of this
or the other communion. For the civil government can give no
new right to the church, nor the church to the civil government.
So that whether the magistrate join himself to any church or
separate from it, the church remains always as it was before—
a free and voluntary society. It neither acquires the power of
the sword by the magistrate's coming to it, nor does it lose the
right of instruction and excommunication by his going from it.
But in all churches the magistrate can forbid that to be done
which is not lawful to be done anywhere, because it injures some
member of the commonwealth in that which it is the business
of the civil government to protect—his life or estate." And a
church, Locke argued, that was against the civil rights of the
community has no right to be tolerated by the magistrate. If it
teach that no faith is to be kept with those who differ from it
in religious doctrine, that kings excommunicated by it forfeit
their crowns and kingdoms, that dominion is founded in grace—
meaning that civil supremacy is vested in those who belong to
their own religious society—"what," said Locke, "do all those

and the like doctrines signify but that they may and are ready upon any occasion to seize the government and possess themselves of the estates and fortunes of their fellow-subjects ; and that they only ask leave to be tolerated by the magistrate so long until they find themselves strong enough to effect it." These are, in Locke's words, the chief principles discussed and maintained in his three letters concerning Toleration. In the first letter he set them forth, and met by anticipation some of the chief objections likely to be urged against them. Locke's second letter, published in 1690, and third, a work of some length, in 1692, both signed " Philanthropus," were replies to the objections actually raised by theologians of Queen's College, Oxford, in three letters, of which the first was entitled, *The Argument of the Letter concerning Toleration briefly Considered and Answered.*

5. Locke's argument for religious liberty, in 1689, was followed by his argument also for civil liberty. In 1689 and 1690 he published *Two Treatises of Government;* one opposed to the arguments of Sir Robert Filmer (ch. viii. § 67) in his *Patriarcha,* which had appeared in 1680, and was applauded by upholders of the absolute supremacy of kings ; the other an essay concerning the true original, extent, and end of civil government. They were described by him as the beginning and end of a discourse concerning government, and he hoped " sufficient to establish the throne of our great restorer, our present King William ; to make good his title, in the consent of the people, which being the only one of all lawful governments, he has more fully and clearly than any prince in Christendom ; and to justify to the world the people of England, whose love of their just and natural rights, with their resolution to preserve them, saved the nation when it was on the very brink of slavery and ruin." He should not, he said, have replied to Sir Robert " were there not men amongst us who, by crying up his books and espousing his doctrine, save me from the reproach of writing against a dead adversary." Sir Robert based his plea for absolute monarchy upon the argument that men are not naturally free. They are born in subjection to their parents, and imperial authority is based on patriarchal. Absolute lordship was vested in Adam, inherited from him by the patriarchs. A son, a subject, and a servant or slave, were one and the same thing at first. It was God's ordinance that the supremacy should be unlimited in Adam, and as large as all the acts of his will ; and as in him

so in all others that have supreme power. Locke, in reply to this, undertook to show : 1. That Adam had not, either by right of fatherhood, or by positive donation from God, any such authority over his children or dominion over the world as was pretended. 2. That if he had, his heirs yet had no right to it. 3. That if his heirs had, there being no law of nature nor positive law of God that determines which is the right heir in all cases that may arise, the right of succession, and, consequently, of bearing rule, could not have been certainly determined. 4. That even if that had been determined, yet the knowledge of which is the eldest line of Adam's posterity has been so long since utterly lost, that in the races of mankind and families of the world, there remains not to one above another the least pretence to be the oldest house, and to have right of inheritance. Wherefore it is impossible that the rulers now on earth should make any benefit or derive the least shadow of authority from that which Sir Robert Filmer and his followers held to be the foundation of all power, Adam's private dominion and paternal jurisdiction. Having disposed of this argument for absolutism in the first treatise, in the second Locke set forth what he believed to be the real basis of civil government. "Political power," he said, "is the right of making laws with penalties of death, and, consequently, all less penalties, for the regulating and preserving of property, and of employing the force of the community in the execution of such laws, and in the defence of the commonwealth from foreign injury, and all this only for the publick good." Men, he said, are by nature subject only to the laws of nature, born equal and free. Hooker's recognition of this (ch. vii. § 90) caused Locke from time to time to quote him, and always as "the judicious Hooker." The influence of this treatise has caused Locke's "judicious Hooker" to become as much a commonplace of speech as Chaucer's "moral Gower" (ch. iv. § 24). But the state of liberty is not a state of licence. Reason is one of the laws of nature, and it teaches that if men are all equal and independent, no one ought to harm another in his life, health, liberty, or possessions. Next to the preservation of himself, the natural law wills that each shall aid in the preservation of the rest of mankind ; and into every man's hand is put the execution of such natural law on those who molest their neighbours, as far as reason allows that power may be used to prevent recurrence of offence or secure reparation for the injury. In this state of nature, Locke argued, all men are, until

by their own consents they make themselves members of some
political society. The state of war is not, in Locke's system,
the state of nature, but that which tends to destroy its first conditions. Thus, he who attempts to get another man into his
absolute power, does thereby put himself in a state of war with
him. To avoid this state of war is one great reason of men's
putting themselves into society and quitting the state of nature.
A man, not having the power of his own life, cannot by compact enslave himself to any one ; nobody can give more power
than he has himself. Slavery is nothing but the state of war
continued between a lawful conqueror and a captive. Though
the earth and its goods are common to all men, each man has a
property in his person, and the labour of his body is his own.
An apple gathered upon common ground belongs to him who
has given labour to the gathering. If the water in the stream
belongs to all, that in the pitcher is the property of him who
drew it out. In this part of his treatise Locke is the first to
point distinctly, as Hobbes had pointed more indistinctly, to
labour as the source of wealth. But God gave the earth to
man's use. When its natural fruits were the chief wealth, none
had property in more than he could use—as much land as he
could labour on, as much fruit as he could consume in his family
distribute to others, or store for a future need. He had no right
in reason to claim land that he could not cultivate, or gather
fruit only to let it rot. But the invention of money, as a sign of
value in itself not subject to decay, made it possible to accumu-
late the wealth derived from labour, and establish large properties, to which the first right was given by labour, and which
grew by the heaping up of durable things; for the bounds of
just property are exceeded not by the mere largeness of possession, but by the perishing of anything in it uselessly. Paternal
power is the right and duty of guiding children till they reach
maturity, because they are not as soon as born under the law of
reason, and this has no analogy with the social compact. A
civil society is formed when any number of men agree to form
a government that shall maintain and execute laws for avoidance
of those evils which lie in the state of nature, where every man
is judge in his own case. Absolute monarchy, said Locke, is
no form of civil government at all ; for the end of civil society
is to avoid the inconveniences of a state of nature, and that is
not done by setting up a man who shall be always judge in his
own case, and therefore himself in the state of nature in respect

Y *

of those under his dominion. For his subjects are exposed to all that can be suffered at the hands of one "who being in the unrestrained state of nature, is yet corrupted with flattery, and armed with power." Political societies, then, are formed by the consent of the majority, chiefly for protection of the property of those who are so united. Each society needs an established law, an impartial judge, and power to support and execute his sentence. Thus arise the Legislative and Executive powers of a state. The commonwealth may be ruled by the majority as a democracy; by a few select men as an oligarchy; or by one as a monarchy, hereditary or elective; or by any form compounded of these, as shall seem best to the community. The supreme power is the Legislative, bounded by the law of God and nature, bound, therefore, to maintain equal justice, to seek only the good of the people, whom it may not tax without their own consent, because then Government itself would deprive them of that which it exists for the purpose of defending. The Legislative is restrained also from transfer of the power of making laws to anybody else, or placing it anywhere but where the people placed it. Legislation need not be continuous, and is best put into the hands of divers persons, who then separate and become subject to the laws they have made. But Execution of the Laws must be continuous. Its power is always in being, and thus the Legislative and Executive power come often to be separated. Another power, the Federative, is that which represents the whole society as one in its relation to the rest of mankind; and an injury done to one member of the body engages the whole in the reparation of it. These two powers, the Executive, which administers laws of the society within itself, and the Federative, which manages the security and interest of the public without, though really distinct in themselves, are almost always united. Throughout, while the supreme power is with the Legislative, it holds this as a trust from the people, which can remove or alter the Legislative if it be found unfaithful to the trust reposed in it. If the Executive break trust by use of force upon the Legislative, it puts itself into a state of war with the people. The use of force without authority always puts him that uses it into a state of war, as the aggressor, and renders him liable to be treated accordingly. The power surrendered by each individual to the society cannot revert to him while he remains a member of it. So, also, when the society has placed the Legislative in any assembly of men, to continue in them and their successors, with direction and authority for providing such successors, the Legislative can never revert to the people whilst that government lasts, unless they have set limits to its duration, or by the miscarriages of those in authority the supreme power is forfeited through breach of trust.

With such argument as this, John Locke gave philosophical expression to the principles established practically by the English Revolution.

6. Locke's *Essay concerning Human Understanding*, in Four Books, was first published complete in 1690. Its object was to lead men out of the way of vain contention by showing, through an inquiry into the nature of the human understanding, what are the bounds beyond which argument is vain. In his First Book he followed into a new field Bacon's principles, and maintained that man has no innate ideas, but is created with a receptive mind and reason, whereby he draws knowledge from the universe without. "The goodness of God," Locke said, "hath not been wanting to men without such original impressions of knowledg, or ideas stamp'd on the mind; since He hath furnish'd man with those faculties, which will serve for the sufficient discovery of all things requisite to the end of such a being. And I doubt not but to show that a man, by the right use of his natural abilities, may, without any innate principles, attain the knowledg of a God, and other things that concern him. God having endu'd man with those faculties of knowing which he hath, was no more oblig'd by His goodness to implant those innate notions in his mind, than that having given him reason, hands, and materials, He should build him bridges or houses." "No innate sense of God himself is necessary," said Locke, "for the visible marks of extraordinary wisdom and power appear so plainly in all the works of the creation, that a rational creature who will but seriously reflect on them, cannot miss the discovery of a Deity." Thus it seemed stranger to him that men should want the notion of God than that they should be without any notion of numbers or of fire. In his Second Book, Locke traced the origin of our ideas from the world about us by sensation or reflection, and argued that our most complex thoughts are formed by various combinations of simple ideas derived from the world about us, suggested to the mind only by sensation and reflection, and the sole materials of all our knowledge. "It is not," said Locke, "in the power of the most exalted wit or enlarg'd understanding, by a quickness or vanity of thought, to invent or frame one new

simple idea in the mind, not taken in by the ways aforemen-
tioned; nor can any force of the understanding destroy those
that are there." Locke then discussed in detail the forms of
simple idea derived from sensation and reflection, the action of
the mind upon them in perception, retention, discernment,
naming, abstraction; and its manner of making complex ideas
out of simple ones. He discussed the source and character of
man's ideas of space, duration, number, and infinity, of pleasure
and pain, the passions, his idea of power and of liberty, with
argument upon the nature of free will. He explained by his own
method the causes of obscurity in some ideas, and pointed out
how, by the association of ideas, men are made unreasonable
who have been trained from childhood to associate with certain
words collections of ideas that do not properly belong to them.
A musician used to any tune, when he hears part of it will have
the ideas of its several notes following one another in his understanding without any act of his own. So whole societies of men
are impeded in the fair pursuit of truth. "Some independent
ideas, of no alliance to one another, are by education, custom,
and the constant din of their party, so coupled in their minds,
that they always appear there together; and they can no more
separate them in their thoughts than if they were but one idea,
and they operate as if they were so. This gives sense to jargon,
demonstration to absurdities, and consistency to nonsense, and
is the foundation of the greatest, I had almost said of all, the
errors in the world; or if it does not reach so far, it is at least
the most dangerous one, since so far as it obtains, it hinders
men from seeing and examining." The Third Book was a distinct
essay upon words as signs of ideas, and enforced the importance
of assuring that, as far as possible, they shall be made to represent clearly the same impressions in the minds of those who
use them, and of those to whom they are addressed. Thus two
men might argue without end upon the question whether a bat
be a bird, if they had no clear and equal notion of the collection
of simple ideas forming the complex idea of a bat, whereby
they could ascertain whether it contained all the simple ideas
to which, combined together, they both give the name of bird.
The Fourth Book of the Essay applied the whole argument to
a consideration of the bounds of knowledge and opinion.
Knowledge can extend no farther than we have ideas, and is
the perception of the connection and agreement or disagreement
and repugnancy of any of our ideas. Narrow as the bounds

may seem, our knowledge does not reach to them. Knowledge comes by the way of reason in comparing clear and distinct ideas definitely named. Knowledge is to be had only of visible and certain truth; where this fails we must use judgment, and regulate our degree of assent by reasoning upon the grounds of probability; the foundation of error lying here in wrong measures of probability, as it may lie also in wrong judgment upon matters of knowledge. The witness of God, who cannot err, makes an assured revelation highest certainty. Assurance that the testimony is indeed from God establishes "faith; which as absolutely determines our minds, and as perfectly excludes all wavering as our knowledg it self; and we may as well doubt of our own being, as we can whether any revelation from God be true." What is deducible from human experience God enabled us by reason to discover. What lies beyond our experience may be the subject of a revelation, which is above reason, but not against it. Locke ended with a threefold division of the objects of human knowledge—1, Study of nature, in the largest sense a man's contemplation of things themselves for the discovery of truth; 2, Practical applications, a man's contemplation of the things in his own power for the attainment of his ends; and, 3, Man's contemplation of the signs (chiefly words) that the mind makes use of, both in the one and the other, and the right ordering of them for its clearer information. "All which three," said Locke, "viz., *Things*, as they are in themselves knowable; *Actions*, as they depend on us in order to happiness; and the right use of *Signs* in order to knowledg, being *toto cælo* different, they seem'd to me to be the three great provinces of the intellectual world, wholly separate and distinct one from another." In this Essay, and in his two letters to Stillingfleet, Bishop of Worcester, in the course of the controversy raised over it, the simple piety of Locke is very manifest. The reason of Locke caused him to maintain (Book IV., ch. x.) "that we more certainly know that there is a God than that there is anything else without us."

Locke had finished, in March, 1690, *Some Thoughts concerning Education*, published in 1693, a treatise wisely designed to bring experience and reason to aid in right training of the bodies and minds of children. It is very practical, beginning with the education that may form a healthy body, passing then to a consideration of the right methods of influencing and guiding the mind, the relation of parents to the children, who "must not be hinder'd from being children, or from playing, or doing as children, but from doing ill ;" relation of teachers to the young, development of character, subjects and methods of formal study, and the ordering of travel. The influence of Locke's treatise on education was direct and whole-some ; and to this day, among sensible customs and traditional opinions that help to the well-being of an English home, there are generally some that may be traced back to the time when Locke's Treatise on Education was a new book with a living power over many of its readers.

In 1695 Locke published a book on *The Reasonableness of Christianity, as Delivered in the Scriptures*, the result of his endeavour to turn aside from contending systems of theology and betake himself to the sole reading of the Scripture for the understanding of the Christian religion. Out of the same spirit came his study of St. Paul in *A Paraphrase and Notes on the Epistles of St. Paul to the Galatians, Corinthians, Romans, Ephesians. To which is prefix'd, An Essay for the Understanding of St. Paul's Epistles, by consulting St. Paul himself.* This was published in 1705, the year after his death, for John Locke died early in Queen Anne's reign, in 1704. In 1706 appeared some posthumous works of his, the chief being an essay *Of the Conduct of the Understanding*, the self-edu-cation of the man in learning to make right use of his mind, which has its natural place between the Essay concerning Human Understanding and Locke's Thoughts on the Educa-tion of Children.

7. **John Dryden** (ch. x. § 60) remaining loyal to King James II., and to his adopted faith, was unable to obey the Act which required oaths of allegiance and supremacy to be taken by all holders of office before August 1, 1689. Dryden, there-fore, suffered in his way, with the non-juring clergy, and lost his offices of poet-laureate and historiographer. **Lord Dorset,** who had aided the Revolution, and was now Lord Chamberlain, was liberal in private generosity to Dryden in this time of his need ; but his vacation of the laureateship was inevitable, and, as a stout Whig, his old antagonist, **Thomas Shadwell,** was presented to William by Dorset himself as Dryden's successor. There was not another Dryden on the Whig side, and it must have been a source of grim content to Dryden when he saw that, all things considered, there really was not a man who had a better claim to be King William's laureate than MacFlecknoe. Wycherley (ch. x. § 38) was a better dramatist,

but in their own time they were paired. The Earl of Rochester wrote of them :

> " None seem to touch upon true comedy
> But hasty Shadwell and slow Wycherley;"

and said also of Shadwell, " If he had burnt all he wrote and printed all he spoke, he would have had more wit and humour than any other poet." **Gerard Langbaine**—son of a learned father of like name, who edited Longinus, and became keeper of the archives and Provost of Queen's College, Oxford—Gerard Langbaine, the younger, born at Oxford, in 1656, took lively interest in the stage. He became senior bedel of the University, and died in 1692. He wrote an appendix to a catalogue of graduates, a new catalogue of English plays, and published at Oxford, in 1691, *An Account of the English Dramatick Poets; or, some Observations and Remarks on the Lives and Writings of all those that have published either Comedies, Tragedies, Tragi-Comedies, Pastorals, Masques, Interludes, Farces, or Operas, in the English Tongue.* Langbaine spoke in this book of Wycherley as one whom he was proud to call his friend, and " a gentleman whom I may boldly reckon among poets of the first rank, no man that I know, except the excellent Jonson, having outdone him in comedy." Of Shadwell, Langbaine said, " I own I like his comedies better than Mr. Dryden's, as having more variety of characters, and those drawn from the life. . . . That Mr. Shadwell has preferred Ben Jonson for his model I am very certain of; and those who will read the preface to *The Humorists* may be sufficiently satisfied what a value he has for that great man; but how far he has succeeded in his design I shall leave to the reader's examination." Of Shadwell's play of *The Virtuoso*, printed in 1676, Langbaine said that the University of Oxford had applauded it, " and, as no man ever undertook to discover the frailties of such pretenders to this kind of knowledge before Mr. Shadwell, so none since Mr. Jonson's time ever drew so many different characters of humour, and with such success." Shadwell had written fourteen plays, and Wycherley his four. Shadwell did not wear his laurels long; he died in December, 1692. **Nahum Tate** (ch. x. § 48) succeeded him as laureate, and **Nicholas Brady** preached his funeral sermon. Tate, therefore, was laureate when the first edition of Tate and Brady's *New Version of the Psalms* appeared, in 1696, after the printing of some specimens in previous years. Tate, who was a friend of Dryden, and had been chief writer of the second part of "Absalom and Achitophel," remained laureate during the rest of Dryden's life, and throughout Queen Anne's reign.

**John Dryden,** obliged to return to the stage as a source of income, produced in 1690 his tragedy of *Don Sebastian* in blank verse, with a little prose, and in the same year a comedy, *Amphitryon,* following Molière, with music by Henry Purcell, an excellent musician, and one of the organists of the Chapel Royal, who died of consumption in 1695, at the age of thirty-seven. Purcell also supplied the music for Dryden's *King Arthur; or, the British Worthy,* written in 1685, and produced as a dramatic opera in 1691. With a quiet touch of good-humoured satire, Dryden said in the preface to this attempt at what he called "the fairy way of writing :" " Not to offend the present times, nor a government which has hitherto protected me, I have been obliged so much to alter the first design and take away so many beauties from the writing, that it is now no more what it was formerly than the present ship of the *Royal Sovereign,* after so often taking down and altering, to the vessel it was at the first building ;" and to deserved praise of the genius of Purcell, he added, " In reason my art on this occasion ought to be subservient to his." In May, 1692, Dryden produced his tragedy of *Cleomenes; or, the Spartan Hero,* finished for him by his friend **Thomas Southern.** Southern's best plays, both tragedies, were produced in the reign of William III. ; *The Fatal Marriage,* in 1694, and *Oroonoko,* founded on Mrs. Behn's novel (ch. x. § 28), in 1696. The play added new strength to the protest of the novel against slavery. Southern was an amiable man and a good economist. By his commissions in the army, which he entered early in James II.'s reign, his good business management as a dramatist, and careful investment of his money, he became rich, and lived to be a well-to-do, white-haired old gentleman, who died at the age of eighty-six in the year 1746. He was the introducer of the author's second and third night, which raised his profit from the players, and he was not above active soliciting, which brought in money from bountiful patrons of the theatre to whom he sold his tickets. He contrived even to make a bookseller pay £150 for the right of publishing one of his plays. When Dryden once asked him how much he made by a play, he owned, to Dryden's great astonishment, that by his last play he had made £700. Dryden himself had been often content to earn a hundred. In 1694

**Dryden** produced his last play, *Love Triumphant,* a tragi-comedy, which was a failure. In its prologue and epilogue he took leave of the stage, for he had now resolved to devote himself to a translation of Virgil. While writing these later plays, Dryden had received, in 1692, a fee of five hundred guineas for a poem—*Eleonora*—in memory of the Countess of Abingdon, and had written a *Life of Polybius* to precede a translation by Sir Henry Shere, with a preliminary Essay on Satire, a trans-lation of *The Satires of Juvenal and Persius,* translating himself Satires 1, 3, 6, 10, and 16 of Juvenal, and all Persius. He edited also, for Tonson, in 1693, a third volume of Miscellanies (ch. x. § 52), *Examen Poeticum: being the Third Part of Miscellany Poems. Containing Variety of New Translations of the Ancient Poets; together with many Original Poems by the Most Eminent Hands.* This was a substantial volume, with an appendix of seventy-eight pages, separately paged, containing a translation by Tate of a famous poem by Fracastorius, upon a subject that all readers might not wish to find included in the volume. It opened with Dryden's translation of the First Book of " Ovid's Metamorphoses," included verse by Congreve and Prior, much verse by **Thomas Yalden,** of Magdalene College, Oxford, then aged twenty-two, and a fellow-student of Addison's ; a trans-lation of Virgil's first Georgic, dedicated to Dryden by Henry Sacheverell, another of Addison's college friends ; and the first published writing of **Joseph Addison** himself, *To Mr. Dryden : by Mr. Jo. Addison ;* dated from Magdalene College, Oxford, June 2, 1693. Addison, aged twenty-one, here exalted Dryden as a translator from the Latin poets. " Thy copy," he said—

> " Thy copy casts a fairer light on all,
> And still outshines the bright original."

Dryden's old publisher, Henry Herringman, had by twenty years of industry made fortune enough to retire upon ; and had for some time been living, says his tombstone, "handsomely and hospitably," at Carshalton, where he and his wife Alice, after fifty-eight years of wedded life, died, within six weeks and two days of each other, in 1703. Jacob Tonson had begun business as a bookseller in 1678, with a capital of only £100, cheerfulness, honesty, and industry. Herringman had already set up his house at Carshalton, and withdrawn much personal attention from his business. Young Tonson, aged twenty-three, short, stout, and pushing, had his way to make, and sought the goodwill of the poets. Otway and Tate came to him, and with help of a partner in the venture, he raised £20 to pay Dryden for the copy of his play of *Troilus and Cressida*, with which he began business relations with the great poet in 1679. Jacob Tonson, thenceforth Dryden's publisher, had produced the Miscellanies, wished to make them annual, and in the next year, 1694, appeared the fourth and last of Dryden's series, as *The Annual Miscellany : for the Year* 1694. *Being the Fourth Part of Miscellany Poems ; Containing Great Variety of New Translations and Original Copies, by the Most Eminent Hands.* Again there was a good deal from Yalden, through whom probably Addison obtained his introduction to the Miscellany, and there was now more from young Addison. The volume, much thinner than its predecessor, opened with the " Third Book of Virgil's Georgicks, Englished by Mr. Dryden," and that was immediately followed by *A Translation of all Virgil's 4th Georgick, except the Story of Aristeus. By Mr. Jo. Addison, of Magdalene College, Oxon.* On other pages were, from the same hand, *A Song for St. Cecilia's Day, at Oxford,* and the *Story of Salmacis,* from the Fourth Book of "Ovid's Metamorphoses;" and the book closed with *An Account of the Greatest English Poets, To Mr. H. S., Apr. 3d.,* 1694. *By Mr. Joseph Addison.* "H. S." stood for Henry Sacheverell.

8. **Joseph Addison** was born on May-day, 1672, in his father's parsonage, at Milston, Wiltshire, and was named Joseph, after Joseph Williamson (ch. x. § 42), the patron who had given that small living. Addison was son and grandson to a clergyman. His mother was a clergyman's daughter, and one of his uncles became Bishop of Bristol. Addison's father, Lancelot, was the son of a poor Westmoreland clergyman, who had begun the world at the Restoration as chaplain to the garrison at Dunkirk, and then held for eight years as poor a position at Tangier. When he lost that office, the small living of Milston, given to him by Mr. Joseph, afterwards Sir Joseph, Williamson, enabled Lancelot Addison to marry ; and he had been made one of the king's chaplains when his son Joseph appeared as the firstborn of a family that came to consist of three sons and three daughters. Joseph Addison's father had also turned to account his experiences in Tangier, and earned credit by a little book, on *West Barbary; or, a Short Narrative of the Revolutions of the Kingdoms of Fez and Morocco. With an Account of the Present Customs, Sacred, Civil, and Domestic,* published in

1671, and dedicated as "An Unfeigned Testimony of my Respect and Affection" to the patron after whom the son presently born was named. Lancelot Addison published also a *Life of Mahomet*, and an account of the Jews. About 1677 the Rev. Lancelot Addison became Archdeacon of Salisbury, and his son Joseph then went to a school at Salisbury. In 1683, Lancelot Addison became Dean of Lichfield; and Joseph, aged eleven, then went to school at Lichfield until 1685, when he was sent, a dean's son, as a private pupil to the Charterhouse. There he found, among the boys on the foundation, one of his own age, Richard Steele, who had been sent to the school a few months earlier, in 1684. Between Addison and Steele, as boys at the Charterhouse, an enduring friendship was established.

**Richard Steele** was not two months older than Addison. He was baptized on the 12th of March, 1672 (old style, 1671, see note on p. 106), as the son of Richard Steele, an attorney in Dublin. His father died when he was not quite five years old, and he was in his thirteenth year when, on the nomination of the first Duke of Ormond, he was received as a foundation boy at the Charterhouse. Steele went home at holiday time with his friend Addison to the Lichfield Deanery, where he was on brotherly terms with the children of the household, and where the father gave his blessing to the friendship between his son Joseph and Richard Steele. **Addison** was only about two years at the Charterhouse. He went to Oxford in 1687. Steele did not leave the Charterhouse for Oxford until March, 1689, the year in which Addison, who had entered Queen's College, was elected a Demy of Magdalene. Steele went to Christchurch; and thus, at the beginning of the reign of William and Mary, their schoolboy friendship was being renewed by Steele and Addison as students at Oxford. Addison's lines in the "Miscellany" for 1694, which addressed to Henry Sacheverell, at his request,

> "A short account of all the Muse-possest
> That down from Chaucer's days to Dryden's times
> Have spent their noble rage in Brittish rhimes,"

were the work of a young man with a bent for criticism, though not yet a critic. He echoed opinions of the French school, and followed the polite taste of the day. Of Chaucer he said that he was "a merry bard,"

> But age has rusted what the poet writ,
> Worn out his language, and obscur'd his wit;

> In vain he jests in his unpolish'd strain,
> And tries to make his readers laugh in vain.
> Old Spencer next, warm'd with poetick rage
> In antick tales amus'd a barb'rous age;
> * * * *
> But now the mystick tale, that pleas'd of yore,
> Can charm an understanding age no more ;
> The long-spun allegories fulsom grow,
> While the dull moral lies too plain below."

Shakespeare was simply left out of Addison's list. His next heroes were Cowley and Sprat—Great Cowley, whose " fault is only wit in its excess."

> " Blest man ! who's spotless life and charming lays
> Employ'd the tuneful prelate in thy praise :
> Blest man ! who now shall be for ever known,
> In Sprat's successful labours and thy own.
> But Milton next, with high and haughty stalks
> Unfetter'd in majestick numbers walks.
> * * * *
> Whate'er his pen describes I more than see,
> Whilst ev'ry verse, array'd in majesty,
> Bold and sublime, my whole attention draws,
> And seems above the critic's nicer laws."

A genuine admiration of Milton, who did not appeal in vain to young Addison's religious feeling, is the most interesting feature of these lines, which went on from Milton to Waller, Roscommon, Denham, Dryden, Congreve, Montague, and Dorset, in the manner of one who was being educated in "an understanding age," trained by polite France in a shallow self-sufficiency. This "understanding age," however, was not quite ignorant of Spenser. There had appeared, in 1687, *Spenser Redivivus: containing the First Book of the Fairy Queen, His Essential Design preserv'd, but his Obsolete Language and Manner of Verse totally laid aside. Deliver'd in Heroick Numbers, by a Person of Quality.* All the old music, with its sweet variety of number, was fled. There were no more sonnets ; they took flight out of our literature at the coming in of the French influence. Narrative was to be after the manner of France, in rhymed couplets ; our old "riding rhyme," so called because it was the rhyme that described the Canterbury pilgrims, was now dubbed "heroic verse," and the predominance of this metre had now become one characteristic of the outward form of English poetry.

**Richard Steele** wrote his earliest published verse a few months after the appearance of Addison's Account of the Poets. But Steele's interest was above all things in life itself, and then in literature as the expression of it. He showed his interest in men by writing a comedy at college, and was content to burn it when a fellow-student thought it bad. His first printed verse .was on the death of Queen Mary, by small-pox, in the Christmas week of 1694; and Steele used more than once one of its opening lines, expressing his sense of the earnest under-tone of life—" Pleasure itself has something that's severe." Since the throne was not vacant, Parliament still sat, and for the first time a procession of the two Houses of Lords and Commons joined in the funeral pomp of an English sovereign. Steele's poem, of about 150 lines, was called *The Procession.*

9. When Mary and her husband had been proclaimed King and Queen of England, Mary sent to ask William Sancroft, Archbishop of Canterbury, for his blessing, and had for answer, " Tell the princess to ask her father's ; without that I doubt mine would not be heard in heaven." He would not transfer to William the oaths he had sworn to James, and was suspended on the 1st of August, 1689, but not deprived till 1690, when four more of the seven bishops whom King James had sent to the Tower—namely, Turner, White, Locke, and Ken—besides Lloyd of Norwich and Frampton of Gloucester, were deprived as Non-jurors. About four hundred clergymen and members of the Universities suffered with them, and many who took the oaths had no sympathy with the Revolution. **Thomas Ken** (ch. x. § 59), when deprived, at the age of fifty-three, had £700 and his books, and was presently housed by an old college friend, Thomas Thynne, Lord Weymouth, in a suite of rooms in his mansion of Longleate, in Wiltshire. Lord Weymouth took Ken's £700, and paid him an annuity of £80 a year. From Longleate he paid occasional visits to friends, went abroad at first on his old white horse, and, when that was worn out, on foot, preaching, and collecting subscriptions for distressed Non-jurors and their families. At Longleate House he died, in March, 1711.

Among the non-jurors was **William Sherlock,** a divine then high in repute, born in 1641, educated at Eton and Peter-house, Cambridge; in 1669 Rector of St. George's, Botolph Lane, and Prebendary of St. Paul's; then Master of the Temple, an active preacher and writer against the Roman Catholics. At the time of his deprivation, Sherlock published, in 1689, the most popular of his books, *Practical Discourse concerning Death.* His deprivation was soon followed by his acceptance of the established authority in 1691, when he was restored to his office of Master of the Temple, and made Dean of St. Paul's. In 1692 appeared his *Practical Discourse concerning Future Judgment;* and he was involved in a long and bitter controversy with **Robert South,** a learned, zealous, and good-natured divine, upon the Trinity. Sherlock died in 1707 ; South, who had conformed to all Governments of his time, died in 1716, aged eighty-three. The amiable **John Tillotson,** who took in 1691 the archbishopric of which Sancroft had been deprived, lived only until 1694, and his funeral sermon was preached by **Gilbert Burnet,** who had been regarded by the Stuarts as an enemy since 1682, when he showed his sympathy with Lord William Russell during his trial and before his execution. Burnet was abroad, and much with the Prince and Princess of Orange during the reign of James II. He came over with William as his chaplain. In 1690 he was made Bishop of Salisbury. He had published, in 1686, at Amsterdam, *Some Letters containing an Account of what seemed Most Remarkable in Switzerland, Italy,* &c. They are five letters addressed to the Hon. Robert Boyle. The information in them is compactly given, and their tone is very strongly Protestant. Burnet published, in 1692, *A Life of William Bedell, D.D., Lord Bishop of Kilmore, in Ireland, with his Letters,* and *A Discourse of the Pastoral Care.* **William Penn** (ch. x. § 41) published, in 1694, *A Brief Account of the Rise and Progress of the People called Quakers,* and an *Account of his Travels in Holland and Germany in* 1677, *for the Service of the Gospel of Christ, by way of Journal.* Fox (ch. ix. § 16) and Barclay (ch. x. § 21) had been Penn's companions on that journey. The *Journal* of **George Fox,** who died in 1690, was published in 1694.

10. **John Strype,** born at Stepney in 1643, was educated at St. Paul's School and Jesus College, Cambridge. In 1669 he was presented to the living of Theydon Boys, which he resigned for that of Low Leyton, in Essex. He lived to the age of ninety-four, and was incumbent of Low Leyton for sixty years. He was an accurate student of Church history and biography, and began, in 1694, with a folio of *Memorials of Archbishop Cranmer.* In 1698 appeared his *Life of Sir Thomas Smith* (ch. vii. § 24), and in 1701 his *Life and Actions of John Aylmer, Bishop of London* (ch. vii. § 32).

**Humphrey Prideaux** was born in 1648, at Padstow, in

·Cornwall; was educated at Westminster School and Christ-church, Oxford. In 1676 he wrote an account of the Arundel Marbles. Then he obtained the living of St. Clement's, Oxford, and in 1681 a prebend at Norwich. In 1697 he published a *Life of Mahomet*, and in 1702 was made Dean of Norwich.

11. **Sir George Mackenzie,** of Rosehaugh, who died in 1691, aged fifty-five, was a good friend to English writers of his time, and himself a good writer. He was born at Dundee, of a known family, in 1636, studied Civil Law at Bourges, in 1659 began life as an advocate, and next year published *Aretine; or, The Serious Romance.* Then he became justice depute, after-wards was knighted. In 1667 his *Moral Gallantry* established moral duties as the principles of honour. He was one of the men most active in establishing the Advocates' Library, founded at Edinburgh in 1682, and had a high literary and social repu-tation when he died, in the reign of William and Mary.

12. **John Evelyn** (ch. ix. § 18) was appointed one of the Commissioners of Greenwich Hospital when William III., after the death of Mary, actively carried out her wish to found a home for old sailors, and made this hospital, of which Evelyn became treasurer, the noblest monument to her memory. When the Czar Peter came to England, in 1698, he lived at Sayes Court, to be near the Deptford Dockyard. In 1699, John Evelyn succeeded to the paternal estate, by the death of his elder brother; and in May, 1700, he left Sayes Court for Wotton. Evelyn's famous garden at Sayes Court was described in the Philosophical Transactions of the Royal Society. Among his numerous writings were "*The French Gardiner:* Instructing how to Cultivate all Sorts of Fruit. Trees and Herbs for the Garden" (1658); "*Fumifugium;* or, the Aer and Smoak of London Dissipated" (1661); "*Sculptura;* or, the History and Art of Chalcography and Engraving in Copper" (1662); "*Kalendarium Hortense;* or, the Gardiner's Almanac" (1664); "*Sylva*" (1664), a Treatise on Forest Trees, the first book printed for the Royal Society, and the book with which his name is most associated; "*Terra*" (1675), also printed for the Royal Society; "*Navigation and Commerce:* their History and Pro-gress" (1672), this being an introduction to the History of the Dutch War, written at the request of Charles II.; *Public Em-ployment and an Active Life preferred to Solitude and all its Appanages* (1667), an answer to one of Sir George Mackenzie's books, which was a "Moral Essay preferring Solitude to Public

Employment." Under William III., Evelyn produced, in 1690, a satire on the frippery of ladies, *Mundus Muliebris; or, the Ladies' Dressing Room Unlock'd, and her Toilette Spread. In Burlesque. Together with the Fop Dictionary, Compil'd for the Use of the Fair Sex.* In 1697, Evelyn published *Numismata: a Discourse of Medals;* with a digression concerning Physiognomy; and in 1699, *Acetaria: a Discourse of Sallets.*

13. **John Ray** was the chief botanist of the time. He was a blacksmith's son, born in 1628 at Black Notley, near Braintree, Essex. He was sent from Braintree School to Cambridge, where he obtained a fellowship of Trinity; in 1651 was Greek Lecturer of his college, and afterwards Mathematical Reader. In 1660 he published a Latin Catalogue of Plants growing about Cambridge, and then made a botanical tour through Great Britain. His Latin *Catalogue of the Plants of England and the Adjacent Isles* first appeared in 1670. Ray took orders at the Restoration, but refused subscription, and resigned. In 1663 he spent three years with a pupil, Mr. F. Willoughby, on the Continent, and published an account of his travels in 1673, as *Observations made in a Journey through Part of the Low Countries, Germany, Italy, and France, with a Catalogue of Plants not Natives of England.* Ray married, in 1673, a lady twenty-four years younger than himself; educated the children of his friend Mr. Willoughby, who had died in 1672; and finally. in 1679, he settled in his native place, and lived there till his death, in 1705. Among his chief books was *A Collection of English Proverbs, with Short Annotations*, first published in 1670; and in the reign of William III. he produced, in 1691, *The Wisdom of God Manifested in the Creation;* in 1692, *Miscellaneous Discourses concerning the Dissolution and Changes of the World;* in 1693, *Three Physico-Theological Discourses concerning Chaos, the Deluge, and the Dissolution of the World;* and in 1700, *A Persuasive to a Holy Life.* Ray was one of Nature's naturalists—wise, modest, and unassuming —with the sense of God that comes of a full study and enjoyment of His works. The mathematical works of **John Wallis** —*Opera Mathematica et Miscellanea*—were published in three folios between 1693 and 1699. Wallis died in 1703, aged eighty-eight. **Ray's** *Physico-Theological Discourses* belong to a course of scientific speculation on the Cosmos, which formed part of the new energy of scientific research, and received impulse in 1681 from the "Sacred Theory of the Earth" (*Telluris Theoria*

*Sacra*), by **Thomas Burnet**, who, in 1685, was made Master of the Charterhouse.  Thomas Burnet discussed the natural history of our planet, in its origin, its changes, and its consummation, and the four books contain—(1) The Theory of the Deluge by Dissolution of the Outer Crust of the Earth, its Subsidence in the Great Abyss, and the Forming of the Earth as it now Exists; (2) Of the First Created Earth and Paradise; (3) Of the Conflagration of the World; and (4) Of the New Heaven and the New Earth.  This new attempt made by a Doctor of Divinity to blend large scientific generalization with study of Scripture, more imaginative than scientific, stirred many fancies, and was much read and discussed.  But under William III., Thomas Burnet's speculations in his *Archæologiæ Philosophicæ Libri Duo* drew on him strong theological censure; and he was called an infidel by many because he read the Fall of Adam as an allegory.  This not only destroyed his chance of high promotion in the Church, but caused him to be removed from the office of Clerk of the Closet to the king, and he died at a good old age, in 1715, still Master of the Charterhouse.  **William Whiston**, who was thirty years or more younger than Thomas Burnet, was chaplain to a bishop when, in 1696, he published *A New Theory of the Earth, from its Original to the Consummation of all Things.*  This fed the new appetite for cosmical theories with fresh speculation.  In Burnet's system, fire, in Whiston's, water, played chief part as the great agent of change.  In 1698 Whiston became Vicar of Lowestoft, and in 1700 he lectured at Cambridge, as deputy to Newton, whom he succeeded in the Lucasian Professorship.  Whiston lived till the middle of the eighteenth century.  In Queen Anne's reign his search for a primitive Christianity affected his theology, and brought on him loss of his means of life in the Church and University.  He taught science; lived, as a poor man, a long and blameless life, until his death, in 1752; and in his writings blended love of nature with the love of God.

14.  **William Congreve**, thirty-two years younger than William Wycherley, wrote all his plays in the reign of William III.  His first play, *The Old Bachelor*, appeared in 1693, sixteen years after Wycherley's last play, "The Plain Dealer."  Congreve was born at Bardsey, Yorkshire, in February, 1670; was educated at Kilkenny and at Trinity College, Dublin: entered the Middle Temple; in 1693, at the age of

twenty-three, produced a novel *Incognita; or, Love and Duty Reconciled*, and at Drury Lane his play of *The Old Bachelor*, which he professed to have written several years before " to amuse himself in a slow recovery from sickness." The success of the play was great, and it caused Charles Montague, then a Lord of the Treasury, to make Congreve a commissioner for licensing hackney coaches. In the following year, 1694, Congreve produced, with much less success, *The Double Dealer*. The two theatres at Drury Lane and Lincoln's Inn had joined their forces about · 1682, and there was then only one great theatre, that at Drury Lane, with Thomas Betterton the greatest of its actors. Irritated by the patentees at Drury Lane, Betterton, then a veteran actor, sixty years old, seceded. He carried other good players with him, as well as the new dramatist, and obtained a patent for a new theatre, which opened in Lincoln's Inn Fields, in 1695, with William Congreve's comedy of *Love for Love*. This had a brilliant success, and the company gave Congreve a share in the new house, on condition of his writing them a play a year if his health allowed. His next play appeared in 1697. It was his only tragedy, *The Mourning Bride*, the most successful of his pieces. In the same year **John Vanbrugh** (b. 1666, d. 1726) produced at Drury Lane his first play, *The Relapse;* and the first play of **George Farquhar** (b. 1678, d. 1707), *Love and a Bottle*, was acted in the following year, 1698. **Vanbrugh** was of a family that had lived near Ghent before the persecutions by the Duke of Alva. His grandfather came to England, and his father acquired wealth as a sugar-baker. After a liberal education, finished in France, John Vanbrugh was for a time in the army, and in 1695 he was nominated by John Evelyn as secretary to the Commission for endowing Greenwich Hospital. His *Relapse* was followed by *The Provoked Wife*, produced in 1698 at Lincoln's Inn Fields. **George Farquhar**, the son of a poor clergyman, was born at Londonderry. He left Trinity College, Dublin, to turn actor for a short time on the Dublin stage, came young to London, and got a commission in a regiment under Lord Orrery's command in Ireland. Young Captain Farquhar was but twenty when his first play, *Love and a Bottle*, won success. Congreve's plays were the wittiest produced by writers of the new comedy of manners, but their keenness and fine polish were least relieved by any sense of right. Vanbrugh's style was less artificial and his plots were simpler, but his ready wit and coarse strength were as far as Congreve's finer work from touching the essentials of life. Farquhar had a generosity of character that humanized the persons of his drama with many traces of good feeling. Vanbrugh's "Relapse" was a sequel to *Love's Last Shift; or, The Fool in Fashion*, produced in 1696 by **Colley Cibber** (b. 1671, d. 1757), the son of Caius Gabriel Cibber, a sculptor from Holstein, sculptor of the bas-relief on the Monument by which the fire of London was commemorated. After education at Grantham Free School, Colley Cibber took to the stage within a year after the Revolution ; first giving his services as an actor for the privilege of seeing plays, then rising to twenty shillings a week, and marrying upon that, with £20 a year from his father. His first play, *Love's Last Shift*, had not advanced him as an actor ; but when Vanbrugh, in 1697, made his own first play a sequel to Cibber's, he secured Cibber as actor of its leading part, Sir Novelty Fashion, newly created Lord Foppington.

15. In March, 1698, **Jeremy Collier** (b. 1650, d. 1726) published *A Short View of the Immorality and Profaneness of the English Stage : Together with the Sense of Antiquity upon the Argument*. It spoke clearly and sharply the minds of many, passed through several editions within the year, and raised a controversy in which the wits were worsted. Jeremy Collier, a divine educated at Cambridge, who had been Rector of Ampton, Suffolk, and then Lecturer at Gray's Inn, was one of the Non-jurors at the Revolution, and had been imprisoned in Newgate for maintaining the cause of James II. He had earned credit by writing *Essays upon Several Subjects*—Pride, Clothes, Duelling, General Kindness, Fame, Music, &c.—when he made his plain-spoken but intemperate attack on the immodesty and profaneness of the stage of his own time, with evidence drawn from Dryden, and from the last new plays of **Congreve** and **Vanbrugh**. Vanbrugh's *Provoked Wife* appeared at Lincoln's Inn Fields early in 1698. Later in the year, he produced at Drury Lane, without success, the moral *Æsop*, from the French of Boursault, with a second part wholly his own. In 1700, Congreve's wittiest comedy, the *Way of the World*, was produced, without success, at Drury Lane ; and **Farquhar** produced there, with success, his *Constant Couple*, which he followed up next year with its sequel, *Sir Harry Wildair*.

16. **John Dryden** published, in July, 1697, his *Translation*

*of Virgil*, the subscription and Jacob Tonson's payment giving him about £1,200 for the work. In September, 1697, he wrote *Alexander's Feast*, that "Ode for St. Cecilia's day" which was at once received as the best poem of its kind. It was written at request of the stewards of the Musical Meeting which had for some years celebrated St. Cecilia's day, and it was first set to music by Jeremiah Clarke, one of the stewards of the festival. Early in 1698 Dryden prepared a new edition of Virgil, and was beginning to translate the "Iliad." In March, 1700, in fulfilment of a contract to give Tonson 10,000 verses for 250 guineas, appeared Dryden's *Fables*. These were modernized versions from Chaucer of "The Knight's Tale," "The Nun's Priest's Tale" (with the Fox a Puritan), and "The Wife of Bath's Tale," "The Flower and the Leaf," and "The Character of a Good Parson," adapted to Bishop Ken; versions from Bocaccio of "Sigismonda and Guiscardo," "Theodore and Honoria," and "Cymon and Iphigenia," with much translation from Ovid, and Dryden's version of the First Book of the "Iliad." Referring, in his preface, to attacks upon the immorality of his plays, Dryden spoke severely of the impertinences of Sir Richard Blackmore; but of Jeremy Collier he wrote, "I shall say the less, because in many things he has taxed me justly; and I have pleaded guilty to all thoughts and expressions of mine which can be truly argued of obscenity, profaneness, or immorality, and retract them. If he be my enemy, let him triumph; if he be my friend, as I have given him no personal occasion to be otherwise, he will be glad of my repentance. It becomes me not to draw my pen in the defence of a bad cause, when I have so often drawn it for a good one." But of Collier's style Dryden added, "I will not say, 'The zeal of God's house has eaten him up;' but I am sure it has devoured some part of his good manners and civility." Dryden, afflicted with painful disease, was working to keep house, when his eldest son, Charles, who was at Rome, chamberlain of the household of Innocent XII., was obliged in 1698 to return to England invalided. Dryden, labouring to meet the new expense thus caused, wrote to Tonson, "If it please God that I die of over-study, I cannot spend my life better than in preserving his." Early in 1700, when Vanbrugh revised Fletcher's comedy of "The Pilgrims" for Drury Lane, the profits of the third night were secured for his son, Charles, by Dryden's addition to the piece of a Prologue and Epilogue, and a *Secular Masque* on the Close of the Seventeenth Century. Twenty days after the writing of the Prologue and Epilogue, Dryden died, on the 1st of May, 1700.

17. **Sir Richard Blackmore** (b. about 1650, d. 1729) was educated at Westminster School, and Edmund Hall, Oxford, where he took the degree of M.A. in 1676; graduated in medicine at Padua, and became a prosperous physician in Cheapside. In 1695 he published *Prince Arthur*, an epic poem in ten books. In his preface Blackmore attacked the abuse of wit upon the stage, said that in its other departments the poetry of the day had become impure ; and that for this reason, among others, he had, in the intervals of business, written " Prince Arthur." " I was willing," he said, " to make one effort towards the rescuing of the Muses out of the hands of those ravishers, and to restore them to their sweet and chaste mansions, and to engage them in an employment suitable to their dignity." He then prosed upon epic poetry, of which, he said, the purpose was "to give men right and just conceptions of religion and virtue;" and told his public that he had endeavoured to form himself on Virgil's model, substituting Christian for pagan machinery—that is to say, he used Lucifer, Raphael, Uriel, &c., instead of heathen deities. His Arthur sailed to the Saxon coast ; devils and angels affected the weather; but at last he and his people landed on Hoel's shore of Albion, where

> " Rich wine of Burgundy and choice champagne
> Relieve the toil they suffered on the main ;
> But what more cheered them than their meats and wine
> Was wise instruction and discourse divine
> From godlike Arthur's mouth. "

The Fury Persecution stirred Hoel; but an angel sent him to Arthur, from whom he heard a sermon. In Book III., Hoel asked for more, and Arthur preached him another sermon. In Book IV., Lucius, at a supper of Hoel's, being asked to tell Prince Arthur's story, began in Virgilian style,

> " How sad a task do your commands impose,
> Which must renew insufferable woes."

Finally, an Ethelina and a kingdom awaited the result of single combat between Prince Arthur and King Tollo, and the poem closed thus :

> "So by Prince Arthur's arms King Tollo slain
> Fell down, and lay extended on the plain."

Blackmore became a butt of the wits whom he attacked. He

was a common-place man with an amiable faith in himself, and
without intellect to distinguish between good and bad in poetry.
His religious purpose was sincere, and it gave dignity to his
work in the eyes even of Locke and Addison. Blackmore's
*King Arthur*, in twelve books, appeared in 1697, the year in
which he was knighted and made one of the physicians to King
William. In 1700 appeared Blackmore's *Paraphrase on the
Book of Job, the Songs of Moses, Deborah, and David, and on
Four Select Psalms, some Chapters of Isaiah, and the Third
Chapter of Habakkuk;* and in the same year he defied his
satirists, and continued his attack upon immoral verse with a
*Satire on Wit.*

18. **Samuel Garth**, born of a good Yorkshire family about
1660, became M.D. of Cambridge in 1691, and Fellow of the
London College of Physicians in 1693. He was a very kindly
man, who throve both as wit and as physician, and he acquired
fame by a mock heroic poem, *The Dispensary*, first published in
1699. The College of Physicians had, in 1687, required all its
fellows and licentiates to give gratuitous advice to the poor.
The high price of medicine was still an obstacle to charity; and
after a long battle within the profession, the physicians raised, in
1696, a subscription among themselves for the establishment of
a Dispensary within the college, at which only the first cost of
medicines would be charged to the poor for making up gratuitous
prescriptions. The squabble raised over this scheme, chiefly
between physicians and apothecaries, Garth, who was one of
its promoters, celebrated in his clever mock-heroic poem. It
was suggested to him, as he admitted, by Boileau's mock-heroic,
*Le Lutrin*, first published in 1674, which had for its theme a hot
dispute between the treasurer and precentor of the Sainte
Chapelle at Paris over the treasurer's wish to change the position
of a pulpit. Garth, a good Whig, was knighted on the accession
of George I., and made one of the physicians in ordinary to the
king. He wrote other verse, and died in 1719.

19. **John Pomfret**, who died in 1703, aged thirty-six, was
Rector of Malden, and son of the Rector of Luton, both in Bedfordshire. His *Poems* appeared in 1699, the chief of them a
smooth picture of happy life, *The Choice*, first published as "by
a Person of Quality." As one part of "The Choice" was "I'd
have no Wife," it was promptly replied to with *The Virtuous
Wife; a Poem.* **William Walsh** (b. 1663, d. 1708), whom
Dryden, and afterwards Pope, honoured as friend and critic,

was the son of a gentleman of Worcestershire. He wrote verse, liked poets, was a man of fashion, and sat for his own county in several Parliaments. He published, in 1691, a prose *Dialogue concerning Women, being a Defence of the Sex, written to Eugenia.* **William King** (b. 1663, d. 1712) was born in London to a good estate, graduated at Oxford, became D.C.L. in 1692, and an advocate at Doctors' Commons. He acquired under William III. and Queen Anne the reputation of a witty poet, who idly wasted high abilities and good aids to advancement in the world. In 1699 he published a *Journey to London,* as a jest upon Dr. Martin Lister's *Journey to Paris.* In 1700 he satirised Sir Hans Sloane, then President of the Royal Society, in two dialogues called *The Transactioner.* At the end of William's reign, Dr. King obtained good appointments in Ireland. **Thomas Brown** (b. 1663, d. 1704), a Shropshire man, after an Oxford training, became a schoolmaster at Kingston-on-Thames, and left his vocation for that of a licentious wit in London. He wrote satires, two plays, dialogues, essays, declamations, letters from the dead to the living, translations, &c. **George Granville** (b. 1667, d. 1735), second son of Bernard Granville and nephew to the first Earl of Bath, went early to Cambridge, wrote verse as an undergraduate, was at the Revolution a young man of twenty-one, loyal to the cause of King James. Under William III. he lived in retirement and wrote plays—*The She Gallants* (1696) ; a revision of Shakespeare's " Merchant of Venice," as *The Jew of Venice* (1698), with Shylock turned into a comic character ; and *Heroic Love,* a tragedy upon "Agamemnon and Chryseis." George Granville was made Lord Lansdowne, Baron Bideford, in 1711, when the Tories came into power. **John Oldmixon** (b. 1673, d. 1724), of a Somersetshire family, who became a violent Whig writer and a narrow-minded literary critic, was little more than a boy at the date of the Revolution. In 1698 he published a translation of Tasso's *Amyntas,* and in 1700 produced *The Grove; or, Love's Paradise,* an opera. **John Dennis** (b. 1657, d. 1733), son of a London saddler, after education at Harrow and at Caius College, Cambridge, travelled in France and Italy, and began his career as a writer in the reign of William III., with *The Passion of Byblis* in 1692, and in the same year " *The Impartial Critick;* or, some Observations on Mr. Rymer's late Book, entitled a Short View of Tragedy." In 1693 Dennis published " Miscellanies in Verse and Prose."

In 1695 he published a poem, *The Court of Death*, on the death of Queen Mary; and in 1696, *Letters on Milton and Congreve*, and *Letters upon Several Occasions, Written by and between Mr. Wycherley, Mr. Dryden, Mr. Moyle, Mr. Congreve, and Mr. Dennis*, also adverse "Remarks" on Blackmore's "Prince Arthur." In 1697 he published *Miscellaneous Poems;* in 1698 *The Usefulness of the Stage to the Happiness of Mankind, to Government, and to Religion, occasioned by a late Book written by Jeremy Collier, M.A.;* in 1701 a little treatise on the *Advancement and Reformation of Modern Poetry;* and in 1702 an *Essay on the Navy*, a tract against Sacheverell's party, *Priestcraft dangerous to Religion and Government*, a volume of collected *Works*, and, on the death of William III., a poem sacred to his memory, *The Monument.* There was a vein of good sense and liberality of thought in Dennis's writing; and he was a good critic to the extent of his moderate ability. He produced plays also, poor ones: *A Plot and No Plot*, in 1697; *Rinaldo and Armida*, in 1699; in 1702, *Iphigenia*, and *The Comical Gallant; or, the Amours of Sir John Falstaff, with an Essay on Taste in Poetry.* Thus Dennis's literary industry had earned him a foremost position among critics by the time of Queen Anne's accession. He was then forty-five years old.

20. **Matthew Prior**, joint author with Charles Montague of *The Town and Country Mouse* (ch. x. § 58), obtained in 1690, through the influence of the Earl of Dorset and Mr. Fleetwood Shephard, the appointment of Secretary to the Embassy at the Congress held at the Hague, and opened by King William in January, 1691. In September, 1688, Louis XIV., instigated by his minister Louvois, declared causeless war against the Emperor, claimed permanent sovereignty of France on the left bank of the Rhine, and sent an army over the Rhine to live upon and devastate the country. This left the way more open for the establishment of William III. as King of England. In November William's fleet arrived at Torbay. England and Holland became allied under one chief. Louis presently was condemning to flames Ladenburg, Heidelberg, Mannheim, Speyer, Worms, Oppenheim, Frankenthal, Bingen, and many helpless villages, driving a hundred thousand people from their homes. By June, 1690, the Grand Alliance was complete which banded the German Empire, Holland, Spain, and England against Louis XIV. To raise war money, Louis struck to the heart of commerce and agriculture, ground his people with taxa-

tion, sent to the melting-pot works of art fifty times more
precious than the metal in which they were executed, sold
revived offices of royal barber, periwig-maker, and the like.
" Every time," said his finance minister, Pontchartrain, "your
Majesty creates an office, God creates a fool to purchase it."
While in France, as Voltaire said, the people were "perishing
to the sound of Te Deums," the war between Louis and the
Grand Alliance lasted till the Peace of Ryswick, in 1697. After
the resolve of the Conference at the Hague, which ended in
March, 1691, not to make peace until all grievances were
redressed, in April Louis took Mons; at the beginning of 1692
he had in army and navy more than half a million in arms, and,
with some hope of a counter revolution, was planning invasion
of England. This attempt cost France, at the beginning of
June, the disaster of La Hogue. At the end of June, 1692, after
a memorable siege, the French completed the capture of Namur
and its forts. Boileau then celebrated the glory of Louis XIV.
in a Pindaric ode, which served the purpose also of a shot
at Perrault in the Battle of the Ancients and the Moderns.
**Matthew Prior** afterwards returned Boileau's fire with a
laughing comment upon his ode, which he followed stanza for
stanza, in *An English Ballad on the Taking of Namur by the
King of Great Britain*, 1695; for in that year there was
another siege of Namur, and, on the 31st of August, William III.
took the citadel by open assault in daytime, and in presence of
Villeroi's army of a hundred thousand that would not risk
battle.

21. **Joseph Addison** (§ 8), aged twenty-three, addressed to
King William from Oxford a paper of verses on the capture of
Namur. They united evidence of ability with declaration of
Whig principles, and were sent through Sir John Somers, a
lawyer and patron of letters, who had been counsel for the seven
bishops, under James II. Somers was William's first Solicitor-
General, had become Lord Keeper, and was made in 1695 Lord
Chancellor and a peer. Addison, then destined for the Church,
sought, as was usual, to advance his fortunes by the way of
patronage; and it was not without effect that, in lines sent with
the poem, he credited Somers with "immortal strains;" spoke
of Britain advanced "by Somers' counsels, and by Nassau's
sword;" and sought the Lord Keeper's good word—" For next to
what you write is what you praise." Thus Addison secured one
patron. He had already, in 1694, aimed a shaft of compliment,

z

in his Account of the Poets, at the noble Montague "for wit, for for humour, and for judgment famed." In 1697 he addressed to Montague, who was a good Latin scholar, and then Chancellor of the Exchequer, some patriotic Latin verses on the Peace of Ryswick (*Pax Guglielmi Auspiciis Europæ Reddita,* 1697). Thus he completed the capture of another patron. At the negotiations for the Peace of Ryswick, **Matthew Prior** was again employed as Secretary of Embassy. **Charles Montague** (ch. x. § 58), himself brought into public life by the good offices of the Earl of Dorset, had, after the publication of the *Town and Country Mouse,* been one of those who invited William of Orange to England. Under the new king, the Earl of Dorset was Lord Chamberlain of the Household, and procured Montague a pension of £500 a year from the Privy Purse. In a year or two Charles Montague's ability had made him prominent in the House of Commons. The Earl of Dorset then secured his appointment to a vacant office of Commissioner of the Treasury, by virtue of which he became a Privy Councillor, and had such good opportunity of showing his value to the Government that he was rewarded, in 1694, with the office of Chancellor and Under-Treasurer of the Exchequer. Then it was that Addison praised the noble Montague.

> " For wit, for humour, and for judgment fam'd ;
> To Dorset he directs his artful muse,
> In numbers such as Dorset's self might use."

Montague and Somers, who were fast friends, now urged on King William the policy of calling in and re-coining the clipped silver money. This was opposed by Robert Harley and others, on the plea of inconvenience in war time; but more strongly supported, as necessary to maintain the credit of England abroad, and save the wasting of supplies voted for the army, by a rate of exchange heavily against us. Montague carried not only that measure, but went on also to provide security for the public debt by a sinking fund; saved from ruin the Bank of England, which had just been established by the energy of William Paterson—it only began business January 1st, 1695—and in other ways Charles Montague economised and increased the resources of England. William made him First Commissioner of the Treasury ; then, during his own absence, in 1698, and again in 1699, one of the Lords Justices of England; and in 1700 raised him to the peerage, as Baron Halifax.

**Joseph Addison** was induced by Somers and Montague to

give up thoughts of taking priests' orders, and accept a pension
of £300 a year while travelling to prepare himself for diplomatic
life.   Before starting, Addison brought out at Oxford, in 1699,
dedicated to Montague, a second volume of *Musæ Anglicanæ*,
Latin poems by members of the University.   The first volume
appeared in 1692.   Eight Latin poems of his own were in
Addison's collection ; one of them on *Machinæ Gesticulantes*
(*Anglicè, a Puppet Show*), another on the "Bowling Green." In
the summer of 1699, Addison left Oxford for Paris, stayed some
weeks there, then lived for a year at Blois to learn French,
and, among other studies, work at Latin authors, with especial
reference to Latin geography, before he passed on into Italy.
When he returned to Paris from Blois, Addison was introduced
to Boileau, of whom he wrote to a correspondent, " He is old,
and a little deaf, but talks incomparably well in his own calling.
He heartily hates an ill poet, and throws himself into a passion
when he talks of any one that has not a high respect for Homer
and Virgil."   In December, 1700, Addison left Marseilles for
Genoa, in company with Mr. Edward Wortley Montague.   He
spent a year in Italy, and was at Geneva by December, 1701,
after what he called " a very troublesome journey over the Alps.
My head is still giddy with mountains and precipices; and you
can't imagine how much I am pleased with the sight of a plain."
It was during this troublesome journey that Addison addressed
to Charles Montague, then become Lord Halifax, his metrical
*Letter from Italy*, with its patriotic apostrophe to liberty and
British thunder.   King Louis, he wrote, strives in vain

> " To conquer or divide,
> Whom Nassau's arms defend and counsels guide."

Addison, aged thirty, was waiting at Geneva for a coming
appointment as secretary for King William with the army in
Italy under Prince Eugene, when he received news of the king's
death on the 8th of March, 1702.  With the life of the sovereign
Addison's pension dropped ; his friends were out of office.

22.  **Richard Steele** (§ 8) did not seek advancement in
life by the way of patronage.   Enthusiasm for the Revolution
caused him to quit Oxford, and enlist as a private in the Duke
of Ormond's regiment of Coldstream Guards.   He said lightly
afterwards that when he mounted a war-horse, with a great
sword in his hand, and planted himself behind King William
III. against Louis XIV., he lost the succession to a very good

estate in the county of Wexford, in Ireland, from the same humour which he has preserved ever since, of preferring the state of his mind to that of his fortune. Lord Cutts, the colonel of the regiment, who was writer of verse as well as soldier, distinguished Steele, made him his secretary, got him an ensign's commission, and afterwards the rank of captain in Lord Lucas's regiment of Fusiliers. While ensign in the Guards, Steele wrote *The Christian Hero*, as he afterwards said, "with a design principally to fix upon his mind a strong impression of virtue and religion, in opposition to a stronger propensity to unwarrantable pleasures." It was in four parts :—(1) Of the Heroism of the Ancient World; (2) of the Bible Story as a Link between Man and his Creator; (3) of the Life a Christian should lead, as set forth by St. Paul; (4) of the Common Motives of Human Action, best used and improved when blended with Religion. There was a closing eulogy of William III., as a great captain, and, still better, "a sincere and honest man." *The Christian Hero*, dedicated to Lord Cutts, was published in 1701, and was so well received that by 1711 it was in a fifth edition. Steele's next work was a comedy, *The Funeral; or, Grief à la Mode*, first acted in 1702. It was—with satire against undertakers and dishonesties of law—a comedy of a lord whose death was but a lethargy, from which he recovered in the presence of a trusty servant, who, for good reasons, persuaded him to wait awhile, and watch unobserved what went on in the house of mourning. The wit of the comedy was free from profanity; it was emphatically moral in its tone, and Steele's warmth of patriotic feeling also found expression in it.

23. **Jonathan Swift** was born in Dublin, November 30, 1667. His grandfather, a Herefordshire vicar, married an aunt of Dryden's, and left six sons, of whom two were Godwin and Jonathan. Jonathan, who married a Miss Abigail Erick, of Leicester, had one daughter, and then died a few months before the birth of his one son. His income had been from law agencies, and he left little to his widow, who returned to Leicester about two years after her husband's death, leaving the two children in charge of their uncle, Godwin. By him young Jonathan was sent to school at Kilkenny, and then to Trinity College, Dublin, where he failed when he first went up for his B.A. degree, and obtained it afterwards "by special grace," a phrase implying, at Trinity College, Dublin, special disgrace. In the year of the Revolution, Swift's uncle, Godwin, failed in

intellect, lost speech and memory, and was unable to do more for his nephew. Jonathan Swift went therefore to his mother, at Leicester, and by her advice presented himself to **Sir William Temple** (ch. x. § 39), whose wife was distantly related to her. Sir William became young Swift's friend, enabled him to study at Oxford, where he was admitted at once to the degree obtained at Dublin, and where he graduated as M.A. He then lived with Sir William, at Moor Park, near Farnham, in Surrey. After about two years with Sir William, **Swift** had a long and serious illness. It left him subject to fits of giddiness, first symptoms of the disease of brain that modified his character, and towards the close of life destroyed his reason. He went for change of air to Ireland, and then returned to Sir William, who had left Moor Park for Sheen.

About this time Sir William was taking lively interest in an argument over the Epistles ascribed to Phalaris, who was Tyrant of Agrigentum, B.C. 565. **Richard Bentley,** born in 1662, the son of a small farmer near Wakefield, in Yorkshire, had become a foremost scholar, and was king's librarian when, in 1695, the **Hon. Charles Boyle,** then an undergraduate of Christchurch, Oxford, second son of Roger Boyle, and nephew to Robert Boyle, made a pettish reference to him in the preface to an edition of the Epistles of Phalaris. **William Wotton,** in 1694, had published *Reflections upon Ancient and Modern Learning.* To a second edition of that book Bentley added, in 1697, an attack on the authenticity of the letters ascribed to Phalaris. Charles Boyle being no great scholar, other Christchurch men, chief of them **Francis Atterbury** (b. 1662, d. 1732) answered Bentley in his name, and published, in 1698, *Dr. Bentley's Dissertations on the Epistles of Phalaris, and the Fables of Æsop Examined.* Then followed a famous battle of books. Sir W. Temple took interest in the quarrel ; and **Swift** began to write his " Battle of the Books." In 1699 **Bentley** published an enlarged *Dissertation on the Epistles of Phalaris,* and won his battle.

At Sheen, King William sometimes paid unceremonious visits to Sir William Temple. In one conversation, the king offered to make young **Swift** a captain of horse. But Swift took orders, and went to Ireland, where Lord Capel, on Sir W. Temple's recommendation, gave him a prebend worth £100 a year, which he gave up to return to Sheen. Sir William would use interest to get him something better, and

Swift's heart was touched by the wit and kindness of Hester Johnson, daughter of Sir William's steward.  Sir William died in 1700, leaving £1,000 to Hester Johnson, and a legacy also to Swift, who was made his literary executor.  Swift dedicated Sir W. Temple's works to the king, and went to Ireland as secretary to the Earl of Berkeley, who had been appointed one of the two Lords Justices of Ireland.  His office of secretary Swift did not long hold, but he obtained from Lord Berkeley the livings of Laracor and Rathbeggan, together worth about £260 a year.  He went at once to Laracor, and invited Hester Johnson with a female friend, named Dingley, to make her home in the same village.  She did so ; and while Swift had the society of the woman he loved, he took care that they should never be alone together.  He was violently angry when his sister married, about this time.  He would not marry himself; and when at last he did go through a private ceremony of marriage with Hester Johnson, whom he called " Stella," marriage was only a form. Their relations with each other remained as before, and they lived on opposite banks of the Liffey.  Uncharitable reasons have been given for this.  One reason, that Swift could hardly proclaim to the world, was sufficient.  The seeds of insanity were in him ; that terrible disease can be inherited.  He died as his Uncle Godwin died.  Might not Swift feel that he and his sister had no right to marry ?  And, for himself, if he thought so he was surely right, whatever unsoundness of judgment he may have shown in the way he took, nevertheless, to satisfy his best affections.

Swift's first publication was at the close of William's reign. When Tory reaction then caused the House of Commons to impeach John, Lord Somers, Charles Montague, Earl of Halifax, the Earl of Orford, and the Earl of Portland, Swift published, in 1701, with covert reference to the political situation, *A Discourse of the Contests and Dissensions between the Nobles and Commons in Athens and Rome.*  In this pamphlet Lord Somers figured as Aristides, Halifax as Pericles.  The Earl of Orford was Themistocles, and the Earl of Portland Phocion.

24. **Daniel Defoe** (ch. x. § 55) in those last days aided King William with his doggrel poem of the *True-born Englishman.* Defoe, under William III., had married—he married twice in his life.  His family had been ruined by a venture ; and, to escape the prison threatened by one rigid creditor, he withdrew

for two years to BristoL   There he wrote his *Essay on Projects*,
which was published two or three years afterwards, in 1697.
It suggested many things—improvement in roads, reforms in
banking, a savings' bank for the poor, insurance offices, an
academy like that of France, a military college, abolition of
the press-gang, and a college for the higher education of women.
" A woman," said Defoe, " well-bred and well-taught, furnished
with the additional accomplishments of knowledge and behaviour, is a creature without comparison.   Her society is
the emblem of sublimer enjoyments ;  she is all softness and
sweetness, love, wit, and delight."   One project, also, was for
improvement of the law of debtor and creditor.   When he had
compounded with his creditors, and thus secured for himself
liberty to work, he returned to London, and worked on till he
had paid voluntarily beyond the composition the last penny of
his debts.   His patriotic suggestions of projects for raising
war-money caused  Defoe  to  be  employed from 1694 to 1699
as accountant to the Commissioners of the Glass Duty.

   To the cry raised by the Opposition that King William was no
true-born Englishman, especially represented by the bad poem
of one Tutchin, called *The Foreigners*, Defoe replied, in 1701,
with his satire on *The True-born Englishman*, rhymes of which
80,000 copies were sold in the streets.   Among their home-
truths are vigorous assertions of the claims of the people
against persecution in the Church or despotism in the State.
In these he finds as dangerous a thing

> " A ruling priesthood, as a priest-rid king :
> And of all plagues with which mankind are curst,
> Ecclesiastic tyranny's the worst."

While of the kings false to their trust he says :

> " When kings the sword of justice first lay down,
> They are no kings, though they possess the crown.
> Titles are shadows, crowns are empty things,
> The good of subjects is the end of kings."

   Then came to the throne Queen Anne (1702—1714), and hard
words hailed on the Dissenters.   A substantial blow was aimed
in a bill that was to disqualify them from all civil employments.
It passed the Commons, but failed with the Lords.   Sacheverell,
preaching at Oxford, had denounced him as no true son of the
Church who did not raise against Dissent " the bloody flag and
banner of defiance."   But, in 1702, Defoe spoke boldly on behalf
of liberty of conscience, in his pamphlet called *The Shortest Way*

*with the Dissenters.* He wrote, as in all his controversial pieces, to maintain a principle and not a party. He began his satire with a quotation from Roger l'Estrange's Fables. A cock at roost in a stable, having dropped from his perch, and finding himself in much danger among restless heels, had a fair proposal to make to the horses—that we shall all of us keep our legs quiet. This fable Defoe applied to the Dissenters, who were then asking for equal treatment, although they had been intolerant enough themselves not long since, when they had the upper hand. Professing, in his assumed character of a bigoted High Churchman of the day, to show the vice of Dissent before teaching its cure, he dealt, in the first place, a fair blow to his own side for past intolerance. The Dissenters ought not, perhaps, to have been blind to the irony of the second half of the pamphlet ; but in the first half the irony is not all against ecclesiastical intolerance. Defoe was against all intolerance, and to the bigotry of his own party Defoe gave the first hit. The succeeding satire, since it could not easily surpass the actual extravagance of party spirit, had in it nothing but the delicate, sustained sharpness of ironical suggestion to reveal the author's purpose to the multitude. Several reasons, he said, are urged on behalf of the Dissenters, "why we should continue and tolerate them among us," as, "They are very numerous, they say; they are a great part of the nation, and we cannot suppress them. To this may be answered, They are not so numerous as the Protestants in France, and yet the French king effectually cleared the nation of them at once, and we don't find he misses them at home." Besides, "the more numerous the more dangerous, and therefore the more need to suppress them ; and if we are to allow them only because we cannot suppress them, then it ought to be tried whether we can or no." It is said, also, that their aid is wanted against the common enemy. This, argues Defoe, is but the same argument of inconvenience of war-time that was urged against suppressing the old money ; and the hazard, after all, proved to be small. "We can never enjoy a settled uninterrupted union and tranquillity in this nation till the spirit of Whiggism, faction, and schism is melted down like the old money." The gist of the pamphlet, the scheme set forth on the title-page as the Shortest Way with the Dissenters, is propounded in this passage :—" If one severe law were made, and punctually executed, that whoever was found at a conventicle should be banished the nation, and the preacher be hanged, we should soon see an end of the tale ; they would all come to church, and one age would make us one again.　To talk of five shillings a month for not coming to the sacrament, and one shilling a week for not coming to church— this is such a way of converting people as never was known, this is selling them a liberty to transgress for so much money. If it be not a crime, why don't we give them full licence ?　And if it be, no price ought to compound for the committing it ; for that is selling a liberty to people to sin against God and the Government. . . . . We hang men for trifles, and banish them for things not worth naming ; but an offence against God and the Church, against the welfare of the world and the dignity of religion, shall be bought off for five shillings.　This is such a shame to a Christian Government that 'tis with regret I transmit it to posterity."

The pamphlet delighted men of the Sacheverell school.　A Cambridge Fellow thanked his bookseller for having sent him so excellent a treatise—next to the Holy Bible and the Sacred Comments, the most valuable he had ever seen.　Great was the reaction of wrath when the pamphlet was found to be a Dissenter's satire ; nevertheless, the Dissenters held by their first outcry against the author.　Defoe, aged forty-two, paid for this service to the English people in the pillory, and as a prisoner in Newgate.　But his *Hymn to the Pillory*, which appeared on the first of the three days of the shame of the Government in his exposure, July 29, 30, and 31, in the year 1703, turned the course of popular opinion against the men who placed him there — men, as his rhyme said, scandals to the times, who

> " Are at a loss to find his guilt,
> And can't commit his crimes."

Defoe returned from the pillory to Newgate, whence he was not released till August, 1704.　It was in Newgate, therefore, that he began his career as the first critical and independent journalist, by producing his *Review*.　This was begun on the 19th of February, 1704, came out on Saturdays and Tuesdays until 1705, and then three times a week till May, 1713.

25. Defoe's *Review* was established in the year of the battle of Blenheim.　Before the death of childless Charles II. of Spain, there had been negotiations in Europe, and two Treaties of Partition, to reconcile rival interests and maintain " balance
z *

of power," before the King of Spain died in November, 1700, leaving a will that made the Duke of Anjou, second son of the Dauphin, his heir.   Louis XIV. having to choose between the share allotted to him by Treaty of Partition and a throne for his grandson, chose the throne, and his grandson entered Madrid, as King Philip V., in January, 1701.   In the following September James II. died, and Louis openly named James's son, James Edward, King of England.   In all negotiations between England and France before and after the death of the King of Spain, until the breaking out of the War of the Spanish Succession after the death of James II., **Matthew Prior,** secretary to Lord Jersey, was confidentially employed.   He was so employed when he wrote, in the century year, his finest ode, the *Carmen Seculare,* in praise of William.   In 1701 the war began in Italy, where Prince Eugene drove the French behind the Adda, and defeated Villeroi at Chiari. France suffered more and more.   The coin had been debased five times in eight years.   Everything was taxed for war expenses, and the tax on wine had become so high that many ceased to cultivate the grape.   In the winter of 1701 Louis raised a hundred new regiments.   In the following March, King William died.   Queen Anne went on with the war.   The Dauphin was generalissimo in Flanders, Villeroi in Italy; and they were pitted against Marlborough and Prince Eugene.   By 1704 the struggle had become a series of sieges and reliefs; but Marlborough's victory of Blenheim, August 13, 1704, by which he saved Austria, secured also a party triumph over those who in England and Holland opposed the policy that Marlborough personified.   War meant for men like Steele and Addison resistance to the spread of despotism in Europe by the domination of Louis XIV., and more especially a crushing of the hope of English partisans of the Divine right of kings, who were disposed to undo the work of the Revolution, and, with French help, some day make a king of the Pretender.

26. One of those who, in 1705, published their poems on Blenheim, was John Philips, born December 30th, 1676, at Bampton, in Oxfordshire, where his father, Dr. Stephen Philips, Archdeacon of Salop, was vicar.   John Philips, of delicate constitution and great sweetness of character, was sent from home education to Winchester School, where he was excused much roughness of school discipline, and often read Milton in play-hours.   He had written imitations of Milton before he was sent,

in 1694, to Christchurch, Oxford. There his simple, modest cheerfulness, and his quick wit, surrounded him with friends. Milton still was his favourite study, and he knew Virgil almost by heart. He traced out Milton's imitations of the classics, and himself imitated the blank verse of his master poet. He was destined for the profession of medicine, and delighted in natural science, but his weak health made him unfit for active duty. At college he wrote in playful mood, to suggest to a careless friend the value of a shilling in the pocket, his *Splendid Shilling*, a burlesque poem representing, in about 150 lines, the commonest images in high-sounding Miltonic verse. In style as in subject it was small coin glorified, perhaps the best piece of burlesque writing in our literature. This was read in manuscript, praised, copied, printed without authority. It gave Philips a reputation for wit when he came to London, and was hospitably received into the house of **Henry St. John** (afterwards Lord Bolingbroke), who was two years his junior. St. John had entered Parliament for Wootton Basset in 1701, and became one of the best speakers in support of Robert Harley. When Halifax and Lord Godolphin set Addison writing a poem upon Blenheim, their rivals, Harley and St. John, asked for a poem on the same theme from **John Philips**, and it appeared in 1705 as *Blenheim : a Poem inscribed to the Right Honourable Robert Harley, Esq.*, a strain of blank verse, with echoes in it of the roll of Milton's music. In the same year appeared the authorised edition of " *The Splendid Shilling : An Imitation of Milton.* Now First Correctly Published." In 1706, John Philips published, also in blank verse, at a time when the orthodox measure was " heroic" couplet, his carefully-written poem in two books, *Cyder.* This is a good example of a form of poem which in modern literature had its origin in Virgil's "Georgics," and which had been especially cultivated in Italy by Alamanni, Rucellai, Tansillo, and others ; indeed, Philips's " Cyder" was presently translated into Italian. John Philips was preparing to rise to a higher strain, and attempt a poem on the Resurrection and the Day of Judgment, when his health entirely failed, and in February, 1708, he died of consumption in his mother's house, at Hereford, when he was not yet thirty-three years old.

27. **Joseph Addison** (§ 21), at the beginning of Queen Anne's reign, with his pension lost and college debts unpaid, had only the income of his fellowship. He was at Vienna in November, 1702, where he showed to Montague's friend, George

Stepney (ch. x. § 52), then British Envoy at Vienna, what he had sketched of his *Dialogues on the Usefulness of Ancient Medals*, written after the model of Fontenelle's "Dialogues on the Plurality of Worlds." They were not published until after his death. Addison probably travelled as tutor, but in June, 1703, he was at Hamburg, and politely declined to be travelling tutor to the son of the Duke of Somerset for the insufficient pay of a hundred a year. About September, 1703, he had returned to London, and was lodged up three pair of stairs in the Haymarket. But his friend **Richard Steele** was again by his side. Addison was with Steele when he was finishing his second comedy, *The Tender Husband*, produced in 1703; and Steele afterwards wrote, "I remember when I finished *The Tender Husband*, I told him there was nothing I so ardently wished as that we might some time or other publish a work written by us both, which should bear the name of the 'Monument,' in memory of our friendship.". In 1704, Steele's third comedy, the *Lying Lover*, was produced, and failed, because his strong sense of responsibility as a writer would not allow him, while adapting the story, to treat lightly the romancing of the hero. He took the hero from Corneille's *Menteur*, itself an adaptation from the Spanish of Alarcon. Steele felt bound to uphold the sacredness of truth, and therefore opened his last act with the hero in Newgate. Thus he spoilt the comedy. The Earl of Godolphin, who was Lord Treasurer, and a close friend of Marlborough's, and who was passing gradually from the Tories to the Whigs, having had the abilities and claims of Addison urged on him by Halifax during the rejoicings over Blenheim, gave him at once the post of a Commissioner of Appeal in the Excise, vacated by John Locke's removal to the Board of Trade, and asked him to write a poem on the battle. The result was Addison's *Campaign*, in the usual heroic couplets, a piece much praised, with especial admiration of the use made of a recent great storm, for likening of Marlborough in battle to the angel who

> "Pleased th' Almighty's orders to perform,
> Rides in the whirlwind and directs the storm."

Addison followed up the success of this piece by publishing his *Remarks on Italy*, with a dedication to Lord Somers. They chiefly treat travel in Italy as a way of illustrating passages from Latin poets. A copy of it Addison gave inscribed "to Dr. Jonathan Swift, the truest friend, and the greatest genius of his age."

**28. Swift**, who had graduated as D.D. in 1701, was in London in 1704, and then published his *Tale of a Tub*, and *Battle of the Books* (§ 23). "Tale of a Tub" is a very old English phrase for a nonsensical story, and had been used by Ben Jonson for the title of a play. Swift's tale was a satire on behalf of charity and good works among men of different forms of faith, represented by Peter (Church of Rome), Martin (Church of England), and Jack (Dissent), and ("let the priests be clothed with righteousness") how they dealt with the coats their father had bequeathed to them and bidden them keep clean. In its main plan the "Tale of a Tub" is a wise book, and essentially religious, but its uncontrolled wit handled sacred things in a way shocking to many, and Swift was too good a partisan of his own Church to make a book that should be itself a great example of the charity it recommended. If Swift had not written the "Tale of a Tub" he would have died a bishop.

**Addison**, early in 1706, was appointed Under-Secretary of State to Sir Charles Hedges, a Tory, who was, before the end of the year, succeeded in office by Marlborough's son-in-law, the Earl of Sunderland. In that year Addison produced, with music by Thomas Clayton, *Rosamond*, an opera that was to match the Italians with English genius. It only lived three nights, although Addison had chosen the subject to enable him to bring on the stage a compliment to Marlborough; for Woodstock had been lately granted by the Crown to the great general, and Addison put Henry II. to sleep in order to edify him and the public with a vision of the rising glories of the palace of Blenheim, voted by the nation, and then being built by **Vanbrugh** (§ 14). It was in this year, 1706, that Vanbrugh gave up writing for the stage.

**29. Farquhar** (§ 14), under Queen Anne, produced his *Inconstant* in 1703, *The Twin Rivals* in 1705, *The Recruiting Officer* in 1706, and his last and best play, *The Beaux Stratagem*, written in six weeks when he was dying. He died, but thirty years old, during the height of its success. A woman who loved Farquhar had entrapped him into marriage by pretending to possess a fortune. When undeceived he never in his life reproached her. From his death-bed he commended his two helpless daughters to his friend Wilks, the actor, who got them a benefit. His widow died in extreme poverty. One of his daughters married a poor tradesman, the other became a maidservant.

30. **Daniel Defoe**, while still writing his *Review*, and, among other works, publishing, in 1706, a long poem in folio, *Jure Divino*, in favour of limited monarchy, and against the doctrine of Divine right in kings, was actively employed in Scotland as a promoter of the Union of the legislatures of Scotland and England, which became law on the 1st of May, 1707. In 1709 Defoe published a *History of the Union*.

31. Addison having received from Oxford a poem in praise of his "Rosamond," sought out the author, and found him to be **Thomas Tickell** (b. 1686, d. 1740), son of a Cumberland clergyman, and undergraduate of Queen's College, Oxford. Tickell thenceforth became Addison's friend and follower. In 1707 **Richard Steele** was appointed Gazetteer, and the value of the office was presently raised for him from sixty to three hundred pounds a year. He was made also a gentleman usher to the Prince Consort, with salary of a hundred a year. He had about this time an estate in Barbadoes, yielding over six hundred a year after payment of encumbrances upon it. This had been left him by a first wife, who died only a few months after marriage. In September, 1707, Steele was married to Miss Mary Scurlock.

Addison, besides his public work, was acting in some way as friend and tutor to the ten-year-old son of the Dowager Countess of Warwick, the last Warwick of the family of Rich (ch. vii. § 61). At the end of 1708 the Earl of Sunderland was dismissed from his secretaryship, and Addison, his under-secretary, was transferred to the office of chief secretary to the Earl of Wharton, just appointed Lord Lieutenant of Ireland. Addison was returned to Parliament, through Lord Wharton's interest, as member for Malmesbury, but was too nervous to speak in the House. He rose once, but, embarrassed by his welcome, stammered and sat down. Addison took with him to Ireland his first cousin, **Eustace Budgell** (b. about 1685, d. 1736). Budgell and Addison were sisters' sons. Budgell inherited a good fortune from his father in 1711, was advanced by Addison in life and literature, afterwards ruined himself by the South Sea Bubble, and at last escaped from the life of a hack writer by drowning himself under London Bridge. Addison had gone to Ireland, where his cousin Budgell lived with him, when **Richard Steele** issued the first number of the *Tatler* on the 12th of April, 1709.

32. Doubtless it had occurred to Steele, as a reader of Defoe's "Review," that its little supplement of advices from

the "Scandal Club," dealing lightly with characteristics of the common daily life in comments and imaginary letters, represented a good form of service to society.   Defoe said of this light matter, which some censured him for blending with his discussion of great public questions, that many "care but for a little reading at a time," and "thus we wheedle them in, if it may be allowed that expression, to the knowledge of the world, who, rather than take more pains, would be content with their ignorance, and search into nothing."   Upon this hint, or, at any rate, in this spirit, Steele acted when he planned and began the *Tatler*, without taking his friend Addison into his councils.   The *Tatler*, planned to give a little of its space to news, was a penny paper, published three times a week ; and it was not until eighty numbers had appeared, and its success was complete, that Addison returned to London, became a contributor, and was drawn by Steele into a form of writing that brought all his powers into use.   An accident made Isaac Bickerstaff the hero of the *Tatler*.   Swift, then in London seeking fortune, had issued under that name, at the beginning of 1708, a jest against the superstition that maintained prophetic almanacks, in *Predictions for the Year* 1708, which included a prediction of the death of John Partridge, the chief maker of these almanacks, on the 29th of March next.   After the date had gone by, Swift published an account of *The Accomplishment of the First of Mr. Bickerstaff's Predictions, being an Account of the Death of Mr. Partridge, the Almanack Maker, on the 29th inst.*   Other wits kept up the joke.   Partridge, in his next almanack, declared that he was "still living, in health, and they are knaves that reported it otherwise."   In the first number of the *Tatler*—Swift, Addison, and Steele being then intimate friends—Steele, in the name of Bickerstaff, continued the joke, and explained to Partridge that if he had any shame he would own himself to be dead ; "for since his art was gone, the man was gone."   The name of Isaac Bickerstaff, thus accidentally assumed at the beginning, was retained throughout the *Tatler*. Addison's return to London was at the end of July or beginning of August, 1710.   It was the time of the dismissal of Godolphin from office, when Harley came into power, and the tide of events was running against Marlborough, the Whigs, and the war party.   Matthew Prior had left the Whigs, and was conducting, in the Tory interest, a paper called the *Examiner*. Addison, therefore, set up a *Whig Examiner*, "to give all

persons a re-hearing who have suffered under any unjust
sentence of the *Examiner.*"  This paper of Addison's began
on the 14th of September, 1710, and ended on the 8th of
October following.  On the 2nd of November, Swift began to
write in the *Examiner.*  Steele had also lost his place of
Gazetteer, by writing against Harley, but retained the office of
Commissioner of Stamps, which had been given to him a few
months before.  Nos. 190, 191, and 193 of the *Tatler* were the
offenders.  Of No. 193 it was said that Steele wrote political
satire, while he professed only to be talking about the stage.
Steele closed the *Tatler* at No. 271, on the 2nd of January,
1711, and it was re-issued in four volumes.

33. On the 1st of March appeared the first number of its
successor, the *Spectator*, which excluded politics, and, like the
*Tatler*, was Steele's paper, but in which he had, from the first,
Addison's co-operation.  The *Spectator* was published daily,
and its price was a penny, until the 1st of August, 1712, when
a halfpenny stamp duty killed many journals.  It reduced
the sale of the *Spectator*, which then had its price raised to
twopence.  Steele and Addison's *Spectator* ended at No. 555,
December 6, 1712.  The other numbers, to 635 (June 18 to
December 20, 1714), forming afterwards the eighth volume,
represent Addison's unsuccessful attempt to revive it, about
a year and a half after it had ceased to appear.  Steele's
hearty interest in men and women gave life to his essays.
He approached even literature on the side of human fellowship; talked of plays with strong personal regard for the
players; and had, like Addison, depths of religious earnestness
that gave a high aim to his work.  He sought to turn the
current of opinion against duelling.  Some of his lightest papers
were in accordance with his constant endeavour to correct the
false tone of society that made it fashionable to speak with contempt of marriage.  No man laboured more seriously to establish
the true influence of woman in society.  Addison's delicate
humour, and fine critical perception, produced essays with
another kind of charm.  The Saturday papers in the *Spectator*,
which many would read on Sunday, were, as a rule, on subjects
that would harmonise with thought on sacred subjects, and the
series of eighteen papers in which Addison brought Milton into
fashion, by his criticism of "Paradise Lost," begun on Monday,
Dec. 31, 1711, were the *Spectators* for the first seventeen Saturdays of 1712.  Eleven essays on the pleasures of Imagination

(Nos. 411—421) were another important series of his, appearing every day, from June 21 to July 3, 1712. To the sketches of Sir Roger de Coverley and other members of the Spectator Club, both friends contributed, but they owed most to the fine humour of Addison.

34. In the *Spectator* for December 20th, 1711 (No. 253), Addison heartily commended the newly-published "Essay on Criticism," by young **Alexander Pope**. Pope was born in Lombard Street, May 21, 1688. He was the only child of Roman Catholic parents. His father was a linendraper, who retired from business about the time of his son's birth, and presently went to live at Binfield, about nine miles from Windsor, on the border of the forest. Sickly and frail from birth, Pope got instruction at home from a family priest, named Banister, was sent for a short time to school at Twyford, then to London, where he contrived to see Dryden, who had interest for him both as poet and as Roman Catholic. Pope, still a boy, went home to Binfield, studied in his own way, and tried his skill in verse upon translations and imitations of Latin and English poets—some of them done, he said, at fourteen or fifteen years old. The popularity of Dryden's "Fables" (§ 16) also caused him to try, in Dryden's manner, adaptations of Chaucer. At the age of sixteen, in 1704, Pope wrote his "Pastorals;" but as they were not printed until he was twenty-one, they had, of course, the benefit of later revision. This was the case with all juvenile work of the poet, who wrote of himself ("Epistle to Arbuthnot"):

> "As yet a child, nor yet a fool to fame,
> I lisped in numbers, for the numbers came."

Pope first appeared as a poet at the age of twenty-one, in Tonson's *Poetical Miscellanies*, of which the series had been begun by Dryden (ch. x. § 52), and a former volume had contained the first published writing of Addison. The sixth part, issued in 1709, opened with the Pastorals of Ambrose Philips, and closed with *Pastorals* by Mr. Alexander Pope. It contained, also, Pope's *January and May*, from Chaucer's "Merchant's Tale," and his *Episode of Sarpedon*, translated from the Twelfth and Sixteenth Books of Homer's Iliad, with two poems in praise of Pope's Pastorals, one of them by Wycherley. The same volume contained translations from Lucan, by Nicholas Rowe; and eight poems by Tickell, one of which was that on "Rosamond," which made Addison his friend. Also there were some pieces by Lawrence Eusden, and there was a pastoral dialogue by the author of the poem on *The Spleen.* This was **Matthew Green**, whose cheerful, thoughtful octosyllabics dealt with remedy for the depression of spirits which was said to have its source in the spleen.

35. **Nicholas Rowe** (b. 1673, d. 1718), son of a serjeant-at-law, was bred to the law, but, on the death of his father, turned to literature. He produced several plays—*The Ambitious Step-mother*, in 1700; *Tamerlane*, in 1702; *The Fair Penitent*, in 1703; *The Biter*, an unsuccessful comedy, in 1705; *Ulysses*, in 1706; and, in 1708, *The Royal Convert;* afterwards, *Jane Shore* (1713), the best of his tragedies. Rowe had a reverence for Shakespeare, and was the first editor of his works. After the four folio editions of Shakespeare's Tragedies, Comedies, and Histories, in 1623, 1632, 1664, and 1685, came, in 1709-10, in seven volumes, *The Works of William Shakespeare; Revised and Corrected, with an Account of his Life and Writings, by Nicholas Rowe.* Rowe's "Life of Shakespeare" preserves to us the traditions current in Rowe's time. Upon the death of Nahum Tate (ch. x. § 48), in 1715, Nicholas Rowe succeeded him as Poet Laureate, and held that office in the reign of George I., when he published his translation of *Lucan's Pharsalia.* There were two future Laureates writing with Pope in Tonson's "Miscellany" for 1709, for upon Rowe's death, in 1718, his successor was the Rev. Lawrence Eusden.

36. **Ambrose Philips**, born in 1671, was seventeen years older than Pope. He was of a good Leicestershire family, and educated at St. John's College, Cambridge. He came to London, was a zealous Whig, and published, in 1700, the *Life of John Williams, Archbishop of York*, celebrating him as an opponent of the policy of Laud. Ambrose Philips became, next to Steele, Addison's most familiar friend. In 1709, when his Pastorals were published, he was in Copenhagen, and wrote thence to the Earl of Dorset a *Winter Piece*, much lauded by Addison in No. 393 of the *Spectator.* Addison was over-zealous on his friend's behalf, and greatly magnified in the *Spectator* Philips's translation of Racine's "Andromaque," as *The Distrest Mother*, acted in 1711. **Pope's** *Pastorals* were four, entitled "Spring,' "Summer," "Autumn," "Winter," and their shepherds had names from the ancient classics. **Ambrose Philips, in his six pastorals, included Spenser's "Shepherd's Calender" (ch. vii. § 31) among his models, and had among his shepherds Lobbin, Thenot, Colinet, Cuddy, and Hobbinol.

37. In the *Spectator* for May 15, 1711, appeared the advertisement, " This day is published *An Essay on Criticism.* Printed for W. Lewis, in Russell Street, Covent Garden." Lewis was a Roman Catholic bookseller. Published in 1711, the Essay had been written in 1709. It was writing about writing, in the fashion of the day. Young Pope was following the lead of Boileau. But the " Essay on Criticism," though suggested by *L'Art Poetique* (ch. x. § 23), was the work of a fresh mind, with native vigour of its own ; and Pope surpassed all preceding attempts to write couplets that packed thought, with brilliant effect of antithesis and shrewd aptness of word, within the compass of a line or couplet. Almost every truth is associated, in a thoughtful mind, with considerations modifying any one abrupt expression of it ; therefore, whoever seeks to express thought by a succession of bright flashes of speech must frequently say more or less than he means. For many of us, ever now, the unaffected style of a true thinker is like the daylight that we work in, and don't stay to praise. Yet Pope, while perfecting an artificial style, was in his own way very much in earnest. In his " Essay on Criticism," while he followed the lead of Boileau in setting up for models the Latin writers of the Augustan time as the true artists who formed their style on nature, he dwells more than Boileau dwelt on the fact that nature is " at once the source, and end, and test of art." The spirit of the " Essay on Criticism" is, as a whole, thoroughly generous. Pope saw no critic in

> " The bookful blockhead ignorantly read
> With loads of learned lumber in his head."

He knew the weak side of the legislation upon literature that had its source in Paris, for critic-learning flourished most in France.

> " The Rules a nation born to serve obeys ;
> And Boileau still, in right of Horace, sways."

In Pope's ideal critic

> " Good nature and good sense must ever join ;
> To err is human, to forgive divine."

There was no ill-nature in the poem, unless it were ill-nature to pair in a line Blackmore and Melbourne for their attacks on Dryden, and laugh at Dennis, who, with real merit, rather too much assumed the God, and was, in politics, intolerant of that which was to Pope most sacred. The wise, he said, can bear to be told their faults.

" But Appius reddens at each word you speak.
    And stares, tremendous, with a threat'ning eye,
    Like some fierce tyrant in old tapestry."

John Dennis had produced, in 1709, a play of *Appius and
Virginia.* His stare was a characteristic. "He starts, stares,
and looks round him at every jerk of his person forward," said
Steele ; and he had an affection in his writing for the word
"tremendous," that became a joke against him. Dennis, who
had been referred to by name favourably in another line of the
poem, resented this lesson in critical temper, and produced,
towards the end of June, *Reflections Critical and Satyrical upon a
late Rhapsody called "An Essay on Criticism."*    Dennis's attack
made Addison's good word in December the more welcome.
Pope repaid it by contributing to the *Spectator* for May 14, 1712,
(No. 378), his *Messiah : a Sacred Eclogue, in Imitation of Virgil's
"Pollio."*    The fourth eclogue of Virgil, predicting the birth of a
wonderful boy while Pollio is consul, and said by Virgil to have
been founded on Sibylline verses, has a parallelism with parts of
Isaiah, which Pope therefore formed into a Virgilian eclogue.

The artificial gardening of the time had its match in the
ornamental cultivation of the fields of poetry. But there is
elevation in Pope's *Messiah,* though it does write "dewy
nectar" where Isaiah had written "righteousness," and refine
sheep into "the fleecy care." Pope contributed also to the
*Spectator* of November 4, 1712, a short letter with some lines
on "Cephalus and Procris," and another letter upon the Emperor
Adrian's lines beginning, "Animula, vagula, blandula," to the
*Spectator* of November 16. Out of this correspondence came,
by Steele's suggestion, Pope's poem called *The Dying Christian
to his Soul.*    One of its stanzas was a close imitation of a
stanza by Thomas Flatman, a barrister of the Inner Temple,
who published "Songs and Poems," in 1674, and painted
pictures, and who died in 1688. Steele did not receive Pope's
lines until just after December 6th, 1712, the date of the last
number of his *Spectator.*

38. In 1712, Bernard Lintot, the publisher, imitated Tonson
by producing a volume of "Miscellaneous Poems and Translations." Pope may have been its editor. It contained translations of his from Statius and Ovid, with smaller original
pieces, and *The Rape of the Lock* in its first form, in two books.
One of the smaller pieces, "To a Young Lady with a Volume
of Voiture," recalls Pope's intimacy with Teresa and Martha

Blount, two daughters of a Roman Catholic family at Maple Durham, near Reading. Martha Blount, two years younger than Pope, probably would have become Pope's wife if his bodily infirmities, a chief cause of the irritable mind, had not kept him unmarried. She had his love till death, and when he died he left her £1,000, all his household effects, and the residue of his estate after payment of debts and legacies. Was there not here a point of fellow feeling between Pope and Swift? The "Rape of the Lock" arose out of a suggestion made to Pope by his friend, Mr. Caryll, that a family quarrel arising out of the liberty taken by Lord Petre, aged twenty, in cutting off a lock of the hair of Miss Arabella Fermor, daughter of Mr. Fermor, of Tusmore, might be made the subject of a playful poem that perhaps would restore peace. The result was an airy satire on the vanities of fashionable life, which Pope thought he could enlarge into mock heroic by providing an epic machinery, lively and slight enough to be in harmony with its design. The reading of a French story, " Le Comte de Gabalis," by the Abbé Villars, which talked about Rosicrucians, and four kinds of spirits of the four elements—sylphs, gnomes, nymphs, and salamanders—suggested to him what he called a Rosicrucian machinery of sylphs in place of the interposition of heathen gods and goddesses. Addison told Pope that his poem, as it stood in Lintot's "Miscellany" in 1712, was *"merum sal,"* a delicious little thing, that he would not be likely to improve; and Pope, then irritable towards Addison, ascribed honest and natural advice to a mean motive.

39. In 1713, before March 9th, Pope's *Windsor Forest* appeared as a separate publication. In 1713, on the 12th of March, appeared No. 1 of **Steele's** *Guardian,* the successor to his *Spectator.* The change of name indicated one of his reasons for having dropped the *Spectator* three months before. He did not wish to be bound to neutrality, but would be free to speak, if he pleased, on public affairs. " The parties amongst us," he said, " are too violent to make it possible to pass them by without observation. As to these matters I shall be impartial, though I cannot be neuter." The *Guardian* was sketched as a Mr. Nestor Ironside, an old gentleman, guardian to the Lizard family, and thus in association with a Lady Lizard, widow of Sir Marmaduke Lizard, and her sons and daughters. As a daily half-sheet, the *Guardian* was continued through 175 numbers, ending on the 1st of October, 1713. Pope was a

contributor to it of eight papers.  In No. 22 of the *Guardian*, for April 6th, **Thomas Tickell** began a series of five papers (Nos. 22, 23, 28, 30, 32) on pastoral poetry, which led up to a glorification of Addison's friend, Ambrose Philips ; the last paper, on the 17th of April, ending with the dictum that Theocritus "left his dominions to Virgil, Virgil left his to his son Spenser, and Spenser was succeeded by his eldest-born, Philips."  Of Pope's pastorals there was only implied condemnation.  **Pope** resented this, and, as Tickell was Addison's retainer, Pope would rightly believe Addison privy to the slight thus put upon him.  He took prompt revenge cleverly in the *Guardian*, for April 27th (No. 40), with a paper professing to be one more of the series.  This paper proceeded to compare Pope and Philips, and did so with ironical praise of all that Pope thought worst in Philips, and ironical condemnation of himself in company with Virgil.

In 1714 Pope reproduced *The Rape of the Lock*, as "an Heroi-Comical Poem in Five Cantos," separately published. Lintot paid £7 for the original two cantos, and £15 for the enlarged poem, in February, 1714.  Success was immediate. The poem went through three editions in the year.  In some sense inspired by Boileau's "Lutrin," as the "Essay on Criticism" was inspired by "L'Art Poetique," "The Rape of the Lock" was a poem that surpassed all former writing of the kind. The fairy machinery was handled daintily ; the style suited the theme.  As in the Essay on Criticism, there was a predominant good humour ; and substance was given to the work by underlying English seriousness, that makes the whole a lesson summed up by Clarissa's speech in the fifth canto, which has for its closing lines :

> " Good humour can prevail
> When airs, and flights, and screams, and scoldings fail.
> Beauties in vain their pretty eyes may roll ;
> Charms strike the sight, but merit wins the soul."

There is more than idling in such lines as those which represent the lady's toilet table as an altar, the toilet itself as a religious rite ; and place the lady's Bibles by her looking-glass, among puffs, powders, patches, and billet-doux.

40.  **John Gay** was of Pope's age, born near Barnstaple, in 1688, and educated in that town before he was sent to London as apprentice to a silk weaver.  In 1712 he passed from behind the counter into the service of the Duchess of Monmouth, as her secretary ; and in 1713 he first won credit with his *Rural*

*Sports,* a Georgic, with a dedication to Pope. Thenceforth Pope and Gay were friends, and to his new friend, who had begun his career in verse with rural themes, Pope, with Tickell's trumpeting of Ambrose Philips fresh in his ears, suggested the writing of a set of pastorals that should caricature Philips's lauded rusticity. This was the origin of Gay's six pastorals called *The Shepherd's Week,* published in 1714, with a proem in prose to the reader, and a prologue in verse to Bolingbroke. But though the proem burlesqued Philips, and the purpose of censure and caricature was evident enough, yet simple speech is better than the false classicism that condemned it; and Gay, being much more of a poet than Ambrose Philips, and in himself, as Pope said, "a natural man, without design, who spoke what he thought," *The Shepherd's Week* made its own mark as pastoral poetry, and, in spite of its Cloddipole and Hobnelia, by its own merit went far to disprove its case. At the end of Queen Anne's reign Gay went to the Court of Hanover, as secretary to the Earl of Clarendon.

· 41. **Addison** saw his tragedy of *Cato* first acted at Drury Lane, where Colley Cibber was joint patentee and manager, in April, 1713, when the *Guardian* was a few weeks old. He had thought of a play on the subject before leaving Oxford, and wrote the greater part when on his travels. He gave all profits of acting to the players, who, therefore, spared no cost in putting " Cato " on the stage. Pope had written a prologue for it, Garth an epilogue. The very great success of the play was due to the fact that it was received as a patriotic manifesto; and as each party claimed to be as patriotic as the other, factions strove who should applaud it most. Bolingbroke, indeed, wickedly drew from it a hit at Addison's own hero, Marlborough, who had so long had his own way. He sent between the acts for Booth, who acted Cato, and gave him fifty guineas, "for defending the cause of liberty so well against a perpetual dictator."

**John Dennis** appeared as a hostile critic, with *Remarks upon Cato, a Tragedy;* and Pope then, upon a question not personal to himself, took occasion to pay off an old score of his own by *Dr. Norris's* (a mad-doctor's) *Account of the Frenzy of J. D.,* a form of advocacy which Addison repudiated as one to which " he could not in honour or conscience be privy."

42. When Steele abruptly stopped the *Guardian,* **Sir R. Blackmore** (§ 17), with **John Hughes** (b. 1677, d. 1720), endeavoured to continue its work by establishing another series

of essays, published under the name of "The Lay Monk," but collected under the name of *The Lay Monastery.* This appeared, with little success, three times a week, for forty numbers, from Nov. 16th, 1713, to February 15th, 1714. **John Hughes** is said to have caused Addison suddenly to finish Cato, by accepting an invitation to write the last act of it for him. Since his poem, "The Triumph of Peace," on the Peace of Ryswick, Hughes had written much that was creditable, including three or four letters in the *Spectator.* He had a situation in the Ordnance Office, was made afterwards, by Lord-Chancellor Cowper, Secretary for the Commission of the Peace, and died of consumption on the first night of his most successful play, "The Siege of Damascus."

43. Among contributors to the *Guardian*, besides Addison, was **George Berkeley**, born at Kilcrin, in Kilkenny, in 1684. He was educated at the Kilkenny Grammar School and Trinity College, Dublin, of which he became a Fellow in 1707. In 1709 appeared Berkeley's *Theory of Vision ;* in 1710, his *Principles of Human Knowledge ;* and, in 1713, his *Dialogues between Hylas and Philonous.* He opposed the materialist tendencies of the time with a metaphysical theory that represented an extreme reaction from them. The existence of matter could no more, he said, be proved, than the existence of the spirit could be disproved. We know only that we receive certain impressions on the mind. Berkeley was made Bishop of Cloyne in 1735, and died in 1753.

44. **Richard Steele** made his interest in the political life of his time very conspicuous by his paper on the demolition of Dunkirk, in the *Guardian* for August 7th, 1713. When the *Guardian* had been brought to an end, it had a sequel in the *Englishman*, which appeared (from October 6, 1713, to February 15, 1714) three times a week, forming 57 numbers, and in which the essays were chiefly political. **Swift**, whom Harley and St. John had this year (1713) made Dean of St. Patrick's, violently attacked Steele for his paper in the *Guardian*, urging the fulfilment of that stipulation in the Treaty of Utrecht which required the demolition of the harbour and works at Dunkirk. Steele replied with a pamphlet, *The Importance of Dunkirk Considered.*

When, in 1710, Robert Harley (made, in 1711, Earl of Oxford) became Secretary of State, there followed a Dissolution of Parliament, and a Ministry weary of war and taxation, and weary also of tolerance.   It was ready to make peace at the expense of Holland.   The preceding Ministry had of late years been making war at the expense of Holland, by tempting the unwilling Dutch with promises.   Both parties were in the wrong. One had continued the war when all its ends could have been accomplished by an advantageous peace ; the other was now ready to end it with a peace that was discreditable and disadvantageous.   Louis XIV. negotiated with new hope, and greatly reduced his offers.   **Matthew Prior** was now employed as a negotiator for the Tories.   The English were bribed with commercial advantages over the Dutch, and the Dutch felt themselves betrayed.   Prince Eugene had come to London in 1712, and in vain sought to influence Queen Anne.   Warm controversies over complicated questions preceded the signing of the Peace of Utrecht, on the 11th of April, 1713.   The Treaty of Commerce was rejected in the House of Commons by a small majority.   The House was dissolved in July, and there was great party violence at the elections.   Many wore emblems of allegiance to the Pretender.   Jacobites were busy.   The Pretender, inflexibly Romanist, claimed for himself the liberty of conscience he offered.   The new Parliament met in February, 1714.   **Steele** sat in it as member for Stockbridge, in Dorset. He put forth a pamphlet which is described by its long title : *The Crisis; or, a Discourse Representing from the most Authentick Records, the just Causes of the late Happy Revolution : and the several Settlements of the Crowns of England and Scotland on Her Majesty; and on the Demise of Her Majesty without Issue, upon the most Illustrious Princess Sophia. . . . With some Seasonable Remarks on the Danger of a Popish Successor.*   The Queen, in her speech on opening Parliament, said, "There are some who are arrived to that height of malice as to insinuate that the Protestant Succession in the House of Hanover is in danger under my Government."   The Lords, mostly Whigs, summoned before them the printer and publisher of *The Public Spirit of the Whigs*, and committed them to the custody of the Black Rod.   Harley, Lord Oxford, had given **Swift** £100 for writing it, but now affected indignation at its tone.   The House of Commons, mostly Tory, fell upon **Steele** as author of the *Crisis* and of a pamphlet called *The Englishman*, being the close (No. 57) of the paper so called. Steele defended himself well, but he was expelled the House on the 18th of March, 1714, by a majority of 245 against 152.

The Princess Sophia, aged eighty-four, died of apoplexy, on the 28th of May; and her son George, Elector of Hanover, or rather of Brunswick and Lüneburg, aged fifty-four, then became heir apparent. Queen Anne had a stroke of apoplexy on the 30th of July, and died on the 1st of August; so the Hanoverian became King George I.

<hr>

## CHAPTER XII.

### FROM ANNE TO VICTORIA.

1. AT the beginning of the reign of George I. (1714—1727) the oldest living writer was Thomas d'Urfey (ch. x. § 26), aged about eighty-six, who lived on to within a few years of a hundred. John Locke had been dead ten years, Sir Isaac Newton, aged seventy-two, was still living, and lived to the close of the reign of George I., dying March 20th, 1727, two or three months before the king. Bishop Ken had been dead three years, Bishop Sprat three months, Gilbert Burnet (ch. xi. § 9), whom William III. had made Bishop of Salisbury, was seventy-one years old, and died in the next year. **Jeremy Collier** (ch. xi. § 15) was sixty-four. He published in the year of Queen Anne's death the second of the two folio volumes of his *Ecclesiastical History of Great Britain, chiefly of England, from the First Planting of Christianity to the End of the Reign of Charles the Second, with a brief Account of the Affairs of Religion in Ireland, collected from the best Ancient Historians.* In 1721 appeared the original supplement to his translation of Moreri's *Great Historical, Geographical, Genealogical Dictionary,* which he had issued in three volumes folio in 1701 and 1706. Jeremy Collier died in 1727, at the close of the reign of George I. But Joseph Butler, whose "Analogy of Religion" appeared in the reign of George II., was a young man of twenty-two at the accession of George I., and John Wesley was a boy of eleven. William Wycherley (ch. x. § 38) was then seventy-four years old, and had but a year to live. Elkanah Settle (ch. x. § 26) was sixty-six, with ten years of a life of poverty before him. Thomas Southern was fifty-five. Farquhar had died in the middle of Queen Anne's reign. Congreve (ch. xi. § 14) was forty-four, and lived through the reign of George I., dying in 1729. Colley

Cibber was forty-three, Vanbrugh forty-two, and died the year before the king. Nicholas Rowe was forty-one, and had four years to live. Richard Bentley (ch. xi. § 23) was fifty-two. The critic, Thomas Rymer, died in the year before Queen Anne, having chiefly spent his time during her reign in publishing the great collection of public treaties, known as Rymer's *Fœdera*. The first of the ten folios issued by him appeared in 1704. Critic John Dennis (ch. xi. § 19) was fifty-seven; **Charles Gildon**, born in 1665, of a Roman Catholic family in Dorsetshire, who failed as an actor, and became critic of the narrowest French school, was forty-nine, and produced, in the reign of George I., his *Complete Art of Poetry* (1718), a *Satirical Life of Defoe* (1719), and *The Laws of Poetry* (1720). He died in 1724. Daniel Defoe (ch. xi. § 24, 30) was about fifty, of like age with Matthew Prior (ch. xi. § 25). Jonathan Swift (ch. xi. § 32), and Samuel Garth (ch. xi. § 18), who was knighted at the accession of George I., were both forty-seven years old ; Steele and Addison both forty-two ; Gay and Pope both twenty-six ; James Thomson and John Dyer both fourteen. **John Oldmixon** (ch. xi. § 19) was forty-one, and had begun to take especial interest in history. He produced, early in the reign of George I., *Memoirs of North Britain* and *Memoirs of Ireland from the Restoration,* and he began, towards the end of the reign, *A Critical History of England.* Among friends and helpers of Pope, John Arbuthnot was thirty-nine, Thomas Parnell thirty-five, Elijah Fenton thirty-one. Addison's friend, who became also his secretary, Thomas Tickell, was twenty-eight, Samuel Richardson, the future novelist, was twenty-five, and Henry Fielding, seven, at the accession of George I., when Edward Young was thirty, Allan Ramsay twenty-nine, Richard Savage sixteen, Samuel Johnson a child five years old, David Hume three, Lawrence Sterne but a year old, and Shenstone newly born.

2. The chief writings of the reign of George I. were Defoe's " Robinson Crusoe " (1719), and the novels of his that followed it ; Swift's " Drapier's Letters " (1724), and his " Gulliver's Travels " (1726) ; Pope's " Iliad " (1715—1720), and " Odyssey " (1723—5) ; Allan Ramsay's " Gentle Shepherd " (1725), and Thomson's " Winter," and Dyer's " Grongar Hill," which were both published at the close of the reign, in 1726, and represented in the work of young men a reviving sense of nature. There were some indications, also, of coming social changes in Mandeville's " Fable of the Bees " (1723).

3. **Joseph Addison**, on the death of Queen Anne, was made secretary to the Regency, until the arrival of George I. Then Marlborough's son-in-law, the Earl of Sunderland, being made Lord-Lieutenant of Ireland, appointed Addison Chief Secretary. **Richard Steele** had, only the day before the last number of the *Englishman* appeared, started, February 14th, 1714, a paper called the *Lover*, dedicated to Garth as "the best-natured man," and published three times a week until its close, on the 27th of May. Whilst that was running he published nine numbers of another paper, called the *Reader*, through which he replied to the *Examiner*. Steele wrote, also, another pamphlet upon the Dunkirk question, and one on behalf of religious toleration, after his expulsion from the House of Commons.

The accession of George I. brought the Whigs again into power. Steele was made surveyor of the royal stables at Hampton Court, and a deputy-lieutenant in the Commission of the Peace for Middlesex. Through the death of the sovereign, the licence of the royal company at Drury Lane required renewal. Steele was applied to; his name was, at their request, inserted in the patent as Governor of the Company, and, in kindly relation with the players, he began to receive an income of six hundred a year from the theatre. He was returned also to the first Parliament of George I., as member for Borough-bridge in Yorkshire; and in April, 1715, he was one of three deputy-lieutenants who were knighted upon going up to the king with an address.

In this year Steele published a translation of an Italian book on *The State of Roman Catholic Religion throughout the World*, with an ironical dedication to the pope. At Drury Lane he produced his friend **Addison's** one comedy, *The Drummer*, written some years before. It was not successful, and is noticeable chiefly as another illustration of the religious feeling that was a mainspring of the literary work of Steele and Addison. A mock ghost of a drummer brings out a lively dread of the supernatural from below the surface of a fop who sets up for an atheist.

In September, 1715, rebellion in favour of the Pretender, James Stuart, broke out in the North. It was suppressed, but there were many Jacobites of the party that had felt its strength during the last years of Queen Anne, and Addison was chosen by the Ministry to maintain the cause now identified with the Hanoverian Succession. He did this in a series of fifty-five papers called the *Freeholder*, which appeared between December 23rd, 1715, and June 29th, 1716. In August, 1716, the Earl of Sunderland resigned his office of Lord Lieutenant, and Addison ceased to be the Irish Chief Secretary after ten months' tenure of office. In the same month Addison married the Countess Dowager of Warwick (ch. xi. § 31.), and thenceforth he lived chiefly at Holland House, in Kensington. In April, 1717, Addison's steady friend, Lord Sunderland, became Secretary of State, and made Addison his colleague. Failure of health caused Addison to remain in office only eleven months. He resigned in March, 1718. In 1719 the Ministry to which he had belonged brought in a Peerage Bill, limiting the king's prerogative in establishing new peerages, except to replace such as should become extinct. The strong objections to such a measure were felt by many of the Whigs ; and Sir Richard Steele attacked it in papers connected by the name of the *Plebeian.* Addison, then near his death from asthma, replied as the *Old Whig.*

**Sir Richard Steele,** appointed one of the Commissioners for Forfeited Estates, had a hearty welcome at Edinburgh, in November, 1717. He had a patent device, called *The Fishpool,* for bringing salmon and other fish alive from Ireland to the London market, and published an account of it in 1718. In December, 1718, Steele's wife died, aged forty, leaving him with a son and two daughters. Then came, in 1719, on the 14th of March, the first number of his *Plebeian,* against the Peerage Bill. **Addison,** on the 19th, replied with the *Old Whig.* On the 6th of April appeared the fourth and last number of the *Plebeian ;* and Addison died on the 17th of June, aged forty-seven, leaving one daughter, who did not marry.

4. **Susanna Centlivre** (b. about 1680, d. 1723), was the daughter of a Mr. Freeman, of Holbeach, in Lincolnshire, who was ruined by resistance to the Stuarts. She was married at sixteen to a husband who died in a twelvemonth, then to an officer who, after eighteen months, was killed in a duel ; then she supported herself by writing plays and acting. As actress she fascinated Mr. Joseph Centlivre, the king's head cook, who married and survived her. She wrote, between 1700 and 1721, nineteen lively plays, with good plots and frequent expression of her political feeling as a hearty Whig. The most successful of her plays were *The Busy Body* (1709), *The Wonder* (1713), and *A Bold Stroke for a Wife* (1718).

5. To punish Steele for his opposition to the defeated Peerage Bill, his patent at Drury Lane was threatened by the Government, and he started a paper called the *Theatre*, continued from January 2nd to April 5th, 1720, to protect his own interests and those of the stage. Steele's patent was revoked, whereby he was deprived of his £600 a year, and three years' continuance of that income after his death. This act proceeded chiefly from the ill-will of the Duke of Newcastle, who was Lord Chamberlain. In May, 1721, Steele was restored to his office by the good-will of Robert Walpole, then at the head of the Treasury; and in the following year, 1722—the year of the death of his only son, Eugene—he produced, with very great success, his fourth and last comedy, *The Conscious Lovers.* This was founded upon Terence's "Andria," designed, Steele said in the preface, "to be an innocent performance," and written chiefly for the sake of a scene in the fourth act, in which the younger Bevil so deals with a challenge from a friend as to enforce once more Steele's doctrine that Christian duty rises far above, and utterly condemns, the point of honour worshipped by the duellists. The old tenderness of Steele's love for Addison appeared also this year in a letter to Congreve, prefixed to a new edition of Addison's comedy of "The Drummer." Steele began two more comedies, "The School of Action" and "The Gentleman," but his health failed. He withdrew from London to the West of England, and about 1726 settled on a mortgaged estate of his, derived from the Scurlock family, at Llangunnor, near Carmarthen. There he was at home, with failing health and struck with palsy, at the end of the reign of George I. One who knew him, and received kindness from him in his last days, said of Steele, "I was told he retained his cheerful sweetness of temper to the last, and would often be carried out of a summer's evening where the country lads and lasses were assembled at their rural sports, and with his pencil give an order on his agent, the mercer, for a new gown to the best dancer." Steele died on the 1st of September, 1729, having survived Addison about ten years. Of his two daughters, the younger died in 1730, of consumption; the other married a Welsh judge, who became Lord Trevor of Bromham. Steele had paid every creditor before his death, and his children were not left in want. He had been a tender husband, a good father, a devoted friend, was open and kindly, while imprudently generous in the fellowship of men; and taking his place in

literature with a high sense of responsibility, he was throughout a faithful servant of God and his country.

6. **Daniel Defoe** (ch. xi. § 24, 30), was under persecution for his independence of thought, both at the close of Queen Anne's reign, and after the accession of George I. For a time, at the close of Anne's reign, he had withdrawn to Halifax, where he lived in Back Lane, at the sign of the " Rose and Crown." Against the claims of the Pretender he wrote *A Seasonable Caution,* which he distributed gratuitously among the ignorant country-people in different parts of England; and he wrote two other pamphlets, with titles designed to catch Jacobite readers, *What if the Pretender Should Come?* and *Reasons Against the Succession of The House of Hanover.* For writing these, Defoe was arrested and prosecuted in 1713. His enemies declared him Jacobite. They might as well, he said, have made him Mahometan. Nevertheless, he had to thank Harley for the queen's pardon. The persecution was continued under the new reign; for Defoe, with sturdy independence, had opposed false cries of every party in the State, and had never flinched from upholding what he thought sound policy because it came from his political opponents. Thus he had incurred a sort of infamy by asserting the soundness of what we should now all hold to be sound in the treaty of commerce which the Tories had associated with their treaty of peace with France, while he opposed the terms of peace; for at the last elections in Queen Anne's reign, the Whigs raised their battle-cry hotly against the commercial treaty. In 1715, Defoe, failing in health, and attacked on all sides, wrote his *Appeal to Honour and Justice, being a True Account of his Conduct in Public Affairs.* He had reason, he said, to think that his death might be near, and wished, before he embarked on his last voyage, to " even accounts with this world, that no slanders may lie against my heirs, to disturb them in the peaceable possession of their father's inheritance, his character." Defoe was, in fact, struck with apoplexy before the " Appeal " was finished; and the publisher, after waiting six weeks, issued it as it then stood, with the note that " in the opinion of most who knew him, the treatment which he here complains of, and others of which he would have spoken, have been the cause of this disaster." Defoe said here, " It has been the disaster of all parties in this nation to be very hot in their turn, and as often as they have been so, I have differed from them all. and ever must and shall do so." He cited seven chief

occasions of such differences with his friends. Against intemperate party warfare, Defoe urged that to attain harmony in the State there must be moderation in the exercise of power by the Government, and that " to attain at the happy calm which is the consideration that should move us all (and he would merit to be called the nation's physician who could prescribe the specific for it), I think I may be allowed to say, a conquest of parties will never do it ; a balance of parties may." With such last words as these, Defoe retired from political strife, and lived at Newington with his wife and six children. There, with a keen sense of his own political isolation, he now wrote " *The Life and Strange Surprising Adventures of Robinson Crusoe*, of York, Mariner, who lived Eight-and-twenty Years all alone in an Uninhabited Island on the Coast of America, near the Mouth of the great River of Oronooque ; having been Cast on Shore by Shipwreck, wherein all the Men Perished but Himself. With an Account of how he was at last as Strangely Delivered by Pyrates. Written by Himself." The two parts of *Robinson Crusoe* were published one at the beginning and the other at the close of the year 1719, with prefaces affecting to present them to the world as a true narrative of fact. The book had no relation whatever to the existing novel of the French school, or to any other kind of novel. It was an imitation of those simple and graphic records of adventure by sea which, since the days of Elizabeth, had quickened the delight of England in her sailors. If we would bring to mind how much imagination went to Defoe's exact suggestion of the real in this thoroughly English story-book, let us think how a man of weak imagination would have solved the problem : given one man and an island, to make a story. In Defoe's story, all is life and action. There is no rhetorical lament, or waste of energy upon fine writing ; attention, from first to last, is bound to the one man, only the more after the man Friday has been added to the scene, and the reader is made to feel that healthy life consists in trusting God, and using steadily with head and hand whatever faculties He gave us. Some part of the charm of the book springs from a reality below the feigned one, Defoe's sense of the fellowship of his own life with that of the solitary worker. The suggestion of the story was found in Captain Woodes Rogers's account of his " Cruising Voyage Round the World," published in 1712, which told how, in February, 1709, he took from the island of Juan Fernandez a seaman, named Alexander

Selkirk, who, when out on a piratical voyage, had been left ashore on that uninhabited island, after a quarrel with his captain, in September, 1704. Selkirk had been furnished only with a few books, nautical instruments, a knife, a boiler, an axe, and a gun, with powder and ball. Captain Rogers had brought him to England in 1711.

Robinson Crusoe was followed by Defoe's other novels, which still imitated forms of literature distinct from fiction, and sometimes included pictures of the coarse life of the time. *The Life and Piracies of Captain Singleton*, and *Duncan Campbell* appeared in 1720; *Moll Flanders* in 1721; *The Life and Adventures of Colonel Jack*, included commonly in genuine accounts of highwaymen, and the *Journal of the Plague*, which Dr. Mead quoted as the narrative of an eye-witness, both in 1722; the *Memoirs of a Cavalier* in 1723; *Roxana* in 1724; *The New Voyage Round the World* in 1725. At the beginning of the reign of George II., Defoe produced, in 1728, *The Life of Captain Carleton*, which Dr. Johnson fastened upon as an addition to English history. Defoe's health then failed completely, when he had begun another book. His last letter was to a son-in-law, when looking forward to his rest after life's troubled journey. "By what way soever He please to bring me to the end of it, I desire to finish life with this temper of soul—*Te Deum laudamus.*" Defoe died on the 24th of April, 1731.

7. **John Arbuthnot** (b. 1667, d. 1735) was the son of a Scotch Episcopal clergyman. The Revolution having deprived the father of Church preferment, the son, M.D. of Aberdeen, came to London and taught mathematics for a living. He obtained notice in 1697, by an examination of Dr. Woodward's account of the Deluge; was witty, learned, and a good talker, and was rising into medical practice. Then he chanced to be at Epsom when Prince George was in sudden need of medical attendance, was called in, treated him successfully, and became his regular physician. In 1709 he was made also Physician to the Queen, and Fellow of the College of Physicians. Already he was F.R.S., and a friend also of the wits and poets. In 1713 he wrote one of the cleverest of English political satires, *Law is a Bottomless Pit; or, the History of John Bull*, after the fashion of Swift's "Tale of a Tub," an allegory on the political disputes associated with the French War to its close in the Treaty of Utrecht. In 1714 he amused himself with Pope, Swift, Gay, Parnell, as members of a Scribbler's Club, and began with Pope

2 A

and Swift a satire, after the manner of Cervantes, upon the abuse of human learning.   The death of Queen Anne stopped them, when there had been produced only Book I. of the *Memoirs of Martin Scriblerus.*   Swift went back to Ireland, and Arbuthnot was deprived of his post and of his official residence at St. James's.

**Thomas Parnell,** born in Dublin in 1679, and M.A. of Trinity College there, took priest's orders in 1700, and in 1705 was made Archdeacon of Clogher.   He married, was intimate with the wits of Queen Anne's time, and towards the end of her reign went over to the Tories.   The queen's death destroyed his hope of advancement by the change.   Parnell obtained a prebend through the influence of Swift, and in 1716 was Vicar of Finglass.   He died in 1717, aged thirty-eight, and his friend Pope published, in 1722, a collected edition of his poems. The best of them was *The Hermit,* modernised from an old moral tale.

8. **Jonathan Swift** (ch. xi. § 23), about 1712, began to give, when in London, some instructions to a Miss Esther Van Homrigh, daughter of Bartholomew Van Homrigh, a Dutch merchant, who had settled in Ireland after the Revolution, married an Irishwoman, and bequeathed £16,000 to his widow and four children, two of them sons, who soon died.   The widow and daughters lived in London beyond their means, and ran away to Ireland.   The mother and one sister died, leaving Esther sole possessor of the remaining fortune.   She had an ill-regulated mind, and no personal beauty, and it pleased her to become enamoured of Swift. Turning her Dutch Van into Vanessa, and transposing the syllables of his dignity as Decanus or Dean, he wrote a poem on *Cadenus and Vanessa,* which, if it treated her delusions with unwise compliment to herself, was clearly intended to represent it as delusion.   The girl overlooked the counsel in the poem, and magnified the compliment.   Swift's vanity was, no doubt, flattered.   He did not deal firmly with the young lady's diseased imagination.   In Ireland, in 1716, he was privately married in his garden to the one woman who had his love, but the marriage made no difference in their relations to each other.   In 1720 Swift was recommending to the Irish the use only of Irish linen manufactures.   Miss Van Homrigh, who had settled at Selbridge, a house of her father's, ten or twelve miles from Dublin, drove him, by an excess of impor-

tunity, to over-harshness, and, being sickly, died in 1723 in the course of nature, considering herself a victim of love, and leaving the Dean's letters and " Cadenus and Vanessa " to be published after her death.   An age especially delighting in low scandal took the meanest view of the case, and Stella had to run away for a time from the tattle that surrounded her. Surely, it was said to her, the Dean must have loved Vanessa very much to write of her so beautifully.   " It is well known," replied Stella, " that the Dean can write very beautifully on a broomstick."   This referred to the " Meditations on a Broomstick," with which he had in earlier life edified Lady Berkeley, when she expected him to go on reading one day aloud to her Robert Boyle's "Occasional Reflections upon Several Subjects" (ch. x. § 29).

In 1724 Swift published *The Drapier's Letters*, against Wood's halfpence.   Copper coin having become so scarce in Ireland that the chief manufacturers were paying their workmen with tin tokens, a patent was granted to William Wood, an ironmaster, of Wolverhampton, to make £80,000 worth of farthings and halfpence during fourteen years, for supply of copper coin to Ireland.   Swift denounced the patent as an enrichment of William Wood at the expense of Ireland, which was to have its good money taken in exchange for copper coin of less than its nominal value.   Sir Isaac Newton, as Master of the Mint, and two of the assayers, testified that Wood's halfpence not only contained more copper than any before sent to Ireland, but also excelled former coinages "in goodness, fineness, and value of the metal."   No matter.   Writing as an Irish trader, M. B Drapier, Swift raised a storm in Ireland.   The "Drapier's Head" became a patriotic sign, and the Dean an idol of his countrymen.   Government offered in vain a reward of £300 for evidence to prove who was the writer of the fourth letter, dated Oct. 13, 1724.   The printer was arrested, but when the grand jury was to find a true bill against him a paper of the Drapier's, called " Seasonable Advice to the Grand Jury," had found its way to the hands of each of them, and they threw out the bill, though the Chief Justice sent them back several times to revise their return.   Swift prevailed, Wood's patent had to be revoked, and the Irish sang the praises of their Dean :

> " Now we're free by nature,   .
> Let us all our power exert ;
> Since each human creature
> May his right assert.

*(Chorus.)*  Fill bumpers to the Drapier,
        Whose convincing paper
        Set us, gloriously,
        From brazen fetters free."

Swift was now at work upon his *Travels into Several Remote Nations of the World, by Lemuel Gulliver, first a Surgeon, and then a Captain of several Ships.* Of this book he had the first suggestion from a passage in the "Memoirs of Martin Scriblerus" (§ 7); but it was also of the school of Cyrano de Bergerac's "Comic History of the States and Empires of the Moon," which had been twice translated into English (1659 and 1687), and Joseph Hall's "Mundus Alter et Idem" (ch. viii. § 15). Swift brought "Gulliver" to London in April, 1726; was with Pope till August, while the book was being printed, and recalled to Ireland by illness of Stella when it appeared, in the beginning of November, without the author's name. The first edition was sold in a week. Cleansed of impurities, it is now for its bright wit and bold flights of fancy read by children as a delightful tale of wonder. As a new book it was read by statesmen and men of the world as bitter political and social satire. Like "Robinson Crusoe," it takes the form of a sailor's book of adventure in strange lands; but there all likeness ends. Lemuel Gulliver's four voyages were: (1) To Lilliput, where English politics of the Court of George I. are satirized in a people who are as men and women seen through a diminishing glass, and where Blefuscu stands for France; (2) To Brobdingnag, where men and women are seen as through a magnifying glass, and the satire is continued with reference, particularly in the sixth chapter, to the politics of Europe; (3) To Laputa, &c.—satire against the philosophers; and (4) to the country of the Houyhnhnms—satire upon the whole human race. Although Swift lived until the middle of the reign of George II., the chief work of his life was done before the death of George I. Stella being better, he was in London again with Pope in 1727, collecting three volumes of "Miscellanies," but had again to hurry back. He was ill himself in October, and Stella, then within a few weeks of her own death, denied ease to herself that she might be his tender nurse. Lines of his "To Stella Visiting Me in my Sickness, October, 1727," end thus:

" Best pattern of true friends, beware;
You pay too dearly for your care,
If while your tenderness secures
My life, it must endanger yours.

> For such a fool was never found
> Who pulled a palace to the ground,
> Only to have the ruins made
> Materials for an house decayed."

Stella died in January, 1728, and all joy went out of Swift's life. His character lost what had softened its harsher lines. Disease of mind slowly increased upon him. In 1736 he was seized with a fit while writing, and he wrote no more. In 1741 he was insane beyond hope, and in charge of a legal guardian until his death, at the age of seventy-eight, in 1745.

9. **Alexander Pope** (ch. xi. § 38, 39), at the accession of George I., was at work on his translation of the " Iliad." His literary life falls into three periods, corresponding to three reigns. Under Queen Anne he produced his own earlier poetry ; under George I. he was translator of Homer and editor of Shakespeare ; and the later period of his own verse falls under the reign of George II. After publishing, at the beginning of 1715, his version of Chaucer's *Temple of Fame,* Bernard Lintot published, in January the same year, the first of the six volumes of Pope's *Iliad,* containing four books with prefatory matter. In the same week Tonson published, as a verse pamphlet, *The First Book of Homer's Iliad. Translated by Mr. Tickell.* It had this notification : " To the Reader,—I must inform the reader that when I began this First Book, I had some thoughts of translating the whole ' Iliad ;' but had the pleasure of being diverted from that design by finding the work was fallen into a much abler hand. I would not, therefore, be thought to have any other view in publishing this small specimen of Homer's ' Iliad,' than to bespeak, if possible, the favour of the publick to a translation of Homer's ' Odysseis,' wherein I have already made some progress." In spite of this courteous note, Pope resented the rivalry, ascribed it to Addison, who was supposed to have polished Tickell's verse, and who took part in the inevitable drawing of comparisons. Addison had established, in 1712, Daniel Button, an old servant of the Countess of Warwick, in a coffee-house in Russell Street, Covent Garden, opposite Will's, made it his place of resort, and drew the wits to it. When Steele set up the *Guardian,* he set up its letter-box at Button's in the form of a lion's head, said afterwards to have been designed by Hogarth, though Hogarth was but sixteen when the *Guardian* was appearing. Of talk at Button's, when the first volume of Pope's " Iliad" was new, Gay told Pope, "Mr. Addison

says that your translation and Tickell's are both well done, but
that the latter has more of Homer." Pope now expressed his
annoyance in that satire which lays a bitter emphasis on the
defects of Addison,

> "Who when two wits on rival themes contest
> Approves of both, but likes the worse the best,"

but not without generous recognition of his worth as one

> "Blest with each talent and each art to please,
> And born to live, converse, and write with ease.

This piece of satire was first printed in 1723, then among
Pope's "Miscellanies," in 1727, and finally incorporated in the
Epistle to Arbuthnot, in 1735. Addison was so free from ungenerous feeling in this matter, that he went very much out of his
way in the *Freeholder*, for May 7, 1716, to say that, as the illiterate could judge of "Virgil" from Dryden's translation, "those
parts of Homer which have already been published by Mr. Pope
give us reason to think that the 'Iliad' will appear in English
with as little disadvantage to that immortal poem." Addison
added a generous word for Nicholas Rowe, then translating
the "Pharsalia" of Lucan, "the only author of consideration
among the Latin poets who was not explained for the use of the
Dauphin, for a very obvious reason ; because the whole 'Pharsalia' would have been no less than a satire upon the French
form of government."

In April, 1716, Pope's father and mother having sold their
little house and ground at Binfield, the family removed to one of
a row of houses—Mawson's New Buildings—at Chiswick. In
October, 1717, Pope's father died, and Pope wrote these few
words to Martha Blount : "My poor father died last night.
Believe, since I don't forget you this moment, I never shall."

About the same time, Colley Cibber produced his *Non-
juror*, a version of Moliere's "Tartuffe," directed against the
Roman Catholics and Non-jurors who had sympathised with the
Jacobite insurrection of 1715. It had a great success, and its
loyalty marked Cibber for the post of Poet Laureate, to which
he succeeded on the death of the Rev. Laurence Eusden (ch.
xi. § 35), in 1730. But its bitterness towards those who were
of the faith of Pope's household stirred Pope's resentment
against Cibber, and marked him for the post to which he was
afterwards promoted in "The Dunciad." Pope expressed his
feeling at once in a satirical *Key to the Non-juror*, with a touch

in it of serious indignation. This trifle was suggested by his former "Key to the Lock," published in 1715, when he expounded the piece as a political allegory, the Lock being the Barrier Treaty, Belinda Queen Anne, and so forth. Cibber himself ascribed Pope's dislike of him to resentment of a piece of personal impertinence, introduced by Cibber as actor of the character of Bayes in the "Rehearsal."

In 1718 Pope took a long lease of a house, with five acres of ground, at Twickenham, the house thenceforth known as Pope's Villa. An underground passage connecting the land on opposite sides of the public road, Pope, otherwise careful of money, spent much in transforming into an ornamental grotto. He lived at Twickenham with his mother, to whom he was a devoted son, upon his small patrimony, increased substantially by the profits of translating Homer. A volume of the "Iliad" appeared annually after the first in 1715, until there was a pause in 1719, and in 1720 the work was completed by the issue of the fifth and sixth volumes. Pope was paid £200 a volume by his publishers, and 660 copies to supply subscribers. Pope's friend, Parnell, wrote the Life of Homer, Broome and others found material for notes; but Pope, after deducting payment for aid, must have received at least £5,000 for his translation of the "Iliad." All his original work in Queen Anne's reign had not brought him £100; and Dryden had not obtained more than £1,200 for his translation of Virgil. Pope next undertook to supply Tonson with an annotated edition of Shakespeare, and Lintot with a translation of the "Odyssey." For each there was to be a subscription list. In the proposals for a translation of the "Odyssey," Pope said he had undertaken it, but that the subscription was also for two friends who would assist him in his work. These were Broome and Fenton.

10. **William Broome** had been educated at Eton as a foundation scholar, and at Cambridge by the subscription of friends, and was Vicar of Sturston in Suffolk. He had a turn for verse, and, with repute as a Greek scholar, had begun his literary life by taking part in a prose translation of the "Iliad." Introduced to Pope at Sir John Cotton's, in Cambridgeshire, Broome pleased the poet, and was employed in selecting extracts for notes to the "Iliad." Upon the "Odyssey" Broome was a chief helper. He translated eight books, the 2nd, 6th, 8th, 11th, 12th, 16th, 18th, and 23rd, and compiled all the notes. The 11th and 12th books he had translated some years before, for his diversion.

**Elijah Fenton,** who, after a Cambridge education, had been
usher in a school, afterwards master of the school at Seven-
oaks, then secretary to Lord Orrery and tutor to his son, Lord
Boyle, had published verse in 1709 and 1717, and in 1723, while
at work for Pope, produced a tragedy, *Mariamne.* He also
edited Waller, and wrote a Life of Milton.   Fenton, as fellow-
worker on the "Odyssey," translated four books, the 1st, 4th, 19th,
and 20th.   Pope translated the other twelve, and his knack of
translating Homer was so easily caught that, when he had
touched over the work of his assistants, few readers could
observe in the Odyssey a difference between the books translated
by him and those done by his colleagues, Broome and Fenton.
Pope's reputation made the profit of the undertaking, and his
share of the earnings by the Odyssey, produced in 1723-4-5,
was £3,500, after paying Broome £400 for the eight books and
£100 for the notes, and Fenton £200.   Thus Pope earned eight
or nine thousand pounds in the reign of George I. by that work
of his life which is least valuable to posterity.   But it was the
age of French classicism, when Homer and Virgil were the
names to conjure by.   Addison knew that he enjoyed the
"Babes in the Wood" and "Chevy Chace," when he wished to
make others do so by commending them in the *Spectator.*   But
to do that, or justify to himself his own enjoyment, he must
needs show how they reminded him of Virgil and Horace (see
the *Spectator,* Nos. 70, 74, and 85).   While the "Odyssey"
translation was in progress, **Broome** wrote of Pope to Fenton,
"he turns everything he touches into gold."   When it was
ended, he obliged Pope by appending a note, in which he
claimed for himself the translation of only three books, and for
Fenton only two ; with expectation that the rest of their work
was to be praised as Pope's by the public, and its glory then
claimed for the authors.   But Broome's relation to Pope ended
in just discontent ; and, with a sense of fraud upon his reputation,
he wrote of Pope to Fenton as a King of Parnassus, who held
"all its gold and silver mines as privileges of his supremacy,
and left coarser metals to the owners of the soil."   Broome
published a volume of Miscellaneous Poems in 1727, married a
rich widow, and became LL.D. at the beginning of the reign
of George II.   He was afterwards Vicar of Eye, in Suffolk,
and died in 1745.

11. In 1725 Pope's *Edition of Shakespeare* appeared, in six
volumes.   Only 750 copies were printed, and of these 140

remained unsold, until their price was much reduced. Shake-
speare was not then a name to conjure with, and Pope received
little more than £200 for his work upon him.  But he brought
Shakespeare into notice at a time when a writer on the Laws
of Poetry, editing the "Essay on Poetry" by John Sheffield
(Lord Mulgrave, who died Duke of Buckinghamshire, in 1720),
Lord Roscommon's "Essay on Translated Verse," and Lord
Lansdowne on "Unnatural Flights of Poetry," said, in 1721,
"To go through all the soliloquies of Shakespeare would be to
make a volume on this single head.  But this I can say in
general, that there is not one in all his works that can be
excused by reason or nature."

When Swift brought "Gulliver" to town, and was with
Pope at Twickenham, in 1726, with aid from Gay and
Arbuthnot, of whom Swift said that if the world contained
twelve Arbuthnots he would burn "Gulliver's Travels," the
friends began to collect many pieces, chiefly of Swift's, into
three volumes of *Miscellanies*, of which the last appeared in
1727.  Among Pope's contributions were a satire on Burnet's
"History of His Own Times," in which Gay took part, called
*Memoirs of P. P., Clerk of this Parish*, and a *Treatise on Bathos;
or the Art of Sinking in Poetry*, in which Pope dealt satirically
with many of the minor poets of the day, and did not spare his
dissatisfied colleague, William Broome.  The next step from
this was to the "Dunciad."

12. **Lewis Theobald**, son of an attorney, at Sittingbourne,
in Kent, and bred to the law, published, in 1714, a translation
of the *Electra* of Sophocles ; and produced in the following
year an acted tragedy, the *Persian Princess*, written before he
was nineteen.  His *Perfidious Brother*, acted in 1716, was on
the model of Otway's "Orphan."  In 1715 he published trans-   –
lations of the "Œdipus" of Sophocles, and versions from Aristophanes of *Plutus* and *The Clouds*.  To these he had added opera,
melodrama, and, in 1725, when Pope issued his "Shakespeare,"
the pantomime of *Harlequin a Sorcerer*, before his attack
upon Pope's "Shakespeare," in 1726, with a pamphlet, called
"Shakespeare Restored; or, Specimens of Blunders Committed
and Unamended in Pope's Edition of this Poet."  Theobald
understood Shakespeare better than Pope did, and lived to
show it ; but this did not lessen the annoyance of his attack,
and, fresh from the smart of it, Pope made Theobald the hero of
his "Dunciad."  In 1727 Theobald gave work to the critics by

2 A *

producing at Drury Lane, as a play of Shakespeare's, *The Double Falsehood; or, the Distrest Lovers.*

13. **Bernard de Mandeville** represented in the reign of George I. the rising tendency to speculate on the corruptions of society. Great principles still underlying public contests were now buried under party feuds and personal ambitions. Men were growing up with little in the public life about them to inspire a noble faith or stir them to the depths. Polite life became artificial ; with small faith in human nature, negligent of truth. The fashionable world had the king's mistress for a leader; and the prevailing influence of French fashion, which had been low at its best, was degraded since the death of Louis XIV., in 1715. Louis XV. became King of France from 1715 to 1774; until 1723, under the regency of the Duke of Orleans. The Court of France was sinking into infamy. Polite society in France was the more tainted, and the nation suffered many tyrannies. Mandeville, born at Dort, in Holland, about 1670, graduated as a physician, and practised in England. After a coarse, outspoken book, in 1709, he published, in 1711, a treatise on Hypochondriacal and Hysterical Affections, in three dialogues, with amusing strictures upon medical follies ; and in 1714 appeared a short poem of 500 lines, called *The Grumbling Hive; or, Knaves Turned Honest.* There was a volume, in 1720, of " FreeThoughts on Religion, the Church, and National Happiness," and the " Grumbling Hive " reappeared, in 1723, with a full prose commentary, as *The Fable of the Bees.* This book outraged conventional opinion, by working out an argument that civilisation is based on the vices of society. The bees lived in their hives as men, " millions endeavouring to supply each other's lust and vanity;" lawyers, physicians, priests, thriving upon the feuds, follies, and vices of mankind. Luxury employed its million, pride its million, envy stirred men to work. Fickleness of idle fashion was the wheel that kept trade moving. But the hive grumbled at the vice within it, and the knaves turned honest. In half an hour meat fell a penny a pound ; masks fell from all faces. The bar was silent, because there were no more frauds ; judges, jailors, and Jack Ketch retired, with all their pomp. The number of the doctors was reduced to those who knew that they had earned their skill. Clergy who knew themselves to be unfit for their duty resigned their cures. All lived within their incomes, and paid ready money. Glory by war and foreign conquest was laughed at by these honest bees,

"who fight but for their country's sake, when right or liberty's at stake." Then followed fall of prices, extinction of trades founded upon luxury, and of the commerce that supplied it. These glories of civilisation are gone, still Peace and Plenty reign, and everything is cheap, though plain. At last the dwellers in the honest hive appeared so much reduced as to become a mark for foreign insult, and they were attacked. Because there was no hireling in their army, but all were bravely fighting for their own, their courage and integrity were crowned with victory. But they suffered much loss in the conflict. "Hardened with toils and exercise, they counted ease itself a vice ; which so improved their temperance that, to avoid extravagance, they flew into a hollow tree, blest with content and honesty." This satire, with the remarkably plain speaking in the appended notes and dissertations—one "A Search into the Nature of Society"—startled many people ; and in 1723 the book was presented by the Grand Jury of Westminster as one "having a direct tendency to the subversion of all religion and civil government, our duty to the Almighty, our love to our country, and regard to our oaths." Bernard Mandeville, who certainly meant none of these things, but whose book was as a first faint swell before the rising of another mighty wave of thought, published a second volume of it in 1728. He was partly supported by some Dutch merchants, and had for his patron the first Earl of Macclesfield. In 1732 he published *An Inquiry into the Origin of Honour, and Usefulness of Christianity in War;* and he died in 1733. Before the close of the reign of George I. there were other indications of a slowly-coming change.

14. **Allan Ramsay,** born in 1685, at a hamlet of a few cottages among the hills between Clydesdale and Annandale, was the son of a poor worker in Lord Hopetoun's lead mines. He worked there himself as a child, washing ore. Then he was sent to Edinburgh, apprenticed to a barber, and worked at that trade some years. But he delighted in old songs and ballads of his country, and could sing himself. His interest in literature made him a bookseller ; and his cheery nature, his gift of verse and innocent pride in it, made his shop popular. In 1721 he published, by subscription, a volume of *Poems,* partly in his native dialect, and, in 1724, *The Evergreen : Scots Poems Written by the Ingenious before* 1600. These were mostly taken from George Bannatyne's MS. (ch. vii. § 16), and included pieces by Henryson, Dunbar, Kennedy, Lindsay, and the true

old ballad of "Johnnie Armstrong," never before printed. It
was one of the first signs in our literature of the coming revival
of nationality, and it began among the people, for correction of
false classicism.   In the same year followed Allan Ramsay's
*Tea-table Miscellany*, and in 1725 *The Gentle Shepherd*, of
which the first sketch, only a short dialogue, had already
appeared in 1720, as *Patie and Roger: a Pastoral by Mr. Allan
Ramsay, in the Scots Dialect; to which is added an Imitation of
the Scotch Pastoral; by Josiah Burchett.* Ramsay's admirer,
Mr. Burchett, was Secretary of the Admiralty.   Allan Ramsay's
*Gentle Shepherd* is a pastoral play in five acts, with rustic
humour and rustic sentiment breaking often into delightful
lyric forms.   Duplicate dialogue was provided in the lyric
parts lest any performer should be unable to sing; for the
*Gentle Shepherd* has, from Ramsay's time to this day, been
accepted by Scottish peasantry as a play of their own, and
may even yet be seen acted by them in barns on holiday
occasions.   The true and homely sense of life is in the piece,
although its author was not yet so free from the literary
influences of the time as to venture on a Patie, for his hero,
who was not to turn out well-born at the end.   Therefore he is
a "gentle" shepherd, that is, a shepherd in appearance, but
really the son of a Sir William Worthy; and his Peggy also
proves to have been born a lady.   But Allan Ramsay's home-
bred poetry is so simple and true that it is little damaged by
contact with his more formal strains, and by his surface
adoptions of the taste of a polite world that helped him to keep
house in comfort.   He wrote occasional verses for rich friends,
and loved the poets.   He sang praise of Pope's Iliad; wrote
a Scottish ode to Gay; a pastoral, "Sandie and Richie," on the
death of Addison; another on the death of Prior; lamented, in
verse, Newton's death in 1727.   For Allan Ramsay had broad
sympathies, looked upon himself also as a man of genius, and
spoke with a free, musical and hearty voice.   He died in 1758.

15. In Roxburghshire there was born, in September, 1700,
another poet, who was harbinger of a new time.   **James
Thomson**, eldest son of the minister at Ednam, and educated
at Jedburgh, became, in 1719, Student of Divinity at Edinburgh,
where he had David Mallet among his fellow-students; and, in
1720, contributed to the *Edinburgh Miscellany* an essay "On a
Country Life, by a Student of the University."   In March,
1725, Thomson, aged twenty-five, embarked at Leith for London.

He arrived almost without money ; what was to have been sent
to him could not be sent. His letters of introduction, wrapped
in a handkerchief, were stolen from him, and presently he
received news of the death of his mother. In July he was at
East Barnet, teaching the five-year-old son of Lord Binning to
read, and writing his *Winter.* This little appointment was
obtained for Thomson by his college friend, **David Mallooh**
(b. about 1700, d. 1765), who had smoothed his name into
**Mallet,** become tutor to the sons of the Duke of Montrose,
and was able to help in finding friends. Mr. Duncan Forbes, of
Culloden, who had seen some of Thomson's poetry in Scotland,
and Mr. Aikman, a good friend also to Allan Ramsay, were
helpers who had influence in London society. Thus **Thomson**
became introduced to Pope, Arbuthnot, and Gay, and his
*Winter,* the first published section of his *Seasons,* appeared in
March, 1726. Its author went to be tutor to a young gentleman in an academy in Little Tower Street ; but "Winter"
was soon in a second edition, and opened a better career to
the poet. *Summer* appeared in 1727, and the other seasons
followed in the beginning of the reign of George II. There
is more of the artificial and rhetorical in Thomson's poetry
with its triple adjectives than we should now associate with
a true sense of nature. His English is very Latin, but his
words are apt, and he paints with a minute truth of detail.
Until French classicism was overthrown, young poets who
were growing into a new sense of beauty, found a quickening
influence in Thomson's " Seasons." Even Burns drew, in his
youth, inspiration from the book which came out in the days
of Swift's " Gulliver " and Pope's "Dunciad," alone of its kind
with one remarkable exception.

16. **John Dyer,** a young Welshman of Thomson's age,
published his "Grongar Hill" in the year 1726, when Thomson's
" Winter " first appeared. Dyer was born at Aberglasney, in
Carmarthenshire, and educated at Westminster School. He
abandoned law for painting, found himself a poor artist, took
orders, got some preferment, and wrote, not in the orthodox
ten-syllabled couplet, but in octosyllabic verse, his *Grongar
Hill,* celebrating the charms of that hill near his birthplace in
a strain of the simplest natural poetry.

> " Be full, ye courts, be great who will ;
> Search for peace with all your skill
> Open wide the lofty door,
> Seek her on the marble floor.

> In vain you search, she is not there;
> In vain ye search the domes of care!
> Grass and flowers Quiet treads,
> On the meads and mountain heads,
> Along with pleasure, close ally'd,
> Ever by each other's side:
> And often, by the murm'ring rill,
> Hears the thrush while all is still,
> Within the groves of Grongar Hill."

**Isaac Watts,** born at Southampton in 1674, son of a Nonconformist schoolmaster, became first a tutor, then pastor of a congregation in Mark Lane; and after the failure of his health in 1712, retained his pastoral charge, preaching when he could, and lived as guest with his friends, Sir Thomas and Lady Abney, at Theobalds, until 1748, the year of his death and of James Thomson's. In 1728 he had been made D.D. by the Universities of Edinburgh and Aberdeen. He published *Horæ Lyricæ* in 1706, *Hymns* in 1707, *Psalms and Hymns* in 1719, *Divine and Moral Songs for Children,* 1720; and, among various other works, a volume of *Logic,* in 1725. There was a supplement on *Improvement of the Mind,* in 1741.

17. In the reign of George II. (1727—1760) we find our national life advancing still to a new vigour of expression, and the fourth of the periods into which our literature may be divided—*The Period of Popular Influence*—slowly gaining strength as the *French Influence,* although strong throughout the reign, loses its hold upon the faith of our best writers. The most vigorous advance made in this reign was by the development of the great English novelists, Richardson, Fielding, and Smollett. At the same time the revolt against all despotism was rising throughout Europe. Authority was questioned with increasing boldness.

**John Gay** made the great success of his life just after the accession of George II. with *The Beggars' Opera.* The publication of his *Poems* in two volumes by subscription in 1720 had produced him a thousand pounds. In 1726 he published his *Fables,* with a dedication to the Duke of Cumberland, for whom they professed to be written. In January, 1728, his *Beggars' Opera,* written on Swift's suggestion, with Newgate characters to caricature Italian Opera, was produced with wonderful success. Gay was a bright, natural poet. Captain Macheath, Polly, and Lucy were for the public a welcome escape from the conventional, and Gay's profits from his author's rights came to £700. The Court considered itself satirized. The Archbishop of Canterbury thought that robbery was recommended. The performance of a sequel, *Polly*, was therefore interdicted. But Gay got all the more from his bookseller for the publishing of " Polly," and the Duke and Duchess of Queensberry took care of him until his death in 1732, when he left £6,000 to his sisters.

**William Somerville,** a gentleman of property at Edston, in Warwickshire, who loved literature and field sports, died in 1742, aged fifty, having produced in 1735 his poem of *The Chase*.

18. **Pope** in this third period of his life worked in accord with the new energy of the time. Even through the small pique and personal bitterness of *The Dunciad* there flowed a deeper current, that did work of its time in scouring out the channel through which better literature was to flow than that of the small critics and weak poets who claimed to represent the "understanding age." As first published in three books in May, 1728, " The Dunciad " had Lewis Theobald (§ 12) for its hero. In the first book, the goddess of Dulness chose Theobald to be Settle's successor, and carry diversions of the rabble from Smithfield to the polite West. In the second book, poets, critics, and booksellers contended in games to honour the new king. In the third book the new king, sleeping on the lap of Dulness, was transported in a vision to the banks of Lethe ; where Settle's ghost having discoursed to him of the glories of Dulness past and present, prophesied the triumph of her empire in the future. In April, 1729, " The Dunciad " appeared with the " Prolegomena of Scriblerus and Notes Variorum," to which Swift and Arbuthnot had contributed. There was, of course, much outcry ; and in January, 1730, a *Grub Street Journal* was established, which appeared weekly unto the end of 1737, Pope contributing. It professed to be written by certain Knights of the Bathos, who under guise of attack on Pope, fought his battle, and really attacked his adversaries.

19. In 1731 Pope wrote his Epistle to the Earl of Burlington, *Of Taste*, including a satire of the false luxury of the Duke of Chandos at Canons. In August of that year he had finished three books of his "Essay on Man." In 1732 appeared his Epistle to Lord Bathurst, *Of the Use of Riches*, including his famous character of the Man of Ross, and his moralising on the deathbed of George Villiers, Duke of Buckingham. In the same year he published, as an experiment, the first part of his *Essay on Man*, containing the *first two Epistles* inscribed to Boling-

broke as Lælius.   There was no author's name, and for a little
while nobody—not even Swift—supposed this to be Pope's
work.   In 1733 Pope published the *third Epistle of the Essay
on Man*, and an imitation of Horace (Satire 1 of Book. II.) in
dialogue between Pope and his friend Fortescue, a lawyer in
good practice, soon afterwards a Baron of the Exchequer.   To
the same year belonged the *Moral Essays, Characters of Men.*
In the summer of this year, Pope lost the mother so long
witness to the successes of the son who cheered her with un-
failing love.   In 1734 appeared the *fourth Epistle of the Essay
on Man*.   In January, 1735, Pope published the *Epistle to Dr.
Arbuthnot*, in which he defended himself against aspersion.   His
friend Arbuthnot died only a month later.   In the same year
appeared the *Moral Essays, Characters of Women;* in 1737 five
of the *Imitations of Horace;* and in 1738 the *Universal Hymn*,
closing the Essays on Man, and the satirical dialogue, " 1738,"
which afterwards formed an Epilogue to the satires.   Pope's
ethical writings in the reign of George II. indicate not only
the thoughtfulness of advancing years, but in some degree also
new tendencies of thought in Europe.   The Essay on Man, an
argument for God's goodness, as Father of all mankind, excited
warm controversy.   It was, and is ascribed to the influence
of Bolingbroke.   Its doctrines really came from Leibnitz's
*Théodicée.*

20.   **Henry St. John** (ch. x. § 26), who, in 1712, was
called to the House of Lords as **Viscount Bolingbroke**, was
dismissed after the death of Queen Anne from the office of
Secretary of State, which he had held four years.   In 1715 he
was impeached for high treason by Robert Walpole, attainted,
and had his name erased from the roll of peers.   He became
for a time Secretary of State to the Pretender, who gave him a
paper earldom, dealt treacherously with him, entered upon the
Scottish rebellion against his counsels, and dismissed him
summarily after his return.   Bolingbroke had seen enough of
Jacobitism at head-quarters, knew that its last chance of success
was lost, and gave it up.   Bolingbroke lived for the next seven
years in exile at La Source, near Orleans.   His wife died in
1718, and in May, 1720, he privately married the widow of the
Marquis de Villette, with whom he had been living.   At La
Source, in harmony with the new tone of French thought,
Bolingbroke began his philosophical writings, and was visited
by young Voltaire.   His French wife managed his return to

England in 1723, through the Duchess of Kendal, with a bribe of £11,000. In 1725 he obtained a grant of restored property, but not the reversal of attainder, which would restore him to the House of Lords and political life. He bought an estate at Dawley, near Uxbridge, within easy ride of Twickenham. There he affected philosophical contempt of ambition and played at farming. He was much visited by Pope; and by Swift also when, in 1726, Swift came to England. But Bolingbroke had ambition, and took his place as the most vigorous writer against Sir Robert Walpole, by his letters in *The Craftsman*, after 1726; and a series of letters, called *The Occasional Writer*, begun in January, 1727 : there was also *A Dissertation on Parties*, in nineteen letters, and a series of letters on *The History of England*, signed *Humphrey Oldcastle*, and ironically dedicated to Walpole. Bolingbroke's writing gave *The Craftsman* a sale far exceeding even that of "The Spectator." After this, in 1735, he retired again to France, until the death of his father called him home in 1742. He died himself in 1751. The religion expressed in Bolingbroke's essays on Human Knowledge, and the *Philosophical Writings*, published by David Mallet, in 1754, was contained in his parting words to Lord Chesterfield, after he had given orders that none of the clergy should visit him in his last moments : "God, who placed me here, will do what He pleases with me hereafter ; and He knows best what to do. May He bless you."

21. Pope's "Essay on Man" sprang from an endeavour to meet and grapple with the rising want of faith in France, that came of the corruption of the Church and of Society. *Pierre Bayle*, who died in 1706, published, in 1697, at Rotterdam, the first edition of his "Historical and Critical Dictionary ;" the second edition, in four volumes, appeared in 1702, and in 1710 it was translated into English. It raised many doubts and questions embarrassing to theologians ; and to these, in the book of which Pope adopted the teaching in his "Essay on Man," Leibnitz undertook to reply. GOTTFRIED WILHELM LEIBNITZ (b. 1646, d. 1716), son of a Professor of Moral Philosophy at Leipzig, wrote on jurisprudence and mathematics at the age of twenty-two, came afterwards to England, knew Newton and Boyle, was made F.R.S. ; was a leader of science also in Paris, claiming priority as discoverer of the differential calculus, when, in 1710, he wrote in French his *Théodicée*, to justify God in His works by showing Τὴν τοῦ Θεοῦ δίκην. Boyle having lately died,

Leibnitz began by putting him in heaven, where he now saw Truth at its source ; and having spoken in his preface of forms and ceremonies as only the shadows of the truth, he argued that naked truth would easily bring Faith into accord with Reason. But we are in love, he said, with superficial subtleties. Leibnitz held by the continuity of nature, and sought to blend the truths of different schools of philosophy.

Pope, following Leibnitz, argued in his *Essay on Man* that Man being only part of the great Universe, linked to it by nice dependencies and just gradations, which he cannot understand until he see the whole plan of creation, we must have faith, while we see but in a glass darkly, that " our proper bliss depends on what we blame ;" must know that there is in discord harmony not understood, in partial evil universal good. He argued that God's goodness may be found in passions and imperfections of the individual man. On self-love social love is built, and self-love, pushed from social to divine, " gives thee to make thy neighbour's blessing thine." He argued that God for man in society " on mutual wants built mutual happiness," and traced from the state of nature the development of government. Here there was abnegation of the old faith of his party in the Divine right of kings, " For Nature knew no Right Divine in men." Advance of thought was indicated when from Pope the question came :

> " Who first taught souls enslaved, and realms undone,
> Th' enormous faith of many made for one ?"

Thus, while injuring the expression of his mind by the constant labour for a brilliant antithesis not reconcileable with full sincerity of style, Pope wrote his " Essay on Man" in the spirit of his lines,

> " In Faith and Hope the world will disagree,
> But all mankind's concern is Charity :
> All must be false that thwart this one great end ;
> And all of God that bless mankind, or mend."

His fourth epistle on the source of happiness placed it in virtue alone, and in the sympathies of life :

> " Abstract what others feel, what others think,
> All pleasures sicken, and all glories sink ;"

placed it in love of God and love of man, open to each who can but think or feel,

> " Slave to no sect, who takes no private road,
> But looks through Nature up to Nature's God ·

> Pursues that chain which links th' immense design,
> Joins heav'n and earth, and mortal and divine ;
> Sees that no being any bliss can know,
> But touches some above and some below ;
> Learns, from this union of the rising whole,
> The first, last purpose of the human soul ;
> And knows where faith, law, morals, *all* began,
> All end, in love of God, and love of man."

Whatever we may think of the sufficiency of Pope's doctrine, it was assuredly not irreligious in design or temper. Our best poet even of a corrupt and artificial age did what he could to meet the scepticism it produced. In Milton's day it had been the aim of the great poet to " justify the ways of God to man," by answering doubts of His goodness that touched doctrines of the national religion. A bolder spirit of doubt now asked whether the daily experience of life was consistent with man's faith in an All-wise and Almighty Ruler. Therefore, even adapting Milton's line, Pope, to the best of his own lower power, sought to meet this doubt and " vindicate the ways of God to man." It is easy to misunderstand, away from its context, the formula twice repeated in the fourth epistle, " Whatever is is right ;" but Pope meant only what Milton meant when he wrote :

> " All is best, though oft we doubt
> What the unsearchable dispose
> Of highest Wisdom brings about,
> And ever best found in the close."

22. In 1736 **Joseph Butler** (b. 1692, d. 1752), son of a Presbyterian at Wantage, and first educated at a school for Dissenters, and then at Oxford, had become one of the chief preachers in the Church of England, and in that year he sought to satisfy the questioner by his *Analogy of Religion, Natural and Revealed, to the Constitution and Course of Nature.* In 1738 Butler was made a bishop. In 1739 Wesley began to preach. **John Wesley** (b. 1703, d. 1791) and his brother Charles (b. 1708, d. 1788) produced in 1738 their *Collection of Psalms and Hymns.* John Wesley was a clergyman's son, educated at the Charterhouse and Christchurch, Oxford, where his brother Charles followed him from Westminster. Charles persuaded some undergraduates to join with him in seeking religious improvement, living by rule, and taking the sacrament weekly. They were laughed at as " Bible Moths," " The Godly Club," &c. Then somebody, noticing their methodical ways, said that, like the old school of physicians so called, here was a new school of

*Methodists.* This name abided by them. John, when he returned to Oxford, became leader of the little society established by his brother. Then there was added strong influence upon his mind by the Moravians, and by his associate, **George Whitefield** (b. 1714, d. 1770), and in 1739 **John Wesley** began to influence the people as a preacher, with an enthusiasm that gave life to their religion. In 1749 Wesley published at Bristol, where he had built a meeting-house, *A Plain Account of the People called Methodists.* Among Wesley's other writings was, in 1763, *A Survey of the Wisdom of God in the Creation.* Methodism under John Wesley became an organized association, with himself for its directing head. The conditions of membership were prayer, and study of Scripture, with a resolved attempt to avoid vices and follies, practise Christian virtues, and bear in patience the reproach of men, for Christ's sake. Wesley sought, in fact, to join men in one grand endeavour to be true, without fear of the world and its conventions.

23. In 1740 **Pope** sketched the plan of a "History of the Rise and Progress of English Poetry." In 1741 he began a fourth book of the "Dunciad," completed during six weeks, in the house of Ralph Allen, at Bath. Ralph Allen, the friend of many writers of the time, and the Mr. Allworthy, the ideal good man, of Fielding's "Tom Jones," was a man of little education, great simplicity and kindliness, and a shrewd practical mind, who, as postmaster at Bath, had seen serious defect in our postal system from the absence of direct communication between country towns, so that a letter from Birmingham to Manchester had to be sent through London. "Quickened and improved correspondence is the life of trade," Allen wrote to the Lords of the Treasury, when offering to provide direct communication between certain towns. As farmer of cross posts he made a large fortune by his energy and enterprise, greatly improved the whole postal system, and added much to the material well-being of his country. In March, 1741, Pope published *The New Dunciad, as it was Found in the Year* 1741, with the original three books modified, a fourth book added, and Colley Cibber, who had been since 1730 Poet Laureate, replacing Theobald as its hero. **Theobald** had made good his claim to criticise Pope's "Shakespeare," by producing, in 1733, his own *Edition of Shakespeare,* in seven volumes. The literary controversy had brought Shakespeare into notice. Pope had replied to Theobald's strictures in a second edition of his own "Shake-

speare," in 1728; but Theobald's edition, in 1733, destroyed Pope's, and 13,000 copies of it were sold.  **Colley Cibber,** hero of the "Dunciad" in its second form, and then more than seventy years old, had, in an *Apology for his Life,* published in 1740, referred to Pope's hostility, of which the source lay deeper than he understood (§ 9).  He took his place in the "New Dunciad" good-humouredly, published *A Letter from Mr. Cibber to Mr. Pope Inquiring into the Motives that might Induce him in his Satirical Works to be so Frequently Fond of Mr. Cibber's Name;* and then *Another Occasional Letter from Mr. Cibber to Mr. Pope, wherein the New Hero's Preferment to his Throne in the "Dunciad" seems not to be Accepted, and the Author of that Poem his Rightful Claim to it is Asserted; with an Expostulatory Address to the Rev. Mr. W. W——n, Author of the New Preface, and Adviser in the Curious Improvements in that Satire.*  The Rev. Mr. W. W——n was **William Warburton,** who joined a commentary to the edition of Pope's "Essay on Man" and "Essay on Criticism," published in 1743. **Pope** died on the 30th day of May, 1744.

**Colley Cibber** had given up acting, but occasionally played fops and feeble old men for £50 a night.  In 1745 he played, at the age of seventy-five, Pandulph, in his own version of Shakespeare's "King John," as "Papal Tyranny."  He died in 1757.

24. **William Warburton,** born in 1698, son of the town clerk at Newark-upon-Trent, was educated at the grammar school there, and then articled to an attorney, with whom he served five years.  In 1723 he took deacon's orders, and published *Miscellaneous Translations, in Prose and Verse, from Roman Authors,* with a Latin dedication to Sir Robert Sutton, who gave him a small Nottinghamshire vicarage in 1726.  He then came to London with a few introductions, one to Theobald, whom he helped a little in his Shakespeare.  In 1727 he dedicated to Sir Robert Sutton, whose wife was the Countess of Sunderland, *A Critical and Philosophical Inquiry into the Causes of Prodigies and Miracles, as related by Historians, with an Essay towards Restoring a Method and Purity in History.* Sir Robert caused Warburton to be put on George II.'s list of Masters of Arts, created when he visited Cambridge in 1728; and procured for him the better living of Barnet Broughton, in Lincolnshire, where Warburton lived some years with his mother and sisters.  In 1736 he produced a book on the

*Alliance between Church and State,* which went through four
editions in his lifetime; and in 1738, *The Divine Legation of
Moses,* proved from absence of reference to a future state. This
led to controversy, and was followed by a *Vindication.* In the
same year, 1738, Warburton was made Chaplain to the Prince
of Wales.   When M. de Crousaz, Professor of Philosophy
and Mathematics in the University of Lausanne, attacked the
" Essay on Man," Warburton defended Pope in six letters,
published together in 1739, followed by a seventh in 1740.
This established the friendship between Pope and Warburton.
In 1741 Pope introduced his friend to Ralph Allen, at Prior
Park, near Bath.   Warburton afterwards added a commentary
to Pope's " Essay on Man " and " Essay on Criticism," and was
left, in 1744, Pope's literary executor.   In the following year he
married Ralph Allen's niece and heiress, Miss Gertrude Tucker,
and thenceforth lived chiefly at Prior Park, which became his
own when Allen died, in 1764.   In 1747 Warburton followed
Theobald in the series of *Editions of Shakespeare.*   Pope's
edition, in 1725, and Theobald's, in 1733, had been followed, in
1744, by the edition of **Sir Thomas Hanmer,** thirty years
Member, and at last Speaker of the House of Commons.   Now
came that of **Warburton,** in 1747, with much rash and dog-
matic change, but not a few happy suggestions.   These were
the editions preceding that of Samuel Johnson, in 1765, all
from Pope's downward resting their claim to credit on con-
jectural dealing with the text, but all helping to fix attention on
the greatest of all poets.   Warburton became King's Chaplain
in 1754; got, in 1755, the Lambeth degree of D.D. from Archbishop Herring; in 1757 became Dean of Bristol, and in 1759
Bishop of Gloucester.   He died in 1779, aged eighty-one.   Two
years afterwards his wife married again, and gave Prior Park to
her late husband's chaplain.

25. **James Thomson,** who had published his " Winter "
in 1726, and " Summer " in 1727 (§ 15), added *Spring* in 1728.
He failed on the stage in 1729, with his first tragedy, *Sophonisba,*
though it went through four editions in 1730, when his *Seasons*
first appeared in a complete edition, with *Autumn* and the closing
*Hymn* of praise from all the works of Nature :—

> " These as they change, Almighty Father, these
> Are but the varied God.   The rolling year
> Is full of Thee."

In 1730 and 1731 Thomson travelled in France and Italy

with a young gentleman, Charles Richard Talbot, who soon afterwards died, and to whose memory he inscribed his poem on *Liberty*. Part I. of " Liberty " the poet published in December, 1734, when his pupil's father had become Lord Chancellor, and gave Thomson the office of Secretary of Briefs in the Court of Chancery. Parts II. and III. appeared in 1735, Parts IV. and V. in 1736. The poem deserved, perhaps, more credit than it received, but " Liberty" was no fresh topic, while a real sense of the charm of natural objects, almost gone out of our literature, had been revived in *The Seasons*. Lord Chancellor Talbot's death, in 1737, caused Thomson to write a poem honouring his memory. He now lost his office as Secretary of Briefs. In 1738 another play of Thomson's, *Agamemnon*, was acted without success. In 1739 the acting of his play of *Edward and Eleonora* was prohibited, because it took part, in marked political allusions, with the Prince of Wales against the king. His love of liberty caused Thomson to write a preface, in 1740, to a new edition of Milton's " Areopagitica ; " he wrote also in that year, with Mallet, the masque of *Alfred*, which contains the now national song of *Rule Britannia*. In 1744 Thomson received the sinecure office of Surveyor-General of the Leeward Islands, worth £300 a year. In 1745 his most successful play, *Tancred and Sigismunda*, was acted at Drury Lane. In 1747 he visited Shenstone at the Leasowes, and afterwards worked at a poem begun years before, *The Castle of Indolence*, in Spenser's manner. Shenstone had then written his " School-mistress," in Spenserian stanza. **Gilbert West**, who was made LL.D. of Oxford in 1748, and who died in 1756, published in 1749 a translation of *The Odes of Pindar*, and wrote *Imitations of Spenser*. **John Armstrong** (b. 1709, d. 1779), a physician, published in 1744 a poem on *The Art of Preserving Health*, and contributed to Thomson's " Castle of Indolence " four stanzas at the close of Canto I, describing the diseases indolence has caused.

26. **William Shenstone** (b. 1714, d. 1763) was the eldest son of a gentleman farmer, who owned an estate worth about £300 a year, called the Leasowes, near Hales Owen, in a bit of Shropshire set in Worcestershire. He was educated as a commoner at Pembroke College, Oxford ; and after his fathers death ceased to farm the small property as before, but wasted its resources in the work of turning it into ornamental ground. He suffered house and land to go to ruin, that he might make

beautiful gardens, with grottos, temples, and inscriptions, according to the invalid taste of his day. Shenstone left Leasowes to be sold after his death for payment of the debts incurred in beautifying it. His love of natural beauty was blended, far more than in Thomson, with the conventional life of his time; but he wrote pleasant verse, often with tender simplicity, and, in his *Essays on Men, Manners, and Things*, pithy prose. Perhaps the origin of his inactive life is told by his *Pastoral Ballad in Four Parts*, written in 1743. The four parts are four love-poems, entitled " Absence," " Hope," " Solicitude," " Despair." Of the fickle fair one, in the strain of " Hope," he wrote :

> " One would think she might like to retire
> To the bow'r I have labour'd to rear ;
> Not a shrub that I heard her admire,
> But I hasted and planted it there."

And in the strain of " Disappointment :"

> " Yet time may diminish the pain ;
> The flow'r, and the shrub, and the tree,
> Which I reared for her pleasure in vain,
> In time may have comfort for me.
>     *     *     *     *
> " O ye woods, spread your branches apace ;
> To your deepest recesses I fly !
> I would hide with the beasts of the chase,
> I would vanish from every eye."

Perhaps this was not an empty sentiment. But in a healthy man there is no plea that can make inactivity respectable. Shenstone's *Schoolmistress* was first published in its complete form in 1742, developed from some early verse of his. It sketches a village schoolmistress in thirty or forty Spenserian stanzas, with kindly humour and poetic feeling, and is only bad as an imitation of Spenser. In that respect it is feeble, with mock antique phrases, and eighteenth century affectations of rusticity.

27. But Shakespeare was coming to his own ; the popularity of " The Schoolmistress " indicated a returning relish for Spenser ; and when, in 1748, **Thomson's** *Castle of Indolence* appeared, begun fifteen years before as satire on the poet's own indolence, and since developed with much care, there was evidence of a rich fancy at work, playfully imitating an old master poet, with a true sense of his worth. The *Castle of Indolence* was the last work published by Thomson. It appeared in May, and the poet died on the 27th of August, 1748.

28. **John Dyer** (§ 16) became Rector of Belchford, and afterwards of Kerkby, in Lincolnshire ; then Sir John Heathcote gave him the rectory of Coningsby in the same county; and there, in 1757, he died of consumption. His *Ruins of Rome*, published in 1740, was a poem suggested by his wanderings and sketches in Rome as an artist. *The Fleece*, in four books, published in the year of his death, was the longest of Dyer's three poems. Beginning with a sketch of sheep upon the English downs, he described, in his four books, (1) the shepherd's craft, and the sheepshearing ; (2) passed to the wool, its qualities and treatment, and the trade created by it for the well-being of men ; (3) spinning and weaving, roads and rivers by which merchandise is conveyed about our own country ; (4) export and far trade with the world. Dyer's *Fleece* is an elevation of the Georgic to the praise of commerce, and shows how the contemplative mind of a good natural poet can find a soul of things in the wool-pack. " Trade," Dyer sang,

> " Trade to the good physician gives his balms ;
> Gives cheering cordials to the afflicted heart ;
> Gives to the wealthy delicacies high ;
> Gives to the curious works of nature rare.
> And when the priest displays, in just discourse,
> Him, the all-wise Creator, and declares
> His presence, pow'r, and goodness unconfin'd,
> 'Tis trade, attentive voyager, who fills
> His lips with argument. To censure Trade,
> Or hold her busy people in contempt,
> Let none presume."

29. **Samuel Richardson** was born in 1689, in Derbyshire, one of the nine children of a joiner who had been in business in London, and who could afford him only a common school education. As a boy he liked letter-writing, and wrote their love-letters for three damsels of his village. In 1706 he was apprenticed to a printer in London, served seven years, and corresponded with a gentleman of fortune who "was a master of the epistolary style." When out of his time, he worked five or six years as compositor and corrector of the press, married his late master's daughter, and set up for himself in a court in Fleet Street. Richardson's first wife died in 1731, and he married afterwards the sister of a bookseller at Bath. By his first wife he had five boys and a girl, and by his second, five girls and a boy. He lost all his sons and two of his daughters ; the remaining four daughters had much work in transcribing his

letters. By ability and steady industry Richardson advanced in life, removed to Salisbury Court, and was employed by booksellers not only to print but also to make indexes and write prefaces and dedications. Two booksellers, Mr. Rivington and Mr. Osborne, asked the good printer to write for them a volume of " Familiar Letters," in a common style, on such subjects as might be of use to those country readers who were unable to indite for themselves. Then writes Richardson, " ' Will it be any harm,' said I, ' in a piece you want to be written so low, if we should instruct them how they should think and act in common cases, as well as indite ?' They were the more urgent with me to begin the little volume for this hint. I set about it, and in the progress of it writing two or three letters to instruct handsome girls who were obliged to go out to service, as we phrase it, how to avoid the snares that might be laid against their virtue," a story occurred to him that he had heard from a friend many years before. He thought that this, if told by letters, "in an easy and natural manner, suitably to the simplicity of it, might possibly introduce a new species of writing that might possibly turn young people into a course of reading different from the pomp and parade of romance-writing; and dismissing the improbable and marvellous, with which novels generally abound, might tend to promote the cause of religion and virtue." The book, as first complete in two volumes, was written in two months, from November 10th, 1739, to January 10th, 1740, published at once, received with great applause, and immediately translated into French and Dutch. Richardson, as well as he could, brought simple nature into the novel, from which it had been altogether banished (ch. x. § 1), and led strong reaction against the faith in princes and princesses as the only true heroes and heroines. I will take, he said to himself, a poor servant girl, make her the namesake of one of the choicest of romance princesses—the Pamela of Sidney's " Arcadia"—set my Pamela corresponding artlessly with her low-born father and mother, Goodman Andrews and his wife, and make you feel that human sympathies are broader than conventional distinctions. It was another step from the conventional towards that clear light of nature which for most writers was still lost in the cloud of French classicism. But as Allan Ramsay must needs give a titled father to his Gentle Shepherd, and as Thomson's young Lavinia could not make Palemon happy without turning out to be the daughter of his noble friend Acasto,

"Whose open stores,
Though vast, were little to his ample heart;"

so in Pamela the conventional homage to rank was still conspicuous. Pamela, left by the death of her mistress subject to a
young master who was a worthless libertine, resisted infamous
practices upon her, in the hope that she might thus become his
wife; and the second title of Richardson's book, *Pamela; or,
Virtue Rewarded,* means that in the end she did, with pious
gratitude, marry the scoundrel. As for Goodman Andrews, when
he heard the glad tidings, his "heart was full; and he said, with
his hands folded and lifted up, ' Pray, sir, let me go—let me go to
my dear wife, and tell her all these blessed things while my breath
holds; for it is ready to burst with joy.'" The success of the
book caused Richardson to write two more volumes, which were
superfluous, the work having been completed as first published.

Richardson's "Pamela" struck new life into literature, not
only by its bold and direct challenge to the romance-writing
hitherto in fashion, by what was new and right in its plan, but
also by what was wrong in its plan; for the flaw in its morality
—obscured by the prevalence of the low social tone it represented—was obvious to Henry Fielding, and in ridicule of this
he began to write his "Joseph Andrews." He would pair the
virtuous serving-maid with a virtuous serving-man. Before he
had gone far he felt his strength, and produced not a mere
caricature, but a true novel. Thus Fielding, our greatest
novelist, received his impulse from Richardson.

30. **Henry Fielding** was born on the 22nd of April, 1707,
at Sharpham Park, near Glastonbury, Somersetshire, son of a
Lieutenant-General Fielding, who was youngest son of the
youngest son of a George Fielding, Earl of Desmond, who was
second son of the first Earl of Denbigh. Young Henry Fielding
was educated at Eton and at the University of Leyden, where
he was to study civil law, and did study, until the supplies from
home failed. His father lived with careless extravagance, had
married again, and was adding a young family to the five or six
children of his first wife. At twenty Henry Fielding had to
leave Leyden and live by his wits, with a nominal allowance
from his father of £200 a year. At twenty-one (in 1728) he
wrote his first comedy, *Love in Several Masques;* then followed
*The Temple Beau* and *The Author's Farce,* in January and
March, 1730; in 1731, *The Coffee-House Politician* and *Tom
Thumb.* This, published as *Tragedy of Tragedies; or, the Life*

*and Death of Tom Thumb the Great, with the Annotations of Scriblerus Secundus,* was a burlesque on the conventional fine writing of the stage, having an aim like that of Buckingham's "Rehearsal" (ch. x. § 17), and was richly illustrated with ironical notes, showing the passages burlesqued. Another burlesque on stilted tragedy, "Chrononhotonthologos," was produced in 1734, by Harry Carey, a musician, who, says Dibdin, "led a life free from reproach, and hanged himself October 4th, 1743." Among the dramatic pieces of Fielding were, in 1732, *The Covent Garden Tragedy,* a jest on Ambrose Philips's version of "Andromaque" as "The Distrest Mother," also versions from Molière of "Le Medecin malgré Lui" and "L'Avare ;" and, in 1734, *Don Quixote in England.* During his first nine years in London, Fielding was among the players at Bartholomew Fair, and kept a booth in the George Inn Yard, usually with John Hippesley. The fair was a great institution then, and the theatres closed that the players might appear in it. In 1735 Fielding married a Miss Craddock, one of three sisters who were beauties of Salisbury. The lady had £1,500, and he had from his mother a small country house at East Stour, in Dorsetshire. Fielding had married for love. He would live at East Stour and feel the peace of a country life. But country life, with open hospitality, horses, coach, and livery servants, soon made an end of £1,500. Fielding and his wife then came to lodgings in London with a single maidservant, and Fielding worked for bread. He formed, in 1736, a "Great Mogul's Company of Comedians," and produced with great success *Pasquin : a Dramatic Satire on the Times,* its plan a mock rehearsal of two plays. In 1737 he continued his free dramatic criticism upon life and politics with a piece called *The Historical Register for* 1736, Sir Robert Walpole figuring in the piece as "Quidam." The result of this was the passing, in June, 1737, of the Act which forbade any play to be represented before it had obtained the licence of the Lord Chamberlain. The Licensing Act broke up the Great Mogul's Company, and in November Fielding entered himself as a student of the Middle Temple. To a paper of periodical essays, called the *Champion,* Fielding became an active contributor from November, 1739, to June, 1740, creating representatives of the chief subjects of discussion in a Vinegar Family. In June, 1740, he was called to the bar, and began practice on the Western Circuit. In June 1741, his father died, but there was nothing to inherit. In

February, 1742, Fielding published the novel suggested by Richardson's " Pamela," *The Adventures of Joseph Andrews and of his friend Mr. Abraham Adams.* In Mr. Abraham Adams, Fielding drew, with exquisite humour and a healthy sense of what is pure and true, a scholar and a Christian, who had external oddities, as absence of mind, which might bring him into ridiculous situations, but whom nothing could lower in our respect, simply by reason of his essential purity and truth. Parson Adams was a clergyman dignified with the best graces of his office, and in Parson Trulliber his opposite was shown. Through Parson Adams, Fielding, in his first novel, spoke out of the depths of his own heart not seldom, and it is pleasant to find him in a first novel, that, under genial disguise of Abraham Adams, expresses so much of his own sense of religion, noticing the character of Richard Steele's work, when he makes Parson Adams, in talking of the theatre, say, " I never heard of any plays fit for a Christian to read but ' Cato ' and ' The Conscious Lovers ;' and, I must own, in the latter there are some things almost solemn enough for a sermon." Fielding, who was not all himself as an eighteenth century dramatist, quitted the stage in 1743, after the not unmerited failure of his last comedy, *The Wedding Day.* In the same year he published three volumes of *Miscellanies.* These contain some verse, a few essays—on " Conversation," on " Knowledge of the Characters of Men," on " Nothing,"—and two works of mark, *A Journey from this World to the Next,* and the *History of the Life of the Late Mr. Jonathan Wild the Great,* a thieftaker who came to be hanged. Fielding's " Jonathan Wild " was written with masterly irony, as " an exposition of the motives which actuate the unprincipled great in every walk and sphere of life, and which are common alike to the thief or murderer on the small scale, and to the mighty villain and reckless conqueror who invades the rights or destroys the liberties of nations." At this time Fielding lost the wife to whom he was devotedly attached. He had lost a child but a few months before, and was himself suffering much from gout. He wrote a preface for his sister, **Sarah Fielding,** to her clever novel, *The Adventures of David Simple ; Containing an Account of his Travels through the Cities of London and Westminster, in the Search of a Real Friend,* published in 1744. She published another, *The History of Ophelia,* in 1760. **Henry Fielding** and his sister Sarah were much together after his wife's death.

On the 5th November, 1745, Fielding began a paper, the *True Patriot*, to oppose the Jacobitism stirred into activity by the Rebellion of that year. After the final ruin of the Stuart cause at the battle of Culloden, in April, 1746, among eight victims who suffered the capital penalties of high treason was a young Jacobite officer, James Dawson, the day of whose expected pardon was to have been his wedding day. The young lady who loved him could not be dissuaded from witnessing his execution ; and, says a letter of the time, " she got near enough to see the fire kindled which was to consume that heart which she knew was so much devoted to her, and all the other dreadful preparations for his fate, without being guilty of any of those extravagances her friends had apprehended. But when all was over, and that she found he was no more, she drew her head back into the coach, and crying out, ' My dear, I follow thee—I follow thee ! Sweet Jesus, receive both our souls together !' fell on the neck of her companion, and expired the very moment she was speaking." The incident, as thus described, was made by Shenstone (§ 26) the subject of a little ballad, *Jemmy Dawson*, which endeavoured to reproduce its simple pathos. Fielding about this time defied conventional opinion by taking for second wife the Mary Mac Daniel who had been his first wife's one faithful servant, and had been the nurse of his children ; with whom, therefore, he could still live in memories of her, and whom his children from their birth had learned to love. In this, if he was unwise, at least he acted upon principles above the sense of many who laughed at him.

The work of Fielding's *True Patriot* changed only its form when, in December, 1747, he started the "*Jacobite Journal;* by John Trott-plaid, Esq.," to throw cold water of jest and satire upon the yet smouldering embers of rebellion. This paper appeared every Saturday until November, 1748, and about that time, by the good offices of his friend, George Lyttelton, then Lord of the Treasury, Fielding was made a justice of the peace for Middlesex and Westminster. In those days such an office had been brought into contempt by men like Justice Thrasher, in his "Amelia," who had drawn dishonourable profit out of it. Henry Fielding, by taking the highest view of his duty, " reduced," as he says, " an income of about £500 a year of the dirtiest money upon earth to little more than £300, a considerable portion of which remained with my clerk ; and, indeed "
—(observe the kindliness of what follows)—" if the whole had

done so, as it ought, he would be but ill-paid for sitting sixteen in the twenty-four in the most unwholesome as well as nauseous air in the universe, and which hath in his case corrupted a good constitution without contaminating his morals."

31. In 1748 **Samuel Richardson** took his place in literature by publishing, when his age was fifty-nine, the second of his three novels, *Clarissa Harlowe*, in eight volumes, with an interval of several months before the publication of the second half. Here, as always, Richardson told his story in the form of correspondence. Clarissa Harlowe, a young lady of birth and fortune, pressed by her family to marry against her inclination, left home, and threw herself on the generosity of her lover, Sir Robert Lovelace, an attractive libertine. He persecuted her, and treacherously wronged her to the uttermost ; she refused then his offer of marriage, and died broken-hearted. Lovelace left England, not reformed, and was killed in a duel by one of Clarissa's relations, Colonel Morden. Clarissa's correspondent was Miss Anne Howe, a widow's lively daughter, with a formal but estimable suitor, Mr. Hickman. Lovelace had for his correspondent a friend, Mr. John Belford ; this party of four answering the place of hero and he-friend, heroine and she-friend in the mock classical French tragedies. The moral of the piece was that the most unhappy home is shelter for a young girl safer than she may succeed in finding by quitting it to trust herself among the snares of life. The book is full of improbability ; it contains, like "Pamela," scenes unfit to be read by the young, and no page of it is like the work of a man of genius in texture of thought or vigour of expression. Yet the whole effect produced is equal to that of a work of high genius. If Richardson's mind was not large, his story filled it. His nature, even with all its little pomps and vanities, was absorbed in his work ; the ladies about him, who, as the least critical of his admirers, were his chosen friends, fed him with sweet solicitudes and enthusiasms about the persons of his story ; his fictitious characters and situations lived and were real for him ; and he became the great example, in our literature, of the might that comes of giving all one's powers—even if they be not great powers—to whatever one has to do. By thoroughly believing in his work, and giving all his mind to it, Samuel Richardson, as novelist, secured the full attention of his readers, and sometimes even by importunity of tediousness, by the drop after drop that in time hollows the stone, compelled his readers

to see as he saw, feel as he felt, and not seldom to weep where he wept—and he wept much himself—over the sorrows of Clarissa.

32. The first novel of **Tobias Smollett** appeared in the same year as Richardson's "Clarissa," and the year before "Tom Jones." Smollett, born in 1721, in the parish of Cardross, was left dependent on his grandfather, Sir James Smollett, of Bonhill, sent to school at Dumbarton, where he wrote satirical verse, and a poem on Wallace, went from Dumbarton to Glasgow, where he studied medicine and was apprenticed to a surgeon, the Potion of his first novel. He came to London with a tragedy, "The Regicide," written before he was eighteen It was rejected by managers, but ten years afterwards published with a preface. In 1741, when Pamela was a new book, Smollett, aged twenty, was surgeon's mate on board a ship of the line, and sailed in the expedition to Carthagena. This experience of life was also used as material for his first novel. He quitted the service when in the West Indies, lived some time in Jamaica, and met the lady whom he afterwards married. He was back in London in 1746, and then published anonymously *The Tears of Scotland*, expressing from his heart, though no Jacobite, his just indignation at the cruelties that disgraced the suppression of the Rebellion of 1745; also *Advice*, a satire which gave offence. He wrote "Alceste," an opera, for Covent Garden, quarrelled with the manager, published in 1747 *Reproof*, a sequel to "Advice," married, and produced in 1748, when his age was twenty-seven, his first novel, *Roderick Random*. Richardson, who in the same year published "Clarissa," was eighteen years older than Fielding, and thirty-two years older than Smollett. "Roderick Random," written in the form of autobiography, was a bright story, rich in mirth and a quick sense of outside character, that painted life as Smollett had seen it, blending his own experiences with his fiction. It became immediately popular, and helped much in establishing the new form of fiction in which writers dealt immediately with the life of their own time, and the experience in it of common men and women.

33. **Henry Fielding** did not laugh at Richardson's "Clarissa," but he also had been long at work on a great novel, and when his age was forty-two, in 1749, the year after "Clarissa" and "Roderick Random," published his *Tom Jones*. No critic has over-praised the skilful construction of the story of "Tom Jones;" but the durability of the work depends on something

even of more moment than its construction—upon the imperishable character of its material, and on the security with which its foundations are laid, deep in the true hearts of Englishmen. Fielding's first novel was provoked by an affectation, and it was prefaced with a distinct explanation of his own "idea of romance." In the first pages of his first novel he taught that "the only source of the true ridiculous is affectation." His jest was against insincerity in all its lighter forms ; his power was against untruth. In all his novels, and in *Tom Jones* most conspicuously, a generous and penetrating mind, familiar with the ways of men, dealt mercifully with all honest infirmities, sympathised with human goodness, and reserved its laughter, or its scorn, only for what was insincere. In *Tom Jones* a work was planned upon the ample scale to which readers had become accustomed. There was room for a wide view of life. The scene was divided fairly between country and town. The story was built out of the eternal truths of human nature, and was exquisitely polished on its surface with a delicate and genial humour that suggested rather than preached censure on the follies of society in England, not unmixed with the directest Christian condemnation against crime. The very soul of the book enters into the construction of *Tom Jones*. The picture of a good man, coloured by Fielding with some of the warmth of living friendship for Ralph Allen of Bath (§ 23), is presented at once in Squire Allworthy ; and there is a deep seriousness in the manner of presenting him, on a May morning, walking upon the terrace before his mansion, with a wide prospect around him, planning a generous action, when " in the full blaze of his majesty up rose the sun, than which one object alone in this lower creation could be more glorious, and that Mr. Allworthy himself presented—a human being replete with benevolence, meditating in what manner he might render himself most acceptable to his Creator, by doing most good to His creatures." The two boys bred by Allworthy, Tom Jones and Blifil, about whom the whole story revolves, are as the two poles of Fielding's mimic world. One of them is everybody's friend but his own ; the other nobody's friend but his own. One is possessed of natural goodness, with all generous impulses, but with instincts, as we are once or twice distinctly reminded, wanting the control of prudence and religion. He lies open to frequent heavy blame, and yet more frequent misconstruction ; yet we have faith in him because he is true, his faults are open,

**2 B**

his affections warm. We know that time and love will make a noble man of him. The other conceals treachery under a show of righteousness and justice. His fair outside of religion and morality, the readiness with which he gives an honest colouring to all appearances, are represented wholly without caricature. His ill deeds are secret, his affections cold, and he is base to us by reason of his falsehood. Appreciation is not only due to the sterling English in which this book is written, and the keen but generous insight into human character that animates every page, but also to its brave morality. Scenes of incontinence, which the corrupt manners of his age permitted Fielding to include among his pictures of the life about him, were not presented as jests by their author. Fielding differs in this, as in many things, essentially from Smollett, that in his novels he has never used an unclean image for its own sake as provocative of mirth in ruder minds. In Fielding's page evil is evil. In " Tom Jones," Allworthy delivers no mock exhortations ; whenever Jones has gone astray, the purity of Sophia follows next upon the scene, a higher happiness is lost, and his true love is removed farther from his reach. At last the youth is made to assent to Sophia, when she replies, very gravely, upon his pleading of the grossness of his sex, the delicacy of hers, and the absence of love in amour : " I will never marry a man who shall not learn refinement enough to be as incapable as I am myself of making such a distinction."

The episodes of the book are as true limbs of it. It is not merely variety that they supply. It is completeness. It is true that the Man of the Hill's story is not a part of the direct mechanism of the plot ; but it is equally true that it is a vital part of the whole epic history. Only by episode could there have been interpolated between Jones's generous and Blifil's ungenerous principle of intercourse with other men, the picture of one who has wholly withdrawn himself from human intercourse, and dares to solve the question of life's duties by looking from afar with scorn upon his fellows.

It is a minor excellence that this part of the work has been contrived also to supply to the large study of English life those chapters, excluded from the main action of the tale by the peculiar education and the characters of Jones and Blifil, which paint the follies of youth at the University and the life of the gambler. Partridge once breaks upon the narrative of the Man of the Hill with a characteristic story of his own, in which

Fielding commands wise reflection on the undefended state of criminals tried for their lives.

In June, 1749, Henry Fielding, who had been elected by the Middlesex magistrates their Chairman of the Sessions, delivered a *Charge to the Grand Jury* touching seriously upon many faults in the condition of society; and in January, 1751, he published *An Inquiry into the Causes of the late Increase of Robbers, &c.; with some Proposals for Remedying the Growing Evil*, in which he urged the checking of intemperance, and denounced the new vice of gin-drinking. This led to an Act of Parliament that placed restrictions on the sale of spirits. It was also in the year 1751 that Fielding, aged forty-four, published his *Amelia*. For "Tom Jones" the publisher had paid £100 beyond the stipulated price of £600. For *Amelia* he paid £1,000. Thus, by the middle of the eighteenth century, Richardson and Fielding, with Smollett for new ally, had destroyed the faith in royal Arcadians, had carried a large body of the people on from reading of short papers, to the reading of substantial works of fiction that dealt with the life they knew and cared for, and had made the novel of real life a great recognized power. French classicism was decaying, and there was no influence above that of the main body of the people influencing the form of our best literature. Fielding's *Amelia*, dedicated to his kind friend Ralph Allen, of Bath (§ 22), has for its theme the beauty of true womanhood. He constantly identified his first wife with Amelia, while condemning often his own failings in the character of her husband, Mr. Booth. Fielding dealt also in his novel with those evils of society against which he had been contending, and brought pathos and sharp satire in his jail scenes against what were in his day the iniquities of criminal law.

On the 4th of January, 1752, Fielding began *The Covent Garden Journal; by Sir Alexander Drawcansir, Knight, Censor of Great Britain*, which lasted until the end of the year. His health was still failing, but he stayed in London to complete the breaking up of an organised gang of street ruffians; took, morning and evening, half a pint of the tar-water recommended by Bishop Berkeley's "Siris" in 1744; and, when hope of life was gone, left England with his wife and eldest daughter for Lisbon. The account of his *Voyage to Lisbon* was Fielding's last work. He arrived in the middle of August, and died, aged forty-eight, on the 8th of the following October, 1754.

34. **Samuel Richardson** published his third and last novel,
*Sir Charles Grandison*, a year before the death of Fielding.
He had accused his lady correspondents of liking Lovelace too
well. They replied that he had given them nobody else to like.
Thereupon he resolved to give them his ideal of a good man in
Sir Charles Grandison, well-born, rich, accomplished, travelled,
and always right, in Richardson's view, though he has two
heroines in love with him, and is in love with each—the one
who did not marry him went mad—and though he fought
duels. Richardson could not rise like Steele above convention
(§ 5); but as he knew duelling to be wrong, and reasoned
against it in his novel, he compromised by making Sir Charles
so skilful a swordsman that he could disarm without murdering
an antagonist. Richardson's three novels painted life respec-
tively in the lower, middle, and higher classes of society. *Sir
Charles Grandison* was published in 1753. Richardson, meanwhile, throve in business. His printing-offices and warehouses
at Salisbury Court covered the site of eight houses which he
had pulled down. In 1755 he removed from his country house
at North End, Hammersmith, to a house at Parson's Green. In
1760 he bought half the patent of Law Printer to the King; and
in July, 1761, the first year of the reign of George III., he died,
at the age of seventy-two.

35. **Tobias Smollett** graduated as physician in 1750, at
Marischal College, Aberdeen, but was a doctor with few patients.
In the summer of 1750 he visited Paris, and probably wrote there
his *Peregrine Pickle*, published in 1751. Its brightness, and
the hearty fun of many of its chapters, like that (ch. xliv.) which
describes an entertainment in the manner of the ancients, made
the book widely popular and Smollett famous. The pompous
gentleman caricatured by Smollett, as the giver of this banquet
was **Mark Akenside** (b. 1721, d. 1770), son of a butcher at
Newcastle-on-Tyne. He was sent to the Edinburgh University, with aid of a fund for the purpose, to be educated as a
Dissenting minister; but he made medicine his study, was proud
of his oratory in the debates of the Medical Society, and aspired
to a seat in Parliament. After three years at Edinburgh
Akenside went to Leyden, where he stayed another three years,
took his degree as M.D., and found a friend in a student of
law, Mr. Dyson, who came home with him. *The Pleasures of
Imagination*, in its first form, appeared in 1744, when Akenside's
age was twenty-three. Its subject was suggested by Addison's

Essays on Imagination, in the *Spectator.* Akenside wrote odes also, and worked at the elaboration of his chief poem throughout his life, publishing the enlargement of his First Book in 1757, and of the Second in 1765 ; the enlargement of Book III., with an unfinished fragment of Book IV., appeared after his death. Akenside had less feeling for the sense of poetry than for its sound. His style was artificial. In life he affected a false dignity, and his pompous manner laid him open to Smollett's ridicule. He was ashamed of a lameness caused in childhood by the fall of a cleaver in his father's shop. He never married, and was greatly indebted to the liberality of Mr. Dyson for income while he was endeavouring to make a practice.

36. **Smollett's** *Peregrine Pickle* was followed, in 1752, by a study of depravity in an adventurer chosen from the purlieus of treachery and fraud, the *Adventures of Ferdinand Count Fathom.* In 1755 he published a free *Translation of Don Quixote*, then visited his mother and friends in Scotland, and when he came back, accepted the invitation of booksellers to edit the *Critical Review*, set up in 1756, to oppose the Whig *Monthly Review*, that had been started in 1749. Smollett was genial, but irritable, and now submitted himself to vexation by the irritable race of the small authors. At this time Smollett began *A Complete History of England, deduced from the Descent of Julius Cæsar to the Treaty of Aix-la-Chapelle*, 1741, *containing the Transactions of One Thousand Eight Hundred and Three Years.* He is said to have written it in fourteen months. It was published in four volumes in 1758, and reprinted next year in numbers, extending to eleven volumes, with a weekly sale of 12,000. For a paragraph in the "Critical Review," Smollett was fined £100 and imprisoned for three months, at the suit of Admiral Knowles, and worked in prison at *The Adventures of Sir Lancelot Greaves*, an imitation of Cervantes, published in "The British Magazine" in 1760 and 1761. Smollett then worked at the *Continuation of the History of England* to 1765, published in 1769, in two volumes 4to. After the loss of his only child, Smollett had travelled for health, and in 1766 he published his *Travels through France and Italy.* In 1769 appeared his *Adventures of an Atom*, dealing, under Japanese names, with English politics, from 1754 to 1768. In 1770 he went to Italy with broken health, and while there published, only a few months before his death, his last, and perhaps his best novel,

*The Expedition of Humphrey Clinker.* Smollett died, at the age of fifty, near Leghorn, in October, 1771.

37. **George Lyttelton,** born in 1709, at Hagley, Worcestershire, friend to Fielding and to some of the best poets of his time, was educated at Eton and Oxford, and became secretary to Frederick Prince of Wales, when he was in opposition to George II. He became a Lord of the Treasury after Sir Robert Walpole's resignation, and was Chancellor of the Exchequer in 1757, when he resigned and took a peerage. He printed verses, also *Letters from a Persian in England to his Friend at Ispahan,* in 1735 ; *Dialogues of the Dead;* and in 1767, *The History of the Life of King Henry the Second and of the Age in which he Lived,* a book upon which he had been at work for thirty years. He died in 1773.

38. **George Lillo** (b. 1693, d. 1739), a London jeweller, had a turn for writing plays. He was a Dissenter, who, said Fielding, had the spirit of an old Roman joined to the innocence of a primitive Christian. There was more of moral purpose than of genius in his tragedies. One of them, " George Barnwell," produced in 1731, for a long time kept the stage. Another citizen, **Edward Moore,** bred as a linendraper, had an earnest purpose in his three plays, of which one, *The Foundling,* produced in 1748, was condemned for its resemblance to Steele's " Conscious Lovers;" and the tragedy of, *The Gamester* had imperfect success, because of the righteous severity with which it attacked a fashionable vice of the day. **David Mallet** (§ 15), besides writing the tragedies of *Eurydice,* in 1731, and *Mustapha,* in 1739, and working with Thomson, in 1740, at the masque of *Alfred,* published also, in 1740, the *Life of Lord Bacon,* in which, as Warburton says, he forgot that Bacon was a philosopher. Among Mallet's poems is the ballad of *William and Margaret,* a sentimental double to the old ballad of " Sweet William's Ghost," which had been given by Allan Ramsay in his " Tea-table Miscellany." In the original ballad the tormented ghost of an unworthy Sweet William visits Marjorie, and shows her at his grave that which makes her give back to him the plight of troth he suffers for having broken.

> " And she took up her white, white hands,
>     And struck him on the breast,
>   Saying, ' Have here again thy faith and troth,
>     And I wish your soul good rest.' "

In Mallet's ballad, Margaret, killed by William's faithlessness,

comes to the living William and draws him to her grave, where
"thrice he called on Margaret's name, and thrice he wept full
sore; then laid his cheek to her cold grave, and word spoke
never more." Mallet said that th : ballad was suggested to him
by lines in Fletcher's " Knight of the Burning Pestle :"

> When it was grown to dark midnight,
> And all were fast asleep,
> In came Margaret's grimly ghost
> And stood at William's feet."

The reviving taste for simple writing is indicated by this piece,
as by Shenstone's " Jemmy Dawson " (§ 30). **Vincent Bourne**
(b. about 1697, d. 1747), a sub-master of Westminster School,
who was the best Latin poet of his time, turned " William and
Margaret " into Latin, as *Thyrsis et Chloe.* Vincent Bourne's
Latin poems were collected in 1772. **William Whitehead**
(b. 1715, d. 1788), son of a baker at Cambridge, was educated
at Winchester School and Cambridge, became tutor to the son
of Lord Jersey, wrote poems and plays, prospered by the good-
will of the Jersey family, and, in 1757, succeeded Cibber as Poet
Laureate. **Paul Whitehead** (b. 1710, d. 1774), was of another
family, born in London, and apprenticed to a mercer before he
entered the Temple. He lived by his writings till he obtained
a place worth £800 a year. Among his verse was the *Gymnasiad*,
a mock heroic against the taste for boxing. **Richard Glover**
(b. 1712, d. 1785), son and partner of a London merchant trading
with Hamburg, published, at the age of twenty-five, in 1737, a
serious epic poem on *Leonidas.* It appealed to patriotic feeling,
and was very popular. In 1739 he produced another poem,
*London; or, the Progress of Commerce;* and the ballad of *Hosier's
Ghost,* to rouse national feeling against Spain. He was a leading
patriotic citizen; produced, in 1735, a tragedy, *Boadicea,* and
afterwards *Medea.* He entered Parliament at the beginning
of the reign of George III. **Christopher Pitt,** educated at
Winchester School and New College, Oxford, was Rector of
Pimpern, in Dorsetshire. He wrote some original verse, published in 1725 a *Translation of Vida's Art of Poetry,* and in
1740 a *Translation of the Æneid.* He died in 1748.

39. **Joseph Spence,** born in Northamptonshire, in 1698,
and educated at Winchester School and New College, Oxford,
published in 1727 an *Essay on Pope's Odyssey.* In 1728 he
became Professor of Poetry at Oxford; and, in 1742, Professor
of Modern History, and Rector of Great Horwood, in Bucking-

hamshire. In August, 1768, he was found accidentally drowned in his garden. Spence's chief original work was *Polymetis* (1747), an inquiry into the relations between Roman poets and remains of ancient art. But, as Professor of Poetry at Oxford, he expressed a rising sentiment of the time by introducing to the public, in 1730, **Stephen Duck** as "a poet from the barn, though not so great a man, as great a curiosity as a dictator from the plough." Stephen Duck, who began life as a thresher, had a turn for verse, which was developed in his early manhood by the reading of Milton, who inspired him with a deep enthusiasm. His chief pieces were drawn from his work and his religion, "The Thresher's Labour," and "The Shunamite." Spence's good offices obtained for Stephen Duck a pension of £30 from Queen Caroline, and afterwards, when he had prepared himself for holy orders, the living of Byfleet, in Surrey. Like his friend Spence, Stephen Duck died by drowning. He fell into religious melancholy, and committed suicide from a bridge near Reading, in 1756.

40. **Joseph Warton**, born in 1722, son of an Oxford professor of poetry, was educated at Winchester School and Oriel College, Oxford. He wrote verse; went to France, in 1751, as companion to the Duke of Bolton, and obtained from him the Rectory of Wynslade, to which that of Tunworth afterwards was added. In 1755 he became second master of Winchester School, and was head master from 1766 to 1793. He published, in 1756, an *Essay on the Genius and Writings of Pope*, to which a second volume was added in 1782. In his latter days he had more Church preferment, and he died in 1800. His brother, **Thomas Warton**, six years younger, educated at Winchester School and Trinity College, Oxford, also wrote poems, and, in 1753, aided the reviving taste for our best literature by critical *Observations on the Faerie Queene*. In 1756 he was elected Professor of Poetry at Oxford for ten years; and, in 1774, produced the first volume of his *History of English Poetry*, followed by a second volume, in 1778, which brought the account down to the time of Elizabeth. Thomas Warton succeeded William Whitehead as Poet Laureate, in 1785; published in that year Milton's Minor Poems, with notes; and died in 1790. **Richard Hurd**, born in 1720, who became Bishop of Lichfield and Coventry in 1775, and died in 1808, was a friend of Warburton; and, among other works, wrote, between 1758 and 1764, his *Dialogues Moral and Political*, and *Letters on*

*Chivalry and Romance.* **Edward Young**, also, was a Winchester boy, son of a chaplain to William III., and born at Upham, near Winchester. He passed from Winchester School to New College, obtained a fellowship at All Souls, and published his first verse in Queen Anne's reign, in 1712, an *Epistle to Lord Lansdowne* on the Creation of Peers, and a poem on the Last Day in 1713. He produced, in the reign of George I., his tragedies of *Busiris, King of Egypt*, and *The Revenge*, both acted at Drury Lane, in 1719. In 1725-6 appeared his *Universal Passion*, in seven satires, on the Love of Fame. He took orders in 1727, became Chaplain to George II., and was presented by his college to the living of Welwyn, Herts. In 1730 he published two epistles to Mr. Pope, concerning the authors of the age, satires in aid of Pope against the Dunces. Dr. Young—he had graduated as LL.D.—married, in 1731, the daughter of the Earl of Lichfield, and widow of Colonel Lee. She died in 1741. While in grief for this, he began to write his "Night Thoughts." *The Complaint; or, Night Thoughts on Life, Death, and Immortality*, in eight parts, first appeared in 1742-3. In 1745 followed *The Consolation;* and in 1755 Young published a prose-book, *The Centaur not Fabulous; in Six Letters to a Friend on the Life in Vogue,*—the Centaur being the profligate seeker of pleasure, in whom the brute runs away with the man. Young died in 1765. The subject of Young's "Night Thoughts" is the Immortality of the Soul, but, with aim to produce good lines that very often hit the mark, the treatment of the theme has a gloom not proper to it, although characteristic of much of the literature of his time. Robert Blair (b. 1700, d. 1746), the minister of Athelstaneford, in Haddingtonshire, published his poem of *The Grave* in 1743, at the same time as Young's "Night Thoughts."

41. **William Collins** (b. 1721, d. 1759), the son of a hatter at Chichester, was another Winchester boy. He passed from Winchester to Oxford in 1740; published, in 1742, his *Persian Eclogues*, written at Winchester; and, having taken his degree of B.A., came to London with genius and ambition, but an irresolute mind, not wholly sound. He suffered much from poverty. In 1747 he published his *Odes* polished with nice care, and classical in the best sense, rising above the affectations of the time, and expressing subtleties of thought and feeling with simple precision. The "Ode to Evening" is unrhymed, in a measure like that of Horace's "Ode to Pyrrha." The *Ode on*

2 B *

*the Passions,* for music, rose in energy of thought and skill of expression to the level even of Dryden's "Alexander's Feast." But the volume was not well received. When Thomson died, in 1748, William Collins wrote an ode upon his grave at Richmond. In 1749 Collins was released from want by the death of his mother's brother, Colonel Martin, who had often helped him, and now left him about £2,000. But in another year, his reason began to fail. He had been in a lunatic asylum at Chelsea before he was removed to Chichester in 1754. There his sister took charge of him, and he died, at the age of thirty-nine, in June, 1759. When the great cloud was coming over him, he carried but one book about with him—a child's school Bible. " I have but one book," he said, " but that is the best ;" and when he suffered most, in his latter days at Chichester, a neighbouring vicar said, " Walking in my vicaral garden one Sunday evening, during Collins's last illness, I heard a female (the servant, I suppose) reading the Bible in his chamber. Mr. Collins had been accustomed to rave much, and make great moanings ; but while she was reading, or rather attempting to read, he was not only silent, but attentive likewise, correcting her mistakes, which, indeed, were very frequent, through the whole twenty-seventh chapter of Genesis."

42. **David Hartley** (b. 1705, d. 1757) was a physician educated at Cambridge, who, in 1749, published *Observations on Man ; his Frame, his Duty, and his Expectations,* arguing that vibrations of the nerves produce all intellectual energy, by causing the association of ideas.

43. **Thomas Gray,** born in 1716, was son of a money-scrivener on Cornhill, and the only one of his twelve children who survived their infancy. His father was morose and indolent, neglected business, and spent money in building a country house at Wanstead, without telling his wife what he was about. Mrs. Gray, on her part, had joined Miss Antrobus —one of her sisters—in business, and made money by a kind of India warehouse, on Cornhill. Gray was sent to school at Eton, because his mother had a brother among the assistant masters there. At Eton he formed a friendship with **Horace Walpole** (b. 1717, d. 1797), youngest son of Sir Robert. His uncle at Eton being a Fellow of Peterhouse, Cambridge, Gray entered there as a pensioner, in 1734. In 1738 he left without a degree, and in the spring of 1739 set out for travel in France and Italy, as the companion of **Horace Walpole.** In Italy the friends dis-

agreed.   **Gray** left Walpole at Reggio, went on before him to Venice, and returned to England about two months before his father's death, in 1741.   Gray and Walpole were not reconciled till 1744.   After the death of his father, Gray's mother and her maiden sister (and late partner in business), Miss Antrobus, went to live at the house of their other sister, Mrs. Rogers, who was also a widow, at Stoke Pogis, near Windsor.   Thenceforth, Gray's home was with his mother and two aunts, at Stoke Pogis. Being urged by them to make law his profession, Gray went to reside at Cambridge again, and took the degree of B.C.L. At Stoke, in 1742, he wrote his. "Ode to Spring"—much of his verse was written in the spring and summer of this year— and in the autumn his *Ode on a Distant Prospect of Eton College*, the first published verse of Gray's, although it did not appear until 1747.   From 1742 until his death, in 1771, Gray lived chiefly at Cambridge, where, in 1768, he was made Professor of Modern History.   His Aunt Antrobus died in 1749; and in 1750 he had written his *Elegy in a Country Churchyard*, suggested by the churchyard at Stoke Pogis.   In February, 1751, Gray wrote to Horace Walpole that the proprietors of a magazine were about to publish his Elegy, and said, "I have but one bad way left to escape the honour they would inflict upon me ; and therefore am obliged to desire you would make Dodsley print it immediately (which may be done in less than a week's time) from your copy, but without my name, in what form is most convenient to him, but on his best paper and character.   He must correct the press himself, and print it without any interval between the stanzas, because the sense is in some places continued beyond them ; and the title must be, 'Elegy Written in a Country Churchyard.'   If he would add a line or two to say it came into his hands by accident, I should like it better."   Walpole did as was wished, and wrote an advertisement to the effect that accident alone brought the poem before the public, although an apology was unnecessary to any but the author.   On which Gray wrote, "I thank you for your advertisement, which saves my honour."   Gray's fame has its deepest foundations in the simplest of his poems—that on the sight of his old Eton playground, and the Elegy, which in all revisions he sought to bring into simple harmony with its theme. He expunged classicism    In one familiar stanza he put Hampden in the place of Gracchus, or some other ancient worthy. Milton and Cromwell, for Tully and Cæsar, improved the lines—

" Some mute, inglorious Tully here may rest,
   Some Cæsar guiltless of his country's blood."

In March, 1753, Gray's mother died, as his father had died, of
gout, from which he himself suffered severely; and in the same
year appeared *Six Poems*, with designs by R. Bentley.   In 1754
he wrote his *Ode on the Progress of Poetry*, and *The Bard*,
published in 1757, at Strawberry Hill.   The first collected
edition of Gray's *Poems* was not published till 1768, three years
before his death.

44. **Horace Walpole** had a large income from posts given
him by Sir Robert, his father.   He entered Parliament in 1741,
but seldom spoke, though for many years a member.   In 1747
he bought the estate of Strawberry Hill, near Twickenham, and
lavished money upon its adornment.   There he set up a printing
press, from which, in 1757, Gray's "Bard" and "Ode on the
Progress of Poesy," were the first works issued.   In 1791, he
became Earl of Orford, and he died, aged eighty, in 1797.   His
chief works were *A Catalogue of the Royal and Noble Authors
of England* (1758); *Anecdotes of Painting in England*, with
some accounts of the principal artists, by George Vertue,
digested from his MSS. (1762-71); *The Castle of Otranto*, a
romance, published in 1765; and *Historic Doubts on the Life
and Reign of King Richard the Third* (1768).   Publications of
Horace Walpole's *Letters* began to appear in 1818, and were
finally arranged in nine volumes in 1857.   The small talk of
their time is also illustrated by the letters of **Lady Mary
Wortley Montague,** born in 1690, eldest daughter of Evelyn
Pierrepont, Duke of Kingston.   She married, in 1712, Addison's
friend, Edward Wortley Montague, went with him, in 1716, to
Constantinople, and after their return lived near Pope, at
Twickenham.   In 1739 Lady Mary left her husband and con-
nections, to live abroad, and did not return to England for twenty
years.   She was in Venice when her husband, with whom she
had corresponded, died in 1761.   She came home in January;
and died in August, 1762.   There was, in the following year, an
unauthorised publication of her letters.   They were collected by
her grandson, in 1803.

45. Let us now see how we passed out of the bondage of dead
forms into the truer life of our own time.   War against despotism
in life, and in the literature through which life speaks, was rising
throughout the eighteenth century.   In Germany, revolt against
what was called the *à la mode* age had for its leaders men in-

fluenced by the freer English thought. Simple truth of life in
Defoe's "Robinson Crusoe" (1719) pleaded so strongly against
false classicism to many a German mind, that the book was not
only translated in Germany, but had there more than forty
imitators. There were two Westphalian Robinsons; there was
a Saxon, a Silesian, a Franconian, a Bohemian Robinson; there
were Robunse and Robinschen, Robinsonetta, the Moral Robinson, and the Invisible Robinson. Two young men of like age,
Bodmer and Gottsched, both of them pastor's sons, became
leaders of literature, and represented the two forms of thought
now coming into battle-array one against the other. *JOHANN*
*JACOB BODMER* (b. 1698, d. 1783), son of the Swiss pastor of
Greifensee, shrank from the gloom of his father's theology, and
instead of becoming himself a pastor, learnt silk manufacture.
His interest in literature was strong, especially in the old life and
literature of his own country. In the year when "Robinson
Crusoe" appeared, young Bodmer became a clerk in a Zurich
Government office. In the following year, he expressed to a
friend his wish to improve the German taste in letters. For
this purpose he joined Hagenbusch, Breitinger, and others, in
1721, in establishing a weekly journal on the model of Addison's
*Spectator*, called the *Painter of Manners* ("Mahler der Sitten").
It was revised and re-issued in 1746. *JOHANN CHRISTOPH*
*GOTTSCHED* (b. 1700, d. 1766), a year or two younger than
Bodmer, was son of a pastor near Königsberg, was tutor there,
and thence went to Leipzig, where he became Professor of
Eloquence, and a leader of literature with a true enthusiasm,
but his faith was in strict obedience to rules drawn from the
ancient classics. In 1729 Gottsched published a *Critical Art*
*of Poetry* ("Kritische Dichtkunst"). Between 1730 and 1740
he was supreme as a German critic. In 1737, in a second
edition of his "Art of Poetry," he attacked Milton. This
raised *BODMER* against him, and the battle for free nationality in German literature was fought in the name of Milton.
Bodmer's reply to Gottsched was a treatise published in 1740,
on *The Wonderful in Poetry* (Über das Wunderbare in der
Poesie). Gottsched mocked. Bodmer replied again. Young
literary Germany gathered itself to one side or the other. On
the side of Bodmer, with his battle-cry of "Milton!" were
Klopstock, Wieland, Haller, all the young men who represented the advance of the great blossom-time of German
literature. *GOETHE* was born in 1749, *SCHILLER* in 1759, when

the battle was won, and Gottsched deposed from his critical dictatorship. Bodmer not only defended Milton's choice of subject, and the details of his plan, but he translated from the *Spectator* Addison's essays upon Milton; finally he translated " Paradise Lost " itself. He went back to early German literature, published, with a glossary and critical remarks, the text of " Fables from the Suabian Period ; " following that up at once with a main part of the old German saga of the "Nibelungenlied," and its sequel, the " Klage." In his old age he was translating early English ballads.

46. In France, MONTESQUIEU (b. 1689, d. 1755) published, in 1749, based upon studies of England in England, his fourteen years' labour upon the theory of government, *De l'Esprit des Loix,* and the conditions necessary to the welfare of the subject. In 1751 appeared the first volume of the " Encyclopédie," completed in 1765, which was to be a free review of all knowledge, by men who were in no field of it slaves to authority. It was planned by DENIS DIDEROT (b. 1712, d. 1784), who had been imprisoned two years before for his " *Lettre sur les Aveugles, à l'Usage de Ceux qui Voient.*" Diderot offered to sell his library in aid of the costs of the great dictionary, but Empress Catherine gave him a high price for it, appointed him its librarian, and left it in his hands. The Preliminary Discourse to this encyclopædia was by JEAN LE ROND D'ALEMBERT (b. 1717, d. 1783), who had charge of its mathematical department. D'Alembert sprang out of the profligacy of the time, the son of a nun who became, as Madame de Tencin, a noted wit and beauty. He was bred by a glazier's wife, who found him, a deserted infant, laid at a church door.

Authority in France had forfeited respect. It was represented in religion by self-seeking men, notoriously corrupt. At Court it was despicable, while terrible throughout the land for its oppressions. In the earlier days of Louis XV., under the Regency of the Duke of Orleans, there was a fashion for cutting up engravings, that the figures in them might be stuck on fans and fire-screens; a fashion for making ribbon-knots; for playing with a cup and ball. The Duke of Gesures kept open house for forty; twenty, in green suits of his giving, were alone admitted to his presence in green magnificence making green ribbon knots. The Duke of Epernon had a bold fancy for performing surgical operations on his vassals. After the Regency there was the twenty years' rule of Madame de Pompadour, a person of low birth, who maintained influence when she had lost beauty by encouraging the infamous seraglio of the Parc aux Cerfs. What wonder if the revolt was fierce, and men of intellect were urged to deny all that rested on authority alone, and seek to build afresh on other ground? What wonder if the intellectual reaction led to an excess of scepticism, and men, weary of cold formalism, broke loose, defied it all, and gave a passionate expression to their feelings? In France, Voltaire chiefly represented the intellectual reaction, Rousseau the emotional.

47. *VOLTAIRE*, twenty years older than Rousseau, was born in 1694, son of a notary, educated by Jesuits, and early introduced into the salon of Ninon l'Enclos, who left him two thousand francs to buy books. He left law for literature. In 1716 he was sent to the Bastile, on suspicion of having written a satirical poem against Louis XIV. In 1718 his tragedy of "Œdipe" was acted. Afterwards he was in the Bastile again; then was for three years in England, where, in 1728, he published his "Henriade;" then came his "Lettres Philosophiques," and other writings of all kinds. In 1750 Voltaire settled at the Court of his friend, Frederick the Great, but left him after three years; presently settled with Madame Denis, near the territory of Geneva, at Ferney, which was raised by him from a hamlet to a town of watchmakers, and where he lived until his death, in 1778. He died, aged eighty-four, of excitement caused by the enthusiasm with which he was received when he paid a visit to Paris. *JEAN JACQUES ROUSSEAU*, born in 1712, son of a watchmaker at Geneva, had his taste for literature, his romance-reading, and republicanism encouraged by his father; was placed to no purpose with an attorney and with an engraver, from whom he ran away before he was sixteen; and, after many adventures, first made his mark as a writer when he won, in 1750, the prize offered by the Academy of Dijon for an essay on the question whether the Revival of Learning had contributed to the Improvement of Morals. His argument was that it had not; and so said many. Three years later Rousseau, in another essay, attacked society for its irregularities, and praised the state of nature. Voltaire, in thanking him for a copy of it, said, "Really, the reading of your work makes one anxious to go on all-fours." It did represent a weariness of wigged and powdered civilization that led many to glorify natural man as something greater than the same animal as he had been perverted by culture. Glorification of "the noble

savage" now came into literature as one form of the reaction against despotism of conventionality. Rousseau rejected the positive idea of duty, and took sensibility for the rule of conduct. The heart is good, he said; listen to it : suffer yourselves to be led by Sensibility, and you will never stray, or your strayings will be of a creditable sort. A stream of sentiment, unwholesome at its source and becoming yet more sickly as it flowed, now poured into literature. It was the excess of a good thing ; another form of the excess that marks reaction. Rousseau, persuaded that virtue was incompatible with wealth or dependence, gave up a place under a receiver-general of finance, put off his sword, left off white stockings, took to a round wig, sold his watch, and said, " Thank God, I shall never again be obliged to know what o'clock it is!" He attached himself to an ignorant maidservant, Thérèse Levasseur, and five children were born to him between 1747 and 1755, but he sent them all to the Foundling Hospital, and, when writing six months before his death, gave as reason that, " unable to educate them himself, they would have been left to their mother, who would have spoilt them, or her family, who would have made monsters of them. I tremble still to think of it." But he had said, in " Émile," " No toils, no poverty, and no respect of men absolve a father from the duty of being himself the educator of his children." Rousseau's "*Émile, ou Traité sur l'Education,*" appeared in 1762 ; in the same year with his sentimental elaboration of the principles of the Dutch Declaration of Independence and the English Settlement of 1689, into an ideal of the Social Contract —*Contrat Social*—which had a most powerful influence on the subsequent course of the French Revolution. In the preceding year, 1761, he had published his sentimental novel, the " *Nouvelle Heloise.*" Rousseau's theory of the Social Contract established the sovereignty of all, and that the general voice might ordain articles of religion, " not as dogmas, but as sentiments of sociability," banishing those who refused to accept them, and punishing with death those who, after acceptance, violated them in practice. But he said that " the most just revolution would be bought too dearly by the blood of a single citizen." Such was the stir of thought abroad, gathering intensity during and after the days of our George II., and having for one of its signs the French Revolution of 1789. Our Revolution of a hundred years before had been so far sustained and turned to right account that while we felt strongly the

impulse from abroad, it only quickened the old English sense
of duty.  We pass into the new times with Samuel Johnson and
with David Hume.

48. **Samuel Johnson** was born on the 18th of September,
1709.  His father was a bookseller at Lichfield, and he was
named Samuel, as godson of a friendly lodger in the house, Dr.
Samuel Swinfen.  He was born scrofulous, and as in his earliest
days the Tory party was re-asserting the doctrine of Divine
right, by reviving in the person of Queen Anne the pretence to
cure scrofula, therefore called " king's evil," by touch of a royal
hand, he was taken to London to be touched by Queen Anne.
The disease remained, and it was part of the hard work of
Johnson's life to battle with it.  In 1716, at the age of seven, he
was sent to Lichfield Grammar School; and in 1724, aged
fifteen, to a school at Stourbridge, as assistant pupil.  In 1726
he came home for two years, and in October, 1728, aged nineteen, went, by Dr. Swinfen's advice, and with some assistance
from him, to Pembroke College, Dr. Swinfen's own college, at
Oxford.  There the hypochondriacal oppression of the brain, to
which he had been subject, increased.  Johnson's scrofulous
constitution made itself felt by him chiefly in the brain, and
might have reduced another man to the insanity of which he
never lost the dread.  He feared it at college, and wrote in
Latin for Dr. Swinfen an account of his symptoms.  Dr.
Swinfen, proud of the Latin, and forgetting that Johnson was
revealing to him a very secret dread, showed the report to
others, and made Johnson less willing to accept help from him.
Johnson remained at Oxford, even during vacation, from the
31st of October, 1728, to the 12th of December, 1729; he then
left, probably because of illness, and did not return, because of
poverty.  His father died in 1731.  Johnson, then twenty-two
years old, received £20, all he could hope for from his father's
effects, laid by eleven guineas of it, and in 1732, aged twenty-
three, went to be usher in the school at Market Bosworth.  He
gave that up in a few months, and went to stay with a friend
and schoolfellow, Edmund Hector, who was seeking practice in
Birmingham as a surgeon, and lodged at the house of a bookseller.  For the bookseller Johnson translated, for five guineas,
*Father Lobo's Voyage to Abyssinia*, which was published in
1733.  In 1734 Johnson was at home with his mother, who
kept the shop at Lichfield, proposing to print the Latin poems
of Politian by subscription.  In November of that year he

wrote to Edward Cave, who in the preceding year, 1733, had
established "The Gentleman's Magazine," offering to supply it
with a literary column ; and Cave answered the letter.  In July,
1736, Johnson, aged twenty-seven, married Elizabeth, aged
forty-eight, widow of Mr. Porter, who had sons and a daughter,
Lucy.  Her first husband, a mercer, had died insolvent.
Johnson loved the wife thus chosen, who was twenty-one years
older than himself.   Through life she was his " dear Tetty ;" and
eighteen years after her death he wrote of her in his "Diary,"
" When I recollect the time in which we lived together, my grief
for her departure is not abated ; and I have less pleasure in any
good that befalls me, because she does not partake it.  On many
occasions I think what she would have said or done.  When I
saw the sea at Brighthelmstone, I wished for her to have seen it
with me.  But with respect to her, no rational wish is now left
but that we may meet at last where the mercy of God shall
make us happy, and, perhaps, make us instrumental to the
happiness of each other.  It is now eighteen years."  After his
marriage Johnson set up school in a large house at Edial, near
Lichfield.  He had been refused the mastership of the grammar
school at Solihull, because it was found, on inquiry, that he was
so independent in spirit that he might " huff the feoffees;" and
" yᵗ he has such a way of distorting his fface (wʰ though he can't
help) yᵉ gent. think it may affect some young ladds."   The
want of control over his face and gestures sprang from that
affection of the brain against which Johnson battled through
life.  And he was grateful to an old wife for the love that, with
his visible ungainliness, he had not ventured to seek among the
young.  There came to Johnson's school at Edial only the two
sons of Captain Garrick, of Lichfield, who had known and
respected Johnson at home, and one other boy.   Here the
foundation was laid of a lifelong friendship between Johnson
and **David Garrick** (b. 1716, d. 1779).  The school failed,
and in March, 1737, Johnson, aged twenty-eight, and Garrick,
aged twenty-one, came to London together, Mrs. Johnson being
left at Edial or Lichfield, while a new start in life was being
looked for.  Garrick studied a little more, then joined his
brother as wine merchant, but after the death of an uncle, who
left him a thousand pounds, and the deaths of his father and
mother, he followed his natural bent, and in 1741 took to the
stage, became the greatest actor of his time, and author, translator, or adapter of about forty plays.  **Johnson, while school-**

keeping, had begun a tragedy, *Irene.* Having come to London
with Garrick in March, 1737, in July he was lodging at Greenwich, to work at his play, and offered to translate for Cave a
" History of the Council of Trent." He went back for three
months to Lichfield, where he finished " Irene," and next year,
1738, aged twenty-nine, returned to London with his wife, to do
or die. His tragedy was refused. He looked again to Cave,
and in March appeared his first contribution to " The Gentleman's Magazine," Latin verses to Sylvanus Urban. In June
he began to contribute to the Magazine " Debates of the Senate
of Lilliput." Report of proceedings in the English Parliament
was unlawful, but a Mr. William Guthrie provided Johnson with
accounts of them, which he worked up in his own way. These
became famous, and were dropped by Johnson when in full
success, because they were accepted as faithful reports, and he
would not be even indirectly party to a fraud. In May of 1738
appeared Johnson's first poem, his *London,* a poem in imitation
of the third satire of Juvenal, for which Dodsley gave £10.
It came out at the same time with Pope's, 1738 (§ 19), expressed
the depth of Johnson's own feeling as a lonely struggler in the
great city, and had printed in capitals one line,

> " This mournful truth is everywhere confessed,
> SLOW RISES WORTH BY POVERTY DEPRESSED."

It was in a second edition within a week. Pope caused
inquiry to be made for the author, and recommended him to
the good offices of Lord Gower, who would have made him
master of a grammar school at Appleby, in Leicestershire, with
a salary of about £60 a year ; but the degree of M.A. was a
necessary qualification. This was asked in vain for the author
of " London " from his own university at Oxford, and also from
Dublin. In the following year, 1739, Johnson, aged thirty,
received advances from Cave, as small as half-a-crown, for
work to be done. One letter was signed "Yours *impransus*"—
without a dinner ; for Johnson sturdily sought to pay his way,
and dined or hungered as his means required. As a good Tory
he published this year a small satirical pamphlet, " *Marmor
Norfolciense;* or, an Essay on an Ancient Prophetical Inscription in monkish rhyme, lately discovered near Lynne, in
Norfolk" (the county of Sir Robert Walpole), " by Probus
Britannicus." The next four years were years of work and
poverty. In 1744 he was thirty-five years old, still struggling,

and it was at this time that he wrote his *Life of Savage*, who had died in 1743.

49. **Richard Savage**, born in 1698, was a natural son of the Countess of Macclesfield. When he accidentally discovered who was his mother she repelled him. He wrote plays, and was befriended by Steele, lived an ill-regulated life, killed a man in a tavern brawl, was found guilty, and had his mother active in opposing the endeavours made to obtain mercy for him. He was pardoned, and stayed from writing against his mother by a pension of £200 a year from Lord Tyrconnel, who also received Savage into his family. He published, in 1729, a moral poem called *The Wanderer.* Lord Tyrconnel found Savage's wild way of life unendurable, and Savage, asked not to spend all his nights in taverns, resolved to "spurn that friend who should presume to dictate to him." They parted. Savage attacked his mother in a poem ; in another poem, *The Progress of a Divine*, described a profligate priest who rose by wickedness, and who found at last a patron in the Bishop of London. He received £50 a year from the queen, and when he received the money annually disappeared till it was spent. After the queen's death his friends promised to find him £50 a year, if he would live quietly in Wales. He went to Wales, but was coming back to London when he was arrested for debt, died in prison, and was buried at the expense of his gaoler. Johnson, who knew and pitied him—as poor as he, and knowing what the struggle was in which Savage had fallen, while he rose himself in dignity —said, "Those are no proper judges of his conduct who have slumbered away their time on the down of plenty." He told Savage's sad tale with the kindliness of a true nature, while he drew from it the lesson "that nothing will supply the want of prudence; and that negligence and irregularity, long continued, will make knowledge useless, wit ridiculous, and genius contemptible."

50. In 1745, **Johnson**, aged thirty-six, published *Miscellaneous Observations on the Tragedy of Hamlet, with Remarks on Sir Thomas Hanmer's Edition of Shakespeare*, to which he added proposals for a new edition of Shakespeare. In 1747 his friend Garrick opened Drury Lane, and turned at once to. Johnson for the opening prologue. In the same year Johnson issued the *Prospectus of his Dictionary*, addressed to Lord Chesterfield. In 1748 he wrote "The Vanity of Human Wishes," chiefly at Hampstead, where his wife was staying for

her health; and in 1749, the year of the publication of "Tom Jones"—Johnson being then forty years old—Garrick, as patentee of Drury Lane, brought out Johnson's *Irene*, and, though it was not successful, forced its run for nine nights, that Johnson might not lose his three author's nights. They brought him in £195 17s., besides £100 from Dodsley for the copyright. In the same year Dodsley gave but £15 for Johnson's second poem, published in May, *The Vanity of Human Wishes*, which has in it, like "London," depths of feeling stirred by a long conflict with adversity.

In 1750 Johnson began *The Rambler* on the 20th of March, and continued it every Tuesday and Saturday till its close, on the 17th of March, 1752, about a fortnight before the death of his wife. The deeply religious nature of Johnson animated his work in joining himself to the number of those who had followed the track of the "Tatler" and "Spectator." The Latin style of "The Rambler," and its studied avoidance of common words, represented only a full working out of the fashionable theory of the time, derived from France. Johnson did for the style of his own day what Lyly had done in his time, and identified his name with it. But he lived on and outgrew it, as his neighbours did; so that the style of his "Lives of the Poets" differs altogether from that of "The Rambler." His wife's death left Johnson with none but his old mother at Lichfield dependent on him. In 1754 Cave died with his hand in Johnson's, and Johnson wrote his life for the next number of the "Gentleman's Magazine." To the *Adventurer* a series of 140 papers, issued between November 7, 1752, and March 9, 1754, by his friend, **Dr. John Hawkesworth,** Johnson contributed. From January 31, 1754, to September 30, 1756, appeared, in 140 numbers, *The Connoisseur*, by Mr. Town, critic and censor-general, its editors being **George Colman** (b. 1733, d. 1794) and **Bonnel Thornton.** Colman became an active dramatist, and was succeeded in that character, and in his management of the little theatre in the Haymarket, by his son, **George Colman the Younger** (b. 1762, d. 1836). In *The World*, by Adam FitzAdam, a series of essays in 210 numbers, published between January, 1753, and December, 1756, the **Earl of Chesterfield**—Philip Dormer Stanhope (b. 1694, d. 1773), whose *Letters to his Son* were published the year after his death—praised Johnson's Dictionary. Chesterfield's two letters appeared in *The World* just before the Dictionary came out,

and on the 7th of February, 1755, Johnson addressed a letter
to him, repudiating the patronage of one to whom seven years
before he had looked for aid, and who during his seven years of
labour against difficulties had not given him one word of encouragement or one smile of favour.   In 1755, Johnson being
forty-six, his *Dictionary* appeared.   To supply letters after his
name upon the title-page, for satisfaction of the booksellers,
Oxford had now conceded to Johnson the degree of M.A., and
Dublin spontaneously added that of LL.D.   Johnson received
for the "Dictionary" in all £1,575, which was payment at the
rate of £225 a year while it was in progress, out of which he had
to buy books for reference and pay six amanuenses.   He was
so poor that in March next year he was arrested for a debt of
£5 18s., and was helped by Samuel ·Richardson.   To avoid
debt, he did any honest work—wrote sermons for clergymen
and prefaces for authors.   It was at this time that he issued
*Proposals for his Edition of Shakespeare.*   In April, 1758, he
began *The Idler,* a weekly essay in "The Universal Chronicle,"
continued for two years.   In 1759 his mother died, at the age
of ninety.   His poverty had kept him from her, because he
could not spare from his aid to her the money it would cost
to go to and from Lichfield.   There were her little debts to pay,
and there would be the funeral expenses.   To provide these he
wrote his moral tale of *Rasselas,* for which he was paid £100,
with £25 afterwards for a second edition.   Johnson had now
neither wife nor mother to support, and "The Idler" was dis-
continued in April, 1760.   In that year his influential friends
obtained for him, from Lord Bute, a grant of £300 a year.   It
required courage to tell him that they had done so.   In his
"Dictionary," as in all works of his, he had set the mark of his
mind.   Its religious spirit was in his careful choice of illustrative extracts, which should be in themselves worth reading, and
tempt nobody to read a book that he believed could be injurious.
Its spirit of independence broke out in some of his definitions,
and he had defined Pension, "a grant made to any one without
an equivalent;" Pensioner, "a slave of state, hired by a stipend
to obey his master."   When told of the grant of a pension to
himself, and assured that this was not said to him in joke, he
remained silent for a time, and then assented.   His after course
of life showed that he had resolved to take this part of the money
usually wasted on unworthy men, not for his own enrichment,
but in trust for those whom it could relieve from unmerited

suffering. He always carried money for occasional charities, and he had, in Bolt Court, these house companions, rescued from distress :—Robert Levitt, a poor, awkward and helpless surgeon to the poor, had shown his need of a protector, and for the last thirty years of his life found shelter under Johnson's roof. Miss Williams, a friend of his wife's, daughter of a Welsh doctor, who ruined himself, had, in Mrs. Johnson's time, come to London for an operation in her eye. She became blind. Poor creature! Johnson must take care of her. She stuttered, and had a vile temper. Johnson bribed the maid to bear with that by the addition of half-a-crown a week to her wages. Mrs. Dumoulin; for her claim it was enough that she was Dr. Swinfen's daughter, now the widow of a writing-master, and in want. Another of his pensioners and hearth-sharers was Miss Carmichael; another, a negro, Francis Barber, whom Johnson took when his old master, Dr. Bathurst, had been unable to support him. Disdainful of so poor a bar to human fellowship as colour of the skin, Johnson treated this negro servant with friendship, was at some cost to educate him, and addressed him in letters as "Dear Francis," signing himself "Affectionately yours." Johnson lived among these people as their friend, not as their benefactor, and did not affect patronage. "No man," said Mrs. Thrale, "loved the poor like Dr. Johnson." His outside rudeness covered the tenderest heart. His own experience of poverty quickened his sympathies, while it roughened his spirit of independence. "He had nothing of the bear but his skin," said Garrick.

51. It was not till 1763 that **James Boswell** (b. 1740, d. 1795) then a young man of twenty-three, first saw Dr Johnson in the back-parlour of Thomas Davies, actor, bookseller, and author of some useful books upon the stage. Boswell had studied law in Scotland, and was afterwards called to the English bar. His minute chronicling, thenceforth, of Johnson's sayings and doings is made interesting by a rare vigour of thought in the man whose common talk is thus recorded. Such hero-worship as Boswell's has its weak side, but there was no meanness or self-seeking in the young gentleman's choice of an object of reverence. Boswell's *Life of Johnson* was first published in 1791, seven years after Johnson's death. **Mrs. Thrale,** who, before she married the rich brewer, had been a lively Welsh girl—Miss Hester Salusbury—first met Johnson in 1764, when he was brought to her house at Streatham to meet a poetical shoemaker

named Woodhouse who was then being talked about. He soon became the most honoured friend of the house, and the centre of attention at Mrs. Thrale's literary parties. In 1765 Johnson's mind suffered so much that he wrote in his diary on Easter day, " My memory grows confused, and I know not how the days pass over me. Good Lord deliver me !" In that year his *Edition of Shakspeare* appeared, and he wrote to Joseph Warton that, as he felt no solicitude about the work, he felt no comfort from its conclusion. In 1766 he was confined to his room for weeks together, and declared himself on the verge of insanity. In 1770 he was sixty-two. His failing health had obliged him to feel that he was himself benefited by his pension, and as he resolved that he would not take the benefit without giving an equivalent, he began to write political pamphlets. His first, in 1770, was called the *False Alarm*, on the commotion caused by the expulsion of Wilkes from the House of Commons. This was the year of the birth of Wordsworth.

52. **David Hume,** about a year and a half younger than Johnson, was born in April, 1711, of a good Scottish family. His father died when he was young. His mother bred him to the law, but he cared most for literature. In 1734, at the age of twenty-five, he was sent to Bristol with letters to merchants. Proving unfit for commerce, he went to France to economize and write. In 1737 he came to London, and in 1738, when Johnson published his " London," David Hume published his *Treatise on Human Nature*, written in France. It was unsuccessful. In 1742 he published at Edinburgh, *Essays, Moral, Political, and Literary*, in which he discussed politics as a science, superstition and enthusiasm, civil liberty, national characters, the rise of arts and sciences. Among studies of different solutions of the social problem, Hume expressed inclination rather to dispute than to assent to the conclusions of the philosophers. He upheld the dignity of human nature, and held " that the sentiments of those who are inclined to think favourably of mankind are much more advantageous to virtue than the contrary principles, which give us a mean opinion of our nature." In 1745 Hume, aged thirty-four, came to England to live with the young Marquis of Annandale, who was weak in mind and body. In the following year General St. Clair made him secretary in an expedition against France. In 1747 he was with St. Clair on a military embassy to Vienna and Turin. He recast his first part of the treatise concerning Human Nature, and it was published in 1748

while he was abroad, as an *Enquiry concerning Human Under-standing.* In 1749 and 1750 Hume was in Scotland with his brother in the country, writing. In 1751 he removed to Edin-burgh, and published there his *Political Discourses,* which were well received. In the same year he published in London, with less success, an *Enquiry concerning the Principles of Morals,* which he considered to be his best work. In 1752 he was made Librarian to the Faculty of Advocates at Edinburgh, and had an access to books which suggested the writing of his History. The first section appeared in 1754, as a *History of the Reign of James I. and Charles I.,* in a quarto volume, which was decried and neglected. There were only forty-five copies sold in a twelvemonth. In 1755 Hume published his *Natural History of Religion,* and in 1756 a continuation of his *History of England,* from the death of Charles I. to the Revolution. This was better received. He then went back in time, and published, in 1759, the *History of the House of Tudor,* which was clamoured against; and in 1761, the year after the death of George II., he went back to a still earlier time, and com-pleted his History of England from the Conquest to the Revo-lution. Smollett's History (§ 36), from that date to the death of George II. is usually printed as a continuation of Hume. As a philosopher, Hume denied miracle, and drew from Locke's doc-trine, that knowledge comes to us only from the outside world, an argument that the experience we reason from is based only on custom, without assurance that we see cause and effect. Our notion of necessity, he said, rests only on the association of ideas. From a combination of swiftly-succeeding ideas which arise from and cease with movements of the body, we form, Hume argued, an imaginary entity which we call the soul, and assign to it immortality. In 1763 Hume went with the Earl of Hertford, who was ambassador, to Paris, became secretary to the embassy, and remained in Paris as Chargé d'Affaires till 1766, when he returned to England. He brought with him ROUSSEAU (§ 47), who was made much of in England, and pensioned by George III.; but he listened to the ill-con-ditioned grumblings of Thérèse Levasseur, looked upon Hume as an agent of his enemies, quarrelled with him and with the gentleman who had placed a country house at his disposal, and when the wind was against his prompt departure, harangued the people of Dover on the shore in French. Rousseau left England in May, 1767, after a stay of thirteen months. He had then begun to write the "Confessions" which appeared after his death in 1778. Hume, between 1767 and 1769, was an under-secretary of state. In 1769 he retired to Edinburgh, possessed of a thousand a year, and died in 1776, aged sixty-five.

53. **Thomas Reid** (b. 1709, d. 1796), a Scottish clergyman, who became, in 1752, Professor of Moral Philosophy at King's College, Aberdeen, was the first who attempted a philosophical answer to Hume's scepticism. This was by his *Inquiry into the Human Mind*, which appeared in 1764, and was submitted to Hume's friendly criticism before publication. Reid's *Essays on the Intellectual Powers of Man*, in 1785, and *Essays on the Active Powers*, in 1788, completed an argument which Reid sought to pursue by Bacon's method of investigation, carefully distinguishing between observation and reflection, while he endeavoured to vindicate against attacks of scepticism those fundamental laws of belief which base human knowledge upon what Reid called the common sense of mankind.

54. **William Robertson** (b. 1721, d. 1791) was a popular pulpit orator, who published, in 1759, a *History of Scotland, in the Reigns of Mary and James VI., until his Accession to the Throne of England*, a work of labour and pains rather than genius, and written with artificial dignity. It went through fourteen editions in his lifetime. In 1761 Robertson was made King's Chaplain; in 1762, Principal of the Edinburgh University; and in 1764, Historiographer Royal for Scotland, a post revived for him, with a salary of £200 a year. In 1769 he published a *History of the Reign of Charles V.*, with a View of the Progress of Society from the subversion of the Roman Empire to the beginning of the sixteenth century; and in 1777, a *History of America*. Robertson had the natural insight of good sense with patient industry, but none of Hume's freshness of thought, and his Latin style wants the wealth of mind and richness of expression that gives life to the pomp of a Latin style in **Edward Gibbon** (b. 1737, d. 1794), the first volume of whose *Decline and Fall of the Roman Empire* appeared, when its author was thirty-nine years old, in 1776, the year of the death of David Hume. Gibbon had been a delicate child, and had been educated chiefly at private schools before he went to Magdalen College, Oxford. When he had been there fourteen months he turned Romanist, and to wean him from his new opinions his father placed him under a Calvinist minister at Lausanne, by whom he was re-converted. In 1758, aged twenty-one, he returned to

England ; in 1761 he published, in French, his *Essai sur l'Etude de la Litterature.* In 1763 he travelled through France and Switzerland to Italy, and in 1764, aged twenty-seven, when musing among the ruins of the capital, it first occurred to him to write a history showing the cause of the Decline and Fall of the great Roman Empire. In 1770, the year of the birth of Wordsworth, Gibbon was thirty-three years old, and the death of his father gave him property. He was in Parliament for eight years after 1774, finished his history at Lausanne, and published the close of it on his birthday in 1788. In those parts of his History that dealt with the Church, Gibbon sometimes brought the scepticism of the time into sharp contact with Christianity.

55. **Laurence Sterne** (b. 1713, d. 1768), grandson of Richard Sterne, Archbishop of York, and son of Lieutenant Sterne in a marching regiment, was born at Clonmel barracks. After education at Halifax in Yorkshire, and at Jesus College, Cambridge, his uncle, Dr. Sterne, obtained for him, in 1738, the vicarage of Sutton, near York, and in 1741 a prebend in York Minster, with a house in Stonegate. In that year Sterne married. The first two volumes of *Tristram Shandy* were published at York, in December, 1759, witty and whimsical, suiting the spirit of the time in their defiance of convention, and sometimes of decency. Their success brought Sterne to London, and he thenceforth weakly sacrificed himself to the shallow flatteries of London society. The second edition of this part of "Tristram Shandy" was followed at once by two volumes of the *Sermons of Mr. Yorick*. Oliver Goldsmith, in his " Citizen of the World," condemned Sterne's affectations of freedom in dashes and breaks, with the worse licence of indelicacy, and was so far displeased by the superficial tricks of the book that he was unjust to the true genius of the writer, and missed the charm of his Uncle Toby and Corporal Trim. In 1761 appeared volumes iii. and iv. of "Tristram Shandy ; " in 1762, vols. v. and vi. ; in 1765, vols. vii. and viii. ; in 1767, vol. ix. In 1768, after a visit to France, appeared Sterne's *Sentimental Journey*, of which the style reminds us that 1761 and 1762 were the dates of the chief sentimental writings of Rousseau. In the same year Sterne died, on the 13th of September, at lodgings in Bond Street, with no friend near ; the only sign of human affection the knock of a footman, sent by some of his grand friends from a neighbouring dinner party to learn how Mr. Sterne was. A single mourning coach, with two gentlemen inside, one of

them his publisher, followed his body to the grave. It was dug up after burial, and recognised in a few days on the table of the Professor of Anatomy of Cambridge. Sterne left no provision for his widow and daughter at York, but died in debt, and his family were aided by a collection made at next York races. His daughter, Lydia, married a Frenchman, and is said to have been among the victims of the French Revolution.

56. **Oliver Goldsmith** (b. 1728, d. 1774) was producing his best works in the years immediately before the birth of Wordsworth. He was one of eight children of the clergyman of Kilkenny West; was educated at the village school; entered, with aid from an uncle, Mr. Contarine, in 1745, as a sizar at Trinity College, Dublin, and there graduated as B.A. in 1749. From 1752 to 1754 he was studying medicine at Edinburgh, and continued like studies in 1754 at Leyden. He then travelled on foot about the Continent. In 1756 he was in London again, and tried many ways of earning bread. He had no skill in managing outward affairs of life, but had within him a pure breath of genius. He wrote criticisms for the *Monthly Review*, and then for the *Critical Review;* published, in 1759, an *Enquiry into the Present State of Polite Learning in Europe*; produced eight numbers of a paper called *The Bee;* and contributed in 1760, to Newbery's new daily paper, the *Public Ledger*, two articles a week for a guinea a-piece. These essays, collected in 1762, as *The Citizen of the World*, are full of the kindliest humour, and in prose written with the unaffected grace of a true poet. In 1763 Johnson, who felt the worth of Goldsmith, and was his firm friend, sold the MS. of the "Vicar of Wakefield" for £60, to relieve Goldsmith from immediate distress and debt. In December, 1764, his poem of the *Traveller; or, a Prospect of Society*, appeared, and Goldsmith rose in fame. Its success caused the purchaser of the *Vicar of Wakefield* to produce it, at last, in February, 1766; and it went through three editions before the end of August. Goethe tells us that when, aged twenty-five (and in the year of Goldsmith's death), he was a law-student at Strasburg, Herder read to him a translation of the "Vicar of Wakefield." More than half a century after Goldsmith's death, when the German poet was by many regarded as the patriarch of contemporary European literature, he ascribed, in a letter to his friend Zelter, the best influence over his mind to the spirit of that wise and wholesome story as it was made known to him "just at the critical moment of mental develop-

ment." In 1768 Goldsmith's first comedy, the *Good-natured Man*, was produced ; in 1770 appeared his other poem of great mark, *The Deserted Village;* in 1772, his other comedy, *She Stoops to Conquer*, was acted ; and Goldsmith died on the 4th of April, 1774. He did much other work of the pen, wrote histories of Greece, Rome, England, and of Animated Nature. His "Vicar of Wakefield" brought idyllic grace into the novel of real life, and his *Traveller* and *Deserted Village* calmly reflect some shadows of the life and thought of Europe in his day.

57. In the year of the birth of Wordsworth, 1770, George III. had been ten years on the throne. In August of that year, **Thomas Chatterton** committed suicide. He was a youth of eighteen, who had been taught at a charity school in his native town of Bristol, and articled to an attorney. The boy, with a poet's genius, and a turn for antiquities, played upon the reviving taste for our old national literature among men who had still but a faint critical sense of its form of thought or language, by inventing a series of mock antique poems, which he ascribed to an imaginary monk of Bristol, named Thomas Rowley. Rowley lived, he said, three centuries before the poems were discovered by his father in an old chest in the church of St. Mary Redcliffe, where he and his forefathers had been sextons for many generations. Chatterton came to London in 1770, with the confidence of genius, warmed by young hope and ambition ; found himself starving in the midst of plenty, with a defiant sense of power. He was but a boy; his was not yet a sustaining power ; and he poisoned himself in the agony of his despair.

58. In the year of the birth of Wordsworth, 1770, Pope had been dead twenty-six years ; Fielding had been dead sixteen years, Richardson nine, and Smollett had but another year to live. Thomson had been dead twenty-two years ; Dyer and Allan Ramsay twelve, Shenstone seven. Collins had been dead fourteen years. Gray died in that year, and Akenside the year before. **Charles Churchill** had died six years before, at the age of thirty-three. He had been ordained without a degree ; had a wife and two sons, and lived by a poor school when he succeeded his father as curate and lecturer of St. John's, Westminster, and added to his little income by teaching English to young ladies at a boarding-school. He delighted in the theatre, and in 1761 published at his own cost, as a shilling pamphlet, the *Rosciad*, a critical satire on the stage, in thought bold, in verse masterly. Other keen satires in verse followed. Churchill

turned to the larger stage, supported Wilkes, wrote, in 1762, *The Ghost;* in January, 1763, *The Prophecy of Famine,* a satire on Scotland and the Scotch; lived a wild life, wrote other satires, and died after four years of a brilliant intellectual career, that caused Garrick to say of him after his death, "Such talents, with prudence, had commanded the nation."

59. **James Grainger** died three years before the birth of Wordsworth, aged about forty. He was a Scotch physician, who left practice in London, and, finding a wife on his way out, settled in the island of St. Christopher, where he wrote his poem of the *Sugar Cane,* published in 1764. Another Scot, **William Falconer,** published in London, in 1762, a touching poem, called *The Shipwreck,* and himself died by shipwreck in 1769. **James Beattie** (b. 1735, d. 1803) was the son of a village shopkeeper at Lawrencekirk. He became an usher in the Aberdeen Grammar School, published *Original Poems and Translations* in 1760; in 1770 an angry *Essay on Truth* against Hume; and in 1771 the first canto of *The Minstrel.* That won him strong friends in London, a pension of £200 from the king, and the professorship of Moral Philosophy and logic in Marischal College, Aberdeen. Another Scotsman, **James Macpherson** (b. 1738, d. 1796), published, in 1762, poems attributed to Ossian, or Oisin (ch. i. § 5), founded in part on Gaelic traditional poetry, but so modern in form and expressive of the sentimental gloom then fashionable, that they owed their great success to the reproduction in new form of living tendencies of thought. The controversy as to their genuineness was, like that over the Rowley Poems, sign of a sympathy with the past, that was not yet informed by any critical understanding. **Thomas Percy** (b. 1729, d. 1811), son of a grocer at Bridgenorth, was sent from his town grammar-school with an exhibition to Oxford, and was from 1753 to 1778 Vicar of Easton Maudit, in Northamptonshire. He married in 1759, and had six children; had a turn for literature, and amused himself as a collector of old ballads, having for the basis of his collection a folio MS. collection in a handwriting of about the time of Charles I. The result was his *Reliques of Ancient English Poetry,* published in 1765, in which he meddled with the old ballads to bring them into some accord with the conventional taste of his age, and still was condemned by many as an antiquary. But his book struck a true note, and was food for young minds in the coming time. Walter Scott remembered

the spot where he read Percy's "Reliques" for the first time, and believed that he read no book "half so frequently, or with half the enthusiasm." Percy became chaplain to the Duke of Northumberland, with whose house his name of Percy inspired him to claim kindred ; he was blessed also with a wife whose pride it was to have once nursed a prince ; Percy became Dean of Carlisle in 1778, and, in 1782, Bishop of Dromore, in Ireland. William Cowper, who had not yet published verse, was thirty-nine ; and Joseph Priestley (b. 1733, d. 1804) was thirty-seven in 1770. Thomas Paine (b. 1737, d. 1809), was then, like Gibbon, thirty-three years old ; John Horne Tooke (b. 1736, d. 1812) was twenty-four ; and John Wolcot (b. 1738, d. 1819), afterwards satirist in verse as Peter Pindar, thirty-two ; Hannah More (b. 1745, d. 1833) was twenty-five ; William Paley (b. 1743, d. 1805) was twenty-four.

60. In 1770 **Samuel Foote** (b. at Truro about 1720, d. 1777) was satirizing men of his time in the series of comedies begun in 1752. Garrick also was among the dramatists; and **George Colman** (b. about 1733, d. 1794) and **Richard Cumberland** (b. 1732, d. 1811), who begun their dramatic careers in 1760. **John Home** (b. 1724, d. 1808), ordained, in 1750, minister of Athelstaneford, in East Lothian, had produced, in 1756, at Edinburgh, his tragedy of "Douglas," whereby he so much offended the Presbytery, that, to avoid Church censure, he resigned his living and became a layman.

**Adam Smith** (b. at Kirkcaldy in 1723, d. 1790) was from 1752 to 1764 Professor of Moral Philosophy at Glasgow, and published, in 1759, his *Theory of Moral Sentiments*, but his *Inquiry into the Nature and Causes of the Wealth of Nations* did not appear till 1776. This famous book developed Locke's doctrine that labour is the source of wealth. **Sir William Blackstone** published the first volume of his *Commentaries on the Laws of England* in 1764, and finished in 1768. Among the youths and children, in 1770, who were to express the thought of England for a coming generation, were Jeremy Bentham, aged twenty-two; Richard Brinsley Sheridan, nineteen; Fanny Burney, eighteen ; Elizabeth Inchbald, seventeen ; Sophia Lee, twenty ; Harriet Lee, fourteen ; Joanna Baillie, eight ; Maria Edgeworth, five ; George Crabbe, sixteen; William Godwin, fourteen ; William Gifford, thirteen ; Robert Burns, Richard Porson, and Richard Beckford, eleven ; Wm. Cobbett, eight ; Samuel Rogers, seven ; and Robert Bloomfield, four.

Intensity of thought and feeling, in the days before and after the French Revolution, roused men who were young during the stir of it to new sense of life.   Wordsworth (d. 1850) was born in 1770; Walter Scott (d. 1832), James Montgomery (d. 1854), Sydney Smith (d. 1845), and John Lingard (d. 1851), were born in 1771; Samuel Taylor Coleridge (d. 1834) and James Hogg (d. 1835) in 1772.   Francis Jeffrey (d. 1850) was born in 1773. Robert Southey (d. 1843) in 1774.   Jane Austen (d. 1817) and Charles Lamb (d. 1834) were born in 1775; Jane Porter (d. 1850) and James Smith (d. 1839) in 1776; Thomas Campbell (d. 1844) and Henry Hallam (d. 1859) in 1777; William Hazlitt (d. 1830) and Mary Brunton (d. 1818) in 1778; and in 1779 Thomas Moore (d. 1852), Henry Brougham (d. 1868), John Galt (d. 1839), and Horace Smith (d. 1849).

61. **Richard Brinsley Sheridan,** whose wit revived English comedy towards the close of the eighteenth century, was born in Dublin in 1751, son of an actor who taught elocution.   After education at Harrow, he eloped from Bath with Miss Linley, a famous singer, then eighteen years old, and daughter of a composer; fought two duels; and then, having to live by his wits, produced his comedy of *The Rivals*, in January, 1775, when he was twenty-four years old.   *The Duenna* followed at the close of the same year; in February, 1777, *The Trip to Scarborough*, an alteration of Vanbrugh's "Relapse;" and in May, 1777, *The School for Scandal*.   Sheridan's last piece was *The Critic*, in 1779.   He died in July, 1816.

62. **William Cowper,** though he lived longer and wrote later in life, was of the same age as Charles Churchill, and about three years younger than Goldsmith.   He was born in November, 1731, son of the Rev. John Cowper, rector of Great Berkhamstead, and chaplain to George II.   His mother died when he was six years old.   After early experience of a rough school and two years' suffering from inflammation of the eyes, Cowper was sent, aged ten, to Westminster School, where he had Charles Churchill (§ 58) and Warren Hastings among his schoolfellows. The kindness of schoolfellowship made Cowper afterwards recognise in his verse the good of Churchill when the world only condemned him for his faults.   In 1748 Cowper left Westminster, was entered of the Middle Temple, and articled for three years to law.   An uncle had two daughters.   One of them, Theodora, touched his young fancy; the other, Harriet, was his friend afterwards as Lady Hesketh.   A nervous melancholy,

shadow of evil to come, had weighed on Cowper. When he was called to the bar in 1754, Theodora's father refused sanction to his daughter's engagement with Cowper, and he saw her no more. Two years later, his father, who had married again, died. Cowper's means diminished. He was made a Commissioner of Bankrupts, which brought him £60 a year. In 1763, a cousin, Major Cowper, offered him the offices of Clerk of the Journals of the House of Lords, and of Reading Clerk, and Clerk of Committees, to which he had a right of presentation. He flinched from taking more than one ; and when the major's right of nomination to that was questioned, and the fitness of the nominee was to be tested, Cowper's nervous excitement passed into lunacy, and he was placed, in December, 1763, in an asylum at St. Albans. When he recovered, Cowper gave up his small office of Commissioner of Bankrupts, and was chiefly dependent on his friends. In June, 1765, he went into retired lodgings at Huntingdon, where he became acquainted with the Rev. Mr. Unwin and his wife, and their son, a young clergyman. He went to live with them as friend and lodger. Mrs. Unwin became a widow in June, 1767, and presently removed, Cowper with her, to Olney, Buckinghamshire, where the Rev. John Newton, once master of a slave-vessel, was curate. The influence of Mr. Newton, and the death of his own brother, in 1770, increased Cowper's melancholy. In 1771 Cowper joined Newton in the composition of a hymn-book, for which Cowper wrote those signed " C." in the volume published in 1779, as *Olney Hymns*. In 1773 Cowper had another attack of insanity, in which he attempted suicide. Mrs. Unwin watched over him. He took to gardening. A friend gave him three hares, which he cherished, and which live yet in his verse. He had also five rabbits, two guinea-pigs, two dogs, a magpie, a jay, a starling, canaries, pigeons, and goldfinches. In 1779 Mr. Newton left Olney. Mrs. Unwin then suggested to Cowper that he should write some sustained work in verse, believing that this occupation would preserve health for his mind. He wrote the *Progress of Error*—found health in the occupation—and wrote on *Truth*, *Table Talk*, *Expostulation*, these pieces being all written between December, 1780, and the following March. They were sent to a publisher who asked for more. Then *Hope* and *Charity* were added ; *Conversation* and *Retirement* while the book was being printed ; and in March, 1782, William Cowper, aged fifty, first joined the company of English poets. Lady Austin, a

2 c

baronet's widow, sister-in-law of a clergyman near Olney, had then become Cowper's friend.   Her liveliness cured his low spirits; she set him laughing with the story of John Gilpin. When he went to bed, it amused him half through the night, and next morning it was turned into the best of playful ballads. Lady Austin advised him to give up the couplet, and write something in blank verse.   " Set me a subject, then," said he. " Oh, you can write on anything.   Take the Sofa."   So Cowper began the best of his poems, and called it *The Task*, begun in the summer of 1783, finished in 1784, and published in 1785. In 1784 he began his *Translation of Homer*.   Mrs. Unwin's jealousy had obliged Cowper to deny himself the wholesome friendship of Lady Austin.   Work at Homer was his chief security for health.   The Homer, in blank verse, was published in 1791, and £1,000 paid for it.   Then Mrs. Unwin was seized with palsy.   Cowper's mind suffered again.   He battled with insanity ; planned work upon Milton ; but sank again into painful sickness of mind, from which, after Mrs. Unwin's death, in 1796, only revision of his Homer gave relief.   "I may as well do this," he said, "for I can do nothing else ;" and worked on sadly till his death in 1800.   The rising spirit of the time speaks even from the pure strain of Cowper in his solitude. He denounced the Bastile.   " My ear is pained," he said,

> " My soul is sick with every day's report,
> Of wrong and outrage with which earth is filled."

63.  **William Wordsworth** was born at Cockermouth, on the 7th of April, 1770, second son of John Wordsworth, attorney and law-agent to Sir James Lowther, afterwards Earl of Lonsdale.   His mother, Anne, was only daughter of William Cookson, mercer, of Penrith.   Wordsworth's grandfather had come into Westmoreland out of a Yorkshire family.   From 1770 to 1778, when his mother died of consumption, Wordsworth spent his infancy and early boyhood at Cockermouth, and sometimes with his mother's parents at Penrith.   He was the only one of her five children about whom she was anxious; for he was, he says, of a stiff, moody, violent temper.   He was bold in outdoor sports ; and, free to read what he pleased, read Fielding through in his boyhood, "Don Quixote," "Gil Blas," "Gulliver's Travels," and the "Tale of a Tub."   After home teaching at a dame school, and by a Rev. Mr. Gilbanks, Wordsworth was sent, in 1779, to Hawkshead School, in the Vale of Esthwaite, in Lancashire.   Boys at the school lodged in neighbouring cottages,

and Wordsworth lodged with an old dame, Anne Tyson, who lived to be eighty, and whom he honoured afterwards with loving recollection in his " Prelude." Wordsworth was a boy in the days of the American War of Independence, by which, and by the later struggle of the French Revolution, the chief energies of Burke were stirred into action.

64. **Edmund Burke**, the son of an attorney at Dublin, was born in 1730, educated first at a famous school kept by Abraham Shackleton, a member of the Society of Friends, at Ballitore, in Kildare, then at Trinity College, Dublin, where he was fellow-student with Goldsmith, and graduated as B.A. in 1748, M.A. in 1751. In 1750 he came to study law in London. To aid his means of entering into society he contributed to periodicals. In 1756 he published as a satire upon Bolingbroke (§ 20), whose works Mallet had published in 1753, and against the new turn of thought in France (§ 46, 47), *A Vindication of Natural Society, or a View of the Miseries and Evils arising to Mankind from every species of Artificial Society. In a letter to Lord * * * , by a late Noble Writer.* This piece of irony was followed in the same year by Burke's *Philosophical Inquiry into the Origin of our Ideas of the Sublime and Beautiful.* This continued the form of speculation of which 'Addison had given the first example in his Essays on Imagination (ch. xi. § 33), and worked out with ingenuity and eloquence of style, a theory that sense of beauty is associated with relaxation, terror with contraction, of the fibres of the body. Burke's health suffered; there were signs of consumption; and he was received at Bath into the house of an Irish physician, Dr. Nugent, whose daughter he married in the spring of 1757. In January, 1758, his only son Richard was born. Burke resumed work in London, and on Christmas Day, 1758, first dined with Dr. Johnson, thenceforth his warm friend, at Garrick's house. In June, 1759, he started the *Annual Register*, and was its chief writer and editor for several years. In 1761 he was appointed Private Secretary to William Gerard Hamilton, then become chief Secretary in Ireland. For his help to the Irish Government Burke received in 1763 a pension of £300 a year, which he resigned when he had held it two years, because he found it was regarded as a pledge of servitude. Burke became one of the first members of the literary club founded in 1764 at the Turk's Head in Gerrard Street, Soho: Goldsmith and its founders, Johnson and Sir Joshua Reynolds, were among the

other members. A Mr. William Fitzherbert was so much impressed by Burke's powers, as shown at the Turk's Head Club, that he recommended him to the Marquis of Rockingham, who became Premier in July, 1765, as private secretary. Another of Burke's admirers at the same time gave him a seat in Parliament for Wendover. Lord Rockingham felt Burke's power and used his counsel in dealing with the American difficulty. Parliament in the beginning of 1764 had voted its right to tax the colonies; it proceeded to tax sugar and other articles of colonial import, and passed a Stamp Act which had been proposed some time before. The American colonies protested vigorously, and the first Congress of the colonies produced a " Declaration of Rights and Liberties " on the 19th of October, 1765. Burke, who dreaded revolution in all forms, reverenced all old institutions, and was by nature a conservative, advised the avoidance of collision by a compromise. Great Britain should assert the right to tax, but at the same time abstain from using it. Accordingly, the Stamp Act was repealed, and an Act was passed asserting the legislative power of Great Britain. Lord Rockingham's ministry then gave place, in July, 1766, to that of Pitt, Earl of Chatham, and Burke defended its policy in *A Short Account of a late short Administration.* To the liberality of Lord Rockingham Burke owed the means of buying in 1768, for £23,000, the estate at Beaconsfield. His heart was set upon founding a family, his hope all rested upon his one son Richard. Burke was among those wrongly suspected of authorship of the *Letters of Junius,* which appeared in the *Public Advertiser,* with bold denunciation of the men in power, between 1769 and 1772, and are now often ascribed to Sir Philip Francis. His policy of conciliation caused Burke to be appointed in 1771 agent for New York, while the English Government was making the breach with the colonies more hopeless. In 1773 he published *Thoughts on the Cause of the Present Discontents,* in which he maintained that government ought to be in the hands of an aristocracy. On the'19th of April, 1774, he made a famous *Speech on American Taxation,* including a history of the question for the last eleven years. "Again and again," he said, " revert to your old principles; seek peace and ensue it . . . Be content to bind America by laws of trade; you have always done it. Let this be your reason for binding their trade. Do not burden them by taxes; you were not used to do so from the beginning. Let this be your reason for not taxing.

These are the arguments of states and kingdoms.  Leave
the rest to the schools." In 1774 Burke became member for
Bristol, and his colleague, who had to follow him as orator on
the hustings, in thanking the electors, contented himself with,
" Gentlemen, I say ditto to Mr. Burke ! ditto to Mr. Burke ! "
On the 22nd of March, 1775, Burke laid before the House of
Commons thirteen resolutions for reconcilement with America,
and made a famous *Speech on American Conciliation.*  He was
opposed by his friend **Samuel Johnson**, who in this year published *Taxation no Tyranny.*  In June, 1775, George Washington
was appointed commander-in-chief of the forces of the United
Colonies.  On the 2nd of July, 1776, the colonies declared their
independence, and established as free and independent the United
States of America.  The American War then followed to its
end in the recognition of American Independence by treaties
signed on the 3rd of September, 1783, when Wordswórth was
thirteen years old.

65. **Samuel Johnson** (§ 51) died in the following year.  He
had paid a *Visit to the Hebrides*, and described it in the year
before he wrote his pamphlet on the American question.  In 1777,
when he was sixty-nine years old, the booksellers asked him to
write lives of the poets since the Commonwealth, to be prefixed
to new editions of their works in a series of volumes.  The *Lives
of the Poets* appeared in 1779-81, and represent the clearness of
Johnson's critical power, and the natural force of his style in later
life.  He had his own strong predilections, and was himself in
his judgments, but he tried honestly to be fair.  " They will ask
you to write the life of some dunce," Boswell said : "will you do
that, sir ?"  "Yes, and say he was a dunce."  When Johnson was
asked to name his own price for his work, he fixed it at £200 ;
the publishers gave more, but still much less than the work was
worth.  Johnson, true to his own maxim, "I hate a complainer,"
was thoroughly content.  " It is not," he said, "that they gave
me too little, but that I wrote too much."  In 1782 his friend
Levitt died.  In 1783 his friend Mrs. Williams died, and he had
a stroke of palsy.  In 1784 he died himself.  Opium was given
to him in his last illness to relieve pain ; he asked if it could
restore health, and being told that it could not, said, "Then I
will take no more, for I wish to meet my God with an unclouded
mind."  The dread of loss of intellect remained to the last.  He
turned his prayers into Latin to assure himself that he was still
master of his faculties.  On the 13th of December he whispered,

"Jam moriturus" (Now I am about to die), and fell into a quiet sleep. In that sleep God took the soul of a true servant, who had lived in his own different way, like Milton, as ever in his great Taskmaster's eye.

66. **William Wordsworth** (§ 63) was then at school at Hawkshead, become an orphan by his father's death in 1787. The father bequeathed only a considerable debt from his employer, paid to his children long afterwards, when Lord Lonsdale died. In October, 1787, Wordsworth's uncles sent him to Cambridge, where the university life of that time fell below his young ideal. He spent his first summer vacation, 1788, in the old cottage at Esthwaite with Dame Tyson ; his second vacation he spent with his uncles at Penrith, who were educating him, and who designed him for the Church. But that was the year when the Fall of the Bastile (July 14th, 1789) resounded through Europe, and young hearts leaped with enthusiastic hope. It was with young Wordsworth as with his Solitary in the *Excursion.* Men had been questioning the outer and the inner life,

> "The intellectual power through words and things
> Went sounding on, a dim and perilous way,"

and men were roused from that abstraction ;

> "For lo ! the dread Bastile,
> With all the chambers in its horrid towers,
> Fell to the ground ; by violence overthrown
> Of indignation and with shouts that drowned
> The crash it made in falling ! From the wreck
> A golden palace rose, or seemed to rise,
> The appointed seat of equitable law
> And mild paternal sway. The potent shock
> I felt : the transformation I perceived,
> As marvellously seized as in that moment
> When, from the blind mist issuing, I beheld
> Glory, beyond all glory ever seen,
> Confusion infinite of heaven and earth,
> Dazzling the soul. Meanwhile, prophetic harps
> In every grove were ringing ' War shall cease ;
> Did ye not hear that conquest is abjured ?
> Bring garlands, bring forth choicest flowers to deck
> The tree of Liberty.' My heart rebounded ;
> My melancholy voice the chorus joined—
> " Be joyful all ye nations in all lands,
> Ye that are capable of joy be glad !
> Henceforth, whate'er is wanting in yourselves
> In others ye shall promptly find ; and all,
> Enriched by mutual and reflected wealth,
> Shall with one heart honour their common kind."

His next holiday Wordsworth took in France, with his

friend Robert Jones, each carrying a stick, his luggage in a
handkerchief, and £20 in his pocket. They landed at Calais on
the eve of the fête of the Federation, July 14, anniversary of the
Fall of the Bastile, when the king was to swear fidelity to the
Constitution. All that he saw raised Wordsworth's enthusiasm
as they travelled through France to the Alps.

> "A glorious time,
> A happy time that was; triumphant looks
> Were then the common language of all eyes;
> As if awaked from sleep, the nations hailed
> Their great expectancy."
>
> (*Prelude, Book VI.*)

67. Wordsworth came home, graduated as B.A. in 1791;
visited his friend Jones in the Vale of Clwydd, and made an
excursion in North Wales. In November he was in Paris again,
went thence to Orleans, to learn French where there were fewer
English. At Orleans, where he formed intimate friendship with
the Republican general Beaupuis, at Blois, and at Paris, where
he arrived a month after the September massacres, he spent
thirteen months. In events terrible to him he saw the
excesses of reaction, but he sympathised so strongly with the
Brissotins that he would have made common cause with them,
and perhaps have perished, if he had not been compelled to
return to London before the execution of the king, January 21,
1793. After that event England prepared war against the
Revolution, and **Edmund Burke** was leader of the war-cry.
Burke had been twice a minister as Paymaster of the Forces,
and was foremost prosecutor in the seven years' trial of Warren
Hastings, which ended with his acquittal, in April, 1795. He
first expressed in the House, in February, 1790, his desire to
check the French Revolution by armed interference. In October,
1790, he published his *Reflections on the Revolution in France.*
This pamphlet was answered by **Thomas Paine** with the
first part of *The Rights of Man;* by **James Mackintosh,**
afterwards Sir James, then a young man of twenty-six, with
his *Vindiciæ Gallicæ.* In December, 1791, Burke published
*Thoughts on French Affairs.* In 1794 occurred the calamity of
Burke's life, that crushed all his energy. He had lived in his
son Richard, then thirty-six years old, a barrister, for whom,
in July, 1794, he vacated his seat at Malton. Richard was to
outshine his father, who was anxious to become Lord Beaconsfield, that he might transmit the title to his son; and that his
son, uniting himself with the aristocracy, might realize his own

highest ideal. Because it crossed this hope, Burke had forbidden his son's marriage to a young lady who had lived in the house as companion to his mother, and whom he loved. Richard obeyed. On the 26th of July there was a dinner party at Burke's house, to celebrate his son's return as member for Malton—father and mother alike blind to the fact that he was dying of consumption. The truth was urged on them. Richard was taken to a house at Brompton, and, as he lay there dying, he heard his father and mother in loud lament in the next room, rose, dressed, and tottered in to them, that he might seem well and cheer them. He spoke comfort, heard the rustle of the trees outside, said, "What is that—does it rain?" then, seeing what it was, he repeated twice the lines of Milton that his father had delighted in:

> " His praise, ye winds, that from four quarters blow,
> Breathe soft or loud; and wave your tops, ye pines,
> With every plant, in sign of worship wave,"

then bowed his own head in sign of worship, sank on his mother's lap, and died. Burke cared no more to be Lord Beaconsfield. He was a broken man for the remaining three years of his life, and died in July, 1797.

68. **Wordsworth** and other young men of the day were bitterly indignant at the alliance of their country with despotic powers to put down the Revolution. That war of the Revolution, which began on the 1st of February, 1793, and ended at the Peace of Amiens on the 27th of March, 1802, was in his eyes an unholy war, and laid the foundations of the patriotic war against Napoleon which followed, from the 29th of April, 1803, to the battle of Waterloo, on the 18th of June, 1815. In 1793, after his return from France, Wordsworth published *Descriptive Sketches during a Pedestrian Tour on the Italian, Swiss, and Savoyard Alps;* also, *an Evening Walk, an Epistle in Verse.* In May, 1794, he was in London, planning a literary and political miscellany, called "The Philanthropist," which was to be Republican, not Revolutionary. In November, he was looking for employment on an Opposition newspaper, that he might pour out his heart against the war. But presently he heard of the sickness of a young friend at Penrith, Raisley Calvert, like himself the son of a law agent. Wordsworth went to Penrith and nursed him. Calvert was dying. He had £900 to leave, and determined to make Wordsworth master of his fortunes. He died in January, 1795, and left Wordsworth

his money. Then Wordsworth resolved, by frugal living, to secure full independence, and to be a poet. In the autumn he and his sister Dorothy settled at Racedown, near Crewkerne, a retired place with a post once a week. And thus Wordsworth began his career at the time when that of Burns was ending.

69. **Robert Burns** was born on January 25, 1759, two miles south of the town of Ayr. His father, William Burness, had been a gentleman's gardener near Edinburgh, went to Ayrshire, married Agnes Brown, in December, 1757; was then gardener and overlooker to a Mr. Ferguson, of Doonholm. Robert was his first son. In 1766, when Robert Burns was six or seven years old, his father, with £100 lent by his master, took the farm of Mount Oliphant, in the parish of Ayr. He was unsuccessful, and Mr. Ferguson's death left him in the hands of a harsh factor. Robert Burns was sent, at six years old, with his next brother, Gilbert, to a school at Alloway Mill for a few months; then taught with children of neighbours by a Mr. Murdoch ; then by their father, a devout, hardheaded Scot, with a touch of obstinacy in him. Then they were sent to school on alternate days for a quarter, at Dalrymple, two or three miles off, for writing-lessons. About 1777 the lease of Mount Oliphant was broken, and William Burness went to Lochlea, in the parish of Tarbolton, where his temper embittered litigation as to the conditions of the lease. Robert was sent to Kirkoswald parish school to learn mensuration, and passed his nineteenth summer on a smuggling coast. At home he and his brother worked on the farm, and had £7 a year each as wages from their father, with which to clothe themselves and meet other expenses. In 1781-2 Robert went for six months to Irvine to learn flax-dressing. In 1783, at the end of the year, three months before their father's death, he and his brother Gilbert had taken the farm of Mossgiel, of 119 acres, at £90 rent, in the neighbouring parish of Mauchline. Robert was there four years, during which the farm did not prosper, but the poet's genius developed fast. He found a friend in Gavin Hamilton, writer, of Mauchline, from whom the farm was sub-leased, and joined in a feud of his with Mr. Auld, the minister of Mauchline, who was fierce against all heterodox opinions. Thus Burns came to write *The Holy Fair*, the *Twa Herds*, and *Holy Willie's Prayer*, a scathing satire against self-righteous intolerance. To the same period belong *Hallowe'en* and the *Cotter's Saturday Night*, in which his father was the pious

2 c *

cotter.  Burns drew his notion from *The Farmer's Ingle* of
**Robert Ferguson,** a Scottish poet, nine years older than himself, son of a draper's clerk at Edinburgh, who had poured out
his native strain of verse between 1771 and the date of his death
·in a lunatic asylum, in 1774, when he was only twenty-four years
old.  **Burns** sang to himself also in the days at Mossgiel as he
drove the plough (completing the verses in his head and writing
them down when he went home in the evening) his touching
poems to the *Mountain Daisy*, that lay in the path of his
plough, and *The Mouse*, whose home the ploughshare laid in
ruins.  In the unprosperous farm Burns was thinking of emigration from his native land when he wrote—

> " But, Mousie, thou art no thy lane,.
> In proving foresight may be vain :
> The best laid schemes of mice and men
>   Gang oft agley,
> And leave us nought but grief and pain
>   For promised joy.

> " Still thou art blest, compared wi' me !
> The present only toucheth thee :
> But, och ! I backward cast my e'e
>   On prospects drear,
> And forward, tho' I canna see,
>   I guess an' fear ! "

Hopeless of Mossgiel, Robert Burns thought of trying his
fortune as manager of a plantation in the West Indies, if he
could raise money to pay for his passage.  Then his brother
Gilbert suggested that the money might be raised by printing
the poems he had written.  He added a new piece or two, including *The Twa Dogs*, and the Poems of Robert Burns first
appeared, printed at Kilmarnock, in the autumn of 1786.  At
the last moment, when Burns was about to leave Scotland,
a generous letter from **Dr. Thomas Blacklock** changed his
destiny.  Blacklock was the son of a Scotch bricklayer ; had
been blinded by small-pox in his infancy, and had developed
unusual powers through being much read to by his friends.
When he was nineteen, his father was crushed by the fall of a
kiln ; and in his desolation he was befriended by Dr. Stevenson,
of Edinburgh, who enabled him to develop his powers.  He
became a scholar and a poet, was a man of the finest tone of
mind, and having been made easy by a post in the University,
he took orders and became D.D.  The gentle Blacklock, who
had also published verse, brought **Burns** to Edinburgh, and
found him friends in the University.  In April, 1787, a second

edition of his poems was published at Edinburgh, by subscription.  Burns was supplied with money, but although then and
always he yielded too readily to temptation, he held to his
vocation as a farmer, sent £200 to his brother to help him at
Mossgiel, and after a little tour agreed for a farm at Ellisland,
in March, 1787.  Johnson's "Museum of Scottish Song" was
started in 1787, and to this Burns, whom Nature had made
greatest among lyric poets, sent lyric after lyric in pure love
of song, taking no payment, and disdaining the thought of being
paid for singing.  In August he married Jean Armour, who had
been refused him by her father when he was poor and there
was scandal in their love ; and then he sang to her :

> " She is a winsome wee thing,
> She is a handsome wee thing,
> She is a bonny wee thing,
>     This sweet wee wife o' mine
>         •     •     •     •
> * The warld's wrack we share o't,
> The warstle and the care o't ;
> Wi' her I'll blithely bear it,
>     And think my lot divine."

The wild, wilful, defiant verse, the wanton lines cast in the
teeth of censure, belonged partly to Burns's own nature, partly to
the tumult of his time ; but out of the depths of his soul came
many a strain of thought and feeling that had taken root there
in the poor farm at Mount Oliphant, when, "the cheerful supper
done, with serious grace the saint, the father, and the husband
prayed."  Burns asked for and got a place in the Excise, in aid
of his income from the farm at Ellisland, but it took him away
from his farm-work.  Captain Grose, the antiquary, came to
his farm when gathering materials for his *Antiquities of Scotland*,
published in 1789-91.  Burns told him a Galloway legend, and
gave it him in verse for his book as *Tam o' Shanter*.  In the
winter of 1791 Burns was promoted to the Dumfries division of
the Excise, with £70 a year, and went with his family to
Dumfries.  Parted from the Nature of which he was poet,
exposed to the temptations that he was weak to resist, Burns
failed in health and spirits.  War with France was impending.
Burns felt all the revolutionary fervour and the hope that sprang
out of the ruins of the Bastile.  He had gallantly seized an
armed smuggling craft, and when her effects were sold he
bought four small carronades, and sent them as a gift from
Robert Burns to the French Convention.  They were stopped

at Dover, and the too zealous exciseman was admonished. The rest is a sad tale of poverty and failing health, until the poet's death on the 21st of July, 1796.

70. **William Wordsworth**, when, in 1803, he visited the grave of Burns, sang of him, in one of his own favourite measures, derived from Allan Ramsay and Robert Ferguson,

> " Fresh as the flower, whose modest worth
> He sang, his genius ' glinted ' forth,
> Rose like a star that touching earth,
>      For so it seems,
> Doth glorify its humble birth
>      With matchless beams.
>
> " The piercing eye, the thoughtful brow,
> The struggling heart, where be they now ?
> Full soon th' aspirant of the plough,
>      The prompt, the brave,
> Slept with the obscurest, in the low
>      And silent grave.
>
> " I mourned with thousands, but as one
> More deeply grieved, for he was gone
> Whose light I hailed when first it shone,
>      And showed my youth
> How Verse may build a princely throne
>      On humble truth."

Wordsworth was newly settled with his sister at Racedown when he heard of the death of Burns. He had just written his tragedy of *The Borderers* (first published in 1842). At Racedown, in June, 1797, Coleridge, who had read the " Descriptive Sketches," looked in upon Wordsworth and his sister. Each young poet felt the genius of the other, and there was soon a warm friendship between them.

71. **Samuel Taylor Coleridge**, two years and a half younger than Wordsworth, was born October 21, 1772, the son of the vicar and schoolmaster at Ottery St. Mary. His father died when he was nine years old. In the following year he had a presentation to Christ's Hospital from an old pupil of his father's, and was educated there till 1791. Then he was sent to Jesus College, Cambridge, and obtained, in the summer, Sir W. Brown's gold medal for a Greek ode on the Slave Trade. In 1793 he passed the summer at Ottery, wrote " Songs of the Pixies;" and returned, in October, to Cambridge. In December, being in despair over his poverty and £100 of college debt, he left Cambridge, and enlisted as Private Silas Titus Comberbach, in the 15th Light Dragoons. He was found

at last, his discharge was obtained in April, 1794, and he went
back to Cambridge, gave up hope of a fellowship, but could not
take orders because he had become a Unitarian.. He resolved
to join Citizen Southey, and turn author. After a ramble in
Wales he went to see Southey at Bristol.

72. **Robert Southey,** nearly two years younger than Coleridge, was born at Bristol, August 12, 1774, the son of an unprosperous linendraper. He was educated by help of his mother's
maiden aunt, Miss Tyler, until 1788, when Miss Tyler, and an
uncle, the Rev. Herbert Hill, chaplain to the English factory at
Lisbon, sent him to Westminster School. He was expelled from
the school for a jest on the head master's faith in flogging, contributed to a school magazine called the *Flagellant.* His uncle
Hill thought he had been hardly treated, and resolved that
Robert Southey should still have justice done to his unusual
abilities. He was sent, therefore, to Balliol College, Oxford, in
1792, soon after his father's death. There he distinguished himself by his fervent zeal for the cause of the French Revolution, the
general overthrow of tyrannies, and the re-establishment of the
world on a right basis. At Easter, 1794, Coleridge came to him,
and sympathized with all his aspirations, joined him afterwards
at Bristol, was introduced to Robert Lovell, George Bennett, and
other kindred spirits. In this year Southey published his
revolutionary dramatic poem of *Wat Tyler,* and joined Coleridge
in his writing of the *Fall of Robespierre.* The new associates
agreed that as the old state of things in Europe would impede
prompt settlement in social questions, the wisest thing they could
possibly do would be to proceed to the New World, and there,
on virgin soil, establish a community in which all should be
equal and all good. From three Greek words meaning "all-
equal-government," they called their proposed state a Pantisocracy. Wives, of course, would be needed, and there were the
three Miss Frickers, eligible wives. One of these ladies was an
actress, one kept a little school, one was a dressmaker. Lovell
would marry one, Coleridge one, and Southey one. They would
and they did. Sarah Fricker became Mrs. Coleridge, and Edith
Fricker was to become Mrs. Southey, when Aunt Tyler had
been told of the young enthusiast's intentions. Aunt Tyler
raged, and discarded Southey. Good-natured Uncle Hill held
by the youth, in whom he saw "everything you could wish a
young man to have, excepting common sense and prudence,"
and as (for want of funds) the Pantisocrats could not get to the

Susquehannah, tempted him with the offer of a visit to Lisbon.
Change of scene, and absence from Bristol, might suffice to
cure his fever. Southey went with his uncle, but privately
married Edith Fricker the day before he started. When he
came home, in 1796, he claimed his wife, and at once began to
seek his living as an indefatigable writer. He produced at
Bristol his first epic, *Joan of Arc*, and as he worked on with
patient industry, and saw much to disenchant him, he became,
in time, a supporter of the old order of things.

73. **Coleridge**, after the break-up of the Pantisocracy, wrote
patriotism, preached and travelled to obtain subscribers for a
periodical outpouring of thought, to be called *The Watchman*,
which appeared from the 1st of March to the 13th of May,
1796, in which year also there were Poems of his published. He
earned money by writing verse in a newspaper. In September
of that year, his son, Hartley, was born. Coleridge had rare
powers as poet and thinker, and a gift of speech that made
them felt in daily intercourse by those about him. To be near
a substantial helper, Mr. Thomas Poole, he went to live in a
cottage at Nether Stowey, on the Bristol Channel. There was
his home when he called on **Wordsworth** and his sister, and
so strong a friendship was established that the house at Racedown was given up, and William and Dorothy Wordsworth
went to live at Alfoxden, to be near Coleridge. In the autumn
of 1797, **Coleridge**, with Wordsworth and his sister, started
from Alfoxden for Linton, and in the course of the walk *The
Ancient Mariner* was planned as a poem to be sent to the
*London Magazine*, and bring five pounds towards expenses of
the little holiday. Coleridge made the story out of a dream of
his friend, Mr. Cruikshank. Wordsworth suggested introducing
into it the crime of shooting the albatross, because he had been
reading about albatrosses in Shelvocke's Voyage (1726) a day or
two before. Wordsworth also suggested the navigation of the
ship by dead men, and furnished here and there a line. The
poem grew till it was too important to be given to a magazine.
The friends then began to plan the volume of *Lyrical Ballads*,
first published in September, 1798. It included the "Ancient
Mariner," with Wordsworth's "We are Seven," the "Idiot Boy,"
&c., written with distinct sense of a principle that deliberately
condemned and set aside the poetic "diction" of the eighteenth
century. As much pains was taken by Wordsworth to avoid the
diction as other men take to produce it. The poet, he argued,

thinks and feels in the spirit of human passions, and differs from others in a greater promptness to think and feel without immediate external excitement, and a greater power in expressing such thoughts and feelings as are produced in him in that manner. His painting of men and nature must show his perception of deep truths; but to do that fitly, it must be true itself to the life of his fellow-men in every imagined incident, and speak the common language. A selection, he said, of the language really spoken by man, wherever it is made with taste and feeling, will itself form a distinction far greater than would at first be imagined, and will entirely separate the composition from the vulgarity and meanness of ordinary life. For if the poet's subject be judiciously chosen, it will naturally, and upon fit occasion, lead him to passions the language of which, if selected truly and judiciously, must necessarily be dignified and variegated, and alive with metaphors and figures. In their common work, Coleridge was to give the sense of reality to visions of the fancy, Wordsworth to make the soul speak from the common things of life. The first edition of the "Lyrical Ballads" was published by Southey's friend, Cottle, at Bristol. The second edition, with a second volume all Wordsworth's, was published in London, in 1800, as *Lyrical Ballads, with Other Poems.* After the founding of the *Edinburgh Review* in 1802, Wordsworth had to fight for his doctrine, and stormed all the positions of the hostile critics.

74. For the first edition of the "Lyrical Ballads," in September, 1798, there was some money paid. Wordsworth had thirty guineas for his part, and a holiday abroad was resolved on. Wordsworth and his sister, with Coleridge and a friend of his, crossed, in the autumn of 1798, from Yarmouth to Hamburg, where they stayed a few days, and met Klopstock several times. Coleridge went north, to Ratzburg; Wordsworth and his sister went south, and wintered, for cheapness, at Goslar, near the Hartz mountains. There, in the spring, Wordsworth wrote the opening lines of that autobiographical poem which was published after his death, in 1850, as *The Prelude, or Growth of a Poet's Mind.* His purpose was to review thoughtfully the course of his own mind through surrounding influences, and now that he had, with the "Lyrical Ballads," fairly begun work as a poet, to determine what his aim should be, what was the highest duty he could hope to do in his own calling. This work of retrospect and self-examination was not complete until the winter of 1805-6. Meanwhile he married. After his return from Goslar, in the spring of

1799, his first visit was to the family of Mary Hutchinson, his cousin, his old playmate and companion at dame school, and his future wife. He then settled with Dorothy in a small cottage at Grasmere, to which, in 1802 he brought his wife. It was then that he finished the " Prelude," and after tracing his life from childhood to the days of his enthusiastic sympathy with the French Revolution, showed how, after his return, the influence of his sister Dorothy, and communion with nature, brought him calmer sense of the great harmony of creation and of the place of man in the great whole. His interest in man grew deeper, as he cared less for the abstract questions about life, and more for the real man ;

> " Studious more to see
> Great truths, than touch and handle little ones. "

We have fought our battle, and won freedom enough to work on and show the use of freedom—to what end the powers of civil polity were given. All we have now to do is to remove hindrances and furnish aids to the development of each individual Englishman and Englishwoman. Let each unit become better and wiser, and the whole nation will grow in strength and wisdom by the growth of its constituent atoms. There are millions helpless or mischievous because not born to conditions which have made the lives of others happy. We are not idly to lament "what man has made of man," but actively to mend the mischief. Whoever makes his own life and its influence wholesome, or in any way helps to make lives about him wholesome, adds thereby to the strength of England, and is doing the true work of the nineteenth century. Having gained, said Wordsworth,

> " A more judicious knowledge of the worth
> And dignity of individual man ;
> No composition of the brain, but man—
> Of whom we read, the man whom we behold
> With our own eyes—I could not but inquire,
> Not with less interest than heretofore,
> But greater, though in spirit more subdued,
> Why is this glorious creature to be found
> One only in ten thousand ?  What one is
> Why may not millions be ?"

Upon this thought Wordsworth rested. Here, also, this narrative draws to its close, touching the key-note of the days in which we live. Wordsworth made it the one work of his life as a poet to uphold the "dignity of individual man," strengthen tne sense of all the harmonies of nature, and show how, among them all, when taking its true place,

> "The mind of man becomes
> A thousand times more beautiful than the earth
> On which he dwells, above this frame of things
> (Which, 'mid all revolution in the hopes
> And fears of men, doth still remain unchanged)
> In beauty exalted, as it is itself
> Of quality and fabric more divine."

As the storm of revolution rolled through Europe, hearts beat high. The United States became independent. Poland rose. Even in St. Domingo Toussaint l'Ouverture led the vain fight for freedom. Then the Greeks struggled to be free. Belgium won independence. Great Britain abolished slavery in her possessions. The Italians, the Hungarians rose. Stirred by the living energies about him, **Thomas Campbell**, a young man of two-and-twenty, sang, in 1799, closing the eighteenth century, *The Pleasures of Hope :*

> " Ye that the rising morn invidious mark,
> And hate the light, because your deeds are dark ;
> Ye that expanding truth invidious view,
> And think, or wish, the song of Hope untrue ;
> Perhaps your little hands presume to span
> The march of Genius and the power of man ;
> Perhaps ye watch, at Pride's unhallow'd shrine,
> Her victims newly slain, and thus divine :—
> Here shall thy triumph, Genius, cease, and here
> Truth, Science, Virtue, close your short career.
> Tyrants ! in vain ye trace the wizard ring :
> In vain ye limit Mind's unwearied spring."

The couplet through which young Campbell poured his new music, and through which, in all their naked wretchedness, the sorrows of the poor were uttered to the rich by **George Crabbe**, who had lived among them and felt what they were —that measure, dear to former critics of the time now ended, was put to new use. It was cast aside, too, for bold freedom in the revival of old measures and fearless experiment with new. There were not only the free measures of **Coleridge** in *Christabel* (1806), of **Walter Scott** in *Marmion* (1808), of **Byron** in the *Giaour* (1813), and their like, but, in his *Thalaba* (1802), and *Curse of Kehama* (1810), **Southey** revelled in defiance of all past metrical rule, and quoted from Wither :

> " For I will for no man's pleasure
> Change a syllable or measure.
> Pedants shall not tie my strains
> To our antique poet's veins

> Being born as free as these,
> I will sing as I shall please."

Reaction against a too formal life led many with ill-regulated minds to an extravagant defiance of conventional law or conventional opinion. But their strength was the truth that was in them. Whatever **Byron's** faults, the soul of his time stirred in him. The pages in his *Childe Harold* (1812–18) that won him fame were those in which he represented his own time with an enthusiasm that sent him to die among the Greeks at Missolonghi. It speaks from his *Ode on Waterloo:*

> " But the heart and the mind,
> And the voice of mankind,
> Shall arise in communion—
> And who shall resist that proud union ?
> The time is past when swords subdued—
> Man may die—the soul's renewed."

The deep stir of life was again filling the land with song. **Young John Keats**, in his short journey to the grave (1796—1821), began to seek expression for the thought that the reign of the old gods, the Titans, must pass away as the new life glows in *Hyperion:*

> " As Heaven and Earth are fairer, fairer far
> Than Chaos and blank Darkness, though once chiefs ;
> And as we show beyond that heaven and earth
> In form and shape compact and beautiful,
> In will, in action free, companionship,
> And thousand other signs of purer life ;
> So on our heels a fresh perfection treads,
> A power more strong in beauty, born of us
> And fated to excel us, as we pass
> In glory that old Darkness."

Disdaining bondage to imperfect forms, and stung by tyranny, the pure spirit of **Percy Bysshe Shelley** defied God, yet declared Him in his verse. He lived for a far ideal of beauty in which love and truth should be supreme :

> " The one remains, the many change and pass ,
> Heaven's light for ever shines, Earth's shadows fly ;
> Life, like a dome of many-coloured glass,
> Stains the white radiance of Eternity,
> Until Death tramples it to fragments. Die,
> If thou wouldst be with that which thou dost seek."

What Shelley sought was love like that of Heaven, and a justice that remembers mercy. He died in 1822.

As the tumult lessened, the calm voices spoke. A poet who sings to us still, sang in his youth of the life and work of men.

In the second of his two poems, *Paracelsus* (1835) and *Sordello* (1840), **Robert Browning** wrote .

> " God has conceded two sights to a man—
> One of men's whole work, time's completed plan ;
> The other of the minute's work, man's first
> Step to the plan's completeness."

He taught, as **Elizabeth Barrett Browning**—the best English poetess—afterwards taught, in *Aurora Leigh* (1856), that we must be content to do our day's work in our day, and the more quietly for the far vision of what may be, which should include conviction that

> " No earnest work
> Of any honest creature, howbeit weak,
> Imperfect, ill-adapted, fails so much,
> It is not gathered, as a grain of sand
> To enlarge the sum of human actions used
> For carrying out God's ends."

**Alfred Tennyson**, in his *In Memoriam* (1850), has based upon a human love a strain that rises step by step from the first grief of the bereaved to the full sense of immortality and of the upward labour of the race of man, each true soul being

> "A closer link
> Betwixt us and the crowning race
> Of those that, eye to eye, shall look
> On knowledge."

Tennyson's *Idylls of the King* (1859–73) is one great allegory of a divine voice in each man's soul that should be king over his passions and desires.   In prose and verse there is one mind. **Jane Austen**, painting only from the life she knew, was contrasting *Sense and Sensibility* (1811), attacking *Pride and Prejudice* (1813) in novels, of which **Scott** wrote in his " Diary" after their writer's death in 1817, "That young lady had a talent for describing the involvements, feelings, and characters of ordinary life, which is to me the most wonderful I ever met with.   The big bow-wow I can do myself like any one going, but the exquisite touch which renders common-place things and characters interesting from the truth of the description and the sentiment is denied me."   And there was the bright romance and poetry of " the big bow-wow " in Scott himself, the shrewd humour, the genial sense of life that made the sequence of his novels, from *Waverley*, in 1814, to his death, in 1832, as one of the powers of Nature for the health of men.   Then **Charles Dickens** sought to undo wrong and quicken goodwill among

men ; **William Makepeace Thackeray** attacked the petty
vanities and insincerities of life, and with a cynical air upheld an ideal opposite as his own inmost simplicity and kindliness to the life of the men who scorn their neighbours and
consider themselves worldly wise.   Now, too, **George Eliot**
in all her novels instils her own faith in "plain living and high
thinking," by showing that it is well in life to care greatly for
something worthy of our care ; choose worthy work, believe in
it with all our souls, and labour to live through inevitable
checks and hindrances, true to our best sense of the highest
life we can attain.   If **Thomas Carlyle** involves more
in his condemnation of the times than may deserve his
censure, his war is the true war of his century, with the host
of false conventionalities that yet remain, with all that stands
in the way of the work now chiefly left for us to do.   " Men
speak," he says, " too much about the world.   Each one of
us here, let the world go how it will, and be victorious or
not victorious, has he not a life of his own to lead?   One
life, a little gleam of time between two eternities, no second
chance to us for evermore.   It were well for us not to live as
fools and simulacra, but as wise and realities.   The world's
being saved will not save us, nor the world's being lost destroy
us.   We should look to ourselves : there being great merit
here in the duty of staying at home.   And on the whole, to
say the truth, I never heard of worlds being saved in any
other way.   That mania of saving worlds is itself a piece of
the eighteenth century with its windy sentimentalism ; let us
not follow it too far."

To these notes on the spirit of our Literature in the nineteenth century I must be content to add some indication of its
substance in the form of Annals.

———

# ANNALS.

Henry Mackenzie (b. 1745, d. 1831), *The Man of Feeling*, 1771.   Sir Joshua
Reynolds (b. 1723, d. 1792), *Discourses*, 1772.   Edmund Burke, *Thoughts on the
Present Discontents*, 1773.   Joseph Priestley (b. 1733, d. 1804), *Natural and Re-
vealed Religion*, 1774.   Burke, *Speech on American Conciliation;* Johnson,
*Taxation no Tyranny*, 1775.   Adam Smith, *Wealth of Nations*, 1776.   Sheridan's
*School for Scandal*, 1777.   Frances Burney, *Evelina*, 1778.   Johnson's *Lives of the
Poets*, 1779—1781.   Hannah Cowley (b. 1743, d. 1809), *The Belle's Stratagem*,

1780. Erasmus Darwin, *The Botanic Garden*, 1781. William Cowper, *John Gilpin*, 1782 ; *The Task*, 1783. Charlotte Smith, *Elegiac Sonnets*, 1784. George Crabbe, *The Newspaper*, 1785. Robert Burns, *Poems* (*printed at Kilmarnock*), 1786, (*printed at Edinburgh*) 1787. Edward Gibbon, *Decline and Fall of the Roman Empire*, completed 1788. Gilbert White (b. 1720, d. 1793), *Natural History of Selborne*, 1789. Henry James Pye (b. 1745, d. 1813) succeeds Thomas Warton as Poet Laureate, 1790. Edmund Malone (b. 1741, d. 1812), *Edition of Shakespeare*, 1790. Elizabeth Inchbald (b. 1753, d. 1821), *A Simple Story*, 1791. Mary Wollstonecraft, *Vindication of the Rights of Women*, 1792. William Wordsworth, *Descriptive Sketches*, and *An Evening Walk*, 1793. Robert Southey, *Wat Tyler*; S. T. Coleridge, *The Fall of Robespierre*, 1794. Matthew Gregory Lewis, *The Monk*, 1795. Walter Scott, translation of Bürger's *Leonora and the Wild Huntsman*, 1796. William Gifford begins editing the *Anti-Jacobin*, 1797 (*Poetry of the Anti-Jacobin*, 1801). Wordsworth and Coleridge, *Lyrical Ballads*, 1798.

---

**1799.** Thomas Campbell (b. 1777, d. 1844), *Pleasures of Hope*. Robert Southey, (b. 1774, d. 1843), *Poems*, with Robert Lovell. Walter Scott (b. 1771, d. 1832), *Translation of Goethe's Götz von Berlichingen*. Matthew Gregory Lewis (b. 1775, d. 1818), *Tales of Terror*. William Cobbett (b. 1762, d. 1835), *Works of Peter Porcupine*. William Godwin (b. 1756, d. 1836), *St. Leon*. Richard Brinsley Sheridan, *Pizarro*, from Kotzebue. Erasmus Darwin (b. 1731, d. 1802), *Phytologia* [*Botanic Garden*, 1781].

**1800.** William Wordsworth (b. 1770, d. 1850), *Lyrical Ballads*, 2nd Ed. Robert Bloomfield (b. 1766, d. 1823), *Farmer's Boy*. Samuel Taylor Coleridge (b. 1772, d. 1834), *Translation of Schiller's Wallenstein*. Walter Scott, *Eve of St. John*. Thomas Moore (b. 1779, d. 1852), *Anacreon*.

**1801.** Robert Southey, *Poems*, 2 Vols. M. G. Lewis, *Tales of Wonder*. Dugald Stewart (b. 1753, d. 1828), *Life of W. Robertson* [*Philosophy of the Human Mind*, Vol. ii., 1792]. James Hogg (b. 1772, d. 1835), *Scottish Pastorals*. James Henry Leigh Hunt (b. 1784, d. 1859), *Juvenilia*. Maria Edgeworth (b. 1767, d. 1849), *Early Lessons, Belinda, Castle Rackrent*. Amelia Opie (b. 1769, d. 1853), *Father and Daughter*. T. Moore, *Little's Poems*.

**1802.** Charles Lamb (b. 1775, d. 1834), *John Woodvil, a Tragedy* [*Rosamond Gray*, 1798]. R. Bloomfield, *Rural Tales*. R. Southey, *Thalaba*. W. Scott, *Minstrelsy of the Scottish Border*, Vols. i., ii. William Paley (b. 1743, d. 1805), *Natural Philosophy* [*Horæ Paulinæ*, 1790; *Evidences*, 1794]. Thomas Paine (b. 1737, d. 1809), *Letters to the Citizens of the United States* [*Rights of Man*, Part i., 1791 ; Part ii., 1792]. William Gifford (b 1757, d. 1826), *Juvenal in English Verse* [*Baviad*, 1791 ; *Mæviad*, 1795]. Maria Edgeworth, *Moral Tales*. William Lisle Bowles (b. 1762, d. 1850), *Sonnets*, 8th Ed. [*Fourteen Sonnets*, 1789]. *Edinburgh Review* established.

**1803.** W. Scott, *Minstrelsy of the Scottish Border*, Vol. iii. R. Southey, *Tr. Amadis of Gaul. Ed. Chatterton*. Charles Dibdin (b. 1745, d. 1814), *Autobiography, with Words of 600 Songs*. W. Godwin, *Life of Chaucer*. James Hogg, *The Mountain Bard*. Jane Porter (b. 1776, d. 1850), *Thaddeus of Warsaw*.

**1804.** W. Scott, *Ed. Sir Tristrem*. R. Bloomfield, *Good Tidings*. Charlotte Smith (b. 1749, d 1804), *Conversations* [*Sonnets*, 1784 ; *Emmeline*, 1788]. Anna Seward (b. 1731, d. 1809), *Memoirs of Darwin*. James Grahame (b. 1765, d. 1811), *The Sabbath*. Maria Edgeworth, *Popular Tales*. Amelia Opie, *Adeline Mowbray*. Anna Maria Porter (b. 1781, d. 1832),

*Lakes of Killarney.* W. L. Bowles, *Spirit of Discovery by Sea.* Joanna Baillie (b. 1762, d. 1851), *Miscellaneous Plays.*

**1805.** W. Scott, *Lay of the Last Minstrel.* R. Southey, *Madoc.* W. Godwin, *Fleetwood.* Mary Tighe (b. 1773, d. 1810), *Psyche.* James Hogg, *Pilgrims of the Sun.* James Grahame, *Sabbath Walks.* Hannah More (b. 1745, d. 1833), *Hints for the Education of a Young Princess.* William Roscoe (b. 1753, d. 1831), *Life of Leo X.* [*Life of Lorenzo de' Medici,* 1795]. Sophia Lee (b. 1750, d. 1824) and Harriet Lee (b. 1756, d. 1851), *Canterbury Tales,* 5 Vols., 1797—1805. William Hazlitt (b. 1778, d. 1830), *Essay on the Principles of Human Actions.*

**1806.** S. T. Coleridge, *Christabel.* W. Scott, *Ballads and Lyrical Pieces.* James Hogg, *Mador of the Moor.* James Grahame, *Birds of Scotland.* Maria Edgeworth, *Leonora, and Letters.* Amelia Opie, *Simple Tales.* T. Moore, *Epistles, Odes, &c.* W. L. Bowles, *Ed. Pope's Works.* James Montgomery (b. 1771, d. 1854), *Wanderer of Switzerland.*

**1807.** George Crabbe (b. 1754, d. 1832), *The Parish Register* [*The Newspaper,* 1785]. W. Wordsworth, *Poems,* 2 vols. S. T. Coleridge, *Zapolya, Sybilline Leaves.* A. M. Porter, *The Hungarian Brothers.* Sydney Smith (b. 1769, d. 1845), *Peter Plymley's Letters on the Catholics.* R. Southey, *Espriella's Letters, Tr. Palmerin of England.* Henry Kirke White (b. 1785, d. 1806), *Remains,* Edited by R. Southey, 1807—1822, in 3 vols. T. Moore, *Irish Melodies,* 1807—1834. George Gordon, Lord Byron (b. 1788, d. 1824), *Hours of Idleness.* C. and M. Lamb, *Tales from Shakespeare.* Elizabeth Carter (b. 1717, d. 1806), *Memoirs of. by M. Pennington.* J. H. Leigh Hunt, *Dramatic Criticism, Classic Tales.* Thomas Robert Malthus (b. 1766, d. 1834), *Letter on Poor Laws* [*Principles of Population,* 1798].

**1808.** W. Scott, *Marmion. Life and Works of Dryden.* R. Southey, *Tr. Chronicle of the Cid.* W. Godwin, *Faulkner, a Tragedy.* Henry Mackenzie (b. 1745, d. 1831), *Works,* 8 vols. Jeremy Bentham (b. 1748, d 1832), *Scotch Reform.* Hannah More, *Cœlebs in Search of a Wife.* Anna Letitia Barbauld, *Lessons for Children. Quarterly Review* established.

**1809.** Byron, *English Bards and Scotch Reviewers.* S. T. Coleridge, *The Friend,* June 1st, 1809, to March 15th, 1810. T. Campbell, *Gertrude of Wyoming.* Reginald Heber (b. 1783, d. 1826), *Palestine.* James Grahame, *British Georgics, Africa Delivered.*

**1810.** W. Scott, *Lady of the Lake.* G. Crabbe, *The Borough.* R. Southey, *Curse of Kehama, History of Brazil.* James Hogg, *The Forest Minstrel.* Dugald Stewart, *Philosophical Essays.* Jane Porter, *The Scottish Chiefs.*

**1811.** Jane Austen (b. 1775, d. 1817), *Sense and Sensibility.* W. Scott, *Vision of Roderick.* R. Bloomfield, *Banks of the Wye.* Leigh Hunt, *The Reflector.* Dugald Stewart, *Biographical Memoirs.* Maria Edgeworth, *Tales of Fashionable Life.* David Ricardo (b. 1772, d 1823), *Price of Bullion.* Hannah More, *Practical Piety.* Mary Brunton (b. 1778, d. 1818), *Self-Control.* A. M. Porter, *Ballad Romances.* John Wilson (b. 1785, d. 1854), *Elegy on J. Grahame.* Isaac Disraeli (b. 1767, d. 1850), *Despotism, a Novel.*

**1812.** Byron, *Childe Harold,* Cantos i., ii. ; *Curse of Minerva.* Samuel Rogers (b. 1763, d. 1855), *Poems* [*Pleasures of Memory,* 1792]. Jane Austen, *Pride and Prejudice.* G. Crabbe, *Tales in Verse.* R. Southey, *Omniana, Attempts in Verse by John Jones.* Isaac Disraeli, *Calamities of Authors.* Reginald Heber, *Poems and Translations.* J. Wilson, *Isle of Palms.*

John Galt (b. 1779, d. 1839), *Tragedies, &c.* Joanna Baillie, *Plays on the Passions*, Vol. iii. James Smith (b. 1775, d. 1839), Horace Smith (b. 1772, d. 1849), *Rejected Addresses.* Frances d'Arblay (b. 1753, d. 1818), *Traits of Nature* [*Evelina*, 1778, *Cecilia*, 1782]. Amelia Opie, *Temper.* Samuel Rogers, *Poems* [*Pleasures of Memory*, 1792].

**1813.** W. Scott, *Rokeby, Bridal of Triermain.* Byron, *Waltz, Giaour, Bride of Abydos.* S. T. Coleridge, *Remorse, a Tragedy.* Percy Bysshe Shelley (b. 1792, d. 1822), *Queen Mab.* W. Gifford, *Ed. Massinger.* James Hogg, *The Queen's Wake.* Barbara Hofland, *Son of a Genius.* J. Montgomery, *World before the Flood.* Southey succeeds Pye as Poet Laureate.

**1814.** W. Wordsworth, *The Excursion.* Byron, *Ode to Napoleon, Corsair, Lara.* Walter Scott, *Lord of the Isles, Waverley.* R. Southey, *Roderick.* W. L. Bowles, *Spirit of Discovery by Sea.* Jane Austen, *Mansfield Park.* Leigh Hunt, *Feast of the Poets.* Dugald Stewart, *Philosophy of the Human Mind.* Vol. ii. T. R. Malthus, *Effect of Corn Laws.* F. d'Arblay, *The Wanderer.* Mary Brunton, *Discipline.* S. Rogers, *Jacqueline.* I. Disraeli, *Quarrels of Authors.*

**1815.** Wordsworth, *White Doe of Rylstone; Poems with New Preface and Supplementary Essay.* Scott, *Guy Mannering, Paul's Letters, Field of Waterloo.* Byron, *Hebrew Melodies.* Heber, *Bampton Lectures.* D. Ricardo, *Price of Corn.* Mrs. Opie, *Simple Tales.* Henry Hart Milman (b. 1791, d. 1867), *Fazio, a Tragedy.*

**1816.** Scott, *The Antiquary, Black Dwarf, Old Mortality.* Byron, *Childe Harold*, Canto iii. ; *Siege of Corinth; Parisina; Prisoner of Chillon.* Jane Austen, *Emma.* Coleridge, *A Lay Sermon.* Southey, *Pilgrimage to Waterloo, Lay of the Laureate.* P. B. Shelley, *Alastor, and other Poems.* Leigh Hunt, *Story of Rimini.* John Wilson, *The City of the Plague.* W. Gifford, *Ed. Ben Jonson.* Jeremy Bentham, *Chrestomathia.*

**1817.** John Keats (b. 1796, d. 1821), *Poems.* Byron, *Manfred, Lament of Tasso.* Scott, *Harold the Dauntless; Border Antiquities*, Vol. ii. (Vol. i., 1814). Moore, *Lalla Rookh.* Coleridge, *Biographia Literaria.* W. Hazlitt, *Characters of Shakespeare's Plays.* Mrs. Barbauld, *Hymns in Prose for Children.* Maria Edgeworth, *Comic Dramas.* Felicia Hemans (b. 1794, d. 1835), *Modern Greece.* I. Disraeli, *Curiosities of Literature*, Vol. iii. [Vols. i., ii., 1791-3]. *Blackwood's Magazine* established.

**1818.** Keats, *Endymion.* Shelley, *Revolt of Islam, Laon and Cythna.* Scott, *Heart of Midlothian, Bride of Lammermoor, Legend of Montrose, Rob Roy.* Byron, *Childe Harold*, Canto iv.; *Beppo.* H. H. Milman, *Samor.* Moore, *The Fudge Family in Paris.* Jeremy Bentham, *Parliamentary Reform Catechism.* Henry Hallam (b. 1778, d. 1859), *Europe during the Middle Ages.* James Mill (b. 1773, d. 1836), *History of British India.* James Morier (b. 1780, d. 1849), *Second Journey through Persia.*

**1819** Wordsworth, *Peter Bell.* Byron, *Mazeppa, Don Juan*, Cantos i., ii. Crabbe, *Tales of the Hall.* Shelley, *The Cenci, Rosalind and Helen.* Thomas Hope (b. 1770 (?), d. 1831), *Anastasius.* Jeremy Bentham, *Radical Reform.* Rogers, *Human Life.* Bryan William Procter (b. 1790), *Dramatic Scenes.* James Montgomery, *Greenland.* Felicia Hemans, *Tales and Historic Scenes.*

**1820.** Wordsworth, *The River Duddon.* Scott, *Ivanhoe, Monastery, Abbot.* Southey, *Life of Wesley,* Keats, *Lamia, Isabella, Eve of St. Agnes, &c.* Thomas Brown (b. 1778, d. 1820), *Philosophy of the Human Mind.* I

Lytton Bulwer (b. 1804, d. 1873), *Ismael, an Oriental Tale.* B. W. Procter. *A Sicilian Story.* H. H. Milman, *Fall of Jerusalem, a Dramatic Poem.*

**1821.** Scott, *Kenilworth.* Byron, *Marino Faliero, Prophecy of Dante, Sardanapalus, The Two Foscari, Cain, Don Juan,* Cantos iii., iv., v. Southey, *Vision of Judgment.* Shelley, *Prometheus Unbound, Adonais, Epipsychidion.* W. Gifford, *Persius in English Verse.* John Galt, *Annals of the Parish, Ayrshire Legatees.* Jeremy Bentham, *On the Restrictive Commercial System.* Letitia Elizabeth Landon (b. 1802, d. 1838), *The Fate of Adelaide.*

**1822.** Scott, *Fortunes of Nigel, Pirate.* Wordsworth, *Ecclesiastical Sketches.* Byron, *Werner, Vision of Judgment, Heaven and Earth.* Rogers, *Italy.* James Montgomery, *Songs of Zion.* Charles Lamb (b. 1775, d. 1834), *Essays of Elia* (in *London Magazine*). John Wilson, *Lights and Shadows of Scottish Life.* Thomas Lovell Beddoes (b. 1803, d. 1849), *The Bride's Tragedy.* H. H. Milman, *Martyr of Antioch, Belshazzar.*

**1823.** Scott, *Peveril of the Peak, Quentin Durward.* Byron, *Don Juan,* Cantos vi.—xiv.; *The Island; Age of Bronze; Morgante Maggiore Tr.,* Canto i. Moore, *Fables for the Holy Alliance, Loves of the Angels.* Southey, *History of Peninsular War,* Vol. i. John Gibson Lockhart (b. 1794, d. 1854), *Ancient Spanish Ballads.* Harriet Martineau (b. 1802), *Devotional Exercises for the Use of Young Persons.* John Foster (b. 1770, d. 1843), *Essays.* John Wilson, *Trials of Margaret Lindsay.* Mary Howitt (b. 1800), *The Forest Minstrel.* Charles Knight (b. 1791, d. 1873), *Quarterly Magazine.* C. Lamb, *Elia* (in a volume).

**1824.** Byron, *The Deformed Transformed.* Scott, *St. Ronan's Well, Redgauntlet.* Southey, *Book of the Church.* Thomas Campbell, *Theodric, with other Poems.* C. Lamb, *Elia,* and Series, in *London Magazine.* Thomas Carlyle (b. 1795), *Tr. of Goethe's Wilhelm Meister.* J. G. Lockhart, *Reginald Dalton.* Heber, *Life of Jeremy Taylor.* James Morier, *Hajji Baba.* Robert Chambers (b. 1802, d. 1871), *Traditions of Edinburgh.* Walter Savage Landor (b. 1775, d. 1864), *Imaginary Conversations,* Vol. i.

**1825.** S. T. Coleridge, *Aids to Reflection.* Scott, *Betrothed, Talisman, Lives of British Novelists.* Southey, *Tale of Paraguay.* Thomas Carlyle, *Life of Schiller.* James Hogg, *Queen Hynde.* Robert Plumer Ward (b. 1765, d. 1846), *Tremaine.* Moore, *Memoirs of Sheridan.* Henry Brougham (b. 1779, d. 1868), *Education of the People.*

**1826.** Scott, *Woodstock.* Elizabeth Barrett Browning (b. 1809, d. 1861), *An Essay on Mind, and other Poems.* Harriet Martineau, *Principles and Practice, The Rioters.* Horace Smith, *Brambletye House.* H. H. Milman, *Anne Boleyn.* Benjamin Disraeli (b. 1805), *Vivian Grey.*

**1827.** Alfred Tennyson (b. 1809), with Charles Tennyson, *Poems by Two Brothers.* Scott, *Tales of a Grandfather, Life of Napoleon, Two Drovers, Highland Widow, Surgeon's Daughter.* T. Carlyle, *Specimens of German Romance.* John Keble (b. 1792, d. 1866), *The Christian Year,* Heber's *Hymns.* E. Lytton Bulwer (afterwards Lytton), *Pelham.* James Montgomery, *Pelican Island.* Dugald Stewart, *The Philosophy of the Human Mind,* Vol. iii. Moore, *Epicurean.* Thomas Hood (b. 1798, d. 1845), *Plea of the Midsummer Fairies.*

**1828.** Scott, *Fair Maid of Perth, Tales of a Grandfather,* 2nd Series. E. L. Bulwer, *The Disowned.* T. Moore, *Odes upon Cash, Corn, and Catholics.* Alexander Dyce (b. 1798, d. 1869), *Ed. Peele.* W. Hazlitt, *Life of Napoleon.* W. S. Landor, *Imaginary Conversations,* Vol. iii. [*Gebir,* 1798]

**1829.** A Tennyson, *Timbuctoo.* Scott, *Anne of Geierstein, Tales of a Grand-father*, 3rd Series. Southey, *All for Love.* Douglas Jerrold (b. 1803, d. 1857), *Black-Eyed Susan.* George Robert Gleig (b. 1796), *Chelsea Pensioners.* E. L. Bulwer, *Devereux.* R. Chambers, *The Scottish Songs.* H. H. Milman. *History of the Jews.*

**1830.** A. Tennyson, *Poems chiefly Lyrical.* Scott, *Tales of a Grandfather*, 4th Series; *History of Scotland*, 2 Vols.; *Demonology and Witchcraft; Doom of Devorgoil; Auchindrane.* W. Godwin, *Cloudesley.* T. Moore, *Life of Byron.* Thomas Arnold (b. 1795, d. 1842), *Christian Duty of Granting the Claims of the Catholics.* *Hood's Comic Annual* (1830 to 1839).

**1831** Scott, *Count Robert of Paris, Castle Dangerous.* Ebenezer Elliott (b. 1781, d. 1849), *Corn Law Rhymes.* B. Disraeli, *The Young Duke.* Mary Somerville (b. 1792, d. 1872), *Mechanism of the Heavens.* Caroline Elizabeth Norton (b. 1808), *The Undying One.* Letitia E. Landon, *Romance and Reality.* Sir James Mackintosh (b. 1765, d. 1832), *History of England.* John Payne Collier (b. 1789), *History of English Dramatic Poetry.* Thomas Love Peacock (b. 1785, d. 1867), *Crotchet Castle.*

**1832.** Southey, *History of the Peninsular War*, Vol. iii. Harriet Martineau, *Illustrations of Political Economy.* Douglas Jerrold, *The Rent Day*, &c. E. L. Bulwer, *Eugene Aram.* W. and R. Chambers, *Journal* established. C. Knight, *Penny Magazine* established. B. W. Procter, *English Songs.* Henry Taylor (b. 1800), *Isaac Comnenus.* William Edmonstoune Aytoun (b. 1813, d. 1865), *Poland, Homer, and other Poems.* Anna Maria Hall, *The Buccaneer.*

**1833.** Alfred Tennyson, *Poems.* Hartley Coleridge (b. 1796, d. 1849), *Poems.* Southey, *Lives of British Admirals*, Vol. i. Thomas Carlyle, *Sartor Resartus* (in *Fraser's Magazine*). Elizabeth Barrett (afterwards Browning), *Translation of Prometheus Bound, and Poems.* Robert Browning (b. 1812), *Pauline: a Fragment.* E. L. Bulwer, *Godolphin.* T. Moore, *Travels of an Irish Gentleman in search of a Religion.* Charles Knight, *Penny Cyclopædia* begun. Michael Faraday (b. 1791, d. 1869), *Experimental Researches in Electricity.* B. Disraeli, *Alroy.* Charles Lamb, *Last Essays of Elia.* William Howitt, *History of Priestcraft.* Felicia Hemans, *Hymns on the Works of Nature.*

**1834.** *Remains of* Arthur Henry Hallam (b. 1811, d. 1833). Southey, *The Doctor*, Vol. i. Hartley Coleridge, *Life of A. Marvell.* W. Godwin, *Lives of the Necromancers.* Harriet Martineau, *Illustrations of Taxation.* William Harrison Ainsworth (b. 1805), *Rookwood.* Edward Bouverie Pusey (b. 1800), with John Henry Newman, John Keble, and others, *Tracts for the Times*, 90 Nos. (1834—1841). Frederick Denison Maurice (b. 1805, d. 1872), *Eustace Conway: a Novel.* Felicia Hemans, *Hymns for Children.* A. M. Hall, *Tales of Woman's Trials.* Charles Mackay (b. 1812), *Poems.* Captain Frederick Marryat (b. 1786, d. 1848), *Peter Simple, Jacob Faithful.* Mary Somerville, *Connection of the Physical Sciences.* John Foster, *Essay on Popular Ignorance.* E. L. Bulwer, *Last Days of Pompeii.* Thomas Campbell, *Life of Mrs. Siddons.* Henry Taylor, *Philip van Artevelde.* B. Disraeli, *The Revolutionary Epic.*

**1835** Wordsworth, *Yarrow Revisited.* Robert Browning, *Paracelsus.* Leigh Hunt, *Captain Sword and Captain Pen.* E. L. Bulwer, *Rienzi.* B. Disraeli, *Vindication of the British Constitution.* L. E. Landon, *Lay of the Peacock.* Thomas Noon Talfourd (b. 1765, d. 1854), *Ion*

**1836.** Charles Dickens (b. 1812, d. 1870), *Sketches by Boz.* Captain Marryat,

*Japhet in Search of a Father.* E. L. Bulwer, *Athens.* Henry Taylor, *The Statesman.* Hartley Coleridge, *Lives of Northern Worthies.* Earl Stanhope (b. 1803), *History of England from the Peace of Utrecht.*

1837. Charles Dickens, *Pickwick.* Thomas Carlyle, *The French Revolution.* Robert Browning, *Strafford.* Harriet Martineau, *Society in America.* E. L. Bulwer, *Ernest Maltravers.* Thomas Campbell, *Letters from the South.* Henry Hallam, *Literature of Europe in the 15th, 16th, and 17th Centuries,* 4 Vols. (1837-39) B. Disraeli, *Henrietta Temple, Venetia.*

1838. Wordsworth, *Sonnets.* Dickens, *Oliver Twist.* Thomas Carlyle, *Sartor Resartus* (in a vol.), *Miscellanies.* Elizabeth Barrett (Browning), *The Seraphim, and other Poems.* Douglas Jerrold, *Men of Character.* Frances Trollope (b. 1778, d. 1863), *Widow Barnaby.* E. L. Bulwer, *Alice, Lady of Lyons.* William Ewart Gladstone (b. 1809), *The State in its Relation with the Church.* Martin Farquhar Tupper (b. 1810), *Proverbial Philosophy; Geraldine: a Sequel to Coleridge's Christabel* Francis William Newman (b. 1805), *Lectures on Logic.* Lady Charlotte Elizabeth Guest, *The Mabinogion* (1838 to 1849). Eliza Cook (b. 1818), *Poems.*

1839. Thomas Moore, *Alciphron.* Dickens, *Nicholas Nickleby.* Thomas Carlyle, *Chartism.* Harriet Martineau, *Deerbrook.* W. H. Ainsworth, *Jack Sheppard.* E. L. Bulwer, *Richelieu, The Sea-Captain.* H. H. Milman, *Life of Gibbon.* B. Disraeli, *Count Alarcos : a Tragedy.* Charles Knight, *Pictorial Shakespeare.* Charles Lever (b. 1806, d. 1872), *Harry Lorrequer* Philip James Bailey (b. 1816), *Festus.*

1840. Dickens, *Master Humphrey's Clock.* William Makepeace Thackeray (b. 1811, d. 1863), *Paris Sketch-Book.* John Forster (b. 1812), *Statesmen of the Commonwealth.* Robert Browning, *Sordello.* Leigh Hunt, *A Legend of Florence.* Harriet Martineau, *The Hour and the Man.* Barbara Hofland, *Farewell Tales.* Richard Monckton Milnes, Lord Houghton (b. 1808), *Poetry for the People.* E. L. Bulwer, *Money.* H. H. Milman, *History of Christianity.* W. E. Gladstone, *Church Principles in their Results.*

1841. Thomas Carlyle, *Hero Worship.* Douglas Jerrold, *Cakes and Ale.* *Punch* established. Isaac Disraeli, *Amenities of Literature.* Thomas Campbell, *Life of Petrarch.* E. L. Bulwer, *Night and Morning.* Charles James Lever, *Charles O'Malley.* Samuel Warren (b. 1806), *Ten Thousand a Year.* John Westland Marston (b. 1820), *The Patrician's Daughter : a Tragedy.*

1842. Thomas Babington Macaulay (b. 1800, d. 1859), *Lays of Ancient Rome, Critical and Historical Essays* (from the *Edinburgh Review*). Wordsworth, *Guide to the Lakes.* Alfred Tennyson, *Poems,* 2 Vols. Robert Browning, *Pippa Passes, King Victor and King Charles, Dramatic Lyrics.* John Wilson, *Recreations of Christopher North.* Henry Taylor, *Edwin the Fair.* Leigh Hunt, *The Palfrey.* Thomas Campbell, *Pilgrim of Glencoe, and other Poems.* E. L. Bulwer, *Zanoni, Eva.* Dickens, *American Notes.* Thackeray, *Irish Sketch-Book.* John Payne Collier, *Ed. Shakespeare.*

1843. Dickens, *Christmas Carol.* Thomas Carlyle, *Past and Present.* Robert Browning, *A Blot on the 'Sutcheon, Return of the Druses.* Douglas Jerrold, *Story of a Feather.* Harriet Martineau, *Life in the Sick Room.* Lucy Aikin, *Life of Addison.* Matthew Arnold (b. 1822), *Cromwell ; a Prize Poem.* Alexander Dyce, *Ed. Beaumont and Fletcher.* John Stuart

Mill (b. 1806), *System of Logic.* James Martineau (b. 1806), *Endeavours after the Christian Life.* Hood, *Song of the Shirt.* Wordsworth succeeds Southey as Poet Laureate. John Ruskin (b. 1819), *Modern Painters.*

**1844.** Dickens, *Martin Chuzzlewit, Cricket on the Hearth.* Robert Browning, *Colombe's Birthday.* Elizabeth Barrett Browning, *Poems.* Robert Plumer Ward, *Chatsworth.* R. Monckton Milnes (Lord Houghton), *Palm Leaves.* B. Disraeli, *Coningsby.* Sydney Smith, *Letters on American Debts.* A. Dyce, *Edition of Skelton.* E. Bulwer Lytton, *Tr. Poems and Ballads of Schiller.* Arthur Penrhyn Stanley (b. 1817), *Life of Dr. Arnold.* Alexander William Kinglake (b. 1811), *Eothen.* George Lillie Craik, *Sketches of History of Literature in England* (1844 to 1851). Elizabeth Missing Sewell (b. 1815), *Amy Herbert.* Charlotte Mary Yonge (b. 1823), *Abbey Church.*

**1845.** Thomas Carlyle, *Cromwell's Letters and Speeches.* Robert Browning, *Dramatic Romances and Lyrics.* Charles Dickens, *The Chimes.* Douglas Jerrold, *Mrs. Caudle's Curtain Lectures.* George Henry Lewes (b. 1817), *Biographical History of Philosophy.* Harriet Martineau, *Forest and Game Law Tales.* W. E. Aytoun, *The Glenmutchkin Railway.* Arthur Helps, *The Claims of Labour.* Robert Chambers, *Vestiges of the Natural History of Creation.* Caroline E. Norton, *The Child of the Islands.* Mary Cowden Clarke (b. 1809), *Concordance to Shakespeare.*

**1846.** Dickens, *Pictures from Italy, Battle of Life.* Douglas Jerrold, *Punch's Complete Letter-Writer, Chronicles of Clovernook.* Robert Browning, *Luria, A Soul's Tragedy.* G. H. Lewes, *Biographical History of Philosophy,* and Series. Edward Augustus Freeman (b. 1823), *Principles of Church Restoration.* Robert Bell (b. 1800, d. 1863), *Life of Canning.* James Orchard Halliwell (b. 1820), *Dictionary of Archaic and Provincial Words.* Charles Kingsley (b. 1819), *The Saints' Tragedy.* George Grote (b. 1794, d. 1871), *History of Greece,* 12 Vols. (1846 to 1856). C., E., and A. Bronte, *Poems, by Currer, Ellis, and Acton Bell.*

**1847.** Alfred Tennyson, *The Princess.* Dickens, *The Haunted Man.* Thackeray, *Mrs. Perkins's Ball.* Leigh Hunt, *Men, Women, and Books.* John Keble, *Lyra Innocentium.* G. H. Lewes, *Comte's Philosophy, Ranthorpe.* Arthur Helps, *Friends in Council.* G. R. Gleig, *Story of Waterloo.* E. B. Lytton, *The New Timon.* James Anthony Froude (b. 1818), *The Shadows of the Clouds.* B. Disraeli, *Tancred.* James Martineau, *Endeavours after Christian Life,* Vol. ii. Charlotte Bronte (b. 1816, d. 1855), *Jane Eyre.* Emily Bronte (b. 1818, d. 1848), *Wuthering Heights.* Anne Bronte (b. 1820, d. 1849), *Agnes Grey.*

**1848.** John Forster, *Life of Goldsmith.* T. B. Macaulay, *History of England, from the Accession of James II.,* Vols. i., ii. Elizabeth Cleghorn Gaskell (b. 1810, d. 1865), *Mary Barton.* Mary Somerville, *Physical Geography.* J. S. Mill, *Principles of Political Economy.* Henry Taylor, *Notes from Life.* J. A. Froude, *The Nemesis of Faith.* Ebenezer Elliot, *More Verse and Prose.* Arthur Hugh Clough (b. 1819, d. 1861), *The Bothie of Tober-Na-Vuolich.* Arthur Helps, *The Conquerors of the New World.* Matthew Arnold, *The Strayed Reveller.* R. Monckton Milnes (Lord Houghton), *Life and Remains of Keats.* Thackeray, *Vanity Fair, Our Street.* Dickens, *Dombey and Son.*

**1849.** Charlotte Bronte, *Shirley.* Thackeray, *Pendennis, Dr. Birch.* Robert Browning, *Poems.* 2 Vols. W. E. Aytoun, *Lays of the Scottish Cavaliers,* Douglas Jerrold, *A Man made of Money.* E. B. Lytton, *The Caxtons, King Arthur.* Austin Henry Layard (b. 1817), *Nineveh and its Remains.*

E. A. Freeman, *History of Architecture.* Leigh Hunt, *The Town: a Book for a Corner.* Harriet Martineau, *Household Education.* G. H. Lewes, *Life of Robespierre.* William Hepworth Dixon (b. 1821), *John Howard.* A. H. Clough, *Ambarvalia.* J. Ruskin, *Seven Lamps of Architecture.*

**1850.** Wordsworth, *The Prelude.* Alfred Tennyson becomes Laureate, *In Memoriam.* Robert Browning, *Christmas-eve and Easter-day.* Dickens, *David Copperfield, Household Words* established. Thackeray, *The Kickleburys, Rebecca and Rowena.* Leigh Hunt, *Autobiography.* Douglas Jerrold, *The Catspaw.* Harriet Martineau, *History of England during the Thirty Years' Peace.* Thomas Carlyle, *Latter-Day Pamphlets.* E. C. Gaskell, *Moorland Cottage.* E. B. Lytton, *Harold.* Thomas Lovell Beddoes, *Death's Jest-Book.* Alexander Dyce, *Ed. Marlowe.* W. Wilkie Collins (b. 1824), *Antonina.* Sydney Dobell (b. 1824), *The Roman.* Francis W. Newman (b. 1805), *Phases of Faith.* F. D. Maurice, *Moral and Metaphysical Philosophy,* Part i. Charles Merivale (b. 1808), *History of the Romans under the Empire,* 7 Vols. (1850 to 1861).

**1851.** Elizabeth Barrett Browning, *Casa Guidi Windows.* Thomas Carlyle, *Life of John Sterling.* Arthur Helps, *Companions of My Solitude.* Douglas Jerrold, *Retired from Business.* W. Hepworth Dixon, *William Penn.* E. B. Lytton, *Not so Bad as We Seem.* J. O. Halliwell, *Ed. Shakespeare.* Robert Chambers, *Life and Works of Burns.* W. E. Gladstone, *Two Letters on Neapolitan State Prosecutions.* Charles Kingsley, *Yeast.* G. L. Craik, *The English Language.* Richard Chenevix Trench (b. 1807), *Study of Words.* John Ruskin, *Preraphaelitism.*

**1852.** Thackeray, *Esmond.* Dickens, *Child's History of England.* W. Wilkie Collins, *Basil.* B. Disraeli, *Lord George Bentinck : a Political Biography.* John Earl Russell, *Memoirs of Thomas Moore.* W. Hepworth Dixon, *Robert Blake.* Charles Reade (b. 1814), *Peg Woffington.* Charles Kingsley, *Phaeton.* A. H. Layard, *Nineveh and Babylon.*

**1853.** Charlotte Bronte, *Villette.* Macaulay, *Speeches.* Dickens, *Bleak House.* Thackeray, *English Humourists.* Sydney Dobell, *Balder.* Leigh Hunt, *Religion of the Heart.* Elizabeth C. Gaskell, *Cranford, Ruth.* Matthew Arnold, *Empedocles on Etna, Poems.* E. B. Lytton, *My Novel.* Charles Knight, *Once upon a Time.* J. S. Mill, *Enfranchisement of Women.* Michael Faraday, *Lectures on Non-Metallic Elements.* Charles Kingsley, *Hypatia.* Charles Reade, *Christie Johnstone.* J. Ruskin, *Stones of Venice.*

**1854.** Dickens, *Hard Times.* John Forster, *Life of Goldsmith,* Enlarged Edition. W. E. Aytoun, *Firmilian.* Douglas Jerrold, *A Heart of Gold.* Robert Bell, *Annotated Edition of the Poets* begun. H. H. Milman, *History of Latin Christianity,* Vols. iii., iv. Gerald Massey (b. 1828), *Ballad of Babe Christabel.* William Allingham (b. 1828), *Day and Night Songs.* Thomas Henry Huxley (b. 1825), *Educational Value of Natural History.* Richard Owen (b. 1804), *Structure of Skeleton and Teeth.* F. D. Maurice, *Moral and Metaphysical Philosophy.* John Doran (b. 1807), *Table Traits.*

**1855.** Robert Browning, *Men and Women.* Alfred Tennyson, *Maud.* Dickens, *Little Dorrit.* Thackeray, *The Rose and the Ring.* G. H. Lewes, *Life of Goethe.* Arthur Helps, *The Spanish Conquest of America* (1855—1861). Macaulay, *History of England,* Vols. iii., iv. Charles Kingsley, *Glaucus, Westward Ho.* A. P. Stanley, *Sinai and Palestine.* George Macdonald, *Within and Without : a Dramatic Poem.* George Meredith (b. 1828), *Shaving of Shagpat.* Leigh Hunt, *The Old Court Suburb, Stories in Verse.* Elizabeth C. Gaskell, *North and South.* Anthony Trollope (b.

1815), *The Warden.* Matthew Arnold, *Poems,* 2nd Series. Charles
;Shirley Brooks (b. 1816), *Aspen Court. Saturday Review* established.

**1856.** Elizabeth Barrett Browning, *Aurora Leigh.* W. E. Aytoun, *Bothwell.*
David Masson (b. 1822), *Essays, Biographical and Critical.* Alexander
Dyce, *Ed. Shakespeare, Ed. Table Talk of Samuel Rogers.* J. O.
Halliwell, *Ed. Marston.* J. A. Froude, *History of England from Fall
of Wolsey to Death of Elizabeth,* Vols. i., ii. Thackeray, *Miscellanies.*
Dinah Maria Mulock (Craik), *John Halifax.* E. A. Freeman, *History
and Conquests of the Saracens.*

**1857.** Thomas Hughes (b. 1823), *Tom Brown's School Days.* E. C. Gaskell, *Life
of Charlotte Bronte.* Anthony Trollope, *Barchester Towers.* Alexander
Dyce, *Ed. Webster.* Henry Thomas Buckle (b. 1822, d. 1862), *History of
Civilisation.* Charles Kingsley, *Two Years Ago.* Charles Reade, *Never
Too Late to Mend.*

**1858.** Thackeray, *The Virginians.* "George Eliot," *Scenes of Clerical Life.*
John Forster, *Historical and Biographical Essays.* Thomas Carlyle,
*Life of Friedrich II.,* Vols. i., ii. Anthony Trollope, *Doctor Thorne.*
J. A. Froude, *History of England,* Vols. iii., iv. Arthur Helps, *Oulita
the Serf: a Tragedy.* Matthew Arnold, *Merope: a Tragedy.* E. B.
Lytton, *What will he Do with It?* Robert Chambers, *Domestic
Annals of Scotland.* William Morris (b. 1834), *Defence of Guinevere,
and other Poems.* W. E. Gladstone, *Studies on Homer.* Adelaide Anne
Procter (b. 1824, d. 1864), *Legends and Lyrics.*

**1859.** "George Eliot," *Adam Bede.* Alfred Tennyson, *Idylls of the King.*
Dickens, *A Tale of Two Cities.* Charles Darwin (b. 1809), *Origin of
Species.* Sir William Hamilton (b. 1788, d. 1856), *Lectures on Metaphysics
and Logic.* Anthony Trollope, *The West Indies.* David Masson, *Life of
Milton,* Vol. i.; *British Novelists.* John Payne Collier, *Ed. Shakespeare
revised.* J. S. Mill, *On Liberty.* John Earl Russell, *Life of C. J. Fox.*
Thomas de Quincey (b. 1785, d. 1859), *Works Collected* (1853—1860).

**1860.** Elizabeth Barrett Browning, *Poems before Congress.* "George Eliot,"
*The Mill on the Floss.* G. H. Lewes, *Physiology of Common Life.* John
Forster, *Arrest of the Five Members.* C. Shirley Brooks, *The Gordian
Knot.* W. Wilkie Collins, *The Woman in White.* Macaulay, *Mis-
cellaneous Writings, History of England,* Vol. v. J. A. Froude, *History of
England,* Vols. v. and vi. Charles Reade, *The Cloister and the Hearth.*

**1861.** "George Eliot," *Silas Marner.* Dickens, *Great Expectations.* Thackeray,
*The Four Georges, Lovel.* Anthony Trollope, *Framley Parsonage.* Thomas
Hughes, *Tom Brown at Oxford.* W. E. Aytoun, *Norman Sinclair.*
Charles Knight, *Popular History of England* (1858—1862). Earl Stan-
hope, *Life of Pitt.* Theodore Martin (b. 1816), *Tr. of Catullus.*

**1862.** Thackeray, *Adventures of Philip, Roundabout Papers.* Thomas Carlyle,
*Life of Friedrich II.,* Vol. iii. E. B. Lytton, *A Strange Story.* Sir Henry
Taylor, *St. Clement's-eve.* F. D. Maurice, *Claims of the Bible and of
Science.* David Gray (b. 1838, d. 1861), *The Luggie, and other Poems.*
Caroline E. Norton, *The Lady of Garaye.* Jean Ingelow (b. 1830), *Poems.*
Mrs. Browning's *Last Poems.* John William Colenso, *The Pentateuch and
Book of Joshua Examined,* 5 Parts (1861 to 1865). Theodore Martin, *Tr.
Dante's Vita Nuova.* Charles Darwin, *Fertilisation of Orchids.*

**1863.** "George Eliot," *Romola.* Thomas Henry Huxley, *Evidence as to Man's
Place in Nature.* Edward A. Freeman, *History of Federal Government,*
Vol. i. Charles Kingsley, *The Water Babies.* A. W. Kinglake, *History*

*of the Invasion of the Crimea*, Vols. i., ii.   Elizabeth C. Gaskell, *Sylvia's Lovers*.   John Keble, *Life of Bishop Wilson*.   A. P. Stanley, *History of the Jewish Church*.   Florence Nightingale (b. 1820) *Notes on Hospitals*. George Macdonald, *David Elginbrod*.

**1864.** Alfred Tennyson, *Enoch Arden*.   Robert Browning, *Dramatis Personæ*. John Forster, *Life of Sir John Eliot*.   Algernon Charles Swinburne (b. 1843), *Atalanta in Calydon*.   John Henry Newman (b. 1801), *Apologia pro Vitâ Suâ*.   William Allingham, *Laurence Bloomfield in Ireland*. G. H. Lewes, *Aristotle*.   Thomas Carlyle, *Life of Friedrich II.*, Vol. iv. Alexander Dyce, *Revised Edition of Shakespeare*.   E. B. Pusey, *Lectures on Daniel, An Eirenicon*.   John William Kaye (b. 1814), *History of the Sepoy War*.   John Doran, *Their Majesties' Servants*.

**1865.** Dickens, *Our Mutual Friend*.   Algernon C. Swinburne, *Chastelard*. John Stuart Mill, *Comte and Positivism*.   *Fortnightly Review* established. Thomas Carlyle, *Life of Friedrich II.*, Vols. v., vi.   Elizabeth C. Gaskell, *Wives and Daughters*.   W. H. Dixon, *The Holy Land*.   F. D. Maurice, *Conflict of Good and Evil in Our Day*.   George Grote, *Plato*.

**1866.** "George Eliot," *Felix Holt*.   Lord Lytton, *The Lost Tales of Miletus*. James A. Froude, *History of England*, Vols. ix., x.   W. Wilkie Collins, *Armadale*.   Matthew Arnold, *New Poems*.   Bryan W. Procter, *Charles Lamb: a Memoir*.   Christiana Rosetti, *The Prince's Progress*, &c.

**1867.** William Morris, *Life and Death of Jason*.   Edward A. Freeman, *History of the Norman Conquest*, Vol. i.   Thackeray, *Denis Duval*.   Jean Ingelow, *A Story of Doom*.   G. H. Lewes, *Biographical History of Philosophy* (Enlarged Ed.).   Thomas Carlyle, *Shooting Niagara, and After!*   W. H. Dixon, *New America*.   Theodore Martin, *Memoir of W. E. Aytoun*. Matthew Arnold, *Study of Celtic Literature*.   J. A. Froude, *Short Studies on Great Subjects*.   Augusta Webster, *A Woman Sold*, &c.   John Hill Burton, *History of Scotland*, Vols. i.—iv.

**1868.** "George Eliot," *The Spanish Gypsey: a Poem*.   Robert Browning, *The Ring and the Book*.   William Morris, *The Earthly Paradise*.   Gerald Massey, *Shakespeare's Sonnets Interpreted*.   E. A. Freeman, *History of Norman Conquest*, Vol. ii.   W. H. Dixon, *Spiritual Wives*.   A. P. Stanley, *Memorials of Westminster Abbey*.

**1869.** Matthew Arnold, *Culture and Anarchy*.   E. A. Freeman, *History of Norman Conquest*, Vol. iii.   John Forster, *Life of W. S. Landor*.   Harriet Martineau, *Biographical Sketches*.   W. H. Dixon, *Her Majesty's Tower*. Vols. i., ii.   Alexander Dyce, *Ed. Ford*.

**1870.** Charles Dickens, *The Mystery of Edwin Drood*.   John Stuart Mill, *The Subjection of Women*.   Matthew Arnold, *St. Paul and Protestantism*. Dante Gabriel Rosetti, *Poems*.   Thomas Henry Huxley, *Lay Sermons, Essays and Reviews*.   John Henry Newman, *Miscellanies*.

**1871.** Robert Browning, *Balaustion's Adventure*. *Prince Hohenstiel-Schwangau*. Robert Buchanan, *Napoleon Fallen: a Lyrical Drama*.   Lord Lytton, *The Coming Race*.   David Masson, *Life of Milton*, Vol. ii.   W. H. Dixon, *Her Majesty's Tower*, Vols. iii., iv.   Benjamin Jowett, *The Dialogues of Plato translated, with Analyses and Introductions*.   Charles Kingsley, *At Last: a Christmas in the West Indies*.   John Morley, *Voltaire*. A. C. Swinburne, *Songs before Sunrise*.   Anthony Trollope, *Ralph the Heir*.   William Black, *Daughter of Heth*.

**1872.** "George Eliot," *Middlemarch*.   Alfred Tennyson, *Gareth and Lynette*. Robert Browning, *Fifine at the Fair*.   William Morris, *Love is Enough*.

George Grote, *Aristotle,* edited by Alexander Bain and George Croom Robertson. William Chambers, *Memoir of Robert Chambers.* John Forster, *Life of Dickens,* Vols. i., ii. Edward A. Freeman, *History of the Norman Conquest,* Vol. iv. James A. Froude, *The English in Ireland in the Eighteenth Century.* Charles Darwin, *Expression of the Emotions.*

**1873.** Lord Lytton, *Kenelm Chillingly;* (unfinished last work) *The Parisians.* Anthony Trollope, *Australia and New Zealand.* John Morley, *Rousseau.* E. A. Freeman, *Historical Essays.* Matthew Arnold, *Literature and Dogma.* Robert Browning, *Red Cotton Nightcap Country.* David Masson, *Life of Milton,* Vol. iii. Charles (Tennyson) Turner, *Sonnets, Lyrics,* and *Translations.* John Stuart Mill, *Autobiography.* David Masson, *Life of Milton,* Vol. iii.

**1874.** John Forster, *Life of Charles Dickens,* Vol. iii. William Stubbs, *Constitutional History of England,* Vol. i. J. A. Froude, *The English in Ireland.* George Eliot, *Legend of Jubal.* A. C. Swinburne, *Bothwell.* John Morley, *On Compromise.* Dorothy Wordsworth, *Record of a Tour in Scotland in 1803,* edited by J. C. Shairp.

**1875.** Robert Browning, *Aristophanes' Apology, The Inn Album.* Alfred Tennyson, *Queen Mary.* William Morris, *The Æneids of Virgil done into English Verse.* John Forster, (unfinished last work) *Life of Swift,* Vol. i. Thomas Carlyle, *Early Kings of Norway.* John Richard Green, *Short History of the English People.* William Wordsworth, *Prose Works* edited by A. B. Grosart.

**1876.** George Eliot, *Daniel Deronda.* A. C. Swinburne, *Erectheus.* William Morris, *Story of Sigurd the Volsung.* F. W. Farrar, *The Life of Christ.* George O. Trevelyan, *Life and Letters of Lord Macaulay. Life and Letters of Charles Kingsley,* edited by his wife. Leslie Stephen, *History of English Thought in the Eighteenth Century.*

**1877.** Alfred Tennyson, *Harold.* Lewis Morris, *The Epic of Hades.* Robert Browning, *The Agamemnon of Æschylus transcribed.* William Allingham, *Songs, Ballads,* and *Stories.* Thomas Huxley, *Physiography.* John Morley, *Critical Miscellanies.* Matthew Arnold, *Last Essays on Church and Religion.* Harriet Martineau, *Autobiography.* B. W. Procter, *An Autobiographical Fragment.*

**1878.** William Stubbs, *Constitutional History of England,* Vol. iii., and last. David Masson, *The Life of Milton,* Vols. iv., v. W. E. H. Lecky, *History of England in the Eighteenth Century,* Vols. i., ii. Robert Browning, *Le Saisias.* A. C. Swinburne, *Poems and Ballads,* Second Series. Lewis Morris, *Gwen.* John Morley, *Diderot and the Encyclopædists.* John Robert Seeley, *Life and Times of Stein.*

**1879.** W. E. Gladstone, *Gleanings of Past Years.* Matthew Arnold, *Mixed Essays.* J. A. Froude, *Cæsar, a Sketch.* Robert Browning, *Dramatic Idyls.* Alfred Tennyson, *The Falcon* (acted). Charles Dickens, *Letters.* Algernon C. Swinburne, *A Study of Shakespeare.*

**1880.** David Masson, *Life of Milton,* Vol. vi. (and last, except *Indexes*). Robert Browning, *Dramatic Idyls,* second series. Lewis Morris, *The Ode of Life.* Algernon C. Swinburne, *Songs of the Springtides.* Alfred Tennyson, *Ballads and other Poems.* Justin MacCarthy, *History of Our Own Times.*

**1881.** Charles Darwin, *On the Formation of Vegetable Mould through the Action of Worms.* Thomas Carlyle, *Reminiscences,* Edited by J. A. Froude. John Morley, *Life of Cobden.* Charles Dickens's *Letters.* Vol. iii. Dante

Gabriel Rossetti, *Ballads and Sonnets.* Algernon Swinburne, *Mary Stuart,*
a *Tragedy.* J. H. Shorthouse, *John Inglesant.* John Addington Symonds,
*Italian Literature,* Two Vols., completing a work in Five Vols. on *Renaissance in Italy.*

**1882.** John Anthony Froude, *The Life of Carlyle,* Vols. i., ii. Matthew Arnold,
*Irish Essays and others.* John Richard Green, *The Making of England.*

---

# APPENDIX.

### I.—CHAUCER.

THE Scrope and Grosvenor Roll (see pp. 124, 125) is no authority for the
age assigned to Chaucer as a witness aged "forty and more" in October,
1386. It was William Godwin, in 1803, who first called attention to
the discrepancy detected by himself between the accepted evidence of
Chaucer's age and that of the Scrope and Grosvenor Roll. He had been
led to search for the record by a slight reference to it in the Life prefixed
to Urry's edition of Chaucer. Having obtained a copy of Chaucer's
evidence from Francis Townsend, Windsor Herald, he found, as he said,
not the particulars he looked for, but something that he did not look for;
"and this was a new hypothesis respecting the period of Chaucer's birth."
Mr. Godwin then showed that the reduction of Chaucer's age by eighteen
years or less was in contradiction to Gower's reference to his friend's
"dayés old" and to Chaucer's own 'For I am old," in "The House of
Fame," which was written when he was still Comptroller of Customs, therefore, not later than 1386, the very year when the Scrope and Grosvenor
Roll calls his age "forty and more." Although he was the discoverer of
this new ground for question, Godwin made a right estimate of its value,
and he built no theory upon it.

In 1832, Sir Harris Nicolas printed privately for subscribers the Scrope
and Grosvenor Roll, with a History of the Family of Scrope and Biographical Notices of upwards of two hundred of the Deponents in favour of Sir
Richard Scrope, including Chaucer. The third volume, which was to have
contained biographical notices of the other deponents for Sir Richard and of
the deponents for Sir Robert Grosvenor, did not appear. Sir Harris Nicolas,
in comparing known facts of the lives of deponents with the statements of
their ages on this Roll, had occasion again and again to show, from in-

ternal as well as external evidence, that wrong ages were often assigned to witnesses. No one has studied the Roll so minutely as its editor, who also found that it gave him no authority to disturb the received opinions as to Chaucer's birth year. He said " the many instances which have been adduced of the mistakes that occur respecting the ages of the deponents, of whom some are stated to have been ten, and others even twenty years younger than they actually were, prevents Chaucer's deposition being conclusive on the point." I add a few of these mistakes :—

Sir John Massy, when examined for Scrope at Chester, was aged fifty ; when examined in the same year for Grosvenor he was forty-three " et pluis." Sir George Bryan was entered as 'sixty " et pluis " when his age was over eighty. Sir Richard Bingham, aged sixty-six, was said to be fifty " et pluis," The " and more " is so vague that if we omit it from the age of Sir R. Conyers we must suppose him to have married at the age of eight. But, as Sir Harris Nicolas explains, " the word ' pluis ' is often used with great latitude in the depositions, and sometimes means ten or even twenty years." Sir Robert Marny is said to have been fifty-two (without any " pluis "), and first armed at the first relief of Stirling—that is to say, when he was two years old. He is said also to have been at the siege of Tournay (in 1340), when, by this fallible record, his age must have been six. Sir Bernard Brocas, when his age was really fifty-six, was put at forty, while the record adds that he was first armed at La Hogue, so that the Roll itself represents him as having gone to the wars when he was not yet one year old. Either he did so, or one of the two dates must be wrong. John Schakel also, said to be forty-five in 1386, and to have been first armed in the year of the battle of Morlaix, must (if this record be trustworthy) have gone to the wars aged one. According to this good witness of ages, vigour, which sometimes began early, might last long. Sir Harris Nicolas points out that John Thirlewall, if the record on the Roll be right, must have been begotten when his father was one hundred and thirty-five years old. There can be no stable reconstruction of opinion as to Chaucer's life and works based on a statement of age in the Scrope and Grosvenor Roll.

## II.—Students' Books.

*Old English History.* By Edward A. Freeman, D.C.L. Macmillan. Price 6s. [The best short sketch of English history before the Conquest.]

*The Growth of the English Constitution from the Earliest Times.* By E. A. Freeman. Price 5s. Macmillan and Co.

*Select Charters, and other Illustrations of English Constitutional History,* from the Earliest Times to the Reign of Edward I. Arranged and Edited by William Stubbs, M.A., Regius Professor of Modern History. Price 8s. 6d. Clarendon Press Series. Macmillan. [A thorough manual of early constitutional history, with citation of the whole text of important documents, and many illustrative extracts, chiefly in Latin.]

*The Constitutional History of England in its Origin and Development.* By William Stubbs, M.A., Regius Professor of Modern History. Three volumes (1875—78). Oxford, Clarendon Press. Price 36s. [The best work on its subject.]

2 D

*A Short History of the English People.* By John Richard Green, M.A.
Price 7s. 6d. Macmillan. [Has two qualities seldom found together,
being very popular and very thoughtful.]

*An Anglo-Saxon Reader,* in prose and verse, with Grammatical Introduction, Notes, and Glossary. By Henry Sweet, M.A. Price 8s. 6d.
Macmillan.

*An Anglo-Saxon Primer.* By H. Sweet. Price 2s. 6d.

*A Book for the Beginner in Anglo-Saxon.* By John Earle, M.A., Professor
of Anglo-Saxon, Oxford, Price 2s. 6d. Macmillan.

*A Grammar of the Anglo-Saxon Tongue,* from the Danish of Erasmus
Rask. By Benjamin Thorpe. Second Edition. Price 5s. Trübner
and Co.

*A Compendious Anglo-Saxon and English Dictionary.* By the Rev.
Joseph Bosworth, D.D. Price 12s. J. R. Smith.

*An Anglo-Saxon Dictionary,* based on the MS. Collections of Dr. Bosworth.
By T. Northcote Toller, M.A., Smith Professor of English in the
Owen's College, Manchester. Parts i. and ii., each 15s.

*Bibliothek der Angelsächsischen Poesie,* von C. W. M. Grein. Two Vols.
[Contains " Beowulf," " Cædmon," the poems of the Exeter and Vercelli
Book, and all the chief pieces of First English poetry. There is an elaborate
glossary, First English and Latin, in two companion volumes.]

*Beowulf* alone has been edited with a full glossary (German), by C.
W. M. Grein (price 3s. 6d.) and by Moritz Heyne (price 4s. 6d.).

*Cædmon* has been edited by K. W. Bouterwek, with Glossary, First
English and Latin (price about 7s.).

*Specimens of Early English.* A new and revised Edition, with Introduction, Notes, and Glossarial Index. By the Rev. Richard Morris,
LL.D., and Professor Walter W. Skeat, M.A. Part i., A.D. 1150—
1300 (price 9s.); Part ii. (price 7s. 6d.), *from Robert of Gloucester to
Gower,* A.D. 1298 *to* A.D. 1393. Clarendon Press Series. Macmillan.

*Specimens of English Literature, from the "Ploughman's Crede" to the
"Shephearde's Calendar,"* A.D. 1394—A,D. 1579. With Introduction,
Notes, and Glossarial Index. By the Rev. Walter W. Skeat, M.A.
Price 7s. 6d. Clarendon Press. Macmillan.

*Chaucer: the Prologue to the Canterbury Tales, The Knightes Tale, The
Nonnes Prestes Tale.* Edited by Rev. R. Morris, LL.D., and Prof.
Skeat, who has edited in volumes of the same series, price 4s. 6d. each.
the *Prioresses Tale* and *The Man of Lawes Tale,* with others.

*The Riches of Chaucer.* By Charles Cowden Clarke. Price 10s. 6d.
Lockwood and Co.
[A very good Chaucer for young readers and ladies, with omissions,
and with the spelling modernised.]

*The Vision of William concerning Piers the Plowman, by William Lang-
land.* Edited by Prof. W. W. Skeat, M.A. With Introduction,
Notes, and Glossary. Price 4s. 6d. Clarendon Press. Macmillan.

No books produced in this country give more efficient help than those
of Mr. Skeat and Dr. Morris to the student who begins to make acquaintance with our early English authors. Other good aids to the study of
English literature in the Clarendon Press series are Mr. Kitchin's school

editions (price **2s. 6d.** each) of the First and of the Second Books of *Spenser's Faerie Queene;* the Rev. R. W. Church's edition (price 2s.) of the First Book of *Hooker's Ecclesiastical Polity,* and the fully annotated editions of *Select Plays of Shakespeare,* by Messrs. W. G. Clark and Aldis Wright, which are published at 1s. and 1s. 6d. each, and are the best books of the kind. These editions already include *The Merchant of Venice, Hamlet, Macbeth,* and *Richard II.* Mr. W. Aldis Wright has contributed also to the series a thoroughly good student's edition of *Bacon's Advancement of Learning* (price 4s. 6d.), and I know no compact body of notes upon Milton fuller or more judiciously selected than those in the Clarendon Press edition by Mr. R. C. Browne of *Milton's Poems,* in two volumes (price 4s. and 3s. each). The Rev. Mark Pattison contributes to the same series, in two volumes (price 1s. 6d. each), fully annotated editions of *Pope's Essay on Man* and of his *Epistles and Satires.*

A good annotated edition of *Pope's Works* (price 3s. 6d.) has been contributed by Professor A. W. Ward to the *Globe Edition of English Authors.* Macmillan. In the same series (also price 3s. 6d.) is our best annotated *Dryden,* with a memoir, revised text, and notes, by W. D. Christie, M.A. It has a carefully-corrected text ; and Dr. Morris has secured the same advantage for the *Spenser* in the Globe series, which is not annotated, but has a glossary and an excellent introductory memoir by Prof. Hales. Best of all is a thorough *Milton* by Prof. Masson.

Prof. Hales has also provided teachers and young students with a class-book containing about thirty of the best English poems, each complete, from Spenser, Milton, Dryden, Pope, Johnson, Collins, Gray, Goldsmith, Burns, Cowper, Coleridge, Scott, Wordsworth, Byron, Keats, and Shelley, under the title of *Longer English Poems, with Notes, Philological and Explanatory, and an Introduction on the Teaching of English* (price 4s. 6d.). Macmillan. The notes are very full and good, and the book, edited by one of our most cultivated English scholars, is probably the best volume of selections ever made for the use of English schools.

Older students will find among the *Publications of the Early English Text Society,* which gives a most liberal return of books for the annual subscription of a guinea, many of the chief old romances, including *Havelok,* which may be had separately for 10s.; and Sir David Lindsay's works, *The Satire of the Three Estates,* forming a separate part, price 2s. 6d. Information about the work of the *Early English Text Society* and the *Chaucer Society* may be obtained by addressing the Hon. Sec., care of N. Trübner and Co., 60, Paternoster Row.

The *English Reprints* of Professor Arber (issued by himself from 1, Montague Road, Birmingham) are exact reprints of valuable books, otherwise scarce, with good bibliographical and biographical introductions. The series includes *Udall's Ralph Roister Doister* (6d.); *Sir Thomas More's Utopia,* in Ralph Robynson's Translation (1s.); *Latimer's Sermon on the Ploughers* (6d.); *Seven Sermons before Edward VI.* (1s. 6d.); *Ascham's Toxophilus* (1s.), *Schoolmaster* (1s.); *Tottel's Miscellany* (2s. 6d.); *Lyly's Euphues* (4s.); *Gascoigne's Steel Glass,* and other pieces of his (1s.); *Gosson's Schoole of Abuse* (6d.); *Sidney's Apologie for Poetrie* (6d.); *Puttenham's Arte of English Poesie* (2s.); *King James I.'s Essays of a Prentise in the*

*Divine Art of Poesie, and Counterblast to Tobacco* (1s.); *A Harmony of Bacon's Essays* (5s.)—the texts of Bacon's editions in parallel columns, showing at a glance every successive omission, addition, and correction; *The Duke of Buckingham's Rehearsal* (1s.), &c. &c. Books hitherto unattainable, or reproduced only at high price for a limited number of subscribers, are here made accessible to all students at a price not above that of the best cheap literature of the day. To the single energy of Mr. Arber, who is his own publisher, students of English are indebted for this first attempt to give them free access to books in which the general reader has yet to acquire an interest.

*An Etymological Dictionary of the English Language*, by the Rev. Walter W. Skeat, M.A., Elrington and Bosworth Professor of Anglo-Saxon in the University of Cambridge (price £2 4s.), is the result of a rare union of sound scholarship with indefatigable powers of work.

· *A Concise Etymological Dictionary* is a work by the same author (price 5s. 6d.).

Dr. Edwin A. Abbott, Head Master of the City of London School, has been the first to produce, besides other good aids to the study of English, a Shakespearian Grammar. This has been developed in successive editions, is well arranged, and so indexed as to be handy either for chance reference, or for use in the study of a single play. It is entitled *A Shakespearian Grammar. An Attempt to Illustrate some of the Differences between Elizabethan and Modern English. For the Use of Schools.* Price 6s. (Macmillan.)

*A Brief Biographical Dictionary.* Compiled and Arranged by the Rev. Charles Hole. Price 4s. 6d. Macmillan. [Is a handy and trustworthy little desk-book of reference for dates of birth and death of noteworthy persons, of all times and countries, with a defining word or two on each.]

*The Dictionary of Biographical Reference.* By Lawrence B. Phillips. Price 31s. 6d. Sampson Low, Son, and Marston. [Is an accurate work of the same kind, on a much larger scale. It includes living writers, and contains one hundred thousand names, together with a classed index of the biographical literature of Europe and America.]

An excellent reference *Dictionary of General Biography*, in one volume, is that edited by William L. R. Cates. Price 21s. Longmans.

*Cassell's Biographical Dictionary.* Price 21s. [Is illustrated with woodcut portraits of eminent men, and is especially good in its British-Indian Biographies.]

*Familiar Words.* By J. Hain Friswell. Price 6s. Sampson Low, Son, and Co. [Is a convenient and accurate dictionary of commonly-quoted lines, or phrases; showing from what book they are taken.]

There is also a *Dictionary of Phrase and Fable*, giving the Derivation, Source, or Origin of Common Phrases, Allusions, and Words that have a "Tale to Tell." By the Rev. E. Cobham Brewer, LL.D. Price 3s. 6d. Cassell & Company. [Is an especially good book of reference for words, phrases, and allusions of all kinds, about which a student might be glad of information. It is so full of curious and useful matter, that while it is of constant service to the worker, it is, perhaps, the only dictionary

in the world that any intelligent idler might be glad to read at odd times
for amusement.

Cordial recognition is due to the merit of the "Lessons in English" and
"Lessons in English Literature" which form part of the new edition of
*Cassell's Popular Educator*, a work—in six quarto volumes (price 5s. each)
—that skilfully gives the required assistance to those who are labouring to
help themselves by the enlargement of their knowledge. It is described as
"A Complete Encyclopædia of Elementary, Advanced, and Technical
Education;" but there is a companion series, with a good Index, *The
Technical Educator* (in four volumes, 6s. each), forming a distinct Encyclopædia of Technical Education. These volumes are strong aids to that
development of the individual which it is the chief work of the best men
of our time to maintain as a source of health and strength for England in
the present and the future, and for which the publishers of the book now
in the reader's hand have laboured long and faithfully. They have given
aid to the attainment of a knowledge of the past life of our country by
issuing in nine large volumes (price 9s. each) a history— *Cassell's Illustrated
History of England*—from the Roman Invasion to the year 1871, which
allows space for the detail that helps many to realise the past, associates
the reigns of kings with steady growth of a great people, and gives due
weight to events that especially concern the story of the British Constitution. A characteristic feature of this work is the very large space given to
a narrative of those events of recent history which have the most direct
connection with the political and social life of our own day.

There is suggestive matter in a handsome and well-illustrated book by
Thomas Archer, issued by the same publishers, that looks abroad as well as
at home for *Decisive Events in History* (price 5s.) from Marathon to Sedan,
a book planned for popular use, and apt for the development of thought.

*The Story of English Literature*, by Anna Buckland (price 5s., Cassell &
Company), is a book designed chiefly for young readers. It tells clearly and
gracefully, with a quick sense not only of what is significant, but also of
what will interest the young, those main facts in the story of our Literature
which represent the mind that shaped our History. Miss Buckland's book
might be very usefully employed in home teaching or in junior classes as a
first introduction to English Literature.

In *Cassell's Library of English Literature*, edited by Henry Morley,
there is an endeavour within five large volumes (price 12s. 6d. or 11s. 6d.
each, and each a complete work) to illustrate the history of English thought
by making the wit and wisdom of our English writers speak for itself.
Following strictly in each volume the succession of years from generation
to generation—for there can be no clear recollection of the past when
that is observed carelessly—and with only so much connecting narrative
and annotation as are necessary to secure a proper understanding and
enjoyment of the pieces quoted, an attempt is made to gather into one
volume as many as possible of the best *Shorter English Poems;* to give a
like collection in another volume of *Shorter Works in English Prose;* in
another volume to illustrate by poets and prose writers the course of *English
Religion;* in another *English Plays;* and in another to describe, with help
of abundant extract, the *Longer Works in English Verse and Prose.* All

the pictures in these volumes are taken from contemporary portraits, or reproduce contemporary illustrations of the pieces quoted, or the forms of thought expressed in them.

Another book in aid of the general study of our literature, issued by the same house, is the *Dictionary of English Literature*, being a comprehensive guide to English authors and their works, by W. Davenport Adams. (Price 10s. 6d.) The matter in this book is so well chosen and digested, that in common practical use the general reader will seldom fail to find what he looks for, whether it be date of a book, information about an author, or reference to the source of a phrase or quotation.

The *Encyclopædic Dictionary*, of which the second part of the second volume, just published, reaches to the word "destruction," is published by Messrs. Cassell & Company (10s. 6d. per section). As a dictionary of English words it is unusually full, including Scottish dialect, many obsolete words found in our old writers, and a host of scientific and technical terms. Pronunciation is carefully marked, and etymologies are well given, but the special character of this Dictionary consists in the extension given to the definitions. These are encyclopædic. They are compact in form, show great care to ensure accuracy of detail, and give, with illustrative quotation of authors, and with aid of woodcut sketches and diagrams, the kind of information often hunted for in vain. No other dictionary has explained the various meanings of words with such completeness of exact detail. The student who is finding in it what he wants will often learn more than he looks for.

In *The Leopold Shakspere* (price 6s.), Messrs. Cassell & Company have produced the lay-Bible of England for the English people in a richly illustrated volume, prefaced by Mr. Furnivall. This labour for a wide diffusion of the means of intellectual health does not stop at the lay-Bible, but includes strenuous endeavour to aid thoughtful study of the Bible itself. *The History of the English Bible* (price 2s. 6d.), by the Rev. W. F. Moulton, M.A., D.D., Master of the Leys School, Cambridge, traces the story of successive English efforts to make the contents of the Bible rightly known, from Cædmon's paraphrase to the recent labours on behalf of a revised translation. *The Bible Educator*, in four volumes (price 6s. each), edited by Dean Plumptre, is a storehouse of illustrative and explanatory matter, contributed by some of the best Biblical scholars, that will help many to read with a new interest and quicker understanding the Book that has given its best strength to English literature and still lies at the heart of English life.

# INDEX.

Absalom and Achitophel, 715—719
Academy, the French, 631
Actors, 330, 331, 383—387, 414, 440, 505, 635, 636
Addison, Joseph, 753, 754—756, 769—771, 779—785, 791, 796—798
Advancement of Learning, Bacon's, 517, 518
Ælfric, 37, 38
Aidan, 16
Aikin, Lucy, 890
Ailred of Rievaulx, 64
Ainsworth, William Harrison, 889, 890
Akenside, Mark, 836, 837
Alain de l'Isle, 120
Alcestis in Chaucer, 111, 112, 148, 149
Alcuin, 24
Aldhelm, 21
Alemanni, 288, 289
Alexander, King, Romances of, 77, 78
Alexander, William, Earl of Stirling, 504
Alfred, King, 31—35
— of Beverley, 48
Allegory, Development of, 46, 47, 87, 88, 119, 121, 211, 212, 215, 216, 218 —220, 376, 406
Allegro, L', 553
Allen, Ralph, 820, 822, 833
Allingham, William, 892, 894
Amadis of Gaul, 281, 392
Amyot, Jacques, 379
Ancren Riwle, the, 76
André, Bernard, 221
Andrew, Legend of St., 28
Andrewes, Lancelot, 511, 512
Aneurin, 6
Anglo-Saxon Chronicle, 34
Anglo-Saxons, 11, 12
Annus Mirabilis, 648—653
Anselm, 43
Apollo Club, Ben Jonson's, 536
Aquinas, 92
Arabs, Influence of the, 45—47
Arbuthnot, John, 801, 802
Arcades, Milton's, 555
Arcadia, 278, 279, 392—394, 629
Areopagitica, 581—583
Ariosto, 200, 279—281, 391, 449 ; translated, 469

Arminius, 514, 738
Armstrong, John, 823
Arnold, Matthew, 890—895
— , Dr. Thomas, 889
Arthur, King, 7, 8, 30, 31, 61—64, 456, 562, 765
Ascham, Roger, 305—307, 351
Ashmole, Elias, 621
Assembly of Foules, 119—121
Asser, 35, 36
Astrea, D'Urfé's, 629, 630
— , the Divine, 683
Astrolabe, Chaucer on the, 155
Astrophel and Stella, 421, 422
Athelard of Bath, 45
Atterbury, Francis, 773
Aubrey, John, 653, 654
Aungervyle, Richard, 93—97
Austen, Jane, 883, 886, 887
Authority, Contest about the Limit of, 52—54, 735, 736
Avesbury, Robert of, 98
Ayenbite of Inwit, the, 108
Aylmer, John, 321, 322, 374
Aytoun, William Edmondstoune, 889, 891—893


B

Bacon, Francis, 381—383, 399, 432, 433, 461, 463—468, 517—524, 584
— , Roger, 80—82
Bailey, Philip James, 890
Baillie, Joanna, 886, 887
Balades, 130, 209
Baldwin, William, 337, 338
Bale, John, 300, 339, 340
Ballads, 206—209
Ballot, 611
Bannatyne, George, 349
Barbauld, Anna Letitia, 886, 887
Barbour, John, 145, 146
Barclay, Alexander, 217, 218
— , Robert, 664, 665
Barrow, Isaac, 665, 666
Bartas, G. Saluste du, 379, 405—407, 475, 476

Bath, Athelard of, 45
Baxter, Richard, 612, 613, 664, 709, 726
Beaton, Cardinal, 277, 302, 303
Beattie, James, 862
Beaumont, Francis, 501—504
Becket, Thomas à, 54
Beddoes, Thomas Lovell, 883, 892
Bede, 8, 22—24, 33
Behn, Aphra, 682—684
Bell, Robert, 891, 892
Bellarmin, Cardinal, 511
Bellenden, John, 263, 26,
Benedict's Rule, 36
Bentham, Jeremy, 886—888
Bentley, Richard, 773
Beowulf, 13, 14
Berkeley, George, 792
Berners, Juliana, 187
— , Lord, 250
Bestiary, Metrical, 27, 76
Beveridge, William, 666, 667
Beverley, Alfred of, 48
Bible, the, 14, 17—21, 58, 74, 75, 137,
    175, 194, 233—241, 249, 250,
    253—255, 343, 344, 347
Bilney, Thomas, 248
Bishops' Bible, the, 347, 359
Blackfriars Theatre, 387
Blacklock, Thomas, 874
Blackmore, Sir Richard, 765, 766, 787,
    791
Blackstone, Sir William, 863
Blair, Robert, 841
Blanche, Duchess, 119, 125, 126
Blaneford, Henry of, 98, 183
Blank Verse, 294, 295, 327, 370, 371,
    537, 638—642, 654, 655
Blind Harry, 188, 189
Bloomfield, Robert, 885, 886
Boccaccio, 115—118, 148, 149, 163, 164,
    169, 184, 337
Bodenham, John, 478
Bodley, John, 343, 346, 347
— , Sir Thomas, 343, 508
Bodmer, 845
Boece, Hector, 263
Boethius, King Alfred's, 34, 35;
    Chaucer's, 111
Boiardo, 200
Boileau, 632, 633, 667—669
Bolingbroke, Lord, 779, 816, 817
Boscan, 279
Boswell, James, 855
Bourchier, John, Lord Berners, 250
Bourne, Vincent, 839
Bowles, William Lisle, 885—887
Boyle, Charles, 773
— , Robert, 584, 585, 619, 642, 685—
    688
— , Roger, 584, 622, 638
Bracton, Henry of, 82
Bradwardine, Thomas, 97
Brady, Nicholas, 751
Brandt, Sebastian, 218
Brome, Alexander, 547
Bromyard, John of, 175, 273
Brontë, Anne, 891
— , Charlotte, 891, 892

Brontë, Emily, 891
Brooke, Arthur, 350
Brooks, Charles Shirley, 893
Broome, William, 807
Brougham, Henry Lord, 888
Brown, Thomas, 703, 767
Brown, Dr. Thomas, 887
Browne, Sir Thomas, 585
— , William, 524, 525
Browning, Elizabeth Barret, 363
    889—891, 893
— , Robert, 882, 883, 889—894
Brownists, 462, 587
Bruce, Barbour's, 145
Brunanburh, Battle of, 36, 37
Brunellus, 56
Brunne, Robert of, 92, 93, 101
Brunton, Mary, 886, 887
Brut, 49, 65, 66, 73, 74
Bryskett, Lewis, 369
Buchanan, George, 401—404
— , Robert, 894
Buckingham, George Villiers, Duke
    of, 656—658, 716
— , John Sheffield, Duke of, 669—
    671
Buckle, Henry Thomas, 893
Budgell, Eustace, 782
Bulwer, Lord Lytton, 888—895
Bunyan, John, 615, 616, 661—664
Burgh, Benedict, 188
Burke, Edmund, 867—869, 871, 872
Burley, Walter, 98
Burnet, Gilbert, 667, 758
— , Thomas, 761
Burney, Fanny (D'Arblay), 837
Burns, Robert, 873—876
Burton, John Hill, 894
— , Robert, 509
— , William, 508
Bury, Richard of, 93—97
Butler, Joseph, 819
— , Samuel, 673—676
Byrhtnoth, the Death of, 37
Byron, George Gordon, Lord, 881
    882, 886—888

## C

Cabbala, the Threefold, 570
Cædmon, 14, 17—21
Caeilte M'Ronan, 4
Calderon, 504, 679
Calderwood, David, 566
Calprenède, 631, 632
Calvin, 303, 304, 320, 330, 344
Camden, William, 348, 428, 460, 507
Campbell, Thomas, 881, 885, 836
    888—890
Campion, Edmund, 409, 410
Canterbury Pilgrimage, the, 54
— Tales, Chaucer's, 163—170
Canute, 38

Capgrave, John, 187, 188
Carew, Richard, 460— , Thomas, 541.
Carlyle, Thomas, 884, 888—894
Carter, Elizabeth, 886
Cartwright, William, 546
Cattraeth, Battle of, 5, 6
Cavendish, George, 247
Caxton, William, 195, 196
Celts, 2—11
Censorship of the Press, 431, 474, 581—583 ; of the Stage, 828
Centlivre, Susannah, 797
Cervantes, 427, 503, 504
Chambers, Robert, 888, 889, 891—893
— , William, 889, 895
Chapman, George, 487, 488, 505, 506
Character Writing, 533, 540
Charlemagne and Alcuin, 24, 25
— Romances, 61
Chatterton, Thomas, 861
Chaucer, Geoffrey, 108—112, 117—129, 146—156, 159—161, 163—170, 377, 378, 442, 764, 805, 896, 897
Chaucer's Stanza, 117, 118, 406
Cheke, Sir John, 301, 302, 307, 315
Chester Plays, 102, 103
Chesterfield, Earl of, 853, 854
Chestre, Thomas, 188
Chettle, Henry, 389, 436, 437
Chevy Chase, 208
Cheynell, Francis, 568
Child, Sir Josiah, 689
Chillingworth, William, 568
Chivalry, Romances of, 61—64, 279—282
Chrestien of Troyes, 64
Christis Kirk of the Green, 185
Chronicle, the Saxon, 34: Monastic, 42, 43, 347
Churchill, Charles, 861, 862
Churchyard, Thomas, 338, 339
Cibber, Colley, 763, 806, 821
Cid Campeador, the, 55
Clarendon, Lord, 691
Clarissa Harlowe, 831
Clarke, Mary Cowden, 891
Cleveland, John, 547
Clough, Arthur Hugh, 891, 892
Cobbett, William, 885
Cockayne, Land of, 91
Colenso, John William, 893
Coleridge, Samuel Taylor, 876—879, 881, 885—888
— , Hartley, 889, 890
Colêt, John, 222, 230
Colin Clout, 245, 373, 444
Collier, Jeremy, 763, 794
— , John Payne, 889, 893
Collins, William, 841, 842
— , W. Wilkie, 892—894
Colman, George, Elder and Younger, 853, 863
Columba, 15
Columbus, 198, 230.
Colvil, Samuel, 677
Commission, High Court of, 344, 345, 515

Compendious Book of Godly and Spiritual Songs, 304
Comus, 555—557
Confessio Amantis, 157—159
Congreve, William, 761, 762
Constable, Henry, 458, 459
Constantinople, the Fall of, 192, 193·
Cook, Eliza, 890
Cooper, Thomas, 431
Corbet, Richard, 545
Corneille, 633, 634
Coryat, Thomas, 529
Cotton, Charles, 734
— , Sir Robert, 507, 508
Court of Love, Chaucer's, 109, 111, 112
Courts of Love, 83—85
Courtier, Castiglione's, 354
Covenanters, 564, 565
Coventry Plays, 103
Coverdale, Miles, 249, 253, 310, 314, 346
Cowley, Abraham, 548, 623, 671—673
— , Hannah, 885
Cowper, William, 864—866
Crabbe, George, 881, 886, 887
Craik, George Lillie, 891, 892
Cranmer, Thomas, 247—249
Cranmer's Bible, 254
Crashaw, Richard, 547, 548
Creech, Thomas, 725
Cromwell's Bible, 254
Crowne, John, 679
Crusades, the, 55, 85—87
Cuckoo and Nightingale, the, 152
Cudworth, Ralph, 665, 740
Culdees, the, 15
Cumberland, Richard, 863
Cursor Mundi, 93
Cuthbert, 17
Cymry, the, 2, 3. 5, 8
Cynewulf, 26, 28

D

Daisy, Chaucer's, 148, 149
D'Alembert, 846
Danes, the, 31, 32
Daniel, Samuel, 457, 507
Dante, 86—89, 113, 146, 147
D'Arblay, Frances, 887
Dares, 67
Darwin, Charles, 893, 895
— , Erasmus, 885
Davenant, Sir William, 539, 540, 623—626, 635—637, 640
David, St., 15
Davies, Sir John, 459, 460, 473
Day, John, 340—342
Decameron, the, 118, 163, 167, 168
De Foe, Daniel, 726—729, 774—778, 782, 799—801
Dekker, Thomas, 488, 490, 491, 500, 505
Denham, Sir John, 547, 640
Dennis, John, 767, 787, 788, 792

Deposition of Richard II., Poem on the, 132
De Quincey, Thomas, 893
Devil Tavern, 536
Diana, Montemayor's, 279
Dibdin, Charles, 885
Dickens, Charles, 883, 889—894
Dictys, 66
Dicuil, 29
Diderot, Denis, 846
Diet of Worms, 236
Digby, Sir Kenelm, 621
Dillon, Wentworth, Earl of Roscommon, 667—669
Diodati, Charles, 534, 558, 562
Disraeli, Isaac, 886, 887
— , Benjamin, 888—892
Dixon, William Hepworth, 892, 894
Dobell, Sydney, 892
Dominic, John, 72, 73
Donne, John, 527—529
Doran, John, 891, 892, 894
Dorset, Charles Sackville, Earl of, 651, 655, 750
Dort, or Dordrecht, Synod of, 514, 561, 568
Douglas, Gavin, 215, 216, 258—261
Drake, Sir Francis, 423, 424, 434
Drama, Rise of the, 282—284, 296, 297, 330—335, 369, 383—389, 410, 411, 440, 474—506, 535—539, 633—636
Drapier's Letters, 803
Drayton, Michael, 458, 524
Dream, Chaucer's, 122, 123
Drummond, William, of Hawthornden, 532, 533, 541
Dryden, John, 626, 627, 636—642 648, 658, 697—701, 715—746, 729—731, 735, 750—754, 763—765
Duck, Stephen, 840
Dugdale, William, 621, 622
Dumoulin, Pierre, 603
Dunbar, William, 205, 210—215
Dunciad, the, 815, 821
Duns Scotus, 92
Dunstable, Miracle Play at, 50
Dunstan, 36
D'Urfey, Thomas, 676, 677, 794
Dyce, Alexander, 888, 890—894
Dyer, John, 813, 825

E

Eadmer, 43
Earle, John, 540
Earthquake of 1580, 390
Edinburgh Review, 885
Edgeworth, Maria, 885—887
Edward the Confessor, a Life of, 38, 39
Edwards, Richard, 383, 384
— , Thomas, 588
Eikon Basilikè, 595
Eliot, George, 884, 893, 894
Elizabeth, Queen, Lines by, 430
Elliott, Ebenezer, 889, 891

Ellwood, Thomas, 613
Ely, Thomas of, 64
Elyot, Sir Thomas, 249
Erasmus, 234, 235, 297, 310
Erigena, John Scotus, 29, 30
Essay on Man, Pope's, 815—819
Essays, Bacon's, 464—466, 519, 521
Ethelwold, 36
Etherege, Sir George, 677, 697
Euphuism, 352, 353, 355—361, 394, 400, 415, 526, 527, 529
Evelyn, John, 620, 653, 759, 760
Exeter Book, the, 26—28
— , Joseph of, 65, 66

F

Fabyan, Robert, 220, 221
Faerie Queene, the, 397, 446—457
Fairfax, Edward, 469
Falconer, William, 862
Falls of Princes, 184, 335, 337
Fame, House of, Chaucer's, 146, 147 805
Fanshawe, Sir Richard, 622
Faraday, Michael, 889, 892
Farquhar, George, 762, 763, 781
Faust, John, Printer, 195
Faustus, Doctor, 417, 418
Feltham, Owen, 568
Fenton, Elijah, 808
Fergus Finnbheoil, 4
Ferguson, Robert, 874
Ferrers, George, 338—342
Field, Nathaniel, 505
Fielding, Henry, 827—835
Filmer, Sir Robert, 589, 609, 743
Filostrato, Boccaccio's, 117
Finnesburg, the Fight at, 28
Fionn M'Cumhaill, 4
First English, 11, 12, 41
Fisher, John, 205, 222, 250
Fitzstephen, William, 54
Flecknoe, Richard, 720, 721
Fletcher, Giles, LL.D., 473
— , Giles, 473, 525, 526
— , John, 501—504
— , Phineas, 473, 544
Flodden, 258
Florence of Worcester, 43
Florio, John, 468
Flower and the Leaf, the, 152
Flytings, 214, 242
Foote, Samuel, 863
Ford, John, 536
Fordun, John of, 99
Forster, John, 891—895
Fortescue, Sir John, 189, 190
Foster, John, 888, 889
Fox, George, 616—618, 738
— , John, 314, 340, 486
Francis of Assisi, 72
Frederick II., Emperor, 85, 86
Freeman, Edward Augustus, 891—893

Frobisher, Martin, 423
Froissart, Lord Berners's, 250
Froude, James Anthony, 891, 893—895
Fuller, Thomas, 570, 571, 614, 665
Fysshe, Simon, 311

## G

Gabhra, Battle of, 4, 5
Gaddesden, John of, 98
Gaels, 2—5, 10
Gaimar, Geoffrey, 48, 49
Galahad, 63
Galt, John, 887, 888
Gamelyn, the Tale of, 166
Garcilasso de la Vega, 279
Garrick, David, 850
Garth, Samuel, 766, 795
Gascoigne, George, 369—371, 384
Gaskell, Elizabeth Cleghorn, 891—894
Gauden, John, 594, 595
Gaudia, 76
Gaunt, John of, 118, 119, 121, 123, 125—128, 162
Gay, John, 790, 791, 814, 815
Genesis and Exodus, 76
Geneva Bible, the, 343
Geoffrey the Grammarian, 188
— , of Monmouth, 47—49
— , of Vinsauf, 68
Gerland, 41
Gerson, 174
Gervase of Tilbury, 71
Gibbon, Edward, 858, 859
Gifford, William, 885, 887, 888
Gilbert, Sir Humphrey, 368, 422—424
Gilbertus Anglicus, 98
Gildas, 31
Gildon, Charles, 795
Giraldus Cambrensis, 68—70
Gladstone, William Ewart, 890, 892, 893
Glanville, Ralph, 65
Gleig, George Robert, 889, 891
Globe Theatre, 440
Gloucester Fragments, 36
— , Robert of, 90
Glover, Richard, 839
Gododin, the, 5
Godwin, William, 885, 886, 839
Goethe, 845
Golding, Arthur, 329, 390, 407
Goldsmith, Oliver, 860, 861
Golias Poems, 58, 59
Gomberville, 631
Gongora, Luis de, 526
Googe, Barnaby, 408, 409
Gottsched, 845
Gorboduc, 330—335
Gosson, Stephen, 387, 388
Gower, John, 129, 130, 138—145, 156—159, 160—163
Graal, the Holy, 62, 64
Grafton, Richard, 347, 348

Grahame, James, 885, 886
Grainger, James, 862
Granville, George, Lord Lansdowne, 767
Gray, David, 893
— , Thomas, 6, 842—844
Greek, Study of, 192—194, 199, 200, 223, 224, 301
Green, Matthew, 786
Greene, Robert, 389, 414—416, 434—437
Gregory's Pastoral Rule, 35
Grenville, Sir Richard, 462
Greville, Fulke, Lord Brooke, 464, 539
Grey, Arthur Lord, 369, 395
Grimald, Nicholas, 327
Grindal, Edmund, 375, 376, 470
Griselda, Tale of, 167
Grocyn, William, 199
Grosseteste, Robert, 71, 72, 78—80
Grote, George, 891, 895
Grub Street, 341
Guardian, the, 789
Guest, Lady Charlotte Elizabeth, 890
Guillaume de Lorris, 87
Gulliver's Travels, 804
Gutenberg, John, 194, 195
Guthlac, St., Legend of, 27
Guy of Warwick, 77
Gwalchmai, 71

## H

Habington, William, 540
Hakluyt, Richard, 427
Hales, John, 567, 568
Halifax, Charles Montague, Lord, 732, 770, 780
Hall, Anna Maria, 889
— , Arthur, 408
— , Edward, 300, 301
— , Joseph, 473—475, 510, 567, 572, 573, 576
Hallam, Henry, 887, 890
— , Arthur Henry, 889
Halliwell, James Orchard, 891—893
Hamilton, Sir William, 893
Hampole, the Hermit of, 106—108
Hanmer, Sir Thomas, 822
Harding, John, 182, 183
Harington, Sir John, 469
Hariot, Thomas, 426
Harlaw, Battle of, 177, 178
Harrington, James, 609—612
Hartley, David, 842
Hartlib, Samuel, 583, 584, 619
Harvey, Gabriel, 362, 363, 372, 390, 471
— , William, 517, 544
Havelok, 77, 90
Hawes, Stephen, 218—220
Hawkesworth, John, 853
Hayward, Sir John, 460
Hazlitt, William, 886—888
Heber, Reginald, 886—888
Heliodorus, Æthiopics of, 392

Helps, Arthur, 891, 893
Hemans, Felicia, 887, 889
Hendyng, Proverbs of, 91
Henry of Blaneford, 98, 183
— of Huntingdon, 52.
— the Minstrel, 188, 189
Henryson, Robert, 201, 202
Herbert, Edward, Lord Cherbury, 516, 517, 542
—, George, 542—544
Herrick, Robert, 550
Herringman, Henry, 753
Heylin, Peter, 563
Heywood, Jasper, 327, 328
—, John, 299, 3 0, 315
—, Thomas, 488, 505
Higden, Ralph, 99, 100
Higgins, John, 338
Hilarius, 49
Hilda, Abbess, 16, 17
Hind and Panther, 729—731
—, Transversed, 731, 732
Hobbes, Thomas, 588, 389, 607—609, 619, 620, 691, 692, 745
Hoccleve, Thomas, 179—181
Hofland, Barbara, 887, 890
Hogg, James, 885, 886
Holcot, Robert, 98
Holinshed, Ralph, 348
Holyday, Barten, 540, 541
Home, John, 863
Homer, Translations of, 408, 487, 805, 807, 808
Homilies, Ælfric's, 38 ; the Book of, 310, 375
Hood, Thomas, 888, 889, 891
Hooke, Robert, 685, 686
Hooker, Richard, 469—473, 744
Hope, Thomas, 887
Hopkins, John, 312, 329, 330
Hoveden, Roger of, 67, 68
Howard, Hon. Edward, 638
—, Sir Robert, 638, 641, 655
Howe, John, 613, 614
Howel, Prince, 71
Howitt, Mary, 888 : William, 889
Hughes, John, 791, 792
—, Thomas, 893
Hume, David, 856—858
Hundred Merry Tales, 300
Hunt, John Henry Leigh, 885, 886, 887, 889, 890—892
Hunting of the Cheviot, the, 208
Huntingdon, Henry of, 52
Hunton, Nicholas, 589
Hurd, Richard, 840
Huss, John, 171
Huxley, Thomas Henry, 892--894
Hyde, Edward, Lord Clarendon, 691

I

Idols, Bacon's, 522, 523
Inchbald, Elizabeth, 885
Ingelo, Nathaniel, 622
Ingelow, Jean, 893, 894

Instauratio Magna, Bacon's, 521, 522
Interludes, 298, 299
Iscanus, Josephus, 65, 66
Italian Plays, Early, 282—284
Itinerary of Richard I., 68

J

James I. of Scotland, 176—178, 184, 185
— IV. —, 210, 211, 257, 258
— V. —, 258, 262—270
— VI. —, I. of England, 404—406
Jean de Meung, 87, 88
Jerrold, Douglas, 889—892
Jest Books, 300
Jewel, John, 342, 381
John of Bromyard, 175, 176
— — Fordun, 99
— — Oxnead, 89, 90
— — Salisbury, 59, 60
— — Trokelowe, 98, 183
Johnson, Richard, 449
—, Samuel, 849—856, 869, 870, 885
Jonson, Ben, 489—491, 497—501, 535, 536
Joseph of Exeter, 65, 66
Jowett, Benjamin, 894
Judith, a First English Poem, 28
Junius, Letters of, 868
—, Francis, the Elder, 366
—, —, the Younger, 602

K

Kaye, John William, 894
Keats, John, 882, 887
Keble, John, 888, 891, 894
Ken, Thomas, 733, 734, 757
Kennedy, Walter, 214
Killigrew, Thomas, 635
King Alexander, 77
— Horn, 77
—, William, 767
Kinglake, Alexander William, 891, 893
King's Quair, the, 177
Kingsley, Charles, 891—894
Knight, Charles, 888, 889, 892, 893
Knighton, Henry, 175
Knight's Tale, Chaucer's, 116
Knolles, Richard, 506
Knox, John, 303, 320—326, 399—401
Kyd, Thomas, 389—401, 489
Kynddelw, 71

L

Lamb, Charles, 885, 886, 888
—, Mary, 886
Lancelot, 61—63
Landon, Letitia Elizabeth, 888, 889
Landor, Walter Savage, 888
Langbaine, Gerard, 751

Langland, William, 131—135
Langtoft, Peter, 90, 93
Languet, Hubert, 368, 369
Lansdowne, George Granville, Lord, 767
Latimer, Hugh, 252, 253, 255, 312—314
Latin Quantity in English Verse, 68, 390, 407, 408, 429, 474
Laureate Poets, 204, 635, 751, 786, 806, 839, 840, 885, 887, 891, 892
Layamon, 73, 74
Layard, Austin Henry, 891, 892
Leclerc, Jean, 739
Lee, Harriet, 886
—, Nathaniel, 680
—, Sophia, 886
Legend of Good Women, the, 148, 149
Leibnitz, 817, 818
Leighton, Robert, 666
Leland, John, 255, 256, 289
Leo X., 233—236
L'Estrange, Sir Roger, 710, 711
Lever, Charles James, 890
Leviathan, Hobbes's, 608, 609
Lewes, George Henry, 891—894
Lewis, Matthew Gregory, 885
Licensing of Books, 474, 581—583
— of Plays, 828, 823
Lightfoot, John, 568, 569
Lillo, George, 838
Lily, William, 223, 224
Limborch, Philip van, 738, 739
Linacre, Thomas, 199, 200, 224
Lindisfarne, 15
Lindsay, Sir David, 256—258, 264—278, 302, 308—310
Lindwood, William, 181
Lismore, Book of the Dean of, 4
Llywarch Hen, 6, 7
— ab Llywelyn, 71
Locke, John, 706—709, 725, 726, 738—750
Lockhart, John Gibson, 888
Lodge, Thomas, 389, 435, 438
Lollards, 175, 181, 182, 186, 187
Looking Glass for London and England, 435, 436
Lope de Vega, 504, 679
Lorris, Guillaume de, 87
Lovelace, Richard, 549
Lovell, Robert, 877, 885
Lucan Translated, 537
Luces de Gast, 64
Luther, Martin, 235, 236
Lycidas, 558—560
Lydgate, John, 178, 179, 184, 335
Lyly, John, 355—361, 389, 413, 414, 431, 440, 441
Lyttelton, George, Lord, 838
Lytton, Lord, 888—895

**M**

Macaronic Verse, 284, 285
Macaulay, Thomas Babington, 890—893
Macdonald, George, 892, 894

MacFlecknoe, 720
Machiavelli, 284
Mackay, Charles, 889
Mackenzie, Sir George, 759
—, Henry, 885, 886
Mackintosh, Sir James, 871, 889
Macpherson, James, 862
Maid's Tragedy, the, 503
Mair, John, 260
Maldon, Battle of, 37
Malherbe, 629
Malory, Sir Thomas, 197
Mallet, David, 813, 823, 838, 839
Malmesbury, Aldhelm at, 21, 22
—, William of, 44, 45
Malone, Edmund, 885
Malthus, Thomas Robert, 886, 887
Mandeville, Sir John, 135—137
—, Bernard, 810, 811
Map, Walter, 56—64
Marianus Scotus, 41
Marino, Gianbatista, 526, 527
Marlowe, Christopher, 389, 416—421, 437, 438, 473
Marot, Clement, 279, 304, 305, 330, 376, 377
Marprelate Controversy, 399, 430—432
Marryatt, Captain Frederick, 889, 890
Marsilius of Padua, 143
Marston, John, 473, 488, 490, 500
—, John Westland, 890
Martin, Theodore, 893, 894
Martineau, Harriet, 888—894
—, James, 891
Marvell, Andrew, 605, 606, 627, 692—697, 709
Masques, 298, 331, 332, 519
Massey, Gerald, 892, 894
Massinger, Philip, 505, 536
Masson, David, 893
Matthew Paris, 83
Matthew's Bible, 254
Maurice, Frederick Denison, 883, 892—894
May, Thomas, 537
Mayne, Jasper, 538, 607
Medici, the, 190—192, 196, 200
Merchant of Venice, 479—486
Meredith, George, 892
Meres, Francis, 478
Meilyr, 71
Merlin, 7, 47
Mermaid Tavern, 497
Meung, Jean de, 87, 88
Michael Scot, 82, 86
Michel of Northgate, 108
Middleton, Thomas, 488, 505
Milesians, the, 10, 11
Mill, James, 887
—, John Stuart, 891, 894
Milman, Henry Hart, 887—889, 890, 892
Milnes, Richard Monckton, Lord Houghton, 890, 891
Milton, John, 533—535, 550—565, 572—584, 587, 588, 591, 592, 594—606, 627, 628, 642—648, 658—661, 756

Minot, Laurence, 106
Miracle Plays, 49—52, 54, 100—105
Mirror for Magistrates, 335—338, 509
Molière, 633
Monmouth, Geoffrey of, 47—49
Montague, Charles, Lord Halifax, 732, 770
— , Lady Mary Wortley, 844
Montaigne, 406
Montemayor, George of, 279, 392
Montesquieu, 846
Montgomery, James, 886, 887
Moore, Edward, 838
— , Thomas, 885—890
Morality Plays, 245—247, 271—276
More, Alexander, 603, 604
— , Hannah, 886
— , Henry, 569, 570, 685
— , Sir Thomas, 224—234, 240—242
Moreto, 679
Morier, James, 887, 888
Morley, George, 733, 734
— , John, 894, 895
Mornay, Philip du Plessis, 407
Morris, William, 893, 894
Morton, Cardinal, 224—226
Mother Hubbard's Tale, 442, 443
Moytura, Battle of, 5
Mulgrave, Earl of, 669—671
Mun, Thomas, 689
Munday, Anthony, 409
Myrddhin, 7, 47
Mystery Plays, 51


N

Napier, John, 517
Nash, Thomas, 431, 432, 438, 473
Nassington, William of, 183
Neckham, Alexander, 67
Needham, Marchmont, 710
Nennius, 30, 31
Netter, Thomas, 181, 182
Neville, Alexander, 328
Newbury, William of, 67
Newman, Francis William, 890
— , John Henry, 894
Newspapers, 710, 711, 777
Newton, Sir Isaac, 688, 689, 729, 794
— , Thomas, 328
Nibelungen, the, 55
Niccols, Richard, 509
Nicholas of Clamanges, 144
— Guildford, 75
Nigel Wireker, 55, 56
Nightingale, Florence, 894
Nominalists, 92
Normans, 31, 32, 39, 40
Norris and Drake, Farewell to, 434
North, Roger, 711, 712
— , Sir Thomas, 379, 380
Northumbrian Psalter, 91
Norton, Caroline Elizabeth, 889, 891, 893
— , Thomas, 330

Novum Organum, Bacon's, 522
Nuce, Thomas, 328
Nut-brown Maid, the, 208


O

Occam, William, 92
Occleve, Thomas, 179—181
Oceana, Harrington's, 610, 611
Octave Rhyme, 117
Odoric of Pordenone, 136
Ohthere's Voyages, 33
Oisin (Ossian), 4, 5
Oldcastle, Sir John, 181
Oldham, John, 713, 714
Oldmixon, John, 767, 795
Ollamh, the, 9
Opie, Amelia, 885—887
Opinion, 53, 54
Ordericus Vitalis, 43, 44
Orfeo, Politian's, 197, 198
Orinda, 684, 685
Orlando Furioso, 279—281
Ormulum, 74, 75
Orosius, King Alfred's, 33
Osbern, 41
Otterburn, Battle of, 208
Otway, Thomas, 680—682
Overbury, Sir Thomas, 533
Ovid Translated, 329, 541, 753, 773
Owain, Prince of Powis, 71
Owen, Richard, 892
Owl and Nightingale, 75
Oxnead, John of, 89, 90


P

Pageants, 413
Paine, Thomas, 871, 885
Paley, William, 885
Palladis Tamia, 478
Palmerin, 281, 392
Pamela, Sidney's, 393, 394; Richardson's, 826, 827
Pandosto, 415
Panther, the, 27
Papacy, Schism in the, 142—145, 172—174
Paradise Lost, 563, 644—648, 655, 657
Paris Garden, 440
— , Matthew, 83
Parker, Matthew, 342, 343, 345, 346
— , Samuel, 692, 695, 696
Parnell, Thomas, 802
Parzival, 64
Paston Letters, 188
Pastoral Poetry, 197, 198, 201, 278, 279, 372—377, 786, 788, 790
Paternoster, Metrical, 76
Patrick, St., 5, 15
Patronage, 225, 411, 412
Paynter, William, 350, 351
Peacock, Thomas Love, 889

Pecock, Reginald, 185—187
Peeblis to the Play, 185
Peele, George, 410, 411, 413, 434, 438, 439
Pelagius, 14, 97
Penn, William, 707, 708, 758
Penry, John, 431
Penseroso, 553
Pepys, Samuel, 653
Percy, Thomas, 862, 863
Periods, the Four, of English Literature, 112, 113, 628, 629, 736, 814
Petrarch, 113—115, 167
Petty, Sir William, 620, 689
Phaer, Thomas, 329
Philips, Ambrose, 786
—, John, 778, 779
—, Katherine, 684, 685
Philobiblon, 96
Phoenix, the, 27
Physiologus, 27, 76
Piers Plowman, Vision of, 131—135; Crede, 159
Pilgrim's Progress, 663, 664
Pisa, Council of, 173
Pitt, Christopher, 839
Platonism, 193, 194, 357, 569, 570
Plimsoll, Samuel, 895
Plutarch, North's, 379
Pole, Reginald, 286
Politian, 197, 198
Polychronicon, the, 99, 150
Pomfret, John, 766
Pope, Alexander, 785, 787—791, 805—809, 815—821, 851
Pordage, Samuel, 716—719
Porter, Anna Maria, 885, 886
—, Jane, 885, 886
Prayer, Book of Common, 310, 311, 344, 564
Précieuses, the, 630, 631, 633
Precisians, 345
Prideaux, Humphrey, 758, 759
Priestley, Joseph, 885
Printing, Invention of, 194—196
Prior, Matthew, 732, 733, 768—770, 778, 783, 793
Procter, Adelaide Anne, 893
—, Bryan William, 887—889, 894
Promptorium Parvulorum, 188
Prose, English, 155, 156, 306
Prynne, William, 538, 539, 563, 567, 690, 691
Psalms, Versions of the, 91, 107, 254, 255, 288, 304, 305, 329, 342, 343
Purchas, Samuel, 510
Puritans, 344, 345, 372—376, 513
Pusey, Edward Bouverie, 889, 894
Puttenham, George, 378, 429, 430

Q

Quakers, 618
Quarles, Francis, 532, 542
Quarterly Review, 886
Quixote, Don, 503, 504, 837

R

Rabelais, 278 ; translated, 622
Racine, 633
Raleigh, Sir Walter, 368, 395, 396, 424, 426, 427, 461—463, 509, 510
Ralph Roister Doister, 296, 297
Rambouillet, Marquise de, 630, 631
Ramsay, Allan, 811, 812
Randolph, Thomas, 538, 539
Rape of the Lock, 788—790
Ray, John, 760
Reade, Charles, 892, 893
Realists, 92
Reid, Thomas, 858
Reinaert, 55
Religio Laici, 722—724
Remonstrants, the, 514, 738, 739
Repressor, Pecock's, 186, 187
Revels, Master of the, 331, 384
Reynolds, Sir Joshua, 885
Ricardo, David, 886, 887
Richardson, Samuel, 825—827, 831, 832, 836
Rievaulx, Ailred of, 64
Rishanger, William, 183
Robert of Avesbury, 98
— — Brunne, 92, 93, 101
— — Gloucester, 90
Robertson, William, 858
Robin Hood, 206
Robinson Crusoe, 800, 801
Rochester, Earl of, 667
Rocleve, 181
Roger Infans, 45
Roger of Hoveden, 67, 68
— — Wendover, 82, 83
Rogers, John, 253, 254
—, Samuel, 887
Rolle, Richard, 106—108
Roman de la Rose, 87, 88 ; English Version of the, 110
Romeo and Juliet, 350, 351
Roscoe, William, 886
Roscommon, Earl of, 667—669
Ross, Alexander, 674
Rossetti, Christina, 894
—, Dante Gabriel, 894
Rousseau, 847, 848, 857, 858
Rowe, Nicholas, 786
Rowley, William, 488, 504
Roy, William, 238
Rushworth, John, 622
Russell, John, Earl, 892, 893
Rutherford, Samuel, 588
Rymer, Thomas, 699, 700

S

Sackville, Thomas, Lord Buckhurst, 330—336, 338, 351
—, Charles, Earl of Dorset, 651, 655, 732, 750
Sæwulf, 41, 42
St. John, Henry, Lord Bolingbroke, 779, 816, 817

St. Maure, Benoit de, 40, 66, 67
St. Nicholas, Miracle Play of, 50
Salisbury, John of, 59, 60
Salmasius, 599—603
Saluste, Guillaume, du Bartas, 379, 405, 406, 407, 475, 476
Samson, Agonistes, 658—661
Sanazzaro, 278, 392
Sandys, George, 506, 541
Satire of the Three Estates, 271—276
Satires Burnt, 473
Satiromastix, 490
Savage, Richard, 852
Savile, Sir Henry, 469, 470
Schiller, 845
Schoolmaster, Ascham's, 351—355
Science, Development of, 45—47, 91, 517—519, 521—524, 571, 572, 584—586, 618—621, 685—690, 760, 761
Scot, Michael, 82, 86
Scott, Sir Walter, 881, 883, 885, 886—889
Scotus, Duns, 92
Scriptorium, the, 25, 42, 196
Scuderi, Magdeleine, 632
Secretum Secretorum, 157
Sedley, Sir Charles, 655, 656
Selden, John, 514—516, 590, 591
Senchus Mor, 5
Seneca Translated, 327, 328
Settle, Elkanah, 678, 679, 716
Seven Champions of Christendom, 448, 449
Seward, Anna, 885
Sewell, Elizabeth Missing, 891
Shadwell, Thomas, 677, 678, 751
Shaftesbury, First Earl of, 705—709, 711—715, 726
Shakespeare, William, 380, 381, 397—399, 436, 437, 439—441, 477—487, 493—497, 498, 756, 808, 809, 852, 854, 856
Sheffield, John, Earl of Mulgrave, 669—671
Shelley, Percy Bysshe, 882, 887, 888
Shenstone, William, 823, 824
Shepherd's Calendar, the, 372—380
—, Play, the, 104, 105
Sheridan, Richard Brinsley, 864, 885
Sherlock, William, 756, 758
Shirley, James, 536, 537, 607
Shoreham, William of, 107
Sibbes, Richard, 570
Sidney, Algernon, 724
—, Sir Philip, 364, 365, 368, 369, 371, 372—380, 391—394, 421, 422, 425, 426
Skelton, John, 203, 216, 217, 242—246, 273
Smectymnuus, 572, 573
Smith, Adam, 863, 885
—, Charlotte, 885
—, Horace, 887, 888
—, James, 887
—, Sydney, 886, 891
—, Sir Thomas, 301, 307, 315, 362
Smollett, Tobias, 832, 836—838

Somerville, Mary, 889, 891
—, William, 815
Somnium Scipionis, 120
Sonnets, 84, 85, 88, 114, 293, 294, 421, 422, 445, 496, 497, 551
South, Robert, 758
Southern, Thomas, 703, 724, 752
Southey, Robert, 877, 878, 882, 885—889
Speed, John, 508
Spelman, Sir Henry, 586
—, Sir John, 587
Spence, Joseph, 839, 840
Spenser, Edmund, 361—364, 372, 390, 391, 395—397, 411, 441—457, 475, 756, 808, 809
Spottiswoode, John, 566
Spectator, the, 784
Sprat, Thomas, 686, 687
Stanhope, Earl, 890, 893
Stanihurst, Richard, 407, 408
Stanley, Arthur Penrhyn, 891, 894
—, Thomas, 607
Steele, Richard, 755—757, 771, 773, 780, 782—785, 792, 793, 796—798
Stepney, George, 725
Sterne, Laurence, 859, 860
Sternhold, Thomas, 305, 312, 329, 330
Stewart, Dugald, 885—887
Stanza, Chaucer's, 117, 118; Spenser's, 449
Stillingfleet, Edward, 737
Stow, John, 348, 460
Strode, Ralph, 129
Strype, John, 758
Stuart Dramatists, 493
Stubbes, Philip, 428
Studley, John, 328
Suckling, Sir John, 546
Supplication for the Beggars, 311
Surrey, Henry Howard, Earl of, 290—295
Swift, Jonathan, 772—774, 781, 783, 784, 792, 793, 802, 803
Swinburne, Algernon Charles, 894
Swinford, Catherine, 128, 202
Sydenham, Thomas, 689, 690
Sylvester, Joshua, 475, 476, 526


T

Tain Bo, the, 5, 10
Talfourd, Sir Thomas Noon, 889
Taliesin, 7
Tamburlaine, 416, 417, 474
Tasso, 378, 379, 406, 449; translated, 469
Tate, Nahum, 721, 722, 751
Tatler, the, 782—784
Taverner, Richard, 254
Taylor, Sir Henry, 889, 890, 893
—, Jeremy, 577, 578, 592—594, 614, 615, 661
—, John, the Water Poet, 529, 530, 541

Temple, Sir William, 703—705, 707, 709, 712, 773
Tennyson, Alfred, 883, 888—890, 892—894
Teseide, Boccaccio's, 116
Testament of Cresseid, 201
— of Love, the, 154
Teutons, 3
Thackeray, William Makepeace, 883, 891—894
Theatres, the First, 385—388, 411 412. 440
Theobald, Lewis, 809, 820
Thomas of Ely, 64
Thomson, James, 812, 813, 822 --824, 842
Thorn, William, 99
Thornton, Bonnel, 853
Thrale, Mrs., 855
Throckmorton, Job, 431
Tickell, Thomas, 782, 790, 793
Tighe, Mary, 886
Tillotson, John, 666, 758
Tiptoft, John, Earl of Worcester, 188
Tobacco, 426
Tom Jones, 833, 834
Tonson, Jacob, 753
Tottel's Miscellany, 315, 316, 326, 327
Tourneur, Cyril, 504
Towneley Mysteries, 103
Toxophilus, 306
Tradescants, the, 620
Tragedies, 52, 169, 184, 332—338
Transition English, 41
Traveller's Song, the, 26, 27
Travers, Walter, 470, 471
Trench, Richard Chenevix, 892
Trevisa, John, 150
Tripartite Chronicle, Gower's, 151, 153, 161, 162
Trivet, Nicholas, 90
Troilus and Cressida, Chaucer's, 117, 128, 129
— Verse, 406
Trokelowe, John of, 98, 183
Trollope, Anthony, 892—895
— , Frances, 890
Troubadours, 55
Troy, 49, 65—67
Troynovant, 66
Tudors, 202
Tupper, Martin Farquhar, 8 jo
Turbervile, George, 350
Turgot, 41
Turner, Dr. Francis, 697
Turpin, Archbishop, 61
Tusser, Thomas, 316, 349
Twyne, Thomas, 329
Tyndal, William, 236—242, 248—250


U

Udall, John, 431
— , Nicholas, 295—297, 310, 312, 315, 363
Unities, the Three, 634


Urquhart, Sir Thomas, 622
Usher, James, 512—514, 573, 587
Utopia, More's, 228—233


V

Vaughan, Henry, 548
Vanbrugh, John, 762, 763
Venus and Adonis, Shakespeare's, 439
Vercelli Book, the, 26—28
Vergil, Polydore, 221
Villiers, George, Duke of Buckingham, 656—658, 715
Vinsauf, Geoffrey de, 68
Virgil, Translations of, 259, 294, 295, 329, 407, 408, 763, 764
Virginia, 424, 426, 427
Vitalis, Ordericus, 43, 44
Voltaire, 847
Vox Clamantis, 139—142, 174


W

Wace, 49
Wakefield Plays, 103
Waldenses, 57, 58, 73
Wallace, Blind Harry's, 189
Waller, Edmund, 545, 546, 639, 64:
Wallis, John, 586, 619, 760
Walpole, Horace, 842—844
Walsh, William, 766, 767
Walsingham, Thomas, 183
Walton, Izaak, 623, 733, 734
Warburton, William, 821, 822
Ward, Robert Plumer, 888, 891
Warner, William, 428
Warren, Samuel, 890
Warton, Joseph, 840
— , Thomas, 840
Watson, Thomas, 412, 413
Watts, Isaac, 814
Wavrin, John de, 182
Webbe, William, 429
Webster, Augusta, 894
— , John, 505
Wendover, Roger of, 82, 83
Wesley, John, 819, 820
West, Gilbert, 823
Westminster Assembly, 587
Whale, Myth of the, 27
Wheloc, Abraham, 587
Whetstone, George, 409
Whiston, William, 761
Whitby, 14, 16, 32
White, Gilbert, 885
— , Henry Kirke, 886
Whitefield, George, 820
Whitehead, Paul, 839
— , William, 839
Whitgift, John, 470, 473
Whittingham, William, 343
Whole Duty of Man, 692

Wiclif, John, 131, 137, 138, 171
Wilkins, John, 571, 572, 586, 620, 687
William of Malmesbury, 44, 45
—      — Nassington, 183
—      — Newbury, 67
.—      — Rishanger, 183
—      — Shoreham, 107
Will's Coffee House, 709, 710
Wilmot, John, Earl of Rochester, 667
Wilson, John, 886—888, 890
Wireker, Nigel, 55, 56
Wither, George, 530—532, 541, 542, 627
Wolfram, von Eschenbach, 64
Wollstonecraft, Mary, 885
Wolsey, Thomas, 227, 228, 238, 242—245
Wood, Anthony, 654
Woodville, Anthony, Lord Rivers, 196
Worcester, Florence of, 43
Wordsworth, William, 866, 867, 870—873, 876, 878—881, 885—888, 890, 892
Wotton, Sir Henry, 567
--, William, 773

Wulfstan's Voyage, 34
Wyat, Sir Thomas, 285—290, 303
—  — the Younger, 315
Wycherley, William, 701—703
Wyntershylle, William, 183


X

Ximenez, Cardinal, 233


Y

Yalden, Thomas, 753
Yonge, Charlotte Mary, 891
York, Alcuin at, 24—26
Young, Edward, 841
—, Thomas, of Loncardy, 525, 535

THE END

CASSELL AND COMPANY LIMITED, BELLE SAUVAGE WORKS, LONDON, E.C.
20,783.

Milton Keynes UK
Ingram Content Group UK Ltd.
UKHW020754080124
435661UK00018B/1233